REAMDE

REAMDE neal stephenson

wm

WILLIAM MORROW

An Imprint of HarperCollins*Publishers*

REAMDE. Copyright © 2011 by Neal Stephenson. All rights reserved. Printed in the United States of America. No part of this book may be used or reproduced in any manner whatsoever without written permission except in the case of brief quotations embodied in critical articles and reviews. For information address HarperCollins Publishers, 10 East 53rd Street, New York, NY 10022.

HarperCollins books may be purchased for educational, business, or sales promotional use. For information please write: Special Markets Department, HarperCollins Publishers, 10 East 53rd Street, New York, NY 10022.

FIRST EDITION

Designed by Lisa Stokes

Library of Congress Cataloging-in-Publication Data

Stephenson, Neal.
  Reamde / Neal Stephenson. — 1st ed.
      p. cm.
   ISBN 978-0-06-197796-1
   1. Computer games—Fiction. 2. Virtual reality—Fiction. 3. Money laundering—Fiction. I. Title.
   PS3569.T3868R43 2011
   813'.54—dc22

                                                                        2011020573

ISBN 978-0-06-210642-1 (international edition)

11 12 13 14 15   OV/RRD   10 9 8 7 6 5 4 3 2

REAMDE

PART I

Nine Dragons

THE FORTHRAST FARM
Northwest Iowa

Thanksgiving

Richard kept his head down. Not all those cow pies were frozen, and the ones that were could turn an ankle. He'd limited his baggage to a carry-on, so the size 11s weaving their way among the green-brown mounds were meshy black cross-trainers that you could practically fold in half and stuff into a pocket. He could have gone to Walmart this morning and bought boots. The reunion, however, would have noticed, and made much of, such an extravagance.

Two dozen of his relatives were strung out in clumps along the barbed-wire fence to his right, shooting into the ravine or reloading. The tradition had started as a way for some of the younger boys to blow off steam during the torturous wait for turkey and pie. In the old days, once they'd gotten back to Grandpa's house from Thanksgiving church service and changed out of their miniature coats and ties, they would burst out the doors and sprint half a mile across the pasture, trailed by a few older men to make sure that matters didn't get out of hand, and shoot .22s and Daisies down into the crick. Now grown up with kids of their own, they showed up for the re-u with shotguns, hunting rifles, and handguns in the backs of their SUVs.

The fence was rusty, but its posts of Osage orange wood were unrotted. Richard and John, his older brother, had put it up forty years ago to keep livestock from straying down into the crick. The stream was narrow enough that a grown man could cross it with a stride, but cattle were not made for striding, or bred for intelligence, and could always contrive some way to get themselves into terrible straits along its steep, crumbling banks. The same feature made it an ideal firing range. Summer had been dry and autumn cold, so the crick was running low under a paper-thin glaze of ice, and the bank above it threw up gouts of loose dirt wherever it stopped a bullet. This made it easy for the shooters to correct their aim. Through his ear protectors, Richard could hear the voices of helpful onlookers: "You're about three inches low. Six inches to the right." The boom of the shotguns, the snap of the .22s, and the *pow, pow, pow* of the semiautomatic handguns were reduced to a faint patter by the electronics in the hearing protectors—hard-shell earmuffs with volume knobs sticking out of them—which he'd stuffed into his bag yesterday, almost as an afterthought.

He kept flinching. The low sun shone in the face of a two-hundred-foot-tall wind turbine in the field across the crick, and its blades cast long scything shadows over them. He kept sensing the sudden onrush of a bar of darkness that flicked over him without effect and went on its way to be followed by another and another. The sun above blinking on and off with each cut of a blade. This was all new. In his younger days, it had only been the grain elevators that proved the existence of a world beyond the horizon; but now they had been supplanted and humbled by these pharaonic towers rearing their heads above the prairie, the only thing about this landscape that had ever been capable of inspiring awe. Something about their being in motion, in a place where everything else was almost pathologically still, seized the attention; they always seemed to be jumping out at you from behind corners.

Despite the wind, the small muscles of his face and scalp—the parents of headaches—were relaxed for the first time since he had come back to Iowa. When he was in the public spaces of the re-u— the lobby of the Ramada, the farmhouse, the football game in the side yard—he always felt that all eyes were on him. It was different here, where one had to attend to one's weapons, to make sure that the barrels were always pointed across the barbed wire. When Richard was seen, it was during terse, one-on-one conversations, spoken DIS-TINCT-LY through ear protection.

Younger relations, rookie in-laws, and shirttails called him Dick, a name that Richard had never used because of its association, in his youth, with Nixon. He would answer to Richard or to the nickname Dodge. During the long drive here from their homes in the exurbs of Chicago or Minneapolis or St. Louis, the parents would brief the kids on who was who, some of them even brandishing hard copies of the family tree and dossiers of photos. Richard was pretty sure that when they ventured out onto Richard's branch of the family tree—and a long, stark, forkless branch it was—they got a certain look in their eyes that the kids could read in the rearview mirror, a tone of voice that in this part of the country said more than words were ever allowed to. When Richard encountered them along the firing line, he could see as much in their faces. Some of them would not meet his eye at all. Others met it too boldly, as if to let him know that they were on to him.

He accepted a broken twelve-gauge side-by-side from a stout man in a camouflage hat whom he recognized vaguely as the second husband of his second cousin Willa. Keeping his face, and the barrel of the weapon, toward the barbed-wire fence, he let them stare at the back of his ski parka as he bit the mitten from his left hand and slid a pair of shells into the warm barrels. On the ground several yards out, just where the land dropped into the ravine, someone had set up a row of leftover Halloween pumpkins, most of which were already blasted to pie filling and fanned across the dead brown weeds. Richard snapped the gun together, raised it, packed its butt in snugly against his shoulder, got his body weight well forward, and drew the first trigger back. The gun stomped him, and the base of a pumpkin jumped up and thought about rolling away. He caught it with the second barrel. Then he broke the weapon, snatched out the hot shells, let them fall to the ground, and handed the shotgun to the owner with an appreciative nod.

"You do much hunting up there at your Schloss, Dick?" asked a man in his twenties: Willa's stepson. He said it loudly. It was hard to tell whether this was the orange foam plugs stuffed into his ears or sarcasm.

Richard smiled. "None at all," he replied. "Pretty much every-thing in my Wikipedia entry is wrong."

The young man's smile vanished. His eyes twitched, taking in Richard's $200 electronic hearing protectors, and then looked down, as if checking for cow pies.

Though Richard's Wikipedia entry had been quiet lately, in the past it had been turbulent with edit wars between mysterious people, known only by their IP addresses, who seemed to want to emphasize aspects of his life that now struck him as, while techni-cally true, completely beside the point. Fortunately this had all hap-pened after Dad had become too infirm to manipulate a mouse, but it didn't stop younger Forthrasts.

Richard turned around and began to mosey back the way he had come. Shotguns were not really his favorite. They were rel-egated to the far end of the firing line. At the near end, beside a motorcade of hastily parked SUVs, eight- and ten-year-old children, enveloped in watchful grown-ups, maintained a peppery fusillade from bolt-action .22s.

Directly in front of Richard was a party of five men in their late teens and early twenties, orbited by a couple of aspirant fifteen-year-olds. The center of attention was an assault rifle, a so-called black gun, military-style, no wood, no camouflage, no pretense that it was made for hunting. The owner was Len, Richard's first cousin once removed, currently a grad student in entomology at the Uni-versity of Minnesota. Len's red, wind-chapped hands were gripping an empty thirty-round magazine. Richard, flinching every so often when a shotgun went off behind him, watched Len force three car-tridges into the top of the magazine and then hand it to the young man who was currently in possession of the rifle. Then he stepped around behind the fellow and talked him patiently through the pro-cess of socketing the magazine, releasing the bolt carrier, and flip-ping off the safety.

Richard swung wide behind them and found himself passing through a looser collection of older men, some relaxing in col-lapsible chairs of camo-print fabric, others firing big old hunting rifles. He liked their mood better but sensed—and perhaps he was being too sensitive—that they were a little relieved when he kept on walking.

He only came to the re-u every two or three years. Age and circumstance had afforded him the luxury of being the family genealogist. He was the compiler of those family trees that the moms unfurled in the SUVs. If he could get their attention for a few minutes, stand them up and tell them stories of the men who had owned, fired, and cleaned some of the guns that were now speaking out along the fence—not the Glocks or the black rifles, of course, but the single-action revolvers, the 1911s, the burnished lever-action .30-30s—he'd make them understand that even if what he'd done did not comport with their ideas of what was right, it was more true to the old ways of the family than how they were living.

But why did he even rile himself up this way?

Thus distracted, he drifted in upon a small knot of people, mostly in their twenties, firing handguns.

In a way he couldn't quite put his finger on, these had an altogether different look and feel from the ones who swarmed around Len. They were from a city. Probably a coastal city. Probably West Coast. Not L.A. Somewhere between Santa Cruz and Vancouver. A man with longish hair, tattoos peeking out from the sleeves of the five layers of fleece and raincoat he'd put on to defend himself from Iowa, was holding a Glock 17 out in front of him, carefully and interestedly pocking nine-millimeter rounds at a plastic milk jug forty feet away. Behind him stood a woman, darker-skinned and -haired than any here, wearing big heavy-rimmed glasses that Richard thought of as Gen X glasses even though Gen X must be an ancient term now. She was smiling, having a good time. She was in love with the young man who was shooting.

Their emotional openness, more than their hair or clothing, marked them as not from around here. Richard had come out of this place with the reserved, even hard-bitten style that it seemed to tattoo into its men. This had driven half a dozen girlfriends crazy until he had finally made some progress toward lifting it. But, when it was useful, he could drop it like a portcullis.

The young woman had turned toward him and thrust her pink gloves up in the air in a gesture that, from a man, meant "Touchdown!" and, from a woman, "I will hug you now!" Through a smile she was saying something to him, snapped into fragments as the earmuffs neutralized a series of nine-millimeter bangs.

Richard faltered.

A precursor of shock came over the girl's face as she realized *he isn't going to remember me*. But in that moment, and because of that look, Richard knew her. Genuine delight came into his face. "Sue!" he exclaimed, and then—for sometimes it paid to be the family genealogist—corrected himself: "Zula!" And then he stepped forward and hugged her carefully. Beneath the layers, she was bone-slender, as always. Strong though. She pulled herself up on tiptoe to mash her cheek against his, and then let go and bounced back onto the heels of her huge insulated boots.

He knew everything, and nothing, about her. She must be in her middle twenties now. A couple of years out of college. When had he last seen her?

Probably not since she had been in college. Which meant that, during the handful of years that Richard had absentmindedly neglected to think about her, she had lived her entire life.

In those days, her look and her identity had not extended much beyond her backstory: an Eritrean orphan, plucked by a church mission from a refugee camp in the Sudan, adopted by Richard's sister, Patricia, and her husband, Bob, reorphaned when Bob went on the lam and Patricia died suddenly. Readopted by John and his wife, Alice, so that she could get through high school.

Richard was ransacking his extremely dim memories of John and Alice's last few Christmas letters, trying to piece together the rest. Zula had attended college not far away—Iowa State? Done something practical—an engineering degree. Gotten a job, moved somewhere.

"You're looking great!" he said, since it was time to say something, and this seemed harmless.

"So are you," she said.

He found this a little off-putting, since it was such transparent BS. Almost forty years ago, Richard and some of his friends had been bombing down a local road on some ridiculous teenaged quest and found themselves stuck behind a slow-driving farmer. One of them, probably with the assistance of drugs, had noticed a similarity—which, once pointed out, was undeniable—between Richard's wide, ruddy cliff of a face and the back end of the red pickup truck ahead of them. Thus the nickname Dodge. He kept wondering when he was going to develop the aquiline, silver-haired good looks of the men in the prostate medication ads on their endless seaplane junkets and fly-fishing idylls. Instead he was turning out to be an increasingly spready and mottled version of what he had been at thirty-five. Zula, on the other hand, actually was looking great. Black/Arab with an unmistakable dash of Italian. A spectacular nose that in other families and circumstances would have gone under the knife. But she'd figured out that it was beautiful with those big glasses perched on it. No one would mistake her for a model, but she'd found a look. He could only conjecture what style pheromones Zula was throwing off to her peers, but to him it was a sort of hyperspace-librarian, girl-geek thing that he found clever and fetching without attracting him in a way that would have been creepy.

"This is Peter," she announced, since her boyfriend had emptied the Glock's clip. Richard noted approvingly that he checked the weapon's chamber, ejected the clip, and checked the chamber again before transferring the gun to his left hand and extending his right to shake. "Peter, this is my uncle Richard." As Peter and Richard were shaking hands, Zula told Peter, "He lives pretty close to us, actually!"

"Seattle?" Peter asked.

"I have a condo there," Richard said, sounding lame and stiff to himself. He was mortified. His niece had been living in Seattle and he hadn't known. What would the re-u make of this? As a sort of excuse, he offered up: "But lately I've been spending more time at Elphinstone." Then he added, "B.C.," in case that meant nothing to Peter.

But an alert and interested look was already coming over Peter's face. "I've heard the snowboarding's great there!" Peter said.

"I wouldn't know," Richard said. "But everything else is pretty damned nice."

Zula was mortified too. "I'm sorry I didn't get in touch with you, Uncle Richard! It was on my list."

From most people this would have been mere polite cliché, but Richard knew that Zula would have an actual, literal list and that "Call Uncle Richard" would be somewhere on it.

"It's on me," he said. "I should have rolled out the welcome mat."

While stuffing more rounds into empty magazines, they caught up with each other. Zula had graduated from Iowa State with a dual degree in geology and computer science and had moved to Seattle four months ago to take a job at a geothermal energy start-up that was going to build a pilot plant near Mt. Rainier: the stupendous volcanic shotgun pointed at Seattle's head. She was going to do computer stuff: simulations of underground heat flow using computer codes. Richard was fascinated to hear the jargon rushing out of her mouth, to see the Zula brain unleashed on something worthy of its powers. In high school she'd been quiet, a little too assimilated, a little too easy to please in a small-town farm-girl sort of way. An all-American girl named Sue whose official documents happened to read Zula. But now she had got in touch with her Zula-ness.

"So what happened?" Richard asked. For she had been careful to say "I *was going*" to do this and that.

"When I got there, all was chaos," she said. The look on her face was fascinated. Going from Eritrea to Iowa would definitely give a young person some interesting perspectives on chaos. "Something funny was going on with the money people. One of those hedge fund Ponzi schemes. They filed for bankruptcy a month ago."

"You're unemployed," Richard said.

"That's one way to look at it, Uncle Richard." she said, and smiled.

Now Richard had a new item on *his* list, which, unlike Zula's, was a stew of nagging worries, vague intentions, and dimly perceived karmic debts that he carried around in his head. *Get Zula a job at Corporation 9592*. And he even had a plausible way of making it happen. That was not the hard part. The hard part was bestowing that favor on her without giving aid and comfort to any of the other job seekers at the re-u.

"What do you know about magma?" he asked.

She turned slightly, looked at him sidelong. "More than you, I would guess."

"You can do heat flow simulations. What about magma flow simulations?"

"The capability is out there," she said.

"Tensors?" Richard had no idea what a tensor was, but he had noticed that when math geeks started throwing the word around, it meant that they were headed in the general direction of actually getting something done.

"I suppose," she said nervously, and he knew that his question had been ridiculous.

"It's really important, in a deep way, that we get it right."

"What, for your *game company?*"

"Yes, for my Fortune 500 game company."

She was frozen in the watchful sidelong pose, trying to make out if he was just pulling her leg.

"The stability of the world currency markets is at stake," he insisted.

She was not going to bite.

"We'll talk later. You know anyone with autism spectrum disorder?"

"Yes," she blurted out, staring at him directly now.

"Could you work with someone like that?"

Her eyes strayed to her boyfriend.

Peter was struggling with the reloading. He was trying to put the rounds into the magazine backward. This had really been bothering Richard for the last half minute or so. He was trying to think of a nonhumiliating way to mention this when Peter figured it out on his own and flipped the thing around in his hand.

Richard had assumed, based on how Peter handled the gun, that he'd done it before. Now he reconsidered. This might be the first time Peter had ever touched a semiautomatic. But he was a quick study. An autodidact. Anything that was technical, that was logical, that ran according to rules, Peter could figure out. And knew it. Didn't bother to ask for help. So much quicker to work it out on his own than suffer through someone's well-meaning efforts to educate him—and to forge an emotional connection with him in so doing. There was something, somewhere, that he could do better than most people. Something of a technical nature.

"What have you been doing, Uncle Richard?" Zula asked brightly. She might have gotten in touch with her Zula-ness, but she kept the Sue-ness holstered for ready use at times like this.

"*Waiting for cancer*" would have been too honest an answer. "*Fighting a bitter rear-guard action against clinical depression*" would have given the impression that he was depressed *today,* which he wasn't.

"Worrying about palette drift," Richard said.

Peter and Zula seemed oddly satisfied with that nonanswer, as if it fit in perfectly with their expectations of men in their fifties. Or perhaps Zula had already told Peter everything that she knew, or suspected, about Richard, and they knew better than to pry.

"You fly through Seattle?" Peter asked, jumping rather hastily to the last-resort topic of air travel.

Richard shook his head. "I drove to Spokane. Takes three or four hours depending on snow and the wait at the border. One-hop to Minneapolis. Then I rented a big fat American car and drove it down here." He nodded in the direction of the road, where a maroon Mercury Grand Marquis was blotting out two houses of the Zodiac.

"This would be the place for it," Peter remarked. He turned his head around to take in a broad view of the farm, then glanced innocently at Richard.

Richard's reaction to this was more complicated than Peter might have imagined. He was gratified that Peter and Zula had identified him as one of the cool kids and were now inviting him to share their wryness. On the other hand, he had grown up on this farm, and part of him didn't much care for their attitude. He suspected that they were already facebooking and twittering this, that hipsters in San Francisco coffee bars were even now ROFLing and OMGing at photos of Peter with the Glock.

But then he heard the voice of a certain ex-girlfriend telling him he was too young to begin acting like such a crabby old man.

A second voice chimed in, reminding him that, when he had rented the colossal Grand Marquis in Minneapolis, he had done so *ironically.*

Richard's ex-girlfriends were long gone, but their voices followed him all the time and spoke to him, like Muses or Furies. It was like having seven superegos arranged in a firing squad before a single beleaguered id, making sure he didn't enjoy that last cigarette.

All this internal complexity must have come across, to Peter and Zula, as a sudden withdrawal from the conversation. Perhaps a precursor of senility. It was okay. The magazines were about as loaded as you could get them with frozen fingers. Zula, then Richard, took turns firing the Glock. By the time they were done, the rate of fire, up and down the barbed-wire fence, had dropped almost to nothing. Ammunition was running low, people were cold, kids were complaining, guns needed to be cleaned. The camo chairs were being collapsed and tossed into the backs of the SUVs. Zula drifted over to exchange hugs and delighted, high-pitched chatter with some of her cousins. Richard stooped down, which was a little more difficult than it used to be, and started to collect empty shotgun shells. In the corner of his eye he saw Peter following his lead. But Peter gave up on the chore quickly, because he didn't want to stray far from Zula. He had no interest in social chitchat with Zula's retinue of cousins, but neither did he want to leave her alone. He was swivel-headedly alert and protective of her in a way that Richard both admired and resented. Richard wasn't above feeling ever so slightly jealous of the fact that Peter had appointed himself Zula's protector.

Peter glanced across the field at the house, looked away for a moment, then turned back to give it a thorough examination.

He knew. Zula had told him about what happened to her adopted mom. Peter had probably googled it. He probably knew that there were fifty to sixty lightning-related fatalities a year and that it was hard for Zula to talk about because most people thought it was such a weird way to die, thought she might even be joking.

THE GRAND MARQUIS was blocking an SUV full of kids and moms who had just had it with being out there in the noise and the cold, so Richard—glad of an excuse to leave—moved quickly toward it, passing between Peter and Zula. Not too loudly, he announced, "I'm going into town," which meant that he was going to Walmart. He got into the huge Mercury, heard doors opening behind him, saw Peter and Zula sliding into the plunging sofa of the backseat. The passenger door swung open too, and in came another twentysomething woman whose name Richard should have known but couldn't recall. He would have to ferret it out during the drive.

The young funsters had much to say about the Grand Marquis as he was gunning it out onto the road; they had got the joke of it, decided that Richard was hip. The girl in the passenger seat said she had never before been in "a car like this," meaning, apparently, a sedan. Richard felt far beyond merely old.

Their conversation flew back and forth like the twittering of birds for about five minutes, and then they all fell silent. Peter was not exactly chomping at the bit to divulge facts about himself. Richard was fine with that. People who had job titles and business cards could say easily where they worked and what they did for a living, but those who worked for themselves, doing things of a complicated nature, learned over time that it was not worth the trouble of supplying an explanation if its only purpose was to make small talk. Better to just go directly to airline travel.

Their chilly extremities sucked all the energy from their brains. They gazed out the windows at the frost-burned landscape. This was western Iowa. People from anywhere else, traveling across the state, would have been hard-pressed to see any distinction between its east and its west—or, for that matter, between Ohio and South Dakota. But having grown up here, and gone on many a pirate quest and Indian ambush down along the crick, Richard sensed a gradient in the territory, was convinced that they were on the threshold between the Midwest and the West, as though on one side of the crick you were in the land of raking red leaves across the moist, forgiving black soil while listening to Big Ten football games on the transistor radio, but on the other side you were plucking arrows out of your hat.

There was a north-south gradient too. To the south were Missouri and Kansas, whence this branch of the Forthrasts (according to his research) had come around the time of the Civil War to get away from the terrorists and the death squads. To the north—hard to miss on a day like today—you could almost see the shoulder of the world turning inward toward the Pole. Those north-seeking Forthrasts must have thought better of it when they had ascended to this latitude and felt the cold air groping down the necks of their coats and frisking them, and so here they'd stopped and put down roots, not in the way that the old black walnut trees along the crick had roots, but as blackberries and dandelions grow thick when a lucky seed lands and catches on a stretch of unwatched ground.

The Walmart was like a starship that had landed in the soybean fields. Richard drove past the part of it where food was sold, past the pharmacy and the eye care center, and parked at the end where they stocked merchandise. The parking spaces were platted for full-sized pickup trucks, a detail useful to him now.

They went inside. The young ones shuffled to a stop as their ironic sensibilities, which served them in lieu of souls, were jammed by a signal of overwhelming power. Richard kept moving, since he was the one with a mission. He'd seen a way to contribute to the re-u without stepping in, or turning an ankle on, any of the cow pies strewn so intricately across his path.

He kept walking until everything in his field of vision was camouflage or fluorescent orange, then looked around for the ammunition counter. An elderly man came out wearing a blue vest and rested his wrinkly hands on the glass like an Old West barkeeper. Richard nodded at the man's pro forma greeting and then announced that he wanted three large boxes of the 5.56-millimeter NATO cartridges. The man nodded and turned around to unlock the glass case where the good stuff was stockpiled. On the back of his vest was a large yellow smiley face that was thrust out and made almost hemispherical by his widower's hump.

"Len was handing it out three rounds at a time," he explained to the others, as they caught up with him. "Everyone wants to fire his carbine, but no one buys ammo—and 5.56 is kind of expensive these days because all the nut jobs are convinced it's going to be banned."

The clerk set the heavy boxes carefully on the glass counter, drew a pistol-shaped barcode scanner from its plastic holster, and zapped each of the three boxes in turn: three pulls of the trigger, three direct hits. He quoted an impressively high figure. Richard already had his wallet out. When he opened it up, the niece or second cousin (he still hadn't contrived a way to get her name) glanced into the valley of nice leather so indiscreetly that he was tempted to just hand the whole thing over to her. She was astonished to see the face of Queen Elizabeth and colorful pictures of hockey players and doughboys. He hadn't thought to change money, and now he was in a place with no bureaux de change. He paid with a debit card.

"When did you move to Canada?" asked the young woman.

"1972," he answered.

The old man gave him a look over his bifocals: *Draft dodger!*

None of the younger people made the connection. He wondered

if they even knew that the country had once had a draft, and that people had been at pains to avoid it.

"Just need your PIN number, Mr. Forrest," said the clerk.

Richard, like many who'd moved away, pronounced his name forTHRAST, but he answered to FORthrast, which was how everyone here said it. He even recognized "Forrest," which was what the name would probably erode into pretty soon, if the family didn't up stakes.

By the time they'd made it to the exit, he'd decided that the Walmart was not so much a starship as an interdimensional portal to every other Walmart in the known universe, and that when they walked out the doors past the greeters they might find themselves in Pocatello or Wichita. But as it turned out they were still in Iowa.

"Why'd you move up there?" asked the girl on the drive back. She was profoundly affected by the nasal, singsongy speech pathology that was so common to girls in her cohort and that Zula had made great strides toward getting rid of.

Richard checked the rearview mirror and saw Peter and Zula exchanging a significant glance.

Girl, haven't you heard of Wikipedia!?

Instead of telling her why he'd moved, he told her what he'd done when he'd gotten there: "I worked as a guide."

"Like a hunting guide?"

"No, I'm not a hunter."

"I was wondering why you knew so much about guns."

"Because I grew up here," he explained. "And in Canada some of us carried them on the job. It's harder to own guns there. You have to take special courses, belong to a gun club and so on."

"Why'd you carry them on the job . . ."

" . . . if I wasn't a hunting guide?"

"Yeah."

"Grizzlies."

"Oh, like in case one of them attacked you?"

"That's correct."

"You could, like, shoot in the air and scare it off?"

"In the heart and kill it."

"Did that ever happen?"

Richard checked the rearview again, hoping to make eye contact and send the telepathic message *For God's sake, will someone back there rescue me from this conversation,* but Peter and Zula merely looked interested.

"Yes," Richard said. He was tempted to lie. But this was the re-u. It would out.

"The bear rug in Grandpa's den," Zula explained from the back.

"That's real!?" asked the girl.

"Of course it's real, Vicki! What did you think it was, polyester!?"

"You killed that bear, Uncle Dick?"

"I fired two slugs into its body while my client was rediscovering long-forgotten tree-climbing skills. Not long after, its heart stopped beating."

"And then you skinned it?"

No, it politely climbed out of its own pelt before giving up the ghost. Richard was finding it more and more difficult to resist firing off snappy rejoinders. Only the Furious Muses were holding him at bay.

"I carried it on my back across the United States border," Richard heard himself explaining. "With the skull and everything, it weighed about half as much as I did at that age."

"Why'd you do that?"

"Because it was illegal. Not shooting the bear. That's okay, if it's self-defense. But then you're supposed to turn it over to the authorities."

"Why?"

"Because," said Peter, figuring it out, "otherwise, people would just go out and kill bears. They would claim it was self-defense and keep the trophies."

"How far was it?"

"Two hundred miles."

"You must have wanted it pretty bad!"

"I didn't."

"Why did you carry it on your back two hundred miles then?"

"Because the client wanted it."

"I'm confused!" Vicki complained, as if her emotional state were really the important thing here. "You did that just for the client?"

"It's the opposite of that!" Zula said, slightly indignant.

Peter said, "Wait a sec. The bear attacked you and your client—"

"I'll tell the story!" Richard announced, holding up a hand. He didn't want it told, wished it hadn't come up in the first place. But it was the only story he had about himself that he could tell in decent company, and if it were going to be told, he wanted to do it himself. "The client's dog started it. Hassled the poor bear. The bear picked the dog up in its jaws and started shaking it like a squirrel."

"Was it like a poodle or something?" Vicki asked.

"It was an eighty-pound golden lab," Richard said.

"Ohmygod!"

"That is kind of what I was saying. When the lab stopped struggling, which didn't take long, the bear tossed it into the bushes and advanced on us like *If you had anything whatsoever to do with that fucking dog, you're dead*. That's when the shooting happened."

Peter snorted at this choice of phrase.

"There was no bravery involved, if that's what you're thinking. There was only one climbable tree. The client was not setting any speed records getting up it. We couldn't both climb it at the same time, is all I'm saying. And not even a horse can outrun a grizzly. I was just standing there with a slug gun. What was I going to do?"

Silence, as they considered the rhetorical question.

"Slug gun?" Zula asked, dropping into engineer mode.

"A twelve-gauge shotgun loaded with slugs rather than shells. Optimized for this one purpose. Two barrels, side by side: an Elmer Fudd special. So I went down on one knee because I was shaking so badly and emptied it into the bear. The bear ran away and died a few hundred yards from our camp. We went and found the carcass. The client wanted the skin. I told him it was illegal. He offered me money to do this thing for him. So I started skinning it. This took *days*. A *horrible* job. Butchering even domesticated, farm-bred animals is pretty unspeakable, which is why we bring Mexicans to Iowa to do it," said Richard, warming to the task, "but a bear is worse. It's gamy." This word had no punch at all. It was one of those words that everyone had heard but no one knew really what it meant. "It has almost a fishy smell to it. It's like you're being just steeped in the thing's hormones."

Vicki shuddered. He considered getting into detail about the physical dimensions of a grizzly bear's testicles, but, judging from her body language, he'd already driven the point home firmly enough.

Actually, he had been tempted to rush the job of skinning the grizzly. But the problem was that he started with the claws. And he remembered from his boyhood reading about the Lakota braves taking the claws off after they'd killed the bear as a rite of manhood, making them into a necklace. Boys of his vintage took that stuff seriously; he knew as much about Crazy Horse as a man of an earlier generation might have known about Caesar. So he felt compelled to go about the job in a sacred way. Having begun it thus, he could not find the right moment to switch into rough butchery mode.

"The more time I spent—the deeper I got into it—the more I didn't want the client to have it," Richard continued. "He wanted it so badly. I was down there covered in gore, fighting off yellow jackets, and he'd mosey down from camp and size it up, you know. I could see him visualizing it on the floor of his office or his den. Broker from New York. I just knew he would tell lies about it—use it to impress people. Claim he'd bagged it himself while his chickenshit guide climbed a tree. We got to arguing. Stupid of me because I was already deep into the illegality of it. I'd placed myself in a totally vulnerable position. He threatened to turn me in, get me fired, if I didn't give him the trophy. So I said fuck you and just walked away with it. Left him with the keys to the truck so he could get home."

Silence.

"I didn't even really want it that badly," Richard insisted. "I just couldn't let him take it home and tell lies about it."

"Did he get you fired?"

"Yes. Got me in trouble too. Got my license revoked."

"What'd you do after you lost your job?"

Put my newfound skills to work carrying backloads of marijuana across the border.

"This and that."

"Mmm. Well, I hope it was worth it."

Oh Christ, yes.

They reached the farm. The driveway was full of SUVs, so Richard, pulling rank as one who had grown up on this property, parked the Grand Marquis on the dead grass of the side yard.

THE VEHICLE RODE so low that getting out of it was like climbing out of one's own grave. As they did so, Richard caught Peter scanning the place, trying to identify where the fatal clothesline had stood.

Richard thought about becoming Peter's Virgil, giving the poor kid a break by flatly explaining all the stuff he'd eventually have to piece together on his own, if he and Zula stayed together. He did not actually do it, but the words he'd speak had been loosed in his mind. If there was such a thing as a mind's eye, then his mind's mouth had started talking.

He cast his eye over a slight bulge in the ground surrounded by a ring of frostbitten toadstools, like a boil striving to erupt through the lawn from some underlying Grimm brothers stratum. *That's what's left of the oak tree. The clothesline ran from it to the side of the house—just there, beside the chimney, you can see the bracket. Mom was upstairs dying. The nature of what ailed her created a need for frequent changes of bed linens. I offered to drive into town and buy more sheets at J.C. Penney—this was pre-Walmart. Patricia was affronted. As if this were me accusing her of being a bad daughter. A load of sheets was finished, but the dryer was still busy, so she hung them up on the clothesline. It was one of those days when you could tell that a storm was coming. We were up there sitting around Mom's bed in midafternoon singing hymns, and we heard the thunder rolling across the prairie like billiard balls. Pat went downstairs to take the sheets off the line before the rain came. We all heard the bolt that killed her. Sounded like ten sticks of dynamite going off right outside the window. It hit the tree and traveled down the clothesline and right down her arm through her heart to the ground. Power went out, Mom woke up, things were confused for a minute or two. Finally Jake happened to look out the window and saw Pat down in the grass, already with a sheet on her. We never told Mom that her daughter was dead. Would have made for some awkward explaining. She lost consciousness later that day and died three days after that. We buried them together.*

Just rehearsing it in his mind left Richard shaking his head in amazement. It was hard to believe, even here, where the weather killed people all the time. People couldn't hear the story told without making some remark or even laughing in spite of themselves. Richard had thought, for a while, of founding an Internet support group for siblings of people killed by lightning. The whole story was like something from a literary novel out of Iowa City, had the family produced a writer, or the tale come to the notice of some wandering Hawkeye bard. But as it was, the story was Zula's property, and he would give Zula the choice of when and whether and how to tell it.

She, thank God, had been away at Girl Scout camp, and so they'd been able to bring her home and tell her, under controlled conditions, with child psychologists in the room, that she'd been orphaned for the second time at eleven.

A few months later Bob, Patricia's ex-husband, had popped his head up out of whatever hole he lived in and made a weak bid to interfere with John and Alice's adoption of Zula. Then, just as suddenly, he had dropped out of the picture.

Zula had passed through teenagerhood in this house, as a ward of John and Alice, and had come out strangely fine. Richard had read in an article somewhere that even kids who came from really fucked-up backgrounds actually turned out pretty good if some older person took them under their wing at just the right point in their early adolescence, and he reckoned that Zula must have squirted through this loophole. In the four years between the adoption and the lightning strike, something had passed from Patricia to Zula, something that had made all the rest of it okay.

Richard had failed to mate and Jake, the kid brother, had become what he'd become: a process that had started not long after he'd looked down out of that window to see his dead sister wound up in a smoldering sheet. These accidents of death and demographics had left Alice not only as the matriarch but as the only adult female Forthrast. She and John had four children, but precisely because they'd done such an excellent job raising them, these had all moved away to do important things in big cities (it being the permanent, ongoing tragedy of Iowa that her well-brought-up young were obliged to flee the state in order to find employment worthy of their qualities). This, combined with her perception of a Richard-Jake axis of irresponsible malehood, had created a semipermanent feeling of male-female grievance, a kind of slow-motion trench warfare. Alice was the field marshal of one side. Her strategy was to work the outer reaches of the family tree. John helped, wittingly or not, with things like the firearms practice, which made coming here less unattractive to distantly related males. But the real work of the re-u, as Richard had only belatedly come to understand, took place in the kitchen and had nothing to do with food preparation.

Which didn't mean that the men couldn't get a few things done of their own.

Richard made a detour over to Len's Subaru and left the boxes of cartridges on the driver's seat. Then into the farmhouse by its rarely used front door, which led him into the rarely used parlor, crowded today. But more than half of the shooters had gone back to the motel to rest and clean up, so he was able to move around. A cousin offered to take his ski parka and hang it up. Richard politely declined, then patted the breast pocket to verify that the packets were still there, the zipper still secured.

Five young cousins ("cousins" being the generic term for anyone under about forty) were draped over sofas and recliners, prodding their laptops, downloading and swapping pictures. Torrents of glowing, crystalline photos rushed across their screens, making a funny and sad contrast with the dozen or so family photographs, developed and printed through the medieval complexities of chemical photography, laboriously framed, and hung on the walls of the room.

The word "Jake" caught his ear, and he turned to see some older cousins looking at a framed photo of Jake and his brood, about a year out of date. The photo was disorientingly normal-looking, as if Jake could comfortably flout every other convention of modern American life but would never dream of failing to have such a picture taken of him and Elizabeth and the three boys. Shot, perhaps, by some other member of their rustic church who had a knack for such things, and framed in a birchbark contraption that one of the boys had made himself. They looked pretty normal, and signs of the true Jake were only detectable in some of the minutiae such as his Confederate infantryman's beard.

A woman asked why Jake and his family never came to the re-u.

Richard had learned the hard way that when the topic of Jake came up, he needed to get out in front of it fast and do everything he could to portray his kid brother as a reasonable guy, or else someone else would denounce him as a nut job and it would lead to awkwardness. "Since 9/11, Jake doesn't believe in flying because you have to show ID," Richard said. "He thinks it's unconstitutional."

"Does he ever drive back here?" asked a male in-law, cautiously interested, verging on amused.

"He doesn't believe in having a driver's license either."

"But he has to drive, right?" asked the woman who'd started it. "Someone told me he was a carpenter."

"In the part of Idaho where he's moving around, he can get away without having a driver's license," Richard said. "He has an understanding with the sheriff that doesn't translate so well to other parts of the country."

He didn't even bother telling people about Jake's refusal to put license plates on his truck.

Richard made a quick raid on the outskirts of the kitchen, grabbing a couple of cookies and giving the women something to talk about. Then he headed for what had, in his boyhood, been the back porch and what had latterly been converted into a ground-level nursing-facility-slash-man-cave for his father.

Dad, legal name Nicholas Forthrast, known to the re-u as Grandpa, currently aged ninety-nine, was enthroned on a recliner in a room whose most conspicuous feature, to most of those who walked into it, was the bearskin rug. Richard could practically smell the aforementioned hormones boiling off it. During the porch conversion project of 2002, that rug was the first thing that Alice had moved out here. As symbol of ancient Forthrast manly virtues, it competed with Dad's Congressional Medal of Honor, framed and hung on the wall not far from the recliner. An oxygen tank of impressive size stood in the corner, competing for floor space and electrical outlets with a dialysis machine. A very old console television, mounted in a walnut cabinet, served as inert plinth for a fifty-four-inch plasma display now showing a professional football game with the sound turned down. Flying copilot in a somewhat less prepossessing recliner to Dad's right hand was John, six years older than Richard, and the family's acting patriarch. Some cousins were sitting cross-legged on the bearskin or the underlying carpet, rapt on the game. One of the Cardenas sisters (he thought it was most likely Rosie) was bustling around behind the recliners, jotting down numbers on a clipboard, folding linens—showing clear signs, in other words, that she was about to hand Dad off to John so that she could head off to her own family's Thanksgiving observances.

Since Dad had acquired all these accessory parts—the external kidney, the external lung—he had become a rather complicated piece of machinery, like a high-end TIG welder, that could not be operated by just anyone. John, who had come back from Vietnam with bilateral below-the-knee amputations, was more than comfortable with prosthetic technology; he had read all the manuals and understood the functions of most of the knobs, so he could take over responsibility for the machines at times like this. If Richard were left alone with him in the house, however, Dad would be dead in twelve hours. Richard had to contribute in ways less easily described. He loitered with hands in pockets, pretending to watch the football game, until Rosie made a positive move for the exit. He followed her out the door a moment later and caught up with her on the wheelchair ramp that led down to Dad's Dr. Seuss–like wheelchair-lift-equipped van. "I'll walk you to your car," he announced, and she grinned sweetly at his euphemistic ways. "Turkey this afternoon?" he asked.

"Turkey and football," she said. "Our kind of football."

"How's Carmelita?"

"Well, thank you. Her son—tall! Basketball player."

"No football?"

She smiled. "A little. He head the ball very well." She pulled her key chain out of her purse, and Richard got a quick whiff of all the fragrant things she kept in there. He lunged out ahead of her and opened the driver's-side door of her Subaru. "Thank you."

"Thank *you* very much, Rosie," he said, unzipping the breast pocket of his parka. As she was settling into the driver's seat, smoothing her skirt under her bottom, he pulled out a manila envelope containing a half-inch-thick stack of hundred-dollar bills and slipped it into the little compartment in the side of the door. Then he closed the door gently. She rolled the window down. "That is the same as last year, plus ten percent," he explained. "Is it still suitable? Still good for you and Carmelita?"

"It is fine, thank you very much!" she said.

"Thank *you*," he insisted. "You are a blessing to our family, and we value you very much. You have my number if there is ever a problem."

"Happy Thanksgiving."

"Same to you and all the Cardenases."

She waved, put the Subaru in gear, and pulled away.

Richard patted his jacket again, checking the other packet. He would find some way to slip it to John later; it would pay for a lot of oxygen.

The handoff had undoubtedly been awkward and weird. Much less stressful, for a man of his temperament, was to FedEx the C-notes, as was his practice in years when he did not attend the re-u. But, as he ascended the wheelchair ramp, the Furious Muses remained silent and so he reckoned he had not handled it too badly.

The gravamen of the F.M.s' complaints was Richard's failure to be "emotionally available." The phrase had left him dumb with disbelief the first time a woman had gone upside his head with it. He guessed that many of his emotions were not really fit to be shared with *anyone,* much less someone, such as a girlfriend, he was supposed to be *nice* to, and associated "emotional availability" with unguarded moments such as the one that had led to his getting the nickname Dodge. But several of his ex-girlfriends-to-be had insisted that they wanted it, and, in a Greek mythic sort of revenge, they had continued to be emotionally available to him long past their dates of expiration. And yet he reckoned he'd actually been emotionally available to Rosie Cardenas. Maybe even to the point of making her uncomfortable.

Back to the ex-porch. The place had become more crowded as the football game approached the end of the fourth quarter, and the sound had been turned back on. Richard sidled through the crowd and found a place where he could lean against the wall, which was more difficult than it used to be, since people kept hanging new stuff on it. John, apparently, had been spending enough time here that he'd taken the liberty of decorating it with some of his own Vietnam memorabilia.

In the middle of a big empty space, though, a World War II vintage M1 Garand rifle was mounted on a display bracket with a brass plaque. John knew better than to crowd this shrine with his 'Nam souvenirs.

As a boy, Richard had assumed that this rifle was The One, but later Bud Torgeson—the longest lived of Dad's comrades-in-arms—had chuckled at the very idea. Bud had patiently explained that holding an empty M1 rifle by its barrel and swinging it like a club hard enough to stave in excellent Krupp steel helmets was way out of spec for that particular equipment and generally led to its being rendered unusable. After The One had been duly inspected by whoever was in charge of handing out medals, it had been scrapped. This

M1 on the wall, along with the plaque, had been purchased surplus, cleaned up, and given to Dad by the enlisted men who had served under him and, according to the story, been saved from death or a long stint in a prison camp by said crazy spasm of Berserker-style head bashing.

Without being unduly bitter about it, Richard had always wondered why the offspring of Nicholas who had settled down and lived exemplary, stable, churchgoing lives in the upper Midwest were viewed as carrying on the man's heritage and living according to his example, given that the single most celebrated episode in the man's life had been beating a bunch of storm troopers to death with an improvised bludgeon.

IN THE AFTERMATH of Patricia's death, when long-absent Bob, or a lawyer representing him, had sent them a letter containing the startling news that he'd be seeking custody of Zula, the family had held a little conference. Richard had attended via speakerphone from British Columbia. Speakerphones normally sucked, but the technology had served him well in that case, since it had enabled him to roll his eyes, bury his head in his hands, and, when it got really bad, hit the Mute button and stomp around the room cussing. John and Alice and their lawyers were being perfectly rational, of course, but to him they'd seemed like a town council of hobbits drafting a resolution to demand an apology from the Ringwraiths. Richard, at the time, was in regular contact with motorcycling enthusiasts who had a branch in Southern California, euphemistically describable as "active." Through their good offices, he got a line on some private investigators, unconventional in grooming and in methods. These then made it their business to learn more about Bob's private life. When the Bob dossier had reached a pleasing thickness—heavy enough to make a flinch-inducing thump when casually tossed onto a table—Richard had climbed into his crappy old diesel Land Cruiser and driven straight through from Elphinstone to L.A. There he had checked in to a hotel, taken a shower, and put on exactly the sort of bulky leather jacket he would use to conceal a shoulder holster, had he owned one. He had dropped off the Land Cruiser for an oil change and taken a taxi to a specialty auto rental place that had been recommended to him by an actor Richard had met in the tavern at the Schloss when the actor and his entourage had been up in Elphinstone for a movie shoot. There he had rented a Humvee. Not a Hummer, that being the pissant pseudo-Humvee then (it was 1995) available in the civilian market, but an actual military-grade Humvee, seven feet wide and, once you figured in the weight of the subwoofers, three tons heavy. Blasting Rage Against the Machine's "Know Your Enemy" from its formidable aftermarket stereo, he had showed up half an hour late for the showdown at the Denny's and parked in the handicapped space. He had known, from the moment he'd spotted Bob's slumped profile through the window of the restaurant, that he had already won.

It was a disgrace. A bundle of the cheapest tricks imaginable. That, in and of itself, would have convinced a better man that Richard was only bluffing.

Richard's future ex-girlfriend of the moment had spent several years with her nose pressed up against the glass of Hinduism, and he had been subjected to much talk of avatars, maia, and so on. By showing up in this avatar, Richard was manifesting himself in exactly the way that Bob had always imagined him. And to the extent that Bob was now a declared enemy of the family, Richard was in that way becoming Bob's worst nightmare made flesh.

The gambit had worked. But Richard had not been comfortable in that avatar, to the point of wondering where the hell it had come from. What had come over him? Only later, after talking to Bud and meditating on the story behind the Medal of Honor, had he understood that he had been manifesting, not as an avatar of Richard, but as an avatar of his whole family.

THE FOOTBALL GAME did not exactly end but, like most of them, reached a point where it was simply unwatchable. Almost everyone left. Richard pulled up a chair and sat at his father's left hand. It was just the three of them then: John, Nicholas, and Richard. Patricia was fourteen years dead. Jacob had been born much later than the others, when Mom had been at damn-near-menopausal age, and everyone understood that he had been an unplanned pregnancy. He was neither dead nor here, but in Idaho, a state often confused, by bicoastal folks, with Iowa, but that in fact was the anti-Iowa in many respects, a place that Iowans would only go to in order to make some kind of statement.

Richard had practically no idea as to his father's true state of consciousness. Since the last storm of ministrokes, he'd had little to say. But his eyes tracked things pretty carefully. His facial expressions and his gestures suggested that he knew what was going on. He was pretty happy right now sitting there between his two oldest sons. Richard settled back in his chair, crossed his ankles atop the bearskin, and settled in for a long sit. Someone brought him a beer. Dad smiled. Life was good.

RICHARD AWOKE AND made efforts to silence his phone, only to find that the local climate had sucked all moisture out of his fingertips, which could not obtain virtual purchase on the tiny affordances of its user interface. Through some combination of licking and breathing on his fingers he was able to get them damp enough that the machine now grudgingly recognized them as human flesh, responded to his commands, and became silent.

He groped for his reading glasses and tapped the Calendar button. A green slab rushed out of the darkness and made his white chest hairs glow in viridian thickets. His eyes came into focus and read its label: ROAD TRIP: SKELETOR.

Zooming out to a longer time scale, he saw good color omens: no red at all for the next fortnight, and four solid days of green—the color of business—coming up.

Blue was the color of family and other personal activities. Yesterday, for example, had been a sixteen-hour blue tombstone labeled RE-U.

Following ROAD TRIP: SKELETOR were other enormous green slabs labeled → IOM, which, as Richard knew only too well, was the airport code for the Isle of Man. Then PAY FEALTY D2 and finally → SEA.

Red was for things like medical appointments and doing his taxes. A week that was even lightly spattered with Red was pretty much a write-off when it came to getting anything accomplished. Blue wasn't as bad as Red, but it did tend to infiltrate neighboring regions of Green and mulch them. Rare indeed were the moments

when Blue time could be converted to Green; for example, yesterday when he had realized that Zula ought to be working for Corporation 9592.

Waking up in Green mode, then spending the whole day there,
was really the only way to get anything done. So color physics now
dictated that he must steal out of the hotel without having any interactions whatsoever with the re-u crowd that would already have
filled the Ramada's breakfast room and spilled over into the lobby.

He checked out over the phone and stood in perfect silence, eyeball to peephole, until he could no longer see miniature Forthrasts
in bathing suits, going to or from the pool. He then stole out of the
motel through a side exit and gunned the Grand Marquis to a gas
station half a mile down the road, just to get decisively clear. He
pumped a bathtub-load of gasoline into the thing and bought a cup
of coffee and a banana for the road. He fired up the car's onboard
GPS device and began coping with its user interface.

The Possum Walk Trailer Court was no longer listed in its
"Points of Interest" database, so he had to settle for browsing the
greater Nodaway region of northwestern Missouri. Expecting to
see nothing more than a post office and maybe a county park, he
was dismayed and fascinated when it hurled up a low-res icon of
a pointy-eared humanoid with long blue braids, labeled KSHETRIAE
KINGDOM. Further browsing informed him that it was part of a larger
K'Shetriae-themed complex that included an amusement park and a
retail outlet. He could not bring himself to choose this as his destination and coyly allowed the machine to vector him to the county
seat.

On his way out of town, deeply preoccupied with the fact that
the ersatz quasi-Elven race known as the K'Shetriae were now
embedded (though sans the controversial apostrophe) in the memory
chips of real-world GPS systems, he almost plowed into the back of
what passed for a traffic jam around here: Black Friday shoppers trying to force-feed their vehicles into the parking lot, and their bodies through the doorway, of Walmart. In olden days he would have
pumped the brakes judiciously, bringing the enormous vehicle to a
stop, but nowadays he knew that this could be outsourced to anti-
lock brakes, so he just crushed the pedal to the floor and waited.
The pedal thrummed beneath his foot. The white plastic teat of his

go cup discharged a globule of coffee and his banana boomeranged into the glove compartment lid. He watched dispassionately as the tailgate of a pickup truck grew huge in his windshield, not unlike a calendar item zooming onto the screen of his phone. No collision occurred. The driver gave him the finger. A light changed and traffic seeped forward. Soon enough, he was on the interstate, southbound. That rapidly grew boring, so he switched to two-lane roads, to the mounting chagrin of his GPS.

In spite of his cloak-and-dagger exit from the Ramada, his brain was jammed with family stuff. He had woken up in the wrong color! He had to get all traces of Blue out of his mind and achieve full Greenness before he got anywhere near the Iowa/Missouri line.

For this was not just a friendly meeting. Nuances in today's conversation, things left unsaid, or said in the wrong way, could have expensive consequences. The day after Thanksgiving might have been time off for most of the country, but not for Skeletor. The parochial turkey-eating customs of the United States were of no interest at all to the hyperinternational clientele that he and Richard shared. And even their American players, though they might have taken a few hours off yesterday for family observances, would be devoting most of today to questing for virtual gold and vicarious glory in the world of T'Rain, making this one of the heaviest days of the year for Corporation 9592's servers and the system administrators who kept them running.

But his mind kept drifting into the Blue. It was like a puzzle in a video game: he had to figure out what was *really* bothering him. It wasn't the Furious Muses; after a brief howl of outrage when he'd almost rear-ended the pickup truck, they had been silent for hours.

Somewhere around Red Oak, he finally put it together: it was yesterday's short but uneasy exchange with the Wikipedia-reading in-law.

The actual content of the Wikipedia entry was not at issue. What bothered Richard was the mere fact that such a thing existed and that he had been abruptly reminded of it at a moment when he just wanted to be Dodge, hanging around the old place, doing normal Iowa stuff.

The entry in question started with a summary of what Richard was now, and it filled in biographical details only when they seemed relevant to whatever mysterious stalker/scholars compiled such documents. He was not important enough, and the entry was insufficiently long, to include a biographical section laying out the whole story in narrative form. Which seemed all wrong to him, since the only way to make sense of what he was now was to tell the story of how he'd gotten that way.

WHEN HE HAD lugged that bearskin down the Selkirk Crest, he had done so without a plan—without even a *motive*—and certainly without a map. The ridges were steep and rocky. The sun shone on them like a torch. No water sprang from them. Attempts to descend into the cool-looking valleys were baffled by the density of the vegetation, called "dog fur" by the few people who actually lived in those parts, apparently because it made the hiker know what it must be like to be a flea navigating a dog's hindquarters. Half out of his mind with hunger and exhaustion, he traversed a long talus slope that ramped down into the remnants of a dead silver mine, then descended through a belt of dog fur and, surprisingly, into a grove of ancient cedar trees. Decades later he would learn the term "microclimate." At the time, he just felt that he had stepped through a wormhole to a damp and chilly rain forest perched above the Pacific. The canopy was so dense as to choke off the energy supply to everything beneath it, so the place was mercifully free of undergrowth, and a brook ran through the middle of it from a spring farther up the slope. Maybe it was just heatstroke and low blood sugar, but he felt something holy. He flung off his pack and sat down in the creek and let its cold water explore his clothes, lay down on his back, gasped at the cold, rolled over on his stomach, drank.

His fantasy that he was the first human ever to set foot in the place was shattered moments later when he noticed, just a few yards from the stream, the foundations of an old one-room cabin. It was currently occupied by the wreckage of its own roof. Rot and carpenter ants had reduced it to a splintery mulch that he raked out with his bare hands, until a cold slicing sensation told him he had just cut his finger on something unnaturally sharp. Investigating more carefully after he'd bandaged the cut, he found a crate of whiskey that had been crushed into shards by the collapse of the roof. He had inadvertently followed an old whiskey-smuggling trail from Prohibition days. This cabin had been used as a cache by bootleggers.

What worked for whiskey ought to work as well for marijuana, and he made a business out of that for a few years, sometimes traveling solo, other times as part of a pedestrian caravan. He showed them the bootleggers' shack, and they used it as their base camp in the United States. Half a mile down the slope was a logging road where they would rendezvous with their U.S. distributors, a sodality of motorcycling enthusiasts.

In 1977, President Carter granted amnesty to draft dodgers, so Richard, finally free to do business in his own country under his own name, crossed the border in an actual vehicle for a change and drove down the valley to Bourne's Ford, the county seat, where the records were kept. He found the owner of the property where the cabin stood, and he bought it for cash.

Though this was exactly the kind of subtlety that the Wikipedian herd mind could be relied on to trample, there was much about his later life that could be traced back to the obsession with land that had come over him when he first walked into that cool grove. In the fullness of time, he came to understand that it probably had something to do with the farm in Iowa and his knowing, even at that age, that whatever Dad's last will and testament said—however things were handled after his father's eventual demise—he wasn't going to be part of it. If he wanted to own land, he'd have to go out and find some. And it might be better and more beautiful land than the farm in Iowa could ever be, but it would never be the same; it would always be a place of exile.

He fancied, for a few years in the late 1970s, that he would one day build a cabin on the bank of Prohibition Crick, as he had dubbed the nameless stream that flowed through his property, and live there. But it was much more comfortable north of the border, lounging on the shores of Kootenay Lake with pockets stuffed with hundred-dollar bills, and he lost his gumption for homesteading in the wilderness.

THE MOUNTAINS IN that corner of B.C. were riddled with abandoned mines. Richard and one of his motorcycle gang buddies, a Canadian named Chet, became fascinated by one such property, where, a hundred years ago, a successful miner from Germany had constructed an Alpine-style Schloss whose foundations and stone walls were still in decent shape. The local economy was in the toilet because of the closure of a big paper mill, and everything was cheap. Chet and Richard bought the Schloss. From the moment that they conceived this idea, Richard came to think of the Idaho property as a mere rough draft, a before-thought.

As the Schloss became a more settled and comfortable place to live, and developed into a legitimate resort run by people who actually knew what they were doing, Richard found himself with a lot of free time, which he filled largely by playing video games. In particular, he became seriously addicted to a game called Warcraft: Orcs & Humans and its various sequels, which eventually culminated in the vastly successful massively multiplayer game World of Warcraft. The years 1996 through 2006 were his Lost Decade, or at least that's what he'd have considered it if it hadn't led to T'Rain. His weight crept up to near-fatal levels until he figured out the trick of playing the game while trudging along—very slowly, at first—on a treadmill.

Like many serious players, Richard fell into the habit of purchasing virtual gold pieces and other desirables from Chinese gold farmers: young men who made a living playing the game and accumulating virtual weapons, armor, potions, and whatnot that could be sold to American and European buyers who had more money than time.

He thought it quite strange and improbable that such an industry could exist until he read an article in which it was estimated that the size of the worldwide virtual gold economy was somewhere between $1 and $10 billion per year.

Anyway, having reached a place where he had no more virtual worlds to conquer—his characters had achieved near-godlike status and could do anything they wanted—he began to think about this as a serious business proposition.

Here was where the Wikipedia entry got it all wrong by laying too much emphasis on money laundering. The Schloss was turning a profit *and* appreciating in value *and* giving him free lodging and food, so it had been years, by this point, since Richard had given much thought to all his unspent hundred-dollar bills. In his younger days, it was true, he had spent enough time worrying about money laundering that he had developed a nose for subterranean money flows, like one of those dowsers who could supposedly find water by walking around with a forked stick. So, yes, the quasi-underground virtual gold economy was inherently fascinating to him. But T'Rain was certainly not about him laundering a few tubs of C-notes.

Video games were a more addictive drug than any chemical, as he had just proven by spending ten years playing them. Now he had come to discover that they were also a sort of currency exchange scheme. These two things—drugs and money—he knew about. The third leg of the tripod, then, was his exilic passion for real estate. In the real world, this would always be limited by the physical constraints of the planet he was stuck on. But in the virtual world, it need be limited only by Moore's law, which kept hurtling into the exponential distance.

Once he had put those three elements together, it had happened fast. Canvassing chat rooms to communicate with English-speaking gold farmers, he confirmed his suspicion that many of them were having trouble expanding their businesses because of a chronic inability to transfer funds back to China. He formed a partnership with "Nolan" Xu, the pathologically entrepreneurial chief of a Chinese game company, who was obsessed with finding a way to put Chinese engineering talent to work creating a new massively multiplayer online game. During an epic series of IM exchanges and Skype calls, Richard managed to convince Nolan that you had to build the plumbing first: you had to get the whole money flow system worked out. Once that was done, everything else would follow. And so, just as a way of learning the ropes, they worked out a system whereby Richard acted as the North American end of a money pipeline, accepting PayPal payments from American and Canadian WoW addicts, then FedExing hundred-dollar bills to Taiwan, where the money was laundered through the underground Filipino overseas worker remittance network and eventually transferred from Taiwanese bank accounts to Nolan's account in China, whence he was able to pay the actual gold farmers in local specie.

This Byzantine arrangement, whose complexities, colorful failure modes, multinational illegalities, and cast of shady characters still, all these years later, caused Richard to wake up bathed in sweat every so often, was only a bridge to a more sane and stable venture: Richard and Nolan cofounded a company whose purpose was to construct the new, wholly original game of Nolan's dreams on top of the system of financial plumbing that Richard now felt he was qualified to build.

When their discussion of the company's name consumed more than the fifteen minutes Richard felt it deserved, he pulled some Dungeons & Dragons dice out of his pocket and rolled them to generate the random number 9592.

The game that Corporation 9592 built had any number of novel features, but in Richard's mind their most fundamental innovation was that they built it from the ground up to be gold-farmer-friendly. Gold farming had been an unwelcome by-product, an epiphenomenon, of earlier games, which had done all that they could to suppress the practice, even to the point of getting the Chinese government to ban such transactions in 2009. But in Richard's opinion, any industry that was clocking between $1 and $10 billion a year deserved more respect. Allowing that tail to wag that dog could only lead to increased revenue and customer loyalty. It was only necessary to structure the game's virtual economy around the certainty that gold farmers would colonize it in vast numbers.

He sensed at a primal, almost olfactory level that the game could only be as successful as the stability of its virtual currency. This led him to investigate the history of money and particularly of gold. Gold, he learned, was considered to be a reliable store of value because extracting it from the ground required a certain amount of effort that tended to remain stable over time. When new, easy-to-mine gold deposits were found, or new mining technologies developed, the value of gold tended to fall.

It didn't take a huge amount of acumen, then, to understand that the value of virtual gold in the game world could be made stable in a directly analogous way: namely, by forcing players to expend a certain amount of time and effort to extract a certain amount of virtual gold (or silver, or diamonds, or various other mythical and magical elements and gems that the Creatives would later add to the game world).

Other online games did this by fiat. Gold pieces were reposited in dungeons guarded by monsters. The more powerful the mon-

ster, the more gold it was squatting on. To get the gold, you had to
kill the monster, and building a character powerful enough to do
so required a certain amount of time and effort. The system func-
tioned okay, but in the end, the decision as to where the gold was
located and how much effort was needed to win it was just an arbitrary choice made by a geek in a cubicle somewhere.

Richard's crazy idea was to eliminate the possibility of such
fudging by having the availability of virtual gold stem from the
same basic geological processes as in the real world. The same, that
is, except that they'd be numerically *simulated* instead of *actually
happening*. Idly messing around on the Internet, he discovered the
mind-alteringly idiosyncratic website of P. T. "Pluto" Olszewski, the
then twenty-two-year-old son of an oil company geologist in Alaska,
homeschooled above the Arctic Circle by his dad and his math
major mom. Pluto, a classic Asperger's syndrome "little professor"
personality now trapped in the rather hirsute body of a full-grown
Alaskan bushwhacker, had spent a lot of time playing video games
and seething with rage at their cavalier treatment of geology and
geography. Their landforms just didn't look like real landforms, at
least not to Pluto, who could sit and stare at a hill for an hour. And
so, basically as a protest action—almost like an act of civil disobe-
dience against the entire video-game industry—Pluto had put up
a website showing off the results of some algorithms that he had
coded up for generating imaginary landforms that were up to his
standards of realism. Which meant that every nuance of the terrain
encoded a 4.5-billion-year simulated history of plate tectonics, atmo-
spheric chemistry, biogenic effects, and erosion. Of course, the average person could not tell them apart from the arbitrary landforms
used as backdrops in video games, so in that sense Pluto's efforts
were all perfectly useless. But Richard didn't care about the skin
of Pluto's world. He cared about its bones and its guts. What mattered very much to Richard was what an imaginary dwarf would
encounter once he hefted a virtual pick and began to delve into the
side of a mountain. In a conventional video game, the answer was
literally nothing. The mountain was just a surface, thinner than
papier-mâché, with no interior. But in Pluto's world, the first bite of
the shovel would reveal underlying soil, and the composition of that
soil would reflect its provenance in the seasonal growth and decay

of vegetation and the saecular erosion of whatever was uphill of it, and once the dwarf dug through the soil he would find bedrock, and the bedrock would be of a particular mineral composition, it would be sedimentary or igneous or metamorphic, and if the dwarf were lucky it might contain usable quantities of gold or silver or iron ore.

Reader, they bought his IP. Pluto moved down to Seattle, where he found lodging in a special living facility for people with autism spectrum disorders. He set to work creating a whole planet. TER-RAIN, the gigantic mess of computer code that he had single-handedly smashed out in his parents' cabin in the Brooks Range, gave its name to T'Rain, the imaginary world where Corporation 9592 set its new game. And in time T'Rain became the name of the game as well.

NEAR RED OAK the highway ran past a shopping center anchored by a Hy-Vee, which was a local grocery store chain. Like a lot of the bigger Hy-Vees, this one had a captive diner just off the main entrance, where local gaffers would go in the mornings to enjoy the $1.99 breakfast special. Richard, seeing himself, for at least the next half hour, as a sort of aspirant gaffer, parked the Grand Marquis in one of the many available spaces and went inside.

He was expecting bright simple colors, which would have been true of the Hy-Vee diners of his youth. But this one had post-Starbucks decor, meaning no primary colors, everything earthtone, restful, minutely textured. Big steaming pickups trundled by the window, enhanced, like Lego toys, with bolt-on equipment. Pallets of giant salt bags were stacked in front of the windows like makeshift for-tifications. At the tables: a solitary general contractor rolling mes-sages on his phone. Truckers, great of beard, wide of suspender, and huge of belly, looking around and BSing. Uniformed grocery store employees taking coffee breaks with spouses. Small-town girls with raccoon eye makeup, not understanding that it simply didn't work on pale blondes. Hunched and vaguely furtive Mexicans. Gaffers showing the inordinate good cheer of those who, ten years ago, had accepted the fact that they could die any day now. A few younger cli-ents, and some gentlemen in bib overalls, fixated on laptops. Rich-ard made himself comfortable in a booth, ordered two eggs over easy with bacon and whole wheat toast, and pulled his own laptop out of his bag.

The opening screen of T'Rain was a frank rip-off of what you saw when you booted up Google Earth. Richard felt no guilt about this, since he had heard that Google Earth, in turn, was based on an idea from some old science-fiction novel. The planet T'Rain hung in space before a backdrop of stars. The stars' positions were randomly generated, a fact that drove Pluto crazy. Anyway, the planet then began to rotate and draw closer as Richard's POV plunged down through the atmosphere, which sported realistic cloud formations. The shapes of continents and islands began to take on three-dimensionality. Dustings of snow appeared at higher elevations. Waves appeared on the surfaces of bodies of water, rivers were seen to move. Roads, citadels, and palaces became visible. Some of these had been presupplied at T'Rain's inception, and therein lay a great number of tales. Others had been constructed by player-characters during the Prelude, a period of speeded-up time that had occupied the first calendar year of T'Rain's existence, and still others were being constructed now, though much more slowly since the game world had slowed down into Real Time Lock. At the moment, Richard's main character was twiddling his thumbs in a half-completed fortress in a system of fortifications that, in this part of T'Rain, was roughly analogous to the Great Wall of China, in the sense that everything north of it was overrun by high-spirited horse archers.

Richard hadn't logged on since late Wednesday evening. During the intervening thirty-six hours, of course, an equal amount of time had gone by in the virtual world of T'Rain, which meant that Richard's character had to have been doing *something* during that day and a half—something quiet, innocuous, and inconsequential, such as sleeping. And indeed, according to the minilog that was now superimposed on Richard's view of the world, the character, whose name was Fudd, had slept for eight hours, spent seventeen hours awake, slept for another eight, and rolled out of bed three hours ago. During Fudd's waking hours he had, without any intervention from Richard, consumed a total of four meals, which accounted for two hours, and had devoted the remainder of his time to "meditation" and "training," which had had the effect of making Fudd slightly more magically powerful and slightly better at kicking ass (not that

Fudd needed a lot of improvement in either department). Every race and class of character in T'Rain had such automatic behaviors. Some, such as sleeping and eating, were shared by all. Others were specific to certain character types. Since Fudd was a sort of warrior magician, his "bothaviors" were meditation and training. If he'd been a miner, his bothavior would have been digging up gold, and whenever Richard logged on to that character he would have observed a slightly larger amount of gold dust in its purse.

Of course, being a warrior mage had way more entertainment value than being a miner. Players selected their character types accordingly. Still, the entire virtual economy would collapse unless miners were digging up the gold and other minerals that Pluto's algorithms had salted around the world, and so miner characters had to exist in very large numbers to make the whole thing work. Here was how Corporation 9592 had squared this with making a game that was actually fun to play:

- Warrior mages and other interesting characters were expensive to maintain. Corporation 9592 charged the owners of such characters more money. Miners, hunter-gatherers, farmers, horse archers, and the like cost virtually nothing; teenagers in China could easily afford to maintain scores or hundreds of such characters.

- Miners, farmers, and the like didn't require a lot of intervention by their owners. A miner character would reliably generate gold with no human intervention at all, provided that its player had the good sense to plonk it down in a part of the world that had actual gold mines and to protect it from raids by bandits, invaders, and so forth.

- If you really did feel like *playing* the miner, as opposed to just letting it act out its natural-born bothaviors for the entire duration of its life span, there was usually stuff you could do. There were rich veins of ore scattered around the world that, once discovered, could be mined far more productively than the run-of-the-mill deposits where the vast majority of miner characters toiled. These veins tended to be in rough border regions that could not be reached and explored without having a lot of fun adventures along the way.

- The social structure was feudal. Any character could have between zero and twelve vassals, and either zero or one lord. A character with no lord and no vassals was called a ronin, but, except among rank newcomers, there were few of these; more typical was to set up a moderately sized network of vassals who spent their lives doing things like mining and farming. A character who had some vassals but no lord was called a Liege Lord and, obviously enough, sat at the top of a hierarchy; most Liege Lords were small-timers running one- or two-layered networks of miners or farmers, but some ran deeper trees comprising thousands of vassals distributed among many layers of the hierarchy, and here was where the intragame politicking really became a significant part of the game, for people who cared and could afford to spend their time that way.

By making such provisions and tweaking them over the first couple of years of T'Rain's existence, Richard and Nolan had managed to pull off the not-so-easy feat of making a massively multiplayer game that was as accessible to the all-important Chinese teenager market as it was to the podgy middle-aged Westerners who were dependent upon those Chinese teenagers for virtual gold. From one point of view, the Westerners got to have more fun, since they could purchase gold pieces and use that virtual cash to fund spectacular building projects and wars that were simply out of reach to the kids in China. But on the other hand, those kids in China were actually making money; playing the game, to them, was a source of income rather than an expense, and most of them were perfectly happy with the arrangement.

All of which fell under the general category of "plumbing"; it was the stuff that Richard had figured out very early in the project, the prerequisite for its being a self-sustaining business at all. He had become so fascinated by the gritty stuff, such as bothaviors of bellows-pumpers, that he had failed to pay enough attention to the features of the world that would be most obvious, and therefore most important, to the actual customers. Pluto's world generation code was mind-blowingly awesome. Richard's currency stabilization plan—once he'd hired a couple of people who knew about tensors—was worked out in better detail than such plans for *real* currencies. And the underlying code written by Nolan's programmers to keep the whole system running was as well engineered as any in the industry. But for all that, they didn't actually have a world. All Richard's miners and horse archers and whatnot were just faceless manikins. T'Rain had no races, no cultures, no art and music, no history. No Heroes.

To provide all that, they needed what were known in the business as Creatives.

It seemed logical enough that their first Creatives ought to be writers, since their work would inform that of the artists and composers and architects who would be hired later. They had hired Professor Donald Cameron, a Cambridge don and writer of very highly regarded fantasy fiction, to lay down a few general markers. But Don Donald, or D-squared as they inevitably referred to him in all internal communications, was under contract, at the time, to deliver Volumes 11 through 13 of his Lay of the Elder King trilogy, and Richard really needed to get a lot written in a hurry.

And so it was that Richard, under a certain amount of temporal duress (launch was less than a year away), had conceived Corporation 9592's Writers in Residence Program.

Years later, he was astounded by the naïveté of it. Writers, as it turned out, rather *liked* having residences. Once they had moved in, it was nearly impossible to dislodge them.

Devin Skraelin was the third writer they approached. Negotiations with the first two had run hard aground on various arcane new-media subclauses for which their lawyers had lacked the necessary mental equipment. Richard was desperate by that point, and, as it turned out, so was Devin. As a fantasy writer, he was not highly regarded ("one cannot call him profoundly mediocre without venturing so far out on the critical limb as to bend it to the ground," "so derivative that the reader loses track of who he's ripping off," "to say he is tin-eared would render a disservice to a blameless citizen of the periodic table of the elements"), but he was so freakishly prolific that he had been forced to spin off three pen names and set each one up at a different publishing house. And prolific was what Richard needed at this point in the game. Early in his career Devin had set up shop in a trailer court in Possum Walk, Missouri, because he had somehow determined (this was pre-Internet) that it was the cheapest place to live in the United States north of the Mason-Dixon Line. He had refused to deal through lawyers (which was fine with Richard, by this point) and refused to travel, so Richard had gone to see him in person, determined not to emerge from the trailer without a signed contract in hand.

Just how dirty and squalid that trailer had been, and just how much Devin had weighed, had been greatly exaggerated since then by Devin's detractors in the T'Rain fan community. It was true that his reluctance to travel had much to do with the fact that he did not fit comfortably into an airline seat, but that was true of a lot of people. It was not true, as far as Richard could tell, that he had grown too obese to fit through the doorway of his trailer. Later, when the money started coming in, Devin moved into an Airstream so that he could be towed around the country with no interruption in his writing schedule—*not* because he was physically unable to leave it. Richard had seen the Airstream. Its doorway was of normal width and its sanitary facilities no larger than those of any other such vehicle, yet Devin had used both of them, if not routinely, then, well . . . when he had to.

It was all kind of irrelevant now. Richard had shared with Devin the trick of working (or at least playing) while walking on a treadmill, and Devin had taken it rather too far. Obesity had not been a problem with him for a long time. On the contrary. The nickname Skeletor was at least four years old. There was a web page where you could track his heart rate, and the number of miles he'd logged that day, in real time. He graciously credited Richard with saving his life by telling him about the treadmill thing, and Richard ungraciously wondered whether that had been such a good idea.

FUDD HAD A dozen vassals, each of whom had another dozen: enough to keep him in beer. His lord was another character owned by Richard, who didn't get played that often. Having no particular responsibilities, Fudd had been hanging out in a corner of this fortification that was designated as a Chapterhouse, which only meant that it was a safe place for characters of Fudd's type to be parked, and to practice their bothaviors, for hours, days, or even weeks at a time while their players were not logged in. In the jargon of the game it was called a home zone or simply HZ, by analogy to children's games of tag. For a miner, the HZ would be an actual mine with its associated canteen and sleeping quarters, for a peasant it would be a farm, and so forth. Warrior-mage knights like Fudd had fancier and more expensive HZs in the form of Chapterhouses, most of which were generic—serving any character of that general type—and a few of which were limited to specific orders, by analogy to the Knights of Malta, Knights Templar, and so on, of Earthen yore. A whole set of conventions and rules had grown up around HZs. They were necessary to maintain the game's verisimilitude. You couldn't have characters just snapping out of existence when their player's Internet connection got broken or their mom insisted that they log out, and so most players tried to get their characters back to an HZ when it was time to stop playing. In cases of force majeure (e.g., backhoes, or Mom slamming the laptop shut on the player's fingers), the character would slip into an artificial intelligence (AI) mode and attempt to automatically transport itself back to an HZ. Trotting along like zombies, these were easy pickings for bandits and foemen. Nolan kept it that way to discourage players from simply logging out when their characters were embroiled.

Anyway, now that Richard was in control, it was safe for Fudd to leave the Chapterhouse, and so, as Richard prodded keys on his keyboard, the white-bearded warrior mage unlimbered himself from his meditative pose and headed for the exit of the HZ. The way out led through the tavern where Fudd had been taking his meals in Richard's absence. The tavernkeeper had mail for him: remittances from his network of vassals, which went into Fudd's purse. From there he exited to a sort of arming and mustering room, a transition zone between the HZ and the outside world. Fudd shrugged off an invitation from a trio of characters who had figured out that Fudd was decently powerful and who wanted him to join them on some kind of raiding party. For many who played these sorts of games, going on raids and quests in the company of one's friends—or, in a pinch, with random strangers—was the whole point. Richard had always been more inclined to solo questing. Rather than explaining matters to them, he simply used a magic spell to render himself invisible. Rude, but effective. Angry "WTF?s" rolled up the chat interface as he slipped out the doorway.

Fudd was not going on a quest anyway. Richard didn't have that kind of time. He just wanted to wander around the world a bit and see what was happening. He'd been doing this a lot recently. Something was changing; there was some kind of phase transition or something under way in the society of the game. Richard didn't know much about phase transitions other than it was what happened when ice melted. Working at Corporation 9592, however, had brought him into contact with a sufficient number of nerds with advanced degrees that he now understood that "phase transition" was an enormously portentive phrase that those guys only threw around when they wanted the other nerds to sit up and take notice. Suddenly something happened; you couldn't exactly make out why. Or maybe—an even more haunting thought—it had happened already and he was too dim-witted, too out of touch, to get it. Which was actually why Fudd existed. Richard had other characters in T'Rain that controlled huge networks of vassals and possessed godlike powers, but for that very reason they never had to participate in the same grunt-level questing and moneymaking on which the majority of customers spent most of their time. Fudd was powerful enough to move around the world without getting jumped and killed every ten minutes, but not so powerful that he didn't have to work at it.

Invisible, Fudd jogged around the courtyard of the fortress, which was home to a bazaar or market comprising a number of separate stalls: an armorer, a swordsmith, a victualler, a moneychanger. He eavesdropped on the latter for a minute to make sure that nothing weird was happening with exchange rates. Nothing ever was. Richard's plumbing was working just fine. Something in Devin's department might be fucked, but Corporation 9592 was still making money.

The characters running the market stalls, and the customers browsing them, broke down into three racial groups: Anthrons, which were just plain old humans; K'Shetriae, which were rebranded elves; and Dwinn (originally D'uinn before the Apostropocalypse had forever altered T'Rain's typography), which were rebranded dwarves. Three additional racial groups existed in the world, but they were not represented here, because those three other groups were associated with Evil, and this was a border fort just on the Good side of the border. K'Shetriae and Dwinn were generally Good. Anthrons could swing either way, though all the ones here (unless they were Evil spies) were Good.

He wasn't seeing anything new here. He invoked a Hover spell. Fudd levitated into the air above the square court of the fortress, gazing down at the two dozen or so characters in the market.

A projectile passed beneath him, arcing down into the court from outside the wall. It landed harmlessly on the ground. Richard zoomed closer and moused over it. The thing was cobalt blue and had an ungainly shape. As he got closer he could see that it was an arrow, its warhead and fletching cartoonishly oversized, its shaft much too thick. They had to be modeled in this style if they were to be visible at all. Video screens, even modern high-resolution ones, could not depict a fast-moving arrow from a hundred feet away in any form that would be detectable to the human eye, and so a lot of the projectiles and other small pieces of bric-a-brac in the game— forks and spoons, gold pieces, rings, knives—were done in this big oafish style, like the foam weapons wielded by nerds in live-action role-playing games.

This arrow, however, was even fatter and stupider-looking than the norm, and when Richard zoomed in on it, he saw why: it had a scroll of yellow paper rolled around its shaft and tied with a red ribbon. The interface identified it as a TATAN MESSAGE ARROW.

He gained altitude and looked out to the north to discover a formation of Tatan horse archers cavorting, daring the fort's garrison to make a sally, firing message arrows in high parabolic arcs. Probably Chinese teenagers, each running a dozen characters at a time; horse archers had bothaviors that made it easy to maneuver them in squadrons. Richard's eye was offended by their color scheme. He did not have to consult Diane—Corporation 9592's color tsarina, and the last of the Furious Muses—to know that he was looking at a case study in palette drift.

The horse archers loosed a final volley of arrows, then turned away; crossbow fire from the parapet of the fortress had already felled several of them. Richard turned his attention back to the courtyard, just to see if any of the characters down there had been struck by a message arrow. None had; but one of them had walked over to investigate an arrow that was lying on the ground. As Richard watched, he picked it up. Richard moused over him. The character's name was Barfuin and he was a K'Shetriae warrior of modest accomplishments. Double-clicking to obtain a more detailed summary of Barfuin, Richard was rewarded with a grid of statistics and a head-and-shoulders portrait. He could not help but be struck by the similarity between Barfuin and the dreadfully low-resolution K'Shetriae icon that had come up on his GPS screen this morning, when he had been attempting to browse the points of interest of greater Nodaway. The most obvious fact was that they both had blue hair. Which was palette drift again. He slammed his laptop shut and pushed it out of the way, because a waitress was approaching with his eggs and bacon.

IF THERE WERE going to be K'Shetriae and Dwinn, and if Skeletor and Don Donald and their acolytes were going to clog the publishing industry's distribution channels with works of fiction detailing their historical exploits going back thousands of years, then it was necessary for those two races to be distinct in what archaeologists would call their material cultures: their clothing, architecture, decorative arts, and so on. Accordingly, Corporation 9592 had hired artists and architects and musicians and costume designers to create those material cultures consistent with the "bible" of T'Rain as laid down by Skeletor and Don Donald. And this had worked fine in the sense that every new character came with that material culture built in—its clothing, its weapons, its HZs were all drawn from those stylebooks. But it was necessary to give players some freedom in styling their characters, because they liked to express themselves and to show some individuality. So there was an interface for that. Your K'Shetriae cloak could be made of fabric in one color, fringed with a second color, and lined with a third. But all three of those colors had to be selected from a palette, and Diane had chosen the palettes. So in the game's early years, it had been easy to distinguish races and character types from a distance just by the colors that they wore.

Then someone had figured out that the palette system was hackable and had posted some third-party software giving players the ability to swap out Diane's official palettes for ones that they made up to suit their own tastes. Corporation 9592 had been slow to react, and so this had become quite popular and widely used before they'd gotten around to having a meeting about it. By that time, something like a quarter of a million characters had been customized using unofficial palettes, and there was no way to repalettize them without deeply pissing off the owners. So Richard had decided that the company would just look the other way.

Which you almost *had* to, so ugly were many of the palettes that people ended up using. It had gotten so bad that it had actually led to a backlash. The trend in the last year or so had been back toward Diane's palettes. But out of this, it seemed that an even more strange and subtle phenomenon was going on, which was that people were using Diane's palettes with only *small* modifications. These almost-but-not-quite Dianan palettes were being posted and swapped on fan sites. Players would download them and then make their own small modifications and then post them somewhere else. Since a color, to a computer, was just a string of three numbers—a 3D point, if you wanted to look at it that way—you could actually draw diagrams showing the migration of palettes through color space. Over the summer, Diane had hired an intern to develop some visualization tools for understanding this phenomenon of palette drift, and then for the last two months Diane had been putting in way too many hours messing around with those tools and sending Richard "most urgent" emails about the trends she'd been observing. Another executive would have reprogrammed his spam filter to direct these messages into interstellar space, but Richard actually didn't mind, since this was a perfect example of the hyperarcane shit that he would use to justify his continued involvement in the company to shareholders, if any of them ever bothered to ask. Yet he was having a hard time putting his finger on why it was important. Diane was convinced that the palettes were not just zinging around chaotically but slowly converging on one another in color space, grouping together in regions that she designated "attractors" (borrowing the term from chaos theory).

Cutting into his egg and watching the neon-yellow yolk spread across his plate, Richard considered it. He looked up and gazed around the Hy-Vee. It was a good place to be reminded of the fact that palettes were everywhere, that people like Diane were gainfully employed in many industries, picking out the color schemes that would best catch the eye of target markets. Panning from the cereal aisle (wholesome warm colors for colon-blow-seeking senior citizens) to the checkout lanes (bright sugar bombs in grabbing range of cart-bound toddlers), he saw a kind of palette drift in action right there. He was too far away to read the labels on the boxes, but he could still draw certain inferences as to which customers were being targeted where.

There was a brief interruption as the gastrocolic reflex had its way with him. As he was coming back from the men's room, Richard glanced over the shoulder of a (judging from attire) farmer in his middle fifties who was sitting alone at a table, ignoring a cold mug of coffee and playing T'Rain. Richard slowed down and rubbernecked long enough to establish that the farmer's character was a Dwinn warrior engaged in some high-altitude combat with Yeti-like creatures known as the T'Kesh. And palette-wise, this customer was playing it pretty straight; some of his accessories were a bit garish, but for the most part all the hues in his ensemble had been picked out by Diane.

He went back to his table and called Corvallis Kawasaki, one of the Seattle-based hackers. Reflecting the natural breakdown of skills between Nolan and Richard, most of Corporation 9592's programming work was done in China, but the Seattle office had departments that ran the business, made life good for Creatives, and took care of what was officially denominated Weird Stuff and the weird people who did it. Pluto was Exhibit A, but there were many other arcane R&D-ish projects being run out of Seattle, and Corvallis had his fingers in several of them.

While dialing Corvallis's number, Richard had been checking the IP address of the Hy-Vee's Wi-Fi router.

"Richard" was how Corvallis answered the phone.

"C-plus. How many players you have coming in from 50.17.186.234?"

Typing. "Four, one of whom appears to be you."

"Hmm, that's more than I thought." Richard looked around the diner and found one of the others: a kid in his early twenties. The fourth was harder to pick out.

"One of them's dropping a lot of packets. Look outside," Corvallis suggested.

Richard looked out the window and saw an SUV parked in the handicapped space, a man sitting in the driver's seat, face lit up by a grotesquely palette-drifted scenario on the screen of his laptop.

"One of them's a Dwinn fighting some T'Kesh."

"Actually, he just got killed."

Richard looked up and verified that the farmer had disgustedly averted his gaze from his screen. The farmer reached for his coffee cup and realized how cold it was. Then he looked up at the clock.

"This guy is a study!" Richard said.

"What do you want to know?"

"General demographics."

"His net worth and income are strangely high, considering that you are in something called a Hy-Vee in Red Oak, Iowa."

"He's a farmer. Owns land and equipment that are worth a lot of money. Takes in huge federal subsidy checks. That's why."

"He has a bachelor's degree."

"Ag engineering, I'll bet."

"He has bought seventeen books in this calendar year." Meaning, as Richard understood, T'Rain-themed books from the online store.

"All by D-squared?"

"You called it. How'd you know?"

"Call up his character."

Typing. "Okay," Corvallis said, "looks like a pretty standard-issue Dwinn to me."

"Exactly my point."

"How so?"

Richard pulled the paper placemat out from under his platter and flipped it over. Pulling a mechanical pencil from his shirt pocket, he drew a vertical line down the middle and then poised the tip of the implement at the head of one of the columns.

"Richard? You still there?"

"I'm thinking."

In truth, he wasn't certain that "thinking" was the right word for what was going on in his head, since that word implied some kind of orderly procedure.

There were certain perceptions that pierced through the fug of day-to-day concerns and the confusions of time like message arrows through the dark, and one of those had just hit him in the forehead: a memory of a scene from a generic fantasy world, not Tolkien but something derivative of Tolkien, the kind of thing that a Devin Skraelin would have created. It had been painted on the side of a van that had picked him up in 1972 when he had been hitchhiking to Canada so that he wouldn't have to get his legs blown off like John. In those days—strange to relate—there'd been a connection between stoners and Tolkien buffs. For the last thirty years it simply hadn't obtained; the ardent Tolkien fans were a disjoint set from the stoners and potheads of the world. But he remembered now that they were once connected to each other and that the van-painting types used the same album-cover palette as these people—some Good, some Evil—groping out to find one another with their cobalt blue message arrows and their acid yellow scrolls.

"New research project," Richard heard himself saying.

"Uh-oh."

"You seen all Diane's shit about attractors in palette space?"

"I'm aware of it," Corvallis said, pivoting into a defensive crouch, "but—"

"That's all that matters," Richard grunted. His hand had begun moving, drawing letters at the top of the left-hand column. He watched in dull fascination as they spelled out: FORCES OF BRIGHTNESS. Then his hand skated over to the right column. That one only took a few moments: EARTHTONE COALITION.

"Forget everything you're supposed to know about T'Rain. The races, the character classes, the history. Especially forget about the whole Good/Evil thing. Instead just look at what *is* in the way of behavior and affiliation. Use attractors in color space as the thin end of your wedge. Hammer on it until something splits open." Richard thought about supplying Corvallis with these two labels but thought that if he wasn't completely full of shit, C-plus would discover the same thing on his own.

"What prompts this?"

"At Bastion Gratlog this morning, horse archers were shooting messages over the walls to people inside."

"Why don't they just use email like everyone else?"

"Exactly. The answer is: they don't actually know each other. They are reaching out. Reaching out to strangers."

"Completely at random?"

"No," Richard said, "I think that there is a selection mechanism and that it's based on . . ." —he was about to say color, but again, he didn't want to tip Corvallis off—"taste."

"Okay," Corvallis said, stalling for time while he thought about it. "So your fifty-five to sixty rich farmer with college degree who reads lots of books by Don Donald . . . he'd be on one side of the taste line."

"Yeah. Who is on the other side?"

"Not hard to guess."

"Bring me hard facts though, once you're done guessing."

"Any particular deadline?"

"My GPS tells me I'm two hours from Nodaway."

"De gustibus non est disputandum."

SCHLOSS HUNDSCHÜTTLER
Elphinstone, British Columbia

Four months later

"Uncle Richard, tell me about the . . ."—Zula faltered, then averted her gaze, set her jaw, and plowed ahead gamely—"the Apostropo . . ."

"The Apostropocalypse," Richard said, mangling it a little, since it was hard to pronounce even when you were sober, and he had been hanging out in the tavern of Schloss Hundschüttler for a good part of the day. Fortunately there was enough ambient noise to obscure his troubles with the word. This was the last tolerable week of skiing season. All the rooms at the Schloss had been reserved and paid for more than a year ago. The only reason that Zula and Peter had been able to come here at all was that Richard was letting them sleep on the fold-out couch in his apartment. The tavern was crowded with people who were, by and large, very pleased with themselves, and making a concomitant amount of noise.

Schloss Hundschüttler was a cat-skiing resort. They had no lifts. Guests were shuttled to the tops of the runs in diesel-powered tractors that ran over the snow on tank treads. Cat skiing had a whole different feel from Aspen-style ski areas with their futuristic hovering techno-infrastructure of lifts.

Though it was less expensive and glamorous than heli-skiing, cat skiing was more satisfactory for truly hard-core skiers. With heli-skiing, all the conditions had to be just right. The trip had to be planned out in advance. With cat skiing, it was possible to be more extemporaneous. The diesel-scented, almost Soviet nature of the experience filtered out the truly hyperrich glamour seekers drawn to the helicopter option, who tended to be a mixture of seriously fantastic skiers and the more-money-than-brains types whose frozen corpses littered the approaches to Mt. Everest.

All of which was water long, long under the bridge for Richard and for Chet, who, fifteen years ago, had had to suss out all these tribal divisions in the ski bum market in order to write a coherent business plan for the Schloss. But it explained much about the style of the lodge, which might have been flashier, more overtly luxurious, had it been aimed at a different segment of the market. Instead, Richard and Chet had consciously patterned its style after small local ski areas of British Columbia that tended to be more rough-and-ready, with lifts and racks welded together by local people who happened to be sports fanatics. It was designed to be less polished, less corporate in its general style than south-of-the-border areas, and as such it didn't appeal to all, or even most, skiers. But by the same token, the ones who came here appreciated it all the more, felt that merely being in the place marked them out as truly elite.

In one corner was a group of half a dozen ridiculously expert skiers—manufacturers' reps for ski companies—very drunk, since they had spent the day up on the high powder runs scattering the ashes of a friend who had ODed on the same drug that had killed Michael Jackson. At another table were some Russians: men in their fifties, still half in ski clothes, and younger women who hadn't been skiing at all. A young film actor, not of the first rank but apparently considered to be really hip at the moment, was taking it easy with three slightly less glamorous friends. At the bar, the usual complement of guides, locals, and cat mechanics had turned their backs on the crowd to watch a hockey game with the sound turned off.

"The Apostropocalypse is to the current realignment in T'Rain what the Treaty of Versailles was to the Second World War," said Richard, deliberately mocking the tone of a Wikipedia contributor in hopes that the others would get it.

Zula showed at least polite attention, but Peter missed it on every level, since he had been spellbound by his phone ever since he had tramped into the place about fifteen minutes earlier, wind- and sunburned and deeply satisfied by a day's snowboarding. Zula, like Richard, was no skier and had ended up turning this trip into a working vacation, spending several hours each day in the apart- ment, jacked in to Corporation 9592's servers over the dedicated fiber connection that Richard had, at preposterous expense, brought up the valley to the Schloss. Peter, on the other hand, turned out to be a very hard-core snowboarder indeed, who, according to Zula, had spent a lot of time since the re-u shopping for special high-end snowboards optimized for deep powder; he had finally purchased one from a boutique in Vancouver just a few weeks ago. He now treated it like a Stradivarius, all but tucking it into bed each night, and Zula was not above showing a trace of jealousy.

Peter and Zula were making a long weekend of it. They'd left Seattle after Zula had got off work and had fought traffic up to Sno- qualmie Pass, where most of the skiers peeled off to ride the con- ventional lifts. Feeling more elite by the minute, they had blasted across the state to Spokane and then headed north toward Metaline Falls, a tiny border station up on a mountain pass that just happened to coincide with the forty-ninth parallel. Crossing about an hour before midnight, they drove through the pass to Elphinstone, and then turned south along the poorly marked, bumpy, meandering mountain track that inclined to the Schloss. This plan actually did not sound insane to them, and thus reminded Richard once more of his advanced age. During the hours they'd been on the road, he'd found himself unable to stray from his computer, calculating which dangerous road they were driving down at a particular time, as if Zula were a part of his body that had gone off on its own and that needed to be kept track of. This, he supposed, was what it was like to be a parent. And as ridiculous as it was, he found himself haunted by thoughts of the re-u. For if Zula and Peter did have a crash on the way over, then later, when the story was told and retold at the re-u, laid like a brick into the family lore, it would be largely about Richard, when he'd learned of it, what actions he'd taken, the cool head he'd displayed, the correct decisions he'd made to manage it all, Zula's relief when he had showed up at the hospital. The moral was preordained: the family took care of itself, even, no, especially in times of crisis, and consisted of good, wise, competent people. He might have to steer to the required denouement on slick and turning ways, through a whiteout. Just when he had been getting ready to pull ski pants over his pajamas and go out looking for them, they had arrived, precisely on their announced schedule, in Peter's annoyingly hip, boxy vehicle, and then Richard had stopped seeing them as crazy wayward kids and thought them superhuman with their GPS telephones and Google Maps.

Now they were getting ready to do it again. Not wanting to waste a single hour of snowboarding, Peter had spent Monday afternoon on the slopes and intended to drive them back to Seattle tonight.

When Peter had first come in and sat down next to Zula, Richard had forgiven his close attention to the phone on the assumption that he was checking the weather and the road conditions. But then he started typing messages.

He seemed like a barnacle on Zula. Richard kept telling himself that she wasn't a stupid girl and that Peter must have redeeming qualities that, because of his social ineptness, were not obvious.

Zula was looking at Richard through the big clunky eyeglasses, hoping for something a little more informative than the Treaty of Versailles joke. Richard grinned and leaned back into the embrace of his massive leather-padded chair. The tavern was a good place for telling stories and, in particular, for telling stories about T'Rain. Richard had been so impressed by a Dwinn mead hall drawn up by one of T'Rain's retro-medieval-fantasy architects that he had, as a side job, hired the same guy to make a real version of it at the Schloss. This was a young architect who had never had an actual job building a physical structure. Coming out of school into a market smashed flat by the real estate crash, he'd been unable to find work in the physical universe and had gone straight into the Creative department of Corporation 9592, where he'd had to forget everything he knew about Koolhaas and Gehry and instead plunge himself into the minutiae of medieval post-and-beam architecture as it might have been practiced by a fictitious dwarflike race. Actually building such a thing at the Schloss had made him very happy, but the stress of dealing with real-world contractors, budgets, and permits had convinced him that he'd made the right move after all by confining his practice to imaginary places.

"I see vestiges of it when I go through Pluto's old code," Zula said. "The D'uinn." She spelled it out.

"So the chronology is that we brought Don Donald in as our first Creative, but he didn't have a lot of time to work on the project."

"More high-level discussions is what I heard," Zula put in.

"Yeah. I had to cram for these discussions by reading my Joseph Campbell, my Jung."

"Why Jung?"

"Archetypes. We were having this big discussion about the races of T'Rain. There were reasons not to just use elves and dwarves like everyone else."

"You mean, like—creative reasons or intellectual property reasons?"

"More the latter, but also from the creative standpoint there's something to be said for making a clean sweep. Just creating an entirely new, original palette of races without any ties to Tolkien or to European mythology."

"All those Chinese programmers . . ." Zula began.

"You'd be surprised, actually. The politically correct, campus radical take on it would be just what you'd think—"

"Elves and dwarves, c'mon, how could you be so Eurocentric?" Zula said.

"Exactly, but in a way it's almost *more* patronizing to the Chinese to assume that, just because they are from China, they can't relate to elves and dwarves."

"Got it."

"Turned out, though, that when we got Don Donald in here, he had good reasons why elves and dwarves were not just arbitrary races that could be swapped out for ones we made up but actual archetypes, going back . . ."

"How far?"

"He thinks that the elf/dwarf split was born in the era when Cro-Magnons coexisted in Europe with Neanderthals."

"Interesting! *Way* back, then, like tens of thousands of years."

"Yeah. Before even language, maybe."

"Makes you wonder what we could find in African folklore," she said.

This stopped Richard for a few moments, while he caught up

with her. "Since there might have been even a greater diversity of, of . . ."

"Hominids," she said, "going back maybe farther."

"Why not? Anyway, we didn't get much beyond this level in the initial set of D-squared talks. Then it all got handed off to . . ."

"Skeletor."

"Yeah. But we didn't call him that in those days, because he was still fat." Saying that, Richard felt a brief spike of nervousness that Peter might be twittering or, God forbid, live-video-blogging this. But Peter's attention was entirely elsewhere; he had begun keeping an eye on the tavern's entrance, his eyes jumping to it whenever someone came in the door.

Richard turned his gaze back to Zula, not without a certain feeling of pleasure—avuncular, noncreepy—and went on: "Devin just went nuts. His official start date was two weeks before our initial meeting—but by the time he walked in the door, he already had a stack of pages *this thick* with ideas for historical sagas based on the very sketchy outlines provided by Don Donald. There actually wasn't much point to the meeting. It was a formality. I just told him to keep it up, and I got an intern cataloging and cross-referencing all his output . . ."

"The Canon," Zula said.

"Exactly, that was the beginning of the Canon. Forced us to hire Geraldine. But with the key difference that it was all still fluid, since we hadn't actually released any of it to the fan base yet. It was kind of scary, the way it grew. Later in the year is when we started to feel a little creeped out by it, like Devin was taking our world and running away with it. So we announced, and I'm not too proud to say that this was a retroactive policy change, that the Writers in Residence program operated on an annual basis and that when Devin's year was up, he was welcome to continue writing stuff in the T'Rain world but that he would in fact have to share authorship of that world with the *next* Writer in Residence."

"Which turned out to be D-squared."

"No accident. Devin had become so dominant over the world that any other writer just would have been buried under his output. There was only one other writer who had, (a) the prominence in the world of fantasy literature to rival Devin's, and (b) the priority—"

"He'd been there first," Zula said.

"Yes. Just long enough to run around and pee on all the trees, but that still counted for a lot."

"Hey, I just saw someone I know," Peter announced, nodding toward the entrance. A man in an overcoat had just walked in from the parking lot and was scanning the tavern, trying to decide where he wanted to sit.

"Friend of yours?" Richard asked.

"Acquaintance," Peter corrected him, "but I should go over and just say hey."

"Who is it?" Zula asked, looking around, but Peter was already on his feet, headed over to a table by the fire, where the new arrival had just taken a seat. Richard watched as the man looked up at Peter's face. His expression did not show anything like surprise or recognition. And certainly not pleasure. He had expected to meet Peter here. They had been texting each other about it. Peter was lying.

Richard now sort of forcibly turned the conversation back, because the thing with Peter troubled him and his first instinct with things that troubled him was to wall them off, and then wait for them to grow bad enough to threaten the structural integrity of the wall, and then, finally, to get out a sledgehammer.

"We brought both of them out here," Richard said.

"To the Schloss?"

"Yeah. It didn't look like this in those days. It was before the Dwinn mead hall remodel. They came in the summer, when this place has a whole different vibe. We brought some chefs up from Vancouver to prepare meals, and we held a retreat here, sort of to mark the formal handoff from Skeletor to D-squared. That was when the Apostropocalypse happened."

"ONE IS BEMUSED by the notion of convening a *retreat* in order to get work done," said Don Donald, while they were still just milling around on the terrace, sipping pints and getting used to the views of the Selkirks. "Should it not in that case be denominated an *advance*?"

Richard was lost from the very beginning of that sentence, so gave up altogether on trying to parse it and just watched D-squared's face. Donald Cameron, then fifty-two, looked older than that, with swept-back silver hair and an impressive honker, swollen from the rich liquid diet of the ancient Cambridge college where he lived about half the time. But his complexion was pink and his manner was vigorous, probably because of all the brisk walks that he took around the castle on the Isle of Man where he lived the *other* half of the time. He'd checked in to his suite a few hours earlier, rested up for a bit, gone for one of those brisk walks, and stepped out onto the terrace only thirty seconds ago, whereupon he'd been surrounded by about four nerds, sufficiently highly ensconced in Corporation 9592's food chain that they felt entitled to approach him. Richard knew for a fact that most of these people had stacks of Donald Cameron fantasy novels in their rooms in hopes of getting them signed, and that they were just sucking up to him long enough to feel comfortable with broaching such a request.

"Maybe you need to coin a new word for it," Richard said, before any of the fanboys could laugh or, worse, try to enter into repartee with the Don.

"Heh. You have noticed my weakness for that sort of thing."

"We depend on it."

D-squared raised an eyebrow. "We have already *advanced* to the point of doing work! One imagined that this was to be a purely *social* gathering, Mr. Forthrast." But he was only kidding, as he now indicated by winking, and nodding in the direction of—

Richard turned around and stepped clear of the rapidly growing fan cluster to see Devin Skraelin making his entrance. He wondered whether Devin had been twitching the curtain in his suite, waiting for Don Donald to emerge onto the terrace so that Devin could arrive *last*. As usual, he was trailed by two "assistants" who seemed too old and authoritative to merit that designation. Richard had been able to establish that the female "assistant" was an intellectual property lawyer and that the male was a book editor who had been sacked in the latest publishing industry cataclysms: he was now Devin's captive scribe.

"Thank you," Richard said. "More on this later, if you please."

"I can't wait!"

Richard moved to intercept Devin but was cut off by Nolan Xu, who was just about the worst Devin Skraelin fanboy in the whole world. Nolan had, until now, been largely marooned behind the

Chinese border by visa and exchange-rate hassles, but during the last year or so he'd been finding it easier and easier to make long forays out to the West. Some men in that position would have headed straight for Vegas, but Nolan, for a combination of personal and business reasons impossible to sort out, went to science-fiction and fantasy conventions.

Richard pulled up short and spent a few moments watching the interaction. Devin had lost 211 pounds (at least that was the figure posted on his website as of six hours ago) and now looked hefty, but not so obese as to draw attention to himself. He paid due attention to Nolan but never let more than about five seconds expire without casting a glance in Don Donald's direction. If Richard had been a random observer of the scene, he'd have guessed that one of the two writers was an assassin and the other his intended victim. He'd have been hard-pressed, though, to know which was which.

Professor Cameron, for his part, remained supremely affable and civilized until he was good and ready to acknowledge Devin's presence, then pivoted on the balls of his hand-tooled loafers and swept—there was no other word for it—across the terrace to extend a hand of greeting to his rival.

"As if he owns the place," Richard muttered.

"The Schloss?" asked Chet, who was just hanging around keeping an eye on things. All Chet knew of fantasy literature was that it was a useful source of van art.

"No," said Richard. "T'Rain."

LATER THEY DINED in the Schloss's banqueting hall, which was fairly standard-issue Bavarian fortress architecture. Several tables had been joined end to end to make a single very long one. "Just like Shakey's Pizza Parlor!" remarked Devin, when he saw it. "Just like High Table at Trinity," said D-squared. Richard, the only man in the room who had dined at both of those places, could see merit in both points of view, so—trying to be the agreeable host—he signaled agreement with each, while hiding a growing feeling of unease over what would happen when these two men ended up sitting across the Shakey's/Trinity table from each other. For seats had been assigned. Richard was at the head of the table. Devin and Professor Cameron were adjacent to him, facing each other. Nolan was next to the latter, so that he could gaze lovingly across the table at the former, and Pluto was next to Devin, on the theory that Don Donald would feel more at home if somewhere in his field of view was a ridiculously intelligent geek of limited social skills. Pluto's chair faced the glass windows that opened out onto the terrace, so that he could relieve his boredom by inspecting the shape of the mountains that rose up on the opposite side of the valley.

So much for all the people who'd be in earshot of Richard. From there the seating arrangement propagated down the table according to someone's notion of hierarchy and precedence. The menu was middle-European hunting-lodge cuisine as reinterpreted by the culinary staff that Richard and Chet had drawn to the place over the years. The venison, for example, was farm raised, therefore certifiably prion-free, ensuring that Corporation 9592 would not go belly-up in a few decades as its entire senior echelon was struck down by mad cow disease. The wine list made a diplomatic nod or two in the direction of British Columbia's nascent viticultural sector and then lunged decisively south of the border. D-squared made some insightful remarks about a nice dry Riesling from the Horse Heaven Hills and Devin requested a Diet Coke. Lots of curiosity was expressed, on all sides, about the Schloss and how Richard and Chet had come to build it. Richard explained that it had originally been put together from bits and pieces of three different structures in the Austrian Alps, which had been bought by a certain Austro-Hungarian mining baron (*literally* a baron). He'd caused the pieces to be shipped down the Danube to the Black Sea and thence all the way around the world to the mouth of the Columbia, then up to a place where the stuff could be loaded onto a narrow-gauge mining railway that no longer existed, whose right-of-way, now a bike and ski path, ran through the grounds of the Schloss. Then fast-forward to its discovery and prolonged rehabilitation by Richard and Chet. Richard left out all material having to do with drug money and motorcycle gangs, since that was amply covered by the Wikipedia entry that all present had presumably read and perhaps even edited.

For in the late 1980s the marijuana thing had started to get darker, more violent; or perhaps Richard, after his thirtieth birthday, started to notice the darkness that had been there all along. He had cashed out and gone back to Iowa, where he had enrolled in courses in hotel and restaurant management at Iowa State University. This was the point where the story became wholesome enough that he felt he could relate it in polite company. After a few months in Iowa, he had come to his senses, realizing that people with such skills could simply be hired, and had returned to B.C. He and Chet had then begun to fix up the Schloss in earnest.

All of which made for perfectly pleasant conversation as they sampled some light predinner wines and popped colorful amuse-bouches into their mouths and spooned up soup, but as the dinner stretched on into dishes that looked more like main courses and that were accompanied by red wine, Richard found himself wishing that they could just grab the Band-Aid and rip it off. The formal purpose of this retreat and this dinner was to celebrate the conclusion of Devin's year as Writer in Residence and to hand the torch to Don Donald, who had finally polished off his trilogy-turned-tetrakaidecalogy and was ready to devote some time to further development of the backstory and "bible" of T'Rain.

During the last three months of Devin's tenure, he had been almost disturbingly productive, leading to an email thread at Corporation 9592 (subject: "Devin Skraelin is an Edgar Allan Poe character") spattered with links to websites about the psychiatric condition known as graphomania. This had led to a new piece of jargon: Canon Lag, in which the employees responsible for cross-checking Devin's work and incorporating it into the Canon had been unable to keep pace with his output. According to one somewhat paranoid strain of thought, this had been a deliberate strategy on Devin's part. Certainly it was the case that, as of this dinner, the only person who had the entire world in his head was Devin, since he had delivered a thousand pages of new material at one o'clock this morning, emailing it from his room in the North Tower of the Schloss, and no one had had time to do more than scan it. So he had everyone else at something of a disadvantage.

Talk of the Schloss led naturally to a conversation about Don Donald's castle on the Isle of Man, which had also been the target of heavy renovation work. In that, Richard perceived an opening and made a gambit. "Is that where you anticipate doing most of the T'Rain work?"

Silence. Richard had probably crossed a boundary, or something, by mentioning "work." He had found that barreling on ahead was better than apologizing. "Do you have a study there—a suitable place to write?"

"Most suitable!" the professor exclaimed. He went on to describe a certain room in a turret, "with prospects, on a fair day, west to Donaghadee and north to Cairngaan," both of which he pronounced so authentically that visible frissons of pleasure radiated down the table. It had been fixed up, he said, in a manner that made it "both authentic and habitable, no easy balance to strike," and it awaited his return.

"Devin's given you a lot to work with," said Geraldine Levy, who was the mistress of the Canon, seated down the table from Pluto. "I can't help but wonder if there is any particular part of the story of T'Rain that you'd like to hone in on first."

"Home in," Cameron corrected her, after an awkward few seconds trying to make sense of it. "The question is perfectly reasonable. My answer must be indirect. My method of working, as you may know, is to compose the first draft in the language actually spoken by the characters. Only when this is finished do I begin the work of translating it into English." Like a tank rotating its turret, he swung around to aim at Devin. "My *collaborator,* quite naturally, prefers a more . . . efficient and direct method."

"I am in awe of what you do with all the languages and everything," Devin said. "You're right. I just . . . wing it."

"So your world," said D-squared, continuing the pivot until he was aimed at Richard, "*has* no languages at the moment. You are more fascinated by *geology*"—he nodded Pluto's way—"and consider that to be fundamental. I would have started rather with words and language and constructed all upon that foundation."

"You have a free hand in the matter now, Doctor Cameron," Richard pointed out.

"*Almost* free. For there have been *some*"—Cameron turned his eyes back toward Devin—"coinages. I see words in Mr. Skraelin's work that do not appear in English dictionaries. The very word T'Rain, of course. Then the names of the races: K'Shetriae. D'uinn.

These I can work with—can incorporate into fictional languages whose grammar and lexicons I shall be happy to draw up and share with—Miss—Levy." A hesitation before the "Miss" as he checked her left ring finger and found it vacant.

Miss Levy was only a "Miss" because lesbians couldn't get married in the state of Washington, but she was willing to let it slide. "That would be huge for us," she said. "That part of the Canon is just a gaping void right now."

"Happy to be of service. Some questions, though."

"Yes?"

"K'Shetriae. The name of the elven race. Strangely reminiscent of Kshatriya, is it not?"

Everyone at this end of the table drew a blank except for Nolan. Halfway down the table, though, Premjith Lal, who headed one of their Weird Stuff departments, had pricked up his ears.

"Yes!" Nolan exclaimed, nodding and smiling. "Now that you mention it—very similar."

"Mind explaining it?" Richard asked.

"Premjith!" Nolan called out. "Are you Kshatriya?"

Premjith nodded. He was too far away to talk. He reached up with both hands, grabbed his ears, and pulled them up, making them pointy and elven.

"It is a Hindu caste," Nolan explained. "The warrior caste."

"One cannot help wondering if the person who coined that name might have heard the word 'Kshatriya' in some other context and later, when groping for an exotic-sounding sequence of phonemes, pulled it back up, as it were, from memory, thinking that it was an original idea."

Richard tried ever so hard not to look at Devin, but it was as if someone had put a crowbar into his ear and kicked it. Within a few seconds everyone was looking at Devin, who was turning red. He killed time for a few moments by sipping from his Diet Coke and fussing with his napkin, then looked up with great confidence and said, "There are only so many phonemes, and only so many combinations of them that you can string together to make words in imaginary languages. Any name you come up with is going to sound like the name of a caste or a god or an irrigation district somewhere in the world. Why not just put your head down and get on with it?"

Premjith was just barely in range. "There are something like a hundred million Kshatriya who are going to be bemused by this aspect of the Canon," he pointed out. He wasn't upset, just . . . bemused. Richard made a mental note to take Premjith out for sushi and find out if there were any other things he'd noticed seriously wrong with T'Rain that he hadn't felt like mentioning.

"Hundred million . . ." Devin repeated, not loudly enough for Premjith to hear him. "I'll bet within five years of T'Rain going live, we'll have more K'Shetriae than there are Kshatriya."

"Now, that is—if memory serves—spelt with an apostrophe between an uppercase K and an uppercase S, is it not?" Don Donald asked.

"That's right," said Devin, and glanced at Geraldine, who nodded.

"Now the apostrophe is used to mark an elision."

"A missing letter," Pluto translated. "Like the o in 'couldn't.'" He snorted. "The *second* o, that is!"

"Yes, just so," the Don continued. "Which leads me to ask why the S in 'K'Shetriae' is capitalized. Should one infer from this that 'Shetriae' is a separate word that is a proper noun? And if so, what are we to make of the K-apostrophe? Is it, for example, some sort of article?"

"Sure, why not," said Devin.

D-squared, having set the hook, was content with a few moments' discreet silence, but Pluto erupted: "Why not? *Why not?*"

Richard could only watch, like staring across a valley at an avalanche overtaking a skier.

"If it is an article," said Don Donald, "then what is the T-apostrophe in T'Rain? What is the D-apostrophe in D'uinn? How many articles does this language have?"

Silence.

"Or perhaps the K, the T, and the D are not articles but some other features of the language."

Silence.

"Or perhaps the apostrophe is being used to indicate something other than elision."

Silence.

"In which case, what *does* it indicate?"

Richard couldn't bear it anymore. "It just looks cool," he said.

Don Donald turned toward him with a bright, fascinated look. Behind him, Richard could see everyone else collapsing; things had gotten a bit tense.

"I beg your pardon, Richard?"

"Donald, look. You're the only guy in this particular sector of the economy who has the whole ancient-languages thing down pat to the extent that you do. Everyone else just totally makes this stuff up. When some guy wants a word that seems exotic, he'll throw in a couple of apostrophes. Maybe smash a couple of letters together that don't normally go, like Q and Z. That's what we're dealing with here."

Silence in a different flavor.

"I am aware that it doesn't exactly jibe with your M.O.," Richard added.

"M.O.?"

"Modus operandi."

"Mmm," said the Don.

"If you want to make up some languages," offered Devin, "knock yourself out."

"Mmm," the Don said again.

Richard glanced at Geraldine, who was thinking so hard that coils of smoke were rising from her sensible hairdo.

"Mr. Olszewski," the Don finally said, "may I plant a volcano here?"

"Here!?"

"Yes, on the site of this property."

"Any particular type of volcano you had in mind?"

"Oh, let's say a Mount Etna. I've always favored that one."

"No way," said Pluto. "That is a highly active, young stratovolcano. The Selkirks aren't that geologically active. The type of rock here—"

"It simply wouldn't make sense," said the Don, summing up and cutting short what promised to be a long and devastatingly particular tour of the world of volcanology. "It would be incoherent."

"Totally!"

"I fear that an analogous situation may obtain in the case of all these apostrophes. My colleague has refrained from coining words, it is true. But it has been necessary, hasn't it, to coin names for the races of T'Rain, and indeed for the world itself. And in some cases, such as 'K'Shetriae,' the apostrophe is followed by a capitalized letter, while in others, as 'D'uinn,' the following letter is lowercase, a situation that requires some sort of coherent explanation. At least if I am to proceed with my work in the manner to which I am accustomed."

Richard noted the implicit threat there.

"THANKS FOR COMING all the way out from Vancouver," Peter said. They had not introduced themselves, or shaken hands, just sized each other up and confirmed with nods that they were who they were.

"*This* is a hell of a place," said Wallace. He did not seem like the kind of man who was utterly confounded—or would admit to it, anyway—very often. For a good half minute he had eyes for nothing but the interlocking timbers that pretended to hold up the roof. "Where have I seen those before?" Then his eyes dropped to regard Peter, who was eyeing him somewhat warily. He turned his attention back to the tavern: its rustic furniture, its leaded glass windows, its floor of pegged wooden planks. But finally it was the silverware that tipped him off. He picked up a fork and stared in amazement at the motif stamped into its handle: a raw geometric pattern inspired by Nordic runes. "Jesus fucking Christ," he said. "Dwinn!"

"I beg your pardon?" Peter said, aghast at how this was going.

Wallace cracked up—another thing that, one suspected, he didn't do often—and cast a glance at his laptop bag, which he'd left sitting on the empty chair next to him. "I could show you," he said. "I could go to this place right now, in T'Rain."

"You play T'Rain?" Peter inquired, seeing in this an opportunity for, at least, a conversational gambit.

"We all have our vices. Each brings its own brand of trouble. That connected with an addiction to T'Rain is less dangerous than many I could name. Speaking of which, what does a man have to do to get a club soda in this place?" Wallace spoke with a Scottish accent, which came as a surprise to Peter and created a one-second time lag in all Peter's responses as he worked to understand what

Wallace had just said. But once he'd parsed "club soda," he turned in his chair, half rose, and secured the attention of a waiter.

Peter did not yet like the way the conversation was going. Wallace had thrown him completely off-balance by making the conversation about T'Rain and had pressed him into service as drink fetcher. Now, though, Wallace changed his attitude a bit, explaining himself, as if educating Peter. Doing him a favor. "This is the feast hall of King Oglo of the Northern Red Dwinn. I've been in it ten, maybe fifteen times."

"You mean, your character's been in it."

"Yes, that is what I mean," said Wallace, and he didn't have to add *you fucking shite-for-brains.*

Wallace had come into the place wearing an overcoat, a garment that Peter had seen only in movies. Probably the only overcoat within a two-hundred-kilometer radius. A gentleman's garment. About him were various other faint traces of white collarness. His red-going-white hair had been slicked back from his sun-mottled forehead, which sported a divot above the left temple where a skin cancer had been rooted out. Reading glasses hung on a gold chain from his neck. His shirt was open at the neck. Its sheer fabric would look good beneath a sharp suit but would afford him very little protection if he had to stop and change a tire. His right hand was anchored by a fat gold signet ring.

"I don't play T'Rain myself," Peter said, though this seemed pretty obvious by this point.

"What games do you play?"

"I like snowboarding. Shooting. Sometimes I—"

"That's not what I'm asking. I'm asking, what's your vice and what brand of trouble does it lead to?" Wallace tapped his signet ring on the table.

Peter was silent for a few moments.

"And don't try to tell me that there is none, because we both know why we're here." *Tap tap tap.*

"Yeah," said Peter, "but that doesn't mean it's because of a vice."

Wallace laughed, and not in the delighted way he'd laughed when he had recognized that he was sitting in the feast hall of King Oglo. "You reached me through certain individuals in Ukraine who are not exactly solid citizens. I checked you out. I have read all the postings you made, starting at the age of twelve, in hacker chat rooms, written in that ridiculous fucking spelling that you all use. Three years ago you went on record under your real name calling yourself a gray-hat hacker, which is as good as admitting that you were a black-hat before. And a year ago you signed on with this security consultancy where half of the founders have done time, for Christ's sake."

"Look. What do you want me to say? We're here. We're having this meeting. We both know why. So it's not like I've been lying to you."

"Very true. What I'm trying to establish is that *you have been lying to everyone else,* including, I'd guess, your cappuccino girlfriend over there. And it's helpful for me to know what vices or troubles led you to tell those lies."

"Why? I've got what you came for."

"That's what I am trying to establish."

Peter reached into a large external pocket of his coat and pulled out a DVD case containing a single unmarked disk, white on top, iridescent purple on the bottom. "Here it is."

Wallace looked disgusted. "That's how you want to deliver it?"

"Is there a problem?"

"I brought a notebook computer. No DVD slot. Rather hoped you'd bring it on a thumb drive."

Peter considered this. "I think that can be arranged. Hold on a second."

"THAT GUY JUST tasked your boyfriend," Richard remarked, shortly after Peter had sat down across from the stranger by the fire.

"Tasked?"

"Gave him a job to do. 'Get the waiter's attention. Order me a drink.' Something of that nature."

"I don't follow."

"It's a tactic," Richard said. "When you've just met someone and you're trying to feel them out. Give them a task and see how they react. If they accept the task, you can move on and give them a bigger one later."

"Is it a tactic you use?"

"No, it's manipulative. Either someone works for me or they

don't. If they work for me, I can assign them tasks and it's fine. If they don't work for me, then I have no business assigning them tasks."

"So you're saying that Peter's friend is manipulating him."

"Acquaintance."

"It's some kind of business contact," Zula guessed.

"Then why didn't he just come out and say so?"

"That's a good question," Zula said. "He's probably afraid I'd be mad at him if he interrupted our vacation for a business meeting."

So he lied to you? Richard thought better of actually saying this. If he pushed too hard, he might get the opposite result from what he wanted.

Besides, Peter was now headed back over to the table.

"Does either of you have a thumb drive I could use?"

The question hung there like an invisible cloud of flatulence.

"I want to transfer some pictures between computers," he explained.

Richard and Zula and Peter had all been lounging around the place for a while, occasionally checking email or messing around with vacation photos, and so Richard had his laptop bag between his feet. He pulled it up into his lap and groped around in an external pocket. "Here you go," he said.

"I'll get it right back to you," Peter said.

"Don't bother," Richard said, peeved, in a completely school-marmish way, by Peter's failure to use the magic words. "It's too small. I was going to buy a new one tomorrow. Just erase whatever's on it, okay?"

PETER RETURNED TO the table, pulled out his laptop, and inserted the thumb drive. His computer, a Linux machine, identified it as a Windows file system, which was just what he needed since Wallace's machine was also a Windows box. Finding several files in it, Peter erased them. Then he popped the DVD out of its case and pushed it into the slot.

"Why don't you just use the local copy on your machine?" Wallace asked him.

"Ooh, good trick question!" Peter said. "It's like I told you. There is only one copy. It's on the DVD. I am not about ripping you off."

The DVD appeared as an icon on his desktop. He opened it up, and it showed but a single file. He dragged that over to the thumb drive's icon and waited for a few seconds as the files were transferred. "Now, two copies," he said. He dismounted the thumb drive and removed it. "Voilà," he said, holding it up. "The goods. As promised."

"Not until I agree that it is what you have claimed."

"Go ahead and check it out!"

"Oh, I've looked at the sample you sent. They were all legit credit card numbers, just like you said. Names, expiration dates, and all the rest."

"So what are you getting at?"

"Provenance."

"Isn't that a city in Rhode Island?"

"Since you are an autodidact, Peter, and I have a soft spot for autodidacts, I'll forgive you for not knowing the word. It means, where did the data come from?"

"What does that matter, if it's good data?"

Wallace sighed, sipped his club soda, and looked around the feast hall. As if willing forth the energy needed to go on with this stupid conversation. "You are misconstruing this, young man. I'm trying to help you."

"I wasn't aware I needed any help."

"This is *proactive* help. You understand? *Retroactive* help—the kind *you're* thinking of—is throwing a drunk the life preserver after he's fallen off the pier. *Proactive* help is grabbing him by the belt and pulling him to safety before he falls."

"Why should you even give a shit?"

"Because if you end up needing help, boy, owing to a problem with the *provenance* of these credit card numbers, then I'm going to need it too."

Peter spent a while working it out. "You're not in business for yourself."

Wallace nodded, managing to look both encouraging and sour at the same time.

"You're just running the errand—acting as an agent, or something—for whoever it is that's *really* buying this."

Wallace made expressive gestures, like an orchestra conductor, nearly knocking over his club soda.

"If something goes wrong, those people will be pissed off, and you're afraid of what they'll do," Peter continued.

Wallace now went still and silent, which seemed to mean that Peter had at last come to the correct conclusion.

"Who are they?"

"You can't possibly imagine that I'm really going to tell you their names."

"Of course not."

"So why do you even ask, Peter?"

"You're the one who brought this into the conversation."

"They are Russians."

"You mean, like . . . Russian mafia?" Peter was too fascinated, yet, to be scared.

"'Russian mafia' is an idiotic term. An oxymoron. Media crap. It is vastly more complicated than that."

"Well, but obviously . . ."

"Obviously," Wallace agreed, "if they are purchasing stolen credit card numbers from hackers, they are by definition engaging in organized criminal activity."

The two men sat there silently for a minute while Peter thought about it.

"How these people come to engage in organized criminal activity is quite interesting and complicated. You'd find it fascinating to talk to them, if they had even the faintest interest in talking to you. I can assure you it has nothing in common with the Sicilian mafia."

"But you just got done threatening me. That sounds like . . ."

"The cruelty and opportunism of the Russians are greatly overstated," Wallace said, "but they contain a kernel of truth. You, Peter, have chosen to trade in illegal goods. In doing so, you are stepping outside of the structures of ordinary commerce, with its customer service reps, its mediators, its Angie's List. If the transaction fails, your customers will not have any of the normal forms of recourse. That's all I'm saying. So even if you're a complete shite-for-brains with no regard for the safety of yourself or your girlfriend, I'll ask you to answer my question as to provenance, because I still have a choice as to whether I'll proceed with this transaction, and I'll not go into business with a shite-for-brains."

"Fine," Peter said. "I'm working with a network security consultancy. You already know that. We got hired by a clothing store chain to do a pen test."

"What, their pens weren't writing?"

"Pen*etration* test. Our job was to find ways of penetrating their corporate networks. We found that one part of their website was vulnerable to a SQL injection attack. By exploiting that, we were able to install a rootkit on one of their servers and then use that as a beachhead on their internal network to—to make a long story short—get root on the servers where they stored customer data and then prove that their credit card data was vulnerable."

"Sounds complicated."

"It took fifteen minutes."

"So these data you're trying to sell me are already compromised!" Wallace said.

"No."

"You just told me that the client has been tipped off to the vulnerability!"

"*That* client has been tipped off. *Those* numbers were compromised. *These* numbers are not *those* numbers."

"What are they, then?"

"The website I've been telling you about was set up by a contractor that subsequently went out of business."

"No wonder!"

"Exactly. I looked through archived web pages and shareholder disclosures to learn the names of some of the other clients who'd hired the same contractor to set up retail websites during the same period of time."

Wallace thought about it, then nodded. "Reckoning that it was all cookie-cutter."

"Yeah. All these sites are clones of each other, more or less, and since the contractor went belly-up, they haven't been keeping up with security patches."

"Which is probably why you got hired to do the pen testing in the first place."

"Exactly. So I did find a lot of cookie-cutter sites that shared the same vulnerabilities, including one big one. A department store chain that you have heard of."

"And you then repeated the same attack."

"Yeah."

"Which is now traceable to that consultancy you work for and its computers."

"No no no," Peter said. "I worked with some friends of mine in Eastern Europe; we ran the whole thing through other hosts, we anonymized everything—there is absolutely no way that this could be traced to me."

"These friends of yours work for free?"

"Of course not, they're getting part of the money."

"You trust their discretion?"

"Obviously."

"That explains why your initial contact with me came through Ukraine."

"Yes."

"It's good to have that loose end tied up," Wallace said primly. "But the biggest loose end of all is still loose."

"And that is?"

"Why are you doing this?"

Peter was stuck for an answer.

"Just tell me you're addicted to cocaine. Being blackmailed by your dominatrix. It's perfectly all right."

"I'm upside down on my mortgage," Peter said.

"You mean on that hacker dump where you live?"

"It's a commercial building in Seattle . . . an industrial neighbor-hood called Georgetown . . ."

Wallace nodded and quoted the address from memory.

Peter's face got hot. "Okay, you've been checking me out. That's fine. I acquired the space before the economy crashed. I use part of it as live/work space and lease out the rest. When the economy went south, vacancy rates went nuts and the property lost a lot of book value *as well as* not bringing in rent. But with this, I can make it right. Avoid foreclosure, fix a few things, sell it, be in position to buy . . ."

"A real house where a female might actually want to live?" Wallace asked. For Peter, in spite of willing himself not to, had let his eyes stray momentarily in the direction of Zula.

"You have to understand," Peter began.

"Ah, but Peter, I don't *wish* to understand."

"Seattle is full of these people—no smarter than me—no harder working than me—"

"Who are zillionaires because they got lucky. Peter! Listen to me carefully," Wallace said. "I've already told you who I work for. How do you think I feel?"

That left Peter silent long enough for Wallace to add, "And did I make it clear enough that I don't give a shite?"

"You give a *shit* about tying up those loose ends."

"Ah, yes. Thank you for bringing me back to important topics," Wallace said. He checked his watch. "I got here about half an hour ago. If you'd been watching the parking lot, you'd have seen two vehicles pull in. One is mine. Nice little ragtop, not so well adapted for these roads, but it got me here. The other a black Suburban with a couple of Russians in it. We parked on either side of your orange 2008 Scion xB. One of the Russians, a technical boy not much less talented than you, opened up his laptop and established a connection to the Internet using the lodge's Wi-Fi network. He is sitting there now waiting for me. If we go through with this transaction, I'll be in the backseat of that Suburban about thirty seconds later handing him this thumb drive. And he has got, what d'you call them, *scripts* that can go through your data and check those credit card numbers *fast*. And if he finds anything wrong, why then the retribution that I was warning you of, a few minutes ago, will have been completed before your liver has had time to metabolize that swallow of Mountain Dew you just enjoyed."

Peter took another swallow of Mountain Dew. "I have the same scripts," he said, "and I just ran them on this data a few hours ago. My friends in Eastern Europe have been keeping an eye on things too; they'd let me know if there was a problem. I'm scared of the people you work for, Mr. Wallace, and I wish I had never gotten into this; but one thing I'm not worried about at all is the integrity of the data I'm selling you."

"Very well then."

Peter set the thumb drive on the table and slid it across to Wallace.

Wallace drew a laptop from his bag and opened it up on the table. He inserted the thumb drive. Its icon appeared on the screen. He double-clicked it to reveal a single Excel file entitled "data." Wallace dragged that folder into his "Documents" icon and watched for a few seconds as the little on-screen animation reassured him that the transfer was taking place. As this was happening, he remarked: "There is another way that this could go wrong, of course. Already alluded to in this conversation."

"And that is . . . ?"

"Perhaps this is not the only copy of the data? Perhaps you'll double your money, or triple it, by selling it to others?"

Peter shrugged. "There's no way I can prove that this is the only copy."

"I understand. But your Ukrainian colleagues—?"

"They've never even seen this stuff. When we ran the exploit, the files went straight to my laptop."

"Where you have retained a copy, just in case?"

"No." Then Peter looked a bit uncertain. "Except for this." He ejected the DVD from his laptop. "Would you like it?"

"I would like to see it destroyed."

"Easy enough." Peter bent the disk into a U and squeezed it hard, trying to snap it. This required a surprising amount of effort. Finally it made an explosive *crack* and fell apart into two halves, but several shards went flying onto the table and the floor. "Fuck!" Peter said. He dropped the two jagged semicircles onto the table and held up his right hand to display a cut on the base of the thumb, about half an inch long, with blood welling out of it.

"Do you think you could try to be a little more conspicuous?" Wallace asked. He had opened up the new "data" file and verified that it consisted of line after line of names, addresses, credit card numbers, and expiration dates. He scrolled all the way to the end and verified that it contained hundreds of thousands of records.

Then he pulled the thumb drive out of his machine and flicked it into the fire burning a few feet away from them. Peter, who was sucking on his self-inflicted laceration, couldn't help glancing over in the direction of Richard and Zula.

With his foot, Wallace shoved a small duffel bag across the floor until it contacted Peter's ankle. "Should pay for a few Band-Aids with enough left over to buy Uncle Dick a new thumb drive. But how you'll pay off your mortgage with hundred-dollar bills I'll never know."

"Turns out Uncle Dick knows something about it." Peter had

taken his hand from his mouth and now pressed the bleeding wound against the icy cold side of his Mountain Dew glass.

"You know this of your own personal knowledge, or Wikipedia?" Wallace asked.

"Just so you know, he has a lot of problems with his Wikipedia entry."

"As would I," Wallace said, "were it mine. Answer my question."

"Richard doesn't talk about the old days. Not to me anyway."

"What, he doesn't think you're worthy of his niece?" Wallace said in a tone of mock wonderment. "Richard Forthrast went straight a long time ago. He'll not help you with your embarrassment of hundred-dollar bills."

"He found a way," Peter said. "So can I."

"Peter. Before we part ways, hopefully forever, I'd like to speak with you briefly about something."

"Go ahead."

"I can see that you've spoken forthrightly. So now I want to respond in kind and tell you that all that stuff about the Russians was just BS. A scare tactic, pure and simple."

"I figured that out already."

"How, exactly?"

"A minute ago you said you were going to give the thumb drive to a Russian hacker in the backseat of the Suburban. But just now you threw it in the fire."

"Clever boy. So I needn't tell you that there is no Suburban in the parking lot. You can look for yourself."

Peter did not look. He was almost excessively ready to believe Wallace.

"I am in business for myself," Wallace said. "A small-timer without the muscle to back up my business, and so I have to play these mind games sometimes, as a way of judging people's sincerity. It worked in this case. I can see that you have played me straight. Otherwise it would have come through in your eyes."

"That's okay," Peter said. "We used to watch this stupid program called *Scared Straight*. I think you scared me straight just now."

"Oh really!" Wallace drawled. "You've turned a new leaf! This was your last big score! You're getting out now. Going on the straight and narrow path, like Richard Forthrast."

"He did it . . ." Peter began.

" . . . so can you," Wallace finished. "I think that is all bollocks, but I shall take my leave now and wish you luck."

"IS PETER A drug user?" Richard asked.

"No, he's straight edge," Zula said with a quick roll of the eyes and air quotes. "Why?"

"Because that looked like a drug transaction to me."

She looked back over her shoulder. "Really? In what way?"

"Just something about the psychological dynamic."

She gave him a penetrating look through her glasses.

"Which I admit doesn't explain the antics with the thumb drive and trying to kill himself with a DVD," he allowed.

She averted her gaze and shrugged.

"Never mind," he continued.

"So D-squared lowered the boom on Skeletor about the apostrophes."

"Yeah. A well-planned attack, I'd say. And it led to, among other things, the change where D'uinn became Dwinn."

"Gosh, the way people talk about it on the Internet . . ."

"You'd think it was a much bigger deal. No. Not at the time, anyway. But this is how history is done now. People wait until they have a need for some history and then they customize it to suit their purposes. A year ago? Only the most hard-core T'Rain geeks would have heard of the Apostropocalypse and it would be considered a footnote. Maybe amusing at most."

"But ever since the Forces of Brightness went all Pearl Harbor against the Earthtone Coalition—"

"It's become important in retrospect," Richard said, "and it's been blown up into this big thing. But really? It was just an excruciatingly awkward dinner. D'uinn got changed into Dwinn. Supposedly for linguistic reasons. But it set a precedent that Don Donald had the authority to change things that Devin had done in the world."

"Which he then went on to abuse?"

"According to the Forces of Brightness," Richard said. "But the fact is that D-squared has been discreet, restrained, only changed things in places where Devin really pissed down his leg. Things that Devin himself would have changed, had he gone back and reread his work and thought about it a little harder. So it's mostly not a big deal."

"To you maybe," Zula said, "but to Devin?"

Richard thought about it. "At the time, he really acted like he didn't care."

"But maybe he really did," Zula said, "and has been plotting his revenge ever since. Hiding things deep in the Canon. Details of history that Geraldine and her staff wouldn't necessarily put together into a bigger picture. But his fans—to them it was like a dog whistle."

Richard shrugged and nodded. Then he noticed that Zula was gazing at him. Waiting for more.

"You don't care!" she finally exclaimed. Then a smile.

"I did at first," he admitted. "I was shocked at first. One of my characters got ganked, you know. Attacked without warning by other characters in his party. Cut down while *he* was defending *them*. So of course that was upsetting at the time. And the furor, the anger over the last couple of months—how could you not get caught up in that, a little? But—I'm running a business."

"And the War of Realignment is making money?"

"Hand over fist."

"Who's making money hand over fist?" asked Peter, breaking in on them. He unslung a black nylon duffel bag and placed it on his lap as he sat down. He was gripping a rolled-up wad of paper napkins, applying direct pressure to his DVD wound.

"You ask an interesting question," said Richard, looking Peter in the eye.

"Just joking," Peter said, immediately breaking eye contact.

"Well," said Zula, and tapped her phone to check the time. "Could you take a picture of me and my uncle before we hit the road?"

AS GOOGLE MAPS made dispiritingly clear, there was no good way to drive from that part of B.C. to Seattle, or *anywhere* for that matter; all the mountain ranges ran perpendicular to the vectors of travel.

The Schloss's access road took them across the dam and plugged them in to the beginning of a provincial two-laner that followed the left bank of the river to the southern end of the big lake Kootenay: a deep sliver of water trapped between the Selkirks and the Purcells. It teed into a larger highway in the middle of Elphinstone, a nicely restored town of about ten thousand residents, nine thousand of whom seemed to work in dining establishments. A gas stop there developed into a half-hour break for Thai food. Peter talked hardly at all. Zula was used to long silences from him. In principle she didn't mind it, since between her phone, her ebook reader, and her laptop she never really felt lonely, even on long drives in the mountains. But usually when Peter was quiet for a long time it was because he was thinking about some geek thing that he was working on, which made him cheerful. His silence on the drive down from Schloss Hundschüttler had been in a different key.

From Elphinstone they would go west over the Kootenay Pass. After that, they would have to choose the lesser of two evils where routing was concerned. They could go south and cross the border at Metaline Falls. This would inject them into the extreme northeastern corner of Washington, from which they could work their way down to Spokane in a couple of hours and thence bomb right across the state on I-90. That was the route they'd taken when they'd come here on Friday. Or—

"I was thinking," said Peter, after he'd spent fifteen minutes twirling his pad thai around his fork and attempting to burn a hole through the table with his gaze, "that we should go through Canada."

He was talking about an alternate route that would take them across the upper Columbia, through the Okanagans, and eventually to Vancouver, whence they could cross the border and plug in to the northern end of I-5.

"Why?" Zula asked.

Peter gazed at her for the first time since they'd sat down. He was almost wounded by the question. It seemed for a moment as if he'd get defensive. Then he shrugged and broke eye contact.

Later, as Peter was driving them west, Zula put away her useless electronics (for phone coverage was expensive in Canada and the ebook reader couldn't be seen in the dark) and just stared out the windshield and replayed the encounter in her head. It pivoted around that word "should." If he'd said, *It would be fun to go a new way*, or *I'd like to go through Canada just for the hell of it*, she would not have come back with *Why?* since she'd been thinking along similar lines herself. But he'd said, *We should go through Canada*, which was an altogether different thing. And the way he'd deflected her question afterward put her in mind of the way he'd behaved around that stranger in the tavern. Uncle Richard's question about a drug deal had irritated her at the time. Peter's look, his clothing, the way he acted, caused older people to make wrong assumptions about who he was. But she knew perfectly well that he was a sweet and decent guy and that he never put anything stronger than Mountain Dew into his body.

Should. What possible difference could it make? The Metaline Falls border crossing was rinky-dink to be sure, but by the same token, it was little used, and so you rarely had to wait. The border guards were so lonely they practically ran out and hugged you. The Vancouver crossings were among the largest and busiest on the whole border.

He was avoiding something.

That was the one thing about Peter. If something made him uneasy, he'd dodge around it. And he was good at that. Probably didn't even *know* that he was dodging. It was just how he instinctively made his way in the world. He wasn't an Artful Dodger. More of an Artless Dodger, guileless and unaware. As a young child Zula had seen some of that behavior in Eritrea, where confronting your problems head-on wasn't always the smartest way; the patriarch of her refugee group had devised a strategy for getting even with the Ethiopians that revolved around walking barefoot across the desert to Sudan, checking into a refugee camp long enough to make his way to America, starting a life there, getting rich (at least by Horn of Africa standards), and sending money back to Eritrea to fund the ongoing war effort.

But the Forthrasts came out of a different tradition where, no matter what the problem, there was a logical and levelheaded behavior for dealing with it. *Ask your minister. Ask your scoutmaster. Ask your guidance counselor.*

Peter had been really troubled on the drive down the lake shore to Elphinstone, then hugely relieved when they had opted for the western route. By going west, he had effected some sort of dodge.

To avoid some scary-looking, switchbacky stuff in the Okanagans—perhaps not the best choice, in the middle of the night, and at this time of year—they shot up north and connected with a bigger, straighter highway at Kelowna. There they stopped at a gas station/ convenience store, and Peter took the exceptional step of buying coffee. Zula made the hopeless suggestion that she be allowed to drive and Peter offered her an alternative role: "Talk to me and keep me awake." Which she could only laugh at since he hadn't said a word. But from Kelowna onward she did try to talk to him. They ended up talking mostly about nerd stuff, since that was the only area where, once he got going, the words would really tumble out of him for hours. He was perpetually interested in the underlying security apparatus of T'Rain and how it might be vulnerable and how, therefore, he might be able to improve it, while charging them money for the service and making him look very good to his new employer. Zula was perpetually unable to talk about it much because she had signed an NDA of awesome length and intimidating detail, something on which no minister, scoutmaster, or guidance counselor could ever have given sage advice. She could talk about what had been made public, which was that her boss, Pluto, was the Keeper of the Key, the sole person on earth who knew a certain encryption key that was changed every month and that was used to digitally sign all the fantasy-geological output of his world-generating algorithm. It was sort of like the signature of the Treasurer of the United States that was printed on every dollar bill to certify that it was genuine. Because the output of Pluto's code dictated, among other things, how much gold was in each wheelbarrow of ore dug out by Dwinn miners. Zula had not been hired to work so much on the precious-metals part of the system—her job was computational fluid dynamics simulations of magma flow—but she had to touch those security measures every day, and Peter was forever posing hypothetical questions about them and how they might be breached—not by him but by hypothetical black-hat hackers that he could be paid to outwit.

That got them awake and alive to Abbotsford, still something like an hour outside of Vancouver, but grazing the U.S. border, and in some ways a more logical place to cross. They stopped, not for gas, but because Peter's bladder was full, and the stop turned into a long one as Peter used his PDA to check the waiting times at various border crossings. Meanwhile Zula went in and bought junk food. When she came out, he had the back of the vehicle open and was fussing with something back there. She heard zippers, the rustle of plastic. "You want to drive?" he asked her.

"I've been telling you for six hours that I'd be happy to drive," she pointed out mildly.

"Just thought you might have changed your mind or something, but I would really like to rest my eyes and might even go to sleep," he said, which Zula did not intuitively believe since to her he seemed to have a pretty serious buzz on. But something clicked in her head to the effect that he was dodging again. The act of driving across the border was triggering his dodging instinct. It had happened as they had neared the fork in the road at Elphinstone and was now happening again. She agreed to drive.

"It's the Peace Arch," he said. "We want the Peace Arch crossing."

"There's one, like, two miles from where we are now."

"Peace Arch has less traffic."

"Whatever then."

So she began driving them the last few dozen kilometers west, to the Peace Arch crossing, which was actually right on salt water: the farthest they could go, the longest they could delay the crossing. Peter, after a few minutes, leaned his seat back and closed his eyes and stopped moving. Though Zula had slept with him more than a few times and knew that this was not his pattern when it came to sleeping.

The electronic signs on the highway said that the so-called Truck Crossing—just a few miles to the east of the Peace Arch crossing—was actually less crowded and so she went that way. Only two cars were ahead of them in the inspection lane, which probably meant a wait of less than a minute.

"Peter?"

"Yeah?"

"Got your passport?"

"Yeah, it's in my pocket. Hey. Where are we?"

"The border."

"This is the Truck Crossing."

"Yes. Less wait time here."

"I was kind of thinking Peace Arch."

"Why does it matter?" Only one car to go. "Why don't you get out your passport?"

"Here. You can give it to the guard." Peter handed his passport to Zula, then settled back into a position of repose. "Tell him I'm asleep, okay?"

"You're not asleep."

"I just think that we're less likely to get a hassle if they think I'm asleep."

"What hassle? When is there ever a hassle at this border? It's like driving between North and South Dakota."

"Work with me."

"Then close your eyes and stop moving," she said, "and he can see for himself that you're asleep, or pretending to be. But if I state the obvious—'he's sleeping'—it's just going to seem weird. Why does it matter?"

Peter pretended to sleep and did not respond.

The car ahead of them moved on into the United States, and the green light came on to signal them forward. Zula pulled up.

"How many in the car?" asked the guard. "Citizenship?" He shone the flashlight on Peter. "Your friend's going to have to wake up."

"Two of us. U.S."

"How long have you been in Canada?"

"Three days."

"Bringing anything back?"

"No," Zula said.

"Just a bag of coffee. Some junk food," said Peter.

"Welcome home," said the guard, and turned on the green light.

Zula accelerated south. Peter motored his seat back upright and rubbed his face.

"Want your passport back?"

"Sure, thanks."

"It's like two hours to Seattle," Zula said. "Maybe that's long enough for you to explain why you have been fucking with me all day."

Peter actually seemed startled that she had figured out that he was fucking with her, but he made no attempt to protest his innocence.

A few minutes later, after she had merged into traffic on I-5, he said, "I did something hyperstupid. Maybe even relationship-endingly stupid, for all that I know."

"Who was that guy in the tavern? He had something to do with it, right?"

"Wallace. Lives in Vancouver. As far as I can tell from his trail on the Internet, he's an accountant. Trained in Scotland. Immigrated to Canada in the 1980s."

"Did you do some kind of job for him? Some kind of security gig?"

Peter was silent for a little while.

"Look," Zula said, "I just want to know what is in this car that you were so nervous about taking across the border."

"Money," he said. "Cash in excess of ten thousand dollars. I was supposed to declare it. I didn't." He leaned back, heaved a sigh. "But now we're safe. We're across the border. We—"

"Who is 'we' in this case? Am I some sort of accomplice?"

"Not legally, since you didn't know. But—"

"So was I ever in danger? Where does this come from, this 'we're safe' thing?" Zula did not often get angry, but when she did, it was a slow inexorable building.

"Wallace is just a little weird," he said. "Some things he said— I don't know. Look. I realized I was making a mistake even while I was doing this. Hated every minute of it. But then it was done and I had the money and we were on the road, headed for the border, and I started to think about the implications."

"So you *wanted* to find a border crossing that was busy," she said.

"Yeah. So they'd be more pressed for time, less likely to search the car."

"When you checked the crossing times at Abbotsford—"

"I was looking for the crossings that were busiest."

"Unbelievable."

She drove for a while, thinking through the day. "Why did you do it at the Schloss?"

"It was Wallace's idea. We were trying to match up our travel schedules. I mentioned I'd be there. He jumped at it. Didn't seem to mind driving all the way out from Vancouver in the winter. Now I realize that he didn't want to cross the border with the cash. He wanted to saddle me with that little problem."

"What kind of an accountant pays for security consulting services in cash?"

Peter said nothing.

Zula was working through it. Hundred-dollar bills. One hundred of them would make ten thousand bucks. That would be a bundle roughly how thick? Not that thick. Not that difficult to hide in a car.

He was carrying more than that. A lot more. She'd seen odd behavior connected with his luggage. Rearranging something at Abbotsford.

"Hold on a sec," Zula said. "You charge two hundred bucks an hour. It would take fifty hours of work to add up to ten thousand dollars. My sense, though, is that you are carrying a lot more than ten thousand. Which means a lot more than fifty hours of work. But you just haven't been that busy lately. You've been fixing up your building. You just spent a whole week *hanging drywall*. When could you have logged that many hours?"

And so then the story did come out.

ZULA'S PREDICTION WAS right. It did give them something to talk about all the way back to Seattle.

Peter was right too; it was a relationship termination event. Not so much what he'd done in the past—though that was pretty stupid—but what he'd done today: the ridiculous drama about crossing the border.

The real kiss of death, though, was that he invoked Uncle Richard.

It happened when they were somewhere around Everett, about to enter into the northern suburbs of Seattle. He sensed that he had ten, maybe fifteen miles in which to plead his case. Which he attempted to do by bringing up all the weird stuff that Richard Forthrast had done, or was rumored to have done, in his past. Zula seemed to get along just fine with Uncle Richard, so—the argument went—what was her problem with Peter now?

It was then that she cut him off in midsentence and said that it was over. She said it with a certainty and a conviction in her voice and her face that left him fascinated and awed. Because guys, at least of his age, didn't have the confidence to make major decisions from their gut like that. They had to build a superstructure of rational thought on top of it. But not Zula. She didn't have to decide. She just had to pass on the news.

Day 1

On Friday Zula had skipped out of work early and driven straight to Peter's space (he always called it his "space"). She had parked her car inside the more warehousey part of the building, which was accessible through a huge, grade-level, roll-up door off the back alley, and left a few of her work things there. So despite the relationship termination event, she had to go back to his place to get her car and collect her things. From I-5 she exited onto Michigan Avenue, which ran diagonally along the northern boundary of Boeing Field, and after following it toward the water for a couple of blocks, doubled back north into Georgetown.

A hundred years earlier Georgetown had been an independent city specializing in the manufacture and consumption of alcoholic beverages. It was bounded by major rail lines and industrial waterways. Early in the twentieth century it had been annexed by Seattle, which couldn't stand to see, so close to its city limits, an independent town so ripe for taxation.

When airplanes became common, the regional airport had been built immediately to the south. This was nationalized around the time of Pearl Harbor and then used by Boeing to punch out B-17s and B-29s all through the war. Georgetown's quieter and narrower streets had become crowded with riveters' bungalows. Still the neighborhood had preserved its identity until late in the century,

when it had come under attack from the north, as dot-coms looking for cheap office space had invaded the industrial flatlands south
of downtown, preying on machine shops and foundries that had
lost most of their business to China. The mills and lathes had been
torn out and junked or auctioned off, the high ceilings cleaned up
and rigged with cable ladders creaking under the weight of miles
of blue Ethernet wire. Truck drivers had had to get used to sharing the district's potholed streets with bicycle commuters in dorky
helmets and spandex. It was during that era that Peter, sensing an
opportunity, had acquired his building. He had talked himself into
it largely on the strength of a belief that he and some friends would
launch a high-tech company there. This had failed to materialize
because of changes in the financial climate, so he had ended up
using part of it as live/work space and renting the rest of it to artists and artisans, who, as it turned out, didn't pay the same kind
of rent as high-tech companies. But what was bad for Peter had
been good for Georgetown—at least, the aspect of Georgetown
that was about actually making things as opposed to playing tricks
with bits.

It was an old brick building. The ground floor had high ceilings
supported by timbers of old-growth fir, which would have made it a
fine setting for a restaurant or brewpub if the building had been on
a more accessible street and if Georgetown hadn't already had several of those. As it was, he'd subdivided that level into two bays, one
leased by an exotic-metals welder who made parts for the aerospace
industry, the other serving as Peter's workshop. It was there that
Zula's car had spent the weekend. Above was a single story of finished space with nice old windows looking out toward Boeing Field.
This too was subdivided into an open-plan live/work loft, where
Peter lived, and another unit that he had been fixing up in the hopes
of renting it to some young hip person who wanted to live, as Peter
put it "in the presence of arches."

The remark had made little sense to Zula until she had spent a
bit of time in the neighborhood and started noticing that, yes, the
old buildings sported windows and doorways that were supported
by true functioning arches of brick or stone, the likes of which were
never used in newer construction. For Peter to have noticed this was
a bit clever, and for him to have understood that it would be attrac-

tive to a certain kind of person reflected somewhat more human insight than one normally looked for in a nerd.

So, that night, when they got back to his space at about 2 A.M. and she went upstairs to collect the stuff she'd left scattered around during the months that she'd been quasi living with him, and she saw the brick window arches that he had left exposed during the remodel, a lot went through her head in a few moments and she found herself unable to move or think very clearly. She stood there in the dark. The lights of Boeing Field shone up against a low ceiling of spent rain clouds and made them glow a greenish silver that filled the apertures of the windows smoothly, as if troweled onto the glass.

She was strangely comforted. The natural thing for Zula to be asking herself at this moment was *What did I ever see in this guy?* Other than his physical beauty, which was pretty obvious. Those occasional left-handed insights, like the arches. Another thing: he worked very hard and knew how to do a lot of things, which had put her in mind of the family back in Iowa. He was intelligent, and, as evidenced by the books stacked and scattered all over the place, he was interested in many things and could talk about them in an engaging way, when he felt like talking. Being here now, alone (for he was down in the bay unpacking his gear), enabled her to walk through the process of getting a crush on him, like reenacting a crime scene, and thereby to convince herself that she hadn't just been out-and-out stupid. She could forgive herself for not having noticed the relationship-ending qualities that had been so screamingly obvious for the last twelve hours. Her girlfriends had probably *not* been asking each other, behind Zula's back, what she saw in that guy.

Which led her to question, one last time—as long as she was alone in the dark and still had the opportunity—whether she should have broken up with him at all. But she was pretty certain that when she woke up tomorrow morning she'd feel right about it. This was the third guy she had broken up with. Where she'd gone to school, mixed-race computational fluid dynamics geeks didn't get as many dates as, say, blond, blue-eyed hotel and restaurant management majors. But, like a tenement dweller nurturing a rooftop garden in coffee cans, she had cultivated and maintained a little social life of her own, and harvested the occasional ripe tomato, and maybe enjoyed it more intensely than someone who could buy them by the sack at Safeway. So she was not utterly inexperienced. She'd done it before. And she felt as right about this breakup as she did about the other two.

She turned on the lights, which hurt her tired eyes, and began picking up stuff that she knew was hers: from the bathroom, her minimal but important cosmetics, and some hair management tools. From her favorite corner, some notes and books related to work. A couple of novels. Nothing important, but she didn't want Peter to wake up every morning and be confronted with random small bits of Zula spoor. She piled what she found at the top of the stairs that led down into the bay and looped back through the living quarters, gleaning increasingly nonobvious bits of stuff: a baseball cap, a hair clip, a coffee mug, lip balm. She went slower and took longer than necessary because when this was over she'd have to carry it all downstairs to the bay where Peter was fussing with his snowboarding gear, and that would be awkward. She was too tired and spent to contend with that awkwardness in a graceful way and did not want Peter's last recollection of her to be as a fuming bitch.

When she returned to her stuff pile for what she estimated was the penultimate time, she heard voices downstairs. Peter's and another man's. She couldn't make out any words, but the other man was vastly excited. A cool draft was coming up the stairs from below: outside air flowing in through the open bay door. It carried the sharp perfume of incompletely burned gasoline, a smell that nowadays came only from very old cars, precatalytic converter.

Zula looked out a small back window on the alley side of the building and saw a sports car parked there with its lights on, the driver's door hanging open, the engine still running. The driver was arguing with Peter down in the bay. She assumed that this was because Peter had left the Scion blocking the alley while he unloaded. The convertible was stopped nose to nose with the Scion; its driver, or so Zula speculated, was pissed off that he couldn't get through. He was in a hurry and drunk. Or maybe on meth, to judge from the intensity of his rage. She couldn't quite follow the argument that was going on downstairs. Peter was astonished by something, but he was taking the part of the reasonable guy trying to calm the stranger down. The stranger was shouting in bursts, and

Zula couldn't understand him. He had (she realized) some sort of accent, and while her English was pretty much perfect, she did have a few weak spots, and accents were one of them.

She was just about to call 911 when she heard the stranger mention "voice mail."

". . . turned it off . . ." Peter explained, again in a very calm and reasonable voice.

". . . all the way from fucking Vancouver," the stranger complained, "rain pissing down."

Zula moved to the window and looked at the stranger's car again and saw that it had British Columbia license plates.

It was that guy. It was Wallace.

There had been some kind of problem with the transaction. It was a customer service call.

No. Tech support. Wallace was complaining about a "fucking virus or something."

The tension somehow broke. The adrenaline buzz on which Wallace had blasted down from Vancouver had abated. They had agreed to talk about this calmly. Wallace shut off the convertible's engine, killed the lights, came into the bay. Peter pulled the door down behind him.

"Whose car is this?" Wallace demanded. Now that the big door was closed, the sound echoed up the steps and Zula was better able to follow the conversation. Her ear was tuning in to the Scottish accent.

"Zula's," Peter said.

"The girl? She's here?"

"I dropped her off at home." Zula noted the lie with grudging thanks and admiration. "She parks it here when she's not using it."

"I have to take a vicious piss."

"There's a urinal right over there."

"Good man." The freestanding urinal in the middle of his shop was one of Peter's proudest innovations. Zula heard Wallace's zipper going down, heard him using it, thought it would be funny to come down the stairs and make her exit at that point. But her car was now blocked in by Wallace's. "I've been assuming that you deliberately fucked me," Wallace remarked, as he was peeing, "but now I entertain the possibility that it is something other than that."

"Good. Because it was totally on the up-and-up."

"Other than being a massive identity theft scheme, you mean to say."

"Yes."

"Convincing me of that is easy enough. Already done. But the people I work with are another thing." Wallace finished and zipped up again. Zula could hear the timbre of his voice change as he turned around.

"I thought you said you worked alone."

"I was telling the truth the first time," Wallace said.

"Oh," Peter said after a noticeable pause.

"I've already had three fucking emails from my contact in Toronto wanting to know where the hell are the credit card numbers. As a matter of fact, I'd better send him an update right now. If lying through my teeth can be so called."

The conversation lapsed for a few moments, and Zula guessed that Wallace was thumb-typing on a phone.

"I guess I don't understand why you haven't just sent him the numbers," Peter said. "So maybe you should just take this from the top, because everything you were shouting when you pulled up a few minutes ago left me totally confused."

"Almost finished," Wallace muttered.

"The password to my Wi-Fi is here," Peter said, and Zula heard him sliding a piece of paper down the counter.

"Never mind, I used something called Tigmaster."

"You should use mine; it is way more secure than Tigmaster."

"What is that anyway, an animal trainer?"

"Welder. My tenant. He should put a password on his Wi-Fi, but he can't be bothered."

"Right, he's not security conscious like you and me."

Peter didn't answer since that must have sounded to him, as it did to Zula, like a trap.

Zula had thought better of calling 911 when she understood that it was Wallace and not some random enraged crankhead. Now she considered it again. But Wallace was much calmer now. And Peter was the only person here who had actually broken the law. Zula was satisfied just to have broken up with him. Sending him to prison would have been overkill.

"Take it from the top? All right, here we go," said Wallace, then paused. "Any beers in that fridge?"

"I thought you didn't drink."

Silence.

"Be my guest."

Fridge-opening and beer sound effects as Wallace went on: "As you saw, I transferred the file to my laptop right there in the tavern. Verified its contents. Closed the laptop. Went to my car. Drove back to Vancouver, stopping only once for petrol, never left the car, never let the laptop out of my sight. Parked in the garage at my condo building, went to my flat, hand-carrying the laptop. Set it down on my desk, plugged it in, opened it up, verified that everything was just as I'd left it."

"When you say 'plugged it in,' could you please tell me every-thing you plugged into it?" Peter had now dropped, improbably, into a polite, clinical mode, like a customer service rep in a Banga-lore cubicle farm.

"Power, Ethernet, external monitor, and FireWire."

"You say Ethernet—you don't use Wi-Fi at home?"

"Are you fucking kidding me?"

"Just asking. You have some kind of firewall or something between raw Internet and your laptop?"

"Of course, it's a corporate firewall solution that I pay a fucking mint for every month. Have a lad who maintains it for me. Totally locked down. Never a problem."

"You mentioned FireWire. What's on that?" Peter asked.

"My backup drive."

"So you're backing up your files locally?"

"You're not getting this, are you?" Wallace asked. "I told you who I worked for, yes?"

"Yes."

Peter had not mentioned to Zula that Wallace worked for any-one and so she did not understand what this was about, but the way both men talked about Wallace's employer had certainly attracted her notice.

"There are a couple of things I would never, ever like to have to explain to him," Wallace said. "First, that I lost important files because I forgot to back them up. Second, that his files have been accessed by unauthorized persons because I backed them up to a remote server not under my physical control. So what choice do I have?"

"Keeping the hardware under your physical control is the only way to be sure," Peter said soothingly. "What is the backup drive exactly?"

"A rather pricey off-the-shelf RAID 3 box, which I have placed inside of a safe that is bolted into the concrete wall and floor of the condo. When I am home, I open the safe and pull out the FireWire cable and connect it to my laptop long enough to accomplish the backup, then close it all up again."

Peter considered it. "Unconventional but pretty logical" was his verdict. "To physically steal the box, someone would have to do huge damage to the safe and probably destroy the RAID."

"That's kind of my thinking."

"Okay, so your first move on getting home was to open the safe and make a backup just like you said, so that if your laptop's drive just happened to crash at that particular moment you'd still have a copy of the file I sold you."

"You convinced me that it was the only copy extant," said Wallace, sounding almost defensive.

"So in a world governed by Murphy's law, making an immediate backup was the right move," Peter agreed.

"He was expecting the file to show up on a particular server in Budapest no later than . . . translating to West Coast time, here . . . two A.M., and it was only midnight."

"Plenty of time."

"So I thought," Wallace said. "Having set the backup in motion, I left the room, took a piss, and listened to the voice mail on my landline while I unpacked a few items and mixed myself a drink. I sorted through the mail. This might have taken all of about fifteen minutes. I went back to my study and sat down in front of my laptop and opened up a terminal window. When I am undertaking operations of this sort, I prefer to use SCP from the command line."

"As you should," Peter agreed.

"My first move was to check the contents of 'Documents' to remind myself of the filename and approximate size of the file that you sold me. And when I did that, I saw—well, see for yourself."

Evidently Wallace's laptop was already open on Peter's workbench. There was a brief pause and then Peter said, "Hmm."

"You need to understand that yesterday, 'Documents' contained a dozen or so subdirectories and maybe two score of files," Wallace said.

"Including the file in question."

"Yes."

"And now it contains two files and two files only," Peter said, "one of which is called troll.gpg, the other—"

"README," Wallace said. "So I read the fucking thing."

Peter snorted. "I think it's *supposed* to be called README," he said, "but there's a typo. They transposed two letters, see?"

"REAMDE," Wallace said.

"You've already opened it?"

"Perhaps stupidly, yeah."

Peter double-clicked. There was a pause while (Zula imagined) he examined the contents of the REAMDE file.

The name had jogged a vague memory. Zula's bag was leaning against the wall right next to her. Moving quietly, she reached into the padded laptop slot at its top and pulled out her computer. She set it on the floor, sat down next to it, and opened it up. Her first move was to hit the button that muted the sound. Within a few seconds it had attached itself to Peter's Wi-Fi network. She clicked an icon that caused a VPN connection to be established to Corporation 9592's network.

"We already established that you're not a T'Rain player," Wallace said.

"Never got into it," Peter admitted.

"Well, that picture you're looking at is of a troll. A particular type of mountain troll that lives in a particular region of T'Rain, rather inaccessible I'm afraid. Which might help you make sense of the caption."

" 'Ha ha noob, you are powned by troll. I have encrypt all your file. Leave 1000 GP at below coordinates and I give you key.' Ah, okay, I get it."

"Well, I'm pretty fucking glad that you get it, my friend, because—"

"And now," said Peter, cutting him off, "if we check out the contents of the other file, troll.gpg, we find that"—miscellaneous clicks—"one, it is huge, and two, it is a correctly formatted gpg file."

"You call that correctly formatted!?"

"Yeah. A standard header and then several gigs of random-looking binary content."

"Several gigs you say."

"Yeah. This one file is big enough to contain, probably, all the files that were originally stored in your 'Documents' folder. But if we take the message in REAMDE at face value, it's all been encrypted. Your files are being held for ransom."

Zula had brought up Corporation 9592's internal wiki, and now went to a page entitled MALWARE. Several trojans and viruses were listed. REAMDE wasn't difficult to find; it was the first word on the page, it was large, and it was red. When she clicked through to the dedicated page for REAMDE and checked its history, she found that 90 percent of its content had been written during the last seventy-two hours. Corporation 9592's security hackers had been toiling at it all weekend.

"How is this possible?" Wallace demanded.

Upstairs, Zula was already reading about how it was possible.

"It's not just possible, it's actually pretty easy, once your system has been rooted by a trojan," Peter said. "This isn't the first. People have been making malware that does this for a few years now. There's a word for it: 'ransomware.'"

"I've never heard of it."

"It is hard to turn this kind of virus into a profitable operation," Peter said, "because there has to be a financial transaction: the payment of the ransom. And that can be traced."

"I see," Wallace said. "So if you're in the malware business, there are easier ways to make money."

"By running botnets or whatever," Peter agreed. "The new wrinkle here, apparently, is that the ransom is to be paid in the form of virtual gold pieces in T'Rain."

"So until now, this has been a technical possibility, but few people have used it on a large scale," Wallace said, working it through. "But these fuckers have figured out a way to use T'Rain as a money-laundering system."

"Yeah," Peter said. "And I'm guessing, since you drove all the way down here and left, as I now see, eight voice mails on my phone, that your backup drive in the safe also got infected."

"Yeah, it fucked everything it could reach," Wallace said. "It must have passed into my system from that fucking thumb drive you handed me, and then—"

"Don't try to make this my fault. I use Linux, remember? Different OS, different malware."

"Then how did this fucking virus get on to my laptop?"

"I don't know," Peter said.

Zula did know, because she was skimming pages of technical analyses of the REAMDE virus. One of the ways it propagated was through thumb drives and other removable media. And Peter had borrowed one of Richard's old thumb drives so that he could transfer something into Wallace's computer. Richard's machine must be infected with REAMDE; but he wouldn't know or care, since he was protected by corporate IT.

"But it doesn't matter," Peter continued. "All that matters is—"

"It *does* matter for establishing culpability," Wallace said. "Which may be of interest to him."

"All I'm saying is, we have to address the problem," Peter said.

"Brilliant analysis there, Petey boy. It's quarter to three. I'm already forty-five minutes late. I bought myself a bit of time by sending an email with some bullshit to the effect that my car broke down in the Okanagans. But the clock is ticking. We have got to decrypt that file!"

"No," Peter said, "we have to pay the ransom."

"Fuck that."

"It is not possible to decrypt the file," Peter said. "If we had the NSA working on it, we could probably decrypt it. But as matters stand, you're screwed unless you pay the ransom."

"*We're* screwed," Wallace corrected him, "since this is all much too complicated to explain to him. He is *not* a computer guy. Has never heard of T'Rain, or any other massively multiplayer online game, for that matter. *Might* just barely understand the concept of a computer virus. All he'll understand is that he doesn't have what he paid for."

"Then it's like I said. We pay the ransom."

Quite a long silence.

"I was hoping," Wallace said, "that there was another copy of the file."

"I already told you—"

"I know what you fucking told me," Wallace said. "I was hoping that you were lying."

"Is this all just another ruse to find out whether or not I *am* lying?"

"You're just clever enough to be stupider than if you weren't clever at all," Wallace said. "This is quite real. I very badly want you to tell me, right now, Peter, that you lied to me earlier and that you have a backup copy of the file on one of your machines here."

And then Wallace dropped his voice to a low growl and talked for about two minutes. During this time, Zula could not make out a single word that Wallace was saying.

When he was finished, all Peter could say, for a minute or so, was the f-word. He said it in about a dozen different ways, like an actor searching for just the right reading.

"Well, it doesn't matter," he finally said, very close to sobbing, "because I was telling you the truth before. There really is no other copy!"

Now it was Wallace's turn to say the f-word a lot.

"So we have to pay the ransom," Peter said. "A thousand gold pieces?"

"That's what it says," Wallace answered.

"How much is that in real money?"

"Seventy-three dollars."

Peter, after a moment, let out a burst of laughter that sounded eerie to Zula. He was close to hysteria. "Seventy-three dollars? This whole problem can be solved for *seventy-three bucks*!?"

"Raising the funds isn't the hard part," Wallace said.

Something about the sound of Peter's laugh told Zula it was time to call 911. Best to do it from a landline so that the dispatcher would have the building's address. She got up as quietly as she could and padded around to the corner where Peter had all his kitchen stuff. A cordless phone was bracketed to the wall. She picked up the handset and turned it on, then put it to her ear to check for a dial tone.

Instead of which, she heard a series of touch-tone beeps.

Someone else was on the line, on another extension, dialing a different number.

"Welcome to Qwest directory assistance," said a recorded voice.

"Good morning, Zula," said Wallace on the other extension. "I know you're in the building because your computer suddenly popped up on Peter's network. I've been keeping an eye on the phone down here. It's got a handy little indicator, tells me when another extension is in use."

The phone went dead. Down below, Zula could hear ripping and snapping noises as Wallace did something violent to the line. "What are you doing!?" Peter exclaimed, more confused than anything else.

"Getting us all on the same level," Wallace said. She could hear him bounding up the stairs.

ZULA CARRIED A bike messenger shoulder bag rather than a purse. She'd left it on the floor at the top of the stairs. Wallace stirred a hand through it, plucked out her phone, then her car keys. With his other hand he closed the lid on her laptop and picked it up. "When you're feeling more sociable, I'd be pleased to see you below," he announced, then turned and walked back down the stairs.

She heard her Prius beep as he unlocked it with the key fob. For some reason that broke her out of her paralysis. She walked over to her bag. She was starting to wish she'd listened to all her relatives in Iowa who thought of Seattle as being only one step above Mogadishu and who kept importuning her to get a concealed weapons permit and buy a handgun. In an outside pocket of the bag she did have a folding knife, which she now found and slipped into the back pocket of her jeans. Then she came down the stairs to see Wallace slamming the passenger door of the Prius and hitting the lock button. He pocketed the key chain. "Your mobile and Peter's are safe and sound inside the car," he announced. Zula didn't understand this use of "mobile" until she reached the base of the steps and saw two phones resting side by side on the car's dashboard.

"Fucking rude of me, ain't it?" Wallace said, looking her hard in the eye. "But for us to solve this problem we need to trust each other and to focus, and you kids nowadays substitute communicating for thinking, don't you? So let's think."

She could feel Peter's gaze on her, knew that if she turned to face him, a channel would open up between them and he would try to say something, by a gesture or a look on his face, probably by way of apology. She did not do so. Peter needed to issue an apology much more than she needed to receive one, and, in keeping with Wallace's suggestion, she wanted to focus on solving the problem and getting out of here.

"We need to deliver a thousand GP to a location in the western Torgai Foothills?" she said.

"And then pray that our virus writer is a nice honest criminal who'll cough up the key promptly," Wallace said.

"If we're going to travel with that much gold, we are going to be a target for thieves," she pointed out.

"It's only seventy-three dollars," Peter said.

"To a teenager," Zula said, "in an Internet café in China, it's huge. And stealing it from travelers on a road is much faster than mining it."

"Not to mention more fun," Wallace added.

"How will their characters even know that you're carrying that much gold?" Peter asked.

"I have an idea," Wallace announced brightly. He turned to face Peter and aimed a finger at him. "You: shut the fuck up. If you can make yourself useful in some other way, such as making coffee, please do so. But Zula and I don't have time to explain every last fucking detail of T'Rain to you." Wallace turned back to Zula. "Shall we make ourselves comfortable upstairs?"

"WHAT IS YOUR most powerful character?" Zula asked as she was plugging in her power adapter in what passed for Peter's living room. Peter was in what passed for a kitchen, making coffee.

"I only have one," Wallace said. "An Evil T'Kesh Metamorph." He was logging on to T'Rain using Peter's workstation.

"Let me see him," Zula said. She launched the T'Rain app on her laptop and logged in. She was sitting in an office chair, which she now rolled over in Wallace's direction as far as the power cord would let her go. Wallace's T'Kesh Metamorph was visible on the screen of the workstation.

"What have you got?" Wallace asked, taking a peek at her laptop. "A whole zoo of characters, I'll bet?"

"Employees don't get in-game perks. We have to build our characters from scratch just like the customers."

"Probably a wise corporate policy," said Wallace, sounding a bit disappointed.

"I have two. Both Good," Zula said. "But of course it doesn't matter anymore."

"The one on the left," Wallace said, craning his neck sideways to look at her screen, "is a better match in these times, is it not?"

He was talking, of course, about palettes.

Until the week before Christmas, it would have been quite difficult for Zula's and Wallace's characters to do anything together in T'Rain, because hers were Good and his was Evil. Hers would not have been able to travel very far into Evil territory, or his into Good. They could have met up in some wilderness area or war zone, but that would not have helped them on this mission, since the western Torgai Foothills were an island of firmly Evil territory most easily approached from Good zones to the west.

But then, as millions of students had gone on Christmas break and found themselves with vast amounts of free time for playing T'Rain, the War of Realignment had been launched. This had been carefully prepared, for months in advance, by parties still unknown. It basically consisted of a hitherto unidentified group, consisting of both Good and Evil characters, launching a well-laid blitzkrieg against a different group, also mixed Good/Evil, that wasn't even aware it was a group until the hammer fell on them. The aggressors had been dubbed, by Richard Forthrast, the Forces of Brightness. The victims of the attack were the Earthtone Coalition. These terms, initially used only for internal memos in Corporation 9592, had leaked out into the player community and were now being printed on T-shirts.

Wallace's character was identifiable from a thousand yards away as belonging to the Earthtone Coalition. Zula's first character—the one on the left—was also Earthtone. Her other character was markedly Brighter. She had created it on Christmas Eve when it had become obvious that large parts of the world of T'Rain were being rendered inaccessible to her Earthtone character because of the huge advances being made on all fronts by the numerically superior legions of the Forces of Brightness. In consequence, her Bright character—being newer—was much weaker. How *much* weaker was a matter of interpretation. In a radical break with role-playing game tradition, T'Rain did not use numerical levels to indicate the power of its characters; rather, it used Aura, which was a three-part score calculated from a number of statistics including the character's rank in its vassal network, the size and overall power of that network, the amount of experience it had racked up, the number of things it knew how to do, and the quality of its equipment. As a character's Aura expanded it acquired certain perks, but never in a wholly predictable way.

The world that Pluto's software had created was almost exactly the same size as Earth, which meant that traveling around it using thematically appropriate (i.e., medieval) forms of transportation required a lot of time. In theory that might have been fixable by messing around with the very definition of time itself; one could imagine, for example, jump-cutting from the beginning of a three-month sea voyage to its end. This was fine in single-player games but totally unworkable in a multiplayer setting. The progress of time in T'Rain had been locked down to that of the real world.

Pluto's solution had been to computer-generate a system of ley lines that crisscrossed the world with density comparable to that of the New York City subway system. This had been used as the basis of a teleportation system that worked by routing characters to intersections of ley lines. The number of lines and intersections was incredibly colossal and made far more complex by the fact that certain lines could only be accessed by certain types of characters. No one could really use the system without the aid of software that kept track of everything and provided suggestions on how to get from point A to point B.

And so with a few moments' work, Zula and Wallace were able to teleport their characters to a city in the flatlands below the Torgai Foothills. Wallace's character went to a moneychanger and acquired a thousand gold pieces, which would show up as a $73 charge on Wallace's credit card. From there they teleported to the closest ley line intersection that they could find to the coordinates specified in the REAMDE ransom note, which, from there, would be a fifteen-minute ride on the swift mounts that both of them owned.

The ley line intersection point was marked by a simple cairn. This shimmered into view on both of their screens. Zula turned her character (a K'Shetriae mage) until she saw Wallace's T'Kesh standing about a hundred feet away (the teleportation process involved some positional error).

The most notable feature of the landscape was that it was littered—no, paved—with corpses in varying stages of decomposition.

A boulder, about the size of an exercise ball, plunged out of the sky and struck the ground nearby. Since meteorites were no more common in T'Rain than they were on Earth, Zula suspected some artificial cause. Turning toward the nearest of the Torgai Foothills, a small peak a couple of hundred meters distant, she saw a battery of three trebuchets, one of which was being reloaded. The other two were just in the act of firing. Their dangling weights and hurling slings seemed ungainly, chaotic, and unlikely to work. But they did a fine job of hurling two additional boulders in her direction. Zula had to dodge one. Not far away was an outcropping of stone that looked like it might provide shelter. She ran to it and immediately came under fire from a squadron of horse archers hidden in tall grass nearby. She invoked some spells that should have protected her from the barrage of arrows, but one of them scored a lucky hit and killed her. Her character disappeared from the screen and went to Limbo.

Zula turned her head to see how Wallace was faring. Not much better. He was pinned under a boulder and had been surrounded by another squadron of horse archers, riding around him in a ring, firing inward. His health was low and dropping fast. "Don't let yourself get captured," she warned him. "I know," he said, and clicked an icon on his screen, helpfully labeled FALL ON YOUR SWORD.

ARE YOU SURE YOU WANT TO FALL ON YOUR SWORD? asked a dialog box.

YES, clicked Wallace.

A few seconds later his character was in Limbo too.

"It's so obvious," Wallace said, after devoting a few moments to regaining his composure. "This REAMDE thing has infected—how many computers?"

"Estimated at a couple of hundred thousand," said Peter, who'd been sitting in the corner with his laptop, doing research on it. But he could only see Internet rumors in the public domain. Zula, thanks to her access to the VPN, knew that the real figure was closer to a million.

"All the victims have to go to the same fucking place with a thousand gold pieces. So naturally, thieves are going to set up an ambush at the closest ley line intersection."

"It would pay for itself pretty quickly," Zula allowed.

"So those guys stole your money?" asked Peter, violating the rule, earlier laid down by Wallace, that he couldn't ask stupid questions about how T'Rain worked.

"No, because I fell on my sword, and died, and went to Limbo with all my kit," Wallace said. "If I'd gotten weak enough for them to capture me, then they could've made away with the gold and everything else. But I was lucky. What they're doing is probably quite profitable."

"So what do we do?" Zula asked.

"Get out of Limbo," Wallace said. This was easy enough; there were half a dozen ways to bring a character back to life, each with its own pros and cons. "Find a less obvious ley line intersection. Go there and be ready to fight our way through."

"We could recruit a larger party—"

"At three in the morning? Not enough time," Wallace said. "You're sure you can't recruit a more . . . omniscient character?"

"You mean, wake up my uncle?" Zula responded. "Are you sure you want him involved?"

SO THEY GOT out of Limbo and tried again, teleporting to another, much less convenient ley line intersection an hour's ride from the place they were trying to reach. Here they were immediately ambushed, and nearly overcame the thieves, but because of some unluckiness they ended up in Limbo again and had to try it a third time. First, though, Wallace got more gold pieces and used them to buy, at extortionate rates, some spells and potions that would keep them alive a bit longer. They teleported back in again and fought their way through the ambush and withdrew to higher ground

a couple of thousand yards away—where they were set upon by
another party of thieves before they could recover from wounds
suffered in the first ambush. They fought back as hard as they could
but ended up in Limbo once more.

Just before Zula's character perished, though, she saw something a bit odd: some of their ambushers were going down with
spears and arrows lodged in their backs. The ambushers had been
counterambushed by some hostile group that had rushed to the
scene of the fight but arrived too late.

"Let's go back there," she suggested. "I think we have help."

"Saw them. It's just another group of thieves," Wallace said.

"So what? Let them kill each other."

So they attempted to do the same thing, except this time they
didn't even make it past the first group of thieves. Again, though,
their ambushers got ambushed.

Another potion-buying spree led to another attempt at the same
location. This time—now that they knew something of the ambushers' numbers and tactics—they dispatched the first group handily,
and then retreated to a place where they would have a few minutes'
respite before the second group attacked them. And this time—
because she knew what to watch for—Zula was distinctly able to
see two separate groups converging on them: the bandits, and the
bandit fighters. And her theory about the latter group was borne out
when they focused all their fire on the bandits but left Zula's and
Wallace's characters alone. One of them even cast a healing spell on
Zula's character when her health was beginning to run low.

But then they retreated into the woods with no explanation, no
attempts to communicate.

"I get it," Wallace finally said. "They work for the Troll."

"Interesting," Zula said.

"Their job is to help ransom carriers make it through."

"Well," said Zula, causing her character to mount up, "let's
make the most of it."

And so began what they had expected to be an hour-long ride.

In practice, five hours of intense and difficult play got them most
of the way there. The Torgai Foothills—which, only two weeks ago,
had been some of the most desolate territory in all T'Rain—were
tonight overrun by roving bands of characters Good and Evil, Bright

and Earthtone. Every bit of open land was littered with skeletons of departed characters and infested by ransom thieves fighting pitched battles against hastily formed coalitions of ransom carriers. Zula and Wallace joined up with one such group that was carrying a total of eight thousand gold pieces. It was reduced to a quarter of that size by successive ambushes and then joined another coalition with ten members, which later split up because, as they belatedly found out, they were going to different places: apparently, different REAMDE files specified different coordinates. Everything was hard fought and required multiple scouting missions, feints, and probing attacks.

Zula was not a gamer. She avoided people who were (another reason she'd liked Peter). She'd fallen into the job at Corporation 9592 not out of any desire to work in that industry but because of the family connection and the accident of knowing how to do what Pluto wanted. The character she'd created in the world of T'Rain was her first personal exposure to this world, and it had taken some getting used to. She had learned to understand and appreciate the game's addictive qualities without really being addicted herself. Devoting this much time—six hours and counting—to a game session was a new behavior for her. She was only doing it to extricate herself and Peter from this freak situation they had gotten into. She had assumed that it would take about fifteen minutes and that then she would go home and never see Peter again, never see Wallace again.

Now it was light outside. She'd been awake for twenty-four hours. There was something deeply wrong about the situation, and the only thing that had kept her from simply running out the door of the building and flagging down the first car she saw and asking them to call 911 was the addictive quality of the game itself, her own inability to pull herself out of the make-believe narrative that she and Wallace had found themselves in. She'd always scorned people who compulsively played these games when they should have been studying or exercising. Now she was playing the game when she should have been calling the cops. And yet none of this crossed her mind until Wallace's phone began to emit a Klaxon alarm sound, and she looked up and noticed that it was daytime, that her bladder was about to explode, and that Peter was asleep on the couch.

It wasn't the first time that Wallace's phone had rung. He had it programmed to make different ring sounds for different people.

Until now his calls had all been generic electronic chirps, which he had silenced and ignored. But this was the sound of battle stations on an aircraft carrier. He snatched it up immediately and answered "Hello." Not "Hello?" with the rising inflection that meant *To whom am I speaking?* but "Hello" with the full stop that meant *I was wondering when you'd call.*

The sound of the Klaxon had awakened Peter, who sat up on the couch and was dismayed to see that last night hadn't just been a bad dream.

Zula got up and went to the bathroom and peed. She was debating whether she ought to look in the mirror or just shield her eyes from the sight of herself. She heard Peter cursing about something. She decided not to look in the mirror. All her stuff was in the shoulder bag anyway.

She emerged from the bathroom to find Wallace sitting rigidly in his chair, quite pale, mostly just listening, almost as if the phone had been shoved up his arse. Peter was pounding away furiously on his laptop. The T'Rain game had vanished from the screen of the computer that Wallace had been using and from Zula's as well. In its place was a message letting them know that their Internet connection had been lost.

She smelled cigarette smoke.

No one was smoking.

"Tigmaster's down too," Peter said, "and all the other Wi-Fi networks that I can reach from here are password protected."

"Who's smoking?" she asked.

"Yes, sir," Wallace finally said into his phone. "I'm doing it now. I'm doing it now. No. No, sir. Only three of us."

He had gotten to his feet and was lurching toward Peter and Zula. He came very close, as if he couldn't see them and was about to walk right through them. Then he stopped himself awkwardly. He took the phone away from his head long enough for them to hear shouting coming from its earpiece. Then he put it briefly to his head again. "I'm doing it now. I'm putting you on speakerphone now, sir."

He pressed a button on the telephone and then laid it on his outstretched palm.

"Good morning!" said a voice. "Ivanov speaking." He was

somewhere noisy: behind his voice was a whining roar. The pitch changed. He was calling from an airplane. A jet. "Ah, I see you now!"

"You . . . see us, sir?" Wallace asked.

"Your buildink. The buildink of Peter. Out window. Just like in Google Maps."

Silence.

"I am flyink over you now!" Ivanov shouted, amused, rather than annoyed, at their slowness.

A plane flew low over the building. Planes flew low over the building all the time. They were on the landing path for Boeing Field.

"Soon I will be there for discussion of problem," Ivanov continued. "Until then, you stay on line. Do not break connection. I have associates on street around your place."

Ivanov said this as if the associates were there as a favor, to be at their service. Peter edged toward a window, looked down, focused on something, and got a stricken look.

Meanwhile another voice was speaking in Russian to Ivanov. Someone on the plane.

"Fuck!" Wallace mouthed, and turned his head away as if the phone were burning his eyes with arc light.

"What?" Zula asked.

"I have correction," said Ivanov. "Associates are inside buildink. Not just in streets around. Very hard workers—enterprising. Wi-Fi is cut. Phone is cut. Stay calm. We are landink now. Be there in a few minutes."

"Who the fuck is this person on the phone!?" Peter finally shouted.

"Mr. Ivanov and, if I'm not mistaken, Mr. Sokolov," said Wallace.

"Yes, Sokolov is with me!" said Ivanov. "You have good hearink."

"Flying over the building—from where?" Peter demanded.

"Toronto," Wallace said.

"How—what—?—!"

"I gather," Wallace said, "that while we were playing T'Rain, Mr. Ivanov chartered a flight from Toronto to Boeing Field."

Peter stared out the window, watched a corporate jet—Ivanov's?—landing.

"Google Maps? He knows my name?"

"Yes, Peter!" said Ivanov on the speakerphone.

"You might recall," said Wallace, "that when I arrived, the first thing I did was to send an email message using the Tigmaster access point."

"You lied to me, Wallace!" said Ivanov.

"I lied to Mr. Ivanov," Wallace confirmed. "I told him that I was delayed in south-central British Columbia by car trouble and that I would email him the file of credit card numbers in a few hours."

"Csongor was too smart for you!" Ivanov said.

"What the fuck is CHONGOR?" Peter asked.

"Who. Not what. A hacker who handles our affairs. My email message to Mr. Ivanov passed through Csongor's servers. He noticed that the originating IP address was not, in fact, in British Columbia."

"Csongor traced the message to this building by looking up the IP address," Peter said in a dull voice.

Thunking noises from the phone. "We are in car," said Ivanov, as if this would be a comfort to them.

"How can they already be in a fucking car?!" Peter asked.

"That's how it is when you travel by private jet."

"Don't they have to go through customs?"

"They would have done that in Toronto."

Peter made up his mind about something, strode across the loft, and pulled a hanging cloth aside to reveal a gun safe standing against the wall. He began to punch a number into its keypad.

"Oh holy shit," Zula said.

Wallace hit the mute button on his phone. "What is Peter doing?"

"Getting his new toy," Zula said.

"His snowboard?"

"Assault rifle."

"I have lost connection to Wallace!" Ivanov said. "Wallace? WALLACE!"

"Peter? PETER!" Wallace shouted.

"Who is there?" Ivanov wanted to know. "I hear female voice sayink holy shit." Then he switched to Russian.

Peter had got the safe open, revealing the assault rifle in question: the only thing he owned on which he had spent more time shopping than the snowboard. It had every kind of cool dingus hanging off it that money could buy: laser sight, folding bipod, and stuff of which Zula did not know the name.

Wallace said, "Peter. The gun. In other circumstances, maybe. These guys here, down on the street? You might have a chance. Local guys. Nobodies. But." He waved the phone around. "He's brought Sokolov with him." As if this were totally conclusive.

"Who the fuck is Sokolov?" Peter wanted to know.

"A bad person to get into a gunfight with. Close the safe. Take it easy."

Peter hesitated. On the speakerphone, Ivanov had escalated to shouting in Russian.

"I'm dead," Wallace said. "I'm a dead man, Peter. You and Zula might live through this. If you close that safe."

Peter seemingly couldn't move.

Zula walked over to him. Her intention, in doing so, was to close the safe before anything crazy happened. But when she got there, she found herself taking a good long look at the assault rifle.

She knew how to use it better than Peter did.

On the speakerphone, the one called Sokolov began to speak in Russian. In contrast to Ivanov, he had all the emotional range of an air traffic controller.

"Zula?" Wallace asked, in a quiet voice.

Down in the bay, the voice of Sokolov was coming out of someone's phone. Feet began to pound up the steps.

"Clips," Peter said. "I don't have any clips loaded. Just loose cartridges. Remember?"

Peter, that is not a home defense weapon, she had told him when he'd bought himself the gun for Christmas. *If you fire that thing at a burglar, it's going to kill some random person half a mile away.*

"Well then," Zula said, and slammed the door.

They turned to see a great big potato of a shaven-headed man reaching the top of the steps. He swiveled his head to take a census of the people in the room: Peter and Zula, then Wallace. Then his head snapped back to Peter and Zula as he took in the detail of the gun safe. The look on his face might have been comical in some other circumstances. Zula displayed the palms of her hands and, after a moment, so did Peter. They moved away from the gun safe. The big man hustled over and checked its door and verified that it was locked. He muttered something and they heard it echo, an instant later, on Wallace's speakerphone.

Wallace unmuted it. "I am sorry, Mr. Ivanov," he said. "We had a little argument."

"Makink me nervous."

"Nothing to be nervous about, sir."

"This can't just be about the credit card numbers," Peter said. "No one would charter a private jet just because you lied to them in an email about when the credit card numbers would be available."

"You're right," Wallace said. "It's not just about the credit card numbers."

"What's it about then?"

"Larger issues raised by last night's events."

"Such as?"

"The integrity and security of all the other files that were on my laptop."

"What kind of files were those?"

"It's unbelievably fucking stupid for you to ask," Wallace pointed out.

"Explanation is comink," said Ivanov. "We are here."

Zula stepped closer to one of the windows in the front of the building and saw a black town car pulling up.

Two men who had been loitering outside approached the car and opened its back doors.

From the passenger side emerged a stout man in a dinner jacket. From behind the driver emerged a lithe man in pajamas, a leather jacket thrown over the pajama top. Both had phones pressed to their heads, which they now, in perfect synchrony, folded shut and pocketed.

One of the two loiterers escorted the new arrivals to Peter's front door. This opened into a corridor leading back to the ground-floor bay where the cars were parked.

The other loiterer was clad only in jeans and a T-shirt, which made him underdressed for the weather. He went over to a beat-up old van parked in front of the building. He opened the rear cargo doors, leaned in, and then heaved a long object onto his shoulder. He backed away and kicked the van's doors shut. The object on his shoulder was a box about four feet in length and maybe a foot square, bearing the logo of the big home improvement store down the street, and labeled CONTRACTOR'S PLASTIC 6 MIL POLYETHYLENE SHEETING. He carried it into the bay and pulled the front door closed behind him.

THE MAN IN the pajamas came up the stairs first and spent a few moments strolling around the room looking at everything and everyone. "Vwallace," he said to Wallace.

"Sokolov," Wallace said in return.

From the way that Wallace had spoken of him, Zula had half expected Sokolov to be eight feet tall and carrying a chainsaw. She was pretty certain, though, that he was not carrying any weapons at all. He was wiry, looking perhaps like a shooting guard for the Red Army basketball team. His thinness made it easy to underestimate his age, which was probably in the middle forties. He had sandy hair with traces of gray. It looked as if it had been buzz cut about six months ago and little tended since then. His chin was stubbled, but he didn't naturally grow whiskers on his cheeks. He had a big nose and a big Adam's apple and large eyes whose color was difficult to pin down, as it depended on what he was looking at. When he looked at Zula, they were blue and showed no trace of personal connection, as if viewing her through a one-way mirror. Same with Peter. He went into the bathroom and looked behind the door. He checked the closets. He looked behind sofas and under beds. He found the door that led into the adjoining unit where Peter had been hanging sheetrock. He disappeared into it for a few moments, then emerged and said a word in Russian.

The word must have meant "all clear" because the man in the dinner jacket now came up the steps. Right behind him was the T-shirted man who had fetched the roll of plastic from the back of the van. After looking around the place, paying special attention to the vacant unit, Ivanov said something to this man that caused him to turn around and go back downstairs.

Ivanov was blue-eyed but his hair was dark, made darker yet by some sort of pomade or oil that he had used to slick it back from his forehead, which was an impressive round dome. His complexion was pale but flushed by the chilly air outside. Over his dinner jacket he was wearing a black overcoat well tailored to his frame, which, to put it charitably, was stocky. But he moved well, and Zula got the idea that he could have given a good account of himself in a hockey brawl. Probably had done so, many times, when younger, and prided himself on it. He paid considerably more notice to Peter and Zula than Sokolov had done. Wallace he almost ignored, as if keeping the speakerphone off the floor had been the most useful thing that the Scotsman could possibly achieve today. He sized Peter up and shook his hand. Over Zula, he made a bit of a fuss, because he was that kind of guy. It didn't matter why he was here, what sort of business he had come to transact. Women just had to be treated in an altogether different way from men; the presence of a single woman in the room changed everything. He kissed her hand. He apologized for the trouble. He exclaimed over her beauty. He insisted that she make herself comfortable. He inquired, several times, whether the temperature in the room was not too chilly for a "beautiful African" and whether he might send one of his minions out to fetch her some hot coffee. All of this with meaningful glances at Peter, whose manners came off quite poorly by comparison.

The man in the T-shirt came up the stairs with the box of contractor plastic on his shoulder. Behind him was the other one who had been loitering on the street, carrying a staple gun. When they reached the top of the steps, they looked at Ivanov, who gestured with his head toward the door that led to the adjoining apartment. They went into it and closed the door behind them. Sokolov watched curiously.

Finally they were all sitting down together: Wallace, Peter, and Zula on the sofa, facing Ivanov, who was in the largest chair. Behind Ivanov was Sokolov, who sometimes stood with hands clasped behind his back and at other times paced quietly around the loft, gazing out the windows.

"I am confused," Ivanov said, "as to why you send email complaining of car breakdown in southern part of B.C. when car works fine and is actually in warehouse of Peter, in Seattle—a man I have not had pleasure to meet before."

Wallace tried and failed to speak, cleared his throat, tried again: "I lied to you, sir, because I knew that I would not be able to deliver the credit card numbers at the time promised. I could see that they would be a few hours late. I hoped that you would not mind a short delay."

Ivanov pulled his sleeves back to reveal, and to examine, the largest wristwatch Zula had ever seen. "How many is 'few'? Sometimes I have trouble with English."

"The delay has turned out to be longer than I had expected."

"What is nature of delay? Has Peter fucked us?"

Peter flinched.

"I apologize for language," Ivanov said to Zula.

For a while, only a few muffled noises had been heard from the empty apartment next door, but now they heard the whoosh of plastic sheeting being pulled off the huge roll, followed by the sporadic *thud/click* of the staple gun, which came distinctly through the wall. This posed a distraction to Peter and Zula, which Ivanov noticed and misinterpreted. "Makink little kholes," he said. "Not big kholes. Easy to fix. With a little—" He said a word in Russian, then looked to Sokolov. Sokolov, a bit distracted—maybe taken aback—by what was going on in the other room, missed the cue. Ivanov then looked to the giant potato-like man who was standing near the gun safe and asked him a question. This fellow was deeply apologetic that he was unable to help. But he did shout something downstairs to the smoker who was posted in the bay, who called back: "Spackle!"

"Spackle," Ivanov repeated, and spread his hands, palms up, as if requesting forgiveness.

"It has nothing to do with Peter. Actually Peter has been working diligently to help me overcome the problem," Wallace said.

"So Peter has not fucked us."

"That is correct, sir."

"You? Have you fucked me, Wallace?"

"This is not that kind of problem."

"Oh really? What kind of problem is it?"

"A technical problem."

"Ah, so you have drove your car to warehouse of Mr. Technical Genius, here, to get *tech support*."

"Yes."

"And he has given it?"

"Yes. And Zula as well."

Ivanov blushed. "Yes, forgive me, of course, I do injustice."

Silence, except for the *whoosh-rustle-clunk* of the plastic and the staple gun.

"And?" Ivanov asked, raising his eyebrows. "Still is problem?"

"I'm afraid so."

"Something is wrong with file?" This with a dark look at Peter.

"The file was fine."

"*Was* fine?"

"Now it's been rendered inaccessible."

"You did not make backup?"

"I was quite careful to make a backup, sir, but it too has been rendered inaccessible."

"What is this word 'inaccessible'? You have lost computer?"

"No, both it and the backup drive are under my control, but the data were encrypted."

"You forgot key?"

"I never had it."

Ivanov laughed. "I am not computer specialist, but . . . how can you never have key to file you encrypted?"

"I did not encrypt it."

"Peter? Peter encrypted it?"

"No!" Peter exclaimed.

"Zula encrypted it?"

"No," said Peter and Wallace in unison.

"She cannot speak for herself?"

"I did not encrypt it, Mr. Ivanov," Zula said, earning her an appreciative nod, as if she had just stuck her landing at the Olympics.

"Is missink person? Someone not here who encrypted both file and backup?"

"In a manner of speaking."

Ivanov's face crinkled up and he laughed. "Ah, here is good part! Finally we come to part where bullshit starts. Makes me feel needed."

The door to the adjoining space opened and the two men came out, carrying the roll of plastic, considerably depleted. Through the open door Zula could see that the entire apartment had been lined in plastic. One sheet had been unrolled on the floor and folded up the walls, and then other sheets had been draped over that to cover the walls and even the ceiling. The two men walked wordlessly through the room and went downstairs into the bay.

"In a manner of speaking!" Ivanov slapped his thigh. "What fine expression." The smile went away, and he fixed his gaze on Wallace. "Wallace?"

"Yes, sir?"

"How many people have touched your laptop this day?"

"One, sir. Only I."

"How many have touched backup drive in nice expensive safe?"

"One."

"Then khoo—*in a manner of speaking*—khoo encrypted file?"

"We don't know. But we can get the key—" Wallace was trying to talk over Ivanov now. "With these people's help we can get the key—"

Ivanov had put both of his hands to his temples and was staring at the floor between his feet.

One of the plastic staplers came back up the stairs carrying a cordless drill, a blowtorch, a roll of duct tape, and a length of piano wire. He went into the plasticked apartment and closed the door behind him.

"First thing I must understand: has someone fucked us or not?"

"Yes, someone has most certainly fucked us, sir," Wallace answered.

"Apologize to Zula when you say such word!"

"Beg your pardon, Zula," Wallace said.

"How bad?"

"Bad."

"You have on laptop, on backup drive, many important files to us."

"Yes."

"Status of these files?"

"The same."

"All encrypted?"

"Yes, sir."

"Originals and backups?"

Here the tension had become so unbearable that Zula did not know whether she might faint or throw up.

Ivanov laughed.

"I know how to do this," he said. "Someone fucks us extremely badly, I am familiar with situations of this type. Sokolov too. Peter!"

"Yes, Mr. Ivanov?"

"You know of Battle of Stalingrad?"

"No, sir."

Ivanov was crestfallen.

"The biggest battle of all time, probably," Zula said.

Ivanov brightened and gestured eloquently at her. "A wonderful and glorious victory for Mother Russia?" he asked.

"I don't know if I'd call it that."

"Vwy not!?" Ivanov demanded, in such a blustery tone that Zula was certain he was playing her.

"Because the Germans penetrated very deeply into Russia and inflicted horrendous losses."

This was the correct answer. "Khorrendous losses!" Ivanov repeated. He turned to face Wallace, daring him to appreciate how clever Zula was. "Khorrendous losses! You hear Zula? She understands. Where are you from? Not from this ridiculous fucking country."

"Eritrea."

"Eritrea!"

"Yes."

He held out his hand to her again. "Khorrendous losses! This girl understands nature of khorrendous losses. Where are your parents?"

"Dead."

"Dead! Khorrendous losses indeed. But! Eritreans won war."

"Yes."

"You, here, in nice country—a victory of a kind, yes?"

"Yes."

"Russians, after Stalingrad, marched to Berlin. DO YOU UNDERSTAND POINT, Wallace?"

"Yes, sir."

"You said that these two, Peter and Zula, could solve technical problem and win our little battle in spite of khorrendous losses, yes?"

"Yes, we were working on it but—"

Ivanov held up his hand to shut him up. "Wallace, do favor and go through door." He gestured toward the plastic-lined room.

Wallace didn't move.

"Just that door," Ivanov repeated helpfully.

"Can we just get this done quick and simple?" Wallace asked.

"Not if you sit on couch. Quick and simple depends on how fast you move. And on what information I get from Peter and Zula. Now, go wait."

Wallace, watched curiously by Sokolov, stood up and tottered into the adjoining room. One of the men in there stepped forward, moving carefully on the slick plastic, and closed the door behind him. Through it they could hear the screech of a length of duct tape being jerked off a roll.

"Mr. Ivanov," Zula said, "Wallace is innocent."

"You are beautiful girl, smart, I guess you know of computers. Convince me of this," Ivanov pleaded. "Make me believe."

ZULA TALKED FOR an hour.

She explained the nature and history of computer viruses. Talked about the particular subclass of viruses that encrypted hard drives and held their contents for ransom. About the difficulties of making money from ransomware. Explained the innovation that the unknown, anonymous creators of the REAMDE virus had apparently come up with. Ivanov had never heard of massively multiplayer online role-playing games, or MMORPGs, so she told him all about their history, their technology, their sociology, their growth as a major sector of the entertainment industry.

Ivanov listened raptly, breaking in from time to time. Half of the time this was to compliment her, since he seemed convinced that any female who did not receive a compliment every five minutes would stab him with an ice pick in his sleep. The other half of the time it was to ask a question. Some of these were keenly insightful, and others betrayed a disturbing lack of technical understanding.

Once these preliminaries were out of the way, Ivanov began to drill down on the question of Wallace's culpability. Was the infection chargeable to any carelessness on his part? How, in other words, did the virus spread?

Zula told him what she'd learned, which was that REAMDE was actually spread through a security hole in Outlook, an extremely popular piece of software that, among other things, managed calendars, contacts, and whatnot. In order to do anything significant in

T'Rain, you needed to run a reasonably deep vassal network. Coordinated group activities thus became an essential part of game play. Which meant that several of the players in your feudal hierarchy had to be online at the same time, to transact business and conduct war parties, dungeon raids, and the like. Those activities had to be scheduled around Little League practices, dentist appointments, studying for final exams, and so on, and so a stand-alone scheduling system, existing only inside of the T'Rain app, didn't really serve. A third-party add-on had been created that built a tunnel between T'Rain and Outlook. Most T'Rain players used it. The add-on worked by sending messages back and forth, consisting of invitations to participate in group raids and the like. Most of these were pure text, but it was possible to attach images and other files to such invitations, and therein lay the security hole: REAMDE took advantage of a buffer overflow bug in Outlook to inject malicious code into the host operating system and establish root-level control of the computer, whereupon it could do anything it wanted, including encrypting the contents of all connected drives. First, though, it sent the virus onward to everyone in the victim's T'Rain contact list.

There was another detail, mentioned on the internal wiki, that she did not share with Ivanov: the security hole in Outlook had been known for a while and most antivirus programs were hip to it. But hard-core gamers were still vulnerable since they ran T'Rain in full-screen mode and so were oblivious to the increasingly hysterical warnings being hurled onto their screens by their virus-protection software.

Another detail she elected not to share: Wallace had almost certainly gotten the virus from Uncle Richard's computer, spread via the thumb drive.

"So Wallace used this *add-on*," Ivanov said, using air quotes, "and got infected by this virus."

"Completely innocently, yes," Zula said. During the first part of her lecture she'd been surfing on a burst of energy that had carried her most of the way through, but in the last ten minutes or so, exhaustion had come over her, and she had slowed down and begun to mumble her words and to begin sentences she didn't know how to end. Now, she dimly realized that the upshot of all she'd said, in

Ivanov's mind, might be that Wallace had screwed up and deserved to be punished. This now left her almost paralyzed.

To her own considerable surprise and then shame, she began crying. She leaned forward and put her face in her hands.

"I am eediot!" Ivanov exclaimed. "I am stupidest man in world." He stood up. Afraid that he was going to come over and comfort her, Zula tensed and forced herself to hold it in for a moment. She dared not look up. Through her tears and her fingers she could see Ivanov's polished shoes moving around. He stepped out of the room. She let go of a train of little gasps and sobs, mixed now with self-anger and frustration that she was being such a stupid girl. She hadn't cried in a serious way since her mother's funeral.

Ivanov was back in the room after no more than fifteen seconds. She could hear his footsteps behind the sofa. She flinched as something limp and heavy fell across her shoulders. "What is wrong with you?" Ivanov wanted to know. He was addressing Peter. She realized that Ivanov had grabbed Peter's arm and draped it over Zula's shoulders and was now tamping it down into place like wet cement in a form. She got it under control then, certainly not because Peter had his arm around her shoulders but because of a kind of humor, albeit very dark, that was in the situation: the man Ivanov, whoever and whatever he was, jetting in from Toronto to give Peter lessons in how to be chivalrous to his girlfriend, and Peter trapped, unable to explain that they had just broken up.

Ivanov scattered orders to everyone in the room. People went into motion; phones were unfolded. Zula sat up straight, pushing back against the weight of Peter's arm, and Peter, terrified of what would happen to him if he disobeyed Ivanov, left it where it was, a dead weasel draped over her shoulders.

"Only thing I actually believe is that someone fucked me," Ivanov announced, with the customary nod of apology toward Zula. "You know any Russian? *Kto Kvo*. A saying of Lenin. It means 'who whom?' Today I am the *whom*. The one who is fucked. I am dead man. As dead as him." He nodded toward the adjoining room. Zula heard her lungs filling with a gasp. Ivanov continued, "That is not question. Question is *manner* of my death. I have some time remaining. Maybe a fortnight. Would like to spend it well. It is too late for me to die gloriously. But I can die better than him." Another nod. "I can die as a *who*, not as a *whom*. I can show my brothers that I was fighting for them to very end, in spite of khorrendous losses. I think they will understand this. I will be a forgiven dead man instead of a smashed insect. Only thing I need is: who is the *who*?"

Peter finally took his arm off Zula, who sat up fully straight and regarded Ivanov directly. Ivanov looked back at them—but mostly at her—with an interested expression. As if this were a highly formal, academic sort of drawing-room inquiry. "Do you understand question?"

"You want to know who did this to you?"

"I would use different verb but yes."

They all sat there silently for a few moments. They could hear the engine of a vehicle starting down below, they could hear men talking on phones.

"You want the identity of the Troll. The person who created the virus," Peter said.

"Yes!" Ivanov snapped, faintly irritated.

"And if we can give you that information, then . . . we're cool?"

"Khool?" Ivanov demanded, clearly in no mood to be negotiating—if that was what this was called—with Peter.

"I mean, then it's good? Between you and us?"

Now, kind of an interesting moment.

Though the whole situation was laden with implicit threat, Ivanov had not lifted a finger, nor intimated that he ever would, against Peter or Zula. His eyebrows went up and he regarded Peter, now, in a new light: as a man who had just, in a manner of speaking, issued a threat against himself. Volunteered that he owed Ivanov something and that consequences would be due him if he failed to deliver.

Ivanov made a little shrug, as if to say, *The thought had never crossed my mind, but now that you mention it . . .* "You are most generous."

During this whole interlude, Peter had been realizing his mistake and was now trying to backpedal in quicksand. "You understand that the virus writer could be anywhere in the world, that he's probably gone to great lengths to hide his identity, cover his tracks . . ."

"You confuse me," Ivanov said. "Can you find Troll, or not?"

Peter looked at Zula.

"Why you look at Miss Zula? *You* are khacker genius, correct?"

Peter couldn't get anything out.

ZULA WAS VERY tired, and her mind was in several places at once. The word "flashback" was much too fraught to describe what was happening in her mind. But it was the case that the mind pulled up memories that were germane to the impressions flooding into its sensory organs, and the first few years of her life related better to what was happening now than most of what she had experienced in small-town Iowa. She did not have the energy, the clarity, or what nerds denominated the "bandwidth" to deal with all aspects of this situation at once. Certainly the one that dominated was the sense that she was in danger. There was a technical side to it also. But neither of those explained the sick feeling that kept passing in waves through her abdomen. There was a moral aspect to this. She'd failed to see it at all until Wallace had been sent to the other room. For that, a man like Ivanov would probably see her as ridiculously naive. She could perhaps be forgiven that naïveté once.

Now, though, she was being asked to give up another person: a complete stranger, somewhere, who had created REAMDE. She had not volunteered for the job. Peter had betrayed her with a glance.

"Miss Zula? I apologize, I see that you are very tired," Ivanov said. "But. You work at same company? Is possible?"

And the Iowa-girl response, of course, was always yes. Especially to a polite, older man in good clothes who had come such a long way.

For some reason she was remembering a moment when she had been something like fourteen years old, the apex of the crystal meth epidemic in Iowa. She had been home alone and had looked out the window to see a strange van coming down the road, very slowly. It had made a couple of passes by the house and then pulled into the driveway that led to their equipment shed. A couple of men had gotten out of the van, looking around nervously. Not knowing whether they might have come on a legitimate errand, Zula had made a phone call to Uncle John (as she called her second adopted dad), and Uncle John had extremely calmly talked her through the procedure of locking every door in the house, getting a shotgun and a box of shells, and hiding herself in the attic. His matter-of-fact instructions had been accompanied, and sometimes drowned out, by dim roaring, screeching, and thumping noises that, as she later understood, had resulted from his driving at a hundred miles an hour while he talked. Zula had barely gotten the attic stairs pulled up behind her when a lot of disturbing vehicular noises had ensued from outside, and she had peered out a gable vent to see Uncle John's car in the middle of the front yard at the end of a long set of skid marks that completely surrounded the house (for he had orbited it once, checking for signs of forced entry) and John hobbling around it on his prosthetic legs to crouch behind and use it for cover while across the way the van screamed out onto the road with a door hanging open. A cloud of what she took for steam was rising from the side of the shed where they kept the anhydrous ammonia tank. A few minutes later the sheriff's department was there in force, and Zula felt it safe to emerge from the attic. John yelled at her that she did not have permission to come down yet. Then he hugged her and told her that she was his wonderful girl. Then he asked about the whereabouts of the shotgun. Then he told her again how magnificent she was, and then he ordered her to go upstairs and not come out until he gave permission. She went upstairs and, peering out a window, saw what John did not want her to see: the ambulance men putting on their hazmat suits and placing a large brown wrinkled thing into a body bag. One of the thieves, startled, perhaps, by Uncle John's sudden advent, had made a mistake with the anhydrous ammonia line and been sprayed with the chemical, which had sucked all the water out of his body.

It was in that moment, but never before and rarely since, that she had perceived a kind of subterranean through line, perhaps like one of those ley lines in T'Rain, running from her people in Eritrea to her people in Iowa.

"WITH A PHONE call," Zula said, "I might be able to get more information about the Troll."

Ivanov continued to gaze at her in an expectant way and, after a few moments, raised his eyebrows encouragingly.

"Then," Zula added, "you could be on your way."

Ivanov's face stopped moving, as if hit by a blast of anhydrous ammonia.

"To continue solving your problem," Zula added graciously, "or whatever it is you need to do."

"A phone call," Ivanov said, "to whom?"

"The company has a privacy policy."

Ivanov's face screwed up. "This sounds like bullshit."

"There are rules," Zula said. For Uncle Richard had explained to her, at the beginning of her employment at Corporation 9592, that most of the people she'd be working with were burdened with Y chromosomes and that what worked at Boy Scout camp should work here. *Boys,* he said, *only want to know two things: who is in charge, and what are the rules.* And indeed this worked magically. Ivanov nodded. "The company has information about names, addresses, demographics of its customers," Zula continued. "But it doesn't release that information. You don't play the game under your own name—your real name. There's no way that I, as a player, could ever track down the true real-world identity of the Troll or any other player."

"But someone," Ivanov said, "someone at company knows."

"Yes, someone always knows."

"Maybe rule gets broke sometimes, a little."

"Generally not but . . ." Zula truncated the sentence since Ivanov was already making a *this is bullshit* gesture.

APPARENTLY SOMEONE WENT out for supplies, since their Russian was suddenly punctuated with phrases like "venti mocha."

"Peter," said Sokolov; the first sound he had made in a long time.

Peter looked up to find Sokolov nodding significantly at a webcam mounted at the top of the stairs, aimed down into the shop.

"You have two security cameras."

Peter made no response.

"Or perhaps more?" Sokolov went on.

Peter considered it. "Three, actually," he admitted.

"Ah," Sokolov said.

For a few moments, Zula wondered how Sokolov could possibly have missed the third one. They were all pretty obvious: one aimed down the front hall at the street entrance; another in the shop, covering the alley doors; the third at the top of the stairs.

Then she got it. Sokolov was testing Peter.

Sokolov knew perfectly well that there were three cameras; he had gone over the whole place, seen everything. But he had said "two" just to see whether Peter would 'fess up to the existence of a third.

"Motion activated?" Sokolov asked.

"Yes."

"Storing data where?"

"Here," Peter said. "On my server."

Sokolov made no sign that he had heard, but only stared into Peter's eyes for several long seconds.

"And . . . on a backup drive," Peter admitted. "Under the stairs."

Sokolov finally took his gaze from Peter's face and nodded. "Files will need to be erased."

"Okay," Peter said, sounding hugely relieved. He slapped his knees and rose to his feet. "Let's do that."

Watched carefully by Sokolov, Peter busied himself at a terminal for a while. In the meantime, a preposterous amount of car moving was going on. Peter's Scion ended up parked on the street outside. Zula's Prius was shifted deeper into the bay and Wallace's sports car was moved in next to it, clearing the alley.

During these efforts, Zula's phone was retrieved and presented to her, by Ivanov, as if it were a Swarovski necklace.

"ZULA."

"C-plus, hi."

"It's not often that I have the pleasure of talking to someone in the magma department."

"C-plus, that is because I am working on a side project here—long story—that Richard sort of put me on."

"Management by founder," Corvallis said, in a tone of ironic disapproval. Supposedly, "management by founder"—a term of art for Richard doing whatever struck his fancy—had been eradicated from Corporation 9592 a few years ago when professional executives had been parachuted in to run things.

"Yeah. So, an informal project. Call it research. Having to do with some, uh, unusual gold movements connected with a virus called REAMDE."

"Funny. Had never heard of it until I came to work this morning. Now, it's all anyone will talk about."

"It exploded over the weekend. Look, I just need one piece of information."

"Where should I look?"

"My log. Several hours ago."

Typing. "Wow, you died a lot last night!"

"Sure did."

Typing. "Then you unceremoniously logged out."

"Power failure in Georgetown, the Internet went down."

"Okay. You were having some fun in the Torgai hills, looks like."

"Yeah. An ill-fated expedition."

"I'll say. So. What is it you need?"

"During the early part of it, someone cast a healing spell on me. Not a member of my group. It would have happened at maybe three in the morning our time, when my character was near a certain ley line intersection . . ."

"Well, only one healing spell was cast on you all night, so it's pretty easy."

"You've got the log entry?" For in the world of T'Rain, a little sparrow could not fall from its nest without the event being logged and time-stamped.

"Yeah."

"Okay." Zula couldn't help but notice the effect that her half of the conversation was having on Ivanov. He turned and gestured to Sokolov, who stepped nearer, as if the Troll were about to jump out of Zula's phone and make a run for it.

"Who cast that healing spell on me, C-plus?"

"Hard to say."

"What do you mean?" Zula asked, a bit sharply.

"It's *literally* hard to say. My Chinese is a little weak."

"So the name of the character is in Chinese?"

Ivanov and Sokolov looked at each other as only Russians could look at each other when the Chinese came into it.

"Yeah, and he or she didn't bother to slap a Western handle onto it."

This was part of Richard and Nolan's efforts to make T'Rain as Chinese friendly as possible. In other such games, each player had to use a name written in Latin characters, but in T'Rain it was optional.

"He or she—so, no demographics or personal data about the player?"

"It's transparently a load of crap generated by a bot or something," Corvallis said.

"Credit card?"

"It's a self-sus."

Another one of Richard and Nolan's innovations. In most online games, you had to link your account to a credit card number to cover the monthly fees. Not so Chinese teen friendly. But since T'Rain had hard currency money plumbing built into its guts, this too was somewhat optional; if your character was turning a profit, for example, by selling gold, you could pay your monthly fee by having it deducted automatically from your character's treasure chest. These were called self-sustaining accounts.

"Is there any way to get any hard information at all about who runs that character?"

Zula didn't like the effect that this had on Ivanov's face.

"I can give you the IP address that they were connected from."

"That'd be fantastic!" Zula said, hoping that she was really selling its fantastic-ness to Ivanov. She gestured for something to write with. Sokolov wheeled and plucked a Sharpie from a mug on a side table. Perhaps it was a bit odd that he knew the location of every pen in the room better than Peter did, but maybe it was his job to spot everything in his vicinity that could be used as an improvised weapon. Sokolov bit the cap off and held out his palm for Zula to write on. She took the pen and rested her writing hand on Sokolov's, which had taken a lot of abuse and was missing the end of one finger, yet was as warm as any other man's.

"Ready?" Corvallis asked.

"Shoot," said Zula, then cringed at the choice of word.

Corvallis, speaking extremely clearly and crisply, recited four numbers between 0 and 255: a dotted quad, or Internet Protocol address. Zula wrote them down on the palm of Sokolov's hand. Ivanov watched with spectacular intensity, then gave her a wondering look.

He knew what it was.

It was the same sort of thing that Csongor had used to detect Wallace's lie and route him to Peter's place. And having seen it work perfectly once, Ivanov supposed it could not fail to work again.

"Thanks," Zula said, "and my next question—"

Typing. "It's one of a large block of addresses allocated to an ISP in Shyamen."

"Come again?"

Corvallis spelled it, and she wrote it on Sokolov's flesh: X-I-A-M-E-N.

This triggered furious but comically silent activity among Ivanov and his minions.

"You can google it yourself," Corvallis said, and Zula—who was, in spite of everything, still being watched intently by Sokolov—resisted the temptation to say *No, I can't.* "Formerly called Amoy," he continued, in a singsongy voice to indicate that he had googled it. "A port city in southeastern China, at the mouth of the Nine Dragons River, just across the strait from Taiwan. Two and a half million people. Twenty-fifth largest port in the world, up from thirtieth. Blah, blah, blah. Pretty generic, for a Chinese city."

"Thanks!"

"Sorry I couldn't get more specific."

"Gives me something to work on."

"Anything else I can help you with?"

Yes. "No."

"Have a good one!" And he was gone.

The word "Bye" was hardly past Zula's lips when Sokolov had pulled the phone from her hand. He knew how to work it and pulled up its web browser and googled Xiamen.

She had been vaguely aware for a while of some gratifying smells in the room: flowers and coffee.

Ivanov, smiling, approached her with a vast bouquet of stargazer lilies cradled in his arms. They still bore the plastic wrap and barcode from the grocery store up the hill. "For you," he announced, bestowing them on her. "For because I made you cry. Least I could do."

"That is very sweet of you," she said, trying through all her exhaustion to sell it.

"Latte?" he asked. For the T-shirted man was at his side with a cardboard tray crowded with cups from Starbucks world HQ, whose colossal green mermaid loomed over Georgetown like the Stay Puft Marshmallow Man.

"Love one," she said, and she didn't have to lie about that.

Since the visitors were now all busy, she carried the flowers into the kitchen area and laid them on a cutting board so that she could cut the ends off the stems and put them in water. Idiotic. But it, like so many of her nice-Iowa-girl impulses, was like a brainstem reflex. It wasn't the flowers' fault that they'd been purchased by gangsters. The latte was enormously pleasurable, and she popped the lid off and threw it away so that she could sink her lips into the warm foam and gulp from it. Peter owned no vases, but she found an earthenware water pitcher that would support the flowers and filled it with water. Then she set about the messy business of tearing away the plastic wrappers and the rubber bands that held the flowers' stems together.

Seeing large movement while she was doing this, she glanced up to see two of the men carrying a long, heavy, plastic-wrapped bundle out of the adjoining apartment.

She was on the floor before she was fully conscious of being light-headed.

WORLD OF WARCRAFT had been the toweringly dominant competitor in Corporation 9592's industry for what seemed like forever, until you checked the dates and realized that it was only a few years old. Richard and Nolan had passed through several phases in their attitude toward it:

1. Abashed denial that they could ever even dream of competing with such an entrenched power as WoW

2. Certainty, growing into cockiness, that they could knock it off its perch in a coup de main

3. Crushing realization that it was impossible and that they were doomed to abject failure

4. Cautious optimism that maybe life wasn't going to totally suck forever

5. Finally getting their shit together and coming up with a plan

Somewhere between Phases 4 and 5, Richard holed up at the Schloss during Mud Month—the weeks following the end of the ski season—and wrote out some ideas that had been brewing in his mind since the deepest and most lugubrious weeks of Phase 3. Reading them, Corvallis had identified this as an "inflection point," which was another of those terms that meant nothing to Richard but that was—to judge from the vigorous shifts in body language it elicited in meetings—of infinite significance to math geeks. As far as Richard could make out, it denoted the hardly-obvious-at-the-time moment when, seen later in retrospect, everything had changed.

For a while the memo had rattled around the office like a dried-out whiteboard pen. Then Richard, with a bit of jargonic assistance from Corvallis, had given it an arresting title: Medieval Armed Combat as Universal Metaphor and All-Purpose Protocol Interface Schema (MACUMAPPIS).

Since Medieval Armed Combat was the oxygen they breathed, even mentioning it seemed gratuitous, so this got shortened to UMAPPIS and then, since the "metaphor" thing made some of the businesspeople itchy, it became APPIS, which they liked enough to trademark. And since APPIS was one letter away from APIS, which was the Latin word for bee, they then went on to create and trade-mark some bee- and hive-related logo art. As Corvallis patiently told Richard, it was all a kind of high-tech in-joke. In that world, API stood for "application programming interface," which meant the software control panels that tech geeks slapped onto their technolo-gies in order to make it possible for other tech geeks to write pro-grams that made use of them. All of which was one or two layers of abstraction beyond the point where Richard could give a shit. "All I am trying to say with this memo," he told Corvallis, "is that anyone who feels like it ought to be able to grab hold of our game by the technological short hairs and make it solve problems for them." And Corvallis assured him that this was precisely synonymous with hav-ing an API and that everything else was just marketing.

The problems Richard had in mind were not game- or even entertainment-related ones. Corporation 9592 had already covered as many of those bases as their most imaginative people could think of, and then they had paid lawyers to pore over the stuff that they'd thought of and extrapolate whole abstract categories of things that might be thought of later. And wherever they went, they found that the competition had been there five years earlier and patented everything that was patentable and, in one sense or another, pissed on everything that wasn't. Which explained a lot about Phase 3.

The epiphany—if this wasn't too fine a word for some crazy-ass shit that had popped up in Richard's brain—had occurred in a brewpub at Sea-Tac. Richard had been marooned there for a couple of hours after his flight to Spokane had been delayed by a collision between a baggage truck and the plane: a strangely common occurrence at that airport, and one of those folksy touches that helped to preserve its small-town feel. Sitting there quaffing his pint and gazing at the shoeless and beltless travelers penguin-shuffling through the metal detectors, he had been struck by the sheer boringness of the work being performed by the screeners of the Transportation Security Administration: staring at those bags moving through the x-ray machines, trying to remain alert for that once-in-every-ten-years moment when someone would actually try to send a gun through.

Thus far, a commonplace observation. He had done a bit of research on it later and learned that the more sophisticated airports had hired psychologists to tackle the problem and devised some clever tricks. For example, they would digitally insert fake images of guns into the video feed from an x-ray machine, frequently enough that the screeners would see false-color silhouettes of revolvers and semiautomatics and IEDs glide across their visual fields several times a day, instead of once every ten years. That, according to the research, was enough to prevent their pattern-recognition neurons from being reclaimed and repurposed by brain processes that were more fruitful, or at least more entertaining.

The brain, as far as Richard could determine from haphazard skimming of whatever came up on Google, was sort of like the electrical system of Mogadishu. A whole lot was going on in Mogadishu that required copper wire for conveyance of power and information, but there was only so much copper to go around, and so what wasn't being actively used tended to get pulled down by militias and taken crosstown to beef up some power-hungry warlord's private, improvised power network. As with copper in Mogadishu, so with neurons in the brain. The brains of people who did unbelievably boring shit for a living showed dark patches in the zones responsible for job-related processes, since all those almost-never-exercised neurons got pulled down and trucked somewhere else and used to beef up the circuits used to keep track of NCAA tournament brackets and celebrity makeovers.

So the airport luggage scanner epiphany was simultaneously dis- and encouraging. Dis- because some occupational psychologists had already beaten him to it and come up with a fix, but en- because people with Ph.D.s had vouched for the basic idea.

In order to make the case for MACUMAPPIS, Richard had to, (a) find some other desperately boring job to use as his *experimentum crucis,* and (b) figure out a way to map its basic processes onto Medieval Armed Combat. Between his years as a slavering World of Warcraft addict and his years as a founder/creator of T'Rain, he had ripped out probably half of the neurons in his brain and dragged them over and soldered them on to the cortical centers responsible for two-handed axe wielding, shield bashing, arrow shooting, and spell casting. In an evening of random questing around the imaginary world that D-squared and Skeletor had created, Richard could fire more neurons than Einstein had used while coming up with the idea of general relativity. Certainly way more neurons than the average supermarket checkout clerk or private security guard fired during an eight-hour shift. And the power of the Internet ought to make all that neural activity reswitchable; you should be able to patch it all together so that it would work.

Around this time there was an airport security scare in which some fuckwit entered a concourse by walking upstream through an exit portal, bypassing the security checkpoint. As always happened in such cases, the entire airport had to be shut down. Planes waiting for takeoff had to taxi back to gates and unload all passengers and baggage. All the passengers had to be ejected from the sterile side of the airport and then turn around and pass through security again. Flights were delayed, and the delays ramified throughout the global air travel system, eventually racking up a cost of tens of millions of dollars. All of which could have been prevented had the one TSA employee posted by the exit—an employee whose sole purpose in being there was to just keep his fucking eyes open and stop people from walking the wrong way through a door—had actually done his job. Richard was fascinated. How could even the laziest and sloppiest employee screw this up? The answer, apparently, was that it had nothing to do with laziness or sloppiness. It was that Mogadishu copper thing all over again. The neural pathways required to accomplish the seemingly easy task of identifying a pedestrian walking the wrong way through a door had, in the brain of this employee, been uprooted a long time ago and zip-tied onto those used by some other, more important, or at least more frequently used, procedure.

And so they started up the first APPIS pilot project, which went something like this. They shot some consumer-grade video of Corporation 9592 employees walking down a hallway. They spun that up into a demo, which they showed to several regional airports that were too small and poorly funded to afford fancy, expensive, alarm-equipped one-way doors, and thus had to rely on the bored-employee-sitting-in-a-chair-by-the-door technology. They parlayed those meetings into a deal that gave them access to live 24/7 security camera footage from a couple of those airports. The footage, of course, just showed people walking through the exit.

They patched that footage into pattern recognition software that identified the shapes of the individual humans and translated them into vector data in 3D space. This made it possible to import all the data into the T'Rain game engine. The same positions and movements were conferred on avatars from the T'Rain world. The stream of human passengers walking down the corridor in their blazers, their high heels, their Chicago Bears sweatpants, became a stream of K'Shetriae, Dwinn, trolls, and other fantasy characters, dressed in chain mail, plate armor, and wizards' robes, moving down a stone-lined passageway at the exit of the mighty Citadel of Garzantum.

The High Marshal of the Garzantian Empire then made an announcement to the effect that huge amounts of gold could be earned by, honor bestowed upon, and valuable weapons and armor handed out to anyone who nabbed a goblin attempting to sneak in through said passageway. Characters who volunteered for this duty were issued a special instrument, the Horn of Vigilance, and told to blow it whenever they spotted a wrong-way goblin. Extra points were handed out for actually confronting the goblin and (of course) engaging it in Medieval Armed Combat.

Now, in all the entire (real) world's airports put together, the number of people who got into concourses by walking the wrong way through exit doors amounted to maybe one or two per year: not enough to hold the attention, or assure the vigilance, of even the most rabid T'Rain player. So the APPIS system now sweetened the pot by automatically generating fictitious, virtual wrong-way goblins and sending them up that tunnel at the rate of one every couple of minutes, every day, forever. Some balancing had to happen—the value of the rewards had to be tweaked relative to the frequency of wrong-way goblins—but with a minimal amount of adjustment they were able to set the system up in such a way that 100 percent of all the wrong-way goblins were apprehended. The total number of wrong-way goblins that had to be generated per year was about two hundred thousand—which was no problem, since generating them was free. The trick, of course, was that a tiny minority of those one-way goblins were not, in fact, computer-generated figments. They were representations of actual human forms that had been picked up by airport security cameras as they walked the wrong way into airport concourses. In reality, of course, this happened so rarely that testing the system was well-nigh impossible, and so they ran drills, several times a day, in which uniformed, badged TSA employees would present themselves at the exit and show credentials to the bored guard and then walk upstream into the concourse. In exactly 100 percent of all such cases, some T'Rain player, somewhere in the world (almost always a gold farmer in China) would instantly raise the Horn of Vigilance to his virtual lips and blow a mighty blast and rush out to confront the corresponding one-way goblin: an event that, through some artful cross-wiring between Corporation 9592's servers and the airport security systems, would cause red lights to flash and horns to sound and doors to automatically lock at the airport in question.

Corvallis and most of the other techies hated this idea because of its sheer bogosity, which was screamingly obvious to any person of technical acumen who thought about it for more than a few seconds. If their pattern-recognition software could identify the moving travelers and vectorize their body positions well enough to translate their movements into T'Rain, then it could just as easily notice, *automatically,* with no human intervention, when one of those figures was walking the wrong way and sound the alarm. There was no need at all to have human players in the loop. They should just spin out the pattern-recognition part of it as a separate business.

Richard understood and acknowledged all of this—and did not care. "Did you, or did you not, tell me that this was all marketing? What part of your own statement did you not understand?" The purpose of the exercise was not really to build a rational, efficient airport security system. It was, rather (to use yet another of those portentous phrases cribbed from the math world), an existence proof. Once it was up and running, they could point to it and to its 100 percent success rate as vindicating the premise of APPIS, which was that real-world problems—especially problems that were difficult to solve because of hard-wired deficiencies of the human neurological system, such as the tendency to become bored when given a terrible job—could be tackled by metaphrasing them into Medieval Armed Combat scenarios, and then (here brandishing two searingly hip terms from high tech) putting them out on the cloud so that they could be crowdsourced.

The system, despite its bogosity—which was fundamental, evident, and frequently pointed out by huffy nerd bloggers—immediately became a darling of hip West Coast tech-industry conferences. APPIS had to be turned into a separate division and expanded onto a new floor of the office building in Seattle, which conveniently had been vacated by an imploding bank. New ideas and joint venture proposals rushed in, like so many wrong-way goblins, at such a pace that the APPIS staff could scarcely blow their Horns of Vigilance fast enough. The underemployed nerds of the world, impatient with the slow pace at which Corporation 9592's in-house programmers bent to their demands, began to generate their own APPIS apps. The most popular of these was a system that would accept low-quality video of a corporate meeting room, supplied by a phone, and transmogrify the scene into a collection of hairy, armored warlords sitting around a massive plank table in a medieval fortress. Whenever a meeting participant lifted a bottle of vitamin water or a skinny nonfat latte to his or her lips, the corresponding avatar would quaff deeply from a five-liter tankard of ale and then belch deeply, and whenever someone took a nibble from a multigrain bar, the avatar would bite a steaming hunk of meat from a huge leg of lamb. Power-Point presentations, in this scenario, were turned into vaporous apparitions hanging in numinous steam above a sorcerer's kettle. In the first version of the app, the horn-helmeted avatars all said exactly the same things that the corresponding humans did in the real-world conference room, which made for some funny juxtapositions but wore thin after a while. But then people began to create add-ons so that if, for example, someone's clever new proposal got trashed by a grouchy boss, the event could be rendered as a combat scene in which the hapless underling's severed head wound up on the end of a spear. Large swaths of the global economy were, it now seemed, being remapped onto their T'Rain equivalents so that they could be transacted in a Medieval Armed Combat setting. Demonstrable improvements in productivity were being trumpeted every day on the relevant section of Corporation 9592's website (by a medieval herald, naturally, and with an actual trumpet).

Richard insisted, only half in jest, that he wanted to see 10 percent of the global economy moved into T'Rain. Or at least 10 percent of the *information* economy. But since the information economy had now got its fingers into just about everything, this wasn't much of a limitation. Factory workers watching widgets stream off the assembly line, inspecting them for defects, ought to be able to meta-phrase their work into something way more neuron grabbing, such as flying up a river valley on a winged steed, gazing into its limpid waters at the rocks strewn up its channel, looking for the one that contained traces of some magical ore.

Which was *also*, as C-plus patiently explained, a ridiculous idea, since any machine-vision algorithm smart enough to convert a defective widget into an ore-containing boulder in a virtual river valley was smart enough to just sound a buzzer on the assembly line and flag the offending unit without involving human beings or virtual fantasy worlds. To which Richard responded, with equal if not greater patience, that he still didn't give a shit because this was ultimately about marketing, and the crazy apps that random people on the Internet were writing were much better than anything he, Richard, could ever come up with.

Anyway, it had worked, after a shambling and chaotic fashion, and T'Rain had thus become far more intensively patched into the wiring diagram of the real world than a quasi-medieval fantasy world had any right or reason to be. Which was how they had ended up needing a calendar-and-contact-management app and diverse other add-ons that they had never dreamed of when they had been setting up the world *ab initio.*

Richard himself was not a user of the calendar app. He did most of his T'Rain questing solo, or in the company of one or two old friends, and so he didn't need it; and the mere idea of needing to schedule his time that carefully made him dispirited. He used his phone for stuff like that, and the calendar app's integration to the phone was clunky and not really worth putting up with. Even if it had worked, it just would have meant more crap showing up on his schedule, and fewer of the perfectly empty days that always gave him such a nice little endorphin rush when they appeared, as if by some act of divine grace, on his screen. Consequently, he was in no danger of being infected by REAMDE. And so, the morning after Peter and Zula had gone back to Seattle, when Richard woke up in his big, round, quasi-medieval bedchamber at the Schloss and checked his corporate email account, he was able to view the weekend's spate of escalating SECURITY ALERT messages with some kind of detachment. There was a new virus; it was called REAMDE (*sic*), which was an accidental or deliberate/ironical misspelling of README; it had been simmering for a few weeks now, and in the last few days it had gone exponential, as these things commonly did. It was a consequence, really, of APPIS, and of all Richard's efforts to turn T'Rain into a Profit Center above and beyond the mere world of hard-core gamers. As such, it was perfectly all right from a business and marketing standpoint; it would only generate stories in the tech press about how T'Rain had made the jump from a mere niche product for the prohibitively geeky to a business productivity app that mundanes felt that they had to have, along with their Excel and their PowerPoint, and Richard could already predict that at their next quarterly meeting they would see, in retrospect, a surge in sales precisely tracking the spike in free publicity generated by the advent of this terrible virus.

His calendar was clear for today, but prophesying a journey to Seattle tomorrow so that he could get up early on the following morning for another one of his whirlwind journeys to Nodaway and the Isle of Man. He considered using this REAMDE thing as a pretext for going to Seattle now, a day early. And he might have done just that, if more time had elapsed since his last interaction with Zula. But she had only just left, and he didn't want to creep the poor girl out by turning into some kind of hovering stalker-uncle. Better for her to decide on her own that she was ready for a little more Richard time. So he left his schedule alone, reckoning he'd be busy all day anyway, with emails from friends and family members whose personal files were being held hostage by some mysterious troll on the Internet.

THERE WAS NO coming awake but a gradual reassembly of consciousness from parts that, while still functioning, had come unlinked. She was looking down on snow-spackled mountains as though seeing them in the opening screen of T'Rain and, at the same time, having a dream of walking barefoot through them. For it was barefoot that she and her group had walked most of the way from Eritrea to Sudan, and her dreams often took her back to that journey, as though the nerves in the soles of the feet were connected more tightly to the brain than any others. In her dream, the snow on the mountains was warm between her toes, which she knew made no sense; but it was explained as some magic that had been dreamed up by Devin Skraelin based on an oblique reference by Donald Cameron. And then she and Pluto had been given the job of making it real, rendering it from bits, and she was walking across it with a caravan of Eritrean refugees to make sure that it all held together.

When memory started working again, it told her that she had, for quite a long time, been lying on her side with eyes half open, gazing out a window. The mountains were passing by beneath her. The world was roaring and humming.

She was on a plane. Her seat smelled of good leather. It had been leaned all the way back to form a flat bed, and she had been covered with blankets. Nice ones. Not airline blankets.

She had not been raped or otherwise abused. A bandage was on her hand. She remembered the lilies and the knife.

And the latte. They had put Rohypnol in her latte.

She moved a little and found that her parts worked, though she was stiff from lying in one position too long.

She shifted her head away from the window and found herself looking down the barrel of a small plane's fuselage.

Across the aisle was Peter, similarly reclined, gazing at her. She jumped a little when she saw that.

They were at the aft end of the cabin. At the forward end, Sokolov sat in a chair, reading glasses on the end of his nose, reviewing documents.

In the bulkhead that terminated the cabin just aft of them was a single door that, Zula guessed, led to a separate compartment. Since she couldn't see Ivanov anywhere else, she assumed he must be in there.

"How long have you been awake?" Peter asked.

"A minute," Zula said. "You?"

"Maybe half an hour. Hey, Zula!"

"What?"

"Do you have any idea where we're going?"

Zula tossed off the blankets, got to her feet, and walked, a little unsteadily, up past Sokolov to the head of the plane. The cockpit door was closed, but beside it was another door leading to the lavatory.

Something scraped and thumped to the floor at her feet. She looked down to discover her shoulder bag. Sokolov had tossed it her way.

She looked up and locked eyes with him. "Thanks," she said.

He gazed at her for a three-count and went back to his documents.

She went in, sat down, put her face in her hands, and peed.

Think.

How had Ivanov and company gotten them out of the country?

Uncle Richard sometimes flew in private jets when he went to the Isle of Man to pay court to Don Donald and wouldn't stop talking about how easy, how "zipless" it was. No check-in. No security frisk. No wait. Just go straight to the plane and get on and go.

Zula didn't know how the drug had affected her—had she been out cold? Merely groggy? Or in some compliant zombielike state? Anyway, the Russians could have bundled her and Peter into vehicles without anyone noticing and driven them straight onto the tarmac at Boeing Field and (if Uncle Richard was to be believed) right up to the side of the plane, where it wouldn't have been that difficult to get them up the stairs and on board.

So really it would have been easy. Huge penalties would have obtained if they'd been noticed or caught, but these guys weren't the type to concern themselves with such matters. In a sick way, she kind of liked that about them.

She went through her bag. Her passport was gone. The knife had been removed from her pocket. No car keys (not that they would have been of any use) or phone. There was a book she'd been reading, some of the odds and ends she'd collected from Peter's place—cosmetics, tampons, hair stuff, hand sanitizer. A standard-issue Seattle fleece vest. Pens and pencils were all gone—because they were potential weapons? Because she could have used them to write a note calling for help? Someone had gone through her luggage—the larger bag she'd taken on the ski trip—and pulled out (thank God) underwear, a couple of T-shirts, a pair of shorts, and stuffed them into this bag.

So they were going someplace warm.

Think. When would her absence be noticed? It was common knowledge at work that she had gone skiing for the weekend. When she failed to show up for work today, people would assume she was sleeping in.

But eventually—in a few days, maybe?—people would get worried.

Then what?

Eventually they might look for her at Peter's and find her car there, unless the Russians had taken it out and driven it into the murky waters of the Duwamish. But they would find no trace that anything had gone wrong.

She had vanished off the face of the earth.

That was upsetting, to the point of making her nose run a little, but she didn't cry. She had cried at Peter's place when things had gotten bad. Then she had stupidly believed that the problem was solved. As if you could really get out of such a bad situation so cheaply. Now she was back to square one, the place she'd been when she'd stopped crying at Peter's and had started thinking about what to do.

She cleaned up and did a little bit of maintenance on the mascara. Didn't want anyone to notice that she had been putting energy into makeup but didn't want to visibly degenerate either, wanted to make the point, even if she made it subliminally, that she still had some pride, wasn't falling apart. She performed a comb-out on her hair and then ponytailed it back. Changed into the cleanest clothes she could glean from the bag and went back to her bed, which she made back into a seat. Sat down and looked at more mountains.

"You know the time?"

Peter shook his head. "They took my phone."

She sat there for a while.

"We're going to Xiamen," she announced.

"That's on the other side of the Pacific!" he hissed.

"So?"

"So we've been flying over mountains the whole time!"

"A great circle route from Seattle doesn't go across the Pacific. It goes north. Vancouver Island. Southeast Alaska. The Aleutians. Kamchatka." She nodded out the window. "All mountains like those. Young. Steep. Subduction zone stuff."

Sokolov, without looking up, spoke one word: "Vladivostok."

"See?" Zula said.

"What's that?"

"A city. Extreme eastern Siberia."

"Siberia. Fantastic."

"We're going to Xiamen," she insisted. "It's the only thing that makes sense."

"Maybe they'll just take us into Russia and—"

"What?" Zula asked. "Kill us? They could have done that in Seattle."

"I don't know," Peter said, "sell us into white slavery or something."

"I'm not white."

"You know what I mean."

"You saw the way Ivanov was. There's only one thing he cares about. Find the Troll. And"—she hesitated on the threshold of the word, but there was no point in being prissy—"kill him."

"It would make sense," Peter said, finally getting into the spirit. "Stop in Vladivostok. Take on supplies or whatever. Then on to Xiamen."

For Zula the thread of the conversation had snapped when she had said "kill." She was now party to a murder plot. The memory of the events in Peter's apartment was seeping back. When she had made the phone call to Corvallis, she had felt certain that it was the only thing she could do, but now she was replaying it in her mind, questioning her decision.

The aft door opened and Ivanov burst out, wrapped in a bathrobe. Ignoring everyone else, he went to the toilet.

Peter pulled his feet up onto his seat so that his knees were in front of his face, wrapped his arms around them, and put his head down.

Zula had been irked by his overall attitude at first. But he had a head start; he'd awakened earlier, been thinking about their situation longer. As minutes went by and the novelty of being on a private jet wore off, Zula began to understand the same thing that Peter did, which was that they were not meant to get out of this alive.

Ivanov emerged from the bathroom groomed and walked down the aisle, sliding his eyes over Zula's face but making no connection. All his courtesy in Peter's apartment had been to serve a purpose that no longer existed.

Peter had turned his head to the side and was watching Zula watch Ivanov. After Ivanov had gone back into his compartment, he said, "I'm sorry."

"No one could have foreseen it."

"Still."

"No. The thing with REAMDE was totally random. Bad luck is all."

After a couple of minutes, she said, "Maybe it's not what you think it is."

"Huh?"

"You're thinking, once they've got what they want—" And she made a subtle flicking motion of her thumb across her throat.

"That's pretty much what I'm thinking, yes."

"But that assumes that this thing is sort of . . . *normal*. Kind of an orderly procedure. I don't think it's that."

Peter flicked his eyes back toward Sokolov, warning her to shut up. The plane began to descend over more snowy mountains.

THEY LANDED ON a long and well-paved runway in a place that was otherwise forested, with lozenges of snow splattered among the trees. It seemed to be a serious commercial airport serving passenger jets both regional and intercontinental, with some cargo traffic as well. Various hangars and utility structures were visible from the runway, but they didn't get a good view of the terminal building per se. The plane taxied to an apron where a few other smaller planes were parked, and the pilot chose a place as far as possible from the others. Sokolov walked up and down the aisle pulling down the shades on all the windows. The pilots, who spoke Russian, emerged from the cockpit and opened the door, letting in fresh but chilly air. Ivanov and Sokolov exited the plane, leaving Zula and Peter there alone.

"So those other guys in Seattle—" Peter began.

"Were just local yokels," Zula said.

"Temps."

"Yeah."

They heard a vehicle pull up next to the plane. Some men got out, and Sokolov talked to them. The vehicle drove away. After that, they didn't hear Ivanov's voice, but the voices and the cigarette smoke of the new guys continued to infiltrate the cabin.

Zula said, "Ivanov said he was a dead man. Remember?"

"Yeah, I remember that."

"So all I'm saying is that this might not be a normal example of what he does for a living."

"You think it's what, then?"

"A suicide run."

"Makes me feel a lot better."

"No, seriously, Peter. It *should*."

"How do you figure?"

"If he expected to survive this, he'd need to get rid of us to cover his tracks. But if he's expecting to end up dead, then he's not thinking that far ahead."

"Maybe we can jump clear before the blast?"

"Why not? We don't matter except insofar as we can help him find the Troll."

"Correction. He *believes* we can help him find the Troll."

"Well," Zula said, "that is your department."

"Yeah. And I'm telling you that it is pretty much hopeless unless we can somehow get inside that big ISP and look at their logs. Which would be difficult even in Seattle. For a bunch of Westerners to attempt that in China? Are you kidding me?" A trace of a smile came onto his face. "This is why I never wanted to work in a technology company."

"What do you mean?"

"It is a classic Dilbert situation where the technical objectives are being set by management who are technically clueless and driven by these, I don't know, inscrutable motives."

"Then we just need to scrutinize them harder. Do what those guys in the high-tech companies do."

"Which is what? Because that's *your* department."

"Set expectations. Look busy. File progress reports."

"And when they lose patience?"

"How should I know?" Zula said. "I'm not claiming I know the answer."

ANOTHER PLANE TAXIED alongside them and cut its engines. A few people came out of it, and there was more talking and smoking. Their plane began to flinch as heavy objects were loaded into its cargo space.

The whole aircraft shifted on its suspension as someone put his weight on the front stairway, and they could feel it bobbing slightly as he mounted each step.

He entered the plane. Zula's instantaneous judgment was that the guy was another of Ivanov's goons, like the ones who had showed up at Peter's place in Seattle. This was based entirely on appearance: his size, build, and extremely close-cropped copper-blond hair, his coat—dark green canvas, hanging to midthigh, with a vaguely military cut about it, looking like it could conceal just about anything short of a bazooka—and his scuffed black steel-toed boots. As he reached the top of the steps he swung a large shoulder bag down to the deck. It was a somewhat hip bike messenger bag with a broad padded strap meant to go diagonally across the body.

The first thing he wanted to look at was the cockpit, and so all they could see for a few moments was the back of his head, supported by an unusually thick neck.

After he'd gotten his fill of looking at the plane's control panel, which took a while, he turned to inspect the door of the lavatory. He pushed at it curiously, causing it to accordion open, and then gave it a curious up-and-down look. He had been standing in a somewhat hunched posture, as if afraid he would bang his head on something, and now tilted his head back, opening his mouth to reveal a set of stained, gapped, but structurally rock-solid teeth, and felt above him with one hand, checking the height of the ceiling, verifying that if he straightened his posture the top of his bristly, bullet-shaped head would slam into it. Then he noticed Zula and Peter and turned toward them. His eyes were pale blue and broad set in a wide, bony skull. But his complexion was florid and just a bit toasty. He was surprised, interested, but not at all troubled, to see Zula and Peter looking back at him.

"Hello," he tried, and Zula understood that English was not his native tongue; but he was trying to find out whether Peter and Zula could communicate that way.

"Hello," they responded.

"I am Csongor."

"Csongor the hacker?" Peter inquired.

"Yes," Csongor answered, amused, or at least bemused, that Peter had been able to identify him in this way. He stepped into the passenger cabin. He and his luggage were too wide to move abreast down the seat-row, so he held the messenger bag out at arm's length and allowed it to precede him.

"I'm Peter. You've apparently heard of me," said Peter in a tone that was sour, verging on openly hostile.

Csongor, seeming to take the matter very seriously, stepped forward and extended his hand. Peter, incredulous, shook it. Csongor then turned toward Zula and waited for his cue.

"This is Zula," Peter announced, in a tone of voice suggesting that Csongor really ought to drop dead.

Zula extended her hand. Csongor bent forward and kissed it, not in an arch way, but as if hand kissing were a wholly routine procedure for him. He set his bag down on one of the leather-upholstered seats, carefully, suggesting that it contained something valuable and delicate, such as a laptop. Then he sat down next to it, facing Peter and Zula.

Peter shifted in his seat in a manner just short of writhing that spoke of discomfort with the new seating arrangement. He ended up squarely facing Csongor. Zula could almost smell his tension. He did not like facing people, he was an introvert, it wasn't his way.

There was a long, awkward moment.

"Who wants to begin?" Zula asked.

Csongor looked at Peter, who apparently didn't want to begin. So, with a small *by your leave* sort of gesture, he began to speak in distinctly accented but essentially perfect English. "Yesterday . . . this thing happened with Wallace's email. A couple of hours later, I was asked to go to Moscow for a meeting. I went. There was no meeting. Instead I was *recommended* to get on this plane." He nodded in the direction of the plane that had parked next to them. "I followed the *recommendation*. It was full of certain types of people. Now I am here. I know nothing."

Neither Peter nor Zula said anything in response.

Csongor found this somewhere between funny and irksome. "You said who wants to *begin*," he reminded Zula, "not *end*."

Still nothing.

Csongor tried, "You guys have a similar story, I guess?"

"Not really *that* similar," Zula said. "It started with Wallace being murdered in Peter's apartment."

Csongor's blue eyes snapped over to appraise Peter. "You murdered Wallace?"

Zula was astonished to hear herself laughing. But it seemed that whatever neurological circuits were responsible for laughing took no account of what the higher brain might consider inappropriate. "No, no," she said. "Some Russians murdered him. Then they brought us here."

"Well, that's not very good," Csongor said.

"I know," Zula said. "Whatever it was that Wallace did, he didn't deserve—"

"No, I mean it's not very good *for us.*"

Peter snorted. "We weren't under any illusions that this was anything other than unbelievably bad for us."

"Yes, but perhaps I was," Csongor said. And now that he said this, Zula saw that he was quite sincerely taken aback.

As he might well be. He had just been made aware that he was complicit in a murder.

"That is too bad," Peter said, "because I was kind of hoping that maybe you could tell us what *the fuck* is going on. Who are these people? We know *nothing.*"

Csongor's face reconfigured itself in a way that suggested his wheels were turning now, he was thinking instead of merely reacting. "Nothing? Really?"

Peter drew breath as if to answer, then checked himself.

"You know nothing about playing certain types of games with other people's credit card numbers?" Csongor asked. "Or is that rather the specialty of Zula?"

Peter sighed. "Zula has nothing to do with it. I did sell Wallace a database of credit card numbers."

"The one that Ivanov is so angry about."

"Yes."

"Well then," Csongor said. "Now we have basis for conversation. These kinds of guys—how much do you know about them?"

"You mean, Russian, er . . ." Having spit out the adjective, Peter couldn't bring himself to utter the noun.

"Mafia or organized criminals or whatever you want to call them," Csongor said, turning hands momentarily palms up to say it didn't matter. "They are not like how you see them on TV and movies . . ."

"Really? Because showing up in the private jet, killing Wallace in my apartment, it all seems pretty much straight from the script."

"Ah, but this is *extremely unusual,*" Csongor said. "I am amazed, frankly."

"Comforting."

"Almost all of what they do is very boring. They are trying to make a living in the context of this unbelievably fucked-up system.

This is their only motive. Not excitement, not violence. How they got most of their revenue in Russia was not crazy shit like drug deals or arms trafficking. It was overcharging for cotton from Uzbekistan. And when they moved into the States and Canada, it was health insurance fraud, avoiding gasoline taxes, and credit cards. Lots of credit cards."

"What's your involvement with all this?" Zula asked. "If you don't mind my asking?"

"No, I don't mind your asking," Csongor said. "But I do mind *answering,* since it is somewhat embarrassing. Not a thing to be proud of."

"Okay, don't answer, then."

Csongor considered it. Zula had pegged his age in the early thirties at first, but now that she was getting a better look at him—the elasticity of his face, the openness of his feelings—she understood that he was more like a big-boned twenty-five. "I will answer a little bit now, maybe more later. How much do you know of the history of Hungary?"

"Nada."

"Zip."

Apparently Csongor was unfamiliar with these slang terms, so Zula just shrugged hugely. He nodded and looked a little dismayed, unsure where he should begin. "But you at least know it was a Warsaw Pact country. Until about 1999 or so. Controlled by Russians in a very severe way." Peter and Zula had begun nodding as if they did know all these things, which encouraged him. "Today, it is fine. It is totally modern, with a high standard of living. But in the nineties, when I was a teenager, the economy was terrible—the Communist system had been dynamited, like an old statue of Stalin, but it took some years for a new system to be created. Bad unemployment during those years, inflation, poverty, and so on. My father was a schoolteacher. Overqualified for it. But that is another story. Anyway, in our family, we had very little money, and the only way we knew to make a living was using our brains. As it happens, I was not the smart one. My older brother is the smart one."

"What does he do for a living?" Zula asked.

"Bartos is pursuing a postdoc in topology at UCLA."

"Oh." Zula looked at Peter and told him, "That's a kind of math."

"Thank you," Peter snapped.

Csongor continued, "But I could tell that I was not like Bartos, so I looked for other ways to make a living using my brain. The teachers in my academy only wanted me to play hockey for the school team. I ignored my classes and taught myself to program computers. Then suddenly I was making money this way. When the economy got better, programmers were needed all over the place. Especially doing localization."

"What is localization?" Zula asked. Peter sighed, letting her know it was a stupid question.

"Translating foreign software into Hungarian, making things work correctly in the special environment of Hungary," Csongor explained, and Zula thought that she could glimpse, here, in the way that he contentedly explained things, Csongor's father the schoolteacher. "As an example, because of inflation, Hungarian currency is debased." Warming to the task, he pulled a wallet out of his pocket and produced a sheaf of bills from Magyar Nemzeti Bank, illustrated with engravings of men Zula had never heard of with crazy hats and florid mustaches. The denominations were enormous; the smallest was 1,000, and some of them bore five digits. "So if you have some trivial app that is used in retail, like for a cash register, foreign software might not be suitable because it wants format consisting of decimal point followed by some number of cents. But we don't have a decimal point or cents, just an integer. So minor rewriting of software is needed. I did this kind of thing for merchants."

"Which led to credit card readers?" said Peter, who was finally showing some patience.

"Exactly. In Warsaw Pact times, merchants did not have credit card readers, but when the economy came to life in the late 1990s, everyone suddenly had to have them, and so when people learned that I could program such machines, I had lots of work to do. My father had died from cigarettes and my mother could not make so much money, so I made money to put Bartos through school and so on. All fine. But there is a little snag. You see, the last Soviet soldier left Hungary in 1991. But there were other Russians who came in during the Cold War who took a little bit longer to leave."

"These guys," Zula said, cocking her head in the direction of the neighboring plane.

"Mafia, yes," said Csongor. "So Step 1 of the new economy was that everything got very bad. Step 2 was that things got better and everyone obtained credit cards. And Step 3—"

"Step 3 was credit card fraud," said Peter.

"Yes, and this was attempted in a number of different ways. Some better than others. The best of all ways is like this. A waiter in a restaurant has a little credit card reader in his pocket. The customer wants to pay his bill. He hands his credit card to the waiter. The waiter takes it back to a place where he is not observed and swipes it once to pay the bill. So far, totally legitimate."

Peter was already nodding, confident that he knew this material, so Csongor finished the story for Zula's benefit. "However, then the waiter swipes the card through the illegitimate reader in his pocket and makes a copy of the credit card data. The reader stores the data of many such cards. These data are aggregated and then sold on the black market."

"So you got involved in that racket," Peter said.

Csongor hesitated, not completely happy with the phrasing. "I took a job to program the firmware of a device. I was perhaps naive. It became clear to me only slowly what the device was used for."

Peter let out a tiny snort. Csongor caught it immediately, thought about it, finally shrugged his huge shoulders and met Zula's eye. As if she had somehow been named the judge of all such matters. "So I am just the latest in a very long line of Hungarians being talked into extremely stupid adventures by Germans, Russians, whatever. But it took me into this culture"—he shifted his gaze onto Peter, and Zula understood that he was now talking about international hacker culture—"where I was cool. Respected. Powerful drugs for a teenager."

Peter did not meet Csongor's gaze, and so Csongor went on as if the point had been conceded.

"Then later the same client came back to me with a new problem: there was too much data. Thousands of these machines had been mass-produced and distributed to waiters, not only in Hungary but all over Europe, and the data storage problem was becoming an issue, there were security problems, and so on. Could I help with this? And by the way, if the answer was no, perhaps they would report me to the police or cause other trouble for me. So I became a systems programmer. I built the systems these people needed. And after that, they needed someone to keep the system running in a secure and reliable way. So, over years, I morphed into a kind of mostly freelance systems administrator. I run servers, set up email systems, websites, wikis—"

"I know what a systems administrator is," Peter said.

"My clientele are small companies or sole proprietors who are not big enough to hire someone just for this purpose. But my specialty, my niche, is situations where privacy and security are very important."

"You work for gangsters," Peter said.

"As do you, Peter."

"This part of it is boring for me," Zula said.

Csongor turned to look at her, his face a mixture of curiosity and regret. "Systems administration?"

Zula shook her head and made a gesture of two fists banging into each other, looking between Peter and Csongor. They seemed to take her point. Zula continued, "So I'll bet Wallace contacted you and said 'I need secure email, no questions asked.'"

"Exactly," Csongor said. "I knew he worked for Ivanov. But. A Scottish accountant in Vancouver. What could possibly go wrong?" He chuckled and slapped his thigh, hoping that the others would join him in a little round of ironic laughter, but Peter was having none of it.

"Who is Ivanov? What did Wallace do for him?" Peter asked.

Csongor leaned back in his seat, suddenly feeling tired, and rubbed his eyes. "I had been working for these people for six years before I ever met Ivanov. Then he showed up in Budapest one day and took me to a hockey game and dinner, and then it was obvious who was really the boss."

"But it was too late then."

"Yes, I already knew too much and so on. In Russia there are a few such groups as the one that Ivanov is part of. Some are ethnic Russians. Ivanov belongs to one of those. Others are Chechens or Uzbeks or what have you. The Russian ones are very old, dating back to perhaps Ivan the Terrible. If you are a member of such a group, you live your whole life in it."

Peter snorted. "That's not saying much."

"I beg your pardon?"

"If you're a mobster, your life expectancy is what, thirty years?"

"On the contrary," Csongor said. "Precisely because so many of their activities are routine and boring, many of the members die of old age. Which is the problem."

"What problem?"

"It's a problem for Ivanov, that is."

"How so?"

"It has always been the practice for groups like this to have a fund, called the *obshchak,* which is a common pool of money that they use for all kinds of purposes, including benefits."

"*Benefits!?* Are you telling me that Russian mobsters get *dental!?*"

Csongor shrugged. "I don't see why you are so surprised. A man who gets a toothache must have it seen to, no matter what he does for a living. In the system of these groups, the money for the dentist is paid out of the *obshchak.* When a member reaches the age of retirement, the *obshchak* takes care of him. And, of course, the *obshchak* is also used to fund . . ."—and Csongor looked around at the plane—"operations."

"So we are guests of the *obshchak* right now," Peter said.

"Yes, but I do not think that we are *authorized* guests," Csongor returned.

"What do you mean?"

"I think that Ivanov is basically stealing the funds that are being used to rent this plane," Csongor said. "Because this is not how these guys operate. They are extremely conservative investors for the most part. They don't do crazy shit like this."

Peter snorted.

Zula said, "A pension fund is a pension fund."

"Precisely," said Csongor, turning to her. "Most of the *obshchak* is invested in proper financial instruments. Wallace is a, here my vocabulary fails me—"

"Money manager?" Zula guessed.

"He is one who manages the money managers," Csongor said. "He distributes his clients' funds among several different professional managers, evaluates their performance, moves money from one account to another as necessary."

"That's not all he does," Peter said. "When I met him, he was buying stolen credit card numbers from me."

"This is unusual for Wallace."

"I sort of got that impression."

"Wallace's boss is—*was*—Ivanov. I believe that Ivanov made some mistakes. Of the money he controlled, some was supposed to be invested legitimately. This he entrusted to Wallace. Other money was put into schemes that we would call organized crime. I can only guess, but I think that Ivanov got into trouble."

"Some of his schemes failed," Zula said.

"Or perhaps he simply embezzled from the *obshchak*," Csongor said. "Maybe he was not the right man to be managing this money."

Peter laughed.

Csongor allowed himself the barest trace of a wry smile and continued: "The quarterly numbers were looking not so good. He knew he was in trouble, needed to take some risks in order to bring those numbers up. Guys like him are maybe addicted to taking risks anyway. He and Wallace set up some complicated transactions and at the same time invested some of the money Wallace controlled in schemes such as your stolen credit card numbers. When Wallace lost all his files—"

"The house of cards collapsed," Zula said.

"Yes."

"So why haven't they come down on Ivanov yet?"

"They don't know," Csongor said. "Ivanov has a long leash and has moved with too great speed. By the time his bosses know that something strange is going on, we'll be in Xiamen."

"So we *are* going to Xiamen," Zula said.

"This is what I was told," Csongor said. "To find the Troll."

"Are they going to kill us?"

Csongor thought about it rather too long for Zula's taste. "I think this depends on Sokolov."

"What is the deal with him?"

"Another private contractor, like Wallace. Except that he does security."

"I'm afraid to even ask about his background."

"Twice a hero," Csongor said. "Once in Afghanistan and once in Chechnya."

"Military," Peter translated. "Not a gangster."

"There is a bit of a, what do you call it, revolving door. It's complicated."

"But if it's true that Ivanov has gone off the reservation," Zula said, "then a military man isn't going to approve of that, is he? He doesn't have to keep following orders if it's clear that his boss has gone bananas."

"I don't know Sokolov" was all that Csongor said to that.

SOKOLOV STEPPED ABOARD and then backed halfway into the cockpit to let others go by him. One by one, short-haired Russian security consultants came aboard and distributed themselves around the cabin according to suggestions from Sokolov. These were younger than Sokolov, but not precisely *young;* their ages seemed to range from late twenties to late thirties. They all had interesting faces, but Zula was disinclined to gaze directly at them since she did not want to be caught looking. Peter, Zula, and Csongor were allowed to keep their own space in the aft part of the cabin. Sokolov's crew filled up the other available spaces and, when all seats were taken, resorted to sitting on the floor in the aisle. There were seven of them including Sokolov.

A car pulled up alongside. The two Russian pilots came aboard and began doing paperwork. More stuff was loaded from the vehicle to the plane's cargo hold, and when that got full, additional items were handed up from below and passed down into the passenger cabin and stuffed wherever they would fit. Ivanov came aboard, smelling of alcohol, and went into his compartment in the back. Sokolov handed Zula a shopping bag that turned out to contain a pair of Crocs, a few T-shirts, and underwear.

The pilots closed the door. Sokolov issued a directive to raise the window shades. The plane taxied to the runway, took off north, and banked south. Several minutes later, as they were climbing toward cruising altitude, Zula got a good long view of what she took to be Vladivostok: a sizable port city built around a long inlet, shaped like a crooked finger, at the end of a beefy peninsula.

They flew for a while in silence. The security consultants smoked: a behavior that Zula had never seen aboard an airplane.

"So if we are to find the Troll, perhaps we should conceive of a plan?" Csongor offered.

The security consultants looked at him curiously, but then their attention began to drift away, and they began to make wry comments and crack jokes in Russian. Every so often Sokolov would tell them to shut up and they would be quiet for a while. Or perhaps Sokolov was ruling out certain topics of conversation. Zula preferred not to speculate on what those topics might be.

"Well, for starters, do you know anything at all about Xiamen?" Zula asked.

"I had the opportunity to do a little googling," Csongor said.

"We didn't," Peter said.

"It is a curious place," Csongor said. "Maybe a little like Hungary."

"What does that mean?"

"Too many neighbors."

"I had never heard of it until yesterday," Zula said.

"It's the place with the terra-cotta warriors, right?" Peter said.

"You are thinking of Xi'an," Csongor said, with a rueful smile indicating that he had made the same error. "That is inland. Xiamen is on the coast. A little bit up from Hong Kong. Directly across a, what do you call it, a narrow bit of water—"

"Strait," Zula said.

"Yes, from Taiwan. So. Xiamen is the place where the Spanish silver used to come into China. Spanish brought it on galleons from Mexico to Manila, and from there, Chinese merchants brought it up to Xiamen, and then up the Nine Dragons River to the interior. But the Dutch found out about this, and so the place became infested with Dutch pirates who would hide behind all the little islands and come out and steal the silver. When they weren't doing that, they would rob the Chinese people. Then Zheng Chenggong came and chased them away. This was an amazing man. His mother was Japanese. His father was a Chinese pirate. He was born in Japan. But he was raised by Muslim ex-slaves, freed by his father; so some people think he was secretly a Muslim. Anyway, he chased the Dutch out of Taiwan and made it part of China again. He's a hero to both the mainland Chinese and to the Taiwanese. There is a huge statue of him in Xiamen."

"And this relates to our problem how?" Peter asked, making an elaborate show of patience.

Csongor gave Peter an appraising look. "Like I said, I only had Internet access for a few minutes. Long enough to download some old books. Then they cut me off. So I have been reading the books on the plane."

"So all your information is from old books," Peter said.

"Yes. But there is a point, which is that the links between Xiamen and Taiwan are very old and complicated. Right in the harbor of Xiamen are two islands that actually belong to Taiwan! They are less than ten kilometers from Xiamen, but they are part of a different country and during the Cold War the Red Army used to shell them all the time with artillery."

"So I'm getting the picture that Xiamen has got all kinds of links to Manila, Hong Kong, and Taiwan, it is a major port, et cetera," Zula said. "Is this all just touristy background stuff or does it tell us anything regarding the Troll?"

Csongor shrugged. "Maybe not about the Troll but maybe about us. About our situation. I was trying to figure out how these guys were going to get us into the country. You need a visa to enter China. Did you know this?"

"No," Zula said, and Peter shook his head.

"It's not hard but it takes a little while, you have to do some paperwork, send in your passport. Obviously we do not have visas. So I was wondering, how are these guys even going to get us into the country?"

Zula and Peter were watching Csongor interestedly, waiting for the punch line.

"You ask why this is relevant to us. The answer, I think, is that if they were trying to get us into some place in the interior of the country they would have a more difficult time. But Xiamen is famous for smuggling and corruption. Something like ten percent of all foreign goods sold in China are smuggled in to the country. Traditionally a lot of that smuggling has happened through Xiamen. There was a huge smackdown there ten years ago—"

"Crackdown," Peter and Zula said in unison.

"Yes. Many officials executed or sent to prison. But it is still the kind of place where a man like him"—Csongor, not wanting to utter the name, flicked his eyes toward the door of Ivanov's compartment—"would be able to make connections with local officials who control the ports, the customs, et cetera, and get away with smuggling, shall we say, human cargo into the country."

"Fine, so let's suppose you're right about all of that and he can get us in," Peter said. "What do we do then?"

Csongor considered it for a few moments. Not just the technical problem of finding the Troll, but, perhaps, what he could get away with saying out loud. Ivanov could not hear them through the bulkhead, but the security consultants could, and at least one of them—Sokolov—spoke some English. As Csongor made these calculations his head remained still, and turned away from the Russians, but his eyes wandered about in a way that Zula found hugely expressive.

"The address that we are working with," he began, referring, as Zula understood, to the dotted quad written on the palm of Sokolov's hand.

"Is part of a huge block controlled by an ISP," Peter said. "This we know."

"What if we attempted to narrow it down geographically?" Csongor said.

"We can't exactly break into the headquarters of the ISP and interrogate their sysadmins . . ." Peter said, following Csongor's line of thought.

"But those sysadmins must have some scheme for allocating all those addresses to different parts of the city," Csongor said. "It might not be perfect, but . . ."

"But it probably won't be *random*," Peter said. "We could at least get an *idea*."

It was Zula's turn to feel like kind of a dunderhead, but working in a tech company had taught her that it was better to just come out and ask the question than to play along and pretend you understood. "How are you going to get that information?" she asked.

"Pounding the pavement," Peter said, and looked to Csongor for confirmation.

Zula could tell from the look on Csongor's face that he was not familiar with the idiom. "Going out on the streets," she said, "and doing what?"

"I've heard they have Internet cafés all over the place there," Peter said, "and if that's true, we should be able to go in, pay some money, log on to a computer, and check its IP address. We write it down and move on to the next Internet café."

"Or we could wardrive," Csongor said.

Zula was vaguely familiar with the term: driving around with a laptop, looking for and logging on to unsecured Wi-Fi networks.

"Hotel rooms," Peter said, nodding.

"Or just lobbies, even."

"We could then build a map giving us a picture of how the ISP has allocated its IP addresses around the city. And that should make it possible for us to zero in on a neighborhood where the Troll lives. Maybe, if we get lucky, an Internet café that the Troll uses."

Zula thought about it. "What I like about it," she said, "is that it is kind of systematic and gradual, and so it should prove to our host that we are working on the problem in a steady way and getting results."

This—keeping Ivanov happy, keeping his paranoia in check— was an aspect of the problem that Peter and Csongor had evidently not been thinking about very hard, and they gaped at her. She shook off a wave of mild irritation. "In management-speak, there are metrics that we can use to set expectations and show progress toward a goal."

They weren't sure whether she was joking. She wasn't sure herself.

Why was she annoyed with them?

Because they were actually trying to solve the technical problem of locating the Troll. Which might have been Ivanov's problem, but it wasn't theirs. Theirs was Ivanov.

If they succeeded in finding the Troll, they'd have a worse problem: they'd be complicit in a murder plot.

But she did not make any further trouble, because there was something about their plan that she liked: it would get them out on the street, where they might be able to summon help or even escape. It was not clear to her what would happen to them if they went to the police and admitted that they had entered the country without visas, but it was unlikely to be worse than whatever Ivanov had in mind.

During this, she had been watching Sokolov from the corner of her eye. He still had a document on his lap, but he had not turned a page in a long time. He kept shushing the members of his squad, sometimes angrily. He was listening to them, trying to follow their conversation.

"Do you think they'll allow us to go out on the street like that?"

"That's the question," Csongor admitted.

"They have to," Peter said, "if they want to find the Troll."

"Then I'll try to sell it," Zula said. "I'll try to make him understand that this is the only way." She made sure Sokolov could hear that much.

IN CSONGOR, ZULA had begun to recognize something that she had also seen in Peter and, indeed, that probably accounted for her having been attracted to Peter in the first place. Neither of these men had much in the way of formal education, since each had decided, during his late teens, to simply go out into the world and begin doing something. And each of them had found his way from there, sometimes with good and sometimes with bad results. Consequently, neither had much in the way of money or prestige. But each had a kind of confidence about him that was not often found in young men who had followed the recommended path through high school to college and postgraduate training. If she had wanted to be cruel or catty about it, Zula might have likened those meticulously groomed boys to overgrown fetuses, waiting endlessly to be born. Which was absolutely fine given that the universities were well stocked with fetal women. But perhaps because of her background in refugee camps and the premature death of her adoptive mother, she could not bring herself to be interested in those men. This quality that she had seen in Peter and now saw in Csongor was—and she flinched from the word, but there seemed little point in trying to distance herself from it through layers of self-conscious irony—masculine. And along with it came both good and bad. She saw the same quality in some of the men of her family, most notably Uncle Richard. And what she knew of him was that he was basically a good man, that he had done some crazy shit, hurt some people, felt bad about it, that he had gotten lucky, that he would die to protect her, and that his relations with women, overall, had not gone well.

THE PLANE DESCENDED for a while and then made a series of turns that seemed like a landing approach. In another half hour the sun would be down, but presently the light was shining almost horizontally across the landscape below them, casting distinct shadows and throwing the landforms and buildings into relief. That it was hot and humid was obvious even from up here. The physical geography was bewilderingly complicated: a lot of multipronged peninsulas groping toward a stew of large and small islands in a sprawling bay formed by the confluence of at least two major estuaries. With the exception of some silted-in bits and slabs of artificial land around the water's edge, the landforms tended to be steep, mountainous, and green. As they descended it became easy to pick out Xiamen, which was a generally circular island, separated from the mainland by straits narrow enough that modern bridges had been thrown across, connecting it to what looked like industrial suburbs.

It was by far the largest island in the bay, with the exception of one, farther from the mainland, that rivaled it in size if not in population. For the round island of Xiamen was almost entirely developed, only the steepest bits in the interior remaining green. The big island east of it was shaped like a sponge that had been squeezed almost in half. It had some built-up areas, but they were scattered, low-lying towns separated by broad flat regions devoted to agriculture. Other parts of it were mountainous and appeared to be wilderness, albeit scarred by winding roads and speckled with curious installations, heavy on domes and antennas. "That's the Taiwanese island, isn't it?" Zula said.

"I would guess so," said Csongor. "All that stuff is military; it looks like the crap that the Soviets used to build in Hungary."

Another, smaller island passed under their wing. It too was notably underdeveloped compared to everything else. "The other one," Csongor said. "One is Quemoy, the other is Matsu. I don't know which is which."

Moments later they were above Xiamen, and after another series of turns they came in for their landing.

The plane did not head for the terminal but instead taxied to a more low-slung part of the airport. This was crowded with other small private jets, and it was necessary to taxi past a score of them before finding a parking spot. Zula, of course, had no idea what Xiamen's private jet terminal looked like on a normal day, but the scene that presented itself out the window looked extremely busy to her. Beyond the chain-link security fence, there were enough black cars jockeying for position that it was necessary for men in uniforms to stand about waving their arms and blowing whistles. Some of them were admitted onto the tarmac to pull up alongside parked jets.

The security consultants had taken an interest in the proceedings and were pressing their faces against windows. *"Germaniya,"* said one of them. *"Yaponiya,"* said another.

"Names of countries," Csongor explained. For Zula was on the wrong side of the plane and having a difficult time getting a clear view. "Some of these jets belong to governments. There's yours right there." And he rolled clear of a window and pointed toward one marked UNITED STATES OF AMERICA.

"What's going on?" Zula asked.

Csongor shrugged. "Some kind of conference maybe?"

"Taiwan," Peter said. "I heard about this! It's something to do with Taiwan."

Zula goggled, not out of skepticism but because she didn't normally look to Peter to be up to speed on current events. He shrugged. "Slashdot. There's been some kind of hassle, connected with this. Denial-of-service attacks against Taiwanese ISPs."

"Okay, yes! I did hear something about this," Csongor said. "They are having diplomatic talks. But I didn't realize it was happening in Xiamen."

But this was the last they saw before Sokolov ordered that all the shades be pulled down.

After they came to a stop, Ivanov emerged from the aft cabin, talking on a phone, and exited the plane.

They turned off all the lights and sat there for an hour before Zula fell asleep.

When she woke up, it was still dark. People were up and moving around, but not talking. Everyone was getting their stuff. Zula followed suit. Sokolov was lodged in the cockpit door again, slapping each of his men on the shoulder as they filed off.

Csongor, who had an actual wristwatch, said that six hours had passed since the plane had landed.

When Zula reached the head of the aisle, Sokolov held out a hand to stop her, then handed her a black bundle. It smelled like new clothing. She took it in both hands and let it unfold. It was a black hoodie printed with the name of a fashion designer, flagrantly bootleg.

"Not my style," she said.

"Later we get you fur coat," Sokolov said.

She locked eyes with him. He had perhaps the best poker face she had ever seen; she could not get the slightest hint as to whether he was engaging in deadpan humor, cruel sarcasm, or actually intending to get her a fur coat.

"That's not my style either."

He shrugged. "Put this on; we worry about style later."

She put it on. He reached around behind her neck, grasped the hood, and pulled it up to cover her head, then forward so that her face was shrouded. Then he gave her a pat on her shoulder to let her know she could proceed. In a strange way that made her hate herself, she enjoyed the sensation of the pat.

Descending the stairs, she saw that two vans were idling right next to the plane. Standing next to the first one was a security consultant, watching her carefully. At the base of the stairs was another, who did not touch her but walked next to her as she proceeded to the van.

She was directed to the backseat where she sat in the middle between two security consultants who made sure that her seat belt was tightly fastened. Csongor ended up in front of her and Peter was, apparently, in the other van.

Sokolov gave a directive. The vans went into motion, driving through a gate in the security barrier and out onto an airport road. A black Mercedes pulled in ahead of them. Zula kept waiting for the moment when they'd roll up to a security checkpoint, but it didn't happen. They never got checked at all. At some point they merged into traffic on a highway. They were in China.

CHET HAD TO drive into Elphinstone to pick up some supplies for the Mud Month shutdown, so he gave Richard a lift to the town's one-runway airport. A twin-engine, propeller-driven airplane awaited him there, and Chet, who knew the drill, simply drove right up to it, rolled down his window, and exchanged some banter with the pilot while Richard pulled his bag out of the back of Chet's truck and heaved it through the plane's tiny door. Thirty seconds later they were in the air. Richard, who made this journey a couple of dozen times a year, had set up a deal with a flying service based out of the Seattle suburb of Renton, and so all this was as routine as it could be. The amount of time he would spend in the air was less than what some Corporation 9592 employees would spend in their cars this morning, stuck on floating bridges or bottled up behind random suburban fender benders.

The first and last thirds of the route were entirely over mountains. The middle third traversed the irrigated basin around Grand Coulee Dam. No matter how many times Richard flew it, he was always startled to see the ground suddenly level out and develop a rectilinear grid of section-line roads, just like in the Midwest. Early on, the pattern was imposed in fragments scattered over creviced and disjoint mesas separating mountain valleys, but presently these flowed together to form a coherent grid that held together until it lapped up against some terrain that was simply too rugged and wild to be subjected to such treatment. The only respect in which these green farm-squares differed from the ones in the Midwest was that here, many of them sported inscribed circles of green, the marks of center-pivot irrigation systems.

Richard could never look at them without thinking of Chet. For Chet was a midwestern boy too and had grown up in a small town in the eastern, neatly gridded part of South Dakota where he and his boyhood friends had formed a proto-motorcycle gang, riding around on homemade contraptions built from lawnmower engines. Later they had graduated to dirt bikes and then full-fledged motorcycles. The world's unwillingness to supply Chet with all the resources he needed for upkeep and improvement of his fleet of bikes had led him into the business of small-town marijuana dealing, which must have seemed dark and dangerous at the time, but that now, in these days of crystal meth, seemed as wholesome as running a lemonade stand. Chet had logged a huge number of miles riding around on those section-line roads, which he preferred to the state highways and the interstates since there was less traffic and less of a police presence.

One evening in 1977 he had been riding south from a lucrative rendezvous in Pipestone, Minnesota. It was a warm summer night; the moon and the stars were out. He leaned back against his sissy bar and let the wind blow in his long hair and cranked up the throttle. Then he woke up in a long-term care facility in Minneapolis in February. As was slowly explained to him by the occupational therapists, he had been found in the middle of a cornfield by a farmer's dog. It seemed that his nocturnal ride had been terminated by a sudden westward jog in the section-line road. Failing to jog, he had flown off straight into the cornfield, doing something like ninety miles an hour. The corn, which was eight feet tall at that time of the year, had brought him to a reasonably gentle stop, and so he had sustained surprisingly few injuries. The long, tough fibrous stalks had split and splintered as he tore through them, but his leathers had deflected most of it. Unfortunately, he had not been wearing a helmet, and one splinter had gone straight up his left nostril into his brain.

The recovery had taken a while. Chet had gotten most of his brain functions back. He had not lost any of his wits, unless discretion and social skills could be so designated, so he had devoted a lot of attention to the question of why the transit-brandishing pencilnecks who had laid out the section lines a hundred years ago had been so particular about sticking to a grid pattern and yet had perversely inserted these occasional sideways jogs into the grid. Examining maps, he noticed that the jogs only occurred in north-south roads, never east-west.

The answer, of course, was that the earth was a sphere and so it was geometrically impossible to cover it with a grid of squares. You could grid a good-sized patch of it, but eventually you would have to insert a little adjustment: move one row of sections east or west relative to the row beneath it.

It being the 1970s, and Chet being a high school dropout with a damaged brain, he could not help but perceive something huge in this discovery. Nor could he avoid coming to the conclusion that the mistake he had made on that beautiful moonlit night had been a sort of message from above, a warning that, during the grubby, day-to-day work of small-town pot dealing, he had been failing to attend to larger and more cosmic matters.

He had moved west, as Americans did in those days when they were searching for the cosmic. A few hundred miles short of the Pacific, he had fallen in with the biker group that collaborated with Richard on his backpack smuggling scheme. Among them he had acquired a sort of shamanistic aura and become the high priest of a breakaway faction calling itself the Septentrion Paladins to distinguish themselves from their predominantly Californian parent group. They had moved north of the border and established themselves in southern B.C. A second, near-fatal crash had only enhanced Chet's mystical reputation.

Not long after Chet had been released from the hospital after the second crash, the Septentrion Paladins had embarked on a project to, as Chet put it, "get in touch with our masculinity."

When this policy initiative had abruptly been made known to Richard in the middle of a barroom conversation on seemingly unrelated topics, awe and horror had struggled for supremacy in his mammalian brain as his reptilian had begun to tally all exits, conventional and un-, from the bar; lubricated his whole body with sweat; and jacked his pulse rate up into a frequency range that had probably jammed Mounties' radar guns out on Highway 22. For he had known these men all too well in their premasculine days and could not imagine what they were about to get up to *now*. Over the course of the next few minutes' marginally coherent discussion, however, he pieced together that what Chet really meant was that they would *stay* in touch with their masculinity but with a more modest body count. The change in emphasis seemed to coincide with some of the surviving principals' getting married and having kids. They got rid of most of their guns and took advantage of Canada's surprisingly easygoing sword laws, riding around the provincial byways with five-foot claymores strapped to their backs. They met in forest clearings to engage in mock duels and jousts with foam weapons, and they went to Ren Faires to hoist tankards with their newfound soul brothers in the Society for Creative Anachronism. Roaring down the byways of southern B.C. with the cross hilts of their claymores projecting above their shoulders, they had become a familiar feature of that self-consciously quirky part of the world. Barely visible behind concentric shells of tinted glass and perforated sunscreens, children in minivans had pointed to them and waved with lavish enthusiasm. The Septentrion Paladins had become the subjects of offbeat-slash-heartwarming featurettes on regional television news broadcasts, and they had ceased to commit crimes.

. . . .

TURNING HIS ATTENTION back to matters inside the plane's cabin, Richard resumed reading the *T'Rain Gazette,* a daily newspaper (electronic format, of course), created by a microdepartment operating out of the Seattle office, which summarized what had been going on all over T'Rain during the preceding twenty-four hours: notable achievements, wars, duels, sackings, mortality statistics, plagues, famines, untoward spikes in commodity prices.

TORGAI MORTALITY HITS 1,000,000% MARK

(compiled from reports by Gazette correspondents Gresh'nakh the Forsaken, Erikk Blöodmace, and Lady Lacewing of Faërie)

Torgai Foothills—The mortality rate in this unexpectedly war-ravaged region today skyrocketed through one million percent. Local observers attributed the unusual figure to an "epochal" influx of outsiders, compelled, by as yet unexplained astral phenomena, to pay tribute to a local troll. The visitors or, as they have come to be known to locals, "Meat," are laden with tribute and hence make tempting targets for highwaymen (the one million percent benchmark is considered by analysts to be an important psychological barrier that separates a war-ravaged inferno from a chiliastic gore storm).

Steadying himself on an eight-foot wizard's staff as he waded through a knee-high river of blood washing down the market street of Bagpipe Gulch—a community that once prized its status as the "Gateway to Torgai"— Shekondar the Fearsome, a local alchemist, denied that the trend was a negative influence on the town's image, insisting that the influx of "Meat," and the bandits, land pirates, and cutthroats who had come to prey on them, had been a boon to the region's economic development and a bonanza for local merchants, especially those who, like Shekondar, dealt in goods, such as healing potions and magically enhanced whetstones, that were in demand among the newcomers.

In the Wayfarer Inn, a popular local watering hole situated on the precipitous road leading up out of Bagpipe Gulch into the foothills, a more nuanced view of the situation could be heard in the remarks of a muffled voice barely audible through a wall of corpses stacked all the way to the taproom's ceiling, and identifying itself as Goodman Bustle, the barkeep. Suggesting that all the visitors and attention might be "too much of a good thing," the voice identifying itself as Bustle complained that many customers, citing as an excuse the towering rampart of decaying flesh that had completely blocked access to the bar, had departed the premises without paying their tabs.

The compilers of this document all sported advanced liberal arts degrees from very expensive institutions of higher learning and wrote in this style, as Richard had belatedly realized, as a form of job security. Upper management had grown accustomed to reading the *Gazette* every morning over their lattes and would probably have paid these people to write it even if it hadn't been an official part of Corporation 9592's budget.

The phrase "as yet unexplained astral phenomena" was a hyperlink leading to a separate article on the internal wiki. For it was an iron law of *Gazette* editorial policy that the world of T'Rain as seen through the screens of players must be treated as the ground truth, the only reality observable or reportable by its correspondents. Oddities due to the choices made by players were attributed to "strange lights in the sky," "eldritch influences beyond the ken of even the most erudite local observers," "unlooked-for syzygy," "what was most likely the intervention of a capricious local demigod," "bolt from the blue," or, in one case, "an unexpected reversal of fortune that even the most wizened local gaffers agreed was without precedent and that, indeed, if seen in a work of literature, would have been derided as a heavy-handed example of deus ex machina." But of course it was one of the *Gazette* staff's most important tasks to report on player behavior, that is, on things that happened in the real world, and so such phrases were always linked to non-*Gazette* articles written in a sort of corporate memo-speak that always disheartened Richard when he clicked through to it.

In this case, the explanatory memo supplied the information that the Torgai Foothills were the turf of a band calling themselves the da G shou, probably an abbreviation of da G[old] shou, "makers of gold," where the truncation of "Gold" to "G" was either due to the influence of gangsta rap, or because it was easier to type. They had been running the place for years. All pretty normal. There were many little enclaves like this. Nothing in the rules prevented a sufficiently dedicated and well-organized band of players from conquering and holding a particular stretch of ground. The "Meat" were there because of REAMDE, which had been present at background levels for several weeks now but that recently had pinballed through the elbow in its exponential growth curve and for about twelve hours had looked as though it might completely take over all computing power in the Universe, until its own size and rapid growth had caused it to run afoul of the sorts of real-world friction that always befell seemingly exponential phenomena and bent those hockey-stick graphs over into lazy S plots. Which was not to say that it wasn't still a very serious problem and that scores of programmers and sysadmins were not working eighteen-hour shifts crawling all over the thing. But it wasn't going to take over the world and it wasn't going to bring the whole company to a stop, and in the meantime, thousands of characters were racking up experience points slaying each other in Goodman Bustle's pub.

CORVALLIS KAWASAKI PICKED him up on the tarmac of the Renton airport. He was driving the inevitable Prius. "I could have had a friggin' Lincoln town car," Richard complained, as he stuffed himself into its front seat.

"Just wanted to bend your ear a little," C-plus explained, fussing with the intermittent wiper knob, trying to dial in that elusive setting, always so difficult to find in Seattle, that would keep the windshield visually transparent but not drag shuddering blades across dry glass. They were staring straight down the runway at the southern bight of Lake Washington, which was flecked with whitecaps. It had been a choppy landing, and Richard felt a bit clammy.

Corvallis had grown up in the town after which he was named, the son of a Japanese-American cog sci professor and an Indian biotech researcher, but culturally he was pure Oregonian. No one at the company knew exactly what he did for a living. But it was hard to imagine the place without him. He shifted the Prius into gear, or whatever it was called when you pulled the lever that made it go forward, and proceeded at a safe and sane speed among the parked airplanes, dripping and rocking against their tie-downs, and out through a gate and onto something that looked like an actual street. "I know you're going to see Devin tomorrow and mostly what's on your mind is the war."

He paused slightly before saying "war," and he said it funny, with a long O and heavy emphasis.

"Woe-er?" Richard repeated.

"W-O-R," C-plus explained, "the War of Realignment."

"Is that what the cool kids are calling it now?"

"Yeah. I guess it works better in email than in conversation. Anyway, I know you're going to be prepping for that, but also you need to know that there are some interesting techno-legal issues coming up around REAMDE."

"God, that sounds like just the sort of can of worms that I retired to get away from."

"I don't think you are actually retired," Corvallis pointed out mildly. "I mean, you just flew in from Elphinstone and tomorrow you're taking a jet to Missouri and from there—"

"It's a selective retirement," Richard explained, "a retirement from boring shit."

"I think that's called a promotion."

"Well, whatever you call it, I don't want to 'drill down'—is that the expression you use?"

"You know perfectly well that it is."

"Into nasty details of REAMDE's legal consequences. I mean, we've had viruses before, right?"

"We have 281 active viruses as of the last time I checked, which was an hour ago."

Richard drew breath but C-plus cut him off. "And before you go where you're going, let me just point out that most of them don't actually make use of our technology as a payment mechanism. So REAMDE is not just another virus. It presents new issues."

"Because our servers are actually being used to transfer the booty."

"Turns out," Corvallis warned him, "that federal law enforcement types haven't yet bought into the whole APPIS mind-set, and so they aren't real big on terms like 'booty,' 'swag,' 'hoard,' 'treasure,' or anything that is evocative of a fictitious Medieval Armed Combat scenario. To them, it's all payments. And since our system uses real money, it's all—well—*real*."

"I always knew that that was going to swing around and bite me in the ass someday," Richard said. "I just didn't know how or when."

"Well, it's bitten you in the ass lots of times, actually."

"I know, but each one feels like the first."

"The creator of the REAMDE virus has made some . . . interesting choices."

"Interesting in a way that's bad for us?" Richard asked. Because this was clearly implied by Corvallis's tone.

"Well, that depends on whether we want to be the avenging sword of the Justice Department, here, or sort of cop out and say it's not our problem."

"Go on."

"The instructions in the eponymous file just state that the gold pieces are to be left at a particular location in the Torgai Foothills. They do *not* say that the gold is to be mailed or transferred to any one specific character."

"Obviously," Richard said, "because in that case we could just shut down that character's account."

"Right. So the way that the virus creator takes possession of the gold is by simply picking it up off the ground where it has been dropped by the victim."

"Which is something that any character in the game could do."

"Theoretically," Corvallis said. "In practice, obviously, you can't pick the gold up unless you can actually get to that location in the Torgai Foothills. And in order to turn those gold pieces into real-world money, you have to then physically get them out to a town with an M.C."

"Not 'physically,'" Richard corrected him. "You guys always make that mistake. It's a game, remember?"

"Okay, physically in the game world," Corvallis said, his tone of voice suggesting that Richard was being just a little pedantic. "You know what I mean. Your character has to be capable of surviving the journey from the drop point, through the foothills, to the near-est town or ley line intersection, and to an M.C."

For, as C-plus didn't need to explain to Richard, virtual gold pieces in the game could not be converted into real-world cash with-out the services of a moneychanger—an M.C.—and you couldn't find those guys just anywhere. For techno-legal reasons Richard had forgotten, they had limited the number of moneychangers, inserted some friction and delay into the system.

Richard said, "So the creators of the virus were leveraging their physical control of the—goddamn it!" For Corvallis had gotten a mischievous look on his face and raised an index finger from his steering wheel. Richard corrected himself, "They were leveraging their *virtual,* in-the-game-world military dominance of that region to create a payment mechanism that would be more difficult for us to shut down."

"As far as we can tell, they are using as many as a thousand dif-ferent characters to go into that region and pick up the gold and act as mules."

"All self-sus, no doubt."

"You got it."

"But how are they extracting real money from self-sus accounts?" Because the usual way of turning your pretend gold pieces into real money was to have it show up as a payment to a credit card account.

"Western Union money transfers, through a bank in Taiwan."

Richard got a blank look.

"It's an option we added," Corvallis explained. "Nolan's always looking for ways to make the system more transparent to Chinese kids who don't have credit cards."

"Fine. Where is the drop point?"

"Drop point?"

"Where are the victims depositing the ransom money?"

"Interesting question. Turns out that there's not just one place for that. The REAMDE files are all a little bit different—apparently they were generated by a script that inserts a different set of coordi-nates each time. So far we have identified more than three hundred different drop locations that are specified in different versions of the file."

"You're telling me the gold is scattered all over the place."

"Yeah."

"They anticipated we might make moves to shut them down," Richard said, "so they spread things out."

"Apparently. So it's analogous to a situation in the real world where caches of gold have been scattered all over a rugged wilderness area, hundreds of square kilometers."

"If that happened in the real world," Richard said, "the cops would just cordon off the area."

"And that is exactly what cops of various nationalities are asking us to do in this case," C-plus said. "Just write a script that will eject or log out every character in the Torgai Foothills and prevent them from logging back in. Then go in there and collect evidence."

"By 'go in there' you just mean run a program that will identify all gold pieces, or piles or containers thereof, in that region."

"Yes."

"And are we telling them to fuck themselves?" This seemed the obvious thing to do, but Richard wouldn't put anything past Corporation 9592's current CEO.

"We don't have any choice!" C-plus said.

Richard was struck mute with admiration at the way C-plus had answered the question while imputing nothing except helplessness to the CEO.

Corvallis went on, "REAMDE has affected users from at least forty-three different countries that we know about. If we say yes to one, we have to say yes to all of them."

"And then our company is being micromanaged by the United Nations," Richard said. "Awesome." He was way too old to use this all-purpose adjective sincerely but was not above throwing it into a sentence for ironic effect.

"The legal issues are just fantastically complex," C-plus said, "given all the different nationalities. So I'm not here to tell you that we've got an answer. But it helps that each individual event is a very small crime. Seventy-three dollars at current exchange rates. Under the radar as far as serious criminal prosecution is concerned."

"I have a headache already," Richard said. "Is there anything you actually need me to do? Or are you just . . ."

"Just cluing you in," C-plus said. "I'm sure that the PR staff will want some quality time with you before you go on the road."

"They just want to tell me to shut up," Richard said. "I already know that."

"That is not the actual point. They just want to be seen as having done their jobs."

Richard fell silent for a while, wondering whether there was any way that he could delegate to an underling all meetings whose sole purpose was for the people he was meeting with to demonstrate that they were doing their jobs. Then he realized he should have just stayed in the Schloss if that was what he really wanted.

Half an hour later they were at Corporation 9592's headquarters, chilling out in a small conference room with an oversized LCD video screen. Corvallis offered to "drive," meaning that he would operate the mouse and keyboard, but Richard asserted his prerogative, dragging the controls over to his side of the table and then logging in using his personal account. All his characters were listed on the splash screen. Compared to some players, he didn't have that many: only eight. Even though he understood, intellectually, that they were just software bots, it made him feel somehow guilty to know that they were all sitting in their home zones twenty-four hours a day, executing their bothaviors, and waiting for the master to log in and exercise them.

He scanned the list of names and decided, what the hell, he would just unlimber Egdod.

Egdod was the first player-character that had ever been created in T'Rain, not counting a number of titans, gods, demigods, and so on that had been set up in order to build the world and that were not owned by any one player. He had his own personal home zone, a towering fortress of solitude constructed on the top of one of T'Rain's highest mountains and decorated with artifacts that Egdod had looted from various palaces and ruins that he'd had a hand in conquering. Egdod was so famous that Richard could not even take him out of doors without first concealing his identity behind a many-layered screen of spells, wards, disguises, and enchantments whose purpose was to make him look like a much less powerful, but still way-too-puissant-to-fuck-with character. Even the simplest of these spells was far beyond the powers of all but a few hundred of T'Rain's most powerful denizens. Richard had written a script that invoked them all automatically, with a single keystroke; otherwise it would have taken him half an hour. Each spell triggered its own custom-designed light show and sound effects extravaganza, the latter propagating through the building thanks to the oversized subwoofers with which this conference room had been supplied, and so awareness that Egdod was being aired out spread through neighboring offices by subsonic vibration and then throughout the rest of the building by text message, and curious employees began to congregate in the doorway of the conference room, not daring to cross its threshold, just wanting to catch a glimpse of the event, in somewhat the same spirit that navy veterans would gather on the shore to watch the battleship *Missouri* being towed to a new berth. Which was not to imply that a warship of that class would have stood much of a chance against the firepower of an Egdod. A direct hit from an ICBM might have mussed Egdod's hair—which, predictably, was white, in a God of the Old Testament do. Richard longed to swap it for something a little more against-the-grain, and when Egdod was in disguise, he always did. But once in a blue moon, Egdod had to appear in his true avatar to kill a god, divert a comet, or carry out some ceremonial function, and at those times it was necessary that he look the part. As the successive magic wrappers were laid down, however, this awe-inspiring figure and his harbingers and vanguards, his encloaking energy-nimbi and meteorological accoutrements, got stripped away and snuffed out, and finally Egdod himself altered his appearance to that of a somewhat pixieish, vaguely elven-looking young female with spiky dark hair. At this point the crowd in the doorway dispersed, except for a few who wanted to linger and get a view of Egdod's fortress from inside.

Gravity was of no more concern to Egdod than crabgrass to an archangel, so he could have taken flight directly from any balcony or open window, but the Torgai Foothills were six thousand miles away, which was a long trip even at the supersonic velocities of which Egdod was capable. So instead he made use of the ley line intersection that was directly beneath the mountain. Wary of being followed out of the Bagpipe Gulch intersection, he went to another LLI about a hundred miles away, underneath a large city that bestrode a great river flowing down out of the mountain range above the Torgai. But even this place had been thrown all out of whack by REAMDE, with long queues outside the moneychangers' kiosks and healing potions at such a premium that they were being auctioned in the town square for ten times their usual market price. On his way to the city gates, Egdod was accosted several times by bands of warriors who assumed that he, or rather the spiky-haired pixie he was pretending to be, had come here to pay ransom in the Torgai Foothills. *Don't even think of going up there alone,* was the general tenor of their remarks; *pay us enough and we'll escort you to the proper coordinates.* Richard got rid of them quickly just by claiming that his/her errand had nothing to do with REAMDE. At the first opportunity, he made the character invisible and then, just in case he was being followed, superinvisible and then double-super and then hyperinvisible. For run-of-the-mill invisibility spells could be penetrated by countermeasures of varying strengths. Satisfied that no one could plausibly see him/her, he/she took to the air and flew the hundred miles to Torgai in a few minutes, plunging to treetop level at the end and flying nap-of-the-earth to get a better view of what was going on down there.

A lot was the quick answer.

Not that Richard didn't already know this; but there was something about actually seeing it.

And besides, this was almost kind of like his job now. The CEO, who had actual responsibilities, could get by with reading the summaries and maybe allow himself to be seen checking out the *T'Rain Gazette* during his coffee break. But actually going to the place was a waste of his shockingly expensive time. Richard, however, as founder/chairman, receiving only token compensation, was almost expected to go and view spectacles of this kind, in roughly the same way that the Queen of England was expected to fly over derailments in a chopper.

A key difference was that he got to have inappropriate emotional responses. "This is fucking cool," he remarked, gazing down from an altitude of perhaps a thousand feet at a corpse- and skeleton-strewn meadow where something like twenty different Medieval Armed Combat encounters were going on simultaneously. "We should pay these guys to do this all the time."

"Which guys?"

"Whoever created this virus."

"Oh."

"Who *did* create it, by the way?"

"Unknown," C-plus said, "but thanks to your niece, we're pretty sure he's in Xiamen."

"The place with the terra-cotta soldiers?"

"No, you're thinking of Xian."

"Zula's been helping you track these guys down?"

C-plus looked a bit taken aback. "I thought you were aware of it."

"Of what?"

"Her participation. She said it was a side project that you had put her on."

Had it been anyone else, Richard would have said, *I have no idea what the hell you are talking about,* but since it was family, his instinct was to cover for her. "There may have been some mission drift," he speculated.

"Whatever. Anyway, we have an IP address in Xiamen, but nothing else."

Richard put Egdod into auto-hover mode, then leaned back and took his hands off the controls. "Are the Chinese cops among those who have been pestering us to do something about this?"

"They were among the first to do so, is my understanding."

"Then one way to shut them up—"

"—is to ask them to trace down this IP address for us. Yes, I agree; we would never hear from them again."

"So are we going to do that?"

"I doubt it," C-plus said, "because we'd be giving up information about our own internal procedures. And I'm pretty sure Nolan doesn't want to do that."

"And, come to think of it, I'm sure Nolan's right," Richard said. "I'm an idiot. Let's not tell the Chinese government anything."

"Are you asking me to pass that on to our CEO?" Corvallis said, in a tone of voice making it clear that, if flat out asked, he'd flat out refuse.

"Nah," Richard said, "I have other reasons to ruin his day."

Day 2

In the dark, driving through Xiamen was like driving through any other modern city, save that they were more exuberant, here, about lighting things up; the highway was illuminated with dashed lines of blue neon, and bright signs, some familiar corporate logos and others unreadable by Zula, erupted from the tops of buildings.

They stopped at a brand-new Hyatt not far from the airport and dropped off the two pilots. Then they followed what she took to be a ring road, since water was always on their right, until they were in the middle of what had to be the most crowded and built-up part of the island. This was more than a match for Seattle. The waterfront to their right was an unbroken series of low-slung passenger ferry terminals. To their left was a mixture of buildings: some brand-new skyscrapers, some pre-economic-miracle hotels and office structures rising to perhaps ten or fifteen stories, some vacant lots-cum-construction-sites, and a few tenacious patches of old three- to seven-story residential neighborhood buildings.

They turned off the ring road into a place that had been land-scaped recently. A huge steel door raised, and they descended into a parking structure beneath an office tower. The parking spaces hadn't been striped yet, and the lighting was temporary. Construction tools and supplies were piled around.

The two vans had caravanned the whole way behind the black

Mercedes. A Chinese man, dressed informally, but seeming to wield great authority, climbed out of the backseat of the Mercedes. Ivanov, who had been sitting next to him, climbed out of the other side. The Chinese man used a key card to summon an elevator. He held the door open as Ivanov, the seven security consultants, Zula, Peter, and Csongor crammed themselves aboard. Then he pushed himself in, swiped his card, and hit the button for the forty-third floor. All told, the building seemed to have fifty stories.

Standing in an elevator with a bunch of strangers felt a little awkward even in the best of circumstances. Never more so than now. Zula, and most of the others, stared at the control panel, which was ostentatiously high tech; above it was an electroluminescent screen that flashed the numbers of the floors as they went by and occasionally displayed Chinese characters as well, synchronized with a lush female voice speaking canned phrases in Mandarin.

Floor 43 sported a reasonably nice elevator lobby, lined in expensive-looking polished stone and equipped with men's and women's bathrooms. Beyond that, it consisted of two large office suites of equal size. The one to the left, as they stepped off the elevators, was completely unfinished. The floors were bare concrete. The ceilings were just the underside of Floor 44: corrugated steel deck frosted with foamy stuff and supported at wide intervals by huge zigzagging trusses. The suite to the right seemed to have been built out recently but never occupied. Double doors of plate glass, set in a plate-glass wall, gave way to a reception area containing a built-in desk but no furniture. Beyond that was an open space about the size of a tennis court, obviously destined to become a warren of cubicles. Around the perimeter were glass-walled offices of various sizes, each with a window. The largest of these was a conference room with a large built-in table and sprays of unconnected Ethernet cables hanging out of hatches in its center. Other than that there was no furniture in the whole place. The floor was covered in brown-gray carpet, and the ceiling was a grid of acoustical panels interrupted here and there by light fixtures and vent louvers.

It was, in other words, the most perfectly generic office environment that could be imagined.

"Safe house," Sokolov announced, and he indicated by gestures that Zula, Peter, and Csongor might wish to make themselves comfortable in the middle of the open space.

Ivanov departed in the company of the Chinese man.

Three of the security consultants set to work bringing up all the cargo that had been flown in on the plane and packed into the vans. They had been supplied with elevator key cards and so were free to come and go as they wished.

One of the security consultants was stationed at the reception desk, thereby controlling entry to and exit from the suite. As soon as all the cargo had been brought up, he connected the entry doors together with a cable lock.

One security consultant went into the men's room, which was off the elevator lobby, and apparently bathed as best he could in the sink. Certain of the bags coming up from below contained bedrolls and personal effects. He selected one of these and carried it into a vacant office, where he rolled out a sleeping bag and lay down and stopped moving. Two of the cargo movers followed his lead as soon as they were finished with their job, while the third, after rooting around in bags for a while, distributed some thick black plastic packets that turned out to contain military rations. He assembled a portable stove on the floor, ignited it, and began to heat water.

Sokolov and one other security consultant made a thoroughgoing reconnaissance of the forty-third floor. They began by clambering up on the conference table. The consultant gave Sokolov a leg up, enabling his boss to pop up through a ceiling tile and commence an exploration of the crawl space above the ceiling. The ceiling grid itself was made of flimsy aluminum extrusions, suspended from the true ceiling by a web of wires, and completely incapable of supporting a person's weight. Assuming that this half of the building was a mirror image of the vacant suite next door, however, there were heavy steel trusses at regular intervals, consisting of T-shaped beams connected by zigzagging rods of steel, and a reasonably acrobatic person could use those as monkey bars to travel around above the ceiling. Zula, Peter, and Csongor, sitting on the floor and eating their rations in the middle of the vacant space, heard Sokolov and scraping and clanging as he made his way overhead, and heard him thumping in an exploratory way on the walls that defined the boundary between this suite and the elevator lobby/bathroom core. The conclusion seemed to be that those walls went all the way up to the underside of Floor 44 and that this suite, therefore, could neither be escaped nor infiltrated by the common action-movie trick of moving around above the ceiling. In the same spirit, Zula looked around at the ventilation louvers and noted that they were all far too small to admit a human body.

Apparently satisfied that there were no tricky ways out of the safe house, Sokolov allocated offices. Zula got one all to herself. Peter and Csongor each got to share one with a security consultant.

"I need to use the bathroom," Zula announced. Sokolov drew himself up and made a sort of bow and escorted her to the lobby, where the guard undid the cable lock and opened the doors. Sokolov went into the women's room ahead of Zula, vaulted up on the counter, popped a ceiling tile, and reconnoitered. Apparently he did not entirely like what he saw because he came back down in a pensive mood. After thinking about it for a few moments, he withdrew into one of the toilet stalls, closed the door, made himself comfortable on the toilet, and said, "Okay, I wait. Is okay!"

She went into a different stall and peed. She could hear Sokolov thumbing away on a PDA or something. She emerged from the stall, stood before a sink, and took off all her clothes. Using a bar of soap from her bag and a roll of paper towels issued by Sokolov, she gave herself a stand-up sponge bath. Then—fuck it, Sokolov was trapped—she bent over and shampooed her hair. This took a good long time because of the difficulties entailed in rinsing. As she was finishing up she jumped a little, hearing male voices, but then she realized that Sokolov had opened up communications on some kind of walkie-talkie system.

The result of this procedure was going to be extreme frizziness, but there was little point in concerning herself with that. A now useless instinct warned her that if Peter took a picture of her tomorrow, it would make a hilarious and embarrassing Facebook posting. She wondered how long she would have to go without posting on Facebook before that silence, in and of itself, warned her friends that something was amiss. Then she remembered it would boot her absolutely nothing even if they did realize that something was wrong.

That, she now realized, was the point of the black hoodie. The airport probably had security cameras. Supposing that her friends and family were able to put out a worldwide all-points bulletin for her, the Xiamen authorities would not be able to pick out her face on their security footage.

She pulled on some clean clothes, brushed her teeth, pulled all her stuff together, and called out "Okay." Sokolov emerged from the stall. They went back into the office suite. The cable lock was reinstated behind them. Zula had noted the location of a door off the elevator lobby that apparently led to a fire stair, and she wondered how many flights down she could get before a security consultant would catch up with her. They were probably practiced at vaulting over the railings, or some other high-speed stair-descending technique that she didn't know about.

Peter had tried to talk her into taking a parkour class in Seattle. She wished she'd said yes.

Sokolov extended a hand, reminding her of the location of her private office, and she heard "Thank you" coming out of her mouth before it occurred to her how stupid that was.

The office had floor-to-ceiling windows with views inland, though if she got her face close to the glass she could also see toward the water. The closest building of comparable height was half a mile away, and she reckoned she might be able to get someone's attention by dancing naked in front of the window, or using her light switch to blink S-O-S in Morse code. Since her office had a glass wall on its inner side, though, any such antics would have been obvious to the security consultants drinking coffee a few feet away.

So for now she decided that she would actually try to sleep instead of hatching any Nancy Drew/Scooby-Doo-style escape plots. And to her surprise she found herself being rousted out of bed some time later by Peter. As usual she had no idea what time it was, but it was broad daylight outside. "In twenty minutes we are havink meetink," Peter said.

She made another trip to the bathroom, supervised using the same procedure as before. While she was standing in front of the mirror, changing into a different T-shirt, she caught sight of herself for a moment, and this for some reason caused an irresistible wave of grief and melancholy to break over her. She turned on both faucets, rested the heels of her hands on the counter, and put her weight on them, then allowed herself a sobbing fit that went on for maybe half a minute.

Then she splashed water on her face and announced, to her own reflection, "Okay."

SOKOLOV HAD BEEN doing a lot of thinking about insanity: what it was. Its causes. When Ivanov had begun to suffer from it. Whether it had completely taken Ivanov's mind or rather came and went in waves. Every so often Ivanov would blink and look about him with a surprised, almost childlike expression, as though a sane part of his mind had come awake, regained control of the body, and found itself in a predicament concocted, while it had been asleep, by the part of Ivanov that was completely out of his fucking mind.

But on the other hand Sokolov owed his life—his survival in Afghanistan, in Chechnya—to his ability to see things through the eyes of the adversary, and in this case that meant trying to put himself in Ivanov's shoes. This reversal of perspective was not always easy. One frequently had to work at it for some days, observing the other, gathering data, even conducting little experiments to see how the other reacted to things. His men in Chechnya had thought that he, Sokolov, was crazy because he had sometimes taken actions that made no evident tactical sense, solely as a way of proving or disproving a hypothesis as to what the Chechens were thinking, what they wanted, what they were most afraid of.

What they considered *normal*.

This was always the hard part. If you knew what was normal to the enemy, then everything became easy: you could lull them to sleep by feeding them normal, and you could scare the hell out of them by suddenly taking normal away. But normal to Afghans and Chechens was so different from normal to Russians that it took a bit of work for a man like Sokolov to establish what it was.

Applied to the current situation, the question was: Could it be considered normal to divert rather large amounts of *obshchak* funds to charter a private jet from Toronto to Seattle and thence to Xiamen in order to track down and liquidate a person—probably a kid—who had written a virus and held some files hostage for $73?

UNTIL SOKOLOV WOKE up that morning in the safe house and literally smelled the coffee—for the day shift had awakened at 0600 local time and begun to brew it on the camp stove—he did not understand how completely fucked he was, how *interesting* the situation had become. And then he felt astonished and ashamed that he'd let events get so far ahead of him. He had been defeated by Ivanov at the game of Normal. Getting on a plane and flying somewhere to do a job: What could be more normal than that? But Ivanov had not shared with him any information about how they would actually get into the country. Now men nominally under Sokolov's control had done murder in the United States and they were in China illegally, and at the mercy of whatever local gangsters or officials Ivanov had cut a deal with.

Though, to be fair, those people were at Ivanov's mercy as well, because they didn't understand that Ivanov was crazy. And once they came to understand that Ivanov was not only crazy but traveling in the company of seven warriors and three hackers, they would begin having nightmares about all the consequences that would fall on their heads if those people actually began to do the sorts of things that they were in the habit of doing.

What kind of bullshit had Ivanov told them? Probably that he wanted to smuggle some high-value goods into the country through the private jet terminal. Two vanloads' worth of stuff. Bootleg caviar or something else expensive enough to justify leasing a private jet.

No. Prostitutes. High-value specialty prostitutes. That's what he must have told them.

The office in which Sokolov was sleeping had a whiteboard mounted to its wall, and he longed to stand up and begin drawing a diagram of the situation. It would be a complicated diagram. Fortunately, no markers were available; drawing diagrams probably was not a smart idea. He had to carry everything in his head. He lay there, smelling the coffee and staring up at the ceiling tiles. There were nine of them, a three-by-three grid, making up most of the office's ceiling. He assigned himself the one in the middle. The rest of the grid looked something like this:

Ivanov	Ivanov's Chinese contacts	The Troll
Sokolov's employer	Sokolov	The Squad
Csongor	Peter	Zula

This grid didn't come into existence without some iterations, some failed attempts. Wallace, for example, and the local talent Ivanov had called up in Seattle. Zula's uncle. None of these was worth thinking about right now.

So he went through the grid evaluating each part of it in turn.

IVANOV:

Sokolov badly wanted to get connected to Vikipediya and learn about strokes. Also about certain medications he had seen among Ivanov's personal effects, whose names he had memorized. He knew that Internet usage in China was monitored by the PSB, the Public Security Bureau, and wondered whether the mere act of accessing Vikipediya as opposed to Wikipedia would cause a red thumbtack, or its modern, digital equivalent, to be stuck into a map at the local PSB headquarters as a way of saying *Russians here*. How many Russians were in Xiamen legitimately, that is, with visas? Probably not all that many, and so if the red thumbtack appeared in an unexpected part of town, it could lead to trouble. Pavel Pavlovich, one of his platoon-mates in Afghanistan, had taken mortar shrapnel in the forehead, going into his brain, and had seemingly recovered; but afterward his personality was different: he seemed a little crazy, unable to control certain impulses, and after a regrettable incident involving a rocket-propelled grenade, they had sent him home. Sokolov was developing a theory that Ivanov suffered from high blood pressure—a theory that could easily be confirmed if he could look up the names of those medications—and that it had been worse than usual recently because of the trouble he had gotten into with the *obshchak*. When he had received the phone call from Csongor, alerting him to the inconsistency in Wallace's story, his already high blood pressure had spiked and—according to this theory—he had suffered a little stroke that had damaged him in the same way as the shrapnel had done poor Pavel Pavlovich. On the flight from Toronto to Seattle, Ivanov had slept most of the way, and Sokolov, looking at him, had thought he seemed sunken, damaged, exhausted. But when he was awake, he was a demon.

IVANOV'S CHINESE CONTACTS:

Probably no longer relevant, but they deserved a ceiling tile all their own because they were mysterious. Had they simply arranged for Ivanov to drive those two vans through security and then forgotten about him, moving on to other corrupt activities? Or were they now actively paying attention to Ivanov and his crew, *worrying* about Ivanov? Because if these faceless, nameless Chinese were *worried* about Ivanov, then they would soon have plenty to worry *about;* and if they became sufficiently worried, there might be some effort to liquidate Ivanov and everyone with him. Since Sokolov knew nothing of how Ivanov had managed all this, there seemed little he could do about it other than make certain that their activities remained innocuous for as long as possible. The very strangeness of their errand would be enormously helpful in that regard. Speaking of which . . .

THE TROLL:

Nothing to worry about in and of himself, since he was almost certainly just a lone teenager working out of his bedroom, and so this ceiling tile was more a placeholder for Troll-related issues and questions; for example, what the hell would they do when they actually found him? Perhaps even more worrisome: What would they do if they *couldn't* find him?

SOKOLOV'S EMPLOYER:

Sokolov worked for a security consultancy based out of St. Petersburg, with discreet branch offices in Toronto, New York, and London, that derived much of its income from working for people like Ivanov. As in any business, customer satisfaction was of paramount importance. Usually this meant doing whatever one was told to do by the client to whom one was assigned. At least in theory there ought to be exceptions in the rules for brain-damaged clients. But, to keep things simple, the company's founders, all retired Spetsnaz brass, had carried over the chain of command, culture, and traditions from the military unit where they had built their careers and from which they hired most of their employees. Going over the boss's head was frowned on and could lead to miserable repercussions on Sokolov. He might find out the hard way, for example, that Ivanov wasn't crazy at all and was actually carrying out direct orders from higher up. If so, the mission—whatever the hell it was—was important, and screwing it up would cause only that much more trouble for Sokolov.

SOKOLOV:

He had taken this job because he thought it would be simple and easy compared to being active-duty military. Until recently he had not been wrong. For exactly that reason he had been somewhat bored. Now he was far from bored but feeling many of the same stresses that had caused him to retire from active duty in the first place. Was it possible to find a station in life with just the right level of interest? Was it possible to be *normal* without being someone's dupe?

THE SQUAD:

Sokolov had worked with most of them before, and they would carry out his orders professionally and with no questions asked. Though rumors did circulate that sometimes the higher-ups would plant a spy in such a unit, reporting home via a back channel, and this might be especially true in very strange situations like this one. He had summoned them on extremely short notice and had been unable to supply an explanation of where they were going or what the mission might be.

CSONGOR:

The least of Sokolov's worries. Obviously the Hungarian did not want to be here, but he knew the rules of the game, had been tangled up with Ivanov for a long time, and would be docile as long as he believed he would get out of the situation alive.

PETER:

Sokolov put the odds at 100 percent that Peter would, sooner or later, do something stupid and cause enormous trouble. Peter would do this because he believed he was clever and because he thought only of himself. It would be safer to take him out and shoot him now, but disposing of the body would be difficult and the shock of it would probably disturb the equilibrium of Zula.

ZULA:

The only person here whom Sokolov might be able to deal with productively. "Productive" being the operative word here in that she seemed like one who might do something not utterly predictable and not capable of being done by Sokolov himself.

She was also a problem of large proportions in that Ivanov would almost certainly want to liquidate her, and she was the only person involved in this clusterfuck who didn't actually deserve it. Waging war on his enemies had been Sokolov's habit and his profession for a long time, but being chivalrous to everyone else was simply a basic tenet of having your shit together as a human and as a man. He had always been worried that he might get into a situation like this one. It had never happened until now.

HE GOT COFFEE and went into the meeting room before anyone else got there. He spent a while looking out the window, appraising the battleground.

From this remove it did not look hugely different from other places; just more crowded. Humidity and smog caused buildings that were only a few blocks away to be shrouded in mist, like matte paintings in the background of an old Soviet movie, creating the feeling that everything was farther away than it really was. This made it difficult to get a sense of how far the city sprawled. The hot and humid climate was inconvenient, since it limited the sorts of things that one could carry in one's clothing, or else forced one to go about conspicuously and suspiciously bundled up. This, however, would not really be a problem until they set out to liquidate the Troll, and based on what Zula and Peter and Csongor had been saying on the plane, they wouldn't have that information for a few days at least.

This building was situated on the inland side of the six-lane avenue that ran along the waterfront. Across that avenue was an arcade of ferry terminals that stretched along the shore for at least a kilometer, fronting on a waterway that was as busy as any that Sokolov had ever

seen. Because he had been looking at maps, he knew that this body
of water was a strait separating Xiamen from a smaller island about a
thousand meters away, but it was impossible not to read it as a river: a
mighty river like the Volga or the Danube. But the docks were linked
to the terminals by hinged gangways, confirming that this water
was salt and that it rose and fell with the tides. Plying the strait was
an astoundingly dense and various traffic, ranging from skiffs up to
freighters, but dominated by two types of craft: tubby, double-decker
passenger ferries, and a type of vessel that he hadn't seen before but
that was evidently the traditional working craft of these waters: an
open, flat-decked boat rising no more than a meter above the waterline, shingled along both sides with old tires, averaging maybe ten
meters long, with a little boathouse, or at least an awning, toward
the stern, sheltering the engine, the steering gear, and the operator.
These were so densely packed in some areas that it was a wonder they
could move at all, and each was carrying something different: passengers, a drum of lubricant, a pallet of shrink-wrapped cargo, a cooler
packed with ice and fish. Weaving and zipping among these larger,
slower vessels were white speedboats carrying passengers in orange
life vests: fast water taxis for the well-heeled, he guessed. Some of
them were headed directly across the strait to the little island, which
was steep and green and seemed to consist largely of parks and villas.
Obviously it was older and more affluent than the suburbs that Sokolov could see reaching toward Xiamen from every direction, difficult
to resolve through the haze, but much more heavily built up.

All of which was unusual and picturesque but probably did not
bear directly on the mission. Sokolov turned his attention to the picket
line of buildings like this one that stood along the inland side of the
big avenue. There were a few other modern blue-glass skyscrapers,
and some construction sites where new ones were being erected. But
at least half of the frontage was claimed by buildings of older vintage,
sporting the logos of hotels and Western food chains. Directly below
them was a building of perhaps a dozen stories with a huge KFC sign
on its top. Its entryway was choked by taxis, which made Sokolov
think that it must be a hotel, probably catering not to Westerners but
to Chinese business travelers. It fronted on a traffic exchange. In the
center was a raised circle in the middle with traffic lights on it, but
other than that, this was just a hectare or so of pavement that—as

was obvious from Sokolov's point of view—had, over and over again, been slit open and trenched and cabled and repaved. It supported a steady flow of taxis, buses, motor scooters, the occasional Lexus or Mercedes. On the opposite side of the exchange was a curving building with a panoramic billboard, colorful photos of fashion models and liquor bottles, offices fronting on the intersection, their nature unguessable by Sokolov since they didn't have any English in their signs. The architects of these buildings had lavished a huge amount of attention on rooftop antenna masts, which were far more massive and squat and wide-stanced than was really called for by pure engineering considerations. They must have been trained in the Soviet Union and been steeped in the mid-twentieth-century statist mindset that a building without a radio transmitter was like a battleship without guns. It was a technology and a reason largely forgotten now but preserved in the architecture in the same way as church steeples. What really mattered to the mission at hand was not radio transmitters. It was that zany web of patched pavement cuts splattered all over the streets below, where Internet had been laid down.

He kept noticing basketball courts and realized that, from where he stood, he could see four of them, all new and well tended.

On patches of open ground here and there, he saw people executing slow, formalized movements, then recalled that Chinese liked to do calisthenics.

Not far away, a broad street led away from the water for at least two kilometers. It was lined with expensive-looking Western-style storefronts. It ran along ground that was table flat, but off to its right a kilometer or so, spines of gray stone rose out of the ground, supporting tufts and copses of dark green vegetation. Remnants of ancient fortifications, steep and ivy matted, were grafted onto the rock, and newer buildings grew out of those.

These parts of the city—the ferry terminals, the skyscrapers and skyscrapers-to-be, the older generation of high-rise buildings, the basketball courts, the shopping street, the outcroppings of stone—were the special bits. All told, they accounted for perhaps 25 percent of the city's surface area. The remainder was all the same: an undifferentiated expanse of close-packed buildings, four or five stories high, often with blue roofs (why blue?) built on a warren of streets so narrow that, in general, he could not see the pavement, but had to infer, from the pattern of crevices between buildings, that streets must exist. In the rare places where such streets aligned with his sight lines, enabling him to see all the way to the bottom, they appeared to be paved not with asphalt but with human beings in motion, and vehicles marooned in the sea of people.

He felt certain that the Troll lived in a neighborhood very much like one of these. He needed to know what it would be like to move and fight in such a place. His initial thought was "more like Grozny than Jalalabad," but he would have to do much better than that. He did not even know, for example, whether Xiamen had any sort of underground mass transit system that could be put to use.

A faint humming sound alerted him to the approach of wheeled luggage. He turned to see Ivanov approaching from the direction of the elevator lobby, towing a black rollaway bag. One of the squaddies jumped up and offered to help him with it, but Ivanov brushed him off with a flicking gesture and came straight for the conference room. Sokolov opened the door. Ivanov entered without breaking stride, heaved the bag up, and slammed it down on the conference table. "You may open it."

Sokolov unzipped the top flap and peeled it back. The entire bag was filled with magenta currency.

"Our *obshchak*," Ivanov joked. At least Sokolov hoped he was joking.

All the notes were the same denomination: 100 RMB. They were printed in an uneasy mixture of purplish reds, and each bore a portrait of the young Mao Zedong. None of the bills was loose; they had been stacked into bundles of various sizes. Sokolov picked up a small one.

"Ridiculous country," Ivanov said. "One hundred is the largest denomination that exists. You know how much it is worth? *Fourteen dollars*. They print nothing larger because if they did, it would be counterfeited instantly. So changing money is a huge problem. I am already tired."

The small bundle consisted of nine 100-RMB notes with a tenth wrapped around it.

"So that is the local equivalent of a C-note," Ivanov said.

Sokolov replaced it, reached deeper into the bag, and pulled out a stack of bills having the approximate proportions of a brick. He looked questioningly at Ivanov.

Ivanov shrugged. "Ten thousand dollars or something." Then he shook his finger at Sokolov. "But remember: money goes a long way in China!"

"How do they carry it around?" Sokolov asked wonderingly.

"Purses," said Ivanov.

Sokolov replaced the brick.

"What are your orders?" he asked.

"Get the hackers in here and make a plan for finding the Troll."

"They have been talking about it," Sokolov said. "They want to go out on the streets. Pound the pavement." He gave the expression in English.

"Will they make trouble? Try to run off?"

"Peter might."

"Always keep one here as insurance."

"That one can't be Csongor," Sokolov, "since they don't really know him."

"Then either Peter or Zula always stays here. Unless—?"

"Zula will not create trouble if she knows Peter is hostage," Sokolov began. "However, if the situation is reversed—"

"I knew it!" Ivanov slammed the table, and his face turned red. To him, Sokolov's vague suspicion that Peter *might* be the kind of guy who would betray Zula was ontologically the same as a YouTube video of him actually doing it. He seemed ready to kill Peter on the spot. Sokolov, for his part, was gratified that Ivanov trusted his intuitions in this way, but he could not help wondering if he'd judged Peter unfairly.

"This is just my guess," Sokolov said.

"No, you are right! Peter stays here then. Zula goes out with Csongor. And you send two of your men with them at all times."

"Sir, I request permission to go out with them alone," Sokolov said.

"Why?"

"Because I have seen nothing of the city other than what I can see from this window."

"Fine. Good idea. Go out and learn more of the place. You'll see more than you want to see, I can tell you that."

Sokolov turned toward the window. The hackers, as Ivanov called them, were standing outside, awaiting orders. He indicated with a movement of his head that they should enter.

Csongor, Zula, and Peter filed into the room and stood across the conference table from Ivanov, pretending they had not noticed the sack full of currency. Ivanov switched to English. "Much time has gone by sleepink, flyink, sleepink. Easy to forget nature of mission. Do you recall mission?"

"Figure out who the Troll is," Peter said.

Ivanov stared at Peter as if he had said something deeply offensive. And in truth, there was nothing Peter could have said that would have helped him.

"Find motherfucker who *fucked* me!" Ivanov shouted, so loudly that he could have been heard in Vladivostok.

He let that one ring in their ears for a few moments. The hackers were physically shriveling, like raisins.

"You need to pound pavement!" Ivanov asserted.

Peter's eyes flicked toward Sokolov.

"You look at me!" Ivanov shouted.

"Yes, sir," Peter said. "Yes. We need to move around the city, get on the Internet in different places, check the IP addresses—"

"And send distress call home to mama!?" Ivanov inquired.

Peter's face had been red from the beginning, but now it got redder.

"You, stay here," Ivanov said. "Help make map or somethink." He looked at Zula. "Lovely Zula, you pound pavement in company of Csongor." He turned his attention to Csongor. "Csongor, you are only person who touches computer." He shook his finger. "No email, no Facebook, no Twitter. And if there is some other such thing I have not heard of yet—none of that either!"

In Russian, Csongor said, "What if we need to go into the world of T'Rain?"

In English, Ivanov said, "Only exception to rule: Zula can play T'Rain if necessary. Csongor, Sokolov will watch carefully, make sure nothink funny happens."

Zula and Csongor nodded.

Ivanov half turned and extended a hand toward Sokolov. "Sokolov will be present at all times to protect you from harm and ensure rules are followed. If rules are broken in serious way, if Zula goes to powder room and never comes back, any other such problem, then I must have extremely serious conversation with Root of All Evil here." He extended his hands toward Peter in a gesture whose natural conclusion would have been out-and-out strangulation.

"Everyone understand rules?" Ivanov said.

Everyone nodded.

"Go pound pavement." He reached into the bag, pulled out as many stacks of bills as he could grab in a single hand, and slid them down the table to Sokolov. "Except for Peter. You." He gestured toward Peter as if the room contained more than one person of that name. "Stay for brief discussion."

Sokolov picked up the money, then backed to the door and held it open as Zula and Csongor exited the room. No one could look at Peter, who had become a nearly unbearable sight on grounds of posture alone: shoulders drawn together, body trembling, back of neck brilliant red. Sokolov was favorably impressed by the fact that he had not yet shit his pants. Men always made crude jokes about people pissing their pants with fear, but in Sokolov's experience, shitting the pants was more common if it was a straightforward matter of extreme emotional stress. Pants pissing was completely unproductive and suggested a total breakdown of elemental control. Pants shitting, on the other hand, voided the bowels and thereby made blood available to the brain and the large muscle groups that otherwise would have gone to the lower-priority activity of digestion. Sokolov could have forgiven Peter for shitting his pants, but if he had pissed his pants, then it really would have been necessary to get rid of him. In any case, Peter had done neither of these things yet.

A minute or two later, though, after they had gathered near the reception area with their water bottles and day packs, Sokolov noted Zula—who had kept a stony face through most of this—looking with concern through the glass wall of the conference room at Peter, who was still being arraigned, or something, by Ivanov.

Something had changed, though. Ivanov was still gesturing, but instead of punching and strangling, his hands were making neat little chopping gestures on the tabletop, sketching concentric circles, reaching out toward the city beyond the window and gathering in imaginary stuff and pouring it out on the table. Peter was nodding his head and even moving his jaw from time to time.

Peter was *interested*.

"Is okay," Sokolov said. "He works for Ivanov now."

. . . .

IVANOV HAD OFFERED to rent them a car and driver, but Sokolov guessed they would learn more by using taxis. They took the elevator down to the parking garage, found a fire exit, climbed up a windowless concrete stairway, and emerged into a strip of landscaping. This led along the side of the building out to the edge of the waterfront avenue. Sokolov pivoted and took a phone picture of the building from which they had just emerged. Later, when he wanted to go back to the safe house, he could show it to a taxi driver. They were already perspiring freely, or perhaps that was just the humidity condensing on their artificially chilled skin. Sokolov had acquired a blazer from an airport shop in Vladivostok, which he now removed, folded, and placed in his shoulder bag on top of the magenta bundles.

The drivers of the taxis that flocked and schooled in the plaza before the KFC-topped hotel were confounded by, and almost indignant at, the manner in which the three Westerners had seemingly teleported into existence in this normally unfrequented corner. It was clearly their habit to keep an eye on every place from which a possible customer could sortie. Westerners on foot, unnoticed and unpestered, were as much an affront to civic order as gushing fire hydrants and warbling car alarms. Sokolov had the feeling that the next time they came out of that fire exit, there would be at least one taxi waiting for them. It was not a good feeling.

He took pictures of the plaza and the hotel. Ostensibly. In truth, of course, what he was really doing was using the viewfinder of his phone to stare back at all the Chinese people who were staring at them.

Sokolov had never been a spy per se, but he had undergone a bit of training in basic spycraft as part of his transition into private commerce. Spies were supposed to have a strong intuitive sense of when they had been noticed, when someone else's eyes were on them. Or at least that was the line of bullshit that the spycraft trainers liked to lay on their students. If true, then no Western spy could tolerate even a few seconds' exposure to a Chinese street, since that internal sense would be setting off alarms continuously—and by no means false alarms. If they had dressed up in clown suits, strapped strobe lights to their foreheads, and sprinted out into traffic firing tommy guns into the air, they would not have drawn more immediate and intense scrutiny than they did simply by entering this public space as non-Chinese persons. Sokolov could only laugh. He had thought it might be otherwise, simply because Xiamen had such a long history of contact with the outside world.

Of course, it would be that way everywhere. They were not merely noticed. They were *famous*.

And, because he did everything in the backseat of a car with tinted windows, Ivanov did not understand these realities. Sokolov would never be able to explain to him the difficulty of doing anything discreetly in this city.

"Into hotel. Use Internet," Sokolov said. Shrugging off propositions from taxi drivers, they trudged along the edge of the plaza to the hotel, leaving in their wake a hundred ordinary Chinese citizens who stopped in their tracks to stare at them as they went by. A fair proportion of these literally had their mouths hanging open. Sokolov, determinedly not meeting their eyes, looked at other things and counted eight security cameras *that he could see.*

Observed from various distances by at least six uniformed members of the security forces, operating in pairs, they trudged up the steps of the hotel. Two dozen taxi drivers, sitting in their vehicles outside, watched their every move through the hotel's glass doors, in case they might change their minds and come back out.

As he'd expected, most of the hotel's clientele were Chinese, and so their little party came in for further inspection as they stood around uncertainly in the lobby. He'd imagined that they might be able to sit down on some comfortable chairs and order tea and look at newspapers. But this was not that sort of lobby. Rather than make an ongoing spectacle of themselves, Sokolov led the others straight to the elevators and hit the button with the image of Colonel Sanders next to it. A minute later they were on the roof. But the restaurant wasn't open yet.

"I got Wi-Fi," said Csongor, looking at the screen of his PDA.

"Fine," Sokolov said. "We leave."

They took the elevator back down, walked out the front doors, and got into a taxi. "Hyatt," Sokolov said. He knew there was a Hyatt because the pilots were lodged there. It was out near the airport.

"Okay, so we have one IP address at least," Csongor said, during the drive.

Sokolov was taking phone pictures out the window, getting shots mostly of hotels. This five-minute adventure had told him that Western-style business hotels were the only places in Xiamen where they could do so much as draw breath without being the talk of the town for weeks afterward.

"Anywhere near the address space we're interested in?" asked Zula.

"In fact, yes!" said Csongor. "They use the same ISP. Which isn't saying much, of course."

"It's a start," Zula said.

They went to the Hyatt and ordered breakfast.

In the vicinity of the airport, vast development projects were under way: a number of commercial real estate parks and one international conference center with a giant windowed sphere in front of it. Sokolov longed to hide himself in their anonymity and emptiness. But they were so disconnected from the city proper that he might as well have tried to hunt down the Troll from a shopping mall in Toronto.

Banners on every lamppost sported pictures of the local hero, Zheng Chenggong. A similar but much larger banner had been mounted to the front of the new conference center. Apparently this image was the official logo of the conference that had attracted the multinational fleet of small jets: something to do with patching up relations between Taiwan and mainland China.

As they picked at their omelets, Sokolov asked Csongor (who had logged on to the Hyatt's Wi-Fi network) to google up a list of four- and five-star hotels. Csongor not only did that; he figured out a way to patch in to the Hyatt's business center and printed out the list. A member of the hotel staff brought it to their table on a little tray.

They went outside and got in a taxi. Sokolov pointed to a hotel on Csongor's printout, and the taxi took them there. It was back in the middle of town, closer to the waterfront. They went into the lobby and found a place to sit down. While Csongor got on the Internet, Sokolov watched the way guests interacted with the front desk staff and the concierge.

They did the same thing eight times at eight different hotels. It took them until midafternoon.

Then they took a taxi back to the hotel that had the best concierge. Sokolov had Zula go to the concierge, a young woman who spoke excellent English and gave every impression of actually enjoying her job. Zula explained that she and her friends wanted to go on a leisurely drive around town and see some of the less touristy sites, maybe go shopping in local markets.

The concierge led them out front and explained as much to a taxi driver. Sokolov, Zula, and Csongor crammed themselves into the taxi's backseat. The driver offered to let Sokolov ride up front, but Sokolov wanted to remain partly concealed behind the tinted windows in the rear.

Until now they had never seen anything other than modern commercial districts, but within twenty seconds of their pulling out of the hotel drive, the taxi was deep in one of those older neighborhoods that had attracted Sokolov's interest.

Csongor had a laptop open and was continually scanning for available Wi-Fi stations. Most of these were password protected, but every so often he found one that was open and checked its IP address.

Zula meanwhile was using Csongor's phone, which had built-in GPS, to keep track of their latitude and longitude. This wouldn't have been necessary in New York or some other city where they could have made sense of the street grid, but here it was the only way that they could tally Csongor's observations against the physical geography of the city.

If the taxi moved much faster than walking pace, Wi-Fi stations came and went too quickly for Csongor to establish connections, but this rarely happened. Whenever a clear place opened up in traffic, it would be seized by a gaunt man in a conical hat pulling a two-wheeled cart. Those guys were all over the place; they seemed to have a stranglehold on transport of all goods weighing less than a ton. If the taxi driver honked for long enough, the offending carter would eventually pull aside and make way.

After they had been driving around somewhat aimlessly for twenty minutes, the taxi driver made a phone call and then handed his phone back to Zula. With a nervous glance toward Sokolov, Zula accepted the phone.

Then she smiled and took the phone away from her head. "It's the concierge," she explained. "She hopes we are enjoying the tour so far, and she wants to know what sorts of things we would like to shop for."

"Some of the men carry small bags, like purses," Sokolov said. "I want one."

Zula relayed that into the phone and then handed it back to the taxi driver, who listened for a few moments, then snapped the phone shut and effected a course change. Ten minutes later they had pulled up in front of a little storefront piled high with leather goods. Sokolov and Zula got out of the taxi, leaving Csongor in the vehicle with his laptop.

As Sokolov had come to expect, this was the most sensational thing that had happened in this district of Xiamen since Zheng Chenggong had chased away the Dutch pirates and so, as they shopped for luggage, they were enjoyed by a vast audience of fascinated neighbors, aged family members of the proprietors who had been hastily summoned from upstairs via phone, random passersby, flabbergasted carters, and professional beggars who carefully tracked their every movement, talked about them, and found sudden humor in details so minor that Sokolov was not entirely sure what they were reacting to. He quickly settled on a leather man-purse that looked as if it could comfortably accommodate several currency bricks, with plenty of room left over for some ammo clips and a couple of stun grenades, and he was about to pay the quoted price when Zula intervened and proposed a somewhat lower figure. This led to haggling, which, as it turned out, Zula was good at. Not in the sense of being an absolute bitch about it but in the sense of remaining on good terms with the proprietor even while firmly insisting that the price was too high. And so finally Sokolov was granted an unbroken stretch of twenty or thirty seconds in which he could actually turn his attention to the neighborhood and try to gather in some impressions of the place.

All the buildings were made of concrete, or perhaps bricks or stone blocks with mortar troweled over them. It didn't really matter. The point was that the walls would stop low-velocity rounds and shotgun pellets, and you couldn't kick your way through them. They would not burn very easily. Depending on how much rebar had been used—and his guess was that the builders had cut plenty of corners in that department—these structures, compared to wood- or steel-framed ones, would be more vulnerable to collapse under the exceptionally stressful conditions that frequently obtained when men like Sokolov were earning their pay. They were four or five stories high, which meant that they did not have elevators and that, if it was like Europe, the highest floors would house the poorest people. Ground floors tended to be retail; upper stories were offices (on larger streets) or apartments (smaller). Apartments quite frequently sported small balconies, but these had invariably been retrofitted with grids of steel bars, even on the upper floors— apparently burglars here climbed walls and abseiled from rooftops. The grids themselves looked eminently climbable and so might be handy for gaining access to a roof when doors were locked, or to depart from a building when stairwells were filled with products of combustion or men with guns who wanted to kill him. Some ropes might come in handy. But really, when wasn't that the case?

Street widths ranged from one meter (pedestrians only) to perhaps eight meters (all traffic).

Wiring was external and informal in the extreme. Some of the bundles strung across streets were as thick as his torso, and it was obvious that they had begun as one individual wire that had accreted more wires over time.

"Okay," Zula said, "one hundred." She was looking at him. So was the shopkeeper.

Sokolov pulled a C-note equivalent ten-stack from his pocket, peeled off a bill, and handed it over. The man-purse was his. The audience began to disperse. Show was over.

Back in the taxi, Sokolov said: "Same procedure. Buy some other stuff."

"What would you like to buy?"

"Does not matter."

"Tea? There seem to be a lot of people selling tea."

"Tea then."

"Teapot to make it in?"

"Yes."

"I need to hit a drugstore."

"Why?"

"Because I'm a girl."

"Fine. Hit drugstore. Repeat procedure."

They repeated procedure for a while. Zula bought tea from a small, energetic woman in blue boots and a tea service from an old lady in a side alley. It became somewhat routine, and Sokolov even began to feel somewhat comfortable standing in the open bays of the shops as Zula haggled. It seemed to work for Csongor, who reported that he was gathering more data the whole time. But Sokolov did not see much more during the last hour than he had during the first ten minutes. The physical layout of these neighborhoods did not vary much from one block to the next. But it would be easy to get lost, and only a lifelong resident would be able to find his way out. The hazy conditions made it difficult to get a fix on the location of the sun, so celestial navigation was out.

He had the taxi driver take them back to where they'd started, and he slipped the concierge a C-note wad. Then they walked home along the waterfront, giving Sokolov a chance to see how the ferry lines operated and Csongor a chance to wardrive some of the Wi-Fi hotspots in the terminals' various waiting rooms and snack bars. When Colonel Sanders hove into view, Sokolov called ahead to warn his squad that they were coming, and when they reached the office building, the steel door was already open for them.

"Home sweet home," Zula said.

HOME SWEET HOME looked a bit different. Some chairs—injection molded, bright pink—had been brought up. Peter was ensconced behind a brand-new computer, still reeking with the ammoniacal smell of new electronics. To all appearances, this was connected to the Internet.

"I worked out a deal with Ivanov," he explained, after Zula had taken another stand-up sponge bath and grabbed a slice of pizza (for there was a Pizza Hut somewhere within delivery range). "He's got a sysadmin back in Moscow that he trusts. This machine is connected over a VPN to that guy's system in Moscow, so he can monitor my use of the Internet and make sure I'm not sending out any distress calls."

Zula was divided between thinking that this was a clever solution and finding it weird that Peter would put up with it. And indeed the look on his face was not proud. But he had an explanation ready. "We are totally handcuffed if we don't have access to Internet," he pointed out. "We can't even use Google Maps. I've been able to make a lot of progress this way."

"Such as?"

"Well, for one thing, I downloaded a copy of the REAMDE executable that someone posted on a security blog," he said. "And I decompiled it."

"How'd that work for you?" she asked. Peter was proud, almost desperately so, of what he'd done, and she felt obligated to let him speak of it.

"Well, I was afraid that they might have used obfuscated code," he said, "but they didn't."

"Meaning?"

"Some compilers will mess with the object code to make it harder to decompile. Whoever created REAMDE didn't do that. So I was able to get some pretty clean source code files. Then I looked for unusual character sequences in those files and googled them."

"You wanted to see if anyone else had gone down the same path before you," Zula said, "and posted their results."

"Exactly. And what I found was a little unexpected. I found a security discussion group where someone had indeed posted some decompiled code that matched what I got. But it wasn't from REAMDE. It was another, older virus called CALKULATOR that made a little bit of a splash about three years ago."

"Okay," Zula said, "so you're thinking that the creators of REAMDE recycled some of the source code from CALKULATOR."

"They must have. There's no way this could have happened by accident. And the interesting thing is that the CALKULATOR source code was never found—it's never been posted."

"So it's not the case," Zula said, "that the Troll just downloaded the CALKULATOR source files from a server somewhere and then incorporated them into REAMDE."

Peter was nodding, and a smile was on his lips. Zula continued: "REAMDE and CALKULATOR were made by the same people."

"Or at least people who know each other, who privately exchange files with each other."

"So the obvious question then becomes—"

"What do we know about the creators of CALKULATOR?" Peter said. "Well, it was a far more devastating virus than REAMDE because it infected anyone who used Outlook—whereas REAMDE is endemic to hard-core T'Rain users. For about a week, it was the virus du jour, it made quite a sensation, and there was a big law enforcement effort devoted to tracking down its creators. They weren't nearly as clever about hiding their tracks as the Troll has been, and so it was eventually traced to a group in Manila."

"Hmm. That's a twist."

"Yeah, we're focusing on Xiamen and suddenly we get this clue in Manila. But here's the thing. A couple members of the Manila group were caught and prosecuted. But everyone knows that most of those involved were never identified, never caught. And then the other thing is that a lot of Filipinos are ethnic Chinese and still have family ties to China."

"So maybe the Troll is a Chinese hacker living in Xiamen," Zula said, "but he's got family ties in Manila . . ."

" . . . and that's how the source code ended up here and got recycled into REAMDE."

Zula had been keeping an eye on the safe house as this conversation had proceeded. Csongor was closeted in an office with today's notes, doing some data entry work on his laptop. Sokolov was in the conference room being debriefed by Ivanov. Two of the security consultants were sleeping, two were playing Xbox, and two were on duty. But all the Russians who were awake were casting occasional glances in their direction. Keeping an eye on the hackers, wondering what they were talking about. Perhaps guessing from their body language and the expressions on their faces that they were focused on the problem at hand and making some progress.

And that, as she kept having to remind herself, was the only thing that mattered. Not catching the Troll. But making Ivanov believe that they were making progress toward catching the Troll, stringing him along, long enough for them to think their way out of this.

Long enough for Zula to do so, anyway. Because she didn't get any vibe at all from Peter that he was interested in leaving. He had become too fascinated by the Troll hunt.

He believed that if they caught the Troll, Ivanov would be nice to them.

And maybe he was right. Maybe this was how Ivanov recruited.

Or maybe making them think so was how he kept people docile until it was time to kill them.

"What's next?" she asked. "What do we do with this information?"

"One of my thoughts was, we have a jet at our disposal, we could shoot down to Manila and try to find some of the CALKULA-TOR crew, ask them questions."

When Zula considered the meanings of those verbs "find" and "ask," all she could think of was Wallace and the 6 mil polyethylene sheeting. Was that what Peter had in mind? Or did he really think that the hackers in Manila would voluntarily rat out their blood relatives in Xiamen? Zula didn't want to ask that hard question of Peter because she was afraid of what she might learn about the man she'd been sleeping with. "To Ivanov that's going to feel like a wild-goose chase," she pointed out. "He prefers the direct approach."

This was meant as kind of a joke, but Peter nodded soberly. "We might also look for a Filipino expat community in Xiamen. In Seattle they have their own grocery stores and hair salons. Maybe it's the same here."

Zula, who unlike Peter had actually seen Xiamen, was pretty sure that this was hopeless. But she stifled the urge to say as much. "Have you reported this to Ivanov?"

"I've been feeding him little updates."

Zula tried to ignore the way he'd phrased this. "He knows about the possible Manila connection?"

"Not yet."

"If we can turn it into an excuse for more pavement pounding," Zula suggested, "it might help us."

"Help you how?"

"Help *us*," she repeated.

She realized that she kind of wanted to kill him. She was sure that the feeling would pass. But she was also sure that it would come back. "Do whatever you want with the information," she said, and walked away.

. . . .

"ARE YOU INSANE?" Ivanov asked him.

Sokolov was flummoxed. Ivanov accusing *him,* Sokolov, of being insane. So unexpected. He could not think of anything to say.

He had been telling the story of the day. At first he had merely summarized, which was generally what superiors wanted their subordinates to do for them, but Ivanov had insisted on hearing everything in great detail. And so, after suffering quite a few interruptions, Sokolov had settled into a much more detailed storytelling style, and Ivanov had listened carefully all the way through the account of the "shopping" expedition, tipping the concierge, and walking home along the waterfront.

It would not be the first time Sokolov had been tongue lashed by the boss, so he just stood there at attention and waited for it.

Ivanov laughed. "I do not care," he said, "what the fucking buildings are made of. Whether the walls can, or cannot, be penetrated by number 4 buckshot. About the options for escaping the building in the event of a tactical retreat. What the *fuck* are you thinking, Sokolov? Are you thinking that this is the Siege of Grozny? This is not the Siege of Grozny! It is very simple. Find the Troll. Go to where he lives. Enter his apartment. Take him out of there and bring him to me."

Sokolov had nothing to say.

"Did I hire the wrong guy?"

"That is possible, sir," Sokolov said. "Those guys you found in Seattle—the ones who did Wallace—they are more the type for this kind of job."

"Well, those guys in Seattle ARE NOT HERE!" Ivanov said, crescendoing, during that sentence, from a mild conversational tone to a shout that could detonate stored ammunition. "Instead, I have YOU! And your extremely expensive guys out there!"

Sokolov might have pointed out that he and his expensive guys were security consultants and that Ivanov had lately been asking them to do some pretty weird things. But he didn't see how it would improve Ivanov's mood.

"Another thing," Ivanov continued, "what the fuck was the point of coming back along the waterfront? Are you under the impression that the Troll lives in a ferry terminal?"

"Reconnoitering the ground," Sokolov said. "Getting to know the field of operations."

Ivanov was nonplussed. "The ground—the field of operations—is where the Troll lives. And he doesn't live in a ferry terminal."

Sokolov said nothing.

"I don't get it, Sokolov. Explain your thinking to me."

"Tactical maneuver in this city is going to be nearly impossible," Sokolov said. He nodded at a window. "Just look at it. All the space is taken up. But the water is a different story. It's crowded, yes. But it's the only option we've got if we need to—"

"To what, Sokolov?"

"To fall back. Improvise. Move creatively."

There was now a silence of perhaps thirty seconds as Ivanov marshaled every resource of energy and strength at his disposal to control his rage.

Sokolov wasn't the least bit worried about what would happen when Ivanov lost that struggle and blew his stack. He was much more worried about what was going on in the boss's circulatory system in the meantime. For during all their comings and goings today, he had managed to spend a few minutes on some hotel lobby Internet terminals, and he had confirmed that Ivanov was on two varieties of blood pressure medication.

Assuming, of course, that he was still actually taking his pills.

So what really worried Sokolov was that this visible struggle to hold in his fury was driving Ivanov's blood pressure up to levels normally seen only in deep-sea oil wells. Flaking off more bits of stuff that were going straight to his brain.

If Ivanov dropped dead, how the hell would they get out of this country?

So lost did Sokolov get in these ruminations that he forgot that Ivanov was still alive, still in the room, and still in the middle of a conversation with him.

"Your job," Ivanov finally said, extremely quietly, "is not to move creatively. There will be no falling back. No improvising."

"I understand, sir," Sokolov said, "but it is simply a normal practice to be familiar with the area and to have some kind of backup plan."

It felt like a reasonable thing to say, but it seemed to disturb

Ivanov more deeply than anything Sokolov had done during the entire interview. It was not merely that Ivanov thought a backup plan was *unnecessary*. He actually thought Sokolov was up to something *fishy*. Sokolov's interest in a backup plan made him *actively suspicious*.

But Sokolov was not above doing some tactical maneuvering, some falling back, even here. He shrugged, as if the backup plan remark had been mere whimsy. "Anyway," he said, "I got an idea."

"Yes? What kind of idea?"

Sokolov took a few steps over to the window and looked down toward the waterfront. It was only about seven in the evening and so people were still flooding and surging by the thousands in and out of the ferry terminals' gates. Ivanov turned to the window as well, tried to see whatever it was that Sokolov was looking at.

"Yes?" Ivanov prompted him, after a few moments.

"I can't see any just now," Sokolov said. "They are not that numerous compared to the commuters, the students, and so on."

"Who are these people you can't see any of?"

"Fishermen."

"They would use a different terminal," Ivanov growled.

"No, I'm not speaking of commercial fishermen. I mean hobbyists. Anglers. I saw a few of them earlier. Just regular Chinese guys. Retirees. They were coming home from a day out fishing, I suppose on one of those little islands out there." He turned to Ivanov and caught his eye. "They wear funny hats."

"I have seen them. Coolie hats," Ivanov said.

"No, not those. The guys I'm talking about wear huge hats made out of light-colored cloth. Big bills sticking out the front to keep the sun off their faces. With skirts hanging down the sides and the back, all the way to the shoulders. Like what an Arab would wear in a sandstorm. The head and face are almost totally hidden. More so if they wear big sunglasses."

"They sit out in the sun all day," Ivanov said, getting it. "You can't hold a parasol while you are fishing."

"Yes. The other thing about them is that they have these fancy cases to hold their rods." Sokolov held his hands about a meter apart, indicating the length. "With a bulge at one end to make room for the reel."

Ivanov's face relaxed and he began to nod.

"Better yet," Sokolov said, "each one of them is carrying a little cooler."

"Perfect," Ivanov said.

"Everyone ignores these guys."

"Of course," Ivanov said, "just like you or I would ignore an old fisherman on a bridge in Moscow."

"Sometimes you see one all alone," Sokolov said, "but it's not unusual for them to travel in a group—they'll hire one of those boats to take them to their favorite fishing hole."

"I see."

"Now. We can't walk around all day in such costumes without someone figuring out that we're not Chinese," Sokolov said. "But we don't need to. We just need to get from a vehicle into a building, or to walk down a street for half a block, without every fucking Chinese person in a kilometer radius taking phone pictures of us and calling home to Mama."

"Very good," Ivanov said. "Very good."

Sokolov decided not to mention his other observation, which was that the only other category of person who went completely ignored were the beggars who lay down flat on the ground in crowded pedestrian districts.

"We will make a plan," Ivanov said. "One plan. And it will work."

There'll be no more talk of backup plans.

"Yes, sir."

"Bring in the others," Ivanov said. "We will discuss, and make preparations for tomorrow."

THEY HAD ALL—FOUNDERS, executives, engineers, Creatives, toilers in Weird Stuff—been trying to think about big long-term issues raised by the Wor: the War of Realignment. Without a doubt T'Rain was making money from the Wor in the short term, but the question that was bothering the hell out of all of them was: Will it last? Because they had making money *before,* when the story of the world had actually made *sense.* Now it had mutated into something that seemed to lack exactly the kind of coherent overarching narrative that they had hired the likes of Skeletor and D-squared to supply.

All their meetings since the beginning of the Wor had been circular and pointless, even more so than meetings generally. Much of it came down to idle speculation about the internal mental states and processes of Devin Skraelin. Could the Wor really be laid at his feet? Suppose they could prove that he had orchestrated the whole thing, should they charge him with breach of contract? Or should they just lean on him to write his way out of the problem? In which case, Skeletor had only succeeded in drumming up more business for himself. Or was Devin helpless in the toss of cultural-historical forces beyond his ken? In which case, should they fire him and hire one of the thousands of ambitious, eager, and perfectly qualified young writers all hoping for an opportunity to take his place?

These meetings tended to start out with confident PowerPoint presentations and gradually trail off into quasi-philosophical management-speak aphorisms, more and more eyes turning to Richard as if to say, *Please O please help us.* Because Corporation 9592, at bottom, didn't *make* anything in the way that a steel mill did. And it didn't even really *sell* anything in the sense that, say, Amazon.com did. It just extracted cash flow from the players' desire to own virtual goods that would confer status on their fictional characters as they ran around T'Rain acting out greater or lesser parts in a story. And they all suspected, though they couldn't really prove, that a good story was as foundational to that business as, say, a blast furnace was to a steel mill. But you could slap a white hard hat onto an investor and take him into the plant and let him verify that the blast furnace was still there. Whereas a fantasy world was—well—a fantasy world. This had not prevented a lot of investors from entrusting many steel mills' worth of capital to the board of directors of Corporation 9592 and the CEO they had hired to look after the business. And in normal times, it made money and everyone was happy, probably because they weren't thinking about this potentially troublesome fantasy-world-based aspect of the business. But now they were thinking about it quite hard, and the more they thought about it, the more troubled they became. Corporation 9592 seemed to be undergoing an ontogenical retroversion to something like a start-up company. Richard was the only link back to that phase of the company's development, the only one who could think and function in that environment. The rabid dog they kept locked in the basement. Most of the time.

Anyway, now Richard was on the plane over eastern Montana. Pluto was sitting across the aisle in a backward-facing seat, regarding the eastern foothills of the Rockies like a plumber gazing into a torn-open wall. Not that Pluto could really be of much direct use when it came to story issues. But it comforted Richard to have a God of Olympus on the plane with him. Pluto was a reminder that there were more elemental principles even than whatever it was Devin Skraelin did for a living. Pluto tended to view all Narrative Dynamics as nothing more than benign growths on his work, kind of like those microbes embedded on Martian meteorites. And indeed Richard supposed that, if it came down to that, Pluto could probably summon up a planetary catastrophe that would eradicate all life and history on T'Rain's surface, and then start over again. But he would have a hard time sliding that one by the board of directors.

Enough of this woolgathering. He forced himself to look back down at the Devin Skraelin novel open on his lap.

Gnawed to a perilous weakness by the ravening flames, the drawbridge juddered under the footfalls of the massive Kar'doq. Its clenching talons pierced the carbonized wood of the failing timbers like nails driven into cheese. Peering down through a swirling nimbus of smoke, dyed all the lurid hues of Al'kazian silk by the particolored tongues of eldritch fire that lapped all around, its thin lips drew back to expose a silvery rictus of gibbering fangs. Staggered by the heat, which blasted his flesh like that of a swordsmith's forge, Lord Kandador—knowing that his loyal guardsmen and guardswomen suffered yet worse agony—yet knowing that they would uncomplainingly go to their deaths before showing even the smallest hint of fear—gave the order to fall back. No sooner had the command escaped his parched throat than his young herald, Galtimorn, raised the glittering Horn of Iphtar to his cracked and bleeding lips and began to sound the melancholy tocsin of retreat. A few notes rang forth above the din of battle, then faltered, and Lord Kandador looked down to see Galtimorn crumpling to the smoking planks like a marionette with its strings cut, a

stubby black iron arrow projecting obscenely from his chest.
Had his guardsmen and guardswomen heard the signal? A
sudden drawing-back, felt, rather than seen, suggested that
they had. Transferring the full weight of his double-handed
sword Glamnir to his right hand, Kandador reached down and
in a single mighty gesture heaved the stricken young herald up
onto his back. "To the keep!" he bellowed; and turning toward
a phantom that had suddenly loomed in the corner of his eye,
severed a Wraq's bestial head from its gristly neck with a
casual-seeming flick of the hungry blade.

This (Volume 11 of *T'Rain Origins: Chronicles of the Sundered: The Forsaken Magicks*), and the many others like it, had to be understood as Devin's implementation of a general world mythos that had been drawn up on the back of a napkin, as it were, by Don Donald after a five-hour lunch, heavy on liquids, with Richard and Pluto, way back in what Richard now thought of as the good old days of the company.

The original plan had been that it was just going to be Richard and D-squared getting to know each other, serious meetings to happen later. But D-squared had ended up going from zero to seven hundred miles an hour in two pints. Richard ought to have foreseen this. But he'd had no idea, in those days, how guys like Don Donald and Devin Skraelin actually worked. He had guessed that they must be kind of like engineers, meaning that you had to have lots of meetings with them and explain the problem in PowerPoint presentations and get preliminary scoping meetings and contractual hoo-ha out of the way before they would actually begin to ply their trade per se.

Richard picked Don Donald up at Sea-Tac and drove him to his downtown hotel, assuming he'd want to crash for at least a day to recover from jet lag and whatnot, but he ended up leaving his Land Cruiser at valet parking and stepping into the hotel restaurant with his guest for "a bite," which, after D-squared noticed the row of tap handles projecting above the bar, improved to "a pint," during which Richard basically explained the entire premise of the game. This led to a second pint during which Don Donald, showing zero symptoms of jet lag or intoxication, achieved missile lock on what he had identified as the central matter of interest, namely Pluto's terrain-generating code, and plunged into that topic so deeply that Richard had been obliged to begin making phone calls to Pluto and eventually sent a taxi around to collect him. Pint number 3 was all about getting to know Pluto (who drank club soda). After a pause for a trip to what D-squared identified as "the W.C.—it is an abbreviation for water closet—*the toilet,* if you please," he devoted pint numbers 4 and 5 to disgorging an entire cosmogonical schema that he had either just made up or been carrying around in his hip pocket in case someone asked for one.

During the first part of this feat or whatever you wanted to call it, Richard, somewhat addled, labored under the misconception that he was listening to the plot of a book that D-squared had already written. But the Don kept working in details from what he had just learned ten minutes ago about T'Rain, which obliged Richard to the belated, stuporous recognition that D-squared was just making it all up on the spot. He was *doing it. Now.* At 12:38 he had been waiting in line at Sea-Tac to have his retina scanned by Homeland Security, and at 2:24 he was slamming back pints in the hotel restaurant and getting the job done. The job that they had paid him for. Or rather, that they were *proposing* to pay him for, since no actual written agreement was in place.

Donald Cameron was sort of a one-stop shopping operation in that he supplied critical exegesis of his own work even as he was hurling it into the space around him. "You will have noticed that many if not most works of fantasy literature revolve around physical objects, usually ancient, imbued with numinous power. The Rings in the works of Tolkien being the best-known example."

Richard, hiding his face behind his pint for a moment, made a plausible guess as to the meaning of the word "numinous" and nodded agreement.

"There is nearly always a chthonic link. The object-imbued-with-numinous-power tends to be of mineral origin: gold, perhaps mined from a special vein, or a jewel of extraordinary rarity, or a sword forged from a shooting star. I am merely describing," D-squared added, with a flick of the fingers, "pulp. But the vast popularity of, say, a Devin Skraelin, attests to the power of these motifs to seize the reader's attention, down at the level of the reptilian brain, even as the cerebrum is getting sick."

"Who or what is Devin Skraelin?" Richard asked.

"A colleague who has distinguished himself by the sheer vastness of what you computer chaps like to call his *output*."

Richard looked down into his pint and rotated the glass gently between the palms of his hands, wondering how much stuff a person would have to write to be pegged, by Donald Cameron, of all people, as remarkably prolific.

"You were saying something about the mineral origin," said Pluto, crestfallen and maybe even a bit offended by the digression.

"Indeed yes," said D-squared. "I daresay it is an archetype." He paused for a swallow. "One can only speculate as to its origins. Why is the serpent an archetype? Because snakes have been biting our ancestors for millions of years: long enough for our fear of them to have been ensconced in our brainstems by the processes of natural selection." Another swallow. Then a shrug. "Hominids have been making stone tools since long before *Homo sapiens* existed. They must have noticed that certain types of stone made better tools than others."

"Granite doesn't fracture the right way," Pluto allowed. "The grain size is—"

"Even troglodytes must have noticed that certain outcroppings of stone made wondrously effective weapons."

"*Especially* troglodytes!" Pluto corrected him.

"For them it would have been a commonplace observation of the natural world, not nearly as ancient as 'snakes are dangerous,' and yet ancient *enough* that it must have played some role in the processes of natural selection that led to the development of human consciousness. Culture. And, loosely defined, literature."

Richard was more than happy to sit and listen. It was the weirdest business meeting of his career so far, even using an elastic definition of "business," and he saw that was good.

"The point is," said Don Donald, "that *it works*. Put a magic gem in a story and it grabs the reader. This can be done shamelessly, or with more or less artfulness, according to the tastes and talents of the author. I should say that Tolkien got it right by layering atop it a story about good and evil. The numinous mineral object is now also a *technology*; it has been imbued with power by a sentient will who possesses some sort of arcane wizardry. It can only be unmade by exposing it to a certain geological process that, being geological, is prior to, and takes precedence over, any work of culture."

Don Donald was clearly accustomed to addressing people whose only way of responding was to nod worshipfully and take notes. He did not, in other words, leave a lot of breaks in his testimony to allow for discussion. For the moment, that was fine, since it made it easier for Richard to drink.

"If I have correctly understood your company and its technology, you possess a command of the geological underpinnings of your world that far exceeds that of any competitor. It would seem the natural and obvious step, then, to capitalize on this, by creating, or providing a facility for the creation of, numinous objects of mineral origin."

"NOMOs," coined Pluto.

D-squared looked taken aback until he got it.

Richard put in: "Among geeks, the cool-soundingness of the acronym is more important than the existence of what it refers to."

"I might then be of service," said D-squared, "by erecting a cultural (ahem) story atop that geological basement. The cultures would have artisans, metallurgists, gemologists, and so forth who would create the—er—NOMOs that would presumably be of central importance to the game."

"I was thinking about the formation of the moon the other day," Pluto put in.

"Pluto, would you care to expand on what you just said, since we do not understand it?" Richard asked.

"There's a theory that the moon was made when young Earth got sideswiped by something huge, almost planet sized. We don't know where that thing went." He shrugged. "It's kind of weird. You'd think that if we got hit by something big enough to knock the moon off, it would still be around somewhere, orbiting the sun. But I was thinking: what if it fell back into Earth later and merged with it?"

"What if it did?" Richard asked.

"It would be a very strange situation," Pluto said. He pointed out the window of the restaurant, up into the sky. "A piece of Earth is up there. Sundered. Separated forever. Not coming back." Then he lowered his aim and pointed down at the floor. "While down inside the earth is alien stuff. Stuff that doesn't belong. The residue of the thing that hit us and sundered the world."

Richard had been worried that D-squared would find Pluto incomprehensible and that the entire interview would be one long series of excruciating faux pas. But, perhaps because Cameron lived and dined with Premier League nerds at Cambridge, he seemed perfectly at ease with the shaggy Alaskan demiurge. He was either fascinated by Pluto's idea, or putting forth a commendable effort to feign fascination, and it didn't matter which. "Is it your idea that this alien planetesimal remains intact and hidden below the surface?"

"Way deep down, a big chunk of it might be intact," Pluto said, "but some of it would have been melted and carried away by magma flows. But not dissolved. It would manifest on the surface of T'Rain as veins of special ores and so on."

"Of course!" said Don Donald. "And the cultures that arose on the planet's surface, knowing nothing of the geological facts, would come to recognize the special properties of these ores, whatever they might be."

"If the physics of the planetesimal were different, like because it came through a wormhole from another universe or something, then that would provide a basis for what we call magic," said Pluto, "and the metallurgists, or whatever, who learned how to exploit it would become alchemists, brewers of potions, sorcerers—"

"And they would get busy manufacturing lots of NOMOs," Richard put in, just in case anyone was losing sight of this. Because he had played enough games to know that NOMOs equaled valuable virtual property which equaled cash flow for Corporation 9592. "I think my work here is done," he said, rising to his feet by the always-safe drunken expedient of leaning against a wall as he straightened his legs. "I shall leave you two to work out the details."

Not for the first time, the future survival and prosperity of the company was secured by Pluto's memory. After talking to D-squared for another couple of hours, he went home and wrote it all down in an emacs document entitled "it.txt," which was later transmogrified into "it.docx" and thereby founded a lineage of more discursive documents and wiki pages, and a project and then a department that were all called "it" until one of the professional managers who had begun to infiltrate the company raised her eyebrows and it all had to be renamed Narrative Dynamics. The first major initiative of which had been to hire Devin Skraelin.

The gist of "it," as Richard only found out much later (he was a big believer in delegating responsibilities to people who actually cared about them), was that the T'Rainian biosphere supported two distinct types of DNA, one made exclusively out of original T'Rain elements, the other commingled with trace amounts of stuff from the swallowed planetesimal and therefore imbued with "magic," where "magic" was now a social construct invented by T'Rain's sentient races to explain the different physics that governed the alien atoms. Some species were made entirely of the mundane DNA, some were hybridized with a bit of the alien stuff, and a very few were made of 100 percent alien material and consequently had angelic/demonic/ godlike qualities, though these had trouble reproducing since it was difficult to round up a sufficient biomass of the right kind of stuff.

Of course. it was way more complicated than this made it sound; and it wasn't long before tables and tree diagrams had to drawn up to keep it all straight, but this was the gist of it.docx, which, in its fully fledged, nine-point-seven-megabyte incarnation, they had handed off to Devin when they had made him the first, and the last, Writer in Residence.

"HOW'S ZULA DOING?" Richard asked, trying to get a conversation started with Pluto. They were over the High Plains now and he supposed that his traveling companion might have less to gaze at.

"I haven't seen her in a few days," Pluto said, without taking his eyes off the window. Perhaps his attention had been seized by the meanderings of the Platte.

So that gambit had failed. Richard considered his options. Other people would want to sentimentalize about the old days, but the great thing about traveling with Pluto was that he only cared about you to the extent that you were interesting to him *now*. In that way he kept you on your toes. No aspect of the relationship could be counterfeited when it was being minted anew from moment to moment.

"I meant," Richard said, "how's she doing in the job?"

"As best as anyone can given the nature of the problem," Pluto said, finally glancing Richard's way for a fraction of a second.

During the Titanian phase of the game's development, when they had been laying down great slabs of world and story from one day to the next, Richard had pushed Pluto, hard, to supply them with material even before it was "ready," which, for Pluto, meant that every cubic millimeter of solid matter in the world had to have a detailed backstory stretching 4.5 billion years. Pluto's diligence in this and other matters had become a bottleneck delaying millions of dollars' worth of efforts by other contributors. Richard had demanded that Pluto supply maps stipulating the locations of certain ore veins and gem deposits by fiat. In a thirteen-hour meeting, the memory of which still sent palpable horrors running up and down Pluto's spine, Richard had stood at a whiteboard drawing out maps of the mineral deposits by hand. Photographs of the whiteboard had then been used to generate the actual maps used in the game. Much of Pluto's work since then had been in the newly created discipline of Teleological Tectonics, meaning that he started with Richard's maps and then ran the tectonics and the magma flow simulations *backward* in time so that everything could be knit together into a lava narrative that made sense by Pluto's lights. This project had perked along in the background for several years and only recently got to the place where serious computing resources could be thrown at it. That job had fallen to Zula. "The nature of the problem" was Pluto petulantly reminding Richard that Richard had been the originator of said problem.

"How's the Divine Intervention Queue looking?" said Richard, trying another tack.

For there were limits to what Teleological Tectonics could achieve. They had discovered a number of irresolvable conflicts between what the simulations insisted ought to be there, and what was already present in T'Rain. These were simply going to have to be fixed through acts of divine intervention. In and of itself, this wasn't a problem. There were lots of divinities in T'Rain. But even the craziest divinity didn't just go around altering landforms at random, and so it had become part of Zula's job to act as a liaison between the Departments of Teleological Tectonics and of Narrative Dynamics, cajoling the latter into cranking out storylines to explain why this or that god had decided to move a volcano three miles to the south-southeast, or transmute a vein of copper into limestone.

"You know the URL," Pluto pointed out, meaning the link that Richard only needed to click on if he wanted to inspect the Divine Intervention Queue himself.

Pluto seemed to be in an extrapissy mood, so Richard asked the flight attendant for another tray of sushi and turned to gaze out the window. It was a clear day. They were well into square-road-grid territory now. From here—he guessed Nebraska—the grid would continue eastward until it lapped up against, and discharged into, the finer scratchings of the Great Lakes' industrial conurbations: places that Richard's people never went to, save as beggars or conquerors. But before getting there the jet would plunge down into thicker air and home in on the K'Shetriae Kingdom.

SOMETIMES HE USED the FBO, the private jet terminal, at Omaha, and drove from there to the Possum Walk Trailer Park, a trip of about two hours. Today, however, they were pressed for time, and so they landed at a small regional airport only about half an hour from their destination.

Richard was oppressed by a desire to get clear of the airport and out into open country. In a big place like Omaha they could slip out of the FBO and quickly blend in with the mundanes, but here the arrival of a private jet was a big deal, and everyone in the place knew about it. Just inside the little pilots' waiting room in the terminal, a plate of Rice Krispie Treats had been set out for them. Richard absentmindedly stuffed one into his mouth as they waited for their ride. Presently they were collected by a very polite young man named Dale, who drove them on a hilariously tortuous route around the airport to the car rental lot. Dale guessed out loud that they had come to pay a call on "Mr. Skraelin," and Richard agreed that it was so. Dale paid Richard an elaborate compliment on the success and the sheer entertainment value of his game and, warming to the task, told Richard a few things about his band of raiders, a group of local kids who had gone to high school together and now spent every Friday evening sitting around in someone's basement conducting bloodthirsty incursions against the Earthtone Coalition, whom Dale hated so much that he seemed almost offended that he had to go to the trouble of killing them. Almost all Dale's friends' characters belonged to the Var' species.

Richard knew better than to draw actionable conclusions from this one chance encounter. Corporation 9592 had an entire department full of people with advanced degrees in statistics, managing a code base that monitored a million Dales per second, analyzing them six ways from Sunday. Any wisdom that proceeded from this sketchy conversation with Dale would be listened to, politely but incredulously, and then classified as "anecdotal" and forgotten. But Richard couldn't help himself. Unlike the K'Shetriae, which were basically elves, and the Dwinn, which were basically dwarves, the Var' had no discernible antecedents in folklore, unless you counted focus groups of nerds as folk. They were technologically primitive but capable of channeling the forces of weather, for example, shooting lightning bolts at their enemies but only during thunderstorms, freezing them to death but only during blizzards, and so on. A perfect match, in other words, for midwesterners. Just like Republicans or Democrats who spent so much time socializing with others of their kind that they could not believe any normal-seeming, mentally sound person could possibly belong to the opposite faction, Dale was a rock-ribbed Forces of Brightness man. As such, he exemplified a trend that had already been analyzed to exhaustion by the demographers. The Earthtone Coalition was 99 percent Anthrons, K'Shetriae, and Dwinn: the old-school races found in the works of Tolkien and his legion of imitators. Players who opted to belong to the newfangled races such as the Var', on the other hand, tended to join up with the Forces of Brightness.

He was working on a theory that it was all related to the Rice Krispie Treats.

Bear with me, he said (not out loud, of course), showing his palms to the Furious Muses. Just hear me out.

Having now lived for a few decades in parts of the United States and Canada where cooking was treated quite seriously, and having actually employed professional chefs, he was fascinated by the midwestern/middle American phenomenon of recombinant cuisine. Rice Krispie Treats being a prototypical example in that they were made by repurposing other foods *that had already been prepared* (to wit, breakfast cereal and marshmallows). And of course any recipe that called for a can of cream of mushroom soup fell into the same category. The unifying principle behind all recombinant cuisine seemed to be indifference, if not outright hostility, to the use of anything that a coastal foodie would define as an ingredient. Was it too much of a stretch to think that the rejection, by the Dales of the world, of traditional fantasy-world races such as elves and dwarves was motivated by the same deep, mysterious cultural mojo as their spurning of onions and salt in favor of onion salt?

The recombinant food thing was a declaration of mental bankruptcy in the complexity of modern material culture. Likewise, Dale and his friends, living in a world where libraries were already stuffed with hundreds of thousands of decaying novels that would never again be read, where any television program or movie ever filmed could be downloaded and viewed, simply did not have the bandwidth to absorb a vast amount of detailed background material about fictitious races on a made-up planet. They just wanted to kick ass.

Anyway, Dale got them to their rental car, not before pumping Richard for a few tips about the latest from the Torgai Foothills. Weather in that region could be violent, which was a good thing for Var' raiders, and so Dale's group had been hanging out on some windy crag and staging raids on the freebooters who had been raiding the ransom bearers. Richard allowed as how "nothing lasts forever" and "the situation is fluid" before shaking Dale's hand and thanking him and closing the rental car's door.

The largest and newest billboard on the airport access road sported a huge picture of a blue-haired elf and said KSHETRIAE KINGDOM in ten-foot-high block letters. Beyond that, the roadsides were mercifully free of T'Rain-related clutter until they hove in view of the theme park itself. Taking advantage of the digital map on the car's GPS device, Richard diverted onto a gravel road about half a mile short of the main entrance and gave the whole complex a wide berth; he had remembered that the park included some fiberglass terrain features—mountains with painted-on snow, dotted with fanciful K'Shetriae temple architecture—that most certainly would not pass muster with Pluto, and he didn't want the rest of the day to be about that. The GPS unit became almost equally obstreperous, though, over Richard's unauthorized route change, until they finally passed over some invisible cybernetic watershed between two possible ways of getting to their destination, and it changed its fickle little mind and began calmly telling him which way to proceed as if this had been its idea all along.

A straight shot down a paved state highway took them to the

gate of the Possum Walk Trailer Park, which had been beefed up and connected to an electronic security system. Childish as the emotion was, Richard could not help but feel resentful over being interrogated by an electronic box thrust out on a pipe. He had come to this place several years ago when it had still reeked of exploded meth factories and hog confinement facilities. In those days, Devin had been a mere tenant, living alone in a thirty-year-old mobile home that gave and groaned beneath his weight whenever he troubled himself to get up and move around. Of course, he had long since bought the entire property, as well as a couple of adjoining lots, and evicted his erstwhile neighbors and sold their trailers on eBay. His original trailer stood alone, a weird hybrid of *Little House on the Prairie* and *Grapes of Wrath*. A prefab steel roof had been erected above it to protect it from vengeful elements. Farther back from the highway, concrete pads had been poured and steel buildings erected to form a U-shaped compound embracing the small, separate building, little different from a mobile home in size and layout, where Devin worked and lived. The purpose of the U was to house his lawyers, accountants, managers, and sous-novelists.

The gate droned aside. As Richard drove through it, the GPS unit announced: "You have arrived!" Idling past the old mobile home, Richard gazed at its front door for a few moments and let himself be that guy from several years ago who had come up those rotten wooden steps to knock on that door and offer Devin a job. Then he snapped out of it and turned his attention to a woman just emerging from the closest prong of the U. She was struggling with her weight, and was dressed and coiffed in a way that, seen on the streets of Seattle, would have been incontrovertible proof of Sapphism. But Richard knew he had to be careful about making such assumptions here. As he parked in one of about seven thousand available spaces, she drifted over toward the driver's side of the car and began simpering at him through the window. Richard prepared himself to receive disagreeable news manfully.

"Good afternoon, Mr. Forthrast, I'm Wendy."

"Nice to meet you, Wendy." Until a couple of years ago, he'd have gone through the ritual of insisting that she address him as Richard, but the fact was that he had flown here from Seattle in a private jet and she had driven her Subaru.

"He just went into F.S. about fifteen minutes ago," she said apologetically. "Would you like to come in and make yourself comfortable?"

The first of these sentences meant that, according to the biometric sensors on Devin's body, he had just entered into what psychologists referred to as the flow state, and he was not to be disturbed until he emerged from it of his own volition.

The second of these sentences meant sitting around and eating. As Richard knew all too well, there was a waiting room stocked with bowls of Chex Party Mix and recombinant gorp, with fridges along the walls replete with soft drinks, and a coffee urn. Sitting in that room, using the free Wi-Fi, was an inevitable prelude to any meeting with Devin, who had an uncanny knack for ascending into the flow state only minutes before any scheduled visit. As a way to head off tiresome, repetitive objections from visitors who could not be placated with gorp and sugar water, Devin's staff had printed up copies of a complimentary handout sheet, "Flow State FAQ," and scattered them around the feeding troughs. Pluto, who had never been here before, picked one of them up and went into the flow state himself as he learned all about this amazingly productive psychological/physiological regimen and how all history's greatest artists and geniuses had done their best work while immersed in it. Richard, who'd had plenty of opportunities to familiarize himself with the document's contents, knew that it contained only one operative phrase, which was that interruptions were inimical to the flow state and had to be prevented at all costs. It was the most passive-aggressive way imaginable for Devin Skraelin to tell people that he was in the middle of something and fuck off.

Having already committed an unpardonable sin against his body by eating the Rice Krispie Treat at the airport, Richard forced himself to ignore the proffered food. He opened his laptop and checked his email.

- As far as T'Rain was concerned, he saw nothing that couldn't wait. Everyone who mattered at Corporation 9592 knew that he was doing this and so they weren't bothering him.

- There was a little uptick of traffic on his Schloss Hundschüttler email address. The weather had turned warm during the last few days, as they'd expected, and the skiing, which had been marginal during Peter and Zula's visit, had gone decisively to hell. The long-range forecast looked worse. So Chet had declared that Mud Month would commence in two days. This was a mandatory four-week break in the Schloss's operations, when all the employees got to go home, and the place sat empty.

• Brother John had posted an update on Dad's latest round of visits to medical specialists. Nothing huge to report on that front.

Richard closed his laptop. He reached over and took one of the free "Flow State FAQ" handouts and flipped it over so that he was looking at its back side, which was blank. He reached into his shoulder bag and pulled out a Sharpie and used it to write

DEVIN
FUCKING KNOCK IT OFF

on the back of the FAQ. Then he got up and walked out of the waiting area and back across the parking area, passing the old trailer again, all the way to the entrance gate. He slapped an override button that caused the gate to pull open, then went outside and positioned himself in front of the video camera that monitored incoming cars. He held up the sheet of paper in view of the video camera and stood there while he counted to twenty. Then he walked back through the gate and returned to his position in the waiting area.

Five minutes later, Wendy came in and announced that Devin had emerged from the flow state earlier than was his wont and that they were welcome to go in and see him.

"I know the way," Richard said.

THE SPACE WAS windowless. Or, if you were willing to consider giant flat-panel screens as being windows into other worlds, it was a greenhouse. In the middle was Devin's elliptical trainer, or rather one of a pool of treadmills, elliptical trainers, and other such gadgets that were swapped in and out as he ruined or got sick of them. Depending from the ceiling was a massive articulated structure: an industrial robot arm, capable of being programmed to move along and rotate around a myriad of axes with the silence of a panther and the precision of a knife fighter. It supported an additional large flat-panel screen and a framework that held up an array of input devices: an ergonomic keyboard, trackballs, and other devices of which Richard knew not the names. Devin, naked except for a pair of gym shorts emblazoned with the logo of one of his favorite charities, was stirring the air with his legs, working the reciprocating paddles of the trainer. Invisible streams of cool wind impinged on his body from perfectly silent high-tech fans, not quite evaporating a sheen of perspiration that caused all his veins and tendons, and his twelve-pack abs, to pop out through his skin, as though the epidermis were shrink wrap laid directly over nerve and bone. According to this morning's stats, Devin's body fat percentage was an astonishing 4.5, which placed him into a serious calorie debt situation that in theory should extend his life span beyond 110 years. The slight up-and-down bobbing of his head and upper body was compensated for by equal movements of the robot arm, which used a machine vision control loop to track his attitude through a camera and to calculate the vector of translations and rotations needed to keep the huge screen exactly 22.5 inches away from his laser-sculpted corneas and the keyboard and other input devices within easy and comfortable reach of his fingers. A custom-made headset, with flip-down 3D lenses (currently flipped up and out of the way) and a microphone enabled him to dictate ideas or take phone calls as necessary. A chest harness tracked his pulse and sent immediate notification of any flipped T-waves to an on-call cardiologist sitting in an office suite two miles down the road. A defibrillator hung on the wall, blinking green.

You laugh, Richard had once said to a colleague, after they'd visited the place, but all he's doing is applying scientific management principles to a hundred-million-dollar production facility (i.e., Devin) with an astronomical profit margin.

"Hello, Dodge!" he called out, only a little short of breath. The system was programmed to keep his pulse between 75 percent and

80 percent of its recommended maximum, so he was working hard but not gasping for air.

"Good afternoon, Devin," said Richard, suddenly wishing he'd remembered to bring a hat, since it was chilly in here. "I apologize if our arrival came as a surprise."

"Not a problem!"

"I had been assuming that with all your support staff and what-not, someone here might have made you aware of the schedule." This for the benefit of the half-dozen members of said staff who, unaccountably, had crowded into the room.

"No worries!" And he sounded like he meant it. If it was true that exercise jacked up one's endorphin levels, Devin must live his whole life on something like an intravenous fentanyl drip.

"You remember Pluto."

"Of course! Hello, Pluto."

"Hello," said Pluto, looking put out that he was actually being chivvied through this meaningless program of social pleasantries.

"Can we talk about something?" Richard said.

"Sure! What's on your mind?"

"*We*," Richard stressed, "as in, *you and me*."

"You and I are both here, Richard," said Devin.

Richard held eye contact for a few moments, then broke it and scanned the faces of everyone else in the room. "This is not *material*," he said. "Devin and I are not going to be generating *intellectual property*. And neither is it some kind of a brainstorming or strategizing effort in which we will be wanting ideas and input from amazingly bright and helpful people whose job it is to supply that. No record of the conversation needs to be made." Richard could see people's faces falling as he ticked his way down the list. Finally he looked back at Devin. "I'll see you in the trailer," he said, "just for old time's sake."

THE TRAILER WAS cleaner and, at the same time, even more of a dump than he remembered. Someone had definitely hit all its surfaces with a diluted bleach solution. The place probably did not contain a single intact strand of DNA. As always, the information technology had aged badly: the plastic shell of Devin's elephantine cathode-ray-tube monitor had turned the color of dead algae. To his credit, he had a cheerful red diner table in the kitchen, and three chairs to go with it. Richard sat down in one of these and looked out the window as Devin, now in a tracksuit, strode across the lot followed by a train of rattled and nettled assistants. The caboose of that train was Pluto, forgotten and bemused.

Devin's sleek elven frame made scarcely an impression on the structurally compromised stairs. He banged the door shut and came in looking pissed.

"I'm sorry," Richard said, "but there is some stuff that we have to sort out."

Skeletor had not been expecting Richard to lead off with an apology and so this shortened his stride. "The wo-er," he said.

"Yeah. You know, the last time I came here, the day after Thanksgiving, I was playing the game at a Hy-Vee on my way down and I saw some stuff going on that looked funny to me at the time. But a month later, when the Wor started, it was obvious in retrospect that I had been seeing certain preparations. The creation of a fifth column. Probing attacks on what would soon become the Earthtone Coalition's front lines. Which leads to the question, if certain people had been preparing for the Wor *one* month in advance, who's to say they weren't preparing for it *six* months or even *twelve* in advance?"

Devin shrugged. "Beats me." Not the most adroit answer and yet Richard was wrong-footed by its sincerity. He had known Devin for a long time and thought he could read the man's body language reasonably well.

Another tack. "The thing is," Richard said, "not half an hour ago I'm pulling out of the airport with Pluto and I see that huge billboard for K'Shetriae Kingdom, with the blue-haired guy on it, and in the light of all that has been going on, I can't help seeing that as dog whistle politics."

"Dog whistle politics?"

"A signal that only certain people can hear. The very blueness of that hair is a shout-out to the Forces of Brightness. Earthtone Coalition people see it and don't go any further than to shudder at its tastelessness and look the other way. But Forces of Brightness people see it as a rallying point."

"I think it's just that a blue-haired humanoid is more eye-catching. And the purpose of a billboard is to be eye-catching."

Richard could hardly contest those points. He leaned forward, put his elbows on the red Formica of the diner table, clamped his head between his fingertips. "What bothers me is the trivialization," he said. "T'Rain is one huge virtual killing machine. It is just warriors with poleaxes and magicians with fireballs fighting this endless series of duels to the death. Not real death, of course, since they all just go to Limbo and get respawned, but still, the engine that makes the whole system run—and by that, I mean generate revenue—is the excitement and sense of competition that comes out of these mano a mano confrontations. Which is why we had Good vs. Evil. Okay, it wasn't very original, but at least it was an explanation for all the conflict that drives our revenue stream. And now, because of the Wor, Good vs. Evil has been replaced by—what? Primaries vs. Pastels?"

Devin shrugged again. "It works for the Crips and the Bloods."

"But is that the story you've been writing?"

"It's every bit as good as what we had before."

"How so?"

"What we had before wasn't really Good vs. Evil. Those were just names pasted on two different factions."

"Okay," Richard said, "I'll admit I've often had similar thoughts myself."

"The people who called themselves Evil weren't really doing evil stuff, and the people who called themselves Good were no better. It's not like the Good people were, for example, sacrificing points in the game world so that they could take the time to help little old ladies across the street."

"We didn't give them the opportunity to help little old ladies across the street," Richard said.

"Exactly, we set them certain tasks or quests that had the 'Good' label slapped on them; but, art direction aside, they were indiscernible from 'Evil' tasks."

"So the Wor is our customers calling bullshit on our 'Good/Evil' branding strategy, you're saying," Richard said.

"Not so much that as finding something that feels more real to them, more visceral."

"Which is what exactly?"

"The Other," said Skeletor.

"Say what!?"

"Oh come on, you did it yourself when you saw the billboard at the airport. 'Ugh! Blue hair! How tasteless!' When you did that, you identified, you categorized that character as belonging to the Other. And once you have done that, attacking it, murdering it, becomes easier. Perhaps even an urgent need."

"Wow." Richard was seriously taken aback because Furious Muse number 5, a comparative literature graduate student at the University of Washington who had toiled in Corporation 9592's creative salt mines for a summer, had barely been able to make it through a paragraph without invoking the O-word. Hearing it from the mouth of Skeletor had taken Richard right out of the here-and-nowness of the conversation and left him wondering if he had fallen asleep on the business jet and was only dreaming this. He made a mental note to google F.M. number 5 at the next opportunity and find out if she had moved to Nodaway.

Richard had always writhed uncomfortably during O-word conversations, since he had the general feeling, which he could not quite prove, that certain people used it as a kind of intellectual duct tape. And yet any resistance to it on Richard's part led to the accusation that he was classifying people who liked to talk about the Other as *themselves* belonging to the Other.

And so the general result of Skeletor's invocation of the O-word at this point was to make Richard want to pull the rip cord on this whole conversation.

But no. There were shareholders to think of. At some level he had to justify spending a bazillion dollars on jet fuel just to translocate his ass to this diner chair.

On one level this was stressful and pressure-laden, but on another he could not have been more comfortable. Richard knew a few people who, like himself, basically could not stop making money no matter what they did; they could be kicked out the door of a moving taxi anywhere in the world and be operating a successful business within weeks or months. It usually took a few tries to get the hang of it. Beyond that, it was possible to succeed beyond all reasonable bounds if one kept at it. Some found an adequately successful business early enough in life that they were golden-handcuffed; others only figured out how to make money as they were approaching the age of retirement. After the smuggling and the Schloss, Richard had gotten to the place where he just knew how to do it, in the sense that every teenaged tinkerer who played with electricity knew that in order to make anything happen you had to connect a wire to each terminal of the battery. At some level, making any business run was that simple. Everything else was fussing with the knobs.

"Say more about the Crips and the Bloods," Richard said, stalling for time while he tried to get his mental house in order.

"To us they look the same. Urban black kids with similar demographics and tastes. Seems like they all ought to pull together. But that's not where they're at. They are shooting each other to death because they see the Other as less than human. And I'm saying it has been the case for a long time in T'Rain that those people we have lately started calling the Earthtone Coalition have always looked at the ones we now call the Forces of Brightness and seen them as tacky, uncultured, not really playing the game in character. And what happened in the last few months was that the F.O.B. types just got tired of it and rose up and, you know, asserted their pride in their identity, kind of like the gay rights movement with those goddamned rainbow flags. And as long as it's possible for those two groups to identify each other on sight, each one of them is going to see the other as, well, the Other, and killing people based on that is way more ingrained than killing them on this completely bogus and flimsy fake-Good and fake-Evil dichotomy that we were working with before."

"I get it," Richard said. "But is that all we are? Just digital Crips and Bloods?"

"What if it's true?" Devin shrugged.

"Then you're not doing your fucking job," Richard said. "Because the world is supposed to have a real story to it. Not just people killing each other over color schemes."

"Maybe you're not doing yours," Devin said. "How can I write a story about Good and Evil in a world where those concepts have no real meaning—no consequences?"

"What sort of consequences do you have in mind? We can't send people's characters to virtual Hell."

"I know. Only Limbo."

They both laughed.

Devin thought about it a little more. "I don't know. I think you have to create an existential threat to the world."

"Such as?"

"Comparable to a nuclear holocaust or what would have happened if Sauron had gotten his hands on the One Ring."

"I'm going to have all kinds of fun getting that idea past the shareholders."

"Well, maybe the shareholders have a point. The company is making money, right?"

"Yeah, but the reason I'm here is that there is some concern that this may not continue to be the case. If the F.O.B. kill all the Earth-tone Coalition, which they are likely to do, then what is there left to do in that world?"

Devin shrugged. "Kill each other?"

"There's always that."

Day 3

"Homegirl, this is the third time you come by here, let me put you out of your misery!"

The voice was a confident alto: someone with an excellent ear for pronunciation, even if her command of certain idioms was a little shaky. Zula spun around on her heel, then dropped her gaze twenty degrees to discover a face—somewhat familiar—smiling back at her from five feet and two inches above street level.

This was the woman—no, girl—no, woman—who had sold her a kilogram of green tea on the street yesterday afternoon. A kilogram being a rather huge amount. But she had made it seem like such a reasonable idea at the time.

The girl/woman confusion was irresolvable. She was petite and trim, traits hardly unusual among Chinese females. She had a pixie haircut, which *was* unusual. But this did not seem to be a fashion statement, given that she was wearing blue jeans and a pair of knee-high, bright blue pull-on boots—the kind of boots that working people used when scrubbing a boat deck or sloshing around in a rice paddy. A black T-shirt and a black vest completed the ensemble. No makeup. No jewelry except for a man's watch, clunky on her wrist. She was rooted to the ground in a way that kept catching Zula's eye: she planted those boots shoulder width apart on the pavement and stood square to whomever she was talking to, occasionally bounced a little on the balls of her feet when she was amused or excited by something. Her confidence made her seem forty but her skin was that of a twenty-year-old, so Zula concluded that she was young but odd in some way that would take Zula a little while to sort out.

Not *all* young women around here wore high heels and dresses, but it was certainly common enough that this tea-selling woman was placing herself miles outside of the mainstream by looking the way she did. And yet Zula didn't get any sense of in-your-face nonconformism. She was not consciously making any kind of statement. This was who she was.

She had approached Zula and struck up a conversation yesterday afternoon. Zula, Csongor, and Sokolov had found their way to a street where a number of tea sellers had their shops, and Zula had been eyeing them, trying to decide which one she would approach, psyching herself up for another round of bargaining. And then suddenly this woman had been in front of her, blue boots planted, smiling confidently, and striking up a conversation in oddly colloquial English. And after a minute or two she had produced this huge bolus of green tea, seemingly from nowhere, and told Zula a story about it. How she and her people—Zula had forgotten the name of the group, but Blue Boots wanted it understood that it was a separate ethnicity—lived way up in the mountains of western Fujian. They had been chased up there a zillion years ago and lived in forts on misty mountaintops. Consequently, no one was upstream of them—the water ran clean from the sky, there was no industrial runoff contaminating their soil, and there never would be. Blue Boots had gone on to enumerate several other virtues of the place and to explain how these superlative qualities had been impregnated into the tea leaves at the molecular level and could be transferred into the bodies, minds, and souls of people condemned to live in not-so-blessed realms simply by drinking vast quantities of said tea. A kilogram of the stuff would vanish in no time and Zula would be begging for more. But it would be hard to buy more in America. Speaking of which, Blue Boots was keen on finding a Western Hemisphere distributor for this product, and Zula seemed like a fine candidate . . .

If Zula had actually been a tourist, just wanting to be left alone, she'd have grown tired of Blue Boots. But as it was she felt so happy to see a quasi-familiar face that she had to hold back an impulse to gather the tiny thing in her arms.

"Good morning," Zula said. "You were right. I drank all that tea."

"Ha, ha, you are full of *shit!*" said Blue Boots delightedly.

"You're right. I don't need any more today, thank you."

"You want a distributorship?"

"No," Zula began, but then perceived that Blue Boots was only teasing her and broke it off.

"You are so fricking lost it's sad," said Blue Boots. "Everyone on the street is talking about it."

"We are trying to find a *wangba,*" Zula said.

"A turtle egg? That is a very bad insult. Be careful who you say it to."

"Maybe I'm pronouncing it wrong."

"In English?"

"We are trying to find an Internet café," Zula said.

Blue Boots wrinkled her nose in a way that from most other females her age would have seemed like an effort to be cutesy but from her seemed as pure as the mountain waters of her native region. "What does Internet and coffee have to do with each other?"

"Café," Zula said, "not coffee."

"Café is a place where you drink coffee!"

"Yes, but—"

"This is China," said Blue Boots, as if Zula might not have noticed. "We drink tea. Have you forgotten our conversation of yesterday? I know we all look the same to you but—"

"I'm from Eritrea. We grow coffee there," Zula said, thinking fast.

"Here instead of a café we would have a teahouse."

"I get it. But we are not looking for something to drink. We are looking for Internet."

"Come again?"

Zula looked to Csongor who wearily held up a piece of paper with the Chinese characters for *wangba* printed on it. They had been showing it to random people on the street for the last half hour or so. Everyone they talked to seemed to have at least a vague idea of where such a thing could be found and pointed them in one direction or another while speaking earnestly, usually in Chinese but sometimes in English.

"Why didn't you say so?" said Blue Boots. She pointed. "It's that way, just above the—"

Zula shook her head. "How do you think we got so fricking lost?"

"Come on, I'll take you there." And she took Zula's hand in hers and began walking with her. The gesture was a bit familiar but, at least for now, it felt nice to be holding anyone's hand and so Zula laced her fingers together with her guide's and let her arm swing freely.

It seemed inconceivable that any of them, even Sokolov, would defy her, so Csongor and Sokolov dutifully fell in behind.

The pixie haircut was shaking in dismay. "You need translator, man."

"Agreed."

"Excellent!" And Blue Boots let go of Zula's hand, stopped, pivoted, and thrust out her right. Zula, out of habit, began to extend her hand, then realized she was about to enter into a binding contract and hesitated.

"Awwa!" said Blue Boots, and snapped her fingers in frustration. "Almost had you over a barrel."

"We don't even know your name."

"I don't know yours."

"Zula Forthrast," said Zula quietly. She looked back at Sokolov, who was distractedly gazing around with his habitual, posttraumatic, thousand-yard stare. A trace of a grin came onto her face.

"What?" Blue Boots wanted to know.

Zula killed the smile and shook her head. She had passed her name on to someone. And if that someone were to google the name, what might come up? Perhaps an article from the *Seattle Times* about a young woman who had inexplicably gone missing.

"I am Qian Yuxia."

Zula, who had spent her life with her nose pressed up against the window of the straight-haired world, was growingly obsessed with Qian Yuxia's haircut, which was one of those wedgy, short-on-top, longer-on-the-bottom productions. Someone who loved Qian Yuxia and who was very good with sharp objects had been maintaining this, and Qian Yuxia had just as determinedly been ignoring it.

"Is that a common name where you are from?" Zula asked, just making conversation.

"Yongding," Yuxia reminded her. "Where the Big-Footed Women make the *gaoshan cha*. High mountain tea."

"Are you a Big-Footed Woman?"

Yuxia looked at her like she was an idiot and extended a blue boot.

Zula shrugged. "But you might have a very small foot inside there!"

"I am Hakka," said Qian Yuxia, as if that should put this entire part of the conversation to rest immediately. "I told you yesterday."

"Sorry, I forgot the name."

"What is up? Why are you here?"

Sokolov had now drawn close enough that Zula felt it best to stick to the script. Because they had worked out a script yesterday. "You've heard about the conference? About Taiwan?"

"Yes, what are you, the ambassador of Eritrea?"

"I'm here with the American delegation," Zula said. "Csongor, here, is with the Hungarians and—"

"Ivan Ivanovich," said Sokolov, with a courtly nod.

"Ivan is with the Russians. We have a couple of days off and so we are just—"

"Chillin'?"

"Yes. Chillin'."

"Is one of these guys your boyfriend?"

"No. Why?"

Qian Yuxia gave Zula a playful backhanded slap on the arm, as if to chide her for being a slow pupil. "I want to know if it is cool to flirt with them!"

"Sure, go ahead!" Zula had been kind of assuming that Qian Yuxia was a dyke. Maybe she wasn't. Or maybe she was a dyke who found it amusing to flirt with heterosexual males.

"Your hotel doesn't have Internet!?"

"Of course it does." Which did not answer the implicit question. "Csongor is such a nerd that he can't go a whole hour without checking his email."

"Hmm. Well, here is a place."

Yuxia had led them across an intersection and down a side street lined with little shops. Next to one of these, a stairway led up and into the interior of a building. It was unmarked except for an old piece of World of Warcraft paraphernalia, the head of a creature called a Tauren, pasted to the wall. Like a medieval tavern sign, almost.

They paused there for a moment.

"They are called stairs," said Qian Yuxia.

YESTERDAY IT HAD seemed as though they were harvesting an impressively large number of IP addresses and latitude/longitude pairs. When Csongor had actually produced a map of these, though, and overlaid it on an image of Xiamen, it had looked discouraging: their data somehow managed to be sparse and clumpy at the same time. A few trends had been evident, though, and had given them reason to believe that the IP address still written in fading ink on Sokolov's hand was assigned to an access point, not way out in the suburbs, not near the university, and not even in one of the more far-flung parts of the island, but within a kilometer or two of the safe house.

They could probably see the Troll's building from their window. Which was a little bit like saying that you could see Earth from the moon. But it was a kind of progress.

The general plan for today, then, was to visit all the Internet cafés they could find that lay in the general zone of interest, and try to get some finer-grained data.

While making this plan in the presence, and under the close supervision, of Ivanov, they had all spoken confidently of Internet cafés, as if it were a subject on which they were knowledgeable. And why not? They were hackers; they were from Seattle; Peter's loft was all of about a mile from the world headquarters of Starbucks, an organization that had shotgunned the planet with coffee bars featuring Wi-Fi.

They had, in other words, been assuming three things of Chinese Internet cafés: (1) that they were all over the place, (2) that they were easy to find, and (3) that they served coffee; that is, that they were literally cafés, as in small cozy places where customers could curl up with a laptop to check their email.

The pathetic naïveté and Seattle-centrism of these assumptions had already begun to infiltrate Zula's awareness but clobbered her in the teeth as she followed Qian Yuxia to the top of the stairs. The helpful strangers who had been giving them useless directions always seemed to be saying that the Internet café was "upstairs of" or "in the back of" such-and-such a business, and this had given Zula the idea that they were talking about tiny backroom enterprises.

Now she understood that these business *had* to be upstairs of, or in the back of, other enterprises *because they were so enormous*. This one occupied an entire floor of the building. Brand-new PCs with flat-panel screens were packed in together as tightly as the laws of thermodynamics would allow, and essentially all of them were in use. There were at least a hundred people in here, all wearing headphones and therefore weirdly silent.

"Holy Jesus," Csongor said.

"What?" asked Yuxia.

"It is ten times as big as the biggest one we have ever seen," Zula explained.

"This is only half of it," said Yuxia, nodding toward another stair that led up to an additional story. "How many you want?"

"I beg your pardon?"

"How many of you want to use computer?"

"One," said Zula, "unless—?" She looked at Sokolov, who had been staring at more decorative swag posted on the wall. It was one of a series of promotional posters that Corporation 9592's marketing department had produced shortly after the launch of the game, when they were making a ferocious effort to steal customers away from World of Warcraft. They were fake travel posters, rendered in photorealistic detail. This particular one showed a Dwinn perched on a boulder at the edge of a pristine mountain lake, fishing rod in hand, battling it out with a toothy, prehistoric-looking beast that could be seen breaching from the surface in the middle distance with a lure hooked through its lip. The real purpose of the poster had been to show off the incredible realism of Pluto's landform-generating software, which was on spectacular display in the mountain slopes on the far side of the lake. But the riggers and animators, not to be outdone, had lavished a lot of time and energy on getting the Dwinn's posture exactly right: leaning back against the tension on the line, one foot planted, the other just coming up off the ground. It was as good, for Zula, as seeing a snapshot of home and hit her hard; she'd not been ready for it here.

Conveniently, Sokolov chose this of all moments to wax talkative. He slowly turned his head to gaze at Zula, then Yuxia. "Maybe I google fishing equipment store."

Zula was still contending with a sizable knot in her throat, and Yuxia had no idea what to make of Sokolov.

"Fishing," Sokolov repeated, nodding at the poster and pantomiming a cast and a reel-in. "My boss wants to go fishing. But we did not bring matériel."

"When?" Yuxia asked.

Sokolov shrugged. "Maybe tomorrow. Maybe next day. Depends. But today I could be getting equipment. Need to google store."

"That's not going to work," Yuxia said, "if you can't read Chinese."

"Need help then. Need to buy special hats. Little iceboxes. Case for rod." He shrugged. "Usual."

Yuxia turned away and approached the front counter of the *wangba,* which was a pretty sizable installation in its own right, spanning about twenty feet and sporting two tills. The wall behind it was filled with a couple of glass-fronted refrigerator cases, jammed with beverages, and some shelves stocked with instant dried noodle bowls, sealed with disks of foil and printed all over in eye-grabbing colors. Behind the counter were three people: two employees, both men in their twenties, and one Public Security Bureau officer in his light blue shirt, necktie, and dark slacks. The latter was seated with his back to them and was paying attention to a pair of flat-panel screens subdivided into four panes each. Zula assumed that these were showing security camera footage, but on a second look she saw that each one of them was showing a half-size image of a computer screen. Some of those were displaying windowed user interfaces, such as a person might use to surf the web or check Facebook, but most were running video games. Each pane changed every few seconds.

She looked at Csongor, who had become fixated on the same

thing. He turned to look at her. Their eyes met and they both laughed.

"What is funny?" Sokolov asked.

Csongor turned to him. "This guy is looking over everyone's shoulder," he said. "Making sure they don't look at porn, or whatever."

Sokolov got it but didn't see the humor.

Qian Yuxia had in the meantime stomped up to the counter and addressed one of the employees in the style of a drill sergeant greeting a trainee who had showed up drunk and disheveled. The employee, for his part, began and ended the conversation by looking her carefully up and down, which confirmed in Zula's mind that Yuxia was a bit of an unusual customer, and yet not wholly unprecedented. The PSB officer turned away from his screens long enough to examine the three Westerners, then glanced at Yuxia, then turned back to the screens. Apparently being a Westerner wasn't such a big deal if you had a Chinese minder to lead you around; it was the unaccompanied and clueless Westerners who drew all the attention.

Some kind of transaction took place. Yuxia summoned Sokolov forward with a snap of the fingers and compelled him to produce money, which disappeared into the till. The employee handed over two strips of paper with alphanumeric strings printed on them: user IDs and passwords.

They proceeded into the main floor of the *wangba*, which reminded Zula of the part of a casino where the slot machines are lined up, except without the noise: densely packed humans in a dark, low-ceilinged room, sitting on identical chairs and focused on machines. And indeed the slot machine comparison was not a bad one in that most of these people were playing video games. A few of them were playing World of Warcraft, Counterstrike, and Aoba Jianghu, which was the all-Chinese game that Nolan Xu had created prior to cofounding Corporation 9592 and that lived on in the *wangba* world as an oldie but goodie, frequently imitated, always pirated (its copy protection scheme had been annihilated twenty-two hours after its release), never equaled. But the clear majority of them were playing T'Rain, which meant that most of them were here for business and not pleasure. Zula had enough experience with the game by this point that she could identify, at a glance, most of the landscapes and situations that passed beneath her eye as she followed Yuxia down an aisle toward the stairway. Taking in a longer view of the *wangba,* she saw just a few heads that had popped up, gopher style, above the low half walls that separated one row of workstations from the next. Some of these were young men slurping noodles from bowls and watching their friends play games, but she also saw another PSB officer making his rounds.

The next floor up was a repeat of the first, with more terminals vacant. A third PSB officer was stationed here, sitting on a chair at the top of the stairs, drinking tea from a big glass thermos and bored out of his mind. Csongor sat down at one terminal and Sokolov sat at the next. Csongor pretended to check his email while Yuxia helped Sokolov search for fishing gear providers in downtown Xiamen.

Once Csongor was logged on to a computer it took him only a few moments to establish its IP address and a few moments more to snoop around the local network getting an idea of what IP addresses might be assigned to neighboring machines. So "checking his email" took only a few seconds, and then he was logged off and ready to go. He walked toward Zula, breaking stride as soon as he got within about a meter of her, and then turned sideways. For he had not approached her to talk, or for any reason other than to be in her presence. This had become his habit. Zula had grown accustomed to it. She felt better when he was there, just on the edge of her personal space. It appeared that he felt better there too.

Sokolov had taken some phone pictures of fishermen traipsing out of a ferry terminal yesterday afternoon and showed them to Yuxia, zooming in on their heads and urging her to get a load of their hats. They were the most retarded-looking hats Zula had ever seen, and she didn't believe for a moment that Sokolov wanted to go fishing. He had some other plan in mind and had realized on the spur of the moment that Yuxia could help him with it.

The somewhat comforting feeling she got from Csongor's proximity was now wrecked by a sort of icicle-through-the-heart sensation as she realized that Yuxia was about to get tangled up in this. And that was at least partly Zula's fault.

Yuxia and Sokolov finished their business and logged off. "We go to buy hats," Sokolov announced, and then he stood to one side, as was his habit, waiting for the ladies to go first.

. . . .

YUXIA WAS GOING to make finding *wangbas* a million times easier, but there was a price to be paid, which was that they could not simply go straight from one to the next while maintaining the pretext that they were only doing it so that Csongor could check his email. No one needed to check his email that frequently; and if he did, it would be easier to just hang out in one *wangba* rather than flitting from one to the next.

Sokolov's plan—whatever the hell it was—concerning the fishing equipment helped to solve this problem. For they devoted about forty-five minutes now to walking to a store where it was possible to buy the goofy-looking cloth hats favored by septuagenarian Chinese anglers. During the walk, Zula got to know Yuxia a little better. In fact, she pestered Yuxia with questions, because she was a little bit nervous that Yuxia might start asking *her* questions that, given the circumstances, would be difficult to answer. The script that they were working from was flimsy and would not stand up to scrutiny from the lively mind of Qian Yuxia.

She learned that Yuxia lived in a town up in Yongding that was something of a tourist attraction because of its *tulou*: huge round fortresslike buildings of rammed earth, constructed centuries ago by the Hakka people. Most of the tourists were Chinese who came up in buses from Xiamen. But the place did attract some Western travelers, mostly backpacker types, and so during the tourist season she worked for a hotel that catered to such people. She hung around at the bus station and wandered about the main tourist game trails, and when she saw Westerners who looked lost, she greeted them, talked to them, and steered them to the hotel. She drove them around the region in a van so that they could see some of the off-the-beaten-track *tulou*s. That, and watching movies, and reading books left at the hotel by the backpackers, was how she had learned her English. During the off-season she drove the van to the distant outskirts of Xiamen and made arrangements to park it somewhere, then rode the bus into Xiamen, stayed at a hostel, and plied her trade as an itinerant tea merchant. Mostly this was a matter of wholesaling tea to established retail shops, but she was not above approaching end users directly, as she'd done yesterday with Zula.

That got them as far as the hat shop, where Sokolov purchased an even dozen of the shapeless hats that he wanted. Then it was time for Csongor to "check his email" again. So they found another *wangba* and Csongor did that while Zula slurped noodles and Yuxia helped Sokolov find a store that traded in rod-and-reel cases.

Then they repeated the cycle: they set out on foot to a place where Sokolov was able to purchase some rod-and-reel cases, and then they found the nearest *wangba* so that Csongor could "check his email" yet again.

Zula asked Yuxia what a Hakka was and learned that they were the only Chinese who had refused to take up the practice of foot binding. So "Big-Footed Woman" was not just a throwaway line. Not only that, but they would buy the unwanted female children of their Cantonese-speaking neighbors and raise them. Yuxia was not the type to deploy terminology like "feminist" or "matriarchal," but the picture was clear enough to Zula. She was able to draw comparisons to her early years being raised by Marxist-feminist teachers in caves in Eritrea, which provided a safe topic for time-consuming chitchat as they wandered about in the streets.

This third *wangba* was on the top story of a four-story commercial building that fronted on a side street, perhaps wide enough to carry a car going in each direction if uncomplicated by pedestrians, bicyclists, or carters. It was a bit smaller than the first two they'd visited and had a younger clientele and a somewhat seedier vibe about it. There was a single PSB officer stationed at the entrance, but he didn't have the high-tech system for monitoring what was shown on the customers' terminals. A few mirrors were planted about the place, theoretically making it possible for him to look over people's shoulders, but in order for it to work, he would have to care and he would have to look up from his glossy magazine (in Chinese, but exclusively concerned with the personnel and doings of the National Basketball Association), neither of which obtained. This *wangba* was considerably louder, not with music or with game sound tracks but with conversation. As they perceived after they paid their way in, the hubbub all emanated from one corner, where a dozen or so teenagers had locked down a cluster of terminals and were playing a game together, looking over each other's shoulders and calling out warnings, orders, encouragement, mockery, and wails of despair.

As usual, Csongor went to one terminal while Yuxia and Soko-lov went to another. Zula drifted over toward the corner where the young men were all playing. As soon as their screens came into view she recognized that they were playing T'Rain. The style in which they were communicating told her that they must all be part of a raiding party going on an adventure together; their characters were all in the same place in the T'Rain world, probably conducting a dungeon raid or fighting it out with a rival gang, and so a warrior might be calling out to a priest that he needed to be healed or a mage might be requesting protection from a menacing beast while he cast his spells. It was a common enough play style.

She could tell that they were badass. This was confirmed when she got into position for a better look at their characters: massively powerful and expensively equipped.

The landscape in which they were fighting looked strikingly familiar.

It was the Torgai Foothills.

They were fighting near the ley line intersection with the tre-buchets.

She became aware, suddenly, that she had been watching for a few minutes and that Sokolov was right next to her, close enough that she could sense his warmth. He'd read the look on her face, come over to see what had transfixed her.

Feeling suddenly conspicuous, she turned away and walked back toward where Csongor was sitting. He was looking aghast at the screen of his terminal.

"What is going down?" Qian Yuxia wanted to know. "What is you guys' problem?"

Sokolov turned to look at her. "Tomorrow we go fishing," he announced. "Need iceboxes."

HALF AN HOUR later Zula was chained to a sink in the women's bathroom at the safe house.

When Sokolov had understood that the young men in the cor-ner were in league with the Troll—that one of them might even *be* the Troll—when Csongor had beckoned him over and shown him an IP address on his screen that matched the one written on Sokolov's hand—the Russian had acted with a combination of extreme dispatch and perfect calm that in other circumstances Zula would have admired. He had made a phone call. A few minutes later he had escorted Zula out to the street just as a taxi containing four security consultants had pulled up. One of these had remained in the taxi, and the others had stood around Zula in a manner that was not overtly threatening but that made it obvious she had no choice but to climb into the backseat. A few minutes later she and the security consultant were in the parking garage of the skyscraper, and a minute after that they were in the ladies' room. The Russians, tired of escorting her to the bathroom and waiting in a stall, had somehow procured a length of chain about twenty feet long and padlocked one end of it to the U-bend of a drain trap beneath one of the sinks. The other end of the chain had a handcuff locked onto it, which ended up snapped around Zula's ankle. Her luggage and her sleeping bag had already been deposited on the floor, along with a stack of rations, a modest heap of junk food, and a roll of paper towels. She had enough slack to reach the toilet, and she could get water from the sink. What more could a girl ask for?

This was the one time that she just went out of her mind crying. Fetal position, head banging on the floor. It was being chained that did it. She'd been through a lot of weird stuff, but no one had ever thought to chain her before.

Eventually she came up onto her hands and knees and made use of the paper towels.

Then she escaped.

During college she'd rented a house with some other girls. The kitchen drain kept getting clogged. They didn't have money to hire a plumber. Zula had not grown up on an Iowa farm for nothing. The key thing you had to know was that the pipe nuts that held drain traps in place, though they looked huge and immovable, were generally applied finger-tight, since all that was necessary was to compress an internal O-ring around the pipe, and cranking it down with a wrench would not make it seal any better, in fact would only inflict damage.

The plumber who had installed the drain trap to which Zula had been chained had stronger hands than Zula did, but she was eventually able to move the nuts and yank out the U-bend.

She piled the loose chain into her shoulder bag and then slung that over her shoulder.

She then climbed up on a toilet and from there to the top of one of the partitions between the stalls and moved a ceiling tile aside. She had a flashlight in her bag—another Iowa-farm-girl residual habit—and used it to look around for whatever it was that had made Sokolov so concerned when he had first seen it.

This was not totally obvious at first, and so she clambered up into the space above the ceiling and got a grip on one of those zig-zaggy trusses and used it to crab-walk away from the safe house and toward the core of the building. The elevator shafts were nearby, but they were clad in concrete and there was no obvious way to get inside of them; even if she had been able to do so, it wasn't clear how that would have helped her.

When she was certain that she must have passed beyond the limits of the ladies' room, she reached down, pried up a ceiling tile, and looked into the space below. It seemed to be a utility corridor, dark at the moment.

She let herself down onto the upper surface of the metal grid in which the ceiling tiles were fixed. This supported her weight but was destroyed in the process: the flimsy extrusions bent downward and the adjoining tiles folded and cracked. It didn't matter. She got a grip on the ruined grid and let herself down until her feet were dangling maybe three feet above the floor, then let herself drop.

As she had guessed from looking at the arrangement of the concrete verticals passing through the ceiling space, the fire stairway was just on the other side of a wall, and all she had to do, in order to get into it, was to exit from this corridor into the elevator lobby and then pass through an adjoining door. During those few moments she would be in clear view of any guard who was posted at the reception desk of the safe house—but she knew that at least four of the seven security consultants were deployed outside the building, and she hoped that the desk might be unattended. It was easy enough to check this by pushing the door open slightly and peering through the crack.

No one was there. Deeper inside the suite she could see other security consultants pacing around, talking on phones, ransacking their luggage, but no one was looking out into the elevator lobby.

She exited, made two strides across the polished marble floor, opened the doorway to the fire stairs, and slipped in. Restraining the urge to just make a break for it, she used her butt to soften the closure of the door. Then she began to descend the stairway as fast as she could with twenty pounds of chain jangling in the bag around her neck and one end of it cuffed to her ankle.

The descent of forty-three floors gave her plenty of time to think about this in a way she hadn't when she had just made the decision to do it. To the extent she'd thought about it at all, she had been thinking, *What would Qian Yuxia do?* or perhaps, *What would Qian Yuxia think of me if she could see me curled up on the floor sobbing like a little girl?*

Until now her complicity in all of this had been based on a certain kind of unspoken bargain that had been struck between her and Ivanov, a bargain that amounted to "we are treating you badly and will probably kill you but we could treat you a lot worse and we could kill you sooner." Not much of a bargain, but then she hadn't had much choice in negotiating the terms. The way she had been sucked into this terrible situation was bad enough, but the thought that she was now partly responsible for getting Yuxia ensnared in it too was intolerable.

In theory, Peter was being held hostage and might be answerable for her escape, but she doubted it. Peter had gone over to the other side. He was being useful to them. Killing him wouldn't get her back. And as for Csongor—she hoped nothing bad would happen to Csongor, but she was also entitled to think of herself and her own survival.

Which was all she was thinking of when she hit the bottom of the stairwell, rounded a corner at speed, and caromed off a man who was standing right there for some reason. She spun away from him instinctively. He grabbed at her but had to settle for her shoulder bag. She left it in his grasp and kept running, the chain dragging out behind her as it uncoiled from the bag.

Then her leg was yanked out from under her, spinning her back and around as she fell so that, as she went down on the concrete floor, she could see a man standing twenty feet away, holding her empty shoulder bag, one foot stomped down on the end of the chain.

Sokolov.

He picked up the end of the chain. With his free hand he then made a one-word call on his mobile phone.

And then back up to the ladies' room where the chain was detached from Sokolov, passed up into the ceiling space, and padlocked around a cast-iron pipe six inches in diameter.

RICHARD WAS IN the hammerbeam hall of a red sandstone castle on the Isle of Man, being announced by D-squared's herald in a language that sounded vaguely French.

Once again his arrival had been unexpected (though not, as it turned out, unheralded). This time, the element of surprise was down to a backup that had developed in D-squared's email pipeline. Don Donald used email when he was at Cambridge and when he was traveling, but he had banned Internet in his castle, and even installed a phone jammer in the dovecote. He came here to read, to write, to drink, to dine, and to have conversations, none of which activities could be improved by electronic devices. And yet he had this awkward problem that much of his livelihood was derived from T'Rain. And even though he did not play the game himself, professing to find the very ideal "frightful," he couldn't really ply that trade without communicating rather frequently with people at Corporation 9592.

Richard had once looked D-squared up on Wikipedia and learned that he was a laird or an archduke or something. This castle, however, was not his ancestral demesne. He had bought it, cash on the barrelhead. At first his staff had made use of a trailer parked outside its south bastion, placed there to serve as a portable office for the contractors who were fixing the place up. It was equipped with Internet and a laser printer on which emails that merited the attention of the lord of the manor could be printed up on A4 paper and conducted into the donjon in a leather wallet. Later the white paper was discontinued in favor of light brown pseudoparchment. This was a simple matter of taste. Modern paper, with its eye-searing 95 percent albedo, simply ruined the look that was slowly coming together inside the walls. The sans-serif typefaces were swapped out for faux-ancient ones. But it was not as if a man of Donald Cameron's erudition could be taken in by a scripty-looking typeface chosen by an assistant from Word's mile-long font menu. And the style and content of these messages from Seattle were every bit as jarring as the paper they were printed on. A medievalist, he quite liked being in a medieval frame of mind; in fact, *had* to be, in order to write. Sitting in his tower "with prospects, on a fair day, west to Donaghadee and north to Cairngaan," writing with a dip pen at a thousand-year-old desk, he entered into a flow state whose productivity was rivaled only by that of Devin Skraelin. Suddenly to be confronted by a hard copy of an email in which a twenty-four-year-old Seattleite with a nose ring wrote something like "we r totally stressing out cuz chapter 27 is not resonating with 16 yo gamer demographic" was, to say the least, inimical to progress. Some way needed to be devised for important communications to get through to him without disturbing the requisite ambience.

Fortunately he had, without really trying, attracted a coterie of people who, depending on the point of view of the observer, might have been described as hangers-on, lackeys, squatters, parasites, or acolytes. They were of divers ages and backgrounds, but all of them shared D-squared's fascination with the medieval. Some were blue-collar autodidacts who had made their way up through the ranks of the Society for Creative Anachronism, and others had multiple Ph.D.s and were fluent in extinct dialects. They had begun to show up at his doorstep, or rather his portcullis, when word had got out that he was considering the possibility of turning some parts of the castle into a reenactment site as a way to generate a bit of coin and to keep the castle from falling victim to the subtle but annihilating hazards of desuetude. In those days the plan had been to maintain a sort of firewall between the part of the manor where he lived and the part where the reenactment was to happen. But a few years' experience had taught him that as long as one paid a bit of attention to weeding out the drunks and the mental defectives, the sorts of people who were willing to live in medieval style 24/7 were just the ones he needed to have around.

As easy and as tempting as it was to have some fun at the expense of D-squared and his band of medievalists, Richard had to admit that several of them were as serious and dedicated and competent as anyone he'd ever worked with in twenty-first-century settings; and in some very enjoyable conversations shared over mead or ale (brewed on-site, of course) they had managed to convince him that the medieval world wasn't worse or more primitive than the modern, just different.

And so the email pipeline now worked like this: down in Douglas, which was the primary city of the Isle of Man, the girlfriend of one of the medievalists, who dwelled in a flat there ("I happen to rather *like* tampons"), would read D-squared's email as it came in, filter out the obvious junk, and print out a hard copy of anything that seemed important, and zip it up in a waterproof messenger bag. When it came time to walk her dog, she would stroll up the waterfront promenade until she reached the wee elven train station at its northern end, where she would hand the bag to the station agent, who would later hand it over to the conductor of the narrow-gauge electrical train that wound its way from there up into the interior of the island. At a certain point along the line it would be tossed out onto the siding and later picked up by D-squared's gamekeeper, who would carry it up the hill and place its contents on the desk of the in-house troubadour, who would translate it into medieval Occitan and then sing and/or recite it to D-squared at mealtime. The lord of the manor would then dictate a response that would follow the reverse route back down the hill to the girlfriend's laptop and the Internet.

Ludicrous? Yes. All done with a straight face? Of course not. Having taken a few meals there, Richard could tell, from the reactions of those present—at least, the ones who understood Occitan— that the troubadour was a laff riot. Much of the laughter seemed to be at the expense of American cubicle fauna who thought in Power-Point and typed with their thumbs, and so Richard was now careful to phrase all his emails to Don Donald in such a way as to make it clear that he was on to the joke.

The one in which he'd announced his imminent arrival at IOM was still being translated.

And yet for Don Donald to receive a surprise visit was much less of a problem than it was for Skeletor. This was the medieval world. Communications were miserable. *Most* visits were surprise visits. As long as the visitors didn't have poleaxes or buboes, it was fine. There was plenty of room in the castle, and there were buffers in place, which was to say, servant-reenactors, who made Richard and Pluto comfortable as word percolated inward to the donjon.

When D-squared next descended his perilous, zillion-year-old stone spiral staircase to the hall to take a meal, Richard and Pluto were announced, courteously and a bit pompously, by the herald—actually (since the place was a bit understaffed) a man who shuttled among the roles of Herald, Brewer, and Third Drunk.

"THERE MIGHT BE a need to confer extraordinary powers upon the Earthtone Coalition," Richard proposed.

Don Donald leaned back in his chair and began messing around with his pipe. When Richard had been a boy, all men had smoked pipes. Now, as far as he could discern, D-squared was the only pipe smoker remaining in the entire world.

"To keep them from being wiped out, you're saying."

"Yes."

"How could such a thing be done," D-squared wondered, biting his pipe stem and squinting at something above Richard's right shoulder, "without ratifying an invidious distinction?"

"Are you speaking Occitan? Because I have to tell you that between the jet lag and the delicious claret—"

"There is no basis in the game world," said D-squared, "for any of what has happened during the last four months. Town guards, military units, raiding parties fissured, without warning, into two moieties, at daggers drawn. Or perhaps I should say *dagger* drawn since, if the reports I've heard are to be credited, a good many of what you call the Earthtone Coalition found themselves suddenly and inexplicably in Limbo with particolored bodkins in their backs."

"There's no doubt it was a well-planned Pearl Harbor–ish kind of event," Richard said.

"And many of your customers appear to be having great fun with it. Bully for them. But it poses a problem, doesn't it, in that this extraordinary fission of the society is in no way justified, prefigured, even hinted at, in any of the Canon that Mr. Skraelin and I and the other writers have supplied."

D-squared's feelings were hurt, and he didn't care who knew it. He went on, "I daresay you ought to just roll it back. It is really a hack, isn't it? As though someone hacked into your website and defaced it with childish scrawlings. When such a thing happens, you don't incorporate the vandalism into your website. You set it to rights and carry on."

"Too much has happened," Richard said. "Since the beginning of the Wor we have registered a quarter of a million new players. Everything they know about the world and the game has been post-Wor. To roll the world back would be to unmake every single one of their characters."

"So your strategy is to put your thumb on the scale. Grant special powers to the characters you'd see win. Like Athena with Diomedes."

Richard shrugged. "It's an idea. I am not here to lay stuff on you ex cathedra. This is a collaboration."

"All I mean to say is that, if you help the Earthtone Coalition, then you are, implicitly, admitting that such a thing as the Earthtone Coalition exists. You are conferring legitimacy on this ridiculous distinction that has been created by mischief makers."

"It was a groundswell. An enormous flocking behavior, a phase transition."

"No respect shown for the integrity of the world."

"All we can do," Richard said, "is move faster than the other guys. Lunge ahead of them. Surprise them with just how cool, how adaptable we can be. Delight them by incorporating their creation into the Canon. Show them what we're made of."

"Well *that* puts me on the spot, doesn't it? How can I decline, on those terms?"

"I apologize for my choice of words," Richard said. "I am really not trying to corner you. But I do believe that with a bit of thought you could actually come up with something that you would not be so unhappy with."

Don Donald looked like he was thinking about it.

"Otherwise, it's just going to veer. Like an airplane with its control surfaces shot off."

"Oh. I'm the empennage?"

Richard threw up his hands.

"The tail feathers on the arrow," explained D-squared, "that make it fly straight. Made of quills. Like the ones—"

"That writers used to write with, I get it."

"Trailing behind . . ."

"But guiding the warhead. Yup. Hey, are you a writer or something?"

D-squared chuckled forcibly.

"They want it," Richard said. "They didn't at first. They were thrilled to be off on their own, making up their own story."

"The players, you mean."

"Yes. This was very clear in the chat rooms, the third-party websites. Now that's faded. They're saying they want some direction back, they want the story of the world to make sense again."

Something occurred to Don Donald, and he jabbed the stem of his pipe at Richard. "What language do they speak, in these chat rooms? Is it all English?"

"Why do you ask?"

"I'd like to know who these people are. The instigators, the ringleaders. Are they Asians?"

"That is a common misconception," Richard said. "That the Asians, less fluent in English, less conversant with European mythology, don't cotton to the sorts of stories and characters that you like to write—but they are attracted by bright colors." He shook his head. "We have analyzed this to death. It's completely without foundation. Between the Chinese, with their Confucian background, and the Japanese, they are second to no one in their respect and maybe even awe for COBS."

"COBS?"

"Crusty Old Brown Stuff. Sorry."

"Another one of your internal acronyms?"

"A whole department. When you go into the world—which you never do—but when you go, for example, to the hut of Galdoromin the Hermit, at the End of the Fell Path, and get past his two-headed wolf and go inside and look around, all that shit hanging on the walls was produced by COBS." Richard decided not to share the fact that the decor of Galdoromin's hut had been inspired by a T.G.I. Friday's in Issaquah. "Top-level design happens in Seattle, but the detailed modeling of the actual stuff all happened in China. They did a great job of it too."

Don Donald appeared to be thinking about it. Richard tried shutting up for a change. He drained his tankard and stepped out to the garderobe. Then, back with an idea: "I was sleeping on the plane and a line came into my head: 'We've all been made fools of!' Kind of reflected the whole way I felt about the Wor. But later I was thinking, *Why not turn it around and put it into the mouths of those people we find most annoying?*"

D-squared, sitting in profile to Richard, one elbow on the table cradling his pipe, turned to meet his eye. The pipe, supported by the hand, remained motionless, making it look as though cartoon character physics was in effect. "Make them out to be the dupes?"

"Yes, erect some kind of backstory where they had been seduced into this massive act of betrayal by fast talkers of some stripe who later turned out to be not what they seemed."

"What about the blue hair?"

"We might have to finesse that a little, but the gist of it is that the people who signed up for this rebellion were told to wear gaudy clothes and adornments as a badge, so that they would know who was in on the conspiracy."

"'We've all been made fools of!'" the Don repeated. "Seems almost like sour grapes, doesn't it, when you put it into the mouths of people you're not especially fond of."

"Again. Finesse."

"What sorts of emergency powers might you be willing to put in the hands of the—it pains me, Richard, to hear these words coming from my own lips—Earthtone Coalition?"

"A full answer could get obnoxiously technical. The game stats are very complicated. So, if we wanted to be sneaky about it, there are all sorts of ways we could put our thumb on the scale, as you said earlier. Or we could just be obvious about it and invoke some new deity or previously unknown deep feature of the world's history."

"Which would need to be written."

"Which would need to be written."

Day 4

A side effect of being chained in the powder room was being out of the loop. Zula had no idea what was going on. She ate her military rations and slept surprisingly well and woke up in good spirits. Not that her situation had improved. But at least she had tried something. She could hear people coming and going via the elevators. Since she had no windows, no phone, and no watch, she couldn't tell what time it was.

She had managed to sneak a ballpoint pen into her pocket yesterday, so she wrote a letter to her family on paper towels, rolled it up, and stuffed it into the drainpipe she had disconnected yesterday. Maybe some plumber would see it when he came to fix the drain, and bring it to the attention of a supervisor, and eventually it would make its way to someone who could read English. She hoped so. She was proud of that letter. It was not devoid of humor.

Sokolov knocked once, then entered the ladies' room and bid her good morning. He removed the handcuff from her ankle and escorted her out. "Leaving forever," he said, "bring your stuff."

They took the elevator to the ground floor and walked out the main entrance of the office building onto the front drive, a sweeping horseshoe partially covered by an awning, where a van was waiting for them with its engine idling and its rear doors splayed open. Standing behind it were four of the security consultants, wearing stupid hats, variously smoking or fussing with a stack of plastic coolers and rod-and-reel cases that had been packed in the back. As was invariably the case, they were being observed by a thousand Chinese people and an unknowable number of security cameras. But all the people doing tai chi in the shade of the trees, the uniformed schoolgirls streaming out of the ferry terminals, the taxi drivers killing time in the adjoining square, the paired PSB officers, the carters, the construction workers showing up to work on the skyscraper, all these people just looked at the scene around the van for a few seconds and reckoned that it was a bunch of crazy foreign visitors going fishing.

Peter and Csongor were in the backseat. Qian Yuxia was behind the wheel. Next to her, riding shotgun, was Ivanov, talking to Yuxia in the charming style of which he had exhibited flashes during the interview in Peter's loft in Seattle. They were talking about *gaoshan cha,* high mountain tea, and Ivanov's plan to distribute it in Russia, where he was certain it would be enormously successful.

Zula was strongly encouraged to enter the van by its side door and sit in the back between Peter and Csongor. As she climbed in Yuxia greeted her with, "Good morning, girlfriend, you ready to catch some lunkers?" and Zula nodded back at her, wondering if there was anything she could say at this moment that would persuade Yuxia to put the van in gear and shove the gas pedal all the way to the floor. That would lead to a situation where they were far away from the security consultants but Ivanov would still be in the van with them. It seemed almost inconceivable that he wasn't carrying a weapon of some kind. So what would it boot them unless Yuxia had the presence of mind to drive straight to a Public Security Bureau station and crash its front gates?

"Lots to talk about," Peter remarked, fixing her with a dirty look.

"What the hell is she doing here?" Zula asked Csongor.

"For this operation, a van was necessary," Csongor said. "When Ivanov heard about Yuxia, he said, 'She's perfect, give me her phone number,' and then he called her and talked her into this."

"Okay." Zula said, not in the sense of *I accept this* but rather *I see how horrible this is.* She had a fretful feeling, now, of having missed a hell of a lot during her captivity in the ladies' room. "But yesterday—what happened?"

"After Sokolov put you in the taxi at the *wangba,* he told Yuxia that it was time to buy ice chests now, and so the two of them left." Csongor paused, maybe looking for a way to say the next part diplomatically. "I think it was on his way back from that errand that he ran into you."

"Actually, I ran into him," Zula said, "but go on."

"What was that about anyway?" Peter demanded. "You could have gotten us killed!"

A new thing happened now, which was that Csongor torqued his great barrel-shaped torso toward Zula and leaned forward so that he could get a clear view of Peter. He braced one hand against the seat in front of him. The other he let fall on the top of the seat close to Zula's head, carefully not touching her but making her feel half enveloped. He fixed Peter with a gaze that Zula would have found intimidating had it been aimed at her. Csongor's head seemed as big as a basketball and his eyes were wide open and unblinking and aimed at Peter's face as if connected by steel guy wires. "It was about her having her shit together," Csongor said.

"But the Russians—" Peter began, shocked by the sudden turn in Csongor's personality.

"The Russians loved it," Csongor said flatly. Then, looking at Zula: "They were talking about you half the evening. You can be sure there are no hard feelings on their account. Or on mine."

"What about *him,* though!?" Peter demanded, with a glance up at Ivanov. "His are the only feelings we have to worry about."

"I'm not so sure that is the case—"

Zula held up both hands between them, then made the fists-crashing-together gesture again. "Let's go back to the *wangba* if you don't mind, since I know nothing."

"Okay," Csongor said. "The other Russians came upstairs and hung around with me for a while and kept an eye on the T'Rain players you spotted. We were there for *six hours* watching those guys. It became sort of obvious that one of them was the boss. Tall guy, a little older than the others, in a Manu jersey."

"Manu jersey?"

"Manu Ginobili," Peter said, almost angry that Zula did not understand the reference. "He plays for the Spurs."

"Manu, as we called him, never played T'Rain himself, he didn't get into it emotionally, just watched what was going on and talked on his phone constantly and told the other guys where they should send their characters and what they should do. So one of those guys"— Csongor pointed with his chin at the security consultants behind the van—"went down to the street and kept hailing taxis until he got one whose driver spoke a little bit of English. He handed the driver a stack of money and said, 'You can keep this if you help me.' And what he told the driver was that they were going to sit there for a while, possibly all night long, but that eventually a kid in a Manu jersey was going to emerge and then they were going to follow him."

"I've never heard of Manu Ginobili," Zula said. "Is he really such a common cultural referent that—"

"Yes," said Peter and Csongor in unison.

"So," Csongor continued, "after another few hours, Manu came out of the *wangba,* and the taxi driver followed him into one of those backstreet neighborhoods and Manu went into a certain building. The Russian and the taxi driver stayed there for another couple of hours, just watching the building, and Manu didn't come out again. But later we did see him up on the roof shooting hoops with some other young men."

"There's a basketball court on the roof?"

"Not a court," Peter said, again fuming over what he saw as an inane question. "Just a hoop! We can see it clearly from the safe house."

"Really?"

"Really. It is all of half a mile from here, as the crow flies."

"We can look right down on it. We were up half the night watching them through binoculars," Csongor said.

"So it's an office building? Apartments?" Zula asked.

"Strictly apartments," Csongor said.

"A dump," said Peter. "Half the block is vacant."

"How can anything be vacant in this town?"

"One block away is a construction site," Csongor said. "The area is under development. The building and the ones around it are probably going to be demolished within a year."

"The taxi driver was extremely helpful once he saw the wad of cash," Peter said. "He got out of the taxi for a smoke, asked around on the street a little bit, learned some more about the building."

"And?"

"And it has kind of a seedy reputation. The landlord can't write long-term leases in a building that he's itching to tear down. But he hates leaving money on the table. So he rents on a month-to-month basis to anyone who's willing to pay in cash, no questions asked."

"I get the picture," Zula said.

"So, as an example, there are various foreign tenants," Csongor said.

"Like Filipinos?"

"No," Csongor said with a laugh, "*internal* foreigners."

"What does that mean?"

"Chinese people who come from parts of China that are so far away and so different that they might as well be foreign countries."

"Economic migrants," Peter said. "Their equivalent of Mexicans."

"Okay," Zula said, "but Manu is not one of those."

"It appears that Manu and a few other young guys are living together in one of the units. We don't know which one," Peter said. "They put up the basketball hoop on the roof. They go up there and hang around drinking beer and smoking and playing ball until all hours."

"With laptops," Csongor said, shaking his head in disbelief.

"Yeah, even at two in the morning they have the laptops going. Their real office is somewhere down below, but they've obviously set up Wi-Fi to the roof."

"So it's believed that the Troll is one of these guys," Zula said, trying to put this all together, "or that maybe they all, collectively, are the Troll. They're running REAMDE out of this apartment. They're having a problem with bandits attacking their victims when they go to the ley line intersection with ransom and so they are paying mostly younger kids to hang out at the *wangba* all day killing the bandits. Manu goes to the *wangba* to oversee them, but he's constantly in touch with the apartment by phone."

"Five minutes after Manu departed from the *wangba*," Csongor said, "another guy showed up *dribbling a basketball* and took his place."

"The bandit-killers work in shifts around the clock," Zula said, translating that.

During the last minute or so, the security consultants had been climbing into the van and taking seats one by one. There weren't enough seats and so one of them ended up sort of wedged into the space between the driver's and passenger's buckets up front. Sokolov slammed the rear doors closed and got in last and claimed a space that had been reserved for him.

"Everyone ready?" Yuxia called out, in a voice that easily penetrated to the back row.

Response was muted but affirmative.

Ivanov looked to the security consultant seated between him and Yuxia, and they exchanged a nod. Ivanov reached out with his left hand and placed it over Yuxia's right hand, clamping it in place on the steering wheel. At the same moment, the security consultant reached forward and slapped a handcuff down over Yuxia's wrist. A moment after that he had snapped the other half of the cuff over the steering wheel. Ivanov removed his hand.

"What the *fuck*!?" Yuxia exclaimed, pulling her hand back, testing the cuff, still convincing herself that this was really happening.

"For your benefit," Ivanov explained.

"*Benefit!?*"

"When there is investigation by PSB, they will see handcuff, see that you had no choice, find you innocent."

"Innocent of *fishing?*"

Ivanov opened his jacket, letting Yuxia see a shoulder holster. "Huntink." He snapped his fingers and Sokolov handed him a map printed, apparently, from Google. It showed a satellite photo of Xiamen with streets superimposed.

"Zula! What is going on, girlfriend?" Yuxia called.

"They kidnapped me," Zula said. "I tried to escape last night and warn you but they caught me. I am sorry you got mixed up in this." She had told herself last night that this would be the last of crying, but tears came freely to her eyes now.

Yuxia caught that detail in the rearview mirror. "I am going to fuck you up, motherfucker!" she told Ivanov.

"Perhaps later," Ivanov said dryly.

"It won't help to talk to him like that, Bigfoot," Zula said.

"We go now," Ivanov said, "and all will be fine at end of day, exception being for Troll." He reached over and shifted the van into drive, then gave Yuxia an expectant look.

"Who is Troll?" Yuxia said in a sullen voice. But she gave it some gas and pulled out onto the waterfront road.

Now that they were in movement toward a destination only half a mile away, a fairly basic question occurred to Zula: "Why are we even being brought along on this? Anyone know?"

"Apparently the building contains something like eighty separate units," Peter said. "Some vacant, some not. These guys don't know which unit the Troll is living in. They can't just go down the hallways kicking in eighty doors; somebody will call the cops."

"That still doesn't answer my question," Zula said.

"They have convinced themselves," Csongor said, "that if the three of us get inside the building, we can determine which unit contains the Troll."

"Why do they believe that?"

"Because we are hackers," Csongor said, "and they have seen movies."

THE DRIVE TOOK a little while; they could have done it faster on foot. Sokolov was in occasional touch with other Russians on his walkie-talkie, which Zula had to assume was some kind of whiz-bang encrypted device, otherwise the PSB would be all over them. Since two of the Russians were missing from the van, she reckoned that Sokolov had sent out an advance party.

Csongor, who had reasonable command of Russian, supplied running translation of the walkie-talkie traffic: "He sent two guys there when it was still dark. They found a way into the building. They have been hanging out in a room in the cellar that no one uses. Accessible by a back entrance. That is where we are going."

Yuxia, following directions from Sokolov, steered them down a street so narrow that both rearview mirrors had to be folded in against the sides of the van, and local residents had to run out into the street to pull caged poultry and large flat baskets of green tea out of their path. After a few agonizingly slow and controversial minutes of this kind of progress, they came athwart of an alley, no wider than a doorway, on their right side. The Russian on the other end of the walkie-talkie connection yelped out a single word. "Stop," Sokolov said.

They opened the right side door of the van. The Russians filed out of it into the alley and made a bucket brigade: Peter reached behind the seat and pulled out coolers and other gear, which he handed forward to Sokolov who tossed them a few feet to one of his men in the alley, and in this fashion the equipment was moved into the building's back entrance. This was impossible to see clearly, back there in the darkness, but seemed to be twenty or thirty feet distant, on the alley's left side. Meanwhile Zula tried to make sense of her surroundings as best she could from twisting around in her seat and craning her neck out the windows.

If the alley to their right was the back entrance, then this street ran along the side of the Troll's building, and they were now parked at its back corner. The ground floor sported some large openings sealed off by grimy steel roll-up doors. Above those were some corrugated metal awnings, holed with rust, that stretched partway across the street above the van and made it impossible for her to see much of the upper stories.

Looking out the windshield, she could see an intersection about fifty feet ahead of them where this side street was crossed by a wider one that was crammed with the usual flow of mostly pedestrian and bicycle traffic. That street seemed to belong to a more well-illuminated part of the universe, and Zula guessed it was because construction was under way on the far side of it: the building across the street was covered with scaffolding and blue tarps, and beyond it was a gaping cavity in the city's fabric where an arcology or something was being thrown up.

That was all Zula could see before Sokolov indicated it was time for them to make themselves useful. Csongor, Zula, and Peter clambered out over a folded-down van seat and exited into the alley. Sokolov closed the side door of the van, then followed them down the alley toward the back entrance. Yuxia, presumably following instructions from Ivanov who was still riding shotgun, pulled forward and out of view.

A minor controversy was under way in the alley, where an old lady was leaning out of her second-floor window hollering some kind of invective down at the Russians. Zula enjoyed a moment's hope that this woman would call the PSB. Sokolov looked up at her for a few moments, then reached into his man-purse, pulled out a half-inch-thick stack of money, let her see it—this shut her up—and then hurled it at her. It shot past her through the window and thumped against something inside. She withdrew her head and closed the window. Sokolov never broke stride.

A half flight of concrete stairs descended into a basement corridor lit by a few bare lightbulbs. The security consultants waved them down a corridor for twenty paces or so, and into a room filled with blue-gray light sifting in through a couple of dirty sidewalk-level windows. This was situated adjacent to the bottom of what Zula guessed was the building's main stairway. It wasn't difficult to see that the building had been designed around a central core that included not only the stairway but all the other stuff that had to run vertically: the plumbing, the power, the sewer lines. So this room was replete with pipes, valves, meters, crazy electrical wiring, and fuse panels. There was no Internet gear—in fact, no post–Second World War technology at all—which was hardly surprising, but did raise the question as to where the REAMDE guys were getting their connectivity. But all the buildings in China were webbed together with improvised wire and so they were probably pirating it from somewhere else.

"Can we go to the roof?" Peter asked.

A scout ascended to the roof and reported back via walkie-talkie that none of the REAMDE boys were hanging out there at the moment. So Peter and Zula, accompanied by Sokolov, climbed six stories to the top of the stairway. Access to the roof had formerly been sealed off by a door, but the lock had been jimmied.

The Troll's terrace consisted of half a dozen plastic injection-molded chairs, a rusty folding table, a basketball hoop held up by a scaffolding made from plumbing parts, a tea service, a plastic tub containing a stack of magazines about the NBA, and an extension cord that trailed across the roof into the stairwell and was patched into the remains of a light fixture.

From that same light fixture, a length of cheap two-strand lamp cable ran up to the roof of the little shack that topped the stairwell, where it disappeared under a plastic bucket held in place with a brick. A blue Ethernet cable also went under that bucket.

Peter got a leg up from Sokolov, vaulted to the top of the shack, squirmed over to the bucket, removed the brick, and tilted it back to reveal a Wi-Fi device, green LEDs twinkling merrily.

The blue Ethernet cable ran from it across the roof to the front of the building, then disappeared through a drain hole in the roughly meter-high parapet. Zula followed the cable to the edge, leaned over the parapet, and peered down. She was now standing near the corner of the building diagonally opposite to where they had exited the van.

Sixty feet below her, she could see the van parked in front of the building's main entrance, blocking traffic and creating controversy.

The blue cable had been tucked in alongside a vertical drain-pipe that ran from the drain hole in the parapet down the front of the building. At some point the cable presumably peeled away from the drainpipe and entered the building through a window or some other opening, and that would mark the location of the Troll's apartment. In a perfect world they would have been able to see that place from this vantage point and immediately pick out the apartment in question, but no such luck; it must be hidden beneath some horizontal feature that was blocking their view. And what with all the balconies, clotheslines, awnings, and external plumbing, there were plenty of those.

Not for the first time, Zula corrected herself: no, it was *good* luck, not bad, that they couldn't figure it out; turning the Troll over to Ivanov would be a *bad* thing. She was a little perturbed by how easy it was for her to get caught up in the excitement of the hunt.

Peter drifted over to her, fixated on the screen of a PDA. "The name Golgaras mean anything to you?"

"It is the name of one of the continents of T'Rain," Zula said.

"How about Atheron?"

"Same."

"I'm picking up four Wi-Fi access points," Peter said. "Two of them are set to the default names and have really weak signals—I'll bet they are in that building across the street. Golgaras is very strong, and Atheron is considerably weaker."

"Try unplugging that Wi-Fi unit under the bucket," Zula suggested, "and see if one of them goes dead."

Peter turned and headed back to the stairwell to try the experiment.

Zula had become interested in a bundle of improvised wiring that joined this building to the one across the street with the scaffolding and the blue tarps. It was connected to the front wall almost directly below her between the fourth and fifth stories. It was not attached at any one point but rather involved with the building through a spreading and ramifying root system. Zula was able to make out a single strand of blue Ethernet cable spiraling lazily around the outside of the bundle: the last piece of wire to have been added.

"Ivanov requests status report," said Sokolov, who had crunched up behind her on the pea gravel. He had plugged an earpiece into his walkie-talkie.

"I think it's in this corner of the building," Zula said. "Below us somewhere. I'm going to guess it's on the fourth or the fifth floor."

Sokolov relayed this into a microphone clipped to his shirt collar.

"Golgaras went dead," Peter reported. "Atheron is still transmitting."

"Meaning?" Sokolov asked.

"We think that they have two WAPs," Peter said. "One up here on the roof and probably one in their apartment."

Sokolov put his hand to his ear and listened, then asked: "Ivanov asks: What is basis for guess of this corner?"

Zula directed his attention to the wire bundle below them. Peter and Sokolov bent over the parapet and saw what she had seen.

"We could narrow it down more," Peter volunteered, "if we could get a look at the building from the front. See where the blue wires enter the structure."

Sokolov relayed that. There was a short pause.

"Fuck," Sokolov said in English, and looked down. On his face, anger was mixed with something like embarrassment.

Zula and Peter followed his gaze and saw Ivanov emerging from the passenger seat of the van. He went around to the side door, opened it up, rummaged around for a minute, and pulled out a pair of binoculars, which he pressed to his face and aimed up their way.

Sokolov recoiled from the parapet and reached out to grab Peter and Zula, but they were already following, dropping down low where they couldn't be seen from the street.

"He is insane," Sokolov said, quite matter-of-factly, as though remarking that Ivanov was 1.8 meters in height. He certainly did not say it in the ironic admiring way that a certain type of young American male might have done. But before he could elaborate on the topic, his eyes went out of focus as he received a transmission from Ivanov.

"We go down now," Sokolov said.

They met Ivanov in the cellar. He had taken a phone picture of what, from his standpoint, had been the upper left quadrant of the building's façade. Of course the screen of his phone could not even come close to resolving an object as slender as an Ethernet cable from that distance, but he was able to point out the place where, with the help of his binoculars, he had seen both of the blue wires entering the building: a small hole, most likely a vent for a kitchen fan, above the fourth story and below the fifth.

They counted the windows between the corner of the building and the location of that hole. Then they sent a security consultant up to one of the lower floors (assuming that they all had the same layout) and had him go all the way to the end of the corridor and then count doors back from there, noting the apartment numbers on the doors.

As this was going on, Zula managed to peel Csongor off from the center of discussion. "Yuxia is out there alone in the van!" she exclaimed. "If we could get to her—"

Csongor shook his head. "Ivanov took the keys from the ignition," he said. "They are in his pocket."

"Oh."

"His left front trouser pocket, should that information become somehow relevant."

"Still, she could honk the horn—call for help—"

"One of the Russians raised the same issue," Csongor said, and fell silent.

"And?"

"Ivanov is not worried."

"Why not?"

"Yuxia called you 'girlfriend.'"

"So?"

"So they think maybe you and Yuxia are lesbians." Csongor blushed to an extent visible even in the dimly and bluely lit basement.

"Holy crap," Zula said. "Tomorrow remind me to have a good laugh about that if I haven't been tortured to death."

"But I think that this 'girlfriend' is a way that black women greet each other, even if they are heterosexuals." Something about the look on Csongor's face indicated that this wasn't just a foray into urban American slang but that it was of possible direct bearing on his future happiness. Zula permitted herself a moment of amazement on how the male reproductive drive could obtrude on situations where it was worse than useless. She even considered telling a little white lie.

"You are correct," Zula finally said. "She just picked up the expression from a movie or something."

"You and Yuxia are just friends," Csongor said with relief so evident that Zula felt her face heat up.

"Just friends who have known each other for all of, like, twenty-four hours," Zula said.

"Ivanov believes otherwise," Csongor said, "and he told Yuxia that if she made any trouble, he would do bad things to you."

"Well," Zula said, "that much might be true."

Csongor didn't enjoy hearing this.

"But even though Yuxia and I are not lovers," Zula pointed out, "threatening me might still change the way she makes decisions."

The door-counting Russian came back with a rough sketch. From this and the phone image of the front of the building, they were able to figure out which door would give access to the unit in question, supposing they knew whether it was on the fourth or the fifth floor. But there was no way to settle that question by looking at the building from the outside. The upshot was that the Troll probably lived in unit 405 or unit 505.

This seemed like excellent progress (if you wanted to look at it that way) to Zula, considering that they had been in the building for all of about twenty minutes. But it only seemed to make Ivanov more pissed off.

She stepped over to the large, rusty steel box that, as anyone could see from all the cables and conduits diving into it, served as the building's main electrical panel. Its door was hanging askew. She kicked it open. Uncle John had taught her to keep her hands in her pockets when approaching mysterious electrical equipment. She did so now.

The panel sported an array of flat round objects with little windows in them. These were planted in round sockets. Some of these were empty, revealing screw threads and electrodes similar to light-bulb sockets. Most of them, though, were occupied by the little win-dowed buttons. These tended to be labeled with strips of paper on which Chinese characters had been written by hand.

"What are those?" Peter asked. He had followed her over.

"Fuses," Zula said. "I've heard of them."

"Instead of circuit breakers?"

"I think so."

"Okay, I see where you're going," Peter said, with a rush of geek energy.

Zula hadn't been going anywhere, just wandering around look-ing at stuff. She looked at Peter. He had pulled out his PDA again. "Yup," he said, "I can still see Atheron." He looked up at her brightly, then glanced back to see whether Sokolov and Ivanov were paying attention. They weren't. He checked the PDA again and his faced clouded over. "Shit, I lost it. Signal's really weak."

Csongor had drawn closer, so Peter explained: "Zula and I did this before, up on the roof. Atheron is their WAP in the apartment. I can't log on—they put a password on it—but I can see the signal. If we cut the power by pulling the fuse, it should go off the air."

Csongor's eyes flicked over to the fuse panel. "Each apartment has a unique fuse?"

"So it would seem," Zula said. "Labeled in Chinese."

"Can anyone here read Chinese numbers?"

"Sort of," Zula said.

Ivanov came over and asked a question in Russian. His eyes jumped from Peter to the fuse panel to Zula as words poured out of Csongor. Peter added the caution that his PDA could not quite pick up Atheron from here in the cellar and so, with a lot more talk-ing than really seemed necessary, the following arrangement was worked out. Most of the security consultants stayed in the cellar doing what they'd been doing the whole time anyway, which was tinkering with weapons and ammunition from the rod-and-reel cases and the coolers. Peter ascended partway up the stairs with the PDA, getting more centrally located in the building so that he could pick up a consistent signal from Atheron. Ivanov was sticking to Peter; he wanted to see this thing happen with his own eyes and so he would be looming over Peter's shoulder through the entire experiment. Csongor remained at the base of the stairs where he could see and talk to Zula, who was stationed at the fuse panel, and Sokolov was in the stairwell somewhere between Csongor and Ivanov, so that he could exchange hand signals with both of them.

While all of this was being worked out, Zula prepared to bullshit her way through the project of reading, or pretending to be able to read, Chinese numerals.

The numbers actually mounted on the doors of the apartments were Arabic. But whatever electrician or custodian had labeled these fuses in the cellar had used the Chinese system.

Zero was a circle. One, two, and three were represented by the appropriate number of horizontal lines. Four could be remembered because it was a square with some extra stuff inside of it. Beyond that, however, the numerals were nonobvious. With a bit of help from Yuxia, she had been trying to learn them. In some contexts, where numbers were arranged in a predictable order, this was easy. Reading random numbers would have been impossible for her. The situation with this fuse box was somewhere between those extremes. At the top of the box she was seeing some labels that weren't numbers at all—she guessed that they must say things like "cellar" or "laundry room." Below that she began to see numbers that began with a single horizontal line, meaning 1, and after several of those she saw some with two horizontal lines, and after that a bunch with three lines, and so on. So it seemed that the fuses were laid out in a somewhat logical fashion according to floor and apartment number. But all of this was more in the nature of general trends than absolute rules; it was obvious that the building had been rewired several times and that available fuse sockets had been put to use willy-nilly. She had to carry out a kind of archaeological dig in her head to reconstruct how it had come to be this way. Toward the bottom of the panel she began to see the squarish character that meant four, and below that, the less obvious glyph that she was pretty sure meant five. So the fuse that would kill the Atheron signal was probably in the bottom half-dozen or so rows of the grid. But this was the part of the box that had been most heavily exploited by opportunistic rewirers in more recent decades and so there was a lot more noise and misdirection for her to sift through here.

"They are ready," Csongor said. "You can begin pulling fuses."

"Explain to them that the box is a mess, and it's just going to take me a little bit longer to make sense of it."

Csongor looked as if he really didn't want to be the bearer of that message.

"If I just start pulling fuses indiscriminately," Zula pointed out, "tenants are going to start coming down here to find out what's wrong."

Csongor went up the stairs and relayed that to Sokolov.

Zula was noticing that the newer circuits all had fuses in them but that several of the sockets for what she took to be fifth-floor apartments were vacant. She reckoned that empty sockets were probably a marker for vacant apartments. To discourage squatters and to prevent other tenants from pirating electricity, they would pull the fuse, thereby shutting off the power, to any unit that was not occupied. Scanning the whole panel, she saw that every floor had at least one or two vacant units but that they were most common on the fifth floor: not surprising since, in a building with no elevator, those were the least desirable apartments.

Her eye fell on a socket labeled with the character for 5, then 0, then the 5 character again; 505 was one of the two most likely candidates, the other being 405. But this socket didn't have a fuse plugged into it.

She scanned up the panel until she found the sequence of characters that, she was fairly certain, represented 405. It had a fuse.

She reached out and unscrewed the fuse, then turned to Csongor and held the fuse up in the air. He gave a hand signal to Sokolov, who apparently relayed it up the steps.

But none of this was even necessary. Peter and Ivanov were already on their way down.

Zula screwed the fuse back in as they descended, restoring power to 405.

"Got it on the first try!" Peter announced, wiggling the PDA in the air in a triumphant style that Zula found a little chilling. "We found the Troll!"

"Zula," said Ivanov, "nicely done." As if she had removed a brain tumor. Then Ivanov drew up short, in a way that was almost funny. "Which apartment?" For he had realized that this information was still lacking. Only Zula knew the answer.

It had been a while since that many people had looked at her that raptly.

"It's 505," she said.

Sokolov spoke to Ivanov in Russian, raising some kind of objection. Or perhaps that was too strong a word. He was mentioning an interesting point.

Ivanov considered it and discussed it with Sokolov, but he had his eye on Zula the whole time.

He knew. She had done something wrong—given herself away somehow.

"Sokolov worries," explained Csongor, "that the procedure is imperfect. Some additional scouting is recommended. But Ivanov counters that if we are too obvious, we may give warning to the Troll who might escape."

Ivanov nodded, though, as if he had taken Sokolov's point. He then spoke in Russian to the security consultants.

Three of them put their hands to their belts, unsnapped little black pouches and pulled out handcuffs. One of them approached Zula. He snapped a cuff around a heavy steel conduit that ran out of the floor, carrying power cables up to the fusebox. He grabbed Zula's left hand and whacked the other manacle down across her wrist. Meanwhile Csongor was being handcuffed to a cold water pipe in another part of the room. A third consultant cuffed Peter to the iron banister at the base of the stairs.

The other security consultants were on their feet, checking their gear and concealing their weapons. "We go to visit Troll in 505," said Ivanov. "If you have spoken truthfully, then we achieve our goal and be on our way, everyone happy. If you have made little mistake, then we shall return to this room and have discussion of consequences. So. Is 505 the correct place? Or is it perhaps 405?"

"It's 505," Zula said.

"Very well," said Ivanov, and issued orders. Sokolov, all the security consultants, and Ivanov began to ascend the stairs.

THE BIG FAT Russian had been trying to create feelings of terror in Qian Yuxia's heart and had been partly successful, but as she sat there alone, handcuffed to the steering wheel, the terror receded quickly and she was left feeling disappointed and offended. When he had called her yesterday and asked her to go fetch the van and organize a fishing trip, she had been flattered to have been chosen, from all the people in Xiamen, to be given such a responsibility. She had been up half the night riding buses into the little town in the country where she had parked the van, driving it back into Xiamen, and making preparations. As a special gesture to demonstrate how much she appreciated this opportunity, she had showed up early this morning with cups of coffee and muffins from a Western-style bakery.

The worst part, though, was that the big man had sweet-talked her by telling big stories about how he would help her sell *gaoshan cha* in Europe, and she had fallen for it completely. These people, it seemed, had sized her up as some sort of country bumpkin. An *opportunistic* country bumpkin who would swallow any sort of lie if she thought it would help her sell tea.

That much was merely offensive. But what *really hurt* was the fact that they had been *right*.

All she had to do was roll the window down and start screaming and those people would spend the rest of their lives in prison.

But the big man was powerful—he had money, he had soldiers, and all of them were armed.

But if he was all that powerful, why did he have to get help from someone like Qian Yuxia in order to perform the simple act of borrowing a van?

Because she was disposable. That was why. She was a nobody, all alone in the big city. No one would notice she had gone missing.

So it was time to roll the window down and start screaming.

But if she did that, the big man would do terrible things to Zula. He had promised it. Yuxia liked Zula and felt a sort of loyalty to her simply based on the fact that tears of shame had come into Zula's eyes when she had spoken of her failure to warn Yuxia.

Maybe there were some small things that she could do, short of screaming, to improve the situation a little bit. She surveyed her surroundings. Not her immediate surroundings, which tended to consist of people screaming at her for blocking the street, but more the middle distance. It was busy with people plying their trades and going about their errands. Carters went to and fro pulling their two-wheeled wagons piled with all sorts of goods. One carter, whose wagon was empty, had pulled up a couple of meters away from the van and had been keeping a close eye on Yuxia. Like a certain number of these guys he was gaunt and looked about ninety years old, which probably meant that it was difficult for him to compete against the younger, burlier carters. He had to make up for that with street smarts. He had seen them earlier, unloading stuff from the back of the van and passing it down the alley. He had seen the big man climb out of the van a minute ago and look at the front of the place with his binoculars. He knew that there were several Westerners inside the building and that something was going on in there. Like everyone else on this street he was always thinking about how to make things work to his advantage, and he had made the calculation that if he hung around in the vicinity of the van, flaunting his availability, then someone connected with this operation might dispatch him on some sort of errand.

Yuxia rolled down the window. She didn't need to catch the carter's eye because he was already staring right at her. "I need a locksmith," she complained. "But my phone is dead."

Then she glanced at the front of the apartment building just to make sure that the big man wasn't seeing any of this. When she turned her attention back, the carter was gone.

WHEN IVANOV'S HEAVY footsteps had receded, Peter muttered, "Thank God. We did it. Yes! We did it. This thing is *over.*"

Zula just could not summon the energy to break the news to him that they hadn't done it and that it wasn't over. She found the fuse for Apartment 405 again and started to unscrew it.

"What are you doing, Zula?" Csongor asked.

Peter swiveled to look at her. "Yeah," he said, "what are you doing?"

"Warning them."

"Warning *who!?*"

"The hackers in Apartment 405." She pulled the fuse out, then stuck it back in. Then repeated. Each time she reestablished contact, she heard a little pop as a spark bridged the gap. "I wonder if they know Morse code," she said, and began to jiggle the fuse in and out, making a little pattern: dot dot dot, dash dash dash, dot dot dot. Just like Girl Scout camp.

"You just told Ivanov that they were in 505," Peter said in a freakishly calm and thick voice, as though he had been gargling molasses.

"Understandable confusion," Zula said. "This panel is a mess. And who can read these Chinese numbers?"

She found it impossible to talk and do the Morse code thing at the same time, and so she pulled the fuse away and looked around the cellar.

Peter and Csongor were both just staring at her. Hoping, perhaps, that she was just pulling their legs? Hard to tell.

It was important for them to understand. Zula sighed and looked at each of them in turn. "First of all, Ivanov is planning to kill us no matter what happens. That's just obvious." She let that hang in the still air of the cellar for a few moments. "Which doesn't mean that we are going to die. Because Sokolov thinks Ivanov is crazy and he will intervene to prevent Ivanov from killing us. All of that is out of our hands. We've been asked to give up these hackers, who are basically just a bunch of harmless kids, so that Ivanov can kill them. And we just simply can't do that. It's just wrong. It's not how people behave. So I lied to the Russians."

Peter said "Shit!" and dropped to his hands and knees—or rather *hand* and knee since one hand was fixed to a banister—and began feeling around on the floor like a man who'd lost a contact lens. But he couldn't seem to find it. "Zula!" he hissed. "You have a bobby pin in there?"

"You mean, *in my hair?*"

"Yeah."

Zula could not hold back a sigh and an eye roll, but then she pulled a bobby pin from her hair and flung it at Peter.

"Do you have any more?" asked Csongor.

Zula threw him another one.

People who watched too many movies about hackers had all sorts of ludicrous ideas about what they were capable of. In general, they hugely overestimated hackers' ability to do certain things. But there was one area in which hackers were routinely underestimated, and that was lock picking. For them, picking locks was a nice way to kick back and relax after a long day of doing pen tests on corporate networks. No hacker loft was complete without a shoebox full of old locks, handcuffs, and so on, that these guys would sit around and pick just for the fun of it. Zula had always been a spectator, not a participant, and now wished that she had paid more attention. But she was pretty sure that Peter and Csongor would have this part of the problem solved rather soon and that they could then run out the door and free Yuxia from her captivity in the van.

"The Russians will go to 505 and kick the door down and probably make some noise," Zula said. "I am hoping that this will alert the kids in 405 and that they'll have a chance to get out of there." Having nothing else to do, she went back to jiggling the fuse in the socket.

"What about the people who are actually living in Apartment 505?" Peter asked. "Did you ever think of that?"

"It's vacant," Zula said. But Peter's question had made her nervous that she might have made a mistake, so she found the label that, she was pretty sure, read "505" and verified that the fuse socket was empty.

Which it was. But this time she noticed a detail she'd missed the first time around. There was no fuse screwed into the socket, that much was true. But there was *something* gleaming in there, something other than an empty socket. She dropped to one knee to get a better look at it.

A disk of silver metal was lodged in the socket.

The fuse had been bypassed; someone had jammed a coin into it, which was a very unsafe thing to do for a number of reasons.

"What are you seeing?" Csongor asked.

"I wonder if 505 might actually have some squatters living in it?" Zula said. "Can I borrow your flashlight?"

Csongor tossed her the tiny LED flashlight that he carried in his pocket. She aimed it into the hole and verified that the gap between the contacts had in fact been bridged by a silver coin stuffed into the hole.

It was not a Chinese coin, or any kind of coin that Zula had ever seen. It was stamped, not with an image of a person's profile or any other sort of normal coin art, but a crescent moon with a little star between its horns.

. . . .

THE CARTER RETURNED after a few minutes. A small, bald man was trotting behind him, carrying a bag of tools.

As he drew closer Yuxia got his attention through the windshield and waved him over toward the passenger's seat. She unlocked the door. He opened it and climbed in, a bit tentatively, since it might be considered improper for a strange man to enter a vehicle with a solitary female.

"Close the door please, I need to talk to you for a moment," Yuxia said.

He closed the door, giving her a weird look, as if Yuxia might be running the world's most complicated and opaque scam. Which perhaps she was. For the time being, though, she was not allowing him to see her handcuffed wrist.

The carter had pulled up close along the driver's side of the van. "Go over there please and wait," Yuxia said, nodding at the front of the building. "I will pay you for your trouble once my problem is solved."

The carter, somewhat suspicious and somewhat reluctant, withdrew a couple of meters.

Yuxia turned to the locksmith and gave him a big smile. "Surprise!" she exclaimed, and displayed the handcuff.

She was afraid that the poor man might have a heart attack. Yuxia had her left hand on the lock button, ready to lock him in the van if he tried to bolt. He probably would have done exactly that if she had been a man, but because she was a young woman he apparently felt that the decent thing was to hear her out.

"A bad man did this to me," she said, "and so, as you can see, it is probably a matter for the police. I will call them once I am free. But right now I really need to get this thing off my wrist. Can you help me, please?"

He hesitated.

"It's hurting me very badly," she whined. Talking this way was not her style, but she had seen other women do it with effect.

The locksmith cursed under his breath and unzipped his bag.

LIKE ANY RUSSIAN, Sokolov enjoyed a game of chess. At some level he was never not playing it! Every morning he woke up and looked at the tiles on the ceiling of the office that was his bedroom and reviewed the positions of all the pieces and thought about all the moves that they might make today, what countermoves he would have to make to maximize his chances of survival.

He had heard somewhere, though, that, mathematically speaking, the game of Go was more difficult than chess, in the sense that the tree of possible moves and countermoves was much vaster: far too vast even for a supercomputer to work through all the possibilities. Computer chess programs had been written that could challenge a Kasparov, but no computer program could give a high-level Go player a game that was even moderately challenging. Supposedly you couldn't even think about Go as a logical series of specific moves and countermoves; you had to think visually, recognizing patterns and developing intuitions.

As of thirty seconds ago—when Zula had done whatever the hell she had done—this had changed from a game of chess into a game of Go.

It might be that Zula had made the decision to give Ivanov what he wanted, sell out the Troll, and hope for Ivanov's mercy. If that were the case, then a few seconds from now they would be invading an apartment full of terrified Chinese hackers and something regrettable was going to happen. Why, oh why, had Ivanov come in from the van? Why was he following them up the stairs? If he'd simply stayed down in the van, Sokolov might have been able to finesse the situation, perhaps emerge from the building with one hacker in tow while letting the others escape. Perhaps Ivanov would have been satisfied with scaring the hell out of that one hacker, roughing him up a little bit. After which Sokolov would have had to divine the boss's intentions regarding Zula. He'd already made up his mind that he would, if necessary, physically intervene to protect her. Even if it meant killing Ivanov.

On the other hand, it might be that Zula had sent them on a wild goose chase. That they were about to break into a vacant apartment. In which case all hell was going to break loose when Ivanov realized that Zula had fucked him and that the hackers who had fucked him *earlier* were escaping from the building. That was really the point where it turned into a game of Go, because Sokolov couldn't even begin to think rationally about the tree of moves and countermoves that would branch out from such an event.

So he didn't. He gave it up and accepted the fact that he would have to work intuitively, like a Go player. Even though he had never played Go in his life.

For now he had to operate on the assumption that Zula had given them correct information and that Apartment 505 would contain something like ten young male hackers, mostly asleep. They would not be armed in any significant way. He had gone over this with his squad the night before and reminded them of it this morning before leaving the safe house: their tactical approach must be to flood the apartment in the first five seconds after breaching the door. Every one of those hackers had to be found and divested of his phone and his computer before he could send out distress calls. The landlines had to be found and cut. The entire apartment had to be explored. It might be one single space or it might be a warren of smaller rooms. Some of those back rooms might have means of escape: ways out onto fire escapes or balconies. The plan, then, was to pile through the door the moment it was knocked down and leave one man to secure the center while the other six scattered as far and as deep into the apartment's recesses as they could go. Once they had found and secured the periphery they would work their way back into the center, driving the hackers before them. Everyone would end up in the same place, and then a conversation could begin.

All the men knew that plan, were equipped for it, were ready for it. From the stairs they trooped out into the fifth-floor corridor, which conveniently for them was empty at the moment. Sokolov was leading the way, but as they passed 503 he looked over his shoulder and made room for Kautsky, the biggest man in the squad, the door breaker. Kautsky was armed with a combination sledgehammer/ax/crowbar that could make short work of any door. The ones in this building looked particularly flimsy, so Sokolov had no worries about getting through rapidly. Kautsky would be their man in the middle, the first one through, who would hold the center and block the exit while the others flooded in behind him and flowed to the edges. Ivanov had no scripted part in this plan, since he was supposed to be waiting down in the van, but Sokolov hoped that he would have the good sense to stay well to the rear, in the hallway, long enough for things to get under control. Then he could come in and wreak whatever revenge it was that he had been dreaming of.

Kautsky planted himself in front of 505 and wound up with the hammer, then looked back at Sokolov, awaiting his cue. Sokolov looked back toward Ivanov. He needn't have worried. Climbing stairs was not Ivanov's strong point, and he was only just now emerging from the stairway, breathing heavily, still a good twenty meters away from them. Before Ivanov could catch up with them and fuck up the entire operation, Sokolov gave Kautsky a nod, and the hammer fell.

AS THE LOCKSMITH worked on the manacle around Yuxia's wrist, she chewed the nail of her free thumb and scanned the street and the front of the building.

In a minute, she'd be free to get out of the van. The easiest thing then would be simply to disappear into the crowd on the street and hope that the PSB did not somehow follow her. A dubious gamble, considering that a PSB officer had been standing half a block away looking suspiciously at the van for the last couple of minutes.

But the van belonged to the family enterprise in Yongding. If she abandoned it here, it would be traced to her immediately.

She could go into that building and try to figure out what was going on. That was what a plucky heroine would do in a movie, but it didn't seem like a very wise idea in real life.

Or she could summon the PSB herself. But funny things sometimes happened when the PSB got involved. It wasn't always about punishing the wrongdoers and helping the victims. Everyone knew that there were all sorts of connections between criminal groups and the government. Yuxia knew very little about these Russians. Less than an hour had passed since they'd put the cuff on her wrist and she hadn't had time yet to sift through her memories of them and piece together a theory as to what they were really up to. But they had to be either spies or gangsters. If they were the latter, they might have connections with local gangsters, and if that were the case, there was no telling what bad things might happen to Yuxia if she ratted them out to the PSB and some mole within the PSB ratted her out in turn.

She had to get the van out of here.

The manacle came off her wrist.

"Thank you, sir. Now can you start the engine?" she asked. "I don't have the keys."

The locksmith's eyes jumped down to the ignition switch on the steering column, then back up to hers. He said nothing, but she could see in his face that he could do it. Just as plain, though, was that he really didn't want to. He knew that something was profoundly wrong about this situation and he wanted out of here.

"No," he said, and he began putting his tools back in his bag.

She glanced out the windshield to see the PSB cop looking her way, ignoring an angry woman who was haranguing him while gesturing irritably at the van.

Yuxia waved at him in the windshield and beckoned him over.

The locksmith was closing up his bag now. "I am doing this one for free," he said. "I am getting out of here now and I don't want to see you again, I don't want to hear from you again."

The van's power windows did not function with the engine off, so Yuxia half opened the door, forcing the cop to step around it. "Good morning, Officer!" she said brightly, which had the effect of freezing the locksmith. She pushed the door a little farther open, turning toward the cop, and blocking his view of the handcuff dangling from the steering wheel while giving him a nice big smile to look at. But he was not much taken with the smile. He looked her up and down, paying special attention to the blue boots.

"Move this van!" he said.

"I lost my keys," she said.

"How could you lose your keys!?"

Everything about this cop was reminding Yuxia of another reason why she didn't want any dealings with the PSB. She was a Big-Footed Woman from the mountains and they were Han lowlanders and that did not make for easy dealings.

"The keys fell out of my hand and went down there," she answered, pointing at a sewer grate a few meters up the street. "The locksmith is starting the engine for me. As soon as he's finished, I'll be on my way."

The cop stepped toward her, wanting to look inside the van. Yuxia scooted back on the seat and leaned against the steering wheel, concealing the handcuff but giving the cop a clear view of the locksmith's face and his bag of tools. The cop nodded. This was his beat; he recognized the face of every merchant in the neighborhood, including this one.

"What are you waiting for!?" the cop demanded. "This vehicle is blocking traffic! Stop sitting around flirting with this girl! Get the engine started and get it out of here or we'll have it towed!"

The locksmith made some calculation of his own as to whether he should cry for help and turn this into a full-fledged PSB investigation. Yuxia had no way of knowing what elements went into that calculation.

"Yes, Officer!" the locksmith replied. "It should only be a couple of minutes!"

"Very well." The cop stepped back from the van and sauntered out in front of the vehicle to direct traffic and keep an eye on things. Yuxia closed the door.

THE DOOR GAVE after two blows, and Kautsky blew through it. The rest of the squad, poised like sprinters at the starting line, rushed through after him, diverting around him like water flowing around a derelict tank in an Afghan river.

Sokolov had spoken to them of the need to sever the loop: the loop of observing, thinking, deciding, and acting. In normal circumstances the loop was a good thing but not now; they had to act without thinking for a few moments, and only then could they observe and think and decide. Sokolov, never one to ask his men to do something he wouldn't do himself, followed the rule pretty faithfully even though some part of his brain was already telling him that something was wrong, something didn't make sense. The apartment was indeed a warren of smaller rooms, which was bad for them, but not unexpected, nothing they couldn't cope with. But he wasn't seeing computers and he wasn't seeing young Chinese men. He was seeing sleeping bags and mattresses on the floor, rather closely spaced, with men sleeping on them. Lots of men. Some looked Chinese but some didn't. A migrant laborer squat? They were hairy and somewhat older than he'd been expecting. Stuff was piled all over the place: burners, thermometers, pots and pans, jars of ingredients he couldn't identify just now, big rectangular cans of the type used to hold industrial solvents. God, there were a lot of people living here! Sokolov's squad was certainly outnumbered, perhaps by as much as two to one. Not that it mattered since the Russians were all strapped with multiple semiautomatic weapons and, in Kautsky's case, an autoloading shotgun. Whereas China was not one of those places where ordinary people had weapons.

Which only made him more surprised and disoriented when, after that first five seconds had passed, and the loop had started running again, Sokolov noticed that the apartment was full of Kalashnikov assault rifles. These, and their banana-shaped ammunition magazines, were simply all over the place.

You couldn't look at everything at once, and so Sokolov ended up looking at one noteworthy thing in particular. He was in a relatively large room, cut almost in half by a long table consisting of planks set up on oil drums. His mind had first pegged the table as a kitchen counter, since it looked as though things were being mixed up there in bowls, but on second thought, the stuff they were mixing up was not food. It was a concoction he had seen and smelled before. Hell, he'd even *made it* before. It was fuel oil and ammonium nitrate. Everyone's favorite cheap simple high explosive. Standing on the opposite side of the table was a rather tall man, a Negro with a beard, wearing the T-shirt and jeans he had apparently just been sleeping in. But now he was up on his feet and looking around brightly. Behind him, an inconveniently placed window had been sealed off by covering it with a cheaply printed poster of Osama bin Laden.

There was a silence throughout the apartment as all the Russians' loops started running again and as the occupants, who had mostly been sleeping, came awake to discover the Russians among them.

Sokolov must have had an astonished look on his face because the tall Negro was looking at him with a certain degree of amusement. The Negro's hands and arms were largely concealed by the clutter of explosives-making stuff on the table, but they went into motion now, and Sokolov heard the very familiar *snick-chunk* of a Kalashnikov being charged; this being the last thing that one generally did preparatory to pulling the trigger.

Two very loud booms sounded from another room: Kautsky opening up with his semiautomatic shotgun.

Swinging the rifle upward, the Negro spoke in a calm, quiet, and matter-of-fact tone: *"Allahu akbar."*

"I JUST CAN'T fucking believe it," Peter muttered, as he worked the bobby pin in the manacle. "I can't believe what you did."

"Really."

"Yeah, really."

"Well, I can't believe what everyone *else* is doing," Zula said. "As far as I'm concerned I'm the only one here being reasonable."

"You think it's reasonable to fuck with a guy like Ivanov?"

"What kind of a guy *is* Ivanov anyway?" Zula asked. "What do we really know about him?"

"He's a pretty tough guy," Csongor put in. Zula glared at him, and he looked somewhat apologetic for having taken Peter's side.

"Do you know that of your own knowledge, or just by reputation?" Zula asked.

Csongor didn't answer.

"Did you not see what happened to Wallace in my building?" Peter demanded.

"That's a good way of putting it. I did not see what happened to Wallace. I saw Wallace go into a room. I saw a long bundle being carried out. Obviously we were meant to think it was Wallace's dead body. I'll bet it was fake."

"Fake!?"

"Yeah. They took him in there and said, 'Listen, Wallace, we need to scare the crap out of these two Americans, so play along. Shut up and go limp for a minute and we'll roll you up in a piece of plastic and carry you out and make it look like we just killed you.' He's probably sitting in his flat in Vancouver right now playing T'Rain."

"I doubt it," Csongor said.

"I suppose that is theoretically possible," Peter said, "but I think it is insane and irresponsible of you to bet our lives on it."

"None of this is real," Zula said. "It is all gangster theater."

A couple of loud booms echoed down the stairway.

After a brief silence, they heard several different fully automatic weapons firing at the same time.

Peter swiveled his head around and fixed Zula with a look.

"Either that, or I'm wrong," Zula said.

"THAT'S ENOUGH!" THE locksmith exclaimed, barely audible above the sound of gunfire and of stray pieces of broken glass and debris rattling down onto the roof of the van. "I've had it!" He was half lying, half sitting on the floor of the van, legs folded up in front of the passenger seat, body wedged in under the radio, reaching up to work on the ignition lock. His brain was telling him to hurl himself out of the vehicle and run as fast as he could, but it was going to take a little while to extricate his body.

Yuxia looked out the windshield. The PSB cop was backing away from the building, looking up just like everyone else on the street.

Something really bad was happening, and Qian Yuxia was an accomplice to it.

She reached down and slipped her hand into the locksmith's as if she were going to help pull him up. Instead of which she pinned it against the steering wheel. She used her other hand to grab the dangling manacle and snap it over his wrist.

"You can try to pick that handcuff while I've got my fingernails in your eyes," she said, "or you can start the engine while I sit here quietly. Your choice."

IN THE WHOLE world, there might have been as many as ten thousand people who were better than Sokolov at falling and rolling around on hard surfaces. Circus acrobats and aikido masters, mostly. Also included in that group would have been many of the younger Spetsnaz men. The remaining six billion or so living humans did not even enter the picture.

Sokolov had come to it a bit late, since he had not been recruited into Spetsnaz until after serving a couple of tours in Afghanistan. But for exactly that reason his trainers had been ruthless with him, making him dive and fall and roll on concrete floors over and over again until blood had seeped through the fabric of his uniform wherever there'd been bone anywhere near the skin. The point being that if you did it right, there shouldn't be blood, or even bruises.

Different special forces units around the world had different philosophies as to what was the best way to conduct close-quarters fighting. In Spetsnaz, it was a fixed doctrine that you should be in continual motion and most of that movement should take place at an altitude of considerably less than a meter. Standing there like an asshole looked good in cowboy movies but was not a viable tactic in a world filled with fully automatic weapons. Knees, hips, shoulders, and elbows should be used as fluidly as the soles of one's boots. Hands, though, should be reserved for holding things, such as guns. Sokolov had been trained accordingly and had maintained that standard of training for as long as he had stayed in Spetsnaz. After he had moved into the private sector, he had continued to practice SAMBO: a Soviet martial art, similar in many respects to jujitsu, that involved a huge amount of falling and rolling. He had done this because, when you were working as a security consultant, trying to keep things safe for private clients—clients who might be, say, movie stars at ski resorts or CEOs' wives at shopping malls—there were times when you just wanted to get someone on the ground or place them in a submission hold as opposed to riddling their corpse with bullets and shotgun pellets.

Usually, of course, he warmed up a bit first and swept the floor to make sure it was clean and free of little bits of hard stuff that could cause minor injuries. Those niceties were lacking here, but the fact that a tall black man—evidently an Islamic militant of some type—was swinging a loaded and cocked AK-47 over the table at him gave him all the motivation he needed to skip the preliminaries and go into motion.

First, though, he put four bullets into the wall just next to the door toward which he was diving. He did this because he had seen, in his peripheral vision, someone furtively poking his head around the corner and then drawing it back: behavior that triggered whole networks of neural circuitry built up in his brain during his work in Afghanistan and Chechnya.

How could he put four bullets through a wall when his hand was empty? The answer was that he had a pistol in his hand, with a round chambered and ready to go, before he was consciously aware of it. Though his employer would have bought him any sort of fancy gun and holster he had asked for, Sokolov had elected to stay with a Makarov: the standard-issue Russian sidearm, which was a smallish and rather simple semiautomatic pistol that lived in an odd and ingenious type of holster. Unlike most holsters, which were dead ends—you could only get the weapon out by *pulling* on it, butt first—the Spetsnaz holster was a sort of rail that the pistol moved *through*. When bad things were not happening, you inserted the weapon into the top of the rail, where it stayed, safe and secure. When bad things started to happen, you brought your hand down onto the butt of the pistol and *pushed* it down and through the end of the device. As you did so, lugs built into the rail engaged the slide of the pistol and pushed it back, chambering a round, so that by the time the weapon was free of the holster it was ready to fire. About a tenth of a second after the black man said *"Allahu akbar,"* Sokolov discovered his pistol in his hand in exactly that condition. He aimed it just to one side of the door frame and fired four rounds as quickly as that was possible while initiating a dive and roll. A burst from the AK-47 might have passed through the general area where he had been standing, but it was hard to tell; the apartment had become rather noisy, and all he could hear was ringing in his ears. He tumbled fluidly into the next space, which turned out to be a sort of back storage room, perhaps a pantry, with a sleeping bag, now empty, on the floor. The former occupant of the bag had gotten stealthily to his feet, picked up an AK-47 of his own, and made that furtive glance into the room where the black man had been mixing up the ANFO. Now he was slumped on the floor, not doing much. Sokolov could not see where bullets had gone through him, but he could tell from the sheepish, glazed look on the man's face that he was hit. While making these admittedly hasty observations Sokolov began firing back into the room from which he had just escaped, but the black man had had the presence of mind to change his position and so nothing was there. Sokolov, now lying flat on his back in a spreading puddle of the other man's blood, holstered his pistol and took the AK-47. It was a bit large and cumbersome for these environs, but its bullets would penetrate brick walls and it had a larger magazine.

Some idiot was spraying AK rounds through the wall above him, causing shattered plaster to rain down into his face. Sokolov verified that his rifle was ready to fire, then rolled into the doorway and discharged three rounds at a man—not the black man, but a

Central Asian type with a beard—who was doing the spraying. The man went stiff and just as quickly went floppy, and Sokolov hit him with one additional shot, more carefully aimed at his center of mass. The Central Asian went down. There was no doubt in Sokolov's mind that he had been stationed at that position by the black man with orders to cover Sokolov. This implied that the Negro was, (a) in charge, and (b) trying to make his way out of the apartment. A very deeply buried instinct, the lust for the hunt, made Sokolov want to go after him. Then some higher part of his brain weighed in. Thirty seconds ago he had been in the hallway getting ready to scare the hell out of a Chinese hacker and now he wanted to pursue a black Islamic militant through the middle of a pitched AK-47 duel in a bomb factory?

Looking past the supine body of the Central Asian, Sokolov could see one end of a larger room that looked almost like a disco because of the muzzle flashes. Whatever was going on there—and he could see very little of it—could not possibly last for very long. He could already see the feet of one of his men lying motionless on the ground, sticking out into the doorway.

The light was brightening and flickering.

From where Sokolov lay he could have belly-crawled like an infantryman across the ANFO-mixing room, but this would have made him easy prey for anyone who happened to step into the doorway. So he pushed himself up and crossed the room with a dive and a roll and came up just short of the doorway with his rifle at the ready.

He was greeted by a tongue of yellow flame reaching across the floor. He flinched back, not before some of it had lapped around his boot and set it on fire. He stomped his boot on the floor and managed to get the fire out, and a powerful smell of acetone came into his nostrils. A can of the stuff had been punctured.

Four completely motionless bodies—two of them Russians— were sprawled on the floor. Three wounded men—one of them Russian—had given up all thought of continuing the fight and were trying to roll or crawl clear of the rapidly spreading lake of burning solvent. The exit lay on the opposite side of the flames; Sokolov was trapped in this end of the apartment. All the gunfire was happening at the other end. Through the rippling air above the fire, Sokolov saw men on their feet and knew them as enemy, since his Spetsnaz boys would never expose themselves so stupidly. Aiming and firing over the flames, he brought down five with as many shots. But the mere fact that they were standing there in that attitude all but proved that Sokolov's men were either dead or had withdrawn into the corridor.

A can of something went up in a great whoosh of flames that forced him back out of the room and into the place where they mixed the ANFO. He began to push the door closed. All the windows in the space behind him had been destroyed by stray rounds, and the fire, ravenous for oxygen, was sucking a torrent of air through them. The wind got its teeth in the door and slammed it closed. Small round holes began to appear in it, and splinters flickered around the room.

THE AMOUNT OF noise emanating from the apartment above was literally shocking in the sense that Marlon and his friends reacted to it in a physical way, as though giant hands were squeezing their viscera. Their instinct was to squat down on the floor. A line of craters appeared across their ceiling. It took them a surprisingly long time to get it through their heads that these had been made by bullets.

If strangers had begun pounding on their door, they might have reacted a little more quickly. They had always speculated as to what they might do if the virus project led to a police raid. Most of that discussion had been in the same vein as "What if Xiamen got taken over by zombies?" Because the odds that the PSB would trouble itself over the activities of a nest of virus writers were not much higher than those of a zombie plague. But they had talked through it anyway and agreed that departing via the building's main stairway was out of the question. The cops, or the zombies, would be there in force. More important, it was not nearly clever or cool enough; it was lacking in hacker flair.

Power in the building was undependable, and so they had uninterruptible power supplies—UPSes—on their computers, to provide battery backup during blackouts. The UPSes had alarms that would squeal whenever the power was out; this was a warning to shut down the computer before the battery died.

This morning, Marlon had been awakened by the sound of several UPSes buzzing and squealing. Nothing terribly unusual about that. Usually, though, when the power went down, it stayed down for a while, and the squeals continued. But not today. Today there had been a brief outage, lasting well under a minute. Enough to wake Marlon up. But a few minutes later there had been a whole series of brief ones that had made the alarms squeal in a repetitive pattern: groups of three beeps, sometimes shorter, sometimes longer.

Someone had been trying to send them a signal. He had no idea who was doing it, or what the message was, but something about it had triggered every paranoid nerve in Marlon's body. He had thought back to their evacuation plan. He knew his roommates quite well and thought it likely that they had arrived at the same state of mind.

If a zombie attack had actually materialized, then they might have had a clue as to how to respond. But a stupendous machine-gun free-for-all in the apartment above them was not an eventuality that they had ever thought of and so it froze them for a time.

They really didn't want to know, or to be bothered by, their neighbors; and so they had always tried to do unto their neighbors in exactly the same way. This was a fixed policy of Marlon's. He was the oldest, at twenty-five. He had been living in places like this for about ten years, or ever since he had dropped out of middle school to become a *zhongguo kuanggong,* a Chinese gold miner, and to pursue the trade of *dailian,* or level grinding, in World of Warcraft and selling high-level characters to clients in *Omei:* Europe-America. At first he had only bunked—not worked—in places like this. Every day he'd get up and dribble his basketball through the streets of Xiamen to an office building that housed a medium-sized gold-mining operation: seventy-five computers used in shifts by a couple hundred miners. But since anyone could do this from any computer on the Internet, there was no reason to work for a company that would take part of your earnings, and so after a couple of years, he and a dozen other *zhongguo kuanggong* had split away and set up their own group in an apartment where all of them had worked and most of them had lived.

This had lasted for less than two years. Marlon's current group—the ones in *this* apartment—had been launched out of a slow divergence that became too wide to be papered over between two factions. One got more conservative over time as some of them got married and began to seek a more stable lifestyle. They began to see a steadier and safer return in the domestic market, where they could diversify among a number of China-based games, predominantly Aoba Jianghu, so that they would not have to worry about getting cracked down on by Blizzard, the company that ran World of Warcraft and that made active efforts to put gold miners out of business. Marlon's faction, on the other hand, thought they saw bigger opportunities, albeit with higher risk, in concentrating on WoW for the foreign market.

Or at least that was what they *argued* about; it was the *ostensible* reason for the split-up. But really it boiled down to pride. Some of the miners were ashamed that they were living in crowded apartments and doing this kind of work for a living. They wanted to get out, or if they couldn't get out, to change the essential nature of the work. Marlon's group, on the other hand, was fine with what they were doing. They saw it as no worse than any other occupation, even better than most; they were making a product and selling it to a market, they didn't have to put up with asshole bosses or dangerous working conditions, and they were ever alert for ways to seek new opportunities.

Thus the split and the move to a different apartment. At about the same time, T'Rain came along. They jumped to it, liking the fact that there was less risk; it had been created by the founder of Aoba Jianghu, it was designed from its tectonic plates upward to be friendly to the da G shou, as they now called themselves: the Makers of G(old). And they had been very happy with T'Rain for a while.

But along with less risk came more management, in a sense. It was harder for them to make a big strike when their moves were being so meticulously watched, analyzed, and controlled by number crunchers in Seattle.

Either that, or they'd gone into it with the teen illusion that they could somehow make a big strike, and then they had grown up.

In any case, after the da G shou been at it for a couple of years, they had begun to get resigned to the fact that they were going to be grinding away at this possibly for the rest of their lives, and they had developed a strain of resentful ideology. Clever Chinese people had created this gold-mining industry and sustained it in the face of

Blizzard's most determined onslaughts, but the makers of T'Rain, using Nolan Xu as their running dog, had co-opted them and turned them into a resource extraction colony.

During the WoW days, it had been common for the *zhongguo kuanggong* to fall victim to griefing attacks—relentless persecution in the game world—from players in *Omei* who had found it amusing to KoS (Kill on Sight) any character they suspected of belonging to a Chinese player. The in-game identities of these griefers had become well known. Marlon and several of his comrades had formed an all-Chinese guild called the Boxers: a powerful, nay unbeatable gang of raiders who would hunt down their enemies and grief them to the point where they'd have to liquidate their characters and create new accounts under assumed names. The Boxers had gone dormant when everything had moved over to T'Rain. More recently, though, they had revived it. In its new incarnation, though, it didn't have to settle for roaming around and griefing the griefers. Instead it carved out a chunk of territory in the Torgai Foothills region and defended it against all comers, slowly expanding and improving it. REAMDE was only the latest—but by far the most lucrative—moneymaking scheme that they had launched from their rebel enclave. They had easily been pulling in enough gold to get a lease on a bigger apartment—maybe even an office suite—but Marlon, the grizzled veteran, who had seen many such schemes come and go, had been slow to make any such move. This place was a dump, but it was a cheap dump, it was conveniently located with respect to a *wangba* with an easily bribable cop, the landlord didn't ask questions or give them any hassles, and there was no compelling reason to move. Many of the other tenants seemed to view the place in the same light.

Until the high-velocity rounds began to pass down into their apartment from above, Marlon had never troubled himself to think about the possible drawbacks of having neighbors who shared his attitude about what constituted suitable real estate. He had the vague sense that the apartment above them was crowded, but that was frequently the case in buildings like this one. From time to time, as they climbed the stairs to play basketball on the roof, they would see people who seemed to be *waidiren*—"not from around here" types, internal foreigners—and perhaps even *waiguoren*—

non-Chinese. If the wind was blowing the right way, they would sometimes get a whiff of chemical odors, but it was difficult to pin down their origin.

But now those chemicals were dribbling down into their apartment through bullet holes, and the dribbles were *on fire*.

Marlon stared in fascination at a puddle of burning acetone that was forming on a pile of magazines. Then it penetrated his awareness that the other guys, the younger ones, were looking at him wondering what to do.

"Zombies," he announced, and turned toward the nearest window.

The windows along the front of the building had shallow balconies projecting no more than a meter from the wall; these were fully caged in iron grids as a security measure, but some of the grids had swing-out hatches. These they kept padlocked. But one of the outcomes of their zombie-attack planning sessions had been a decision that the keys to those padlocks should be hung on nails, far enough inside the grids that no burglar could reach them, but close enough to be easily found in the event of a panicky departure (a little more realistically, they were worried about being trapped inside the building in the event of fire). There were three hatches, three padlocks, and three keys. Marlon noted that one was already in use by a member of the group, so he grabbed his closest roommate by the arm and pushed him over to another and made sure he understood what to do. Then Marlon proceeded to the third, which was in the kitchen, and took the key and unlocked the padlock and swung the hatch open.

He stuck his head out the window. It seemed a long way down to the street. A van was parked down there—the gangsters' ride? Never mind. Incredibly bad things were happening upstairs— fragments of glass and plaster were raining down right in front of him—and his apartment was on fire. Younger da G shou, boys he felt responsible for, were queuing up behind him. He debated whether he should be the last one to depart, like a captain on a sinking ship, or should lead them forth like a sergeant going into battle. He decided on the latter approach. Turning his back to the grid he leaned back, stuck his head out, reached up, got a grip on the bars, and swung out into the open. Then he got his feet on the bars beneath him and crab-walked out of the way, making room for the next guy.

EVEN DOWN IN the basement, the gun battle had been shockingly loud from the get-go; but it actually kept getting louder. Zula, relegated to infuriating uselessness by the handcuff and her inability to pick it, could only stand there and wait for something to change.

Think, Zula.

Did skinny teenaged Chinese hackers have a *lot* of automatic weapons lying around their apartments?

If so, were they so skilled at using them that they could actually put up that much of a battle against a crew like Sokolov's?

Peter had gotten himself free. Seeing this, Zula turned toward him, expecting that his first move would be to cross the floor and begin work on her handcuff. She even rotated her wrist into a more convenient position for him.

He did not approach.

"I'd better see what's going on," he said, after a silence. A silence that had gone on for too long. He'd had too much time to think during that silence.

"Peter?" she said. Standing there with her wrist poised in what she'd hoped would be an inviting position, she felt like a girl in a prom dress, being stood up by her date.

"Just going to scope it out," he assured her.

He had that same look about him, the same tone of voice, as the night they had driven back from B.C. He was in full dodging mode.

"Whatever is going on up there," Zula said, "it has nothing to do with hackers. This is something bigger than that."

"Back in a sec," Peter said, and walked to the base of the stairs. He hesitated for a few moments, unable to meet her eye. "Whatever," he muttered. He hunched his shoulders and began walking up the stairs.

MARLON COULD SEE four other da G shou clinging to various grids like spiders, looking for ways down. There were only three left in the apartment.

Moving around this way was not difficult. At least 50 percent of the building's frontage consisted of grids just like the one Marlon was hanging from. The only aspect of this that was remotely problematic was finding ways to make the transition from one grid to the next. In many cases, this was made considerably easier by other features that had been attached to the outside of the building: awnings, brackets for external air-conditioning units, bundles of cables, plumbing, downspouts, and quasi-European architectural bric-a-brac, cast in concrete.

Looking straight up, Marlon could see the bundle of wires that ran above the street to the building across the way. He could clearly make out the blue cat-5 cable that he and his partners had added to it when they had moved in. If he could climb up to it, he could shinny across the bundle to the opposite building. That seemed unnecessarily risky, though, when he could just climb down.

The window above him, on the fifth floor, exploded and showered him with glass. Marlon closed his eyes and bowed his head and let it rain down all over him. Then he began moving sideways as fast as he could, because the glass breaking was not just a one-time event: someone was up there systematically demolishing the window with a hard, heavy object. Risking a quick look up, he glimpsed that object and recognized it as a rifle butt. He moved sideways as rapidly as he could. His roommates were emerging from the same hatch he had used and looking his way; their instinct was to follow the leader. Marlon waved them furiously in the other direction, making significant glances up at the flailing rifle butt, and they quickly took his meaning.

People were screaming down on the street. He ignored them.

A shot sounded directly above him, then another, each one threatening to knock him loose with its shock wave. Metal flew, and he understood that the lock on a window grille had been shot out from the inside. Not knowing what this might portend, he began moving faster, more recklessly, and in a few moments reached the building's corner. Below him, a narrow side street plugged into the large one that ran along the front. One floor below, an awning had been constructed sufficiently far in the past that the corrugated metal was thoroughly rusted and holed. Which was a good thing; he'd have slid off a new roof. This one would afford plenty of friction and numerous handholds. Marlon used the window grids to descend to that level and then used an air-conditioner bracket and a downspout as handholds to make the move around the corner and get onto that awning. Following that horizontally for about ten meters he came to the midline of the building's side wall, which was marked by a vertical column of small windows that shed light onto an internal stairway. Running parallel to that was a vertical cable bundle, very thick and dense, with many handholds. Marlon sank his fingers into it, got a solid grip, and then planted his shoes against the brick and began to walk down the side of the building like a human fly.

As he was passing the window on the second floor, he nearly lost his grip. A face had appeared briefly in the window, so close that he could have reached out and touched it had a dirty pane of glass not been in the way. It was the face of a white man, round, heavy, dark hair slicked back, the skin flushed with excitement. It was only there for a second. Then it disappeared as the man proceeded down the steps to the floor below.

But even through the glass and above the noise, Marlon could hear the man bellowing a single English word: "YOU!"

Curiosity, for Marlon, had now become a more powerful force than self-preservation. He'd been planted in one location for a few moments and now turned his attention back to the wire bundle, looking for his next set of handholds. He wanted to get down to the level below and see who YOU was.

But his attention was drawn by renewed movement in the window: another face, dimly seen through the dirt on the window, descending the stairs, rounding the turn at the landing. But this one was different in several ways. To begin with it was a dark-skinned face, something rarely seen in these parts. A couple of the other da G shou had mentioned seeing a black man in the building's upper hallway, and Marlon had made fun of them for watching too much hoops on television. But there was no denying that Marlon was now seeing a black man, and a fairly tall one at that. He was carrying a rifle that Marlon recognized, from video games, as an AK-47. But unlike the first man, he was moving carefully, even furtively.

Rounding the turn on the landing, the black man turned his back to Marlon, descended a couple of steps, and crept to a halt.

Marlon had remained frozen through all of this, not wanting to draw notice by making any sudden movements, but now he let himself down so hastily that he lost his grip and found himself briefly dangling by one hand before he was able to regain his grip and plant his feet again.

Coming in view of the first-story window, he saw the first man, the big white fellow, standing with his back to Marlon, confronting another white man who had apparently been coming up the stairs from the basement. This second man was young, slender, with longish hair and a heavy beard-shadow. His facial features were difficult to make out, but it was obvious from his body language that he was in a state of terror so advanced that he had become physically unstrung. He was leaning back against the wall of the stairwell as if getting that extra inch of distance from the big man would somehow improve his situation. He had turned his head down and to one side and was holding his hands up in front of him.

The big man was shouting at him in English. Marlon couldn't make out a word he was saying. This was partly because of the window and the ambient noise (though the gun battle seemed to be over) but also, as he came to realize, because the big man had a heavy accent of some type.

And also because the big man was completely out of his mind with rage. A rage that only seemed to grow the more he bellowed and gesticulated.

The big man was talking himself into something.

He was talking himself into doing something dreadful to the younger man.

Marlon noticed, now, that a pistol had appeared in the big man's hand.

When he was ready, the big man aimed his gun directly at the young man, who tried to hide behind the white palms of his hands. There were three enormous booms. The big man made some contemptuous remark and then walked past the younger man, who was still collapsing to the floor, and proceeded down the next flight of stairs.

After a few moments the black man stalked after him.

IT HAD BEEN with mixed feelings that Olivia Halifax-Lin had learned that Abdallah Jones had absconded from Mindanao and turned up in Xiamen. For Olivia had just devoted the better part of a year, and MI6 had spent half a million quid, on setting her up with a false Chinese identity so that she could work under deep cover within the borders of the Middle Kingdom. And she really hated Abdallah Jones a lot. But hunting Islamic bombers was not supposed to be her job.

As any Halifax-Lin family photograph would demonstrate, one could never predict the outcome of what used to be called miscegenation. Olivia had two siblings. Her older brother looked Welsh to Welsh people, but on a trip to Portugal he'd been mistaken for Portuguese, and when he went to Germany, Turks came up to him on the street and greeted him in Turkish. Their younger sister had classic mixed-race looks. Olivia, on the other hand, could walk down any street in China without drawing undue notice. In a small town, she would likely be pegged as *waidiren,* but in a big city she would never be identified as *waiguoren.*

Their father was an economist, born and raised in Beijing but relocated to Hong Kong in his late teens and eventually to an academic post in London, where he had married Olivia's mother, a speech therapist. They had grown up speaking English and Mandarin interchangeably. Olivia had read East Asian history at Oxford. It was considered good form to pick up at least one language you didn't already know, and so she had taken a couple of years of Russian.

Preferring to hang with a more international crowd, she had spent a lot of time in the student bar at St. Antony's College, and it was there that she had first been approached by a member of the faculty who suggested in a deniable and genteel—almost subliminal—way that (ahem) MI6 knew of her existence. While flattered, she had deflected the overture—supposing that's what it was—by mentioning that she had plans to pursue a master's degree in international relations at the University of British Columbia, with an eye toward coming back to St. Antony's to pursue a Ph.D.

The professor, by this point, had bought her a drink. After allowing a few minutes to pass, he had made a whimsical suggestion. The Chinese community in Vancouver was huge: a city within a city, populous enough that the appearance of an unfamiliar Chinese-looking and -acting person in a store or an apartment building would not arouse any particular notice. Olivia's memory of the conversation was a bit hazy—she was a lousy drinker—but she was pretty sure he had used the term "spy Disneyland." And when she had asked for an explanation, he had pointed out that a girl like Olivia could go to a place like Vancouver's Chinatown and try to pass as Chinese and see if anyone detected the subterfuge. It would give her a feeling for what would be entailed in working as a deep cover agent in China, but it would be as safe, and as fake, as Disneyland.

The idea of Olivia as an MI6 agent had seemed comical at first, and yet she had to admit that it appealed to the same part of her personality that enjoyed acting in amateur theatrical productions—which, aside from sporadic and desultory participation in field hockey and kung fu, was her main extracurricular activity.

She had performed sixteen speaking roles in a dozen different productions. The numbers looked funny because she tended to get cast in roles so small that, with a change of costume, she could easily do more than one in the same play. With time and experience she had graduated to sidekick and girlfriend roles in small productions around Oxford. Beyond that, she had no ambitions in the theatrical world. But she had come to understand that the decisions of casting directors reflected the way that people in general, and men in particular, looked at her. New men who swam into her environment ignored her at first. Some then began to gaze curiously at her. Then they either went back to ignoring her or else found some way of letting her know that they thought she was beautiful; that this was by no means obvious; and that they deserved some reward or appreciation for having been so ingenious as to notice it. Different directors had awarded her greater or lesser roles depending on where they fell in the continuum of Olivia-face-appreciation, but starring roles had eluded her for the reason mentioned.

But in the deep cover agent game, bit players, girlfriends, and sidekicks were precisely what was wanted. No James Bond types need apply.

There were about half a dozen photographs in the world—mostly candid shots taken on phones—that made Olivia look really beautiful. And she had learned that she could make people look for, and eventually see, that beauty by looking as if she expected it. But she could just as well make them fail to see it by looking otherwise. She thought it might be a good skill for a spy.

· · · · ·

AFTER SIX MONTHS in Vancouver, she had suddenly been over-come by a craving for winter melon soup that resulted in a sponta-neous trip to Chinatown. Not the old one downtown, but the new one out in the suburbs. A haggling session with a greengrocer had led to Olivia's taking possession of a winter melon as long as her arm. As they had finished the transaction, the grocer had made a bit of small talk with Olivia, asking her how long she had been in Canada. "Six months," Olivia had told him, and he had then politely inquired which part of China she had come over from. And rather than try to explain everything about her parents, she had just said, "Beijing." He had accepted that with no trace of skepticism, and nearby onlookers had joined in the conversation, accepting her as a pure Chinese woman from China.

During her second year, then, she had moved to an apartment building in a mostly Chinese neighborhood and had passed, with very little difficulty, as a graduate student from Beijing. The clos-est she ever came to being outed was when someone made a com-ment—a flattering one, she hoped—about her unusual looks. But then, Yao Ming probably got a lot of comments about his unusual height. No one doubted Yao Ming was Chinese.

After a while she had been invited to tea (the English kind) by a woman based at the British consulate in Vancouver, who again in a very genteel and deniable way wanted to know how it was all going and whether a Ph.D. from St. Antony's were still in her future, or might she consider taking a bit of time off first and gaining some experience in the world of work? Olivia had not ruled it out, and after that, the teas had become a regular thing and had led to lun-cheon interviews in nice London restaurants when she went home for the holidays.

She had begun *not* doing certain things that, had she done them, would have made it impossible for her to work for MI6 in the future. She had not put up a Facebook page. She had not posted photos of herself on Flickr. She had not visited China, meaning that the government of that country had no photos of her, no record of her existence. She had not done these things for the simple reason that the MI6 plants who kept popping up in her path kept asking her whether she had ever done them. And when she said no, the news was always greeted with impressed eyebrow raising.

And so to London and MI6, where she had toiled as an analyst for two years, developing her cover identity and writing reports on miscellaneous topics. One of which had been the Welsh terrorist Abdallah Jones, who was of particular interest to Olivia because he had once blown up Olivia's great-aunt's bridge partner on a bus in Cardiff.

He was (as she learned) of West Indian ancestry, that is, the descendant of slaves brought to the Caribbean to work on sugar cane plantations. He had grown up in a Cardiff slum where he had acquired an addiction to heroin. He had kicked that addiction with the assistance of a local mullah who had converted him to Islam. Chemically unshackled, he had taken an undergraduate degree in earth sciences at Aberystwyth and followed that up with graduate instruction at the Colorado School of Mines, where he seemed to have learned a hell of a lot about explosives. Returning to Wales, he had fallen in with a radical cell of Islamists and cut his teeth blowing up buses in Wales and the Midlands before migrating to London and graduating to tube stations. When those activities had rendered him the object of intense police curiosity, he had moved to Northern Africa, then Somalia, then Pakistan (the site of his largest single exploit, killing 111 people in a hotel blast), then Indonesia, the southern Philippines, Manila, Taiwan, and now—strange to relate—Xiamen. All those steps had made perfect sense except for the last two.

To say, as people frequently did, that Abdallah Jones was to MI6 what Osama bin Laden had been to the CIA was to miss a few important points, as far as Olivia was concerned. It was true that Jones was MI6's highest-priority target. So to that point, the comparison served. Beyond that, as Olivia took every opportunity to point out, comparing Jones to bin Laden was dangerous in that it minimized the danger posed by Jones. Bin Laden's best days had been over on September 12. One of the most famous men in history, he'd spent the rest of his life huddled in various hiding places, watching himself on TV. Jones, on the other hand, was little known outside of the United Kingdom, and even though he had blown up 163 people in eight separate incidents before his thirtieth birthday, there was little doubt that he would kill many more than that in the future.

Since he was out of the United Kingdom, and unlikely to return, he'd have to be caught in some other country.

Awkward, that.

Fortunately there was this thing MI6, an entity whose purpose was to operate in places that did not happen to belong to the United Kingdom. And so when Olivia's bosses there asked her to write reports about Abdallah Jones, it was not simply because they wanted to fatten his already huge dossier. It was because they wanted to work out some way of catching him or killing him.

Olivia had assumed it was all academic, at least to her. Her languages were English, Mandarin, (less so) Russian, and (even less so) Welsh. This made it unlikely for her to get an undercover posting in the places where Abdallah Jones tended to hang out. So all her flawlessly gardened memos and PowerPoint presentations about what a bad actor Jones was and how important it was to go after him had seemed free of any taint of self-interest; MI6 could throw its entire annual budget after Jones and it wouldn't bring Olivia Halifax-Lin any more budget authority or any chance at operational glory.

After a shoot-out in Mindanao that had left several American and Filipino special forces troops dead, Jones had moved to Manila for a couple of months and then breezed out of town hours before a police raid, leaving behind a fully operational bomb factory that he had thoughtfully booby-trapped. Circumstantial evidence suggested that he must have gotten passage to Taiwan on a fishing vessel. The Chinese-speaking world was not a normal locus of Islamic terror, and so why he had gone to Taiwan, and what he had done there, could only be guessed at.

After six months of lying very low, he had made the jump across the straits to Xiamen, of all places.

Vague as it might have sounded, this was incredibly precise and specific intelligence that hinted at the existence of extraordinary sources and methods. Though Olivia had not been told this explicitly, it was easy enough to guess that MI6 must have an informant in Pakistan who was privy to messages being passed between Jones and his al-Qaeda contacts.

She did know this much for certain: through that channel, MI6 had obtained the name of a city (Xiamen) and a couple of mobile numbers. Radio frequency devices had been used to scan for the digital signature of those mobile phones and slowly zero in on the place where they were being used. Much of this had been done in collaboration with American three-letter agencies, through pure signals intelligence technology: satellites, listening posts on the nearby Taiwanese island of Kinmen, and remote-control devices dropped in Xiamen by contract operatives who, of course, had no idea what they were doing or who they were working for.

That whole phase of the operation had been based on the premise, first put forth by Olivia, that Jones had to be sitting in one place most of the time. A tall black man simply couldn't move around in a Chinese city without attracting a huge amount of attention. He must have a safe house somewhere and he must spend virtually all his time in it, communicating via phone. All of which was perfectly obvious to anyone who'd ever been in China, or even in Chinatown, but it had apparently come as a useful insight to some people in MI6 who had assumed that, because Xiamen was a big international port city, Abdallah Jones could wander about in the same way he might have done in Paris or Berlin.

Through these technical means, anyway, the signals intelligence geeks had narrowed Jones's location down to roughly one square kilometer before Jones had had the good sense to throw away his phones and swap them out for new ones.

The day after those phones had gone dark, Olivia had been put on a plane to Singapore.

No particular orders awaited her there, and so she just wandered around Chinatown for a few days, reassuring herself that she really could pass for Chinese.

Then, in the abrupt and enigmatic style she was beginning to get used to, she was flown to Sydney, and from there to an airport on some place called Hamilton Island, where she was met by John, a sunburned Brit, formerly of the Royal Marines' Special Boat Service, now working, or pretending to work, as a recreational scuba diving instructor. From the airport, John and Olivia walked (the first time in her life she had ever departed from an airport as a pedestrian) to an anchorage only a few hundred meters away, where a diving boat awaited. Olivia made herself at home in a cabin while John motored to a smaller island a few kilometers away.

Then John spent three days teaching Olivia all that he could about scuba diving.

Then he took her back to the airport, gave her a great big salty/sandy hug, and put her on another plane. She was sad to see the last of him but also a little bit relieved. Less than twelve hours after she'd first come aboard his boat, Olivia and John had started having sex, and hadn't stopped until ten minutes before the stroll to the airport. This was by far the fastest time Olivia had ever gone zero to sixty with any man; she was thrilled, shocked, and embarrassed by it and understood that if she had stayed on that boat for even one more day, the whole situation would have started to go sour and maybe even blown up her career.

Flying back into Singapore with John's handprints almost palpable on her, she followed instructions to go and dine at a particular restaurant. There she met a man named Stan, whose attempts to dress like a tourist did very little to hide the fact that he was a lieutenant commander in the U.S. Navy. Stan and Olivia ate noodles together and then proceeded by taxi to Sembawang Wharves, where Olivia boarded an American destroyer in a long raincoat with the hood up while carrying a large umbrella. It wasn't raining.

The destroyer seemed impatient for her to arrive, and cast off its lines and headed out to sea even while she was being shown to her accommodations. Somewhat to her relief, Olivia did *not* find herself having impulsive sex with Stan or any other members of the destroyer's crew.

A day and a half later, under heavy clouds just before daybreak, she was transferred to a Royal Navy submarine that had been waiting for them out in the middle of nowhere. Here the accommodations were the tiniest imaginable, and she saw all sorts of circumstantial evidence that men and stuff had been hastily and grudgingly moved aside for her benefit. A waterproof pouch awaited her. It contained a cheap but reasonably presentable business suit from a Shanghai tailor who had evidently been supplied with her measurements. There was also a purse, prepacked with her Chinese identity card; her Chinese passport; a somewhat used wallet containing credit cards, money, photos, and other plausible wallet contents; half-used-up containers of the same cosmetics she used normally, mostly Shiseido stuff that could be obtained in any city in the world; and other purse junk, such as used train tickets, receipts, candy, cough drops, breath mints, tampons, dental floss, hotel giveaway sewing kit, Krazy Glue, and, inevitably, a condom, expiration date three years ago, artfully timeworn so it would look like she had thrown it into her purse after a mandatory safe sex workshop and forgotten about it.

The captain of the sub handed her a sealed envelope, half an inch thick, covered with warnings as to its secrecy. She opened it up to find three items:

- A letter from her boss telling her to establish the precise whereabouts of Abdallah Jones. This document did not bother to point out, or even hint at, the terrible things that would happen to Jones soon afterward. This only made it feel heavier in her hands, as if it had been typed out onto a sheet of uranium.

- The dossier of her Chinese alter ego. Most of this she had written herself and had memorized, but they'd apparently included it in case she wanted to do some last-minute cribbing.

- An addendum explaining how the hell her alter ego had suddenly found herself in Xiamen. This she read closely, since it all came as a surprise to her.

Aboard the sub was a squad of Special Boat Service men. One of them showed her a place where an extra pod had been welded onto the hull of the submarine, like a wen on a camel. This could be accessed through a system of hatches. Olivia was quite certain that it was the most expensive single object she had ever seen in her life. The pod was a tiny submarine, capable of holding up to half a dozen men. "Or five men and one woman, if it comes to that," the SBS man said. In some ways it was a simple vessel. It was not made to be filled with air or to withstand the pressure of the ocean. The seawater filled it, and the occupants wore scuba gear. But in other respects it was loaded with what she took to be fantastically complex navigation and stealth technology.

She spent a day on the sub, mostly alone, though they did throw a nice dinner for Olivia in the officers' mess and made several toasts to her, to her fine qualities, to her mission, to her good luck, et cetera, et cetera.

And that was when she started to get scared.

You'd think it would have happened earlier. It wasn't as though hints had been lacking as to the nature of the plan. But the thing that got to her emotionally about that dinner was precisely the tradition of it: hundreds of years of Royal Navy men going out to strange parts of the world to do spectacularly imprudent things. It was a way for those who *weren't* going to show their appreciation—a precursor of survivor's guilt.

It hadn't occurred to her before, but: she had to cross the Chinese border *somehow*. Crossing at any legal port of entry would leave traces impossible to reconcile with her cover story. Even if she did it with fake papers and then threw them away, they'd have photos of her, and you had to assume they were using digital face recognition software now. Theoretically she could have hiked across the border from some place like Laos or Tibet, but that seemed awfully Victorian. They simply didn't have time. So it was going to be this. At three in the morning she put on the scuba gear and carried her waterproof pouch to the miniature pod-sub, where, as promised, five of the SBS men were waiting. Some kind of long and tedious procedure followed, involving lots of checklists. The thing filled with water and started to move independently of the big submarine.

Then there was nothing but darkness and silence for an hour. The men controlling the sub's movements were working hard, reading instruments, looking at electronic maps. She began to see landforms she recognized: the big round island of Xiamen nudged its way onto the screen.

They drew very near to one of the outlying islands, and one of the SBS men spent a while peering through the electronic equivalent of a periscope. Then the decision was made and the order given. Accompanied by one of the divers, she swam the last hundred meters and belly-crawled up onto a garbage-strewn beach in an unfrequented cove and kept crawling until she and the diver were concealed in foliage. They pulled off their masks and lay there motionless for a while, until certain that no one was nearby. Olivia peeled off her wetsuit. Modestly looking the other way, the diver opened the waterproof pouch and pulled out garments one by one, starting with panties, and handed them over his shoulder to her. When she was fully clothed, he turned around and saluted her—another detail that almost killed her—then crawled down through the garbage into the water, dragging behind him a bag containing her scuba kit. A wave lapped over him and he was gone.

Olivia applied mosquito repellent and squatted in the woods for two hours, then walked uphill to a little road and then down the road for a kilometer to a place where hundreds of people, mostly young women, were streaming out of a huge new apartment complex to a bus stop. Like them, she took a bus to the ferry terminal, and from there she joined in a flow of thousands across the wide aluminum gangplanks onto a crammed passenger ferry. An hour later she was in downtown Xiamen. Following instructions memorized from that envelope, she went to a FedEx office and picked up a large box that was waiting for her. Slitting it open with a penknife from her purse, she found that it contained an altogether typical-looking rollaway suitcase of the type currently making the rounds of every airport luggage carousel in the world.

A five-minute taxi ride took her to a middling business hotel near the waterfront. She walked into the place looking as if she had just breezed in from the airport, presented her Chinese ID card, and rented a room. Settling into it, she opened the rollaway to find a laptop that she recognized, since she had bought it and set it up herself, making certain that every detail of its hardware and software configuration was consistent with her cover story. She booted it up, connected to the hotel's Wi-Fi, and discovered several days' messages from anxious clients in London, Stockholm, and Antwerp.

She was now Meng Anlan, working for a fictional Guangzhou-based firm called Xinyou Quality Control Ltd., founded and owned by her fictitious uncle Meng Binrong, who was trying to set up a branch office in the Xiamen area. Xinyou Quality Control Ltd. acted as a liaison between clients in the West and small manufacturing firms in China. That was a common way to make money nowadays, and many firms were doing it. The only thing the least bit unusual about the cover story was Meng Anlan's gender; except in some very unusual cases, women simply didn't do things like this in China.

Or at least they didn't do it *openly*. There were any number of firms that, for all practical purposes, were controlled by women; but they were always fronted by men. So the plausibility of Olivia's cover story was founded on her fictitious uncle Binrong in Guangzhou, who was (according to the story) the real boss. Meng Anlan was just running errands for him, acting as a sort of personal assistant. All decisions of significance had to be referred to Binrong.

This was a bit more complication than was really desirable in a spy's cover story. But there simply weren't that many plausible excuses for a young woman in China to be out on her own, far away from home and family. There were millions of them doing low-level factory jobs and living in company dorms, but there was little point in MI6 sneaking her into China so that she could adopt that lifestyle. She was only useful as an agent if she had the money and the freedom to move around. They had even considered making Olivia into a high-priced call girl or a kept woman. This needn't have involved actually having sex with anyone; the clients could have been imaginary. They had settled on the industrial-liaison story because it would give her excuses to do things like travel around the region, make contacts with people in industry, and lease office space.

They had used various forms of electronic misdirection to set up Guangzhou telephone and fax numbers that would ring through to a subterranean room at MI6 headquarters where a small Chinese-British staff was available: a woman playing the role of receptionist and a blond, blue-eyed Englishman, fluent in Cantonese and Mandarin, playing the role of Meng Binrong. So the story would hold up as long as the people she talked to in Xiamen went no further than contacting her uncle by phone, fax, or email. But if anyone got curious enough to visit the offices of Xinyou Quality Control in Guangzhou, they'd find nothing, and the whole story would unravel. And there were any number of other ways in which Meng Anlan's identify could be picked apart. When that happened, the best possible outcome would be that she'd have to leave, never to come back, never to work in this kind of role again. Other possible outcomes included serving a long prison term or being executed.

She was being spent. There was no other way to put it. Her combination of looks, background, and command of language made her a one-of-a-kind asset. Someone at MI6 must, at one time, have had high hopes for her—must have planned to use her for something big and important. Her identity had been created, at enormous expense and trouble, to serve that purpose, whatever it might have been. But that original purpose had been forgotten when Abdallah Jones had moved to Xiamen and thrown away his mobile. Someone had made the decision that Olivia must be redeployed and put on the job of finding this one man.

She found a nice Western-style apartment on Gulangyu Island, just across a narrow strait from downtown Xiamen, and got it furnished and decorated in a style that was consistent with her cover story. She began taking the ferry into downtown every day and "looking for office space." But the search for office space was really a block-by-block reconnaissance of the square kilometer where Abdallah Jones was believed to have his safe house.

She went through several huge emotional swings in her assessment of the level of difficulty. A thousand meters simply wasn't that great a distance. Ten football pitches. And so, viewed from a comfortable remove, the job hadn't seemed that difficult. During her first couple of weeks of wearing out shoe leather in downtown Xiamen, though, she became inordinately depressed about her chances of making any headway. The population of the square kilometer in question was probably between twenty and thirty thousand. The number of buildings ran to several hundred. She felt overwhelmed, wandering around all day getting lost in the district's tortuous, crowded streets and then lying half awake all night in her Gulangyu apartment, retracing the steps she'd taken during the day and having hallucinatory dreams about all that she'd seen.

The apartment, at least, was nice. Gulangyu Island was small, steep, green, largely vehicle-free, and covered with sinuous, narrow roads that switchbacked through its little enclaves. A finer mesh of alleys and stone staircases webbed its parks and courtyards together. It was where Westerners had built their villas and their consulates in the post–Opium War period, when Xiamen had been known by its Fujianese name of Amoy. Though that era had long passed, the buildings remained.

Just barely. To look around Gulangyu Island was to be reminded that Fujian had been a tropical jungle and wanted, in the worst way, to be a tropical jungle again. If humans ever walked away from it, or stopped fighting it back with pruning shears and bucksaws, the creepers and lianas, the root systems, runners, spores, and seed pods would, in the space of a few years, overrun everything they had ever built. She did not know the detailed history of the place, but it was obvious that something like this must have happened to Gulangyu during the time of Mao, and that post-Mao real estate developers had gotten to the island just in the nick of time. From place to place you could still see an old Western-style building that was being torn to pieces in slow motion by foliage, rendering it so structurally unsound that only rats and wood-munching bugs could live there. But quite a few of the old buildings had been rescued—Olivia imagined a D-day-style invasion of the island, gardeners with saws and shovels parachuting out of the sky and storming the beaches—and were being liberated from the thorny or flowery embrace of climbing vines, deratted, reroofed, fixed up, and condoized. Her apartment was small but nicely located on the top floor of what had once been a French merchant's villa and now served as home to a couple dozen young professionals like Meng Anlan. Her bed looked out onto a small balcony with a view across the water to the brilliant downtown lights of Xiamen, and during those nights when sleep eluded her, she would sit up and hug her knees and stare across the water, wondering which of those scintillae was the screen of Abdallah Jones's laptop.

But as weeks went by and she got the square kilometer sorted out in her head, it began to seem doable. Ninety percent of the buildings could simply be ruled out. They were commercial properties or private residences. Unless Jones had some sort of an arrangement with a shop owner or a prosperous family, which seemed most unlikely, he had to be living in an apartment building, and not just any, but one that catered to transients and economic migrants. There were only a few of those in the search zone, and by various means she was able to cross several of them off the list. So those first few weeks of confusion and misery culminated, suddenly, with a short list of plausible Jones hideouts.

On rational grounds, she could not make a choice from among these, but her gut feeling was strongly in favor of a large, locally notorious dump of a place, five stories high, enmeshed in the finely reticulated streets of an old neighborhood but close enough to its edge that it was probably fated for demolition and skyscraperization. It had been a proud building during the era that the city was called Amoy and rich Europeans maintained wine cellars on Gulangyu. A hotel, perhaps. But long since repurposed into a workers' apartment building.

Olivia pretended to be interested in leasing an office in a building directly across the street. The two buildings were of equal height and similar vintage, webbed together by particolored skeins of improvised wiring. The landlord wanted to steer Olivia to offices in the lower floors, where access was easier and rent was higher. But Olivia had become expert in prolonging her "search for office space" to ridiculous lengths by making claims about the nutty miserliness of her uncle in Guangdong. She had a whole line of patter ready to go, and a war chest of anecdotes about how cheap Meng Binrong was. She used these to prod the landlord ever higher in the building and cajoled him to pry open old dusty doors and let her see offices that were being used as storage dumps for maintenance supplies and doors, toilets, and ventilators that were awaiting repair. In each office that she inspected, Olivia was careful to go and look at the view, forcing stuck windows and thrusting her head out into the hot muggy breeze. As she explained, her only compensation for working in an office so many flights of stairs above street level was the nice view she could get, and the natural ventilation. In truth, of course, she was looking at the building across the street, gazing into its windows, hoping to see a glimpse of a tall black Welshman.

An irregular thumping noise was emanating from somewhere, not inside this building but nearby. At first she heard it only subliminally, since it was buried in ambient sound from the street. But as she dragged the exhausted and irritable landlord skyward, this sound began to break clean from the clamor of the street and to enter her consciousness. The thumping started and stopped. It would go for three or six or ten beats, like the pounding of a heart, then cease for a little while, then start again, sometimes faster and sometimes slower. Sometimes it terminated in a faint crashing noise. She knew the pattern well because she and her colleagues in London had heard it in the background of Abdallah Jones's recorded phone conversations and had devoted many hours to wondering what it was. Their first thought had been construction noise from a neighboring apartment, but it didn't really fit that pattern; what sort of construction used only hammers but never a saw? Perhaps Jones lived upstairs of a butcher shop where heavy cleavers were being used to whack apart big carcasses? Or a martial arts dojo where students were hitting a punching bag? They had never really been able to pin it down, and it drove them crazy.

But the higher that Olivia climbed in that office building, the more certain she became that she was hearing exactly that pattern of sounds from the apartment building across the street. It was becoming more distinct, and she was growing more excited the higher she climbed.

Reaching the top floor, she entered an office and found her view blocked by a tattered blue tarp that had been hung down in front of the windows. She strode across the room, hauled the window open—they were huge, old-school, double-sash windows—and pulled the hem of a blue tarp to one side.

Directly across the street, perhaps twenty meters away from her, on the roof of the apartment building, half a dozen young men were playing basketball.

She watched one of them dribble through the defenders— *thump, thump, thump, thump, thump*—and take a shot. *Crash.*

"This might be acceptable," she said to the landlord, a bit distractedly since she was taking phone video of the hoopsters. "I'll get back to you."

The landlord made a phone call. Olivia continued to enjoy the view. The apartment directly below the makeshift basketball court had sheets or posters or something covering most of its windows. Olivia badly wanted to make a call of her own: *I have found him.* But she didn't want to repeat Jones's mistake. She had other ways of communicating with her handlers in London.

She found her way to the nearest *wangba*, logged onto a terminal, surfed the Internet at random for a while, then visited a certain blog and left a comment containing a prearranged phrase.

The next day she received a message encrypted in the least significant bits of an image file, telling her what to do next.

Some part of her hoped that MI6 would yank her straight back to London, buy her dinner at a nice restaurant, and give her a promotion. That fantasy was based on her guess that they would move on Jones immediately, either by tipping off the Public Security Bureau to his presence or by sending a hit squad.

The encrypted message, however, told a different story about how Olivia would be spending the next weeks or perhaps months.

They were congratulatory, in the devilishly understated manner that you would expect. But they seemed to have decided that

Abdallah Jones would be worth more to them if he could be milked for intelligence before being dispatched to reap his quota of black-eyed virgins. They wanted her to find a place from which Jones's apartment could be placed under surveillance, and then report back.

Olivia called the landlord, went back to the building across the street, took phone pictures of the office, and negotiated a lease. Using her cover identity, she sent an email to Meng Binrong, containing all the pictures and full details as to the terms of the lease. The message went to a mailbox registered in Guangzhou but was automatically encrypted and forwarded to London.

Another message, purring with satisfaction, reached her the next day. She was told to work on her cover and await further contacts.

Working on her cover was good advice; she had let that slide for a couple of weeks as she'd got herself established in Xiamen. She caused a desk and a chair to be moved into the new office, then buckled down to her pretend work, swapping volumes of email with her pretend clients and her pretend uncle, arranging trips to small factories up and down the estuary of the Nine Dragons River, and keeping one eye, always, on Apartment 505 across the street. The tenants were careful to keep most of the windows blocked, but sometimes they had to open them up for ventilation, and when they did, Olivia could see exciting details: lots of mattresses on the floor, and containers of what looked like industrial solvents, and men who did not seem to be from around here. She never saw Jones; but then it was inconceivable that a man as careful as him would actually show his face in an open window.

Equipment began to show up via FedEx, disguised as proto-types of consumer electronics devices that her pretend clients wanted to have mass-produced in China. The disguise was pretty easy to maintain; all electronic devices looked the same under the hood, being just circuit boards with chips on them. It was known that Chinese intelligence had begun to embed custom chips in circuit boards that were being shipped to the West, chips that were programmed to phone home and send back intelligence, and Olivia suspected that her original destiny—the one she'd been groomed for—had been to investigate that problem. So there was some symmetry, and a bit of satisfaction, in turning the tables. Following elaborate instruction sheets, sent to her, encrypted, by boffins in London and Fort Meade, she got these devices running in the office, listening in on any elec-tromagnetic signals emanating from the apartment building. Data streamed in and got compressed and encrypted and squirted back to London and Fort Meade, where people who actually understood this stuff could pick it apart and make sense of it.

This provided the first real setback in the investigation. The devices were picking up a lot of data, but it seemed (to make a long story short) that Abdallah Jones's safe house was located directly above a nest of Chinese hackers whose gear radiated a huge amount of electronic noise into the ether. These hackers, as far as Olivia could make out, were the basketball players, who also seemed to do a lot of work on the building's roof—so Jones's nest was actually sandwiched *between* two levels of hacker activity. This made it dif-ficult to tell Jones's noise apart from the hackers'. So much so as to suggest that Jones might have chosen the site *deliberately* as a trick to hide his own emanations in his neighbors' noise.

More stuff was FedExed, and Olivia made a foray into the apart-ment building and planted a device behind a radiator in the corridor just outside of Jones's apartment. She was not privy to details, but she gathered that this somehow made it easier to sort out the ter-rorists' bits from the hackers' bits. Then MI6 flew in a signals intel-ligence boffin, using the name Alastair and pretending to be one of Xinyou Quality Control's clients. Alastair and Olivia held lengthy "meetings" in the office, during which Alastair tweaked the equip-ment that was already there and installed a new box: a system for bouncing invisible lasers off the windowpanes of Apartment 505. Any sound inside the apartment would cause the windows to vibrate slightly, and the laser rig could pick up the vibrations and translate them back into surprisingly intelligible sound recordings. He also hooked up an automated video recording system that would turn on whenever movement was detected; that is, whenever the terror-ists (for there was absolutely no doubt, now, that they were terror-ists) opened a window.

The fact that the office building was under renovation provided huge advantages in using it as a surveillance platform. Its façade was obscured by a tangle of scaffolding, ropes, tarps, lashed bam-boo, extension cords, work lights, and pneumatic hoses. Amid all that clutter, Alastair's equipment—which was really quite modest in size—could easily go unnoticed. Their primary camera peered out through a hole, no larger than the tip of Olivia's finger, in the blue tarp.

Olivia did not have to read any ecstatic memos from London to know that she had found a gold mine. What feedback she did get from London suggested that the value of the information they were getting was so high that they now wished that Abdallah Jones would pursue a very lengthy career of blowing things up, or preparing to, in Xiamen, just so that they could go on milking him. Reading the foreign newspapers, Olivia saw occasional reports of Predator drone strikes in Waziristan and could not help getting the impression that the stuff she was sending back to London was directly correlated with some of those.

She was running one of the most high-value installations in the global war on terror. And she was the only person who *could* run it. The operation was a colossal success—much more important than whatever now-forgotten job they'd *originally* wanted her to do. Euphoric as she might have been about this, at some level she knew that it couldn't last. Eventually Jones would have to do something. He couldn't just live there for month after month constructing bombs to no purpose. Sooner or later they would learn, from the lasers on the windows, that Jones was about to go blow something up. And then MI6 would have an interesting decision to make. If they did *nothing*, the explosion would happen and the PSB would investigate it and eventually find their way to Apartment 505. And working outward from there they would eventually come and check out Olivia's office and find all the high-tech surveillance gear, arrest her, and subject her to God only knew what sort of treatment. If it came to that, Olivia would have to destroy the equipment and get out of town first.

Or, in a spirit of international cooperation, MI6 might tip off the Chinese authorities and thereby prevent Jones from carrying out his plan. But in so doing they would *also* tip their hand as to the sources and methods they'd used to learn all these interesting things, which would lead to the same or similar consequences for Olivia.

Or they could send in some kind of hit squad to kill Jones or even abduct him and get him out of the country. This, to put it mildly, would be a challenging operation.

In any case, Olivia had been supplied with detailed instructions as to how to shut down her little safe house, should it come to that. There were no papers to shred, no tapes to burn. Everything was electronic. So the shutdown procedure came down to frying the electronics. This they had made easy. Everything in the place had a kill switch; all she had to do was hit that, and a jolt of high voltage would go through all the chips and destroy the information stored in them. The PSB could still recover the circuit boards, but, according to Alastair, these were devoid of useful information; they were just stock chips, off-the-shelf stuff that anyone could buy from electronics retailers on the Internet, connected together in an obvious way. The important stuff—the unique stuff—was all in how they were configured, the bits that they contained, and this was easy to scramble. It would be *nice,* he stressed, if she could prevent the stuff from falling into their hands—for example, by throwing it over the railing of a ferry or burning down the building (she couldn't tell whether he was being serious about this last suggestion)—but the most important thing was to hit all those kill switches.

In a properly manned safe house, there would have been at least three people, working in shifts, looking after the gear, always ready to hit the kill switches and shut the place down on a moment's notice. A few decades earlier MI6 might have had the resources to maintain that many deep cover agents in China. If the operation had been in almost any country, they could have found a way. But in China it was just too difficult. Once Alastair had flown home, she was the only person there, and she could only spend so much time in the office. Meng Binrong sent her many pretend emails making him look like a total slavedriver, and this gave her the excuse she needed to clock twelve, fourteen, sometimes sixteen hours a day in the office, but sometimes she had to go back to Gulangyu and get a few hours' sleep in her apartment, if only to keep up appearances with the landlord and the neighbors.

Because of those long hours and the tunnel vision that tended to set in as a result, perhaps she could be forgiven for being so oblivious, for so long, to the obvious target of Abdallah Jones's preparations. Xiamen was hosting an international conference, bringing in diplomats from all over the globe. Ostensibly this was to celebrate the 350th anniversary of Zheng Chenggong's liberation of Taiwan from the Dutch. But everyone knew that the real agenda was to discuss relations between Taiwan and mainland China and that very significant developments might be announced there. Some radical Islamists claimed Zheng Chenggong as one of their own, and accordingly considered Taiwan to be part of the Islamic Caliphate. It was a forlorn pretense, but anyway they were furious about oppression of Muslims in western China, so any excuse would suffice.

Olivia had noticed banners going up on lampposts, featuring heroic images of Zheng Chenggong, but did not really become aware that the conference was happening until it began to cause traffic jams on her way to work in the morning. At which point she understood, far too late, that there must be some connection between this and a recent spike in chatter from Apartment 505. The crisis must be nigh.

ONE MORNING SHE was returning to the office, having just enjoyed a few hours of sleep at home, when she noticed a minor oddity: a van parked on the street between the apartment building and her office. It was messing up the flow of traffic and creating a minor sensation among street vendors and passersby. If it hadn't been for the diplomatic conference and her awareness that something big was about to happen, she might have ignored it. But as it was, her first thought was that the jig was up: it was a squad of PSB investigators come to knock on Abdallah Jones's door and ask him what he and his friends were doing in there. Or worse: they were coming to arrest Olivia.

On further inspection, though, it didn't look like an official vehicle, and the driver was a young woman in blue boots who seemed to be having some trouble with keys. But it had been enough to get her heart pounding, so after walking slowly and calmly into the office building and getting into the stairway where no one could see her, she ascended the steps two at a time and got into her office as soon as she could. Resisting the temptation to gawk out the window, she pulled on the headphones that she used to monitor the sounds in Abdallah Jones's apartment.

Everything sounded routine: some snoring, a few sleepy men getting up and making tea, listening to an Arabic podcast. The very normality of this calmed her down quite a bit and made her feel a fool for having become so excited. She blotted perspiration from her forehead, sat down, set her purse on the desk, woke up her computer, and checked her email.

A huge thud came through on the headphones, followed by a great deal of excited talking.

Then some loud pops, clipped by the electronics so that they just came through as dropouts in the stream of noise.

Then the sound went dead entirely. She pulled off the headphones and realized that she could hear more pops *directly* from across the street. She went to the window and checked the laser device. It seemed to be in good repair. Then she peered through a peephole in the blue tarp and saw the problem: it worked by bouncing a laser off a windowpane. But the windowpane in question no longer existed.

She was startled by crashing and splintering noises from inside the office, just to her right. Pulling her head back inside, she noticed that half of her windows were now shards on the floor. There was dust in the air and craters in the wall opposite the windows. Her mind, slowly catching up, told her that she had just heard a long burst of automatic weapons fire and that a good bit of it had come directly across the street and sprayed the office.

She dropped to hands and knees, reached up, and hit the kill switch on the laser device.

MI6 had sent in a hit squad. They were doing it now. But they had forgotten to advise her.

Or perhaps they had just decided that she was expendable.

SOKOLOV HAD SEEN many strange things already this morning, and yet still he was taken aback when he swung out of the shattered window and scanned the front of the building to find it cluttered with young Chinese men crawling around on it like spiders.

Then he remembered that, sixty seconds earlier, his greatest concern in the world had been what to do about a cabal of Chinese hackers. These must be them.

He understood and approved of the decision that the hackers had made to avoid the building's stairwells and escape via its exterior surface. It would have been easy enough to follow their lead down to the street, and in a sense this was the obvious decision to make, since they knew the terrain much better than he did. Often, in unfamiliar territory, it was wisest to pattern one's movements after the locals'.

On the other hand, there was this thick bundle of wires running from a point on the building's facade not far from where Sokolov was now, across the street to an office building under construction. The wires, in aggregate, must be a lot heavier than Sokolov, and so would probably support his weight. He favored the idea of using them as an escape route, for two reasons. First of all, simply getting down to the street might not help him that much, since, unlike the hackers, he could not blend in. He would be noticed and arrested very quickly. But if he could get into the other building he would have some chance of hiding somewhere, long enough, at least, to devise a plan.

Second, the apartment he had just left was full of high explosives and was on fire.

Now, compared to the typical layman, Sokolov was not especially worried about the proximity of ANFO and open flames. Like most high explosives, the stuff was difficult to set off. Fire alone would not suffice. Some sort of primer was needed: a detonator, such as a blasting cap. So it was quite possible that the entire building could burn to the ground without any sort of explosion taking place.

And yet this was a simplistic reading of the situation. There was a lot of other stuff in that apartment besides ANFO. During the few, frenzied moments he had spent there, Sokolov had not been able to make a systematic inventory. But if they were planning to use the ANFO, as seemed likely, then they must have some blasting caps in the place; and if they were planning to use it soon, then it was likely that they had already assembled some complete explosive devices in which the detonators had been mated with the ANFO. And anyway, in that devil's kitchen he had just left behind, there was no telling what other stuff they might have mixed up: the terrorists had recipes for other explosives besides ANFO that were much less stable. And so there was a strong argument for getting away from the building as fast as he could. The wire bundle offered him that.

The main argument against it was that the terrorists could easily shoot at him as he was suspended in the air above the street right outside their windows.

But he could hand-over-hand his way along a stretched wire about as fast as most men could run. And the few terrorists who were still alive must be rather preoccupied. So that made the decision easy. He clambered over a series of window grates and other stuff to the wire bundle, reached out with one hand, grabbed, and slowly transferred his weight. The bundle didn't rip loose from the wall. Good. He let go of the apartment building altogether, swung out into space, reached, and made another grab. Then another. Then another.

Then felt himself descending and saw the bundle receding into the sky.

This wasn't like crossing a stretched steel cable in a military training camp. The bundle was a skein of perhaps two dozen separate wires, as gaily colored as a maypole. Some of the wires were electrical, some telephone, some data, some not clearly identifiable. He couldn't get his hand around the whole bundle, and so every time he swung forward he had to thrust his fingertips like a blade into the heart of the thing and get a grip on whatever presented itself. This had worked the first few times, but on his last grab he had aimed wrong, missed the bundle, and snatched one single wire, a blue Ethernet cable that spiraled around all the other wires, and now his weight was pulling all the slack out of that one wire and peeling it loose from the bundle. He reached up with his free hand, whipped it around the taut blue line, and pulled himself up enough to get that first hand free, then repeated, ascending the wire but not gaining altitude since the blue wire was still giving up slack. He was only an arm's length below the bundle but couldn't quite reach it. Finally the wire stopped giving way and held fast and he kicked up with his legs, making himself upside down for a moment, and got both legs wrapped around the whole bundle. The rifle, and a CamelBak water pouch that he was wearing on his back, fell to the ends of their straps and dangled. He allowed himself a few seconds to catch his breath before he began shinnying along the bundle as rapidly as he could manage. This was much slower than the hand-over-hand technique and made him feel like an incompetent civilian, but he could not risk doing it the other way. In any case, he was not too worried about being shot at since the apartment was now completely engulfed in flames. Solvent cans burst open and vomited storms of combustible vapor from windows.

YUXIA WAS BEMUSED by the length of time it took the locksmith to work on the van's ignition. Her family's hotel in the mountains of Fujian was well stocked with DVDs of Western action movies, which could be had for next to nothing in Xiamen. From watching these, Yuxia had learned that any vehicle in the world could be started in a few seconds just by striking at the steering column until wires fell out and then touching the wires together until a spark was observed. And yet this locksmith turned it into an elaborate procedure that centered around picking the lock itself. It was quite obvious from the look on his face that he was extremely disturbed by all the gunfire taking place above, and that this was not making him get the job done any faster.

Yuxia was, of course, rather disturbed herself. She had reacted somewhat impulsively in handcuffing the poor locksmith to the steering wheel. At the time, only a few shots had been fired, and she had assumed that this would be the last of it, and that he would have the engine hot-wired in a few moments anyway. He was over-reacting—using this as a pretext to abandon Yuxia, and, by extension, Zula and Csongor and Peter. But since then it had developed into what sounded like a full-scale war, and pieces of debris kept clattering down onto the van's roof. Every time it happened the locksmith was startled and seemed to lose his place in the lock-picking project. It dragged on for what seemed like a year, and Yuxia began to lose her nerve, as she felt both terrified to be in this predicament and guilty over what she had done to the locksmith. Nothing prevented her from exiting the van and running away. And yet every time she thought about it seriously, something big would slam down onto the van's roof and remind her that it was a good thing to have steel over her head. And life really would be much easier for her if she could get this van out of here.

So preoccupied did she become with such thoughts that she was startled when she heard the van's engine come to life. The dashboard lights came on and the tachometer needle rose off its pin.

The locksmith let out a curse, threw down the tools he'd been working with, and attacked the manacle with something else. This time it took him only a few seconds. Then he was gone, leaving the handcuff dangling from the steering wheel and half of his tools on the floor of the van. He didn't bother to shut the passenger door.

Yuxia reached over, pulled the door shut, then settled herself in the driver's seat again and put the vehicle into gear.

Then she took one last look back at the apartment building. What about Zula and her two hacker boys? The one who was bad for her, and the one who was good for her?

CSONGOR WAS A bit slower than Peter when it came to picking his handcuff. Zula noticed that he was sticking his tongue out as he worked. Somehow, from that, she concluded it was best to remain absolutely still and not distract him.

She, however, was growingly distracted by a sound that was echoing down the stairwell and getting louder every second. It was a human voice, repeating the same utterance, again and again, as if the speaker were an actor trying to memorize an elusive snatch of dialog. At the beginning she could only make out a few of the more percussive consonants, but as the speaker got closer, one flight at a time, she was able to piece the sounds together into words.

He was saying: "You FUCKINK bitch! You FUCKINK bitch! You FUCKINK bitch! . . ."

It was Ivanov and he was saying this in a tone, more of astonishment than of anger, as if the degree of fucking-bitchness exhibited today by Zula went far beyond all known historic precedents, to the point where Ivanov himself almost could not credit the testimony of his own senses. As he proceeded, his astonishment only mounted, and when he said "FUCKINK" his voice would flutter, for a moment, up into a falsetto before collapsing back into "bitch."

In spite of all her efforts not to, she glanced at Csongor to see how he was doing. He reacted immediately, which told her that he could hear it too and that he understood its significance.

Then the chant was interrupted with a sudden "YOU!"

Ivanov was only two, perhaps three flights above them. His footfalls had stopped.

He had to be talking to Peter; but Peter made no response that Zula could hear.

"All by yourself?" Ivanov asked. He had to repeat the question and insist that Peter supply an answer. Finally Zula was able to make out some sort of faint response, kind of a yelping sound, from Peter.

"And where is your lovely girlfriend then?"

The conversation, if that was the right word for it, was nothing more than a series of utterances from Ivanov:

"Ah, brave Peter goes ahead to scout for danger? Zula waits behind, ready to follow? Shall we go and have conversation with Zula? No? Vwy not? Perhaps story is lie? Yes? Is lie? Zula is in cellar for other reason? Maybe because she is CHAINED TO PIPE!? Because BRAVE BOYFRIEND left her behind? TO DIE? While BRAVE BOYFRIEND ran away LIKE FUCKINK RAT?"

A hand came down gently on Zula's shoulder, and she jumped away so violently that she practically split the skin on her wrist when the manacle pulled her up short. But it was only Csongor. He had gotten free. He put a finger to his lips, then dropped to one knee, in the attitude of a man proposing marriage, and went to work on her handcuff with the bobby pin. At first he tried to get access to the keyhole on the manacle that encircled her wrist, but this was pointed downward and it was difficult for him to get the right angle on it, so he gave up on that and began working on the one that was locked around the pipe, which was tilted toward him conveniently.

"How does BRAVE GIRL like Zula get such piece of shit boyfriend!?" Ivanov was hollering. "What would your parents think of you, Peter!? Who raised you anyway? Wolves? Gypsies? Answer question! Not just sob like little girl. Ah, you FUCKINK . . . PIECE . . . of SHIT!"

Each of the three words was punctuated by a boom. Csongor jumped at the first one and dropped the bobby pin. Soon enough he had snatched it up and resumed work on the manacle.

At the sound of Ivanov's gun, Zula had instinctively turned away from the door at the base of the stairs and now she stayed in that position, focusing all her attention on Csongor's hands, like a little kid who thinks that the monster will go away if she pretends it isn't there. This was some really stupid shit, but nothing that had happened in the last few days had really prepared her for anything like what had apparently just happened to Peter.

"Csongor!" called a soft voice.

Zula and Csongor both startled and turned around to discover Ivanov in the room with them, a semiautomatic pistol in one hand, pointed at the floor.

"This is good," Ivanov said. "Finally, someone is real man."

Csongor gave up on picking the manacle and rose to his feet, standing at Zula's side, facing Ivanov from perhaps eight feet away. Ivanov was gazing on Zula's face in a way that made Csongor want to intercept the eye line; he took half a step forward and got between Zula and Ivanov.

"Yes," Ivanov said. "This is proper. I always knew you were proper gentleman, Csongor. Now, move aside so that I can put bullet in head of lying bitch."

"No," Csongor said.

Ivanov rolled his eyes. "I understand you must continue gentleman behavior. Is all quite proper. But situation is as follows. I told Zula she must tell truth about apartment or I would kill her. Zula lied. Now I must carry out end of deal as promised. Surely you understand."

Ivanov now raised the weapon so that he could sight along its barrel and sidestepped a little bit so that he could draw a bead on Zula. But Csongor moved to get in the way.

"Is not game of hockey. Is not puck. Is fuckink *bullet,* Csongor. You cannot stop it."

"Yes, I can," Csongor pointed out.

"Csongor! You are only man in whole building who deserves to be alive," Ivanov pointed out. "Please stop being fuckink asshole. Don't you want to get old and grow the mustache? Drive the bus?"

Zula could only interpret those questions as further proof of Ivanov's derangement, but they seemed to mean something to Csongor, who shrugged.

"Zula wants you to live. Don't you, Zula?"

It was an odd question. Csongor turned around to look at her.

As he did, Zula saw Ivanov lunge forward with unexpected speed. The look on Zula's face told Csongor that something was wrong and Csongor began to swivel his head back—just in time to receive a crushing blow on the jaw from the butt of Ivanov's gun. Csongor spiraled toward the floor. Zula was able to get half underneath him and cushion the impact. She got her free hand under his head and cradled it until it reached the floor.

Then she was stuck, sitting on the floor with Csongor's full weight on her lap. He must have weighed well over 250 pounds.

Zula wet her lips and opened her mouth to make the last speech of her life, in which she would try to explain to Ivanov why it didn't make sense to kill Peter for not treating Zula chivalrously and then shoot Zula in the head while she was handcuffed to a pipe.

There was a series of deafening bangs. The side of Ivanov's head was ripped off by an invisible shovel and flung across the room. He dove sideways as if trying to catch his brains before they hit the floor.

Zula now noticed that there was another person in the room: a tall black man. He was carrying a long weapon that Zula recognized from the re-u as an AK-47.

His eyes met hers.

"English?" he asked.

"American," she said.

"Your confusion is understandable, but I was inquiring, not as to *nationality*, but as to *language*," said the man with the assault rifle. "I'll endeavor to make my questions less ambiguous in future." He was speaking with some sort of British accent. He squatted down next to Ivanov's corpse and began slapping it all over. "This the dude who cuffed you?" he asked, switching seamlessly to Ebonics.

A faint jingle sounded from one of Ivanov's pockets. The man reached in and drew out a handful of change, sorted through it, and pulled out one item that was not a coin: a handcuff key. "Bingo," he said. Slinging the assault rifle over his shoulder, he stood, strode over to Zula's side, and unlocked the end of her handcuff that was locked around the pipe. "Freedom!" he proclaimed brightly.

"Thank you!" Zula exclaimed.

"Is an illusion," he continued, and snapped the manacle shut around his right wrist, chaining his right arm to Zula's left. Then he pocketed the key.

"Who are you?" she asked, squirming out from beneath Csongor.

"You can call me Mr. Jones, Zula," he answered. He now let

the assault rifle slip down off his shoulder, grabbed it by the barrel, and looked at it wistfully. "Difficult to fire with one hand," he pointed out. He turned to look at her. His face was intelligent and not unattractive. "What's the only thing more attention getting, on the streets of Xiamen, than two niggers handcuffed together?"

"I give up."

"Two niggers handcuffed together with a Kalashnikov." He laid the weapon on the floor. Then his eye fell on Ivanov's semiautomatic. He picked it up with his unencumbered left hand. "Nice piece," he said. "A 1911, if I'm not mistaken."

Even in the midst of so many distractions, some part of Zula's mind found it curious that Mr. Jones could be anything less than totally certain that Ivanov's gun was a 1911. *Obviously* it was a 1911. He transferred it to his right hand, then put his thumb on its hammer, which was drawn back in ready-to-fire position. He pulled the trigger and carefully let the hammer down so that it wouldn't fire. Then he reached across with his left and racked the slide once, ejecting a live round, chambering a fresh one, and automatically recocking the hammer. "Cocked," he muttered. With a bit of fumbling, he taught himself how to apply the safety. "And locked." Then, clearly wishing that his right hand were not encumbered, he transferred the weapon back into his left and stuck it in his pants. "Come on," he said, "some kind of fascinating destiny is waiting for us out there. *Inshallah*."

He grabbed her hand and started walking toward the exit. She tried to peel away and drop to Csongor's side, but Mr. Jones simply let go of her hand and allowed the handcuff chain to go taut, so that the metal bit into her already-raw wrist and jerked her along in his path. She sprawled and staggered in his wake and bounced off a wall, where a filthy window, set in a well below street level, grudgingly allowed dim, confused gray light to seep in through several layers of bars and mesh, and thick lashings of rain-driven dirt.

Framed in that window was the face of a man, a young Chinese man, staring into her eyes. No more than arm's length away. How long had he been watching events in the cellar?

But he might as well have been a talking head on a television screen for all that he could help her now. Jones gave another yank, pulling her closer, then reestablished his grip on her hand and began pulling her up the stairs.

AS HE WAS shinnying along the cable bundle, Sokolov had more time than was really good for him to develop that theme of the high explosives and the detonators in the burning apartment just a few meters away. Old instincts began to take over, and he noticed that his mouth was frozen in a yawn; this was so that his eardrums would not burst in the event of an explosion. Every time he advanced his hands to a new position, he took care to sink his fingers deeply into the wire bundle so that he could not be jarred loose by a shock wave. He kept his chin tucked against his chest, though every so often he would let it hang back so that he could get an upside-down view of the office building. For an agonizingly long time, this did not seem to be getting any closer, and so he forced himself not to check for a while. Then he looked again and saw that it was no more than two meters away. He reached forward as far as he dared, got a good solid grip into the guts of the wire bundle, and let go with his legs. He was now hanging a little more than arm's length from the point where the wire bundle penetrated a gap between two hanging tarps.

The tarps flashed as if someone were taking a photograph from across the street. Sokolov began to open his mouth and to tighten his grip on the wires during the fraction of a second that elapsed between then and the arrival of the shock wave. This struck him like a wrecking ball and hurled him bodily into the tarps.

AFTER THE BURST of fire that had broken out the windows of Xinyou Quality Control Ltd. and sent Olivia sprawling to the floor, the gun battle across the street had died down rapidly. Olivia remained on hands and knees for a while, staying below the level of the window-sill. The office contained eight separate devices with kill switches. She was able to take care of three of them before she got to a place where the floor was covered with shattered glass: not the modern tempered stuff that crumbled into nice cubes, but jagged shards of the old school. Crawling on hands and knees through it didn't seem like a good idea. She had not received a *lot* of combat training but she had received a *little,* and one of the more vivid lessons had demonstrated that the stuff civilians tended to hide behind—car doors, brick walls—was almost completely useless when it came to stopping high-velocity rounds. The walls of this building were brick. So it was pointless to hide behind them in any case. Olivia stood up and began crunching over the glass to reach the other five devices that needed to be killed. Footing was treacherous since her Chinese career-girl costume involved high heels, and the glass shards liked to slip over each other when she put her weight on them. At any rate she made it to all the devices and hit their kill switches. She was making a conscious effort not to be distracted by what was going on across the street. Abdallah Jones's apartment had gone up in flames with preposterous speed, as if it were made out of flash paper. Either he was dead or had been flushed from cover into the streets of Xiamen, where he could not possibly last for more than a few minutes.

The initial shock of the gun battle had begun to clear from her mind, and she now realized that the situation was not as dire as she had believed at first. Of course she still had no idea who had invaded Jones's apartment or why. Certainly there were many who wanted him dead. Speculating about it now would get her nowhere. No one was bashing down the doors of Xinyou Quality Control Ltd. So the correct thing for her to do was to gather up all the spy gear and destroy it. She thought she could manage this rather easily by collecting all of it into a garbage bag and then, during the ride home, throwing the bag into the strait between Xiamen and Gulangyu. It would look a little bit odd, but there was nothing radically unusual about Chinese people throwing garbage into the ocean, so it would probably go unnoticed. Even if someone did decide to make a fuss about it, such a crime hardly merited bringing out scuba divers to comb the murky bottom of the strait.

So she yanked the liner out of her wastebasket and made the rounds of the office, pulling the electronics loose from their cords and cables and dropping them into the sack one by one. Somewhat reluctantly she threw her laptop in there too.

She knotted the bag shut. It had become so heavy that she had to carry it slung over her shoulder, Santa Claus style. She turned her back to the vacant windows and began walking across the office to fetch her purse from the desk. She would walk calmly down the stairs and make her way on foot to the waterfront, where she would splurge by hiring a water taxi to take her across to Gulangyu. Halfway there, she would drop the sack overboard. Once she got to her apartment she would pack her bag, make a coded phone call announcing that she was blowing town, then proceed to the airport and grab the next flight capable of getting her out of the country.

As she rehearsed this plan in her mind, she was bewildered by the sudden awareness that she was crumpled against the wall of the office with the breath knocked out of her. Her view of the windows was sideways—no, it was upside down. Then the view disappeared altogether as a roiling cloud of gray dust hurled itself in through the shredded tarps and expanded to fill every corner of the room, including her open mouth.

She tried to spit, but her mouth was dry. The dust had penetrated all the way down her throat, and this made her esophagus go into spasms that only ended when she retched. An instinct to get away from the pool of sick forced her up onto hands and knees. This small movement sent electric knitting needles down all her limbs and made her so dizzy that she became sick again.

She had to get out.

She tottered back against the wall of the office, knees still bent under her.

Her eye fell on the garbage bag, which had come to rest next to her. She grabbed the knot she'd tied in it. Then she gathered her feet under her and pushed herself up, leaning against the wall. With her free hand she groped to the side until she had found the door. Or rather the doorway, since the door had been blown open.

Where was her purse? She looked back into the office, but it was just a gray murk with indistinct shapes in it. Everything had been rearranged. Much of the ceiling had collapsed.

The vacant windows, denuded of their tarps, formed four large hazy gray rectangles across the opposite wall.

A shadow appeared in one of them: the silhouette of a man. He vaulted in over the windowsill, performed a shoulder roll, and alighted on the office floor in a low crouch. In the same movements he unslung a Kalashnikov from his shoulder and brought it up ready to fire.

Ready to fire at *her*. For he had taken dead aim at her face. She knew this because her eyes locked with his through the weapon's iron sights. His were blue.

He had shouted something. Through her confusion and fear and the ringing in her ears it took her a few moments to place it: *"Ne dvigaites'!"* which in Russia was a rudely familiar way of saying "Don't move!" Realizing his mistake, he then added, in English: "Freeze!"

"Ne streliaite!" she said, a bit more formally: "Don't shoot!"

The two of them remained frozen thus for a count of three. Then the Russian exhaled and lowered the weapon's barrel until it was pointed at the floor.

Olivia spun through the vacant doorway and ran.

THE STREET OUTSIDE Yuxia's van got very bright and then just as quickly got very dark and then it was clobbered by what sounded and felt like the entire contents of the apartment building.

As soon as Yuxia could see more than arm's length beyond the windshield—which took a few seconds—she floored the gas pedal. The van jumped forward less than a meter and stopped hard.

There was a loud noise from behind her. She turned around to see that half of a cast-concrete window lintel had fallen through the vehicle's sheet-metal roof like a knife thrust through a sheet of aluminum foil and come to rest on the crushed remains of the middle seat. Dust and sand and gravel were raining into the gap in the van's roof.

She gunned the engine again and again and heard the rear wheels spinning uselessly on the street. Something was chocked under the front wheels.

MARLON'S TENDENCY TO get fascinated by things and for fascination to then override the normal human instinct of self-preservation had been getting him in trouble since the age when he was old enough to crawl to an electrical socket and shove something into it. Having seen the big white man shoot the younger white man in the stairwell and the black man follow him down into the cellar, Marlon could not fail to follow them down one more level and see how it all turned out. Descending to the alley and dropping to his knees before the window well, he'd been able to peer in and see everything that played out there: the burly white man trying to help the handcuffed black girl and getting pistol-whipped for his trouble, some sort of confrontation between the white killer and the black girl, the decisive intervention of the black stalker, and then the departure of the two blacks, handcuffed together. The girl had looked Marlon in the eye on the way out, and he had been terrified for a moment that she would call out to him and alert the black man to his presence and that Marlon would thus become the next victim, but it hadn't happened.

They had left the young white man unconscious or dead on the cellar floor. Marlon was tempted to leave the matter at that and simply get out of there.

But, though the details were incredibly confusing, he had the strong idea that he and his mates had all just escaped death because of action taken by *someone* to warn them by switching the power to their flat on and off. The obvious candidates, since they were down in the room with the fuse box, were the black girl and the big white man. Now it seemed as though they were being made to suffer for what they had done. He felt bad that he was unable to help the black girl, owing to her being handcuffed to an armed killer—and not just any killer, but a killer who had killed *another* killer—which, in the video-game-based metric that Marlon used for keeping score in the world, conferred an elite status—but the white guy was just lying there all by himself, unguarded, and Marlon had the idea that he could get into the cellar through the building's back entrance and see if the guy was okay.

Normally the back door was, of course, locked. But today someone had left it hanging wide open.

Marlon was just stepping through it when the building exploded. And though his first instinct was to run outside and get away from it, he was glad that he didn't. A huge amount of the structure collapsed into the basement and caused a piston of dust to shoot up the corridor right toward his face. He spun away from it and took it in his back, facing out into the back alley, and there he saw perhaps a thousand loose pieces of brickwork rain down from above. Any one of them, had it struck him on the top of the head, would have killed him. But the doorway—according to seismic lore, the strongest part of a building—held above him and protected him.

THE MAN CALLING himself Mr. Jones was quite clearly making it up as he went along. Just as clearly, he was comfortable doing so. He did not appear to be aware that the cellar had an exit on the back alley and so, pulling Zula along with him, he went up one flight of stairs to the ground-floor landing. As they approached it he reached across his body with his free hand and clamped this over Zula's eyes and did not let her see again until they were in a corridor. Zula knew why and didn't fight it.

From there he made for the building's main entrance in the front. After a couple of turns in narrow corridors, they reached a place where Zula could look straight down a hallway, across what she took to be the lobby, and out the front doors to the street. Parked squarely in front of those doors was the van. At first Zula could not see Yuxia in the driver's-side window, but then she noticed movement and realized that Yuxia had leaned over to pull the passenger-side door closed. Then Yuxia sat up behind the wheel again, shifted the van into gear, and turned to look toward the building. Zula enjoyed a moment of hope that Yuxia might see into the corridor and catch Zula's eye. But this would have been very difficult because the interior of the building would have seemed very dark to anyone looking at it from outside. And not only dark but crowded, since tenants, spooked by the gun battle, were getting out of the place as fast as they could.

They almost reached the lobby. Then Jones, apparently acting on a whim, dodged to his left into a door that he had noticed ajar. It was the apartment that fronted on the street and it seemed to have been abandoned in a hurry; no one was in here, but the television was still going and the smell of hot food was coming from the kitchen. Jones headed for the front window, approached it sidelong, yanked the shade down, then peeled the edge of it back an inch or two and sighted through the gap into the street.

"There's our ride," he remarked after a second or two, and Zula thought he might be talking about the van until she noted that he had pressed the side of his head against the wall and was looking some distance down the street.

Then there was a fantastic noise and the limp window shade slammed against the glass and then, an instant later, flailed out into the empty space beyond, since the entire window had been blown out of its frame. Zula cringed instinctively as the shock came up through her feet. But the shocks kept coming.

Jones did not seem in the least surprised.

"The building is collapsing from the top down," he remarked. "Perhaps we should get out of it."

"But Csongor!"

"If Csongor is the man in the cellar," said Jones, "he picked the right place to ride this out."

HAD THE CHINESE woman not spoken to him in Russian, Sokolov would not have given her a second thought. But now his curiosity had been piqued, and so he devoted a little more time to departing the destroyed office than he might have otherwise. The place had been utterly devastated, with most of the damage caused by a collapsed lath-and-plaster ceiling that Sokolov had to tromp over and wade through as he made his way to the door. Conspicuously located near the exit was a garbage bag tied in a knot, which the Russian-speaking Chinese woman had apparently meant to take with her until Sokolov had vaulted in and scared her to death. He found that it was surprisingly heavy and that it contained a number of discrete rectangular objects.

Turning back to survey the office, he was struck by the sheer number of wires and cables strung about the place. Most of them were not connected to anything; their plugs were splayed on the floor, covered with plaster but not with glass. The shattered glass formed the lowest layer of debris. The cords and plugs had been thrown down after the glass had broken and the ceiling had fallen down afterward. In the rush and confusion of the moment, Sokolov could not draw any definite conclusions from that, only make a note of it as a perplexing bit of data that he would have to make sense of later.

Raising his sights a little, he scanned the office as he was slowly backing out of it and noticed that some wires had been tacked and/ or zip-tied to window frames or anything else that would hold them up. At least one of those wires led to what was quite obviously an antenna, and not the sort of antenna that one could buy in an electronics shop but something that said "military" to Sokolov.

His heel struck something heavy but yielding. He looked down and kicked some loose shards of plaster away to reveal a woman's purse. The blast had knocked it off a table, and a few items had spilled from its open top when it struck the floor. Sokolov gathered those up and shoved them back into the purse and zipped it shut. Then he went to the door. He unknotted the garbage bag and saw that it contained a laptop and several electronic boxes, but nothing that was intrinsically useful to him right now. Besides, it was heavy.

Suspiciously heavy.

He reached in and pulled out one of the boxes at random and wiggled it in the air. All its weight was concentrated in the base. There was a steel plate, or something, in there.

It was meant to sink when thrown into water.

It was spy gear and this was a spy nest, and the Russian-speaking Chinese woman worked here and was trying to shut the place down.

But she must not be Chinese or else she would not need to be so furtive. She was a foreign agent.

Sokolov dropped the purse into the garbage bag, reknotted it, and slung it over his shoulder. Then he walked down the hallway until he found the stairs. He descended a couple of flights, walked into another devastated and abandoned office, approached its blown-out windows, and made a reconnaissance of the street. The van—Sokolov's ticket out of here—was still there, though there was a gap in the roof where something big had cratered it.

His eye was drawn by movement at the building's front entrance. Two people wanted to leave the building. To that end, they were standing framed in its doorway. But they were somewhat torn between fear of what was behind them and fear of what was ahead. Behind them the building was undergoing a gradual, staged collapse, or settling, as one failed floor accordioned into the one below it and the weight of the structure was cruelly redistributed. Each of these events led to a vast exhalation of dust from all the building's orifices including the front door; so the two people Sokolov was looking at tended to vanish at random intervals, for a few seconds at a time, as a nebula of dust puffed out of the door and then subsided. Nothing was quite horizontal or vertical anymore, so big messes of debris tended to skid off the top of the pile and accelerate toward the street and strike it with impacts that Sokolov could feel in his gonads and that must be even more impressive to those people in the doorway.

There was another great settling, another one of those horizontal mushroom clouds of dust; and when it cleared, the two people were gone. They had made their move. Sokolov scanned up and down the street, forcing himself to remain calm and do a proper job of it. He saw them running hand in hand away from the building, headed for an intersection about a block away where a vast crowd of spectators had gathered: cars that had simply come to a stop, and pedestrians crouching behind them to look back at the spectacle of the burning and collapsing building.

There was something familiar about each of the two runners. In other circumstances Sokolov would have known them by the color of their skin, but now both of them were chalk-white since, like so many other people in the neighborhood, they were coated with dust.

The tall one was the leader of the mujahideen from Apartment 505.

The short one was Zula.

Why were they running hand in hand? Were they somehow working together? He could not conceive of a way that this would make sense.

Then their feet struck each other, and both of them stumbled and staggered for a few paces, drawing apart. They let go of each other's hands, and Sokolov saw that they were handcuffed together.

The rifle was at his shoulder. He advanced to a position where he could brace himself against the frame of the window, and he drew a bead on the tall black jihadist. From this distance the shot was feasible, assuming that the former owner of this rifle had taken decent care of it, but he would have to watch his breathing and he would have to wait for the target to stand still. Until then all he could do was track him and think about the fundamentals of the shot: how he was bracing himself and what obstructions might get in the way.

It suddenly became obvious where they were heading: a taxi had pulled to a stop, two wheels on the sidewalk and two on the street, and the driver had climbed out of it and was standing in the open door facing the scene of the disaster with his mouth hanging open and a cigarette dangling from his lower lip.

The man in Sokolov's sights had noticed. Putting on a burst of speed and practically dragging Zula along behind him, he closed on the taxi, stopped his momentum by crashing into the rear driver's-side door, bounced back, hauling the door open as he did so, wrapped Zula in a bear hug, and with a thrust of the legs dove sideways into the taxi's backseat, pulling Zula in with him so that the two ended up lying there side by side.

This was perhaps the only thing that could have torn the taxi driver's attention away from the collapsing building. He turned around and gazed in almost equal astonishment at the sight of four dust-caked legs protruding from the open rear door of his taxi. He tried to say something, discovered he had a cigarette glued to his lip, pulled it loose, stuck his head into the driver's-side door, and stiffened up.

Sokolov knew why, even though he couldn't see it: the jihadist was aiming a gun into his face.

After a short discussion, the taxi driver sagged into the driver's seat, closed the door, put the vehicle in gear, and got it moving. Such was the chaos in that intersection that Sokolov could have caught them by walking. Hell, by crawling on hands and knees. But killing the jihadist and helping Zula, as desirable as both of those things might have been, were not his main concerns now. He had to get out before the PSB threw a cordon around this whole area.

UNTIL QUITE RECENTLY, as Csongor had considered his position in the world, he had never thought of himself as the sort of person who would end up in any situation even remotely like this one. Which might seem odd given that he had been employed, to a greater or lesser extent, by criminals since the age of fourteen. But as he had been at such pains to explain to Zula, most of what criminals did was in fact quite boring and they tended to go to great lengths to avoid such outcomes.

The fact that he was the most stable and levelheaded person in the family said more about the recent history of Hungary than about Csongor himself.

His family, at least on the patrilineal side, had dwelled in Kolozsvár, the capital of Transylvania, since the Middle Ages. The city had for centuries been the object of a vicious and sustained tug-of-war between Hungarians and Romanians, who knew it as Cluj. After the First World War, Hungary had lost it, along with the rest of Transylvania, to Romania. Csongor's family had suddenly found themselves living in a foreign country. This had not gone well for them, and so when Hungary had allied itself with the Axis in the late 1930s, Csongor's grandfather had enthusiastically joined the Hungarian Army. He had married a Hungarian woman in Budapest, brought her back to Kolozsvár, impregnated her, and then gone off to help Hitler invade Russia. Along with many of the other Hungarians who participated in the Battle of Stalingrad, he vanished like a grain of salt dropped into the Pacific Ocean, and so his infant son—Csongor's father—never even laid eyes on him. His mother retreated to her family home in Budapest, where they survived the out-and-out Nazi occupation and the eventual onslaught of the Soviet Red Army with the usual litany of horrors, deprivations, and scrapes with sudden violent death. After things settled down a bit, and Hungary and Romania became, at least in theory, sister nations living in harmony under the umbrella of the Warsaw Pact, Csongor's grandmother moved back into the family's old house in Kolozsvár, which was now Cluj again since it had been handed back to Romania. There Csongor's father had endured the remainder of his childhood, and there he had attended the university and become a graduate student in the mathematics department. But circa 1960 the university, which was predominantly Hungarian, had come under the heel of Romanian chauvinists who had subjected the place to a thorough ethnic cleansing. His adviser had committed suicide. Acting now as the man of the household—for his mother had become a bit sick in the head—Csongor's father had sold the old family residence and picked up stakes and moved to Budapest, where, lacking an advanced degree, he had found work as a schoolteacher.

A bachelor schoolteacher for a long time, since the combination of poverty and living with a difficult, needy mother had made it difficult for him to attract steady girlfriends. But his mother had passed away in the mid-1970s and he had struck up a relationship with a much younger woman—one of his former students, whom he had encountered by chance on the subway, years after her graduation. They had gotten married in 1979. Bartos had been born in 1982 and Csongor in 1985. Father was a lovely man, but already in his midforties. Smoking several packs a day, he had burned his body out like a meat cigarette and died when Csongor was ten years old. Though not before he had succeeded in downloading most of what he knew of mathematics into the mind of Bartos and, to a lesser extent, Csongor.

Hungarians had a thing for math. Contrary to rumor, this was not genetic. It couldn't be. As anyone could see from walking down the streets of Budapest, they were absolute mongrels—the Americans of Europe. Lots of blue eyes in faces where one would otherwise not expect to see them. Expensive billboards, all over Budapest's airports, touted the expertise, the might, the global reach of German engineering and construction firms. Engineering! Another luxury of nationalities with huge populations and intact landmasses. Hungary, severed from half of the population and most of the natural resources that it had once claimed, had now to practice a sort of economic acupuncture, striving to know the magic nodes in the global energy flow where a pinprick could alter the workings of a major organ. Mathematics was one of the few disciplines where it was possible to exert that degree of leverage, and so the Hungarians had become phenomenally good at teaching it to their children. Part of that was awarding recognition to those who excelled at it. Bartos had participated in mathematics contests that were broadcast on national television as if they were football championships. He even *looked* like a mathematician.

Meanwhile Csongor, who didn't, was skulking through the corridors of his school trying to avoid the coach of the wrestling team, who tracked him down at least once a day and did everything short of putting him in a headlock to make him show up for practice. Csongor had just barely managed to keep the athletic department at bay by joining the hockey team. But he could not bring himself to skate backward, so they made him the goalkeeper. This he was actually good at, because of an unusual combination of puck-blocking bulk with extremely fast reflexes (he had once tried to capitalize on the latter by becoming a saber fencer, but, as the coach explained to him, "There is too much of you to hit").

He could not have known, during his young puck-stopping years, that this would provide so much conversational fodder for his eventual boss: a Russian organized crime figure and hockey fanatic who wanted to be addressed as Ivanov.

Don't you want to get old and grow the mustache? Drive the bus?

Ivanov insisted that he was a great admirer of the Hungarians and was always marveling over the miracle of their continuing to exist at all, which at first Csongor naively took as a compliment but later came to understand as an implicit threat. His way of bonding with Csongor had been to make all sorts of remarks about Csongor's appearance. "You do not look like hacker. Seeink you on street, I would say captain of water polo team. Then, bouncer in nightclub. Then, bus driver. When you going to grow the big mustache?" For it seemed as though Hungarian men, though they looked all sorts of different ways when young, converged on a few basic body shapes when old. The Grizzled Bullet Head. The Highbrow, with receding silver hair swept back. The Carpathian Wild Man, preceded everywhere by his eyebrows. Csongor, a classic Bullet Head, knew it was only a matter of time before he grew the Mustache. But for now it was his practice to just mow his hair down to stubble on the first Tuesday of each month and to keep his face, which he thought unobjectionable but far from handsome, clean-shaven.

He had learned that certain women were drawn to big men, and he had not been above taking advantage of this from time to time. He had had only one serious girlfriend, a year ago. Yesterday, he had decided that Zula was the woman for him.

He had not exactly lost consciousness when Ivanov had pistol-whipped him across the jaw, but become, as it were, extremely distracted and somewhat disconnected from control of his body during the moments that the other gunman had made his surprising intervention. He had felt, and profoundly appreciated, the feel of Zula's hand on his cheek as she broke his fall, but he was a little fuzzy as to what else had happened, largely because his head had been aimed in the wrong direction and he'd been unable to move it.

Now he was not the least bit fuzzy. He knew that he was in the cellar of a building that was in the process of collapsing. That the immensely strong stairway core was holding up well and creating a pocket of relatively safe breathing space around it. And that he was trapped in that pocket with the semidecapitated corpse of Ivanov and a Kalashnikov assault rifle. And while on one level the situation was, obviously, ridiculously chaotic and dangerous, the Hungarian in him said, *I was wondering when I was going to end up like this.*

From time to time he had wondered how his grandfather had died, since no one had a clue where, or even in what year, it had happened. Maybe he had been in the cellar of some building in Stalingrad, just like this.

During moments when the building was not actively in a state of avalanche, he would call out "Hello! Hello!" as loud as he could manage.

It was almost totally dark. Groping around, Csongor felt buttery leather coated with filthy grit: Ivanov's man-purse, which had fallen to the floor and was lying right next to him. Csongor pulled it to him and opened it up, in case it contained a flashlight or anything else that might be useful. His hands told him that it was almost completely full of Chinese money. There were two extraordinarily dense rectangles of cold metal: full ammunition clips, he realized, for a pistol that was no longer in evidence. Next to them a black box, shaped at one end like a pair of yawning jaws, with small metal pegs as fangs. Csongor picked it up and his finger fell naturally onto a button that was obviously a trigger. He pulled it and a purple lightning bolt leaped between the fangs and danced and twisted about crazily until he let go of the thing. Stupid! If there were a gas leak in this place, the spark would have set it off.

But there had been no explosion; there was no gas leak.

It was some kind of a nonlethal weapon: a stun gun. Maybe Ivanov had brought it for torturing the Troll. Csongor pulled its trigger again and used the dancing light of the arc for illumination. As he had expected, the bag was filled with Chinese money. But stuffed in around the edges were Ziploc bags containing important stuff: passports and phones.

He heard movement from not far away.

"Help!" he cried.

The movement stopped.

"Hello?" Csongor called.

"Hello," said a voice in the dark. "Come this way, please."

"I'm coming," Csongor said. He dropped the stun gun into the bag and zipped it shut. Then he began crawling toward the voice, dragging the bag behind him.

"AIRPORT!" SHOUTED MR. Jones. Then a look of remorse came over his face, Zula guessed, because he had realized how out of control he was. "Airport," he repeated, much more calmly and distinctly.

Because Mr. Jones's right hand was cuffed to Zula's left, they had perforce arranged themselves so that Zula was on the right side of the rear seat and Mr. Jones was on the left, directly behind the driver, who had torqued himself all the way around to stare in paralytic dismay at Mr. Jones.

"Air . . . port," Jones said for a third time, in a tone of just-barely-contained fury, accompanied with a little tossing movement of the pistol in his left hand. The driver finally turned around and shifted into gear. The taxi moved about three inches and then stopped to avoid hitting a staggering, dust-covered refugee. But at least it was moving; the taxi driver had something to think about besides the strange pair in his backseat. A few moments later, he claimed a full arm's length of pavement. And from there, it only got easier. As if the crowd, having conceded the taxi's right to move one meter, could no longer begrudge it the next ten, or the next hundred.

SOKOLOV WATCHED THE slow dissolution of the taxi into the crowd with professional admiration. He was a highly trained and experienced warrior, operating completely on his own, free to hide in this building for a while or emerge at a time of his choosing. Even so, he had rated his chances of escaping from this situation at essentially zero. And yet this Muslim Negro, the victim of a surprise raid, handcuffed to an unwilling hostage, and squarely in Sokolov's rifle sights, had apparently managed to make good his escape simply by taking advantage of an opportunity that had presented itself at random. Of course, the distraction posed by the explosion and collapse of the building had helped him enormously, but it was admirable nonetheless. From long experience in places like Afghanistan and Chechnya, Sokolov recognized, in the black jihadist's movements, a sort of cultural or attitudinal advantage that such people always enjoyed in situations like this: they were complete fatalists who believed that God was on their side. Russians, on the other hand, were fatalists of a somewhat different kind, believing, or at least strongly suspecting, that they were fucked no matter what, and that they had better just make the best of it anyway, but not seeing in this the hand of God at work or the hope of some future glory in a martyr's heaven.

And so what moved him onward and down the office building's stairway was not any sort of foolish hope that he could actually be saved, but competitive fury at the fact that he had been outdone by the suicidal improvisations of this fanatic.

CSONGOR RECOGNIZED HIS savior as one of the hackers: Manu, as they had been referring to him. "Manu" showed Csongor how to make his way out of the cellar to the back door on the alley. Csongor then followed him down the alley to the side street and down that to its intersection with the bigger street that ran along the building's front. This got them far enough away from obvious danger that "Manu" felt comfortable turning around to look curiously at Csongor.

"Thank you," Csongor said.

"I am Marlon," said the other.

"I am Csongor." They shook hands in a curiously stiff, formal way.

"What happened?" Marlon wanted to know.

Csongor, not fully trusting their ability to communicate in English, shrugged to indicate he hadn't the faintest idea.

Not far away, someone had been honking a car horn. First it had been a series of long blasts, and now it was a long string of random taps, culminating in "shave and a haircut, two bits." The neighborhood afforded many distractions at this time, but finally Csongor turned to look and noticed the van sitting there about ten meters away. Projecting below the open driver's-side door was a pair of blue boots. Yuxia's head poked up in the vacant window frame, to see if she had gotten their attention yet.

"Would you like a ride?" Csongor asked, extending one hand toward the van, like a limo driver welcoming a movie star at the airport.

Marlon shrugged and grinned. "Okay."

As they drew closer, Yuxia ran out from behind the door and got in front of the van, crouched, and grabbed a snarled length of rusty rebar that was torquing up into the air in front of the bumper. It was rooted in a sizable chunk of busted-up concrete that was preventing the van from moving forward and that was too heavy for her to move alone. Marlon and Csongor helped her drag this obstruction out of the way, then climbed into the back of the vehicle as Yuxia got into the driver's seat. She put it in gear and started to rumble forward over smaller debris that, while it made for a bumpy ride, didn't prevent the wheels from rolling. Marlon and Csongor busied themselves for a few moments pushing the concrete lintel out the side door. The door wouldn't latch because the entire frame of the van had been distorted by impact, and so Csongor just held it shut. Marlon lay on his back in the wreckage of the seat, got his feet braced against the punched-in roof, and pushed up with all his might, shoving the sheet metal up quite a distance, partly sealing the hole in the roof and greatly increasing the amount of space inside the van. Beyond that, his strength did not suffice to move the metal any farther, and so he and Csongor both ended up on their backs kicking at the ceiling, pounding the metal up like blacksmiths. It gave them something to do and it took their mind off the way Yuxia was driving, which, had they paid attention to it, might have been the most frightening thing they had seen all day.

"Where are we going?" Csongor finally thought to ask. For he could not make sense of Yuxia's decisions.

"To the same place as that taxi," she answered, nodding indistinctly at a mote in the sea of people and traffic ahead of them.

"Why?"

"Because my girlfriend is in it," Yuxia answered. She turned to fix him with a look. "My girlfriend, and yours."

"I wish!" Csongor remarked, before he could haul the remark back.

"Then don't you want to know where she is going?"

SOKOLOV REACHED THE ground floor, ejected the clip from his rifle, cleared its chamber, and threw it down the stairwell. He stepped into the hall that led to the building's main entrance and broke into a run. When he reached the lobby, he slowed to a brisk walk, pushed through a pair of inner doors, strode across the entry-way, and shouldered his way through one of the outer doors.

Just in time to watch the van drive away. Like a horse dropping a turd, it disgorged a large piece of concrete as it accelerated.

There seemed little point now in wondering how the Chinese girl had managed to start the engine. Sokolov swiveled his head to left and right, checking the sidewalk, then withdrew into the lobby to consider his options. A number of people had taken cover beneath the shelter of the scaffolding, and all of them had been far too inter-ested in events across the street to take any note of Sokolov. Even so, he preferred not to stand out in the open any longer than he had to.

He had seen something, though. Off to the right.

He pushed the left-hand door open with his foot. Its window was cracked but still hanging together in the frame. At first he could see his own reflection in it, but as he shoved it open, the angle changed and the reflection careered around. When he got it open about forty-five degrees, he was able to see down the sidewalk to his right and verify what he had noticed moments earlier: at the corner of the building, one of those cart-pulling guys had taken shel-ter under the very end of the scaffolding. Sokolov could practically read the man's mind. He had been caught in the middle of the disas-ter and had run to a place where he could get some shelter. Now the worst was over, police vehicles and fire trucks were loudly and rapidly converging on the neighborhood, and he smelled an oppor-tunity to make some money. Because a hell of a lot of shit was going to have to be carted out of here.

Sokolov ascended to the second floor, shouldered his way into a vacant office, strode to the front, and kicked broken glass out of a window, giving him a clear exit to the scaffold. He swung the gar-

bage bag out onto the platform, then clambered out onto the planking. A blue tarp, much the worse for wear, was dangling there. He
was richly supplied with knives and used one of those to cut a tarp
loose with a few quick strokes. Rather than take the time to fold, or
even wad, it up, he just threw it over his shoulders like a cape. He
picked up the garbage bag and began striding toward the corner
where he had seen the carter.

When he reached the end of the scaffolding, he set the garbage
bag down, grabbed the bamboo rail, vaulted over it, and found purchase for his feet. Leaning out and looking down, he was just able
to see the edge of the carter's conical straw hat, a few feet below
him. Sokolov grabbed the garbage bag, dragged it off the end of the
platform, and let it drop into the side street, just a meter or so out of
the carter's reach.

The carter stepped into the street to investigate. Sokolov could
only see the top of his hat.

When the carter looked up to see where the mystery bag had
come from, Sokolov nailed him in the forehead with a stack of currency two inches thick. It tumbled down his nose, bounced off his
chin, and ended up trapped between his hands and his gaunt belly.

It took the carter a few moments to believe his eyes. Sokolov had
no idea how much money a carter made, and only a vague notion
of the value of that brick of bills, but he assumed that the disparity
between those two figures was noteworthy.

When the carter looked up again, he found himself staring into
the barrel of Sokolov's pistol.

Sokolov pointed to the cart, then made a gesture indicating that
the carter should pull it into the side street.

The carter made a move somewhere between a nod and a bow,
scurried back under the platform for a moment, then pulled his
cart out so that it was directly beneath Sokolov. Sokolov dropped
into it. In the same movement, he swept the blue tarp over him.
He reached out for the garbage bag, but the carter, understanding
his intent, had already picked this up. Sokolov pulled it in under the
blue tarp. He and the carter were now staring at each other through
a tunnel that Sokolov had made in the tarp, about the size of his
hand. Sokolov jerked his head down the side street, indicating the
direction he wanted the carter to travel.

The cart began to move. Sokolov unzipped another pocket, pulled out his phone, brought up the photo gallery app, and flipped through pictures until he had found an image of one of the big Western-style business hotels along the waterfront: one of those places where it was possible to be a white person without attracting one's own personal Stonehenge of cataleptic, openmouthed gapers. He got the carter's attention with a loud *psst,* then showed him the image. The carter took a moment to focus on it—his eyes weren't so good, perhaps—but then he seemed to understand. He changed his course and pulled Sokolov onto a larger street that was even more hysterically crowded than usual. Police and aid vehicles were coming toward them in echelons. Sokolov pulled the edges of the tarp inward and got his weight on them so that his shelter could not be stripped off by a velleity of the wind or the hand of a curious boy. Blue light shone through the tarp. It was warm under there, but he would just have to survive that. His heart was pounding at something like 180 beats a minute, which meant that his body was generating an enormous amount of heat. He rested his head on his arm and closed his eyes and began making a conscious effort to slow his breathing. He had water in the CamelBak pouch strapped to his back. He rubbed some into his hair so that it would evaporate and cool off his head, then put the end of the tube in his mouth and began taking little sips every ten seconds or so. The cart started and stopped, pivoted and lunged through the throng. He was alive, and he was putting distance between himself and the epicenter.

"MY BAD," YUXIA kept saying, as the van pulled up the ramp onto the ring road, in hot pursuit of the dust-covered taxi that contained Zula. "My bad, my bad, my bad."

"There is no bad," Csongor said. He had to shout to be heard, since, as they accelerated to freeway speed, the wind began howling through the crack in the van's roof. "You did nothing bad."

"But I saw her," Yuxia keened. "She ran right past me! I honked but she did not look back. Aiyaa!"

They seemed to be passing a lot of traffic. Marlon, seated next to Csongor in the second row of seats, directly behind Yuxia, leaned forward and made a sharp remark. Yuxia glanced at the speedometer for the first time since the journey had begun, and the blue boot pulled back from the gas pedal.

And only just in time, since they had nearly shot past a dust-covered taxi in the right lane. Yuxia let it gain some distance on them, then cut back into the right lane, drawing stentorian protests from car and truck horns all around.

"So," Csongor said. For he really had no idea what was going on. "Zula ran past you. You honked at her. She ignored you. She got into a taxi—?"

"Bottom line, got thrown into one."

"Who threw her into a taxi? What are you talking about?"

She opened her mouth and shook her head hopelessly.

"The tall black man?" Marlon guessed.

"No, tall white man."

Marlon and Csongor looked at each other.

"White like paper," Yuxia went on. She licked a finger, wiped a streak of concrete dust off her cheek, then held it up for them both to see. "Basic color of this."

Marlon said, "If you had tried to do something, that dude would have killed you." But this just sent Yuxia into another paroxysm of steering wheel pounding.

"My head was confused," Csongor said. "I saw nothing clearly. But after Ivanov struck me, someone else came into the cellar—the same man as you are talking about?"

"Yes, the same," Marlon confirmed. "He shot at the man who hit you and—" Seeing what had happened in his mind's eye, Marlon shook his head in a combination of disbelief and nausea. Csongor, who spoke no Chinese at all, was impressed, thus far, by Marlon's fluency in the universal English of action movies and chat rooms.

They were threading a huge interchange where the ring road connected with a colossal, new-looking bridge thrown across a strait to what Csongor conjectured was the mainland: a zone of tidal flats supporting immense high-rise apartment complexes still under construction, and equally tall standards to support power lines hung across the water.

"Anyone who kills Ivanov is my loverboy," Yuxia remarked.

Csongor had a strong feeling that Ivanov's killer would make a terrible loverboy. He turned and looked at Marlon.

A human figure, outside the car, caught his eye. He looked out the dust-hazed windshield to see a uniformed PSB officer standing in the median strip, just by the side of the road, facing traffic. Both hands in front of him.

Aiming a gun.

Right at them.

Csongor twitched so hard that he kicked Ivanov's man-purse under the passenger seat. But as the cop was flashing by, he perceived that it was actually a manikin, planted there on a concrete base, and that the thing in its hands was a mockup of a radar gun. He put his hands to his face and leaned back and tried to compose himself.

First things first. "You have a phone?" Csongor asked.

Marlon hadn't noticed the manikin. He had been gazing curiously at Csongor's strange reactions and movements. He nodded, sat up out of his slouch, produced a phone, and yanked its battery. Csongor felt a wave of good feeling pass through him. Not only had Marlon guided him out of hell, but he was the kind of guy who didn't have to be told how to render his phone silent and untraceable.

"Yuxia?"

"No! Dr. Evil took it."

"Then it's probably in Dr. Evil's bag," Csongor said. He extricated it from beneath the passenger seat, hauled it up onto his lap, and began zipping it open. The unmistakable lurid pink of Chinese currency gleamed in the gap, and he thought better of opening the thing wide. So he opened it just enough to get his hand inside and began groping around. This went slowly, since he couldn't see what he was doing. Marlon watched with a mixture of curiosity and nervousness.

"Who was that guy?" Csongor asked, trying to get Marlon thinking of something else. "That black man?"

Marlon's eyes snapped up from the bag to glare at Csongor. "Who the fuck are *you*!?" he demanded.

Then Marlon and Yuxia got into an argument. Csongor had the impression that Yuxia had reprimanded Marlon for his bad manners.

"Don't worry about it," Csongor said. "It is a reasonable question." He grinned, trying to convey that he was not offended. Any kind of pronounced facial expression made his head hurt, though.

Perhaps in response to something Marlon had said, Yuxia got an interested look on her face and turned to scrutinize Csongor. Then her eyes dropped to the bag.

Marlon tapped her on the shoulder and nodded toward the windshield, trying to draw her attention to the road, since she had drifted back into the left lane and was passing a lot of cars.

"Marlon is right," she concluded, turning back around and dropping speed. "Who the fuck are you?"

It was obvious that Csongor's behavior with the bag had set their nerves on edge. So he dropped it to the floor of the van, in the middle of the space between himself and Yuxia and Marlon. He unzipped it all the way and pulled back its top flap to expose its full contents.

It had some kind of internal stiffeners that held it open in a box shape. Its main central cavity was filled with money: as many as a dozen rubber-banded bricks that, along with the ammunition clips and the electric stun gun, floated around in a stew of loose bills and ten-bill packets. Sewn to the inside walls of the bag were a number of little mesh pockets, filled with clutter. Csongor, recognizing the purplish-red hue of a Hungarian passport, opened one of these and pulled out a clear Ziploc bag containing his passport, his phone, and most of the contents of his wallet. He pulled the battery from the phone and put the other stuff on the seat next to him. Continuing to explore the other pockets, he found two other Ziploc bags, one containing Peter's stuff and the other containing Zula's. He made certain that their phones were deactivated.

Yet another phone, a Chinese model, had been thrown into one of the pockets. Csongor pulled it out and held it up. "Is this yours?" he asked, popping out the battery.

No answer came from Yuxia, and he looked up for the first time to discover her and Marlon gazing into the bag in silent astonishment. She, at least, had the presence of mind to glance up at the road from time to time.

"This is Ivanov's bag," Csongor said. "Do you guys understand that? It is not mine."

"It is now," Marlon said.

"Are those bullets?" Yuxia asked.

Csongor placed Yuxia's phone and its battery in the cup holder next to her elbow, then reached into the bag and held up one of the ammunition clips. The top couple of cartridges were clearly visible at its top. "Yes."

"You have a gun?" Her tone of voice was not: *It would be really cool and useful if you had a gun.* It was, rather, *If you have a gun, we are in even worse trouble than I had thought.*

"No. Only these. Maybe the other guy took Ivanov's gun."

"What is in the end part?" Marlon asked, eyeing a separate compartment on the end of the bag, big enough to hold a couple of paperback books. Something was definitely making it bulge. Csongor unzipped it, reached in, and, to his own shock, pulled out a pistol. This one was smaller than the one Ivanov had been carrying, with woodgrained grips. He recognized it: this was the basic sidearm that Soviet and Russian military had always carried. He simply could not believe that one of them was in his hand.

"OMG," Marlon said.

In Hungary, Csongor had had very little access to guns. But on a trip to a hacker conference in Vegas two years ago, he had spent a couple of evenings at firing ranges that catered to foreign visitors, and he had learned a few basics. He figured out how to eject the clip from this weapon, then maneuvered it into a shaft of sun coming in through the crack in the roof and pulled back the slide just enough to verify that no rounds were in the chamber. Then he found the safety and flicked it back and forth a couple of times just to get a feel for when it was on and when it was off. When he was certain that the weapon contained no cartridges and that it was inert, he set it on the van's seat next to him, then reached back into the bag pocket to see what other treasures might be contained in there. He came up with a spare clip for the pistol, fully stuffed with cartridges. Then he pulled out a pair of heavy black cylinders with steel rings affixed to their tops.

He looked up and locked eyes with Marlon. Neither of them had ever seen anything like this before, outside of a video game, but Csongor was pretty certain, and Marlon's expression confirmed, that these were grenades.

"Make some noise if you are alive," said Yuxia. Traffic had become complex, and she was doing a lot of lane changing.

"Now we have a pistol and a couple of hand grenades," Csongor announced.

Marlon had taken one of the grenades and was examining it. The sides of the canister were perforated with large holes, revealing some internal structure. "These are not real grenades," he announced. "Look. No shrapnel. Holes instead."

"Stun grenades?" Csongor guessed.

"Or smoke or tear gas." Marlon and Csongor could communicate very clearly as long as they hewed to vocabulary from video games.

Yuxia intervened. "Csongor's supposed to be telling us who he is," she reminded Marlon. "Grenade can be explained later."

"I'll tell you who I am," Csongor promised. "But first please tell me what just happened. What do you know about that tall black guy?"

Marlon was glaring at him. Csongor realized that he had insulted Marlon, or more likely just spooked him, by implying that he, Marlon, might know something about who the guy was. He looked into Marlon's eyes. "It might be important," Csongor pleaded.

"He lived upstairs with dudes from the far west," Marlon said. "We only saw him a couple of times."

"Did you know that these dudes from the far west had AK-47s?"

"What do you take me for, man?"

"Okay, sorry."

Csongor leaned back in his seat, hoping that this would ease the throbbing in his head. There was a significant silence: their way of reminding him that he had yet to explain himself. "Okay," he said. "Do you guys know anything about Hungary?"

Neither of them did. But neither would come out and admit it, perhaps worried about being impolite. Marlon, somewhat surprisingly, made a reference to the 1956 Olympic water polo team. But that was where his knowledge of Hungary began and ended.

Whenever Csongor found himself in an airport, he would go to the newsstand and browse the endless racks of glossy English- and German-language magazines, bemused by the phenomenon of cultures that were large enough to support monthly publications in which people would dither in print over the minutest details of makeup, high-performance motorcycles, and model railways. Hungarians learned those languages so that they could feign membership in that world when it suited them. But their isolation and tininess were nothing compared to what it would have been if Hungary had been part of China. Here, if Hungarians survived at all, they would be trotted out once a year to perform folk dances, simply to prove to the rest of the world that they hadn't yet been exterminated. Csongor had never heard of Yuxia's ethnic minority, the Hakka, and yet he didn't have to look them up on Wikipedia to guess that there were probably ten times as many of them as there were Hungarians.

So where to begin?

"It is a long story. I could start with the Battle of Stalingrad," he said, "and go on from there. But." He stopped, sighed, and considered it.

"First, I am an asshole who made a lot of wrong decisions."

Hungary was an embedded system. It was idle to dream of what it would be like, and of all the brave and noble decisions Hungarians would have made, had it been a thousand times larger and surrounded by a saltwater moat. He paused to rest.

Yuxia checked him in the rearview.

Marlon fixed him with a somewhat incredulous look as if to say, *If you're an asshole who made wrong decisions, what am I?*

Csongor couldn't help chuckling at this. Somewhat to his astonishment, Marlon's face cracked open with a smile. Cool, tough, world-wise, but unquestionably a smile. He turned back toward the window to hide it.

"And because of certain fucked-up remnants of the past, which we are now getting rid of," Csongor continued, "things were actually simple and easy for me as long as I kept making the wrong decisions. However"—he checked his watch, and found that its crystal was shattered and its hands had stopped—"something like half an hour ago, I made the correct decision and did the right thing. Look where I am now."

Another nervous mirror-glance from Yuxia. Csongor realized he'd better explain that remark. "In a car with nice people," he said.

That was better, but he was still planting his big feet in the wrong places. To Csongor, Marlon would always be the guy who risked his life to enter a collapsing building and lead a stranger to safety. But Marlon, he sensed, didn't want to be thought of that way. He had the cool insouciance of the skate rats performing their

death-defying leaps in the Erszébet Tér, the hackers showing off
their latest exploits at DefCon in Vegas.

"Or at least one nice person," Csongor corrected himself.

Marlon turned around and gave him that smile again, then
reached back with his right hand. Some kind of complex basketball-
player handshake ensued. Csongor was pretty sure he muffed his
end of it; Central European hockey players didn't go in for such
things. But he no longer had that awful feeling that he used to get
when he was trying to skate backward, and so he let it rest there.

MR. JONES SAID nothing further in English until an hour into the
journey, when he looked at Zula and said, "I give up."

By that time they had completed a couple of circuits of the ring
road that lined the island's shore. Contrary to the first instruction
given, they had not gone to the airport. Zula had been confused by
this until she had understood that her companion—if that was the
right word—didn't speak a word of Chinese, and that he assumed
(correctly as it turned out) that the taxi driver spoke no English; so
he had just shouted the one English word that every taxi driver in
the world had to know. This had been just to get him moving. Once
that driver had nudged and honked his way clear of the chaos surrounding the exploded building, Mr. Jones had produced a phone,
dialed a number, and spoken in Arabic. Zula had known that it was
Arabic because she had heard a fair bit of that language while living in a refugee camp in the Sudan. After a brief exchange of news,
which Zula could tell had been extremely surprising to the person
on the other end of the line—for Mr. Jones had soon grown weary
of insisting that every word was true—he had handed the phone up
to the taxi driver, who had listened to some instructions, nodded
vigorously, and said something that must have meant "yes" or "I
will do it."

Mr. Jones had then exchanged a few more terse Arabic sentences
with his interlocutor and hung up. And the taxi driver had begun to
drive laps around the ring road.

Zula had been resting her free elbow on the frame of the taxi's
window, turning her hand out, from time to time, to press her fingertips against the tinted glass. There was something about the

manufactured environment of a car that engendered a completely bogus feeling of safety.

When Mr. Jones said those three words: "I give up," Zula opened her eyes and startled a little. Could it really be that she had gone to sleep? Seemed a strange time for a nap. But the body reacted in odd ways to stress. And once they had gotten out onto the ring road, there had been nothing in the way of shootings or explosions to demand her attention. Exhaustion had stolen up on her.

"He was Russian, yes? The big man?"

"The man you . . . killed?" She couldn't believe that sentences like this one were coming out of her mouth.

Surprise, then a trace of a smile came over the gunman's face. "Yes."

"Yeah. Russian."

"The others too. Upstairs. Spetsnaz."

Zula had never heard the word "Spetznaz" until a couple of days ago, but she knew what it meant now. She nodded.

"But there were three others . . . different." He raised his cuffed hand, dragging hers with it, and stuck his thumb up in the air. "You." His index finger. "The one that the big Russian killed in the stairwell. I think he was American." His long finger. "And the one in the cellar who tried to protect you . . ."

"He did more than try."

"He was maybe Russian too—but somehow different from the others?"

"Hungarian."

"The big man—organized crime?"

"More like *dis*organized," Zula said. "We think he was on the run from his own organization. He screwed something up, big-time. He was trying to cover it up. Make amends."

"You say 'we.' What do you mean by 'we'?"

She twisted her cuffed hand up and around and mimicked his counting-on-the-fingers gesture.

"The three of you," he said.

Mr. Jones thought about it for a while. His mood seemed to be improving, but he was cautious all the same. "If I take what you say at face value," he said, "then this is not what I assumed at first."

"You assumed what?"

"Covert special ops raid, of course." The phrase was familiar enough, being the fodder of countless newspaper articles and summer movie plots, but he spoke it with an emphasis, an inflection she had never heard before, as one who actually knew of such things firsthand, had seen his friends die in them. "But if this is really what you say—" He blinked and shook his head, like a man trying to fight off the effects of a hypnotizing drug. "Impossible. Stupid. It was absolutely a special ops job. In fancy dress."

"Fancy dress?"

"What you would call a costume party," he shot back, slipping into a parody of a flat midwestern accent. "To make it deniable." Back to the usual British accent now, the one she couldn't quite place. "Because it would make a hell of a diplomatic mess to send a military team into China. This way, though, they can shrug their shoulders: 'It's those crazy Russian mafia guys, we have no control over them, there was nothing we could do.'"

It sounded so convincing that Zula was starting to believe it herself.

"What was your role?" he asked.

Zula laughed.

His eyes widened slightly. Then he laughed too. "The three," he said, making the hand gesture again. "Why does a deep cover Russian hit squad need to be dragging around the Three We? Handcuffing them to pipes and shooting them in the head?"

At the reminder that Peter was dead, Zula's face collapsed and she felt a momentary sick shock that she'd been laughing only a moment earlier. They were silent for a while, just driving.

"So you guys are in the virus-writing business?" she tried.

She now learned what Jones looked like when he was utterly dumbfounded. This would have been satisfying had Zula not been every bit as confused.

"The Russians," she explained. "That's why they—we—went to that apartment building. To find someone who had written a virus."

"A *computer* virus," Jones said, stating the question as a fact.

Zula nodded and was left with the unsettling notion that Jones's group might be working with other kinds of viruses.

"We have nothing to do with writing computer viruses," Jones announced. "Come to think of it though, might be a good line to get into." Then his mind snapped into focus. "Oh," he said. "That lot downstairs. Boys with computers. Always wondered what they were doing."

Zula swallowed hard and went silent. She had just remembered a fleeting image from just before the start of the gunfire: a coin shoved into the fuse socket, a crescent moon and a star. Someone—perhaps Jones himself—had put that coin in there when they had invaded the vacant flat and set up a squat.

This was all her doing. What would Jones do to her when he understood that?

"So the big Russian—" Jones began.

"Ivanov."

"He was royally pissed off at those lads."

"You might say that."

"How did you get involved?"

"It is a long story."

Jones let his head hang down and laughed. "Look at me," he said. "Your man Ivanov has forced me to cancel certain arrangements. To make other plans. I've nothing but time. And unless I am quite mistaken, you have even more time on your hands than I do. So why on earth should I object to a long story at this juncture?"

Zula gazed out through the taxi's window.

"It is your only possible way out," Jones said.

Zula's nose started to run, a precursor of crying. Not because her situation sucked. It had sucked for a long time. And it couldn't suck worse than it had with Ivanov. It was because she couldn't tell the story without mentioning Peter.

She took a few slow, steadying breaths. If she could just get his name out without cracking, the rest would be fine.

"Peter," she said, and her voice bucked like a car going over a speed bump, and her eyes watered a little. "The man in the stairwell." She looked at Jones until he understood.

"Your beau?"

"Not anymore."

"I'm sorry," Jones said. Not the least bit sorry. Just observing the proper formalities.

"No, I mean—not because he's dead." There. She'd gotten it out. "Not because Peter's dead." Trying the words, like easing out onto thin ice covering a farm pond, wondering how far she cold go before she felt it cracking beneath her. "We had broken up previously. On the day that everything went crazy."

"Then perhaps it would be more informative if you could rewind to the day that everything went crazy, since that sounds like an interesting day," Jones suggested.

"We had been snowboarding."

"You live in a mountainous area?"

"Seattle. Actually we were several hours outside of Seattle, in B.C."

"How does a Horn of Africa girl pick up snowboarding?" For the fact that Zula was from East Africa was written on her face plainly enough for a man like Jones to read.

"I never did. I just hung around."

"Your lad drags you off into the mountains so that he can snowboard while you do nothing?"

"No, I would never put up with it."

"I believe you just told me that you *did*."

"There was plenty for me to do."

"What? Shopping?"

She shook her head. "I'm not that way." The question was still unanswered. "My uncle lives up there, so it was a chance for a family visit. And I could work; I brought my laptop."

"Your uncle lives in a ski resort?"

"Part of the time."

"You have a lot of family in B.C.?"

She shook her head. "Iowa. He's the black sheep."

"I'd have thought *you* were the black sheep."

Zula could not fight off at least a hint of a smile.

Jones was delighted by this.

She was disgusted. Disgusted that he had played the black card so early and that it had worked on her.

How could he have guessed that she was adopted? Being from Iowa was definitely a clue. That, and her accent.

"So, the *two* black sheep are visiting while Peter snowboards. Is that where everything went crazy?"

"No. It's where it started."

"How did it start?"

"A man walked into the bar."

"Ah, yes. A lot of good stories start that way. Pray continue."

And Zula continued. Had Jones given her time to consider her options, to work through the strategy and tactics of what she ought or ought not to divulge, would she have done the same? There was no telling. She began to relate her memories of Wallace in the tavern, and the rest of the story just unfurled, like the wake behind a boat. Mr. Jones listened to it carefully at first, but as she advanced to the point where he could figure out the connections himself, his mind wandered, and he became more and more active on the phone.

He seemed to get along okay in Arabic, but it was gradually becoming clear to her that it was not his native language; he spoke slowly, stopping and starting as he worked his way through sentences, and from time to time, as he listened to the man on the other end, he would get a bemused grin on his face and, she thought, request clarification.

None of which seemed to be standing in the way of his making a plan. The first part of the conversation had been start-and-stop, with a lot of wandering down blind alleys and then suddenly backing out of them. Or so Zula judged from the tone of Jones's voice, his gestures. But suddenly in the last few minutes Mr. Jones and his interlocutor seemed to have hit on a plan that they liked; he finally lifted his eyes from the back of the seat in front of him and began to look around brightly and to drop "Okay" into his utterances.

They were on the eastern curve of the island. This was its least built-up part, but no one would mistake it for an unspoiled natural space. Part of the road was built on reclaimed land, running over the top of a seawall, so along those stretches the water was right below Zula's window. In other sections, a broad sandy beach stretched between road and shore. Occasionally the road would divert inland, ceding the waterfront to a golf course or residential complex. They had been going clockwise around the island for a long time—Zula didn't have a watch, but she judged it must have been at least two hours. Now, at a command from the phone, the taxi driver executed a U-turn and began to head north, going counterclockwise up the eastern limb.

. . . .

"OMYGOD," YUXIA SAID, "he's turning around."

"Why would he do that?" Csongor asked rhetorically.

"He fears we are following him," Marlon theorized.

They blew by the taxi, which had pulled into a crossover lane in the median strip and was waiting for an opening in the oncoming traffic. Its rear windows were so deeply tinted that they could see nothing through them. But the driver was clearly visible, holding the steering wheel in one hand, pressing a phone to his ear with the other. And paying no attention at all to them.

"Why is he talking on the phone?" Yuxia asked, shouldering the van into a gap in traffic and getting into the left lane.

"I think I am wrong," Marlon said. "He did not look like a man who thought he was being followed."

Csongor, the foreigner, was the first to put it together: "He doesn't speak English," he said. "And Zula and the terrorist don't speak Chinese. They have someone on the phone who is translating."

Yuxia braked hard, triggering a storm of furious honking, and veered onto the next crossover.

"Which raises the question," Csongor continued, "who is helping this guy?"

A gap in traffic presented itself fortuitously, so instead of coming to a full stop Yuxia just rolled across the oncoming lanes and pulled around on the shoulder, waited for a few cars to blow by, then accelerated. They had not lost much ground on the taxi, which had had worse luck with the traffic and was being driven more conservatively in any case. But if anyone was looking back through those tinted windows, it would have to be obvious, now, that the battered van was tailing them.

Marlon shrugged, telling him that the answer was obvious: "He has friends around here."

"But they're all dead."

"Not all. There must be some others. In another building."

"Then why did they not simply go straight to that building?" Csongor asked. "Why drive around the island for hours?"

"He wanted to see if he was being followed?" Marlon said. "But we have been obviously following him and he did not notice."

"Not *that* obvious," said the offended Yuxia, triggering a brief exchange of recriminations in Mandarin.

"He's been organizing something. Some kind of drop-off or exchange," Csongor said, tamping down the argument. "Using the backseat of that taxi as his office."

"Fuck, man," Marlon said. "I should never have got into this van."

"You're just getting that now?" Yuxia asked. Still a little irked at him.

"You said you were going to give me a ride," Marlon said, looking at Csongor.

"You can get out whenever you want," Csongor said.

Yuxia said something in Mandarin that appeared to reinforce Csongor's offer with considerable vigor.

"Seriously," Csongor said, "you saved my life, that is enough for one day."

"Who saved mine?" Marlon asked. "Mine, and my friends'?"

Csongor turned to look at him curiously.

"By flashing the power on and off. Warning us."

"Oh," Csongor said. He had quite forgotten this detail in the midst of so many other happenings. "That was Zula." He nodded in the direction of the taxi, a couple of hundred meters ahead of them.

"And that is why the big man—Ivanov—was so angry," Marlon said, working it out. "Because he knew that Zula had messed up his plan to kill us."

"Yes."

"I see." Marlon nodded, then drew in a deep breath and began stroking his beardless chin absentmindedly. Finally, he came to some sort of decision and sat up straighter. "I have done nothing wrong today. The cops can't charge me with anything."

"Except REAMDE," Csongor reminded him.

"For that," Marlon said, "I'm already fucked anyway. But that's a small thing in all of this. So I will go with you for a little while longer and see what happens."

"You sure will," Csongor said.

WHENEVER THE LOOKING was good, Mr. Jones looked out across the water. Zula tried to follow his gaze. But there wasn't much to see. Directly across a narrow strait, close enough that a good swimmer could have reached it in a few hours, was the smaller of the two Taiwanese islands. Perhaps that accounted for the barrenness of the coast, and the lack of shipping traffic. Over the course of a few minutes, their orbit turned them away from that fragment of foreign territory. A larger, more built-up headland came into view off to their right, and they began to see more maritime traffic, since the water to their right was now a strait, about a mile wide, between Xiamen and another part of the People's Republic. The road diverged from the shore to make room for a container port built on flat reclaimed land, indistinguishable, to Zula's eye, from the same facility on Harbor Island in Seattle, with all the same equipment and the same names stenciled on the containers. A series of huge apartment complexes hemmed them in to landward. Then the sea rushed in to meet the road again, and all traffic was funneled onto a causeway-and-bridge complex that they had already crossed a few times today; it spanned an inlet, an arm of the sea that penetrated the round shell of the island and meandered off into its interior.

Looking perpendicularly out the window as they hummed across the bridge, Mr. Jones saw something. He seemed to be focusing on a typical Chinese working vessel that had peeled off from the longshore traffic and was cutting beneath the bridge to enter the inlet: a long flat shoe in the water, a pilothouse built on its top toward the stern, cargo stacked and lashed down on the deck forward. A man had clambered to the top of one such stack and was standing with his elbows projecting to either side of his head; Zula realized he was looking at them through binoculars. His elbows came down and he made a gesture that she could recognize as whipping out a phone and pressing it to his head.

Mr. Jones's rang. He answered it and listened for a few moments. His eyes swiveled forward to lock on the back of the taxi driver's head. After listening to a long speech from the man on the boat, he said, "Okay," and handed the phone to the taxi driver again.

They pulled off the ring road at the next opportunity.

"A BOAT," YUXIA said, taking her foot off the gas and getting ready to exit. "They are getting on a boat. This explains everything."

"Don't follow them so close!" Marlon chided her.

"It's okay," Csongor said. "They're not even looking. Think. All the Russians are dead. And if the cops were following them, then they would have been arrested a long time ago, right? So the fact that they are not arrested yet proves that no one is following them."

"But very soon it will get obvious," Marlon insisted, "and we know that the black one has a gun, and if he has friends on a boat, they will probably have guns too." And he glanced down nervously at the pistol that Csongor had left unloaded on the seat of the van.

Was he nervous because it was there at all?

Or because Csongor had not loaded it yet?

It was a question Csongor needed to start asking himself.

THE TAXI DROVE for a few hundred yards down a big four-laner that seemed to have been constructed for no particular purpose, since it was running across reclaimed land, perfectly flat, only a few feet above sea level, and utterly barren: silt that had been dredged up from the strait and that was too salty or polluted to support life. Soon, though, they doubled back on a smaller street that cut through some kind of incipient development, platted and sketched in but not yet realized. This connected them to the road that lined the shore of the inlet. Zula had lost track of directions in the last few sets of turns but now caught sight of the bridge, spanning the inlet's connection to the sea, that they had crossed a minute earlier.

The inlet ballooned to a width of maybe half a mile. Sparse outcroppings of docks and marinas lined its shore, but boat traffic was minimal. After more discussion on the phone, the taxi turned back toward a system of buildings that were being erected along its shore, laced together by pedestrian walkways that ran over the shallows on pilings. The whole complex appeared to be under construction, or perhaps it was a development that had been suspended for lack of funds. Nearby, a broad, stout pier, strewn with empty pallets, was thrust out into the inlet. Jones projected his free hand over the seat and used his gun as a pointer, directing the driver to turn onto it. The taxi slowed almost to a stop, the driver nervously voicing some objection to Jones.

Mr. Jones pointed one more time, emphatically, and withdrew his hand. Then, making sure that the taxi driver could see him in the rearview, he disengaged the pistol's safety and then rested it on his knee, aiming straight through the back of the seat into the middle of the driver's back.

The driver turned gingerly onto the pier, which was wide enough to support three such vehicles abreast, and proceeded at an idling pace. The boat carrying Jones's friends was headed right for them, churning up a considerable wake.

"Okay. Stop," Jones said.

FOLLOWING THE TAXI was no longer necessary, since it had arrived at a dead end on the pier. Yuxia pulled the van into a space between two waterfront buildings, a couple of hundred meters away, whence they could spy on it from semiconcealment. Obviously it was waiting for something, and obviously that something had to be a boat, and by far the most likely candidate was right out before them in the inlet, chugging along in plain sight, carrying several young male passengers who were suspiciously overdressed for today's hot, muggy weather.

Csongor heaved a great sigh that developed into a laugh. He picked up the semiautomatic pistol. There were two clips. He slipped one of them into a pocket, then shoved the other into the pistol's grip until it clicked into place.

Marlon and Yuxia were watching him closely.

"There is an English expression: 'high-maintenance girlfriend,'" Csongor remarked. "Now, of course, Zula is not my girlfriend. Probably never would be, even if all this shit were not happening. And I think that if she *were* my girlfriend? She would not be high maintenance at all! She is just not that type of girl. However. Because of circumstances, today she is the most high-maintenance girlfriend since Cleopatra."

If this pistol worked like most of them, he would have to do something, such as pulling the slide back, to chamber the first round from the newly installed magazine. He did so. The weapon was live, ready to fire.

"What are you going to do?" Marlon asked, with admirable cool.

"Walk over there, unless you want to give me a ride, and fucking kill that guy," Csongor said. He reached for the door handle and gave it a jerk. But because of damage sustained earlier, it did not give way easily. Before he could get it to move, Yuxia had started the engine, shifted the van into reverse, and started backing out of the space where they'd been hiding.

"I'll give you a ride," she said, though Csongor suspected she was just trying to complicate matters. And indeed, the next thing out of her mouth was, "Why don't we call the PSB?"

"Go ahead if you want," Csongor said, "but then I will spend a long time in a Chinese prison."

"But you are good guy," Yuxia said sharply.

Marlon snorted derisively and, in Mandarin, gave Yuxia a piece of his mind about (Csongor guessed) the effectiveness of the Chinese judicial system in accurately distinguishing between good and bad guys in the best of circumstances, to say nothing of the case where the good guy was a foreign national, in the country illegally, connected with murderous foreign gangsters, with his footprints all over the basement of a collapsed terrorist safe house and his fingerprints all over a cache of weapons and money-bricks. Or so Csongor surmised; but toward the end of this disquisition Marlon also began pointing to himself, suggesting that the topic had moved around to his own culpability. And, as if that weren't enough, he pointed a finger or two at Yuxia as well. For during their drive around the ring road, Yuxia had told the story of how she had handcuffed some poor locksmith to the steering wheel, while telling any number of lies to the neighborhood beat cop.

Whatever Marlon was saying, it struck home keenly enough that Yuxia had to pull the van over to the side of the road and weep silently for a few moments. Csongor simultaneously felt grateful for Marlon's acuity and sad about its effect on poor Yuxia.

But just as Csongor was taking advantage of this uncharacteristic moment of weakness on his driver's part by making another grab for the door handle, he was slammed back against his seat by powerful acceleration as she gunned the van forward.

Marlon shouted something at her, and Csongor could guess its meaning: *What the hell are you doing?*

All of this violent stopping and starting had made Csongor nervous about an accidental discharge of the pistol. He felt for its safety lever and flicked it.

Marlon switched to English and looked at Csongor. "I would like to get out of the car."

"Fine," Csongor said. He shoved the Makarov into a cargo pocket on his trousers, then made yet another grab for the door handle.

"I thought you wanted to help the girl who saved your ass," Yuxia said, with a wicked glance over her shoulder.

"I do," Marlon said. "Maybe in a way that doesn't suck."

Csongor had managed to get the van's side door open. Marlon lurched to his feet, crouching low to avoid gouging his scalp on the jagged metal of the van's torn roof. He reached into his pocket and pulled out his phone and its battery, which he jacked back together. This he dropped into the cup holder next to Yuxia. In the same motion he grabbed Yuxia's phone and battery, which Csongor had left sitting there, and stuffed those into his pocket. Yuxia, bowing to the inevitable, allowed the van to slow down. Marlon spun around on one foot, passing in front of Csongor, and reached down into the open bag and grabbed a small cash-brick. He raised this to his face and clenched it between his teeth, then backed out of the van, slapping the seat next to Csongor as he half fell out. He tumbled and rolled in the dust on the side of the road and then fell away to aft as Yuxia gunned the vehicle forward.

Csongor noticed that one of the two stun grenades was now missing. He picked up the remaining one and put it into his jacket pocket. He had lost track of where they were: moving down a woebegone street lined with small businesses that all seemed to have something to do with marine stuff: knowledge he gained not by careful observation but through momentary glimpses and reeks of sparks, smoke, fish, turpentine, gas. But then they crossed an invisible plane into some other property, and the buildings fell away to reveal a clear path to the pier. The taxi still waited and the boat was almost there.

JONES COULD NOT show himself outside of the taxi, and so they sat, engine running, for several minutes, watching the boat approach. The taxi driver was motionless, staring straight ahead, sweat running from beneath his short haircut and trickling down the back of his neck. Zula was aware, of course, that between the two of them, they might be able to overpower Jones, or at least belabor him to the point where the taxi driver might be able to run away and summon help. But that would require some communication between the two of them—which, with Jones sitting right there listening, would have been impossible even if they'd had a language in common.

The boat glided up along the end of the pier and cut its engines. Its pilot had judged matters perfectly and so it eased to a stop directly before them. The difference in altitude between pier surface and boat deck was only a few feet: a minor obstacle, it seemed, for three men who scrambled up onto the pier and walked up to meet the taxi. One of them came alongside the driver's-side door and let the driver see the grip of a pistol projecting from the pocket of his trousers. Then he gave a little toss of the head that meant *Get out*. The driver popped his door latch, and the gunman pulled it open. Moving in fits and starts, the driver pivoted on his seat, got his feet on the ground, looked up at the gunman for his next cue.

A second man flanked the door on the passenger's side. The third came round and opened Jones's door and greeted him in Arabic. Jones responded in kind while groping for Zula's hand. He interlaced his fingers with hers and then scooted toward the door, pulling her along as he went.

Getting on that boat—which was obviously what would happen next—seemed like an overwhelmingly bad idea to Zula. She gripped the doorside handle with her free hand, anchoring herself there, and refused to be pulled out.

Jones paused on the threshold and looked back at her. "Yes, we can do it kicking and screaming. There *are* four of us. Someone *might* notice, *might* summon the PSB. The PSB *might* respond and *might* get here in time to get a good enough look at yonder boat that they could distinguish it from the thousands of other boats just like it. But you should understand, Zula, that this is a close-run affair. Narrow margins. We can only afford so many unwilling passengers. If you don't let go of that fucking handle and come nicely, we will shove the taxi driver into the trunk of his vehicle and push it into the water."

Zula let go of the door handle and gripped Jones's hand. She slid sideways across the seat until she had reached the place where she could rotate on her bottom and get her feet aimed out the door. Jones was strong and she learned that she could rely on his grip. She got her other hand wrapped around his forearm and then executed a sort of chin-up to get her feet clear of the taxi. As she rose to a standing position on the surface of the pier, she glimpsed his face, gazing, not so much in amazement as simple curiosity, at something that was approaching them from the road.

At that moment—for the brain worked in funny ways—Zula suddenly recognized him as Abdallah Jones, a big-time international terrorist. She'd read about him in newspapers.

Following the gaze of Abdallah Jones, Zula turned her head just in time to see a van come roaring in and crash into the rear bumper of the taxi.

SOKOLOV TOOK INVENTORY. In combat there was this tendency to divest oneself of objects at astonishing speed, which was why he and all others in his line of work tended to attach the really important things to their bodies. Less than an hour ago, in the cellar of the apartment building, he had shed his retired Chinese angler costume and changed into a black tracksuit, black trainers, hard-shell knee pads, an athletic supporter with a plastic cup to protect his genitals, and a belt with the Makarov holster and some spare clips. A bulky windbreaker covered a black vest-cum-web-harness from which he had hung a variety of knives, lights, zip ties, and other things he thought he might need. On his back was a CamelBak pouch full of water. Why carry water on a mission that was supposed to last only fifteen minutes? Because once in Afghanistan he had gone out on a fifteen-minute mission that had ended up lasting forty-eight hours, and when he had made it back to his base, having remained barely alive by drinking his own urine and sucking the blood of rodents and small birds, he had made a vow that he would never be without water again.

He unknotted the garbage bag of stuff he had taken from the office. He had to move in tiny increments lest it become obvious, to the people in the crowd all around him, that there was a living creature underneath the carter's tarp. He felt around inside the bag and identified the miscellany of heavy electronic boxes and then found the soft and squishy leather purse.

Most of the purse's contents were of zero to minimal usefulness. As an example, there was a condom, which he considered fitting over the muzzle of his Makarov to keep dirt out of the barrel, but there was little point in doing so now. He did, however, find a wallet with a government identity card bearing a photo that more or less matched the face of the Russian-speaking, Chinese-looking woman—the spy—he had seen in the office. And so here was a case in which a seemingly trivial aspect of the women's fashion industry had profound consequences, at least for Sokolov. For a man would have carried the contents of this wallet on his person and would have departed with them. But women's clothes made no allowances for such things, so it all had to go in the purse.

The photograph was on the right side of the ID card. A serial number, in Arabic numerals, ran along the bottom. The remaining space was occupied by a set of fields, each field labeled in blue and the actual data printed in black. The top field consisted of three characters, and he assumed that it must be the woman's name. Below it were two other fields, arranged on the same line since each of them consisted of only a single character. He assumed that one of these must be gender. Below that were three fields on the same line, printed in Arabic numerals. The first of these was "1986," the second "12," and the third "21," so it was obviously the woman's date of birth. The last field was much longer and consisted of Chinese characters running across one and a half lines, with additional room below, and he assumed that this must be the woman's address.

In his vest he carried a small notebook and a pen. He took these out and devoted a while to copying out the address. Because of his cramped position in the rattling cart, this took a long time. But he had nothing else to do at the moment.

Also in the purse was a mobile phone, which he of course checked for photographs and other data. He did not expect to find much. If the woman was a spy of any skill whatsoever, she would take the strictest precautions with a device such as this one. Indeed, the number of photos was rather small and seemed to consist mostly of snapshots of real estate. Most of the pictures depicted office buildings, and most of these were of the block where this morning's events had taken place. But a few were of a residential building in a hilly neighborhood with a lot of trees. Interspersed with these were some shots of the interior of a vacant apartment, and the view from its windows: across the water to the downtown core of Xiamen.

This was all very diverting, but he needed to have a plan for what to do when the carter finally got him to the hotel. For by now they had made it to the big boulevard that ran along the waterfront, and from here progress would be quicker. Sokolov flipped open his mobile and refreshed his memory of the place by flipping through the snapshots he had taken a couple of days ago. There was not much here to help him: it was the front entrance of a big Western-style luxury business hotel, and as such it was indistinguishable from the same sort of place as might be seen in Moscow, Sydney, or L.A.

He kept flipping back and forth through the same half-dozen photos, looking for anything that might be of use. Most of the people around the entrance were, of course, bellhops and taxi drivers. Guests went in and out. Some were dressed in business suits, others in casual tourist attire. He did not see any commandos in tracksuits.

Still, something about *tracksuit* nagged at him. He flipped through the series a few more times until he found it: a man entering the hotel. He appeared in two successive pictures. In the first his naked leg and bare arm were just swinging into the frame. In the second, he was nodding to a smiling bellhop who had pulled the door open for him. The man was probably in his early forties, tall, slender, blond hair with bald patch, wearing a skimpy pair of loose shorts and a haggard tank-top shirt emblazoned with the logo of a triathlon. Track shoes completed the ensemble. Strapped around his waist was a fanny pack, with a water bottle holstered in a black mesh pocket.

Sokolov was carrying three knives, one of which sported a back-curving hook at the top of the blade, made for slicing quickly through fabric. Working in small, fidgety movements, he got it caught in the fabric of the tracksuit at about midthigh and then made a circumferential cut, slashing off most of one trouser leg. He repeated the same procedure on the other side. Now he was wearing what he hoped would pass for a pair of athletic shorts. With painstaking care he divested himself of his windbreaker, his gear harness, and his gun belt, leaving his upper body clad only in a T-shirt.

He sucked the CamelBak as dry as he could make it. This was a ballistic nylon sack about the size of a loaf of bread, with a circular filling port at its top. The port was large—about the size of the palm of his hand—which made it easier to fill the thing up. He threw in the woman's mobile, her ID card and most of the contents of her wallet—everything that might be used to identify her. This amounted to a few credit cards and slips of paper and didn't take up much room. He added his little notebook and a couple of his knives. He removed the slide from the Makarov pistol and then threw all the gun's parts in, as well as two spare clips that he had been carrying on his belt. He crammed the remaining volume with currency, partly because he might need it and partly to make it bulge as though it were full of water. Then he closed the CamelBak's port again.

Neatly folded in a pocket of his vest he kept a towel—actually half of a diaper, sufficiently threadbare that it could be compressed into a little packet. This was another thing that he had learned never to be without. He extracted this from its compartment and stuffed it into his waistband.

All his other stuff he crammed into the garbage bag. He was moving a little less stealthily now because the carter had made his way out onto a street that was not so crowded. Sokolov had saved out one zip tie, which he used to knot the bag shut.

He risked a peek out from under the tarp and saw the tower of the hotel a couple of hundred meters ahead.

Even if his jogger disguise were perfect, it wouldn't do for him to jump out from under a tarp on a cart in plain view of the bellhops, or of anyone for that matter. And he still had to get rid of the garbage bag. He flipped his mobile open again and reviewed his snapshots one more time. The other day, after looking at this hotel, they had crossed the street to the waterfront and done some reconnoitering there. Though much of it was built-up and crowded ferry terminals, some of it, farther to the north, was a slum of seedy docks and rubbishy stretches of disused shoreline. He found a snapshot of that general part of the waterfront, then got the carter's attention by hissing at him.

They were now peering at each other through a little gap under the edge of the tarp. Sokolov made a finger-crooking motion. The carter reached his hand under the tarp. Sokolov handed him the phone. The carter pulled it out and looked at it for a few moments, then nodded and thrust it back underneath. Sokolov took it and shoved it into a small external pocket on the CamelBak.

He had worked out a way that he could look out from under the edge of the tarp and thus keep an eye on where they going. From the heavy traffic of the boulevard they moved off onto a smaller and quieter frontage road that ran between it and the shore and got to a place where there was surprisingly little traffic. He could hear water lapping and smell the unmistakable stink of waterfront. He risked pulling the edge of the tarp back, but the carter, without looking back, shook his head and spoke some kind of warning that made Sokolov freeze. A few seconds later, a bicyclist whizzed past them from behind.

But a minute later the carter diverted onto a ramp that ran down onto a rickety pier, brought the cart to a stop, and lit a cigarette. After puffing on it for a minute or so, he suddenly peeled the tarp back and muttered something.

Sokolov rolled out onto his feet, pulling the garbage bag behind him. He executed a 360-degree pirouette, scanning in all directions for witnesses. Seeing none, he completed another spin, moving faster, and let go of the garbage bag. It flew about four meters and sank in water that probably would not have come up to the middle of his thigh, had he been so unwise as to wade into it. But that was enough to conceal the bag perfectly, since this water was not easy to see through, and the bag was black.

Turning his back on the splash, Sokolov noted that the carter had already discovered his tip waiting for him in the bottom of the cart: another brick of magenta bills. This disappeared instantly into the man's trousers. He was saying something to Sokolov. Thanking him, probably. Sokolov ignored him and broke into an easy jog. In less than a minute he was out on the waterfront, headed for the hotel tower, loping from one patch of shade to the next, and trying not to listen to the screaming alarm bells that were going off in his mind. For he had spent the entire day hoping that no one would see him. And now he was being watched, pointed out, remarked on, gawked at by a thousand people. But they were not—he kept reminding himself—doing it because they knew who or what he was. They were doing it in the same way they'd stare at any Western jogger crazy enough to go out in the midday sun.

OLIVIA MADE IT all the way down to street level before she fully took in the fact that she was barefoot. She had been blown out of her shoes. They were up in the office with the Russian dog-of-war.

In a hypothetical footrace between Olivia barefoot and Olivia in high-heeled career-girl shoes, over uneven, rubble-strewn ground, it was not clear which Olivia would stand the best chance of winning. It probably depended on how long it took barefoot Olivia to step on a shard of glass and slice her foot open. Not very long, unless she was careful.

The building had an old front that faced toward the building that had just blown up, and, on the opposite side, a new front, still under construction, facing toward a commercial district in the making. Access to the latter was complicated by its being an active construction zone, but she knew how to get there, because the people who had trained her in London had drilled it into her that she must always know every possible way of getting out of a building. So instead of taking the obvious exit through the front, which she envisioned as an ankle-deep surf zone of broken glass, she doubled back and followed the escape route she had already scouted through the construction zone. This changed from day to day as temporary barriers were erected and removed between the various shops and offices that the workers were creating. Today, though, they had left all the doors open as they had fled the building, so all that Olivia really needed to do was pursue daylight while scanning the floor ahead of her for dropped nails.

There were none. Western construction workers might leave dropped nails on the floor, but it seemed that Chinese picked them up.

And so she made it out into the relatively undevastated side of the building, which backed up onto the rim of a man-made crater several hundred meters in diameter, guarded by temporary fencing. Visitors to China often spoke of a "forest of cranes," but this was more akin to a savannah, being largely open ground with a few widely spaced cranes looming over it. Its natural fauna were construction workers, and right now, a couple of dozen of them were gazing, with horrified expressions, in her general direction.

No, they were gazing in her *exact* direction.

Feminist thinkers might argue with social conservatives as to whether women's tendency to be extremely self-conscious about personal appearance was a natural trait—the result of Darwinian forces—or an arbitrary, socially constructed habit. But whatever its origin, the fact was that when Olivia walked out of a building to find a large number of strange men staring at her, she felt self-conscious in a way she hadn't a few seconds earlier. Lacking a mirror, she put her hands to her face and her hair. She was expecting them to come away caked with dust. They came away glistening and red.

Oh dear.

She was not a fainter, and she doubted that the wounds were going to cost her an important amount of blood. The voice of a first aid instructor came back to her: *If I were to take a shot glass full of tomato juice and throw it into your face . . .* But there was no way that these guys were going to let a bleeding, barefoot woman simply wander off alone into the streets. Two of them were already running toward her with hands reaching out in a manner that, in normal circumstances, would have seemed just plain ungentlemanly. What would have been designated, in a Western office, as a hostile environment was soon in full swing as numerous rough strong hands were all over her, easing her to a comfortable perch on a chair that was produced as if by magic, feeling through her hair to find bumps and lacerations. Three different first aid kits were broken open at her feet; older and wiser men began to lodge objections at the profligate use of supplies, darkly suggesting that it was all because she was a pretty girl. A particularly dashing young man skidded up to her on his knees (he was wearing hard-shell knee pads) and, in an attitude recalling the prince on the final page of Cinderella, fit a pair of used flip-flops onto her feet.

Getting an ambulance during this particular half-hour window of time was completely out of the question, so they shoved a couple of bamboo poles through the legs of her chair, lashed them in place, and turned it into a makeshift palanquin on which Olivia was borne, like a Jewish bride, around the edge of the crater to a place where it was possible to hail a taxi. The chair ride was fun if only because Olivia could not stop thinking about the Brits who had trained her at MI6 and their insistence that she avoid any situation that might draw undue attention to herself. Fortunately she had so many first aid supplies wrapped around her head at this point that no one would be able to pick her out from a random lineup of mummies and burn victims.

THE TAXI BOLTED forward and disappeared off the end of the pier. The ensuing sound effect—a crash, rather than a splash—told Zula that it had nose-dived into the deck of the boat.

The van's velocity dropped to almost zero, which gave Zula a clear look through the windshield—or as clear as was possible, given that it was coated with dust and had just been spiderwebbed by the impact. Behind the wheel, she saw nothing but a white balloon: the airbag. But she was certain that in the moment just before impact, she had got a subliminal glimpse of Yuxia's face.

The van kept rolling forward, passing no more than arm's length from Zula, and as it went by she got a direct view, through the driver's-side window, of Yuxia in profile. The airbag was deflating and peeling away from her face, but she was staring dully ahead, stunned by its impact, and the weight of her foot must still be on the gas pedal. "Yuxia!" Zula cried, and she thought that Yuxia stirred; but the van accelerated and followed the taxi off the end of the pier.

It did not, however, completely disappear. For crashed vehicles were beginning to accumulate on the deck of the boat, and so the van only nosed over and ended up with its rear wheels projecting into the air above the pier's deck.

This was not something that one saw every day, and so it held the attention of everyone: Zula, Abdallah Jones, his two surviving accomplices (for the gunman by the driver's-side door had been leaning into the taxi at the moment of impact, had fared quite poorly, and was lying motionless on the pier), and the taxi driver. And so a peculiarly long span of time elapsed before they all came fully aware that they had been joined by a new participant. Before she had even turned to look at his face, Zula recognized him, in her peripheral vision, simply by the shape of his body, as Csongor. He was staggering toward her and Jones. He was considerably the worse for wear and making a visible effort to snap himself out of a kind of stunned and woozy condition. He must have tumbled out the van's side door just after the impact. Zula began raising her arms to hug him, then stifled the impulse as she felt the handcuff's chain go tense. Csongor was reaching into his trouser pocket.

Zula felt a painful jerk on her left wrist as Jones's hand reached up and across her body. He snaked the back of his hand across her right breast and shoved rough fingernails into the gap between her armpit and her upper right arm, the steel of the cuff digging into her flesh. Since her left arm had no choice but to follow his right, it ended up pulled sideways across her belly.

His grip closed around her bicep. His elbow jammed into her chest as he flexed his arm, spinning her about so that he was face-to-face with her and her back was to Csongor. He was using her as a shield.

Jones's left hand came up bearing the pistol and he put its barrel against her neck, torquing it awkwardly in his hand, aiming through her. She heard the safety come off. And at the same time, Csongor reached around the side of her head with his right arm, and she was surprised to see a pistol in his hand. Except for that, she could not see Csongor, but she could feel him. The pressure of Jones's gun's muzzle against her throat made her want to get away from it, so she leaned back and soon found her head resting comfortably against the heaving, thumping, sweaty barrel of Csongor's chest. The two men were of roughly equal height, and Zula now found herself tightly sandwiched between them.

"Is that the true Makarov or the Hungarian variant?" Jones asked, in a light, conversational tone. "Difficult for me to make out the markings at this distance." He was alluding to the fact that Csongor was holding the weapon's muzzle directly against his brow, just above one eye.

"I got it from a Russian."

"Probably the real thing then," Jones remarked. "I'll give you the benefit of the doubt and assume that you had the presence of mind to chamber a round." He was gazing (Zula guessed) into Csongor's eyes, hoping to read a clue there.

Which he apparently did. "I see less than perfect certainty on your face," Jones said in a tone of drawling amusement. "Still, it would be imprudent for me to assume that there's no round in the chamber. I happen to be quite familiar with the Makarov, since they are all over Afghanistan. I sense that you are a newcomer to it. I'm curious: Did you put the safety on?"

"The safety is most certainly not on at this time," Csongor said.

"Oh, but that's not what I asked. I asked whether you *had* put it on, *at any point,* after you chambered a round and cocked it. You seem like the sort who would. The way Ivanov spoke of you. Your protectiveness of Zula. You are thoughtful, careful, deliberate."

Csongor said nothing.

"I only ask," Jones continued, "because the Makarov has an

interesting quirk: when you put the safety on, it decocks the hammer. Taking the safety off doesn't re-cock it. No. You're left with a weapon that's loaded but not yet in a condition to fire. Quite unlike Ivanov's fine 1911 here, which is both loaded and fully cocked. If *I* apply even the slightest amount of pressure to the trigger, I'll put a rather large piece of metal all the way through Zula's neck and from there into your heart, killing you both so rapidly you'll never even know it happened."

Sirens were approaching: more than one cop car, making its way around the inlet, headed their way. Jones glanced in their direction for a moment, then centered his gaze on Csongor's face again and continued: "You're not even going to get the romantic experience of lying there bleeding to death with her decapitated corpse on top of you, because a hydrostatic shock wave is going to travel straight up your aorta into your brain and render you unconscious and maybe even pop out your eyeballs. You, on the other hand— should you decide to take any action—have a very long trigger pull ahead of you. It's that first round out of the Makarov's magazine that is the bitch. Because the hammer isn't cocked, you're going to have to pull *hard* on that trigger for what seems like *forever* in order to get it drawn back for the first shot. And since your finger is about two inches in front of my left eyeball, it's going to be *bloody* difficult for you to do this in a way that's going to surprise me, isn't it?"

Csongor said nothing. But Zula could sense in his breathing that Jones's words were hitting home. Between that, and the approaching cop cars, the fight was draining out of him.

"What are the odds that you can make it to the end of that trigger pull while you and Zula are still alive, Csongor?"

Jones was staring straight into Csongor's eyes, unblinking, awaiting his submission. "Did I mention, by the way, that being handcuffed to this bitch is a serious pain in the arse? I should like nothing more than to be rid of her."

"Csongor," Zula said. "Listen. Can you hear me? Say something."

"Yes," Csongor said.

"I'd like you to have a look at the pistol that Mr. Jones is holding up to my neck. Do you see it?"

A pause, then, "Yes, I am looking at it."

"Do you note anything remarkable about the condition of its hammer?" Zula asked him.

Jones, still looking at Csongor, had been surprised by Zula's entry into the conversation. Now, though, he smiled broadly. Zula, it seemed, was doing his work for him. Reminding Csongor, in case he'd failed to appreciate it the first time, that the 1911 was only a microsecond away from killing both of them.

Then the grin was replaced by astonishment as Csongor's trigger finger went into motion, executing that long hard pull that Jones had only just warned him of.

THE BELLHOPS WHO would see Sokolov running *in* had never seen him run *out* of the hotel. In a smaller place, this might have aroused suspicion. But this place was forty stories high, and he knew that they would think nothing of it as long as he didn't act in a way that would arouse suspicion. If working as a security consultant had taught him nothing else, it had taught him how to walk in and out of expensive hotels. He jogged up the street, turned into the hotel's huge curving entry drive, slowed to a trot, and entered the shade of its awning, which was big enough to shelter twenty cars. There he dropped to a brisk walk, checked his wristwatch, and pretended to press one of its little buttons. He pulled his towel out of the Camel-Bak's external pocket, unfolded it, wiped his face, and then draped it over his head like an NBA player just sent to the bench. He put the CamelBak's drinking tube into his mouth and pretended to suck on it while pacing back and forth for half a minute or so along a line of potted shrubs that had been planted along the edge of the drive. These grew in big rectangular boxes of concrete, surfaced with pebbles and filled with dirt. Interspersed with them were waste receptacles, constructed in the same manner, with sand beds on top where waiting taxi drivers could stub out their cigarettes, and open slots below where refuse could be deposited.

At this point he had no particular plan, other than that he would enter the hotel and then try to think of something. But now, glancing into one of the waste receptacles, Sokolov noticed something that looked like a credit card, though emblazoned with the logo of this hotel. It was a key card that some departing guest had thrown away; or perhaps a taxi driver had found it abandoned in his back-seat and had tossed it there. On the pretext of throwing away some small bit of debris, Sokolov picked it up and palmed it. Then, using his other hand to wipe his face with the towel—he hoped that this might complicate future analysis of the surveillance video—he approached the hotel's entrance. He bent down, letting the towel drape around his head, and pretended to pull the key card out of his sock. A bellhop opened the door for him and gave him a cheerful greeting. Sokolov nodded and entered the lobby.

What was their ridiculous word for *gymnasticheskii zal*? He was scanning the directional signs, trying not to be too obvious about it.

Fitness Center. Of course.

It was on the third floor, a nice one, with windows overlooking the waterfront. Key card access only. He swiped the card he had stolen and got a red light. Rapped the card against the window and got the attention of an attendant, a young woman, who smiled and hurried to the door to let him in.

They had tiny bottles of water and bananas. Thank God. But he had to pace himself or it would look very strange indeed. A grid of pigeonholes, just by the entrance, served as a place for guests to stash their belongings while they worked out. Sokolov slid his CamelBak into one of these. Stuffed with cash, it did not sag and wobble the way a water-filled one should have, and so he pulled it out and put it on the top shelf where it might not be so conspicuous. Half a dozen other pigeonholes were occupied, two with women's bags, the rest with only a few small items such as key cards and mobile phones. Sokolov went into the men's bathroom, made sure he was alone, turned on a faucet, bent over, and drank from it for a while. Dust from this morning's activities was frozen into the hairs on his arms. He rinsed them clean and splashed water on his face. Exiting the bathroom, he plucked two bottles of water and a banana from the display and carried them over to a bank of treadmills. This was served by three large flat-panel television sets, two showing CNN and one showing a Chinese news channel. Sokolov got on a treadmill that was closer to a CNN screen but in view of the Chinese one, and walked on the thing for a while, drinking water, eating the banana, and monitoring local news coverage. Most of this seemed to be about the diplomatic conference. There was a brief story that seemed to be about a fire in Xiamen. But that was only a guess, based on the graphics and a few fleeting video clips of fire trucks and ambulances in a crowded street, people caked with dust, limping and stumbling, supported by astonished bystanders.

Of course they would claim it was a gas explosion. Everything was always a gas explosion. But Sokolov knew that the PSB investigators now working on the case were under no illusions.

He spent forty-five minutes on the treadmill and half an hour lifting weights. Guests came and went. As they did, Sokolov tallied them: gender, nationality, size, shape, age. Which pigeonhole they put their stuff in.

An Asian man came in; Sokolov guessed Japanese or Korean. He was trim, well put together. He shoved his wallet and a phone into one of the pigeonholes. Sokolov, moving from one machine to another, walked past him and judged him to be of the same height. Shoe size was more difficult to judge at a glance. After wandering around the Fitness Center and taking an inventory of its machines and facilities, this man boarded an elliptical trainer and set it up for a half-hour program, then turned his attention to a magazine.

Sokolov went to the entryway and set a half-empty water bottle down on the counter, then got his CamelBak down, shoved one arm through a shoulder strap, and let it swing free while he poked the other arm through the other strap. It knocked the water bottle off the counter. He cursed and ran to pick it up, but it had already leaked most of its contents into a puddle on the floor. The attendant, delighted to have something to do, ran over, assessed the situation, and then went to grab some towels, assuring Sokolov that it was all okay and she would take care of it.

While she had her back turned, Sokolov turned to face the pigeonholes. He pulled out the Asian man's wallet and flipped it open. His key card was right there in the easiest-to-reach pocket. Sokolov pulled it out and replaced it with the one he had stolen from the wastebasket outside, then put the wallet back.

He then went into the sauna, which was unoccupied, and slipped the stolen key card into his sock. He sat in the sauna for twenty minutes.

When the Japanese or Korean man finished his exercise routine, he retrieved his belongings from the pigeonhole and exited the Fitness Center with Sokolov a few paces ahead of him. They ended up in the elevator lobby together. Sokolov, pretending to be distracted by a phone call, was slow to get on the elevator; the other courteously held the door for him. Sokolov scanned the button panel, reached to hit the button for 21, then hesitated, startled to find that his floor had already been selected. He hit the button again anyway. During the elevator ride, he pretended to lose his connection and, after uttering a couple of mild curses, began fiddling with the buttons, trying to make a new call. He was still doing so when the doors opened and the other man exited. Trailing well behind him, Sokolov ambled down the corridor. The man stopped before the door to Room 2139 and swiped his key card, only to get a red light. Sokolov kept on walking and disappeared around the next corner.

A few moments later he peeked back around the corner to see the man's retreating back. He was headed for the elevators, going down to the lobby to get a new key card made.

Sokolov went to Room 2139, opened the door, and made a quick inventory of its closet and dresser. The guest's name was Jeremy Jeong and he was an American citizen (he had left his passport in a desk drawer). Sokolov established that the best place to hide was under the bed. In most hotels this would not have been the case because the bed was just a box, with no "under," but this was a luxury place with real beds, and the bedspread hung down far enough to hide him. Once he was well situated there, he opened the CamelBak, pawed out the wads of money, and retrieved the pieces of the Makarov, which he quickly assembled into a functioning and loaded weapon. He hoped to God he would not need it, but to leave it in pieces would have been foolish.

He was stuffing the money back into the CamelBak when he heard the door opening and Jeremy Jeong coming in.

ABDALLAH JONES PULLED the trigger of his own weapon, causing its hammer to fly forward and pinch down painfully on the little finger of Zula's right hand, which she had inserted into the gap between it and the weapon's frame. This prevented it from striking the firing pin. Nothing happened.

Jones did not have time to take in and understand his own weapon's failure to fire. The sight of Csongor's trigger finger in motion had thrown him into an involuntary movement. He snapped his head around to the left, pushing the Makarov's muzzle away. Zula saw and heard it discharge and saw Jones's head jerk away from it.

A minute earlier Jones had grabbed her right arm and coiled her body up against his to make her a human shield. Now they uncoiled. Jones pivoted away from her, pulling the pistol loose from her finger, leaving an icy sensation in her fingertip that she knew meant serious damage. His left arm, still holding the gun, flailed back as he rotated away from her. His right hand let go of her arm and trailed away until the handcuff chain brought it up short like a dog that had run to the end of its leash, and then she felt a few more layers of wrist skin being macerated by the steel bracelet, and she toppled forward. Jones was near the end of a full one-eighty, and was collapsing to the surface of the pier. He ended up spread-eagled on his back, his right hand pulling Zula down—she had no choice, now, but to fall down on top of him— and his left sprawled out on the pier, still maintaining a grip on that pistol.

Zula fell. But as she did she launched herself as best she could in the general direction of that gun arm. Her right shoulder happened to come down on Jones's breastbone, forcing the air out of his lungs, and as she was bouncing off it she flung her right hand out and planted it on Jones's forearm, pinning the gun hand to the surface of the pier.

Only after she had reinforced that with a knee against his elbow did she dare to look at the side of Jones's head. She saw red there, but it was the red of burns and abrasions, not of pumping blood. The pistol had gone off right next to the side of his head, but the bullet had not penetrated his skull.

Csongor didn't know this; he was still standing there watching Jones and Zula come to rest, unwilling to fire the pistol again lest he accidentally strike Zula, and probably under the impression that it wasn't necessary. He'd already shot Jones in the head once, and, she sensed, he was a little stunned by his own behavior.

Loud banging noises began to sound from nearby, and Csongor

looked up in alarm. Zula followed his gaze back over her shoulder and saw one of Jones's comrades, perhaps ten meters away, firing a pistol wildly, holding it in one hand so that it bucked with each recoil, and not bothering to sight over the barrel.

The taxi driver chose this moment to make a break for it, and the shooter, following some kind of dumb reflex to attack whatever was moving, turned and fired a couple of rounds that knocked the man flat on his stomach.

Csongor's eyes went to Zula; she had taken the highly imprudent step of removing her free hand from Jones's gun arm and was using it to wave him away and down. He backed up a couple of steps, raising the pistol.

Noting violent movement in the corner of her eye, Zula turned her attention to the other surviving jihadist, who was making a dive for a loose gun that had fallen from the pocket of the man who had earlier run afoul of the taxi.

"Get out, the cops are coming anyway!" Zula shouted.

Csongor backed up two steps toward the edge of the pier, then, just as the other jihadist was opening fire, turned around and jumped off. Unlike the taxi, he did make a splash.

Zula heard a step behind her and then felt something hard pressing into the back of her neck. She removed her knee from Jones's elbow.

"Thank you," Jones said, a bit groggy, but coming around fast. He bent his arm, raising the gun, and then used it to gesture at the prone taxi driver, and then in the direction of where Csongor had jumped. He shouted a command in Arabic. This was acknowledged respectfully by the first gunman to have opened fire, who walked over to the taxi driver and shot him casually in the back of the head. Then he walked over to the edge of the pier and looked down into the water.

A series of booms sounded from below, and the man quietly toppled over the edge and disappeared.

"Polar bears and seals," Jones remarked. He reached up with his cuffed hand, collapsing Zula's arm, and grabbed her hair, which was frizzed out and eminently grabbable. He wrenched her head around with a violent sweeping movement of the arm and slammed her face into the pier, then rolled over on top of her, pinning her full-length to the deck with his body on top of hers. "I'm not shielding you, by the way," he explained, "you're shielding me. You know how polar bears hunt?"

"From below?"

"Very good. It's *so* nice having an educated person around. Your man Csongor can see up, just barely, through the cracks between the planks. He knew exactly where my man was."

The other gunman seemed to have arrived at the same realization and was now moving around nervously, edging toward the end of the pier where the boat was waiting and the water was deeper.

The sirens were getting very close. Jones propped himself up on his elbows, taking some of his considerable weight off Zula, and gazed curiously down the pier, then, for some reason, checked his watch. Blood dribbled from the wound on the side of his head and spattered the side of her face. She turned away from it and let it drain down the side of her neck. Her pinky was starting to throb. She glanced at it and saw the nail ripped out at the base, hanging on by a few shreds of cuticle, and blood coursing out.

The pier jerked beneath them. A few moments later, a massive thud sounded from somewhere. It wasn't especially loud, but one had the impression it had traveled from an event, far away, that had been very loud indeed.

Zula couldn't see what the cop cars were doing, but she knew that they were close, no more than a couple of hundred feet away. There were two of them. One, then the other, turned off its siren.

Then nothing happened for half a minute. Jones just watched, fascinated, and checked his watch again.

Then the sirens came back on again, and the cars went into motion. Their frequency Dopplered down, and their volume began to diminish.

The cops were driving *away* from them at high speed.

"Mere anarchy is loosed upon the world," said Jones, switching into a posh accent. He looked down at her, as if suddenly surprised to find her underneath him. "That bang was the sound of a very brave man martyring himself. Somewhere near the conference center. It seems to have drawn the cops' attention. Which was the whole idea, of course. We have had to do rather a lot of improvising today. Speaking of which, you and I are now going to execute a very nonimprovised long walk off a short pier. If you work with me and come along nicely, I shall permit you to keep your teeth."

JEREMY JEONG DOUBLE-BOLTED his door, which Sokolov approved of. One could not be too careful. Then he stripped off his gym togs and entered the bathroom and turned on the shower.

Sokolov rolled out from under the bed, stripped naked, and stuffed what was left of his clothes into a hotel laundry bag that he found clipped to a hanger. He dropped the CamelBak into the same and then rolled it up into a neat bundle. Having already marked the locations of the clothes he wanted, he was able to find and put on underwear, socks, shirt, and a business suit in less time than it would take Jeremy to shampoo his hair. He stuffed a necktie into his pocket and shoved his feet into a pair of shoes—a bit tight, but tolerable—and then slipped out the door, letting it close softly behind him. He took the elevator down to a mezzanine level, went into a men's room, entered a stall, sat on a toilet, and put on the necktie, then tied his shoes. From the CamelBak he retrieved the little notebook where he had written the address of the spy woman. He exited the stall and checked his appearance in the mirror. The tie was a little askew, so he fixed it. Then he took the elevator to the lobby and approached the concierge, smiling helplessly.

"Sorry, English not so good."

The concierge, a dazzling woman of about thirty, tried a few other Western languages on him, and they decided to stick with English.

"There is nice Chinese lady here. Extremely helpful to my company. I wish to say thanks. When I get back to Ukraine, I send her nice present, you understand?"

The concierge understood.

"Is to be surprise. Nice surprise."

The concierge nodded.

"Here is address of woman. I try to write down correctly. Not good at writing Chinese as you can see. I think this is it."

The woman's eyes scanned the rudely fashioned characters, passing easily over some of them, snagging on others. Once or twice she allowed her flawless brow to wrinkle just a little. But in the end she nodded and beamed. "This is an address on Gulangyu Island," she said.

"Yes. The little island just over there." Sokolov waved toward the waterfront. "Problem is, when I get back to Ukraine, I cannot write woman's address in Chinese on FedEx document. Need to have it in English. So my question for you is, can you please translate this address into English words for FedEx?"

"Of course!" said the concierge, delighted to be part of sending a lovely surprise gift to a nice Chinese lady. "It will be just a moment."

And now a minute or two of moderate anxiety as Sokolov watched her write out the words on a hotel notepad, while handling two interruptions. He thought it very likely that Jeremy Jeong would not even notice that one of his suits was missing (he had three of them) for hours; and even then it would seem so bizarre that he would hesitate to mention it. But there was always the possibility that he was hypervigilant and prone to summoning the law at the slightest pretext, in which case Sokolov really needed to be out of here.

The concierge gave him another smile and slid the paper across the counter to him. Sokolov accepted it with profuse thanks, walked out the door, climbed into a taxi, and took it to another Western business hotel half a mile up the road. There, he availed himself of a free computer in the lobby, where he typed the spy's English address into Google Maps.

This yielded a close-up view of an irregular street pattern, which told him nothing, so he zoomed out until he could see the whole island. He checked the scale and verified his general impression that Gulangyu was no more than a couple of kilometers in breadth. He tried to get a sense of its layout, its cardinal directions: basically, how to get to and from the ferry terminal even if he were lost. Then he turned on the satellite imagery. From this a few things were obvious. First of all, its transportation system was much more finely meshed than was hinted by the street plan, which only depicted perhaps 10 percent of the roads and rights-of-way. Or perhaps those were not roads, but alleys and walkways, private footpaths among the buildings. Second, the buildings were all roofed in tasteful earthtones, contrasting with the garish tile and sheet metal that tended to protect Xiamen's buildings from the rain. Third, there was a lot of greenery. Fourth, the place names tended to be schools, academies, colleges, and the like; and the presence of large oval running tracks and so on suggested that they were rather nice schools.

To paraphrase Tolstoy, all rich places were alike, but each poor place was poor in its own way. The slums of Lagos, Belfast, Port-au-Prince, and Los Angeles each would have presented a completely different and bewildering panoply of risks. But just from looking at this map, Sokolov knew that he could go to Gulangyu and walk its streets and make his way in the place just as well as he could in a parky suburb of Toronto or London.

He did not want to arouse undue attention by printing it out, so he sketched a rudimentary map onto the back of the note he had received from the concierge and spent a while examining the satellite view of the building in question, getting a rough idea as to its layout and the general shape of its grounds. He noted that there was a hotel nearby, standing on considerably higher ground. Its website informed him that it had a terrace where drinks were served in the afternoons.

He bought a man-purse from a store in the hotel lobby and dropped his CamelBak and other few possessions into it, then carried it down to the waterfront where he took the next ferry to Gulangyu.

BY NO MEANS had the planning of the taxi-ramming operation developed to an advanced state during the fifteen seconds between its conception in Yuxia's mind and its execution. She had not, as an example, had time to communicate any part of it to Csongor. Consequently he'd been forced to figure it out by himself and to brace for impact by putting his head against the seat in front of him. Like a lot of good plans, though, this one was extremely simple. The bad men were up to something involving a boat. Yuxia could put the sole tool at her disposal (the van) to use in wrecking same, and thereby prevent them from doing whatever.

High mountain girl that she was, she didn't know much about boats. She was now learning that all her intuitions about them were considerably off base. There had been no question in her mind that having a taxi—to say nothing of a taxi followed by a minivan—crash into the top of one of these things would completely destroy it. Now she was dumbfounded to see that the boat was not destroyed. It still floated; it was still a boat.

Not to trivialize what had happened. Undoubtedly it had been a very bad day for the boat. It might be damaged beyond repair. *But it still floated.* Gazing out the destroyed windshield while hanging facedown in the safety belt, she could kind of see how it worked: the deck might be wood, but the hull was steel. And because it was floating, when things crashed into it, the water acted like a shock absorber of basically infinite capacity. The comparative frailty of the wooden deck planks actually worked to its advantage, since in snapping and bending they soaked up a lot of damage. And the stacks of empty wooden cargo pallets on top of the deck had collapsed as the taxi had fallen through them, further cushioning the impact.

Another amazing fact: *Qian Yuxia had ended up on the boat!* This had not been the plan at all. The idea had been to stop on the pier. But she had not reckoned on the air bag. There must have been a few moments of inattention, following the crash, when she had let her foot press down on the gas.

"Csongor?" she called. But he was no longer in the vehicle.

A phone started ringing. Not hers. It was down somewhere near her foot. . .

It was in her boot! It had gone flying, bounced around the interior of the vehicle, and ended up dropping into the open top of her blue boot. It was now wedged against her right ankle bone. She tucked her foot closer, reached in, and pulled it out.

"*Wei?*"

"*Wei?* Yuxia?"

"Who's this?"

"Marlon."

"Why are you calling your own phone?" For she had recognized this one as his.

"Never mind. Are you okay?"

"I'm talking on the phone, aren't I?"

"Are you still in the van?"

"Yes, but the van is—"

"I know. I'm looking at it. You'd better get out of it."

"Why?"

"Because bad shit is going down on that pier—ohmygod."

Marlon didn't have to explain why he was saying this, because Yuxia could now hear gunfire behind her. Gunfire and sirens.

Bracing her right elbow against the steering wheel to support the weight of her upper body, Yuxia reached out with her left, found the door handle, and jerked back on it. Something went *snick* inside the door, but it didn't open. It must have been jammed by one of today's many violent impacts. Bashing her shoulder into it made no difference. She transferred the phone into her other hand so that she could reach down with her right and undo the seat belt. This caused her to fall forward into the steering wheel and sound the horn. "I'll call you back," she shouted, and snapped the phone shut and, for lack of a better place to put it just now, dropped it into her boot again. Then, using various hand- and footholds in the van's interior, she clambered up into the backseat and across to the open side door.

Beyond this point, her way forward would take her across an exceedingly dangerous-looking terrain of crumpled taxi and splintered wood. Some combination of being struck in the face by the air bag and the boat's gentle bobbing made her queasy and unsure of her movements. She crouched in the door frame while trying to recover her balance. She saw, and was seen by, an older man who had come forward from the boat's pilothouse to inspect the damage. She considered saying something but got the idea, based on the man's appearance, that he might not speak Mandarin. Drawing slowly on a cigarette, he gave her a most unpleasant look. She felt aggrieved by this, until she remembered that she had just done everything in her power to destroy his boat, which was probably the source of his livelihood.

It might have developed into an exchange of curses or even of blows had they not been distracted by the appearance of two figures above them on the edge of the pier: the tall black man and Zula. Yuxia controlled a sudden, ridiculous impulse to wave and call hello.

The black man said, "I am going to count to three and then jump. You may jump, or not." Yuxia understood that, since the speaker was handcuffed to Zula and was much bigger than her, this was both a mean sort of joke and a threat.

In the end they jumped together and landed awkwardly on an open and uncratered stretch of deck. Zula cried out in pain and held a bloody fist protectively against her stomach. This finally got Yuxia moving; she clambered down out of the van's door frame, thinking to go and see what was wrong. The black man looked at her curiously, but then turned his attention to the pissed-off skipper and gave him an order in a language Yuxia did not recognize. The skipper trotted back in the direction of the pilothouse.

Whatever pain had caused Zula to cry out was now subsiding. She looked up and spied Yuxia. A happy and grateful look came onto her face, but only for the briefest moment; then she looked anguished, horrified. "Yuxia! Get off! Jump into the water now!"

Yuxia hesitated, then realized that her girlfriend was probably giving her some good advice. But during that interval, another man had jumped down onto the deck from the pier. He was carrying a gun. At a word from the tall black man, he leveled the weapon at Yuxia, holding it in both hands and staring at her down the length of its barrel. Once his eye had connected with hers through its iron sights, he gave it a little twitch indicating that she should approach. She still had thoughts of taking Zula's advice, but then the boat's engine roared and it surged forward, causing the van to settle. Yuxia had no choice but to scamper away as the van toppled sideways off the crushed taxi. This only brought her closer to the gunman, who showed admirable focus in mostly ignoring the slow-motion vehicular avalanche taking place only a few meters away from him.

She was only a couple of meters away from Zula at this point, so she just walked over to her. Zula threw her bloody right fist around Yuxia's shoulder, and Yuxia put both of her arms around Zula's waist. "Thank you," Zula said, starting to cry. "I'm sorry."

"I'm sorry it didn't work," Yuxia said.

The tall black man stuck his handgun into his waistband, then reached into his pocket. "Since the two of you are on such affectionate terms," he said, pulling out a silver key, "let's make it official." He unlocked the manacle from his right wrist, then peeled Yuxia's left arm away from Zula's waist and snapped it onto her. The two women were now joined at their left wrists, which, as they immediately discovered, meant that they couldn't face in the same direction. If one of them walked forward, the other had to walk backward, or else they had to do something awkward with their arms, and move shoulder to shoulder. Their captor understood this very well. Seiz-

ing the manacle's chain with one hand, he towed them aft, around
the side of the pilothouse, to an open space on the stern that was
shaded under a canvas awning. Rummaging around in a toolbox, he
produced a hammer and a large nail. He drove the nail about halfway into a deck plank, then dragged them over, forced them down,
pressed the chain to the deck right next to the nail, and pounded
on the nail until it had been bent over the chain and its bowed head
driven deeply into the wood.

Having thus secured them, he moved forward again and assisted
the remainder of the crew—half a dozen men, all told—in shoving first the van and then the taxi off the side of the boat and into
the water. The boat by now had crossed to the middle of the inlet
and had laid in a direct course toward the great bridge that crossed
over the channel by which it connected to the sea. Though most of
the inlet was quite shallow, this part of it seemed to be a dredged
ship channel. Both vehicles sank immediately and disappeared into
murky water.

Above them, it seemed as though every police and emergency
aid vehicle in the People's Republic of China was screaming across
the bridge, all headed in the same direction, and all ignoring them
completely.

As the men busied themselves throwing the vehicles overboard,
Yuxia felt a momentary buzzing sensation against her ankle. She
reached into her boot, pulled out Marlon's phone, and checked the
screen. It was showing a text message: TURN OFF THE RINGER.

As she stared at it, a second message came in: RED BUTTON ON SIDE.

She flipped the phone over and found a tiny red button with
a picture of a bell on it. She flicked it to the off position and then
dropped the phone back into her boot.

CSONGOR OBSERVED THE departure of the boat from a squatting
position in the shallow water beneath the pier. Only his head was
above the water. He was peeking from behind an old piling. The
rhythmic surge of the waves rocked his body to and fro. He had
already learned that it was inadvisable to hug the piling for balance,
since it was covered with barnacles that turned it into a sort of 3D
saw blade, and the general effect of the waves was to rub him against

it. Little wavelets fetched up against the gray-white carapaces of the barnacles and stained them pink, for blood was emerging in impressive volumes from the semifloating body of the man Csongor had shot a few moments ago.

His entire body was shaking uncontrollably, but not because he was immersed in water. Much had happened in the last few hours that went far beyond any of his past experiences, but the one that he couldn't get out of his mind was that he had put a gun to a man's head and pulled the trigger. Somehow this was far more upsetting than having been shot at. And actually having shot and killed this other fellow had made curiously little impression on him, though he reckoned it would come back to occupy his nightmares later.

His jittery reaction was not doing him any favors now. He was simply watching, from a few meters away, as a band of terrorists ran off with someone he cared about. And yet no amount of thinking could make the situation any better. He had already tried a frontal assault. Only Zula's quick thinking—how did she know so much about guns!? had saved him. The advantage of surprise had been pissed away. The only action he could take now was to wade in closer and start blasting away with the Makarov. But they would be waiting for that; and from this distance, with shaking hands, he was as likely to hit Zula or Yuxia as he was to hit one of the terrorists. He had heard the tall black man speaking about the suicide bomber, and he had watched with his own eyes as the cops in the two squad cars had listened to orders on their radios, turned around, and raced away to more important duties. So even if he had been willing to simply summon the police and hand himself over to the law, he would not have been able to get their attention.

The exchange of gunfire on the top of the pier had, of course, been witnessed by everyone in the neighborhood, and so all other small craft had darted into shore and the inlet had gone perfectly still except for the churning wake of the terrorists' boat, laboring out toward the open sea, listing and wallowing under the weight of two wrecked vehicles. The shoreline itself was deserted.

The only exception was a small open motorboat that buzzed out from a slip a few hundred meters away and turned to run parallel to shore, headed for the pier where Csongor had been hiding. The noise of its outboard motor quavered up and down like a tone-deaf person trying to carry a tune, and it took a somewhat meandering course at first. But its pilot—a tall slender fellow in a *douli,* or the traditional cone-shaped hat of the Chinese workingman—seemed to be a quick learner. He gained confidence as he went along, and as he drew up alongside the pier he nudged the big hat back on his head to reveal his face: it was Marlon.

Csongor stood up and smiled, which, if you thought about it, was a perfectly idiotic thing to do under the circumstances. Marlon grinned back. Then the grin went away as he realized that he was headed for the muddy shore with no way to stop himself and not enough room to turn around.

Csongor stepped out in front of the boat, leaned forward, and put his hands against its bow, which was covered with scraps of bald tires. Its momentum forced him to back up a few steps, but very soon he brought it to a stop and then swiveled it around so that it was pointing outward again. It was made of wood, perhaps four meters long, more elongated than a rowboat, yet not quite as slender as a canoe. Its most recent paint job had been red, but the one before that had been yellow, and in its earlier history it had been blue. Made to carry things, rather than people, it was not abundantly supplied with benches: there was one in the stern for the operator of the outboard motor, and one at the prow, more of a shelf than a seat.

Ivanov's man-purse was strapped diagonally across Csongor's shoulder. The whole time he had been squatting beneath the pier, it had floated next to him, gradually sinking as it took on water. He peeled it off over his head and threw it into the boat, then got his hands on its gunwale, flexed his knees, jumped, and vaulted in, pitching forward headfirst, praying the little craft wouldn't simply capsize. It seemed excitingly close to doing exactly that but righted itself. Marlon gave it some throttle, and it groaned out along the pier and into the open water of the inlet. "Get down," he suggested. Csongor slid off the vessel's front seat and into the dirty water slopping around in the bottom of the hull. He still felt ridiculously exposed. But when he peered forward over the bow, he noted that he could no longer see the terrorists' boat, which meant that they could not see him. And that was all that mattered. If they looked back, all they would see was a skiff being piloted by a man in a very common style of hat. No large armed Hungarians would be visible unless Marlon drew very close to them, which seemed unlikely.

"Did you buy this, or steal it?" Csongor asked, in a tone of voice making it clear that he didn't actually care.

"I think I bought it," Marlon said. He was piloting with one hand and texting with the other. "The owner didn't speak much *putonghua*."

Csongor was familiarizing himself with some random stuff in the bottom of the boat that its ex-owner had not had the presence of mind to remove during what must have been an extraordinarily hasty and poorly-thought-out transaction. There was a blue umbrella, battered to the point where it could no longer fold up. Experimenting with this, he found that he could get it mostly open and use it to shade his stubbled head from the direct light of the sun. Two oars served as backup propulsion. A plastic container of the type used in the West to contain yogurt served as a bailing device. Csongor, having nothing else to do, went to work bailing. He was thirsty. He looked around and noted that Marlon hadn't had time to procure drinking water.

AFTER THEY HAD put about half a mile of distance between themselves and the Xiamen shore, Jones knelt down and opened both halves of the handcuffs. A box of first aid supplies was produced from somewhere. Most of its contents were claimed immediately by Jones, who, with help from a member of the crew, pressed a stack of sterile pads against the side of his head and then turbaned it into place with a roll of gauze. With what remained, Yuxia went to work on Zula's pinky. Zula had become used to keeping this balled up and pressed to her stomach, and so peeling it away from her belly and straightening the finger was a painful and bloody undertaking. It hurt and bled all out of proportion to the actual seriousness of the wound. Yuxia poured water onto it from a bottle, washing away the blood that had gone all dry and sticky. The nail wasn't quite ready to come off and so they left it on. Then they wrapped gauze around it until her pinky had become a clumsy white baseball bat of a thing.

Meanwhile, just next to them, men were making tea. Zula had been here long enough to recognize all the elements of the ritual. The local procedure involved a lot of spillage, which here was taken care of by a baking sheet that looked as if it had once been used as a shield by riot police. A flat perforated rack was set into this, and resting on the rack were tiny bowls, smaller than shot glasses, old and stained. It seemed terribly important to the men on the boat that Zula accept one of them and drink. So this she did. The first sip of tea only reminded her of how desperately thirsty she was, so she tossed the rest of it back; when she set the bowl down, it was replenished immediately. Yuxia was next. Then Jones had his. Apparently they were considered guests.

She had never really understood the tea thing until this moment. Humans needed water or they would die, but dirty water killed as surely as thirst. You had to boil it before you drank it. This culture around tea was a way of tiptoeing along the knife edge between those two ways of dying.

The men on the vessel were not Middle Eastern and they were not Chinese, but depending on how light and emotion played over their faces, they showed clear signs of both ancestries. They spoke some other language than Chinese or Arabic, but there was at least one—the more competent of the two gunmen, also equipped with binoculars and the phone—who could switch to Arabic when he wanted to communicate with Jones. Zula got the sense that they were burning a lot of fuel during the first fifteen minutes of the voyage, probably trying to put distance between themselves and trouble. The place where they'd shot it out with Csongor could be seen from any number of high-rise apartment buildings; perhaps some curtain twitcher on an upper story had seen the whole thing and was watching their getaway. But even if this were the case, Jones had little to worry about, since there was nothing about this boat to distinguish it from all the others. They churned out into open water, then cut around the northern limb of the island, going right past the end of the runway, where a jetliner on its landing run passed so close overhead that Zula could count the wheels on its landing gear. A slow turn to the south brought them into the busiest zone, the strait between Xiamen and its industrial suburbs on the mainland, spanned by huge bridges and chockablock with much larger vessels.

"To the Heartless Island," said Jones, apparently sensing Zula's curiosity as to where they might be going.

"Come again?"

The skipper had cut the throttle, and the boat, after being

slapped on the stern one time by its own wake, had slowed to a much more leisurely pace. They had merged comfortably into a stream of traffic—mostly boats just like this one, and passenger ferries—that weaved among huge anchored freighters like a stream flowing around boulders.

Jones nodded indefinitely toward a southern horizon cluttered with small islands, or perhaps some of them were headlands of the Asian continent, gangling out into the harbor. "Hub of the commercial fishing fleet," he explained. "Economic migrants from all over China go there because they've been promised jobs. When they arrive, they find that there's nothing for them and they can't afford to go back. So they work as virtual slaves." He nodded toward one of the crew members, who was refilling the teapot. "The place has an official name, obviously. But Heartless Island is what these people call it."

If this had been a real conversation, Zula might now have made further inquiries. It seemed unnecessary though. She could piece it together easily enough. These men on the boat belonged to some Muslim ethnic group from the far west. They had been drawn to Heartless Island in the way that Jones described. Having no other way to make sense of their lives, they had been recruited by some sort of radical group, part of a network that was in touch with whoever Abdallah Jones hung out with. And when Jones had decided to come to China, these men had provided him with the support system he needed.

But she got the sense that he wasn't finished. So she held her gaze on him. In turn, he regarded her with a look that was somewhat difficult to interpret, as one side of his face was distorted by swelling, and he was hardly the most easy-to-read man to begin with. "These men work with me," he said, "because they choose to. I have no power over them. If they began to ignore my commands, or simply threw me overboard and left me to drown, the only consequences, for them, would be that their lives would suddenly become much simpler and safer. And so even if I were the type of man who was capable of forgiving and forgetting your attempt, just a few minutes ago, to get me shot in the head, I would have to be some kind of a fool to allow myself to be seen, by these men, as having shown such weakness. It is not the sort of thing that gains a man respect and influence in the Heartless Island milieu, if you follow me."

Zula did not want to admit that she was following him, but she found that she could no longer hold his gaze, and so she looked to Yuxia instead. The face of Qian Yuxia had gone still and devoid of expression, and she would not meet Zula's eye. Zula reckoned that she had already made some kind of adjustment to what Jones was describing as the Heartless Island milieu.

"And so," Jones concluded, "things are about to get ugly. Not that they were pretty to begin with. But, during the journey, you might wish to consider how you can keep them from really getting out of hand. I would suggest an end to pluck, or spunk, or whatever label you like to attach to the sort of behavior you were showing back on that pier, and a decisive turn toward *Islam:* which means submission. Just a thought."

OLIVIA, THE PRIVILEGED Westerner, was outraged at the amount of time she had to wait at the hospital. Meng Anlan, the hard-bitten Chinese urbanite, wondered who she'd have to pay off, then remembered she didn't have any money. More to the point, no government ID, the sine qua non of Chinese personhood. No connections to speak of either. She could get her uncle Binrong to patch a call through to some hospital administrator and holler at him for a while; but Meng Binrong, as a fictional character based in London, had no pull here either, and, at the moment, a lot of people were probably queued up wanting to say unpleasant things to the people who ran this place.

As time went on, though, the Meng Anlan side of her began to see a kind of simple logic at work here: she had been injured several hours ago, and she was actually fine. The wound—an inch-long laceration in her scalp, well above the hairline—had stopped bleeding. She had a headache, perhaps indicative of a mild concussion, but no blurred vision, no cognitive deficits. Perhaps just a bit of memory loss around the time that she had suddenly found herself crumpled against the wall of a devastated office. But that might not have been memory loss at all; maybe it just reflected the fact that explosions in the real world, as opposed to in movies, happened very quickly, like camera flashes.

It occurred to her that she might just get up and leave without bothering to get any medical treatment at all—which was obviously what the overburdened staff were hoping she would do.

The only obstacle, then, was squaring things up with the two remaining construction workers who had sat it out with her the whole time. They seemed to feel that they were under some sort of obligation to bring the adventure to a satisfactory conclusion—a story they could tell to their coworkers the next day. Or perhaps they were hoping for a reward? She figured out a way to satisfy both requirements by taking down their names and numbers, borrowing a bit of cash to pay for a ferry ticket, and promising to pay it back at the next opportunity, along with a little something for their trouble. They protested at the latter, but she suspected they would not turn it down.

In an epic hospital-hallway haggling showdown, she then talked an orderly out of a roll of gauze, largely by making it clear that if this were given to her, she would disappear almost immediately and never trouble them again.

She then cleaned herself up as best she could in the lavatory and rebandaged the wound with a white headband of gauze that could almost pass for some kind of deliberately chosen fashion-forward accessory, at least until blood began to leak through it. She made good on her promise to leave the hospital and walked in her free set of flip-flops down to the waterfront, where she used her donated construction-worker money to buy a ferry ticket back to Gulangyu.

During the walk, she had undergone the transformation from Meng Anlan, career girl, back to Olivia Halifax-Lin, MI6 spy. During the brief ferry ride, the latter asked herself several times whether going back to her apartment was the right thing to do. But there was no reason to suspect that the PSB would be on to her yet. And if they *were,* then what could seem more suspicious than a failure to go back to her own apartment when she was so badly in need of clothes and rest? She had to get out of China, that was for certain. But lacking money and documents, she would have to summon help from her handlers. Lacking a phone or laptop, she would have to do that by going to a *wangba* and sending a coded message.

But she couldn't rent a terminal at a *wangba* without her ID card. She didn't even have the keys to her own place. So after a ten-minute trudge up the steep winding ways of Gulangyu Island in those oversized flip-flops, which were making the most of every opportunity to escape from her feet, she had to track down the building manager, interrupting his dinner, and get his wife to let her into her own apartment.

The wife was unsettled by her messed-up state. But in a long and polite interrogation session right there on her threshold, Olivia managed to convince her that all was well and that the only thing she needed right now was to be left alone. She did not mean to make it seem as though she were physically blocking the entrance, but this was in fact what she was doing. Body language didn't work on the woman, and so she had to use the other kind of language. But finally Olivia gained the upper hand and reached the point where she felt that she could close the door and double-bolt it without giving offense.

She got a bottle of water out of the refrigerator and began to sip from it, then pulled out a bag of frozen *baozi* from the freezer, opened it, and verified that her Chinese "Meng Anlan" passport was still there.

This, of course, was not meant to pass for spycraft. It wasn't where a spy would hide incriminating fake documents. But it was the sort of place that a young woman who *wasn't* a spy might hide her *legitimate* passport to keep it out of the hands of common burglars. So she now had a way to identify herself as Meng Anlan even if her ID card was lost.

Those few sips of water had been enough to get her kidneys working again, so she set the bottle down, left the passport on the kitchen counter, and went into the bathroom.

As soon as she walked in she felt and heard the door being kicked shut behind her. She turned around, straight into an oncoming wall of white. A pillow slammed into her face as a hand took her by the back of the neck. She cried out once, but the sound went nowhere. Then she heard a quiet voice in her ear: "Don't make any sound. Do you understand?"

He was speaking in Russian.

She nodded.

The pillow came away, and she found herself looking into the blue eyes of the man who had crashed into her office earlier today;

but now he was wearing a suit, and he had shaved his head. Judging from evidence near to hand, he had done so in her bathroom sink, using a pink plastic girl-razor that he had borrowed from her stuff.

"Many apologies," he said.

She made some gesture combining elements of shrug, nod, and shiver.

"We have nice talk?" he said in English.

She would look anywhere except at his eyes.

"I know you are spy," he said, sticking to English for now; maybe he was unsure of her abilities in Russian.

Now she did look him in the eyes. She was expecting, or fearing, a triumphant look. Gloating. *I have you in the palm of my hand.* But that wasn't it. It was more like—professional courtesy.

"Maybe you are only person in Xiamen who is more fucked than me," he said. "My name is Sokolov. We should talk."

What the hell. "My name is Olivia."

IT WAS AN hour into the boat journey. The city was far behind. They were out in the open, ranging through a territory of broadly spaced, rocky islands. Jones had devoted much of the time to discussing matters in Arabic with the one Zula had come to think of as his lieutenant: the gunman with the binoculars and the phone. At a certain point, both men had begun to shoot glances in the direction of Zula and Yuxia, and then the lieutenant had come back and stood in front of Yuxia and caught her eye, then jerked his chin forward, as if to say, *Come with me.* Yuxia had in no way been receptive to the proposal. Jones had approached, sizing up the situation, and had stepped between the lieutenant and Yuxia and squatted down and explained to her in the mildest possible language that he, Jones, wanted to have a private conversation with Zula, and so Yuxia needed either to move peaceably to the bows or else jump off the boat and die—which, from his point of view, would be much preferable. "If we wanted something bad to happen to you, it would have been done already."

And so Yuxia had gone forward with the lieutenant and found a place to sit up in the boat's prow.

"I don't want to have to endure any more of your Nancy Drew

shenanigans," Jones began. "It makes the cost of having you around very high, and since your value is essentially zero—well—as the saying goes—do the math."

"*Essentially* zero," Zula asked, "or zero? Because—"

"Ah, I forget you are a bright girl and inclined to parse my statements closely. Very well then. Look about yourself. Consider your situation. And then cooperate with me. Cooperate by answering my questions. Later, the same questions will be asked of Yuxia. It would be best for all concerned if the answers matched."

Then nothing for a while. He was willing to wait all day.

Zula shrugged. "Ask away."

"Describe the leader of the Russian military squad."

She began to describe Sokolov's appearance. Soon Jones was nodding, tentatively at first, then more emphatically, as a way of telling her to shut up already.

"Did you see him?" Zula asked, but it was a stupid question; she could tell that he had.

Jones looked away and ignored the question.

Her next question would have been *Is he still alive?* but she stifled it.

Jones went on to ask any number of other questions about Sokolov. It wouldn't be an efficient use of his energies to show so much curiosity about a dead man. So she had her answer.

This, she realized, was what Jones and his lieutenant had been talking about. Jones had related the story of this morning's events, as he'd seen them, and at some point, a gap had become obvious: they had not seen Sokolov die, they had not observed his body.

The notion that Sokolov was still alive gave her a thrill of irrational excitement and a sense of weird hope. He was the only person she had seen in the last few days who seemed to be equal to the situation. Was it idiotic to think that he might want to help her? But even if he did, this did her no good if he didn't know she was alive, didn't know where she was. He must be on the run now, even more hard-pressed than she was.

They had gone past a couple of smaller islands and seemed to have set their course for another one, slightly bigger, yet still no more than a couple of miles long.

She needed to start thinking like Uncle Richard. Not Uncle Richard when he was at the re-u but Uncle Richard when he was doing business. She had only watched him in that mode a couple of times—she didn't get invited to meetings where he did important-guy stuff—but when she had, she'd been fascinated by the way he slipped into a different persona and zipped it up over his regular personality. *What does this person want? How does it conflict, or not, with what I want?* And yet never fake, never dishonest. Because people could see through that.

Right now, Jones badly wanted to know about Sokolov. Something had happened between those two men, something that had made an impression on Jones.

"I don't know much about his background, other than the medals and so on . . ."

"Medals?"

" . . . but I interacted with him a fair amount when we took the jet down to Xiamen, and at the safe house, and while we were hunting down the virus writers."

"Hold on, hold on," Jones said. For his eyes had gotten a little wider, his gaze a little more intense, at each of these disclosures.

She had not mentioned, until now, the fact that Ivanov's jet was in Xiamen.

Good. Answering his questions about those would kill another hour.

What would happen when she ran out of material?

All he had to do was google her name and he would know about Richard. Then the logical thing for him to do would be to hold her for ransom.

Of course, he didn't know her last name yet.

The curse of having a distinctive first name: if he just googled "Zula," combined with the name of the company where she worked, he'd probably come up with something.

But there was no Internet on this boat, and, from the looks of where they were going, that wasn't going to change any time soon.

"Are you telling me that the Russians had a safe house?" The question Brit inflected, falling rather than rising at the end.

"Yes."

"In Xiamen?"

"Yes."

"Where?"

"In a—" Zula was getting ready to describe the building. Then she turned and looked back to the city. It was a few miles aft by this point, but the tall downtown towers were clearly visible. "That one," she said. "The new modern tower. Curvy floor plan. Yellow crane sticking out of the top of it."

Jones called for the binoculars. Trading them back and forth with Zula, he made sure he knew precisely which building she was talking about.

He wanted to know which floor. That gave Zula pause, for as she'd looked through the binoculars, she'd wondered whether Sokolov was up there, gazing out the window. Was she putting him in danger by divulging so much?

But Sokolov knew perfectly well that he was in danger, and he would be taking precautions.

It was a way to communicate with him. If Jones sent someone to the forty-third floor of that building, Sokolov would wonder how they had known the location of the safe house, and he might conclude that they'd gotten the information from Zula.

"Forty-three," she said.

"Describe the—" Jones began, but they were interrupted by a few words from the skipper. Jones listened, nodded, then fixed his gaze on Zula and jerked his head toward the pilothouse. "Things are about to get crowded," he said. "You'll be a good deal less conspicuous in there."

Zula wondered to herself, not for the first time, just how cooperative she ought to be. But Jones seemed to enjoy her company and to want information from her, so she had a general sense that things were merely bad and not all the way desperate. Jumping off the boat and swimming for it would certainly make them desperate. Cooperating now might lead to more trust later. So she stood up and walked into the cramped, loud, and ferociously hot confines of the pilothouse. A minute later she was joined by Yuxia. They stayed there for the remainder of the voyage.

She guessed that the word "teeming" must have been coined to describe places like the harbor on this little island. Since then, though, it had been hopelessly diluted by application to such subjects as Manhattan traffic, jungles, and beehives, none of which really approached the level of activity and jam-packed-ness that was belaboring Zula's eyes as they chugged deeper and deeper into the harbor. You'd think that having so much in such a small space would lead to less, rather than more, activity, since crowding made it harder to move, but none of the people who lived here seemed to be aware of any such equation. The outskirts of the bay were gridded over with raftlike structures about the size of city blocks, each consisting of numerous square pens, separated by gangplanks, and covered with stretched netting. The gangplanks were supported by various kinds of floats, including plastic tanks filled with air, giant sausages of closed-cell foam, or simply large plastic bags stuffed with Styrofoam peanuts. Each of these rafts supported a little shack. Zula reckoned that they were fish farms.

The number of fishing boats defied belief or estimation. They exceeded available dock space by a factor of many hundreds, so they had been pushed up onto the beach until the beach was full and then they had been rafted together, side by side, in long arcs stretching across the harbor. When one arc ran out of space, a new one would get started, and in the outskirts of the bay there were a few consisting of only half a dozen or so boats.

Somewhere beyond all of this there must be actual land, and some kind of port town, but Zula saw it only in glimpses. For there was a cleft in all this improvised rafting that penetrated to a dock: just a single pier, where at the moment a passenger ferry was drawn up. From it a road rambled up the hill, forming the spine of a town. The road was lined with low buildings and half choked with people in *doulis* squatting on the hot pavement to mend stretched-out fishnets or string bald tires onto cables. Welding arcs and cutting torches glinted everywhere, bluer and brighter than the sun. Smaller boats like the one that they were on circulated through every patch of water large enough to float them, like mitochondria in cells. The sheer complexity of the rigging and the traffic and the patterns of movement baffled the mind and faded into the haze and humidity long before it started to make sense.

The look on Yuxia's face told Zula that it was equally foreign to her.

All the fishing vessels had been constructed to exactly the same plan, mass-produced in some shipyard somewhere, and all of them were painted the same shade of blue. It was a wonder to

Zula that the people who lived and worked here could tell them apart. There was one, though, that stood apart simply because it literally did stand apart, being anchored a little farther out in the bay and not rafted to any other vessel. That was the one they headed for. They came up along its seaward flank, where fewer eyes could see them, and scaled a ladder to its deck. Like all of them, it had a heavy-looking prow, jutting high out of the water and laden with technical gear. Just aft of that was an expanse of open deck cluttered with gray plastic tubs nested together in stacks. Over that loomed a superstructure that occupied most of the aft half of the vessel. This was two decks high. The cabins in its lower story had only a few small portholes. The upper level sported a few windows and a couple of hatches opening out onto a narrow walkway that ran around its periphery. These were nothing more than brief impressions that Zula gained while she was being hustled straight back to a cabin, apparently used as a berth by fishermen who lived aboard the vessel, since the next thing that happened was that two men came in and dragged all their stuff out of it, leaving her alone in a stripped room with no decoration except a Middle Eastern rug on the steel deck, and two faded posters with Arabic lettering, featuring men in turbans and beards, pointing to the ceiling and unburdening themselves of some profound thoughts about (wild guess here) global jihad. The cabin had a single porthole that, fifteen minutes after her arrival, was unceremoniously sealed off by the simple expedient of taping a piece of paper over it on the outside. Openings and closings of the cabin door were accompanied by clanging sound effects that she interpreted as signifying that the hatch was chained shut on the outside. In a wordless, somewhat poignant act of chivalry, someone opened the door and handed her a bucket. Yuxia had also been taken aboard, but Zula had no idea where she was, or what might be happening to her.

"THERE'S VODKA IN the bar." The spy Olivia said that in Russian. Sokolov guessed now, from her accent and from her freewheeling approach to dispensation of alcoholic beverages, that she was British.

"Thank you, but I am a Russian of somewhat unusual habits

and will not be taking this opportunity to get drunk."

She was a little slow to take that sentence in, but she got the gist of it. Her Russian was, perhaps, slightly better than his English. They would have to switch back and forth and watch each other's faces.

"I am going to take every opportunity I can find," she responded, and went over to the bar—really just a cabinet with a few bottles in it—and took out a bottle of Jack Daniel's.

"You should not become heavily intoxicated," he said, "since further action may be required soon."

The look she gave him made it evident that she was at some pains to avoid laughing in his face.

Where had he gone wrong?

By assuming that she would trust him.

It was a logical assumption. If the spy Olivia were more experienced, she would know right away that trusting him was the correct move. She could trust him because he was completely fucked and he needed her—a Chinese-looking person who could pass for a local—to help him.

Why then no trust?

Because he had crashed through her office window at a particularly difficult moment and aimed an assault rifle at her and then broken into her apartment, probably.

"How did you get in here?" she asked.

"Plan D," he said in English.

"And what is Plan D?"

"The fourth plan that I attempted. It took me all afternoon."

He could have explained it, but it was idiotic to be discussing things in the past when they needed to discuss the future.

Still she was giving him the evil eye over the rim of her whiskey glass.

Pulling these items, one by one, from the pockets of Jeremy Jeong's suit, he placed her ID card, her phone, her keys, and a few other items on the kitchen counter. Each one produced a little exclamation of surprise and delight from Olivia. "To prove I am not fucking asshole," he explained.

She went for the phone first and checked the "Recent Calls" menu to see whether Sokolov had been so stupid as to use it. The answer, as he could have told her, was no.

"This is huge," she said, slapping the ID card off the counter and pocketing it.

"Name on card is not Olivia?"

"Name on card is Meng Anlan."

"Ah."

"So you can't read any Chinese at all."

"Correct."

"How did you even get here? Never mind. Plan D." Still jumping back and forth between Russian and English. Sokolov could tell that she'd learned her Russian in an academic setting, was more comfortable with abstractions and formal sentence structure, had no idea how to express herself colloquially.

"You were conducting surveillance on the jihadists?" he asked. "Or the hackers who lived in the flat below them?"

"The jihadists."

"The name of the leader? The Negro?"

"Abdallah Jones."

Sokolov nodded. He had heard of Jones, seen his photograph in newspaper articles.

"You are employed by MI6?"

She made a visible effort to maintain a poker face, then seemed to realize its futility and nodded.

"MI6 has emergency extraction procedure?"

"Resources," Olivia corrected him, "that they could call on. To improvise such a procedure."

That sounded like a procedure to him. "You activate this procedure how?"

"If I had no other choice, I would make a certain phone call," she said, "but that's to be avoided if I can use Internet."

"You have computer here?"

"Not anymore," she said. "And even if I did, I wouldn't do it from here. I'd go to a *wangba*."

"Have you done this?"

She shook her head. "No government ID, no *wangba* access," she said. "But now that I have this . . . ?" She wiggled the ID and smiled.

"We go to *wangba*?"

It looked like she was about to say yes. Then her face hardened. "Who's 'we,' white man?"

"I beg your pardon?"

She closed her eyes, shook her head. "It's an old American joke."

"I enjoy jokes. Tell me joke."

"You know the Lone Ranger?"

"Cowboy in mask? Has Indian friend?"

"Yes. So the Lone Ranger and Tonto get ambushed by some Comanches and they get chased up into a box canyon and they end up hiding behind some rocks shooting at the Indians, and the Lone Ranger looks at his friend and says, 'Well, Tonto, it looks like we're surrounded.' To which Tonto replies—"

"Who is 'we,' white man?"

"Yes."

"Is funny joke," Sokolov said.

"That's a strange thing for you to say since I don't see the slightest trace of amusement on your face."

"Is Russian sense of humor. What you call dry."

"Okay."

"Joke has meaning."

"Yes, Mr. Sokolov, it has meaning."

"Why should you help poor fucked Russian? That is the meaning."

"More importantly," Olivia said, "why should MI6 help you? Because at the end of the day it doesn't matter what I want or am willing to do. It matters what MI6 is willing to do. And while they might be willing to pull out all the stops to get my arse out of China, I can't necessarily persuade them to do the same in your case."

"Tell them I have useful information."

"Do you?"

Sokolov shrugged. "Probably not. But that is beside the point."

"If I tell them you have useful information, and it turns out that you don't, I look like an idiot."

"Perhaps more important things are to be worried about now than whether you look like idiot when safe in London eating fish and drinking beer."

She spent a while thinking about it.

"I know British," he said. "Looking like idiot is part of being British. Happens all the time. They understand. Have procedures."

"Can you get access to Internet later?" she asked him.

"Hmm, difficult," Sokolov said. "Why?"

"Right now I need to take the ferry back into town and go to a *wangba* and send out my little distress call," she said. "Later I'll probably get instructions on where to go, what to do. I'll need to convey that information to you somehow."

Sokolov balked.

"Were you thinking you were going to stay here? Because you are not going to stay here," Olivia told him. "For obvious reasons, Meng Anlan can't have a Russian commando mercenary sleeping on her fucking sofa. You need to find a place to spend the night, and you need to figure out how you are going to access the Internet. Because if you can do that, then I can send you a message in a chat room or something."

"Mmm," Sokolov remarked. "There is solution."

"Yes?"

"I have place to stay. With Internet. I will go there. Wait for instruction."

A pause. "Really?" she asked.

"Dangerous," he admitted. "Perhaps fucking stupid. But maybe will be fine."

"Does it involve tying up or killing any of my neighbors?"

"Not unless you have neighbor you don't like."

She didn't know how to take that.

"Humor," he explained. Then he nodded out the window. The sun was getting low over Fujian, and orange light was gleaming in the windows of the skyscrapers across the water. "Is over there," he explained. "No problem for you."

"Then let's go," she said. "Obviously we have to leave this building separately. I can be a lookout for you. Tell you when the stairwell is clear, when it's safe for you to move."

"Very good."

"We will walk to the ferry terminal separately and take separate boats," she said. "After that, I can promise nothing."

"Maybe you get me out of China," Sokolov said. "Maybe not. Maybe I am captured. Interrogated. Have to tell them location of British spy equipment and documents from office."

She just stared at him.

"Details," he went on, "for you to share with your boss when you go to *wangba*."

. . . .

LATER, WHEN ONE of the crew opened the hatch to bring her a bowl of noodles and empty her bucket, Zula saw that it was dark outside.

She had tried to use the time to think. Nothing came.

Seemed as though grieving for Peter would be in order. She got ready to cry. Sitting on the edge of a steel-framed bunk bed, elbows on knees, ready to let it come. And some tears did come. Enough to blur her vision and give her the sniffles but not enough to break free and run down her face. She was sad that Peter was dead. Sad enough to forgive, but not enough to forget, the fact that Peter had ditched her in the cellar moments before Ivanov had basically executed him for doing so. That was the truly miserable part about Peter's death: what he had done right before it.

But her mind drifted away from this forced and self-conscious grieving procedure, and she found herself worrying about Csongor. About Yuxia.

A memory came to her, almost as shocking as the first time around, of the young Chinese man's face in the stairwell window, inches from hers.

It seemed as though prayers were in order. Prayers for the dead, for the missing, and for herself. Given that she had been raised by churchgoing folk, it was a bit odd that this hadn't occurred to her before. No aspect of what was going on seemed as though it might be improved by communication with a deity. With the possible exception, that is, that it might make her feel better. That, as far as she could tell, was the purpose of the religion she had been brought up in: it made people feel better when really horrible things happened, and it offered a repertoire of ceremonies that were used to add a touch of class to such goings-on as shacking up with someone and throwing dirt on a corpse. None of which especially bothered Zula or made her doubt its worthwhileness. Making sad people feel better was a fine thing to do.

That kind of religion did not have the power to make one give all of one's money to a charlatan, drink poison Kool-Aid, or strap explosives to one's body, but at the same time it did not seem equal to the challenges imposed by a situation such as this one. Since it had seemed perfectly acceptable to her before, she didn't feel that it was entirely proper, at a moment like this, to suddenly change over into something more fervent.

It was the praying-for-outcomes part she didn't get. Since when did she get to have a vote? This boat would go wherever they pointed it.

And it *could* go anywhere. That was obvious. The whole point of a fishing boat was to go out to sea—out to international waters. She didn't have a map, but she had a vague idea that this thing could take them anywhere in Southeast Asia in a few days. This had to be Jones's plan.

The door hardware started clanging again. The hatch creaked open and Jones came in. He closed the hatch behind him, then sat cross-legged on the rug, leaning back against a steel bulkhead. She sat on the edge of a bunk.

"Tell me about the jet."

"They came from Toronto."

"I know that. Where is the jet now?"

"Short-tempered this evening."

He glared back at her. "The adrenaline has worn off," he said. "Ten of my comrades died today. I think fully half of them were done by your man Sokolov. There was a wall of fire in the apartment. He was trapped on one side of it. No way out. Killed one of my men to get his rifle and then fired through the flames. Drilled several of my mates in the head. Really pisses me off."

"How many of Sokolov's men survived?"

"Not a one."

"Well then."

"In the hours after something like that, you're on a chemical high. When that wears off—well—that's when a Christian would go and get dead drunk."

"What does a Muslim do?"

"Says his prayers and dreams of vengeance."

"Well, I have no idea where Sokolov might be, or even if he's alive."

"He's alive," Jones said. "I'm not asking you to tell me where he is. I agree you can't know that. I'm asking you about the jet."

"And I'm thinking out loud," Zula said. "I don't think that Ivanov owned it. I think he leased it."

"And this is based on what?"

"Some of the others seemed shocked by his actions. Like what he was doing was way out of line."

"I'm willing to believe that," Jones said, and Zula was encouraged to hear him say something positive. "I don't care how much money these Russians make, they can't be flying around on private jets as a matter of routine."

"Well. I don't know anything about that world. But I've heard that even if you don't own one of those jets, you can lease it. I think Ivanov leased it."

"It's at the Xiamen airport?"

"I have no idea. That's where I last saw it."

"The pilots?"

"We dropped them off at the Hyatt, near the airport."

"You've been in Xiamen for three days."

"This is the end of the third full day," Zula said.

"Did you get any sense from Ivanov or Sokolov as to what the plan was for today? Other than grabbing the hackers?"

"We were told to get all our stuff out of the safe house."

"So the plan was to leave. To fly out of here today."

Zula shrugged, letting Jones know that she did not care to speculate.

"It's still there," Jones said. "The jet is still there."

"I'd have absolutely no way of knowing."

"Count on it. The big expense in aviation is fuel. Everything else is a pittance by comparison. There is absolutely no way that they would fuel that plane up and fly it somewhere else for three days, just to save on the pilots' hotel bill. No. Believe you me, the flyboys have been sitting in the Hyatt, watching pornography and running up their bar tab the entire time you've been in Xiamen, and they were probably told to be on call for a departure today. They are probably sitting there right now wondering when the hell Ivanov is going to show up."

Zula was content to let Jones run his mouth. She saw no relevance to her in all of this.

"But Ivanov's not going to show up, because I killed him," Jones went on.

He got to his feet and began pacing around, thinking. The cabin was so tiny that his pacing was soon reduced to a kind of irritable shifting of weight from one foot to the other. He would not meet her eye. He was on the trail of an idea, trying to work something out. "So," he continued, "what would be their orders, if the boss fails to show up? They can't just leave. They have to wait for him. That's all these guys do, is sit around and wait for their masters to snap their fingers."

The idea that had been gestating in Jones's head was so big and crazy that Zula was slow to perceive it. Then she had to bite the words back before blurting them out: *You want the jet!*

What was he thinking? He would need the pilots to fly it out of here for him. Which meant he had to obtain power over the pilots in some way.

She was conscious, suddenly, that Jones was staring at her.

"They would remember you," he said. "They would recognize your voice on the phone."

Zula tried to turn her face to stone. But she knew it was too late. He had seen the truth.

LESS THAN THIRTY minutes after the conclusion of the chat in Olivia's apartment, Sokolov was back in the safe house on the forty-third floor of the skyscraper.

Everything was gone except for the trash they'd left behind, and the computer they'd purchased while they were here. When Peter's advice not to leave this behind had fallen on Ivanov's deaf ears, Peter had begun a project of opening its case to remove its hard drive, which he planned to take with him. But this had proceeded too slowly for Ivanov's tastes and had been interrupted halfway through.

Sokolov was now confronted, therefore, with a partially dismantled machine, whose hard drive—a steel brick about the size of a sandwich—had been unplugged but not yet physically removed from the case. Reconnecting it was idiotically simple, since the plugs only fitted into the sockets one way. He rebooted the machine and it came up as normal. The Internet seemed to work, but he did not do any surfing, since almost anything he looked at might tip off the PSB. Olivia had written out the URL of a popular Chinese chat site that featured occasional English language conversations. He typed it into the browser's address bar and went there, then navigated to the room she had specified. It seemed very quiet, and he didn't see any of the coded phrases that she had told him to look for. This was hardly surprising since she probably had not even made it to the *wangba* yet.

What he really needed to do was sleep, so that he could be sharp tomorrow. He hated to waste the hours of darkness, during which it was easier for him to move about without drawing too much attention. But there was no reason to move about, nothing to be doing. He strolled up and down the length of the office suite a couple of times, looking out at the galaxy of colored lights spread below, the neon letters he didn't know how to read.

He knew already that in spite of his immense tiredness, he would not sleep well.

His command had been wiped out today. All of the men under him were dead. They had wives, mothers, girlfriends back in Russia who were waiting to hear from them and who did not know, yet, that they were gone forever. He had pushed this out of his mind until now, since thinking of it was useless. He had been leading men for a long time, since he had been promoted to the rank of corporal and assigned responsibility for a squad. Given the nature of the places where he had been sent, casualties had been frequent and severe. He had written letters home to those grieving mothers and wives. He had used the same old tired verbiage about how these men had fallen while fighting for the motherland: a difficult claim to make during the invasion of Afghanistan, only slightly easier in Chechnya.

If he had pen and paper here, and the addresses of the bereaved, what comforting lies would he write? These men had been mercenaries working for a shady organization whose sole motive was profit.

As was he.

Even if it were possible to instill a sense of personal loyalty to an organized crime cartel—which, come to think of it, must not be all that difficult, since men fought and died for such groups all the time—the fact was that this had not been a bona fide operation but a colossal mistake, undertaken by a man who had defrauded that group and gone half mad.

Even that could be explained. It would take an ingenious bit of explaining, but it did add up to a coherent state of affairs, as far as it went. What he'd never be able to put into a letter was the fact that they had accidentally stumbled into a bomb factory run by a cell of jihadists.

No wonder the Chinese authorities were calling it a gas explosion. It wasn't that they were trying to cover anything up. It just made for a simpler explanation.

If he were going to tell the families anything, it would have to be that they had died in a gas explosion, or a car accident, or some other such meaningless and random eventuality of war. Like the American soldiers who were getting electrocuted while taking showers in their shoddily constructed military bases. Who wrote *those* letters?

As he paced back and forth gazing out over the streaming and pulsing lights of the city, he saw that there was really only one way to make sense of the entire situation, if by "make sense" was meant "bring it to a conclusion such that proper letters could be written to the mothers of the men who had died this morning." And that was to hunt down Abdallah Jones and kill him.

He squatted down on his haunches, stretching the sore and battered muscles of his legs in a way that hurt but felt good, and crossed his elbows atop his knees and rested his chin on his forearms and stared out at China.

Everything was clear to him, except how he was going to get out of this country. That all depended on Olivia. Helpless as a baby in her bare feet, her aloneness. And yet infinitely more powerful, more capable than Sokolov in this context.

There had been an odd moment there, toward the conclusion of their interview, when she had insisted that he was not welcome to stay in her apartment. A strange thing for her to bring up. As if Sokolov would have expected any such consideration. And yet she had felt it important to make this explicit. Why? Because she was attracted to him, as he was to her, and that made it imperative that scruples be observed, rules followed.

He tucked his chin, let himself fall back on his buttocks, rolled out flat, whipped his arms behind him and slapped the carpeted floor to break his fall, as in SAMBO. It would not be the worst place he'd ever slept. Even better if he got the Makarov out of his waist-band. So he did that, placing it up next to his head, and he pulled the spare clip out of the breast pocket of the suit jacket and a little flash-light from the back pocket of the trousers and placed them all right next to each other. He unlaced Jeremy Jeong's shoes. But rather than slip them off, he decided to learn from the lesson of Olivia and keep them on his feet loosely, just in case there were any more gas leaks.

Sleep did not come, though, since he could not stop thinking about how vulnerable he would be if someone came into the safe house.

He slung his CamelBak over his shoulders and went into the conference room. The big table was wired for Internet, a trunk line of gray wires zip-tied together beneath it. With some quick knife work he peeled loose a run of cable a few meters long and draped it over his neck. He planted a chair in the middle of the table, stood on it, reached up, and pushed a ceiling tile out of the way.

Above him, as he remembered, was a zigzagging steel truss. It was out of his reach, but in a couple of tries he was able to toss the end of the cable through it and then feed more cable up so that the loose end bent down of its own weight and came within his reach. He jerked it down and tied the ends together to form a loop that dangled through the ceiling hole to about a meter above the table's surface.

Then he placed the chair back on the floor, lay down in the mid-dle of the conference table, and slept soundly.

"THE POINT TO be conveyed by this little demonstration should be obvious to anyone with a bit of imagination. And you are obvi-ously that kind of girl. So I, personally, consider it a waste of time. But my colleagues here are earthy chaps. They like concreteness. They don't trust their ability to communicate across cultural and language barriers."

Jones was preceding Zula down a steel-runged ladder into the ship's hold.

"Or," he added brightly, "perhaps they are just sadists."

At this, Zula whipped her head around and got a brief whirling impression of a large, poorly illuminated space with several men in it, and Yuxia seated on a chair in the middle. Her instincts, of course, told her to get out of there. But Jones's lieutenant—she had figured out that his name was Khalid—was above her on the stairs, practically treading on her hands.

The ship's engines had started up some minutes ago, anchor had been weighed, and they had pulled out of the crowded cove and begun swinging around to the back side of the island, which seemed to be completely unpopulated. It was exposed to weather from the sea and it lacked a natural harbor, so it was probably accounted worthless. In this space belowdecks, the engines made a maddening racket. But as Zula cleared the bottom rung and touched down on the deckplates, the throttle was eased back to a low idle, just enough to make a bit of headway and keep the vessel under control.

Yuxia's legs had been tied together at the ankles and knees, and her arms were pinioned behind her back.

A crew member came down the ladder after Khalid, bent sideways under the load of a five-gallon plastic bucket filled to the brim with seawater. A lot of it slopped out as he staggered across the cabin, but when he set it on the deck in front of Yuxia, it was still filled to within a couple of inches of the top.

"Stop," Zula said, "this is just totally—"

"Unnecessary. Yes. I just finished saying that," Jones said. "For you and me, yes. And for *her,* certainly. But it seems terribly important for everyone else."

Khalid had moved around behind Yuxia, and for a moment the tableau presenting itself before Zula's eyes looked just like one of those grainy webcam videos in which a helpless hostage gets butchered.

But this was not to be one of those. Not exactly. "Your friend!" Khalid announced, and then nodded to the men standing to either side of Yuxia. They converged on her and, in a display of clumsiness and ineptitude that would have been funny in other circumstances, eventually managed to get her turned upside down, feet in the air, head down, whereupon they maneuvered her head into the bucket. Displaced water flooded over the rim and washed across the deck.

"No," Zula said quietly.

"Think of it as a performance," said Jones.

"Please tell them to stop it," Zula said.

"You misunderstand," Jones went on. "*You* are the one who

needs to be performing. They want to reduce you to blubbering hysteria. And the longer you continue to play it cool, the longer she goes without oxygen."

Zula launched herself forward and almost made it. Jones kicked out and tripped her. She fell full-length across the deck, her outstretched right hand only a few inches from the base of the bucket. She gathered herself to spring forward again, but a booted foot descended and trapped her hand. She twisted and looked up into the face of Khalid, staring directly down at her with a look of fascinated ecstasy. With her left hand she pawed at his ankle. He was wearing military-style boots with speed lacing hooks. One of them caught the bandage wrapped around her pinky; this spiraled away from her flailing hand and took the fingernail with it. His other foot stomped down on her left forearm, trapping it too. She had twisted around so that she was lying full-length on her side, both hands pinned, only inches away from the bucket within which Yuxia was now struggling for her life, her nicely cut black hair washing against the translucent plastic as she thrashed to and fro trying to knock it over, the surface of the water burbling as her lungs emptied.

Zula was not feeling anything like what they wanted her to feel. She simply wanted to kill them. And had it not been for Jones's helpful suggestion, she might have failed to give them the performance they wanted: the only thing that could save Yuxia's life. But a couple of the details—Yuxia's swimming hair, and the blood streaming freely from the end of Zula's pinky—were enough to send Zula over the edge, into some kind of community-theater method-acting headspace in which she finally let go of all the grief and rage that had been accumulating in her emotional buffer during the last several days and let herself fly out of control and degenerate into the weeping, wailing, messed-up, out-of-control basket case that these guys apparently wanted to see.

She understood what Jones had been trying to tell her. These men needed to know that she was broken. Because only then could they trust her.

Which raised the question: Trust her to do what? Because if they just wanted to kill her, well. . .

What could Zula possibly do for these men that would be worth all of this trouble?

"Please, please, please," she heard herself blubbering, "please, please, please, let her go!"

Khalid took his foot off her hand and gave the bucket a kick. It rotated out from beneath Yuxia's head and emptied its contents onto the deck, which meant that Zula got soaked. Yuxia's head was still hanging upside down just out of Zula's reach. She coughed water out of her lungs, gasped once, and then vomited. When she was finished with that, they upended her again and sat her back down on the chair. The first thing Yuxia must have seen was Zula lying stretched out on the deck at her feet with blood pouring from her trashed pinky. Zula couldn't really get a good look at Yuxia until Jones had hauled her back up onto her feet. She wanted to go and throw her arms around Yuxia and tell her how horribly sorry she was that all this had occurred, simply because Yuxia had, a few days ago, taken it upon herself to befriend a group of lost Western- ers wandering around the streets of Xiamen. "No good deed goes unpunished" was one of Uncle Richard's favorite aphorisms. But Jones was gripping both of Zula's upper arms from behind and was dragging her back toward the ladder. "Time to go," he was saying. "The sooner we get under way, the sooner she is free." He spun her around to face the ladder, then shoved her into it hard enough that she had to bring both hands round in front of her to stop herself from slamming teeth-first into a rung.

She looked back at him over her shoulder. Some sort of uncom- prehending look must have been on her face, because he suddenly looked disgusted. "The entire point of what you have just seen," he said, "is that your friend will be kept here as a hostage, and that if you do not behave perfectly at all times during what is to happen next, she will simply be thrown overboard with something heavy attached to her and suffer the fate just now intimated."

Zula looked past Jones at Qian Yuxia, sitting there in her chair, still breathing rapidly, gazing ahead at nothing in particular. It was hard to imagine how any person could be calmer, more unruffled, by the experience of torture and near drowning. Perhaps Yuxia was just stunned, or brain damaged, or holding in some deep emotional trauma that would later emerge in dramatic and unpredictable fashion.

But that was not how she looked. She looked as though she were calculating how best to revenge herself on these bastards.

"Girlfriend, I'll do whatever I can to make sure you don't get hurt anymore," Zula said.

"I know," Yuxia muttered.

Then Jones shoved Zula up the ladder, and she began climbing toward the light of the stars.

A smaller vessel, similar to the one that had brought them in from Xiamen, but without a taxi crater in its cargo deck, had met them and tied up alongside. Zula was made to understand that she should climb down into it. She did so and found a place to sit where she would not be in the way.

At least half an hour passed in discussions and preparations. It seemed to her as though a lot of gear was being collected from the larger vessel's various cabins and holds and lockers and that it was being gone through, sorted, checked, repacked. And having spent her whole life around guns, she knew from the sounds, from the weight of the stuff, and simply from the posture of the men carrying it, that some of it was weaponry. She was intensely interested in what the men were saying to one another and was maddeningly close to being able to follow the Arabic. She definitely heard the words for airplane and airport, which delighted some little-girl part of her soul ("Yay, going on a trip!") even as her higher brain was ticking off all the bad things that could happen when men like Jones came into proximity with jet aircraft.

She was pretty certain she heard the word for "Russian" too. But it was difficult to make anything out, since all of the conversations were sotto voce, and anyone who raised his voice to a conversational level was glared at and shushed.

Some kind of sorting process seemed to be under way. She had noticed that some of Jones's men had more of a Middle Eastern look about them and preferred Arabic to whatever it was that the other, more Chinese-looking men spoke to each other. The latter were staying behind while the former took places on the smaller boat.

In a manner familiar to anyone who had ever packed a car for a family trip, genial confusion gave way to impatience, then furious ultimatums, then ill-advised snap decisions. Finally the lines were untied, and the smaller vessel began to move away.

Having apparently delegated Khalid to boss the skipper around and generally run the show, Jones disengaged himself from the main group and came over and sat down next to Zula. "Earlier," he said, "I had been looking for some way of telling you that you've fallen in among men who are happy to stone young women to death as a penalty for wrong sorts of behavior." And he nodded in the direction of Khalid's crew, who had busied themselves sorting through and repacking all the gear they'd brought on board. "But you have probably guessed that already." He turned and looked at her brightly. "Then I remembered something about Khalid. You know which one he is?"

"The one who's glaring at me right now?"

Jones looked. "Yes. That one." Then he turned his attention back to Zula. "When Khalid was fighting the Crusaders in Afghanistan—"

"Meaning what? Knights with red crosses on their shields?"

"The Americans, in this case," Jones said. "He and his group were driven, for a time, out of a district that they had controlled for some years. The Americans occupied it and began to impose their culture on the place. Things changed. A school for girls was established."

"Let me guess—Khalid didn't approve?"

"Not at all. But there was nothing he could do except watch from the hills and bide his time. Of course, nothing prevented him and other members of his group from slipping into town occasionally, just to conduct espionage operations. They would disguise themselves—you'll like this—by putting on burqas, so that people would think that they were women. Now, Khalid had a lot to think about beside just the girls' school, but he did make inroads from time to time. Two men on a scooter, one driving, the other carrying a squeeze bottle full of acid. Wait until you see a group of girls walking down the street on their way to school, ride past them, aiming for the faces—*squirt, squirt*—" Jones pantomimed it, aiming an imaginary squirt bottle at Zula's face, and she tried not to flinch. "It scared some of them off. And the poison gas attack very nearly closed the place down altogether. But the teacher was a tough lady. Indomitable. Irrepressible. The kind of woman you only aspire to be, Zula. And so, with plenty of help from the Americans, the school kept on going in spite of all of Khalid's best efforts. But eventually the Americans decided, as they always do, that they had pacified the place quite enough and that they were tired of seeing their young men picked off one by one by snipers and IEDs. So they declared the job finished and they pulled out of that town. You know what Khalid did then?"

"Given the way you're telling the story," Zula said, "I have to guess that he closed down the girls' school and had the teacher stoned to death or something."

"It's what he did *before* stoning her to death that's especially interesting," Jones said.

"And what was that?"

"He raped her."

"Okay," Zula said, "so what is the point of the story? That he's not as much of a Muslim as he claims to be?"

"On the contrary," Jones said, "he did it for the most Islamic of reasons. By his lights, anyway. I happen to disagree with him on a fine point of theology here."

"You're saying there's a theological justification for what he did?"

"More like a theological *motive,*" Jones said. "You see, by raping that schoolteacher, he made her into an adulteress. And you know what happens to an adulteress after she gets stoned to death?"

"She goes to hell?" Zula was trying to play this very cool, but her voice cracked.

"Precisely. So, in Khalid's mind, he wasn't *merely* killing the schoolteacher—he was doing it in a way that condemned her to—"

"I know what hell is."

"I am merely trying to impress on you the danger of being in the power of people like Khalid."

"I reckoned," she grunted.

"You may have *reckoned,* but now you have gone beyond mere *reckoning.* Now you *feel* it so that it will guide your actions."

"Guide, or control?"

"That's a Western distinction. Anyway. They have now got what they wanted from you: blubbering hysteria. Nicely played. For me, its patent fakeness almost made it more moving."

"Thanks."

"I, on the other hand, Westerner that I am, need something that is a little more intellectual."

"Namely?"

"*Islam*," he said, "submission."

"You want me to submit."

"That bit of cleverness in the cellar this morning," he said. "Sending Sokolov to the wrong apartment. It cost me a lot."

"How do you think I feel right now?"

"Not as bad as you deserve."

She had known men like this, lurking at the outer branches of the family tree. Men who seemed to attend the re-u for the sole purpose of making the small children feel bad about themselves. Fortunately Uncle John and Uncle Richard had always been around to keep them at bay.

Her uncles were not, of course, here.

She was getting tired of this. "I submit," she said.

"No more plucky stuff?"

"No more plucky stuff."

"No more clever plans?"

"No more clever plans."

"Perfect and total obedience?"

This one was harder. But really not that hard, when she thought of Yuxia and the bucket. "Perfect. And total. Obedience."

"Well chosen."

WHEN THEY HAD turned Yuxia upside down, her greatest fear had not been being stuck headfirst into a bucket of water—for she sensed, somehow, that this was nothing more than a demonstration—but that the phone would fall out of her boot.

She had been wondering if these men had ever seen a movie. Because in the movies, prisoners were always being frisked to make sure that they didn't have anything on them. But no such treatment had been meted out to Qian Yuxia. Perhaps it was because they were Islamists and had a taboo against touching women. Perhaps it was because she was female, therefore deemed harmless. Or maybe it was because she was wearing a snug-fitting pair of jeans and an equally snug sleeveless T-shirt, making it obvious that she was not carrying anything. Whatever the reason, they had never bothered to inspect her for contraband; they had merely taken her into a large cabin on the main deck and handcuffed her to the leg of a table. The cabin was a busy place, serving as the galley and the mess for the ship's crew, and the table she had been chained to was the one where they took meals and drank tea. Someone was always in the place, and so she had not thought it advisable to pull the phone out of her boot and use it for anything. From time to time a buzz against her ankle would inform her that she, or rather Marlon, had just received another text message. If the place had been a little quieter, she'd have worried that someone might hear the buzz, but with the grumbling of the engines, the slap and whoosh of waves against the hull, the clanking and hissing of cookware, and bursts of static and conversation emerging from the radio's speaker, she was safe from that. Zula had been put somewhere else, apparently in a separate cabin, and Yuxia had wondered: If their positions had been reversed, and Yuxia had been alone, what would she have done with the phone? The two basic choices being: communicate with Marlon, or call the police and tell them everything.

When the men had come in to tie her up, one of them had knelt down in front of her, and she had stifled a gasp, thinking that he knew about the phone in her boot and that he was about to reach in there and snatch it out. She had crossed her ankles to hide it. But the man had paid no attention to the contents of her boots. Instead he had passed a rope behind her ankles and brought its ends around to the front and tied them in a knot *above the phone,* which meant that it was trapped in there. So securely that even being turned upside down had not shaken it loose.

After the terrible thing with the bucket, they dragged her back up to the galley. One of the crew members—the one who seemed responsible for most of the cooking—put a cup of tea in front of her. She was sick and quivering, coughing and raw chested, but basically undamaged, and so she picked up the cup, pressing it hard between both of her hands, which were shaking uncontrollably, and sipped. It was actually pretty good tea. Not as good as *gaoshan cha* but sharing some of the same medicinal properties, which were just what the doctor ordered for someone who had recently been upside down breathing seawater.

Until now, the main thing driving her actions had been concern for Zula. And she was still very concerned about Zula. But that emotion had now been forced out by something much more intense and immediate, which was a desire to see every man aboard this vessel dead. Not even a desire, so much as an absolute nonnegotiable requirement.

Her hands were not shaking with fear. This was rage.

After a few minutes, they moved her to a cabin: the same one, she guessed, where Zula had been held earlier. Which raised the question, What had they done with Zula?

They must be taking her into Xiamen for some reason. The whole purpose of the affair with the bucket had been to force Zula to run some errand for them.

She became so preoccupied by this that she failed to notice for a long time that the phone was buzzing against her ankle. Not just once, to announce a text, but over and over again in a steady rhythm.

She snatched it out in a panic, worried that it would go to voice mail before she could answer it. The number on the screen was hers; this was Marlon, calling her with her own phone.

"*Wei?*" she whispered.

In the background, she could hear a rhythmic squeaking noise.

"What is that sound?" she asked.

"Csongor rowing," Marlon said.

DURING THE LONG run to Heartless Island, Marlon and Csongor had learned from direct observation what every waterman knew from experience, and what engineers knew from wave theory: that longer vessels inherently go faster than shorter ones. They had given the larger vessel something of a head start, since they didn't want to follow it obviously. Not long after the beginning of the voyage, they had noticed that their quarry was pulling away from them, in spite of the fact that they were running the outboard at full throttle and felt as though its frail-seeming wooden hull would be smashed to pieces by the waves at any moment. The boat they were following did not appear to be running at high speed and yet it was gradually outdistancing them.

As they had slalomed around a few small islands along the way, they had been able to regain some lost ground by cutting straight across tidal shallows where the big boat had been obliged to swing wide. But by the time they'd hove in view of the crowded island that seemed to be their destination, the terrorists' boat had become a nearly invisible dot, and it had required all of Csongor's powers of concentration to maintain his focus on it and to prevent its getting lost against the background of countless other vessels.

But of course it had slowed down as it had neared its destination, and so Marlon and Csongor had finally been able to gain on it. The problem of tracking it had become slightly easier, and easier yet when it had elected to swing clear of most of the harbor's clutter and tie up alongside a fishing vessel that stood aloof from the myriad others.

Csongor couldn't be certain that he hadn't become confused and lost it during those anxious minutes, so it had been with a slowly building sense of relief that he made out the damaged deck planks, the crushed pallets, and certain other identifying marks that he had memorized during the first few minutes of the chase.

Whereupon they had run out of gas and been forced to break out the oars.

Much of the remainder of the day had then been consumed with hugely important, yet infuriatingly trivial matters such as obtaining water and food. Without Csongor, Marlon would have found this easier, but still not easy. Easier because he would not have had to explain the presence of a large white man in the boat with him. But still not easy because it would have been obvious to the waterfront society of this little island that Marlon was by no stretch of the imagination a boat person. Had he shown up in a gleaming new white fiberglass runabout, they might have pegged him as a nouveau riche with a freshly acquired toy and taken little note of his obvious lack of nautical acumen. But instead he was in an old and, to put it charitably, well-broken-in working boat that had had no business making the run across open water from Xiamen in the first place. The easiest possible explanation for this combination of clues was that Marlon had stolen the boat from an honest Xiamen waterman and was now a fugitive from justice.

That had all been obvious, and so it had not seemed like a smart move to simply row the boat into the most crowded part of the harbor. Instead, although they had already been suffering from thirst and from a general feeling of being at the end of their ropes, they had taken turns rowing the boat in a wide arc around the island, looking for a less obvious place to put in. Along the way, they had swung past the fishing vessel to which the terrorists' boat had been tied up, never coming closer than several hundred meters and trying not to stare directly at it. There had been nothing to see anyway. A couple of men had been visible through the windows on the bridge, and two more had been loafing on the main deck just aft of the superstructure, but beyond that there had been nothing to suggest that the vessel was occupied by anyone other than run-of-the-mill fishermen.

During their endless, creeping approach to this island, it had become obvious that it must have a sort of dog-bone shape, since there was a hill, covered with dark green vegetation, at each end, and the town spread across the saddle between. It was oriented roughly north-south and the terrorists' boats were anchored toward the southern end of the harbor, where the rafts of conjoined fishing vessels petered out into grids of floating fish farms. As they crept southward, the town abruptly ceased to exist and was replaced by inhospitable terrain consisting of ancient, weathered brown sedimentary rock sloping up out of the water to be colonized by olive-drab succulents on the lower slopes and a scruffy mat of green-black tropical vegetation higher up. Csongor remarked on the fact, which to him seemed odd, that in China some places were unbelievably crowded and others were totally uninhabited but there was no in between. Marlon thought it curious that anyone should find this remarkable. If a place was going to be inhabited, then it should be used as intensively as possible, and if it was a wild place, all sane persons would avoid it.

Csongor guessed that the slope of the ground here was exactly wrong. It was gentle enough that dangerous rocky shallows extended a considerable distance from the tide line, making it a death trap for ships, and yet steep enough that, above the waterline, it was difficult to build on. And so even though they were moving at what seemed an agonizingly slow pace, they went, over the course of perhaps five minutes, from being in a place where ten thousand eyes could see them to a place where they were perfectly invisible. The strata of the bedrock, eroding at different rates, reached into the water with long bony fingers separated by deep shadowed clefts, and the hill rose above them, no man-made objects on the thing except for a radio tower at the summit.

After another half an hour, it became evident that they had worked their way around the southern end of the island and were now looking up its eastern face. Stretched between the hills at either end, like a taut sail between two spars, was a long beach that was absolutely deserted. Driblets of heavily eroded stone were strewn across it from place to place, but for the most part it was an almost perfectly flat expanse of sand that had been dropped by some long-shore current as it tripped over the headland they had just circumnavigated. Above it rose a dune held together by some low green vegetation sparkling with yellow flowers and studded with random pieces of garbage that had apparently been hurled off the edge of the bluff above. For backing up against the top of the slope was a jumbled skyline of low houses that, as they now realized, was simply the other side of the island's one and only town. They had gone halfway around the island and were now looking at the town's back, huddling against the incoming weather from the South China Sea.

They pulled the boat up onto the beach, which was littered with garbage of a more seaborne nature, and left it among some half-dissolved boulders where it might be slightly less conspicuous. Csongor sat down nearby in the shade of a rock, shading himself under the parasol, and waited, hoping that Marlon would get back soon and that no one would come to ask him what business he had here. Marlon hiked up into the town, carrying a small amount of cash from Ivanov's man-purse, and returned half an hour later with two shrink-wrapped bricks of water bottles and some noodles in Styrofoam bowls, already lukewarm but exquisitely satisfying to Csongor. Marlon had already eaten, and so he took a turn at the oars now and rowed the boat back south again while Csongor filled his belly. On their first swing around the southern end of the island, they had noticed a few deep clefts in the rocks: corridors of water no more than a couple of meters wide, where soft layers of rock had been eaten away by the waves. It was late afternoon and these were already deep in shadow. They rowed the boat into one of them and let an incoming wave carry them forward until its keel skidded against the bed of gravel and jetsam that was trying to fill this crevice up. It was cool in here, and they felt invisible and safe. So much so that both men were almost overcome now by a powerful need to sleep. But they took turns keeping each other awake until their stomachs had digested the food and the feeling had passed. Then Marlon clambered up out of the slot and disappeared again for a while.

Csongor was awakened by someone shaking his shoulder. It was Marlon. The sky overhead was deep twilight.

"The boat is moving," Marlon announced.

Csongor was still coming to terms with the fact that he was where he was; it had not all been just a bad dream.

"Back to Xiamen?"

"No. Toward us!"

The tide had receded, and so both men had to get out of the boat and shove it down the rock chute for a few meters to refloat it. The space was too narrow to deploy the oars, and so they had to push it out against wave action by pawing at the rock walls. But eventually they got out to a place where they could row again, and then Csongor saw the boat in question immediately. The smaller vessel—the one with the taxi crater in its cargo deck—was not in evidence. The fishing boat was motoring along directly in front of them, only a few hundred meters off their bow, headed for the dark, uninhabited side of the island.

Without gas for their motor, it was, of course, out of the question for them to follow this vessel. Csongor assumed that it was about to turn into the open sea and disappear. But instead it cut its engines to a low growling idle and kept station in front of the beach for a while—long enough for them to row halfway to it. Then they were scared out of their minds by a smaller vessel, similar in its general lines to the one that had earlier absorbed the hits from the taxi and the van, which came motoring around the north end of the island and made straight for the fishing boat, eventually tying up alongside it. Marlon and Csongor meanwhile backed water and pulled toward the shelter of the rocks. It was dark enough by this point that there was little chance of their being seen, as long as they maintained a prudent separation.

An hour passed. Muffled thuds and voices told them that people and goods were being moved from the fishing vessel to the launch. Then the launch revved its engine and made off to the south, rapidly disappearing around the end of the island, which suggested that it might be headed back toward Xiamen.

After a little while, the fishing vessel too began to head south, moving at an extremely slow pace, perhaps just as a way to save fuel. But by this time Marlon and Csongor had rowed back out into the open water and placed themselves directly in its path.

THE BOAT CARRYING Zula, Jones, and Jones's crew retraced the course taken earlier up the strait between Xiamen and Gulangyu. But just as they were clearing the northern end of the battery of passenger ferry terminals, the skipper cut the throttle and began to steer a course toward shore, aiming for a dark patch along the waterfront. As they drew in closer, ambient light from the buildings of downtown made it possible to see a few mean little piers hosting a motley assortment of smaller craft. Nevertheless, they were sturdy enough to support vehicles. A taxi was waiting on one of them. Leaning against it, a dark human form suspended between the bluish pane of a phone screen and the bobbing red star of a cigarette.

In addition to the skipper, Jones, and Zula, there were six men on the boat. Two of them scrambled up from its prow onto the pier and made the boat fast, then padded over to the taxi and greeted the man who had been waiting for them.

Following, as instructed, one pace behind Jones, Zula disembarked. He led her to the taxi. The two of them climbed into the backseat where tinted windows would make them invisible. It was the same taxi they'd been in earlier in the day.

One man climbed, quite cheerfully, into the vehicle's trunk. An additional two crammed themselves into the backseat along with Zula and Jones, and another got into the front passenger seat. The others stayed with the boat.

They drove to the skyscraper that contained the safe house. The men asked questions, which Jones translated into English for Zula; he then translated her answers back into Arabic. They were all mundane but very practical questions about fire exits, guard stations, the underground parking garage, and so on. The interrogation went on for longer than the drive, and so the driver circled the block a few times as Jones's men satisfied their curiosity.

Finally the taxi pulled into the same covered entrance where, a very long time ago, Zula and Peter and Csongor and all of the Russians had climbed into the rented van and bantered with Qian Yuxia.

The man in the passenger seat climbed out and entered the lobby, where he engaged in conversation with a security guard seated behind a sweeping marble-clad desk.

After a few minutes, he turned half around, while keeping his eye fixed on the guard, and made a little wave back toward the taxi.

The entrance to the underground garage was just ahead of them, down a ramp that was sealed off by a steel door. This now groaned into movement and lifted out of their way. The taxi pulled into it and navigated to an elevator bank, where the two men in the backseat hopped out and liberated the one in the trunk. As they were doing this, the doors of one of the elevators slid open to reveal the first man standing next to the security guard. The guard had his hands behind his back, and he had a pistol to his head. All of them crowded into the elevator, and the doors closed.

The taxi then pulled back out of the skyscraper's basement and onto the waterfront boulevard. A few minutes later they were back at the pier. Khalid and one of the other jihadists now joined them in the taxi, and Jones told the driver to head for the Hyatt by the airport. Once the taxi had pulled out onto the main road, he pulled out his phone, looked at Zula, and said, "Here is where you are going to be magnificently cooperative."

"WHAT ARE YOU asking her?" Csongor demanded.

"Which side of the boat she is on," Marlon said, taking the phone away from his head for a moment. Then he put it back and listened. "She is on that side." He waved his hand out toward the open sea.

Csongor looked at the fishing vessel. It was perhaps a hundred meters away from them. If he stopped rowing, and it kept going on a straight course, it would pass just in front of them, leaving them on its starboard side—which was to say, the side facing toward the island. Marlon was telling him that Yuxia was in a cabin on the port side.

To say that they were trying to intercept the larger vessel would have been to imply, somehow, that they had a plan. Which, in turn, would have been to imply that Marlon and Csongor had been communicating with each other as to what they ought to do. Neither of these was true. Earlier, they had made use of the cover afforded by darkness, and the fact that their out-of-gas boat was incapable of making noise, to move around and keep an eye on the terrorists' activities. This had nearly brought them to grief when the faster launch that had met the fishing boat had suddenly come roaring toward them. Since then Csongor had been rowing with all his might. And when he had rehydrated with a few bottles of water and filled his belly with noodles, his might was considerable, and he was able to jerk the little boat across the flat water like a water skater. But why was he doing it? What was the plan? No idea.

"What are we—" Csongor began, but Marlon cut him off. He was hanging up the phone. "I told her *gao de tamen ji quan bu ning*," he said.

"What does that mean?"

Marlon grinned, stalling Csongor while he worked through the translation. "Make it so that not even their dogs and chickens are at peace."

"Meaning?"

"Raise hell, more or less."

"Okay. Then what?" Csongor stopped rowing and looked at Marlon.

Marlon nodded significantly toward the oncoming vessel. "The wheels," he said.

Csongor turned and looked. Marlon had used the wrong English word, but it was obvious what he was referring to. Every discarded tire in the entire industrialized world seemed to have ended up here on the Chinese coast, where they were used by the locals in the same way that their landlubber cousins used bamboo: as the Universal Substance out of which all other solid objects could be made. Sometimes they had to be hugely reprocessed in order to serve their intended function. In other cases, they still looked like tires. Every boat—nay, every floating object—in this universe was protected on all sides by tires slung from its gunwales on ropes, lined up in rows like shields on a Viking ship. This one was no exception. They dangled just above the waterline. It would be easy to reach up from the rowboat, grab one, and use it to climb aboard the larger vessel. *The wheels.*

"This is not a video game," Csongor said. "It is real."

"Then get real, asshole!" Marlon suggested.

It was neither polite nor well phrased, but Csongor took the meaning.

"You want to take that boat," Csongor said. Just to make sure that he and Marlon understood each other.

"You know of any other way to get out of China?"

"Where are we going to go?"

"Wherever!"

"How are we going to—"

"Listen!" Marlon said. "She's doing it."

Csongor turned back toward the fishing vessel, which was now startlingly close to them, and heard banging and screaming and the voices of angry men. A steel latch clanked, a door was hauled open, and the cacophony, which had been muffled, radiated out over the water: a woman's voice, hardly recognizable as Yuxia's, shouting and, he guessed, cursing, and the sound of glass smashing. Men telling her to knock it off.

"Remember this?" Marlon asked.

Csongor looked at Marlon, becoming a little more visible to him now because of the light diffusing from the fishing boat's windows, and saw him holding one of the objects that they had earlier marked as stun grenades.

"Take two," Csongor said. He reached into his pocket, took out the second stun grenade, and handed it to Marlon. He looped the strap of the purse over his shoulder, just so he wouldn't lose track of it in whatever was to follow, and pulled out the pistol. Jones had identified it, earlier, as a Makarov. He drew back the slide just to verify that there was a round in the chamber.

Then he slipped it into his waistband, grabbed the oars, and began to pull like hell. He had glimpsed an opportunity, however unlikely, to get himself out of China.

SOKOLOV AWOKE TO a perfectly silent office. And yet lodged in his short-term memory was the sound of an elevator door opening.

He willed himself not to go back to sleep and soon heard faint voices.

Feeling in the dark, he verified that his pistol and flashlight were where he had left them, next to his head. He drew one knee, then the other up to his chest so that he could tie his shoes. Whoever they were, the visitors were moving cautiously, reconnoitering, discussing. It was not a break-the-door-down-and-barge-in type of visit.

They would have been stopped by the glass doors. Sokolov had sealed them with the cable lock. They would be trying to find a way around those doors, debating whether to just break the glass. The noise would be stupendous, but it was the middle of the night, and the building was mostly vacant.

Not knowing how many there were or what their intentions might be, Sokolov decided to retreat and lurk. He stood up and got one foot into the loop of Ethernet cable he had tied earlier, then put his weight on it and straightened the leg, thrusting his head and shoulders up through the vacancy in the ceiling.

He let the gun, the clip, and the flashlight rest for the time being on top of an adjoining tile. Then he reached up and got a grip on the heavy steel. Once that was done, it was easy to raise his knees up and go completely upside down, hanging by his hands while endeavoring to thrust his lower legs through the triangular openings in the truss. That accomplished, he was able to hang by his knees, head down, hands free.

He pulled up the cable loop after him and let it rest off to one side atop the ceiling grid.

From the direction of the entrance came a couple of exploratory thumps, followed by a tremendous crash and a long decrescendo of high-pitched clattering as glass fragments sprayed all over the floor of the lobby. He listened for a few moments, just to get some sense of how many there were and how they were moving. Then he picked up the loose ceiling tile from where he had laid it and set it into its position.

As he was doing so, something caught his eye on the table below: his phone, and a scrap of paper. They'd been in the back pocket of his suit trousers. Normally he wore pants with zip pockets and kept them zipped. That way, he never had to worry about things falling out of them when he was something other than upright and vertical, and this in turn left him free to make use of all of his hard-earned diving and rolling skills.

But Jeremy Jeong's business suit had turned that training into bad habits.

There was nothing to be done about it; he could hear the intruders making their way into the office. He carefully fitted the missing tile back into its place. Then he picked up his flashlight and put it into his mouth, leaving it turned off for the time being. He picked up the Makarov and chambered a round with a slow careful movement of the slide, muffling the sound as best he could with his hand. The spare clip was a bit of a problem, since he was still hanging upside down and none of his pockets could be relied upon. He left it where it was for now, but practiced laying his hand on it in the dark until he could touch it on the first try.

And then he could do nothing, for perhaps a quarter of an hour, except listen. And even the listening was not especially good, since he was separated from what he was listening to by a deck of ceiling tiles that had been designed specifically to muffle sound. And the intruders, at least for the first little while, were trying to move stealthily; they had no idea whether anyone was in this office or what sort of reception they should expect, and so they had to clear the place. Clear it, in the sense of a military or police unit going through every room of a house to make sure that no attackers were hiding anywhere. From what little Sokolov could infer based on sounds, they seemed to know what they were doing; they were not just walking around like idiots, clumped together, poking their heads into offices, but rather leapfrogging each other from doorway to doorway and communicating in single-word utterances, or perhaps through sign language. They had, in other words, been through some sort of training. And they had to be armed; it would not make sense for them to do what they were doing unless they had guns and had them out and ready to fire.

But finally there came a point when they began to converse in normal voices. Sokolov heard the faint metallic clicks of guns being put back in safe conditions.

The intruders—Sokolov guessed four or five of them—were not speaking Chinese. Having heard a lot of Central Asian languages, he guessed it was one of those, but he couldn't understand a word of it. One time he heard a man speak roughly in Chinese and heard a meek Chinese voice answering back. They must have a hostage.

A lot of attention was paid, for a few minutes, to the computer. Sokolov had left this switched off, since it gave him the creeps to be sharing space with an intelligent machine that was connected to the Internet all the time. They booted it up and spent a little while clicking around. This rapidly grew boring for whoever was not actually doing it, and so at least one of the men began roaming around the office—Sokolov could see occasional reflected glints from his flashlight.

This man ended up directly below Sokolov. He was quiet for a few seconds, then he called out to his comrades.

A few of them now congregated below, and Sokolov knew that they were looking at the phone he had dropped.

A curious kind of conversation now took place, in which several voices would call out a few words in approximate unison, followed by a pause, followed by a repetition of the same. Sokolov was unsure what to make of it until he heard "Westin." Then he understood that they were going through the photographs on the phone, looking at each one and trying to identify it.

Once they got to the end of the photos, there was general discussion for a while, which did not seem to lead anywhere. Nor would it. There was nothing interesting on the phone. Only the numbers of some dead men.

Then one of them began speaking in Chinese. Haltingly. As if reading.

Sokolov clearly heard the word "Gulangyu."

It was the piece of paper: the one that had fallen to the table alongside the phone. It was the scrap on which he had copied out Meng Anlan's address.

This got them excited in a way that the phone hadn't and actually led to one of them taking out his own phone and making a call to someone. There was discussion in a language that Sokolov recognized as Arabic. Of this he knew a few words, but again the only thing he could distinguish through the ceiling tiles was "Gulangyu."

That, and "Okay," repeated several times.

Some calculation here. He could just slide the ceiling tile out of the way and begin shooting. No doubt he'd be able to get a few of them before they got their weapons off safety and began to shoot back. But when they did shoot back, it would be very difficult for him to move from this incredibly exposed position; and all they'd have to do would be to empty clips toward his general direction and he'd be dead soon.

Moreover, he was certain now that Jones was not among the men down there. These men were speaking a Central Asian language that Jones wouldn't know. But when they made the phone call, they switched to Arabic. They must have been talking to Jones at that point. So even if, by some miracle, Sokolov could kill every man down there, he wouldn't get Jones.

Now, maybe they were now planning an expedition to Olivia's apartment. If so, he wanted to stop them before they got there.

Maybe he could wait until they were out of the room, then let himself down, track them to some place from which he could launch an attack, and get them all.

But they had just given Olivia's address over the phone to Jones. So that cat was out of the bag. Even if he could stop all of these guys, that might not protect Olivia, if Jones was now on his way to her place independently.

Now *there* was a thought. If Sokolov went to Gulangyu now, was there a chance he might be able to intercept Jones there, and finish this thing tonight?

His mind was made up as soon as this thought entered it.

The men below were moving purposefully now, in a hurry to be quit of this place and to embark on their next mission. Sokolov waited until he was fairly certain that they were gone, then moved the tile a little and looked around. Nothing.

But they might have suspected he was up there, left someone behind to kill him when he emerged.

So he grabbed the steel girder, pulled himself up, got his legs free, swung them down and simply dropped straight through the ceiling tile, landing on the conference table and then executing a dive and roll from there toward the doorway. Somersaulting through that, he came up in a low crouch, weapon up, and turned and looked both ways. Nothing. But—

Scared the hell out of him. A man was lying on the floor no more than ten feet away.

But he was motionless, hands zip-tied behind his back. And he was naked.

On second thought, not exactly motionless. Still twitching. A huge stain was spreading out from the vicinity of his head, which was tilted back at a funny angle. His throat had been cut.

Sokolov retrieved his spare clip and other goods from the wreckage now strewn around the conference table, but paused on his way out of the suite to shine his flashlight over the dead man's face. He was ethnic Chinese.

Why had they taken his clothes?

Because something about them made them useful.

A uniform. The guy was a cop, or a security guard.

"*NI YAO GAO de tamen ji quan bu ning.*" Easy for Marlon to say. Hard for Yuxia to accomplish, locked as she was in a steel-walled cabin where everything of consequence seemed to be welded down. There was little in here that a person could smash or break. She tried smacking the glass of the porthole and nearly broke her hand. But there was a wooden chair that wasn't nailed down, and she found that she could pick it up by its back and smash it into things. Her first few attempts went wild and crashed into the steel door, hard enough that the chair itself began to disintegrate and to send fragments of dry, broken wood bouncing back into her face. She brushed kindling out of her hair, then shifted to a double-handed grip on the largest part of the chair that was still in one piece and went back to work, finally beginning to strike home on the glass of the porthole itself. The glass wasn't impressed. She hit it harder. Still nothing. Somehow this made her more enraged than Ivanov's deception, being handcuffed to the steering wheel, Jones abducting Zula, being shoved facefirst into salt water.

She just wasn't screaming enough. She began to let go with a deep grunt from her belly with every blow. Like that American tennis player, the big black woman, who screamed whenever she hit the ball. Anyway, to scream was part of raising hell, right? She wound up like a baseball player and lashed out with what was rapidly being reduced to a single short club of wood and screamed as loud as she could and just missed the porthole with a vicious blow.

This made her even more angry, so she sucked in a breath and let go another scream and struck another wild blow that missed; and she began now to mix her screaming with curses that she had learned from the women of her village when they were very angry at the men in their lives, and finally she landed a strike on the porthole glass so hard that it cracked. The men of the boat had covered the porthole with paper and someone on the other side now snatched it down and looked through the broken glass just in time to see another chair-leg attack headed right for his face. He ducked out of the way as chips of glass flew out from the spreading fracture, and when he bobbed back up, he was screaming right back at her.

A few more strikes and a pie-wedge-shaped chunk of porthole glass was knocked out, and the one man had been joined by three others. Four of them! There were only six men on the whole boat. She gripped the chair leg like a mortar and began to use what was left of the glass as a pestle, jabbing at it with short sharp blows. This was, as much as anything, a way of catching her breath. She had forgotten to breathe. She saw the door handle move and knew they were coming; she stepped back from the door, sucked in as much air as she could, and greeted the first man into the room with a blast of invective that, had he understood the dialect she was using, would have shriveled his genitals into something like raisins. Other men followed the first one in through the narrow hatch and then spread out to either sides, backed up against the walls, out of range of the flailing chair leg. The look on their faces was genuine fear. Yuxia had turned into a crazy woman, a witch. Because only a crazy woman or a witch would behave this badly when she was totally in the power of a group of men who could rape her and kill her any time they felt like it.

A man entered the cabin with such force that he practically knocked the other men down. It was the boat's captain. He hated her. He came right at her. She instinctively swung the chair leg at him, but he must have known some martial arts because he caught it on the fly and twisted it right out of her hand and hurled it contemptuously out the door and into the sea.

Yuxia reached into her boot and pulled out the phone and held it up for all of them to see. "I have already called the police!" she announced. "You are all dead men."

This was perhaps the only thing that could have stopped the captain in his tracks. He stood perfectly still for a count of three.

A small, cylindrical object bounced in over the cabin's threshold and landed in the middle of the floor. This was not the first time Yuxia had ever seen one. Earlier today, Marlon and Csongor had discovered a couple of them among Ivanov's personal effects, and they had discussed them briefly, using some English terminology that she vaguely recognized. Not commonly used English words but ones she had heard before. "Stun" and "grenade." From movies, she understood the grenade concept well enough. The thing on the floor didn't look like the grenades from movies and so she would not have recognized it had it not been for the lucky coincidence of the chat in the van a few hours ago.

Or maybe not such a coincidence.

It occurred to her that the grenade was missing its ring.

Yuxia turned away from it, closing her eyes, and clapped her hands to the sides of her head.

ZULA COULD NO longer remember a time when she hadn't felt extremely conspicuous. Sitting alone in the bar of the Hyatt in damp clothes that were very much the worse for wear, she felt no more or less out of place than usual. She had gotten used to it. She was being eyed by several businessmen who, she could only suppose, were wondering how a crack whore had managed to find her way to Xiamen.

The only men in the place who weren't looking at her were the pair at the next table: a couple of Middle Eastern/South Asian–looking guys in bulky windbreakers. Even they, however, were keeping Zula in the corners of their eyes, in case she had any thoughts of making a break for it.

Anyway, she didn't have to wait for long before the two pilots came down. Uniformed and everything. Carrying their special pilot briefcases and dragging their rollaway bags behind them like cubical pets. They had been ready. She had talked to them on Jones's phone. Called the hotel's operator, asked to be patched through to the two Russians who had checked in at the same time three days ago. It had taken them a while to find the right rooms, but the first of the pilots she'd called, Pavel, had picked up the phone on the first ring. Contrary to what Jones thought, he hadn't been lounging around watching pornography and drinking. He had been waiting.

Of course, what he'd been waiting for was the voice of Ivanov, speaking Russian. Zula speaking English had come as a distinct surprise. But she'd been able to convince Pavel that, yes, she was that girl who had been on the flights earlier in the week. That something had gone awry with the plan. And that it really would be in his best interest to come down and meet with her in the hotel bar.

Pavel and the other pilot, Sergei, approached her somewhat warily, looking her up and down. As just about any sane person would.

"Please," she said, with a gesture. "Sit down."

Even that took some persuading.

But that was okay. She didn't have to persuade Pavel and Sergei of anything else. Just to sit down at this table.

As soon as Pavel and Sergei had taken their seats, the two men in the windbreakers got up and brought their club sodas over and joined them. Five now at the table. Pavel and Sergei were now even more taken aback than they had been to begin with. But proceedings were interrupted by a waitress who came over to take their orders. Zula noted with approval that both pilots asked for nonalcoholic drinks.

One of the men in the windbreakers—Khalid—announced, "Tonight, you will fly to Islamabad."

He then smiled sweetly as Pavel and Sergei broke out into nervous laughter.

"Where is Ivanov?" Pavel wanted to know. He had asked it several times during the phone call. But Zula had never answered it directly until now.

"Dead," she said, and looked significantly at Khalid.

Pavel and Sergei didn't believe it for a moment. But only for a moment.

"Who is this man?" Pavel asked her.

Khalid set down his drink, reached up, grasped his zipper pull, and drew it down to his belly. The garment parted to reveal a sort of vest, sewn out of canvas, sporting a row of long, slender vertical pockets around the midriff. Each of the pockets was bulging full. From the top of each protruded a cylinder of clear plastic, like a piece of kitchen wrap that had been rolled around a flattened tube, about the size of a jumbo burrito, of amorphous yellowish-white stuff, a little bit like pie crust dough that hadn't been rolled out yet. Electrical wires emerged from the top of each dough-tube. They were all linked together and ran up to Khalid's shoulder and then down the sleeve of his windbreaker. He had his hand in his lap, but now coyly displayed it to Pavel and Sergei, letting them see a black plastic object topped with a red button.

Pavel and Sergei couldn't make sense of it for a few moments. Of course it was obviously an explosive vest. Yet to see one right there on a person's body was so shocking that the mind couldn't accept it at first. As if you had found Hitler in your kitchen.

"I've been instructed to tell you a lot of gruesome stuff about what happens when it goes off," Zula said. "Do I need to? I mean, the gist of it is that it'll not only kill us but basically bring down half of the building."

Neither Pavel nor Sergei had anything to say.

The windbreaker was zipped back up.

The waitress brought them their drinks. Zula asked for the check.

"I've also been instructed to tell you that there are two taxis waiting outside. Pavel goes in the first, Sergei in the second. One of these guys with the vests will ride in each taxi, to preserve, I guess, the threat. We'll go straight to the airport and depart for Islamabad as soon as you can get through your preflight checklist. Are there any questions?"

There were no questions.

Leading the four men out across the lobby, Zula felt like a terrorist.

It felt sort of cool.

Not that she was in danger of signing up with these guys any time soon. The burqa requirement, the stoning, and so on pretty much ruled that out. But she had been so powerless for so long (and yet not *that* long—less than a week). Striding out of the Hyatt with enough PETN in her wake to take down the building gave her some weird vicarious feeling of power. The tired businessmen checking in at the registration desk were still giving her the same up-and-down body scan look. And yet she didn't care what they thought of her any longer. She had gone beyond all that, was part of a reality much bigger and more intense than anything they could possibly imagine. They and their opinions of her were irrelevant. Puny.

To be a man who had been helpless his entire life? And to have this power? To be able to access this feeling that she was just tasting now? It must be the most potent drug in the world.

When she climbed into the backseat of the taxi, she could see from the look on Jones's face that he was high on that drug too. "I badly want to turn this thing around and go back into town," he remarked. He was fiddling with the screen of his phone.

"Why?"

"We found Sokolov."

Suddenly she wasn't high on the drug anymore. She hoped it wasn't too obvious in her face.

"Or at least, we know where he went. Place on Gulangyu."

So what's going to happen now? she wanted to ask. But she didn't want to get in trouble for putting her nose where it didn't belong.

He was looking at her as if reading her mind. He *wanted* to tell her. *Wanted* her to ask.

She refused to give him that satisfaction.

"They're going there now," he said, "and they're going to take care of him."

IF HIS EXPERIENCE as the creator of REAMDE had taught Marlon anything at all, it was that something always got massively screwed up with any plan, and you never knew what that something was until it happened. In this case, it was that Csongor rowed too hard. Marlon had first encountered the Hungarian in extremely chaotic circumstances, and for most of their acquaintance he had been too distracted to really pay close attention to the man's physical presence. At 190 centimeters, Marlon considered himself unusually tall. But in looking at Csongor, he'd had the unaccustomed experience of seeing one who was taller. And he was tempted to guess that Csongor was twice his weight, but he knew that couldn't be possible. He carried some weight around his midsection, but none of it was what you'd call flab; his head was big and wide, but it did not support any redundant chins. The power with which he pulled on the oars gave Marlon the nervous feeling that the boat was being jerked out from under him, and that was just in *normal* rowing. During the last minute or so before their collision with the fishing boat, Csongor had finally gotten it into his head that he was rowing for his life, and possibly for Zula's, and had hauled on the oars with so much power that Marlon had instinctively crouched lower in the boat and put a steadying hand on each gunwale.

Csongor, of course, could not see where he was going and so in the final moments Marlon, not trusting his ability to communicate in English, began pointing this way and that, telling him which way to steer. He had neglected to allow for the fishing boat's bow wave, which caused their prow to pitch up sharply at the very end; then one of the tires slung along its sides bashed into them and flipped the boat over in an instant. Marlon, who saw it coming, jumped straight up off his bench even as the little boat was spinning out from under him and managed to snag the rim of a tire with one hand. The other hand followed it an instant later, which was a good thing because otherwise he'd have lost his grip. The larger vessel was moving faster than he'd estimated, and it positively yanked him forward. This drew all of his attention for a moment, but then he looked back along the side and saw the capsized rowboat rapidly falling away to aft, and no sign of Csongor.

Then a hand broke the water and groped up and pawed uselessly at the upturned hull. Another hand joined it. The boat jerked straight down, as if grabbed from beneath by a shark. Csongor was trying to find a way to get his weight on top of it, but it was rapidly falling away to aft. Finally Csongor's torso rose partway out of the water and a hand shot up and grabbed the rim of the last tire. Instantly Csongor was buried in a bow wave of his own making, the same thing that had hit Marlon a few moments earlier: he was being pulled through the sea by the tow rope of his arm, and his head was breaking the waves. But with some more struggling and wrestling, he was able to get the second arm out of the water and grip one of the ropes by which the tire was suspended, and then do a pull-up that got his head out of the water so that he could breathe.

Marlon looked away and tended to his own problems for a moment. His upper body was out of the water, but his legs were being dragged along, creating powerful suction that threatened to rip him off the tire. Inching, like a rock climber, to a slightly better grip, he was able to lift a leg out and drape it over the adjoining tire, and this both reduced the suction and gave him leverage to clamber up and get better handholds. He worked his way to a place where he was standing with one foot on the tire's rim and reaching up over his head with both hands to grip the boat's gunwale.

He risked a look back and saw that Csongor had achieved similar results. The little rowboat was nowhere to be seen. Csongor was holding on with one hand, using the other to pat himself down, verifying that the gun was still where he had put it, the shoulder bag still slung across his body.

Then he began climbing, and Marlon followed suit. In a few moments, he was able to vault over the gunwale and land in a crouch on the main deck. There didn't seem to be anyone around. From the sounds of it, Yuxia was still doing an excellent job of raising hell on the other side.

Csongor, squatting back at the stern, looked across to the opposite side, then turned to Marlon and shrugged, indicating that he saw nothing. He rose to his feet, took the pistol out of his pocket, checked it, and then began to walk around the back of the superstructure.

Marlon took one of the stun grenades out of his pocket and got his finger into its ring. Then he walked across the front of the superstructure, sticking close to its front bulkhead in case anyone might be looking down from the bridge, and peeked around the corner. Perhaps three meters aft, light was shining from an open hatch. Two men, a large one and a smaller one, were standing on the catwalk outside, looking in. The larger of the two got a snarling look on his face and strode over the high threshold into the cabin. As soon as he was out of the way, Marlon was able to look all the way aft to the stern of the boat and see Csongor's bulky form there.

Marlon began to walk aft. Csongor began to walk forward. The smaller man who was still out on the gangway noticed Marlon first, and his whole body went into a kind of spasm. There was no helping it; he couldn't prevent himself from being astonished at the sight of a stranger on his boat. Marlon caught his eye and pointed suggestively aft. The man turned to look in the direction indicated and saw Csongor raising a pistol and aiming at his face. While this poor fellow was thus distracted, Marlon pulled the pin out of the stun grenade—this was surprisingly difficult—and then reached around and chucked it into the cabin. He noticed, then, that the door opened outward, and so he gave it a shove and clanged it shut and leaned against it just in time to feel a mighty boom through his butt and feel a blast of hot air and shattered glass smack him in the back of the head.

SOKOLOV HAD A key card that would enable him to summon an elevator, but he reckoned that the jihadists might be down in the lobby, in view of the indicator panel. They might notice one of the lifts going into motion and stopping at 43. If so, they could simply kill him when the door opened. So he took the stairs instead, just as Zula had done the other day. He took them fast, bounding over banisters and caroming off walls. But he was still moving a hell of a lot slower than those guys in the elevator.

Fearing that the fire exit to the outside might set off an alarm, he took a chance on the door to the lobby, pushing it open slightly first to check for an ambush. No one was there.

They might be waiting to ambush him from the plantings outside, but if they really knew he was here and wanted to ambush him, they'd have gone about it differently. So he walked stolidly out of the building, down the drive, and out to the street. Then he broke into a jog, headed toward the ferry terminals, less than a kilometer away. He was keeping an eye out for the jihadists the entire way but saw nothing.

A ferry was loading at the terminal for Gulangyu. Sokolov swung wide around it, avoiding streetlamps, and made his way down to a smaller and lower dock nearby, where several speedboats were tied up, and their drivers sitting around smoking cigarettes and talking. These were the high-speed water taxis for moneyed passengers, and Sokolov had been eyeing them with interest the whole time he'd been in Xiamen.

On the way over he had made a large withdrawal from the Bank of CamelBak. He let them see the wad of magenta bills in his hand. This got their attention. Not in a favorable way. It made them nervous and suspicious. He could not concern himself with their emotional state just now. He nodded across the water and said, "Gulangyu."

One of the boatmen was just a little quicker than the others; Sokolov ended up in his boat. This was a kind of small pleasure craft seen by the millions on lakes and rivers all over the world: an open white fiberglass skiff with a big outboard motor on its back, capable of seating maybe six people comfortably. Orange life vests were stored in an open bin, probably in obedience to some regulation, and disposable plastic rain ponchos were available for lightly dressed passengers caught in sudden downpours.

The ferry had already pulled away from its dock. At this time of night there were not too many people headed for Gulangyu. Most of the passengers remained in the ferry's roofed, illuminated, Plexiglas-walled interior, perhaps to avoid a faint suggestion of a chill in the air; though around here, "chill" meant that a woman in a spaghetti-strap dress might experience goose bumps when exposed to the full force of the wind.

Not the least bit chilly were four male passengers grouped on an open deck up at the ferry's bow, gazing toward Gulangyu, pointing and talking.

As the boat came abreast of the ferry—for it was going twice as fast as the larger vessel—Sokolov picked up a plastic poncho, swept it over his shoulders, and poked his head through the hole in the middle, then pulled the hood up over his head. He left it on, and did not look back, until a couple of minutes later, when the boatman cut his engine and let the little vessel glide the last few meters toward the Gulangyu terminal.

As he was disembarking, Sokolov glanced back and saw that the ferry was not as far behind them as he had hoped it would be. The little boat had accelerated more quickly at the beginning of the journey and jumped out to a lead, but the ferry, once it got going, moved faster than it appeared to.

Still, there was a reason why people paid more for the speedboats, and Sokolov reckoned it had to do with the congestion in the terminals. Gulangyu Island sported a number of parks, tourist attractions, and bars that attracted a younger crowd, many of whom were trying to make their way back to Xiamen at the moment, and so the terminal on this end was much more crowded.

He made as if to shrug off the plastic poncho, then thought better of it. The boatman was giving him an odd look. Sokolov held out his hand, palm up, and looked to the sky, trying to pantomime: *Does it look like rain to you?* He could not tell whether he was getting through to the boatman at all. Finally he plucked at it and dangled a couple of the magenta bills. These were accepted and the boatman turned away. Transaction finished.

Sokolov flipped the hood up over his shaved head. He'd removed his hair to make himself harder to identify, in the event that the PSB had found a witness to this morning's events or caught something on a surveillance camera. But now it was making him stand out in a way that wasn't to his advantage.

He strode through the waterfront park for a distance, startling a few pairs of young lovers, then cut uphill on a steep street channeled between old stone walls. This was one of the few roads that actually showed up on the map. It wound from side to side, following the island's steep contours, dodging huge outcroppings of gray stone that were plastered with vines, clutched in the monstrous root systems of outlandish trees, and occasionally incised with staircases. From time to time, just after rounding a corner, Sokolov would stop and peer behind to see if anyone was coming up the same way. He saw nothing obvious. But the island's road network was a maze, and Olivia's building could be approached from more than one direction.

As a matter of fact, he wasn't entirely sure he knew where he was; he felt that he should have been there by now, but in the dark he couldn't see any of the landmarks he had picked out earlier.

His view was blocked for a while by a rank of tall trees growing on the inside of a wall, marking the edge of a compound: some school or government institution. Then he came into a crossroads and saw the landmark he'd been searching for: a hotel built atop a high stony rise, with terraces and gardens that afforded a fine view over Gulangyu, the strait, and the city beyond. He had sat there for a while earlier today, gazing down into the courtyard of Olivia's building, watching people come and go, and trying to come up with a Plan C for getting into her apartment after Plans A and B had exposed him to unacceptable risks of detection.

So now he understood where he was and where he needed to go: up a street that forked to the left. But coming down that street toward him, filling its width from wall to wall, was a group of half a dozen young men who he could tell had been enjoying a few drinks and were now ambling toward the ferry terminal. They were in the cheerful and gregarious stage of drunkenness, accosting everyone they saw and trying to strike up conversations in a way that pretended to be friendly but was in truth quite aggressive. One of them had already seen Sokolov, absurdly conspicuous in his shaved head and plastic poncho, and was pointing him out to a fellow. Sokolov cruised into the other fork and, as soon as he was out of view, sprinted flat out for a hundred meters or so, just to get out of hailing range.

An alley presented itself on his left, and he ducked into it. Following it back toward the looming hotel, he began to see landmarks he recognized. Running up a stone stairway overarched with big old trees, he emerged into the somewhat larger street that ran past Olivia's building. Standing right there were a couple of old ladies out for a walk who looked at Sokolov as if he were a marmoset in a zoo. He nodded to them politely and turned in the direction of Olivia's building. Two young women emerged from a gate and pursued him up the street for a short distance, giggling and pantomiming picture-taking gestures. They wanted to get a snapshot of him to show their friends. He quickened his pace and declined the offer.

He had to get out of this fucking country *now*.

Then, there it was. The gateway to the compound that housed Olivia's building, absolutely distinctive because of a tree that had taken root on top of the adjoining wall and spread its weird molten limbs all over the stonework, trying to find some actual dirt to grow in, possibly seeking refuge from the relentless attentions of three different kinds of flowering vines that were using it as a trellis. Sokolov checked in all directions and saw nothing untoward on the street. He walked through the gate into the walled garden that surrounded the building.

The place was constructed in a generally European style as reinterpreted by whatever local artisans the owner had been able to hire a hundred years ago. It was vaguely Classical, with a row of four spindly pillars supporting a veranda and, above it, a balcony. Ahead of him, on the veranda, silhouetted against the lights of the entryway, were four men, checking the place out, talking on phones. Darting their heads this way and that. Sokolov, feeling like a little kid playing some kind of ridiculous game, stepped behind a tree so that they wouldn't see him if they looked back. It had been a hell of a long time since he had been reduced to hiding behind a tree, and he did not view it as much of a professional achievement.

One of the four men was dressed in a bulky, ill-fitting uniform.

Sokolov squatted and peered through a bush.

The one in the uniform ascended the steps and pushed his way through one in a row of four wooden doors, glass-windowed but guarded with ironwork. Beyond these was a broad entrance hall, probably a foyer back in the days when it had been some important businessman's villa. In its new incarnation, this had been lined with mailboxes and provided with a few benches and low tables. A set of inner doors sealed it off from the stairs that gave access to the various units, but Sokolov knew from earlier reconnaissance that these were not locked. The building wasn't secured at all; the only lock between these men and the inside of Olivia's flat was the one on her door.

The other three men took a last look around and went inside.

Sokolov broke from cover and ran around to the side of the building that faced the water and the city lights of Xiamen. Olivia's little terrace was two stories above his head. A tree sprouted from the ground near the building's corner, too close to the building. It had probably been a volunteer seedling at the outbreak of the Second World War. It had grown up wild during the decades when no one was looking after the place, until the new owners, finding this mature, fifteen-meter tree on their property, had gone after it with pole saws, lopped off the lower limbs, and pruned it up into something that looked a little closer to proper landscaping. It was neither the easiest nor the hardest climbing tree that Sokolov had ever seen; the only reason he hadn't gone up it earlier was that, in broad daylight, anyone could have seen him out the window of flats on lower levels.

He climbed it now, not with a lot of grace or dignity, but he didn't fall and he didn't kill a lot of time. A surviving limb arched away from the trunk toward the building's corner. He shinned out on it, finding himself a couple of meters above the building's roof and a couple of meters away. The jump was not especially difficult, though Jeremy Jeong's dress shoes betrayed him as he was shoving off and he ended up catching the eave in his belly rather than landing flat on the tiles as he had envisioned. He lashed out with his left hand and grabbed the bracket of a satellite dish antenna. With his right he gripped the coaxial cable that ran up to it. Getting both hands then on the cable, he let himself slide down until his flailing feet found what he was pretty sure was the concrete railing around Olivia's terrace. Placing his weight on that, he leaned back to clear the building's eave, then pivoted and dropped to a squat on her terrace. This was barely large enough to support one chair and a tiny table. From here, access to her flat was barred by a glass door with an iron grille. Through it, he could see all the way through her bedroom and into the little sitting room beyond it.

The door was locked. Earlier today, he had gotten it open by jerking out the hinge pins. For he had noted on one of her phone pictures that the installers had committed the grievous error of situating these on the outside. Still, it had taken several minutes of screwing around.

He could not see Olivia, but he could see her shadow moving on the wall and the floor. He was fairly certain that she was standing near the flat's door.

He pulled his little flashlight out of his bag, slid it between the bars, and rapped sharply on the glass. Then he turned it on and aimed it at his face.

The shadow froze, then went into slow movement. Olivia peered around the corner for an instant, then drew her head back sharply. He could see her hand coming up to her mouth. Then she risked another look.

What would she do when she recognized him? Calling the PSB would be a perfectly rational option.

Instead she moved his way decisively and unlocked the terrace door, then stood aside to let him enter the bedroom.

"Someone's knocking at the door—says he's a security guard," she said.

"Get dark, warm clothes," Sokolov said. "Put them in a bag with water and food. Other than that, ignore everything."

"What does that mean?"

"*Everything.*"

Sokolov shoved the Makarov through its rail, chambering a round. He then put it back into his waistband.

He strode to Olivia's door, undid the lock, and hauled it open.

The man in the security guard uniform was standing there, hand raised to knock again. Two of his friends were lurking a couple of paces behind him. The third was farther away, keeping a lookout at the top of the stairs.

Sokolov grabbed the "security guard" by the hair, hauled him inside the apartment, slammed the door, and locked it.

The guard pulled a knife—Sokolov could discern this from the way he had chosen to move—and tried to hit him with a direct overhand stab. Sokolov blocked it to the outside with his left forearm, wrapped his arm around the other's like a vine, getting him just above the elbow, then jerked up until he heard a crack. This left the security guard standing very close to Sokolov, a little bit sideways. Sokolov brought his right knee up into the other's groin. When he doubled over, Sokolov jammed his thumb into the man's throat to bring him upright again, then brought his forehead down on the bridge of the man's nose, shattering it. Finally, Sokolov pulled his knife from his trouser pocket, gathered his arm above the opposite shoulder as if to deliver a backhanded chop to the neck, and swung the blade all the way through the security guard's throat.

Before the man could fall down, Sokolov opened the apartment door again and pushed him straight out the door, directly into the arms of one of his friends, fountaining blood from both carotids.

The other friend was standing just off to the side. Sokolov grabbed the man's jacket, pulled him forward, and rammed his knife straight up into the underside of the man's chin until the handle stopped against the point of his jaw.

The sound of a weapon being cocked: the man at the top of the stairs. Sokolov stepped back, slammed the apartment door closed, locked it, then fired half of a clip through the wood, aimed toward the man who was burdened with the security guard's body.

Seeing as how gunfire had started, Sokolov checked his watch, wondering how many minutes it would be before the authorities shut down the ferry terminal.

A few rounds came through the door in his general direction, but this was the man at the top of the stairs firing down the hallway; the bullets were passing into the wall at a shallow angle and getting lost as they felt their way around its internal structure. The weapon was a submachine gun, firing pistol rounds with nothing like the kinetic energy of a rifle cartridge. But in a few moments this man would probably be standing squarely in front of the door firing straight through it, and Sokolov wanted to have himself and Olivia in a different place by then. He turned and strode into the bedroom, where Olivia was cramming things into a bag on her bed. He pulled the bag out of her grasp without breaking stride, stepped onto the terrace, and dropped it over the railing. With his other hand he had taken Olivia by the upper arm, and he now drew her onto the little balcony and got her to sidestep away from the open door and stand with her back to the exterior wall, which was made of brick; it would suffice to stop the type of ammunition that the surviving jihadist would soon be pumping through her front door. Sokolov then climbed up on the terrace railing and got his hands into some ivy that he had noticed climbing thickly up the wall. Jerking on this as hard as he could, he found that it would come away from the wall if he applied enough force but was well attached. So, lacking other options, he sat his butt on the railing, swung his legs over the edge, and jumped off. The ivy peeled away, showering him with mortar dust and vegetable debris, and he fell, jerkily, but only so fast, for a couple of meters, before it finally held fast and stopped him. From there he was able to get a grip on some window bars and clamber down to an altitude where it became possible to jump the rest of the way, striking the ground in a somersault. Rolling back up to his feet he ran around the side of the building to its front entrance, came into the entry hall, and ascended the stairs. People were shouting and screaming in their apartments. He tried not to think about what this portended, and he resisted the temptation to nervously check his watch. First things first. Looking up the stairwell he saw no one; the gunman had moved away from his earlier perch and probably gone to Olivia's door. He heard another burst of fire from the submachine gun. So he took the remaining stairs three at a time and, after checking the Makarov, stepped out into the hallway on Olivia's floor.

The gunman was right in front of her door, which he had just finished kicking open. Seeing Sokolov in the corner of his eye, he performed a classic double-take. During the second half of this, Sokolov fired two rounds into his head. He could tell by the way that the man collapsed that the rounds had gone into his brain and that he was dead, but as he approached he fired two more just to be sure, then picked up the submachine gun, which the man had dropped on the floor. Its clip was probably very close to being empty. Scanning the man's body he noticed an extra clip protruding from a pocket, so he grabbed that. He noticed a phone too, so he took that as well. And finally, best of all, he found his own phone, which this man had taken from the safe house and dropped into a pocket.

He then walked through the apartment, announcing himself so that Olivia would know who he was.

He was dismayed to find that she was no longer on the terrace, but looking down he saw that she had made her way to the ground, apparently without breaking any bones, and was gathering up the items that had spilled from the bag when Sokolov had tossed it. He whistled. She looked up. He pointed to the gate that led out to the street. She saw it and nodded. He spun on his heel and strode out of the apartment. He peeled off the bloody poncho and threw it on the floor, then sprinted down the stairs, burst out the front of the building, and ran down its front steps in time to see Olivia's form silhouetted in the gate.

"To the ferry terminal," he said. "Avoid big streets." His hearing was recovering to the point where he could hear sirens now.

She led him *uphill,* which he hadn't expected, since water was generally *down*—but only so that she could dart into the grounds of a school across the street. They ran across its playing field and out a back gate, then followed a series of alleys and staircases that took them eventually to one of the big parks that spread along the side of the island facing Xiamen.

As they came in view of the ferry terminal, Sokolov checked his watch and found that four minutes had elapsed since the onset of gunfire. Most police departments could not respond that quickly; but if the local cops had been put on some kind of alert because of this morning's disaster in Xiamen, they might have a heavier than normal presence in the ferry terminals. And indeed, through the glass doors of the terminal Sokolov could see PSB officers, at least half a dozen of them, paying close attention to their walkie-talkies.

His pace faltered.

Olivia turned toward him, seeing the same thing.

"We need fast water taxi," Sokolov said.

Olivia pointed into the adjoining park. "Go that way," she said, "wait at the foot of the big statue."

There was no mistaking what this meant, any more than a tourist in New York Harbor could fail to understand what "the big statue" was. She was talking about a huge stone rendering of Zheng Chenggong, which stood on a pedestal at the edge of the water and was lit up with spotlights so that it could be seen from miles away.

"I'll hire a water taxi and meet you there," she explained.

He thought he saw sincerity in her face. Trusting her was a risk, but walking anywhere near the ferry terminal at this moment was a risk too. He nodded, then turned away and walked into the park.

It was a big park, and it took him a few minutes to get near the statue of Zheng Chenggong.

The pedestal itself rose sharply out of the water and was not a good place to board a boat, but below it was a little stretch of sandy beach. He saw a white water taxi rounding a turn into the bay. So he ran down some tiers of stone steps that afforded access to the beach and waited for it to come in closer so that he could wade out to it. But the driver cut his engine and seemed disinclined to come in closer; Sokolov could hear an unpleasant conversation between him and Olivia.

The problem, perhaps, was that normal people didn't wade out into the ocean to board a water taxi, and the mere fact that this was being proposed had aroused his suspicion.

He looked about. The pedestal of the statue was perhaps a hundred meters down the beach to his right. Running along its base was a walkway that developed into a short causeway, extending over shallow, rocky water to a house-sized boulder just a stone's throw away from the shore. Some sort of little temple or gazebo had been constructed on top of that. From it, another little causeway stretched out to an even smaller rock that supported a navigation light. Sokolov flashed his flashlight at the water taxi to get their attention, then waved suggestively in that direction. He did not want to say anything since this would reveal that he was non-Chinese. Willing himself not to break into a dead sprint, he quick-walked up the beach, took a little stone stairway up to the level of the causeway, and then walked across it to the boulder. The causeway skirted this and then headed out to the navigation light. By the time Sokolov got out to that second stretch of causeway, he could see the water taxi approaching and hear the argument continuing.

He had probably aroused the suspicions of the local watermen with his earlier behavior. Word had gotten around. Perhaps they'd even heard the gunfire from up the hill.

The boat would come up just beneath him here. He turned his back on it as it drew closer.

Olivia broke into English. "He refuses to take us," she announced. "So I asked him, 'What do you want me to do, jump overboard and swim to shore?' And he at least agreed to come and let me off here. Can you give me a hand up?"

"Of course," Sokolov said, and turned to face the boat.

The look on the driver's face was everything Sokolov had hoped for. But he had already cut his engine and drifted in close. He reached down to shift his propeller into reverse gear, but Olivia hooked her arm into his and prevented it. The boat drifted closer. Sokolov vaulted over the causeway's railing and slammed down onto its prow, then dove over its windscreen and came up onto his feet in time to intervene in a physical squabble between Olivia and the driver. He got the latter in a very simple armlock, just to focus his attention, and then let him see the submachine gun.

At that point, the driver saw reason and sat down.

"Tell driver to go north around Xiamen," Sokolov suggested.

Olivia said something. The driver backed the boat away from the causeway and then turned it out into the open channel. Once they were well clear of shallows, he made a new course with Gulangyu on the left and downtown Xiamen on the right, and throttled it up.

Sokolov sat down in the back, pulled a life vest out of a storage bin, and set to work strapping it to Olivia's bag.

This did not take especially long, so when it was finished, he leaned back and enjoyed the view of the city, the colossal bridges thrown over the straits that separated it from the mainland, the container port, the big freighters riding at anchor. He would never see Xiamen again, that was for certain.

Something trembled against his leg. He reached in and pulled out the phone he'd taken from the dead jihadist. It had a new text message, consisting of three question marks.

Sokolov flipped through the "recent calls" menu and found seventeen consecutive phone calls to or from the same number, all during the last ten hours or so.

He debated whether he should do this. It was not the safest, most conservative measure for him to take. But they were well clear of the most developed part of the city, rounding the northern curve of the island, the flat open land where they'd built the airport. In another few minutes, Taiwanese territory would come into view.

He hit redial.

"ARE YOU OKAY? Where is Zula?"

"Are you okay? Where is Zula?"

"Are you okay? Where is Zula?"

Even through closed eyelids with her back turned, the grenade's flash had left huge purple patches floating around in the middle of Yuxia's vision, obscuring her view of Csongor's face. But she knew who it was.

"They took her," she said.

He had been holding her by her upper arms. Now he let go. She realized that she was only standing up by virtue of the fact that Csongor had hauled her to her feet. So there were a few moments, now, when she half fell down and had to catch herself and get her legs working and her balance back again. She ended up half leaning against the corner post of a welded steel bunk bed. The cabin was full of smoke, and more smoke was rising from a thousand tiny little embers that had been strewn across the bedspreads and were burning or melting their way down into the blankets. She coughed and pressed her free hand against her mouth. Csongor, meanwhile, was on the move, stepping back and forth over the threshold. She saw him step into the cabin and pick up a man who was lying on the floor. He heaved the man over his shoulder like a sack of rice and stepped outside. There was a splash. Then he stepped back into the cabin and repeated the procedure.

From outside she heard Marlon registering a mild objection. "Those men are stunned!"

"This will wake them up," Csongor said.

As far as Yuxia was concerned, the only thing wrong with what

Csongor was doing was that it might fail to result in these men's deaths. She wanted to throw them off *herself.*

She couldn't hear the ship's engines and supposed it was because the bang of the grenade had deafened her. But neither, she realized, could she feel their vibration. Some kind of hasty and anxious conversation took place between Marlon and Csongor. Yuxia stepped outside to get some fresh air. She saw the cook—the man who had given her tea earlier—cringing against the rail. He had been watching Csongor throw men overboard and assumed he was next. "This guy was nice to me," Yuxia announced in English, and then she said to the man in Mandarin that it was going to be okay. But she wasn't sure he understood Mandarin.

Neither Csongor nor Marlon heard her, since they were, with a lot of banging, running up a steel stairway to the bridge, one level above. Some kind of shouting festival ensued. "Let's go see what is happening," she suggested to the tea man, and made a *you first* gesture in the direction of the stairs. With great trepidation, he preceded her up the stairs and onto the ship's bridge.

Csongor was standing in one corner aiming a pistol at a crew member who had, apparently, remained at the controls through everything that had just happened. Marlon was talking to the guy in Mandarin: "You don't have any choice," he said, as if he were repeating something that he'd said before and that this pilot had been too stupid to take in. "You have to take us out of here. Get us to Taiwan or the Philippines or something. We don't have any time to waste!"

The pilot seemed unable to make any decision until finally the cook spoke up in Fujianese and informed him that all the other men on the vessel had been flung overboard. This seemed to make a considerable impression on the pilot. Finally he turned to the control console and shoved on a handle that caused the engines to rev up. Yuxia felt the boat begin to accelerate beneath her, which was a good feeling. "Get us clear of the shore!" Marlon demanded, apparently fearing that the pilot might make a deliberate attempt to beach the vessel. The pilot made a tentative course shift that caused the bow to swing out away from Heartless Island. It wasn't enough for Marlon who stepped forward and wrenched the wheel farther in the same direction. This elicited a stream of panicky Fujianese from the pilot, which Yuxia translated into English: "He says that you just aimed the ship directly toward Kinmen. If we stay on this course, we will be blown out of the water."

Marlon backed away from the wheel and let the pilot change the course back to one that was more southerly, but he was clearly in a suspicious and jumpy frame of mind and made a point of walking around the cabin and looking out all of the windows to verify that they weren't headed toward land.

"GPS," Csongor said, and nodded at one of the array of little screens and electronic devices mounted to the console.

Within a few moments they had gathered around the device that Csongor had noticed. Identifying it as a GPS unit had actually required some careful observation. It was crude and industrial-looking compared to the units with big color screens that some people had in their cars. This one's screen was tiny and gray and showed only those details of interest to mariners: coastlines, shallows, and buoys. But the latitude and longitude were clearly displayed as long strings of digits across the bottom, and the crude outlines and symbols on the screen were creeping upward as the boat moved south.

"I cannot fucking believe this," Csongor said. "Four days ago I am in Budapest drinking beer. Now I have hijacked a boat in China and I have fallen in love and I have killed people."

No one had much to say about that. Marlon turned to Yuxia and said in Mandarin, "Is there anyone else?"

"I don't think so," she answered, "but we should look around."

They agreed that Csongor should remain on the bridge holding the gun while Marlon and Yuxia familiarized themselves with their new boat.

The cook followed them out and down onto the main deck, then told Yuxia, "There is a gun up on the bridge, hidden under the control panel."

So they went back up to the bridge and had the pilot stand well back while Marlon got down on hands and knees and groped around and found the gun: an ancient revolver, rusty around the edges, but loaded and ready to use. This he threw into the ocean. Then, just to be sure, they had both the pilot and the cook strip all the way down to their drawers and sifted through their clothes and found a phone and two knives. Marlon pulled the battery from the pilot's phone, then did likewise to his phone and to Yuxia's.

. . . .

FOLLOWING INSTRUCTIONS FROM Khalid, the pilot Pavel climbed into the backseat of the stolen taxi, where Jones had been waiting behind tinted glass the entire time. Zula joined them. Khalid got into the passenger seat. A similar arrangement was made in a second taxi behind them, which they had simply hailed from the queue in the hotel drive; Sergei ended up in that one along with the other bomb vest wearer.

Once they had pulled out onto the highway, and the second taxi was squarely in their rearview mirror—for apparently its driver had been instructed simply to follow—Jones said to Pavel, "In normal circumstances I would plan what is about to happen very carefully. Maybe we would build a mockup of a jet out in the middle of Yemen and train on it. But because of the way things are today, we are just going to wing it and trust to Allah. Call it fatalism if you like; I believe that is the traditional spin put on it by Westerners."

Pavel did a pretty good impression of not having understood a single word.

"So," Jones continued, "tell me about what it is like at the private jet terminal in Xiamen. I have never enjoyed the luxury. Will someone be there to stamp my passport?"

Still nothing from Pavel.

"I am quite serious," Jones said. "I need to know whether we have to pass through an immigration barrier. To show documents. Because"—and here he smiled in a way that Zula would have found charming had she known nothing else about him—"you see, I'm afraid that my British passport has been quite misplaced. As has her American one." He nodded Zula's way.

"If you want to know *normal*," Pavel said, "then, *normally*, I would file a flight plan to the destination city. Also passenger manifest. If the destination is in same country, then obviously there is no need to deal with immigration. If destination is in other country, then you should get passport stamped on way out."

"But the sort of bloke who flies about on a private jet is too busy to stand in line to get his passport stamped, isn't he?" Jones said.

"Frequently, yes. Depends on country. Depends also on type of airport."

"Say more."

"Some places, there is no FBO—"

"Come again?"

"Fixed base operator. Special terminal for private jets."

"Ah, thank you for the clarification."

"If is no FBO, you stand in line with everyone else at emigration."

"And if there is an FBO?"

"Then many times it is handled on plane. You go direct to FBO. Get on plane. Wait for official. Official comes on plane. Counts passengers. Checks against manifest. Stamps passports. Goes away. Plane takes off."

"Is this one of those places that has an FBO?"

"Of course, our plane is parked at FBO since three days."

"How did you get into the country in the first place? Did all of you have visas?"

"No," Pavel said.

Zula provided a brief explanation of how they had done it.

Jones considered it. "What if you filed a flight plan for some city in China and then flew to Islamabad instead?"

"Some places it would be noticed. Other places—" Another shrug.

"All right then. What's out there in the general direction of Islamabad?"

"Dushanbe?"

"I'm talking about airports in China—so that there'd be no need for an international flight plan."

"I see."

"Do correct me if I'm wrong. But I think you just got done telling me that, if you file a flight plan for another city in China, the immigration officials need not come on board to stamp passports."

"Generally correct."

"So where would that be?"

"Urumqi?" Pavel guessed.

"How about Kashgar?"

"Yes, of course, Kashgar."

"Never been there," Jones admitted, "but I've been close to it, on the Tajikistan side."

Pavel waited.

Jones smiled. "I daresay that if we file a flight plan to Kashgar, and then overshoot it, and dogleg down to Islamabad, no one will notice. Or if they do, it'll be too late for them to take any action."

"It is only few hundred kilometers from western border of China," Pavel allowed.

"Then I suggest that you get out your laptop, or whatever it is that you use, and make it happen," Jones said.

"Departure when?"

Jones looked at Pavel as if he were a blithering idiot. "Departure *now*. We are driving directly to the airport *from here*."

"Is not possible."

"What do you mean is not possible?"

"Rules in China are that flight plan must be filed six hours in advance."

"Hmm."

"Used to be three to six *days*, is much easier now."

They drove in silence for a few minutes as Jones considered it. Then, just as Zula was beginning to wonder if he had nodded off, he spoke up again: "You were sitting in your hotel waiting for Ivanov."

"Yes," Pavel said.

"If Ivanov had come to the hotel, as planned, today, and picked you up, you'd have gone to the FBO and boarded the jet and then what?"

"We would have flown to Calgary."

"What's in Calgary?"

"Fuel."

"So you're saying Calgary would be a mere refueling stop."

"Yes."

"What would the final destination be?"

"Toronto. Where we started."

"Why not fly directly to Toronto, then?"

"Great circles."

"I beg your pardon?"

Pavel sighed, then held his hands out in front of him as if gripping a globe about the size of a pumpkin. "You see—"

Jones interrupted: "I know what a bloody great circle route is."

"Okay, good. Is much easier to explain then."

"Then explain it."

"If you draw a great circle from here to Calgary, it passes up along the coast of China. South Korea. Sakhalin Island. Kamchatka. Then along the coast of Alaska and British Columbia for some distance. Then it cuts across the mountains and down into Calgary. All of this is a very commonly used air travel corridor, you understand? All of the jets between Asia and North America follow such a route. It does not pass over any sensitive areas. However. If you draw a great circle from here to Toronto, is totally different. It goes up across China. Then North Korea—very bad. Then a large part of Siberia that is definitely not a normal air traffic corridor. To get approval for such a flight plan is impossible. So we must follow the normal corridor until we are over western Canada. From there things get easier. But then we are so far from following a great circle route that it becomes necessary to refuel. Most efficient place to refuel is Calgary. That is where we filed the flight plan."

"You say it has already been filed?"

"Of course."

"You say 'of course,'" Jones said, working it out, "because of that six-hour delay you mentioned. Ivanov was a man in a hurry. He wanted to be ready to get out of here at a moment's notice. Which is a difficult thing for you to reconcile with the six-hour delay mandated by the Chinese government. So you had a flight plan all set up and ready to go in advance."

"This is what I do," Pavel said, "when I am waiting in hotel. My job."

"So it *would be* possible for you to go directly to the airport now and get on that plane and start flying in the general direction of Calgary *immediately.*"

"Not in general direction. Exact direction. But yes. No problem for us to get clearance for this."

"But that is obviously an international flight."

"Yes."

"So the immigration officials will want to come on board and stamp passports."

"Yes."

"Did you say something about a passenger manifest before?"

"Yes. We supply such document to officials."

Jones winced. "I'll bet it has the names of a lot of Russians on it. That would be unfortunate, since all those Russians except for one are now dead."

"Not a problem," Pavel said. "Passenger manifest is separate document from flight plan. Goes to different officials. Does not have to be filed in advance. You see, manifest changes all the time. Someone changes plans at last minute, decides not to fly, or someone is added. We file manifest immediately before departure."

"All right," Jones said, "so the worst case is that by playing some games with the manifest we might be able to take off and head in the direction of Canada."

"Maybe. Depends on officials and passports."

Jones waved this off. "We'll worry about that later. Right now I want to talk about flight plans."

Another long period of him thinking.

"I would *really* like to make a stopover in Islamabad," he concluded. "Let's go over the steps involved in the Kashgar gambit."

"This depends on what you want to do after Islamabad. If you just want to abandon plane there, then your plan would work fine. We could file a plan for Kashgar and divert to Islamabad and no one could stop us."

"Ah, but Islamabad is not the final destination," Jones said. "After a brief stopover there, I would most definitely want to fly somewhere else."

"What is brief?"

"A day or two. Maybe three."

Pavel considered it. "Could work," he finally allowed.

But Pavel had been thinking about it for so long that he had attracted the attention, and then the suspicion, of Jones, who now drew something out of his pocket and reached down and did something that made Pavel jerk uncomfortably. Zula looked down and saw a passing streetlight reflected in the polished metal of a blade, which Jones was holding against the side of Pavel's hand. "You can fly an airplane with nine fingers, can't you?" Jones asked.

Pavel said nothing.

Jones went on: "I'm just a bit concerned. Until now, you've been answering my questions without hesitation, which is how I like it. But the last answer was a long time in coming. Which makes me think that you are starting to play chess with me. I don't want you playing chess. You need to understand that the success of my endeavors, and your personal survival, are now one and the same thing, Pavel. It would be a terrible shame, and a very bad thing for you personally, if I found out, a few days from now, that you had done something clever and fucked me. Fucked me, that is, by exploiting some technical nicety in the world of private jet travel that I can't possibly know about."

"I was thinking about consequences of staying in Islamabad for several days," Pavel allowed.

"And that is very good," Jones returned, "provided you share all those thoughts with me honestly."

"It is a modern airport. You cannot simply fly a jet airplane into such an airport and park it like a car at a shopping mall. It will be noticed. Records will be made of it."

"I encourage you to keep alerting me to such complications," Jones said. "But the fact of its being noticed might not be a bad thing. After Islamabad, I only need to make one more flight."

"To where?"

"Almost any major city in the United States of America would do. I rather have my heart set on Vegas, but I'm prepared to be flexible."

Khalid, who had been sitting quietly in the front seat this entire time, now made a remark over his shoulder, entirely in Arabic, except for the words "Mall of America."

"My comrade makes an excellent point," Jones said, "which is that, if we don't have the range for Vegas, Minneapolis would be brilliant. That would be easier, right? Because farther north."

"Depends on great circles," Pavel said stolidly. "May I use laptop?"

Jones considered it. "This is going to take longer than I had hoped," he said. "We have a bit of business to attend to first. But after that, yes, you may use your laptop."

They arrived at the dock they'd used earlier. The boat had been loitering out in the channel but came in to meet them again.

The driver of the second taxi was ushered onto the boat at gunpoint, and his place behind the wheel was taken by the bomb vest wearer who'd been riding in his passenger seat. The trunks of both taxis were stuffed with cargo. The last two Middle Eastern–looking jihadists, who had been cooling their heels aboard the boat this entire time, climbed into the second taxi along with Sergei. The two taxis pulled back onto the ring road and proceeded to the airport and then to the private jet terminal—what Pavel had referred to as the FBO. Access to this was controlled by a gate with a security guard, but Pavel, in his pilot's uniform, seemed to know the right things to say, and so they were allowed to pull through and drive right up to the side of the jet. Jones and Zula and the two pilots went directly aboard while Jones's men, under the direction of Khalid, began loading gear from the taxis into the plane's cargo hold.

The interior of the jet had been cleaned and spruced up to the level that people who could afford to travel in this style would naturally expect, complete with flower arrangements, chocolates, and drinks in wee fridges. The wood-paneled interior gleamed softly under artfully designed halogen lights, and after the rigors of the last few days, the leather seats gave one the feeling of nestling in a giant baby's lap. Jones did not sit down right away but spent a few minutes walking up and down the length of the thing, alternating between awe, outrage at the sheer level of luxury, and cackling amusement.

He was up in the cockpit, ogling the state-of-the-art displays, when his phone rang. He checked the screen.

"Ah," he said, "the only thing that could possibly make this moment sweeter." He flipped it open, raised it to his head, and spoke in a delighted tone of voice. Zula didn't understand his Arabic, but she could guess what he was saying: "Hey, man, you'll never guess where I'm calling from!"

Then he spun on his heel and stepped back out of the cockpit, a look of astonishment on his face. He moved into the plane's open doorway, as if trying to get better reception. Switching to English, he demanded: "Who's this?"

"SOKOLOV," SAID THE Russian into the phone. "We met earlier when I killed half of your men. Ten minutes ago I killed the other half. Now there is just you, motherfucker. A fucking piece of shit who uses phone to send better men to die. Then runs away to airport."

Olivia, watching interestedly from the opposite side of the boat, wondered how Sokolov knew that the person he was talking to was at the airport. Maybe he could hear jet engines in the background. As it happened, they were just now swinging around the northern end of Xiamen, where the airport was; and realizing this, Sokolov started looking around, just in time to see a 747 come rocketing up off the tarmac and angle up into the night sky. Sokolov's arm jerked toward the place where he had stashed the submachine gun and Olivia shrank down lower on the fiberglass bench, anticipating with a mixture of terror and awe and delight that he might pick up the weapon and try to bring down the plane. But then his rational mind seemed to get that particular bad idea under control. "Running away like fucking rat while brave men are dead in city below. What a fine man you are, Jones. Still have Zula? Are you being nice to her? I suggest you be nice to that girl, Jones, because when I find you, I will kill you fast if you have treated her well and if you have harmed her in any way, I will do it in a way that is not so nice. I have sent a thousand jihadists to heaven to be with their virgins, but you I am going to send to hell." And he hung up the phone and threw it into the sea.

Now there was a few minutes' lull during which Olivia tried to review in her mind all that had happened today. Perhaps this was a mistake. She suspected that men like Sokolov did not devote much time to this sort of introspection. It seemed, though, to be part of her academic/analytical programming, which was all that she really had to offer to this ad hoc partnership. Sokolov's talents and abilities had been on conspicuous display during the last half hour and had made Olivia feel, from time to time, like a side of beef that he was obligated to carry around with him as part of a hazing ritual (though she had saved his life by hiring the water taxi and then talking its driver into driving it to a place where Sokolov could jump on board, and she wondered whether Sokolov understood that fact). There was a temptation to just dissolve her will into his and look on while he did stuff. But the kinds of things Sokolov was extremely good at were useful in specific, limited circumstances that, in normal life, simply didn't arise that often. A time was coming when he would be as helpless and as dependent on her as she had been on him during the escape from the mysterious assailants on Gulangyu.

Speaking of which, she had seen but not quite believed what he had done to those men. It had to have been real, since they had fallen down and not gotten up. But for the moment it was just a pattern of sensory impressions painted on the screen of her memory, not soaked in yet, not understood, not even granted the dignity of having really happened.

Sokolov's phone had GPS and maps, which he had been watching with interest ever since they had left the airport in their wake. They were roaring down Xunjianggang, a strait about three kilometers wide that ran between Xiamen Island and the northeastern district of Xiang'an. It was aimed like a gun at a dark island about ten kilometers away: Kinmen, the "Quemoy" of Cold War propaganda. Though she had never discussed it with Sokolov—they had not discussed *anything* really—it was obviously their destination. For another minute or so they'd be in easy reach of PRC territory to both port and starboard, and so anyone tracking their bogey on radar—supposing they were even discernible against the clutter of giant containerships and small working vessels—would see their movements as unexceptional. But once they debouched from the Xunjianggang into the more open seas, they would come in for all sorts of attention, since there was nothing in that direction that wasn't Taiwanese.

The shore to port—the mainland suburb of Xiang'an—was less built up than the Xiamen shoreline to starboard, and it extended farther to the east and therefore brought them closer to Kinmen. Sokolov said he wanted to track along that shore, and Olivia relayed that instruction to the driver.

Sokolov now moved up and sat in the seat next to the driver. He had his bag with him. He turned on his flashlight and put it in his mouth like a cigar, then shone it down into the bag, which he had zipped open. It was stuffed with a miscellany of junk, but the predominant color was the queasy red/magenta of large-denomination Chinese currency. Much of it was crumpled loose bills, but Sokolov stirred through these and then pulled out a wrapped brick about one inch thick. He let the light shine on it and glanced up at the driver to make sure that it had been noticed. Then he pulled out a plastic sack—a white laundry bag blazoned with the logo of a luxury hotel. He dropped the money stack into this and then carefully rolled it up into a neat packet.

Then he looked at Olivia. "Please drive boat," he said.

"I am going to drive the boat now, please get out of the way," she said to the driver in Mandarin.

He was slow to move.

"I have been watching this man for a while now, and I don't think he hurts people who are not his enemies," she said. "I think it is going to turn out all right."

Watching Sokolov carefully, the driver stood up and vacated the controls. Olivia clambered over the back of his seat and settled in behind the wheel. She picked out a light in the distance and used it to steer by for the time being.

They had exited the strait and come into the fetch of broad ocean waves that were bashing the little boat around. Keeping his center of gravity low, the driver took a seat on one of the benches. Sokolov dropped to his knees in front of the man and thrust the wrapped money-brick at him, then pantomimed a gesture of shoving it into his pants. The driver, whose mood was shifting from abject fear to extreme curiosity, complied. Sokolov then handed him a life vest and made gestures indicating that he should put it on. "Closer to beach please," he said to Olivia, and she steered the boat in closer to some tidal flats that, since the tide was low, reached out a great distance from the shore of Xiang'an and dully reflected its pink-orange lights.

The driver put the life vest on and snapped its strap around his waist. Sokolov, inspecting him like a squad leader checking a trooper's parachute, tugged at the strap and gave it a yank to make it tighter. He then held up his fist, thumb and pinky akimbo, to his jaw. The driver, understanding this universal gesture, reached into his pocket and produced his phone, which Sokolov confiscated.

Then Sokolov made a little gesture with his head and stared expectantly into the driver's eyes.

The driver did not want to go but soon reached a place where he would rather drown than suffer that gaze anymore, so he reached up, pinched his nose, and vaulted over the side.

"Kinmen," Sokolov said. "Top speed."

Olivia swung the wheel hard to starboard and pushed the throttle lever forward as far as it would go. The engine howled, the boat surged forward into the darkness and began pounding across perpendicular wave crests. Sokolov moved up and sat next to Olivia and flipped switches on the dashboard until he found the one that turned off the running lights.

Then he spent a while trying to read the tiny screen of his phone despite the jarring impacts of the hull on the waves.

"Taiwan military will shoot at boat?"

"Maybe."

"You swim?" he shouted.

"Very well," she said.

"Better than me," he admitted. He crawled back and returned a few moments later with a pair of life vests, one of which he placed across her lap. He put one on, then took the wheel while she did the same.

She had gotten into the habit of thinking of Kinmen as being farther away than it really was, because of the military and political barrier; but crossing into its waters took so little time that they were barely able to get themselves strapped into the life vests before they closed to within swimming range. Sokolov experimented with taking his hands off the wheel and found that the boat was rigged in such a way that it would basically keep going straight.

And so at some point, much earlier than she felt ready for, he suddenly nodded at her and she—since it seemed to be expected of her—nodded back. Sokolov spun the wheel around and got the boat aimed toward open water, then took her hand and got one foot up on the gunwale. With his free hand he picked up the bag he had earlier rigged with a life vest. Another exchange of nods and then they went over the side.

The water was warm by the standards of oceans, but her immediate and powerful impression was of being cold. Then she got over it and started swimming.

They seemed to be in the lee of Kinmen. The waves were not as powerful, but they came from many directions and clashed into sudden pyramids of water that just as suddenly collapsed. She just tried to get a bearing on the moon and to keep swimming at all costs. The main thing that she was worried about was being swept out to sea by some unseen current, and indeed when she pulled her head up out of the soup to look at the lights of the island, she got the impression that they were moving sideways at least as fast as forward. She was not much of a nautical person but was enough of a Brit to have absorbed, by osmosis, certain terminology such as "slack water," and she was pretty sure that this was the condition that obtained now: the tide was low, neither incoming nor outgoing, and the water wasn't moving much. But huge rivers emptied into the sea around Xiamen and their flow had to divert around these islands, and there must be currents associated with that.

After passing through a few emotional swings, she came to the realization that they simply hadn't been in the water for that long, she hadn't given this nearly enough time, and just had to keep swimming. She and Sokolov both resorted to the sidestroke and the backstroke when they got fatigued. In the latter position, she watched a helicopter make several passes over the waters nearer to Kinmen than to Xiang'an, probing the seas with a spotlight, and reckoned that the boat must have been noticed on radar. It was natural to feel vulnerable and obvious and exposed. But she tried to imagine what it must be like to be sitting in the cockpit of that chopper with many square miles of dark water beneath and only a needle-thin spotlight beam. If she were a shipwrecked mariner, desperately hoping to be seen and rescued, she would despair of ever being found; so why should she concern herself about it?

Sokolov doffed his life vest and disappeared beneath the water for perhaps half a minute, then resurfaced gasping for breath. "Maybe three meters," he said, apparently giving an estimate of the water's depth. She liked the sound of that.

It was perhaps half an hour later that something grazed her fingertip during a deep stroke, and she realized that she could stand up. Probably could have stood up a while ago.

A moment later she was looking down into the astonished face of Sokolov, who was doing the backstroke. He got his legs under him, then gestured with one hand in a way that clearly meant *Get down, idiot!*

They squatted with only their heads above the water and surveyed the shore ahead of them as best they could in the faint light of the moon. Olivia had the impression of gazing through the broken teeth of a ruined comb.

"Tank traps," Sokolov said. "To stop amphibious landing. No problem for us. As long as we stay out of tank."

Humor. She was too shattered to appreciate it. When she had

made it back to her apartment after the gun battle and explosion, an improvised bandage on her head, she'd planned to crawl into bed and not come out for a long time. With some effort, and with Sokolov's help, she had goaded herself into making a trip out to the *wangba* to send out a distress call. Adrenaline had propelled her through the last hour's events. But as soon as she felt land under her feet and exited swim-or-die mode, the bottom fell out. She dropped to all fours in the shallow surf, not just as a way of keeping her head down but because she did not think herself capable of standing up. Like a prehistoric fish dragging itself up onto the strand by its floppy, vestigial fins, she followed Sokolov up into shallower and shallower water and finally onto a sandy beach guarded by a vast defensive works: a double picket line of spikes angled toward the mainland. As became clear when they got closer, each spike was a railroad rail that had been planted in a massive tub of concrete and cut off at an angle to make it sharp. A fat eye bolt projected from the top of each cement block, which was apparently how they'd been lifted from a barge and dropped into place, one by one, during some long-forgotten Cold War defensive buildup. Rust had thinned the steel, barnacles thickened and furred it. The blocks had settled into diverse angles. Sokolov was right that this was no impediment to them.

A couple of meters beyond the tank traps they encountered a region of hexagonal blocks that had been sunk into the sand, apparently to stop beach erosion; these formed a strip of wildly uneven pavement maybe ten meters wide, running as far as they could see (which was not very far) in either direction.

Beyond that it was just a beach like any other. Alive, though, under her hands. For thousands of tiny crabs, no larger than beetles, were scuttling about, going in and out of pencil-sized holes in the sand.

Sokolov hissed at her, and she realized she'd gone too far. She flattened herself against the sand, glad of an opportunity to lie down and stop moving, even if she were wet and cold. He was a few meters behind her, draped over the dark hexagonal blocks, invisible even to Olivia who knew where he was.

They lay there for a few minutes, waiting and watching. Olivia had begun to shiver upon coming out of the water and was now doing so convulsively. Her teeth literally chattered together for the first time since she'd been four years old. She opened her mouth wider to stop the noise.

Moonlight and long, careful looking revealed that the beach gave way, above them, to a long glacis of what she could only assume was sandy soil, held together by low foliage dotted with yellow flowers. Above that loomed a row of crude, blocky structures that were completely dark. A few hundred meters away from them to the left was a small white blockhouse raised above the beach and supporting an array of antennas and lights. But the lights were not aimed in their direction, and it did not seem likely that they would be visible, supposing anyone was even looking for them.

When he was satisfied, Sokolov slithered down out of the jumble of hex-blocks and crawled on his elbows until he had reached the boundary between bare sand and the carpet of yellow flowers. Olivia followed him as he passed under a steel cable that had been stretched along a row of posts.

"Stay back," he said. She stopped short of the cable.

He did a push-up, drew his knees up under him so that he was sitting on his haunches, pulled out his knife, and stuck it into the sand. After a few moments he drew it out, inched forward, and stuck it in again. Then again. Then again. "Follow in my steps," he said.

"What are you doing?"

"Read sign," he suggested.

Pulling herself up into a squat, she looked straight into a red triangle, suspended from the cable, sporting a skull and crossbones and reading DANGER MINES.

She wondered if a mine could be detonated by shivering.

Sokolov had been dragging the bag behind him. As neither it nor she were yet in the minefield, she duckwalked over to it, opened it up, and pulled out a sweater she'd stuffed into it earlier. This was damp, but because it was wool it would be warm anyway. She pulled it on and immediately felt somewhat better. Then she slung the bag over her knees and inched forward under the cable, stepping in Sokolov's wake.

They now spent what felt like an hour creeping across the minefield.

"Mines very old," Sokolov mentioned, after a while.

"Oh good," she said.

"No, bad. More dangerous."

So much for conversation.

Perhaps sensing Olivia's mood, Sokolov essayed the following: "You could perhaps make phone call?"

"My phone is gone." She'd lost it during the swim.

"Good."

She agreed. The PSB would be all over her apartment by now. They'd find nothing there that was the least bit incriminating, in and of itself: just the personal effects of one Meng Anlan. But a little bit of footwork would make it obvious that Meng Anlan was a fabricated person. They would discover that she had leased a space directly across the street from the epicenter of this morning's excitement, and she would become the object of intense interest, and they would be listening in on all activity involving her phone number. Not that it mattered quite as much now that she and Sokolov had made it to a different country, but sending up a flare didn't seem like the right next step.

"Look in CamelBak," Sokolov suggested.

She had not seen one of these before, but she figured out how to get it open and discovered a couple of phones inside of it. "Which one should I use?" she asked.

"Little Samsung."

"Whose is it?"

"No one's. Bought yesterday. Never used."

She turned it on and observed a weak signal. Apparently it had succeeded in picking up a cell tower across the strait in Xiang'an.

She thumbed out a brief text message and sent it to a number she had memorized but never used before. Part of her training. What to do when everything turned to shit. Don't use any of the usual email addresses or phone numbers. Don't use your own phone. Send a message to this special number, the oh shit number, which you have memorized and which you rememorize every single day before you go to bed and when you wake up in the morning. Use the oh shit number once and never use it again.

The message said HAVE GONE TO HAICANG TO CHECK IN ON GRAND-MOTHER; and it meant *I am on Kinmen and my cover is blown.*

Then she shut the phone off.

Half an hour later they made it out the other side of the mine-field and entered into a more lushly vegetated zone of aloe and flowering cacti growing around old half-buried concrete boxes that she reckoned were bunkers, made to withstand artillery from the mainland. The floors of these were scattered with military debris, but they were otherwise stripped, with rusty, bent brackets dangling from the walls where wiring harnesses had been ripped out. Beyond them, the foliage rose up in a wall, completely untamed. Sokolov ventured into it and came out trailing huge volumes of green vines that he had cut and torn out of the tangles. They piled it on the concrete floor of the bunker until it came up to midthigh. They put on all the clothes they had and then lay down next to each other and pulled more of the foliage on top of them to make a sort of comforter. Sokolov put his arms around Olivia and she burrowed her head into his chest. They interlocked their legs. A quarter of an hour later, she stopped shivering. Then she was gone into a sleep so profound that it verged on death.

JONES HADN'T SAID much during his mysterious phone conversation. He had mostly listened. Whatever he had listened to had really changed his mood. There had been no gloating since then. Instead he had demanded, peevishly and insistently, that they move on to business.

And business, of course, was exactly what this plane was designed for. The main cabin could be configured as a meeting room; a data projector had been concealed in the aft bulkhead and could throw an image up the length of the cabin to a retractable screen at the forward end. So they pulled down all of the window shades and got Pavel's laptop connected to the projector.

The two jihadists who had been driving the taxis drove them away from the plane and apparently parked them in the parking lot of the FBO and then walked back to come aboard. So there were now nine people aboard the jet: the pilots Pavel and Sergei, Abdallah Jones, Zula, Khalid, and four whom Zula thought of as soldiers: the one who had spent the entire day driving the stolen taxi around Xiamen, the second bomb vest wearer from the Hyatt, and two more who had only recently been collected from the boat. The latter two seemed younger, more junior. Certainly more obsequious. In any case, these four soldiers all crammed themselves into the private sleeping cabin at the back of the plane, leaving the main cabin available for this meeting. Zula was not invited to it, but neither was she told to move, and indeed, short of locking her into the lavatory, they could not really have put her anywhere else.

And so, shortly before midnight, they resumed the earlier conversation about flight plans and great circle routes, this time with visual aids. For Pavel had a piece of software that could calculate and plot such routes on a map of the world, and he now used it to shape possible courses from Islamabad to various cities in the United States.

The jet's maximum range was 10,700 kilometers. The pilots wanted Jones to understand that some distance had to be subtracted from that figure to allow for unexpected headwinds and for maneuvering in the vicinity of the airports at either end of the flight plan.

The picture that emerged was that Islamabad was basically located on the opposite side of the world from Denver, and so a great circle route plotted directly over the North Pole would take the jet to the Mile High City, if it had that much range, which it didn't. In fact, if they were to fly the jet on that heading, it would be lucky to reach as far south as Regina, Saskatchewan. More likely, they'd have to set down in Saskatoon for refueling.

This kind of talk seemed to put Abdallah Jones into a foul mood. After some angry pacing up and down the aisle, he appeared to calm himself down and then divulged something to the pilots. Or at least he *acted* as if he were divulging something. Zula had seen enough of the man and his wiles, by this point, to doubt that he ever sincerely divulged anything.

All he wanted, he claimed, was to get the jet across the forty-ninth parallel and land it on U.S. soil. It didn't have to be a big airport. As a matter of fact, he much preferred a smaller, more rural destination. The ideal landing site would be an unmanned dirt strip out in the middle of nowhere. His only goal was to smuggle a few of his brethren into the United States where they could disappear into the general population and then await future orders. But if the jet could only make it as far as Saskatoon, this wouldn't work.

There followed a lot more screwing around with maps and

detailed calculations. The gist of it was that the middle of the United States was actually the worst part to aim for. Because of the mathematics of the great circle calculations, it turned out that the northeastern and northwestern corners of the Lower Forty-Eight were significantly closer to Islamabad—close enough that the jet might be able to reach them without the need to refuel.

They then began to plot and examine great circle routes from Islamabad to various New England and Northwest destinations. Jones was fascinated by the differences between these. The route from Islamabad to Boston, for example, passed over the western Russian heartland, Finland, Sweden, Norway, threaded between Iceland and Greenland, then passed over the Canadian maritime provinces and Maine. Each of these places seemed to give rise to its own set of misgivings in Jones's mind. The route to Seattle, on the other hand, cut across the least populated swath of Siberia, traversed the Arctic Ocean, made landfall again in Canada's extreme northwest, and followed the mountainous wilderness of the Yukon and western British Columbia before crossing the U.S. border only a few miles from its destination. The trajectory was an unbroken swath of the most desolate and unpopulated places on the globe. A small diversion to one side or the other would bring the jet down in the wilderness of Washington's Olympic Peninsula, or the mountains or deserts of eastern Washington State.

Once this was understood, there was no question in Jones's mind as to how they would proceed.

"When we get to Islamabad," he said, "we'll file a flight plan from there to Boeing Field in Seattle. We can reach it without the need to refuel. I like this idea because it's not going to arouse any suspicion in the minds of the authorities; Boeing Field is where you departed from the last time you left the United States."

"But if you land there—" Pavel began.

"—we'll be arrested, obviously, by Homeland Security," Jones said. "But we're not actually going to land there. We're going to divert at the last minute and land out in the middle of nowhere and scatter. So you'll need to reserve enough fuel for that."

"You want to get from Islamabad to Seattle without refueling?" Pavel asked.

"Is that not the entire point of this exercise?"

"We have been plotting great circle routes," Pavel told him. "This is not the same thing as a flight plan."

"I understand that," Jones said.

"You cannot simply fly on a great circle trajectory across Russia," Pavel said, astonished that Jones would not already know this. He directed their attention at the red arc that his software had plotted northward from Islamabad, bisecting Siberia on its way to the high Arctic. "There is no such air traffic corridor. The Russian Air Force would shoot us down as soon as we crossed the border. This cannot be done."

"Crap," Jones said. "Crap crap crap." He thought about it for a while. "Can we somehow divert around Russian airspace?"

"I can tell you right now that if we try to get to the U.S. from Islamabad without passing over Russia, we will have to go by an indirect route, and we will not have enough fuel," Pavel said.

"Then we should fly from Islamabad to somewhere else," Jones suggested, "such as Hong Kong, and refuel there, and then proceed along the usual corridor."

"What is so important about Islamabad?" Pavel asked.

"That," Jones said, "is none of your concern. You just need to fly the plane."

Pavel corrected him: "You need *us* to fly the plane." And he exchanged a look with Sergei, who nodded. During the discussion, the two pilots had occasionally broken into Russian for short private conversations, and it now seemed as though they had been talking about other things than just great circle routes. "It is fun to think about Islamabad and flying here, flying there, all over the world, but right now you are stuck in Xiamen FOB and we are the only ones who can get you out."

Jones sighed. "I had hoped that I could avoid being so blunt," he said, "but the deal is that, if you don't file the new flight plan and get us to Islamabad, we will kill you."

"In Islamabad," Pavel continued, perfectly unruffled by the threat, "you have protection from officials that you can bribe, and you have connection to your friends who live in Waziristan, Afghanistan, Yemen. Surely you can find one or two comrades who know how to fly a plane. You intend to kill us there and then use your own pilots afterward."

Jones looked as if he were about to deny this, but Pavel held up a hand to stop him. "Don't," he said. "Is ridiculous. You have got something very bad that you want to pick up in Islamabad. It's totally obvious. You have a nuclear bomb, or some germs, or something. And your plan is to place this on the jet and then deliver this to some American city. You will crash the plane into a building or something and blow up the city, or poison it, or spread some plague. And everyone on that plane will die, one way or the other. It is ridiculous. You must think that Sergei and I are stupid. We are not. We understand. Obviously we are dead men no matter what. And so we have agreed that you should kill us now. Go ahead. Kill us now, and then figure out some way to get your asses out of China."

Jones actually considered it for a while. Either that, or he was simply waiting until his temper was under control.

Finally he said, "Surely you have some counterproposal? Other than immediate, summary execution?"

"We can fly you out of here," Pavel said, "as soon as we can make a plan that guarantees to keep us alive." He exchanged a look with Sergei and then nodded at Zula. "Us, and the girl."

It was the first time that Zula's presence had been acknowledged at all, and she was strangely grateful for it. Jones's reaction was a little bit odd: ashamed and defensive. Similar to the way he had looked at the conclusion of that phone conversation in the door of the airplane.

Why would he be reacting that way?

Probably, she realized, because he *had* intended to kill her. Or at least had not really been caring whether she lived or died. Which was apparently just fine with Jones as long as it was a private matter. But when people drew it to his attention, he didn't like it.

"All right," Jones said, "since this is all about *you* lot now, and what *you* want, have you considered what is going to happen to you if you get arrested in China? Because you are responsible for having flown some rather bad chaps into the country, aren't you?"

"Obviously we would like to get out of China," Pavel allowed.

"And soon, I should think, since before long they'll be pulling Ivanov's corpse out of that basement and figuring out who he is, and then they'll connect him to this plane, which is just *sitting* here, with us in it."

"Agreed."

"We can't get out on an international flight plan because the immigration officials will want to come on board and check our documents," Jones said.

"Yes."

"So we have no choice but to file a domestic flight plan, wait for six hours, and then, for lack of a better word, cheat," Jones said. "In the sense that we can't actually land the plane at another airport in China or we're dead. So we have to divert from that plan, don't we, and get to some place where we have some chance of surviving."

"Something like that, yes," Pavel said.

Jones spread his hands out wide. "Enlighten me, then," he said. "How can we do that?"

Pavel considered it and discussed it in Russian with Sergei. Zula realized, after a point, that the discussion would go on for a little while, so she got up and used the toilet. Once she'd sat down, she realized that she had sort of ducked past the mirror without looking at it, as if her own reflection were a deeply estranged frenemy with whom she could not possibly make eye contact. So she forced herself to turn her head to the side—for in this high-luxe bathroom, the entire bulkhead was a mirror—and look herself in the eye. She was startled to discover none other than Zula Forthrast looking right back at her. Same old girl. A little bit the worse for wear, of course. Older. Not in the sense of old-old, but rather of having seen more during her life. She wondered what others saw in her; why Csongor, of all people, would go to such lengths to protect her. Why Jones was keeping her around. Why Pavel and Sergei had decided—spontaneously, she thought—to include her in the deal they were striking with Jones. But most of all, why Yuxia would do what she had done. Not nose-diving the van into the boat, for that had been an accident, but ramming the taxi on the pier and taking the airbag right in her face.

Because in a sense the only worthy thing Zula had done all day had been to try to help the hackers upstairs. And Yuxia had not seen that. Neither had "Manu" and the other hackers—the beneficiaries. Only Csongor. But maybe he had told the story to the others?

Or maybe none of it had been that rational. Maybe Yuxia didn't know about the SOS with the fuse. Maybe this was all down to some supernatural effect, such as grace, that flowed through people's lives even if they didn't understand why.

Which led her to a moment, there on the toilet, looking sideways into the mirror, of something akin to prayer. Her earlier thoughts on this topic still stood and so it was not a hands-together, now-I-lay-me-down-to-sleep sort of prayer. More of an act of will. Because if there were some power like grace, like the Force, or Providence, or what-have-you, that had been at work in the world today, then it needed to find its way now to the boat where Qian Yuxia was being held captive and it needed to go one step further in whatever mysterious chain of transactions was playing out here. And if it were possible for a conscious effort of will on Zula's part to make that happen, then she was willing it to happen.

She pulled herself together, splashed water on her face, and came back out into the jet's cabin. Pavel and Sergei were still talking in Russian, panning and zooming around digital maps of the world on the big screen. Jones was on his feet, phone clamped to his head, finger in his ear, looking dumbfounded. He talked in Arabic for a while, his voice and his eyes dull. Not defeated, she thought, so much as completely exhausted. Then he hung up.

"You're free to go," he said, looking Zula in the eye.

"What are you talking about?" she said. Because he could show a kind of mean sarcasm, and this seemed like one of those times.

"The boat," he said, "with your girlfriend on it . . ."

"Yes?"

"Has disappeared."

"What do you mean?"

"Dis. Appeared. Without a trace. Not responding on the wireless. Not answering phone calls. No sign of wreckage. No distress call."

"You know this how?"

"Those lads who dropped us off at the dock," Jones said. "They went back to the island, and there is simply nothing there."

Zula badly wanted to show how happy she felt, but certain matters had to be settled first. "Why are you telling me this?"

"Because it doesn't matter," Jones said. "You're going to stay on the plane anyway."

"You think so?"

"Yes. Because you're in China illegally. You're associated with people who have committed more murders in a few days than Xiamen normally sees in a year. And there is only one way for you to get out of this country, and it's to stay on this plane"—Jones extended a hand, in a sarcastic flourish, toward Pavel and Sergei—"with your white knights."

The racial gibe was not lost on Zula. "I'd take knights of any color," she said. Substituting wordplay for action. Because she knew Jones was right. This plane was her only way out.

"Okay," Pavel announced, "we have plan for getting out."

"How's it going to work?"

"File flight plan now," Pavel said. "Explain later."

"File it then," Jones said. "I'm going to take a bloody nap."

Day 5

A jittery and sometimes outrageous series of misunderstandings led, none too soon, to the following arrangement aboard the fishing boat: Mohammed (for that was the name of the pilot who had been left at the vessel's controls) remained at his station, steering the vessel on a course that would, he claimed, get them out of Chinese territorial waters as quickly as possible without arousing any suspicion that they might be heading for Kinmen. Csongor, armed with the pistol, remained on the bridge with him, to keep an eye on the little GPS screen and make sure he didn't do anything tricky. Meanwhile Yuxia and Marlon, accompanied by the cook, who gave his name as Batu, went up and down the length of the vessel, just trying to get a basic sense of where stuff was and how things worked. Batu's name, appearance, and accent made it obvious to Marlon and Yuxia that he was a member of the Mongolian ethnic minority, and it could be guessed that he had been drawn to Heartless Island as an economic migrant. He had accepted the sudden takeover of his vessel by armed strangers with remarkable serenity and seemed to prefer the new management to the old.

They began by climbing to the flat roof of the superstructure, directly above the bridge. A large white fiberglass capsule was mounted here. Batu said that it contained an inflatable life raft. The hushed voice, cringing posture, and sidelong glances with which he explained this as much as told them that this was some kind of statutory requirement, and hence the epicenter of an elaborate complex of rules, penalties, inspectors, and bribes. Other than that, the vessel didn't have anything in the way of a dinghy. It seemed that, in the harbors it frequented, small craft were so numerous that one could be hailed in a few moments with a wave of the hand, and so there was no need to carry one aboard. A disk-shaped enclosure mounted high up on a steel mast was said to contain a radar antenna, but Batu was skeptical about its being in any kind of working order. The same mast sported mount points for additional lights and antennas, only some of which were used. Marlon looked warily at the things that seemed to be antennas, and Yuxia could see his eyes tracing the cables down the mast and into fittings in the roof of the bridge.

One level below that was the bridge, and the narrow catwalk that surrounded it. Bracketed to the catwalk's railing, directly in front of the bridge's forward-facing windows, were two life preservers, formerly bright orange but sun faded to a sort of bilious caramel hue. Threadbare green-and-white poly ropes had been laced through the railing's stanchions and used to support one edge of a plastic tarp that had been stretched across much of the foredeck; it had been under its cover, Yuxia explained, that much work had earlier been done packing and prepping whatever sort of cargo the vessel had been carrying. If the vessel were being used for its intended purpose, this was where the fishermen would work with the nets, pull the fish on board, and do whatever else it was that fishermen did.

They made a cursory tour of the cabins, mostly just checking for dangerous and/or useful articles, and then ventured belowdecks. Things looked different here from when Yuxia had been put through her ordeal. Then, the place had seemed larger, since its contents had been neatly stowed in boxes. But in the hours since, some kind of frenzied unpacking had taken place, and junk was strewn all over, interspersed with slashed-open cardboard boxes. Yuxia remarked on this, which led to a conversation with Marlon in which she explained, as curtly as she could, what had happened in this place during the afternoon. Yuxia held up her wrists to show the damage inflicted by the ropes as she had struggled. This seemed to affect Marlon deeply, and she was astonished to see tears beginning to come into his eyes.

They decided to get out of there and sort through the junk later.

Batu conducted them to the galley and, as a sort of automatic reflex, got busy making tea. Watching Batu fill a kettle from a spigot, Marlon asked him about the ship's supply of potable water, and Batu assured him that there was plenty—hundreds of liters—in its storage tanks; he prided himself on keeping these topped up at all times. "Water is cheap—not like fuel!"

This prompted the obvious question—which, as soon as it was asked, made Marlon feel foolish for not having asked it before—of how much fuel the vessel might have on board.

Batu didn't know the answer, but the look on his face made it obvious that this could be a serious problem.

"I'm going to go up to the bridge and look at the fuel gauge," Marlon said, getting to his feet, but Batu waved him off, saying that there was no such thing on a boat like this; fuel level was estimated by dipping a stick into the tank and seeing how much of it came out wet. So Marlon sat down again, and he and Yuxia waited while the tea was prepared.

"That guy on the bridge," Marlon said. "Mohammed. Was he one of the ones who—"

"Who what?"

"Did that thing to you?"

"Yes," Yuxia said curtly.

That seemed to dampen the conversation, and so they began to sip at their tea, sitting back in their chairs a little. Yuxia's eyes fell closed, then slowly opened. "I am going down," she said in English. Switching back into Mandarin, she asked Batu to pour a larger cup of tea—not just a thimble—so that she could take it to Csongor, who might be having a hard time staying awake up there. Batu rummaged through his bungee-corded cabinets until he found a mug. Meanwhile Marlon asked him, "When was the last time they bought fuel?"

Batu had a difficult time remembering. "They brought out a couple of drums last week," he said. He set the mug on the table, holding it down with one hand, since the boat had begun to roll as they got away from the coast and into higher seas offshore. He poured the mug full, pausing once to refill the little teapot.

"A couple of *drums*," Marlon repeated. "That can't be very much for a vessel this size."

Batu made no comment.

"There's really no reason to fill the tanks unless you're going out on a long sea voyage," Marlon said, working through the logic of it. "And this thing didn't go out on long voyages, did it?"

"Not recently," Batu said, meaning *not since it became the floating headquarters of a terrorist cell.*

Yuxia tossed back the last of her tea-thimble, then picked up Csongor's mug and got carefully to her feet, stepping across the galley in a wide-based gait to compensate for the vessel's movement beneath her. She passed out through the hatch and began ascending the stairs that led up to the bridge.

"What do you think the range of this boat is? Enough to make Taiwan?" Marlon asked.

Batu shrugged, as if to say, *You're asking a Mongolian about boats?*

From above, they heard Yuxia asking a question, then flashing into anger and speaking in a raised voice. There was a massive thud, as of a body hitting the deck, and the crash of a shattering mug. Csongor cried out in a blurry voice. There was more crashing and banging, and then a series of very loud pops.

CSONGOR HAD KNOWN it was a mistake to sit down. The only way he could remain awake was by staying on his feet. But when the boat worked its way out into the big swells, and the deck began to heave and bank underneath him, he finally had the excuse he needed. Until then he'd been standing in the middle of the bridge, looking out the front windows over Mohammed's shoulders. But along the aft bulkhead was a short bench that had been calling to Csongor for a while. Like everything else of consequence, it was welded to the deck; these people used welders as carpenters used nail guns. Csongor backed away from Mohammed, moving slowly as he compensated for the pitching of the deck, and let himself down to the bench.

Yuxia's voice was in his ears, nearby. Odd, since Yuxia was not on the bridge.

Another oddity: Csongor's eyes were closed. He didn't remember allowing that to happen. He got them open and discovered Yuxia just inside the hatchway with a mug in her hand. She was looking across the bridge at Mohammed, whose posture seemed to indicate that he had just spun around to gaze at Yuxia in astonishment.

Astonishment, and fear.

Mohammed was holding something in one hand: a gray plastic microphone, connected by a coiling black cord to a small electronic box mounted on brackets above the control panel. This had been dark when Csongor's eyes had closed, but glowing LEDs shone out of it now.

The pilot was talking on the two-way radio, or getting ready to.

Csongor reached for the pistol in his back waistband while using his other hand to push himself up off the bench. He noticed that his feet were slow to move. At about the same time, Yuxia was throwing the contents of the mug at Mohammed.

Csongor's body weight was now well forward, but his feet still hadn't budged. They were somehow trapped. He realized he was going to fall flat on his face. His hands came forward instinctively to stop his fall. One of these had achieved a partial grip on the pistol. His ankles were getting torqued in a bad way and he was going down in an extremely awkward fashion, and at some risk of taking Yuxia down with him. He came to rest painfully and in discrete sections, like a big tree breaking into chunks as it fell over in a windstorm. The pistol went sliding across the deck. He could not reach it. Mohammed was crying out in rage and wiping hot tea out of his face. Yuxia hurled the empty mug at him, then dropped to her knees and clawed the pistol up off the deck. She aimed it in his approximate direction and pulled the trigger, but nothing happened because the safety was on.

"Yuxia, give it to me!" Csongor cried, with a beckoning motion, and Yuxia turned and slid the pistol across the deck to him.

Mohammed had recovered enough to reel in the microphone, which had been dangling at the end of its cord. He lifted it to his mouth.

Csongor flicked off the pistol's safety and cocked the hammer. He aimed it at Mohammed, but his view along the sights was blocked abruptly by Yuxia, who threw herself across the bridge and made a grab at the microphone. There was a few moments' wrestling match. Mohammed shoved her away, but she dragged him back with her. This happened to give Csongor a clear shot at the radio. One bullet through that box would put an end to the pilot's broadcasting ambitions. Csongor drew a bead on it.

Mohammed reached up and grabbed a flashlight bracketed above the bridge windows and clocked Yuxia in the head with it and she fell backward to the deck, clutching her face and crying out, more in anger than pain. He raised the mike to his mouth again. Csongor squeezed the trigger and went deaf. The pistol snapped his hands back. A hole appeared in the window above the radio, and cracks networked across the glass. Csongor fired a second time and made another hole in the glass, a few centimeters from the first. He lowered his aim just a hair and pulled the trigger three times in succession.

Mohammed had frozen for a moment after the first bullet had been fired. Then, looking across the bridge to see Csongor aiming in roughly his direction, he assumed that Csongor was aiming at him and decided to get out of there. His way out happened to take him directly in front of the radio and so at least one of Csongor's three-round fusillade struck him in the thorax. He went down immediately.

MARLON RAN HALFWAY up the steps and then paused, wondering if he was about to get his head blown off. But then he heard Csongor's voice, and then Yuxia's, and so he climbed up the rest of the way and entered the bridge.

Csongor was lying on the deck, twisted around in an awkward position. Yuxia was sitting in one corner, holding one hand over a bloody laceration on the side of her head and weeping. Mohammed was lying on the deck surrounded by a lot of blood, still gripping a radio microphone. Its cable, now stretched nearly straight, ran almost vertically up from the microphone to a small box mounted to the top of the ship's control panel. The box had been perforated by a bullet, and the window above it sported two more bullet holes and a fan of cracks.

The mike slipped out of Mohammed's relaxing hand and jumped up and bobbed on the end of its cord like a yo-yo.

Csongor did something with the pistol to make it safe, then drew himself back toward a crude bench at the back of the bridge.

Something was amiss with his ankles. Stepping over to get a better look, Marlon saw that both had been lashed to the bench's supporting angle irons by several turns of electrical wire. A reel and a pair of wire cutters rested on the deck nearby.

Marlon fetched the wire cutters and tossed them to Csongor, who went to work snipping himself loose. "I went to sleep," Csongor said. "He wanted to use the radio—to call his friends, I suppose. But he must have been afraid that I would wake up from the sound of his voice. He couldn't attack me because he didn't have any weapons. So he did this. He knew that he would have time to send out a distress call before I could get loose and come stop him. But Yuxia showed up."

"Did she show up in time?" Marlon asked.

"I don't know," Csongor said, "but I think she did."

Marlon, stepping over a broad ribbon of blood that had found a path across the deck, went to Yuxia. A flashlight was rolling around on the floor with blood on it. Controlling a strong feeling of disgust, Marlon picked this up and turned it on. Yuxia was fully conscious but very upset. "Let me see it," Marlon said. "Let me see it."

"It's fine," she said. "It's nothing."

"Let me have a look."

"It's fine."

"I want to see."

He finally understood that she did not care about the wound on her head and just wanted some comfort. He did not feel it was appropriate, just yet, to put his arms around her, or anything like that, and so he reached down with his free hand and rested it on top of her shoulder and gave it a squeeze. "I'll get some ice from Batu," he said.

"Thank you," she said in a tiny voice, like a child. Not like her.

Marlon got up and passed out through the hatch to the gangway just in time to hear a loud scraping and bumping noise from above. Batu was not down in the galley, where Marlon had left him; he was up on the roof of the bridge. Thumping footsteps suggested he had now gone into rapid motion.

A large white fiberglass capsule rolled and banged down from above, nearly catching Marlon in the head. It splashed down into the sea alongside the ship.

Batu was above him, perched like a cat on the railing. A faded orange life preserver was slung over one shoulder. "There's more water down in the hold," he said, "in plastic drums. Use it sparingly. You don't know how long you'll be drifting." And then he sprang from the railing and plummeted about five meters into the water.

The white capsule was bobbing in the ship's wake now. It had fallen open, and something big and orange was blooming on the water: the life raft, inflating automatically. Batu, belly down on his life preserver, was dog-paddling toward it.

Marlon went back into the bridge and stepped gingerly across a remarkably wide pool of blood to the control panel, where he pulled back on the lever that controlled engine speed. Then he swung the wheel around so that the vessel was pointed due east, toward Taiwan.

"Why did you slow us down?" Yuxia asked.

"To conserve fuel," Marlon said.

"You think we're going to run out?" Csongor asked.

"Batu does."

FINE, SEE YOU AT ELEVEN.

This was the text message that Olivia found on the phone when she turned it on while peeing in a thicket at 6:49 the next morning. It was a response to last night's HAVE GONE TO HAICANG TO CHECK IN ON GRANDMOTHER.

Actually the whole island was a thicket; she had found an especially dense part of it for this purpose and checked for snakes and bugs before dropping into a squat.

She and whoever was at the other end of this connection— presumably a handler in London, routed through an untraceable connection to the instant messaging network—were using a completely open and public channel to pass messages in the clear. They had to be coy. HAVE GONE TO HAICANG TO CHECK IN ON GRANDMOTHER was written in a prearranged code, using characters calculated not to arouse the interest of the PSB. She spent a minute or two squatting there and puzzling over SEE YOU AT ELEVEN before realizing that it probably meant exactly what it said. Kinmen was connected to Taiwan by a long-range ferry, used mostly by mainland Chinese tourists, and by regular air service. The ferry wasn't much use in these circumstances, but it would be easy for the British embassy in Taipei to send someone out on a commercial flight to meet with her at the airport.

This was a virgin phone with no traceable connections to Olivia or anyone else, and she was on Taiwanese soil anyway, and so she felt no hesitation about using its Internet connection to surf for airline schedules. It seemed that a flight from Taipei was coming in to the local terminal at 10:45.

She returned to the bunker to find it empty. But after a bit of looking around, she found Sokolov standing near the edge of the minefield, gazing up the length of the beach. Back toward Xiamen. He checked his watch, then turned to look at her.

She reached out with one hand and found his. He did not snatch it out of her grasp, and so she pulled on it and began walking.

She led him back to the bunker. Still not looking at him, she got up on tiptoe and steadied herself with an elbow crooked around the back of his neck and carefully touched her lips to his. Her heart beating hard, more from fear than from passion, since she was afraid that he would turn away, reject her. That his not taking advantage of her last night was simple lack of interest. But his hand came around against the small of her back, and it became clear that he had only been waiting for her permission.

She had wondered how it would feel having sex on the bed of matted vines, which had become flattened during the night, but it ended up not being an issue since they did it standing up, with her back against the wall. After months of hard work in Xiamen, characterized by nothing but loneliness and anxiety, it felt so good that it brought her almost to a kind of weeping and grateful hysteria. For his part, Sokolov, after he had let her gently down, tumbled back onto the floor, slapping it with both hands, and collapsed as if crucified under the beam of sunlight coming in through the door.

"I am no longer poor fucked Russian," he stated, after ten minutes or so.

"I've got news for you, honey—"

"No. Alluding to yesterday's conversation. In flat."

"Well, you're out of China at least," she said, "but—"

"No. I have useful information," he said.

"Really."

"Yes."

"What kind of useful information?" *Your spy Olivia Halifax-Lin is a helpless slut.*

"Information that can help your employer find Abdallah Jones," he said.

"Aha."

Sokolov got his legs under him, rolled up to a low squatting position. He reached for his trousers, which like many other items of clothing had gone ballistic a few minutes ago and remained sprawled in their positions of impact. He stood up and pulled them on. "Because," he said, "you have message, no?"

"How'd you guess?"

"Heard phone vibrate."

He politely looked the other way as she stood up and mounted a search-and-rescue operation for her clothes. Crisscrossing the floor of the bunker on filthy, bare feet, she thought about the amount of effort and money she devoted, every day, to personal grooming, and how completely beside the point all of it had been during her last two sexual liaisons.

"Why did you wait until now to tell me?" she asked.

"Because until now we were fucking," he pointed out.

"No, I mean why didn't you tell me last night?"

"Because last night I did not have information."

"How could you possibly have obtained any information this morning?"

"This must remain a mystery," he said, "for now." But he glanced upward as he said it, as if the answer were written in the sky above the Xunjianggang.

ZULA FELT THE jet thumping and bucking underneath her and startled awake, fearful/hopeful that they had come under some sort of police assault. But in the first moments after she opened her eyes, she was astonished to see buildings and parked planes streaking past them, and bright sunlight glancing in low over the sea.

She was on a plane, or something else that moved pretty damned fast. She didn't even know whether it was landing or taking off.

How could the sun be up? Hours must have passed while she was slumbering.

The fact that she was lying in a king-sized bed did nothing to help her get her bearings.

The ground was definitely falling away.

First things first: she was on a plane. The plane was taking off. It was something like seven or eight in the morning. The bed was in a private cabin in the plane's tail—Ivanov's cabin. She could smell his hair oil on the pillow.

The city dropping away from her was Xiamen. Looking out the windows on the right side, she could see, only a mile or two away, the big inlet where Csongor had confronted Jones yesterday. Yuxia's van and a crushed taxi lay somewhere on its bottom. And a few miles beyond that in the same direction, on the other side of a strait, was the larger of the two Taiwanese islands; she was sighting straight down the length of a beach, prickly with tank traps and shingled with hexagonal blocks.

Not long after it cleared the runway, the jet banked hard to the right, giving her an even better view of the Taiwanese island—Kinmen—as they swung around it in a broad arc, rapidly gaining altitude, and began to head south. Another turn, a few minutes later, brought them on to what she guessed was a southwesterly course. Nothing but ocean was now visible on the plane's left, but on the right was the whole Chinese mainland, slowly getting farther away from them.

She must have fallen asleep in her seat at about one in the morning, when they were still talking of flight plans. Jones or someone must have carried her into the aft cabin and deposited her on the bed. The four "soldiers" who'd been cooling their heels in here must have been evicted and sent up to the main cabin. These men might stone her to death sooner or later, but in the meantime they would go to great lengths to preserve her modesty.

She remembered one figure very clearly: six hours. That was the amount of time it took to file a domestic flight plan in China. Pavel must have filed such a plan at about the time she'd gone to sleep, and they must have secured approval for takeoff only just now.

. . . .

THEY BEGAN TO consider how to arrange transportation to Kinmen's airport. Olivia used her mobile to pull up a map, from which they learned that they were all of about three thousand meters away from it.

Olivia was for going straight there. With a pensive and reluctant Sokolov in tow, she began to bushwhack inland. They passed quickly through what turned out to be a narrow belt of woods running parallel to the island's north shore and emerged into a flat agricultural countryside, gridded with farm lanes. A hamlet, consisting of a couple of dozen closely spaced buildings, was only a couple of hundred meters off to their right; they avoided this instinctively and sidetracked away from it until a somewhat larger hamlet came into view ahead of them. Then they began cutting south across the island and soon came upon a larger road that ran east-west, across their path. Nor did that make it unusual, since it seemed as though the island's centers of population were in its broad east and west ends, and the several roads joining them squeezed together through the island's narrow waist, which they were transecting: a rocky spine tufted with trees and studded at its summit with the geodesic domes of Cold War radar installations.

The place was decidedly more rural than the mainland looming over it a few miles across the water. Rural, anyway, by Chinese standards. At no point were they out of sight of a building. Bicyclists rode past in one and twos, looking at them curiously. Olivia was inclined to ignore them and trudge on, but Sokolov was obviously uncomfortable. After they had crossed over the second east-west road, he noticed a nearby watercourse, thick with trees, and led her down into it. It was a sort of drainage ditch or canalized creek that ran under the road through an arched stone culvert. Before disappearing completely into the foliage that lined its banks, Sokolov took a good look around at the flat countryside. They were completely exposed.

"Good meeting place," he mused.

Olivia realized that the openness of the landscape cut both ways: anyone could see them from a distance, but by the same token, no one could sneak up on them here.

Moving at less than half the speed they could have made in open country, they followed the watercourse south and uphill for almost a kilometer until what had been a narrow stripe of foliage broadened into a wood that merged with the dense quilt of trees spread over the island's central ridge.

They had used all their drinking water last night, and because of Sokolov's precautions they had not come anywhere near a place where they could buy more. "I'm getting really dehydrated," Olivia remarked at one point, and Sokolov turned and fixed her with a curious look. She decided not to complain about this anymore.

The airport's location was now obvious, since from this altitude they were able to watch a plane coming in for a landing and eventually disappearing behind the ridge. Olivia checked her watch and verified that this was the 10:45 flight from Taipei. Her good-girl instincts were telling her to get down there immediately so that she could impress her contact with her punctuality. Sokolov, however, was having none of this. "He will wait," he pointed out.

"But—"

"You are not here to make him have nice day."

Olivia could hardly deny that.

Sokolov took control of the phone, and Olivia watched over his shoulder for a few minutes as he consulted the map. He needed her linguistic help to locate the island's ferry terminal, where regularly scheduled boats came in from Xiamen. She found this at the island's southwestern tip. The most obvious route from it to the airport would be along the fattest of Kinmen's east-west roads, which they had not crossed yet, as it traversed the southern aspect of the ridge.

They were only about a kilometer—a thousand long strides—from the airport. And yet Sokolov insisted that they hike east—which was to say, away from the ferry terminal—through the worst terrain that he could find, darting over little mountain lanes as necessary, until they came in view of a major road intersection. Sokolov found a place where he could monitor this from cover and sent Olivia down alone, insisting that she wait for a bus so that she could enter the airport "like normal person." "See you at meeting place," he said.

"When?"

"When you are there."

Olivia made a final effort to get semipresentable, waited until the coast was clear, and then emerged from the trees, towing a four-meter-long strand of flowering vine behind one ankle until she kicked free of it. The bus arrived forty-five minutes later and took her on a journey that she could have done on foot in ten.

During the wait, she had the presence of mind to check the screen of the phone she'd been using and saw the message OUT RUN-NING ERRANDS—BUYING A WEDDING GIFT FOR NIECE—I THINK SHE WOULD LIKE NEW KITCHEN KNIFE.

"Kitchen knife" and "wedding gift" were not established code phrases. "Out running errands" seemed like a tipoff that her contact had decided to leave the airport and go elsewhere on the island. But Olivia had no way of guessing where. And the next bus that came along was headed to the airport whether she liked it or not. She climbed aboard. There were three seats available. She chose one on the aisle, not wanting to present her face in a window.

She was still puzzling over the message as the bus pulled up in front of the main terminal and disgorged twenty or so locals, mostly airport workers. As Olivia gazed into the terminal building, all her alarm bells went off at once. All the bad things that she'd been trained to look for were there on display, as if this were a spy training film, carefully designed to depict the worst imaginable scenario. Every bench, every snack bar, every security checkpoint had one or two loitering, watchful men, pretending to pay attention to their mobile phones. Some of them even had the temerity to wear sunglasses indoors.

She was seeing precisely what Sokolov had anticipated: the mainland PSB had packed this morning's ferry with plainclothes goons who had flooded the airport and any other place where Olivia and Sokolov might be likely to show up. They were keeping an eye out for any white male—but especially one traveling in the company of a Chinese female.

What those men might actually do, if they sighted the two together, was not clear to her. They had no power to arrest anyone on Taiwanese soil. Gunplay in a public space seemed unlikely. But they could take pictures and make a hell of a stink.

Olivia's contact, getting off the plane, must have seen the same thing and decided to get out of there.

She remained aboard the bus, sinking low in her seat and peering through the lower edge of a dirty window. A stocky, middle-aged man, wearing a bulky suit and mirrored shades, was leaning against an advertising case, smoking a cigarette and barking into a phone. As the bus began to pull away, she noted that the case was filled with kitchen cutlery—the traditional Chinese cleaver-shaped knives. Which jogged her memory, finally. The island was within artillery range of Xiamen, and during the late 1950s, half a million high-explosive shells had been lobbed into the place. Over the next two decades, these had been followed by five million shells packed with propaganda leaflets. Local artisans dug them out of the ground and used the steel to make cleavers.

THE KNIFE FACTORY was an ideal place for a meeting, if one was concerned about being bugged or overheard. It was just a large open industrial structure, filled in the middle with many thousands of old rusted shells, bullet shaped, melon sized. Workers cut them into cigarette-pack-sized chunks using abrasive-wheel saws that shrieked like condemned souls while hurling out showers of sparkling white hellfire. A mechanical hammer beat these out flat, and they were pushed into a roaring furnace for heat treating. Finally, the tempered slabs were ground into knives on stone wheels and finished on belt sanders that looked and sounded as though they could jerk a finger off without noticing. This business of making shells into cutlery was sufficiently unusual that the factory offered tours. Olivia joined a group of five others who had flown in from Taiwan to see the sights and buy knives.

Getting here had taken long enough that the implications of all those goons in the airport had begun to work themselves out in Olivia's mind. It was strongly in MI6's interest to get her safely back to London, and so she had few worries on that score. But Sokolov was a different matter. MI6 did not know, yet, how she had made her way to Kinmen. They didn't know about her travel buddy. Now that she had made it to Taiwanese soil, he was—to use dry British understatement—inconvenient. But if she were to ditch him here— which would be easy—she would have to spend the rest of her life avoiding mirrors.

If this had been the good old Cold War days, and Sokolov had been a possible defector, stuck behind the Iron Curtain, then they might have organized some sort of caper to smuggle him out to the

West and set him up with a new life. In exchange, he would supply them with priceless military intelligence. But from what little she'd been able to learn, Sokolov divided his time between Toronto, London, and Paris. And there was very little in his head that MI6 didn't already know.

"Meng Anlan?"

The speaker was Chinese, or at least Chinese-looking: a hefty man in his fifties wearing shaded glasses and dressed in the loud shirt of a tourist who didn't care if everyone knew that he was a tourist. He had been checking her out through those shades.

She just looked at him. If he had to ask . . .

"May I walk with you?" he asked. Or rather shouted, since they were standing two meters away from one of those abrasive-wheel saws.

It looked like the conversation was going to be in Fujianese-inflected Mandarin. Fine with her.

She fell in step beside him, and they began a slow procedure of falling farther and farther behind the main tour group. He was shouldering a bag. She hoped it might be full of food. But now was the wrong time to ask.

What the hell. "Do you have anything—a candy bar, a bag of peanuts." She had managed to buy water along the way but had not eaten in something close to twenty-four hours.

"Forgive me," he said in English, and rummaged in his bag. The best he could come up with was a bag of almonds.

As she was stuffing these into her mouth, he said: "Bit of a stink." His accent said that he had grown up in England.

"I'm sure lots of people are bloody furious," she said. "Can we sort that out later?"

"Hunger makes you irritable."

"It's not the hunger. It's the not-knowing-what's-going-to-happen."

"You're fine," he said. "You're safe. You're going home. But it has to be done with a decent respect for the feelings of that lot." He nodded toward the mainland, which they could not see from here, but which loomed psychologically over everything. "They watch the ferries. The terminals. If you were to just waltz on board a plane and fly off to Taipei, it would be construed as—"

"Rubbing their face in it."

"Apparently there were a *lot* of bodies."

"Four, to be exact."

"*In your flat,* yes. But there's the matter of the apartment building—or had you forgotten?"

"I remember it well."

"What in God's name happened there?"

"Long story. Not the place for it."

"We agree," the man said.

"Sorry if I'm focusing too much on narrowly practical matters," she said, "but how do I get aboard a plane without seeming to 'waltz on board'?"

"Use a fake name. Change your appearance. And travel with me."

"You think that will fool them?"

"Actually, I do," he said, "but even if it doesn't, the purpose is—"

"To show a decent respect for their feelings."

"Yes." The man—somehow they had skipped over any sort of formal introduction—drew closer to her and transferred his bag to her shoulder. "Clothes," he said. "Money. British passport. Not in your name, of course. A veritable cornucopia of feminine hygiene. A few odds and ends."

"A book or two?" she asked. "Or is that too much to hope for?"

He chortled. "You're already worried about what you're going to do on the flight to London?"

"Never mind. I'm sure I'll be drinking myself senseless."

He turned his attention to the knife tour for a few moments, admiring a trip-hammer that was using hydraulic power to beat the hell out of a piece of hot steel being moved around in it by a tong-brandishing worker, stripped from the waist up.

But then he turned back.

"There are, of course, many questions."

"Of course."

"You'll answer them all in due course."

"So I supposed."

"But there is one in particular that I have been directed to ask you, just in case something goes awry."

"In case I get sucked out of the airplane."

"Rogue wave. Meteor strike."

"All right. What is the one question?"

"Who killed all those men in your apartment?"

She made no answer.

"Was it you?"

She snorted.

"Because we didn't think you were that sort of spy."

"I'm not," she said. "It wasn't me."

"Well, who was it then?"

"You squandered your one question," she said, "on something that would take me a day and a half to answer properly."

"Do we need to *worry* about him—I'm going to make a wild supposition that a Y chromosome is involved and use the masculine pronoun—do we need to worry about him killing a great many *more* Chinese people on Chinese soil at any time in the near future?"

"Those probably weren't even Chinese people," she said, "but the answer is no. And by the way, he's not British."

"Good. Ah yes. One more thing."

"I thought you said there'd only be one more question."

"It's difficult to stop once I've got started."

"Go ahead, then."

"Where is Abdallah Jones?"

"He could be anywhere in the world," she said. "He was at an airport last night."

"Bloody shame."

"Isn't it."

"*An* airport? Odd phrasing."

Olivia shrugged.

"How do you know he was at *an* airport?"

This, then, was the moment. But she didn't know who this guy was. How much power he wielded, what he might, or might not, be able to do for her. Her sense was that he was just acting here as a conduit between her and someone else, someone back in London. "Mr. Y," she said.

"He of the chromosome?"

"Yes."

"I'm all ears."

"Mr. Y talked to Jones on the phone."

"That must have been an interesting conversation."

"Mr. Y's half of it certainly was. In any case, he knew, somehow, that Jones was at an airport. I would guess he heard jet engines in the background, or instructions on how to fasten a lap belt."

"But Mr. Y knows nothing further."

"Funny you should ask," Olivia said. "Mr. Y says he has more information now. Information that could be used to figure out where Jones went."

"And where is Mr. Y? Stuck in China?"

"Probably looking at you from behind a shrub. Don't look around, though."

"I shan't. Can't say how pleased I am that he understands the need to keep his head down."

"He has all sorts of talents."

This elicited a searching look from the man. Olivia, remembering this morning's activities in the bunker, felt her face getting warm and hoped that he would mistake it for the red heat of the case-hardening furnace glowing on her face. Hurrying on, she continued: "If you would like to make an arrangement with him to get him out of the country safely—which is what I recommend and advocate—then I can make a rendezvous with him and let him know where matters stand."

"Obviously, I don't have a ready-made passport for a gentleman of his description," the man said, "since I don't even know what his description *is*. Even if I did, for him to go to the airport today and get on a plane—"

"I understand. I get it."

"Speaking of passports—"

Olivia was nonplussed for a few moments, then took his meaning. She reached into her pocket and took out her Chinese passport. Her million-pound Meng Anlan passport. The man took it from her and, with a flip of the wrist, tossed it through the open maw of the forge. It exploded into flame before it had even touched the coals, and was fully consumed in a few moments.

"Farewell, Meng Anlan," he said. "Hello, whoever's name is on the passport in that bag. I've forgotten it already."

"Obviously, I'm pleased that you can get whoever I now am out of the country," Olivia said. "But I am disinclined to leave until I know what is to come of Mr. Y. I know you can't get a passport for him. But isn't there some way—"

The man was nodding. "We do, in fact, have a backup plan."

"Really?"

"Yes. We're good at such things. It is much more old-school. Very Cold War. Your friend might like it."

"Pocket submarine?"

"Even more old-school than that. There's a containership," he said. "You can actually see it from the north shore of the island. Riding at anchor. Panamanian registered. Filipino crewed. Taiwanese owned. It has been taking on cargo at Xunjianggang. In a few hours, it is departing for the Port of Long Beach. We'd hoped we could get something Sydney bound—which would be quicker—but it's more important to get you and your fantastically homicidal entourage out of here *today*, before the Chinese can get any more furious than they already are. So Long Beach it is. The great circle route takes two weeks or so."

"How do we make this work?"

"He will need to get out to the ship just after dark. This is something that you shall have to arrange yourself, preferably without leaving the waterfront district littered with corpses. As the ship is pulling out of the Xunjianggang, just starting to build up speed, it should be possible to pull up alongside it and come aboard. As long as you stay out of sight, it should be fine."

"Stay out of sight? Are you serious?"

"From the mainland. Come up on its starboard side."

"And they'll be ready for this?"

"They had better be," he said, "considering what we have paid them."

THEY SPENT THE remaining hours of darkness learning the physics of the boat, which was by no means easier given that they had all been awake for going on twenty-four hours now.

Mohammed's body had to be gotten rid of. This meant throwing it overboard, which seemed like a terrible and disgraceful thing, even notwithstanding the Osama bin Laden precedent. They avoided the matter for a little while, but it was simply out of the question that they could share the bridge with a dead man. So, after some dithering and stalling, Csongor went rummaging for something that was dense and heavy enough to pull the body down to the floor of the sea, but not too heavy for them to move, and that they didn't need for any other purpose. He ended up settling on a black steel box filled with 7.62 millimeter cartridges, of which there were several strewn around the cargo hold. He laid this across Mohammed's ankles and held them up in the air while Yuxia lashed it all together with surplus pallet wrap, and then he dragged Mohammed out of the bridge and jackknifed him over the railing. The corpse was poised there for a moment. Csongor felt it would be proper to say something. But he realized that there was nothing he knew how to say that Mohammed and his people would not find grievously sacrilegious. So he tumbled the body the rest of the way over. The shrink-wrapped lashings seemed to hold, and the corpse vanished.

With buckets of seawater, hauled up on a rope, they sluiced the steel floor of the bridge until it was no longer bloody. Learning their way around the vessel, they found scrub brushes and cleaning supplies and gave the place a more thorough washing down, swabbing blood splashes and fingerprints away from some of the bridge's vertical surfaces. Marlon pulled the ruined radio off its bracket and threw it into the sea, trailing its bloody microphone.

The user interface of the GPS was anything but intuitive, but Marlon figured out how to zoom and pan its tiny map. Standing around it in the dark, they began to get a sense of where they had been—for the GPS displayed the boat's past track—and where they were going. It seemed that, for the first hour of their voyage, Mohammed had steered them generally south along the coast, then changed to an easterly heading, making directly for Taiwan at a speed of something like ten knots. This had brought them to a point about thirty nautical miles off the Chinese coast, which was where the confrontation and shooting had taken place.

At that point, Marlon had dropped the vessel's speed to more like five knots. This was not the absolute slowest they could go, but if they went any slower they lost all sense that they were making forward progress, and the boat seemed to wallow and wander (an impression that could be confirmed by zooming in on the track and observing the way it staggered across the screen). The rudder, it seemed, was not capable of doing its job unless water was flowing across it with at least some minimum speed.

Marlon told Csongor about what Batu had said regarding the fuel gauge, or lack thereof, and so Csongor went down to the engine room and spent a while figuring out how the diesels worked, eventually identifying the fuel line and the pump that fed it. From this, plumbing led back through a bulkhead to a space mostly occupied by a pair of cylindrical tanks of impressive and reassuring size, each rather more than a meter in diameter and perhaps three meters long. Each had a fill pipe welded into its top. Csongor traced those up to a pair of fittings on the deck, which he guessed they would use whenever they pulled up to the nautical equivalent of a gas station. Shining his flashlight around that area, working out slowly in concentric circles, he finally found where they kept the dipstick: a piece of (inevitably) bamboo secured under the gunwale with bungee cords, ruled with felt-tip scribe marks and (to him) cryptic annotations. He called Yuxia down to help him interpret the marks, and then they opened one of the fuel fill hatches and shoved the bamboo pole down into it. Then he began pulling it out in a hand-over-hand movement, praying that he would feel cold wet diesel fuel on his palms. This did not happen, however, until the last few inches of the stick emerged. Yuxia read the nearest number marked on the pole. This meant nothing since they had no idea how quickly the diesels consumed fuel. But there was no ignoring the fact that it was the last number on the stick. "We just have to be scientific about this," Csongor said, and he marked the exact location of the fuel level and noted the time.

They then repeated the experiment with the other tank and found that it was completely dry. Csongor went down and fiddled with the valves and confirmed his suspicion that the empty tank had simply been disconnected from the system; the jihadists had only used the one tank, and they hadn't bothered to put more than a little bit of fuel in it, since all they ever did was putter around the harbor at the island.

Yuxia went back up to the bridge to keep Marlon company and make sure he didn't fall asleep on his feet, and Csongor devoted more time to sorting through the hold's contents. It did not take a Sherlock Holmes to read the recent history of this boat. It had been owned, and used hard, for many years by actual fishermen who had accumulated the sorts of gear and supplies one would expect: nets, lines, stackable plastic trays, polyethylene cutting boards, cutlery, whetstones, all manner of tools, paint, lubricants, solvents, and the like. As sustenance on longer voyages they had also laid in white plastic drums of what he took to be potable water, and sacks of rice, and a few other bulk food items such as soy sauce and cooking oil.

Then, at some point, the boat had been acquired by the jihadists, who had turned it into a floating arsenal: probably not enough to run a war, or even an insurrection, but plenty if the only goal was to blow up a building or plan a Mumbai-style shooting spree. So there was a pallet carrying a black steel drum of what Csongor guessed, by smell, to be fuel oil, and another carrying heavy woven-plastic sacks of white powder labeled as FERTILIZER: ammonium nitrate, presumably. Those two ingredients, mixed together, would make a high explosive that, as Csongor knew from reading the newspapers, could be detonated if one had some blasting caps handy. Csongor had no idea what a blasting cap even looked like, but he soon enough found out, as a carton of them had been helpfully stored on a shelf next to a translucent plastic box filled with phones, all of the same make and model.

Other boxes and pallets had been loaded with ammunition, mostly loose rifle cartridges in dark green or black steel boxes. But these had been raided and depleted earlier in the day as Jones and his men had made hasty preparations for their departure. He already knew that the guns were all missing, since they'd carefully searched for them earlier.

Supposing that they got picked up, eventually, by naval or coast guard vessels, he did not want to be found on board with such things, and so he began to consider how most easily to throw them overboard. Looking up, he noted that much of the foredeck consisted of a large cargo hatch, and so he went up and figured out how to get that open, and then spent a few minutes shining his flashlight over the equipment poised above it: cranes and winches and cables that had obviously been put there to facilitate moving things in and out of that hatch, if only he could figure out how to turn them on and use them. Some of the winches sported hand cranks, and so he reckoned he could get it done with muscle power if he had to. Now that he was out of China, he was finally getting a feel for how things were done in the country, and realizing that they had a genius for the kind of simple technology that required no instruction manuals. It was going to help them during this voyage.

Returning to the hold, he began sorting things out into three piles: trash (e.g., empty cardboard boxes), stuff they might be able to use (food), and dangerous or incriminating objects that needed to be jettisoned. He found four boxes, shrink-wrapped together, packed with instant ramen. Then three cartons of military rations: ready-made meals sealed in black pouches. Opening one of these just to see what it was, he discovered that he was ravenous and ate the whole thing standing up, stuffing the food into his mouth with filthy hands.

He found cigarettes and first aid kits and sorted those into the "keep" pile.

He was spending a lot of time maneuvering around the black steel drum of fuel oil, and finally—for perhaps the energy from the food was at last making its way to his brain—realized that the ship's engines would probably burn it. How to transfer it into the fuel tanks? He spun up a sort of harebrained idea that involved using the ship's crane to haul the drum up out of the hold and then somehow funnel its contents into the fuel filler abovedecks. With a little more consideration, though—for perhaps the Chinese way with technology was beginning to catch on with him—he realized that a siphon ought to work, since the ship's fuel tank was actually situated below the altitude of the fuel drum. So he scrounged a hose and got the thing rigged up and after some false starts and spills and spitting out of fuel oil was eventually able to get a siphon working that drained the drum over the course of the next half hour.

He then redipped the tank, hoping to observe a triumphant and dramatic rise in fuel level, and found that all of his labors had made no effect; in the amount of time it had taken him to do it, they'd burned as much as he'd added.

The eastern sky was growing lighter when he was finished with all of this. He went up to the bridge and found Yuxia up there alone, piloting the boat eastward and silently weeping. Marlon was apparently getting some sleep down in one of the cabins.

It required no great leap of imagination for Csongor to understand why Yuxia had tears running down her face. They had taken insane risks and devoted all their energy during the last few hours to the goal of escaping from China. Replaying the story in his memory, Csongor was unable to see any moment when they might have chosen differently. He and Marlon could not have abandoned Yuxia to whatever fate the jihadists might have had in mind for her. Once they had unexpectedly gotten control of this fishing boat, they'd had to do *something* with it, and getting out of the People's Republic of China had seemed like a good idea. In Csongor's mind, this happened to be synonymous with getting closer to home. Marlon didn't seem to be especially broken up by this hasty and unplanned departure from his native land; for him it must be an adventure of the sort that any young man would want to go on. Anyway, he needed to put some distance between himself and the apartment where he had created REAMDE, and this was an excellent way to accomplish that. But Yuxia had originally been drawn into this by nothing more than her desire to befriend some clueless Westerners she had observed wandering lost in the street. She had family back in Yongding, family who must be worried about her, and she must be asking herself now whether she would ever see them again.

Even if she did, how could she explain certain things to them? The fight on the dock? The torture in the bucket of seawater? Aiming a pistol at Mohammed and trying to shoot him?

No wonder she was a wreck.

"I'll do this," Csongor said. "Go get some food. Go to sleep."

She didn't move.

"It's going to be okay," he said. "We will sort it all out somehow. None of this was your fault. You will go back home someday."

This was meant to be comforting, but it sent Yuxia running out of the bridge with a wail escaping from her throat. Csongor followed her halfway, fearing that she was about to throw herself into the sea, but she thumped down the steel steps and ran into a cabin and slammed the door behind her.

Csongor continued steering the vessel into the sunrise while poking at the controls on the GPS unit, trying to get a sense of where they were. The morning light filtering into the front windows made it much easier to see around the bridge, and he noticed a stash of nautical charts that had escaped their notice in the darkness. He began to spread these out and to try to make sense of them. Most were large-scale depictions of complex features up and down the coast of China, and it was difficult for him to figure out their context. But one sheet caught his eye because it depicted a group of small islands, whose shapes jogged his memory; he'd seen them earlier while panning and zooming the GPS. They were identified, on the chart, as the Pescadores. They were out in the middle of the Straits of Taiwan, nearer to Taiwan than the mainland, but still a good fifty kilometers nearer to the boat's current position than the shore of Taiwan itself. And the GPS seemed to be saying that these islands lay rather close to the course that they'd been steering anyway. So it seemed obvious that they should be making for the Pescadores. Csongor altered his course accordingly, steering on a slightly more southerly heading. As best he could make out from the charts and the GPS, they would reach the island group at something like four o'clock this afternoon. Assuming, that is, that they did not run out of fuel along the way.

THE JET CONTINUED to follow what seemed to Zula like an unremarkable flight plan: slowly gaining altitude, following a straight course that took it away from the Chinese mainland and southward over the South China Sea. Some mountains poked their heads over the eastern horizon, and she guessed that these must be on Taiwan; but they rapidly fell away aft.

She could not make up her mind whether to open the door or remain cloistered back here. A strong instinct told her simply to hole up in the dark and private cocoon of Ivanov's cabin. But sooner or later she'd have to pee, and the jet only had one lavatory, which was forward.

As long as she was alone, it seemed sensible to take stock of what was at her disposal. Though small, the cabin had a little dresser. She checked the drawers and found nothing besides spare pillows and blankets. Ivanov would have taken all his stuff with him, of course. There was also a little flip-down desk, just large enough to support a laptop, and above this, built into the cabinetry, an appliance that was obviously an intercom. It had a row of pushbuttons, variously marked CABIN, COCKPIT, PA, and TALK. Next to them was a volume knob.

She turned the volume all the way down, then pressed the COCKPIT button. She found that if she pressed hard enough, it would lock down, causing an LED to illuminate, marked MONITOR. She then experimented with turning the volume up slowly and began to hear speech: Pavel and Sergei communicating with each other in Russian. Of which she, of course, knew not a word. But from time to time she would hear something she recognized, like "jumbo" or "Taipei." And occasionally a voice in English would burst out of their radio: air traffic controllers, she supposed, communicating with them, or with other planes, from towers on the mainland.

She did not really understand the purpose or the content of these transmissions, but after a few minutes she was able to pick out certain patterns. Many of the transmissions began with a Chinese-accented voice saying "Xiamen Center" followed by the name of an aircraft manufacturer such as "Boeing" or "Airbus" or "Gulf-stream" followed by a series of letters and numbers. Then a series of laconic instructions concerning altitude or heading or radio frequency. She reckoned that these transmissions all originated from an air traffic control center responsible for Xiamen's airspace and that they were bossing the pilots of various airplanes around. In almost all cases, another voice would respond directly, frequently speaking in an English or American or European accent, repeating the series of letters and numbers that seemed to be their plane's call sign, and then acknowledging the command with "Roger" followed by repeating the instructions out loud, presumably just to be sure that they'd gotten the details correctly. Occasionally, though, a transmission would go unacknowledged, and then Xiamen Center would have to repeat it; and if that failed, they might ask some other plane to relay the message. All of which was done with absolute, deadpan calm, which made sense given that it was what these people did all day, every day, just like bagging groceries or driving a truck. Twice she recognized the voice of Pavel acknowledging one of these transmissions, and in that way she learned the call sign of the plane on which she was a passenger, or rather a prisoner.

From time to time the instruction would be something like "Contact Hong Kong Center" or "Contact Taipei Center" followed by a series of digits, which she assumed must be a radio frequency.

Whereupon the pilot would identify himself and repeat the instructions as usual, and then sign off with a "Thank you" or "See ya" or "Out," never to be heard from again. At least on this channel. So she figured that these were outbound aircraft being handed off from one air traffic control center to another.

The time came when Xiamen Center called out the ID of the plane that Zula was on and issued the command transferring them to the responsibility of Hong Kong center. Pavel answered in the usual way and bid Xiamen Center adieu. Pavel and Sergei then exchanged a few sentences in Russian.

Suddenly the plane shifted beneath Zula's feet with a crispness that one never experienced on a commercial airliner. She had to throw out both hands to prevent herself from being thrown forward into the cabin door. The plane was not merely descending in the way that airliners did, that is, by throttling back on the engines and shedding altitude in level flight; it was actually pointed down, using the power of its engines to thrust itself directly toward the sea.

The steepness of the dive increased to the point where Zula was lying full-length on the cabin door. Through it she could hear luggage and junk flying around in the cabin, and sleepy men shouting in alarm, and wakeful ones laughing delightedly.

She had thought at first that this was just a temporary maneuver to shed some altitude, but as it went on and on, she came instead to the realization that Pavel and Sergei had decided to commit suicide by crashing the plane into the sea. This couldn't possibly go on any longer; her ears had popped three times.

But then, just as abruptly as it had gone into the dive, the plane pulled out of it, pressing her into the door, and then the corner between the door and the floor, and finally the floor itself with what felt like several Gs of acceleration as its nose came up and it returned to what seemed to be level flight. When she was able to move again, she peeled herself off the cabin floor, popped her head over the edge of the bed, and looked out a window to see blank white, and raindrops streaming across the glass. She elbow-crawled across the bed, put her face to the window, and looked down. The clouds and fog were too dense to allow her to see very much, but through an occasional gap, she was able to glimpse the gray surface of the ocean hurtling past no more than a hundred feet below.

The plane now banked and executed a course change: a long sweeping leftward turn.

There was a flat-screen TV mounted to the bulkhead above the foot of the bed. Zula had not tried turning it on yet, because she didn't like TV, but now it occurred to her that she was being foolish. So she turned it on and was presented with a menu of offerings including an onboard DVD player, a selection of video games, and "MAP." She chose the latter and was presented with a map of the South China Sea, apparently generated by exactly the same software that was used aboard commercial airliners, since the typefaces and the style of the presentation were familiar to anyone who had ever taken a long-haul airline flight. The place of origin had been programmed in as Xiamen, and the destination was Sanya Phoenix International Airport, which was at the southern tip of a huge elliptical island, comparable in size to Taiwan, that lay off China's southern coast. She was pretty sure that this was called Hainan Island and that it was part of the People's Republic of China. A flight plan had been drawn on the map, connecting Xiamen to Sanya by two straight legs of roughly equal length. The first leg headed south-southwest from Xiamen, roughly paralleling China's southern coast. Then it doglegged into a more westerly heading that took it straight to the southern tip of Hainan. Just guessing, it looked as though the course had been laid out to keep it well clear of the Hong Kong/Shenzhen/Macao/Guangdong area, which was right in the middle. Presumably the airspace around it was extraordinarily crowded and a good thing to avoid.

The plane's actual track and current position were also superimposed on the map, and these showed that the flight plan had been followed precisely until a few minutes ago. Now they were headed a little north of due east, on a track that looked as though it would take them just south of Taiwan.

None of this would have made sense to her had she not been party to last night's meeting in the main cabin. Obviously, they had never had any true intention of flying to Hainan Island. They had chosen that destination solely because it was a domestic flight and as such would not draw the attention of the immigration authorities at Xiamen's airport. For that, any destination in China would have sufficed. But Hainan seemed to have another advantage, which was that a flight to there from Xiamen would naturally pass over the ocean; and over the ocean it was possible to get away with tricks such as screaming along at wavetop level to evade radar.

She reckoned that they were playing some kind of game having to do with the workings of the air traffic control system. Though she had never studied such things in any detail, she knew in a vague way that radar had limited range and that the structure of the air traffic control system somehow reflected that fact; a country's airspace was divided into separate zones, each managed from a different control center with its own radar system. Airplanes in flight were handed off from one control center to the next as they made their way across the country. At some point they had stopped being the responsibility of the air traffic controllers in Xiamen and entered into a zone controlled from Hong Kong. Or perhaps by flying out over the ocean they had entered into a no-man's-land that was not monitored or controlled by any authority. At any rate, she guessed that they had, a few minutes ago, reached one of those edges or seams in the system. Pavel and Sergei had then bid farewell to the air traffic controllers in the zone that they were departing and had gone into the power dive before they showed up on the radar screen, and came to the attention, of any other controllers.

Where they were going now she could only conjecture. Once they cleared the southern cape of Taiwan, there was nothing out there but the Pacific Ocean. But she'd seen enough of great circle routes yesterday evening to understand that flying basically east, as they were doing now, was no way to get across it.

It took them about half an hour's flying time to get east of Taiwan. The plane then banked left again, and its little icon on the screen rotated around until it was pointed a little east of north. So it appeared that they were executing a large U-shaped maneuver around Taiwanese airspace.

The radio, which had been silent for a while, came alive again; apparently the pilots had switched over to a different frequency, and apparently that frequency was being used by Taipei Center, since all the transmissions now seemed to originate from there. Taipei Center seemed to be managing a large number of Boeings and Airbuses. These were helpfully identified, not only by their call signs, but by their origins or destinations as well, and so Zula got a clear impression of an extremely busy airport handling jumbo jets coming in from, or flying out to, far-flung destinations such as Los Angeles, Sydney, Tokyo, Toronto, and Chongqing.

It took rather less than an hour for the plane to clear the northern tip of Taiwan, which was where Taipei was located. It then executed a series of maneuvers and began a long steady ascent, which Zula was able to track using the helpful data screens thrown up every minute or so on the TV display. Presumably this would make the plane visible on radar, supposing that any radar stations were in range. But looking at the smaller-scale map that occasionally flashed up on the TV, Zula noted that they were in a region where planes from all over Southeast Asia and Australia might fly northward en route to Japan or Korea. So maybe they were hoping that their bogey would go unnoticed in all the clutter?

Her bladder could not stand any more waiting, and so she finally opened the door and stepped forward into the main cabin. This was crowded and smelled like sweaty men. The four soldiers were seated close together in the back. Two of them were napping, one was reading the Koran, and the fourth was intently focused on a laptop. At the cabin's forward end, a fold-down table had been deployed and was covered with large aeronautical charts on which Khalid and Abdallah Jones had apparently been tracking their progress. Khalid was there now, staring directly at Zula with hate, fascination, or both. Jones was not in evidence until she made her way up the aisle to the lavatory. She then discovered him lying on his back with his feet in the aisle and his head in the cockpit. He was staring almost vertically upward through the cockpit windows. Pavel and Sergei likewise were craning their necks in what seemed a most awkward manner, attending to something that seemed to be above and ahead of them.

Zula used the lavatory. When she emerged, all three men were still in the same positions, though Jones had now begun cackling with satisfaction.

Noticing Zula standing above him, he tucked his chin, rolled to his feet, and beckoned her forward. She squeezed past him into the cockpit, dropped to one knee, and looked up.

No more than a hundred feet above them was the underbelly of a 747.

So that explained why they had felt free to gain altitude. They had timed their flight plan so as to synchronize it with this jumbo's takeoff from Taipei airport. It was headed for (she guessed) Vancouver or San Francisco or some other West Coast destination. Cutting underneath it as it vectored northward from the tip of Taiwan, they had positioned themselves beneath it and gained altitude in lockstep with it, their bogey merging with its bogey on the radar screens of air traffic controllers and military installations up and down the eastern coast of Asia.

She helped herself to a can of Coke and a bag of chips from the plane's miniature galley, then made her way back aft through the cabin, sensing Khalid's eyes on her spine. Jones was now sitting across the table from him, and they were examining a chart of the northern Pacific.

The soldier with the laptop was sitting with his back to her. Looking over his shoulder she saw what was holding his attention so closely: he was playing Flight Simulator. Practicing a takeoff run from a rural landing strip.

She didn't want to make it obvious that she had noticed, so she kept walking without breaking stride and returned to the cabin, closing the door behind her.

THE MAN, WHO was calling himself George Chow, took Olivia into Jincheng: a fishing town at the island's western end. A couple of hotels had been thrown up near the ferry terminal, serving a mix of tourists and businessmen, and George Chow had taken a suite in one of them. He had apparently traveled here in the company of a Thai woman who had some talents as a hairdresser and a makeup artist. The woman had a bob haircut and wore conspicuous designer eyeglasses and dramatic makeup. She had spread newspapers on the floor and laid out her shears and combs and brushes. Olivia took a quick shower and then received a bob haircut exactly like that of the Thai woman, which, under any other circumstances, she'd have been afraid to take a risk on. The eyeglasses turned out to be fake—the lenses didn't do anything. Olivia ended up wearing them. The same makeup too. And a few minutes later, the same clothes. A PRC goon holding a blurry photograph of Meng Anlan would not immediately peg her as being the same person; and if anyone had noticed

George Chow coming off the Taipei flight this morning with the Thai woman on his arm, they'd assume that he was going home in the company of the same lady.

While all of this was happening, George Chow disappeared for about an hour, then came back saying that various matters had been arranged.

One of which, apparently, was a taxi, waiting for them in the alley just off the hotel's loading dock, piloted by a man who, Olivia inferred, had been well paid not to notice or talk about anything. They drove to the place in the middle of the island that Sokolov had identified, earlier, as a good meeting site. Its advantages now became plain. They stopped near the culvert, and George Chow pretended to take photographs of Olivia standing against the backdrop of the wooded ridge. Sokolov was able to remain perfectly hidden, even though only a few meters away, until a moment when the road was free of traffic. He then emerged and did a passable job of concealing his amusement at the new Olivia.

"You are fashion queen," Sokolov observed.

"For two hours. Once I get to Taipei, all of this is coming right off."

"Then where? London?"

"I assume so. Yes. Let's go."

"Where we go?" Sokolov asked, a bit sharply. He was much too worldly wise to imagine that he too would be whisked away to London.

"I'll explain in the car," Olivia said.

The weather had gradually turned gray as the day had worn on, and it was now becoming blustery, with a strong breeze out of the north. This suited their purposes, since it gave Sokolov an excuse to put on a rain slicker that they had purchased for him in Jincheng, and to wear it with the hood up. For now, though, he just slumped as far down as possible in the car's rear seat as George Chow explained what was about to happen. Meanwhile the driver took them west back into town, then north, running parallel to the island's western coast, until they had passed out of the built-up area (which took all of about thirty seconds) and into another of those strange places where no Chinese people went, apparently for the reason that no *other* Chinese people were there. This was a wild beach landscape similar to the one where they had crawled up out of the surf the night before. On higher ground above it, where the sand was held together by the root systems of sparse grass, a man and his son were flying a string of kites. Below, the beach stretched away for at least a kilometer. Olivia thought at first that it was studded with antitank obstacles even more thickly than the one she and Sokolov had washed up on. On closer examination, though, what she was looking at were thousands of concrete pillars that had been planted upright in the tidal zone to give shellfish something to grow on. Workers were picking their way among them. Each had a bamboo pole balanced over his or her shoulders, a basket or a bag dangling from each end. Seen through the thickening air of an incoming shower, it looked like a colossal cemetery: not a modern American cemetery with its polished and neatly arrayed monuments, but a thousand-year-old English churchyard crammed with worn gray stones tilting this way and that.

George Chow seemed to guess that they wanted privacy, or perhaps he felt a need to keep a watch over any traffic coming up the coast road, and so he remained in the taxi while Sokolov and Olivia walked out, trying to find salt water. For they had arrived early. The tide was low. Olivia left her purse in the car and went barefoot. Sokolov was now using a handheld GPS issued to him by George Chow, aiming for a waypoint marked on its screen.

When they reached a place where fog and mist had rendered them invisible from the road, they sat down on a couple of adjacent shellfish-pillars that had been picked clean by harvesters and watched the tide flow in. For they were only a hundred meters from the rendezvous point. Olivia wasn't wearing much, and Sokolov didn't have to ask to know that she was chilly, and so he sat upwind of her and wrapped his raincoat around her so that she could snuggle up under his arm.

"I think I'm going with you," she announced, after ten minutes had passed in silence.

"Not get on plane?" Sokolov said.

"No. Why should I? Nothing prevents me from just getting on this boat with you, and taking the freighter to Long Beach."

He considered it for a good long time. Long enough that she began to worry that she had screwed it all up. Sokolov had enjoyed this morning's rumpus in the bunker, and might enjoy more in the future, provided there was no commitment; but being stuck on a freighter with Olivia for two weeks was a hell of a lot of togetherness. What man wouldn't recoil, just a little, from that?

"Would make two weeks more interesting," he allowed. Then he switched over to Russian. "But this is not the correct choice for you to make."

Part of her wanted to say *Why not?* but, having affrighted him already, she did not want to get pouty on him now.

"What is the correct choice?"

"Find Jones," he said. "Figure out where he is. Tell me."

"But if we find him," she said, "he's dead, or captured, no matter what. We don't need you to kill him."

"I can dream," he said.

"So you want me to spend these two weeks looking for Jones?"

"Yes."

She peeled his arm from her shoulders and ducked out from beneath him, spinning off the pillar to land with both feet in the surf. It came up to her ankles, with waves sloshing over her calves.

"I'm sorry I have this shit on my face," she said. "Makes me feel stupid."

"Is fine," he said, averting his gaze shyly.

"Listen," she continued, "Jones's trail is cold. There's nothing I can do in the next two weeks to find him."

"Unless I give information."

"Yes. Which I think you are free to do now." She glanced over her shoulder, out into the mist that had descended over the strait between Kinmen and Xiamen. They could hear a boat out there, its motor putt-putting away at a low idle, occasionally throttling up as its driver followed the tide in toward them. "Your ride is here," she pointed out. "You've got what you wanted—safe passage out of China. Tell me what you know. I'll use it while you're on that freighter. When you get to L.A., call me."

"Tail number of Jones's airplane is as follows," Sokolov said, and then recited a string of letters and numbers. Olivia had him repeat it several times. "He took off from Xiamen at zero seven one three hours local time and headed south."

"Why do you think he would go south?"

"Maybe headed for Mindanao," Sokolov said, "where jihadists have camps. But I doubt it. Is probably a diversion. He will get over the ocean, drop to low altitude, disappear from radar, turn off transponder, and then do something else."

"That'll make it difficult to find him."

"Not so difficult. You will see," Sokolov said. He planted both hands on the pillar, pushed himself off, dropped into water that was now knee-deep, gazed over Olivia's shoulder, trying to get a fix on the boat's location from its sound. "Intelligence services will have tapes of radar. Now that you know when he took off, which direction he went, you can follow him on tapes for a little while. Get clues. Figure out where he might have gone. Narrow it down. And then"—he turned to look her right in the eye—"tell me where motherfucker went."

"If he's still alive in two weeks," Olivia said, "I'll tell you."

"Good-bye," he said. "I would give you kiss but do not want to damage professional makeup job."

"It's already damaged," she pointed out.

"Okay then." He wrapped his arms around her, gave her a long and quite thorough kiss. Then he spun her around and set her back down carefully on the top of the pillar, out of the inrushing surf. Turning his back on her immediately, he pulled the hood of the slicker up over his head, then began wading toward the sound of the boat that was idling somewhere out there in the fog. "Walk now or swim later," he warned her, as he was disappearing.

In spite of that good advice, Olivia waited, wanting to hear the sound of the boat's motor throttling up, taking him out of there.

What she heard instead was three short bursts of submachine-gun fire. Then a series of sporadic pops. Followed by the sound of the boat screaming away at top speed.

AFTER A COUPLE of hours, Marlon came up to the bridge with tea service and a couple of military ration packets. As they wolfed these down, Csongor showed Marlon the chart of the Pescadores and explained the course he had been following, which he hoped would bring them into the center of the island group in another few hours.

Csongor then went down into a cabin, climbed into a bed, and arranged himself carefully, since he knew that he would fall asleep instantly and not move until awakened.

The thing that awakened him was a sudden heaving and heeling of the vessel. Csongor was unable to tell the time, but he sensed that he had been asleep for some time; his bladder was quite full and he actually felt rested. But daylight was still coming in through the porthole. He got up and staggered into the head and relieved himself, then pushed the cabin door open against the forces of the wind and (because the boat was listing) gravity. Something hit him in the face that was halfway between rain and mist. He could not see more than a few hundred meters in any direction.

The engine was still running. That was good.

He went up to the bridge where Marlon was planted exactly where Csongor had last seen him. According to the digital clock on the bulkhead, it was a little past three in the afternoon, which meant that Marlon had been running the ship alone for seven hours. He turned his face away from the screen of the GPS to look at Csongor, who was unnerved by the look on his face: haggard, wrecked by exhaustion and stress. "This is the worst video game of all time," he said.

"Kind of a boring one," Csongor allowed.

"Boring," Marlon agreed, "and it doesn't work. The user interface sucks ass."

"What kinds of problems are you having?"

"It doesn't shoot where you aim."

It doesn't shoot where you aim. What could that mean? Csongor drew closer and looked at the display on the GPS, showing the track they'd been following during the time he'd been asleep. He was expecting to see a straight line aimed directly at the Pescadores. Instead, he saw a track that gradually curved south, then jogged northward, then curved south again. Marlon, it seemed, had been trying to steer a straight line for their destination, but something had been pushing the boat inexorably southward. Once he had noticed this, he had tried to correct for it by aiming the boat back the other way. But the net result was that they were actually a little bit south of the Pescadores' latitude at this point, perhaps ten kilometers away from the nearest of the islands, driving north-northeast in an effort to work their way back to it.

The mist had developed into rain, which was spattering the forward and port windows. "We are fighting the wind," Csongor said.

"Now, yes." Marlon said. "But that is new. Something else was bending us south."

"There must be a current in the strait," Csongor said.

"Current?"

"Like a river, a flow of water to the south."

"Fuck!" Marlon said. "We would have been there by now, if I had known."

"I thought it was like a car," Csongor said. "It goes where you point it."

"Well, it doesn't," Marlon said. "It goes where it wants."

The vibration that they'd been feeling in their feet the entire time they'd been aboard devolved into a series of coughs and chugs, then reestablished itself for a few moments, and then ceased.

"Out of gas," Csongor said.

"Game over," Marlon said.

"No," Csongor said. "Game continues. We just made it to the next level."

THE HANDLE OF the sledgehammer was bright yellow plastic, a detail preposterous to Richard, who had paced up and down the length of the relevant aisle at Home Depot trying to find something less painfully embarrassing until the department manager had insisted that he make his choice and leave—it was closing time, nine o'clock.

Standing on the doorstep of Zula's apartment at nine fifteen, gripping the ridiculous implement in brand-new, ergonomically designed work gloves (an impulse purchase, yanked from an aisle-end display as the manager had harried him toward the checkout counters), he realized why he didn't like it: the thing looked like a T'Rain sledgehammer. The realization struck him with such force that it queered his first blow, which caromed off Zula's doorjamb and nearly took out his knee. Then he got a grip, not only on the yellow plastic handle, but on himself, and swung again, getting his hips into it and striking true. The door practically exploded. Supposing Zula turned up all right, he would have a talk with her about the virtues of physical security and devote an afternoon to beefing up her door.

Or her replacement door, to be precise, since there wasn't much left of this one.

"You can turn down the stereo now," he said to James and Nicholas, who were five steps below him, cowering as one. James and Nicholas, a gay couple, lived downstairs of Zula and, as it turned out, had taken an almost parental interest in her welfare. Earlier today, back in the—ha!—long-forgotten hours when Richard had attempted to do this through official channels, they had assured Richard that he should get in touch with them at any time of the day or night if there were anything they could conceivably do to help him get to the bottom of Zula's disappearance. Three minutes ago, Richard had put their offer to the test on multiple levels, knocking them up late in the evening to see how they would feel about some really loud banging and splintering noises from upstairs. As it turned out they had been as good as their word and had even offered to turn up their stereo for a while in case that would help cover any noises that might disturb the nocturnal peace of neighboring properties. A foolish reverence for official cop procedures did not, apparently, go hand in hand with gayness.

And neither did having a missing niece.

"I'd really appreciate it if you could turn it down," Richard said, and then James and Nicholas understood that he just wanted them gone for a minute or two. They turned their backs on him and padded down the carpeted stairs. They occupied the first two floors, and Zula the third, of a big old house on Capitol Hill: Seattle's most oddly named neighborhood, in that Seattle was not a capital and had never been graced with anything resembling a capitol.

This bit—walking into the apartment and turning on the lights—was by far the worst for him, just because of what he was afraid he might find. Growing up on a farm had exposed him to a few sudden and unpleasant sights that he had never been able to clear from his memory. But Zula stabbed or strangled on the floor of her apartment would, he knew, be the last thing that came into his mind's eye at the moment of his death; and between now and then it would come to him unbidden at unforeseeable moments.

Instead all he found was a furious cat, yowling and stalking around an eviscerated cat food bag whose contents had spilled out onto the floor. A toilet drinker, by process of elimination. Other than that, all was orderly: no food left out, no lights left on. He checked her closet and noted that her winter coat wasn't there, saw no skis or any of the other stuff she'd brought on the trip to the Schloss. All of which confirmed the suspicion, which had been pretty strong to begin with, that she had never come back to her apartment after that trip.

This didn't mean she was alive, or even well. But it alleviated the most horrible of his fears. Whatever had happened to her couldn't be as bad as what he had been bracing himself for ten seconds ago.

And it gave him something to write home about. Or whatever the Facebook-era equivalent of that was.

He pulled out his phone, ignored four new text messages from his brother John, and thumbed one out: IN Z'S APT. ALL NORMAL.

John, still in Iowa, seemed to think that Richard would forget the seriousness of the situation without frequent reminders. The cursed invention of text messaging had removed any inhibitions John might ever have felt about what he still denominated "long-distance" telephone calls. On the upside, it enabled Richard to fire off status reports like this one without having to make personal contact.

To John's credit, though, he had, after a grumpy word or two from Richard, named himself the family's single point of contact with Seattle. So at least Richard didn't have to explain his progress, or lack thereof, to *everyone,* all the time. That chore was being handled by John, using a Facebook page.

Richard hadn't checked the page yet—it seemed wrong to be facebooking at a time like this—but he supposed it must contain a lot of detailed information about just what the Seattle Police Department were and were not willing to do in response to a missing persons report. For Richard had made what now seemed like an unrecoverable error by contacting the authorities first and filing same. This had placed him into a mode where all he could really do was nag the officer who was responsible for the case; and said officer had already explained that, unless there was evidence of an actual crime, there was not much they could do in the way of direct, proactive investigation.

He thumbed out a P.S.: Z NEVER CAME BACK HERE AFTER B.C.

John was back at him fifteen seconds later: CONTACTING RCMP. For Richard had already mentioned to him—and perhaps this had

been a mistake—that a winter couldn't go by in the Pacific Northwest without at least one car skidding off a mountain road somewhere and getting trapped in a snowbank, where the inhabitants, if
still alive, had to survive on snowmelt while awaiting a rescue that,
in many cases, never materialized. Snow was gone at lower elevations, but if Peter and Zula had decided to take the northern route,
across the Okanagans, they could be marooned off the apex of any
of a hundred hairpin mountain turns.

Next step: figure where that little fuck Peter lived, and take the
sledgehammer to his door.

Too bad Richard couldn't remember his last name.

NIGHT CAME OVER the jet suddenly, from which Zula guessed
that its trajectory had turned decisively eastward, diving over the
terminator into the shadow of the world.

During her occasional runs to the lavatory she spied a new chart
on the table, covering a vast swath of the earth with Newfoundland
in the upper right, Florida in the lower right, the Aleutians in the
upper left, and Baja California at the bottom. Both nations' Pacific
approaches were carved up into polygonal swatches labeled in block
capitals: ALASKAN DEWIZ and DOMESTIC ADIZ and PACIFIC COASTAL
CADIZ and so on.

A line of pen marks, updated every few minutes, was marching
northeast, off the east coast of Siberia and then roughly parallel to
the Aleutians. It tallied with what Zula could see on the television
monitor back in the cabin.

Khalid and Jones were paying close attention to certain details
of Yukon and British Columbian geography, which couldn't have
been very rewarding given the extremely small scale of this map.

The Aleutians and mainland Alaska were all encompassed in
the region labeled DOMESTIC ADIZ. South of that was a swath of blank
ocean labeled ALASKAN DEWIZ, which ran all the way east into what
she thought of as the armpit of Alaska, where its southeastern panhandle was joined to its main land mass by a corridor only a few
miles wide.

The entirety of southeast Alaska lay exposed to the Pacific,
not encompassed in any of these ADIZ or DEWIZ polygons. Zula

guessed that "IZ" must stand for something like "Intercept Zone" and that it was a military designation. She had read about the Distant Early Warning line in a Cold War history class, and so guessed that DEWIZ was Distant Early Warning Intercept Zone and ADIZ was Air Defense Intercept Zone and CADIZ was its Canadian equivalent.

The CADIZ didn't begin until roughly Prince Rupert, which lay just to the south of the southeast Alaska panhandle, and so it seemed that there was a vast gap in the IZ system, at a rough guess maybe five hundred miles wide, between the Canadian and the American zones. Which, from a national defense standpoint, was not such a big deal, since it would only give the Russian bombers access to the upper bit of British Columbia, the Yukon, and the Northwest Territories. They could use their nukes to melt snow or kill mosquitoes, depending upon the season, but they couldn't penetrate to the cities of Canada or the United States without passing through IZs farther south. And to reach that gap in the first place, they'd have to fly along an awkward southerly course that would burn a lot of fuel.

The whole northwestern third of British Columbia seemed to lie above the Canadian IZ and below the American, and this was where Abdallah Jones seemed to be focusing all of his attention. At a glance it appeared to be impossibly mountainous and desolate, but since this was an air chart, very few features were labeled, roads didn't appear, and towns were not marked unless they sported significant runways. So maybe it wasn't as bad as it looked.

Khalid's attention span did not seem to extend beyond about thirty seconds, and so it was his lot to roll his eyes and sigh hopelessly as Jones devoted hour after hour to his cartographic research. Zula had met any number of men like Khalid and so, even though they'd spent very little time together, she felt she knew the man and his ways. The only thing that could hold the attention of this kind of person for very long was direct interaction with another human being. What *kind* of interaction didn't really matter. Since three of the four soldiers had dozed off and the fourth was still fixated on his flight simulator, and since Jones was absorbed in the map and the two pilots were intensely focused on this project of flying in close formation beneath the belly of the 747, there was no one for him to interact with except for Zula. And Zula was spending most of her time in the aft cabin with the door closed. Whenever she opened the door, it was to find Khalid's burning eyes staring directly at her in a way that seemed to demand some kind of a response. Those eyes tracked her every movement. Khalid couldn't help but notice when Zula glanced over Jones's shoulder at the map.

This show of curiosity on Zula's part had astonished Khalid the first time and offended him the second time. The third time he flew into what she thought was a pretty well-rehearsed rage, getting to his feet and invading her space in a way that all but forced her to back away from him. She couldn't parse the grammar of his sentences, but she was able to recognize a few none-too-flattering nouns; if Khalid had been a gangsta rapper, he'd have been calling her a bitch and a ho. This went on until it disturbed Jones's train of thought, at which point he spoke up and told Khalid to pipe down and put a lid on it. Jones spoke in a tired, even dispirited tone of voice, which seemed to match the overall mood of the jihadists.

Returning to her cabin, Zula considered it. A few hours ago, back in Xiamen, Jones had been convinced that they would be able to fly the jet to some friendly location in Pakistan, pick up a cargo of Bad (perhaps a dirty bomb?), then turn the jet around and fly it straight to some kind of Armageddon in Las Vegas. Instead, because of the intricacies of the international rules around flight plans and restricted airspace, and because of the way Pavel and Sergei had shown some backbone at a critical moment, he had been forced to settle for a hastily patched-together plan that had gotten them safely out of China but that would apparently lead to their running out of fuel many hundreds of miles short of the U.S. border. They would have to touch down in the middle of nowhere and then improvise. He had to be feeling as though he'd been handed an incredible opportunity, then squandered it; but there was little else that he could have done. Zula could clearly perceive a struggle in Jones's head between the Western, university-trained engineer and the Islamic fundamentalist; the former wanted to execute carefully laid plans while the latter just wanted to wing it and trust to fate. Most of his comrades were fatalists and looked askance at the decisions he had been making.

She began considering what she might need to survive in northern Canada at this time of year. Though winter was over, it was still going to be cold. She did not know whether the jihadists had packed winter clothes among the gear in the plane's cargo hold. It seemed unlikely, given that they'd been planning to carry out an operation in Xiamen, a hyperurban zone at the same latitude as Hawai'i. On the other hand, they'd been hanging out on a fishing boat, and such vessels usually had foul weather gear.

So they might have something; but Zula had nothing except for the bed linens in this cabin. Which the others would confiscate anyway, as soon as they felt a need for them. And in any case, she had nothing to wear on her feet except for the pair of ersatz Crocs that had been issued to her in Vladivostok, and if she went outside in those things she would, in short order, be crippled and then maimed by frostbite. The best she could do was rip up the blankets and wrap them around her feet, then slip the Crocs over them. This was better than nothing. But it would have been a lot easier with a knife.

She had always found her gun- and knife-obsessed male relatives to be faintly ridiculous. But she would go so far as to admit that a knife was a good thing to have, in a whole lot of different ways. She had, therefore, been looking around for things in her environment that might be convertible into knives. Plan A had been to shatter the glass screen of the television monitor, pull out a shard, and then fashion a handle by wrapping one end in a strip torn from a bedsheet. She reckoned that this would work but that it would be loud and difficult to hide and might produce knives of highly variable quality.

Plan B, then, had been simply to steal an actual knife from the galley: a nook between the bathroom and the cockpit, which she came close to whenever she went up to pee. She had conceived this idea after her first pee trip—the one where she had looked up through the cockpit windows to see the 747 directly above them. She had planned it during her second pee trip and executed it during her third, scoring a large, heavy steak knife from a drawer. She had shoved it into the front pocket of her jeans, piercing the pocket's internal lining so that the blade was between her thigh and her pant leg, and the wooden handle was concealed in the pocket. With a chef's knife, this would have been crazy, but the steak knife wasn't sharp enough to do damage as long as it stayed flat against her skin.

Which only reminded her of a bit of lore she'd picked up in Girl

Scouts, which was that jeans were the worst possible clothing for cold and wet weather. The heavy cotton fabric would soak up moisture and then lose its power to insulate.

Anyway, trapped now in the cabin by Khalid's free-floating rage, unable to sleep, and with absolutely nothing to do, she decided to kill some time by watching a movie. It was a ridiculous urge, but it might be the last movie she'd ever watch and she literally could not think of anything else to do. One of the DVDs on the shelf was *Love Actually*, a romantic comedy, something like ten years old by this point, which she had seen about twenty times; she and her college roommates watched it ritualistically whenever they found themselves in a certain mood. So she turned that on.

The cabin was so arranged that the television monitor was in its aft bulkhead, facing forward, at the foot of the bed. Zula had made a pile of pillows at the head of the bed and arranged herself facing the screen, which meant that her back was to the entrance, off to one side.

Perhaps an hour into the movie, she became aware that she was not alone. The door had been opened a crack. Someone had been peering through, watching the movie with her.

Her first reaction was embarrassment more than anything else, since the film had a couple of ridiculous comic-relief subplots featuring extremely broad sexual comedy, probably meant to be self-mocking and read ironically by most of the intended audience, but which others on this plane might be inclined to take at face value.

She then got a feeling of vulnerability and discomfort from her position: lying on a bed. So she grabbed the remote, paused the video, and swung her feet onto the floor, preparing to stand up and see who was peeking in at the door.

As she was getting to her feet the door swung inward violently and knocked her back. The edge of the bed caught the back of her legs and made her sprawl back onto the mattress. Khalid stepped into the room, closed the door behind himself, and locked it.

She was making to sit up and get back on her feet, but he swung wildly at her face. She recoiled enough to take most of the force out of the blow, but something hard and sharp sideswiped her across the cheek and sent her back onto her ass with tears welling out of her eyes: not out of emotion, but an involuntary response to being struck in the face. Had she just been pistol-whipped? She reached up to wipe the tears from her eyes and felt something hard and cold press into her forehead: the barrel of a gun. It kept coming, obliging her to roll back. She ended up supine with the top of her head against the aft bulkhead, the frozen TV monitor and the control panel of the DVD player above her. The gun came away. She blinked away tears and saw the muzzle of the weapon aimed at her from maybe two feet away, Khalid holding it in his right hand, using his left to undo his trousers and pull them down. A totally erect penis snapped out. Zula was not a huge penis expert, but she knew it took at least a little bit of time for one of them to get that hard, which made her realize that Khalid must have been standing outside the door for a while, getting himself ready for this. All the other men in the cabin must have fallen asleep.

The thing with the gun was ridiculous. If he pulled the trigger, the plane would depressurize. She wondered if he understood this. But she had to assume he really was that stupid. Once the bullet had gone through her head, she would not be able to enjoy the satisfaction of watching these men lose consciousness from lack of oxygen.

Now that Khalid's intentions were clear, Zula wanted nothing more than to get her pelvic region as far as possible from him. But she was trapped in the back of the cabin. She planted her elbows in the mattress and levered herself up, scooted back, got her hands beneath her, pushed up to a sitting position. Khalid read this as lack of cooperation and became incensed, lunged forward, got a knee up on the bed between her knees, pawed at the waistband of her jeans. She pushed his hand away. He wound up to slap her across the face. She blocked the attack with one arm, but its force moved her sideways and made her head bounce against the front panel of the DVD player. A crisp mechanical noise sounded from behind her skull, and she heard the sound of the DVD being ejected from its slot.

Meanwhile Khalid was taking advantage of her disarray to undo the front of Zula's jeans. He was jerking down on the waistband, trying to peel them off her, but this wasn't working. Partly because he was only using one hand. But also, as Zula understood, partly because the steak knife in her pocket was trapped against her thigh and making it impossible to turn the garment inside out. He was yanking wildly, furiously, shaking her all over. She reached up to brace her hands against the bulkhead behind her, just to prevent her head being slammed into it. Her left hand came into contact with the ejected DVD.

Peter in the tavern at the Schloss. Snapping the DVD and cutting his hand.

Khalid seemed to have lost patience with doing everything one-handed and so he did something to his pistol—placing it on safety?—and then tossed it behind him so that it thumped onto the carpeted floor just in front of the door. He then made much more rapid progress on getting Zula's jeans peeled back from her waist and buttocks. The knife swiveled around and made a long scrape on her thigh.

While he was thus distracted Zula had pulled the DVD from its slot and bent it between the thumb and fingers of her left hand, compressing it almost into a U. She was afraid to just snap it in half—it would make a loud noise, he would notice.

The jeans now bridged the space between her thighs and formed a barrier to Khalid's progress. He had only made matters worse for himself. Looking down at her vulva, exposed but temporarily unreachable, he saw the blade of the steak knife jutting out from the pocket.

He let out a cry of rage. Getting back to his feet he gave the garment several terrific jerks, pulling both legs completely inside-out. Her butt was bouncing up and down anyway and so she swung her hand underneath it, let her weight slam down on the bowed DVD, felt it crack in half, the noise muffled by the mattress and by the flesh of her butt.

The jeans were now dangling from her ankles, the knife far out of her reach. Khalid shoved his hand in, groped for the pocket, and drew the weapon out triumphantly. Then he stepped in, ramming a knee down between hers, and then bent forward to plant the heel of one hand against her chin. He shoved her head back and then placed the blade of the knife against her throat.

Zula chose that moment to swing one arm down and around in a broad, blind scything motion, slashing at Khalid's penis with the sharp corner of a DVD half.

She definitely made contact with something. He reflexively moved both hands down to his groin, leaving the steak knife resting on her belly.

Nothing was there to support the weight of his upper body and so his head leaned forward. His eyes bulged in astonishment—conveniently for Zula who rammed up with both hands, aiming for each eye with a DVD shard.

Some instinct told her to close her eyes as she did this and so she didn't see the results. But she heard a howl from Khalid and felt him toppling backward.

Letting go of the DVD halves, she pawed at the knife on her belly but only succeeded in knocking it away; it bounced across the bed and fell into the crack between the mattress and the wall.

Just as well. The important thing was the gun. She rolled up and fell from the bed and crawled on hands and knees toward the door, where she reckoned the gun had come to rest. Khalid was right next to her, pawing at his face and screaming.

She saw the pistol and slapped one hand down on top of it just as the door was being kicked open from the other side. It burst open, trapping her gun hand against the wall.

She was now lying almost full-length on the floor, hobbled by her inside-out blue jeans, one hand free, the other holding a semi-automatic pistol of unfamiliar design, but pinned between the door and the wall, therefore hidden from view, but also immobilized.

The door had been kicked open by one of the soldiers, who was now leaning against it, pinning her arm. Abdallah Jones was right behind him, looking over his shoulder. Everyone was shouting.

Zula began exploring the pistol's controls with her fingertips, trying to figure out which little protuberance might be the safety. She didn't want to hit the clip ejection lever by mistake. Usually, the safety would be within easy reach of the right thumb. She found something that seemed to fit the bill and flicked it.

Jones brought a hand down on the shoulder of the man who was blocking the doorway and pulled him out of the way, then entered the cabin and dropped to his knees, straddling Khalid and making the cabin now a very crowded place indeed. Zula was being ignored for the moment. She pulled herself up to a sitting position, leaning against the door and slamming it shut. This triggered a fresh round of hollering and door beating on the other side. Zula looked at the gun in her hand to verify that it was cocked; she guessed it was, though she wasn't familiar with this style. Khalid was sitting up about four feet way from her, in profile, knees to his chest, hands over his face. Jones was facing him, speaking to him ardently, trying to get him to take his hands away so that he could look at the damage.

Zula pointed the weapon at the center of Khalid's torso and fired three rounds through what she guessed were his heart and lungs.

A loud, high-pitched noise dominated everything: either ringing in her ears or the sound of air escaping through bullet holes in the fuselage. Maybe both. Something huge flew at her: Jones had reacted by snatching the duvet off the bed and hurling it at her face. At the same time, the pressure on her back became immense. Air was escaping from the cabin, and the higher pressure in the front of the plane was forcing the door open. She fired another round in the direction where she guessed Jones might be coming from, but then his whole weight was on her gun arm, pinning it to the floor, and she was being crushed between his body and the door. His knee came down in the middle of her chest. She used her free hand to hurl the blanket out of the way. Jones was unharmed and on top of her, reaching above his head to grab for a yellow object dangling from the ceiling. She had some difficulty making it out, because it was blurry, but then she recognized it as an oxygen mask. Jones pulled it to him, placed it over his mouth and nose, and got the elastic band over the back of his head.

Then he looked down at her.

The instructions in the safety briefing said that you should put the mask on your own face first, then tend to anyone around you who needed help. Jones had done the first bit perfectly, but now he was just gazing at her interestedly as she went to sleep.

AS SOKOLOV WAS wading out toward the sound of the boat, he began to consider all of the ways in which this might go wrong—or *might already have gone* wrong. This kind of thinking had been his habit for as long as he could remember. It had been amplified a thousandfold during his service in the military and transferred quite comfortably to the security consultant business. If security consultants ran the world, militaries would no longer be needed, because all possible contingencies that might lead to the application of violence would have been anticipated and dealt with long before they had developed into actual wars. Or so he had always told himself as a way to justify his choice of a second career.

The fact that visibility had dropped to much less than a hundred meters was both a good and a bad thing. It was good that Sokolov would be able to board the boat and transfer to the containership unobserved by any spies ashore. It was bad that he could not see his ride coming. In the taxi, he had asked several questions of "George Chow" about how he had made these arrangements, how he had chosen this particular boatman, and whether he might have been observed or followed by any mainland Chinese operatives. George Chow had seemed confident—a bit too breezily confident for Sokolov's tastes—that it had all been pulled off perfectly. This sort of self-assurance, in and of itself, was frequently a warning sign. Sokolov knew nothing of George Chow and his history in this sort of business, nor of the extent to which the mainland authorities had penetrated the police and security forces of this island, and so it seemed safest for him to assume that Chow had been followed from the hotel, or (easier and cheaper) observed on security cameras as he had made his way through Jincheng and down to the waterfront to hire a boatman. If that were the case, then it would have been quite easy for a mainland operative to go and talk to the same boatman as soon as Chow departed and, through some combination of bribery and threats, get him to tell what he knew.

("What *does* the boatman know?" Sokolov had asked, in the taxi.

"Only that he is to pick someone up at a certain place and time" had been the answer from the front seat. "You must tell him where you are going.")

Anyway, the boat waiting at the rendezvous point marked on the GPS device Chow had given him might turn out to be full of men who had come over from the mainland this morning specifically to find Sokolov and either kill him or take him back to the People's Republic of China for interrogation and God only knew what other sort of treatment.

If that came to pass and if it developed into a gunfight (which, if Sokolov had anything to say about it, it most certainly would), then how would it look—or sound, since they couldn't see it—to Olivia and George Chow? A series of gunshots, largely muffled by the sound of surf finding its way through the thousands of stone fingers jutting out of the sand. Even if Olivia were foolish enough to attempt to wade out and investigate, she would find nothing; the boat would have departed by then. At the most there might be a corpse or two floating in the water, but it was highly improbable that she would happen upon such direct evidence. Much more likely was that the outcome would remain mysterious to both her and George Chow and that, spooked, they would get to the airport as quickly as possible and get out of this place.

In the taxi, Sokolov had asked George Chow what was going to happen when he reached the end of the voyage in Long Beach. Chow had assured him that friendly agents of the U.S. government would board the containership at that point and whisk him away to a safe place where he could be debriefed of all the information he had to offer about Abdallah Jones and given assistance in making his way through immigration formalities.

But Sokolov was in no way interested in being thus greeted and debriefed and assisted. He already had a B-1 visa, which entitled him to enter the United States any time he wanted. If he were to sneak into the United States from a containership, which, compared to what he'd been doing in the past twenty-four hours, ought to be as easy as pissing off a dock, then the worst thing that anyone could say about him was that he had not had his passport stamped when he'd entered the country: theoretically a problem, but so trivial and so distant that it hardly seemed worthy of his notice at this time. He had already given Olivia all the useful information that he had regarding the whereabouts of Abdallah Jones, and so any further debriefings in L.A. would inevitably center on topics whose elaboration could only make life more difficult for him, such as Ivanov and Wallace and what had happened yesterday morning in the apartment building. If the American authorities believed that he had been killed in an ambush in the fog and mist off the shore of Kinmen, then he would be spared such embarrassments.

There was also the matter of Olivia.

Sokolov quite liked Olivia and wanted her to be happy. He could tell from watching her face that she was unwilling to be honest with herself about the nature of the relationship that she had enjoyed with Sokolov, which had quite obviously (to Sokolov anyway) been based on simple, animal attraction. Sometimes you met someone and you just instinctively wanted to fuck their brains out. It had to do with pheromones or something. Most of the time, the feeling was not reciprocated, but sometimes it was, and then these things happened with a suddenness and intensity that could not help but be disquieting to anyone who believed that his or her life *made sense*. There was nothing more to it than that, though. They'd had their fun in the bunker, and probably could have had quite a bit more if circumstances had put them in a safe place together. But such relationships were unlikely to last. Olivia, a highly cultivated and rational woman, was unwilling to admit that she was the kind of person who could engage in such a liaison, and so she was even now putting her powerful brain to work coming up with a story according to which it was really much, much more than that. If it were somehow the case that they lived next door to each other or worked in the same office, then she'd have had to work through a long and dramatic and ultimately painful process of coming to terms with the fact that it was all strictly animal attraction and that there was no actual basis for a relationship there.

Fortunately, the situation at hand was quite a bit simpler than that. Even if the rendezvous with the boat and with the containership went perfectly, the two of them would likely never see each other again. But if Sokolov were killed in an ambush in the fog and mist off the shore of Kinmen, then she could close the door on this highly satisfying but ultimately meaningless affair, and go on to live the happy and contented life that Sokolov very much wanted her to live.

And so, as he drew closer to the sound of the boat's motor, Sokolov conceived of a plan, which seemed straightforward enough at the time, to greatly simplify both his future life and Olivia's by firing a few shots from his weapon. This would scare the hell out of the boatman, but Sokolov thought he could bring that problem under control without too much difficulty. Once they had effected the rendezvous with the containership, Sokolov would then find some way to induce its captain to claim that the rendezvous had not occurred—that the boat carrying Sokolov had failed to show up and that Sokolov had never boarded the vessel. Two weeks from now, Sokolov would slip off the ship in Long Beach and make use of his connections in that town to lie low for a bit. Then he would make his way back to Toronto, which was where he had started. A thorough inspection of his passport stamps might turn up some inconsistencies, but he had never seen anyone actually look at those things.

As he drew closer to the place where the boat was waiting for him, he drew out both first the Makarov and then the submachine gun that he had taken last night from the jihadist and checked that both of them were in ready-to-fire condition, which was probably a good idea in any case. He reckoned that if he were trying to simulate the sounds of a battle, it would be more convincing if he could fire a few pistol shots and a burst or two from the submachine gun. He would, of course, wait until he was safely in the boat, so that the boatman would not simply run away from him in terror. To that end, he did not want to emerge from the mist with a weapon in each hand, and so he placed the Makarov in its usual push-through belt rail and slung the submachine gun over his back.

The water had become chest-deep, adequate to float a vessel of some size. Sokolov shrank down into it so that only the top of his head was protruding from the water, a somewhat difficult thing to manage since waves kept rising up to break over him. He began his final approach by sidling from one shellfish-encrusted pillar to the next. He could hear the boat's hull rasping against one of the pillars no more than a few meters away.

Finally it began to come into focus: a long shadow riding on the water. As he drew closer the shadow resolved into a line of fat black Os: the tires slung over the boat's side, the only things keeping it from being macerated by the stone pillars. He could see the boatman sitting erect at the stern, waiting, wondering when the mystery passenger would show up. A white rope ladder had been thrown over the port side near the bow; this was the closest corner to shore, and the boatman must have assumed Sokolov would approach from that direction and be glad of the assistance.

But those tires looked as though they would provide convenient hand- and footholds for clambering aboard, and Sokolov could see no advantage in boarding from the expected direction. So he devoted a few more moments to making his way around to the stern of the boat, half wading and half swimming now, and then approached to the point where he could get a good view of the tire and the loops of rope that he would presently be using to get aboard. Then he drew breath, sank below the surface, and covered the last few meters underwater.

When he saw the corner of the hull above him, he gathered his knees to his chest, let himself sink to the bottom, and then exploded straight up with as much force as he could produce. His hands shot out of the water first and got purchase on the tread of a tire. He brought a foot up and planted it in the tire's rim, moved his hands up to the rope from which the tire was suspended, and then pulled with his arms and pushed with his leg, shooting up over the gunwale and sweeping his free leg around into the boat. For a moment, though his momentum was still carrying him forward, he was straddling the gunwale. The boatman was turning to look at the source of this unexpected splashing. Sokolov caught his eye for a moment, then glanced into the cargo area forward and saw three armed men lying on their bellies, all gazing in the direction of that rope ladder.

It was too late to do anything about the momentum that was carrying him over the gunwale, and the manner in which he had swung one leg over the edge and planted it on the deck now obligated him to carry on in a pirouetting movement. He spun around the planted foot, drawing his other leg into the boat, turning his back on the prone gunmen for just a moment. The movement caused the submachine gun to fly outward on its strap. He stopped hard with both feet on the deck, and the weapon swung around him until it was in front of him. He caught it in both hands, dropping to a knee, and fired a burst into the buttocks of the closest man. Half a dozen rounds entered the target's body through the pelvis and proceeded up through his viscera in the general direction of his brain. A second man levered himself up on his elbow and looked back to see what was happening. Sokolov obliterated his face. The third man, closest to the bow, erupted to his feet and dove over the boat's bow in one motion, chased by a fusillade of rounds from the submachine gun. Sokolov let the weapon drop and hang from its strap and shoved his Makarov through its holster. He turned to the appalled boatman and pointed in the direction of open water. Then he threw himself down on his belly and elbow-crawled up the length of the boat, slaloming around the two stricken men who were flopping and writhing vaguely as they died, and peeked between two tires for a second before withdrawing his head. Three pops sounded from a few meters away: the third operative, probably firing at him from behind one of those stone pillars. Sokolov fired a few blind shots just as a way of making this man think twice about exposing himself. He could hear the motor revving up and feel it moving beneath his chest. The next time he popped his head up for a quick look, the standing stones had all vanished in mist that was now developing into rain. The boatman continued in reverse gear until he was well out to sea, then spun the vessel around and headed straight out.

DIRECTLY THE GUNSHOTS were engulfed in the whoosh and clap of the incoming surf, and the drone of the motor dwindled and failed as the boat built distance between itself and the island. Olivia stifled a ridiculous impulse to call out Sokolov's name. She gathered her feet under her and squatted on the flat top of the stone pillar for a minute or so, cupping her hands to her ears, straining to hear—what?—a call for aid? Screams of terminal agony? Walkie-talkie bursts? But there was nothing, and she was left asking herself whether she had really heard anything at all.

A decent, albeit foolish, instinct told her to wade to the sound of the guns. Looking down, she saw that she would have to swim, rather than wade, and that the surf would bang her around like a pachinko ball among the pillars, foamed with knife-edged oyster shells and barnacles. She had only one course of action, which was to turn her back on whatever had just happened and make her way back toward shore. And she needed to act on it now, before the water got any deeper.

She hitched the skirt of her dress up above her waist—not that it was really going to help—and stripped off her panties and, wanting to keep her hands free, shoved one arm through a leg hole and pulled the garment up to her shoulder where it would stay put. She jumped off the pillar into the water, which came up to her navel, and began wading back in the direction of the shore. This involved some guesswork since the atmosphere had become a dense white fog salted with tiny hurtling raindrops, and it was impossible to see any landmarks, let alone the sun. The surf created swirling and unpredictable currents as it found its way among the pillars and tried to knock her legs out from under her. She moved from one pillar to the next, keeping a hand out for balance, yet trying to avoid any forceful contact between her skin and those serrated, shell-slathered columns. In the early going, she feared she might be headed the wrong way, but soon enough she noticed that the water was now lapping at her buttocks, then her upper thighs, and the going was becoming easier. She was headed back toward George Chow, at least approximately.

She then began to ask herself whether she really *wanted* to find George Chow.

The most paranoid explanation she could think of for the last half-hour's events was that Chow was not an MI6 agent at all, but a Chinese agent (or what would amount to the same thing, a double agent) who had bamboozled Olivia into believing that he'd help get her and Sokolov to safety. Instead of which he had sent Sokolov directly into a trap.

The more she thought about it, though, the less she favored this theory. She guessed that Chow was a legit MI6 man but that one of two things must be the case:

1. He had been followed or ratted out during his earlier movements around Jincheng, and some of the Chinese agents who had come over on the ferry this morning had been waiting for Sokolov on the boat.

2. MI6 actually wanted Sokolov dead and had hired some local talent to make it happen.

The latter also seemed a bit paranoid. But there was no doubt that Sokolov was, for MI6, a highly inconvenient and dangerous loose end. Moreover, Olivia could envision a situation in which the Chinese government would get in touch with the British government through some deep, dark channels and say, "We are hysterically pissed off about what went down in Xiamen yesterday and we want to see heads start rolling now; otherwise, we will make things quite difficult for you." In other words, MI6 might have made a deal to get rid of Sokolov in exchange for maintaining the status quo ante with their Chinese counterparts.

Raising the question, Was Olivia too a loose end who needed to be disposed of as part of the same deal?

She guessed not, for the simple reason that, immediately before Sokolov had kissed her good-bye, he had supplied her with information that MI6 wanted as to how Abdallah Jones might be tracked down.

"DID YOU GET it?" was the first thing George Chow said to her as she approached the car. The directness of this question, so much at odds with Chow's usual Cambridge/Oxford diffidence, did nothing to ease her suspicions.

She had paused at the water's edge, out of his sight, to get her underwear on and her dress down where it was supposed to be. So the absolute best that could be said of her appearance was that her fanny wasn't showing. But Chow, who had been standing there the entire time keeping an eye on her purse and her shoes, tactfully avoided looking directly at her.

"I have all the information he has," she said. "Or perhaps the correct form of the word is *had*."

Chow gawped at her, nonplussed.

She turned her head back out toward the sea, trying to judge whether he was just playing stupid. Was it possible that he could have failed to hear the gunfire? Sound traveled in funny ways on days, and in places, like this. For all she knew, he might have sat down inside the taxi and closed the doors and rolled up the windows just to stay out of the rain, in which case it was completely plausible that he might have failed to hear what she had heard.

In any case, she was not going to give him anything useful until she was in a safe place—preferably London. "Can we please get under way?" she asked, lunging for the door handle of the taxi before Chow could open it for her. "Loitering here seems not a good idea."

He climbed in next to her and gazed at her curiously as the taxi pulled a U-turn onto the road and headed for the airport. She stared resolutely out the windscreen for a few minutes, then, finally, turned to look him directly in the face. "Do you have anything to tell me?" she demanded.

"You're going to have to help me out," he said.

"If you're working for the PRC, put a bullet in me now," she said. "Otherwise please try to get a fucking clue because or else you're worse than fucking useless."

"Olivia!" he exclaimed, in an offended-professor tone. "To the best of my knowledge, all has gone exactly according to plan. If you have better information, I should be obliged—"

"Of that I have no doubt," she said. "What I don't know is *what the bloody fuck was the plan!?*"

This silenced him until they reached the airport—which, given the size of the island, wasn't long. Then it was all ticket counters and security checkpoints and boarding lounges for a while. He tried to beguile her into a remote corner where they could talk, but she could see no advantage in telling him anything until they were farther from China.

They took the next flight to Taipei.

There, George Chow pursued her to the departure lounge for her next flight, which was bound for Singapore. From there she was scheduled to fly nonstop to London.

It seemed that he had received an update on his phone. She hoped to God that they were using some kind of bulletproof encryption.

"Mr. Y," he announced, "never turned up."

"Never turned up where?"

"On the containership to Long Beach."

"How fucking stupid would he have to be to actually board that ship considering . . ."

"Which is a good thing," Chow added, "since it was overhauled and boarded by the Chinese navy on its way out of port."

"So the whole operation was blown," she said.

"Yes," Chow said, "a fact you appear to have been aware of from the very beginning."

Shit. He was trying to put this on her now.

"You're seriously trying to tell me you didn't hear that fucking Wild West shootout down there at the beach."

"I heard nothing," he said. "But if you heard something, you should have informed me so that we could . . ."

"Make sure you finished the job properly?"

"*What!?*"

"Or give the poor bastard even more of your professional assistance?"

Silence.

"He's better off making shift for himself," she said, "assuming he's still alive. Which, come to think of it, seems like a rather bad assumption."

George Chow had gotten a bit hot under the collar.

Not that Olivia could throw stones.

"I hadn't realized until now," he said, "to what degree this had become a personal matter for you."

She thought about it for half a minute or so, and then said, calmly: "I just wish we had done a better job."

"It is a common thing to wish," Chow said, "in our line of work. Welcome to the profession."

"My flight is boarding."

"Bon voyage," he said. "Hoist a pint for me, will you?"

"I'll probably hoist a few."

ZULA AWAKENED TO find herself hog-tied with what she guessed were torn strips of bedsheets. A pillowcase had been placed over her head and secured in place with a snug but not tight ligature. Cold pink brightness shone through it. By squirming around and pressing her face against things she confirmed that this was shining in through the jet's windows.

The light began to fluctuate, shuttering on and off. The engines were straining up and down. Something thudded into the bottom of the plane, or vice versa, and they bounced, then sank and thudded again, and proceeded to make the roughest landing that Zula had ever experienced. As they thumped and rumbled to a stop, its noise, and the declining scream of the engines, was drowned out by cries of "Allahu Akbar!" and then a lot of thumping, as if some sort of scuffle were taking place forward.

Someone came in. Jones. She had learned his smell and the way of his movement. He cut through the bindings that joined her ankles to her wrists. Then he grabbed her by the feet and dragged her to the edge of the bed, then pulled her to a sitting position. He untied the thing around her throat and whipped off the pillowcase. She blinked and shook her head, puffed air out of the side of her mouth to blow a loose lock of hair away from her eye. He could have helped her but chose instead to watch in amusement.

A snow-covered pine branch was pressed against the airplane window.

Khalid was still lying on his side on the floor. The amount of blood was beyond her wildest expectations. Jones was standing in it, staring into her face.

"Pavel and Sergei are dead," he announced.

"From the crash or—?"

"Pavel, I should say, was done in by a largish tree branch that came in through the windscreen and clobbered him in the throat. Sergei fared rather better until one of my colleagues entered the cockpit with a large knife and put him down."

He watched her carefully as this little scene played out in her mind's eye.

"You knew it would happen," he said. "And you understand why. Both of them had been in the Russian Air Force, you know. Dropping napalm on people like me. Touching that they made you part of the deal. I must hand it to the Russians. As much as I hate them and would like to see the entire country sterilized, it is true that they know how to treat a lady."

Zula looked him in the eye. Making the obvious comparison.

"Which brings me to the subject of you," he admitted with a sigh. He turned slightly, revealing a semiautomatic pistol in his right hand. She flinched, and he immediately raised the weapon to cover her. Zula had been so carefully inculcated in gun range etiquette that to have any weapon pointed her way was far more shocking than it would have been to any person unused to firearms. "It has been a great pleasure knowing you," Jones said, as if he were seeing her off at the train station. "Really it has. In a perfect world—no—in a *better* world—I would now say to you something like 'Zula, will you please accept Islam and become a *mujahid* and fight alongside us?' and you would answer 'Of course, I have seen the light of Islam' and it would be so. The problem with that scenario being that, not so many hours ago, you made a reasonably sincere-looking commitment to be submissive and cooperative, and then you killed my best man with a DVD."

She averted her gaze. Did it make any sense to feel guilty?

"*Love Actually,* of all things—a film for which I have always secretly harbored a soft spot, but that I will never again be able to enjoy in quite the same way. And that is why, as much as I hate to do it, I must now, for the good of the cause—"

"My uncle has six hundred million dollars," Zula said.

That rocked him back.

"Really," he said after a while.

"Really. If you don't believe me, check it out. And if I'm wrong, you can give me the Khalid treatment."

"Meaning what you did to him, or what he did to the schoolteacher?"

Zula had no answer.

"Because I'm perfectly capable of doing either, or both, with or without your say-so," Jones pointed out.

"It's true," she insisted.

He considered it for a while. Then he caught her looking. "Oh, I believe you," he assured her. "I'm just trying to work out whether it *matters.* You're suggesting some sort of ransom deal? Of course you are. But it's not clear to me how we would set up such a transaction, or what good the money would do us, even if we could take delivery of it without every police and special forces unit in the world descending upon us. It would be difficult enough in Waziristan. In Canada?" He scoffed.

"My uncle can get you across the U.S. border," she tried.

Jones grinned.

She realized that Jones genuinely liked her. Was, at some level, looking for an excuse not to kill her. "No, really?" he asked. "The same uncle?"

"The same one."

"The black sheep," he said, piecing it together. "The one you went to visit in British Columbia."

"We're *in* British Columbia," she reminded him.

"I really must meet this chap," Jones said, switching to his sarcastic-posh accent.

"I'm sure it can be arranged."

"Then if you don't mind," he said, "my four comrades and I are now going to be quite busy for a while, trying not to die. If we are able to string a couple of nonfatal days together, we may then return to your proposal."

"How can I help?" Zula asked.

"Stop killing people," he suggested.

PART II

American Falls

Day 6

Curtis. Peter *Curtis*. It had taken Richard many hours of devi-
ous googling to pin down the surname of Zula's boyfriend. The
lad's insistence on using a different pseudonym on every system
that he accessed had made this maddeningly difficult. If Peter and
Zula had checked in to the Schloss as regular guests, Richard would
have been able to access Peter's credit card data. As it had happened,
though, they had stayed in Richard's apartment as personal guests.

The decisive break in the case had been achieved by Vicki, she
of the Grand Marquis ammo run and the bearskin rug anecdote.
She was currently a senior at Creighton. She apparently had a serious case of insomnia or a large personal stash of Adderall. Vicki
had access to Zula's Facebook page and to her Flickr photo-sharing
page. She also had some of her own photographs that she'd taken
during the re-u. She had put together a portfolio of pictures of Peter
and then made use of an Internet site that employed facial recognition technology to search the Internet for pictures of the same, or
similar, faces. This had produced a lot of false positives, but several
candidates had turned up, including a series of photographs taken at
DefCon three years ago of a presentation given by a man identifying himself as 93+37. Richard had no idea how to pronounce this,
but he could see that if 93+37 were flipped around in a mirror, the
"9" would look a little bit like a "P," the two central "3"s would look

like "E"s, the "+" would still look like a "t," and the terminal "7" would look a little bit like a lowercase "r," yielding "Peter." The sum of 93 and 37 was, of course, 130, and so Richard had gone to work googling various combinations of "130" and "93+37" with "security" and "hacker" and "pen test" and "Seattle" and "snowboard" until he had begun to establish some leads, in the form of message boards and chat rooms, that Peter, or a person weirdly similar to Peter, had been in the habit of using. And in this manner he had begun to establish a sense of what Peter was interested in, who he hung out with, and what he did in his spare time. He was, for example, strangely interested in something called tuck-pointing, which was the process of repairing old brick structures by putting fresh mortar—*historically correct* mortar, it went without saying—into the spaces between the bricks.

Parsing a series of messages posted on a snowboarding site, Richard guessed the name of the shop in Vancouver where Peter had purchased that high-tech snowboard he was so in love with. Some more searching had uncovered the name of the shop's proprietor. Richard had reached him at an hour of the morning that was apparently considered to be punitively early in the snowboarding world. Richard had explained matters to the shopkeeper and persuaded him to go back into his records and dig up the name on Peter's credit card. And this had thrown open the Google floodgates and enabled Richard to get the address of Peter's building in Georgetown from King County real estate records.

At about nine in the morning, almost exactly twelve hours after breaching Zula's apartment, he found himself circling the block in question. The yellow handle of his sledgehammer was projecting vertically from his passenger seat, all but announcing his intentions to anyone who looked into the windshield; like a fourteen-year-old boy trying to tame an erect penis, Richard kept pushing it down and it kept snapping back up. The building was not hard to identify; it had recently been tuck-pointed.

Since he did not have the benefit of sympathetic neighbors in this case, Richard parked on the street and made his first approach to the building as a pedestrian, sans sledgehammer. It was a brilliant sunny morning of the sort that Seattle would occasionally lay before its desperate residents in the early spring; wild rhododendrons in the vacant lot across the street were showing red blossoms, and hobbyist-pilots were taking off from Boeing Field in their little planes. Richard pounded for a while on what he took to be the front door, then wandered around back. Two large roll-up doors fronted on the alley. Between them was a single human-sized door. Richard was knocking on the latter when a pickup truck pulled into the alley and rolled to a stop, close enough that he could have reached out and touched it. The engine shut down and the door swung open. Out came a lean, close-cropped, stubbled Caucasian male in his thirties, dressed in a scarred brown leather jacket over faded and frayed Carhartts. "Looking for Peter?" he asked, stepping to the roll-up door on the right and inserting a key into a massive tamper-proof padlock that dangled from its hasp. Before Richard could answer, he continued, "I haven't seen him in a week and a half."

"Really."

"Pisses me off too, because he's my landlord, and I want him to fix my Internet. Do you have any idea where he is?" The man dropped to a squat, gripped a handle on the front of the big door, and stood up, heaving it open to reveal a dark bay filled with welding machines and the paintless steel tools and tables favored by those who worked with unbelievably hot things.

"I'm investigating his disappearance."

The man straightened and turned to look at him. "You a cop?"

"Private investigator," Richard said, "hired by the family."

"So they don't know where he is either?"

"He and his girlfriend went missing a week ago."

"Exactly a week, or—"

"Last they were seen was Monday afternoon."

"My Internet died Monday night, late."

"Heard any disturbances, or—"

"No."

"But you're only here during business hours?"

"My hours are irregular," the man said, "but I don't sleep here."

Richard nodded at the roll-up door on the left. It was secured by another massive padlock. "Is that his bay?"

"Yup."

"I don't suppose you have a key?"

The welder thought about it. "Yeah, I got one."

"Mind if I borrow it?"

"Sorry, but I don't lend out my equipment."

"I beg your pardon?"

The man stepped forward into the darkness, reached out, grabbed something, and pulled hard, putting his weight into it. He began backing toward the alley. As he came into the light Richard saw that he was towing a two-wheeled cart loaded with a pair of gas cylinders, regulators, a length of hose, and a triple-barreled torch. "My key," he said. "Opens just about anything."

While the welder halved Peter's padlock—a procedure that took all of about three seconds, once he got his torch up and running—Richard ambled around in the alley, looking at the upper-story windows that he supposed belonged to Peter's living quarters. They were old-fashioned multipaned casement windows with metal frames. He noticed that one of them had a missing pane, right next to the latching handle on the inside.

"It's all yours," the welder announced, stepping back. "Mind your hand, it's going to be hot for a while."

Keeping well clear of the hot parts, Richard got the door unlatched and hauled it open.

Damn, but there were a lot of cars in here. As if Peter had been running a chop shop. In a few moments he identified Peter's boxy van—the one he and Zula had taken up to B.C.—and Zula's Prius, which had been parked as far back in the bay as it would go, apparently to make room for a little sports car that had been shoehorned into the remaining space. The latter had B.C. plates. The keys were still in its ignition.

Hands in pockets, Richard ambled around. The welder remained on the threshold of the big door, perhaps wisely declining to trespass.

"There's your problem," Richard announced. He was standing before half a sheet of plywood that had been screwed to the wall and used as a surface for mounting telecom stuff: cable modem, routers, punch-down blocks, phone gear. In two places, cables had been severed, their cut ends carefully pushed back into place so that the damage was not obvious. One was telephone, the other was the black coax line that had formerly run to the cable modem.

This was the first suggestion of actual wrongdoing that Richard had seen. Of course, the fact that Zula (and, apparently, Peter) had disappeared was more than sufficiently alarming that he'd thought of nothing else for the last couple of days. But in all of the investigating he had done so far, he had not seen actual evidence that human maleficence was involved. He suspected it, he feared it, but—as the Seattle detective assigned to Zula's missing persons case doggedly pointed out—he couldn't prove it. The appearance of those two severed wires thus struck him as deeply as a pool of blood or a spent shell casing.

He pulled out his phone and texted John: CALL OFF THE MOUNTIES. PETER'S CAR HERE. ZULA'S TOO. He decided not to mention the third car or the severed wires for now.

"You recognize this sports car?" Richard asked. His voice sounded funny to his own ears: dry and tight.

"Nope."

"Well. I'm going to look upstairs."

"Yup."

He'd hoped that last night's forced entry to Zula's apartment would be the last time he'd have to expose himself to the possibility of seeing something horrible. Now here he was climbing another staircase toward another possible crime scene. This time he considered it much more likely he'd see something that would scar him for life. But it was his responsibility to shove his face into this particular psychological buzz saw and so he reckoned he should get on with it.

What he found, though, was not what he'd expected. Peter's apartment contained no persons, living or dead. Nor were there any signs of violence or struggle, with two exceptions. One—which he had anticipated—was the missing windowpane, which had clearly been used by someone to break into the loft. The shattered glass was still sprayed over the floor below it.

The other was a wrecked gun safe standing against the wall in the corner of the loft. Something comprehensively bad had happened to it. Its finish had been burned away in a line that went all the way around its top, as though it had been attacked with a thermonuclear can opener. The entire top of the safe had been sliced off and thrown on the floor, where hot metal edges had burned into the wood. Instinctively Richard scanned the ceiling for smoke detectors and noted that they were all dangling open, their batteries removed.

This part seemed almost like a waste of time, but he stepped forward and looked down into the safe and verified that it was empty.

He walked back down the stairs and found the welder. "I could use your professional opinion on something."

"Plasma cutter," was the welder's verdict, after he had come up the stairs and got a load of the ruined gun safe.

"Do you have one?"

"No!" said the welder, and shot him a look.

"I wasn't accusing you," Richard said, holding up his hands. "I was just curious what they look like."

"It's a box," the welder said, holding up his hands to indicate size. "About yay big."

"Portable."

"Totally."

"Portable enough to take it through yonder window?"

"That would be a bit of a stretch. I would recommend stairs."

"So someone probably used the window to get inside and get a door open, then carried the plasma cutter up the stairs."

"Yeah," said the welder, "but I don't think your average burglar carries one around on his person."

"Agreed," Richard said.

The welder looked over his shoulder, a little uneasily, at Peter's apartment. "Seen anything else . . . funky?"

"No," Richard said, "nothing funky."

"Fuckin' weird, man," said the welder, and left.

Richard found his way to the front door, which had a deadbolt, a chain, and a pushbutton lock in the middle of the doorknob. The latter was locked, but the other two weren't. After breaking in via the window, the burglar must have unlocked this door from the inside and used it to bring the plasma cutter in and out, and used the button to secure it behind him when he'd left.

So, to all appearances, the plasma-cutter gun-safe caper had happened when the place was already vacant.

But how did its being vacant square with the presence of three cars in the bay? And why would the sports car's owner leave his key chain in the ignition? Generally, people needed their key chains for other purposes, such as getting into their houses.

Turning around, he noticed a red LED gleaming at him from the top of a shelving unit where Peter was in the habit of storing his rain-coats, hats, and boots. He walked closer and found a little webcam, mounted there with a web of white nylon zip ties. An Ethernet wire trailed away from it and disappeared into a hole in the wall. Richard traced it back into the shop area where the cars were parked, and found a place, not far from the plywood panel with the telecommu-nications gear, where a computer must have sat at one time. It had been on the bottom shelf of a workbench. Above it were a monitor, keyboard, and mouse, but their cables dangled into the space below. A power cable and an Ethernet wire were there too.

Richard assumed that the computer must have been taken, until a minute later when he literally tripped over it while circling the sports car. The CPU—a simple rectangular box—had been thrown down on the concrete floor and attacked with the plasma cutter: a single pass cutting down the side of it, slicing through the stack of drives.

Richard cursed. He'd imagined he was on to something. Peter had set up security cameras around his place. Perhaps one of them had captured some footage of interest. But the intruder had antici-pated this and made sure that the hard drive was destroyed.

He orbited all the cars, peering in through their windows, not wanting to disturb the evidence any more than he already had. Peter's had not been fully unpacked; whatever had happened must have hap-pened shortly after they'd gotten back to the place on Monday night.

He was jotting down the license plate number of the car from B.C. when his ears picked up a familiar *clicking* and *whooshing* noise: the sound of a hard drive coming awake and going to work.

Following the sound, and assisted by some conveniently placed Ethernet cables, he got underneath the flight of wooden stairs that led to Peter's loft, and found a little box, mounted to an improvised shelf and plugged into an outlet through a string of extension cords. It was a Wi-Fi access point. A little bigger than most nowadays.

It was bigger, he realized, because it wasn't just a Wi-Fi router. It was also a backup device. It had its own built-in hard drive.

NONE OF THE jihadists was in a great hurry to explain anything to Zula, but she pieced the following data together from looking out the windows and from half-understood Arabic.

They had been saved by the light of dawn, which had shown them a place to touch down: a landing strip that, however, was evidently too short for this kind of plane. It dead-ended in woods. Which seemed an awkward way to lay out a landing strip. But as Zula began to understand, the people who had put it there hadn't been afforded a lot of choice. This was some sort of valley in high mountains. It was spacious enough, wandering across several square miles of high cold territory, but its shape was convoluted, and its bottom was hacked up by gullies and ridged with outcroppings of hard rock, leaving few alternatives as to where a landing strip might be constructed. And culture shock might have been a factor; maybe Pavel and Sergei, accustomed to big international airports and Hyatts, had not made allowances for north woods bush-pilot dash, and had imputed prudence, or at least sanity, to the architects of this strip.

Or maybe they had just been desperate and unable to make any other choice; or maybe they'd had guns to their heads.

The landing strip was part of an industrial complex that, from Zula's point of view, wandered and sprawled aimlessly into parts of the valley that were hidden behind trees. Encouragingly, this included a small compound of buildings only a hundred meters or so from the landing strip. These all looked the same, and it was obvious enough that they were prefabricated structures that had been brought in on trucks and bolted together. Some of them looked like storage units, but one had a rust-fuzzed chimney protruding from the three feet of snow that covered its roof. Its south-facing wall was fortified by at least two cords of stacked wood. Zula watched through a window as one of the soldiers slogged over to it, moving at a pace of perhaps ten feet per minute as his legs broke through hip-deep snow on every step. When he finally reached the front door he destroyed its lock with a burst of submachine gun fire and staggered inside. A few minutes later, smoke began to emerge from the chimney.

THE DISCOVERY OF the hard-drive-equipped Wi-Fi unit under Peter's stairs placed Richard at a distinct fork in the road. He reckoned that this property housed so much evidence of wrongdoing that the police would have to send someone around to investigate.

The physical link between this crime scene and Zula—her car was parked *right in the middle of it*—might pump a bit of energy into the investigation of her disappearance. But Richard had already gone the cop route and found it not nearly as productive as driving around with a sledgehammer and retaining the services of men with oxyacetylene torches.

And yet on the other hand, if the cops did finally get serious about this, they could do things he couldn't, such as get access to phone and motor vehicle records.

So he adopted a hedging strategy. He unplugged the Wi-Fi hub and threw it in his car and drove it to the Seattle offices of Corporation 9592. There was an information technology department there, which had a little lab where they assembled and repaired computers. No one was there; it was Sunday. In a manner that would spark outrage tomorrow morning, when his depredations were noticed by technicians coming in for work, Richard opened up toolboxes and pulled computers from inventory and generally made a mess of things on someone's workbench. He opened up the Wi-Fi hub and removed the drive. Following instructions drawn from all over the Internet, including even a YouTube video, he connected this to a computer and made a copy of all the files on the drive. He then drove the reassembled Wi-Fi device back to Peter's building, where he plugged it in just as it had been before.

Then he called the cops.

As much as he wanted to hang around and watch them investigate the crime scene, he knew that the first thing they'd do would be to eject him from the premises and surround it with yellow tape. So he hung around only long enough to tell a drastically truncated version of the day's story to the first cop who arrived on the scene. He admitted to cutting off the padlock and then walking around the apartment for a while, but he said nothing about his other activities.

Then he drove back to Corporation 9592. Along the way, it occurred to him that he had just confessed to breaking and entering; but somehow he didn't think that Peter would press charges. Wedged in traffic because of an unholy conjunction of a Sounders game and a slow-moving freight train, he called C-plus. He had one of those rigs where his phone Bluetoothed the conversation into his car's stereo system. The volume was turned up too loud; a blast of noise nearly blew the windows out of his vehicle. Some very unusual mixture of bellowing voices, clashing metal, and heavy respiration. He turned it down hastily.

"Richard."

"C-plus. Busy?"

"Am I ever not?"

In the background, some guy was screaming single-word utterances in Latin. There was rhythmic tromping.

"What the *fuck* are you doing?"

"Maneuvers." C-plus said. Then there was some kind of interruption, the sound of a hand shuffling the phone around.

"You're in the National Guard?" But even as he was saying this, Richard was dismissing the possibility; they didn't speak Latin in the National Guard.

"Roman Legion reenactment group," C-plus explained.

"So you're, like, marching around in sandals and a skirt?"

"The Roman *caliga* is far, far more than just a sandal, at least as that term is construed by modern-day persons," C-plus began. "To begin with—"

"Okay, shut up," Richard said.

C-plus sighed.

"Want to get involved with something way more interesting than what you're actually being paid for?"

"Richard, if you are trying to trap me into griping about my job—"

"Furthest thing from my mind."

"Even so, let me say that my normal work is incredibly interesting and uplifting."

"It is so noted," Richard said, "but I need your help with a personal project. Kind of a detective thing."

"That REAMDE project?"

The question struck Richard as a bit odd and stymied him for a few seconds. "No," he said. "If it were about computer viruses, I wouldn't have even tried to con you into thinking it would be interesting."

"What is it about then?"

"Come down to the IT lab and I'll explain it."

Corvallis raised his voice. "My legion has been getting ready for these maneuvers for three months!" he said. "I have responsibilities as the *pilus posterior* of my cohort—"

"It's about Zula," Richard said. "It's important."

"I'll be there in half an hour."

Richard got to the office about fifteen minutes later, retrieved the computer from the IT lab, and took it to a small conference room, where he got it booted up and hooked into a monitor. Corvallis showed up wearing a tunic of off-white, natural-looking wool that Richard was afraid he might have woven himself on a Roman-style loom. He had swapped his *caligae* for cross-trainers. With practically no small talk he made himself at home on this computer and began poking around in the files that Richard had copied over from Peter's Wi-Fi hub. The files and directories had nonintuitive, computer-generated names, and Richard didn't recognize any of the file formats being used.

In the meantime, Richard's curiosity had gotten the better of him. "Hey," he said, "how come, when I told you I had a detective problem, you guessed it was about REAMDE?"

Corvallis shrugged. "I know Zula has been working on that with you."

"Really?" Richard was startled by this; but then he remembered something Corvallis had said a few days ago, in the Prius, to the effect that Zula had somehow helped narrow the location of the virus writer down to Xiamen. "How long have you known of this supposed collaboration between me and Zula?"

"Since Tuesday morning."

"*Tuesday morning!?*"

"Oh my God, Richard, settle down."

"What time Tuesday morning?"

"Earlyish. I could check my phone."

Silence.

"What the F is going on, Richard?"

"It's like I said on the phone: Zula and her boyfriend have vanished. No one has seen or heard from them in almost a week."

This rocked Corvallis back, and he said "Oh my God" in an altogether different tone. "When did they vanish?"

"Well, as it turns out, C-plus, one of the problems with vanishing is that it is difficult to pin down an exact time when it happened.

If you had asked me twenty-four hours ago . . ." Richard paused, groping through the last day's memories.

Twenty-four hours ago, he had not even been made aware, yet, that Zula was missing.

"Let's just say that, as far as I know, you are the last person who talked to her."

"Oh."

"So what the *fuck* did you talk to her about?"

"Let go of my shoulders, please."

"Hmm?"

"It doesn't help, and it makes it hard for me to type."

"Okay." Richard relaxed his grip on the woolen tunic and backed away from Corvallis, hands in the air.

"She had been up all night—Monday night into Tuesday morning—playing." Meaning, as Richard understood, playing T'Rain. "She said she was researching some gold movements connected with REAMDE."

"Seems a little unusual right there," Richard pointed out. "Tracking down viruses isn't her department."

Corvallis heard a rebuke in that and colored slightly. "It's hard to believe, but at the time, I'd never even heard of REAMDE. Had you?"

"No," Richard confessed.

"So I took what she said at face value. It was a special project you'd asked her to undertake."

"Really unlike her to just flat out lie," Richard remarked.

"Anyway, she needed to identify a player who had cast a healing spell on her at some point during her playing session." Corvallis had his laptop out now and began typing on it between utterances; and as he did, they degenerated from sentences to fragments. "In the Torgai Foothills." Type, type, type. "Total mayhem."

"Was it a member of her party?"

"No. Questing with one other. Getting killed a lot. Didn't understand why at the time."

"Because you didn't know about REAMDE and the bandits and so on."

"Yeah," Corvallis said absently. After about fifteen seconds of typing, he said, "Okay."

Richard bent forward, reached into the gully that ran down the center of the conference table, and extracted a video cable, which he threw across to Corvallis, who plugged it into his laptop. The projection screen at the end of the room lit up with a display consisting mostly of a terminal window: just lines of (to Richard) inscrutable text, the results of various queries that C-plus had been typing into a database. At the moment two character profiles were being displayed. These were just long strings of numbers and words. Corvallis typed a command that caused two windows to appear on the screen, each displaying a character profile in a more user-friendly form: a 3D rendering of a creature in T'Rain, the character's name in a nice little cartouche, tables and plots of vital statistics. Like a police dossier as art-directed by medieval clerics. One of the windows depicted a female character, whom Richard recognized as belonging to Zula. The other was presented in a window whose palette, typeface, and art all said *Evil*. The portrait was not fixed, but kept shape-shifting among several different species, one of which was a redheaded T'Kesh.

"Who is the Evil T'Kesh Metamorph?" Richard asked.

"That is the character Zula was hanging out with the whole time she was logged on that night," C-plus said. Speaking slowly and haltingly as he scanned some user's customer profile, he continued: "Belongs to a longtime customer and heavy user named Wallace, based in Vancouver. But on the night in question"—(typing)—"he and Zula were logged on from the same place"—(typing)—"in Georgetown."

"That's consistent with what I saw earlier today. Zula's car and a sports car from B.C. are both parked at her boyfriend's loft in Georgetown."

"So they must have all been there on the night in question—"

"And that is the place from which they 'vanished.' A word I like less the more I use it. Can you tell me anything more about this Wallace?"

"Not without violating the corporate data privacy policy."

Corvallis shrank from the look that Richard now threw him and went back to typing.

A customer profile appeared on the screen, displaying Wallace's full name, his address, and some information about his T'Rain playing habits. One stat jumped out at Richard. "Check out his last login."

"Tuesday morning," C-plus said. "He hasn't been on since." He typed a little more and pulled up a window displaying plots and charts of Wallace's usage stats, covering the entire time he'd been a T'Rain customer. "That's the longest he has gone without playing in the last two years."

"And Zula?"

"Same," C-plus said. "She hasn't been on at all. And another thing? Neither of them logged out cleanly on Tuesday morning. Their connections went down at the same time, and the system logged them out automatically."

"That doesn't surprise me," Richard said, remembering the severed wires in Peter's shop. "Someone walked into the place and cut their Internet cable with a knife while they were playing."

"Who would do that?" Corvallis asked.

"Peter was hanging around with creeps," Richard said.

This now so obviously looked like a classic drug-dealing-related home invasion/mass murder scenario that Richard had to remind himself of why he was even bothering to continue thinking about it. "Zula wanted something from you. Just before this all happened."

"Actually it was *after*," Corvallis said.

"What do you mean?"

"Their connection went dead at 7:51." Corvallis picked up his phone and thumbed away at it for a few minutes. "Zula called me at 8:42."

"Okay. That's interesting. She called you at 8:42 and told you this story about working with me on the REAMDE investigation and said she needed to know who had cast a healing spell on her character."

"Yeah, and it turned out to be some Chinese player logged in from Xiamen."

"Which is how you first became aware that the virus originated there."

"Yeah."

"So you're telling me that Zula was the first person to figure that out."

"Yes."

"That strikes me as superodd."

"How so?"

"Because if you leave out the whole REAMDE and Xiamen part of the story, this looks very simple. Peter was dealing in drugs or something. He got into business with the wrong people. Those people entered his loft and abducted him and took him away and killed him, and because Zula happened to be there with him, they did the same to her. But that doesn't fit with this Wallace guy, and it certainly doesn't fit in with the fact that Zula apparently traced REAMDE to Xiamen at almost exactly the same moment that she and everyone else in the apartment vanished."

"Wallace seems to have kept a very low Internet profile," Corvallis said.

"Yeah." For Richard had been watching on the big screen as Corvallis googled the man and came up with very little: mostly genealogical sites of no use to them. "I'll bet I know what he looks like though." He was remembering the guy Peter had held the mysterious conference with at the Schloss.

"What do we know about the people who created REAMDE?" Richard asked.

"That's not my department," Corvallis reminded him. "That's being investigated by people who specialize in that stuff."

"Hacker kids in China, that's what I heard."

"Me too."

"It just seems unlikely that they'd have the wherewithal to organize a home invasion in Seattle on a few hours' notice."

"Unless they have friends or something who live here. There are some sketchy characters down in the I.D." By this Corvallis meant the International District, not all that far from Georgetown. As West Coast Chinatowns went, it was small—nothing compared to San Francisco's or Vancouver's—but still managed to produce the occasional gambling-den massacre straight out of a Fu Manchu novel.

"But even if the REAMDE gang knew that Zula was on to them, how would they be able to trace her to Peter's loft in Georgetown?"

"They wouldn't," Corvallis said, "unless they had infiltrated Corporation 9592's China operation and had access to our logs."

"Noted," Richard finally said, after thinking about it for a good long while. He pulled out his phone and accessed a little app that helped him figure out what time it was right now in China. The answer: something like three in the morning. He thumbed out an email to Nolan: *Orb me when you wake up.*

"But look," Richard said, as soon as he heard the little swooshing noise telling him that the email was sent. "The reason I actually called you was because of this." He rested a hand atop the PC he'd carried in from the IT lab and told Corvallis the story about the security cameras and the Wi-Fi hub in Peter's place.

They transferred the video cable from the laptop to the PC and got it hooked up to power and a keyboard. Corvallis opened the directory containing the files copied from Peter's Wi-Fi hub. "Hmm," he said immediately. "What was the brand name of the hub?"

Richard told him. Corvallis visited the company's site and, with a bit of clicking around in their "Products" section, was able to pull up a picture of a device that Richard recognized as looking like Peter's. He copied and pasted the model number into the Google search box, then appended the search terms "linux driver" and hit the button. The screen filled up with a number of hits from open source software sites.

"Okay."

"What are you doing?" Richard asked.

"You said Peter was a geek, right?"

"Yeah. Computer security consultant."

Corvallis nodded. "The format of the files from his hub suggests that they were created by Linux. And indeed when I do a little bit of searching I can see that it's easy to download a Linux driver for this hub. It is Linux-friendly, in other words. So I suspect that what Peter did was set up a Linux-based system to manage his security cameras and perform automated backups and so on. And when he bought that hub, he junked the Windows-based software that shipped with it and reconfigured it to work directly under his Linux environment."

"Which tells us what?"

"That we're screwed." Corvallis used a text editor to open one of the files that Richard had failed to open earlier. "See, the header on this file indicates that it is encrypted. All the files that you recovered from his hub have been encrypted in the same way. Peter didn't want bad guys breaking into his system and snooping around in his security camera archives, so he set up his system with a script that encrypted all the video recordings before saving them to disk. And those encrypted files were then automatically backed up to the Wi-Fi hub."

"And those are the files we are looking at now."

"Yeah. But we'll never get them open. Maybe the NSA could break this encryption. We can't."

"Can we know anything else? How old are the files? How big are they?"

With a bit more typing Corvallis produced a table showing the sizes and dates of the files. "Some are pretty huge," he said, "which makes me think that they must be video files from the cameras you spoke of. Some are tiny. In terms of times and dates—"

They both scanned the table for a while, trying to see patterns.

"The tiny ones are regular," Richard said. "Every hour, on the hour."

"And the huge ones are totally sporadic," Corvallis said. "Listen, it's obvious that the tiny ones are being generated by a cron job."

"Cron job?"

"A process on the server that does something automatically on a regular schedule. Those files are just system logs, Richard. The system just spits them out once an hour, and they get automatically backed up."

"But let's talk about the big files. The video files. It's a motion-activated system," Richard said. "Just look at it. There's a file on Friday afternoon, which is when Peter would have been packing for the trip to B.C. Then nothing—except for the hourly log files, that is—until the middle of the night on the following Thursday. Which is weird. Because we know that a lot was going on in the place Tuesday morning. Why didn't it get picked up by the cameras?"

"Actually, there is *nothing at all*—not even hourly log files— between midnight and ten A.M. on Tuesday," Corvallis pointed out. He drew Richard's attention to the table and traced his finger down the column listing the time/date stamps. "See, the cron job was functioning properly all through Friday, Saturday, Sunday, Monday. Monday night, it did its thing at eleven P.M. . . ."

"But then there's a gap," Richard said. "No more little cron job files until ten in the morning on Tuesday."

"After which," Corvallis concluded, "it resumes its usual habits until Thursday at two A.M."

"Coinciding with a big video file," Richard pointed out. "The reason there's nothing after that is because the server that was running the whole system got trashed. Someone came back to Peter's place on Thursday, two days after Peter and Zula had vanished. Bastard probably knew it was empty; he must have been an accomplice, or a friend of one of the bad guys. Broke in through an upstairs window. Went downstairs, triggering the security camera and causing that last big file to be created. Opened the front door from the inside. Carried in a plasma cutter. Opened Peter's gun safe. Stole something from in there. Noticed the computer that was logging the security videos and used the plasma cutter to destroy its hard drives."

Corvallis nodded. "That fits," he said. "As soon as that computer was destroyed, the hourly log files stopped coming in."

"The only part that doesn't make sense is the gap on Tuesday morning," Richard said. "As if the power went out for a while. But that can't be it. The machine had a UPS."

Corvallis was shaking his head. "A power outage would have showed up in these logs. I'm seeing nothing."

"So how do you explain it?"

"There's an obvious and simple answer, which is that the files were manually erased," Corvallis said. "Someone who knew how the system worked went in between nine and ten A.M. on Tuesday and wiped out all files generated since midnight."

"But this is the backup drive we're looking at," Richard reminded him.

Corvallis looked up at him. "That's why I'm saying it had to be someone who was familiar with the system. He knew about the backup drive, and he was careful to erase both the original and the backup files."

"Peter, in other words, is the one who did this," Richard said.

"That's the simplest explanation."

"Either he was working with the bad guys—"

"Or he had a gun to his head," Corvallis said, then winced at the look that came over Richard's face.

"So where does that leave us?" Richard asked, somewhat rhetorically.

"The data from here," said Corvallis, indicating the PC, "is all stuff that the cops should be able to analyze, the same way we have been doing. But unless they can get the NSA to decrypt the video files, it won't go any further than we've already gone. The other stuff—the T'Rain logs that we used to make the connection to Wallace—they can't get unless they come in our front door with a court order."

"But they can establish a connection to Wallace just from the fact that his car is parked in the loft," Richard said.

"I think that all you can really do is wait for them to gather more information about Wallace," Corvallis said. "Let the investigation run its course."

"That's what I was afraid of," Richard said. "Could you do me one other favor, though?"

"Sure."

"Keep checking the T'Rain logs. Let me know if there is any more activity on any of these accounts."

"Zula's and Wallace's?"

"Yeah."

"I'll set up a cron job to do it right now," Corvallis said.

"Once an hour?"

"I was thinking once a *minute*."

"Now, that's the spirit." Richard considered it.

"Anything else?" C-plus asked, flexing his fingers, kind of like a boxer jumping up and down in the corner of the ring.

"There must also be, I would guess, a whole complex of many accounts connected with these kids in Xiamen, right?"

"In theory, yeah," C-plus said. "But they seem to have been pretty savvy about protecting themselves. Like, instead of carrying the gold around on their persons, they have it stashed all over the Torgai Foothills."

"Which would prevent anyone *other than us* from knowing where it was," Richard said. "But because we have admin privileges, we can just search the database and find every pile of gold pieces in that region, correct?"

"Of course."

"And then we can go back through the log files and identify the characters who moved the gold pieces to those stashes."

"Sure."

"So those characters should get placed on some kind of watch list. Whenever they log in, we track them. Watch what they're doing. Check their IP addresses. Are they still in Xiamen? Or moving around? Do they have coconspirators in other places?"

Corvallis said nothing.

"What am I missing here?" Richard asked, starting to get a bit exercised.

"Nothing."

"Why didn't we do this a long time ago!?"

"Because," C-plus said, "it's exactly the kind of thing that the cops would ask us to do as part of an investigation, and official corporate policy is to tell the cops to go fuck themselves."

"Hmm, so we've been hands-off with the REAMDE guys until now," said Richard, talking loudly over a surge of hot shame. Furious Muses were beginning to pop up on his emotional radar like Soviet bombers coming over the Pole.

"Yeahhhh . . ."

"Well, until we can prove that there's no connection between them and Zula's disappearance, corporate policy has to change," Richard said.

THE JIHADISTS' KIT included several Chinese entrenching tools: bare wooden handles about the length of a man's arm tipped with shovel-shaped blades that could be rotated into a few different positions, making them usable as picks or as shovels. Through a combination of stomping the snow down with their feet and using these tools to scrape and shovel a path, they created a lane from the plane's door to the prefab building with the functioning woodstove. They then used it to transfer their baggage from the plane into the building. The jet had been on the ground for a few hours now and the temperature inside of it had been declining the whole time, to the point where Zula had been pulling blankets off the bed one at a time and wrapping them around herself, transforming herself into a semblance of a burqa-clad woman of the conservative Islamic world. She was startled, after a while, to hear loud hacking and ripping noises from inside the plane, then understood that they were wielding their tools to strip its interior of anything they could conceivably use. But this was only a guess since they had kept the cabin door closed, and reacted splenetically when she pulled it open to peek out.

Eventually, though, the time came when Jones shoved the door open, letting in a wash of cold but blessedly clean-smelling air, and beckoned to her, letting her know that her days of private jet travel were finally at an end. And none too soon for Zula's taste.

She emerged to find the cabin darker than she'd expected, since the interior had been wrecked, and shards of plastic wall-stuff and bats of insulation were dangling in front of the windows. Moreover, the cockpit door was closed, blocking any light from that direction. As Zula proceeded up the aisle, staggering and sliding over debris, she perceived that the door had taken heavy damage, perhaps from the same tree limb that had killed Pavel, and that a lake of blood had seeped out from under it to freeze or coagulate in front of the jet's main entrance. She had no choice but to walk through it and track it out onto the snow beyond, which was already stained with red for a distance of several meters from the side of the plane. But when she looked up and away from the terrorists' gore-track, she saw a clean white overcast sky and smelled pine trees and rain. This was not the bitter dry Arctic cold of midwestern winter, with temperatures far below freezing. This was the heavy drenching chill of the northwestern mountains, which somehow felt colder to Zula, even though the temperature was tens of degrees warmer. She drew the blankets tighter around her body and followed the track toward the heated building. No one escorted her. It did not seem that they were even *watching* her. They knew, as did she, that if she tried to make a run for it, she would bog down in deep snow with her first step and freeze to death before getting beyond rifle range.

The building was dark and it was stifling; they had overdone it with the wood-burning stove. The sharp tang of hot iron reminded her of the smell of Khalid's blood, and it did not hide the musty and mildewy funk of the long-shut-up building. The front room occupied the full width of the structure, which she pegged at eighteen or twenty feet, since this was a double-wide. The back right corner of the room was an L-shaped kitchen. Cabinet doors hung open. At whatever time that this facility had been mothballed, abandoned, or shut down for the winter, it had evidently been stripped of all items worth picking up and carrying away. Remaining was a sparse, motley array of cooking and serving ware, mostly consisting of the cheapest stuff that could be purchased at a Walmart. The wood-stove was in the room's left front quadrant. A banged-up aluminum saucepan, packed with snow, was rocking and sizzling on its top. Behind it was a rectangular table seating six: evidently as much for working as for dining, since behind it, against the wall, were a desk and a filing cabinet. To the right, as she walked in, were a sofa, a chair, a coffee table, and an old television set sitting on top of a VCR—a detail that dated the place more effectively than any other clue. In the back wall was a door leading to a corridor that ran back for some distance. She assumed that a lavatory and smaller offices or bunkrooms might branch off from it.

The jihadists had brought food with them, in the form of military rations, as well as rice and lentils, which could of course be cooked with melted snow. One of the soldiers seemed to have been put in charge of that project. Two others were exploring a neighboring building that seemed to have been a maintenance shop. They were looking for tools, and they were finding a situation analogous to what obtained in the kitchen: all the good stuff had been taken, leaving only junk that wasn't worth moving: rusty shovels and worn-out push brooms. But shovels were just what they needed, since the task at hand, apparently, was to turn the jet into a coffin for Pavel and Sergei and Khalid. Zula inferred that they were worried about being spotted from the air. In that case the pilots had done them a large favor by crashing the plane in trees. A long skid mark led to the wreck, but snow had begun to fall during the time they had been here and would soon erase this. It only remained to cover the plane itself with some combination of snow and hacked-off foliage. This project went much faster once they had liberated some tools from the shed, but even so it occupied Jones and the other surviving jihadists for the remainder of the day. They kept themselves warm by working hard, and when they came in for breaks they wanted to eat. Supplying them with food somehow became Zula's responsibility. This was ridiculous, but no more so than anything else that had happened to her in the last week, so she pretended to go about it cheerfully, deciding that it might improve her life expectancy and enlarge her freedom of action if she made herself useful rather than staying in a fetal position under a pile of blankets, which was what she felt like doing. The front room had windows and therefore views out three sides, and so this also enabled her to move about and look around and try to get some conception of where they were.

During the last couple of hours of the flight, Zula had not followed the plane's course on the electronic map, and so she did not know in what part of B.C. they had actually landed. In a vague way, she thought of B.C. as being a vastly scaled-up Washington State, which was to say that the western part was rain forest ramping up to snow-covered but not especially high mountains, and the interior was, generally speaking, a big basin, tending to dryness, with hills and mountains generously scattered about, and the eastern fringe was even larger mountains: the Rockies and their tributary ranges. The place where she and the terrorists now found themselves looked dry and rocky to her, which made her think that they must be well into the interior. But Zula's time in the Pacific Northwest had gotten her used to the concept of microclimates (a considerable adjustment for one who had grown up in a place where the climate was as macro as it could possibly be), so she knew that it was best not to go making assumptions; it was quite possible that they were only a few miles from salt water and that this valley was dry merely because it lay in the rain shadow of coast-facing mountains. From here it might be rain forest in all directions; or it might be desert. They might be hard up against the border of the Yukon or they might be only a three-hour drive from downtown Vancouver. She simply had no idea. And neither, she suspected, did Abdallah Jones.

There was no doubt, however, that this facility was a mine. It would be wrong to call it "abandoned," since the doors had been locked and some low-value infrastructure had been left in place: just the sort of gear that would be needed to reboot the operation if the owners ever had a mind to do so. Her first guess was that it had been shut down for the winter, but various clues suggested that it had gone unused for a number of years. She knew enough of geology to understand that mineral prices fluctuated, and that, depending on the tenor of the underlying ore, a mine that was profitable in some years might not be worth operating in others. This could be one of those.

Busying her hands with stoking the fire, and occupying her brain with such immediate and practical thoughts, she was almost completely unmindful of what had happened at the end of last night's airplane journey. When this did come into her thoughts, she was shocked by how little effect it had had on her, at least in the short term. She developed three hypotheses:

1. The lack of oxygen that had caused her to pass out almost immediately after she'd killed Khalid had interfered with the formation of short-term memories or whatever it was that caused people to develop posttraumatic stress disorder.

2. This was just a temporary reprieve. Later, if she survived, the trauma of last night would come back to mess her up.

3. Possibly because of devastating experiences earlier in her life, she was some kind of a psychopath, a born killer; the comfortable circumstances under which she'd been living until a week ago had made it possible for this to go unnoticed, but now stress was bringing it out.

She considered hypothesis 3 to be quite unlikely, since she didn't feel the least bit psychopathic, but included it in the list out of respect for the scientific method.

One thing had certainly changed, though: she had fought back and she had eliminated one of these guys. What was to say she couldn't do it again?

The answer came to her immediately: after they had landed, Jones had been about to kill her. She had saved her life only by offering herself as a hostage: a resource by which something might be extorted from Uncle Richard. She guessed it was a one-time reprieve and that any future homicides would be dealt with a little more sternly.

. . . .

RICHARD'S PHONE BEGAN to warble an eldritch, theremin-inspired tune. He picked it up and saw a graphic of a crystal ball with a colored miasma swirling through it, partly obscuring a picture of Exalted Master Yang. YOU ARE BEING ORBED, it said.

He was in his office at Corporation 9592, where he had been preoccupied drafting a status report for his brother John. Since he knew it would end up on Facebook, he had been trying to make it as informative as possible without divulging any of Corporation 9592's proprietary information. This was not going very well, and so he was glad of the distraction. He activated the Orb app, which put up a screen that made it look as though he were sitting at a plank table in a medieval castle, holding a grapefruit-sized sphere of magically imbued crystal in one hand and stroking it with the other. The hands in question belonged to Egdod. The face in the orb was that of Exalted Master Yang, Nolan's primary character, the most powerful martial artist in the world of T'Rain, capable of killing a man with his eyebrow. "You called?" he said.

"Isn't it still way early there?"

"I am in Sydney," Nolan said, "two hours later." The cadences of his voice were familiar, but they had been electronically reprocessed by the Orb app to make him sound like Exalted Master Yang, whose age was well into the quadruple digits, and who rarely spoke above a whisper, lest he inadvertently decapitate his interlocutor with his twenty-seventh-level Lion Roar power.

"Why?"

"I felt it was time to be in a place with a legal system."

"Things too hot for you in Beijing?"

"Not hot. Just . . . weird. Harri wanted to get out." Harri, short for Harriet, was Nolan's wife: a black Canadian lingerie model and power forward. Certain things about China she found a bit odd.

"Related to the REAMDE investigation?" Richard would not have spoken so bluntly had Nolan been in Beijing. The Orb app encrypted all voice traffic, so point-to-point communications were secure; but if anyone were listening in on Nolan's apartment, they'd have been able to hear what both he and Richard were saying.

"Until yesterday."

"What happened yesterday?"

"They started asking me questions about terrorists."

Richard had no answer for that.

"And Russians," Nolan added helpfully.

"Wait a sec," Richard said. "You're saying that *the same cops* who had been pestering you about REAMDE suddenly changed the topic to terrorists and Russians?"

"No," Nolan said, "a different set of cops. Like the investigation was handed off to new guys."

"Did you tell them anything?" Richard blurted out. Then he wished he could haul it back.

"What could I tell them!?" Nolan demanded. "The whole thing was totally bizarre!"

Good, Richard thought, *please let it stay that way.* He was dumb-founded to hear about the terrorists and the Russians—this made no sense whatsoever—but he supposed that the Chinese authorities must take a rather dim view of both groups; and if they had somehow dreamed up a connection between them and REAMDE, it would in no way simplify the project of getting to the bottom of Zula's disappearance.

"Are there any terrorists in China?"

"As of the day before yesterday," Nolan said, "there is one less."

"Oh, yeah, that's right," Richard said. For he had done some googling for Xiamen-related news that he could actually read (there was very little available in English) and found all channels swamped by coverage of an event, a couple of days ago, in which a suicide bomber, stopped by security outside the gates of a convention center in Xiamen, had blown himself up and taken two guards with him. He had interpreted the story as sheer noise, of no possible relevance. "But what possible connection could there be between that and REAMDE? Other than the coincidence that they're in the same town?"

"None at all," Nolan said, "but that doesn't stop the cops—you know how they are."

Richard actually had no idea how Chinese cops were, but he decided to let this go. "How long are you going to stay in Sydney?" he asked.

"Until Harri gets finished shopping," Nolan said vaguely. "Then to Vancouver." Meaning their primary Western Hemisphere residence.

A flash of white in the doorway: Corvallis, coming in hot, tunic swinging. His face said that he had news. "Gotta de-Orb you," Richard announced. "Call me when you get to Vancouver." He severed the connection. "Yeah?"

"Got some stats on those guys," said C-plus, and swiveled his laptop around to display a graph: a red line ascending a ski jump and then falling off a cliff.

"Which guys?"

"Like you said. I came up with a sort of watch list of all the da G shou," Corvallis said. "Or people likely to be associated with them. Added up their clicks per minute." Meaning the number of times per minute that these players hit a key or a mouse button. The figure would be zero, of course, for a player who was not logged in, and some frighteningly high number for one who was embroiled in combat, and somewhere in between for someone who was logged in but just wandering around or socializing. "This is summed over about a hundred different da G shou–affiliated characters, showing the last two weeks."

Beyond that, C-plus didn't have to say much, since the graph spoke for itself. It started at a low-to-middling level, then ascended exponentially over the course of several days, then suddenly dropped to almost zero. After that, a few spikes poked up through the noise floor, but there was basically nothing.

"I can't read the time scale from here," Richard said.

"It gets huge last week, when REAMDE was spiking and you were flying over the Torgai," Corvallis said. "It flatlines around five in the afternoon on Friday."

"Seattle time?"

"Yeah."

Richard consulted his time zone app. "Eight in the morning Xiamen time," he said. "Hold on a sec." He used his browser's history menu to pull up one of those English-language stories about the suicide bomber in Xiamen. "That's a couple of hours before the terrorist blew himself up."

"Say *what*!?"

"Never mind."

"Since then, the da G shou have been losing control over the Torgai region to incursions by more powerful factions," C-plus reported. "An army of three thousand K'Shetriae is advancing on its northern border as we speak."

"Bright, or Earthtone?"

"Bright."

"Hmm. Gold must be lying knee-deep on the ground."

"Some places, yes. But a lot of it has been Hidden." A catch in his voice signaled his use of the word's majuscular form. It had not been hidden in the sense of being stashed under a pile of leaves, but Hidden by the use of magical spells. "Basically, all of the gold that the da G shou could recover before they went dark on Friday is Hidden, and everything that has been deposited since then is just lying there for the taking."

"How much has been Hidden?"

"You want that in gold pieces or—"

"Dollars."

"About two million."

"Holy Christ."

"Another three million is lying on the ground."

"That is just the last couple of days' ransom money, you're saying."

"Yes," Corvallis said, "but the drop rate is declining rapidly as the infection gets under control. Ninety percent of our users have now downloaded the security patch. So it's not going to go much beyond that."

"Okay," Richard said, "so what is my situation, if I'm a da G shou? I know where two million dollars' worth of gold pieces is Hidden but I have lost control of the territory where it's stashed."

"You have to sneak in," Corvallis said, "and recover the stuff one stash at a time . . ."

" . . . and then sneak out and get to an MC without being ripped off," Richard concluded. In the back of his mind, he was worrying about how he was going to explain this to John—definitely not a T'Rain kind of guy. "Which could actually be difficult to pull off, if the Torgai falls under the control of people who know what they're doing. I mean, with that kind of money at stake, there would be plenty of financial incentive to set up a heavy security cordon."

"A Weirding Ward costs about one gold piece per linear meter,"

C-plus said, referring to a type of invisible force-field barrier that could be erected by sufficiently powerful sorcerers.

"Cheaper if you harvest the Filamentous Cobwebs yourself," Richard retorted, referring to the primary ingredient needed to cast a Weirding Ward.

"Not as easy as you make it sound, given that the Caves of Ut'tharn just got placed under a Ban of Execration," countered Corvallis, referring, respectively, to the best place to gather Filamentous Cobwebs and a powerful priestly spell.

"Who did that? Sorry, I haven't been keeping up the last couple of days . . ."

"The High Pontiff of the Glades of Enthorion."

"Sounds Earthtone to me."

"You got it."

"Some kind of strategic move in the Wor?"

"I'm not privy to the High Pontiff's innermost thoughts."

"Anyway," Richard said, "that Ban wouldn't prevent Earthtones from getting in there, if they were exempted from the Ban by a Frond of Peace that had been consecrated by the said Pontiff."

"I forgot about the Frond of Peace loophole," said Corvallis, crestfallen.

"It's okay, you're new here."

C-plus considered it. "So you're saying that Earthtones might actually have an advantage over Brights in seizing control of the Torgai."

"Kind of," Richard said.

Corvallis raised an eyebrow.

"More to the point," Richard went on, "this gives us a way to encourage Earthtones. Make them think they have a chance of turning back those three thousand Bright K'Shetriae you mentioned, and getting control of the three million bucks' worth of gold pieces *that they can see*—which would go a long ways toward financing the Wor."

"Could you help me peel back the layers?"

"Beg pardon?"

"Of your Machiavellian strategy? Because I can see that there is way more calculation and cynicism going on here than I can ever possibly comprehend—"

"It's simple," Richard insisted. "There are all of about two layers. We have no way to track down the da G shou. Hell, forget about even tracking them down. We have no way to even gather more data about the little fuckers until we can get them to log on, right?"

"Right. Unless we get into bed with the Chinese police."

"Yeah," Richard scoffed, "which for reasons I won't explain is now even less likely than it was yesterday. So. It seems from your graph that they are scared shitless and unwilling to log on. But they must be aware that they have two million bucks Hidden in the Torgai. Sooner or later, they'll want to come after that money. If it so happens that the Torgai gets conquered by three thousand K'Shetriae, or whatever, who can use the money on the ground to put up all kinds of walls and wards and force fields and shit, and thereby lock out the da G shou, then the da lose all incentive to try to come back. They never log on. We never see them again. On the other hand, if we can keep things nicely unstable in the Torgai region, and turn it into a chaotic battleground, then that gives the da all sorts of opportunities to sneak back into the place and go rooting around for their Hidden gold . . ."

"And then they'll pop up on the watch list," said Corvallis, nodding, "and we can start gathering data on them."

"Exactly."

"Maybe find the Liege Lord," Corvallis went on. "Only he would have access to the whole two million."

"Oh yeah, of course!" Richard said. "I had forgotten about that detail." For, according to the rules of how the Hiding spells worked, if a vassal Hid something, then not only could the same vassal find and unHide it later; but the same privileges were granted to that vassal's lord, and the lord's lord, and so on, all the way up to the Liege Lord of the network. The two million in gold might have been Hidden by hundreds of different vassals within the da G shou's hierarchy, any one of whom would only be able to see and retrieve the gold that he (or his own vassals) had personally Hidden; but somewhere there must be a Liege Lord who would have the power to personally, single-handedly retrieve all of it.

"Do you know who the Liege Lord is?" Richard asked.

"Of course, in the sense of knowing the account number. But the name and address are fake, as with all of these."

"Okay," Richard said, pulling his laptop in closer, adjusting the screen angle for action. "I'm going to get in touch with D-squared. Or rather, his troubadour. And I'm going to make sure he understands that there's enough gold lying around in the Torgai Foothills to finance the Earthtone Coalition for a year. And I'm going to see whether that gets his creative juices flowing."

"What about those three thousand K'Shetriae?" asked Corvallis, nervously eyeing a map. "Could your man Egdod summon a meteor storm or a plague or something?"

Richard gave him a look that, to judge from his reaction, must have been pretty damned baleful. "Just to slow them down a little," C-plus said, holding up his hands.

"*Of course* Egdod could summon a meteor storm or a plague," Richard said, "but I would prefer to avoid deus ex machina stuff, and so as soon as I get done with this email I'll call a meeting for tomorrow morning."

"Agenda?"

"Figuring out some less obvious way to fuck up the Bright invasion of the Torgai Foothills."

The back end of the double-wide was a bunkhouse, divided into half a dozen small rooms each equipped with bunk beds that had been knocked together out of two-by-fours and drywall screws. The beds still had thin foam mattresses. They gave Zula a room of her own, then nailed the door shut behind her and nailed a scrap of plywood over the outside of its window. She spent a long and shivering night under the bare minimum of blankets needed to keep her from perishing outright of hypothermia. When morning came, and they pulled the nails out of her door, she went to the front room, which was warm because of the stove. She curled up on the sofa under as many blankets as she could scavenge and did not move for a long time.

They had destroyed the lock on the filing cabinet and found a lot of papers belonging to the mining company: pay records, receipts, assay reports, hardcopies of spreadsheets. But they also found a survey map of the area, and a road map of British Columbia.

Jones and the most senior-looking of the soldiers, an Afghan named Abdul-Wahaab, took as many of the warm clothes as they could fit on their bodies, bundled themselves up, packed food and water for a couple of days' journey, and, after a lengthy study of the survey map, trekked off into the woods. Zula, peering out through a gap between blankets, watched them go and thought that she understood their strategy: the snow was less deep in the trees, and it seemed that they were able to move a bit more rapidly there.

Nothing else happened for the rest of the day. Zula did not move much from the sofa. The three remaining soldiers took turns going out in pairs to explore the vicinity, but they couldn't stay out for long because of the shortage of winter clothing. One was always left behind, presumably to keep an eye on Zula. Sometimes they came back with trophies scavenged from other buildings: tools, first aid kits, dead flashlights, worn-out hoodies, work gloves, pornographic magazines, bars of soap, cans of oil. The scavenging developed momentum as they found more warm things to wear. During the afternoon, they put considerable effort into moving snow away from a travel trailer that had been left parked about a hundred meters from the headquarters building. This had been visible yesterday as an anomalous snow drift. Now it was revealed as an Airstream trailer, Zula guessed between twenty and thirty feet long. It had been jacked up to take the weight off its wheels and a shed roof of corrugated fiberglass had been affixed to one side, creating a sheltered outdoor space that, when cleared of snow, proved to contain a picnic table and some lawn chairs. From its interior they scavenged more kitchen ware, blankets, a foam mattress, packets of instant coffee and quick-cook oatmeal.

Zula had not really slept in a few days, but that afternoon, out of some combination of exhaustion, depression, and jet lag, she finally did fall into a deep slumber that lasted until some time after sundown. Then she got out of bed and took it upon herself to melt some more snow. Her Crocs had been confiscated and so she had to make her snow-collection forays barefoot. The pain in her feet reminded her of just how impossible it would be to get away from these people until she could solve the equipment problem. When she had a full pot of warm water, she carried it into the lavatory and gave herself a sponge bath using a bar of soap that had been left there years ago by departing miners. When she was done, she dried herself off using paper towels (a bale of them had also been left behind) and then emerged feeling weirdly and inappropriately energetic. She cooked some rice and some lentils, which were eaten, though not relished, by all (the kitchen had salt and pepper but no other seasonings).

The three jihadists made for quite a study. Two of them, Mahir and Sharif, were native Arabic speakers who, she collected, had gravitated from their home countries (Mahir looked pure Middle Eastern, Sharif had a bit of a North African look about him) to Afghanistan where they had become part of Jones's organization. The third, Ershut, was some kind of Central Asian who seemed to speak limited Arabic. Ershut was not tall, but he was stocky and powerful and tended to get saddled with grunt work, which he always seemed to accept as his lot in life. It was he who had loaded much of the heavy gear from the fishing vessel onto the smaller boat that they'd taken into Xiamen, and who had loaded it from the boat into the taxi and from the taxi into the plane. He was pious without showing the demented fanaticism of the late Khalid; during one of her lavatory forays on the jet last night, Zula had found him praying in the aisle of the main cabin, having apparently divined the direction to Mecca by looking at the on-screen map displayed on the flat-screen TV. One of his first acts in this place had been to scavenge a carpet scrap from a back room and get it pointed a little bit south of east.

Mahir and Sharif were almost certainly lovers. If not, then they were certainly taking male friendship to a level rarely seen in Western culture. They always sat together, and when Sharif went out on a scavenging expedition with Ershut, Mahir spent the whole time sitting by the window and sighing.

Zula was free to move around as long as she gave the impression of doing something useful, such as cooking or cleaning. At one point when no one was paying much attention, she took a yellow pad and a few pencils back into her room and hid them under the mattress. Later, when she'd been nailed back into her room for the night (having begged for and been given an extra ration of blankets), she sat by the light of a candle (these, at least, were abundant) and wrote a letter in the same general vein as the one she had scribbled on a paper towel and stuffed into the disconnected drain trap in the safe house bathroom in Xiamen. This one was a little more discursive, since she literally had all night. When she was finished, she slipped it under the mattress. Her body was showing no interest at all in going to sleep. She tried to tire herself out by doing all of the exercises she could think of that would not make a lot of noise: push-ups, dips, squats, and a gallimaufry of half-remembered yoga moves. But this only jacked up her energy level and made matters worse.

Consequently she was wide awake at about four in the morning when the building was slowly pervaded by the rumble of an approaching engine. This was not a steady drone, as of an overflying plane, but a patternless sequence of sharp rev-ups and die-downs. After a while it became loud enough to wake up Ershut. Through gaps around the edge of the wood they'd nailed over her window, Zula could see that they were being strafed by the headlights of, she guessed, some wildly veering and bucking vehicle that was headed toward them. Ershut pounded on the (apparently locked) door of the room where Mahir and Sharif were spooning. Then she heard feet thumping, magazines being jacked into guns, bolts being drawn back.

Then a horn honked just outside the building. A vehicle door opened. Men began to shout in Arabic, but the sound of their voices was buried under an eruption of gunfire. The high-pitched noise was filtered by the walls, but the deep concussion came right through, making her nostrils sting. She dropped to the floor with a thought of crawling under the bed, then came to her senses and understood that this would do her no good whatsoever. But then she heard the men outside laughing giddily and calling out *"Allahu akbar!"*

They were not in a gunfight. This was celebratory fire. The jihadists had themselves a vehicle; and since it had gotten in to the camp, it must be capable of getting them out.

ZULA WONDERED WHETHER the jihadists were simply out of their minds, firing guns into the air as a way of expressing joy when they were deep behind enemy lines. Or did they understand something about this place that she didn't? Could they really be so isolated that random bursts of automatic weapons fire in the middle of the night would go unheard by human ears?

She would find out soon enough. When the cops came and turned this place upside down—which she assumed *had* to happen sooner or later—they'd certainly find her letter. This improved her mood greatly, since she had been fretting the last day or two about the hell her extended family must be going through. They would continue in that state of unendurable not-knowing until the snow melted and the plane was exposed. Someone would notice it. Maybe in a month and maybe in a year. But the letter would ultimately be found and her family would be able to read it and understand what had happened and grieve properly and, she hoped, be proud of her.

They let her out of the room, apparently with the expectation that she'd be happy to prepare breakfast for them. She pretended that this was the case. But it was not until everyone had eaten and she was cleaning things up that the sky grew bright enough to let her see outside and get a load of the vehicle that Jones and Abdul-Wahaab had stolen.

From the axles up, it was simply a pickup truck, albeit of the biggest and heaviest class: the kind that, on her visits back home, she saw driving around in farm country, carrying bags of cement and towing fifth-wheel trailers. From the axles down, though, it looked like nothing she'd ever seen. The wheels had been removed and replaced with contraptions that looked like miniature tank treads. At each corner of the vehicle, where her eye expected to see a round wheel, it was instead baffled by the impossible-looking spectacle of a large triangular object, consisting of a system of bright yellow levers and wheels circumscribed by a caterpillar tread made up of black rubber plates linked together into an endless conveyor belt about a foot and a half wide. This ran along the ground for several feet beneath each axle and then looped up and around the yellow framework that held it all together, which, she perceived, was bolted onto the truck's axle using the same lug nut pattern as would be used to mount a conventional wheel. So it seemed that these things were a direct bolt-on replacement for conventional tires, made to spread the vehicle's weight out over a much larger contact area. Just the thing for an environment that was covered with snow for six months out of each year, and mud for another two. And indeed as the day grew brighter, she saw that the truck's rearview mirrors and upper body were spattered with dried mud. Conditions might be snowy up in this valley, but this truck had been stolen from some place where spring was well advanced.

The whole time that she was tending to food, Jones's crew were spreading out all the gear that they had brought with them, and everything that they had scavenged from the plane and from the mining camp, and making decisions about what to take and how to pack it. Guns and ammunition seemed to get first priority, followed by warm clothing and blankets. Blue tarps and ropes were deemed of inestimable value; perhaps they'd be camping? They seemed to have a passion for shovels, a detail that she could not help but interpret in the most morbid way possible.

The truck was a crew cab model, meaning that it had a second row of seats. They put Zula in the back, sandwiched between Sharif on her left and Mahir on her right. She felt strangely awkward coming between them, as if committing a social faux pas. But perhaps Jones was fed up with their clinginess and wanted them apart. Ershut rode shotgun and Abdul-Wahaab was squeezed into the middle of the front seat. Jones drove. Zula couldn't help but think that they would be just a little conspicuous rumbling around British Columbia in this contraption with that particular lineup of faces glaring out the windshield.

But that wouldn't even be an issue until they actually made it down to a road; and this did not look like it was happening any time soon. During whatever escapades that he and Abdul-Wahaab had enjoyed yesterday, Jones had learned how to drive the thing and had satisfied himself that if he shifted it into a sufficiently low gear (and this truck had some extremely low gears), it would go *anywhere*. Once the truck was packed, they headed up the valley, avoiding its sloped walls and sticking to its bottom, which was flat, but sinuous and multiforked. Jones seemed to be playing a connect-the-dots game on the map. Every few hundred meters was a cleared area, and these were strung together by a road. Or at least by a lane that had been bulldozed through the trees. The road and the cleared sites were marked on a survey map, which Abdul-Wahaab had spread out on his lap, the better for Jones to follow it. Zula caught glimpses of it during their frequent and voluble disputes as to its interpretation. At one point Jones pointed out the windshield into the sky and glared expectantly into the face of Abdul-Wahaab, and Zula understood that he was pointing out the location of the sun, as a trump card.

They fetched up parallel to a mountain stream, mostly buried under ice with snow on it. In some places it was open to the sky, and there it was possible to see that it was running broad and shallow, easily fordable by the truck. They rumbled and juddered across it, crept up its bank for half a mile, then struck out in what seemed to

Zula like a random direction, plowing directly into the woods and attacking a steep uphill slope as a way of getting out of this valley. Tree branches were pushed out of the way by the windshield, bending back until they either snapped off or else whipped in through the open driver's-side window where Jones had to beat them back with his left arm. She wondered why he would not simply roll up the window until she noticed little blue cubes of safety glass that had been sprayed all over the cab, and understood that the glass had been shattered. It seemed obvious enough that this must have happened when they were stealing the truck yesterday. She hoped that they had merely punched out the window so that they could get in and hot-wire it. Then she noted a key chain dangling from its ignition. They must have stolen it from a person who had been driving it. They must have killed that person.

A CB radio was mounted in the dashboard, and after they had got well clear of the camp and reached a decent stopping place—a flat spot in the forest, where they were well sheltered beneath the trees, and the snow wasn't too deep—Jones turned it on. Then, after a glance back over his shoulder toward Zula, he flicked his knife open, severed its microphone cable, and hurled the mike out through the vacant window frame. It skittered away through the undergrowth like a furtive mammal. He turned the volume up and began to scan through the available channels.

Nothing. They really were out in the middle of nowhere.

It had been set to Channel 4 when turned on. Jones put it back on 4 and left it running. Occasionally it would cough out some noise, but nothing that could be identified as words.

Jones put the truck in gear and attacked another slope. It seemed that they were going up more than down, which didn't make sense to Zula. But when they crawled over the next ridgeline, open country suddenly stretched out before them, foothills diminishing and descending into lowlands that were no longer covered in snow.

YESTERDAY, MONDAY, HAD been one of those days when Dodge had got to work early with the intention of getting a hell of a lot accomplished, only to arrive at the realization, just after lunch, that nothing was going to happen. Because it was no longer up to him.

He had a whole company—a whole structure of vassals—to drag along in his wake, and it just took them a long time to get mobilized.

He'd have thought that *$3 million lying there for the taking* would have been able to command their attention. But it took them a long time to grasp this. Egdod had to grab a few vice presidents' characters by the scruffs of their virtual necks and fly them over Torgai and point out the exposed gold caches for them to really get it.

A companywide memo might have gone some ways toward waking people up, but, as his finger was hovering over the Send button, he realized that this would be a terrible mistake. It would be certain to leak beyond the company network and find its way out into the wild, where it would trigger a gold rush. The one thing they had going in their favor was that no one, outside of Corvallis and Richard and a few others, really had any idea how much money was sitting there. Had this knowledge become public, every T'Rain player in the world would have made a beeline, or rather a ley line, for the Torgai, and things would have gone even more completely out of control. The mere Internet rumor that some gold had been seen there had already triggered a fairly well-organized invasion by those three thousand blue-haired K'Shetriae, which was nothing in the big scheme of things and yet still required strenuous work by Richard to beat it back in some way short of dropping a comet on the head of their Liege Lord.

Nothing came in all day from the Isle of Man. But when Richard woke up on Tuesday, he found a lot of company email, subject line "Plot thickens . . . ," which, when he traced it back to its root, turned out to concern a fifty-thousand-word novella that D-squared had posted on the T'Rain site a few hours ago. This to the evident surprise of his manager/editor here in Seattle, who'd had no idea that the Don was even contemplating any such project. Richard clicked on the link and opened the document. Its opening words were "The Torgai Foothills." He stopped reading there, closed his laptop, got out of bed, and put on some clothes. He took the elevator down to the parking garage of his condo tower in downtown Seattle, got in his car, and drove straight to Boeing Field. Not until he was ensconced in a comfy seat on the jet, arcing northward over British Columbia on a direct route to the Isle of Man, did he open his laptop again and commence reading in earnest.

Day 8

She remembered being brought home to her adoptive parents' house for the first time and seeing, among so many other new and amazing things, a complete set of the *Encyclopaedia Britannica* on the bookshelves in the living room. So many large books, identically bound except for the volume numbers printed on their spines, had naturally drawn her attention. Patricia, Richard's sister and Zula's new mom, had explained to her that these contained anything that you could ever possibly want to know, on any topic, and had pulled one down to look up the entry on Eritrea. Zula, completely missing the point, had assured Patricia that she would never on any account touch those books. Patricia had let out a shocked laugh and explained that no, on the contrary, all of those books were there specifically for her, Zula; they and the knowledge in them were, in effect, Zula's property.

Zula had inherited the set and doggedly lugged it around to a succession of dorm rooms, student flophouses, and studio apartments. Her arrival in the United States had coincided pretty nearly with the advent of full-time high-speed Internet, and she had likewise been encouraged to make free use of that, though it had never been quite the same, to her, as the *Britannica*.

From the age of eight onward, then, Zula had been raised in an environment that had been all about the free and frictionless flow of information into her young mind. She hadn't fully appreciated this until she had found herself in this predicament where no one saw any point in telling her anything at all. Traveling with Jones's band of jihadists, she almost felt nostalgic for the good old days of Ivanov and Sokolov, who had at least bothered to supply explanations of what was going on. Those two had bought into a Western mind-set in which it was important for things to make sense; and, needing the services of Zula and Peter and Csongor, they had been forced to keep them briefed.

Csongor. Peter. Yuxia. Even Sokolov. Whenever her mind went back over those events in Xiamen it snagged on those names, those faces. The mere fact of Peter's death would have prostrated her for a week in normal circumstances. She was now asking herself a hundred times a day what had become of the others. Were any of them alive? If so, were they wondering what had become of Zula?

What had become of Zula: this would have required considerable explanation, much of which Zula was not competent to supply, since they weren't telling her much. Circumstantial evidence (the key chain flailing from the ignition) made it clear that this strange truck with tank treads had been carjacked, as opposed to hot-wired. It seemed simplest to assume that the person they'd stolen it from was dead; it would have been crazy for them to leave the victim alive to call the Mounties. What kind of person drove such a vehicle around in the mountains of British Columbia during the mud season? It was quite obviously a working, not a recreational, vehicle and so Zula guessed it must be some sort of a caretaker or property manager. Perhaps that mine was not as abandoned as they had supposed; perhaps a number of such properties were spread around those mountains and they hired a local jack-of-all-trades to look in on each one of them from time to time.

The question on Jones's mind must then be: How long would it take for his victim to go missing? Because this contraption that they were driving around in was about the most conspicuous vehicle imaginable, short of a Zeppelin, and having five jihadists and a black girl crammed into it was not going to make it any easier to blend in with ordinary traffic on the byways of British Columbia.

At about three in the afternoon, according to the dashboard clock, they stopped at a place where they could look for miles down a mostly barren, rock-strewn valley. A broad stream ran down the middle of it, many braided channels finding their way across an expanse of glacier-dropped stones. Running roughly parallel to the watercourse, on its right, was a paved road that, several miles down-valley, hopped over the river on a low bridge. They were still in the forest; for the last two hours they had been traveling at little better than a walking pace, smashing down any foliage that could not stand up to the truck's inexorable advance, diverting around any trees that were too large to knock over, sometimes traversing slopes so steep that Zula braced her hands against the ceiling, ready for the truck to roll over sideways, sometimes avalanching down slopes so steep that little could grow on them. The front end of the truck looked like the inside of a lawn mower, covered with inches of mulch and mud. They had approached this place by following the course of a tribu-tary, sometimes driving right down the middle of the stream and sometimes nosing up into the surrounding woods. They had now stopped at the edge of the trees. Before them the ground dropped away sharply, the tributary leaping down a succession of rapids and waterfalls to the place where it joined in with the larger river. The truck might have survived the plunge to the bottom, and had it sur-vived, it might have been able to make it to the road and go a few more miles before running out of fuel. But if, as seemed likely, it got stuck in boulders or wrecked itself during the descent, it would have been marooned in a place that was utterly exposed to view from the road and from the air. Best to leave it here. Or this was what Zula surmised must be going on in Jones's mind. He shifted it into reverse and backed it deeper into the trees, then killed the engine.

Apparently this was not the first time that the jihadists had cam-ouflaged a vehicle in mountains. Leaving Zula inside for the time being, they smeared mud over all of its windows and mirrors and any other parts that were capable of reflecting a gleam of sunlight. They unloaded some of the gear from the back—just what they could carry under their own power. They foraged through the woods for ferns and huckleberry bushes and cedar fronds, which they uprooted or hacked off, dragged over, and leaned and stacked around the truck's sides. At some point, they remembered that Zula was still in there, so they extracted her through the cab's sliding rear window and dragged her back straight to the open tailgate, many hands on her arms and

ankles, trying to stifle even the mere thought of fighting or running.
Ershut bent over and braced both hands against her right leg, and
Abdul-Wahaab wrapped a chain around her ankle and then snapped
a padlock into place. She was shooed and chivied back off the edge
of the tailgate and onto the ground behind the truck. The chain was
looped around part of the trailer hitch.

There followed one of those comical interludes in which the
jihadists were confused about what to do next and fell to bitter
recriminations.

It seemed that they were short one padlock. At some point during their scrounging activities around the mining camp they had
found this length of chain, and at some other point they had found
this padlock and the key that went with it. So they could lock the
chain around her ankle. Fine. But they were now wanting the second padlock that was needed to connect the other end of the chain
to the trailer hitch. Some of them shouted at each other, some of
them rummaged aimlessly through all the piles of junk that they
had scrounged.

Ershut said, "It's not a problem, we can do it with one padlock.
Look, I'll show you."

He said it in Arabic.

Zula understood it.

Interesting.

Other men might have gathered round to see Ershut's cleverness, but these guys were all pursuing their own strategies. In the
back of the pickup was a toolbox, secured with another padlock, and
Abdallah Jones was going through the key chain, apparently on the
reasonable assumption that it might contain the key needed to open
this thing.

Ershut looped the long end of the chain through the frame of
the trailer hitch and brought it back to Zula's ankle. Then he held
out one hand and asked for the key to the padlock that was already
there. Then demanded it. Then screamed for it. Finally someone
slapped it into his hand. He undid the padlock on Zula's ankle,
swung the body away from the hasp, brought up the loose end of
the chain, pushed a link over the hasp, then snapped it shut again.

At the same moment Jones dropped to one knee right next
to him, holding up an open padlock that he had apparently just

retrieved from the toolbox. Seeing that Ershut had already found a one-padlock solution, he dropped the lock on the ground and walked away.

Zula was left with an arm's length of slack in the loop that secured her ankle to the trailer hitch. A scrap of plastic, a sleeping bag, a bottle of water, and a short stack of MREs were provided before they finished surrounding the truck in camouflage.

At any other time in her life she would have offered more resistance to such proceedings and would have been correspondingly heartbroken when the padlock clicked shut. But slowly growing in her mind was a feeling that the situation was shifting to her advantage. Which seemed an idiotic thing to say given her current situation: ankle chained to a trailer hitch in the wilderness of northwestern Canada, keys in the pockets of suicide bombers.

But she had begun to see hints that cooperation was slowly working in her favor. It was a hell of a lot better being here than in China. She had taken arms and killed that one guy. *Killed him.* Unbelievable. She had made her survival the linchpin of Jones's plan, whatever it might be. Everything was different. The jihadists seemed oblivious to this shift.

The wall of camo being built around her grew dense enough that she could barely make out the men's movements on the other side of it, as they occluded the slits of light that still shone through here and there. She had the horrifying thought that maybe they were actually constructing a huge bonfire and that they were about to burn her alive. But after a while she noticed she could not hear them anymore. They had shouldered their packs, tromped away, and left her alone.

The trailer hitch had become the center of her personal universe. Above was the open tailgate, providing a kind of shelter from the weather. The ground beneath her was a bed of blunt nails, the sheared-off stumps of mowed-down foliage. She devoted some time to kicking at the stalks, shearing them off level with the ground, and stomping them into the earth. Once it had become passably level, she spread the plastic out on the ground and arranged the sleeping bag on top of that, then climbed inside it. The temperature was well above freezing, but the damp chill would kill her in hours if she did not keep moving and working.

You seem to have made quite an impression on Mr. Sokolov. Jones had said that to her, apropos of nothing, the first evening at the mining camp. *I couldn't make out why until you did for Khalid.* She'd been unable to make any sense at all of these statements and had put them out of her mind until now.

How could Jones possibly know what Sokolov thought of her? Jones and Zula had spent hours going over the events in the apartment building. Most of this had been him extracting information from her. But from the nature of the questions he asked, she had been able to piece together a reasonably coherent picture of how the battle had gone. It was out of the question that Sokolov and Jones could have engaged in any conversation. And if they had, they would not have been chitchatting about Zula; even in the incredibly unlikely event that Sokolov wanted to talk about her in the middle of a crazy running gun battle, Jones didn't even know that she existed at that point.

Finally, now, she understood. The answer to the riddle had come to her while her conscious mind had been thinking about other things. Perhaps she'd gotten a clue from the way that Jones had kept an ear cocked toward the squawks coming from the CB radio in the truck. She'd seen a similar look on his face before, on the plane, at the FBO in Xiamen. He had received a call on his phone and whipped it open. His face had lit up with delight, which had immediately collapsed into shock and then settled into some kind of intense murderous fascination.

It must have been Sokolov on the other end of that call. Sokolov had killed, or at least overcome, the men Jones had sent out to murder him, and ended up in possession of one of their phones, and hit the redial button. He had made some kind of a little speech to Jones. And he had mentioned Zula. That had to be it; that was the only time that Sokolov could ever have communicated with Jones.

Why would Sokolov mention Zula in that conversation?

(It took a while to work these things out. But Zula had a while.)

Really that was two questions: first, how could Sokolov have known that Zula and Jones were together? And second, given that he knew this, why would he go to the trouble of mentioning her to Jones during their brief phone conversation?

The answer to the first question was already in her head, and she needed only to pull it up from memory. On the boat, a couple of days ago, after the scene on the pier. Jones interrogating Zula. Zula telling him about the safe house, pointing to the skyscraper, calling out the forty-third floor. And wondering whether in doing so she was sending a message to Sokolov, letting him know that she, or some other member of the group, was still alive. Because if Jones's men went snooping around on the forty-third floor of that building, it would raise the question: How had they learned the location of the safe house?

As to the second question: Jones had answered it, in a way, with his remark *You seem to have made quite an impression on Mr. Sokolov.*

What the hell did that mean?

Maybe Sokolov had said to Jones: *I hope you kill that conniving bitch!* But Zula doubted this. Her interactions with Sokolov had been about as courteous and respectful as it was possible to get in an abductor/hostage relationship. She had felt, in a weird way, as though she were partners with him.

Otherwise, she wouldn't have done it.

She realized this now. Calling out the wrong apartment number, sending them to 505 instead of 405: this was crazy. Suicidal. No wonder Peter had been furious with her. So furious that his next move had been to abandon her to her fate, leaving her handcuffed to a pipe. Csongor had been as shocked as Peter, but he'd taken her side in the matter because of dumb love. Why had Peter and Csongor been so incredulous at this decision that had seemed so easy, so obviously the correct move, to Zula?

Because Peter and Csongor had not been privy to the almost subliminal exchanges of glances and—not even anything as obvious as glances or words, but hidden signals in postures, facial expressions, the way that Zula, getting on an elevator with a group of Russians, had always chosen to stand by Sokolov's side. Zula and Sokolov were allies. He would protect her from whatever fate Ivanov had in mind for them. And, sensing that she was under his umbrella, she had felt safe enough to send them to 505 when she knew that the Troll was in 405.

And she could do it again. She *had been* doing it again, this time with Jones. And part of the way you did it was by keeping your emotional shit together, not kicking and screaming, not suffering emotional breakdowns, showing you could handle it, could be trusted. Getting them used to having you around.

That was why she had relaxed and shown no emotion when Abdul-Wahaab had padlocked the chain around her ankle. A little thing. But a little thing that Jones had noticed, even if—*especially* if—he wasn't aware that he was noticing it.

Could Jones really be that easily manipulated? He seemed so smart in all other ways.

I couldn't make out why until you did for Khalid.

That explained it. Jones was at a loss to understand why Sokolov, his personal bête noire, thought enough of Zula to make her a primary topic of their one brief phone exchange. He had not observed the way that Zula and Sokolov had grown accustomed to each other during the days they'd been together; and even if he had, he might not have sussed it out, any more than Peter or Csongor had. Consequently, ever since hearing Sokolov's voice coming out of that phone, Jones had been chewing on this, trying to figure out what Sokolov saw in her; and when she had killed Khalid, he had reckoned that this was the answer. He believed that Sokolov's respect for Zula was rooted in an appreciation of Zula's fighting spirit or her prowess with weapons or some other such quality: the kind of thing that a man like Jones would suppose that a man like Sokolov would hold in esteem.

And this left Jones wide open. Ready to be blindsided by the same tactics Zula had used with Sokolov. The difference being that in the case of Sokolov they hadn't been tactics, just Zula instinctively trusting the man. The question now was: Could she bring about a similar effect in Jones's mind by doing similar things in a way that was utterly calculated and insincere?

"ONE DAY, MY son, all of this could be yours," Egdod intoned, swooping low over the Torgai Foothills. He was addressing an Anthron—a man, basically—whom he was holding by the scruff of the neck. The Anthron was dressed in the most nondescript possible woolen cloak. Between his bare feet (for he had declined to spend virtual money on shoes or even sandals), the mature coniferous forest of the Torgai streamed by, just a few hundred meters below.

"Far be it from me to question your *database*," the Anthron replied, "but I still don't see—"

"There!" Egdod called out, banking into a tight turn and spiraling down toward an outcropping of basalt. "Just at the base of those rocks."

"I do see a fleck of yellow, but I assumed it was a patch of eälanthassala," said the Anthron, easily wrapping his tongue around the hexasyllabic name of the sacred flower of the montane branch of the K'Shetriae.

"Look again," Egdod said, and he shed altitude until they were poised only a few meters above the "fleck." This was now revealed as a mound of shiny yellow coins. "I'm going to drop you." He did so.

"Heavens!" exclaimed the Anthron, then landed on his feet and fell awkwardly onto his arse, creating little gold-coin avalanches.

"If your character had better Proprioception—which you could get by spending some of your Attribute credits, or by sending him off to undertake certain types of training, or by drinking the right potion—he would have landed a little more adroitly and rolled out like a paratrooper instead of taking minor damage to his butt, as yours just did," Egdod said, sounding a little peevish for a creature of nearly godlike status. For this newly created Anthron had been absurdly stingy with his Attribute credits and still had most of them hoarded in reserve where they were doing him absolutely no good.

The burst of gibberish left the Anthron utterly nonplussed.

"Never mind," Egdod said.

"Who are those creatures coming out of the trees, over yonder?" the Anthron asked, turning his head to the left. Egdod—who was invisible to everyone in T'Rain except for the Anthron—spun in midair to see a pair of Dwinn marauders headed straight for them. One heavily armed and armored cataphract, unslinging a crossbow, and one mage, clad only in robes, but protected by a swirling nebula of colored lights: force field spells that she had thrown up to protect herself from random slings and arrows.

"You could see the answer for yourself if you had spent some of your Attribute credits on Perceptivity," Egdod groused, and lost altitude until he had positioned himself directly in the path of the incoming crossbow bolt.

"I can't see!" the Anthron complained.

"Oh yeah—you're the only person in the world to whom I am opaque," Egdod said. He turned around to face the Anthron. "Check it out."

"Oh my word, you've been shot!" For Egdod actually did have a crossbow bolt projecting from the general vicinity of his liver. But as the Anthron watched, the bolt was spat out by the wound it had made. It flipped backward for about a meter and stuck in the grass. By the time the Anthron's eyes had traveled back up to the wound, it had healed, leaving behind a pink scar that was rapidly fading. "A little trick I picked up about a thousand years ago," Egdod explained. "Hold on a sec while I deal with these guys."

"Deal with them?"

"I could incinerate them just by looking at them funny," Egdod said, "but then they'd know that an extremely high-level character was running around the Torgai, and word might get around. So I'm going to do it the way a lower-level character might." Egdod turned back toward the interlopers, raised his hands, and uttered a phrase in a dead classical language of T'Rain.

Almost. "You used an incorrect declension of *turom*," the Anthron complained.

"It doesn't seem to have reduced the effectiveness of the spell," Egdod returned. The meadow between them and the two Dwinn was sprouting a crop of spears. Helmeted heads emerged next, and then the armored bodies of *turai*, which, in Classical T'Rain mythology, were fast-spawning autochthonous warriors analogous to the *spartoi* of Greek myth. The Dwinn mage was already waving her hands in the air trying to cast a spell that would throw the *turai* into confusion and possibly even cause them to attack one another, but there were too many of them and it was too late; the Dwinn had no choice but to retreat into the woods, pursued by the dozen or so *turai* who had proved resistant to the mage's spell.

"Okay, let's get this done," Egdod said, "because this kind of thing is going to happen over and over again as long as this pile of gold is just sitting here for the taking."

"Get *what* done, exactly?" the Anthron asked, standing there knee-deep in specie, clueless to a degree that was somewhere between funny and outrageous.

"Pick up the fucking money and put it in your bag," Egdod said. "Or just shift-option-right-click on the whole pile."

"Shift . . . option . . . is that some sort of computer terminology?"

"Just hold your horses. I'm coming over there."

"I thought you *were* here."

"In the real world, like."

RICHARD TOSSED HIS laptop aside onto the mattress and swung his legs down off the edge of the Bed That Queen Anne Had Slept In. Its massive frame of pegged timbers gave out a groan almost as if Queen Anne were still in it now. He rose to his feet and gave his blood pressure a moment to equilibrate, then stalked across the room. Which took a bit of stalking. Other bits of England might be cramped, crowded, and cluttered, but only because all the available space had been claimed by this guest suite. It was situated right in Trinity College, and Richard guessed it had been laid out eight hundred years ago so that noble guests could ride their horses directly into the bedchamber and bring all of their squires and wolfhounds with them too. D-squared was standing with his back to Richard about three hundred feet away. The place lacked television and central heating, but it did have a massive stand surmounted by a four-inch-thick Bible signed by the Duke of Wellington. D-squared had set up a laptop of his own atop the Good Book and was hunched over it, peering and pecking.

During the short drive in from the FBO at Cranfield, Richard had ordered the driver of his black taxi to swerve to a halt in front of the first computer store. The sales clerk, eager to be of service and to make sure that Richard ended up with a machine he'd be happy with, had been solicitous to a fault until Richard had finally got it through the man's head that he had way more money than time and could they please get on with it. Five minutes later, Richard had strode out the door of the place and climbed back into the taxi carrying the new laptop (he had left its empty box sitting on the store's counter and a trail of plastic packaging material all the way to the exit) and a boxed set of DVD-ROMs containing the Legendary Deluxe Platinum Collector's Edition T'Rain software with Bonus Materials. The computer had finished crawling through its inter-

minable boot-up as they were skirting Bedford, and he had jammed
in the installation disc somewhere around St. Neots. The bemused
cabbie had dropped him off at the Porter's Lodge of Trinity when
the installation progress bar was creeping along around the 21 percent mark and so Richard had just carried the machine in on his hip
and kept it perched there, whirring and clicking and trying to force
thunderous T'Rain sound track music through its tinny little speakers, as the bowler-hatted staff had dryly greeted him and escorted
him to his cavernous lodgings. It was ten in the morning or something. Richard had found his way to the suite's toilet, which was
located somewhere in Oxfordshire, and showered and shaved, then
fed another disc into the computer, napped for a couple of hours,
enjoyed a liquid lunch with D-squared, and then brought him back
here to teach him the rudiments of T'Rain.

"Like this," he said, reaching in over the Don's arms in a manner that all but forced the poor man to jump out of the way, and
seizing control of the keyboard. Then Richard did the thing that
always pissed him off when Corvallis did it to him, which was
that he manipulated the keys so fast that it was impossible for any
normal person to understand what he had just accomplished. But
D-squared, used to having people do things for him, was unruffled. He was far more interested in what had happened to all that
money.

"The gold!" he exclaimed. "Where did it all get to? Did those
Dwinn take it?"

The accusation was laughable. Far more important, though,
was the look on the Don's face, which was just a bit provoked, and
his tone of voice, which could only be described as avaricious.

Good.

"No," Richard said, "you took it, and put it in your poke."

"But how could I possibly carry so much gold in that wee bag?"

"That's the whole point of a poke. It's magic. Enables you to
carry a ridiculous amount of VP and thereby enhances our profit
margins like you wouldn't believe."

The Don nodded. Even he knew that VP stood for Virtual
Property.

"But that is not the point," Richard went on. "The point is as
follows." And he turned away and hiked back over to the bed. This

took long enough that a little band of Var' skirmishers, almost offensively Bright, had time to scuttle out of the trees to investigate the strange phenomenon of a solitary Anthron, newly created and hence of essentially zero powers, unarmed and unequipped—un*shod*, even—just standing there like an idiot in possibly the most dangerous region of all T'Rain. It was so uncanny that they were approaching him with a kind of superstitious awe.

As well they might, for Richard, after using certain of his powers to verify his suspicion that they were carrying a lot of money, zotted the whole band into pink mushroom clouds.

"Richard, I'm surprised at you; I didn't think you were going to stoop to such methods!"

"I'm trying to make a point. I blew them away so fast that they didn't have time to Sequester any of their belongings."

"What in heaven's name does that mean?"

"It means we get to steal all of the VP that they were carrying. Go and pick up all the gold that's lying on the ground. And while you're at it, why don't you grab yourself some fucking shoes?"

"Are you suggesting I loot corpses!?"

"I know. What would Queen Anne say?"

"I've no idea!"

"You can take your laptop off that Bible first, if it makes you feel any cleaner about it."

"No need. I gather this sort of thing happens all the time, in T'Rain."

Richard resisted the temptation to say *people make their livings off it.*

Once D-squared had at last solved the user-interface problem of how to pick stuff up and put it in his poke, and had caused the Anthron to loot all the gold, plus some Boots of Elemental Mastery and a Diadem of Scrying that he took a fancy to, Egdod grabbed him (the Anthron, that is) by the scruff of the neck again and flew him, with a velocity that the Don described as "faintly sickening," about halfway around the planet to visit a moneychanger who, being situated almost at the antipode of where all the action was, was offering fast service and good rates.

It was possible to interact with an MC verbally, and thereby remain "in-world," which was equivalent to an actor remaining "in character," but the impatient Richard diverted the Don to a user interface window replete with medievally styled buttons and pop-up menus. "You want to make a Potlatch to Argelion. It's the third checkbox down on the right."

"The god of mammon and lucre!?"

"You know perfectly well what Argelion is."

"I should have thought so! But I recall nothing about a Potlatch! Why, that is a concept from Pacific Coast Indian tradition! Such a thing has no place in—"

"It is one of those things that we added to the world so long ago that we forgot it wasn't your idea," Richard said. "We can argue about it during dinner, if you like. Half of those guys at High Table are probably playing T'Rain in secret; they'll enjoy hearing your thoughts on why Potlatches are bad. But for now, if you would just click on the friggin' box . . ."

"All right, I have done so. And now new things!" The Don said this in the wondering tone that he always adopted when confronted by unexpected dynamism in a user interface. "'One-quarter, one-half, three-quarters, all. Or enter an amount.'"

"Giving you options as to how much of your gold is going to Potlatch," Richard explained. "Click 'All.'"

This suggestion only triggered the same miserly tendencies that had caused the Anthron, until recently, to spare himself the expense of footwear. "No! All of that gold!? It's just going to disappear?"

"*From the game world,*" Richard said. "Just please do it. If you're unhappy with the results, I'll get you more."

The Don, looking scandalized and beleaguered, clicked 'All' and then hit the 'Potlatch' button. Then he sighed. "Easy come, easy go."

Richard did not answer for a few moments, as he was busy logging out. "Okay," he said, closing his laptop, and resuming the journey to the Bible stand. Next time he stayed here, he'd bring roller skates. "I'm going to need your credit card again."

"Why!?" the Don exclaimed, as if this was exactly what he'd been worrying about.

"The same one you used to set up the account. Please."

By the time Richard got over there, D-squared had worried the card out of what looked like Queen Anne's wallet and handed it over. Richard flipped the card onto its face, pulled out his phone, set it on Speaker, and then dialed the customer service number printed on its back.

A lovely British voice came on, introducing them to the root of a branching tree of automated service options. Richard navigated to "Check recent transactions" and then punched in D-squared's credit card number.

The most recent transaction, according to this disembodied robot on the other end of the line, was a credit in the amount of £842.69, time-stamped about five minutes ago.

"I guess you owe me a drink," Richard said to the openmouthed and bulging-eyed face of the Don, "because you are now eight hundred quid—you call them 'quid,' right?—richer. Thanks to that little escapade."

"That was the Potlatch?"

"Yes. Money disappears from T'Rain, as a burnt offering to Argelion. It never comes back. But that's just a cover story that we have set up to enable players to extract hard currency."

"I see!"

"I believe that you *do* see, Donald."

"I had known, of course, that such transactions were possible in principle—"

"But there's nothing quite like having money in the bank, is there?"

"I believe I just *might* buy you a drink, Richard."

"And I would happily accept. But what I would really like to do, while we are hoisting that pint, is to talk to you about what might happen in the next couple of weeks to the other three million dollars' worth of gold pieces that are just lying there on the ground. Free for the taking."

ZULA ATE AN MRE, stuffed the empty tray into the tangle of camouflage that had been erected around the truck, burrowed into her sleeping bag, and went to sleep faster than she had thought possible. She dreamed of China: a disconnected and rearranged version of Xiamen that incorporated bits of Seattle and the Schloss and the cave bunkers of Eritrea. It made perfect sense in dream-logic.

She woke up once to a deeply troubling sound that she identified, after a few moments, as the howling of wolves, or perhaps coyotes. Then she was stuck awake for a long time. She ate another MRE, supposing that a full stomach might do her some good. This did not seem to help especially. She was paying, now, for the ease with which she had slipped into sleep earlier. After a while, she gave up any hope of sleeping again and just tried to make herself comfortable. But from the fact that she ended up dreaming later, it followed that she must have drifted away in spite of herself.

The first couple of nights after the thing with Khalid she had not dreamed of it at all, at least that she could remember. But yesterday during the interminable truck ride, she had found herself remembering the moment of those shards being driven into his face by her hands, and the blood, or something, that had been on her fingers after. This night Khalid did come back to her in her dreams, and she devoted some effort to fighting him off. Not physically fighting him but half-consciously trying to erect some kind of psychic defense against ever seeing his image again, sensing that if he appeared in her thoughts during the day and her dreams at night, he would never be gone, she would still be dreaming of him and reliving the moments in the back of that jet in the unlikely event that she lived to the age of ninety.

She was hearing a kind of snuffling, coughing noise and thought that maybe she had begun crying in her sleep and was hearing her own sobs in the disembodied way that sometimes happened around the foggy frontier between sleeping and waking. Something was grabbing her ankle. The chain, of course. Pulling on it urgently. Really it was just her pulling against it as she rolled around in her sleep. But in the dream it was a man pulling on her wrist. Remarkable that, in a dream, a wrist could substitute for an ankle. But she was seeing the face of an old man who had been with them in the caves in Eritrea and who had walked with them on the long barefoot trek to Sudan. The caves were, among other things, a field hospital for casualties from the war against Ethiopia. Young fighters showed up with burns, gunshot wounds, shrapnel. The doctors tried to fix them up. Some of them died. Some of them could not be fixed— they underwent amputations, and hung around until they could find some place to go. But there was this older guy—in retrospect, probably not older than fifty—with a hollow, sucked-in face carpeted with a patchy gray beard, and urgent, avid green-brown eyes, who showed up there, apparently healthy, and never left. They came to understand, in time, that he was a psychological casualty. Any grown-up could see in a few moments that he was not right in the head. Children didn't have that instinct. The man had things he very much wanted to say, and he seemed to learn, after a time, that adults would veer away from him, pretend not to hear him, even shoo him away. But children unaccompanied by adults—as they quite often were—could give him a few moments' company, the social balm that all humans, even crazy old war veterans, had to have. His way of getting you to pay attention to him was to grab you by the wrist and tug until you were obliged to look into his crazy eyes.

After which, he didn't have a lot to say, since he appeared to have suffered a head injury and could not really form words. But he could gesture at things and look you in the eyes and try to get you to understand. And to the extent that young Zula could follow his train of thought at all, he seemed to be trying to warn her, and any other kid whose wrist he was able to grab, about something. Something really big and bad and scary that was out there in the world beyond this valley where they had found refuge in the caves. In this particular dream he was trying to warn her about Khalid and she was trying to explain that she was pretty sure Khalid was dead, but he wouldn't believe her, wouldn't let go of her wrist, just kept yanking. The snuffling and coughing: her crying? But she wasn't crying; the sounds were coming from somewhere else.

The old man insistent. Like she really just weren't getting it. Had no idea. Needed to wake up.

She was obliged, in fact, to wake up by a crashing noise and a thud, not far away, that traveled through the ground and came up through her ribs.

A few moments' ridiculous confusion here as her mind, like a passenger caught straddling the gap between a pier and a departing boat, tried to bridge the dream with reality.

Then she was very awake; the Eritrean man was gone and instantly forgotten.

She wanted to call out "Hello?" but her throat had spasmed shut. If it was Jones and his crew, there was no reason to call out to them; they knew where she was and she certainly felt no need to exchange pleasantries with their like. But whatever was out there did not move—did not *think*—like a human.

It was at least as big as a human, though.

It was circling this strange thicket that had appeared in its hunting grounds, sniffing at it, probing it with swipes of its paws. Discovering that it came apart rather easily.

It was a bear—it could be nothing else—and it was homing in on the back of the truck, where Zula was.

WHEN SHE HAD made the move from Iowa to Seattle, driving a cute little miniature U-Haul loaded with the *Encyclopaedia Britannica* and other things she couldn't be without, Zula had made a small diversion into northern Idaho to look in on her uncle Jacob and his family: wife Elizabeth, eldest son Aaron, and two other sons whose names she had, embarrassingly, forgotten. She had been warned by most of the family to expect serious weirdness, but she was assured by Uncle Richard that they were perfectly normal people. What she'd found, of course, was somewhere in between; or perhaps those aspects of their life that seemed normal only made the weird stuff seem weirder. Elizabeth going about her housewifely chores and homeschooling the boys with a Glock semiautomatic lodged in a black shoulder holster strapped over the bodice of her ankle-length dress. Or were those culottes?

Anyway, conversing over dinner, they had somehow gotten onto the topic of bears. Uncle Richard had warned Zula, once, that bears were the conversational equivalent of a black hole, in the sense that any conversation that fell into that topic could never escape it. Considering how rare bears and bear attacks were in the real world, Zula, the rational-skeptic college kid, had doubted the veracity of Dodge's observation. Maybe it just happened to him a lot, she had reasoned, because he had this one bear incident in his past that people never got tired of hearing about. But then she had seen it happen a couple of times, around tables in dormitory cafeterias: nineteen-year-old kids who had never seen bears in their lives somehow straying onto that topic and then sticking with it until everyone got up and left.

Uncle Jacob had been out building log cabins all day and had sawdust in his beard. He was tired and distracted by his energetic boys, who wanted all of his attention, and he looked like he wanted a cold beer: an indulgence forbidden by his variant of Christianity. So it had taken a while for him to slip into avuncular mode with Zula. She had almost begun to wonder whether he didn't accept her as a real family member. But it slowly became evident over the course of the meal that he was just hungry. So eventually it turned into a real conversation.

The cabin was built three stories high on a small foundation. The cellar was a food storage area giving way to a subterranean bunker that Jake had dug out by hand and lined with reinforced concrete. The ground floor was practical stuff: sort of a garage/ workshop with corners dedicated to such practical matters as slaughtering, butchering, canning, and ammo reloading. The floor above that was one big kitchen/living/dining space and the top story was bedrooms. Both the second and third floors had sliding doors and windows giving way to screened-in decks on what Zula thought of as the back side of the house, since it faced away from the driveway; but she soon learned that Jake and Elizabeth thought of it as the front. It looked out over an area of flat ground extending across a couple of acres, sparsely populated by trees, which lapped up against the base of a steep rise, the southern approach of Abandon Mountain. A mountain stream, Prohibition Crick, tumbled down that slope and ran past the cabin, making a beautiful sound, on its way to a beaver pond about half a mile away. Like-minded neighbors had built homesteads around that, forming a sparse community of five families and a couple of dozen souls distributed across two square miles of flattish, semiarable land at the head of a river valley that ran almost all the way to Bourne's Ford.

During dinner, a storm had come up that valley and washed over them with a few impressive thunder cracks and a sudden gushing of rain from the tin roof. Clear air had blown in behind it, and the sun had come out and made a rainbow that seemed to plunge down into the valley. The scent of rain-washed cedars came in through the screen porch. Jacob spread honey on homemade bread that Elizabeth had pulled from the oven an hour ago. Life was suddenly good. He asked her about how the journey was going and what plans she had for her new life in Seattle and what sorts of things she liked to do in her spare time. She mentioned a number of activities that seemed, since they were sort of urban and high-tech, to go in one of Jacob's ears and out the other. She also mentioned camping. Not that she was really all that interested in camping. She had done it in Girl Scouts and on family trips. It seemed almost obligatory for a healthy young person moving to Seattle to claim that she was interested in camping. That stirred his interest, anyway, and they talked about that for a little bit, just circling the black hole that was sitting there waiting patiently for them, and then, of course, they were talking about bears. Jacob mentioned that there were very few places left in the Lower Forty-Eight that still harbored grizzly, as opposed to black, bears and that northern Idaho was one of them; they were connected, by the Selkirks and the Purcells, to a vastly larger reservoir of grizzles that ran all the way up the Canadian Rockies into Alaska. Jacob dwelled, a little more than Zula was really comfortable with, on the idea that bears were attracted to menstruating women and that Zula really should not go camping in bear country when she was having her period. The modern feminist college-girl part of her thinking it was all just deeply wrong and inappropriate, the refugee/orphan/Forthrast taking a somewhat more pragmatic view.

It sounded like folklore to her. Not that this would get her anywhere in an argument with Jacob; a *lot* of what he believed was folklore, and the more folky it was, the more doggedly he believed it. No great insight was needed on Zula's part to perceive that he had a chip on his shoulder regarding education and science; she'd already been warned not to mention, in his presence, the possibility that the earth might be more than six thousand years old.

All of which was easy for her. She had been dealing with men like this ever since she had come to Iowa. Men wanted to be strong. One way to be strong was to be knowledgeable. In so many areas, it was not possible to be knowledgeable without getting a Ph.D. and doing a postdoc. Guns and hunting provided an out for men who wanted to be know-it-alls but who couldn't afford to spend the first three decades of their lives getting up to speed on quantum mechanics or oncology. You simply couldn't go to a gun range without being cornered by a man who wanted to talk to you for hours about the ballistics of the .308 round or the relative merits of side-by-side versus over-and-under shotguns. If you couldn't stand that heat, you needed to stay out of that kitchen, and Zula had walked right into it by crossing the threshold of Jacob and Elizabeth's house. She smiled and nodded and pretended to be interested in Uncle Jacob's bear lore until Aunt Elizabeth finished putting the boys to bed and came and rescued her.

Anyway, she had looked it up on the Internet (of course) when she had reached Seattle and found much (of course) conflicting information posted by people with varying levels of scientific credibility. She had ended up knowing no more about it, really, than she had before the conversation with Uncle Jacob. And yet the connection to menstrual blood struck heavy psychic resonances (which was, of course, why the myth was so widespread in the first place), and so, that early morning when she was chained to the trailer hitch under the pickup truck and she realized that the thing sniffing and pawing around was a bear, her brain went straight to her uterus and she asked herself whether she might have lost count of the days and started having her period in the middle of the night. Certainly didn't feel that way. It was funny how the brain worked; she even permitted herself a brief excursion into meta/ironical land wondering if anyone else in the world—in *history*—had been in danger from gangsters, terrorists, and bears in the space of a single week. When would the pirates and dinosaurs show up?

But finally she saw and understood what it was that the bear was actually questing for and saw that the entire train of thought concerning menstrual blood had been a dangerous exercise in self-absorption. The bear was coming for what bears always came for: garbage. The empty trays of the MREs. Owing to constraints imposed by the ankle chain and the surrounding wall of stacked brush, she had not been able to dispose of these in the Girl Scout–approved manner of bagging them and hanging them from a tree far from camp.

The animal sounded, seemed, as if he were only arm's length from her, but she told herself that her fear was making the distance seem smaller than it was. She had one more MRE left. She peeled the lid back and shoved it in the direction of that snuffling and panting sound, then withdrew beneath the truck's undercarriage.

On its tank treads the vehicle was jacked up absurdly high, its running boards at the altitude of Zula's hip. She couldn't stand up beneath it but she could easily squat on her haunches with her head projecting into the space between its driveshaft and its frame. The volume beneath it was not empty, but choked with undergrowth, a mixture of shrubs and small coniferous seedlings that had passed safely beneath the truck's bumper as it eased into this position. These remained upright and undisturbed. So she was *both* hiding in undergrowth *and* taking shelter beneath a truck, which she hoped would suffice to keep her out of the bear's clutches. She had the idea that it was a big one. But of course she *would* think that. Perhaps it was too bulky to want to cram itself underneath the truck; it would be satisfied with the easier pickings of the MRE that Zula had tossed in its direction. This it certainly seemed to be enjoying. She tried to think of what she would do if it crept under here to get her. Punch it in the nose? No, that was what you were supposed to do to a shark. Might not work on a bear. With bears you were supposed to make yourself look big. Don't try to run away. The not running away part was taken care of. Making herself look big might be difficult. The chain on her ankle was a good twenty feet long. Less than half of it had been used to connect her ankle to the trailer hitch. The remainder just trailed on the ground. She began gathering it up, wrapping it around her left hand, turning it into a fat steel club. The weight of it threw her off balance, and she threw out her right hand to steady herself against the truck's frame. She thought it would be all solid and strong, and for the most part it was; but something small and flimsy moved beneath her hand there.

She froze and made herself still. The bear was still making hugely satisfied smacking noises, getting the most out of that MRE. But a few moments later, it too became quiet and still, as though listening, wondering about something. Zula's first thought was that she must have made some noise or that a shift in the breeze had betrayed her presence.

The bear went into movement, and she cringed, thinking it might be moving toward her; but it wasn't. The light of the morning was coming in now through the wrecked screen of camouflage, and ducking down, using that hand on the frame to steady herself, Zula peered back between the truck's rear treads to see its hind legs— *only* its hind legs—planted on the ground. It was standing up to sniff the air and to listen. It let out a kind of indignant barking sound, then dropped to all fours and sauntered away.

There was definitely something under Zula's right hand. She explored it with her fingertips and found that she could pry it loose from its lodging against the frame. It was a little plastic box.

She let the chain spiral off her other hand, then crawled out from beneath the truck to where the light was better.

The little box was a hide-a-key, with a magnet on one side. She slid it open and found two keys linked together by a split ring. One of them looked like a spare ignition key for the truck. The other was much smaller and looked like it belonged to a padlock. She tried it on the lock that was holding the chain around her ankle, but it would not even slide into the keyhole; this was made for a different brand.

Her eyes went to the toolbox padlock that Jones had discarded on the ground yesterday.

Voices were approaching from down the slope. This was probably what the bear had been reacting to. Zula pocketed the keys, then retreated beneath the truck again and put the box back in its place against the frame.

It was Abdul-Wahaab and Sharif.

The open padlock had been half trodden into the ground. Zula pulled it out, dusted it off, and looked at it for a few moments. Then she hooked its hasp through the last link on the chain and snapped it shut.

Abdul-Wahaab and Sharif were upon her. She expected them to notice the disturbance to their camouflage, the shredded MRE tray with huge fang holes in it. They didn't. They were exhausted and they were in a hurry. And they only wanted her. They came in through the gap in the camouflage that the bear had made. Sharif dropped to one knee and undid the padlock that held her captive. He released the loop of chain that passed around the frame of the trailer hitch, then snapped it shut again so that it stayed fixed to her ankle. His eyes snagged for a moment on the other lock, the one from the toolbox, dangling from the end of the chain, but he made nothing of it. He didn't have the key and had no time or need to trifle with it anyway. Zipping the long end of the chain loose from the frame, he stood up, backed away from the truck, and gave the chain a preliminary tug, like a dog's leash. "Let's go," he said in Arabic.

Zula stood up, then turned and bent down as if to collect her sleeping bag. "I'll do it! Just go!" said Abdul-Wahaab. So she turned back toward Sharif. He turned his back on her and began walking out of the woods and down the open slope toward the river. On the opposite bank, between the water and the highway, a green Suburban was waiting for them. On its door was a picture of a bear.

Day 9

She didn't have time for a good look at the Suburban before they shoved her into its open rear doors. What came through to her was, for lack of a better term, its art direction: forest green and blazoned with a logo that incorporated a bear's head and a pair of crossed firearms. She inferred that it belonged to a hunting guide company. This was confirmed by the cargo stored in its back: sleeping bags, tents, camp stove, and the like.

To this, her captors added some of the cargo from the pickup truck camouflaged up in the woods. Much of what they had scavenged from the mining camp was trash, usable only in desperate circumstances; now that the jihadists had gotten themselves an upgrade, they were happy to leave most of the junk behind, taking only the weapons and a few other choice items.

Jones was very keen to get going. They closed the rear doors on her, took seats up front, and peeled out. The five jihadists had all survived the night, but they were dirty and exhausted and had a kind of staring gaze that made Zula not want to meet their eyes. She had the strong feeling that they had committed murder very recently, and she wondered if they were on some kind of drug. As usual, nothing was explained to her, but much could be guessed. They had flagged this Suburban down on the road, or crept up on a campsite where it had been parked, and they had murdered the hunters and the guides, concealed the bodies, and then come back to fetch her. Now they were wondering how much time they had before the victims' failure to check in would be noticed. They might have no more than a few hours, or as much as several days. It was impossible to know, and so they had to put as many miles as possible between themselves and the scene of the crime without drawing attention to themselves.

They drove in silence for a quarter of an hour, just getting used to their situation. Then Jones, who was driving, got the attention of Ershut, who was in the middle of the backseat, and talked to him over his shoulder for a little while. Zula could tell that he was talking about her.

Ershut turned around and made it clear that he wished to trade places with Zula. There was some awkward moving around, not made any simpler by the long chain trailing from Zula's ankle.

He rummaged for a while in toolboxes and equipment chests and found, among other things, a roll of black duct tape and some heavy black plastic sheeting. He cut the latter into a strip about an arm's length wide and a few meters long, then arranged this horizontally like a curtain around the side and rear windows of the cargo area, taping its edges to the head liner and the window frames. The entire back half of the Suburban was now hidden behind black plastic. Anyone looking at it from the outside would probably just assume that the glass had been deeply tinted.

She could see where this was going. They were going to be driving on public highways now. The time would come when they would find themselves close to other vehicles and then they didn't want Zula gesticulating for help in the rear window.

Or, for that matter, kicking the windows out. As she was easily capable of doing, whether or not the windows had plastic over them.

They took the chain off her ankle and obliged her to climb into a sleeping bag. Then they wrapped duct tape tightly around the outside of the bag, binding first her ankles and then her knees together. "I suppose going to the powder room is out of the question?" she called, as they were doing this.

"You'll have to just go inside the bag," Jones announced. "It's distasteful, but it won't hurt you."

They duct-taped her wrists together on the outside of the bag, in front of her waist, and then wrapped more tape around her arms, pinning them down to her sides. Sharif had found a watch cap, or perhaps taken it off a dead hunter, so they pulled this down over her eyes and then sealed it with a blindfold of more tape.

Then they drove forever.

Zula tried to think of some way to gauge the progress of time, but she had nothing other than stops for gas. These occurred three times. Before each one, Ershut climbed into the backseat and jammed a sock into Zula's mouth and then bound it in place with a bridle of duct tape. He remained poised over her as, just a few inches away from her head, someone—probably Jones, since he could pass for a Canadian or an American of African descent—jacked the nozzle into the fuel filler pipe and pumped in another thirty gallons of fuel. An absence of electronic beeps suggested that Jones was going inside and paying in cash, rather than using credit cards.

Where would they have obtained Canadian cash?

Probably from dead hunters.

Only a few minutes after the second of these fuel stops, the Suburban pulled off the road into a flat paved space, presumably a parking lot, and Zula heard typing and clicking from the front. Jones had apparently found a truck stop or coffee shop with Wi-Fi and was messing about on the Internet. Perhaps seeing if any missing persons reports had been filed.

The web surfing lasted for about fifteen minutes. They got back on the road again, and Ershut removed the gag from Zula's mouth. Maybe fifteen minutes later, she finally went ahead and pissed herself. This was no picnic, but she felt better—well, less bad, anyway— when she compared it to what had happened to friends in Xiamen: Yuxia's head in the bucket, Csongor pistol-whipped, Peter dead.

This in a strange way helped her feel better about the gory images of Khalid—half remembered and half dreamed—that kept appearing before her blindfolded eyes. Like it or not, this was the league she was playing in now. Her friends—assuming they were still alive—were playing in it too. And she at least had the advantage that she'd been in it before, or at least in its junior auxiliary, back in Eritrea.

They must have traveled for sixteen hours that day. Zula dozed occasionally, perhaps for twenty minutes, perhaps for three hours—there was no way to guess. They were traveling at highway speeds almost the entire time, which suggested that they were covering a vast distance—something on the order of a thousand miles. It was a long day but, in the end, not radically worse than flying between continents in an economy-class airline seat. And like such a flight, it seemed interminable when she was in the middle of it. At the end of the day, though, it seemed to have taken no time at all, since nothing really had happened.

They slowed suddenly, pulled off the highway onto gravel, and began to descend a relatively steep slope. Ershut scrambled over the backseat and hurriedly reinstated the gag; apparently this was a spur-of-the-moment excursion. The ground beneath the Suburban leveled off, and the vehicle eased through a series of maneuvers, then stopped. She heard a zipping noise as Jones stomped the parking brake down. The engine stopped. A door opened and one person—she assumed Jones—got out. She heard his feet crunching away across gravel. A few moments later, he greeted someone who gave him a cheerful greeting back.

Two greetings, actually, almost in unison: a man and a woman.

A conversation began. Zula could not make out words, but it all sounded cheerful enough. A friendly shooting-the-breeze type of chat. Zula could not hear anything else: no other vehicles, no traffic of any kind, none of the noises of a city. Just a low rushing sound that she was pretty sure came from a nearby river, a fast-flowing mountain stream.

After about ten minutes, the conversation paused, then resumed in much more subdued tones. Less than a minute later, she heard a door swing open and feet ascending a short stairway. Then the door thumped shut.

Two other jihadists got out of the Suburban and walked away over the gravel and there was a repetition of the door opening, the *thump-thump-thump* on the stairs, the door closing again.

Nothing seemed to happen for ten minutes, to the point where Ershut and Mahir—the two still in the Suburban—began to exchange a few nervous remarks. But then suddenly they both made happy exclamations. That door opened again. Someone jogged around behind the Suburban and opened its rear doors, then grabbed Zula's feet and dragged her out. She got thrown over some-one's shoulder—Jones's. He carried her across the gravel for some distance and then, with a great deal of effort, up that short stairway and into a place that sounded enclosed and smelled like a house. He pivoted and carried her down a narrow corridor and through a doorway. Then he bent forward at the waist and launched her. She fell back helplessly, unable to stop herself, imagining that she was about to smash the back of her head against something. But she made a soft landing on a bed and bounced. Jones was already out of the room, slamming the door behind himself. The entire structure rocked slightly beneath his footfalls.

They were in an RV, she realized. An RV parked on a flat gravel lot by the side of a mountain river.

The men were running back and forth between it and the Sub-urban, moving cargo. Someone started the Suburban and drove it up alongside to expedite matters.

It took them no more than a quarter of an hour to get the gear sorted and then she heard the RV's engine start up, far ahead, at the opposite end. For this was some kind of a huge RV, one of those bus-length retirement-homes-on-wheels. It began to move across the gravel, slowly as the driver got the feel of it, then picking up speed. She heard the Suburban falling into formation behind and gave up on any thoughts of trying to kick out the rear window.

Only after they had been on the road for half an hour did Ershut come back and remove her gag. Air rushed into her mouth, greatly improving her sense of smell, and she got an unmistakable scent of blood—the cabin in the jet, Khalid bleeding out on the floor.

"Hold still," Ershut said in Arabic, then cut through the lashings of duct tape around her arms and wrists. "Okay." Then he walked out of the room, leaving its door open.

Zula devoted a few minutes to getting her blindfold and her leg tape off and kicked off the urine-soaked sleeping bag. It took her eyes a few minutes to work properly again, but when she could see, she saw Mahir and Sharif on hands and knees in the RV's kitchen area, using rolls of paper towels and a spray bottle of 409 to clean blood off its white linoleum floor.

. . . .

TOWARD THE END of the long day's drive, there had been an interlude that had posed Zula with a minor brainteaser. The Suburban had been cruising down a highway for some time. She could tell it was a two-laner because of the sound made by oncoming vehicles as they zoomed by a few feet away, and by the fact that it wound from side to side more than a freeway. But at one point they had slowed down, without turning off the road, and descended a long straight slope, losing speed the whole way, and finally come to a halt, still sloping downhill. Nothing had happened for a quarter of an hour or so. Then she had heard the engines of other cars and trucks starting up all around. A series of vehicles had passed them coming up the other way. The Suburban had descended some distance farther, then leveled out, clanking over steel plates, and then parked again. Presently a deep rumbling had started and continued for twenty minutes or so.

By this time, Zula had figured out that they were on a ferry. The obvious conclusion would have been that they were headed over to Vancouver Island. But she'd been on those ferries before and she knew that they were gigantic and that the land approaches to their sprawling terminals would have felt and sounded different. They must be on something smaller. And indeed the crossing had not lasted long, and soon the engines of the Suburban and of the other vehicles around them had started up again and they had ascended up a long gentle slope, building speed as it turned back into a highway.

During the visit that she and Peter had made to B.C., she had learned that the southern part of the province sported a number of long, skinny, deep lakes, oriented north-south, presumably gouges left in the earth by glaciers during the most recent Ice Age. They were too long to dodge around and too wide to bridge, so the east-west highways ran right up to them and stopped and then started again on the opposite side. The dead ends were connected by small ferries.

About an hour after they stole the RV, she got to see one of those ferry terminals. Albeit dimly. It was long after dark. The terminal was closed. The lights—if there were any—had been turned off. Jones switched off the RV's headlamps as they cruised past a sign warning them that there'd be no more sailings until six A.M. tomorrow morning. A moment later, the Suburban went dark too. They felt their way down the ramp by starlight. It was just a straight gash blasted through the woods down to the shore of the lake. It ramped straight into black water. The connection to the shore was bifurcated. To the right, the road leveled off onto a platform built out over the lake on pilings and equipped with gates and ramps and huge bitts for mating with the ferry. To the left, the pavement just sloped straight down through the waterline. It was incised with a pair of deep straight channels hardened with iron rails. These ran obliquely up across the road to a broad open lot off to the side of the waiting area, surrounded by equipment sheds with heavy lifting equipment and other gear: a maintenance yard, she supposed, for the ferries, which could be winched straight up out of the water on those rails and brought to dry dock on higher ground. She got a reasonably good look at the place out the RV's windows because that was where Jones got the gigantic vehicle turned around in a long series of back-and-forths. Meanwhile, Abdul-Wahaab—who had been driving the Suburban—had stopped it in the middle of the ramp, nose aimed down toward the water. He had rolled down all of the windows, opened the sunroof, and parted the rear cargo doors, which he now seemed to be wedging open with a stick. She could not see into it from this distance, but she had a good idea as to its contents. In the time she had spent in this bedroom, she had seen copious evidence—in the form of family photographs, toiletries, denture-soaking equipment, and knickknacks—that this RV was owned by a retired couple whose corpses were now in the back of that Suburban.

Having finished his preparations, Abdul-Wahaab made one last orbit around the big SUV, inspecting his work, then reached into the open driver's-side door. Zula heard a distant *thunk* as he released the parking brake. The Suburban began to roll forward down the ramp. He walked, then ran alongside, keeping his right hand on the steering wheel, then peeled away from it just before it nosed into the water. It lost most of its velocity in the first few yards, plashing up a concentric wave that spread out into the lake, but it never stopped moving. Air burbled up out of the engine compartment. It slid forward into the lake, instantly filling with water, and disappeared, leaving a trail of bubbles that slowly moved away from shore as the vehicle found its way down to the lake bottom. The terrain all around was rocky and steep, and Zula had no doubt that the bottom dropped away precipitously beyond the end of the paved ferry-ramp. The lake must be a hundred meters deep, and the Suburban would come to rest at the very bottom of it.

Jones pulled out of the maintenance yard and got the RV pointed uphill. Abdul-Wahaab stormed in through the side door to accept the enthusiastic congratulations and prayerful thanks of his colleagues. Abdallah Jones steered the RV out onto the open highway, turned on the headlamps, and proceeded in some random direction at, Zula guessed, a speed well within the posted limits.

"I mean, did you see what happened to those three thousand K'Shetriae, beginning of this week?" Richard asked.

Skeletor quickly averted his gaze and pretended to study the pattern of the red Formica tabletop.

Richard continued, "The ones who tried to go in and establish some kind of order in the Torgai Foothills?"

"I know the ones you're talking about." Devin Skraelin shook his head and gazed moodily out the window of the trailer. Apparently as a result of Richard's ducking into this place a week ago, fleeing from Devin's staff like a camper trying to get in out of the mosquitoes, it had now become the unofficial Dodge/Skeletor meeting place, a Reykjavik or a Panmunjom. It had only been a week since that meeting, and yet it seemed a lot longer. Hell, it seemed to have happened in some parallel universe. The universe in which Zula had not yet disappeared.

"I was there for some of it," Devin said, snapping Richard's mind back—if not *to* reality, then *from* reality. "Just hovering, invisible." He wanted Richard to understand that he had not wielded any of his characters' superamazing powers to sway the battle. "It was carnage, no doubt about it. Not what we—what *they*—expected."

"You can say 'we,'" Richard said quickly. He held up his hands, palms out. "I am so far past the point of thinking that the writers have to be these, like, neutral, dispassionate forces in the world."

Skeletor was nodding, like he'd been wondering for years when Richard was finally going to get it. "It just doesn't work," he said. "We already talked about Good versus Evil and how that failed."

"Totally ridiculous," Richard said, as if it were some huge admission. "Just a *weak* effort on our part. 'How can we get two groups fighting, competing? I know, we'll have one group be Good and one Evil.' Exactly the kind of thing you'd expect to come out of a corporate committee."

Skeletor was just nodding, still mostly gazing out the window but occasionally flicking his eyes back Richard's way, perhaps looking for signs of sarcasm.

"We should have just left it to you guys," Richard concluded.

"The way I see it, it's really a sport," Devin said. "Maybe not like soccer, but like some combination of fencing and chess. Now, it has to be story driven, of course." He held up his hand like a pupil volunteering to erase the chalkboard. "Happy to help out there."

In exchange for vast sums of money, Richard mentally added. But he just kept nodding. Looking interested. As if there were any doubt as to what would come next.

Devin continued, "But in the end if you don't have that competitive element, you've got nothing, business-wise. And for those who want solo questing and one-on-one competition, it's there. You can do that. But the real attraction is in the team sport angle, the social thing. Being part of an army. An alliance."

"Wearing a uniform," Richard said. "Having a mascot."

"Yeah, and that is what the Bright versus Earthtone thing turned into. Whether we intended it or not." Devin was being a bit slippery there. A week ago Richard would have been furious at his treachery, at this blithe admission. Devin might even have sensed this, the potential for an explosion, and declined to reveal what he had just now come out and said so baldly. Now he'd said it because he could sense somehow that Richard didn't actually give a shit. Richard had moved on.

"I just came from Cambridge," Richard said.

"Mass?"

"England. Where Donald lives half the time."

"Ah."

"I want you to know that he's fine with all of this."

It seemed pretty clear that Devin had not been expecting this turn in the conversation, and he got a preoccupied look about him.

"He's a quick study. You think I'm joking. But no. For a guy who has never played a video game in his life—"

"Donald Cameron has his own character in the world now!?" Skeletor exclaimed, in somewhat the same tone of voice as a tribune might have said, *Hannibal has crossed the Alps with elephants!?*

"Very weak, of course," Richard said reassuringly. "Didn't even have shoes, for a while."

"I don't care about what he's wearing on his feet! I care about his—"

"Vassal tree? Yes. I understand. He's not quite as quick to get going on that front as you'd imagine. Still learning the ropes. I explained how it all works. He was reluctant to swear fealty to a more established character."

"Why the hell should he!? With a few text messages he could be an Emperor!"

"If he knew how to send text messages, yes."

"How many vassals does he have? Are they powerful?"

"I haven't checked since the FBO at Cranfield."

"The huh?"

"In about ten hours. So I have no idea."

"Why would he suddenly start? Why now?"

"Between you and me—and really, Devin, this must never leave this trailer—" Richard leaned in, held up his hands, rubbed his thumb against his fingertips.

"How could he possibly be in need of money?"

"Have you ever paid taxes in the U.K.? Tried to fix up a sandstone castle on the Isle of Man? Not to mention his other properties." Richard just made the last part up.

"What other properties?"

"Palaces and stuff he inherited, I guess. I'm just saying, he looks like a tattered old professor, but behind that façade he burns through specie like a rap star."

Devin was thinking. "You're referring to the money in Torgai. Vast hoards of gold rumored to be just lying there for the taking."

"Don't be coy, man; we all know what those three thousand

K'Shetriae were thinking. No one is going into the Torgai for its scenic beauty."

"It is so obvious," Devin marveled. "So. Friggin'. Obvious. He never cared about playing the game until there was money on the ground. Never went in *once*. Just wanted to"—and here Devin held his hands aloft and made fluttering motions with his fingers, like an airborne faerie sprinkling dew over rose petals—"craft ancient dead languages. Imbue the history of T'Rain with a grammar and a rhetoric."

"And cash royalty checks."

"Egg-ZACT-ly!" Devin snapped, looking around himself in a kind of shocked, prim way, as if he had never accepted one penny of compensation. "But the minute some Troll dumps a few tons of gold on the ground, he gets an account and turns into Ozzy Fucking Mandias."

Richard's instincts told him that, having gotten Skeletor into this state, the most effective way to keep him there would be to show exaggerated nonchalance. "Now, Devin," he said in a perfectly reasonable tone, "you said yourself that it was a team sport. And part of being on a team is having a captain or a pope or what have you."

"I've had characters in the game since the beginning," Devin said righteously. "Over a hundred of them."

"So the database says," Richard said.

"Now I won't sit here and try to tell you that no one has ever sworn fealty to me. I run vassal networks, sure. Sometimes maybe three deep. You can't understand the workings of the game unless you've played it at that level."

Richard just kept nodding, raising his eyebrows from time to time in an *I'm with you, buddy* sort of effort.

"I could be *seven deep*!" Devin said. "Could have been years ago!" Meaning that his hierarchy of vassals would be seven tiers deep, enough to give him tens of millions of followers. Only one player in the game had ever gotten to that level. Richard had been just hours away from sending Egdod down to liquidate him when the player had choked on a bite of wurst, alone before his monitor screen in Ostheim vor der Rhön, no one around to give him a Heimlich.

"I know that about you, Devin, and I do think it's testimony to your, if I may say, midwestern sense of plain dealing and self-effacement that you have showed such restraint. Of course, one of the problems with us midwesterners is that—"

"We just let people run roughshod over us, yeah, I know that," Devin said, with an involuntary flick of the eyes toward his steel building full of lawyers.

"Well," Richard said, after a longish pause, "I don't want to keep you from your training schedule."

"S'okay, my doctor's after me to ease up a little."

"I'm actually on my way up to visit the family, but it seemed only fair to stop by and fill you in a little on my conversation with the Don."

"Appreciate it," Devin muttered, and then his eyes refocused. "Yeah, I heard you had some trouble with your niece?"

"Am still having it, actually."

"She hasn't turned up yet?"

Richard had vague misgivings about this phrasing, since it seemed to imply that Zula had some choice in the matter. He wondered how many other people were assuming that Zula had just decided to go on the lam and put her family through the torments of hell just because.

"Whatever trouble she's in," Richard said, "does not seem to have resolved."

"Well. Let me know if there's anything I can do," Devin offered.

Richard couldn't think of a polite way to say, *You're about to go do it,* and so he just nodded.

AFTER DITCHING THE Suburban, they drove for three hours. Zula reckoned that they would be heading for the hills, but instead they entered into some place whose roads were equipped, in standard-issue North American style, with streetlamps, convenience stores, and stoplights. After cruising through that sort of environment for about fifteen minutes, Jones swung the wheel and trundled the giant vehicle into a vast parking lot. A neon-lit Walmart logo careered across the windshield. Jones pulled into a parking space, or rather a series of several consecutive spaces, and shut off the engine. After taking a last searching look around the parking lot, he reached up and jerked a curtain across the entire eight-foot expanse of the windshield, affording him and his coconspirators privacy.

Earlier in the evening, Ershut and Abdul-Wahaab had been given the assignment to chain Zula by her ankle to the grab bar in the shower stall. Like so many of the routine chores that filled the day-to-day lives of this roving band of terrorists, this one had occasioned a huge amount of what sounded to an Iowan like violent argument. Ninety percent of this had focused on the mysterious padlock that they had found locked to the last link of the chain. No one seemed to know where it had come from. This, of course, was because Zula had put it there when none of them had been looking. But as she had been hoping, they never cottoned on to it. Jones, becoming annoyed by the sheer volume of their debate, had glanced at it and, after a few moments, identified it as the lock that had formerly belonged to the toolbox from the stolen truck. Rummaging around in the external pocket of a knapsack, he had found that truck's key chain and thrown it to Ershut, who, after a few minutes' trial and error (for it had a lot of keys on it) had managed to get the new lock open. He had then used it to fix that end of the chain to the shower stall grab bar and pocketed the key—which, quite naturally, he'd assumed was the only key. The next and final phase of the operation had been to adjust the length of the chain around Zula's ankle, giving her enough slack that she could get to the toilet, or retreat into the bedroom and curl up on the floor, but not enough to climb up on the bed; for that would have put her within reach of the windows. For this they used the padlock for which Zula *didn't* have a spare key.

When it had become obvious that she was going to be kept in this situation for a long time, she had raked blankets and pillows down from the bed and formed a little nest on the floor where she had dozed during the drive. The RV was capable of sleeping at least half a dozen when all of its seats and benches had been folded down and turned into beds, and all the jihadists except for Jones had found places to lie down and were sawing logs, refreshing themselves after a long day of cold-blooded murder and aimless driving around. Curled up in her nest in the back, Zula gazed down a forty-foot-long tunnel to the other end where Jones had pivoted the driver's seat around to face backward and set a laptop across his knees. Its blue-white light illuminated his face, turning it into a constrasty and off-color mask. No sleeping for him, at least not yet.

She would have been mystified by his decision to park in a Walmart were it not for the fact that her great-aunt and great-uncle, based out of Yankton, South Dakota, were inveterate RVers, forever showing slides and telling stories of their wanderings at the re-u, and she knew from them that Walmart had a policy of rolling out the welcome mat for such people, even to the point of distributing the company's own rebranded version of the Rand McNally Road Atlas on which the locations of all Walmarts were highlighted. It was a near certainty that a copy of that very document was lodged in the console up next to Jones where this vehicle's late owners had been in the habit of repositing all such items. Jones, of course, would not know this. But he seemed nothing if not adaptable. It might be that this was a spur-of-the-moment decision: he had blundered into this central British Columbian town, happened to drive by their Walmart, noticed that the only vehicles in the parking lot were overnighting RVs, and decided to adopt a "when in Rome" strategy. Or, what was more likely, he had spent a while interrogating the former owners at gun- or knifepoint before slaying them, had learned about their habits, rifled their wallets, extracted their PIN numbers and passwords by making false promises that he would not harm them.

The laptop was not the same computer that Sharif had been using on the jet. This one was part of the haul of random consumer booty that had fallen into Jones's hands along with the RV. Jones had evidently been able to obtain a Wi-Fi connection from the Walmart, since he was mostly just mousing and clicking: classic web-surfing behavior. There was a fine moment of comedy when he apparently clicked his way onto the website of some casino in Vegas, and the voice of Frank Sinatra boomed out of the computer's speakers, stirring a couple of the men half awake before Jones found the volume control and stifled it.

Again the strange fixation on Vegas. So Jones was finally getting down to business. Based on the conversation she had overheard in Xiamen, she had a pretty good idea of his plan: go into a big entertainment complex in Sin City and kill as many people as possible, similar to what those Pakistani terrorists had done in the luxury hotels and railway station of Mumbai. The tricky bit being to get himself, his comrades-in-arms, and his stash of weapons across the U.S. border. Not that you couldn't buy weapons in the States, but she had witnessed enough loadings and unloadings of their gear, by this point, to have a rough idea of their inventory, and she thought that they had with them certain items like fully automatic weapons and hand grenades that would be difficult to buy even in the Sweet Land of Liberty.

Jones went through a phase of rebooting the laptop several times consecutively, which made her think that he must have down-loaded and installed some new software. An obvious guess was that he was rigging the machine in such a way that he could communi-cate secretly with his fellow jihadists.

The inherently soporific nature of software installation had its way with her, and she closed her eyes and then opened them to find that it was daytime.

Jones had fallen asleep right where he had been sitting, and Abdul-Wahaab was now hogging the laptop. Ershut was up cooking something steamy on the stove; her nose told her it was rice. Pres-ently, some of this was served up to her in a plastic bowl decorated with pastel flowers. She wondered if these guys understood that they were a couple of hundred feet away from a grocery store that was probably a hundred times the size of the largest one they had ever seen in their lives.

As she was eating her rice, a car pulled up and parked next to them, causing the men to twitch curtains and peer out. They looked apprehensive and made reaching-for-weapons gestures, then their expressions became delighted. Mahir began shouting about how great Allah was. This woke up Jones, who took stock of the situation and told everyone to shut up. He pushed himself up out of the big captain's chair, tottered down the steps on stiff legs, and unlocked and opened the door. Then he backed up so that three men could enter the RV. They had beards and huge grins. Jones shushed them and insisted that the door be hove to and relocked.

Then the place erupted with hearty greetings and laughter and a great deal more in the way of kind remarks about Allah. The only thing that could dampen these men's spirits, it seemed, was the pres-ence of Zula, which they found shocking and maybe even offensive when they noticed it.

The new arrivals looked Indian or Pakistani and, like Jones, seemed to use Arabic as a second or third language, which meant that Jones ended up speaking English to them. English they spoke very well and with minimal accents. Zula was able to infer that they had received an email from Jones last night and had come here— wherever "here" was—from Vancouver as soon as they had been able. Sycophants were the same everywhere, apparently; their most verbal member, who kept maneuvering to be closest to Jones, kept apologizing for not having arrived even sooner. This man—Sharjeel was apparently his name—looked, dressed, and acted like a Westernized grad student or high-tech employee. Watching him, Zula could only think of all the nonterrorist South Asians, happily assimilated into North American society, for whom an asshole like Sharjeel was their worst nightmare.

Having Sharjeel and his friends in the picture made her feel terrible, and it took a bit of thinking to work out why. Until now it had seemed that it would be only a matter of time before Jones and his crew would make a mistake and get noticed or caught. Jones had lived in the States, so he knew how things worked in North America. He was quite good at talking like an American black guy and was capable of being charming; evidently he had charmed this RV's owners for a few minutes before pulling a gun on them. But he couldn't stay awake 24/7, and he couldn't do everything. His comrades, by contrast, were now deeply implanted in a culture where they did not speak the language and had no clue as to what was normal behavior. They got along okay in the wilderness, but in a place like this they could not even be allowed out of the RV.

This made Sharjeel and his buddies extremely useful to Jones and therefore distinctly unwelcome as far as Zula was concerned.

They made themselves useful immediately. One of them sat down in the huge rotating Captain Kirk driver's chair at the front. For Jones proposed to venture into the Walmart with Sharjeel and the other of the new arrivals and wanted an English-speaking person to act as their front man. Which was to say that if some gregarious fellow RVer or Walmart security dick came around knocking on the driver's-side door wanting to chat them up, it would be best if the person responding did not still have the dust of north Waziristan in the folds of his turban.

Jones scrounged a Strawberry Shortcake memo pad from the glove compartment and began to draw up a shopping list. Sometimes he wrote silently, other times he thought out loud. "Cooking oil . . . mosquito repellent . . . matches . . . cordless drill . . ."

"Tampons," Zula called out.

"What brand?" Jones asked without skipping a beat. "Lite, Regular, Super, Ultra?"

"You've actually had a girlfriend?"

"I'll get you a multipack and take your snarky answer to mean that you don't much care," Jones said. "Anything else, as long as I'm in the pink-and-pastel aisle?"

"Baby wipes, unscented preferably. Underwear. A pair of pants that hasn't been peed in."

"Sweat pants okay?"

"Whatever. Some socks, please."

"Ah, you're using the magic word all of a sudden."

"Anything you see that's made out of fleece."

"Anything in Walmart that is made out of fleece," Jones repeated fastidiously, copying it down. "That should be several truckloads' worth." Then he looked up at her. "Will there be anything else, or can I get back to planning atrocities?"

"Knock yourself out."

Sharjeel monitored this uneasily.

After a few more minutes, Jones and Sharjeel and one of the newcomers, who was apparently named Aziz, all tromped down the steps out the side door and went scuffing away across the parking lot.

"Your family is very nice," said a voice in English, after a while.

Zula had sunk into a sort of semicomatose state, a listless, timeless despondency in which she had been spending increasing amounts of time lately. Like a computer being awakened from its power-saving state, she was a bit slow to spin up her hard drive and unblank her screen and begin responding to inputs.

She gazed up the length of the RV to see the third of the newcomers, the one ensconced in the big Captain Kirk chair. He had seized control of the laptop and was apparently surfing. Zula guessed that he might have googled her or something.

It took all the will and self-control she had been developing during the last week and a half not to lose control of herself. The only thing that prevented it was a kind of instinctive awareness that this was probably just what the guy wanted; he was trying to say the most provocative thing he could think of. Circling around and poking at her, trying to learn what she was made of. *Your family is very nice.* She couldn't believe he'd said that. What an asshole.

But she had opened the door to this by her improvisation, a few days ago, just after the jet crash, when she had revealed her full name to Jones. Of course, the first thing he would have done upon getting access to the Internet would be to learn everything about her, her uncle, her larger family. And he had probably left a trail of bookmarks on the laptop for this guy to follow. Maybe even set up a Zula wiki where jihadists all over the world were posting every piece of data they could find.

So that was the situation. Zula chained by the ankle, out of the laptop's reach. The man in the driver's seat looking, she had to guess, at her cousins' Facebook pages, their Flickr albums, the websites they must have put up during the last week in an effort to figure out what had become of her.

Ten seconds with her hands on that laptop and she could bring the wrath of God down on these people and end the whole thing. A fact that they understood perfectly well. Hence the chain. One padlock at her ankle, the other on the grab bar in the shower stall.

The latter was special in that Zula happened to have a key to it in her pocket.

She could take the key out at any time and be free within seconds. Free to move about within the RV, that is. But there was always someone awake, someone watching her. The key was her one chance. She had to use it wisely. Her first move had to be a success.

The man with the laptop stared at her for a while, waiting for a reaction. Then his attention drifted back to the laptop. He poked it and stroked it for a few moments, then glanced up to see Zula looking at him. He spread his hands apart and gripped the machine by its edges, spun it around, and picked it up to aim the screen toward Zula. From almost the other end of the RV she could not see very well, but she could make out several pictures of herself, which she recognized as having been taken during the re-u or other family get-togethers. Above them were words in block letters, HAVE YOU

SEEN THIS WOMAN?, and a telephone number with a 712 area code: western Iowa.

The mere sight of this from thirty feet away brought up a welter of emotions. Joy and fierce pride that her family was on the case. Extreme sadness that it had happened at all. Rage that this man was now trying to use it to manipulate her emotional state. Embarrassment that he was, to some extent, succeeding.

"What's your name?" she asked.

"You may address me as Zakir," he answered.

The man who was willing to be addressed as Zakir was big and doughy compared to all the other jihadists Zula had encountered lately. Probably a cubicle dweller in his professional life. A member of an IT support group for an insurance company, she decided. Bored with his job, unable to get a girlfriend, feeling conflicted about the way he had sold himself out to the Western system, he had somehow made contact with a group of al-Qaeda-affiliated wack jobs during a family visit to Pakistan and ended up on a list of guys to call in Vancouver if ever the global movement needed some assistance on the ground there. And now here he was and loving it. No doubt shocked to have been rumbled at three in the morning and put in a car to this Walmart rendezvous, he was killing some time doing the one thing he was indubitably good at, which was screwing around with computers.

The shoppers began to come back in shifts. Apparently they had split up inside the Walmart, each with his own list. Aziz came back with half a dozen plastic grocery bags dangling from each hand. Women's work. Mostly these contained food, but he had also purchased a cheap webcam, shaped like a little eyeball, in a blister pack, and an extension cord for its USB cable. The feminine hygiene supplies were in there too; these were hurled disgustedly back down the length of the RV and ricocheted against the bedroom walls and came to rest, on the bed, somewhat dented around the corners. Sharjeel came with even more camping equipment: sleeping bags, tents, tarps, ropes, and various fleece garments. He tossed the clothing back to Zula, then went back into the store. Fifteen minutes later he and Jones came back, each pushing a big flatbed cart. They brought in a Skilsaw, a cordless drill, construction screws, insulation, two-by-fours, plywood. A full four-by-eight-foot sheet would have been awkward in the RV's confines and so they had presawn them into four-by-four pieces. Aziz was sent back into the Walmart and came back with a roll of black roofing paper and a white plastic package, about the size of a well-stuffed garbage bag, with a Pink Panther cartoon on it: fiberglass insulation.

The group now divided up, the lovers Mahir and Sharif going out and getting into the car along with the miserable Aziz, while fat Zakir and weaselly, efficient Sharjeel remained in the RV. At a command from Jones, Zakir spun his chair around and fired up the RV's engine, then pulled the great land yacht out onto the open road. Jones unboxed the Skilsaw. The RV had a generator that would produce wall power. He figured out how to get it started. Then he began to take measurements in the back bedroom, scooting politely past Zula each time he went in or out. With a fat Walmart contractor's pencil he stroked out long lines on the plywood panels, then fired up the Skilsaw and cut them to shape, two at a time, suffusing the RV's confines with sawdust, smoke, and a screeching din. He carried these back into the bedroom as they were completed, pushed them up against the windows, and then used the cordless drill, with a screwdriver attachment, to screw them into the RV's walls. This was all done with the curtains closed so that anyone outside would see only curtains, drawn for privacy.

In only a few minutes' time, he was able to screw plywood over all the windows. He deputized Sharjeel to put in more screws while he planned out the next phase of the operation. Sharjeel went to it with a will, driving the screws in at intervals of no more than two inches. It was a statement. Those panels were not coming off.

In the meantime, Jones had been cutting two-by-fours into lengths. He tossed these in through the door, flying right over Zula's head like spears, and directed Sharjeel to screw them down on their edges to the plywood underlayment. This he did miserably. The procedure, as Zula could have told him, was called toenailing, and it was tricky.

Abdallah Jones slashed open the package of fiberglass and it began to expand uncontrollably, threatening to completely fill the interior of the RV. Wrestling and stomping and cursing, he cut off batts of it and passed them back to Sharjeel who stuck them up against the plywood with duct tape.

When all of the plywood had been thus insulated, they pulled over to the side of the road where Jones vindictively kicked all of the insulation, save one six-foot batt of it, out onto the shoulder. Once they were back under way, he busied himself again with plywood. When he had cut the first set of panels, he had always worked with double sheets, making two copies of each shape, and keeping half of them in reserve. Now he and Sharjeel put these spares up over the insulation and screwed them down into the studs. The Colorado School of Mines didn't raise no dummies.

So the whole three-sided bay of the bedroom was now a completely opaque arrangement of insulated plywood walls. Presently it became even darker as Jones and Sharjeel unrolled long strips of black roofing paper and staple-gunned them over the plywood, covering the entire interior surface of the room, including the ceiling, with monochrome black, relieved only by the sporadic glint of staples. A few moments' work with a box cutter removed a disk of tar paper from around the overhead light fixture, so that some dingy yellow light was shed into the space.

They then unlocked Zula's ankle and let her know that her place was back there on the bed. She retreated, sat down, and busied herself picking wood shrapnel and loose tufts of fiberglass off the bedspread (a quilt that had quite obviously been hand-stitched by the old lady butchered yesterday) as Jones and Sharjeel applied a similar treatment to the inside of the bedroom door, reinforcing it with plywood and then building it out to a full depth of five inches, with a bat of insulation in the middle. This had the desired side effect of completely covering up the inside doorknob, making it impossible for Zula to open the door even if it were not locked.

Jones chucked a long fat bit into the drill and put a hole all the way through the reinforced door, then fed the little webcam's USB cable through. Using a web of zip ties, duct tape, and drywall screws, he mounted the little eyeball to the inside surface of the door up near the top. Meanwhile Sharjeel had zip-tied the cable and its extension down the length of the RV's central corridor to its kitchen table and plugged it into the laptop. A long adjustment procedure ensued in which Jones would close the door, leaving Zula alone in the room, and walk up to view the camera's output on the laptop, then tromp back and open the door and wiggle the camera this way and that, getting the angle just right so that (Zula supposed) it could see all parts of the room.

The entire procedure had taken perhaps two hours. Like all home improvement projects, it had started with amazing energy and speed and then slowly petered out as Jones and Sharjeel had gotten hung up on details. But now it was done, and Zula was well and truly locked in. They slammed her shut in there and did not bother opening the door for maybe six hours.

Day 15

There was now a train that would take arriving passengers directly from Sea-Tac to a downtown station that was practically in the basement of Corporation 9592's headquarters. In every way it was faster, safer, and more efficient than the antiquated procedure of driving to the airport in a private vehicle to pick up a visitor. Richard had become somewhat cold-blooded about simply telling people to get on the goddamned train. But today the incoming passenger was John, and there was no question that this called for the ancient, full-dress ceremony: checking the flight's true arrival time on the Alaska Airlines website, driving to the airport, napping in the phone lot, the long radio silence suddenly broken by one-word text messages blossoming on his phone (LANDED, TAXIING, STILL TAXIING!, WAITING TO DEPLANE, FAT LADY BLOCKING AISLE), the carefully timed plunge into the moil of the arrivals curb. John, a legless senior citizen/combat veteran, could have gotten special dispensation from airport authorities on at least three pretexts, but he seemed to find it amusing to stomp out the doors under his own power with his bags slung over his shoulders and to navigate on dead stilts through the vehicular mosh pit to the back of Richard's SUV. He had packed for a long trip: a trip to China.

It had only been something like four days since Dodge had left Iowa, which was well under the threshold for hugging. And if they weren't going to hug, there seemed little point in shaking hands. Anyway their hands were busy, pulling the SUV's liftgate down. John, ever the older brother, initiated the move, and Richard, feeling as if he were being some kind of a bad host, reached up only a fraction of a second later and got his hands on the thing just as it was starting to move down. Four Forthrast hands slammed it shut with much more force than was really called for, and then they parted, each walking up his own side of the vehicle, and climbed into the front seats in unison.

"You can scoot that back," Richard said, of John's seat.

"It's fine," John insisted, speaking to Richard from across a cultural divide that never got any easier to navigate. The idea being that even if John's seat *were* positioned too far forward—limiting his legroom and reducing his level of physical comfort—the mere act of scooting it back a few inches was, by midwestern standards, a gratuitous waste of energy as well as an implicit admission that the scooter was the sort of person who could not handle a little bit of trouble.

Richard paused for a moment, sat back, and asked himself whether he should be driving at all. It was noon. He had not slept at all last night. Then he pulled himself together, looked in both mirrors, checked his blind spot, and accelerated smoothly into traffic. Just like in driver's ed.

"You've got most of a day to kill before we leave for China," Richard said, once they had made it out onto I-5. He had adjusted to the cultural thing now, so he didn't say "a few hours to relax" or "freshen up" or "recover from the flight," any of which would have been construed as Richard implying that John was not up to the stress of modern airline travel. Just "kill" implying that things really weren't moving fast enough for Richard's taste. "My condo is just down the street from the office, so you can go there and take a shower if you want, get on the Internet . . ."

"I'd like to sit down with you and look at it again," John said.

"You're not going to see anything new," Richard said.

"Certain words are difficult to make out on my copy. Zula's handwriting was never the best . . ."

"Your copy *is* my copy, John. Listen to me. We are talking about digital files here. What I emailed you is an exact, perfect copy of what I received from the guy in China. Looking at my copy is not going to help."

"On the second page," John insisted, "there's one line that's sketchy."

"It is a handwritten note on brown paper towels," Richard said. "The guy just spread it out on a counter and aimed his phone camera at it and prayed to his gods. The image quality is poor. But your copy is as good as mine. The only way to extract more information is to go to China, and we're doing that in eight hours."

"Why can't we leave sooner?" John asked, though he already knew.

"The visas," Richard reminded him.

FIVE DAYS AGO, directly following the meeting with Skeletor, Richard had told his pilots to take a day off enjoying the delights of the K'Shetriae Kingdom and then to meet him at the Sioux City FBO. He had then jumped into a rented Grand Marquis and started driving in the direction of home. He never referred to, or thought of, John's farm as home unless things were really bad. He imagined that the drive would do him some good. It seemed that his brain needed to be doing *something* and the drive ought to be a good opportunity. He had been intensely occupied the last few days, playing on the worst character flaws of both Don Donald and Skeletor: the former's avarice and the latter's insecurity. A performance that ought to have brought the Furious Muses down on him in full resonance. Yet they were silent. Perhaps they'd at last left him for other ex-boyfriends who stood some chance of being improved by their suggestions. So his brain was strangely empty and inactive during the four-hour drive.

He did not snap out of it until he was on final approach to the farm, driving along the county road where he had gone bicycle riding when he'd been a kid, and staring in fresh amazement at the colossal wind turbines that John and Alice had been putting up. There was a decent breeze today, and the machines were churning along about as fast as they were ever allowed to. All of them were eye-catching because of that movement, to the point where it almost made it a little difficult for him to keep his eyes on the road. But then his gaze fastened on one that happened to be directly ahead, because of a little squiggle that the road had to make to avoid a bend in the crick. It was down for repairs, apparently, because the blades had been feathered and so it was just standing there inert, the one dead thing in this whirling carnival of white blades.

Richard was able to pull over onto the shoulder and stomp the parking brake before he broke down weeping.

That was why his brain had been silent. Because it knew that Zula was dead.

He showed up at John and Alice's front door with red eyes and found them in the same condition. They did not ask him what he had been doing, why all the flying around. It was just as well. From this remove, the gambit with D-squared and Skeletor seemed ludicrously far-fetched and beside the point.

He stayed there for a night, keeping his eyes on the floor whenever he moved about the house so that they would not accidentally light on a photograph of Zula. John didn't talk much; he had a database of possible leads on his computer, which he worked at obsessively. But his computer, as Richard could see at a glance, was desperately sick with malware, running at about a hundredth of its normal speed and freezing up a few times an hour. He considered offering to help. But the fact that John was putting up with it was evidence that he knew it was hopeless, was just running in place. Alice was silent, inactive except for occasional bursts of manic energy, in some stage or another of grieving. The only person Richard felt comfortable hanging around with was Dad, so he spent most of the evening sitting next to him in the man cave, listening to the hissing and beeping of his bionic support system, watching whatever TV Dad felt like summoning up with the remote. People kept calling the house, but they didn't know what to do. It wasn't like an actual death. You couldn't send flowers. Hallmark didn't make disappearance cards. It was sort of like the Patricia lightning strike all over again: too bizarre to pass smoothly along the greased channels of grieving and condolence.

Breakfast was better, with the three of them all talking about Zula, telling stories about her fondly, as people did of the dead. Dad listened to the stories and nodded and smiled at the right parts. Richard hugged them, got in the Grand Marquis, drove to the FBO, and was back in Seattle four hours later. That was Friday. During the weekend he stayed home, online most of the time, hovering over the Torgai in one window while, in others, scanning real-time statistics from T'Rain's databases. He did not care about the details. He doubted that any of this was going to help at all. But he had made a determination, early last week, that it might conceivably help them get more information if the Torgai remained chaotic and did not fall under the control of any one particular Liege Lord. His expedition to Cambridge and to Nodaway had been solely to ensure the requisite level of chaos, and it seemed to have worked. Don Donald, after a slow start, was now five deep, with tens of thousands of tastefully appointed vassals, and he'd apparently had the good sense to delegate military decisions to players who had actually done this before. Skeletor meanwhile had dusted off his most powerful character, which he hadn't played in several months, and had made a fairly impressive bid to penetrate all the way into the middle of the castle where D-squared's character was holed up and assassinate him. At the last minute, he had been detected and killed so fast that he hadn't had time to Sequester all his Virtual Property. So that stuff had fallen into the hands of the Earthtone Coalition (which couldn't use it because it was so tawdry), and Skeletor's character had emerged from Limbo naked and impoverished and considerably diminished in power. Which was probably for the better anyway, since Devin had other characters better suited to play the role of warrior king: less powerful but with deeper and more well-developed vassal networks.

Such entertainments had prevented Richard from thinking much about Zula all through the weekend and for most of Monday, which had been devoted to long, hairy, poorly run meetings about how the company should deal with this latest turn in the Wor. He had come home late with take-out Thai and slammed into the sofa and tried to watch a movie, but kept drifting from it to the screen of his laptop. This was part of Corporation 9592's strategy; they had hired psychologists, invested millions in a project to sabotage movies—yes, the entire medium of cinema—to get their customers/players/addicts into a state of mind where they simply could not focus on a two-hour-long chunk of filmed entertainment without alarm bells going off in their medullas telling them that they needed to log on to T'Rain and see what they were missing.

It was during one such foray, the movie on pause, some Torgai conflagration burning in a window on the screen, when he noticed he had new email, tentatively flagged as spam. Subject heading: some Chinese characters. He deleted it without looking. But something about it was nagging at him. He didn't read Chinese. But in the last few days he had been trying to learn some things about this place called Xiamen, hoovering up random stuff on the Internet. Some of the pages he'd found were in English, others in Chinese, many in a patchwork of both languages. But he had grown accustomed to seeing one Chinese character that stood out because of its simplicity: just a square with its bottom side missing, and a little cross-tick in its top side. It was half of the two-character symbol for "Xiamen." And he might have been imagining things, but he fancied he had seen it in the subject line of that spam email. So he went to his trash folder and retrieved the message and opened it.

It contained no text at all, just three consecutive images, each one a photograph of a brown paper towel with words written on it in black pen.

The first line of the message on the towel was an email address at Corporation 9592 that Richard used only for personal communications. The second line was a date, bracketed in question marks: Friday before last, making it about three days after Zula and Peter had disappeared from the loft in Georgetown. So the note was about ten days old.

> Uncle Richard,
>
> Hope you will forward this to John and Alice if it ever gets rescued from the drain trap where I am going to hide it. I thought your email address was more likely to work than theirs. John's PC has malware.
>
> This is my first damsel in distress letter, so I hope I am striking the right tone. I have a lot of time on my hands and a whole dispenser full of paper towels so I can produce several drafts if need be.
>
> As you probably know if you are reading this, I am on the forty-third floor of an unfinished skyscraper in downtown Xiamen. I am being held captive—hate that word, but it fits—in

a ladies' room next to an office suite that is being used as a safe
house by a Russian identifying himself as Ivanov, though this
is clearly not his real name. I think that he used to be part of a
Russian organized crime group but that he has betrayed them,
or at least disappointed them to an extent that he thinks is going
to end up being fatal. He was running some sort of financial
scam with their pension fund money, working with a Scottish
accountant in Vancouver by the name of Wallace, who was a
very active T'Rain player. Wallace's computer got infected with
REAMDE . . .

. . . and the note went on to tell a story that, while bizarre in a
lot of respects, explained much of what had been puzzling Richard
for the last week. The narrative portion of the letter ended in what
could only be called a cliffhanger: she and Peter and some other
guy had seemingly identified the Troll, and she had the impression
that the Russians were making preparations to go and snatch him.
Assuming that the letter had been written early Friday morning
Xiamen time, this fit perfectly with Corvallis's statistics showing
that the Troll and his minions had suddenly logged off and gone
dark on Friday morning.

The remainder of the letter consisted of a series of personal
notes directed at various family members, clearly based on the
assumption that Zula would never see any of them again. Richard
had attempted to read it about ten times and been unable to get
through it.

He had awakened John and Alice right away, of course, and John
had packed his bags and started driving through the night toward
the Omaha airport, Alice calling ahead to arrange a morning flight
to Seattle. Richard had called his jet leasing company to set up an
ASAP flight to Xiamen, and they had warned him that he'd need a
visa. He had stayed up into the small hours of the morning researching Chinese visa policies and learned that it all had to be done
through a consulate, of which the nearest was in San Francisco, and
so at five in the morning he had dropped an assistant off at Sea-
Tac, sending her down with his passport and all the documentation
needed to get a visa in ultra-super-expedited fashion. Richard had
called John during a layover in Denver and revectored him to SFO

so that he could hand his passport over to the same assistant. John had then caught the next flight up to Seattle. Recent text messages from the assistant suggested that all was proceeding according to plan and that she would probably be able to catch a six P.M. flight back to Seattle, which would get the visas into their hands at about eight and enable wheels up from Boeing Field as early as nine.

"I HAVE BEEN watching the Facebook page with I guess you could say trepidation," Richard said. "No leaks about this yet." He patted a hard copy of the paper towel message draped over the console between the car's front seats.

"I'm sure there won't be," John said. "Your call came in the middle of the night, no one was in the house but me and Alice, no one knows a thing."

For they had agreed that they would not divulge the existence of Zula's note just yet; the news would make its way into the wild very rapidly, where it might complicate the investigation, or whatever this thing they were doing was called.

"Did your friend get any information on the fella who sent the email?" John asked.

"We don't know that it's a fella," Richard reminded him. "Nolan's on it, but it's the middle of the night in China right now, and he doesn't have a lot to go on. He said it's the equivalent of a Hotmail address."

"What do you mean?" John asked peevishly. He had a Hotmail address.

"An easy-to-get anonymous account frequently used by spammers," Richard said. "What I'm trying to tell you is that whoever sent me that email probably wanted to do it in an anonymous, untraceable way."

"Maybe we could trace him through the skyscraper."

"We don't know which skyscraper it is," Richard pointed out. "Zula didn't bother to specify that in the note. She probably assumed that, if the note were ever found, it would be obvious to everyone which building it came from."

John considered it. "Instead what we have here is some kind of leaker or whistle-blower."

"I would guess so."

"How about the Seattle cops?"

"I called the detective and left a voice mail message. Told him we had evidence that Zula was alive and not in Seattle on Friday. Which I think takes it out of his jurisdiction."

"It takes the missing persons part of it out of his jurisdiction," John said. "But it means that crimes happened in Seattle. Murder and kidnapping and assault and God only knows what else . . ."

Richard nodded. "And I'm sure that the Seattle detectives who work on those kinds of crimes are going to be really interested in Zula's note. But none of that has anything to do with us getting her back safe."

"It most certainly does if the responsible parties can be identified, tracked down, extradited—"

"Something major happened in Xiamen on that Friday, only a few hours after Zula wrote that note," Richard said. He had avoided mentioning this to John and Alice until now because he could not be certain it was actually connected to Zula and he didn't want to confuse and upset them and add a vast number of additional bogus leads to John's already torpid database.

"Go ahead, I'm listening," John said, having heard nothing further than the hiss of tires on wet pavement, the washing-machine surge of the windshield wipers.

Richard sighed. "I'm trying to figure out where to begin." He thought about the sheer level of energy he would have to summon in order to explain the investigations he had been pursuing with Corvallis, the state of the battle for the Torgai, and all the rest. And he felt overwhelmingly tired. "I am about to drive this thing right off the road," he said. "Let's get to my place and get some coffee."

BUT AS IT turned out, when they reached Richard's condo, they went in opposite directions to start the coffeemaker, use the toilet, check email, make phone calls. By the time Richard was ready to talk again, John was asleep on the sofa, and by the time John had awakened from his nap, Richard had conked out on his bed. Later, both awake at the same time, they made sandwiches and looked out the window at the sun setting over the Olympics; the clouds were still heavy, but the red light was streaming in beneath them as if China itself were lurking just a few miles offshore, glowing red like a vast forge. Richard could not get out of his mind that they would soon be chasing that red light westward, and John did not seem talkative either. It was morning there now. Nolan, ensconced in his place in Vancouver, was sending emails, making phone calls, pulling strings, making arrangements for translators and fixers to meet the Forthrasts at the Xiamen airport, trying to get some idea of what the PSB there had been doing. The situation was impossibly hard to read. Was the PSB even aware of the existence of Zula's note? Perhaps it had been leaked to Richard by some random plumber who wanted to do a good deed and not be identified. Or perhaps the PSB had known about it all along and had dangled it in front of Richard as a lure to bring him to Xiamen for interrogation. Or perhaps they had meant to keep it secret, but some leaker within the PSB had taken it upon himself to shoot Richard a copy. Nolan vacillated between urging Richard not to set foot in China at all and helping him get there as quickly as possible. Richard felt no qualms whatsoever; a member of his family was in trouble there and he had to go.

Corvallis had been tracking the assistant's flight up from SFO. He showed up at the condo and helped carry John's bag down to his Prius, which was waiting in the pickup/drop-off lane in front of the building. Richard and John ended up cramming themselves into the backseat together so that they could talk on the way down to Boeing Field.

He really didn't want to talk about this, but he owed it to John to give him the information before they got on a plane to China.

"There were two separate incidents that we know about," Richard said. "They seem to have happened a couple of hours apart. Incident number 2 is better documented: a suicide bomber blew himself up at a security checkpoint outside an international conference. A couple of Chinese cops got killed; there were injuries from shrapnel and flying glass."

"How is this connected to Zula?" John asked.

"We have no idea. But incident number 1 is murkier and maybe more relevant. An apartment building blew up not far from downtown. It was put down to a gas explosion. That's the official story. But Nolan has got some sources in Xiamen, sources we may be meeting tomorrow, who have been asking around, and word on the street is that the explosion happened in the middle of a gun battle that took place on the building's upper floors."

Silence for a while. Richard, who had been through all of this before, knew what John was thinking: he was in denial, trying to think of reasons why this had nothing to do with Zula.

"Now," Richard continued, speaking as gently as he could, "we have learned from Zula's note that she was with these Russians who had come into the country illegally and who were armed. We know that they were looking for the Troll."

"The hackers who created the virus," John translated.

"Yeah. If they succeeded in tracking down those hackers, then this Ivanov character might have been crazy enough to go in shooting. Who knows, maybe they even used grenades or satchel charges."

"Why the hell would you use satchel charges?" John demanded. He had long gotten over the fact that Richard was a draft dodger. But he hated it when Richard strayed into topics of which Richard knew nothing and John had personal experience.

"I don't know, John; I'm just trying to think of a reason why the building blew up. Because the building is gone. It is destroyed."

"A satchel charge wouldn't be powerful enough to bring down a multistory building."

"Okay, well, maybe it was a gas explosion then, but it was set off as a result of the gun battle."

"Maybe it had nothing to do with Zula at all!" John protested.

"But John, the thing is—as Corvallis here can explain much better than I—at the same time that this gun battle and explosion took place, the Troll dropped off the Internet. And hasn't come back since."

The back of Corvallis's neck turned red. They drove past Peter's loft. Everyone observed silence for a while. According to Zula's note, a man—Wallace—had died in there.

Only a couple of minutes later, they turned off Airport Way into the frontage road that led to the FBO.

Considering the net worth of its clientele, one might have expected a glitzier place. But it was just a boxy two-story office building that faced the frontage road—a public thoroughfare—on one end and the restricted zone of the airport tarmac on the other. The airfield's tall cyclone fence ran right up to one wall and then continued on the other side. As they pulled off the road, they entered a parking lot with only a few cars scattered about; at its opposite end this was terminated by the fence, or rather by a large rolling gate set into it. Corvallis pulled up to it and stopped. Richard clambered out of the car. As soon as the personnel inside recognized his face, they hit the button that caused the gate to trundle open. Richard waved Corvallis forward, and he drove onto the tarmac and directly to a bizjet that was parked no more than fifty feet away. Richard followed on foot and greeted the pilot by name as he emerged from the cockpit and descended the stairway. Corvallis parked at a respectful distance from the plane's landing gear and then popped the Prius's hatchback, and the men formed a bucket brigade to move the luggage up into the plane's cargo hold. Richard was more than normally aware of these details since he knew that two weeks earlier Zula had passed through the same gate with the Russians.

The pilot, as usual, was ready to go, but they were still waiting for the assistant with the visas. He invited them to come aboard and make themselves comfortable; the flight attendant had brought in some sushi. John, for whom this sort of travel was still novel, took him up on the invitation. Richard strolled back toward the FBO, thinking he might get a cup of decaf and grab a newspaper. The airport-facing end of the building was a lounge, clean and reasonably well appointed but not flagrantly luxurious. At any time of the day or night, one might see a few people, individuals or small groups, sitting there checking their email and waiting for planes. At this particular moment there was only one other person there, an Asian woman in her twenties, short hair, dressed in jeans and sort of a nice jackety getup that made the jeans look slightly more serious. She had been reading a novel and drinking tea. Richard went over to the self-serve latte machine and began pressing buttons. He was keeping one eye out the window, watching for the taxi carrying the assistant fresh in from San Francisco with the visas.

"Mr. Forthrast?"

The words had been spoken with an English accent. Richard turned around, surprised, to see that it was the Asian woman. She was standing about ten feet away in a somewhat prim attitude, wrists crossed in front of her to hold the novel as a shield in front of her pelvis: *Sorry, I know this is a bit awkward.*

"The same." Richard could read the signs well enough: this was either a hard-core T'Rain player who wanted to rap with him about the game, or someone who wanted a job at Corporation 9592. He dealt with both types all the time, pleasantly.

"Don't go to China."

He had been watching the foam dribble from the latte machine, but now his head spun around to fix on her. She looked apologetic. But quite firm.

"How the hell do you know where I'm going?"

"Zula isn't there," the woman said. "It's a dead end."

"How would you know any of this?"

"I was there," the woman said.

IN RETROSPECT OLIVIA had never done more or traveled farther to achieve so little as in the past ten days.

After bidding adieu to "George Chow" in the Taipei airport, she flew to Singapore. Obsessed by the idea that everyone was looking at her funny, she monopolized a sink in the airport for a while, scrubbing away the ridiculous makeup job that Chow's cosmetician had put on her face in the hotel room in Jincheng. She was itching to attack the haircut too, but you couldn't have scissors in airports and she didn't want to make that much of a spectacle of herself. The laceration on the top of her head had never been properly stitched. It tended to open up and start bleeding at odd moments and so it didn't seem advisable to be getting hands-on up there. Maybe MI6 would have people in London who were good at this sort of thing—combat beauticians, trauma stylists. It seemed likely that her MI6 superiors were making hysterical efforts to get in touch with her and pump her for information during this layover, but she didn't have any way of communicating with them that she was willing to trust. And even if someone walked up to her in person, right here in the ladies', someone she recognized as working for the agency, she wasn't sure how much she'd be willing to divulge. Someone had set an ambush for Sokolov out there in the mist off Kinmen, and she didn't know who. Best case was that it had just been Chinese intelligence or local gangsters. Worst case was that MI6 actually wanted him dead. Between those two extremes, perhaps MI6 had been penetrated and Chinese intelligence had access to its secrets. In any case, she didn't feel like spilling any more information about Sokolov until she got back to London and learned more.

Then the nonstop to London. She spent the first bit of it getting drunk and the rest of it sleeping.

The plane landed at Heathrow's Terminal 5 at something like six in the morning. Since her immigration status had become impossible to make sense of, she was met, at the top of the jetway, by a man in a uniform and a man in a suit. She had always read of people being "whisked through" certain formalities, but this was the first time she had ever been personally whisked and she had to admit that it had its charms. Particularly when you were hungover and bleeding. In order to get from Terminal 5's gates to Immigration and Customs, it was necessary to descend a prodigious stack of escalators, beginning well above ground level and terminating deep below. There was a place, about halfway along, where an escalator deposited the newly arrived passengers on a landing that happened to coincide with street level; as you executed a U-turn to get on the next, you could look out through glass doors and walls at a road with cars and trucks streaming along it. Uniformed personnel were forever stationed before those glass doors to make sure that every-one coming down those escalators kept going down into the levels where they were to be processed.

Everyone, that is, except for those lucky few who were being whisked. Olivia was ready to make the U-turn and descend along with everyone else, but her escorts got off that escalator and just kept walking in a straight line. And since Olivia was sandwiched between them, she did the same, expecting that, at any moment, one of the security guards stationed before the doors would wrestle her to the ground and begin blowing on a whistle. Instead of which, a door was opened for her, an alarm was stifled by a series of digits punched into a keypad, and suddenly she was out of doors climbing into a black Land Rover. They were out on the M4 before the stale air of the jumbo jet had even dissipated from her clothes and hair.

Into a London doctor's office, some sort of exceedingly private and specialized practice, a basic tenet of which was never to evince surprise or skepticism. Where had she come from? South China. Health generally good? Until quite recently. What had happened recently? Hurled against a wall by a blast wave, showered with broken glass, half buried in debris, ran through a damaged building barefoot, makeshift bandages, fled from gunmen, swam in the polluted waters of the Nine Dragons estuary, crawled through minefield, slept on a pile of vines. The doctor just nodded absentmindedly, as if she were complaining of vaginal itching, and then ran her through a scanner the size of a nuclear submarine. That accomplished, he prodded her all over, put his fingers every place he could think of, squeezed bones and organs she didn't know were externally accessible, peered into orifices with Dr. Seuss–like equipment, asked her probing questions intended to judge her cognitive status. Or other kinds of status. Had sex recently? Oh yes. Any chance of being pregnant? No. He lidocained the thing on the top of her head and put in a couple of stitches and did things that produced a scent of burning hair. Then he turned her over to an "injectionist," who plied her trade on Olivia's deltoids, forearms, buttocks, and thighs with unseemly diligence, pulling many wee tubes of blood out of her and replacing the lost fluids with vast, neon-colored inoculations. It was made clear to her that the large muscles in question would hurt later and that she would have to come back for more. All this attention paid to her health made her happy at first, until on further reflection she understood that they were getting ready to work her to death and they didn't want her gumming things up by complaining of vague pains or chills. What, you say your ribs are hurting? That's funny, we didn't see anything on the scan.

Notes were jotted and verbal representations made to the effect that she should see certain specialized doctors and therapists at some vague time in the future. A follow-up was scheduled.

Then, off to MI6 for a surprisingly civil brunch and preliminary round of drinking with persons of gratifyingly high rank. Then the windowless conference room she had been anticipating and dreading. Her primary debriefer was none other than "Meng Binrong," the Englishman who had been telephonically playing the role of her uncle during her time in Xiamen. He was blond-going-white, blue-eyed, with the classic florid English drinker's complexion, energetic, mistakable for a man in his fifties or even late forties. But certain giveaways—the fact that he found it necessary to mow his eyebrows, the sheer number of burst capillaries—suggested he was older than that. Not eager to volunteer details about himself, but it was obvious from the sorts of things he knew—and *didn't* know—and from the way he spoke Cantonese and Mandarin (the former with perfect fluency, the latter a bit choppily), that he had spent his young life in Hong Kong. To Olivia he had always been a gruff voice on the phone, her uncle and boss, her one connection to what was for her the real world. But never more than a play-actor. From certain things he now said and certain assumptions he made, it now became clear to Olivia that this man—who never quite got around to stating his name—had been responsible for running the operation.

Where did that put him, she had to wonder? Was the operation considered a success or a failure? Or was it naive to think that MI6 would even bother assigning such facile designations to undertakings of such complexity? Supposedly they had garnered loads of intelligence from tapping Jones's communications. No one could complain about that. The fact that he'd gotten away was unfortunate. But how could they possibly have anticipated—

"What the *fuck* happened?" asked Uncle Meng, careful to say it in measured and melodious tones.

"Everything I know, I know from talking to Mr. Y," Olivia said, using the code name that she and George Chow had employed for Sokolov.

"Do you know his real name?"

"Does it matter right now?"

Uncle Meng just stared at her with his amazingly pale eyes.

"It's just that I thought we were after Jones."

"You know perfectly well that we are."

"The whole situation with Mr. Y is extremely confusing to me," Olivia said. "Because of what happened at the end."

"Mr. Chow said that you claimed to have heard gunfire from out on the water."

"The claim stands."

"Mr. Y seems like quite the trouble magnet."

"Does that put me in the category of trouble?"

"Why? Was he drawn to you?"

"I'd say it was mutual."

Uncle Meng considered it. "So. You have feelings for Mr. Y. You think you heard him exchanging gunfire with unknown persons, somewhere out in the mists of the Orient. You are worried about what has become of him. And so here we are circling round each other and talking to no purpose because the conversation has become all about him."

"Yes."

"So let's talk about Jones."

"All right."

"The entire point of trying to put Mr. Y on that ship to Long Beach was to secure his cooperation—to get some information he supposedly had as to where Jones was going. Did you get that information from him?"

"Jones was able to get control of a business jet parked at the FBO at Xiamen Airport," Olivia said. She stood up, turned to the whiteboard, and wrote down its tail number. "Mr. Y observed it taking off at zero seven one three hours local time." She wrote that down too. "It headed south."

The conference room was well supplied with younger aides, one of whom, at a nod from Uncle Meng, commenced typing furiously.

Olivia said, "You'll find that it's leased to, or maybe even owned by, a Russian national based out of Toronto, and that it had flown into Xiamen a few days earlier."

"Is this Russian national the same person as Mr. Y?"

"No, Mr. Y worked for him as a security consultant."

"That being a euphemism for the sort of chap who leaves a pile of corpses in the hall outside of your flat."

"They deserved it," Olivia said.

Uncle Meng raised his shorn eyebrows at this, but not in a disapproving way.

"Do we know who else is aboard that plane?"

"I don't know the ins and outs of flying," Olivia said, "but I've been turning it over in my mind and I can't but think that its usual pilots must be at the controls. Jones must have coerced them somehow."

"I don't disagree, but I was really asking about the bloody terrorists."

"Not many of Jones's crew could have survived what happened

in that building," Olivia said. "I'm amazed that Jones did. But he can't have been acting alone. So he must have had some other safe house or support network that he drew on later."

"The yacht club," said Uncle Meng, using a bit of jargon that he and Olivia had devised during the course of the operation. They'd been unable to get many details, but they were fairly certain that Jones had traveled by sea from the Philippines to Taiwan and from there to Xiamen, and that he was getting supplies and personnel through some such connection, probably small fishing vessels passing stuff back and forth, literally and figuratively under the radar.

They ended up drawing a time line on the whiteboard. There was a gap of many hours between the explosion of the apartment building and Mr. Y's startling and timely arrival—which seen from this remove had a touching Romeo-esque quality—on "Meng Anlan's" balcony. This was at least tangentially relevant to Jones's movements, since it was assumed that the men who'd been sent to her apartment had been acting at Jones's behest. Olivia made her best guess as to the time of the phone conversation between Mr. Y and Jones, of which she had overheard Sokolov's half while they'd been out on the stolen water taxi. Sokolov had known somehow that Jones was at the airport. He had guessed that some female named Zula was with him. He had threatened to find and dispatch Jones in some exceptionally cruel style if he did anything to Zula.

After that, the time line sported another white space until 0713 in the morning yesterday, China time, when the jet had taken off. Then a very long blank space encompassing the thirty-six hours between that moment and "NOW." A few tentative marks were later drawn into that space, denoting when Olivia had made contact with George Chow, when Sokolov had disappeared into the mist, and the spans of time occupied by Olivia's flights from Kinmen to Taipei, Taipei to Singapore, Singapore to London.

Then a difficult pause.

"It might have been convenient for us to have known," said Uncle Meng, "just a bit earlier than now, that Abdallah Jones was in the air, in a jet with such-and-such tail number."

Olivia was ready for this. Had been thinking about it. "By the time I got that information out of Mr. Y, Jones had already been in the air for eight hours. Because of what happened—the gunfire—

I considered the operation blown and no longer trusted George Chow, so I didn't give him the tail number. We had to get out of Kinmen anyway. By the time we reached Taipei, Jones had been in the air for at least ten hours. I had no secure line of communications from there by which to reach you. By the time I reached Singapore, it had been long enough that Jones's plane was almost certainly no longer airborne."

Uncle Meng seemed unconvinced. But before this awkward topic could be developed further, one of the younger, laptop-smacking analysts piped up with the following news: "Yesterday a missing persons report was filed on someone named Zula. A Yank. Adopted from Eritrea, hence the unusual name. Female, early twenties, lives in Seattle, which is where the report was filed."

"Get us more on her," said Uncle Meng. "I'd love to know how she ended up on a hijacked business jet in Xiamen with Abdallah Jones. Not to mention how it is that Mr. Y, so bloodthirsty in other respects, cares how this random person is treated."

"You're reading Mr. Y all wrong," Olivia said.

They all just gazed at her, hoping she'd say more.

"He's a gentleman," she explained, for want of any better way to put it.

"Oh. Why didn't you just say so?" said Uncle Meng.

MUCH OF WHAT happened after that was out of her purview: they got loads of data about Zula. Loads more about the Russian. They guessed, but Olivia refused to confirm, that Mr. Y was Sokolov. They brought in RAF types who knew a great deal about airplanes and radar and put aeronautical charts up on the whiteboards and hooked up a flight simulator programmed to simulate that exact type of business jet and tried flying it out of Xiamen. Olivia looked out of the simulator's virtual cockpit windows and saw the beach at Kinmen where she had been standing with Sokolov, and almost fancied that if she strained her eyes enough she might see two columns of pixels down there, blurred representations of herself and of "Mr. Y" staring up at this simulated plane. Extremely childish/ romantic. The true and serious purpose of this was to investigate possible flight plans that Jones might have followed after taking off that morning. Several of these were "wargamed," which sounded like fun until it became evident that 90 percent of the wargaming had to do with the internal doings of air traffic control centers and protocols for filing flight plans in various Southeast Asian countries. A faction badly wanted to demonstrate that Jones could have flown the jet all the way to Pakistan, but gaping holes were blasted in this scenario as expert persons pointed out all the restricted military airspace around the disputed border regions of India/China, Pakistan/India, et cetera. Another faction was all for the idea that he had taken the jet all the way to North America. But to justify this they had to piece together a somewhat tangled tale that could explain how he had evaded radar detection while flying up a crowded and well-monitored air traffic corridor, and they had to provide some justification for why the plane had initially taken off southbound— an injudicious use of fuel. They were able to do that by composing an argument having to do with domestic Chinese flight plans. No one could prove that they were wrong, but all were uneasy with the story's complexity. By far the simplest and most plausible scenario was that Jones had simply dropped the plane down to wavetop level and flown it straight to Mindanao and ditched it. Olivia favored that theory if for no other reason than that, if true, it meant that Jones had already been on the ground and the plane sunk beneath the waves by the time Sokolov had given her the tail number, and so she couldn't be blamed for having delayed passing it on.

To hedge their bets against the possibility that Jones had flown all the way to North America, they got in touch with their opposite numbers in Canada and the United States and suggested that it might be prudent to keep an eye peeled for the said business jet. The most likely supposition being that it might have landed on some remote airstrip or stretch of deserted road and been abandoned. Having (to borrow a term from the Yanks) covered that base, they then focused all their energies on the Mindanao scenario.

These proceedings extended over some forty-eight hours, during which time Olivia was at work almost whenever she was awake. The very meaning of "awake" was rendered debatable by the most extreme case of jet lag she'd ever experienced, possibly commingled with posttraumatic and/or postconcussion symptoms. At least half of the time she spent in that room pretending to take part in the meeting, she was devoting essentially all her energies and attention to the project of not simply dropping into a deep slumber right then and there. She found herself shifting position irritably every ten seconds or so, just to ward off sleep, and she heard the others discussing momentous and complicated topics as though eavesdropping through a very long speaking-tube on a dreadnought.

When they took pity on her and sent her "home," she went to a safe house in London: a perfectly anonymous Georgian town house that had been taken over and bent to this purpose. During the very limited amount of time that she was not working or sleeping, she found herself with nothing to do. She could not resume being Olivia Halifax-Lin just yet, could not begin facebooking or whatever it was people did now. She found a hairdresser who catered to Asians and got that business taken care of, ending up with something pageboyish, straight out of a porn film, that she never would have taken a risk on had circumstances not forced her hand. She rubbed her sore, immunized muscles. Warned to expect foreign travel, she bought clothes: enough lightweight, quick-drying synthetic garments to fill a carry-on bag and a blazer that she could throw on when she wanted to make a symbolic nod in the direction of greater formality. A new passport showed up, which made her wonder just now MI6 did these things: Did they have a passport factory of their very own? Or just a special room at the Central British Passport Factory where they could nip in and bang out a few as the occasion demanded?

There was another session with the injectionist, perhaps a bit ahead of the normal schedule, and she was given antimalaria pills and a stern talking to about why mosquito repellent was such a good thing. Uncle Meng picked her up in what appeared to be his personal car and took her out to Heathrow, though they stopped halfway there for a cup of coffee and a scone.

"You are bound for Manila," he said, "by way of Dubai."

"I presume Manila is not my final destination?"

"It is as far as commercial airlines are concerned," he said. "When you are there, you'll have one night in a hotel to pull yourself together and then you'll find yourself in the company of one Seamus Costello, Captain, U.S. Army, retired."

"So he is, what, just a gentleman of leisure now?"

Uncle Meng did not wish to dignify her witticism with a direct response.

"Mostly," Olivia said, "I would just like to know whether he's working for some other branch of the government or a private security contractor."

"Oh no, we wouldn't set you up with a mercenary," said Uncle Meng, a bit pained.

"Right then, so he was a snake eater. They decided he had talents beyond his station in life. They kicked him upstairs."

"The American national security apparatus is very large and unfathomably complex," was all that Uncle Meng would say. "It has many departments and subunits that, one supposes, would not survive a top-to-bottom overhaul. This feeds on itself as individual actors, despairing of ever being able to make sense of it all, create their own little ad hoc bits that become institutionalized as money flows toward them. Those who are good at playing the political game are drawn inward to Washington. Those who are not end up sitting in hotel lobbies in places like Manila, waiting for people like you."

"He must have other duties."

"Oh yes. He spends most of his time on Mindanao, looking after the Abu Sayyaf crowd."

Here, as Olivia knew perfectly well, Uncle Meng was referring to Islamic insurgents in the southern Philippines who had hosted and succored Abdallah Jones for several months. U.S. special operations forces, operating hand in hand with their Filipino counterparts, had launched a raid against a jungle encampment where Jones had been positively sighted. They had found the place abandoned but extensively booby-trapped. Two Americans and four Filipinos had lost their lives. Weeks later, Jones had been traced to Manila, where he had set up a bomb factory in an apartment building and created explosive devices that had been used in a precisely timed series of car bombings. From there his trail had consisted of nothing but hints and rumors until Olivia had found him in Xiamen.

"Costello has been after Jones for a long time," Olivia guessed. "He takes pride in his work, or used to. Jones got the better of him more than once. Killed members of his team in sneaky and cowardly ways. Blew up civilians on his watch. Then left the country—

went where Costello couldn't get to him. Leaving Costello stuck in a backwater."

"He is just your type," Uncle Meng said gently. "Please do try not to fuck him."

"How come it's okay for James Bond?"

THE FLIGHT TO Dubai was all rich Arabs and City types. The Dubai-to-Manila leg was almost entirely Filipina domestic servants headed for home. The racial and cultural crossrip was far too heavy for Olivia to get thinking about, so she watched movies and played Tetris, finally falling asleep thirty minutes before they began their descent into Ninoy Aquino International Airport. It was late afternoon. Four days had now passed since she and Sokolov had parted ways at Kinmen. A car picked her up and took her to a business hotel in Makati where she ate room service steak, cleaned up, took her malaria pills, and went to bed.

She slept through three alarms and wake-up calls and made it down to the lobby fifteen minutes late. Seamus Costello was in the restaurant eating bacon and eggs, over easy. The reddish-yellow color of the runny yolks perfectly matched that of his beard, but even so he self-consciously wiped his chin before standing up to shake Olivia's hand. He looked like a slightly over-the-hill backpacker, the kind of guy you'd strike up a conversation with on a rattletrap bus in Bhutan or Tierra del Fuego, borrow a joint from, ask for advice on where and where not to stay the night. He was lean, like a strip of bacon that had spent too long in the pan, and a bit north of six feet tall. He had green eyes that seemed just a little too wide open—though, she had to admit, any nonblack eyes looked that way after you'd been living in China for a while—and he had a Boston accent that could scrape the rust from a manhole cover. But he'd been to school—anyone in his job would probably have a master's degree or better—and he could dress up his speech when he remembered to make the effort.

Which he didn't, now. "Ya came this close," he said, holding his thumb and index finger an eighth of an inch apart.

Delivered in the wrong tone, it would have been a rebuke or even mockery. But he had a trace of a smile on his face when he said it. The tone was philosophical.

He was congratulating her.

She shrugged. "Not close enough, I'm afraid."

"Still. What was *that* like? Sittin' there, day after day, listenin' to yer man and his crew . . ."

"I don't speak Arabic, unfortunately."

"I'd not have been able to contain myself," he said ruefully, staring out the window and getting a sort of mischievous-boy look on his face as he imagined (she guessed) going across that Xiamen street and walking up to Apartment 505 and gutting Abdallah Jones with a knife. "Ah, that fucking bastard." He turned his eyes back to her. "So. You think he's on Mindanao."

"There is a cove not far from Zamboanga, sheltered enough that it would be a good place to ditch, deep enough that a plane would sink rapidly and become invisible to—"

"I've swum in it," he said.

"Oh."

Olivia was looking a little startled. "I read the report," he explained. "I know what your working theory is. They ditched, just where you said, and went ashore. That whole area is lousy with Abu Sayyaf, it would have been easy for them to hook up with their brothers." He chose to turn the Boston accent all the way up to eleven when pronouncing the word "brothers."

"So what do you think?"

"I think I'm going to take you down there and we are going to check it out."

"But what do you really think?"

"That doesn't matter," he said. "Tell you what, let's go down there, I'll show you around, and in another couple of days, once we've gotten to know each other, established a *trust relationship,* then we can each tell the other what we really think." Then he pitched forward a bit. "What!? What!?" for a look of amusement had crept onto her face.

"I thought you were here," she said, "because you were no good at politics."

He put his palms together, fingertips nestled in his beard, like a Southie boy going to his First Communion. "I like to think I am here," he said, "because I'm good at acquiring new skills. Which comes in handy in Zamboanga. Want some breakfast?"

"Are we going to miss our plane?"

"They'll wait for us."

THE REASON FOR his lack of urgency became plain when they got out the door and into Manila traffic, for which simple words like "bad" or "horrendous" were completely inadequate as descriptors. Two hours into the journey, they had traveled less than a mile from the hotel.

"Up for a stroll?" Seamus asked her.

"I would be up for just about anything that wasn't this," Olivia said. So he paid the taxi driver and they set out on foot, Olivia feeling inordinately proud of herself for having packed light and, moreover, done so in a bag that could be converted into a backpack. Seamus chivalrously offered to carry it for her but she shrugged him off, and they began walking between lanes of stationary traffic for a while until he steered them off to the edge of the road. The heat was fantastic, whooshing out from beneath the stopped vehicles and baking her bare legs. It abated somewhat as they worked their way out of the traffic jam and onto smaller streets. Seamus purchased two flimsy umbrellas from a street vendor, handed one to Olivia, and snapped the other open to keep the sun off his head. She followed his lead in that. Navigating by the sun, he maneuvered them into a residential neighborhood that started out seeming reasonably affluent and became somewhat less so as they got farther from Makati. But she never felt in any danger, out of a possibly fatuous belief that no harm could come to her when she was walking next to someone like him. They were noticed, and watched carefully, by hundreds of people, and followed by dozens. "Miss? Miss?" some of them called.

"It's freaking them out that you're carrying your own bag," Seamus said, and so she finally surrendered it to him, leaving herself with nothing but a belt pack that was now serving in lieu of purse and the parasol. She'd assumed they were trying to get to the airport, which was definitely off to their left, or south; but Seamus kept taking them west, cutting across the occasional cemetery or basketball court, until they struck water: a very unappealing stagnant creek, half choked with plastic debris and smelling of sewage. Olivia couldn't tell which way it was flowing, but Seamus made an educated guess and led her along its bank, occasionally holding out an arm to prevent her from toppling into it, until they got to a place where it widened into a little basin where actual boats were to be seen: long, slender double-outrigger canoes equipped with outboard motors. Seamus had no difficulty hailing one of these and inducing its owner to take them in the direction of Sangley Point. The hull was so narrow that Olivia could bridge it with her forearm. They sat amidships under an awning of sun-blasted canvas, Olivia in front, leaning back against her pack, and Seamus behind.

She knew that word "sangley," at least; it was Chinese, from the dialect that was spoken around Xiamen, and it quite literally meant "business."

They maneuvered down progressively wider channels for a quarter of an hour or so, the densely packed neighborhoods giving way to giant industrial zones and expanses of flat empty territory, then abruptly turned into a blunt channel that disgorged them directly into Manila Bay. For the first time Olivia was able to look about and get a clue as to where they were. They were headed for a claw of land reaching out into the bay a couple of miles ahead of them. A running conversation between Seamus and the pilot, in a mixture of Tagalog and English, led to a series of increases in the throttle, to the point where they were bounding and bouncing over chop, sending occasional gouts of spray into Olivia's face. "He's worried you don't like it. Wants to go slow for you," Seamus explained, and Olivia twisted around until she could make eye contact with the boatman, grinned, and gave him the thumbs-up.

The spray and the cool sea air were a fine antidote for the killing heat of the traffic jam, and so they arrived at a dock on Sangley Point salty and in need of showers but somewhat refreshed. It was a military installation: an airbase, Seamus had explained, formerly of the United States, now of the Philippine Air Force. A pilot in uniform met them at the dock—Seamus had called or texted ahead, apparently—and walked them to a waiting Humvee that took them directly onto the tarmac of the base's single, very long runway. They pulled up next to a simple two-engine passenger plane with military markings and were airborne a few minutes later. They took off to the west, headed straight for the narrow exit of the gigantic bay, and soon banked left and began the long flight south to Zamboanga:

something like five hundred miles, which they expected to cover in a couple of hours. Seamus spent most of it sleeping. Olivia looked out the windows and tried to see the archipelago's countless islands, inlets, and channels through the eyes of an Abdallah Jones.

"What do you think?" Seamus asked her, just as she was finally about to nod off. She jolted awake, looked across at him—they were seated on opposite sides of a small table that occupied most of the plane's cabin—and tried to snap out of the jet-lag torpor that had crept up on her. She wondered how long he'd been watching her. His decision to leap out of the taxi in Manila and set off on foot had been made to look like the spontaneous act of a free spirit, but she had little doubt that it had been calculated as a way of putting her to the test. Not by any stretch of the imagination a difficult or strenuous test, but an unscripted moment in which she might let her guard down and reveal aspects of her personality otherwise difficult to see. By sleeping for most of the flight, Seamus seemed to be telling her that she had passed the test, whatever it was. Now they were starting to get down to work.

"A million places to hide, once you get down on the surface," Olivia said. "But flying in on a business jet in the middle of the day, you'd be absurdly conspicuous."

With the tiniest suggestion of a nod, Seamus broke eye contact and looked out the window. "There it is," he said. "Welcome to the GWOJ."

"GWOJ?"

"Global War on Jones."

THE ZAMBOANGA OUTPOST of the GWOJ turned out to be one corner of an air force base that had been constructed on flat coastal land, otherwise occupied by rice paddies, outside of a middling regional city. The base as a whole was moderately well fenced and defended. The corner occupied by Seamus and his team was a fortress unto itself, surrounded by high chain-link and razor wire bolstered by stacked steel shipping containers. Approaching vehicles had to run a slalom course through containers that Seamus assured her had been filled with dirt so that they could not simply be bashed out of the way by an onrushing truck bomb. Once inside that perimeter, though, they found themselves in a tiny simulacrum of America: a compound of modular dwellings surmounted by howling air conditioners fed by cables from a huge diesel generator situated downwind. Several of the modules were barracks for Seamus and members of his crew, one was guest quarters for people like Olivia, and there was a double-wide with kitchen and dining facilities at one end and a conference room at the other.

Here as everywhere else in the world, everyone hung out in the kitchen. So after Olivia had dropped her stuff in the guest quarters and taken a shower, she went into the double-wide to find Seamus and two other members of his crew hanging out there, lounging on sofas or sitting with erect postures at the dining table, focused on their laptops, sipping American soft drinks. The whole scene in fact looked quintessentially American to her, which, as she would've been the first person to admit, meant nothing, since she had spent practically no time in the United States. Seamus's crew was multiracial to a fault and looked somewhat uneasy in their cargo shorts and T-shirts, as though they'd all much rather be in uniform. They all had lots of stuff strapped to them: holsters with semiautomatic pistols, knives, radios. Even their eyeglasses were strapped to their heads. Earlier, they'd all been perfunctorily introduced to Olivia; none of them now gave her more than a glance and a nod. They were intensely focused on what they were doing: some sort of pitched battle.

"Fuckers are trying to flank us on the left!"

"I see 'em and am pulling. Need backup though."

"Disengaging from the Witch King and pivoting to get your back. Someone finish the bastard off. A few Kingly Strokes would take care of it, Shame."

Seamus said, "Okay, I'll need to rearm, cover me for second . . . got it . . . Fuck!"

All of the men leaned back from their screens in unison and let out roars of anguished laughter so loud that Olivia's ears crackled. "Fuck, man!" called a compact African American. "He toasted you."

"We're all fucked now," said a Hispanic guy. "Sequester your shit while you still can."

Fierce clicking and typing, punctuated by roaring, anguished laughter, as (Olivia guessed) each man's character died in the game world.

Planted around the dining area, on windowsills and kitchen counters, were plastic dolls: troll- or elflike fantasy characters decked out in elaborate costumes and armed to the teeth with fanciful, quasi-medieval weapons. Each one stood on a faux-stone pedestal with a name chiseled into it. Olivia picked one of them up—very carefully, since it seemed that they were important—and flipped it over. Marked on the underside of the base was the logo of Corporation 9592.

So that answered the question she'd been afraid to ask, for fear of seeming like the stupidest person in the whole world: *Are you playing T'Rain?* Because Olivia was not a gamer and could not tell one such game from another.

"Olivia?"

She looked up and locked eyes with Seamus, who was staring at her over the rim of his laptop screen. Seamus spoke with exaggerated calm: "Put . . . the troll . . . down . . . and slowly back away."

Okay, he was joking. She carefully put the doll back and then clasped her hands innocently behind her back. The other men let out loud *fyoosh!* noises as if an IED had just been successfully defused.

"I'm sorry I touched your doll," she said. "I had no idea how important Thorakks was to you."

Silence, as none of the men knew how to cope with her tactical use of the word "doll."

"I'm not a big T'Rain expert," she continued. "Is Thorakks like a major character in the world?"

"Thorakks is *my* character," Seamus said.

"Wow, how do you rate having a doll made of your personal character?"

"It's called an action figure," he said, "and it's nothing special. If you've got a character in T'Rain, all you have to do is fill out a web form and send them fifty bucks and they'll make you one of these on a 3D printer and ship it to you. Discount for active-duty military."

"Are you active-duty military?"

"No, but we have ways of finagling the discounts."

"Are these your own personal laptops?" Olivia asked.

"Why do you want to know?" asked Seamus, wary that she was about to accuse him of misusing government property.

"Never mind," she said. "I was only wondering if there might be a spare computer around here that I might use."

"For, like, secure email?"

"No. For playing T'Rain."

"I thought you said you didn't play."

"I don't," she admitted, "but this needs to change."

"*Needs!?*"

"Professional reasons," she said.

For she now knew that the missing person called Zula was connected to Corporation 9592—was, in fact, the cofounder's niece—and that her abduction from Seattle to Shanghai had been somehow related to the activities of the nest of hackers who had lived in the apartment below Jones's. While she did not feel the need to spend a huge amount of time on T'Rain, and certainly didn't want to go to the point of having her own personal doll created on a 3D printer, she needed to know a little more about the game.

Twelve hours later, she knew more than she needed to—and yet she still wanted to know more. What was the secret hiding place of the Black Pearls of the Q'rith? What combination of spells and herbs was needed to rouse the Princess Elicasse from her age-long slumber beneath the Golden Bower of Nar'thorion? Where could she get some Qaldaqian Gray Ore to forge new Namasq steel arrowheads to shoot with her Composite Bow of Aratar? And were those the right kind of ranged weapons, anyway, to use against the Torlok that was barring her passage across the Bridge of Enbara? She could have obtained answers to all these questions from Seamus and his band of lost boys, but she knew that any answers provided would only lead to more questions, and she had already pestered them far too many times. They seemed terribly busy, anyway, planning something.

Something violent.

Something in the real world. Not far away.

She collected these impressions during brief moments of lucidity when she pulled herself out of the game to ask a question, fetch more junk food, or go to the W.C. At these times the men would all clam up and pointedly look the other way until she had once again ensconced herself in front of the game.

It was something like three in the morning. She went back to her trailer, tossed and turned until dawn, seeing images of T'Rain whenever she closed her eyes, then finally went to sleep and was awakened in midafternoon by Seamus pounding on her door.

He had even more things strapped to him than usual: a Camel-Bak; extra magazines for his Sig; hard-shell knee pads.

He invited himself in and squatted down, leaning back against the wall. Stretching his quads.

"People are going to die tonight because of that theory you and your colleagues spun up in London," he said.

"The theory that Jones flew the jet down here," she said.

"Yeah. That theory. So before people die for it—keeping in mind one of them might be me—I just thought I would pay a little social call, shoot the breeze, and eventually, you know, get around to asking you whether you still believe in that theory. But it turns out that when I am getting ready to go on one of these operations, I'm not much in the mood for small talk."

Olivia nodded. "He took off southbound. If he had turned it into a martyrdom operation—crashed it into something—we'd know. If it had landed somewhere and been noticed, we'd know. So he didn't do either of those things. He flew it somewhere he could land it and hide it without being noticed. This place is easily reachable from Xiamen, he knows it well, has friends and connections here . . ."

"You mentioned all those things before," Seamus said.

Olivia was silent.

"All I'm saying: here I am. Seamus. Alive and well. Not your best friend, but someone you know a little. As far as I can tell, you don't hate me. You tolerate my presence. Maybe even like me a tiny little bit. I'm about to leave. Let's say I come back in a body bag tomorrow morning. Let's say that happens. You get on a plane and fly back to London. As you are sitting on that long, long airplane flight, at some point when you're over India or Arabia or fucking Crete or something, are you going to go, like"—he smacked himself in the face and adopted a look of chagrin, shook his head, rolled his eyes—"'Shit, you know, that theory actually sucked.' Is that going to happen?"

"No," Olivia said. "It's the best theory we have."

"We being the guys sitting around the table in London?"

"Yes."

"How about *you*, Olivia? Is it the best theory *you* have?"

"Does it matter?" That answer had sprung to her lips surprisingly quickly.

His face froze for a few seconds, and then he smiled without showing his teeth. "No," he said, "of course not."

Then he pushed himself away from the wall, rose to his feet, spun on the balls of his black-on-black running shoes, and walked out.

She sat there without moving for twenty minutes, until she heard the helicopters taking off.

Then she went to the empty dining area and opened up Seamus's laptop—he had given her a guest account—and played T'Rain for the rest of the afternoon, through into the evening, and then all night. Every so often she would stop and try to adjudge whether she was tired enough to go to sleep. But she knew perfectly well that no such thing would happen until Seamus and his men had come back.

They were back at about nine in the morning. Olivia had passed out on the sofa, gotten perhaps three hours' sleep in spite of herself. All six of them came in together, filthy and sweaty and in some cases bloody; but none of them was seriously injured. She got the sense that they had been speaking very loudly and uninhibitedly, but the volume dropped to almost zero as soon as her sleepy head popped up from behind the back of the sofa. She caught Seamus's eye. He was staring at her fixedly, peeling things off himself, dropping them on the floor.

The other men drifted out and tromped off to their barracks. She couldn't avoid the impression that they had wanted to throw down their stuff and relax here and that her presence in the room had ruined it.

Seamus sidestepped around. He was carrying a gray plastic laptop under one arm. Not his usual machine. He set it on the coffee table, then sat down in a chair arranged at ninety degrees to the couch. He leaned forward with his elbows on his knees and carefully placed the tips of his fingers together and flexed his hands against each other, as if checking to see whether all the little joints in the fingers still worked. Some of his knuckles had been bleeding.

He looked Olivia straight in the eye and said, in a mild but direct tone of voice, "Do you want to fuck?"

She must have looked a little surprised.

"Sorry to be so blunt," he went on, "but surviving one of these things always makes me incredibly horny. This, and going to funerals. Those are the triggers for me. So I just thought I would ask.

I feel like I could rip off a great one just now. Tip-top. So I'm just checking. Just on the off chance you might be in the mood for something, you know, totally hot and meaningless."

Olivia could well imagine it: the mischievous grin spreading across her lips, scampering back to the guest cabin, crowding into the shower, and getting banged senseless by this hormonally enraged man-child.

"Um, I sort of am actually," Olivia said earnestly, "but I think it's a temptation I can resist for now." Feeling that this required more explanation, she added, "I was specifically told not to, actually."

He looked impressed. "Really!"

"Yeah."

"Someone actually bothered to issue you an order forbidding coitus with me."

"Yeah. More I think directed at me and my reputation than yours."

He looked crestfallen.

"But I'm sure yours is amazing! Your reputation, that is."

He nodded.

"Did it go all right then?" she asked.

"Yeah! Why do you ask?"

"Just coz you've got blood all over you."

"Do you know what I do for a living?"

She no longer felt like bantering back.

Seamus leaned back, reached into a cargo pocket, pulled out a little black case, unsnapped it to reveal a set of tiny screwdrivers. He flipped the laptop upside down, selected a tool, began to undo little screws. "The objective was to enter one of their encampments and grab at least one subject for interrogation. And to get any other evidence that might be useful along the way. Like this." He patted the laptop. "Not really a good helicopter-gunship-assault kind of mission. We had to land some distance away and go in on foot and surprise them."

" 'Surprise' being, I guess, quite a mild term for how you approached these blokes."

"It's an *incomplete* term. They were *definitely* surprised." Seamus had removed all the little screws he could find. He paused, looking at the laptop, still all together in one piece. "Jones has been known to booby-trap these things and then leave them lying around," he said. "But this one was not left lying around. It was being used when we entered the hut." He popped the back off. Olivia couldn't help flinching. But there were no lumps of plastique inside. Seamus chose another screwdriver and began to remove the screws that held its little hard drive into place. "I'll upload this to Langley while I'm taking my shower."

"What about the other part of the mission?"

"Grabbing a subject?"

"Yeah."

"Done."

"Where is he?"

"In the hands of our Filipino colleagues."

SEAMUS DOCKED THE little hard drive into a gadget that inhaled all its contents without altering them and squirted them down a high-bandwidth connection to the United States for, she guessed, decryption and analysis. Then he went back to his quarters and took a shower. Olivia took one of her own, not because she was dirty but because she had that cottony, icky feeling that came from lying on a sofa for a whole day playing a stupid game. She wanted to get some exercise but didn't see how it was possible. In the courtyard of their little compound, Seamus's team had set up some kind of body-weight exercise system involving ropes, and she'd seen them out there going at it yesterday. But that was exercise with a purpose—*This might give me a tiny edge on the next mission*—whereas she wanted to do something wholesome like go for a walk.

There was a couple of hours' hiatus. Food was eaten, email checked. Then Seamus spun his laptop around. It was playing a video window: a reasonably high-definition feed from a small, windowless, brightly lit room. A man, stripped to the waist, was sitting in a wooden chair, hands behind him as if cuffed. His features were Malay/Filipino, but he had been growing a scruffy beard. One eye was closed off by a huge shiner, and at the places where bony ridges had once sat close beneath the skin, butterfly bandages were straining to hold lacerations closed. The swelling extended down toward his chin, and she wondered whether his jaw might have been broken. He was mumbling in some language that Olivia didn't recognize.

One of Seamus's men, whom she had previously pegged as Hispanic, scooted closer, plugged in a pair of large, expensive-looking headphones, and leaned forward to listen. After a few moments, he began to rattle off sentence fragments in English: "It's like I said before . . . honest to God . . . I'll tell you anything you want to hear, you know this now . . . but you want the truth, don't you? The truth is we didn't see him. Didn't hear anything until a few days ago. Then we got word . . . send out emails, you know. They could be anything, just random."

Seamus explained, "According to the analysts at Langley, that laptop was used to send out a bunch of junk emails starting a few days ago."

"Like spam?" someone asked.

"They were just cutting and pasting random scraps of text from instruction manuals, encrypting it, sending it out. Trying to create the illusion of traffic. False chatter." Seamus swiveled his eyes to look at Olivia. Then he made a little jerk of his head toward the door. She got up, headed for the exit, and he followed in her wake, all the way to her quarters.

"This is not about fucking, I assume?" she asked.

He rolled his eyes. "No, I'm in a completely different state of mind now; I regret what I said earlier."

"Very well," she said levelly.

"Though that is a cute haircut."

This was certainly an attempt to bait her, and so she remained silent and, she hoped, inscrutable.

"What I really wanted to tell you was that . . . you've got what you came here for," Seamus said.

"What did I come here for, do you imagine?"

"Evidence to support the theory you *really* believe."

"Which is?"

"You're asking me?"

"I thought I would get your opinion," Olivia said, "before showing my hand."

He stuck his tongue in his cheek and thought about it.

"It's not poker," she said. "There's no disadvantage in your telling me what you think. We're both trying to get the same rat bastard."

"If Jones had something as awesome as a bizjet," Seamus said, "would he use it to scurry like a mouse back into the nearest hole? I think not."

"He'd do something really cool, like fly it into a building," Olivia said, nodding.

Seamus held up one admonishing finger. "Oh, no," he said, "because that would involve dying, wouldn't it?"

"I suppose very likely, yes."

"And he doesn't want to die."

"For a man who doesn't want to die, he puts himself in some quite dodgy situations," she pointed out.

"Oh, I think he's conflicted," Seamus said. "Someday he's going to be a martyr. *Someday*. This is what he keeps telling himself. Then he looks around himself, at the wack jobs and goat fuckers he has to work with, and he sees how much more he has to offer the movement by staying alive. Putting his expertise to work, his languages, his ability to blend in. And so the day of martyrdom keeps getting postponed."

"Convenient for him, that."

Seamus grinned and shrugged. "I actually don't know whether the man is a coward, or really trying to use his skills in the most productive way by staying alive. I'd love to ask him that someday. Before sticking a knife into his belly."

"So. He didn't come here. He didn't crash it into a building. He didn't get caught. Where'd he go?"

"All of his instincts," Seamus said, "would move him in the direction of the United States."

THEY SPENT THE rest of the day writing reports to their respective higher-ups. The next morning, Seamus and Olivia flew back to Manila. Seamus had business there at the U.S. embassy, and Olivia needed to make arrangements to fly home. The route back to Olivia's hotel was almost a perfect reversal of the trip out, complete with the sweaty hike across the city to get around traffic. They reached the hotel at 10:12 A.M. and the hotel bar at 10:13, and after dutifully gulping down glasses of water for technical rehydration purposes, they moved on to alcohol.

"You can't tell me that bizjet doesn't have enough fuel to reach the States," Seamus said.

She twiddled her hand in the air. "Northern tier," she said.

"Bang! Mall of America," Seamus proposed, reenacting the dive and crash with the hand that wasn't holding a drink.

"Northwest corner much more likely," she said. "Seattle, of course."

"Bye-bye, Space Needle."

"But the Space Needle's still there, last time I checked. So if your theory is right—"

"My theory and yours, lady."

"All right, all right. If *our* theory is right, he somehow got in without being picked up on radar and landed out in the middle of nowhere."

"Do your analysts have any ideas as to how he could avoid radar?"

"Come in very low, of course," Olivia said, "which burns fuel at an insane rate. Or else fly in formation with a passenger aircraft. Right under its belly."

He held his hands up. "Why is that so difficult? Why is it so hard to get people to believe that Jones could do something like that?"

"Occam's razor," she said. "The Mindanao theory had fewer moving parts. So it has to be done away with before anything else can even be discussed."

THEY SAID GOOD-BYE with chaste cheek pecks and went their separate ways: Seamus out into traffic, Olivia up to her room where she began trying to change her flight plan. She didn't want to fly back to London. She wanted to go to the northwestern United States.

She wasted a day in that hotel room. First she had to wait a few hours for people to wake up in London. Then she had to push the idea that her time would be better spent following the Jones-went-to-North-America hypothesis. No one that she talked to was overtly hostile to the idea, and yet she could not seem to make any progress. Procedures ought to be followed. It wouldn't do for her to suddenly touch down on U.S. soil and begin doing intelligence work; contact really ought to be made with counterparts in the American counterintelligence establishment. But no one was awake in America yet, so this would have to wait for another few hours. She fired off spates of emails, went down to the fitness center, got exercise, came back, did more emailing, made phone calls. Played T'Rain. Surfed the Internet for more about Zula and the Forthrast clan. Checked out the heartrending Facebook page that they had set up in an effort to find her. Did more emails.

At last, completely blocked on all fronts, she used her own money to purchase a ticket to Vancouver. She had friends and connections there, it was a Commonwealth country, not too many feathers would be ruffled by her parachuting into the place, and from there she could easily get down to Seattle if occasion warranted. It was certainly better than hanging around in Manila, which, she had come to believe, was about as far as she could get from Abdallah Jones without leaving the planet.

Having grown wise in the ways of Manila traffic, she allocated four hours for the three-mile taxi ride to the airport and found herself airborne at nine o'clock the following morning. A vast number of hours later, the plane landed in Vancouver, at eleven A.M. on what she was informed was Tuesday (they had crossed the International Date Line, occasioning some confusion as to this).

Her plan had been to crash and burn at a hotel in Vancouver, but she found herself strangely pert and eager upon landing. Partly it was a consequence of having spent a hell of a lot of money on the plane ticket. All the economy-class seats had been taken, so she had flown business class and actually managed to get some sleep. Awakening from a long nap somewhere over the Pacific, she found that a new idea and a resolve had materialized in her head: she would go talk to Richard Forthrast. She had been reading all about him and had more or less memorized his Wikipedia entry. He seemed like an interesting and complicated man. He must be thinking about his missing niece quite a bit, and obviously he would have insights about REAMDE and T'Rain that would never occur to Olivia.

Waiting in line at Immigration, she checked her messages and received word that contact had indeed been made with American counterintelligence and that they were receptive to the idea of her paying a call on them and that she should go ahead and book a ticket to Seattle. The message was time-stamped only an hour ago, meaning that if she had waited in Manila for official go-ahead she would only now be calling the airlines there. So she had saved herself a full day by taking action. Of course, getting reimbursed for the ticket might not be so easy.

Once she had passed through formalities, she rented a car and began driving south. She'd been reluctant to share with her new American counterparts her idea of talking to Richard Forthrast; like anyone else who works in an organization and who has just come up with a pet idea, she considered it her property and didn't want to share it out. And she was afraid that it would get slapped down or, worse yet, co-opted. But crossing the border a day ahead of schedule and making solo contact with an American citizen probably was not how to get the relationship off on the right foot, and in any case, she had to keep in mind that talking to Forthrast was just a sideshow to the main project, which was looking for Jones in North America. So she pulled over to the side of the road and made some calls.

At about five in the afternoon, she found herself in a secure office suite in a federal office building in downtown Seattle, making friends with her officially approved contact, an FBI agent named Marcella Houston, who was all about tracking down Jones but who said nothing about Richard Forthrast. Olivia spent a couple of hours with her before Marcella went home for the evening with the promise that they would get cracking on the Jones hunt first thing in the morning.

After checking in to a downtown hotel, Olivia found a secure email waiting for her from London, passing on the information that Richard Forthrast and his brother John had, just a few hours ago, obtained single-entry visas to China, and moreover that a flight plan had been filed that would take them from Boeing Field to Xiamen, departing rather soon.

It was, she realized, all a matter of bureaucratic lag time. By jumping on the plane to Vancouver and then bombing down to Seattle, she had appeared in the FBI's offices a full day ahead of when they had been expecting her and, moreover, just at the close of normal business hours. Marcella had stayed late to give her a polite welcome and to promise that something would happen tomorrow.

All of Marcella's attention had been focused on the Jones hunt. Olivia's proposal to contact Richard Forthrast—supposing it had been noticed at all—had been forwarded to some other person's inbox and probably hadn't even been read yet. Because if anyone of consequence had read it, they would have forbidden her to talk to Richard Forthrast, or they would have insisted on sending one of their own with her.

But as it happened, Richard Forthrast's jet was idling on the tarmac at Boeing Field; and there was nothing preventing her from going down there to talk to him.

WHEN ZULA'S MOBILE prison cell was complete and the door slammed shut on her, time stopped moving for several days. This gave her plenty of time to hate herself for having failed to escape when she'd had a chance.

Sort of a chance, anyway. During the time they'd been parked in the Walmart, before the plywood had been bought and the cell constructed, she could theoretically have gone into the shower stall and unlocked the end of the chain that was looped around the grab bar. She could then have made a dash for the side door and perhaps got it open long enough to scream for help and attract someone's attention. Or she might have gone back into the bedroom, kicked a window out, and jumped. Once she had been locked into the cell, she found it quite easy to convince herself that she ought to have done one of those two things, and that having failed to do so made her into some kind of idiot or coward.

But—as she had to keep reminding herself, just to stay sane—she'd had no idea that they were planning to turn the back of the vehicle into a prison cell. She'd assumed that the chain would be in place for much longer and that she could bide her time, waiting for a moment when everyone was asleep or distracted. Making an impulsive run for it might have blown her one and only chance.

On the day following the Walmart stopover, she dimly heard additional sawing and banging noises on the other side of her cell door.

Leading forward was a narrow corridor perhaps eight feet in length, with doors along its side walls giving access to the toilet and the shower. These were separate rooms, not much larger than phone booths. Of the two, the toilet was farther aft. The next time they opened her cell door, Zula discovered that Jones and Sharjeel had constructed a new barrier across the corridor, situated forward of the toilet and aft of the shower stall. It was a sort of gate, consisting of a hinged frame of two-by-fours with expanded steel mesh nailed across it. Now Zula could obtain direct access to the toilet whenever she wanted. The gate prevented her going any farther forward. This relieved the jihadists of the requirement—which they pretended to find most burdensome—of opening the door to let Zula come out and use the toilet from time to time. By the same token, it prevented them from getting into the toilet themselves, unless they undid the padlock on the steel mesh door and entered into Zula's end of the vehicle. This happened only rarely, though, since they had gotten into the habit of using the shower stall as a urinal, and flushing it by running the shower for a few moments. So they only needed to come in through the mesh door for number 2.

This innovation made for a large improvement in Zula's quality of life, since it enabled her to sit in the middle of the bed and look down the entire length of the RV and out its windshield as they drove endlessly around British Columbia. The field of view was not large; it was comparable to looking through a phone screen held out at arm's length. But it was preferable to staring at plywood.

She could not see any faults in Jones's strategy. These men dared not park the RV in a campground or a Walmart for any length of time. RV encampments were, by definition, transient. But they had many of the social dynamics of a small town. Essentially all the residents would be white middle-class retirees. Jones's crew of Pashtuns and Yemenis would draw attention. But an RV in movement on a highway enjoyed a level of isolation from the rest of the world that was nearly perfect. All its systems—electrical, plumbing, propulsion, heating—were self-contained and would continue working indefinitely as long as fuel and water were pumped into its tanks and sewage removed. They stopped occasionally to take on or discharge fluids, and though Zula couldn't see much, she assumed that Jones was careful to select fueling stations out in the middle of nowhere and to pay at the pump, obviating the need to go inside and interact with any humans. He seemed well supplied with credit cards. Some of these had presumably been stolen from the dead RV owners, others perhaps contributed by the trio from Vancouver.

As long as the RV kept running, B.C. was the best place to hide in the whole world. They often drove for many hours without seeing another vehicle. The road was an endless stripe of light gray pavement curving and weaving and undulating across a countryside that was all mountains. Occasionally, for an hour or two, they would parallel railroad tracks, lightly rust filmed. Sometimes they'd run along rivers caroming through zigzag channels of brown-gray rock topped with acid-green moss that looked knee-deep. Rivers and railways came and went, but the road went on eternally. Every so often she would glimpse a gas station, a cabin, a faded Canadian flag snapping in a turbulent cold breeze, ravens flying overhead, a house sitting inexplicably at a wide spot in the road with senseless suburban touches grafted onto it. Intersections with other roads were so remarkable that they were announced beforehand with all the pomp of bicentennials. Sometimes it was rain forest; other times they drove up valleys with great expanses of rocky, bare red soil studded with sagebrush and supporting sparse growths of scrub pines and open meadows of ranch land that might have been in the approaches to the Grand Canyon. Valleys full of Indians, driving old pickup trucks, gave way to valleys full of cowboys, trotting around on horses with their herding dogs. Newborn calves suckling from their mothers' udders. Huge geometric reshapings of mountainsides that she guessed must be mining projects. Canyons lined with marble the colors of honey and blood. Spindly steel-wheeled irrigation systems poised at the edge of barren cleared fields, like sprinters at the starting line, waiting for the season to begin. Mountains marching in queues from directly overhead to the horizon, one after another, as if to say, *We have more where these came from.* Deciduous trees budding out on the mountains' lower slopes, engulfing the lone dark spikes of conifers in a foaming, cresting wave of light green. Above that, the mountains' upper slopes jumping asymptotically into curling cornices of fluffy white clouds, as opaque as cotton balls. Sometimes the clouds parted, giving glimpses of places higher up, the trees dusted as if the fog were condensing and freezing on them, just letting her know that they were only scurrying around on an insignificant low tier, and that above them were stacked many additional layers of greater complexity and structure and drama, both sunlit and weather lashed.

Other people entered the picture. She guessed that Jones had sent out some kind of an email blast as soon as he'd been able, using a trusted, encrypted electronic grapevine. The first to respond had been Sharjeel, Aziz, and Zakir, only a few hours' drive away in Vancouver. But a couple of days later she began to hear other voices and to see other faces going in and out of the shower stall. Jones's email must have reached other jihadist sleeper cells in eastern Canada, and they must have jumped into cars and started driving west to connect up with the caravan. Or, assuming that they had solid cover stories and all the right documentation, they might have been coming up from cities in the United States. The ethnic diversity of the crew was increasing all the time, and so all business was conducted in either English or Arabic. The latter was preferred, but the former was becoming more commonly used as the RV filled up with people who had been living for years in North America. Sometimes, when they were verging on certain topics, they would send someone back to slam the cell door in Zula's face, and it would then remain closed until someone felt like opening it again.

A certain amount of the discussion had to do with mundane topics such as the management of people, vehicles, food, and money. Only so many could fit comfortably in the RV. Excess bodies had to be placed in cars. Occasionally one of these would be visible through the windshield; Zula had the vague idea that there were at least three of them. Sometimes they drove in procession with the RV, but more often they would strike out on some other road for a while and meet up with the RV a few hours later at a campground or a Walmart. And it appeared that one car was acting as a shuttle between the RV and a safe house in Vancouver; Aziz had turned his apartment into a crash pad where tired, grubby jihadists could go and do their laundry and sort themselves out before rotating back to caravan duty.

Each new member of the crew, it seemed, had to spend a certain amount of time standing at the mesh door, staring at Zula, appraising her. The first few times she just stared right back, but after a while she learned to ignore them.

Jones had acquired a printer during one of the Walmart for-

ays and had been printing up images from Google Maps and taping them together into great irregular green tapestries. Discarded
empty ink cartridges littered the floor. Housekeeping was not the
jihadists' strong point.

There came a time when Jones shooed most of his comrades
off into other vehicles and invited Zula forward to the RV's dining area, which had become, quite literally, a war room. Centered
on the table was one of those stuck-together maps. The image was
festooned with little colored Google stickpins. Taped to windows
and walls all around were photographs, also generated by that hardworking printer.

They were Zula's photographs. Many of them featured Peter or
Uncle Richard. She had taken them during the visit to the Schloss
two weeks ago.

"I found your Flickr page," Jones explained. "Evidently you
downloaded the app?"

"Huh?" Zula was too disoriented by the images to muster anything more coherent than that.

"The Flickr app," Jones said patiently. "It automatically syncs
the photo library on your phone with your Flickr page."

"Yeah," Zula said, "I did have that app." Past tense, since she
thought her phone was somewhere in China, buried in rubble or
maybe in a police lab.

"Well, anyway, your story checks out," Jones said, as if she were
to be commended for this.

"Why wouldn't it check out?"

Jones chuckled. "No particular reason. All I mean is, I can go
right to your Flickr page and see photos that went up there two
weeks ago when you and Peter were visiting Dodge at Schloss
Hundschüttler." He rolled his eyes and used air quotes at the name.

"How'd you know his nickname was Dodge?"

"It's mentioned in his Wikipedia entry."

This was the first time they had discussed Richard—or *any* non-
immediate topic, for that matter—since the very brief conversation
immediately after the jet crash, when Jones had been about to put a
bullet in her, and she'd revealed that she had an uncle who, (a) was
very rich, and (b) knew how to smuggle things across the Canada/
U.S. border. She had expected further interrogation. But Jones was

a thorough man, a self-starter, a strategizer. Zula had slowly come to understand that every action he had taken in the days since had been centered around Uncle Richard and the possibility of using him to sneak across the border. The war room he'd constructed in the RV had nothing to do—*yet*—with a Vegas casino massacre. That could all be seen to after they'd crossed the border. This here was all to do with Richard, and Schloss Hundschüttler was its epicenter.

Her brain was slowly making sense of the virtual stickpins printed on the map. Each one of them corresponded to one of the photos that Jones had printed up from her Flickr page. After several days in the cell, it was taking her a little while to get back into the Internet-based mind-set in which she had lived most of her post-Eritrean life. But she remembered she had once had a phone and that it had a GPS receiver built into it as well as a camera, and those two systems could talk to each other; if you gave permission—and she was pretty sure she had—the device would append a latitude and a longitude to each photograph, so that you could later plot them out on a map and see where each picture had been taken. During the visit to the Schloss, she and Peter and Richard had spent a couple of afternoons wandering around the vicinity on ATVs and snowshoes. The pins printed on the map were breadcrumb trails marking out the paths they had taken, a crumb dropped every time Zula had tapped the shutter button on the screen of her phone.

Her face was flushing hot, as if Jones had caught her out in something acutely embarrassing.

And yet, at the same time, it was strangely pleasurable to be reminded that she had once had a life that had included such luxuries as a boyfriend and a phone.

"Most of this is self-explanatory, if one is willing to put a bit of thought into it," Jones remarked. "As an example, in this snapshot of Peter donning his snowshoes, there's a mountain peak in the background, wooded on its lower slopes, but with a barren face—I'm guessing scree beneath the snow. According to the time-stamp, it was taken right around noon—indeed, I can see the remains of your lunch on the seat of the ATV. The shadows should therefore be pointing north. And strangely enough, when we look at the Google satellite image—which was taken during the summer, evidently—we see a peak here, with a scree-covered face turned toward the pin on the map, which is more or less to its south. So it all fits together. Schloss Hundschüttler's website could hardly be more descriptive; I have already taken the virtual tour of the property and had a virtual pint in the virtual tavern. Virtual pints being the only kind that I, as a devout Muslim, am allowed to have . . ." Jones had become somewhat rambling, perhaps because Zula was being a little slow to snap out of this combination of cell-induced ennui and the shock of seeing familiar places and faces so displayed. He slid a page across the table at her, then bracketed it between two more. Each contained an image from her phone. "But there are still certain mysteries that require explanation. What the bloody hell is this?" he asked. "I know *where* it is." He tapped a location on the map, a few miles south of the Schloss, sprouting a cluster of stickpins. "But what the hell? It's not mentioned on the Schloss's site, and even WikiTravel is silent on the matter."

"It was an abandoned mine." Zula paused, a little taken aback by the unfamiliar sound of her own voice. Then she corrected herself: "It *is* an abandoned mine." She had grown accustomed to thinking of her life and everything she'd ever experienced as dwelling solely in the past.

"What were they mining? Trees?"

She shook her head. "Lead or something; I don't know."

"I'm serious," he said. "What sort of mine requires a million board feet of timber?" For the overwhelming impression given by the photographs was of planks and beams, thousands of them, silver with age, splayed and flattened in some sort of slow-motion disaster that ran all the way down the side of a small mountain. As if the world's biggest timber flume, a waterfall of rough-sawn planks coursing down the slope, had suddenly been deprived of water and had frozen and shriveled in place.

"Mines are supposed to be *below* ground, I'd thought," Jones continued.

"Aren't you a graduate of the Colorado School of Mines?" Zula asked.

Jones, for once, looked a bit sheepish. "They should probably change the name. It's not *just* about that. I only went there to learn how to blow things up. I don't know squat about mines really."

"All of this wood was some kind of structure that they built aboveground, obviously. For what purpose I don't know. But it runs up and down the slope for quite a distance. It's got to be some kind of mineral separation technique that uses gravity. Maybe they sluiced water down through it, or something. In some places, it's just these big chutes." Zula pointed to the wreckage of one such in the background of a photograph of Uncle Richard. Then she shuffled papers around until she found a photo of something that looked like a very old house pushed askew by a shock wave. "Other places you'll see a platform with a shack, or even something the size of this, built on it. But they are mostly just flattened, as you can see."

"Well, whatever this thing is, it's eight point four kilometers from the Schloss, and almost exactly the same elevation," Jones said.

"Because of the railway," Zula said.

He looked interested. "What railway?"

She shook her head. "It doesn't exist anymore. But there used to be a narrow-gauge railway that ran from Elphinstone south into this valley. Closest to town was the Schloss, which was the baron's residence and the headquarters of the whole empire. Farther back up the valley were the mines he made his money from . . ."

"And this is one of those," Jones said, flicking his eyes down at the photos they'd been looking at. "But why did you say *because* of the railway?"

"The elevation," Zula said. "You noticed that there's very little difference in altitude. That's because—"

"Trains aren't very good at going up and down hills," Jones completed the sentence for her, nodding.

"Yeah. Neither are bicyclists and cross-country skiers. So—"

"Ah, yes, now I understand. The trail up the valley, so proudly described on the Schloss's website."

Zula nodded. "That trail is just the right-of-way of the old narrow-gauge mining railway, paved over."

"Yes." Jones considered it for a bit, paying more attention to the convolutions of the terrain shown on the map. "How does one connect with that trail, I wonder?"

Zula propped herself up on her elbows, leaned over the table, tried to focus on the map for a while. Then she shook her head. "This is too much information," she said. "It's not that hard." She flipped one of the photographs over to expose its blank back. Then she swiped the fat carpenter's pencil that Jones had picked up at Walmart. She slashed a horizontal line across the page. "The border," she said. Then a vertical line crossing the border at right angles. "The Selkirks." Another, parallel to it, farther east. "The Purcells. Between them, Kootenay Lake." She drew a long north-south oval, north of the border. "Highway 3 tries to run parallel to the border, but it has to zig and zag because of obstructions." She drew a wandering line across the Selkirks and the Purcells. In some places it nearly grazed the border, in others it veered considerably to the north. At one such location, south of the big lake, she penciled in a fat X, bestriding the highway. "Elphinstone," she said. "Snowboarders and sushi bars." Because of the highway's northward bulge, a considerable bight of land was here trapped between it and the U.S. border. Into the middle of it she slashed a line that first headed southwest out of town but then curved around until it was directed southeast: a big C with its northern end anchored at Elphinstone and its southern end trailing off as it approached the United States. Then she sketched in a series of cross-hatches across this arc, cartographic shorthand marking it as a railway line.

Finally, somewhere down south of the border, below the hook-shaped railway, she made another X and told him that it was Bourne's Ford, Idaho. "My uncle is quite the expert on the history of this railway," she said. "He could explain it better."

"I'll ask him when I see him," Jones said.

This hit her like a baseball bat to the bridge of the nose. It took her a few moments to get going again. "Bourne's Ford is in a river valley," she said.

"Most fords are," Jones pointed out dryly.

"Right. Anyway, it's well served by rail and river transport. So it was thought for a while that the way to make the baron's mine profitable was to run the line over the border and connect with other mining railways that had been run up into the mountains on the U.S. side." She sketched in a few lines radiating up toward Canada from Bourne's Ford. "Abandon," she muttered.

"Abandoned mines?"

"Abandon Mountain," she said. "It's up here somewhere." She made a vague circle between Bourne's Ford and the border.

"Nice name."

"They had a talent for these things. Anyway, so there was this competition as to whether all the ore was going to end up going south to Bourne's Ford and Sandpoint, which would have turned this whole region into a dependency of the United States, or whether they were going to tie it into the Canadian transport network instead. It led to sort of a railway-building contest. The baron was smart enough to play both sides against each other. Americans were trying to punch a line up from the south, and he was at least pretending to run his narrow-gauge line down to the border to connect up with it." She tapped the lower arc of the C. Then she moved the pencil up and scratched at its northern end. "At the same time the Canadians were desperately trying to build the last set of tunnels needed to connect Elphinstone with the rest of the country. The Canadians won. So the baron connected his line at the northern end, and Elphinstone developed into a prosperous town. The southern extension of the line—which was probably just a feint anyway, to make the Canadians dig those tunnels faster—was abandoned."

"But it's still there," Jones said.

"It was *surveyed* all the way to the border," Zula said. "They only graded it to within a few miles. At that point you run into the need for trestles and tunnels, and it starts getting really expensive to actually *build* it. So the bike-slash-ski trail goes up basically to the face of a cliff, five miles short of the border, and stops."

"But there's a way through."

"Evidently," Zula said. "When my uncle was carrying the bearskin south—"

"Bearskin?"

"Another story. Not in the Wikipedia entry. I'll tell you some other time. The point is that he needed to walk into the U.S. but didn't know how. He followed the old narrow-gauge railway line up out of Elphinstone, walking on the railroad ties."

"A nice gentle climb."

"Yes, for the reason mentioned. He got to the end. And then he found some way around, or through, the wall of rock that was blocking his path, and covered the last miles south across the border, and picked his way south—"

She sketched a faint, wavy, speculative line down through the circle she'd drawn earlier for Abandon Mountain, and thence down into Bourne's Ford.

"He didn't exactly pioneer it." She glanced up to see Jones staring at her intently. "He was following traces left forty, fifty years earlier by whiskey smugglers during Prohibition."

Prohibition Crick. She wondered if *that* would show up on Google Maps.

"And later by marijuana smugglers."

"That's the rumor, certainly."

Jones was impatient with that. "Rumor or not, he made a lot of trips along this route." He leaned forward and traced it with his finger. "He passed by the ruin of the baron's house many times, and that was how he conceived the idea to buy the property and fix it up into a legitimate business."

"That much of the Wikipedia entry is correct as far as I know," she allowed.

"YOU MEAN, YOU were there in China?" Richard asked the woman.

"I mean, I was there when the apartment building blew up."

Richard just stared at her.

"The one with your niece in the cellar."

"Yeah," he said. "I didn't imagine you were talking about some *other* blown-up apartment in China."

"Sorry."

He looked at her for a while. "You're not going to tell me who you are, are you?"

"No, I'm afraid not. But you can call me . . . oh, *Laura*, if it helps to have a name."

"What is your interest in all this, Laura? What do you have to gain from talking me out of going to Xiamen?"

"Laura" got a wry look on her face. Trying to work out what she could say and what she couldn't.

"Is this to do with the Russians?" he asked. "Are you somehow connected with that investigation?"

"Not in the way you mean," she said. "But just a few days ago I was with one of them. The leader."

"Ivanov, or Sokolov?" Richard asked. And was immediately gratified to see frank shock spread across Laura's face.

"*Very* good," she said. "I had the feeling that unexpected things might happen if I talked to you."

Richard knew the two Russian names because Zula had mentioned them in her note. But he could see that the woman Laura didn't know about that note. "So which of them were you with?" he asked.

"Sokolov," Laura said. And she must have seen some look of hope on Richard's face, because caution then fell down over her own visage like a shutter. "But I'm very sorry to tell you that this doesn't actually help, where finding Zula is concerned. Not directly, anyway."

"How can it not help? My understanding is that Ivanov abducted her and that Sokolov is his henchman."

"Ivanov's dead. Sokolov, if anything, was prepared to help Zula once Ivanov was out of the way. But because of the way it all went down . . . nothing happened right. Zula is no longer with the Russians."

"Who's she with?"

Laura clearly knew the answer but was uncomfortable blurting it out. "Is there another place we can chat?" she asked.

"Not until you talk me out of getting on that plane and flying to China."

"Zula hasn't been in China for something like ten days," Laura said.

"Where is she then?"

"It is my considered opinion," Laura said, "that she's quite nearby."

Day 17

Even after land finally hove into view on her port side, *Szélanya* glided along parallel to a dark coast for the better part of a day before the winds finally shifted round and enabled them to steer her in to shore. The coastline was fractally scalloped, consisting of shallow bays, miles wide, themselves indented with smaller indentations. The big bays were frequently demarcated by headlands or little isles that were connected to the mainland at low tide. Having cleared one of these, the crew of *Szélanya*—unused to navigating in the presence of land, or, for that matter, any solid object—trimmed her sails and adjusted her rudder to make her cut into the next bay. This one eventually hooked around, perhaps ten kilometers ahead of them, into a little island that was linked to the mainland by mudflats, and once they got themselves pointed into it, there was no doubt that they would make landfall somewhere, and soon. They could not now escape from the bay even if they tried. For *Szélanya* had not been designed as a sailing vessel. It had become one almost two weeks ago, but only in the sense that any floating object, devoid of other propulsion, was wind driven. Actually making it into something that would sail had involved a lot of trial and error; mostly the latter.

She had been well supplied with plastic tarps, but they learned soon enough that these could not stand up to the stresses imposed on them by the wind. Fishnets were much stronger but would not hold air. And so they had improvised sails by combining the two: laying fishnets out over tarps and then sewing them together with zip ties, piano wire, needle and thread, tape. The resulting composites were strong enough to stand up to the wind, but their edges and corners—where the wind's power had to be transmitted into lines attached to the ship—ripped out whenever the breeze was appreciable. So there had been a lot more learning and improvising connected with those edges. The results were very far from being pretty, but nothing had torn out in a long time. It was only after they had solved that problem and hoisted their first little sail up on the yards and the rigging intended for manipulating fishnets that their Engineer had fetched a bottle of beer from the ship's stores and, to the consternation of his fellow officers, smashed it against the boat's prow while christening her *Szélanya,* the "Mother of the Wind." "If such a being exists," he explained, "she might be flattered, and decide not to completely fuck us."

The Straits of Taiwan ran northeast-southwest. As they had learned during the first few hours of their journey, a steady current flowed down it, bending all courses southward. And as they learned over the first few days, that current was strongly assisted by the prevailing winds, which blew vigorously and consistently out of the northeast, pushing them down out of the strait into the South China Sea.

The Skipper had never been on a boat, other than passenger ferries, until the day the adventure had begun. Nonetheless he had, during the first, critical forty-eight hours, acquired a command of basic sailing principles with a speed and fluency that had struck the Engineer as being almost supernatural. Much like a teenager who starts playing a new video game without bothering to open the manual, he tried things and observed the results, abandoning whatever didn't work and moving aggressively to exploit small successes. A profusion of ideas spewed forth from his mind. There was no such thing as a bad idea, apparently. But, perhaps more important, there was no such thing as a good idea either, until it had been tried and coolly evaluated. It was clear how he had become the leader of a sort of gang back home: not by asserting his leadership but by being so relentless in his production, evaluation, and exploitation of ideas that his friends had been left with no choice but to form up in his wake. Once he and his fellow officers had built sails that would not immediately fall apart, and once he had learned to make the ship sail after a fashion, the Skipper had begun perusing some of the charts that had been left beyond on the bridge by the vessel's previous owners. Making some rough calculations from the GPS, he had reckoned that the consequences of just letting the wind and current push them around would be landfall in Malaysia or Indonesia in a few weeks' time. Tacking upwind, or even sailing at right angles to the wind, would be out of the question with what primitive rigging they could improvise from found objects on the boat. But the Engineer, who had done a bit of sailing on Lake Balaton, believed that by setting a sail at the correct angle and angling the rudder just so, they could use the northeasterly winds to drive them south and east toward the island of Luzon, and thereby shorten their voyage by one or two weeks. So they bent their course for the Philippines, and though the first day's results were discouraging, they taught themselves over time to make *Szélanya* track south-southeast more often than not.

Then it was just waiting, and watching the sky, and wondering how it was all going to go down when the inevitable storm hit. It occurred to them—far too late, obviously—that they shouldn't have run the fuel tanks completely dry, since it would be nice to be able to operate the generator that supplied power to the bilge pump. A battery system seemed to be keeping the GPS unit and other small electronic devices alive, but none of the energy-hungry stuff was available to them; when they had to haul on a line, they would use a hand-cranked winch, or, if none was in the right location, jury-rig strange aboriginal-looking snarls of cables and levers to get the job done. The entire vessel began to look as if it were lashed together with metal tourniquets.

They rode out a storm that, in retrospect, had not been a storm at all, but just a rainy day with large waves. For some reason the Pilot was least susceptible to seasickness; she tended to spend more time than anyone else up on the bridge, where the pitching and rolling and yawing ought to have been worse. When the sea was flat, the Skipper and the Engineer would go up there and visit her, but they had come to think of it as the Pilot's own private wardroom and hesitated before entering. When the sea was rough, of course, they tended to be busy setting the sails and fixing things that had just broken. The Engineer's response to seasickness was to expose himself to the weather, lying out on the foredeck staring fixedly at the horizon and letting rain and wave crests wash over him. The Skipper's style was to retreat to his cabin where he could revel in his misery without being observed. Neither strategy would have been possible had it not been for the Pilot's ability to stand planted in the bridge for many hours without letup, managing the wheel and keeping an eye on the compass and the GPS.

The rainy-day-with-waves had at least served as a sort of rehearsal for an actual storm. The Engineer, who had a vague recollection of his tiny sailboat being swamped by a motorboat's wake on Lake Balaton, was fairly certain that the correct way to manage such situations was to keep the ship perpendicular to the wave crests. This made it less likely to get capsized when struck broadside. If they'd had engines, of course, they could have pointed *Szélanya* any direction they liked. As it was, the Engineer had reckoned, they'd have to put up a small sail, just enough to drag her downwind, not so large as to be ripped to shreds by thwarted winds. He had set to work crafting such an object out of tarps and nets and other junk that they hadn't already used for other purposes. The mere act of doing this had seemed to revive very old buried memories, fragments of nautical lore that he had picked up when younger, reading Hungarian translations of books like *Moby-Dick* and *Treasure Island*. He woke up with the vague conviction solidifying in his mind that it might be a good idea to throw something big and draggy off the stern and tow it through the water behind them; as the wind pushed *Szélanya* along, this drogue would torque her stern backward and keep her aimed in a consistent direction, which in general should be perpendicular to the wave crests. He sacrificed a small table to the purpose, enveloping it in a cradle of ropes and then shoving it off the transom at the end of a cable. The initial trial, conducted in calmer conditions, suggested that the thing wouldn't last very long in an actual storm and so he and the Skipper, who had come around to his way of thinking, devoted the better part of a day to reinforcing it.

They certainly had nothing else to do.

It had turned out that the calm day spent working on the

drogue and the storm sail had been calm precisely in a calm-before-the-storm sense, and so the following couple of days had been spent in a condition of extreme misery. The storm sail and drogue had been deployed as soon as it became obvious what was about to happen. The Skipper and Engineer had scurried around and closed all hatches where it seemed water might get in, and then they had gone up to join the Pilot. The vessel's steering gear consisted of a system of chains joining the wheel on the bridge to the actual rudder, and when things became rambunctious, it sometimes required more strength than the Pilot could muster—especially when she was exhausted from a long shift. At such times the Skipper would take over until such time as his arms wore out or the torque simply became too much, whereupon the Engineer would take the wheel and do battle, mano a mano, with the Mother of the Wind. There was no time during the storm when the Engineer was unable to supply the requisite amount of brute force. The problem lay in mixing it with intelligence. They could not see a thing. The bridge's windows were sheeted with rain and windblown spume. The one that faced forward, just above the wheel, had a motorized disk set into it that was supposed to spin at great speed and throw off water, but they could not get it to work. So during the part of the storm when they most badly needed to see the waves, so as to make informed decisions about steering, they were blind and had to judge the shape of the sea by feeling the tilting and heaving and plummeting of the deck plates beneath their feet. By that time, of course, it was too late to effect any useful response. The best that the Engineer could do was assume that the *next* wave would be moving in roughly the same direction as the *current* one, and steer accordingly. He had just about convinced himself that all his efforts were a complete waste of time, based on sheer fantasy, when he lost concentration for a few moments and they got broadsided by a crest that laid *Szélanya* on her side for several moments. All three of them, and all the loose stuff in the bridge, telescoped into what had been the port bulkhead and was now the floor, and lay there like crumpled refuse for several moments until the vessel lazily rolled upright again. She was not beautiful but she was, apparently, well ballasted.

It abated and they discovered, to no one's surprise, that the storm sail and the drogue were long gone.

It was six days after the storm that they sailed her into that bay on Luzon.

Giant water-skating insects had begun to clutter the flat, sparkling waters of the bay. Some of them made buzzing noises. Upon closer observation, these proved to be long slender boats with double outriggers. At first they tended to set parallel courses at a safe distance, but as it became evident that *Szélanya* was going to run aground, they began to draw in closer, apparently trying to make sense of what was happening. Each of them carried between one and half a dozen persons, lithe and brown and keenly interested, verging on celebratory.

CSONGOR HAD IMAGINED running her right up onto the beach, but she hissed to a stop in water a few meters deep, a stone's throw from shore. This made it possible for the small boats, which drew much less water, to surround them. Within a few minutes, *Szélanya* had been girdled by a complex of rafted-together boats, and at least two dozen people had invited themselves aboard. They were all so cheerful, so well behaved in a certain sense, that it took a few minutes for him to understand that they were here to sack *Szélanya*. The GPS had disappeared before he even understood what was happening. The bridge was rapidly denuded of electronics, the mast of antennas, the galley of pots and pans. Hacksaw blades were droning all around, ratchet wrenches chirping like crickets. He experienced a welter of incompatible feelings: outrage that his stuff was being stolen, then the sheepish recollection that he and Marlon and Yuxia had stolen the entire vessel to begin with, committed piracy, killed a man. Giddy relief that they had finally reached dry land, combined with rapidly growing alarm that they had found themselves in a strange foreign place among larcenous, albeit polite, natives. Stabbing, paranoid fear that said people might be stealing his own personal possessions at this very moment, followed by the realization that he had no possessions other than what he was wearing on his body and carrying in his pockets.

Except for the shoulder bag. Ivanov's leather man-purse.

He had been pacing about aimlessly on the deck but now turned on his heel and stormed to the cabin where he'd been sleeping, just in time to confront a young man who was just stepping over the threshold with the said bag slung nonchalantly over his shoulder. The youth twisted his body as if to dodge around Csongor, but as Csongor kept coming he blocked nearly the entire opening for a moment before suddenly going chest to chest with the interloper and body-slamming him back into the cabin. This was already drawing attention from passersby on the gangway outside, trafficking in coiled-up wire rope, plastic fish bins, MREs, and other goods they'd fetched up from the hold. Csongor pulled the hatch shut and dogged it, then turned around to see the young man clutching the bag possessively with one hand while brandishing a knife with the other.

He was better dressed than Csongor, in an immaculate Boston Celtics T-shirt and flower-patterned surfer jams with gravid cargo pockets that made his legs look even skinnier than they were to begin with. Until a couple of weeks ago, Csongor would have found it all quite alarming. As it was, with a sour and contemptuous look on his face, he grabbed the hem of his ragged and salt-stained shirt and pulled it up just high enough to expose the butt of the Makarov protruding above the waistband of his shorts. This had less impact, at first, than he'd hoped for, since for several moments the man simply could not get over the spectacle of Csongor's huge, hairy torso. This was not as convex, nor as pasty-white, as it had been two weeks ago, but even in its slimmed and tanned condition, it was a sort of Wonder of the World or sideshow spectacle to this young Filipino, who in any case did not know what to make of the odd gesture: Was Csongor offering his belly to be stabbed? In time, though, the scavenger's eyes wandered down and focused in on the butt of the gun. It was, Csongor knew, a somewhat hollow threat. If the scavenger were serious about using the knife, he could do serious damage to Csongor, maybe even inflict a fatal wound, before Csongor could pull out the pistol and get it ready to fire. But his sense was that the scavenger was not making a serious promise to use the knife, just trying to bluff his way out of a bad situation, and that all Csongor need do was raise the stakes with a bigger bluff.

Anyway, no attack came. Csongor continued to stare into the man's eyes until finally he put the knife away. Then Csongor pointed at the bag and crooked his finger. The man rolled his eyes, sighed, and slung it off his shoulder, then kicked it across the deck plates.

Csongor scooped it up, then moved sideways and let the scavenger go out.

Thirty seconds later, they were aboard one of the boats, having accepted the offer of a ride ashore. Thirty seconds after that they were standing on dry land, haggling with the skipper, who professed to be shocked that they had not expected to pay for his services. Communication was difficult until Yuxia—who, since they'd made landfall, had alternated between jumping up and down on the sandy beach, as if testing its structural integrity, and dropping to her knees to kiss it—realized that the man was speaking a recognizable dialect of Fujianese. She rolled up and pitter-patted over and began to try out words on him, framing syllables with sandy lips. Csongor could see that communication between the two was far from perfect but that they were getting a few concepts across. Marlon—who until a few moments earlier had been lying spread-eagled on the sand, screaming exultantly—sat up, cocked an ear, listened for a bit, but didn't seem to understand what they were saying any better than Csongor did.

Csongor moved several paces away so that the boatman would not be able to look directly into the bag, then set it down on the sand, dropped to his knees, and unzipped it.

A shadow fell. He looked up to see a girl of perhaps eight years, holding a baby on her hip, staring down curiously. Csongor hooked his arm through the bag's shoulder strap and stood back up, elevating it up above the level where she could see it, and then pulled it open. She edged around, standing up on tippytoe, trying to look in, and the baby reached out with one saliva-drenched hand and got a grip on the bag's edge and pulled it down, as if trying to help his big sister satisfy her curiosity. The situation was impossible; Csongor couldn't very well lay his hand on someone else's baby. But he really did not want any of these people finding out how much Chinese money they were carrying around.

The sun shone down into the bag's central cavity, revealing nothing except a few loose magenta bills. All the cash had disappeared.

Csongor remembered now the young man in the cabin. How his cargo pockets had bulged. He turned to look back out toward the beached hulk of *Szélanya*. A hundred people were on it now, and more were on the way. Others had already finished taking whatever they wanted and were dispersing on their little boats. The situation was impossible. Even if Csongor bought passage back to the wreck, or swam to it, and somehow managed to impose his will on a large number of people, most of whom were probably armed with (at least) knives, the odds were very small that the young man who had taken the bricks of money was still anywhere near the thing.

Csongor checked his wallet and found a lot of Hungarian currency and a few stray euro notes.

He glanced up at the boat pilot, who, by the standards of Filipinos, looked almost totally Asian in his racial makeup. What sorts of connections did people here have back to China? Just a vague awareness that their ancestors had come from there, centuries ago? Or did they go back and forth all the time?

"What kind of money is this guy willing to accept?" Csongor asked Yuxia.

"He is willing to take our *renminbi*," Yuxia reassured him.

"Any other kind?" Csongor asked.

She asked the question and Csongor heard him say, "Dollars."

The girl, seeing that there was nothing marvelous to look at in Csongor's bag, had lost interest, pried the baby's fingers loose from it, and backed away to make further observations. Ambling back toward Yuxia and the boatman, Csongor groped his way into one of the bag's internal side pockets and pulled out the Ziploc bag containing Peter's effects. He extracted and opened Peter's wallet, which was made of ballistic nylon. Flipping it open, he observed what he took to be Peter's state of Washington driver's license, trapped beneath a window, and a number of cards and slips of paper stored in a fan of transparent plastic envelopes: some kind of insurance card, a voter's registration card, a rectangle of white paper with several long strings of random letters, digits, and punctuation marks printed on it: passwords, probably. No photograph of Zula, which only confirmed certain uncharitable opinions that Csongor had been harboring about Peter since the moment they had met. Pockets with credit cards and debit cards. A billfold containing two American dollar bills and a great deal of some other, more colorful currency that Csongor did not immediately recognize: Canadian, he now saw. Very odd to be handling this carefully preserved relic of a dead man's life in a completely different world, here on a beach in Luzon.

The conversation between Yuxia and the boatman had lapsed as the latter gazed into the billfold.

As long as he had the fellow's attention, Csongor said to Yuxia, "We need to get to some kind of city where it would be possible to get a hotel room, get on the Internet, buy a bus ticket to Manila or something. How far away is the nearest city like that? Is it easier to go by boat or on land?" For they could hear occasional trucks storming down a road, a kilometer or two inland, raising clouds of brown dust that rose up from the jungle like heavy smoke.

"He's not stupid," Yuxia pointed out. "You know what he's going to say."

"Use any words you like," Csongor returned, "as long as it gets us out of here."

This at least gave Yuxia and the boatman something to talk about while Csongor opened the Ziploc bag that contained Zula's stuff. Opening her wallet laid him open to a kind of shotgun blast of diverse emotions. Shame at his ungentlemanly behavior. Horror at the thought he might be rifling the possessions of a dead person. Intense curiosity about all aspects of Zula's life. A piercing sense of loss followed by a resolve to get on with this and try to find her, supposing she was still alive. Trepidation that he wouldn't find any money, then a ridiculous sense of gratitude when he discovered, commingled with Canadian bills in various denominations, several crisp new American twenties.

"There is a city south of here along the coast with a hotel where tourists go," Yuxia announced.

"Internal Filipino tourists or—"

"He says they are all white men."

"How long to get there?"

"On his boat, three hours in this weather. Or we can walk to the road and try to hitchhike."

Marlon had rolled up to his feet and drawn closer to the conversation. He was covered with sand and grinning. Csongor exchanged looks with him and with Yuxia. There seemed to be a consensus that they should go by boat. So Csongor snapped a twenty out of Zula's wallet, held it up in the air, and handed it to the boatman.

The boatman looked quite pleased, but: "He wants more," Yuxia said, in a frozen voice that told Csongor he had already been outmaneuvered and outhaggled.

Csongor turned and looked back toward the wreck surrounded by boats, many of which were at least as seaworthy as this fellow's. "Tell him he can have another when he gets us there," he said. "And if he doesn't like that, ask him what is going to happen if I wade out there waving twenties over my head."

"Why are you paying with American money?" Marlon asked.

While Yuxia was translating, Csongor showed Marlon the empty bag. In response to Marlon's shocked look, he nodded in the direction of *Szélanya*. "One of those people was a little too clever for me," he admitted.

The boatman put up enough of an argument to save some face, then moved toward his vessel, making gestures to indicate that they were welcome to step aboard.

This boat was of appreciable size, the hull perhaps twelve meters long and a meter in breadth at its widest place, deeply vee-shaped in cross section, so that the planks that made up its hull rose up to either side of them like walls. It seemed an absolute rule in these parts that all watercraft, no matter what their size or purpose, must have double outriggers, and this was no exception; its outriggers were nothing more than skinny logs that, like most of the rest of the boat, were painted blue. Three more blue logs of comparable dimensions had been thrown crosswise athwart the hull, reaching far out to either side to support the outriggers. The boatman's crew, consisting of a boy of perhaps twenty and another half that age, scampered around on the outriggers and the thwarts with the aplomb of tightrope walkers, smiling all the time; it was difficult to know whether this was their normal level of cheerfulness or a reaction to having been hired on favorable terms. They tended to various chores while the patriarch sat in the back and operated the motor. Marlon, Yuxia, and Csongor made themselves at home beneath a blue tarp awning stretched over the middle part. Now that the hard bargaining was in the past, their hosts became almost embarrassingly hospitable, the younger plying them with bottled water and brightly colored sugary drinks in flimsy plastic bottles, the older stoking up a small concrete brazier and using it to cook up a pot of rice.

The journey took closer to two hours than the projected three, in spite of the fact that most of it was done under sail. For as soon as they had motored clear of the shallows and of the crowd of boat surrounding *Szélanya,* the skipper killed the engine, and he and the boys raised some canvas. These were only a little more polished-looking than the ones that Csongor, Marlon, and Yuxia had improvised, but they seemed to work a good deal better and they soon had the boat skimming efficiently down the coast.

Csongor spent most of the journey replaying in his mind the encounter with the young man in the Celtics shirt, savoring all the different ways in which he had been stupid and cataloging the opportunities he had missed to turn the situation around and get their money back.

Marlon seemed to read his mind. Finally he grinned, reached out, and chucked Csongor on the shoulder. "It's cool," he said.

Csongor ought to have been old enough by now not to be affected by cool kids telling him that he was cool, but even so this had a powerful effect on his mood. "Really?" he said. He glanced at Yuxia, but she had slipped into sleep during the journey and was slumbering deeply, her lips slightly parted. She was, he realized, very beautiful, like a madonna in a church. When she was awake, her energy and the force of her personality shone through her face and made it difficult to know anything about what she really looked like, somewhat in the same way that you couldn't see the glass envelope of a lightbulb when it was turned on. In some other universe he might have been attracted to her, but in this one she would forever be his kid sister.

He glanced back up to find Marlon watching him. During the voyage of *Szélanya,* Csongor thought he had observed some tender moments between Marlon and Yuxia; and he had wondered whether the two of them might end up involved romantically. But the ruthless environment in which they had been living had ruled out anything actually happening. Was Marlon hoping, now, that this would change? And if so, might he feel jealous when he saw Csongor gazing for a long time at the sleeping Yuxia? Csongor didn't see anything of the sort in Marlon's face. He, Csongor, had never been especially good at hiding his emotions, and he hoped that Marlon would be able to read him correctly.

"How is it cool?" Csongor asked. "You have a plan?"

"I have to get to a *wangba*," Marlon said, "and see what is happening in the Torgai. But I think I can get a lot of money."

"Enough to get us to Manila?"

Marlon grinned broadly. Sort of an affectionate reaction to Csongor's naïveté. "Much more than that," he said.

RICHARD FORTHRAST TOOK her a short distance up Airport Way to a neighborhood he called Georgetown. He swung around a corner and slowed down in midblock to draw her attention to a building that, he said, was the very one from which his niece and the subject named Peter Curtis had been abducted a little more than two weeks ago. Then he proceeded to a nearby drinking establishment, in front of which was parked a long row of Harley-Davidsons. The barmaid in chief, an intense woman with many tattoos, greeted him by name and asked him "Any news yet?" and then got a brooding look when he shook his head no. They occupied the last available booth. The waitress already knew Richard's order but brought menus for Olivia and John. Olivia had been steeling herself for a bottle of watery yellow American beer but was surprised to find a dozen and a half beers, ales, and stouts of various descriptions, all available on draft. She requested a pint of bitter and a salad. John Forthrast ordered a bottle of Pabst Blue Ribbon and a hamburger. This triggered some kind of ancient sibling grievance between the two brothers. "You're in a city where you could eat anything," Richard reminded him. "Would it kill you to—oh never mind." The latter clause with a glance toward Olivia and a reckoning that this wasn't the time to revive what showed every sign of being a worn-out argument.

"I don't like spicy food," John muttered doggedly.

"Is this a real blue-collar bar or a simulacrum thereof?" Olivia asked.

"Both," Richard said. "It started out as a pure simulacrum, a few years ago, before the economy crashed, when it was hip for twentysomethings to move down here and dress in Carhartts and utili-kilts. But they did such a good job of it that actual blue-collar people began to show up. And then the economy did crash, and the hip people discovered that they were, in actual point of fact, blue collar, and probably always would be. So you've got guys here who run lathes. But they have colored Mohawks and college degrees, and they program the lathes in computer languages. I was trying to come up with a name for them. Cerulean-collar workers, maybe."

"Do a *lot* of people stop by here on their way to the private jet terminal?"

"You'd be surprised."

Food and drink arrived, precipitating a lull, and then Olivia began trying to explain herself with great care to avoid saying who she worked for, though this must have been obvious, and how she knew what she knew. "Since I can't say much," she concluded, "I had been rather hoping that I might get some clues or some insights from you. And the fact that you already know the names of Sokolov and Ivanov suggests to me that I am not barking up the wrong tree."

Richard pulled out an iPad and brought up images of the note that Zula had written on the paper towels, which Olivia, of course, read with fascination.

There was a sense in which all things to do with Zula and the Russians were a red herring. MI6 couldn't care less about them. They just wanted Jones, and any intelligence that they might be able to glean as a by-product of hunting for him. They'd had a quite satisfactory arrangement going in Xiamen, which had been destroyed by the Russians' intervention. Everything to do with T'Rain and REAMDE was a distraction; for Olivia to hang out in a biker bar with the founder and chairman of Corporation 9592 was acceptable as an off-hours diversion but should under no circumstances be confused with actual productive work. Thus the official line. But having just finished a very long and expensive wild-goose chase to Zamboanga, an officially sanctioned mission that had put Seamus's men to a lot of effort and danger and apparently led to several deaths, Olivia was now inclined to view the party line with a great deal of skepticism. She had a vague sense that drinking with Richard Forthrast might in the long run be more productive than flying to Manila had been. But she couldn't explain how, yet, and so she didn't think she'd be filing an expense report. Which turned out to be a nonissue in any case, since Richard picked up the check before giving her a lift back to her hotel.

It was not until eleven o'clock the following morning that she was really able to get down to work on the NAG, the North American Gambit, which was her name for the theory that Jones had found some way to fly his stolen business jet directly from Xiamen to this continent. Here in the Seattle office of the FBI, signs were obvious that her local contacts were being controlled by persons in Washington, D.C., who were quite serious about working this theory in a systematic way. This was both good and bad. Obviously it was helpful that they liked her theory well enough to take it seriously and devote resources to its investigation. But whoever was running this project in D.C. was an Organization Man or Woman, someone with a studious engineer-like mind-set, who spent a lot of time worrying about accountability. No Seamus Costello, in other words. It seemed that a lot of duplication of effort was going on in which that hypothetical flight was being wargamed and flight-simulated in precisely the way that had already been done at MI6 more than a week ago. Ever newer and better "resources" were being "brought online" and ever more "scary-smart" analysts being "looped in" and "brought up to speed." These developments were relayed second- and thirdhand to Olivia, and it was obvious from the tones of the emails and the expressions on people's faces that she was expected to be gratified by each of these improvements. And yet from this remove, thousands of miles from whatever Beltway conference room where all the action was taking place, all these enhancements yielded zero results other than additional delays. It was not until about twenty-four hours after her meeting with Richard Forthrast that she finally began to get access to some of the data she needed to evaluate the NAG in a serious way: lists of the tail numbers of private airplanes that had landed at U.S. airports around the time in question (a week and a half ago now, long enough to give her the sense that she was pursuing a hopelessly cold trail) and high-resolution satellite images of out-of-the-way bits of the northwestern United States where computer-image-processing algorithms had detected white shapes that looked like they might conceivably be jet airplanes.

Early in the afternoon she received a text message from Richard Forthrast informing her that he was just a few blocks away, killing time at the Greyhound station, and would she like to grab a cup of coffee? The honest answer was that she was right in the middle of

something and she didn't have time, but the message was tantaliz-
ingly mysterious, and coffee sounded good, and Richard was generally fun to hang out with. So she took the elevator to the ground
floor and walked to the Greyhound station and found Richard and
John sitting on a bench, reading the *New York Times* and *Reader's
Digest,* respectively, waiting for a bus from Spokane that had been
delayed by weather on Snoqualmie Pass. Jacob Forthrast had decided
to come out from his compound in Idaho and spend a little time
with his two older brothers. "He feels useless" was Richard's explanation—just the sort of bleak and pitiless analysis that could only
happen between siblings—"and when he found out we weren't
going to China after all, he hopped on a bus." He was looking up at
Olivia over his reading glasses and his *New York Times* and must have
seen in her face certain questions she was too polite to ask: *Does he
not have a car? Is he too poor to pay for an airline ticket?* Richard folded
up his newspaper and treated Olivia to a brisk little explanation of
Jake's belief system, delivered in a way that made it seem like he'd
done it lots of times before and wanted it done properly. His tone
was studiedly noncommittal, making it clear that he didn't agree
with Jake about anything, but there was nothing he could do about
it, and so there was no point getting hung up on the essential ridicu-
lousness of it all.

Not long after this little orientation session came to an end, the
bus pulled in, and Jake climbed off in the middle of a long stream
of senior citizens, ethnic minorities, people too young to drive, and
hard-luck cases. Feeling very much the odd woman out despite the
Forthrast brothers' efforts to make her feel welcome, Olivia strolled
down the street with them to a bookstore that Jake wanted to visit.
Given the fact that Jake believed a lot of crazy stuff, Olivia found it
intriguing that the top item on his list was to visit a bookstore. If
nothing else, it served as an icebreaker. She had no idea how such
a man might react to her as a nonwhite female, but he was quite
cordial, even easy to talk to, and went out of his way to describe
himself as a "wingnut" and a "wack job," apparently thinking that
this would help put Olivia—or "Laura," as she was still calling herself—at ease. It was clear that he had been brought thoroughly up
to speed on the latest news regarding Zula, and how "Laura" fit into
the picture. He had been thinking about it during the bus ride and

come up with any number of questions and theories, most of which seemed like the products of an acute and active mind. He was, Olivia realized, at least as intelligent as Richard, and possibly more so.

"Why do you live out there, the way you do?" she finally asked him.

By this point she was sitting across the table from him in the bookstore's coffee shop. Jake had immediately found the book he wanted: a manual on organic farming. Richard and John had wandered off into other parts of the bookstore, aimlessly browsing, and there was no telling when they'd be back. She had bought Jake a cup of coffee, and he had returned to making self-deprecating jests about his lifestyle, which Olivia was now starting to find a little boring—dancing around the unmentionable. Better to just ask him flat out. As a stranger in a strange land, she reckoned she could get away with it.

"I guess I started with Emerson's essay 'On Self-Reliance' and just followed the trail from there," he said. "'Behold the boasted world has come to nothing . . . Let me begin anew. Let me teach the finite to know its master.' I'd already been having thoughts along those lines when Patricia died . . . Dodge might have told you about that?"

She shook her head. "But I did see something about it . . ."

"In his Wikipedia entry, sure. Anyway, at the time I had nothing else going for me, and so I decided to spend a summer trying to build a life around that."

"Emersonian self-reliance, you mean."

"Yeah. The summer turned into a year, and during that year I met Elizabeth, and after that, well, the die was pretty much cast. Dodge had this property in northern Idaho, which he had acquired years before, during a phase of his life that I believe is also covered pretty well in the Wikipedia article."

Olivia smiled at the polite evasion, and Jake seemed to draw confidence from her reaction. Olivia said, "As I understand it, this was the southern terminus of his . . . route. Or whatever you want to call it. Just a few miles south of the Canadian border. But within reach of the U.S. highway network."

"Exactly. But it also just happens to be one of the most beautiful places you can imagine: the head of a little valley, just where the land gets flat enough to build on and cultivate, but only a few minutes' walk from mountains full of wildlife and waterfalls, huckleberries and wildflowers."

"You make it sound marvelous."

"When I got off the bus in Bourne's Ford—which is the closest town—an old man told me 'Welcome to God's country.' I thought it was kind of hokey, but once I had found my way up the valley to Dodge's property, well, then I understood. At first Elizabeth and I were just living in a backpacking tent. I wrote to Dodge and asked him if he wouldn't mind my trying to improve the place a little, and so we began to build, and things just happened."

"But where does the whole Christian right-wing thing enter into it? What's that about?"

Jake's blissful expression became somewhat guarded. "When we had children, religion came back into our lives, as it does for many people, and Elizabeth has been my pathfinder as far as that is concerned. For me it's about being part of a community that is not based just on geographical proximity or money, but on spiritual values. There are no cathedrals in the mountains. You create your own church just as you hunt or grow your own food, split your own firewood. And just like those things, it might seem simple and rude to people who live in places with cathedrals and schools of theology."

"What about the politics?"

He considered it for a moment. The look on his face was a bit hopeless, as if he despaired of ever explaining it to a cosmopolitan outsider like Olivia. "Again," he quoted, " 'behold the boasted world has come to nothing . . . let me begin anew.' What you're seeing isn't politics. It's the absence of politics. It's us trying to live in a way where we never have to put up with politics and politicians again. That means that when the politicians come after us, try to interfere with our lives, we have to defend ourselves, with passive and non-violent measures when we can, but, failing that . . ."

"With guns?"

"We take full advantage of our 2A rights."

"2A?"

"Second Amendment."

"Are you carrying a gun now?"

"Of course I am. And I'll bet there's ten other people within a hundred feet of us who are doing the same. But you'd never be able to guess who by looking around." For Olivia had instinctively begun looking around. She did not see any obvious pistol-packers. But she did catch sight of Richard and John, who had fallen into conversation near the store's exit and were looking at them significantly.

"Looks like we are leaving," Olivia said, beginning to get up.

"Come and visit us," Jake blurted out.

"I beg your pardon?"

"I know it's out of the way. You may never come within five hundred miles of Prohibition Crick, unless you're flying over it. But if you do, I invite you to come up into our little valley and stay with us. Sincerely. You'll see. It won't be weird. It won't be uncomfortable. No one will be rude to you for being foreign, or not looking like us. You'll enjoy it. We won't try to convert you."

"That is very kind of you," she said, "and it actually sounds like something I might rather enjoy."

"Good."

"Now I just need an excuse to visit—what? Spokane?"

"Or Elphinstone. Or Richard's Schloss. There's lots of nice places within a day's drive."

OLIVIA WAS TOUCHED by Richard's including her in the reunion of the three brothers, until she reflected that Richard was anything but a sentimental fool and that he must have done it for tactical reasons. After that, she only pretended to be touched. She told the Forthrasts she could see plainly enough that they had things to discuss. And Olivia had an investigation to pursue. So she parted ways with them at the bookstore and went back to the FBI offices to resume the NAG investigation.

She was still at work late that night, waiting for things to open up in London so that she could confer with some of her colleagues there and suggest some leads for them to pursue while she slept. Her mobile rang and she saw Richard's name on its screen. "Just calling to check in," Richard explained. An awkward pause followed as she waited for him to go on. But then she understood that he was really just trying to find out whether she had unearthed any leads, found any scrap of hope, during the hours since he'd last seen her.

She could only mumble corporate-sounding buzzwords: drilling down, expanding the envelope, going into the corners of the search space. If those phrases sounded as bad to Richard as they did to her, it was a wonder he didn't just borrow his brother's sidearm and put himself out of his misery.

Richard informed her that he and John and Jake had spent the entire day sitting around his condo in a helpless and despondent condition, "driving each other crazy," and that rather than waste any more time thus, they had agreed that they would leave town first thing in the morning, flying direct to Elphinstone so that they could drive one another crazy in the more beauteous environment of Schloss Hundschüttler. Olivia, who had quite enjoyed the drink in the cerulean-collar bar, expressed sincere regret that she would not get another opportunity to see him. But data were now coming in thick and fast from all those resources and scary-smart people in D.C., and since she had devoted much of the preceding day to complaining, albeit politely, about the lack of progress, she could not very well leave the office at this time to go and have another beer with the decidedly irrelevant Mr. Forthrast.

And after that, another twenty-four hours blew by as if it were nothing. It must have been because she was working now, or, like a cerulean-collar worker, putting on an ironical performance of work, and when people worked, time went by fast.

MI6 higher-ups were asking her to supply daily updates on the progress of the NAG, and before going to bed she wrote one that she did not enjoy writing at all. All day she had, in her mind, been "making progress" according to some artificial metric of what that meant: emails read and written, databases scanned, checklists ticked off, images pondered over. But since none of that work had actually led to the identification of the business jet in question, or to any evidence whatsoever that it had entered the United States, it was only progress in a negative sense. Another day of such progress and the NAG would be dead and buried, and she would be on a flight back to London.

And so as she lay awake in bed in her hotel room, her mind wandered north across the Canadian border, all of a hundred miles from here.

It wasn't as if they hadn't discussed this. Canada was bloody enormous, of course. Everyone knew it, but it never really sank in until one spent time looking at the maps. British Columbia alone was one-eighth the size of the whole Lower Forty-Eight. But they hadn't been able to construct a sensible narrative as to why Jones, given his own personal business jet, would choose to land it there. Nothing against Canada, of course, which all agreed was a perfectly lovely country, but there simply wasn't anything in it that would make for a sufficiently juicy target to make the journey worth it for a man like Jones. If Canada had been selling arms to Israel and pounding Pakistan with drone strikes, Jones would take delight in knocking over the CN Tower or car-bombing a hockey game, but as matters stood he would have to get into the United States or else make a laughingstock of himself.

Getting across that border at a legitimate crossing would, of course, be out of the question. He would have to sneak across somewhere. And so if he were barreling south in a business jet, flying below the radar or else shadowing a passenger plane, pulling up short and setting it down north of the border would be nonsensical.

But, but, but. Plans didn't always go perfectly. It was a mistake to get in the habit of thinking of Jones as a superman. Perhaps he'd run short of fuel. Perhaps something had gone wrong en route and forced them to truncate the journey. Both hypotheses were sound. But both brought the NAG into the realm of free-form speculation. Every clever analyst in the CIA and MI6 could probably spend the next year dreaming up scenarios along such lines, none of which could be disproved, all of which were, therefore, equally worthless.

The next day was Friday, the beginning of her third full day in Seattle and, she suspected, her last. The FBI agents and the analysts in D.C. would happily work through the weekend and expect her to do the same, but her early-morning emails from London clearly suggested that if she had not, by the end of the day, been able to dredge up even a single shred of evidence in support of the NAG, then perhaps her talents could be put to other uses.

She still had intelligence contacts up in Vancouver: the nice people she had occasionally taken tea with during her "spy Disneyland" years at the university there. She reached them and began doing a little bit of gardening around the idea of the SNAG, the Shortened North American Gambit; and when they did not turn her down flat, she began to push on it. Her methods were utterly mendacious. When talking to Canadians, she suggested that their national security was being given short shrift by Yanks who believed that nothing north of the border really mattered; and when talking to Brits, she made lots of reference to the frightfully clever American analysts and all of the whiz-bang technology they'd used to search for evidence.

UNDER A VAST blue sky that offered generous space for lively cumulus clouds to gambol and clash, the double-outrigger boat slid southward with little more than a faint burbling noise of bow wave against hull planks, and the occasional slap as the sharp prow reached out over a breaker and dropped into the trough behind it. The coastline to port gradually became more settled-looking, with radio towers breaking the profile of the coastal hills and occasional villages: mosaics of brightly colored tarps and awnings right along the waterfront, and birds' nests of slender brown poles woven among frail pilings in the water before them and festooned with green fishnets. Hilltops had been denuded of trees in some kind of draconian logging campaign and left covered with a khaki-colored pelt of low vegetation gashed with eroded gullies that had stained the formerly white beaches below them with shit-colored muck. A point came when they could no longer remember the last time they had been unable to see any buildings along the shore, and then they rounded a small headland, a beat-up prominence of brown rock shaped like a clenched fist, and came in view of a town of some size: a crescent-shaped beach, still several miles ahead of them, lined with buildings as much as eight stories high, which they gaped at as if they were lifelong jungle dwellers, and, nearer to hand, the usual agglomeration of smaller habitations and makeshift open-air markets along the waterfront, interrupted in the middle by a big pier reaching out into the sea and connected by hinged spans of diamond-tread steel to a facility on the shore that was obviously a ferry terminal. Obviously, anyway, to Yuxia and Marlon, who saw them all over the place in their part of the world, and easy enough for Csongor to figure out even though he had been raised in a landlocked country. The road leading into it was wide, and congested just now with several buses and some smaller vehicles. The boatman gestured out to sea, drawing their attention to a larger vessel that was lumbering up the coast from the south, wreathed in a black nimbus of smoke: a passenger ferry from Manila. This explained the crowd of vehicles that had gathered at the terminal.

The crew struck the sails as the skipper got the motor started again, and a few moments later the boat's prow was knifing into the sand of the beach, and local boys ranging from toddlers to teenagers were running up to it and putting on a great cheerful pantomime of being helpful, perhaps in the hope of earning, or at least receiving, tips. Marlon and Yuxia and Csongor vaulted over the gunwale into warm, knee-deep water and sloshed ashore and then went through an interminable ceremony of smiling and handshaking and nodding and good-byeing, which used up almost all of the time remaining before the large ferry pulled into the terminal. Finally they disengaged themselves and walked up the beach, followed by a fascinated crowd of youths helloing them, and clambered up a low seawall of broken-up concrete rubble and into the paved area before the terminal. The temperature had gone up by ten degrees, and suddenly they were all perspiring. For the first time in weeks, the smells of crowded human places—charcoal and diesel, incompletely treated sewage, cigarette smoke, garlic—came into their nostrils. Marlon raised the question of whether they should just get aboard that ferry right now and ride it into Manila, which was a place where he reckoned he could make connections with his cousins. But a look at the schedule told them that it would not be departing for some hours yet, and they had all seen, on their way in, that row of buildings along the beach south of here, which showed every sign of being hotels. Since they had no real plan and were in no particular hurry, they agreed to ride a bus into the town and find hotel rooms, which would undoubtedly be cheaper here than in the metropolis, and see if this beach town sported any Internet cafés where they might (if Marlon was to be believed) reap enough gold to pay for suites at the Manila Hotel and purchase first-class tickets to whatsoever destination they chose. So they merged with the crowd streaming off the ferry—perhaps a couple of hundred people all told—and tried to sort out which bus they should get on.

Among those passengers was a far higher proportion of Caucasians than one would expect in a somewhat remote provincial town, and it seemed reasonable to guess that they were headed for the hotels along the beach. Most of them acted as if they'd been here before and knew where they were going. These headed, not surprisingly, for the larger buses idling before the terminal. The smaller vehicles—colorful, largely homemade van/bus hybrids—drew a clientele consisting exclusively of Filipinos. Csongor overheard a white man speaking in English as he shouldered his way across a current of passengers toward a bus, and so caught up with him and asked him whether that bus was going to the hotel district. The man turned and looked him up and down carefully, then informed him, none too warmly, that it was so. Csongor nodded back to Marlon, who stood head and shoulders above most of the crowd, and Marlon relayed the news to Yuxia, who was lost in it, and they followed Csongor up the stairs and onto the bus.

It smelled of perfume, diesel, and cigarettes. At least half of the people on the bus were white. But it was now obvious that this population was crazily out of whack demographically: 100 percent of the white persons were males, and most of them were over fifty. They tended to dress as if they thought they were going on some sort of safari, and they liked to wear sunglasses even when they were sitting behind tinted windows on the bus. Their English was accented in a way that Csongor could not place at first. His first guess was that they were British, but that wasn't quite right. "These dudes are from Oz," Yuxia said, after she and Csongor and Marlon had crammed themselves together into the rearmost row of seats. When that made no impression, she explained, "Australia. Or maybe New Zealand." Apparently she knew this because of her experience dealing with backpackers in her former life. So Csongor gazed up the bus's aisle at the Australians-or-maybe-New-Zealanders and tried to figure out what was going on. Maybe some sort of trade convention—a batch of retired plumbers or jackaroos, or something, who had commandeered a block of hotel rooms for a week of very inexpensive fun in the sun. But it didn't feel that way. None of these men was acquainted, none talked to another—which perhaps explained why the guy Csongor had accosted had given him such a look. They tended not to sit next to each other on the bus. Instead, each sat alone, or else shared a seat with a young Filipino woman. The demographics of the bus's Filipina population were just as crazy: all female, every one of them either quite young or well into middle age. The young ones could be mistaken for women in their twenties because of the way they were dressed and made up, but on closer inspection seemed to be in their late or even middle teens. Some of them seemed to be on their own, but most were accompanied, though at a distance, by mature women, old enough to be their mothers, who, by and large, were making no strenuous effort to seem glamorous.

All these impressions sunk in over the course of a fifteen-minute ride to the waterfront district that they had glimpsed from the boat. Csongor, Marlon, and Yuxia all stared fixedly ahead, as if each was afraid to make eye contact with the others and reveal what was going through his or her mind. When the bus pulled up to a terminal in front of a hotel, they waited until it had nearly emptied out, and then got up as one and marched down the aisle with Yuxia sandwiched closely between Csongor and Marlon. No discussion, no exchange of looks, had been necessary to decide upon that arrangement. When Csongor presented himself in the exit of the bus, blocking most of its door as he paused at the top of the steps, he was greeted by the sight of half a dozen Filipina girls looking up at him with widely varying levels of enthusiasm: some flashing big smiles, others pouting and bored or even openly hostile. But as he came down the steps and it became obvious that he was being followed by a petite Asian female who was, in turn, being followed by an Asian man, they all seemed to jump to the same conclusion, and they turned their backs on him and drifted away in the direction of other buses that were pulling in.

And yet it was an orderly place, and none of them felt any particular sense that they had stepped into a slum. To Csongor it felt very little different from Xiamen. The built environment was cheaply constructed three- to six-story buildings jammed in next to one another to form contiguous blocks, separated by crowded streets and fronted by a mixture of colorful signs and makeshift antitheft measures. It was, in other words, the classic streetscape of emerging Asian economies, and the only thing that made it unusual was that the signs were in English. Or, farther from the main drag, a hybrid of English and something that he did not recognize.

There was a strong argument for getting the hell out of there and taking the next ferry to Manila, but Csongor had become fix-ated on the idea that, only a few yards away, looming above them, were a large number of reasonably modern hotel rooms with beds and showers. It was anyone's guess what they'd have in the way of telephones, but on the opposite side of the waterfront drive, facing the row of hotels, he was able to count three Internet cafés in the space of a single block. So, without much discussion, the three grav-itated in the direction of the hotel that seemed largest and newest, and presently found themselves in its dark and cramped lobby, being evaluated by young females in tight dresses who were lounging on the few available seats, as they checked in to a room. The plan at first was to get one room for Csongor and Marlon and another for Yuxia, but halfway through the check-in process, when it became evident that the rooms were going to be situated on different floors, Yuxia changed her mind and announced that she would be sleep-ing on the floor or the sofa of Marlon and Csongor's room. Which meant, of course, that she would have a bed and Marlon or Cson-gor would sleep on the floor. So they got only one room. As it hap-pened, this brought the price down low enough that they were able to pay for it using American dollars from Zula's wallet, and thereby avoid using Csongor's credit card. Csongor had no idea whether any authorities—Chinese, Hungarian, or otherwise—had put a trace on his card, but still it seemed wisest not to use it unless he had to.

The room was up on the fourth floor, small and dark, with stained shag carpet, smelling of tobacco, alcohol, and sex. Yuxia stormed directly to the window and opened it as far as it would go—about six inches—to let in a bit of a sea breeze.

It seemed as though the shower would be busy for a while, and so Csongor went back down to the street and walked to a bureau de change that he had noticed earlier and changed all of the euros from his wallet and the Canadian dollars from Peter's into local currency. He was slightly offended, but hardly surprised, that they would not accept Hungarian forints. He also ducked into four different Inter-net cafés and found them well patronized by Caucasian males who were generally using them to look at dirty pictures. They varied in size, quality of equipment, hours of operation, and general level of friendliness. Only one of them, NetXCitement!, claimed to be open twenty-four hours, which Csongor thought might be useful given that the evening was already wearing on and they would probably be busy, for a few hours yet, getting cleaned up and fed and clothed.

He bought some Chinese food from a stall on the street and took it up to the room, trying to fight back the almost overpowering urge to rip the garlic-scented containers open and plunge his face into them. A hand-lettered DO NOT DISTURB! sign was up on the door of the room, held in place by the door having been slammed shut on it. Csongor opened the door, brought the food in, then went back and carefully replaced the sign. "Why do we need this?" he asked Yuxia, who was sitting on one of the beds with a towel wrapped around her body just below the armpits. Marlon was still finishing up in the bathroom.

"Hos," she announced, "keep coming around to ask if we *want anything*." Making air quotes around the final two words.

Csongor felt as if he should be abjectly apologizing in the name of every white male who had ever lived, but he didn't know quite where to begin. He still had not quite gotten his mind around the nature of this place and what went on here—particularly the middle-aged ladies, who seemed to be acting in approximately the same role as pimps, but who didn't seem like professionals. They seemed almost like chaperones. But singularly ineffectual ones.

"I'm sorry that this is the first place outside of China that you have ever seen," Csongor said. "It's not all like this. Someday I will take you to Budapest and show you around. Very, very different."

"First we have to get the eff out of here," Yuxia pointed out.

"I got some local money," Csongor said. "Enough to buy this." He nodded at the food, whose aroma, by now, had drawn Marlon out of the bathroom with a towel wrapped around his waist. "We can all get some cheap clothes and pay for maybe one more night here."

"Aren't you going to get in touch with your mother?" Yuxia asked, sounding a bit shocked. "Can't she send you money?"

Csongor considered it. You would think that by this time he and Yuxia and Marlon would know everything there was to know about one another, but the rigors of the voyage had left little time for getting acquainted; Yuxia knew that Csongor's father was deceased, but little else about his family. "My mother is a nice lady with high blood pressure who has little strokes all the time. I will send her a note saying I'm out of the country on business, but I can't possibly tell her what has been going on—it would be like throwing her off a bridge. My brother is in Los Angeles working on his dissertation and I talk to him maybe four times a year."

Yuxia seemed taken aback that any family could be so small and poorly organized.

"What I really want to do is some research," Csongor said. "I want to see if there is any information about a black, English-speaking Islamic terrorist whose code name or real name might be Jones."

I'd like you to have a look at the pistol that Mr. Jones is holding up to my neck, Zula had said on the pier.

"For all we know," Csongor went on, "there are pictures of Mr. Jones up on the Internet, and if I can identify him by name, then I could consider going to the authorities and telling them 'So-and-so was in Xiamen a couple of weeks ago and he has a hostage.'"

"Which authorities?" Marlon asked.

"I have no idea," Csongor said.

"Whoever cares," Marlon suggested.

They dove into the food, almost literally, and did not speak much for a while. It was the finest meal of Csongor's life, and he cursed himself for not having bought ten times as much of it.

"Do you want to get in touch with your family, Yuxia?" Csongor asked, when he was able to speak again. This created a pang that was obvious on her face and that left both of her companions somewhat aghast. "It is all I think about," she said eventually, "but I want to wait until we are somewhere that feels safer."

Csongor went into the bathroom and found Yuxia's and Marlon's damp clothes strung up all over the place. All of them had been wearing the same garments for two weeks, rinsing them occasionally in salt water. He turned on the shower and climbed in fully clothed, using bar soap to squeeze lather in and out of the fabric, then stripped down and left it all on the floor of the tub while he washed himself, letting the soapy water run off his body and down into the clothing, treading on it with his feet. Finally he spent a minute squeezing rinse water through them, then turned off the shower and began toweling himself off. He was a hairy man, a living advertisement for the body waxing industry, and it seemed as though his pelt was capable of holding a liter of water. He wrung out his clothing as best he could and hung it up wherever he could find a place, but despaired of its ever getting dry. But under the sink was a hair dryer stashed on a little ledge, which he pulled out and used to dry his underwear, then his trousers—which he had long ago cut off at the knees to make into shorts—and then his shirt.

After he was dressed, Yuxia and then Marlon rotated through the bathroom, drying out their clothes and putting them on, and then they went downstairs and across the street to NetXCitement!, where they devoted a little time to getting themselves situated. The standards and practices here were radically different from what prevailed in a Chinese *wangba*, and this took Marlon a bit of getting used to. Here there was no need to show ID, and there were no PSB cops hanging around to keep an eye on things. The place might be large by the standards of this provincial town but it was tiny compared to a Chinese *wangba*; it had no more than twenty terminals, plus counter space where perhaps another twenty patrons could plug in their own personal laptops. And instead of being filled with Chinese teenagers mostly playing games, it played host to a smattering of old white men mostly looking at racy pictures.

Having negotiated these cultural rapids, Marlon claimed the fastest and most expensive computer in the place, on the grounds that running T'Rain consumed a lot of memory and processing power, and Csongor rented a run-of-the-mill one nearby.

There was yet more culture shock as Marlon discovered that T'Rain was not even installed on his computer and that he would have to download it, a procedure that in some precincts would have consumed a great many hours. Here it took twenty minutes. For whatever reason, NetXCitement! had an extremely fast Internet connection.

Meanwhile Csongor had been thinking about Yuxia's predicament. "I think I know of a way you could send a message to your family without giving away our location," he said.

He had been clicking around on the computer he'd rented and found that it was so riddled with spyware, trojans, and viruses as to be nearly unusable. And so he had begun a project of rebuilding the machine from scratch. He divided its drive into two partitions, a big one and a small one, and reinstated its existing bootleg copy of Windows, and all of its other bootleg software, viruses, and so on onto the big partition. Then he set about downloading Linux onto the small partition. This entailed a seemingly endless number of reboots, during which he had plenty of time to explain matters to Yuxia. "We'll get Tor running on this thing," he said. "It will anonymize all of our IP traffic, provided we use the right browser . . . as long as you don't come out and tell your family where we are, no one will be able to trace us using IP addresses."

The news that she'd soon be able to check in with her family had powerfully affected Yuxia. Csongor was preoccupied for a time with explaining to her why the procedure was taking so long, why he had to keep rebooting the machine, why he insisted on opening up many small files filled with cryptic Unix jargon and making small edits to them, what it meant to get Tor configured and installed. When he finally got the machine up and running a fully secure, firewalled, anonymized installation of Linux—a feat for which he might have charged a commercial client lots of euros—he handed the machine over to her and then got up and strolled five paces over to where Marlon was just in the final phases of getting T'Rain online.

"How does it work?" Csongor asked. "Your character goes to this place—"

"He has been there the whole time," Marlon said, "waiting in his HZ for me to log in again."

"Okay, but anyway he has vassals?"

"About a thousand of them."

"Wow."

"Only twenty, thirty actual players," Marlon said, "members of the da G shou. But each one has a few toons—"

"Toons?"

"Characters. And they have vassals—low-level toons who are basically nothing more than robots running around the world. Anyway. I am the LL—Liege Lord—of all of these. Any gold that they have hidden, I can see, I can pick up—it belongs to me."

"So your toon can go to this place—"

"Torgai."

"Yeah. Where you live. Where the Troll lives."

"He doesn't have to go there. He's there already. His HZ is in a cave, in the middle of it."

"Okay, so he can pop out of his cave and run around and see gold that would be invisible to anyone else. He can pick that gold up and put it in his bag."

"Maybe. If he can go outside at all." Marlon had, Csongor noted, opened a browser window instead of logging immediately into T'Rain. He seemed to be scanning Chinese-language chat rooms. Csongor could not read the text, but it was obvious from the art-work surrounding it that this chat room was all about T'Rain; it was some kind of board where players hung out to exchange informa-tion and opinion, and the Chinese text was studded here and there with "LOL," "FFS," "w00t," and other staples of text messages.

"Why would you not be able to go outside?"

"Someone might be waiting for me. Or the whole place might be conquered by an army who came to grab all the gold. They would pounce on me as soon as I came out of the cave."

"Can't you hide yourself? With invisibility spells or something?"

"It depends on their power. If you let me read for a minute, I can find out what has been happening around this place."

Having been given the brush-off, Csongor went back over to check in on Yuxia, who was composing a message in a browser win-dow. He was eager for her to finish so that he could do some anony-mous browsing of his own, but she was taking her time about it. As well she might. How would she go about explaining herself to her family?

"Remember," he suggested, "even if the cops in China can't trace your location, they can read your email. So don't tell them anything you wouldn't want the cops to know."

"I am not stupid," Yuxia said levelly.

Doubly brushed off, Csongor drifted back to Marlon, who seemed to have made short work of his reconnaissance. "We are lucky," he said. "It is all total chaos there. No one has hegemony. Perfect for me."

"Sounds dangerous."

"I can fight off bandits and raiders," he said coolly, "just not an army."

With that he launched the T'Rain application proper and typed in a username and a password. A gallery of characters was displayed on the screen, all blinking and breathing and scratching themselves. Beneath each one was a parchment-textured scroll labeled, apparently, with its name. Most of these were written in Chinese. Csongor's eye was drawn to one of these, which he had seen before, depicted in the original ransom note. It was a troll. Its name, neatly printed in Latin letters, was REAMDE.

Marlon double-clicked on Reamde. The image grew to fill the screen, taking on resolution and three-dimensionality as the others faded and flattened. Reamde spun around, turning his back on them. They were now looking over the troll's shoulder. He had been sleeping in a cave and had just now stood up to look about his surroundings. In a quick series of preprogrammed movements, Reamde pulled on clothes, armor, weapons, and boots and slung a bag over his shoulder. Then, responding to commands from Marlon's fingers, he broke into a trot, headed down the cave toward the exit: a starry night sky, showing through a rough aperture. A few moments later Reamde stepped out into the world of T'Rain.

"Bingo," Corvallis said. "He is on the system. He just stepped out of his cave. It looks like he's going to be active for a while."

It was 8:23 A.M. Richard was standing next to his Land Cruiser beside the runway at Elphinstone's tiny airport, watching a Cessna climb into the sky and bank south. He had just stuffed John and Jake into it and handed a couple of ancient C-notes to its pilot.

Just twenty-four hours ago, John and Richard and Jake had landed here. A single day of sitting around had been quite enough, so John had volunteered that he might rent a car and drive Jake back across the border and spend a little time with Jake's family in Idaho. Richard—hoping it didn't seem as if he were rushing his brothers out the door—had called a bush pilot of his acquaintance and made it happen on about thirty minutes' notice. The roar of the Cessna's take-off run had drowned out the sound of Richard's phone ringing, but he'd felt it vibrating against his butt and whipped it out moments before it had gone to voice mail.

"Do we know where he is?" Richard asked.

"Still working on that, but we think the Philippines."

"That would kind of make sense," Richard mused. "The shit hits the fan in China, he gets out of the country, lies low for a while, finally pops his head up when he needs cash." The Cessna was just a faintly droning mote in a cloudy pink sunrise. He let his bottom slam down into the ragged seat of the Land Cruiser.

"Shit," Richard said, glancing back and forth helplessly between his phone and the gearshift lever. "I can't drive stick and talk on the phone."

"Probably just as well," Corvallis mused, "on those twisty mountain roads."

"Just keep track of what he's up to, okay? Don't do anything that would spook him."

"I'm not even logged in," C-plus said. "Just tracking him with database queries."

"What's he doing?"

"Mostly looking for his friends. Putting a posse together."

"So that he can go and gather gold," Richard said. "I'll be at the Schloss in half an hour. Call me if that seems warranted." He hung up, stuck his phone into his jacket pocket, then opened the door and dumped tepid coffee out of his travel mug and got that stowed. There was some crap on the dashboard; he swept it off onto the floor, where it was going to end up anyway. Then he peeled out of the parking lot and began to haul ass in the direction of the Schloss.

CSONGOR, WHO WAS no T'Rain player, was struck by how little screen real estate was actually devoted to viewing the world of the game. From what little he could see, it was quite a beautiful place, with highly detailed, realistically rendered landforms, scattered clouds drifting overhead illuminated by a full moon, and trees whose leaves and branches stirred convincingly in the wind. A bat was orbiting in the clear space before the cave's entrance, and crickets, or something, were singing in the undergrowth. But he had to perceive all these things through a sort of rectangular porthole, not much larger than his hand, in the middle of a screen that was otherwise claimed by windows: one showing a full-length portrait of Reamde himself, with an array of statistics plotted in diverse colorful, ever-fluctuating widgets. Large-scale and small-scale maps showing where he was in the world. A sort of radar plot with bogeys of different colors moving about on it. Three different chat windows in which conversations, 75 percent in Chinese and 25 percent in English, streamed upward in fits and starts, like steam rising from boiling pots. Gridded displays that apparently depicted the inventory of weapons, potions, and magical knickknacks that Reamde was carrying on his person. A sort of roster, tall and skinny, running the entire height of the monitor on its far left, each entry consisting of a thumbnail portrait of a T'Rain character; the character's name, sometimes in Chinese and sometimes in European glyphs; and various fields of data that, Csongor guessed, indicated whether that person was logged on, where they were, and what they were up to. Perhaps three dozen entries were packed into the list, and all but three of them were grayed out. Even as Csongor was noticing this, Marlon moved the cursor to the top of the list and clicked a column heading that caused it to be rearranged: the few who were shown in full color were all moved up to the top. He clicked on one of them and began typing in a pop-up window that suddenly appeared next to the character's icon. The process of typing in Chinese was completely mysterious to Csongor; as Marlon's fingers hopped all over the keyboard, a little window flashed onto the screen as some piece of software tried to guess what Marlon was trying to say and suggested possible completions. The sheer quantity and variety of data being rammed into Marlon's face by, Csongor guessed, at least a thousand discrete user-interface widgets on this huge screen, was overwhelming to his tired brain. But Marlon seemed to have been banking his energies during their sea voyage and was at last getting an opportunity to do what he did best.

A red bogey had been approaching on the radar display and Csongor had been worried that Marlon, preoccupied with his chat windows, was not noticing it. But then he fired off a complex command key combination that caused almost all of the windows to vanish, leaving only the ones that were relevant during combat. Something happened very fast, making no sense at all to Csongor, whose ideas as to what video-game combat should look like were, he guessed, hopelessly old-fashioned. The few times he had tried to play popular video games in Internet cafés in Budapest he had been vanquished in microseconds by opponents who, to judge from the nature of their taunting, were very young, possibly still in the single digits. Csongor now got the sense that Marlon was one of those kids who had grown up without losing any of his skills. In any case, the foe who had been sneaking up on Reamde was dead, and his corpse looted, in less time than it would have taken Csongor to reach out and get a sip of coffee from a cup next to the keyboard, and then all the windows verged back on the screen and Marlon resumed his chat.

Csongor had been assuming that absolute, respectful silence was the correct behavior for him to be engaging in, but Marlon seemed so adept at multitasking that this now seemed like ridiculous, fusty, Old World etiquette. "Getting in touch with the da G shou?" he asked.

"Yes," Marlon said.

"So they are okay?"

"At least some of them." He typed for a while. "They have been waiting."

"For you?"

"For a way to get the money out."

"How is that going to work, anyway?" For Csongor had learned enough to know that the da G shou all used self-sus accounts, which was to say that they were not linked to credit cards. This was convenient for Chinese kids just starting out, but made it harder to transfer profits out of the world.

"It can be arranged," Marlon said. "There are money transfer agents who do it. Normally we work with ones in China but we can find others, anywhere in the world. They can send us money here, by Western Union." Marlon looked up from the screen for the first time since he had logged in. "I saw a Western Union sign as we were coming in on the bus. It is only half a kilometer from here."

"So tomorrow morning, when they open up, we could have cash waiting for us."

"I could have cash waiting for me," Marlon corrected him, "but I will be glad to share it with you and Yuxia."

Csongor flushed slightly but kept on talking through his embarrassment: "What is the procedure?"

"Try to find some more of the da G shou and get them logged on," Marlon said. "One of them can go looking for a foreign money transfer agent and the rest of us can create a raiding party and collect gold."

"You have never dealt with non-Chinese money transfer agents before?"

"Why would we?" Marlon asked.

"Let me make some contacts," Csongor proposed, looking over at the computer he had secured earlier. Yuxia had finished typing and now appeared to be web surfing. "I can probably find one in Hungary. If not there, then Austria."

"Are those near—I don't know the name—dot C H?"

It took Csongor a moment to put this together. Then he understood it as a reference to Internet domain names ending in ".ch."

"Switzerland," Csongor said. *Confoederatio Helvetica.*

"The place with the banks," Marlon said.

"Yes, Switzerland is close to Austria and Hungary."

"Try Switzerland," Marlon suggested gently, then turned his attention back to the game; for at almost the same moment, two more creatures' faces had flashed from gray to color and leaped to the top of the roster. Csongor had an image of teenaged boys all over south China—terrified refugees who had spent the last two weeks staying one step ahead of the cops, hiding out in flophouses or cadging spare beds from shirttail relatives in the country—receiving bulletins on their phones, sprinting to the nearest *wangbas,* slamming their arses into chairs, cracking their knuckles, and going into action.

Csongor moved toward Yuxia and looked over her shoulder. She had opened up a web browser and was looking at a Wikipedia page. The title of the article was "Abdallah Jones." It sported a photograph of a man Csongor had once tried to shoot in the head on a pier in Xiamen.

"Mother*fucker!*" Csongor exclaimed.

Yuxia turned around slowly and looked at him. "Fate has given us a totally awesome foe," she observed.

"Then we should do something totally awesome to him," Csongor suggested. "In a bad way."

"Not so easy, from the pervert capital of the world."

She said it loudly. Faces bobbed up and popped around the edges of various computer monitors around the café, but Yuxia took no note of them. She had turned back to face the computer. Taking in some of Jones's exploits, his death statistics, she shook her head convulsively. "This guy really sucks ass."

"But you knew that," Csongor said.

"No foolin'."

· · · ·

RICHARD MADE NO friends during his drive through Elphinstone; but the dirty little secret of Canadians was that they drove like maniacs, so his speeding and light-running were not so far out of the norm as they might have been south of the border. The road that ran up the valley toward the Schloss had, in recent years, become a vector for sprawl and was now lined by the sorts of businesses that were excluded from the middle of town by its famously prim historic-preservation fatwa. But at the end of the day, Elphinstone wasn't that big and could only support so many car dealerships and Tim Hortons, and so this kind of development petered out in the dead zone around the abandoned lumber mill. Beyond that the road funneled to two lanes and angled upward, then, a few miles later, began to wind like a snake and buck like a mule.

So it was inevitable that he would close in on the tail of a gigantic RV no more than thirty seconds after he'd reached that part of the road beyond which passing was completely out of the question. It was not quite the size of a semi. It had Utah plates. It needed a trip through the RV wash. Its back end was freckled with the usual bumper stickers about spending the grandchildren's inheritance. And it was going all of about thirty miles an hour. Richard slammed on the brakes, turned on his headlights just to make it obvious he was there, and backed off to the point where he could see the rearview mirrors. Then he cursed the Internet. This sort of thing had never used to happen, because the road didn't really lead anywhere; beyond the Schloss, it reverted to gravel and struggled around a few more bends to an abandoned mining camp a couple of miles beyond, where the only thing motorists could do was turn around in a wide spot and come back out again. But geocachers had been at work planting Tupperware containers and ammo boxes of random knickknacks in tree forks and under rocks in the vicinity of that turnaround, and people kept visiting those sites and leaving their droppings on the Internet, making cheerful remarks about the nice view, the lack of crowds, and the availability of huckleberries. Normally Richard and the Schloss's other habitués would have at least another month of clear driving before those people began to show up, but these RVers had apparently decided to get a jump on the tourist season and be the first geocachers of the year to make it to the sites in question.

Richard allowed a decent interval of perhaps thirty seconds to pass, then laid on the horn, and kept laying it on until, less than a minute later, to his pleasant surprise, the RV's brake lights came on and it eased its right wheels over onto the road's meager shoulder at a place where it was only a little dangerous for him to pass. Not that anyone was ever coming the other way; but Richard had been taught the rudiments of passing in Iowa, where if you could not see an open lane all the way to the horizon, you bided your time. He barreled past the RV, and he would have rolled the window down and given the driver a friendly wave if he hadn't been preoccupied. As it happened, he did not even look back at it; its driver was ensconced about thirty feet off the ground, and it was difficult to see into its bridge from where Richard was sitting.

Fifteen minutes later he was at the Schloss. He was feeling a powerful urge to get on the computer right away, but he figured he might be busy for a while, so he decided to get his affairs in order first. In normal times, he'd have done this in his private apartment, but this was the middle of Mud Month and no one was here. So he decided to make himself comfortable in the tavern, which had a huge screen that could be connected to a computer. Since the machine had been rigged up for use during Corporation 9592 retreats, it was powerful, fully up-to-date, connected to the Internet by a fat pipe, and assiduously maintained, from Seattle, by the IT department. Its audio outputs were plumbed into the tavern's excellent sound system, and the seating in front of it consisted of very comfortable leather recliners and sofas. Richard raided the kitchen and stockpiled a few thousand calories' worth of snacks and soft drinks, sending the Furious Muses into Condition Red. In his apartment he could have placated them by walking on the treadmill while playing, but the tavern was not so equipped. He deployed his laptop on a side table and got it hooked up to its charger. He made a last trip to the toilet. On his way out, he noticed a bucket that had been left under the counter by Chet or someone while tidying the place. Following an old instinct, he snatched this up and took it into the tavern with him, setting it next to the place where he would be playing. It had been a long time since he had played a game with such commitment that he needed to pee into a receptacle, and it might very well be overkill here. But he was alone in the Schloss, no one would ever know, he was a man in his fifties, and there were a lot of caffeinated beverages within easy reach.

He turned everything on and booted T'Rain. While it was starting up, he noticed an annoying gleam of window light on the screen and went over to drop the wooden blinds. Then, just for good measure, he went all around the room and dropped the blinds on all the windows. For the sun might have the bad manners to move around and shine in from other directions. As he was finishing, movement caught his eye outside, and he noticed the RV he'd passed earlier, creeping up the road, slowing down even more so that its occupants could admire a roadside view of the Schloss. He gave it the evil eye, trying to use some kind of ESP to tell them to get lost. Sometimes such people would come up the drive and want to enter the place and use the facilities. Richard didn't care as long as staff were in the place to deal with them, but he could see it getting unpleasant in a hurry if affable, retired RVers with vast amounts of time on their hands managed to get a foot in the door. To his relief, the giant vehicle picked up speed, leaving the Schloss's driveway behind.

"I'm strapping in," he announced to Corvallis over a Bluetooth earpiece that he had just worried into the side of his head. He slammed down into a leather sofa, glanced around to be sure that all he might need was within arm's reach, and pulled the wireless keyboard onto his lap.

"He's still there," C-plus answered, "assembling a war band."

"How many so far?" Richard asked. But Corvallis's answer, if there was one, was drowned out by a cataract of awesome fanfares, kettledrum solos, pipe organ chords, and pseudo-Gregorian chanting emerging from subwoofers, tweeters, flat-panel speakers, and other noise-making technologies arrayed all about Richard.

"I take it," Corvallis finally said, when it seemed safe to crawl out from under his desk in Seattle, "that you are logging on as Egdod."

"If ever there was a time . . ."

"You know that if the Troll gets the slightest hint that Egdod even knows of his existence . . ."

"Egdod isn't even going to pick his nose until he has surrounded himself with every disguise and cloaking device known to our servers."

"He's really smart. And fast. I've watched him take down a few wandering bad guys. And the kids in his posse are every bit as formidable."

"Ever make a raccoon trap?"

"No," C-plus said. "I was told they carried rabies, and I couldn't see why it would be desirable to catch one."

"You drill a hole into a tree stump, or something, big enough to admit the raccoon's hand. But you drive some nails in around the edge of the hole and bend their heads inward so that he has to thread his little paw between them to get it into the hole. Then you leave a piece of bait in the hole. The raccoon insinuates his hand into this thing and grabs the bait. But he can't pull his hand out between the nails unless he lets go of it. He ends up trapped by his refusal to let go, you see."

"Have you ever actually done that? I mean, I know you had a very rural childhood and everything, but . . ."

"Of course not," Richard scoffed. "What the hell was I going to do with a rabid animal welded to a tree stump?"

"That's why I was asking . . ."

"It probably doesn't even work. It's just a metaphor." But Richard did not follow up on this statement because he had become rather preoccupied with setting up the many layers of shields and disguises and wards that Egdod needed in order to venture out of the house.

"So," Corvallis finally said, "the application of the metaphor, I'm guessing, is as follows. Right now the Troll could log out and lose nothing. He's like a raccoon who hasn't put his hand into the stump yet. But it looks like he's fixing to go out with his posse and Find and unHide a lot of the gold they've stashed around the Torgai. Then he'll try to carry it out to a moneychanger. At that point, he's like a raccoon who has grabbed the bait. If you attack him and he gets killed, or just logs out, he doesn't get the money he needs."

"You got it," Richard said. "And so it's at that moment that I'll try to pin this little prick down for a minute and have a conversation with him."

CSONGOR HAD ALWAYS done his best thinking while pacing irritably back and forth: a trait that probably explained why he had not performed up to his full potential in traditional academic settings. It served him well now. What Marlon was doing was fascinating. More for its intricacy, and for Marlon's fierce attention to its microscopic details, than for what was actually happening on the screen.

For Reamde had not moved more than a few virtual paces from the cave exit. In a way, Csongor could not take his eyes off it, but in another way he could not stand to watch for more than a minute or two at a time, and this led to pacing.

The other computer, the one with the clean Linux install and the anonymized Net connection, was five steps away. Csongor kept wandering back to it. Yuxia seemed to have established some kind of chat-room connection to someone she knew back in China and was carrying on a sporadic exchange of messages. This relieved a huge emotional burden she'd been carrying ever since the beginning of their adventure. But there was a lot of downtime during which she was able to surf the web for information on Abdallah Jones and (as her investigation continued, and she developed leads) Zula Forthrast and Richard Forthrast and, for that matter, Csongor himself and Csongor's brother in L.A. She had probably never used an Internet connection that was not hobbled by the Great Firewall, and she was already finding it addictive.

Csongor almost had to resort to impoliteness to get her to relinquish the machine for a few minutes. Then he carried out some Google searches, looking for pages that contained both "Zula" and "Abdallah Jones." He pulled up a few pages about terrorism in the Horn of Africa, making reference to the Red Sea bay and the Eritrean port after which Zula had been named, but nothing about Zula Forthrast.

So nothing had happened. No information had made it out into the public sphere yet that established any link between those two names. He tried Jones's name in connection with Xiamen and found nothing. With Yuxia's help he was able to find some news stories in the Chinese media about a gas explosion and a failed terrorist attack that had taken place in Xiamen on the morning in question, but none of these made any reference to Jones or Zula or any of the other people Csongor knew to have been involved. So there had been some sort of totally effective clampdown on news.

"A FLARE JUST went up," said a familiar voice on the phone.

Olivia recognized him, after a moment's disorientation, as "Uncle Meng," presumably calling from London.

She was disoriented because she had been talking to Mounties in Vancouver and hadn't expected London calling.

"Hello?"

"I'm here. Sorry," Olivia said. "What sort of flare?"

"We have a new actor in the GWOJ," said Uncle Meng, who had adopted Seamus Costello's acronym for the struggle in which they all—MI6, FBI, Mounties, the Forthrast family—were jointly engaged.

"What's the new actor doing?"

"Google searches linking names like Zula with names like Abdallah Jones. Xiamen. Csongor."

"Who the hell is Csongor?"

"I've no idea," said Uncle Meng, "which makes me wonder whether this new actor has inadvertently identified himself."

"Where is the new actor?"

"No idea," said Uncle Meng. "Whoever he is, he is savvy about computer security, has set himself up with a clean and well-defended Linux installation of extremely recent vintage, is using some kind of hacker software to anonymize his packets. So we can't guess where he might be."

"Is anything showing up on public sites?"

"Not that we've noticed."

"So the new actor isn't blabbing."

"No. Just fishing. Looking around to see if anyone else knows what he knows. And so far I would say that the answer is no."

"Is there any action you would like me to take?" Olivia asked.

"You've already helped by letting me know you have no idea who Csongor is," said Uncle Meng. "If I need anything else, I'll let you know." And he rang off, which was good since another call was coming in from a number that, judging by area code and prefix, was in the Vancouver offices of the Royal Canadian Mounted Police.

Her cross-border telephonic activities had been a sort of repeat, in miniature, of what she had gone through during her first day or two in the United States: starting with people whose names she knew and whose telephone numbers she had, obtaining other names and numbers, blindly groping through labyrinthine org charts until she actually managed to establish relationships with people who didn't think she was crazy and to whom she could divulge a bit of sensitive information. In contrast to the United States, with its Tower of Babel–like security/intelligence apparatus, Canada offered a straightforward one-stop shopping arrangement in the form of the Royal Canadian Mounted Police. There was also an intelligence agency, the Canadian Security Intelligence Service, but when they had got wind of the sorts of questions Olivia was asking, they had simply referred her to the Mounties, who were better equipped to answer.

As she had hoped, this call was from one Inspector Fournier, whom everyone seemed to think was the man she really ought to be talking to. She excused herself from the room where she had been going over aerial photographs with FBI agents and wandered out into an empty office nearby, gazing out the window over the blue waters of Elliott Bay—for it was a perfect spring day, the sky was clear, the mountains were out—and staring at, without really seeing, containerships being jockeyed around at the port. After some polite chitchat with Inspector Fournier, she asked for, and received, permission to use up a quarter of an hour of his valuable time and launched into a summary of the SNAG theory and its possible relevance to Inspector Fournier's sphere of responsibilities.

AFTER THE INITIAL spate of Google searching, Csongor went into a deep funk for a couple of hours. All during the desperate voyage of *Szélanya* he had been imagining that, if he could only get to a computer with an Internet connection, he'd be able to make things happen. In retrospect, it had not been a realistic assumption at all. But it had given him a reason to keep going through the occasional typhoon.

They had never really decompressed from the voyage. That was the problem. If they had beached *Szélanya* in an isolated cove and spent a little while eating coconuts and swimming in limpid waters, Csongor might now be psychologically ready to pivot into whatever the hell was going to happen to them next. But when *Szélanya* had ground to a halt, Csongor had allowed himself to relax for all of about thirty seconds—and during those thirty seconds, virtually all their money had been stolen. Since then it had been nonstop action; and now he was learning that his precious Internet was completely useless in tracking down Zula.

He was taken by sleep as suddenly and as completely as a man being swept off a deck by a wave.

A FEW HOURS into the Troll hunt, Richard's Bluetooth headset began to bleat out a pathetic low-battery warning. He severed the phone connection to Corvallis, which was becoming less and less useful as Richard got up to speed. Embedded in a complex of spells and disguises about twenty deep, he had made his way to the Torgai Foothills by actually flying there directly, eschewing the crowded ley line network, which would have forced him to emerge at a place where his character—or rather the disguised version of it—might be noticed. Here he was fighting certain ineluctable features of the rule system. He didn't want it understood that Egdod was on the move, and so he had disguised himself as one Ur'Qat, a K'Shetriae warrior mage of much lesser powers—but still powerful enough to survive alone in the war-torn Torgai Foothills.

Another reasonable step might be to make himself invisible. Egdod was capable of putting up invisibility spells that almost no one in the game could penetrate. And yet there was always a small probability that such a spell might fail. This was one of the ways they kept the game interesting: low-level characters always had a chance to defeat high-level ones. Even an Egdod could be detected. Better to disguise himself first as the less powerful Ur'Qat, and then have Ur'Qat cast an invisibility spell. Any spell that Ur'Qat could cast would be much less puissant and hence much more likely to be penetrated than one of Egdod's. So there was a good chance that when Ur'Qat rode the ley line into the Torgai, he'd be noticed, invisibility spell or no; and then he might be attacked outright or, what would probably be worse, be covertly followed as he went sneaking around after Reamde. And perhaps the person following him would be one of Reamde's minions. Egdod could always get to the Torgai in a big hurry, if he decided that this was warranted; but all signs pointed to that Reamde was slowly and patiently effecting a battle plan that was going to stretch out over many hours. As long as that continued to be the case, Egdod would content himself with flying from his fortress to the Torgai. Even moving at supersonic veloc-ity, this took a while. But during the flight, Richard had been able to refamiliarize himself with certain spells and magical items that might soon come in handy. And, at least until Richard's Bluetooth headset had croaked, he'd been able to get updates from Corvallis and to learn something about the minions that Reamde was summoning from, it appeared, all over south China.

CSONGOR WOKE UP nagged by the vague sense that there was *something* useful he could be doing and, after a few moments, remembered what it was: he was supposed to be locating a T'Rain moneychanger, preferably in Switzerland, but potentially anywhere in the world outside of China. It was 3:41 A.M.; he had been sleeping upright in a chair for almost three hours. He looked over at Marlon and found him in exactly the same pose as before. Yuxia was sitting in front of the other computer, but she was nodding off. He tried to move, discovered his neck had gone stiff, devoted a minute to stretching himself out. Then he strolled over for a look over Marlon's shoulder. He was astonished to discover that the troll Reamde *still* had not moved from the cave entrance. But it would be wrong to think that nothing had happened this whole time, for the roster window on the left side of the screen was now filled from top to bottom with character portraits in full color, each with its own little continually-fluctuating-and-updating status display. While Csongor had been sleeping Marlon had recruited several dozen other players to help him. Marlon slapped a function key, and the roster window expanded to fill most of the screen, then rearranged itself into a sort of hierarchical tree structure with Reamde ensconced at the top.

"Your org chart?" Csongor asked.

"Orc chart," Marlon said.

INSPECTOR FOURNIER GOT back to Olivia at about three thirty in the afternoon, letting her know that they had conducted a simple search of police records and found nothing about weird private jet landings or roving bands of Middle Eastern terrorists. The only thing that had been flagged as even moderately peculiar was that a group of hunters had gone missing in north-central B.C., about ten days ago.

Forty-five minutes later—having made a quick raid on her hotel room to grab her stuff and check out—Olivia was northbound on Interstate 5, stopped almost totally dead in the inevitable Friday afternoon rush hour jam-up. But she was moving. She was moving, she was convinced, in the general direction of Abdallah Jones.

IN SOME RESPECTS, Abdallah Jones's jihadists were so hapless that they almost—*almost*—aroused feelings of sympathy in Zula's breast, exciting what little she had in the way of maternal instincts. But certain things they were quite good at and went about with commendable efficiency. One of those was camping out. And after more than a week of aimlessly wandering about the highways and byways of British Columbia in an RV, they were clearly *so* ready to camp out.

She had flattered herself that, as they drew closer to the Schloss, they'd move her up to the front of the RV and consult her for directions. But it seemed that they had scored a GPS from one of the many Walmarts they had raided during their wanderings and were now simply using it to zero in on the coordinates of the place where she had taken photographs of the collapsed mining structure a few weeks ago. They closed and locked the door of her cell so she'd not be a distraction; and so she spent the last few hours of the journey alone in the dark, running through the exercise program she had invented for herself and trying to guess their location from what few sensory cues penetrated the insulated walls of the room. They passed through a town; she guessed Elphinstone. They bought groceries; she guessed at the Safeway. Then they left town and began to ascend (her ears were popping) on a winding road. Almost certainly the one that ran up the valley toward the Schloss. Someone honked furiously at them for a while, then sped past; as a little joke to herself, she imagined it might be Uncle Richard. Then she suddenly knew with certainty that it *must have* been Uncle Richard.

They reached a place where the road became gravel and then shut off the RV's engine. Nothing happened, from her point of view, for an hour; she could feel the suspension rocking as men climbed off, presumably going to reconnoiter. Muffled discussions were going on up ahead of her, and stuff was being unloaded. Almost *had* to be given that the RV had become so crammed with camping gear during the last week that it was difficult to move around in it.

Then she heard the sound she'd been waiting for ever since they'd constructed this prison cell and put her in it: the heavy clinking of the chain as someone dug it out of whatever storage bin it had been heaped in.

Scrabbling at the door. Then it was kicked open. Zakir—the big soft-bodied Vancouverite—was standing there, eyeglasses slightly askew, the chain all piled up in his arms. Shaving and bathing had not been such a priority with him these last several days.

"I'll be needing your neck," he announced, with elaborate, sarcastic fake-politeness.

CSONGOR DIDN'T HAVE the faintest idea how to go about making contact with a T'Rain money-laundering specialist, but he supposed that the direct approach couldn't hurt. He began generating some appropriate Google queries and soon enough began to get a sense for the correct buzzwords and search terms.

The problem turned out to be that none of these people had websites per se. They were post-web and post-email. You got in touch with them by catching up with their toons in T'Rain.

So Csongor began downloading the Linux version of T'Rain to this computer; and while that was going on, he began reading up on the game, trying to learn some of the basics so that he would not be utterly helpless when he entered the world.

The download process was a very slick one that had its own theme music, which blasted out of the machine's speakers for a few moments before Csongor figured out how to turn down the volume. Marlon noticed it. "Are you going in?" he asked. He sounded a bit uneasy.

"To find moneychangers."

"But you don't have a toon."

"That is true, Marlon."

"You'll have to start a new one. That's not going to work. He'll just get killed over and over again."

"So what do you want me to do?"

"My homeboys and I used to make our living selling toons to guys like you."

"They weren't like me."

"Anyway, I'll lend you one for free."

"WE HAVE VERY probably identified Csongor," came the voice of Uncle Meng through Olivia's phone, with no preliminary helloing or chitchat about the weather. "Your email was helpful." For Olivia, following their earlier conversation, had sent Uncle Meng an email describing the contents of Zula's paper towel codex.

Nothing then for a few moments. An aid truck, lights flashing, was trying to force its way through the traffic jam, laying on its horn and obliging drivers to creep aside.

"Everything all right?" Uncle Meng asked.

"Fine. I'm on a freeway traveling much more slowly than walking pace." She had been on the road for half an hour and had not even passed out of the city limits of Seattle. "What did you find?"

"Csongor Takács, twenty-five years old, freelance Internet security consultant and sysadmin, based out of Budapest. Known connections to organized crime figures. Has not logged on to any of his usual servers, Facebook, et cetera, in three weeks."

Olivia probably should have been thinking about something else, but she was wondering whether she should call Richard. For the one detail she couldn't get out of her head was that this Csongor had been doing Google searches on Zula's name. He knew who she was. But he didn't know *where* she was. Was it reading too much into a Google search to say that he was worried about her?

That he was, in other words, a good guy?

"Where does this get us?" she asked.

"Like all the other intelligence concerning the Russians, it gets us nowhere," Uncle Meng said. Not harshly. Sounding a bit regretful. "It is interesting background material, helping explain the events leading up to Jones's flight from Xiamen. But the nature of Csongor's Google searches tells us that—"

"He's as in the dark as we are," Olivia said. "Please do let me know if that changes."

"Oh, I most certainly shall," said Uncle Meng, and rang off as abruptly as he had started the conversation.

Olivia chewed on her thumbnail for perhaps thirty seconds,

wondering if she ought to just pull over and run this investigation from the shoulder of the road for a while. But there was nothing she could do about the traffic. She picked up her phone, navigated to the "Recent Calls" list, and punched in Richard Forthrast's number.

It rang a few times. But then finally his voice came on the line. "British spy chick," he said.

"Is that how you think of me?"

"Can you give me a better description?"

"You didn't like my fake name?"

"Already forgot it. You're in my phone directory as British Spy Chick."

"I was thinking of you," she said, "and thought I should check in. How are you and your brothers doing?"

He laughed. "We were about to kill each other, so I put them on a plane to Bourne's Ford this morning."

"Ah. It sounds charming." Olivia heard herself dribbling out meaningless words, trying to make a decision as to what she should or shouldn't tell Richard.

"The Troll is logged on," he announced.

"He is!?"

"And he's on the move. And I'm tracking him. Which means I'm busy. I want you to call this number"—he rattled off a number with a 206 area code—"and talk to Corvallis and get the details."

"Which details are those?" she asked distractedly, trying to impress the number into her memory.

"The Troll's IP address," Richard said. "So you can track him. He's in the Philippines. With your resources you can probably get his exact coordinates and hit him with a drone attack, or something."

"No comment on that."

"But don't," Richard urged her, "because I want to get some information out of him first. After that, you can hit him with all the Hellfire missiles you want."

She didn't know what to say. Was having trouble with Richard's sense of humor.

He tried again: "Track him all you want. Just don't spook him. Most important of all, don't try to follow him in T'Rain. Because he'll know. He'll be on to you in a second."

She hung up and punched in the number of Corvallis about a

tenth of a second ahead of the moment when it slipped from her memory forever.

A new voice came on: "British spy, er, woman?"

"You can say 'chick' if you want, I shan't file a complaint."

"We tried to get him to take sensitivity training, but he kept blowing it off."

"Oh, compared to some I deal with, your boss is exquisitely refined. Don't worry about it."

"Richard said you might call."

"Yes. You think that the Troll is in the Philippines?"

"Yeah, but we don't have the resources here to nail it down better—his IP address is part of a batch that is allocated over a pretty wide geographic area. Would you like to write down the dotted quad?"

"Love to," Olivia said, "but I'm driving. Sort of. So I'm going to do something else instead."

"Uh, okay, what's that?"

"I'm going to give your number to a colleague of mine who is actually in the Philippines. Seamus Costello is his name. He'll know what to do with it."

"Happy to help out."

"And then he'll probably ask you a lot of questions about how to make his character more powerful."

Corvallis had been typing. "Looks like Thorakks is pretty friggin' powerful already."

"How did you know about that!?"

"T'Rain is one big database," Corvallis said, "and it is my—well, let's just say that I am its master."

"Please don't tell me Seamus is logged on right now."

"He signed off three hours ago," Corvallis said. "It is about seven in the morning there."

"Where? Can you tell where he was logged in from?"

Typing. "The Manila Shangri-La Hotel. Club Level. Would you like his room number?"

"I have his cell," Olivia said, "but if I want to fuck with him—which I do—it would be better to call his landline, wouldn't it?"

. . . .

"THIS FRICKIN' PHONE is attached to the wall by an actual *wire*," said Seamus Costello, with a mix of horror and disgust, when he became awake enough to understand such facts. "How the hell are you reaching me over a *wire*!?"

"You have a few things to learn about spycraft," Olivia said sternly. "Really, I'm surprised. I hope you can be trusted with the information I'm about to give you."

"What information is that?"

"I'm not sure actually," Olivia admitted, "but it's a lead. In the Philippines. Which is where you happen to be stuck."

"I check into hotels like this," Seamus said, "specifically not to be reminded of this fact."

"Well, get on this, and maybe it'll be your ticket out of there."

"GWOJ-related?"

"Of course."

"Where the hell are you, anyway?"

"Northbound on Interstate 5 at the blistering velocity of three miles per hour. Whoops, I take it back, now I'm stopped."

"Like Manila all over again, eh?"

"Except I can't just abandon the vehicle."

"Northbound from . . . San Diego? L.A.?"

"Seattle," Olivia said, and gave him a brief summary of what she'd been doing since she'd left Manila.

"All righty," Seamus said, once he'd taken all of this in. "So the main thrust of the investigation, as far you're concerned, is the SNAG, and you're going to Vancouver to follow up a possible lead there . . . but what does that have to do with me?"

"Seamus, you are a highly trained operative with an exceptional skill set. Catlike reflexes and a killer instinct second to none."

Seamus already suspected that he was being set up in some way, so he refused to say a single word.

Olivia continued, "Thousands of foes have fallen under the swingeing impact of your Targadian Bladed War Mace."

"Any time you want to start making sense, I'm ready."

"There's a mission now that requires a warrior of your skills." And Olivia went on to describe what was going on involving the Troll. Most of the important bits were contained in the first few sentences; after that, she sensed herself trailing off to insignificance.

Traffic was beginning to loosen, she found herself changing lanes, multitasking more than she really wanted to.

Finally Seamus interrupted her: "Am I to understand that this kid was living ten feet away from Jones for months? And that he was right in the middle of the Xiamen 'gas explosion'?"

"Yes on both counts."

"That's all you had to tell me. Where is the little fucker?"

"That's for you and your stupendous national intelligence apparatus to figure out." And she gave him the IP address.

"I'm on it," he said.

"Just one thing . . ."

"Yeah?" Seamus, who had been sweetly confused and sleepy-headed early in the conversation, was fully awake now, and impatient, and didn't care if Olivia knew it.

Actually, sort of wanted Olivia to know it.

"The kid is good. Don't try to take him on."

"Thorakks can handle the kid. Good luck with the SNAG." And he hung up.

Which was fine because Uncle Meng was calling back.

It occurred to her that it was now something like one in the morning in London. Uncle Meng sounded some combination of drunk and tired. He was in his club or something.

"We have indications that Csongor—assuming that's who our Tor-using Googler is—might be trying to establish links with a T'Rain moneychanger."

It took Olivia—trying to think, now, of so many things at once—a few moments to understand. "They're together," she blurted out. "Csongor and the Troll." Then, after a couple of lane changes: "Why would they be together?"

"Unknown," said Uncle Meng, "but perhaps your contact can simply ask them. I myself am going to bed."

IT HAD TAKEN Zula a certain amount of time simply to get used to having open space around her, and a sky above.

They were at the turnaround at the end of the road, a few miles past the Schloss, at the base of the avalanche of planks that was the ruin of the old mining complex. It sloped up above their heads at what seemed like a forty-five-degree angle, though she doubted it could really be that steep. Sprays of boards, snaggled at their ends with bent, wrenched-out nails, made black sunbursts against the sky. Blackberries and ivy were trying to lash together what carpenter ants and gravity had torn asunder. A few hundred meters up the slope, she knew, the old railway bed cut across the middle of this wreck. A month ago she and Peter had been snowshoeing on it. A month in the future, mountain bikers would be riding on it. But now it was a mud sluice channeled by seasonal runnels that would have to be packed with gravel and pounded smooth before anyone could use it for anything. In a few weeks, the work crews would be along to begin that maintenance, but for now it was as abandoned as it ever got.

This was exactly where she'd thought they were going, but even so it seemed surreal and dreamlike to her: the sensation of cool fresh air on her skin, the smell of the cedars and of the mud, and, of course, the fact that she was surrounded by jihadists and that she had a chain padlocked around her neck. Now that they were out in the middle of nowhere, the jihadists had finally gone native and begun to carry weapons more openly. One of them was sitting cross-legged on the roof of the RV, which had been parked across the road, barring access to the turnaround loop, which was where they had dumped out and were sorting through their camping gear. This man had a rifle in his lap and a pair of binoculars hanging around his neck, which he picked up from time to time and used to gaze down the valley. To Zula it was clear enough that if any geocaching tourists or local cops came up the road to investigate, he would wait until he could see the whites of their eyes through the windshield and then shoot them dead.

There had been some turnover during the last week. Zula was beginning to lose track of all the players. Of the three who had come out from Vancouver the morning after they'd stolen the RV, Zakir was still here, of course, holding the end of Zula's neck chain as if walking a dog; and Sharjeel, who was the snappy, efficient, vaguely weasel-like one, seemed to have become one of Jones's most important deputies. Ershut, the burly blue-collar man who had come over on the jet, was playing his accustomed role, moving piles of stuff around and sorting things into stacks.

Mahir and Sharif, the lovers, were not in evidence. Neither was Aziz, the third of the Vancouverites. Abdul-Wahaab was strutting around, staring into the distance and talking importantly on multiple phones, checking his wristwatch. But at least four new guys were in evidence: the sniper on top of the RV, another openly armed man who seemed to be pulling guard duty on the ground nearby (he had found a place of concealment in the trees, but Zula could see him), and two wiry, bearded fellows who looked as if they had come for a long big-game hunting expedition. Even then Zula sensed she had not seen all of them, and that others were riding around, somewhere in this general vicinity, in the small fleet of cars that Jones's network had managed to scare up during the almost two weeks he'd been in the country.

They kept faltering in whatever it was they were supposed to be doing, and Sharjeel kept exhorting them to get off their asses and make some progress. Over the course of an hour they packed several backpacks as full as they would go, and roped and lashed and bungeed more stuff to the outsides of them, and put yet more stuff into garbage bags and plastic coolers that they carried in their arms, and then they trudged off into the woods, following a path that one of the more nimble members of the group had scouted. This took them up along the side of the ruin. They made extremely slow progress because of the steepness of the ground, the undergrowth, and the mud. But in perhaps half an hour—though it seemed longer—they emerged, sweating, into a patch of relatively level ground about the size of a badminton court, sparsely occupied by big old trees that, being evergreens, would give them some cover from the air, but open and flat enough that tents and tarps could be pitched and sleeping bags rolled out. Zakir's first act was to pass the free end of Zula's neck chain around a large tree in the middle of this space and padlock it. This freed him to lie down on his back on a blue foam pad until he was rebuked for laziness by Abdul-Wahaab. He got up and went to work. Zula filched his pad and sat down on it. Until now she had tried to pay as little attention as possible to the padlocks at the ends of the chain, since she was afraid that if she showed too much interest in them she'd be giving something away. Hopeless apathy was a much better stance for her to feign. But no one was paying her much attention now, so she let her gaze travel down the length of the chain to the place where it was locked around the tree trunk. There were two padlocks in Zula's universe. One was a big heavy brass thing, made to stand up to the elements, which they had taken from the mining camp. The other had been removed from the tool-box in the back of the pickup truck; it was smaller, made of steel, with a blue rubber ring molded into its base to keep it from banging and clattering as the box was moved around. Zula had a key to that one. For a while she had simply kept it in her pocket, but as it had become clear that something was about to happen, she had found herself lying awake worrying about the possibility that she might be searched and it might be confiscated. She had soaked a tampon in water until it swelled up, then shoved the key into the middle of it and shoved it right up her ass. It was there now.

The padlock fixing the chain to the tree was the big brass one. She couldn't see the one at her neck, but she could explore it with her fingers and feel the rubber ring around its base. This was the lock that she could open.

WHEN THE DA G shou created a new T'Rain character for possible resale to a rich lazy Westerner, they didn't want to spend a lot of time thinking up a clever name for it, so they just mashed together a few word fragments perhaps skimmed from random Google searches and spam; or at least that was Csongor's best guess as to why he was now wandering around T'Rain in the guise of a fat merchant named Lottery Discountz. It was possible to change the name—as well as take care of the fatness—for a modest fee, but he sensed that if he succumbed to the temptation to begin fiddling with such trivialities so soon, hours would pass without his actually getting anything done. He had his hands full just learning how to make his character move around the place.

He had shimmered into existence in a rented room upstairs of an inn at an important crossroads just outside the southwestern gate of Carthinias, which, as he had learned in a spasm of googling and wiki trawling, was one of the five largest cities in T'Rain. It tended to get left alone during wars, since its markets were useful to everyone, and it never took sides—it was too fractious a place to arrive at a firm political consensus on anything, and the last ruler who had tried to involve it in foreign intrigues had been defenestrated and deposed by a well-organized mob of . . .

There he went again, getting all caught up in seductive details. None of this mattered. The point was that Carthinias was a commercial entrepôt. It was the best place to connect with moneychangers. This would happen in a place called the Exchange. Just a few minutes after waking up in the inn, Lottery Discountz had passed through the city's gate in the halting, meandering gait that marked him as an absolute newbie, and since then he had been caroming drunkenly along its narrow streets, trying to find this Exchange. Or rather trying to work out how the navigational user interface worked, which amounted to the same thing.

From all that he'd heard of such games, Csongor was astonished that he had not yet been jumped and killed for sport. There were certainly characters in the streets who looked capable of it. They ignored him. Every so often another merchant, or some lower-status character such as an errand boy, would bow to him, doff his hat, and utter some sort of polite greeting. It appeared that Lottery Discountz had *status*. One of the ways this was manifested in the game was that characters of a generally nonviolent sort would greet him respectfully. Perhaps it also explained why no one had gutted him in the street yet. But he had the idea that he was getting less and less respect the more he blundered about, so after another spate of wiki checking and turning over rocks in the user interface, he found out that indeed his general level of respectability had been declining steadily since the moment he had left his room at the inn. Apparently this was because he'd been failing to bow and doff his hat in return. The people he'd been inadvertently snubbing had been sending in bad reports of him. So he learned how to bow and doff his hat—it was a simple command-key combination—and ran up and down the street for a bit being extremely polite to everyone he met and rebuilding his reputation before he got killed.

Which he did anyway. Forcing him to learn the procedure for getting a character out of Limbo and back in the world of the living. But after that, in fairly short order, he was able to make his way to the Carthinias Exchange and stroll up and down its gilded colonnades, bowing and doffing, and listening in on the almost totally incomprehensible exchanges of chitchat among its denizens. For everything was couched in a highly compressed jargon optimized for non-native-English speakers who liked to type with the Caps Lock button engaged. It was, he realized, the T'Rain equivalent of the cryptic hand signals employed by commodities brokers who needed to communicate pithy instructions across a riotous trading pit.

Being in any virtual world, of course, required some ability to suspend one's disbelief and enter into the consensual hallucination. So far Csongor had only experienced a few moments of this, and it had mostly been during simple activities such as bumping around his room at the inn or walking down the street. In this place he was finding it completely impossible, partly because he couldn't follow what was going on and partly because, of all places in T'Rain, the fictional premise was most threadbare here. The entire point of this market was to move money back and forth between the virtual economy of T'Rain and that of the real world. When money moved out, it had to be destroyed—permanently and irrevocably removed from the T'Rain universe. This was accomplished by sacrificing it to gods. The amount of gold to be transferred would be taken to one of several temples that stood on craggy acropoli around the limits of the city and handed over to priests or priestesses who would employ some sort of ritual to make it cease to exist: in some cases, hurling it into cracks in the earth to be deatomized by supernatural forces; in others, piling it up on elevated sky altars from which it would, after the proper incantations were intoned, simply disappear. Repulsed and dismayed by the jargon-spouting traders in the Exchange, Csongor wandered up into those rocky hills and observed some of those rites. They did everything out in the open, in full view of sparsely attended observation galleries, probably to make it clear that it was all on the up-and-up and that none of the priests was sneaking a bit of extra gold into the pockets of his toga. Over the course of a quarter of an hour's watching, Csongor saw something like half a million gold pieces ceasing to exist on one such altar, which—taking into account the fact that it was just one of half a dozen or so such establishments, and that it appeared to run at this pace around the clock—suggested (doing some math in his head, here) that on the order of $10 billion was passing out of T'Rain every year.

Ten billion a year.

Marlon needed to transfer $2 million out.

Csongor put his face in his hands, which was what he always did when thinking hard about something. Back at the hotel, he had taken the trouble to shave, and it was strange to feel his smooth cheeks. This arithmetic wasn't that difficult, but he was tired and disoriented.

Ten billion a year worked out to something like a million dollars per hour. So they were going to have to monopolize the Carthinias Exchange for something like two solid hours. Either that, or eke the money out in smaller increments over a longer span of time.

Which, he realized, was what the merchants thronging the colonnades must be doing for a living: aggregating tiny transactions into big ones, or taking awkwardly huge ones and breaking them up into chunks of more convenient size, so that the holy money-furnaces could run at a steady pace day and night.

Understanding this much helped break him out of the state of hopeless despair into which he had been plunged by his initial stumblings about. Lottery Discountz was, for a moment, alone and safe on a marble bench in the viewing gallery of a temple where gold was being swallowed, digested, and shat out as worthless manure by a giant mutant beetle. It was safe to be Away from Keyboard for a few minutes.

Csongor got up and paced around to stretch his legs. Yuxia was perched on a chair in a fetal position, sleeping. Marlon was engaged precisely as he had been for a great many hours. But when Csongor circled around behind him to look at his screen, he saw that the "orc chart" had become as ramified as a two-hundred-year-old maple tree. Marlon had mobilized an army. At a glance, Csongor guessed that it couldn't be less than a thousand strong.

Noting a strange glare coming from one end of the café, Csongor turned to look and realized, after a few moments' disorientation, that the sun was coming up.

INSPECTOR FOURNIER WAS startled, and perhaps slightly irritated, that Olivia had made the decision to go bombing up the road to Vancouver without even mentioning it to him. She sensed him wishing that Commonwealth immigration policies could be tightened up a bit, so as to make it more difficult for inquisitive Brit spies to jump back and forth between nations. The Friday aspect of this certainly wasn't helping; presumably Fournier had plans for the evening, even for the whole weekend, and now he was learning that he would be at least nominally obligated to act as this woman's host.

"Where are you now?" he asked.

"Waiting in line at the border crossing." The electronic signs were claiming that she'd be through in another ten minutes, which seemed pessimistic. That would put her directly into Vancouver's outer suburbs; she'd be downtown in an hour. This fact embarrassed her. It had taken maybe fifteen seconds after the end of her first conversation with Fournier to realize that she had to go to Canada *now,* and she had gone into action without explaining to anyone—not even her FBI hosts—what she was doing. It would take too long for her to explain matters to everyone. She would make phone calls from her car as she was driving, explain it then. But then she had ended up managing matters with Richard and Uncle Meng, Seamus and the mysterious Csongor, and had quite forgotten to call ahead. No wonder Fournier was irked. It was a couple of hours past the normal close of business, he was in the office late, delaying his dinner and thinking about getting into a glass of wine, giving her a courtesy call to let her know what was going on—only to learn that she trying to penetrate his borders at this very moment.

"Listen," she said, "I just want to be positioned in Vancouver so that I can follow up on this lead at the next opportunity."

"Truly, it's not a lead," he pointed out, "and the next opportunity will be on Monday; for voilà the weekend begins."

She decided not to press on this for now. "Has anything new been learned?"

"This was a bear hunting party, two guides and three hunters and all the equipment you would expect, packed into an SUV. They departed eleven days ago. They were supposed to be gone for a week. So they are now late by four days and unheard from, disappeared with no trace."

"The first time we spoke, I thought you said they had been missing for ten days."

"Perhaps you heard such a thing, but I did not say it. The trouble might have started for them as early as eleven days ago, or as late as four."

"Because you see the plane I'm looking for would have landed about thirteen days ago."

"So the dates do not match," he pointed out.

"But if they landed and holed up somewhere for a couple of days . . ."

"Where? Why is there no trace of this landing? Of the holing up somewhere?"

Silence. Olivia inched her car forward another length, stopped at the red light. She was next in the queue to cross the border.

What would Jones do? If he found himself stuck north of this imaginary line on the map?

If he had an SUV full of camping equipment?

He had lived in the wilds of Afghanistan for years at a time. Compared to that, a hike down the Cascades would be a piece of cake.

"He's up there," she insisted. "If he hasn't crossed the border already, that is."

Fournier sighed. "If you suppose he might have crossed the border, why do you not stay to the south of it?"

"Because all I can do is follow his trail," she said, "and I'm going to pick that up in Canada."

Silence. She imagined him pulling his glasses off, rubbing tired eyes, thinking of that glass of wine.

The light went green, the car ahead of her glided into another country.

"I must ring off," she said. "I'm crossing the border."

"*Bienvenue à Canada,* Ms. Halifax-Lin," said Inspector Fournier, and disconnected.

EGDOD HAD JUST been joined by one of Corvallis's favorite characters, a K'Shetriae Vagabond aligned (as of a few days ago) with the Earthtone Coalition. A longtime student of the game, Corvallis had developed a keen appreciation for luck, as in the odds of getting a propitious roll from Corporation 9592's random number generators. Some character types and alignments were luckier than others. K'Shetriae Vagabonds were the luckiest of all. Recently Richard had placed his thumb on the scales and made all members of the Earthtone Coalition slightly luckier than their counterparts in the Forces of Brightness, and Corvallis had not been slow to take advantage of it, trading in all of his Bright kit for more tasteful and understated duds.

"He's on the move," Richard announced, speaking now into his computer. This was the only way he had left of communicating with C-plus. The demise of his Bluetooth headset had been followed, a few hours later, by that of his phone; and a man who had been peeing into a bucket for six hours certainly did not have the time to go rummaging around for a charger. But as long as Clover (for that was the name of Corvallis's uncannily fortunate character) was within earshot of Egdod, Corvallis could hear whatever Richard said, albeit digitally transmogrified into the awe-inspiring timbre of Egdod.

"I notice you're not referring to him as 'the little fucker' anymore," said Clover, in a somewhat reedy, high-pitched voice that sounded nothing like Corvallis. Clover had an Irish accent to boot, this being a menu item commonly selected by American players who wanted to sound more like characters in movies.

"Okay, okay, he stopped being a little fucker when he raised an army of twelve hundred high-level characters and deployed them in battle array around his projected route of advance," Richard admitted. "I have to admit I was wondering why he was taking so long to move away from that cave. I didn't reckon that he was going to set the whole thing up like Sherman's march to the sea."

"Did you notice his leapfrogging cavalry screens?"

"Yes, I fucking noticed them."

"I just thought it was a nice detail," Clover added weakly.

"Well, before you get lost in admiration of the virus-writing son of a bitch, know that he might have information about my niece."

"How can I be of service?" Clover sniffed.

"Feed me a running count of how many gold pieces he's snarfed up. No, better yet, convert it into dollars."

"A hundred and fifty. Dollars."

"But that's just floor sweepings he stumbled across. He hasn't really gotten started."

"Agreed. Anything else?"

"Call your buddies and see if you can put together a high-level raiding party. It doesn't have to be as big as what the Troll has got. A few dozen people who know what they're doing."

"That should be easy enough."

"When you're ready, let me know; we'll attack his flank and observe how he reacts. I'll watch from above."

"Like a god of Olympus," Clover said.

"You think that'll be a problem?"

"For a bunch of veteran T'Rain players to go into action, knowing that the eyes of Egdod are upon them? No, I don't think that'll be a problem."

"Good."

"By the way, he now has thirteen hundred dollars."

LONG AGO, ZULA had got to a place where she could not be surprised, let alone outraged, by anything the jihadists did. This, she reckoned, must be the story of all radical groups, be they Taliban, Shining Path, or National Socialist. Once they had left common notions of decency in the dust—once they had abandoned all sense of proportionality—then it turned into a sort of competition to see who could outdo all the rest in that. Beyond there it was all comedy, if only you could turn a blind eye to the consequences. Anyway, they set up the camp stove and the coolers of food, the portable water bags and the sacks of Walmart groceries squarely in front of the tree where she was chained up, and expected her to do the cooking and cleaning.

The same thing had happened at the abandoned mine two weeks ago. Then, however, it had felt different to her. They had just survived a plane crash and their future had seemed uncertain; they had been holed up together in a cozy refuge; and, as ridiculous as it might sound, there had been a sense of shared hardship that had made Zula feel like pitching in. Now, of course, matters were rather different. There was a chain around her neck, for one thing. But the quality of the personnel had declined precipitously from those days. There was a common saying in the biz/tech world that "As hire As, and Bs hire Cs," the point being that as long as you continued to recruit only the very best people, they would attract others, but as soon as you let your standards slip, the second-raters would begin to seine up third-raters to act as their minions and advance their agendas. Zula almost felt as if she'd seen the whole ABC devolution happen in microcosmic form during the two scant weeks she had been rattling around western Canada with Jones and his crew. Jones was indisputably an A, and, in retrospect, those he had chosen to accompany him on the business jet had been As too in their own ways. Sharjeel was the very prototype of a B and he had brought with him Zakir, precisely the kind of C that people who quoted the "As hire As, Bs hire Cs" maxim dreaded bringing into their organization.

But Jones, being an A, seemed to understand this well enough and had sorted matters out accordingly. Their first few hours at the camp had been so quiet that Zula had actually dozed off on her camp pad for a little while; swathed in four layers of cheap fleece, she could sleep practically anywhere without the need for blankets or sleeping bag. She had awakened to find Zakir eyeing her in a manner that, at any time in her life prior to the advent of Wallace and Ivanov, she'd have found creepy. As it was, she found herself wondering whether Zakir could maintain that state of arousal once she had gotten her chain wrapped around his throat and her knee on his spine. During her confinement in the back of the RV, she had done many push-ups and many squats.

Anyway, the thing that had awakened her had been the advent in camp of a sizable contingent of jihadists, something like ten in addition to the three who had been left here to hold the fort. It seemed that several of the cars had arrived at the turnaround point at about the same time, disgorged this cast of characters, and then been driven away by persons who had been deemed redundant by Jones: Cs, or perhaps even Ds. So all of them were now literally at the end of the road, bereft of wheeled transportation (for the RV had been taken away) and supplied with much more in the way of camping equipment, weaponry, and ammunition than they could plausibly carry. The light was growing dim. Zula pulled the hood of her fleece over her head to hide the movements of her eyes and tried to carry on an inventory without being obvious. She did not see any weapons beyond what they had brought on the bizjet and acquired from the bear hunters. That, she reckoned, made sense; much easier to get weapons where they were going, and less weight to carry across the border.

Probably it was more useful to inventory the men than the gear.

All of the original five were now present: Jones, Abdul-Wahaab,

Ershut, and the lovers. The A-team, as it were. Of the Vancouver contingent there were still weaselly Sharjeel and podgy Zakir. The third member of that group, whose name she had forgotten, seemed to have been sloughed off; perhaps he was one of the bit players whose job had been to drive a vehicle away from this place and make himself scarce. So that was seven. But the total number of jihadists now present was thirteen—a figure she was not able to pin down, exactly, until she was made to serve them all dinner.

The additional half dozen were mostly men she had glimpsed or heard at least once during the interminable wanderings of the RV as they had all zeroed in from, she guessed, diverse parts of North America. Two of them were completely new to her. She gathered from the way these were greeted that they had only just managed to join up with the caravan. Most of those present either hadn't seen them in years or had no idea who they were. She pegged them as As. Partly this was because Jones treated them with special respect. But only partly. She could just tell. Erasto was from the Horn of Africa, probably Somalia. He spoke perfect midwestern-accented English and enjoyed looking at her slyly as he was doing so, glorying in her reaction: he must be an adoptee like her, someone who had been raised in some place like Minneapolis but who unlike her had decided to go back to his homeland and dedicate his life to the cause of global jihad. He was six foot four, built like a greyhound, baby-faced, didn't need to shave. A Benetton model.

Abdul-Ghaffar ("Servant of the Forgiver"—she had remembered that much Arabic by this point)—was a blond, blue-eyed American man of perhaps forty-five, though he might have been ten years older than that and in good shape. He had close-cropped hair, was burly but trim, and appeared to work out a lot. A soccer player or a wrestler—a practitioner of some sport, anyway, that didn't require height, for he was maybe five seven. His native language was of course English, and he followed the others' conversations even more poorly than Zula, who could catch perhaps a third of what they were saying. The obvious question that was posed by his choice of name—what was he seeking forgiveness for?—would go unanswered for now. But it seemed clear that he had converted to Islam late in life and was eager to make up for lost time. She got a clue when he turned his head to expose a skin graft on the top of his head, about the size of a postage stamp. She had seen similar damage on her fair-skinned, farm-dwelling relatives. He was under treatment for malignant melanoma, and he probably had less than a year to live. Until she'd seen that, she'd wondered why a man like Jones would look upon this all-American newbie as anything other than an FBI plant.

The power of laziness was a continual wonder to her. Not that jihadists had any monopoly on that. But with so much manpower up in this camp, could they really not cook their own food? Not set up a little buffet line, pile it on their plates without feminine assistance? All the while leaving Zula chained to some other tree, out of earshot. But it seemed huge to them that their captive female perform this work for them. She was being put on display, she decided, like Cleopatra being towed through Rome. Jones wanted the others to see how the infidel girl had submitted to his mastery.

Which she hadn't, of course. But for purposes of this one meal she was happy to act that way. She even kept her hood up over her head like a sort of chador. And she listened to what they were saying, astonishing herself by how much of their conversation she could now understand.

They ate together for a while, satisfying their appetites, chatting and joking. And then Jones began to address them in a now-let's-get-down-to-business tone. And what he said was that he would be hitting the sack very soon, since he needed to rise long before sunrise to begin the next phase of the operation. He would not see them again for several hours after that. In the meantime, they needed to sleep well but rise in good time and make all ready to divide into two camps: the base camp and the expedition. The latter group would be larger than the former and would be moving out on a great adventure. But this in no way diminished the importance of the base camp crew or detracted from the glory that they would achieve and the heavenly reward that they would reap . . .

(It was, Zula realized, just another business meeting. The only thing missing was the PowerPoint presentation. Some of the group— presumably the Cs—were being given the shit work, and Jones had to soften them up first with the meal and the fake camaraderie.)

Staying behind to enjoy Zula's excellent campfire cuisine would be Zakir, Ershut, and two others. One of these, Sayed, Zula had mentally classified as a graduate student: a quiet man, closer to forty than thirty, who seemed markedly uncomfortable in the camping and hiking milieu. It was obvious to Zula why he and Zakir were being left behind—she'd have made exactly the same choice—and both of them looked some combination of disappointed and relieved.

Ershut, though, was dumbfounded. The same went for Jahandar, an Afghan whom Zula had last seen perched on the top of the RV with a sniper rifle and a pair of binoculars. Zula herself had to make a modest effort to hide her own astonishment, for if ever there was a man cut out for a long trek down the length of a mountain range in hostile territory, it was Jahandar. To the point where Zula had some difficulty in imagining how they had smuggled him this deep into a Western democracy. They must have drugged him, packed him into a crate, shipped him over by air freight direct from Tora Bora, and kept him pent up on a mountaintop until now. Everything about his appearance—the hat, the beard, the glare, the battle scars—should have got him arrested on sight in any municipality west of the Caspian Sea. Anyway, never mind how they'd managed it, Jahandar was here, and he was pissed. And this encouraged the normally taciturn Ershut to voice objections of his own to Jones's plan.

They kept glancing over at her. As if to say, *How many people does it take to keep tabs on a girl chained to a tree?*

Jones gave her a glance too: a knowing look, as if to say, *I can tell you understand more than you let on.* He pushed his dirty plate in her direction, then rose to his feet and made gestures indicating that Ershut and Jahandar should come with him. They strolled away from the campfire until they had reached a place from which they could not be easily heard, where they continued the conversation in lower tones. Jones was filling them in on some aspect of the plan that did not need to be shared with the entire group just now.

Or perhaps it was only Zula with whom they did not wish to share it. For at some point, a few minutes into their discussion, the three of them all turned their heads to look her way, paused in their deliberations for a few heartbeats, and then looked back together, turning their backs on her to continue the discussion in a more reasonable timbre. All the tension was gone from their body language.

They had decided to kill her.

It would not happen right away. But at some point after the main group had been launched toward the border, Ershut or Jahandar would cut her throat—not, she guessed, before she'd cooked them a meal and done the dishes—and then they would set out in pursuit of the main body. And knowing the two of them, they'd have little difficulty in catching up. Zakir and Sayed, she guessed, would be left behind to throw dirt on her corpse.

The meal broke up, and the men scattered into the darkness beyond the reach of the firelight, leaving her with a pile of dirty paper plates and some pots that needed scrubbing. Most of them went to bed. Jahandar made himself tea with the water she had been heating for dishes, then retreated to a position a short distance up the hill, whence he could survey the whole camp and all below it. He took his rifle with him.

Zula did the dishes. Imagining Jahandar's crosshairs on her forehead.

SEVERAL HOURS OF despair had given way to the vague notion, more in Csongor's heart than his head, that he was beginning to make sense of the Carthinias Exchange and its diverse actors. There was a trading pit in the middle of the place, a full 360-degree amphitheater of polished stone steps, perhaps thirty meters—the limit of shouting distance—at its top, funneling in and down to a tiny, flat floor no more than three meters across. The thing was split neatly in half through the middle, though there were no screens or fences or visual cues to make this obvious; it could be inferred by noticing that different sorts of people tended to congregate on each side: on the one, merchants who were trying to get money out of the world, and on the other, priests from the temples, trying to make full use of their money-annihilating capacity by undercutting the competing priests.

So much for the side-to-side split. Csongor sensed that there was some kind of top-to-bottom stratification as well, and he was developing a theory that the people down toward the bottom were trading in larger blocs of money, while the upper levels were for small-timers. To outward appearances, none of these merchants was carrying much gold into the pit and none of the priests was carrying much out of it. Accordingly, he had guessed at first that they were only trading in paper and that the actual transfer of specie was happening in a bank or warehouse somewhere. But then he noticed small, sparkly objects trading hands, generally making their way from the small-timers at the top down toward the heavy hitters in the lower pit. Some wiki searching told him that T'Rain had several types of metal even more precious than gold, though the vast majority of characters in the world never even laid eyes on the stuff; it was used only to effect colossal transactions. One sort of coin— Red Gold—was worth a hundred gold pieces. A Blue Gold piece was worth a hundred of those, and Indigo Gold, or Indigold for short, worth a hundred of *those;* which meant, if Csongor's mental calculation was accurate, that a single Indigold coin had a value, in the real world, of something like $75,000.

It seemed of the highest importance to T'Rain's art directors that these coins look as flashy as their high value implied, and so they gleamed, sending out flashes of colored light as they were passed from hand to hand. Plain old yellow stuff was changing hands in the plaza around the amphitheater, frequently being bulk converted, by strolling moneychangers, into Red Gold coins that were making their way over the rim of the pit and transacting lively commerce in its upper reaches, making a flashing red constellation, as if LEDs were blinking all over the place. But farther down, the predominant color was Blue; and at the bottom it deepened to Indigo.

The transaction that Marlon hoped to pull off would amount to something like thirty pieces of Indigold, or three thousand of the Blue stuff. Since carrying around three thousand pieces of anything was not practical, Csongor had little choice but to set up a relationship with one of the big traders down in the bottom of the pit who, (a) dealt in Indigold all the time, and (b) was controlled by players who could wire funds to the Philippines. But precisely because such characters were carrying around such immense amounts of money, security here was suffocating, with the innermost and lowest ring of the amphitheater guarded by a ring of extremely fearsome-looking guards, standing shoulder to shoulder and looking outward, and walled, roofed, and domed by nested layers of shimmering light that Csongor recognized, vaguely, as magical spells. In T'Rain, figuring out how powerful another character was was a far more complicated proposition than in other such games where you could merely compare levels. Csongor lacked the experience to judge another character's abilities, but he knew a few rules of thumb and had little doubt that even the small-time traders around the rim could strike Lottery Discountz dead just by giving him a cross look.

Which gave him the notion that he might be able to get close to the center of the action precisely because he was so harmless. He tried the experiment of simply walking across the plaza to the edge of the pit and then clambering down on to the topmost bench. No one cared. He moved down another. No reaction. Things began to get crowded and he had to sidestep this way and that to find gaps in the crowd of traders, but no one paid him any particular note. He was close to the dividing line between the merchant side and the priestly side, and he heard priests calling out "Benison!" and coming together with merchants to exchange money. Benisons, as he'd learned, were a way for players to transfer real money *into* T'Rain; the character would pray to a god, a charge would be placed on the player's credit card, and the gold pieces would simply appear on an altar somewhere, or turn up at the end of a rainbow in a mountain glade controlled by this or that faction of priests, and then they would transfer it through markets like this one to the prayerful recipients. Csongor eavesdropped on a few such transactions and noted that they were typically in the thousands of GP range, which was to say, a handful of Red Gold pieces. But after he had worked his way down into the middle reaches where Blue Gold changed hands, he still, from time to time, heard a priest calling out, instead of "Benison!" the phrase "Miraculous Benediction." He looked this up and learned that, every so often, when a character prayed for a Benison, he got a hundred or a thousand times as much as he had asked (and as his player had paid) for. It was a lucky break, like finding a hundred-dollar bill in a box of Cracker Jacks.

And this gave Csongor all he needed to form a sort of plan. He worked his way down as close as he could to the ring of guards, the dome of spells. Once he descended to the point where the magic barriers were inflicting damage on Lottery Discountz and the guards were turning their eyes his direction and reaching for their weapons, he backed off a step, sat down, and began to observe the transactions taking place in the innermost circle. Flashes of purple were going off all over the place. He was watching millions of dollars changing hands. The total number of traders within that ring was perhaps twenty, and any one of them could handle the transaction he had in mind.

He was beginning to hear words coming from Marlon's mouth, which pulled him out of the imaginary world and brought him back into the Internet café in the Philippines. Marlon, who had played almost silently for the last couple of hours, was now communicating directly, in Mandarin, with one of his lieutenants. Or perhaps they were generals. Csongor could only speculate at the size of his army now. Marlon's voice was calm, quiet, but insistent, and his hands were prancing around the keyboard like spiders on a hot skillet.

Since Lottery Discountz was doing nothing except observing the trade pit, Csongor rose, stretched, and strolled over to have a look. Yuxia too seemed to have been stirred awake by the sound of someone speaking in Mandarin and opened her eyes slightly, then stiffened, remembering where she was. Her eyes fixed and focused on something across the room. Csongor followed her gaze and saw that the morning shift, if that was the right word for it, was filtering into the café. For the last few hours they'd had the whole place almost to themselves, but there were a couple of new arrivals who had ensconced themselves behind terminals in Yuxia's line of sight. One of them was just in the act of glancing away. Csongor, hardly a stranger to girl-watching, reckoned Yuxia must have caught him looking and was now giving him the evil eye. Not wanting to get caught up in that exchange, Csongor got to where he could look over Marlon's shoulder and view his monitor.

The last half-dozen times Csongor had checked, he had seen nothing on Marlon's screen that looked remotely like a virtual sword and sorcery world. Instead it had been countless overlapping panes containing ramified orc charts, bar graphs, fluctuating statistical displays, and scrolling columns of chat. All that was gone now, replaced by something that looked a little more like it: a melee at the throat of a narrow pass between foothills. Several members of Marlon's army—not the main group, but one of his flank guards—had been attacked as they forded a stream that ran through the pass. It looked like a carefully laid ambush, and half a dozen of them were already lying dead in the shallows. But reinforcements were hurtling into the combat zone on land, in the air, and over the water, engaging the ambushers in many single combats that merged and divided as one fighter came to the aid of another, then wheeled about to contend with some new threat.

"Problems?" Csongor asked.

"No," Marlon said, "we will kick their asses."

"Are you going to do any ass kicking?" Csongor asked. Because he had noticed that Reamde was just biding his time on a boulder in the middle of the stream.

"Not needed," Marlon said. "I am observing."

"What do you see?"

Marlon took a long time to answer. Then he spoke as if these observations were just coming into his awareness: "They are very good. Experienced characters. Not just kids. But they have not fought together before."

"How can you tell?"

"They don't know how to help each other as an experienced raiding party would. And they look different." Marlon raised his hand from the keyboard for the first time in, Csongor guessed, several hours to point out one of the attackers. "See? Definitely Bright." Then he moved to indicate another. "Him? Earthtone. Why are they fighting together?"

Then, as if something had just occurred to him, he brought his hand sharply down to the keyboard and used the keys to spin his point of view around and up. He was looking up into the starry sky now. Hovering up there were two characters, suspended magically in midair, gazing down. Clicking on them brought up little windows showing their portraits and their names. Csongor could not read, from this distance, the microscopic type.

"Who are they?" he asked.

"Doesn't matter. Not who they say they are," Marlon said.

"What does it mean?"

"This is not the real attack," Marlon said. "Real attack is later."

"How much money do you have?"

"Of gold pieces, two million."

Marlon converted it. A hundred and fifty thousand dollars. Five thousand, roughly, for every member of the ambushing party.

Why would that not be the real attack? Who expected to get

more than $5,000 for a few seconds' fighting in a video game?

"You are still hoping for the amount we discussed earlier?" Csongor asked.

"We can't stop now," Marlon said. "We get it all or nothing tonight."

"Actually, the sun has been up for hours."

"Whatever."

BY THE TIME Olivia had reached her hotel in downtown Vancouver, she had thought herself into a deep funk about Inspector Fournier and what she feared was his obstructive attitude toward the investigation. She was therefore pleasantly surprised when the desk clerk, while checking her in, noticed something interesting on the screen of her computer, and then looked up brightly to inform Olivia that she had a message waiting. A manila envelope was produced. Its heft suggested it might contain ten or twenty pages of material. Once she had checked in to her room and sorted herself out a bit, she opened it up and found that it contained faxed copies of police reports, both local and Royal Canadian Mounted Police.

Her higher-ups at MI6 were insistent that she always keep them apprised of her whereabouts. She had been delinquent about that ever since leaving Seattle, so she checked in with them. It would be something like six in the morning in London now.

Then she settled in to read the reports of the missing hunters: a retired oil industry engineer from Arizona and his two sons, aged thirty-two and thirty-seven, from Louisiana and Denver, respectively, all experienced hunters, who had traveled up to B.C. to celebrate the old man's sixty-fifth birthday by bagging a grizzly. They'd hired a guide company that prided itself on catering to serious old-school hunters. To judge from the tone of certain promotional passages on its website, this was to set it apart from competing firms that offered a posher, and presumably much more expensive, experience. Clients were offered a money-back guarantee that they would actually kill a bear at some point during the weeklong expedition.

Apparently this pitch had been convincing to the two sons, who had pooled their cash to purchase the trip as a surprise for their dad. From the police reports, and from the brutally depressing website that the missing men's family had put up, beseeching the universe for information, it was clear that these were no dilettantes; the father had lived all over the world during his career and had lost no opportunity to hunt big game wherever it was to be gone after, frequently bringing his boys along with him. The guides were no tenderfeet either: one of them—a cofounder of the company—had been doing this for three decades, and the other was a First Nations man whose people had been living in the area for tens of thousands of years. They were in a two-year-old, four-wheel-drive Suburban well equipped with tire chains, winch, and anything else that might be needed to drive out of trouble or survive when hopelessly stuck.

Which was part of their method, and part of the problem now faced by the police. For since the guides were not anchored to a cushy lodge, they could roam wherever hunting was best, and since they were offering a money-back guarantee, they had something of an incentive to do just that. In the course of a week's hunting, they might move among several favorite bear-hunting sites distributed over an area hundreds of kilometers on a side, almost all of which was mountainous, and only just becoming passable without snow machines. By far the most reasonable theory was that they had taken the Suburban one kilometer too far, skidded off the road, and become hopelessly lodged in a streambed or snowbank.

Or at least that had seemed the most reasonable theory during the first couple of days that they had been reported overdue. Consequently the search-and-rescue efforts had been all about crisscrossing the region in light aircraft, looking for a crashed vehicle or a distress beacon, and scanning the radio frequencies on which they might send out a distress call. Phone coverage in most of the region was out of the question, but the Suburban had a citizens'-band radio, and presumably they'd fire it up and call for help as soon as they saw an airplane. Or heard one.

"Heard" being more likely, since weather had been overcast almost the entire time. The pilots were by no means convinced that they'd achieved anything like a proper search of the area. Consequently, the investigation had been at a standstill for the last few days. The families—who had flown up to B.C. and who now seemed to be operating some sort of crisis center out of a hotel in Prince George—the nearest conurbation that even remotely resembled a major city—were insistent that something must be wrong and were coming dangerously close to saying impolite things about the RCMP's conduct of the investigation.

Reading between the lines, it was easy enough to make out what was going on. The police—though they wouldn't dream of saying so openly—were almost certain that the hunters and guides were all dead, probably as a result of driving over a cliff in fog. If they were merely stuck, they'd have made their situation known on the radio, or they'd have hiked out to a major road, something they were more than equipped to do. But the police couldn't just come out and say that. So they had to manage the situation by expressing confidence that the aerial search would turn something up sooner or later. Beyond that, there was little that they could do other than make comforting and reassuring noises when cornered by reporters or distraught wives.

Olivia, needless to say, had a different theory altogether. It was difficult to imagine anything crazier-sounding than that a nest of international terrorists had stolen a business jet from Xiamen, crashed it in the mountains of British Columbia, murdered a Suburban-load of bear hunters, and headed for the border.

On the positive side, though, it should be an easy enough hypothesis to investigate. The Suburban might be four-wheel drive, but it was unlikely that Jones and company had driven it off-road for a thousand kilometers. They'd have taken the path of least resistance.

Actually, she reflected as she googlemapped British Columbia, it wasn't merely the path of least resistance. It was *the path*. This region did not have a road grid. It just had a road. Unless they had taken an extremely circuitous route along logging tracks in the mountains—unlikely, this early in the year—or looped around far to the east, into northern Alberta, they'd have had to proceed south on Highway 97.

And why not? If Jones had managed to hijack the Suburban out in the middle of nowhere, he'd have understood perfectly well that he had only a few days—perhaps just a few hours—in which to do something useful with it before some kind of alert was sent out. He would have headed straight for the U.S. border along Highway 97, through Prince George (actually right in front of the hotel where the families of his victims had set up their base camp), and down into the more ramified system of highways that spread across southern B.C. If he didn't make it across the border right away, he'd look for a way to ditch the Suburban where it wouldn't be noticed, and he'd transfer to some other vehicle.

And then he'd think up a way to cross the border, probably out in the middle of nowhere. Something that would be difficult to prevent even if they knew it was going to happen and had a full-scale manhunt under way.

They wouldn't need to buy food, since they could eat camp rations stolen from the hunters. Hell, for that matter they could just go hungry for a day; it wouldn't be the first time.

The only thing they would need would be petrol. Gas.

Another look at the map.

If they had acquired the Suburban up in the region where the search was going on, and if its tank had been reasonably full, they'd have been able to make it all the way to Prince George before having to refuel. Of course, there were other refueling stations scattered along the road north of there—people had to buy gas somewhere—but Jones would have avoided those instinctively, not wanting to make a memorable impression on the proprietors, who might have recognized the Suburban as belonging to a local guide service. No, he'd have taken it all the way to the relative anonymity of Prince George and then he'd have bought his petrol in the largest, most impersonal gas station he could find.

Tomorrow she would be driving north to Prince George. Somewhere in that town there must be a surveillance camera that had caught the image she needed. And if she could only sweet-talk its owners into giving her a copy of that image, then she could use it as a sort of sluice gate to divert a great deal of misdirected Jones-hunting energy into a more profitable channel

Tonight, though, she had to sleep. Was, in fact, sleeping.

MOST OF CSONGOR'S time in T'Rain had been spent blundering about in a state of hapless newbie confusion. Only his long experience as a systems administrator, struggling with Byzantine software installations, had prevented him from plummeting into despair and simply giving up. Not that any of the sysadmin's knowledge and skills were applicable here. The psychological stance was the thing: the implicit faith, a little naive and a little cocky, that by banging his head against the problem for long enough he'd be able to break through in the end. The advances he had made in understanding the Carthinias Exchange had raised his spirits a bit. On the other hand, watching Marlon run a small war was crushing his morale. The immense power of Marlon's character, his inventory of spells, weapons, and magical items, the size of his army, and his facility in soaking up relevant data from the boggling array of displays and interfaces on his screen and acting immediately upon that information, all bespoke many years' experience playing the game and made it clear to Csongor that he was as out of his league here as he would have been on the field at a World Cup soccer match. Nevertheless, the dogged sysadmin in him would not concede defeat and kept gazing stupidly over Marlon's shoulder, trying to make sense of what was happening and to pick up a few tips as to how he might make better use of Lottery Discountz's cruelly limited set of powers.

For that reason he was completely surprised and utterly unprepared when Qian Yuxia stormed across the Internet café and hurled a cup of water into the face of a man who had been sitting there for approximately the last half hour. "I am not a friggin' T-bird!" she exclaimed.

Then she said it again.

"You want a T-bird, go look some other place!"

Csongor had never heard the English expression T-bird before, but Yuxia had now uttered it three times, so he was pretty certain he was hearing it correctly. He had no idea what it meant.

The victim of the assault was a tall, lanky white man with a scraggly blond beard and green eyes that looked alert and more bemused than angry. He had been surprised by the water in the face, but after that he had sprung to his feet and turned to face his assailant. Not in a threatening manner—he was careful to keep some distance—but in a way that made it clear he was ready to address any follow-up assault should Yuxia care to mount one. He was looking at her interestedly and was by no means afraid or even embarrassed. But the moment Csongor went into movement, this fellow noticed it, and he shifted his position as if to make ready for any threat from that quarter. The green eyes gave Csongor a quick head-to-toe scan and locked in immediately on the right front pocket of Csongor's baggy trousers, which happened to contain a loaded Makarov. Somehow he seemed to guess what was banging around in that pocket. And this fact changed everything. The man showed both of his palms to Csongor, a gesture that said both *Look, my hands are empty* and *Stop where you are.* Csongor faltered, not so much out of obedience as because he was nonplussed by the stranger's behavior.

"It'd be a good thing for all of us," the man said in strangely accented English, "if you could keep your hands north of your navel, as you'll note I'm doing, and maintain a little distance. Then we can have a productive conversation. Until then, it's going to be all about what we're carryin'. And since you are new to these parts, let me tell you, we don't want to go there."

If Csongor had heard this correctly, the man had just threatened to pull out a gun and shoot him.

As if to confirm that his interpretation of matters was correct, the two other customers in the café bolted, leaving only Csongor, Yuxia, Marlon, and the newcomer.

While taking the threat quite seriously, Csongor was not as intimidated as he might have been prior to events in Xiamen. "My life has already 'gone there,' so I am not afraid to 'go there' again if you are causing a problem for my friend," he said.

Yuxia, sensing that the situation wasn't what she'd assumed at first, had backed off a couple of paces and sidestepped a bit closer to Csongor. Meanwhile the Filipino man running the front desk had stuck his head into the room to investigate. Csongor's eyes darted toward him. The blond man, noting this, pivoted that way, relaxing his hands, and rattled off a sentence in what Csongor gathered was the Filipino language. He sounded and looked quite cheerful. Whatever he said erased the apprehensive look from the manager's face and caused him to nod and back out smiling.

"What did you say to him?" Yuxia asked.

"Since you are so sensitive about being mistaken for a T-bird, I probably shouldn't tell you," the man said. "But I told him that you and I were having a little tiff, a common sort of dispute in a place like this, and that we had settled it."

"What is a T-bird?" Csongor asked.

"A tomboy," said the man. "In this context, a real or fake lesbian who caters to mongers who get off on that sort of thing."

Far from wanting to pull a gun and shoot the man, Csongor now wanted to stand here and ask him questions all day. It was such a pleasure to be around someone who actually knew what the hell was going on.

"What is your name?" Yuxia asked.

"James O'Donnell," the man decided.

"Are you a monger?" she asked.

"No. But please don't tell anyone."

Yuxia laughed. "Why? You are ashamed to not be a disgusting pervert?"

"Because that's the only reason to be here?" Csongor guessed.

The man calling himself James nodded. "Any Western male in a town like this who is not a sex tourist will only arouse suspicion and curiosity. I'm guessing the locals are fascinated by *him*." And he nodded toward Marlon, who had glanced up from his monitor once or twice during all this but, since there'd been no gunplay, had not seen fit to interrupt his work.

"*You* should talk," said Yuxia, looking at James's monitor. James had also been playing T'Rain. Csongor was interested to note that James's character seemed to be tromping around in an environment very similar to the Torgai Foothills. As a matter of fact, the mountain peak in the background looked awfully familiar; James's character was within a few kilometers of Marlon's.

"You're following us," he said, "in two worlds at the same time."

James nodded. "I cannot tell a lie. I been doing it for a few hours."

"Do you want some of the gold?" Yuxia asked.

"Fuck the gold," said James. "I want to know anything you might know about Abdallah Jones."

"YOU ASKED ME to tell you when he got over the one-million-dollar mark," Clover mentioned, "and I think it just happened."

"You *think*!?"

"It fluctuates up and down as raiding parties steal money from him. He has got a lot of raiding parties coming after him right now."

"Anything major?"

"No, nothing as big as the party we put together. There hasn't been time. But I'd say that word is getting around that something big is happening in the Torgai. Within an hour I'd expect to see some fairly well-organized hundred-man raids homing in on him."

"I think that's actually a good thing," Egdod said, after thinking about it for a while. Richard had been playing T'Rain for something like fourteen consecutive hours, and his conversational skills weren't everything that they could be. "I think it gives him more incentive to get it done now. He's unHidden a million bucks' worth of gold . . ."

"One point one million," Clover corrected him. "He just raked in a big score."

"Anyway, the point is that for him to re-Hide all of it now, with so many people watching him, would be difficult. Easier to make his strike tonight."

"So what does that mean for us? Or for you, rather, since I am about as puissant as a bacterium living in Chuck Norris's bowels."

"It means that the time has come."

"What are you going to do?"

"Are you wearing headphones?"

"Yeah."

"I suggest you take them off."

"I WAS EXPECTING one Chinese virus-writer kid, alone," said the man calling himself James, with a nod in Marlon's direction. "I didn't realize he'd have a girlfriend, and a Hungarian bodyguard with a pistol in his pocket."

They had withdrawn to a corner of the Internet café where they could speak privately and google things. The place was filling up with mongers.

"I'm not his girlfriend," Yuxia said. "I don't think he likes tomboys."

"De gustibus non est disputandem," said the man.

"What does that mean?"

"It means he's a fucking idiot."

Csongor, a bit taken aback to realize that James and Yuxia

were flirting with each other, felt himself receding to the periphery of relevance.

"I like him," Yuxia said, "like a brother. But . . ." and she held out her hand, fingers splayed, and wiggled it in the air.

"Gotcha," said James, looking at her fascinatedly. But then he seemed to remember his manners, and his gaze strayed to Csongor. "What's your story, big guy? Fish out of water, huh?"

While not immune to James's insouciant charm, Csongor could only think of Zula, so he broke eye contact and looked out the window in a way that must have seemed brooding. He noticed that he was drumming his fingers on the counter, each calloused, sun-dried tip bashing the Formica like a ball-peen hammer.

"I shot him in the head," he said finally.

He turned to look at James, who had shut up for once. "I. Shot. Him. In. The. Head."

"Hold on a sec, are you talking about Jones?"

"Yeah. But it was only, what do you call it?" Csongor pantomimed a bullet caroming off the side of his head.

"A graze," James said. "I fucking *hate* that." He pondered it for a few moments. "You shot Abdallah Jones in the head."

"Yeah. With this." Csongor slapped the heavy thing in his pocket.

"From how far away?"

"Too close." And Csongor related the story. This ended up taking a while. He got the impression that this was the longest span of time that "James" had gone without saying anything since he had obtained the power of speech as a toddler.

But before James could follow up on some of the story's very remarkable features—which was something that he clearly wanted to do in the worst way—they were interrupted by a sharp exclamation from Marlon: "Aiyaa!"

It was the first time since all of this had begun that Marlon had expressed even mild concern about anything. But this was more than that: it was a pang of dismay. He had taken both hands off the keyboard—a completely unprecedented lapse—and clapped them to the sides of his head, and was staring at the screen in astonishment.

His face was illuminated by flickering white light.

"James" was on his feet. He ran around to where he could see the screen. "Holy crap," he exclaimed. "This could only be one spell. But I don't think it's ever been used before."

"One time," Marlon said, "it was used to kill a whole dynasty of Titans."

"Who used it?"

"Egdod."

"I'm going to Yank you," said James, running over toward the terminal where his T'Rain session was still open.

"I have wards and spoilers in effect," Marlon warned him. "You can't Yank me."

"Turn them all off and let me do it. My name is Thorakks."

By now Csongor and Yuxia had edged into the space vacated, moments earlier, by James, and were looking over Marlon's shoulder. Marlon had pushed all the little chat windows and status displays to the periphery of his screen, so they were seeing the world of T'Rain over the shoulder of Reamde, which was to say that they were now looking over two shoulders, Marlon's and the Troll's. The latter was standing on open ground in the floodplain of a river, with the tail end of a mountain range visible on the right, giving way to rolling bottomlands tiled with green fields and speckled with villages. He had, in other words, almost made it out of the Torgai Foothills and seemed to be well on his way to reaching some inhabited place where amenities such as moneychangers and ley line intersections could be found. Csongor, who by now had learned how to make sense of the user interface, observed that Reamde was carrying on his person 9 pieces of Indigold, 767 pieces of Blue Gold, 32,198 pieces of Red Gold, and 198,564 of plain old yellow gold pieces: numbers that boggled the T'Rainian mind, since even a few hundred pieces of yellow gold was rated a considerable fortune and well worth fighting over. This absolutely had to be the largest amount of money ever carried by a single T'Rain character at one time. At a quick calculation it was well over a million dollars in real money, probably closer to two million.

Accordingly, Reamde was surrounded by a phalanx of other characters, too numerous for Csongor to count or even to see. The entire formation was marching across the plain as a bloc, so tightly coordinated in its maneuvers that Csongor reckoned they must all be linked together by some sort of computer algorithm; the other players must have slaved their characters to Reamde's movements and taken their hands from the controls, allowing Marlon to drive the entire formation.

These things alone—the vast amount of money in play, the colossal size of the formation—would have absorbed the attention of even the most experienced and hard-core T'Rain player. And yet the scene was visually dominated by something even huger and more attention-getting: an incoming comet. At its core it was as bright as the screen of Marlon's computer was capable of shining, and its brilliance was lighting up all that faced it with ghastly white brilliance while casting everything else into impenetrable shadow. An interesting psychological phenomenon kicked in here, having to do with perception of light and color. They were looking at a monitor screen in a dimly illuminated room. The monitor was a tray of black plastic with some fluorescent tubes in its back and a window covering its front. The window was etched with a few million microscopic light valves, made of liquid crystals, that could be turned on or off, or to various gradations in between. If every single one of those valves was opened up to let 100 percent of the light through, then they would simply be looking at a tray with some fluorescent tubes in the back, and it wouldn't be all that bright. It would be like staring up at a light fixture in the ceiling of an office: certainly an ample amount of illumination, but nothing compared to the amount of light that the sun shed on the ground, even on the most heavily overcast day. Anyone walking indoors and staring at that tray of light going full blast would not perceive it as bright. They might not even be able to tell whether it was turned on.

And yet Marlon and Csongor and Yuxia were all squinting and averting their gazes and even holding up hands to shield their retinas from the light of the imaginary comet being depicted on the screen of this computer monitor. They perceived it as intolerably bright. Admittedly, this was partly because they were in a dark room and so their pupils were dilated. But beyond that, there was a psychological factor at work. They had been habituated to avert their gaze from extremely bright objects that did what the light in this fictional scene was doing, that is, shining out of the sky and casting deep shadows on the ground, and these instincts were kicking in as the comet drew closer. Moreover, the subwoofer attached to Marlon's computer had gone into some kind of serious overdrive and was causing visible nervousness among the porn-watching clientele of the café, who had probably been warned that there were lots of earthquakes, volcanic eruptions, and tsunamis in the Philippines. One of them even jumped up from his monitor and made a run for the door, fearing he might in the next moment be buried in a lahar. Csongor, snapping out of suspended-disbelief mode, stepped forward and twiddled a knob on the speaker, cutting the bass to a more manageable level.

This made it possible to hear James, who was hollering from across the café: "Dude. It is Comet Rider. And it is targeted on your ass. You are going to die. Let me Yank you."

Marlon's hands flickered like firelight over the keyboard, changing some of the interface settings. Csongor was familiar with what he was doing, since he'd been forced to learn similar tricks in order to perceive all the warding spells that were permanently installed around the trading pit at the Carthinias Exchange. These suddenly became visible—though badly washed out by comet-light—around Reamde and his phalanx: at least a dozen concentric layers of colored force fields, some dome shaped, some conical, some open-topped cylinders, all depicted in different hues and shimmering with various textures. Spells for turning aside projectile weapons, for stopping magical fireballs, for making hidden characters visible, and for inflicting damage automatically on any foes who tried to penetrate to the center.

And for preventing the beneficiary from being Yanked. Yanking was a spell, normally used with hostile intent, that abducted the target character and sucked him across space at unthinkable velocity and deposited him at the feet of the spell caster.

Marlon began bringing down the curtains of protective spells. In doing so, he was exposing himself and the members of his army to attack; but his army was dissolving anyway, fleeing on a menagerie of winged, four-footed, and six-footed mounts, magic carpets, numinous motorcycles, and magical currents of air, trying to put as much space as possible between themselves and him upon whom the comet was unmistakably crosshaired.

Just as the screen was going completely white and the subwoofer trying to turn itself inside out, a translucent image of Thorakks appeared square in the middle, reaching toward him with one gloved and mailed fist. The screen became considerably darker, and they were treated to an animation that made it seem as though they were being vomited up an esophagus of eerily colored smoke and twining tendrils.

And then they were on a rocky ledge on the side of a mountain somewhere, looking at Thorakks, who was lit up a blinding white on one side and completely black on the other.

Marlon spun the point of view around so that they were looking in the same direction as Thorakks, that is, into the valley below them. A fireball the size of Staten Island was just that second slamming into the ground. Marlon had to turn the subwoofer totally off.

They stood there for a minute or so just to enjoy the spectacle: a shock wave spreading out from the middle like a ripple in a pond, eventually freezing to create the rim of a crater. Columns of steam rising up from the vaporized river. Rocks and trees raining down (both Thorakks and Reamde cast warding spells to keep from getting crushed by falling debris). The vast bubble of light and smoke gradually focusing into a column, the column resolving into a bipedal figure: a man with a long white beard, gazing about the crater somewhat in the manner of someone who has just turned on the light in his pantry and is looking for cockroaches. For—as Csongor now understood—this being had literally rode in on the comet, like a child descending a hill on a trash can lid.

"Egdod," Marlon said in an interesting combination of reverence, disbelief, and pants-pissing fear.

"Never thought I'd see him in-game," said James indistinctly from across the room. A moment later the words were repeated, in a harsh metallic voice, and with a different accent, by Thorakks.

Marlon was busy invoking new spells, trying to rebuild the defenses he had shut down in order to allow himself to be Yanked and trying, Csongor suspected, to make himself invisible. Noting this, Thorakks said, with mild amusement: "Seriously? You're going to put up a fight?"

"Yes."

"You're going to go on the lam from Egdod."

"I have no choice."

"Do you know who his player is?"

"Of course I know."

"Do you know he's the uncle of your friend Zula?"

Marlon froze for a moment, and Csongor imagined that, in Marlon's mind's eye, he was seeing the image he had described to them during the voyage: a moment, just after Ivanov had been shot and Csongor knocked out, when Zula's face had met Marlon's through a dirty windowpane, and their eyes had connected for a few moments.

Then his eyes refocused on the screen.

"I will talk to the uncle of Zula when I have the money," Marlon said, "and have given it to my friends. Their home has been exploded and they are running from the police and from everyone else, and they are depending on me to finish this."

"Then let's haul ass," James suggested.

Marlon poised his fingers on the keyboard, then glanced up at Csongor. "Are you ready?"

"I will be," Csongor said, "by the time you get there."

"HEY, BIGFOOT," CORVALLIS said. "You are rearranging the planet faster than our servers can update the caches."

"It's good for you," Richard muttered. "Call it a stress test and get on with it."

"It doesn't help that you're doing it at one in the morning when most of our senior staff are asleep."

"It's Saturday. They're partying. What do you think phones are for?"

"I'll try to reach them but—"

"Before you do that, tell me where the little fucker is."

"So he's back to being a little fucker now?"

"There are a lot of crushed and incinerated remains underfoot . . . but he should have survived . . . I cast a protective ward on him immediately before impact."

After a lot of typing, C-plus answered: "He's not there. He got Yanked just in time by one Thorakks. I can give you general coordinates, but they are moving fast and the database is going to lag."

"Just give me a place to start tracking them," said Richard, sounding more and more like Egdod himself with every moment. "No, scratch that."

"Come again?"

"They have to be heading for an LLI," Richard said, using the in-game jargon for ley line intersection. "There's only one place they can move this amount of gold."

AS LONG AS Zula kept herself busy cleaning up the aftermath of dinner, she was able to avoid thinking about keys and padlocks. They had eaten the food from disposable plastic plates, which she collected and stacked, scraping any residue into a garbage bag. She placed the stack of scraped plates into a second garbage bag. The cooking pots she washed using water that she heated up on the camp stove. She left those out to dry. The chain, naturally, confined her to a circular area, and she'd already made up her mind that she would sleep as far away as possible from where she put the garbage, in case it drew vermin or worse. For now, she placed the garbage bags—which were not yet very bulky—into a cooler, just to keep them safe from small critters such as mice. She considered explaining to the men that they should hang their food from tree limbs, then thought better of it. Instead she dragged the cooler as far as she could go in the direction of the tents where the men were sleeping and left it there. Let them deal with the local wildlife. At worst it would give her some entertainment; at best it might cover her escape. Moving as far as she could go in the opposite direction, 180 degrees around the circle from the food dump, she began to arrange her own little campsite. This consisted of a tiny one-person camp shelter, just large enough to house a sleeping bag.

They hadn't said anything about toilet facilities. As far as she could make out, they were just wandering off into the woods when they needed to eliminate. Does a terrorist shit in the woods? Apparently. But Zula did not have that option. They had equipped her with a large steel serving spoon. She went to a place at the end of her chain, equidistant from the garbage place and the sleeping place, and used the spoon to dig out a shallow pit. The going was easy at first, but then she came to a depth, only a few inches below the surface, where interlocking roots of trees and shrubs made it impossible to go any deeper. She stood above it and wrapped a green plastic tarp around herself for privacy, then dropped her pants and squatted over it, creating a little tent lit up on the inside by her flashlight. She hunched her shoulders and drew the tarp over her head so that she could see what she was doing. The pill of damp cotton came out first, and she was able to pluck it clear before the rest came. When she was finished, she pulled the key out and placed it in a zippered pocket on the leg of her trousers before standing up, getting fully reclothed, and tossing the tarp to one side. Then she used the shovel to fill the hole back in and kicked some more loose pine needles and pebbles over the top for good measure. The men had all long since gone into their tents, the only exception being the sniper Jahandar, who had retreated up into the trees after dinner to, she assumed, keep watch while the others slept. Since Zula was the only person moving in the camp, she had to assume that he was watching her. If so, he was seeing her as a little blob of light bobbing around and tending to chores. After she had finished going to the toilet, she kicked off her Crocs—still the only footwear she was allowed to have—and climbed into her sleeping bag fully clothed and zipped the tiny tent closed, except for a gap down at the bottom where the chain emerged.

She lay there for several minutes just listening. Wondering whether Jahandar or one of the other men might bother to come and check on her. But nothing happened. She could hear Jahandar moving occasionally, but he was just shifting his position, standing up to stretch his legs, pacing around, stretching.

Moving as quietly as she could, she slid a hand down to the side of her thigh, slowly worried the pocket's zipper open, found the key with her fingers, and drew it out. She brought it up to her neck, wrapped one hand around the padlock to muffle any mechanical clicking noises that might come out of it, and got the key inserted. The padlock snicked open, and she felt the chain go slack around her throat. Not exactly a surprise; but one of her nightmares had been that for some reason it would fail to work.

It was a mistake, in a way, to have done this. For now she was overcome by an almost physical longing to squirm out of this sleeping bag and make a run for it.

She seriously considered it until, far off in the darkness, she heard the hiss and snick of a lighter, Jahandar's lungs filling with cigarette smoke.

If she got out, went to the end of the chain as if she had to use the toilet again, and then suddenly made a run for it, would he be able to put a bullet in her before she had vanished into the trees? As he sat up there on his perch, was he keeping her in his crosshairs the whole time or just hanging out with the rifle across his lap, keeping casual watch over the camp?

It seemed unlikely that he would be able to plug her on the first pull of the trigger, given that it was dark and that he would be surprised. But the mere fact that he *might* do so focused her attention. Even if he missed, he would wake the entire camp, and then thirteen men with flashlights and guns and good boots would be pursuing her. At least some of them were experienced in hunting and mountaineering. She'd have the choice between remaining still, in which case they could catch up with her and surround her, or moving, in which case she would make obvious crashing and twig-snapping noises.

From nearby, the sound of a long zipper, somewhat muffled. A sleeping bag, she guessed. Then a second long zipper, sharper. A tent being opened. The swish of someone sliding out of his bag. Probably going to take a leak. Footsteps. Someone made himself comfortable on a camp chair. Some plasticky clicking noises and then the whooshy, saccharine jingle made by Windows as it was booting up.

She rolled onto her stomach, propped herself up on her elbows, and opened the tent zipper a minute amount, worrying the pull upward one tooth at a time so as not to make noise. Peering out through the hole just made, she saw Jones, sitting in the camp chair about thirty feet away, his face ghastly in the light of the laptop's screen. He screwed himself around in his chair, thrust out a leg, got a hand into a hip pocket, and pulled out something tiny which he inserted into the side of the machine: a thumb drive. And then he went to work.

Had he not been right there, wide awake, with a pistol strapped into his armpit, this would have been the most difficult decision in her life. As it was, she had little choice: she snapped the padlock shut again. Then she replaced the key in her pocket and zipped it securely closed.

Despair would have been reasonable. But she reminded herself, again and again, that they could not, all of them, remain together in this camp indefinitely. Most of them would soon be leaving, with only a skeleton crew to keep an eye on Zula, and then her odds would go up accordingly. Jahandar could not be expected to stay up all night, every night, keeping watch over the camp. Sooner or later Zakir's turn would come up, and Zakir would fall asleep immediately.

So she tried to rest. Sleep did not seem realistic, but she could at least lie still and give her body an opportunity to relax muscles, digest food, and store energy.

She must have dozed off, since she was awakened by a tinny Arabic pop song coming from someone's phone: an alarm, not an incoming call. There was no way for her to judge time, but it was definitely still dark and she didn't feel that she had been out for very long. She heard shifting around from one of the tents and low voices.

Peering out through her spyhole, she saw Jones exactly as before. But now pools of light were bobbing and veering across the ground as Ershut and the white American Abdul-Ghaffar—emerged from one of the tents. Sharjeel crawled out from another and scurried over to Jones to suck up to him some more, but Jones, deeply involved in whatever he was doing, told him to bugger off. Gradually they formed a little circle on the ground, anchored by Jones looming above them as on a throne. Occasionally they shone their flashlights across her tent, and she had to resist the temptation to flinch away. There was no way that they could possibly see her through this tiny crevice in the zipper. They gathered around the stove, only a few yards from her tent, and began banging pots. She felt an absolutely ridiculous flash of annoyance that they were somehow invading her territory, making a mess of her kitchen. Strange how the mind worked. They filled a pot with water, lit the stove, began making tea, snacking on bananas from a grocery bag.

After everyone had come fully awake, Jones began to talk, saying everything in English and Arabic so that Abdul-Ghaffar could understand it. Sharjeel was another whose Arabic could use some improvement. But Jahandar spoke nothing but Pashtun and Arabic, so the conversation had to be bilingual.

Actually it was not a conversation so much as a briefing.

"It's 3:30," Jones said. "We'll be under way in moments. I estimate half an hour to get there, half an hour to reconnoiter the place and get in and show him this." He yanked the thumb drive out, held it up as if they could all see what was on it, then put it into the breast pocket of his shirt and smoothed a Velcro flap over it. "Then he'll have to pack some items, I should imagine, which might take another half an hour, and then another half hour to get to the rendezvous point below. So figure we meet there at 5:30 and get under way. Sharjeel, give the men another hour to sleep. Wake her up at 4:00 so that when you rouse the men at 4:30, water will be hot and breakfast ready. That's time for eating, for morning prayers, and for packing. Jahandar and Ershut will, *inshallah*, come up here at around 5:30 to let you know that we are ready to go; when you see them, lead the rest of the expedition down to the trail. Ershut, we may need to display her."

A minute later Jones, Abdul-Ghaffar, Ershut, and Jahandar got up and walked away into the woods, headed downhill into the mining complex, leaving Sharjeel the only one keeping watch over the camp. Zula was tempted to make a run for it then. But then she'd be bracketed between the aroused camp and Jones's contingent. Not a good situation. After five thirty, though, most of these men would be gone for good, leaving her with only four guards, two of whom were incompetent. That would be the time to make a break for it.

To be precise, she needed to make her break during the interval between five thirty and whenever it was that they were supposed to kill her. No schedule had been set for that yet, or if it had, they'd been discreet enough to do it out of her hearing.

Even if they intended to keep her alive indefinitely, she had an obligation to get free as soon as possible. After the jet crash, with Jones's gun in her face, she'd blurted out the one thing she could think of that might keep her alive. And she didn't imagine that Richard or anyone else in the family would fault her for it. But soon, as consequence, Richard was going to be in their power; and if he ended up taking Jones down his usual pathway into northern Idaho, it would lead them straight to the cabin where Uncle Jake and his family lived. She was obligated to do whatever she could to help them out of the mess she'd put them in.

To bears, she added boots as something to be thinking about. Zakir was a big lumbering man, but Sayed the graduate student was a good inch shorter than Zula. She made up her mind to have a look at what was on his feet the next time he emerged from his tent.

. . . .

LOTTERY DISCOUNTZ HAD now spent enough time loitering just above the lower reaches of the trading pit to give his owner a loose understanding of how it all worked. He'd been foxed, at first, by the fact that T'Rain was wired for sound. The easiest way to communicate with characters in one's immediate vicinity was simply to talk. But there was, in addition, an old-school chat interface. You could type little messages, like the Internet pioneers of yore, and they would appear in scrolling windows on the screens of anyone who was listening. It was plainly the case that Marlon and the rest of the da G shou couldn't live without it. So the next time Csongor focused his attention on the money-trading pit, he experimented with turning on the chat interface. For one thing he'd noticed about the place was that, for a trading pit, it was strangely quiet. It was *visually* loud, and ridiculously active, but almost no one was speaking.

It all became clear when he interrogated the chat interface and discovered that there were no fewer than a dozen discrete channels to which he could listen here. Doing so, he was treated to waterfalls of jargon-laden statements in as many separate windows.

Snarph: WTS RG 50 BUX PP NOW

Opening a browser window atop his view of the game, he did some googling and learned how to translate such utterances: "WTS" meant "want to sell," "RG 50" meant that the quantity for sale amounted to fifty or so pieces of Red Gold, "BUX" meant that Snarph's player wanted American dollars (other commonly seen options being "EUR," "LBS," "YEN," and "RMB"), "PP" meant that he wanted to clear the transaction using PayPal, and "NOW" meant the obvious.

Working laboriously from a translation key that he found on a wiki, he typed in

Lottery Discountz: WTS IG XX BUX WU 1HR

Which meant "I wish to exchange a yet-to-be-divulged amount of Indigold for dollars in about one hour, settling the transaction by means of a Western Union wire transfer."

But he did not hit the return key, which would have broadcast the message to all the heavy-hitter gold buyers in the deepest recess of the pit—the channel into which he'd been typing. He, a complete nobody, was proposing to launch a transaction worth (at least) hundreds of thousands of dollars, using Indigold pieces that he did not actually have in hand yet. He had already seen other would-be sellers, making much less unusual propositions, being hounded down as mere mischief makers and slain on the spot. Worse yet—since death, in T'Rain, was only a temporary inconvenience—he might get exiled permanently.

So he waited and watched. Because there was an alternative to broadcasting on a channel: you could send the message privately to a specific individual. He only needed to find the right one. And now that he had discovered the chat interface and broken its code, he was beginning to feel he had some plausible hope of doing so. To begin with, he could ignore all the channels except the ones used by the highest of high rollers. Once he had closed all those windows, he began to look for lines that had the right sorts of codes in them. A particularly appealing one being

Dogshaker: WTB IG 2 EUR WU NOW

By mousing over the characters in his field of view, Csongor was able to identify this Dogshaker, a distinguished-looking K'Shetriae merchant in gleaming purple robes—perhaps a fashion statement intended to emphasize the fact that he dealt in the ultra-high-value Indigo coins. After a minute or so, this Dogshaker was approached by another character who apparently had Indigold to sell, and it became plain from their body language that they were whispering to each other. This meant that they had established a private chat channel and were now using it to negotiate terms. The negotiation appeared to stretch out over several minutes, which made Csongor somewhat anxious. But in due time they shook hands with each other and went their separate ways, the seller climbing up out of the pit and wandering off while the buyer remained where he was.

All of this reconnaissance had consumed a considerable amount of time, during which Marlon and James had been shouting at each other almost nonstop across the café, apparently helping each other negotiate some incredibly challenging set of obstacles, ambushes, and setbacks. Their epic adventure seemed to have driven away business at first, as the sword-and-sorcery-themed quest seemed to have destroyed the erotic ambience being sought by the mongers. Csongor had been a bit concerned that they might be thrown out of the establishment. But Yuxia had been at work distracting the proprietor, not so much by charming as by confusing him. When that began to wear thin, she had moved on to plucking money out of James's wallet and purchasing "LDs"—Lady Drinks—shockingly overpriced beverages that were apparently the fiscal mainspring of the local hospitality industry. Thus Marlon and James had been left free to prosecute their virtual adventure. But of late there had been a lull, and when Csongor finally pulled his head out of the game for a moment to ask why, James informed him that they had fought their way to a ley line intersection and were even now in transit to Carthinias.

Now or never. Csongor created a new chat window, an invitation to set up a private conversation between Lottery Discountz and Dogshaker.

"How many Indigo do you have?" he called out.

"Twenty," Marlon answered.

Lottery Discountz: WTS IG 20 BUX WUWT NOW

After a few moments' pause, he saw a response:

Dogshaker: WHERE HAVE YOU BEEN ALL MY LIFE.

Csongor, a bit nonplussed, typed back,

Lottery Discountz: The pleasure is mutual.

Dogshaker: You don't have it on you.

Lottery Discountz: My friend is bringing it.

Dogshaker: But your message said NOW.

Lottery Discountz: They are coming on LLI at this moment.

Dogshaker: They have muscle? Tempting robbery targets.

Lottery Discountz: Some. Maybe not enough.

Dogshaker: Which LLI are they coming to?

(For one of the reasons the Carthinias Exchange stood where it did was that it was within a couple of thousand meters of not just one but four major ley line intersections.)

Csongor repeated the question aloud.

"Who wants to know?" asked James.

"A possible buyer."

"He wants to rob us," Marlon said.

"He seems respectable. He's doing big transactions in the Exchange. He's worried you're going to get ripped off."

"So am I," said James.

"Me too," said Marlon

In the chat window, Csongor's interlocutor was becoming impatient.

Dogshaker: Would they be coming from the Torgai Foothills by any chance?

Csongor announced, "He has guessed you're coming from the Torgai."

"Of course," James said. "These guys must all know that something big is going down there."

"Comet Rider spell is attention getter," Marlon added, perhaps for comic effect.

Dogshaker the moneychanger, apparently fed up with Lottery Discountz's coyness, began to climb up out of the amphitheater, headed (Csongor guessed) in the direction of the ley line intersection that would tend to be used by visitors from the Torgai Foothills. "He's headed for your LLI," Csongor said. "I'm following him." And he got his hands on the keyboard and sent Lottery Discountz running in pursuit.

"Does he have muscle with him?"

"No."

"What class of character is he?"

"Merchant."

"Then we're probably okay," said James, "unless he's only pretending to be a merchant." During this exchange, he had been sitting back from his keyboard, taking the advantage of a lull to stretch his arms luxuriously. Csongor guessed that nothing much happened during a ley line ride. But suddenly his eyes snapped back to the screen, and he sat forward, bringing his hands back to the keyboard. "We're sort of committed now anyway."

"You're at the LLI?"

"Just popped out," James confirmed. Csongor glanced over to see that Marlon too was once again fully engaged with his computer.

"Then I'll lead him to you." And Csongor typed into the chat window:

Lottery Discountz: Follow me, sir.

To which the moneychanger responded immediately with "K," that being the chat abbreviation for the unwieldy two-letter message "OK."

This LLI was a busy one, an area about the size and shape of a cricket oval surrounded by market stalls mostly occupied by small-time moneychangers. Upward of a hundred characters were scattered around it, some just standing there alone, others gathered in social clusters, still others engaged in duels that were frequently accompanied by spectacular magical light shows. Lottery Discountz stumbled to a halt in the middle of it and turned around several times.

Dogshaker: Is that them?

He turned to look the way Dogshaker was looking and identified Reamde and Thorakks coming their way. He replied with a Y, but Dogshaker was already running toward them. Csongor ran after. Their chat window went through some kind of reconfiguration: apparently the moneychanger had added the newcomers to the chat list, so that they could all see one another's messages. This drew Csongor's attention for a few moments. Another one of those crazy light shows flourished on the screen: some high-level character, locked in a duel, must be invoking a powerful spell.

"O M G," said Marlon out loud.

Csongor looked at the screen. The ground was dropping out from beneath Lottery Discountz's feet. Something was lifting him into the air. The others were coming with him.

James just laughed ruefully. "Oh man," he finally said, "we are so fucked."

Reamde, Thorakks, and Lottery Discountz were all together, standing on something translucent and bluish white, a platform that seemed to be about a hundred meters in the air above the ley line intersection. Csongor turned his point of view around and was startled to see a giant face glowering down at them. Utterly confused, he zoomed way out so that he could see his character from a greater distance.

He now perceived that he and Reamde and Thorakks were literally in the palm of a hand the size of a tennis court. The hand belonged to a towering, godlike figure standing like a colossus above the city of Carthinias, one foot planted at the ley line intersection, the other about a kilometer away near the Exchange.

Having gotten over his initial astonishment, Marlon was now furiously hitting keys, apparently trying to invoke various spells. Bubbles of light bloomed around his hands, but each was snuffed out by some sort of counterspell from the giant figure. Csongor finally had the presence of mind to mouse over the giant's head and learned that this was a character named Egdod.

"Asshole," Egdod proclaimed in a voice that once again obliged all three players to grope in panic for their volume knobs, "I could just kill you and take the gold—if that was what I wanted."

Marlon sat back in despair and clapped his hands to the side of his head.

"Let's go somewhere a little more private," Egdod continued, and Csongor noticed that cloud formations were zipping past them, moving downward. He shifted his point of view down and saw that Carthinias was dropping away beneath Egdod's sandaled feet. He was taking them up into the air like a Saturn V. Lottery Discountz's health indicators were dropping at least as rapidly as their altitude was rising: hypoxia and hypothermia, as it turned out, being the main culprits. But then he noted that spells were being cast on him—and presumably the others too—such as "Heavenly Warmth" and "Breath of the Gods," and his indicators began to climb again.

"Aiyaa!" Marlon exclaimed, having moved his hands around to cover his face altogether.

"Let me hear your voices," Egdod commanded.

James, Csongor, and Marlon all reached for their headsets and slipped them on. Meanwhile, Egdod was explaining: "I'll go through with the transaction just as I said. But first I want to hear everything you know about Zula."

"I know nothing," James announced, and a moment later Thorakks said the same thing in a different voice.

"I'll deal with you later, Seamus Costello!" Egdod thundered.

Csongor, Marlon, and Yuxia all turned to look at "James," who was blushing vividly.

Marlon knew more than Seamus, but he was still too taken aback—and perhaps exhausted—to speak coherently. He looked across the café at Csongor.

"Okay," Csongor said. "The story so far." And he launched into an account of what had transpired in Xiamen two weeks ago. Richard Forthrast (for Csongor had googled Egdod and learned that the owner of this godlike character was none other) knew a surprising amount about the safe house that Ivanov had set up in Xiamen and about the cast of characters. Csongor couldn't guess how he might have come by that information and did not want to interrupt the narrative to ask. Until, that is, Richard said, "You must be the Eastern European hacker."

"We think of ourselves as Central European," said Csongor. "How did you know of me?"

"Zula mentioned you in her note."

This silenced Csongor for long enough that Seamus had to break in and explain, "We're still on the line, big guy . . . he's just taking that in."

"You have heard from Zula!?" Csongor finally exclaimed, exchanging a wild look with Marlon and Yuxia.

"She wrote a note," Richard said regretfully, "before it all went down. Nothing since then, unfortunately."

Having allowed his hopes to rise, Csongor had now to observe another silence as his spirits plunged. He looked up to see Seamus giving him a knowing look. "Well then," Csongor finally said, and he went on to relate a brief account of the storming of the apartment building, Zula's trick with the fusebox, and how that had all played out.

Richard listened in silence until a certain point in the story when he said, "So Peter is dead."

"Yes," Csongor said gently.

"You're sure of this."

"Absolutely sure."

"Well, that is a shame," Richard said, "and sooner or later I'll get around to feeling like crap about it. But right now—focusing on practical matters—it is a problem for me because it prevents me from pursuing the only independent lead I have."

"What lead is that?" Seamus demanded.

"Peter had surveillance cameras in his apartment. They probably recorded video of what went down there the night Wallace was killed and Peter and Zula were abducted. Unfortunately, those files were erased. Later, though, someone came back—probably an accomplice to the original crime—and got caught on video. I have a copy of the file. Unfortunately, it's encrypted. I was hoping I could get the decryption key. But if Peter's dead—"

"Hold on for a moment," Csongor said. For Ivanov's leather man-purse was sitting on the floor between his feet. The money had been stolen from it, but Peter's and Zula's wallets and other personal effects were still in there, sealed up in Ziploc bags. In a few moments, he was able to get Peter's wallet out and find a certain compartment, sealed behind a tiny zipper, with a scrap of paper inside.

Something moved on the screen, and he noted that they had been joined by another character named Clover—apparently an invited guest of Egdod's.

Five lines had been written on the paper. Each began with what was apparently the name of a computer and ended with what was obviously a password.

"Do you have a hostname or something for the system you are trying to crack?"

Clover answered: "This was not a server per se, just a backup drive on a network."

"Brand name Li-Fi, by any chance?"

"The same."

"Then here is the password," Csongor announced and read out the corresponding series of symbols.

"On it," said Clover, and then became still, a sure sign that its owner—whoever he was—was tending to something other than playing T'Rain.

"Pray continue," Richard said, and so Csongor went on telling the story. He got some assistance now from Marlon, who was able to relate parts of it that Csongor had not seen or during which he had been unconscious. But just as they were trying to explain the explosion, and Marlon's rescue of Csongor from the cellar, Clover woke up and interrupted: "That was the correct password. I was able to decrypt the file."

"Can you email it to me?" Richard asked. From which Csongor inferred that Richard and whoever was playing Clover were not in the same place.

"I did it on your server," Clover answered. "The files were already there. All I had to do was send the command."

He rattled off the name of a directory.

Csongor and Marlon now resumed the narrative, a bit uncertainly as they sensed that they no longer had Richard's full attention. This suspicion was borne out a few minutes later when Richard broke in: "I can see him." His voice was husky and he spoke slowly, as if mildly stunned. "This guy finds a way to break in. I can't hear anything—it's all just body language—but let me tell you that I have hired a lot of guys in my time, and this guy is a schlub. A palooka. An epsilon minus."

Csongor did not know the meaning of any of these terms, but Richard's tone of voice was easy enough to read.

"I was half hoping it might have been Sokolov," Richard explained. "But I guess that's impossible—you guys were all in Xiamen by this point. A day later he goes missing off Kinmen."

Csongor looked at Marlon and Yuxia, who both threw up their hands. "You think Sokolov survived the explosion?" he asked.

"We know he did," Seamus announced.

"That is hard to believe," Yuxia said. "If you had been there—"

"We have the most direct and convincing possible testimony that he lived through it," Seamus assured her, with a little wiggle of the eyebrows that made Yuxia blush.

"Sokolov is still alive," Csongor repeated, trying to make himself believe it.

"I didn't say that," Richard put in. "He was involved in a gun-fight off Kinmen the next day."

"Let me tell you something," Csongor said. "If he was in a gun-fight, I am more worried about the people he was fighting against." This drew an approving look and a nod from Seamus.

Richard continued, "The palooka comes in the front door car-rying a piece of equipment that, based on other research I've been doing, matches the description of a plasma torch. He takes it upstairs and sets it up next to Peter's gun safe and runs a huge extension cord down the stairs to Peter's shop where he plugs it into a big-ass indus-trial outlet."

"Gun safe?" Csongor asked wonderingly.

"Not from around here, are you?" Richard asked. "Believe it or not, they are as common in the Land of the Free and Home of the Brave as, let's say, bidets are in France. Anyway, the picture now gets completely fucked up as this guy turns on the torch and slices the safe open. Just takes the top right off. Fast-forwarding here—I think he's waiting for the metal to cool down. Then he reaches into the top and pulls out—oh, for goodness' sake. Who knew that our Peter was a gun nut?"

"What are you seeing?" Seamus asked.

"A nice metal case. Inside of it, a really tricked-out AR-15," Richard said, and then he rattled off a lot of verbiage that seemed significant to him and to Seamus but meant nothing to Csongor: "Picatinny rails on all four sides, mounted with Swarovski optics and what might be a laser sight. Tac light. Tactical bipod. Yes, what-ever other shortcomings he might have had, Peter was very good at adding items to his shopping cart."

"So this goon must have noticed the gun safe during the snatch and made up his mind to come back later and see what was inside."

"If so, he hit the jackpot. I'm looking at probably four thousand bucks' worth of rifle. Want to see a picture?"

"Sure."

There was a brief interlude for clicking and typing, and then Seamus said, "Got it," and began paying attention to something on his screen. Csongor, having nothing else to do at the moment, got up and walked around behind him to see what it was. Evidently T'Rain contained some sort of facility for mailing image files back and forth, and Egdod had used it to send this JPEG to Thorakks. It was a surprisingly well-resolved picture of a bulky man with a shaved head, holding an assault rifle, sans clip, and examining his action. "Not my cup of tea," Seamus said after inspecting it for a little while, "but I concur that Peter was a gun nut and that Mr. Potatohead is feeling very pleased with himself at the time this picture is taken."

"Do you recognize him?" Richard asked.

Csongor was obliged to return to his post and put his headset back on. "No," he said. "In none of my dealings with Ivanov, in Xiamen or otherwise, did I ever see this man."

"He's a local freelancer, Richard," Seamus pronounced. "A temp."

"Maybe I'll send the picture to the Seattle cops, then," Richard said. "Help them clear up some loose ends."

"Save yourself the trouble," said Seamus. "I can get it to the cops, and then some. But it's not going to help finding Zula now."

"I know that," Richard said.

And then there was silence for a few moments. Csongor was unwilling to admit this to himself, but, although the last couple of hours' machinations in T'Rain had been diverting, and the opportunity to exchange information with Richard had felt, for a few minutes, like an enormous breakthrough, it was all turning out to be a dead end. The most it might lead to was that Mr. Potatohead would be arrested, and the story of Zula and Peter's abduction, and Wallace's murder, would be explained to the satisfaction of the Seattle Police Department. But none of this would be of any help in finding Zula now or in stopping Jones.

Richard seemed to be reaching the same conclusion. "Interesting," he finally said, "but all kind of useless."

Seamus was ready for it. "You don't know that," he said. "The way it works is, you follow these leads and you work them until something breaks. Everything we have done here is extremely constructive whether or not you can see a way through to the end."

"All I know is, I've been sitting on my ass for close to twenty-four hours," said Richard, now sounding as bad as Csongor felt. "Thinking, hoping, you guys would know where Zula is. Now it's something like four, five in the morning, I'm at the end of my tether, we have come up with nothing very useful. And some asshole tourist is knocking on my door, probably wanting to empty his holding tank or get directions to the geocaching site. So I'm going to break off for a little."

And indeed Csongor now noticed that the clouds were rushing up past them and the city of Carthinias growing larger and larger as they plummeted toward it. Presently they came to a soft landing exactly where they had started, and Egdod shrank to human size.

"The money?" Marlon asked. "Not for me—for my friends in China."

"Clover will see about making the da G shou whole," Richard said, "at competitive rates. Good luck getting the money into China." As he spoke, it was possible to hear a doorbell ringing in the background. The sound radiated incongruously over downtown Carthinias.

RICHARD STRIPPED OFF his headset and threw the keyboard off his lap, leaving Egdod mute and motionless for the time being. He reached down between his knees and found the pee bucket with his hand, then moved it well out of the way so he wouldn't kick it over. He stood up slowly, partly because his body had stiffened up and partly because he didn't want all the blood to rush out of his brain at once. He checked the time: 4:42 A.M. Who the hell was ringing his doorbell? In addition to which they had been pounding the hell out of every door and window they could find for the last couple of minutes. All the signs pointed to some sort of minor emergency: drunken teenaged mountain bikers who had flipped over their handlebars, or campers chased out of their tents by bears, or an RV gone off the road. It happened a few times a year, though rarely so early in the season.

He shambled out of the tavern and into the lobby, moving awkwardly, trying to make out if all of that had been worth it. From Zula's paper towel note he had already known the first part of the story, and from British Spy Chick he'd learned some of the last bit. So all that he'd gained from nearly twenty-four hours' solid game playing was a picture of some asshole stealing Peter's rifle, more detail about what had happened in that apartment building in Xiamen, and a very large quantity of Indigold.

Overall, he decided that it had been worth it. He knew a great deal more now of how Zula had comported herself during the apartment building showdown and in the hours afterward, and all of it made him proud and would make the rest of the family proud when it went up on the Facebook page and when, in future years, they retold the story at the re-u. And that was all true whether Zula was alive or, as seemed likely, dead.

"All right already," he shouted. He approached the main entrance and hit a switch that turned on the lights in the driveway.

Two men were standing there, sort of wrapped around each other. They looked like backpackers. One of them, a burly middle-aged man, was supporting a taller fellow who was all bundled up in warm clothes with a hood pulled up over his head. The latter's leg was encased, from the knee down, in a splint that had been improvised from tree branches, duct tape, and climbing rope. His head was bowed as if he were only semiconscious or perhaps doubled over in pain.

Nothing Richard hadn't seen before. He unlocked the front door and pulled it open.

"Thank God you're here, Mr. Forthrast!" the man exclaimed, very loudly, as if he wished to be heard by someone else—someone who was not standing directly in front of him.

The lights went out.

The injured man, who until this moment had been draped over his comrade's shoulders, stood up straight and took his full weight evenly on both feet.

Richard by now knew that something funny was going on but was too fuzzy-headed from sleep deprivation and T'Rain playing to do anything other than watch it play out before him like a cut scene in a video game. The tall man reached up and stripped the hood away from his face. But Richard could not see much of him because of the darkness.

"Good morning, Richard," he said. His voice sounded like that of a black man, but his accent told that he was not from around here. His companion had unzipped his jacket and pulled something out. Richard heard the sound of a round being chambered into a semiautomatic pistol. This man backed up a pace and aimed it at Richard's face. Richard flinched. In all the time he had spent messing around with guns, he'd never had one aimed at him before.

"You'd be Jones?" Richard said.

"That I would. May we come inside? I've been tracking your website—the one that keeps asking whether anyone has seen Zula—and I've come to give you news and claim the reward."

"Is she alive?"

"Not only is she alive, Richard, but you have the power to keep her that way."

"WELL, THAT HAPPENED," Seamus announced. He crossed his arms over his chest and used his legs to shove his chair back from the computer.

Csongor had already logged out. Never again, he suspected, would Lottery Discountz walk the streets of Carthinias. Marlon was still engaged, typing chat messages—apparently aimed at the character called Clover, who seemed to be Egdod's bagman. On his screen it was possible to see Clover and Reamde standing so close that their heads were almost touching. Thorakks loitered a few meters away and Egdod—suddenly poignant in his smallness and aloneness—just stood there.

Yuxia was perched on a counter near Seamus. "What's next for you guys?" the latter asked. Grammatically, the question was aimed at all of them, but he was looking at Yuxia when he asked it.

Which was just as well since Csongor hadn't the faintest idea how to answer it. Apparently they were going to get some money now. At least enough to buy an airplane ticket. But to where? And could Csongor even get *out* of this country legally? The last stamp in his passport was from Sheremetyevo Airport, Moscow. Since then he'd entered and left China illegally and sneaked into the Philippines. He might be wanted for God only knew what sorts of crimes in China. Did the Philippines have an extradition treaty with China? Did Hungary?

He could only brood and worry and listen to Yuxia giving Seamus the third degree. "Who the heck are you?"

"I already told you," he said innocently.

"A cop? A spy?"

"I'm a sex tourist."

Yuxia laughed in his face. "You would have to travel much farther," she said, "to find someone willing to do it with you."

This seemed to Csongor shockingly rude, and his head swiveled around just to be sure that such words had actually come from Qian Yuxia's mouth. They had.

And Seamus was eating it with a spoon. "Okay. Not a sex tourist."

"Why do you ask what is next for us?"

"Oh, I just feel that we have established the beginnings of a friendship here, and I want to make sure you are all taken care of, that's all."

"You can take care of me," she said, "by getting me back home."

Seamus made a face. "Now, that's going to be tricky," he said. "I didn't know much about you until just now."

By "just now" he meant the conversation that had occupied much of the preceding hour, in which Csongor, assisted somewhat by his comrades, had narrated the remainder of their story.

"So? Now you know all about us," Yuxia said, trying to sound insouciant. But Csongor knew her well enough, by now, to tell when she was troubled. Her eyes wandered and her face fell.

"I know enough to charge you with a list of crimes as long as my arm, if I were a Chinese prosecutor," Seamus said. Reacting, apparently, to a look on her face, he became dismayed and held out his hands as if trying to tamp something down. "Not that they would. What do I know? All I'm saying is, think hard before you go running back to China."

"I'm not going back," Marlon scoffed. "It is my country and I love it, but I can't go back." And he returned to his money-shuffling activities.

"Mystery man," Csongor said, "what can you do to help us?"

"In the next half hour or so, not so very much," Seamus returned. "I need to make at least one phone call about our goon with the rifle. And I want to keep an eye on Egdod. He is worrying me a little. But after that, I will try to put something together. Maybe you guys can help us."

"Who is 'us' and what do you think we can help you with?"

"The good guys and killing Jones."

"I am all about killing Jones," Yuxia volunteered, holding up her hand like a little girl in school.

Csongor, raised from birth to be a little more cautious in his utterances, only took this under advisement. But he did ask, "Why are you worried about Egdod?"

"He has reverted to his bothavior."

"Which is?"

"Trying to walk home," Seamus said. "And home, for him, is, like, five thousand miles away."

"What does this mean?" Yuxia asked.

"It means that Richard Forthrast's computer crashed, or he lost his Internet connection."

"Maybe he just went to sleep," Yuxia said.

"Yes, or maybe he's having coffee with whoever was ringing his doorbell, and his computer went to sleep," said Seamus. "But in the meantime, the most powerful character in all of T'Rain is wandering around the world on autopilot."

"So what are you going to do?" Yuxia asked.

"Maybe tag along. Like escorting a drunk president home after a long night in the bar."

"Didn't you say you had to make a phone call?"

"I have been trained by the United States government," Seamus said, "to do more than one thing at a time."

"TURNABOUT IS FAIR play," said a disgustingly cheerful voice, with a South Boston accent, on the other end of the line.

Olivia groaned. "What time is it?"

"Something like five, where you are. Not that bad. Up and at 'em."

"What is happening?"

"Just a little update for you. I can't say everything I'd like to, because of where I am. But I found them, and I've been hanging out with them, and oh so much has happened in the magical world of T'Rain while you have been getting your beauty sleep."

"You *physically* found them," she said, sitting up in bed. Outside, it was still dark, and she could see the lights of downtown Vancouver out the windows of her room. "You're where they are."

"Yeah. Courtesy of the Philippine Air Force and a lot of favors that had to be called in."

"That is splendid work," she said. "I knew you were smarter than you looked and acted."

"Just as dumb as everyone thinks, actually. Just a matter of following a big fat easy lead."

"Have you had a chance to talk to them?"

"In a manner of speaking. I've heard their story. Quite a yarn. That's not important now, though."

"What *is* important now, Seamus?"

"There may be some action at your end today. Thought I'd let you know."

"In Vancouver?"

A pause. "Shit, I'm sorry, I forgot you went to Vancouver."

"So . . . the action is going to be in Seattle?"

"Maybe. As a by-product of what just happened, we got a photograph of one of Sokolov's henchmen there. A few days after the main thing went down, he went back and broke into Peter's place and stole a rifle out of a gun safe."

"What does that have to do with—"

"Nothing," he said.

"That's what I thought."

"It's a total red herring, as far as finding Jones is concerned."

"So why are you waking me up to tell me about it?"

"Because I thought you were still in Seattle, working with those FBI agents," Seamus said, "and I just wanted to let you know . . ."

" . . . that they were going to be dealing with this."

"Yes."

"That the investigation down there is going to get derailed and distracted by this red herring."

"Yeah."

"Thank you," she said. "As it happens, I'll be doing something else today, though."

"And what might that be?"

"Driving up to Prince George to look for strategically located security cameras. Begging their owners to let me see footage."

"Have fun with that."

"What's on your agenda, Seamus?"

"Figure out what to do with this traveling circus."

RELUCTANT AS SHE was to give the jihadists credit for anything, Zula had to admit that they showed commendable restraint when it came to talking on the radio. Perhaps it was a Darwinian selection thing. All the jihadists who failed to observe radio silence had been vaporized by drone strikes.

There was no walkie-talkie or phone chatter from the time Jones left the camp with his three comrades until two and a half hours later, when Ershut and Jahandar trudged up the hill, looking winded but satisfied. In the meantime, the other members of the expedition—everyone except for Zakir and Sayed—breakfasted, prayed, and packed. The latter activity seemed to consume a great deal of emotional energy. It looked like every family-leaving-on-vacation meshuggas Zula had ever witnessed in the developed world, blended with a healthy dollop of desperate-refugees-striking-out-for-Sudan. The only thing missing was yelping dogs and crying kids. These men were not being helped any by the fact that each of them was obliged to carry lots of weapons. Washing the dishes and tidying the kitchen area at the base of her tree, Zula had a central viewpoint on the resulting arguments and the ruthless prioritization that flowed from them. It all seemed to come down to: pound for pound, what would kill the largest number of people? Bricks of plastic explosive ended up being given high priority. Guns too were highly thought of. Ammunition, somewhat less so; it seemed that they were expecting to purchase a lot of it in the States. Which Zula had to grant was a very reasonable plan. Unless their weapons used really weird bullets, they'd be able to pick up everything they needed in sporting goods emporia. Bullets, being made of lead, were heavy; and it seemed that heaviness was very much on their minds as they hoisted their packs off the ground, staring off into the distance, thinking about what it would be like to carry this up and down mountains for several days.

In another sample of the weird and profoundly distasteful emotional involvement that had been coming over her of late, Zula actually became anxious that they wouldn't be ready in time. She didn't think she had Stockholm syndrome yet, but she was beginning to understand how people got that way.

In any case, Ershut and Jahandar trudged back into the camp to find their comrades perhaps 75 percent finished with packing; and the intensity of their outrage was sufficient to make the remaining 25 percent come together rapidly. Even so, a quarter of an hour must have expired before the others were ready. During that interval, Zula was, for lack of a better word, exhibited. Ershut was the custodian of the keys. He opened the padlock that secured the end of the chain around the tree, then used it as a very long and heavy dog-leash to prevent Zula from straying as he led her down the hill for a short distance. Below their campsite, but above the uppermost reaches of the plank-avalanche, a lump of granite, about the size of a two-story house, protruded from the slope. It saw, and could be seen from, much of the valley below. Much of the Blue Fork's course could be seen from it, beginning in talus- and snow-covered mountains some miles to the south, or left, and running beneath the cliffs of Bayonet Ridge, directly below, to its junction with the White Fork at the Schloss, off to the right. The slope was heavily forested, but when the angles were right, it was possible to get a clear view of the road and of the turnaround at its end.

Standing in the middle of the turnaround were three men. She could not really see faces at this distance, but she knew them from their shapes as Jones, Abdul-Ghaffar, and Uncle Richard. And she knew that they could see her.

A childish thrill shot down her arm, telling her to raise it and wave at her uncle. She controlled that impulse and lost sight of the men below through a screen of tears. Turning her back on her uncle in shame, she began to trudge back to the campsite, heedless of the tug of the chain. Ershut let her go and locked her back up and left her to sit at the base of the tree, curled up and sobbing. A pathetic state of affairs. But better than she deserved. She had just betrayed her own uncle. He was now in the power of men who would certainly kill him as soon as he was no longer useful.

SOKOLOV HAD A moment's irrational fear that he was *never* going to strike the water, but he mastered the urge to look down, since this would have led to getting punched in the face by the ocean. He wouldn't have been able to see anything anyway. He kept his toes pointed and his ankles together, not wanting any water hammer effects on his testicles either, and then suddenly there was a shock in his legs and a searing *whoosh* immediately snuffed out by a deep mechanical throb: the screws of the freighter, churning away just behind him. An old habit told him that he should begin swimming now. But he was zipped up from ankles to neckline in an orange survival suit that knew how to find the surface. He waited. The frigid water, churned into a foaming sluice by the screws, streamed over him.

His head broke the surface and he was breathing again. To get his bearings, he spun in place, treading water as best he could in the unwieldy suit, until he could see the transom of the freighter receding. It was already impressively far away.

He turned his head to the right and saw what he'd seen a few seconds earlier from the ship's fantail: brassy light reflecting against the underside of low clouds. The lights of a city, and perhaps of an impending sunrise. Brighter, sharper lights gleamed along a slope perhaps a kilometer distant, a bluff rising out of the sea, carpeted with trees but densely settled with houses, and a few big avenues aglow with the logos of strip malls and fast-food places.

He drew a bead on a KFC sign and began swimming.

THE APLOMB WITH which the boatman had helped Sokolov throw the dead men off the deck of his vessel, in those misty waters off Kinmen two weeks ago, had convinced Sokolov that here was a fellow with whom he could really do business. He had wondered where "George Chow" had found this man and had begun to develop a hypothesis that this was not just any random boatman who had been, as it were, hailed off the street, but was actually some kind of a local fixer who ran various errands for the local espionage community. Either that, or he was a clinical psychopath, of whom Sokolov was more afraid than anyone else he had dealt with on that day.

It happened sometimes that in the early part of one of these projects, it felt as if you were going up hill into a headwind. Everything was against you; luck was always bad; nothing fell together, nothing worked out right. But beyond a certain point it changed and it was all easy, everything went your way. Thus here. He had rid himself of Olivia, who was an alluring and yet highly inconvenient person to have in his life. He was no longer in the PRC, no longer in the crowded city center of Xiamen, and, to boot, shrouded in dense fog and being assisted by a peppy boatman who, if he had been impressed or scared by the three gun-toting agents who'd comman-

deered his boat, must have been even more so by the way Sokolov
had vaulted aboard and machine-gunned them. Since he seemed
to have passed over that watershed, it had not really surprised him
when he had found himself, only a little while later, ascending a
rope ladder toward an open hatch near the stern of a big containership bound for the open Pacific. He had easily come to terms with
its Filipino crew and bought passage, and even a bunk of his own,
using the remaining cash in his pockets. The next two weeks had
been a sort of vacation on a steel beach, and a welcome opportunity
to rest up and heal from various minor injuries suffered during the
events in Xiamen. Only during the last couple of days had he really
stirred himself from his bunk and begun to exercise again, practicing his falls and rolls on the ship's deckplates to the great amusement of the crew.

A TIDAL CURRENT seemed to drag him alongshore. A beach came
into view, and he made for it as best he could in the suit. He did not
need it for its flotation properties, but dared not shed it lest he die of
hypothermia within sight of land. The sun was far from being up
yet and would be hidden by dense clouds when it got around to rising above the horizon; but the sky was definitely growing lighter,
enabling him to pick out a few details on the beach: strewn logs, and
fire rings, and a public toilet.

Wrestling and kicking his way through a forest of brown kelp,
he got to a place where he could feel a rocky bottom under his feet
and trudged carefully toward a beached log, taking his time, not
wanting to turn an ankle in a moment of thoughtless haste. When
the water became knee-deep, he crouched in the lee of the log, in
case he was being watched from one of the dwellings on the slope
above, and stripped off the suit. Stuffed inside of it he had been carrying a set of clothes wrapped up in a garbage bag. He changed
into these, all except for socks and shoes, which he carried a-dangle
around his neck for the time being. The survival suit might garner
attention if he left it here, so he stuffed it into the black garbage bag
and slung that over his shoulder. Then he climbed a little higher on
the strand and began to make his way south. He had no idea where
he was, but the freighter had been headed south and so it seemed

reasonable to assume that port facilities and a larger city were to be found in that general direction.

Half a dozen teenagers, boys and girls, were huddled together around the remains of a campfire. The empty beer bottles and fast-food wrappers all around them gave a fair account of how they had spent the preceding evening. They'd had enough foresight to bring blankets and sleeping bags and make a night of it. As Sokolov approached, one of them rose and staggered down the beach until he felt he had gone far enough to fish out his penis and urinate without giving offense to any female members of his party who might be awake. In this he seemed to be erring on the side of caution, glancing back frequently over his shoulder. Sokolov approved of this.

He was still pissing, with the enviable vigor of the young, as Sokolov approached within hailing distance. His eyes traveled up and down Sokolov's body. His face bespoke alert curiosity but not fear; he had not identified Sokolov as a derelict or criminal.

"What is this place?" Sokolov asked him.

"This is Golden Gardens Park," the young man answered, in the touchingly naive belief that this would mean something to Sokolov.

"What is name of city, please?"

"Seattle."

"Thank you." Then, as Sokolov went past him, he asked: "You just jump off a train or something?" For, as Sokolov had noticed, this beach was separated from the city by a railway siding.

"Or something," Sokolov affirmed. Then he pointed with his chin down the beach. "Is bus?"

"Yeah. Just keep going to the marina."

"Thanks. Have nice day."

"You too. Take it easy, man."

"Is not my objective. Nice thing to say though. Enjoy piss."

Olivia's plan to bolt out of the hotel and get a hot start on the day turned out to be embarrassingly, stupidly optimistic in more than one way. The night before she had fallen asleep in her clothes and left several things undone, such as taking a shower, checking her email, and touching base with Inspector Fournier, who'd been so kind as to send her those police reports. After Seamus woke her up, she set about doing those things. The shower went quickly and according to plan; nothing else did. What she'd envisioned as a quick check of her work email turned into a slough of despond. The next time she looked at the clock, an hour and a half had disappeared, and she was only getting in deeper; emails she had sent at the beginning of this session had spawned entire threads of responses in which she was now profoundly entangled, and people were threatening to set up conference calls. Her hasty departure from the FBI offices in Seattle had left her colleagues there variously confused and irritated, and these had to be brought up to speed or calmed down. At the same time, these same people were being made aware of the decrypted video images from the security cameras in Peter's apartment, and so she got to watch as awareness propagated across their networks of email lists and they began to discuss what they should do next. It was Saturday morning and FBI agents were thumbing emails from the sidelines of their kids' soccer games. "Out of office" responses were bouncing around the system like pachinko balls. The chan-nel through which these images had reached them was extremely confusing (decryption key pulled out of a dead man's wallet by a Hungarian in the Philippines communicating with an American in Canada, the conversation taking place on an imaginary planet), and Olivia had to intervene and explain matters.

And that was just the Seattle FBI part of it. She had made the mistake of mentioning the idea of the Prince George security cam gambit to some of her colleagues in London, and this had spawned volumes of useless debate and counterproductive efforts to help her.

The only thing that kept her from being stuck in email all day long was a telephone call from Fournier, who had suddenly become hospitable and now wished to have coffee with her. She agreed to meet him in the lobby of her hotel in half an hour, then packed her bags—not much of a chore, since she hadn't unpacked, and half of her crap was still down in the rental car anyway—and, almost as an afterthought, used Google Maps to check out the route to Prince George.

The results caused her to do a double-take. It was 750 kilometers and it was going to take her eleven hours, not counting eating and peeing breaks. The numbers were so enormous that she suffered a spell of disorientation, thinking that Google must have mistak-enly routed her on some ridiculously convoluted route. But no, the map showed a reasonably straight course. It really was that far: the equivalent of driving from London to John o' Groats. She was going to spend the entire day driving, and she was not going to get there until after dark. Tomorrow was Sunday.

She checked the flight schedules, hoping that there would be hourly shuttles. The result: there were a few flights during the day, including one that she might be able to make if she canceled her breakfast with Inspector Fournier and then made a dash to the air-port. Politically, this was not the best move, and so she booked a seat on a late-morning flight instead.

Then down to the lobby to have coffee and a scone with Fournier. For some reason she had been expecting a middle-aged, rumpled Quebecois version of Columbo, but Fournier was trim, probably in his early thirties, and wore a stylish set of eyeglasses that made him seem younger still. What she'd mistaken for hostility had, she suspected, been a Continental formality that contrasted with the American frat boy ambience she had been immersed in during the previous days. She immediately suspected, and Fournier soon confirmed, that he'd spent a few years living in France, which was where he had picked up his professional manners and his taste in eyewear. Olivia's status as MI6 agent, operating on foreign soil, had probably done nothing to loosen him up. But in person he could not have been more charming and attentive.

Under the circumstances, Olivia couldn't not tell Fournier about her plan to go to Prince George and look for strategically located security cameras. He sat back, stroked his fashionably stubbled chin, and gave it serious consideration. "In a perfect world," he said, "you would not have to go there in person and look for such things." Then he gave a hugely expressive shrug and cocked his head to one side. "Matters being what they are, I fear you are correct. Having such a thing done through the usual channels, when we have no evidence that Jones ever came within thousands of miles of Canada, and no particular reason to suspect foul play in the case of the missing hunters, would be . . . how shall I say this politely? . . . time-consuming."

It seemed clear that Fournier had come here expecting to find a sort of madwoman, but that meeting Olivia in the flesh and hearing her side of the story had begun to tell on him. His confidence that the hunters were merely lost, or innocently frozen to death, had been shaken a bit. He was now finding a few minutes' diversion in entertaining Olivia's theory. If nothing else, he seemed to think, it would enliven an otherwise dull investigation.

Olivia, for her part, was finding it exasperatingly difficult to maintain her focus. She should never have checked her email. All she could think about was the torrent of messages even now coming into her inbox. Her adversaries were framing counterarguments that were going unanswered, her collaborators were requesting help and clarification that she was failing to supply. She ought to have been grateful, and gracious, to Fournier, and so have savored every minute of their discussion. Instead of which she was relieved when he glanced into his empty cup and began the end of the conversation with "Well . . ."

She promised to check in from Prince George, shook his hand,

and headed for the airport. She made a willful effort not to take out her phone until she had checked in her rental car and was on the shuttle bus to the terminal.

Then she was confronted by a queue of unread messages whose length exceeded even her worst expectations. Subject headers had become completely deranged by this point, making it difficult to guess what these people were even talking about. But one of them, at the top of the stack—only received a few minutes ago—had the succinct heading "Got him." It had come from one of the FBI agents in Seattle.

She called him directly on the phone. Agent Vandenberg. A red-head from Grand Rapids, Michigan.

"I'm declaring email bankruptcy," she said.

"Happens to all of us, Liv," said Agent Vandenberg, who was decidedly not of the Continental, Inspector Fournier style.

"Just tell me how it all comes out."

"Don't know yet," he said puckishly.

"But I'm seeing 'Got him' in the subject line. Whom did you get?"

"I guess that should have been 'recognized him,'" said Agent Vandenberg after a slight, embarrassed pause. "One of our guys immediately recognized the subject who stole the rifle. We know all about this guy. Igor." He snickered at the name. "Igor has been the subject of many investigations. He's a legal immigrant. But that's the only thing about him that's legal. This is the first time we have got him so dead to rights, though."

"So are you going to pick him up?"

"We don't see him as a flight risk. We don't think he's about to go do something bad. It's been a week and a half since he stole that gun, and he's been pretty inactive that whole time. So we blasted a judge out of bed, got ourselves a court order, and instituted surveillance on his domicile. It's a crappy little house in Tukwila."

"Where's Tukwila?"

"Exactly. He shares it with another Russian, who has been his roommate there for, like, four years."

"Gotten anything good yet?"

"It's taking us a little while to rustle up an interpreter, so we don't know what the three of them are saying."

"Three?"

"Yeah. There's three Russians in the house."

"I thought you said two. Igor and his roommate."

"They have a visitor. Just arrived. Surprised the hell out of them, apparently. We don't exactly know what's going on. Igor and his roommate were lounging around in couch potato mode, watching a hockey game on the satellite, and suddenly there was a knock on the door. Then they're all like, 'Who the hell could that be?' I'm just guessing from their tone of voice. Then one of them goes and looks out the window and says something like, 'Holy shit, it's Sokolov!' and then they sound kind of scared for a while. But eventually they let him in."

It was fortunate that Agent Vandenberg was such a loquacious soul, since he then went on talking long enough to give Olivia a chance to get her composure back.

"I think I get the general picture," she said, when Vandenberg paused to draw breath, and she felt she could keep her voice steady. "Did you say that the name of the surprise visitor was Sokolov?"

"Yes, we're pretty sure of that. Why? Mean anything to you?"

"It is a very common Russian name," she observed. "But you said that they were surprised to see him?"

"Surprised, and pretty seriously freaked out. Sokolov had to ring the doorbell three times. They left him cooling his heels on their front porch for, like, five minutes while they discussed how to handle the situation. I don't know who this guy is—but he ain't no Avon lady."

"Thanks," Olivia said. "That is interesting."

ZULA ENDED UP retreating into her tiny tent and pulling her sleeping bag over her head. A natural reaction to shame. All she wanted was to have a bit of privacy while she finished her blubbering. This had the unintended, but useful, consequence that the others forgot she was there.

Not *literally*, of course. The friggin' chain trailed across the ground and went right into her tent. Everyone knew exactly where she was. But some kind of irrational psychological effect caused them to act as if she weren't right there, just a few yards away from them.

She wasn't sure whether that was a bad or a good thing. It might cause them to blurt out useful information they'd never divulge if her eyes were on their faces. On the other hand, maybe it was easier to command the execution of someone you couldn't see.

Abdul-Wahaab, Jones's right-hand man, was the last of the hikers to depart the camp. Before hoisting his pack onto his shoulders, he gathered the stay-behind group around him: Ershut, Jahandar, Zakir, and Sayed. They were all of about twenty feet from Zula, standing around the stove and drinking tea.

"I'll speak Arabic," said Abdul-Wahaab. Somewhat redundantly, since he was, in fact, speaking Arabic.

Trying not to make obvious nylon-swishing noises, Zula pulled the sleeping bag off her face and rolled toward them, straining to hear as much as she could. She had been in the company of men speaking Arabic for two solid weeks and was continually frustrated that she hadn't learned more of it. And yet she had come a long way; her time in the refugee camp had planted some seeds that had been slow to sprout but that were now growing noticeably from day to day.

"I have spoken with our leader," said Abdul-Wahaab. "He has learned some things about the way south from the guide."

Zula's mental translation just barely kept up. Fortunately Abdul-Wahaab was not a torrential speaker. He uttered short, pithy sentences and paused between them to sip tea. Zula's understanding was largely based on picking out nouns: *leader. The way to the south.* And this word "dalil," which she had heard frequently in the last few days and finally remembered meant "guide."

"The path is difficult, but he knows of shortcuts and secret ways," Abdul-Wahaab continued, actually using the English word "shortcuts."

"He thinks two days for us to cross the border. After that, one more day before we could reach a place with Internet. Maybe two days."

The others listened and waited for Abdul-Wahaab to give orders. After sipping more tea, he went on: "After four days, if you hear nothing, kill her and go where you will. But we will try to get a message to our brothers waiting in Elphinstone. They will then come here and find you. We will send GPS coordinates showing the way south. God willing, you can then join us for the martyrdom operation."

"In that case, should we kill her?" Zakir asked.

"We will give instructions. She might be useful to us." He sipped his tea. "The guide states that there will be no phone coverage, unless we climb to the top of a mountain and have good luck. If this happens, perhaps you will get a text with other instructions."

Beyond that, the talk turned to what they would all do once they had crossed the border: the challenges they would face there and their eagerness to pursue various opportunities for mayhem. Abdul-Wahaab discouraged all such talk, though, insisting that they maintain their focus on getting through the next few days. He seemed to become aware that he was holding up the rest of the group, and drained his tea, and accepted Ershut's help in hoisting his heavy pack onto his back. Then, after exchanging embraces with the four stay-behinds, he turned away and began tromping down toward the trail.

Zula decided that she would make her move after dark tonight.

WHEN SOKOLOV HAD been a little boy growing up in the Soviet Union, he had been exposed to more than a few magazine articles and television programs depicting the misery of life under capitalism. A reporter would travel to some squalid place in Appalachia or the South Bronx and take a few depressing photographs, then jot down, or make up, some equally depressing anecdotes and package it into a story intended to make it clear that people back in the USSR didn't have it so bad. While no one was stupid enough to take such propaganda at face value, all but the most cynical persons assumed that there was some truth to them. Yes, the standard of living could be higher in the West. Everyone knew this. But it could be lower too.

Both ends of that spectrum were on display during Sokolov's hour-long journey from Golden Gardens to the home of Igor. He waited for a bus near a marina crowded with yachts. The bus took him to a sleek modern downtown, where he did a bit of shopping and then boarded a light rail train headed in the direction of the airport. During that journey, the view out its windows became steadily more like a photo spread from a Soviet propaganda article. The railway line had been threaded through the poorest neighborhoods. The urban part was a complex and densely packed mixture of black people and pan-global immigration; it wasn't pretty, but at least it was striving. Then there was a light-industrial buffer zone that separated it from a sort of white ghetto in the suburbs. The train ran high above this on towering reinforced-concrete pylons, and he looked almost straight down into the backyards of tiny, rotting bungalows strewn with detritus.

He climbed out at the last station before the airport and then walked for a mile and a half, wending his way into a neighborhood full of houses like that. He had not acquired a phone yet, but he had been able to purchase a street map at a bookstore downtown, and he had Igor's address written down in a little book that had been with him through all his adventures.

Igor's house stood at the end of a cul-de-sac, backed up against a freeway embankment held together by a felt of blackberries and ivy. This mat of vegetation had covered and killed several trees and was making a bid to take over a shed in the back. But the house that Igor shared with his friend Vlad was actually tidier than many on this street: the two vehicles parked in its driveway both appeared to be in working order, and neither of them had turned green with moss. They did not store junk on their front porch, and they had taken sensible precautions, covering the front windows with expanded steel mesh and beefing up the locks on the front door.

Igor's fear caused Sokolov nothing more than mild irritation at first, since its sole effect was to slow everything down. But he could hardly blame the man for being cautious. Sokolov took his hands out of his pockets and held them out wide, palms up. "A couple of hours," he insisted, "and then I will be gone. Forever."

HIS CHOICE TO come to this place was debatable, to say the least. He had been thinking about it all through the sea voyage.

He had to go *somewhere* and do *something*. His only real means of making a living was doing what he did: security consultant. The fact that he was fluent only in Russian and that he carried a Russian passport placed certain limits on where he could ply that trade. He could make his way back to Russia and retreat into the woods and spend the rest of his life chopping wood and hunting deer, but he had grown rather accustomed to living in big cities and being paid a decent amount of money and, for lack of a better word, being respected for who he was and what he did. Most of his clients had been nothing like Ivanov, and, after this, he would never work for such a person again. But the regrettable incidents of the last few weeks would need to be explained to the owners of the *obshchak* from which Ivanov had stolen the money, and to the families of the men who had been slain by Abdallah Jones. And Sokolov was actually confident that it all *could* be explained. For the owners of the *obshchak* were, at bottom, reasonable people. Courtesy went a long way with them. In what had happened to Wallace and Ivanov, they would perceive a kind of poetry and a kind of justice. Ivanov had, in effect, obtained just the fate he had wanted, in that he had died while trying to get the money back. The story worked perfectly well as a cautionary tale: look what happens to those who steal money with which they have been entrusted. It would all work out just fine if Sokolov could merely relate the story to the people Ivanov had betrayed.

Not that Sokolov had any certainty of being forgiven. There were no guarantees. But this way he had a decent chance. Whereas if he sneaked around and tried to avoid them, they would surely take note of his lack of courtesy and approach him in a more suspicious frame of mind.

That much he had decided during the first half of his voyage across the Pacific. The question, then, was how to go about making contact with the people in question. Simply calling them from a pay telephone on the beach would be indiscreet and would suggest a kind of desperation.

On the other hand, if he climbed on a bus and went straight to Igor's house, it would seem reasonable enough. For this was not the act of a desperate person. Certainly not that of one with something to hide, since it was to be expected that Igor would spread the news of Sokolov's arrival via the grapevine. No, this was a good low-key way to say to those whom Ivanov had betrayed: *I survived, I got out of China, I am not on the run, I have nothing to hide, you'll be hearing from me once I have got my feet on the ground.*

So in a sense this was a make-work visit. Sokolov still had enough dollars in his pocket to pay for a motel room and a bus ticket. He really needed nothing at all from Igor.

It was a social call.

And yet Igor sensed at some level that this made no sense. Which was why he was so worried. So suspicious.

Anyway, he consented, finally, to let Sokolov in his front door. A decidedly awkward exchange of greetings followed. He and Vlad and Sokolov ended up sitting around the kitchen table, which was strewn with Russian-language newspapers, mugs half full of cold coffee, and dirty cereal bowls. The chilly silver light, so characteristic of this part of the world, washed in through a mesh-covered window and made it possible to see everything without actually illuminating it.

"I just got off a containership from China," Sokolov said. For if Igor conveyed nothing else to the grapevine, Sokolov wanted it known that this, and no other reason, was why he had been incognito for two solid weeks. "No Internet, no phone. I've been totally out of touch."

"Made any phone calls?"

"I don't have a phone. I'm telling you, I literally jumped off the fucking ship two hours ago and came straight here."

"So you have heard nothing in two weeks."

"Closer to three. It's not as if we were doing a lot of communicating when we were in Xiamen."

"Well, you need to check in. There are a lot of people confused. Pissed off."

Sokolov grinned. "Heard from them, did you?"

"I thought I was a dead man," said Igor, completely unamused. Sokolov glanced at Vlad, hoping to draw him into the conversation, but Vlad, a somewhat younger man than Igor—skinny, with long unkempt hair—had scooted his chair into the corner of the kitchen and was sitting there with his hands in the pockets of a bulky leather jacket, implicitly threatening to drill Sokolov with whatever was in his pocket. Vlad had been a minor player in the takeover of Peter's apartment, but he was as deeply implicated as anyone else. Sokolov suspected him of being a meth user.

A plane took off from Sea-Tac, flying directly over the house, and made conversation impossible for a little while.

"Well, you look alive to me," Sokolov said finally.

Igor nodded. "There was a sort of investigation, I guess you could call it. Certain people wanted to know where Ivanov had gone, what he had done. They were very suspicious. I tried to explain to them about Wallace. About the virus." Igor shrugged his huge shoulders, a great rolling movement like a barrel falling off a truck. "What do I know about such things? I just told them what I had overheard. The hacker in China. T'Rain. Zula. Tried to make sense of it. After a while they calmed down."

"There you have it," Sokolov said. "I expected as much. Once they had it all explained. You did well." This not so much for Igor's ears as for those he might spread the story to later.

Igor now got an expectant look on his face. Rather than wait for him to say it, Sokolov said: "I'll take care of it from here."

"Good."

"I just need to make my way back to them, you know, without getting in trouble with Immigration, with the law."

"Yes, of course."

"Which is why I came here," Sokolov said. "I won't be much trouble. Just need to take a shower. Get a bite to eat. Pull myself together. Then I'll be on my way."

"You need money?" Igor asked suspiciously.

"Not really."

Igor softened. "Because I can lend you some if you need it."

"As I said, I just need to collect myself for a few minutes. I'll count my money and perhaps take you up on that offer."

"The shower is that way," said Igor, pointing with his eyes.

THE HOUSE'S FLOOR was spongy and uneven—being consumed from beneath, Sokolov guessed, by some combination of insects and rot. The frame of the bathroom door had sagged into a parallelogram, the flimsy hollow-core door was still a rectangle; he bashed it shut with his shoulder and then used the hook-and-eye lock that had been added onto it when the lockset had stopped working. This seemed to be ground zero for the mildewy scent that pervaded the entire bungalow. Sokolov turned on the shower, then jerked the curtain across its front so water wouldn't splash out onto the floor.

He took a seat, fully clothed, on the toilet, which was located behind the door, and got out his Makarov and chambered a round. That Igor would kick the door down and Vlad fire blindly into the shower stall was unlikely. But neither was it out of the question; and if it happened, Sokolov would be quite disappointed in himself if he had failed to be ready for it.

He checked his watch and made himself comfortable for fifteen minutes, during which time he thought about Olivia and Zula, Csongor and Yuxia and Peter.

Since Zula was the only one he'd seen escaping the building, he had been assuming that Csongor and Peter were dead and that Yuxia was in the custody of the Public Security Bureau. These facts were unfortunate, but there was nothing he could do about them.

Of Zula's situation, he could only speculate. He had scanned some newspapers in the bookstore downtown where he had purchased the map. He'd seen no reference to Abdallah Jones. Then he had moved on to some weekly newsmagazines, where he hoped he might see some stories summarizing events of the last week or two. Nothing.

In several places he had noted posters bearing Zula's face, sometimes alone, sometimes paired with Peter's. They were stapled to telephone poles and bus stop bulletin boards, looking a bit yellow and starting to be encroached upon by advertisements for lost dogs and maid services.

A Google search would have told him much more. But he had seen—more to the point, *not* seen—enough in the newspapers to suspect that Jones was still lying low somewhere and that Zula, if alive, was still with him.

As for Olivia, he hoped and trusted that she had found her way safely home and was well on her way to forgetting about him. He had been reassured, back on Kinmen, to see a kind of intelligent guardedness on her face. *I can't believe I'm fucking this guy.* He'd have been worried, on the other hand, if she had thrown hopeful or adoring looks at him. Now that they had been apart for a while, her rational mind would have seized the controls from whatever part of her brain found a man like Sokolov attractive and wrenched her back onto a safe and reasonable course.

He was not entirely happy about this. Under other circumstances, perhaps, it would have been worth pursuing. Sad that it was impossible. Not as sad as many other things in this world.

The bungalow's walls were thin, and beneath the hiss of the shower he could hear Igor's voice as a kind of indistinct throbbing, difficult to make out except when he pronounced distinct words like "*Da, da!*" During the intervals when Igor was silent, Sokolov heard nothing from Vlad. Apparently Igor was talking to someone on the phone. This was not surprising, and, as a matter of fact, Sokolov was pretending to take this shower precisely to give Igor an opportunity to make a next move: try to kill him, or else call people in his network and begin spreading the news.

He turned off the shower, turned on the faucet, pulled a disposable razor out of his bag, and shaved using a sliver of soap that had been left on the edge of the sink. He kept the Makarov handy. But if they'd been going to do it, they'd have done it while they thought he was in the shower.

While he was shaving, he heard Igor place another phone call, this one in English. Igor seemed to be ordering a pizza from Domino's.

This did not seem to be the act of a man who was about to murder his guest, so on one level Sokolov relaxed a little bit. It did raise new questions, though. Why was Igor now showing hospitality? Any man in his right mind would want Sokolov out of the house pronto. Had he been ordered, by someone on the telephone, to stall Sokolov? Keep him in the house until someone else could be sent out to deal with him?

Anyway, he rinsed his face, splashed water into his stubbled scalp to make it look as if he'd actually showered, pulled his stuff together, wrenched the door open, and stepped back out into the bungalow's living room. Vlad was playing a video game on a tricked-out PC that was connected to a large flat-screen monitor. Igor was watching and supplying commentary, but tore his attention away to greet Sokolov. "Please, make yourself comfortable," he said, rolling forward as if he intended to rise to his feet. He had a beer in his hand. "Would you like a beer? I'll get one for you."

"No thanks, not now."

"I ordered pizza. It should be here in forty minutes. I thought you might be hungry."

"Thanks, that sounds delicious. It's been forever since I had pizza."

These words came out of his mouth somewhat mechanically; his mind was going too fast to make genuine conversation.

"Noodles and rice for two weeks, eh?"

"Beg your pardon?"

"On the freighter—Chink food only, I'll bet."

Sokolov shook his head. "The crew was Filipino; they eat different stuff. It was fine. Just no pizza, that's all."

"How the hell did you talk your way on board that thing? From what I've heard, the Chinese cops must have been going crazy."

Sokolov shrugged. "It's a big port. Famous for smuggling. It's always possible to find a way out of such places."

"But you were alone—and you don't speak Chinese?"

So, one thing at least was obvious, which was that whomever Igor had been talking to on the phone had asked him to wheedle more information from Sokolov on how he had made his way from a gunfight in a collapsing apartment building in Xiamen to Igor's house in Tukwila, and to probe for inconsistencies in the story—to the extent that Igor even had the intellectual equipment for such an undertaking. Perhaps the pizza stalling maneuver was solely to keep Sokolov in the house long enough for Igor to ask a series of such questions. Or perhaps a carload of men was on its way to the house right now to fetch Sokolov and subject him to a more rigorous examination. In either case, it wouldn't look good for Sokolov to bolt out of the house, spurning the pizza, as much as announcing that he had something to hide.

He had, of course, been surveying the place for exits and had noticed that, for such a small structure, it was actually rather difficult to get out of. There seemed to be a lot of property crime in the neighborhood, and it was obvious enough that Igor and Vlad were not above dealing in stolen goods, and possibly in drugs as well, so they had been assiduous about putting bars or steel mesh over their windows. The only exits were the doors.

"What the hell," Sokolov said. "I think I will have a beer. It's okay, I can get it myself." For Igor had already sunk back into the depths of his black leather sofa and was not the sort to get up again quickly. Sokolov went back into the kitchen and confirmed his memory that it led to a sort of back porch with an exit to the yard behind the house. He stepped into the porch and examined the door, a flimsy thing that had been beefed up with more steel mesh and a number of extra bolts. He opened all of these and confirmed that he could now yank the door open with a single quick gesture.

Then back to the living room with his beer. He had been a little worried that Igor would be suspicious at the amount of time he had taken to fetch a beverage, but his host was deeply absorbed with the progress of the video game. Sokolov dragged a chair into a position where he could look out the front window of the house and straight down the length of the cul-de-sac.

There followed about forty-five minutes of desultory conversation. Occasionally Igor would ask him a question about what had happened in Xiamen and Sokolov would relate a bit of the story, but sooner or later they always drifted back into video-game watching.

A small car came up the street, but it was just the pizza delivery. "I'll get more beer," Sokolov said, and went into the kitchen. He found a large pot in the cabinet next to the stove, put it in the sink, and began running hot water into it. Then he went to the fridge and got more beers and ferried them out to the living room. Igor was on his feet, undoing the front door locks, greeting the pizza delivery boy. Sokolov set the beers down on the coffee table. Then he went back into the kitchen and took the pot, now containing several liters of warm water, and placed it on the range and turned the burner on high. When the water was boiling, it might serve as a sort of weapon or at least a distraction.

They ate pizza and drank beer. Vlad had paused his video game. This was not running on a console, such as an Xbox; it ran on a personal computer. Not a boring beige box such as you would see in an office. A PC made specifically for young male game players with a tech fetish, all tricked out with multicolored LEDs and complex molded shapes recalling the hull of an alien spacecraft. When Sokolov had first seen this thing, just after walking into Igor's house a couple of hours ago, his mind had snagged on it for a moment, then moved on. Ever since, something about it had been nagging at him. But he'd had other things to think about.

Now, finally, it came to him. He remembered where he had seen this thing before.

This was Peter's computer.

They must have come back to Peter's place at some point while

Sokolov had been embroiled in China and stolen whatever looked good to them.

It must have been very soon after they had gone to Xiamen, because once Peter and Zula had been reported missing, the cops would have gone there, turned it into a crime scene, made it a very hazardous place to carry out a burglary.

Which meant that the cops must have gone there *after* Vlad and Igor had ransacked it.

Which meant that, instead of finding the carefully cleaned-up, evidence-free scene that Sokolov had arranged, they would have found evidence of said ransacking.

"You are making me nervous, with this look on your face!" Igor complained.

Sokolov glanced up to see that Igor was, in fact, looking a little edgy.

Sokolov cleared his throat. "You went back to that place," he said, "and took some things."

Here, Sokolov would not have been surprised to see Igor dart a guilty look at the fancy PC, which was sitting on the floor so close that he could have set his beer on top of it. But instead Igor threw a nervous look into the corner of the room behind Sokolov. By dint of a supreme effort of will, Sokolov resisted the temptation to turn around and look at whatever it was. Some loot from the apartment, obviously, that Igor considered more valuable or that in some sense loomed larger in his imagination than the PC.

What would a man like Peter have in his place that could be that interesting to Igor? It was easy to understand the attraction of the PC. All young men liked to play video games. What else? Peter didn't do drugs.

Then Sokolov remembered Igor standing at the top of Peter's stairs, examining a gun safe. Assuring Sokolov that it was locked.

"I won't deny it," Igor said, with a shrug to say it was really nothing, and a nervous laugh that argued to the contrary.

"Ivanov didn't pay you well enough?"

"Nothing's enough for a job like that one. Shit, I just thought it was going to be security. Bodyguard shit at the worst. Then it turned into—"

Sokolov nodded. "Of course, I can sympathize. I was as surprised as you were. I am just asking. It is important for me to know the facts. That's all. When did you go back to the place?"

"Two days later, maybe," said Igor, and glanced over to Vlad for confirmation. "We staked it out the night before. Made sure there were no cops, no surveillance. Found a way in. Nice and quiet." Another glance into the corner.

"How did you get the safe open?" Sokolov asked, just guessing. "Quietly?"

"Plasma torch," Vlad blurted out. Igor threw him a killing look, but Vlad didn't even understand that he had stepped into a trap that Sokolov had put out for him.

"Weren't you worried that it would damage the gun?"

"He kept it in a metal case," Vlad said, and nodded into the same corner. This gave Sokolov an excuse, finally, to turn around and look. Resting on the top of a bookshelf at about head level was a long case of burnished aluminum, just the sort of thing a gun fancier would use to carry around an especially prized rifle. One end of it was marred with flecks and streaks of darker stuff: molten metal that had sprayed onto it and congealed.

Sokolov turned back around. "This torch didn't set off the smoke alarms?"

Igor said, "We went around, found them all, pulled their batteries."

"When you were going all over the place looking for those smoke alarms," Sokolov went on, "you might have seen some security cameras."

"Two of them," Igor said. "We cut the wires, of course."

Sokolov, who knew that there were actually *three* cameras, bit down hard until the urge to scream had passed. "Of course. But up until the moment you cut those wires, you were visible to the cameras."

"Vlad's good at computers," Igor volunteered.

Vlad nodded, as if to confirm the validity of Igor's assessment. "Obviously we had cut the Internet the first time we went there," he said, "so we knew that the cameras couldn't send data outside of the building."

"What about inside the building, though?"

"Vlad traced the wires," Igor said.

"I traced the wires," Vlad confirmed, "to the server in his workshop. That's where the video files from the camera were being stored. We used the plasma torch to completely destroy the hard drives in that server."

"Did you also trace the wires to the wireless router under the stairs?"

"Of course," Vlad said.

"Did you know that this router had a hard drive built into it? Used to back up all files on the network?"

Silence.

Vlad the computer expert was turning red. Igor noticed this and held out a hand to steady him. "It has been, what, two weeks," Igor said. "Nothing has happened. The police know nothing of these things. They will never think to collect such evidence."

Sokolov sat there impassively, waiting for Igor to figure it out.

"If they had found this, why have they not come to arrest us?" Igor demanded, sounding almost like a self-righteous, upstanding citizen, scandalized by the complacency of the local cops.

"Unless," Vlad said, "they have put us under surveillance."

"Why would they bother if they already have evidence?"

Vlad said, "It would be a major investigation. Not just of burglary but kidnapping, murder, other things. International spy shit. They don't give a shit about people like us. A couple of burglars!" he scoffed. "They would put on the surveillance and hope that sooner or later someone more important would get in touch with us."

Four eyes turned toward Sokolov.

There was a long pause. Igor raised the fingertips of both hands to his temples, making his huge fat hands into blinders, tunneling his vision at Sokolov.

"Fucking asshole!" Igor finally said. "Why did I let you into my house?"

"Stupid, greedy motherfucker," Sokolov said. "The money wasn't enough. You had to go back. Steal some more."

"Hey, calm down!" Vlad squeaked. "We don't even know if the cops found the video."

"The uncle of Zula is a *billionaire*, moron," Sokolov said. "He would bring in investigators of his own. There is nothing they would not find."

Something occurred to Igor and he exclaimed "Fuck!" then made a grab for his phone. Sokolov's hand jerked toward the Makarov in his jacket pocket, but he restrained the urge to draw a weapon—as did Vlad, watching him attentively.

Igor made a one-button call: a redial. "It's better that you don't come," he announced into the phone. Then listened to a blast of verbal abuse that forced him to pull the device away from his ear. "No, it's nothing like that. I'll explain later. Turn the car around. Don't come."

"You invited some others to the pizza party?" Sokolov asked, after Igor had shut off his phone, terminating more furious denunciations.

Igor held his hands out. "I am sorry, Mr. Sokolov, but I must answer to certain people; and when you showed up, I had to make them aware of the fact that you were here."

"Are there any *other* ways you have fucked me that I have not been made aware of yet?"

The fat hands became flesh pistols, index fingers aiming at Sokolov's eyes. "I never should have worked with you. Now, the cops will come, I'll do time. Be deported."

"Doing time. Getting in trouble. All very normal for a man who breaks into another man's house and steals his computer and his rifle. If you had just followed my orders—"

"Why should I take orders from you, motherfucker?"

"Because I actually know what I am doing."

"Then how did you end up in this fucking situation?"

It was a fair question, and it rocked Sokolov for a moment.

In that interval, Vlad noticed something. "They're coming," he said.

Sokolov looked up at him to see that Vlad was gazing out the house's front window.

"Who's coming?" Igor asked.

"How the fuck should I know?" Vlad said.

Instinctively, Sokolov dropped to a crouch and peered over the sill of the front window, down the length of the cul-de-sac. A dark SUV, headlights on, was headed up the street, moving at little better than a walking pace.

"Why headlights?" Vlad asked.

"To blind us!" Igor said.

"It's a rental," Sokolov suggested. "The lights come on automatically."

"Who rents a car for a bust like this?"

"Not cops," Vlad supposed. "Guys from out of town."

"What kind of guys?"

"Maybe private dicks? Hired by billionaire uncle?"

"Fuck!" Igor said, and stomped over to the corner of the living room. He hauled the rifle case down from the shelf.

"What were you thinking of doing with that?" Sokolov asked him. The two options he could think of were to hide it, so that it couldn't be used as evidence, or to take it out and start using it.

"I am not going back to Russia," Igor said. As if this answered the question. Which it didn't. "I've got an escape route out the back."

"Asshole, they'll be covering the back exit!" Vlad pointed out. No doubt correctly. "You won't get more than a couple of steps!"

The SUV came to a stop, directly in front of the house, headlights glaring brightly enough, on this dull overcast day, to make it impossible to count the number of people inside.

Its driver's-side door opened and a pair of blue-jeaned legs dropped to the ground. The driver stepped out from behind the door and slammed it shut. Short hair did nothing to hide the fact that this was a woman. An Asian woman. She stepped out farther from the SUV's headlight glare.

It was Olivia. And she had apparently come here alone.

"What the *fuck*!?" Vlad shouted, holding up his hands. He would have been ready for a whole carload of heavily armed federal agents. But not this.

Sokolov spun around to face Vlad and raised an index finger to his lips, shushing him. Glancing up toward the ceiling in a gesture that any Russian would recognize: *Remember, someone is listening to us.* Vlad, wide-eyed, seemed to take this in. After a moment's hesitation, he nodded. *Okay, I'll shut up.*

They were distracted by a crisp mechanical clunking noise from the other side of the room. Sokolov looked over to see that Igor had pulled the rifle out of the case. It was some sort of AR-15 variant. The sound had been made by him drawing the bolt carrier back, locking the action into an open state. As Sokolov watched, Igor plucked out one of several loose cartridges that had been rattling around loose inside the case, manually fed it into the breech, and slapped the side of the weapon, releasing the bolt and letting it slam the cartridge into firing position.

Sokolov noticed that his Makarov was in his hands, aimed at Igor.

Olivia rang the doorbell.

"Get down!" Sokolov shouted in English. Unsure whether she'd heard him, he pivoted and fired a round through the door, far above Olivia's head. That should give her the general idea.

"Kill him!" Igor shouted, apparently to Vlad. Then he raised the rifle and aimed it at the front door.

Vlad was fumbling in his pocket. But he was poorly trained and was having trouble getting the weapon out. "Run out the back door," Sokolov suggested. "There's no one there."

"How would you know?" Vlad asked.

"Do it or I'll fucking kill you," Sokolov said, aiming his Makarov at Vlad.

"I told you, he's setting us up! Mother*fucker*!" Igor shouted, letting the barrel of the rifle drop and using his free hand to pull a revolver out of the waistband of his trousers.

Sokolov pivoted and fired two rounds into Igor's midsection, waited for him to hit the floor, then fired one more.

Vlad was crouching on the floor next to the PC with his hands on top of his head, completely unmanned. An utterly ruthless, animal instinct within Sokolov told him to simply execute this miserable person, who could only cause trouble for him. But he could not bring himself to do it.

"I suggest you run. Fast," Sokolov said.

"Why bother? Didn't you say we were under surveillance?"

"By someone," Sokolov said. He had crossed the room and picked up the rifle. Setting his pistol down for a moment, he hauled back on the rifle's bolt carrier, ejecting the round that Igor had chambered, then set the rifle into its case, which he slammed shut. He carried it to the front door, which he opened. Olivia was no longer there. The SUV was in motion, making a three-point turn in the middle of the cul-de-sac, getting turned around into position for a getaway.

Then it stopped.

Nothing happened for a few moments.

Then she kicked open the passenger door.

EXCEPT FOR THE part about his niece being held hostage and he himself being the captive of murderous jihadists, this was the best vacation Richard had had in ten years. The *only* vacation, in truth. He had never understood vacations, never really taken them. But sometimes he talked to people who did understand and take them, and the story they seemed to tell had something to do with getting away from one's normal day-to-day concerns, putting all that stuff out of one's mind for a while, and going somewhere new and having experiences. Experiences that were somehow more pure and raw and true—the way small children experienced things—precisely because they were non sequiturs, complete departures from the flow of ordinary life.

Which Richard was totally incapable of, normally. Looking back, he could see that the majority of his breakups with the women who lived on in his superego as the Furious Muses had occurred in conjunction with attempts to go on vacation. He had never gone on vacation in any place that did not have high-speed Internet. Even the private jet in which he flew to those vacation sites had its own always-on Net connection. This probably qualified him as a serious head case, but he liked nothing more than to sit on a beach underneath a palm frond cabana in Bali, stripped to the waist, sipping an exotic drink from a coconut shell, watching waves roll in from a blue ocean, while wandering around T'Rain via the computer on his lap, firing off memos and bug reports to his technical staff. He could think of nothing more relaxing.

Except for what he was doing now. If only the bad parts of it could be done away with. He was seriously thinking that, if he survived this, he might try to launch a new venture: a vacation services provider for wealthy, hardworking people that would work by showing up at their homes without warning and abducting them.

JONES AND COMPANY had done a creditable job of it, maintaining the injured-hiker pretense until the moment Richard had opened the door, then instantly cutting the power and the Internet. Apparently they had scoped out the property and found the utility shed up by the dam, broken into it, and stationed a man there with bolt cutters. Probably Ershut. Richard had been observing Jones's men, learning their names and qualities, and had identified Ershut as a Barney. This being a term from the original *Mission: Impossible* television series that only made sense to people of Richard's vintage, or hipsters who liked to watch primeval TV shows on YouTube. Anyway, if ever there was a man who would be stationed in a utility shed with bolt cutters, it would be Ershut. The other one, Jahandar, had probably been perched in a tree watching the action unfold through a telescopic sight. But once the door was open and the cables severed, Jahandar moved to another perch closer to the building, with a view across the dam and down the road to Elphinstone, while Jones and Ershut and Mitch Mitchell made themselves at home in the Schloss.

Mitch Mitchell was Richard's secret and unspoken name for the gringo who wanted, in the worst way, to be addressed as Abdul-Ghaffar. Having no idea what the man's actual birth certificate name might have been, Richard—who simply could not bring himself to take the Abdul-Ghaffar thing seriously—had to make one up that went with his face and personality.

"How long you got?" had been Richard's first question to Mitch Mitchell, when he'd taken in the melanoma scar.

"*Inshallah,* long enough to strike a blow for the faith," he had responded. Richard had just barely managed to not roll his eyes, but Mitch seemed to have detected some faint trace of mockery. "But it depends," he had added, "on whether it has gone to the brain."

"No comment on that," Richard had said.

"I hate to break in," Jones said, "just when the two of you are getting off on the right foot. But I need to show you an MPEG, if that's all right."

"Is this MPEG going to answer any of my questions about Zula?" Richard asked.

"Many of them, undoubtedly," Jones said.

Until that point Richard had been engaging in a staredown with Mitch Mitchell, who apparently wanted Richard to believe that the melanoma *had* very much gone to his brain, and perhaps wiped out some of his behavioral inhibitions; but this seemed important enough for Richard to shift his gaze to Jones. He had seen various pictures of the man on the Internet and in the pages of the *Economist* and was still experiencing some of that disorientation that sets in when you find yourself in the actual presence of a famous person.

"Well, let's withdraw to the tavern then, if you don't mind being in a place that serves alcohol."

"As long as you're not serving it now," Jones said.

"Are you kidding? It's five in the morning."

The jest fell flat. Richard led them into the tavern, where T'Rain was still displayed on the big screen. A sizable crowd of people had gathered around Egdod. They were all exhibiting minor bothaviors such as breathing, scratching, and shifting their weight from foot to foot. But nothing was happening. This because (as a large dialog box superimposed on the screen was proclaiming) Richard had lost his Internet connection, and so nothing he saw here reflected what was "actually" (whatever that meant) going on in the T'Rain world. He fired off the command-key combo that shut down the game and was greeted by the usual Windows desktop. Jones meanwhile had shoved a thumb drive into a USB slot on the front of the computer. This showed up as a removable drive. Richard opened it to find one file: Zula.mpeg.

"This isn't going to infect my computer with a virus, is it?" he asked. Again, it was difficult to get a laugh out of these guys.

He double-clicked the icon. Windows Media Player opened up and showed him crappy webcam footage of his niece, sitting on a rumpled bed in a black room, reading yesterday's issue of the *Vancouver Sun*.

"Tried to get the *Globe and Mail*," Jones said apologetically, "but they were all out."

So that was it. Jones wanted to be the guy making the smart-ass quips.

Richard broke down weeping, and they had to leave him alone for a couple of minutes.

"FOR NOW, YOUR assistance in getting across the border would do nicely" had been Jones's answer, when Richard had got his composure back and had asked them what they wanted.

This surprised him a bit. He was so accustomed to people wanting his money. Being asked for his services as a smuggler filled him with a kind of pride, and almost made him grateful to Jones—as if Jones had done him a favor by showing respect for certain of Richard's hidden qualities that no one else gave a shit about anymore.

"You're almost there," Richard said. "Go south. You can't miss it."

"I have been led to believe," said Jones through a thin smile, "that it's a bit more difficult than you make it sound, and that you are especially good at getting across without drawing unwanted attention."

The helpful, earnest Iowa Boy Scout in Richard made him want to sketch Jones a map and provide detailed instructions, right on the spot. But that wasn't what Jones wanted. The terms of the transaction didn't really need to be spelled out, and Jones probably didn't want to say them out loud: he had retained at least that amount of British understatement. But he must have left Zula under the control of some people who were supposed to kill her if Jones and his party failed to make it across the border safe and sound.

Which meant that Richard was going on a little hike. Throwing in his lot with these guys, sharing their fate.

"I guess I'd better pack then," he said.

"We have a good deal of what you'll be needing," Jones said. "But if there is any particular equipment you require, clothing, pharmaceuticals—"

"Weapons?"

The thin smile came back. "I believe we have that adequately covered."1P

WHEN THEY HAD displayed her, up at the top of the hill with a chain around her neck, he had gone into another weeping fit. They were tears of joy. A bit odd, that. But knowing was so much better than wondering; and knowing that she was still alive was sweeter yet.

The first day's hike was straight south along the rail line. It got steeper as it went, until it began to push the limits of what nineteenth-century locomotive technology was really capable of. For the watershed of the Blue Fork was terminated, to the south and east, by a vaguely Cape Cod–shaped range of mountains: a beefy bicep projecting eastward from the Selkirks, and a bony forearm running generally north-south, eventually merging into a branch of the Purcells. They were traversing along the flank of the latter, gradually putting more and more vertical distance between themselves and the Blue Fork. The trail began going on little excursions, elbowing its way into mountain valleys to spring over tributaries, then feeling its way around projecting ridges that separated such valleys. As these became more precipitous, the builders had resorted to constructing trestles across the valleys and dynamiting short tunnels through the ridges, which must have been maddeningly difficult and insanely expensive at the time, but now provided the bikers and skiers who used the trail with amusing distractions.

Eventually they got trapped in the crook of the elbow, where progress was barred by the bulging bicep that ran roughly east-west, several miles north of the border, high enough that its upper slopes were devoid of vegetation: just towering, sand-colored ramparts with snow on the tops. They might have been mistaken for craggy dunes. Richard, who had been all over them, knew them as exposed buttresses of granite whose outer surfaces had spent the last few million years being slowly shivered and whittled away by the ridiculously unpleasant climate. Every small victory of element over mountain was celebrated by a small avalanche as a boulder, the size of a house, a car, a pumpkin, or a teakettle, exploded loose and headed downhill until stopped by older ones. The result was a large terrain of slopes, all at roughly the same angle, ramping up to the high, nearly vertical cliffs from which the rocks were being shed. Nothing much would grow in rubble, so there was no shade from the sun or shelter from the elements, and (perhaps just as important, for the psychological well-being of hikers) no variety to relieve the tedium. Walking across it was a nightmare, not just because it was steep but because its irregularity made it impossible to get into any sort of rhythm; indeed, the term "walking" could not even really be applied to the style of locomotion that the place forced on anyone stupid or unlucky enough to find himself in the middle of it.

It was up in this country where the baron had finally given up on his railway project. He had only run the line this far south as a feint, threatening to extend it into Idaho to spur the Canadians to more decisive action around Elphinstone. But here he had reached a point where he could go no farther unless he bored a mile-long tunnel southward through the ridge. To sell the bluff, he had made some progress, widening an existing mine tunnel for some distance, but had abandoned the project once he had gotten what he'd really wanted: a better connection to the Canadian national system at Elphinstone.

The first day of the journey, then, consisted of walking up to the place where the trail terminated at the head of this aborted tunnel project. Jones could have done this much without Richard's help. Zula had apparently explained that to him already. Richard's special knowledge of the terrain would come into play tomorrow.

And so it was an easy enough hike that day, and a sort of vacation: a chance to let his mind, unshackled by the Internet, roam wherever it willed. Mostly he thought about the reactions he had been having to the discovery that Zula was still alive. For during the last several days he had, as it were, been trying the idea that she was dead on for size, and trying to get his head around what that meant. Certainly he was no stranger to people he knew dying. He had reached the age where he had to attend a couple of contemporaries' funerals a year, and even had a special suit and pair of shoes that he kept handy for such events. But all deaths were as different as the persons who had died. Each death meant that a particular set of ideas and perceptions and reactions was gone from the world, apparently forever, and served as a reminder to Richard that one day his ideas and perceptions and reactions would be gone too. It was never good. But it seemed particularly unfair in the case of Zula. If he was now trading his death for hers, well, that was much better overall, and a trade that—as Jones knew perfectly well—he would gladly accept.

But the notion that it might be coming soon brought to the front of his mind a thing that of late he had been pondering, typically while staring out the windows of private jets at the landscape passing beneath him. His religious beliefs were completely undefined. But whether it was the case that his spirit would live on after his body or die with it, he had the nagging sense that, at his age (and especially in his current circumstances), he really ought to be growing more spiritual. For he was certainly closer to being dead than to having been born. Instead of which he was only becoming more connected to the world. He could not even imagine what it would mean to be a whole and conscious being without the smell of cedar in his nostrils. Seeing the color red. Tasting the first swallow of a pint of bitter. Feeling an old pair of jeans as he drew them up over his thighs. Staring out the window of an airplane at forests and fields and mountains. With all of that gone, how could one be alive, conscious, sentient, in any way that was worth a crap?

It was the sort of rumination that on any other day would soon have been cut short by the arrival of an email or a text message, but as he hiked up the valley of the Blue Fork at the head of a column of sweating and muttering jihadists, none of whom especially wanted to talk to him, he had plenty of leisure to consider it. Which seemed to be getting him absolutely nowhere. But he did try to enjoy the smell of the cedars and the blue of the sky while he still had the equipment to do it with.

OLIVIA PROCEEDED WITHOUT incident to a freeway on-ramp. They drove north through a sparse industrial zone that led into the southern outskirts of downtown Seattle. There they joined with I-5, the main north-south freeway, which they took all the way through the city. Half an hour later, after they had passed through another belt of suburbs and entered another, smaller city, she flicked on her turn signal and exited onto an east-going highway of lesser importance that proceeded across an endless series of tidal sloughs on long straight causeways. A range of mountains erupted from the flatlands directly ahead of them. Once it had gotten up onto slightly higher and drier land, the highway diverted south and began to wind to and fro, as if unnerved by the colossal barrier stretched across its path, but after a while it got funneled into a broad valley, clotted with small communities. The valley became narrower, the air colder, the towns smaller, the trees taller, and then it was clear that they were ascending into a mountain pass.

Both of them relaxed. There was no particular reason for this. No reason why, in today's world, they were safer, more anonymous on a winding highway in the mountains than they were on a freeway in the heart of a major city. But some atavistic part of their brains told them that they had effected some kind of escape. Gotten away with something.

"I don't fancy your friends," Olivia said. It was the first thing either one of them had said since Sokolov had climbed into the SUV in front of Igor's house.

Sokolov ignored it. "How did you know where I was?"

"As long as we're asking nervous questions, I've got one: Did you, or anyone else in that house, happen to say anything out loud when I showed up? Like, 'Holy shit, that looks like the MI6 agent Olivia?'"

"Of course I did not say such things."

"Of course not. But the others? Anything such as 'Who is that Chinese chick in the black SUV?'"

"Nothing; I made this gesture," Sokolov assured her, showing her the finger-across lips move and the upward glance.

"Well, that might help. A little."

"Again. How did you know where I was?"

"This morning I was in the Vancouver airport, on my way to Prince George to go looking for Abdallah Jones, when I was made aware that your friend's house had been placed under surveillance."

"Because stupid idiot went to apartment of Peter and was seen on video camera."

"Exactly. And then I was made aware that someone named Sokolov had just made a surprise visit."

"Ah."

"Yes. I felt a bit responsible."

He turned his head to look at her; she kept her eyes dutifully on the road. "How responsible?" he asked.

"The video files were encrypted, you see. No one could open them. Then, because of some things I did this morning, the encryption key was found."

"Found where?"

"In Peter's wallet."

"Peter is dead though?"

"Yes, Peter is dead. Turns out Ivanov shot him in Xiamen. Then Jones shot Ivanov and ran off with Zula."

"So where is wallet of Peter?"

"Csongor took it to Manila."

"Csongor is in Manila!?"

"As of a few hours ago, yes, he should be. Along with Yuxia and Marlon."

"Who is Marlon?"

"The hacker who created the virus."

A bit of silent driving, now, as Sokolov took all of this in.

"Anyway," Olivia continued, when Sokolov's body language suggested he was ready to hear more, "I sort of got everyone talking to one another. Dodge supplied the video file—"

"Dodge?"

"Richard Forthrast."

"Rich uncle of Zula."

"I hadn't pegged you for a T'Rain fan."

"I read about her in newspapers, magazines, this morning at bookstore. I am not surprised that a man of this type would have obtained video file. So. He supplied file, Csongor supplied key . . ."

"And then lots of cops and spies were looking at video of Igor stealing that." Olivia gave her head a little toss, indicating the rifle case in the backseat. "Why did you bring it, by the way?"

"I shoot moose. We have barbecue."

"I would love to have a moose barbecue with you. But we should probably be figuring out our next move."

"Our? We are together? Partners?" Sokolov's tone was rough and skeptical.

"That's what we need to figure out."

Her phone went off. She answered it and spent the next couple of minutes getting an earful from someone on the other end of the line. "All right," she finally said, "I'll check in with you when I'm north of the border." She hung up and handed the device to Sokolov. "Could you destroy that for me?"

"With pleasure." Sokolov began by figuring out how to eject the battery. In case it had some residual power source, he then laid it out on the dashboard, drew out his Makarov, verified that it was in a safe condition, and raised its butt like a hammer.

"Belay that," Olivia said. "I need to send one last message."

Sokolov set the Makarov down on the floor between his feet and slid the battery back into its socket.

Olivia was navigating an especially curvy part of the mountain pass, so she talked Sokolov through the process of getting the phone turned on and navigating its menus. "In 'Recent Calls,' you should see one, early this morning, to someone named Seamus."

"Yes, I have it," he said after a few moments.

"If you would be so good as to send a text to that number. 'Blown and going dark.' Something like that."

Sokolov looked at her incredulously.

"*Exactly* like that," she corrected herself.

Sokolov spent a few moments thumbing it out and sending it. Then he removed the battery again, placed the device on the dashboard, and picked up the Makarov. He looked at her.

"Go for it."

The butt of the Makarov came down on the black plastic puck, producing a nice splintering noise. Sokolov hit it a few more times and then began to sift through the resultant debris, looking for anything that might possibly be still alive. "Someone mad at you?"

"My boss in London," Olivia said, sounding a little tense. "People are talking."

"You were seen at house of Igor?"

"No. But my presence in the States is a bit of an open secret. I've been collaborating with local FBI on the search for Zula and for Jones. They know the name I'm using—the name on my passport. This morning, after I heard that you had showed up at Igor's house, I walked right across the concourse and got on the next plane for Seattle. It is a fifty-minute flight. I was there in no time. Walked out, grabbed a rental car, drove to Igor's."

"How did you know address of Igor?"

"I accessed a PDF of the court order using that." She nodded at the wreckage of the phone, which Sokolov was now primly scooping into a litter bag. "As you know, Igor's house is less than a kilometer from the airport. Elapsed time, from me getting the news in Vancouver to me showing up on the front stoop of Igor's house, less than two hours."

"Why?"

She gave him a look. "What do you mean, why?"

"Is crazy thing to do. Blowing the operation of the FBI."

"They would have gotten *everything*. All the stuff that went down in that apartment—kidnapping, murder—it all would have come to light and you'd have spent the rest of your life in prison."

"Maybe it will happen anyway," Sokolov said, thinking of Vlad, cringing on the floor.

"You and I had a deal," Olivia said, "back in China. Which was that, in exchange for your assistance in helping track down Abdallah Jones, my employer would get you out of trouble. Something went wrong. I don't know what."

Sokolov shrugged dismissively. "Network of so-called George Chow was penetrated by PSB."

"I am still trying to honor the general spirit of that agreement," Olivia said. "And it's to our advantage—MI6's advantage—to keep you from getting hauled into an American court for a sensational trial. Because then a lot of other stuff would come out too."

"China stuff."

"China stuff. With repercussions for international relations among China, the U.S., the U.K. So you had to be gotten out of that house."

"You acted well," Sokolov agreed. "I was afraid—" Then he shut up.

A little too late. "You were afraid I was being a crazy, love-sick stalker chick."

"Yes."

Olivia sighed. "If only I had the time for such recreations."

"Now you are in deep shit?" Sokolov inquired, shaking the bag of phone debris.

"I left enough circumstantial evidence—flying to Seattle, renting the car—that sooner or later the FBI is going to figure out that I went to Igor's house and blew the operation. They have already begun asking difficult questions of my higher-ups at MI6."

"What is best course for you then?"

"It's going to be an awkward pain in the arse no matter what," Olivia said, "but everything would be a hell of a lot better if I were in Canada. This would put me out of the FBI's jurisdiction, and in a country with Commonwealth ties to the U.K.—easier to grease the skids from there, get me home discreetly."

"To Canada then!" Sokolov said. "Canada is better for me too; I have work visa there. *Byiznyess* connections."

"We'll have to cross the border illegally."

"You know place?"

"I don't know a place, exactly. But I know a family that can get us across."

"Smugglers?"

"It's not so much that they are smugglers," Olivia said, "as that they deny the validity of borders altogether."

BLOWN AND GOING DARK.

Seamus had to hand it to the girl. He was getting to the point where he could not get his day started without a dramatic early-morning text message or phone call from Olivia. If he continued working with this person, he was going to have to get into the habit of going to bed early and perhaps even sober.

They had arrived in Manila at midnight and crashed in a chain hotel just up the street from the U.S. embassy, which was where Seamus intended to be the next morning, just as soon as the visa section opened its doors. So this cryptic message served as a convenient wake-up call.

He had laid his credit card down and secured a suite, employing fake credentials that had been issued to him for use when he needed to travel without throwing his real name around. He had given the bed, which was in its own separate room, to Yuxia. Seamus was sleeping on the floor near the suite's entrance with a pistol under his pillow. Marlon and Csongor had flipped a coin for the sofa, and Marlon had won, so Csongor had staked out a patch of floor in the corner.

Seamus had no idea what level of precautions was appropriate here. Apparently these three had left half of the surviving population of China seriously pissed off at them, as well as making mortal enemies with a rogue, defrocked Russian organized crime figure. In their spare time they had stolen money from millions of T'Rain players, created huge problems for a large multinational corporation that owned the game, and, finally—warming to the task—mounted a frontal assault on al-Qaeda. Had their coordinates been generally known, no amount of security would have been adequate. Seamus's sidearm was a nice gun and everything, but it would not be much use should China invade the Philippines, or should one of Abdallah Jones's minions decide to Stuka a fuel-laden 767 into the roof of the Best Western. He had decided to proceed on the assumption that no one knew where the hell they were, and to hustle them into the embassy first thing in the morning. Perhaps something could be sorted out there.

He'd had a talk with Csongor before going to bed: a little private man-to-man in the hallway, while Marlon and Yuxia had been taking turns using the bathroom. The subject of the talk had been guns. Seamus's instincts had told him to confiscate Csongor's pistol, since more bad than good things could come of his having it. But the Hungarian had been carrying it around now for a couple of weeks and had already used it in anger on two occasions, and so it seemed like not the best idea, from an interpersonal relations standpoint, to demand that it be handed over. And, just as a matter of principle, Seamus could not relieve a man of a gun he had used to shoot Abdallah Jones in the head. Seamus had spent enough time with Csongor by this point to get a sense of who he was, and he felt confident that Csongor would behave sanely and discreetly. His only concern was that some bump in the night would wake them all up and that Csongor, disoriented, would freak out, draw the weapon, and do something fucked up.

So that was what they had talked about. The corridor had been empty, so Seamus had stood well back, keeping his hands in plain sight, and had asked Csongor to take the gun out and demonstrate that he knew how to check the action for live rounds, how to make it safe, how to load and unload it. Csongor had done all those things without fuss or hesitation. Seamus had complimented him on his skill, being careful not to make it gushy or patronizing, since Csongor was not some coddled American kid who needed positive feedback all the time.

"I'm going to keep a light on. Dimly. So we can see each other if we wake up in the middle of the night. No mistakes. No shooting at vague forms. Got it?"

"Of course."

"Glad we settled that," Seamus had said.

Then: "What are your plans?" Since the bathroom had still been unavailable.

Csongor had looked extremely tired.

"You know Don Quixote?" Csongor had finally asked, after

thinking about it for so long that Seamus had nearly fallen asleep on his feet.

"Not personally, but—"

"Of course, but you know the idea."

"Yeah. Tilting at windmills. Dulcinea." Seamus hadn't read the book, but he'd seen the musical and he remembered the song.

"I have a windmill. A Dulcinea."

"No shit, really?"

"No shit."

"Who is she, big guy? Not Yuxia."

Csongor had shook his head. "Not Yuxia."

"That's good, because I kind of like Yuxia."

"I noticed."

"Who is she?" This had partly been about making friendly conversation with Csongor but also partly a matter of professional interest; before he spent much more time wandering around in strange places with this armed Hungarian man-tank, it seemed important for Seamus to understand what made him tick—what motivated him, for example, to run about China engaging major international terrorists in gunplay.

"Zula Forthrast."

"Wow." Seamus considered it. "You picked a tough one. Let me see. She lives in a country that's hard for you to get to. She's the niece of a superrich guy. She's being held hostage, in a part of the world we can only guess at, by an incredibly dangerous terrorist who totally hates you for shooting him in the head."

Csongor had spread out his hands, palms up, as if surrendering. "Like I said. Windmill."

Seamus had stepped around beside him and given him a companionable thwack on the shoulder. "I like windmill tilters," he had said.

"Do you have any ideas at all?" Csongor had asked.

"As to where Jones took her?"

"Yes."

Seamus had then supplied Csongor with a brief explanation of the theories that had been investigated so far: the obvious southern Philippines route, which had been exploded; the North American Gambit, which was still under investigation; and Olivia's new SNAG concept, which (as Seamus was quite confident) she was checking out, at this very moment, in Prince George, British Columbia. None of which had seemed entirely satisfactory to Csongor. But he had obviously been comforted to know that people were working on it and discussing it in places like London and Langley.

"How can I get there?" Csongor had asked.

"You mean, to the northwestern U.S.?"

"Yeah."

Strangely, this was the first time they had discussed what they were actually going to do. It had been obvious enough that they needed to get to Manila, so they had done so without putting any thought into what would happen next. Seamus had a vague idea of getting the three wanderers into the United States, and he had taken them to this place near the embassy. But he hadn't actually sat down and talked to them about it yet.

"Got your passport?" Seamus had asked.

"Unbelievable but yes."

"Hungary is a visa waiver country, right?"

"Yes."

"So you just need to fill out the web form, ditch the loaded gun, and you're in. No problem. As for our Chinese friends . . . that's going to be interesting."

"Does it help," Csongor asked, "that Marlon has two million dollars?"

"It doesn't hurt."

NOW IT WAS five in the fucking morning and he was wide awake, surrounded by people who were sleeping as soundly as it was possible for humans to sleep without being etherized. And Olivia—who was supposed to be pursuing her crazy SNAG theory in Canada—had made the announcement that she was blown and going dark.

How could your cover be blown in *Canada*? Why even *bother* going dark there? How could you *tell*?

Not that Seamus, in general, had any great problem with the Great White North. But to be an MI6 agent in that country seemed about as close to a milk run as you could get in the espionage world.

He fired up his laptop, found a wireless network, set up an

encrypted connection, and got in touch with Stan, a colleague and former comrade-in-arms in the greater Washington, D.C., area. It was quitting time there, and Saturday to boot, but Stan was known to work odd hours. Seamus asked Stan whether it wouldn't be too much of a challenge to his intellectual faculties to track down the provenance of a certain instant message, and wondered whether Stan was too much of a pussy to get it done discreetly, without setting the whole counterterrorism network alight.

Then he took a shower. When he came back, a message was waiting for him from Stan, asking what all this had to do with Seamus's metier, viz., eating snakes and molesting ladyboys in the southern Philippines. The message went on to claim that, as a result of Stan's making the inquiry, the Department of Homeland Security's Terror Alert Status had been elevated to Red, and POTUS had been evacuated to a secure facility in Nebraska. Those preliminaries out of the way, Stan divulged that the message had been sent via a cell tower near the summit of Stevens Pass, northeast of Seattle, and squarely within the borders of the United States. Judging from cell-tower records, the phone in question had been eastbound at the time. Nothing more was known, since the device had not popped up on the network since the message had been sent. Was there anything else?

Why yes, Seamus responded, if it wouldn't interrupt Stan's busy schedule of watching gay bondage pornography videos on the taxpayer-provided high-speed Internet connection, he would very much like to know whether a certain young lady had bought any airplane tickets or rented any cars in Washington or British Columbia of late.

A few minutes later came an email assuring Seamus that the lap dancer in question had indeed left an electronic trail a mile wide and that Seamus might be able to make use of the following data in tracking her down and getting his stolen kidney back: she had flown from Vancouver to Seattle this morning and rented a navy blue Chevy Trailblazer.

Seamus sent a polite note back reminding Stan to zip his fly when finished and promising to buy him a drink during Stan's next visit to Zamboanga, supposing that Stan had the testicular fortitude to come within a thousand miles of such a challenging locale.

Then he pulled up a Google map of Stevens Pass. It was on a minor highway, a two-laner that Google didn't even bother to draw on the map once he had clicked the Zoom Out button a couple of times. Seattle, then Vancouver came into view on successive clicks, and then Spokane, farther to the east, near the Idaho border.

Why had she rented a large SUV? Was it the only thing left in the lot? Or was she expecting to do some off-road work?

Something Csongor had said earlier was eating at him. Had been tunneling into his brain during the scant four hours he had managed to sleep: *Does it help that Marlon has two million dollars?*

The flip answer—always the first thing that would come into Seamus's head—was, *Why yes, with that kind of money he could lease a bizjet and fly there directly.*

Which got him thinking about flight paths and border formalities.

This was an asinine idea, worth thinking about only as a thought experiment, but: Supposing they did exactly that? Leased a bizjet and flew it to the Pacific Northwest?

Then they would still have the minor problem that Marlon and Yuxia lacked visas. Which would be a showstopper if they landed at Sea-Tac or Boeing Field or any other international airport with immigration barriers.

Why not just land out in the middle of nowhere? Avoid those barriers altogether?

Answer: they'd be noticed on radar. In theory. But what if they did something tricky to avoid that? What was to stop them, really? Other than the fact that their pilot would refuse to do it because he wouldn't want to get caught and thrown into prison.

So it was just a crazy thought experiment. But it was a thought experiment with a side effect, which was that it forced him to think exactly the same thoughts that Abdallah Jones had been thinking two weeks ago. Jones must have looked at the same Google map, traced the mountain ranges, zoomed in and out on promising border-crossing sites.

He was now, for some reason, fully and utterly convinced of Olivia's theory. Jones *must* have flown to North America. It was *so* doable.

And he must have stopped short for some reason, landed in

Canada. It didn't really matter why, exactly. But if he'd landed in the States, he'd have done something by now. The fact that he'd been silent for so long suggested that he had been maneuvering toward the Canadian border, looking for a discreet way to cross it.

How would he do it, exactly?

"What are you looking at?" asked a voice from behind him. Csongor, lying there awake, gazing dully at Seamus's laptop.

"I've got a windmill of my own," Seamus said.

"Jones?"

"Yeah. And I think he's somewhere on this map." He was looking at the bottom hundred miles of British Columbia, most of Washington State, and the Idaho panhandle. "And I'll bet he's got your Dulcinea with him. Sweet sovereign of your captive heart."

"What are we waiting for?" Csongor asked.

"The embassy to open. And . . ."

"And what?"

Seamus grabbed his hair with both hands and pulled. "A fucking clue as to where exactly he wants to cross the border. Shit man, once you get past the suburbs of Vancouver it's wilderness all the way to fucking Sault Ste. Marie."

And that was when it came to him. Maybe because he was really smart. Maybe because he was lucky. Maybe because, down in the little toolbar at the bottom of his screen, a little tab labeled "T'Rain" was flashing on and off, trying to get his attention.

He clicked on that tab. The window expanded to reveal that Thorakks was under attack. He was out in the middle of a desert somewhere, walking along in a large crowd of characters who had all been following Egdod. That crowd was being assaulted by a horde of horse archers.

"Are you actually going to play video games now?" Csongor asked incredulously.

"Give me a minute to kick the shit out of these guys and then I'll answer your question," Seamus said, going into action, breaking Thorakks out of his robotic stupor, shouldering a shield, throwing up a protective spell. Cutting down one horse archer with a thunderbolt and another with a stroke of his sword.

But Thorakks wasn't the target. Egdod was.

They were riding in to count coup on Egdod. They couldn't

hope to actually hurt a character of such power, of course. But they could earn the fantastic distinction of having struck a blow against the oldest and most powerful character in all T'Rain.

Egdod was doing nothing. Making no move to defend himself. He was still following his bothavior: trying to walk all the way to his HZ, thousands of miles away.

"Where are you?" Marlon asked. He had been awakened by the sounds of T'Rainian combat.

"How the fuck should I know?" Seamus responded. "When we left that place I stayed logged in and told Thorakks to follow Egdod. So we are wherever Egdod wandered to. How long since we left?"

"Something like twelve hours," Csongor said.

"So. Richard Forthrast gets up twelve hours ago to answer the doorbell and never comes back. Never logs out properly. Egdod goes into his bothavior. What does that tell you?"

Csongor shrugged. "Nothing."

"He's sleeping," Marlon suggested. "He was awake for a whole day."

"Goddamn it," Seamus said. "I was afraid one of you would come up with a reasonable explanation such as that."

"You have an unreasonable explanation?" asked Yuxia, who had emerged from her private bedchamber looking sweet and sleepy and heard the last part of the exchange.

"Yeah," said Seamus, after a brief pause to admire Yuxia. He minimized the T'Rain window, brought up his Google map again, and zoomed in on a stretch of border between the Idaho panhandle and a town called Elphinstone. "Abdallah Jones is crossing the border here, now. And Richard Forthrast is helping him do it."

AS THEY DROVE down out of the pass and into more settled areas in the river valleys on the dry side of the Cascades, Olivia began to feel oppressed by the sense that they were absurdly conspicuous, driving along together in this rental car.

She did not have the faintest idea what the police and the FBI might be thinking. But it seemed best to assume the worst and to start behaving as though she and Sokolov were in a hostile country, cover blown, being hunted by the police. In which case, doing what they were doing was the dumbest possible way to proceed, and it was a miracle they hadn't been pulled over and handcuffed yet.

They could ditch this car easily enough and find some other way to proceed eastward. But the mere fact of "short-haired Asian woman traveling with lean, close-cropped blond man" was enough to make them conspicuous, should an APB go out to all the local cops and highway patrol cruisers.

"We have to split up," she said.

"Agreed."

"At least for now," she added, because some ridiculous instinct was telling her that her first sentence had sounded a little too harsh and she didn't want to hurt Sokolov's feelings. She glanced over at him. He did not appear to be hurt.

"The place we're going is in the general vicinity of Bourne's Ford, Idaho," she said.

"Bourne's Ford, Idaho," he repeated.

"I can't give you a specific landmark. I've never been there."

They had become stuck in traffic behind a semitrailer truck that said WALMART.

"Just find the nearest Walmart," she suggested. "There's got to be one within thirty miles. I'll meet you in the sporting goods department between noon and half past. I'll just keep going there every day until you turn up."

Sokolov pulled the long gun case out of the backseat and laid it across his lap. He opened it up to reveal the weapon. By popping out two pins he was able to break it down into two pieces, neither of which was more than about a foot and a half long, and by collapsing the stock he was able to make it shorter yet. He placed both pieces of it into his knapsack—a new purchase from the Eddie Bauer store in downtown Seattle—and then transferred a lot of other odds and ends that were rattling around loose in there: a few cartridges, two empty clips, some cleaning supplies.

"You really think you're going to need that?"

"Is matter of responsibility," Sokolov said. "Can't leave in abandoned car. Anyway, is evidence too—fingerprints of Igor." He zipped the pack shut and looked at her. "You get out at bus stop, I will liquidate car."

"What are you going to do with it?"

"In the forest, back up there, are, what do you call them, places where hikers pull off road, go to beginning of path."

"Trailheads."

"Yes. I think it is normal to park a car in such place for several days. It is legal. Will not draw attention. But it is off the road. Not obvious. I will go back, park at such place, hike down."

"Then what?"

"Hitchhike." Sokolov paused for a moment. "Is dangerous, I know, to take ride from strangers. With assault rifle in backpack, not so dangerous."

They had been passing signs on the road that appeared to designate bus stops. After a few more miles they found one that was conveniently situated next to a parking lot where they could pull out of traffic. Olivia walked over to the bus stop and checked the schedule and verified that a bus would be along in another twenty minutes to take her into the nearby town of Wenatchee. She went round back of the SUV and rapped on the rear window. Sokolov had already moved laterally into the driver's seat. He popped the tailgate. She hauled it open and pulled her bag out of the back. For a moment, their eyes locked in the rearview mirror.

"See you," she said.

"See you."

She slammed the tailgate, hoisted her bag onto her shoulder, and walked to the bus stop. Sokolov put the car in gear, got the SUV turned around, and headed back up the way they had come, keeping an eye peeled for trailheads.

GIVEN THE REMARKABLE length and diversity of Csongor, Marlon, and Yuxia's enemies list, the five-block stroll from the hotel to the U.S. embassy was one of the more stimulating experiences of Seamus's recent life. Not because anything actually happened—he'd have known how to behave, in that case—but because he had no way of telling whether any of the people who passed them on the sidewalk or cruised past them in cars, jeepneys, and motor scooters were gun-toting assassins bent on retribution. He reckoned he could have covered the distance in about half the time if he had simply slung Yuxia over his back in a fireman's carry and hoofed it with the long-legged Csongor and Marlon keeping pace. Not a one of them was under six feet two, and they all seemed to get the idea that hanging around in the open was not the preferred strategy. Yuxia was a different matter, not because she was tiny (she could move as fast as any of them when she had a mind to) but because she insisted on viewing this as a fascinating exploratory junket into a new and unfamiliar world, and an opportunity to establish cross-cultural relations with as many as possible of the hundreds of people she encountered on the street. Most of these conversations were gratifyingly brief, possibly because Yuxia's interlocutors kept stealing uneasy glances at Csongor and Seamus, who tended to bracket the girl and stand with their backs to each other and their hands in their pockets scanning the vicinity with disconcerting alertness. Meanwhile Marlon did his bit by chivvying her along, muttering to her in Mandarin, as though playing the role of a nervous, irritable boyfriend.

The embassy was huge, a city within the city, and given the number of active Islamic terrorist cells in the Philippines, it was not the sort of place you could just stroll into. Seamus came here frequently enough that most of the marine guards recognized him. But his three companions would have to ID themselves and pass through metal detectors like anyone else. Seamus managed to squeeze the whole party into a gatehouse where they could stand and wait in air-conditioned comfort until the duty officer arrived, which took all of about thirty seconds. Seamus was then able to explain the unusual nature of his visitors and his errand. Csongor was briskly but politely disarmed, and everyone was metal detected and frisked. Seamus was then allowed to lead his guests out into the embassy grounds, which sprawled for many acres across reclaimed land along the shore of Manila Bay. Both Americans and Japanese had, at various times, controlled the Philippines, and run major wars, out of this compound. There was an older chancery in the middle, hemmed in from both sides by more recent buildings that housed the embassy's thousands of American and Filipino employees. A great deal of space was given over to all things having to do with visas. Seamus hoped that he could get Marlon and Yuxia in to see some of those people today.

First, though, he had to get them interested in visiting the United

States. Seamus was enough of a naked chauvinist to assume that any non-American in his or her right mind would want to come to America. But he had not spent half of his adult life in strange parts of the world without picking up a few diplomatic skills. He strolled into the shade of a large tree in front of the chancery and convened the others in a little circle around him.

"I'm going to America," he said, "as soon as I can get on a plane. I'm going there because I think that our friend Abdallah Jones is there and that Zula might be with him, as a hostage. Csongor is coming with me; he can get permission to enter the U.S. by filling out a web form, so it's easy for him. You guys, Marlon and Yuxia, are free to do whatever you want. But I feel I should point out that you are in this country illegally. Chinese citizens need a visa to enter the Philippines, and I'm going to take a wild guess that you didn't get visas before you stole that fishing boat from the terrorists and blew away the skipper. I don't recommend that you just go back to China. You really need to get to some country that is not China and where you have some sort of paperwork so you can't be arrested and deported back to China on sight—which is what would happen if you went out there"—he waved his arm vaguely at the traffic on Roxas Boulevard—"and got noticed." He aimed this last comment at Yuxia, who had spent the last half hour doing everything she conceivably could to get herself noticed. She took the meaning and got a slightly pouty look about her, which was quite unlike Yuxia, and nearly killed Seamus.

Marlon and Yuxia were watching Seamus carefully now. They might, or might not, find the idea of a trip to the United States appealing on its own merits. But he'd gotten their attention by mentioning Jones and Zula, and then scared the hell out of them by elucidating their dilemma regarding paperwork.

"Now, I believe that I might be able to arrange something."

Rapt silence.

"I'm going to assume that neither one of you has a Chinese passport."

Marlon shook his head.

"We only get them when we are going to travel outside of China," Yuxia said, "and I have never done so."

"Actually you have," Seamus pointed out, throwing his hands

out to direct her attention to the fact that she was in Manila. She smiled. "Anyway, not having a passport will certainly throw a monkey wrench into the process of getting a visa to enter the United States." He was trying to employ dry understatement here and wasn't entirely certain that they were fully appreciative of his sense of humor. "But I know some people here in the embassy who can make it all right in no time."

"ARE YOU OUT of your fucking mind?" the CIA station chief was asking him a few minutes later.

Marlon and Yuxia and Csongor were cooling their heels in a café in a relatively nonsecure part of the embassy. Seamus and the station chief, an American of Filipino ancestry named Ferdinand ("Call me Freddie"), were conversing in a part of the building that was very secure indeed. They had known each other for a while.

"Freddie, you know that this room is so secret, so well shielded, that I could strangle you here and no one would ever know."

"No one except for the two marines with submachine guns right outside the door."

"Drinking buddies of mine."

"Seriously, Seamus, what are you asking me to do? Produce forged Chinese passports?"

"Real American ones would be a hell of a lot easier."

Freddie actually considered this. "I suppose we could claim that they were American citizens, visiting Manila, whose passports were stolen by pickpockets. That farce would be uncovered the moment the State Department actually bothered to check the records."

"Freddie. Work with me here. The global war on terror leads us into many strange situations. We do stuff all the time that's not technically legal. Hell, my very presence in this country is a violation of Philippine sovereignty. As is yours."

"So you want to play the GWOT card?"

"Yes. Come on, Freddie. That's the whole point of this conversation."

Freddie gave him an *I'm waiting* look. In retrospect, Seamus should have seen this as the trap that it was.

"I know where Jones is," Seamus said. "I can narrow it down to maybe ten square miles. Or kilometers, for our Canadian friends."

"Would this be related to the work you have been doing with"— and here Freddie picked up a folder marked as containing secret information—"that British girl? Olivia Halifax-Lin?"

"That brave, brilliant British girl who single-handedly tracked Jones down in Xiamen and collected priceless surveillance data on him and his cell for months? Yes, I believe we are talking about the same Olivia."

"Maybe she should have taken a little more time off," Freddie said. "Perhaps that sort of work didn't suit her, lifestyle-wise."

"Why are you saying that?"

"In the last day or so, she seems to have gone totally off the rails. She skipped out of a large and expensive FBI counterterror investigation. Just walked out of the room without explaining anything. Hightailed it up to Vancouver, leaving quite the electronic trail. Including communications with you. Crashed in a hotel room there and was bothering some poor Mountie about this same theory."

"By 'this same theory' you mean the excellent theory that she and I have been developing."

"Ah, so you have been working with her."

"Go on."

"Claimed she was headed to some place in B.C. called Prince George. Bought a ticket. Checked in for the flight. Never boarded it. Instead bought a ticket with cash, on short notice, and went back down to Seattle, still not bothering to explain to anyone what the hell she was doing. Did not give the FBI the courtesy of a call. Then, around the time that her plane was landing at Sea-Tac, there was a shootout in a house full of Russians, low-level criminal types, less than a mile away. An FBI surveillance operation was blown. No one knows where the hell she is. One of the guys who was under surveillance has disappeared. Russian security consultant, ex–special forces, apparently related to the whole Xiamen thing."

"Sounds like you've been talking to the FBI quite a bit."

Freddie made no comment, just rolled his eyes up from the secret documents and stared at Seamus over his glasses. "Yes?"

"Anything from the intel community?"

"Why do you ask?"

"Because they can get information that the FBI can't. And sometimes they're not very nice about sharing."

"This Olivia person," said Freddie, "sent you a text message this morning, didn't she?"

Seamus laughed. "I knew it." He sat up, leaning forward across the table. "So the FBI, the cops, they're clueless. They have no idea where she might have gone. But the intel community was tracking her phone. They have a rough idea."

"Very rough," said Freddie. "And getting rougher with every passing minute. But the presumption is that she wants to get across the border into Canada where she'll have a better shot at clearing up her amazingly tattered visa status and getting home in one piece."

"Which is what the intel community would like to happen," Seamus said, "and so no one is going to drop a dime on her."

"As long as she keeps her wits about her, I would guess she'll be back in London in a couple of weeks, looking forward to, oh, about four decades of working behind a desk."

"Okay," Seamus said. "That's all quite amusing. But what I really want to talk about is Jones."

"Yes. You know where Jones is. You figured it out, apparently, while spending all night playing a video game in a provincial Internet café patronized by Australian sex tourists."

"That is pretty much the size of it."

"And the break that enabled you to put all this together came in the form of a telephone call from Olivia Halifax-Lin, made during her *previous* sudden disappearance from the FBI's radar screens."

"There's no PowerPoint presentation, if that's what you're looking for," Seamus said.

"If there were, would it have Olivia's name on it?"

"Only if that would be advantageous."

"It was a rhetorical question. Everyone knows that the idea came from her."

Seamus said, "I'm guessing that is viewed as a bad thing?"

"Unless you have some hard evidence as to Jones's whereabouts, it's going to be treated as a highly speculative theory that was talked about, but never exactly written down, by an agent whose reputation could hardly sink any lower."

"So it *is* about the PowerPoint."

Freddie ignored this. "Seamus, you are a living example of the Peter Principle."

Seamus looked down, mock shocked, toward his own genitalia.

"Not that one," Freddie said. "Never mind. The point is that you have risen as high as you can get in the hierarchy without having to behave like a responsible manager."

Seamus was half out of his chair, but Freddie calmed him by holding up one hand. "I will be the first to attest that you are as responsible as any man who ever lived when it comes to those in your command. If I had to go back to being a snake eater, I would want to be your subordinate. But above the level where you are now, you have to be able to justify your actions and your expenditures by supplying documentation, and you have to engage in all sorts of political maneuvers to make sure that the right people see your PowerPoint presentations at the right times. And you are a million miles away from being able to do this in the case of whatever theory you and Olivia have been cooking up. And consequently no one above you in the hierarchy is going to stick his or her neck out by supporting your theory."

"Even if I were that kind of guy, Freddie, there *isn't time*. We need to act *now*."

"Give me something," Freddie said.

"I got nothing to give, Freddie!"

"What you're asking for right now is a nightmare from my point of view. Handing out fake passports to two random Chinese kids. What are you trying to achieve, Seamus? You want to make these two into American citizens? Put them in the Witness Protection Program?"

"Look," Seamus said, "I just have to fucking get there. So I can check this out."

"I'm not stopping you."

"But these kids are with me, and I can't just abandon them here."

"I'm listening."

"I could get in a taxi and go to the airport now. If they had an ounce of common sense, they would apply for asylum. Now, *that* would be a nightmare."

"Are you threatening me?"

"I'm just saying, they're here, Freddie, and I ain't sending them back to China. Either they go with me, now, or they camp out on your front yard and request asylum. They are *very* Internet-savvy."

Freddie was frozen solid. Beginning to perspire a bit.

"If I wanted to threaten you," Seamus continued, "I'd hit you where you live."

"Where do I live?"

"Abdallah Jones killed a bunch of your guys."

"They were *your* guys, Seamus."

"I'm your subordinate. You gave the orders. Let's call them our guys. Now I know where Jones is. I can get him. But I have this waif problem."

"Wraith?"

"Waif. Waif. I'm being followed around by Chinese waifs. And one not-so-waiflike Hungarian. Prevents me from getting to Jones. Your personal fault."

"You're making this too hard," Freddie said, after thinking about it for a while. "You just need some way to get them on a plane in Manila, and off the plane Stateside, without them being snatched by Immigration."

"That would do, for now," Seamus admitted. "We could work on the details later."

"It's too bad we can't get them on a military flight," Freddie said.

"How would that help us?"

"It would depart from an airbase here and land at a base in the States. Not that they don't check papers. But we could finesse it much more easily."

"Finesse it?"

"For me to get Immigration at a place like Sea-Tac to look the other way while you smuggled a couple of undocumented Chinese into the country, I would have to get a hundred fucking people involved, from several agencies," Freddie said. "People would drag their feet, raise objections, screw it up."

"I thought this was what you were good at. PowerPoint presentations. Consensus building."

"Only when you give me something to work with. And lots of time. But if we could turn it into a military thing, that would be much easier."

"What does it cost to charter a business jet?"

"How should I know? Do I look like the kind of person who charters business jets?"

"No, but Marlon does."

"Who's Marlon?"

Day 20

Once the main party had gone south, the camp was much reduced in number of tents (only two left, not counting Zula's little one-person shelter) but hugely expanded in its solid waste footprint. Much of what they had brought up here had been carried straight from grocery stores or Walmarts, and during the morning's last-minute packing frenzy, they had pulled everything out of its sacks and packaging material, which they had simply dropped on the ground. Now the wind was blowing it around, much of it tumbling away until it snagged in shrubs or tree branches. Zula wondered if it was stupid for her to be offended by this desecration of the natural environment, given the larger goal of the jihadists' mission and the number of people they'd already killed.

Ershut and Jahandar spent much of the afternoon napping. Zula couldn't tell whether this was in consequence of having awakened early or in the expectation of staying on watch tonight.

While they slumbered, Zula went to work cutting up some mutton to make kebabs. Sayed spent his time reading and praying, and Zakir, supine on a camping mat in a patch of sunlight, either stared at Zula from under the brim of his hat or snored. When he was snoring, Zula took trimmings of fat, bones, and even whole pieces of red meat, and put them in paper grocery bags and tossed them down the slope in the direction of the tents. In any proper grad-student-run campsite this would have led to an inquisition on the scale of the Salem witch trials, but here, given the jihadists' insensitivity to litter, it would go unnoticed save by wild animals. Last night had been bear-free, but, given that this wasn't a frequently used campsite, the animals would have no reason to visit the place until they came to associate it with the availability of food.

All the while she was doing this, she was maintaining, in her head, a debate as to whether it was a good idea. If they didn't execute her before sundown, she stood a good chance of getting away from these men, even without the assistance of the local *Ursus arctos horribilis* community. It wasn't as if she were going to sit up all night long, padlock key in her hot little hand, waiting for the arrival of bears before making her move. If they did show up, they'd be as likely to wake up her captors as to help cover her escape; and if they were of a mind to kill and eat humans, they'd be at least as interested in her as in them. But she did it anyway, because it seemed a fine way to show her contempt for these men.

Afternoon seemed to stretch out forever. The nappers awoke when the sun was only about a hand's breadth above the ridge of the Selkirks and began hanging around her little kitchen area in the timeless manner of hungry persons who expected others to prepare their food. Zula displayed the spitted, ready-to-cook kebabs and let it be understood that they would taste better cooked over coals than on the blue flames of a camp stove. Soon Ershut and Sayed were tromping around in the nearby woods gathering firewood.

Zula grew accustomed to hearing their heavy, crashing movements in the trees and so didn't make much of it at first when her ears picked up the faint crunch of dried pine needles being trod upon, the rustle of shrubbery being pushed out of the way by something making its way through the forest. When it *did* finally break the surface of her awareness, she had the immediate feeling that she had actually been hearing it for quite some time. In the back of her head she'd been thinking, *Why is Ershut creeping along so slowly? He'll never gather much firewood that way.* But then she saw Ershut stomping into the campsite from the opposite direction, carrying a double armload of dead branches. So it must be Sayed? But Sayed emerged from the trees only a few paces behind Ershut.

Zakir, then, the creepy one, was sneaking up on her through

the woods. But why bother? She was chained to a tree. She'd already been caught.

Was it Jahandar, getting into position in a new sniper's perch? No, she'd seen him going off into the woods toward the Blue Fork, carrying an empty water bag.

It must be Zakir then.

Two minutes later, as Zula was putting new fuel onto the nearly burned-out remains of the campfire, she heard a loud zipping noise, and looked up to see Zakir dragging himself out of his tent, where he had apparently gone to change into some warmer clothes. Getting ready for temperatures to drop. For the sun was just a red bubble on the Selkirks now.

So who, or what, had been creeping around in the woods up there?

She became very excited for a moment, imagining that it was a rescuer. A sniper from the Royal Canadian Mounted Police, sent to infiltrate the camp in advance of a major, helicopter-borne rescue operation. On that illusion, she made a point of not staring into the woods, not showing any curiosity about what might be back there.

But after a little while, as the fire blazed high and then began to die down, forming beds of coals in the interstices among the tangled logs, she shook her head in a kind of self-embarrassment that she'd ever been so naive as to imagine such a thing. No one was coming to rescue her. She had to do it herself. And it was probably better that way. Running through woods in the dark, she had a chance. Chained to a tree in the middle of a pitched automatic weapons duel, she wouldn't last long. Worse, she wouldn't have the power to change her situation.

None of which answered the question.

She permitted herself to look out into the woods now. None of the men noticed; none of them cared.

But she'd waited too long. The sun was behind the mountains. The fire almost cast more light, now, than the sky. But she was patient, keeping her back to the sunset and the fire and waiting for her eyes to adjust as she stared into the almost perfect blackness of the woods.

She saw nothing. There was nothing to see.

And yet something was bothering her. After all she'd been

through at the hands of humans, it seemed inconceivable that anything of the natural world could hold any terrors for Zula. But there *was* something out there, and it *did* terrify her. Not in the intellectual way of *I hope Jones didn't order them to kill me* but at a much deeper level.

She could feel a tingle at the back of her scalp. This was something that had happened only a few times in her life. Her hair was attempting to stand up on end, like that of a dog who senses it's staring into something big enough to kill it and wants to look bigger.

But no matter how long she stared into the deepening shadows she saw nothing more. Finally she made up her mind to tear herself away from it and attend to the cooking. She planted a heel and spun around it.

A pair of sparks drew faint red traces across the corner of her eye.

She was relearning ancient lessons here: the peripheral vision was more sensitive to movement than the central. She turned back, shaking her head from side to side like a wolf casting for a scent, and caught glimpses of the twin sparks again.

There they were. She had them now. Two points of red light.

She had missed them before because they weren't down at ground level, where she'd been looking. They were up high in a tree.

She had almost convinced herself that they were just drops of sap reflecting the light of the fire when they winked out for a moment and then came on again.

FOR BETTER OR worse, the "attract wildlife to the campsite" strategy bore fruit some hours later. Zula had no idea of the hour—a timepiece would have come in handy—but the eastern sky was not beginning to get light yet. Maybe three in the morning.

She had dozed off but was now awakened by rustling noises in the vicinity of the jihadists' tents.

She reached up and undid the padlock, then made a little prayer or resolution that she'd never have it on her again.

This made it possible for her to peel off some of the fleece pullovers she had been wearing ever since they had put the chain on. On top of those, she had also been wearing some zip-up garments that could be put on and taken off even with the chain in place, but she had removed those a few hours ago when she had gone to bed. Stripped down, now, to a set of navy blue synthetic long johns, she stuffed the bulky fleeces into her sleeping bag, trying to make it look as if she were still in it.

She had prepared a fake head by stuffing handfuls of pine needles into a plastic shopping bag until it was round and head-sized, then stretching a stocking cap over it. She placed that in the hood of a pullover and snugged the drawstring around it, then pulled the top of the sleeping bag over it, arranging things so that a flashlight beam shone into the tent and played over this scene would make it look as if she had curled up and pulled the edge of the sleeping bag over her face. She stuck the end of the chain into place beneath it.

The little tent's exit was already unzipped; she had seen to that earlier. Only after she'd made all these arrangements did she reach up and part the flaps a fraction of an inch to look out.

In the light of the moon, she could see at least two creatures waddling around gathering up the food scraps she'd left. From the amount of noise they'd been making, she'd guessed bear cubs. But they were only raccoons.

She saw, now, too late, that leaving food out had been a mistake. It had attracted animals that were large enough to wake the men up but not large enough to pose an actual threat to them.

In any case, she could not just squat there in her tent's entrance. Sooner or later the men would wake up. She emerged from the tent. The damp air struck a chill in her limbs, but she knew that soon enough she'd be perspiring. Trying to ignore the cold, she walked in a straight line, moving deliberately, toward the tent shared by Zakir and Sayed. The latter's hiking boots—brand-new from Walmart—were standing at attention in front of it. She plucked these off the ground with a quick motion of the hand—a motion she'd been rehearsing in her mind all night long—and pivoted away. She was headed now for the front of the tent shared by Ershut and Jahandar. Her next intention was to grab their boots as well and carry them off into the woods. Zakir she wasn't as worried about, but it would help her immeasurably to leave those two barefoot.

Something streaked across her vision about twenty feet away, dark gray moving fast against darker gray. There was a tussle and then a scream, like a toddler being backed over by a car. Zula froze.

To stop moving was a bad idea, but her mind wasn't working at the level of ideas.

Some kind of struggle was taking place, rattling the walls of Ershut and Jahandar's tent, tumbling across the ground, sending sticks and litter flying.

A raccoon had been attacked by some other creature. Something that had been stalking it.

Zula lit out and ran.

SHE'D NEVER KNOW, and didn't especially care to know, in what order things had then happened in the camp. Ershut and Jahandar could not possibly have stayed asleep. They'd have climbed out of their tent, guns drawn, to see some kind of Wild Kingdom melee in progress, or perhaps just its bloody aftermath. Not knowing that a hundred meters away Zula was sitting on the ground in the trees, pulling Sayed's boots onto her feet. Their adrenaline would have been pumping madly. They might have laughed upon realizing that all the fuss had been nothing more than wild animals banging around in the night. Perhaps that laughter would wake up Zakir and Sayed, if they hadn't been awakened already, and perhaps Sayed would look out and notice that his boots had gone missing. Or perhaps Ershut would go up to Zula's tent with a flashlight, look inside, and notice the deception, or not.

All she knew was that, within perhaps a quarter of an hour of her departure, flashlights were bobbing down the plank-avalanche behind her, making their way toward the trail along which Zula was running as fast as she could.

She ran faster.

A wave of nausea came over her, and she had to stop to throw up. Her hands were tingling. She wasn't taking in enough oxygen. She had been running anaerobically. She had no choice but to take the next couple of miles at a more measured pace. Behind her— something like a mile—she could see a flashlight bobbing rhythmically as its owner sprinted along the trail. This gave her a rough idea of how much time she would have, when she reached the Schloss, to get inside and call the police. Right now it was looking pretty favorable. Shaking a little from the nausea but feeling better as her heart and lungs caught up with oxygen debt, she built speed until she had reached the quickest pace she could maintain.

In her mind the distance from the camp to the Schloss had grown larger with every hour that had passed while she'd been chained to that tree, and so she was startled when she glimpsed one of its roofs in the moonlight. She had covered the distance in very little time. She took the risk of slowing down a little bit so that she could look back over her shoulder and saw the bobbing light still in pursuit, perhaps a bit closer than last time, but still a few minutes away.

She tried the front door just to see whether it was open, but Uncle Richard had apparently locked it on his way out. That was okay. She'd been visualizing the place in her mind and had already decided where to break in. She ran around to the side facing the dam, which was the least scenic part of the property and consequently where they had situated things like utility sheds and parking lots. The rooms facing that direction tended to be meeting rooms and offices. She picked up a round river rock, about the size of a cantaloupe, from some landscaping. Carrying it in both hands she ran toward an office window and projected it into the glass. It burst through with a noise that must have been audible in Elphinstone. She stood on one foot and used the other to kick away projecting shards, then reached around through the opening and unlocked the window.

A few moments later she was inside the office, holding the telephone to her head, hearing nothing.

The lights didn't work either.

All the power, all the phones, all the Internet were dead.

Jones must have cut the lines when he had come to call on Richard.

A very powerful impulse was now pushing her to burst out crying, but she turned her back on it, as it were, snubbing it like an unwelcome guest at a party, and tried to think.

Her whole plan had been predicated on the assumption that she would be able to make a phone call from here. Or at least trigger the alarm system. Flash lights on and off. That was all she needed: to get someone's attention down the valley. Chet being her best hope; he lived in a little homestead about five miles down the road. On a quiet night it might be possible to hear an alarm from that far away.

This bank of the river—the right bank—was impassable beyond this point, because of Baron's Rock, which turned the shore into a vertical stone wall scoured by icy water in violent motion. To get to Elphinstone she would have to cross to the left bank by running across the dam, following the road that ran over its top. From there she'd have twenty miles of bad road between her and Elphinstone. Jahandar—she was pretty sure that the fast-running jihadist was he—was only a short distance behind her at this point, and was running faster. If she merely followed the road, he could drop her with a rifle shot, or simply catch up with her and put a knife in her back.

She would have to run up into the trees and conceal herself.

Two things would then happen. One, the jihadists would control the road. In order for her to get into town, she'd have to clamber up into the forested hills that rose above the left bank and then bushwhack all the way into town. Two, she would start to get cold and to suffer from the effects of hunger and thirst. For she'd gambled everything on this sprint, leaving behind her warm clothes, not bringing water or food.

The only way she could think of to get attention was to set fire to the building and hope that someone might notice the smoke and flames.

Which might or might not work. But it would take a while. And she couldn't wait in a burning building. Again, she'd have to run into the woods and stay alive there for a few hours, possibly more.

She had only a few minutes in which to equip herself for a wilderness survival trek of unknown duration.

She couldn't even *see* in this place. She had groped her way to the telephone by following dim moonlight-gleams. The only source of light in this room was a red LED, down low on a wall, at the height of her knee.

This brought up a vague memory: the Schloss had emergency flashlights plugged into wall outlets, one in each room, charging all the time, except when the power went off.

Forcing herself to move in slow, careful steps—she didn't want to trip and sprawl on broken glass—she crossed the room, felt her way down the wall, and found the flashlight. It came on, dazzlingly bright. She clapped her palm over it, not wanting to present an obvious target for someone peering through gunsights into the building, and allowed a blade of light to escape between fingers, illuminating the path out of the office.

She exited into a corridor and headed away from the main entrance. To the right was a row of offices and of storerooms that mostly contained kitchen equipment. To the left was the main food prep area for the tavern. Making a quick pass through there, she risked taking her hand off the light—the kitchen had no windows—and plucked a long sharp-pointed butcher knife and a smaller paring knife from a magnetic strip on the wall. These she dropped into a white plastic pail that was sitting on the floor beneath a sink. Using that as a kind of shopping basket she swiped a few odds and ends that might come in handy—two oven mitts, for example, that might serve to keep her hands warm if she couldn't find anything better. There was, of course, no perishable food stored in the place, since it had been shut down for Mud Month. From a fridge she collected a bottle of canola oil that had been left there so it wouldn't go rancid, and scored some twenty-ounce plastic bottles of water. Cabinets yielded some sacks of potato chips and other snacks, as well as rice, raisins, pasta. The bucket was approaching full, and she reckoned she had enough calories in there to keep her alive for days, provided she could find a way to cook the stuff.

Which led her to the idea of camping stoves, and other equipment. Was that too much to hope for, in a ski lodge in the mountains?

Someone was banging on the lodge's front door in an exploratory way, trying to figure out how much force would be required to break it down.

Why didn't they just shoot out the locks? They certainly had the means.

Because they were afraid that gunfire might be heard down the valley.

Uncle Richard had guns here. A fine thought. But impossible. They were stored in a safe in his apartment.

She had the general sense that outdoor gear tended to be stored in the building's basement. An emergency map posted on the wall told her where the stairways were. She found one and descended it.

A window shattered somewhere in the front of the building.

She was almost overcome, for a moment, by the impulse to flee.

But that would just end up with her being dead of hypothermia.

Her nose told her that she was right about the camping equipment. It wasn't a bad smell exactly, but all camping gear smelled the same after a while. She shone the light around and found the stuff she needed, strewn all over the floor.

Of course. If Jones had forced Richard to accompany him, Richard would have needed his own backpack, warm clothes, sleeping bag, tent. They must have come down here and ransacked the place.

So this, at least, was going her way. She nearly tripped over an empty backpack: a big rig with an external aluminum frame. She set the pail down, snatched up the pack, and verified that it was in decent repair. She grabbed a sleeping bag, already jammed into a stuff sack, and lashed it onto the frame with a couple of bungee cords. She dumped the pail into the top compartment indiscriminately and was reminded that there were a couple of knives in the bottom. Storing those would be tricky, so she set them aside for now.

Green nylon tarps, neatly folded into rectangles, were stacked on a shelf. She grabbed three of them. One, if she cut a hole through the middle, might serve as a rain poncho. Another could be a ground cloth, the third a makeshift tent. She pawed some hanks of rope from another shelf, a CamelBak from a hook where it had been stored upside down to drain.

The lodge had collected so many old used ski parkas, pants, and gloves that they were stored in garbage bags in the corners. She ripped two of these open and kicked through them, selecting a coat and some snow pants more for their color (black) than their size (too large), and grabbed two pairs of gloves in navy blue. A stocking cap. A pair of ski goggles, since she didn't have sunglasses, and might find herself on snow.

The backpack was stiffening up as she jammed stuff into it. She circled back to the knives and figured out a way to insert them carefully between the pack's aluminum frame and its nylon sack. They'd stay put there, but the blades weren't in a position to hurt her, or damage the other gear. The handles protruded from the top of the pack; she'd be able to reach back over her left shoulder and grab them if she had to.

A sharp scent was in her nostrils: stove fuel. She opened the nearest cabinet door and found a compartment where they kept camp stoves and supplies.

The jihadists seemed to be giving her all the time in the world. Someone was banging around upstairs, but only one person, as far as she could tell.

Then she guessed why. Jahandar had arrived first. But he hadn't entered the building. Instead he had posted himself on the road, on or near the dam, to prevent Zula from crossing over to the left bank. Jahandar might be a fish out of water in British Columbia, but he had more than enough of the Afghan equivalent of street smarts to understand that, if Zula couldn't cross over to the left bank, she couldn't go down the road to Elphinstone. Ershut, probably, had made it to the scene a few minutes later; he'd be the one banging around, trying to root her out of the Schloss so that Jahandar could plug her with a rifle shot. The out-of-shape Zakir and shoeless Sayed would not be here for a little while longer.

The stoves were of the type that screwed directly onto a fuel bottle; they didn't have tanks of their own. Zula threw a stove, a box of waterproof matches, and a handful of candles into a side pocket of the pack. A little cooking kit—a small pot, a frying pan, and a plate, all cleverly nested and locked together—went into the main compartment. Hard to make use of the stove without that.

Fuel bottles—pods of spun aluminum with narrow necks plugged by screw-in plastic stoppers—were strewn around the cabinet like bowling pins after a strike. She opened one, dropped to the floor, pinned it upright between her knees, then grabbed a brick-shaped gallon can of stove fuel from the lower shelf, spun its cap off, and learned just how difficult it was to decant white gas from one narrow-necked receptacle into another with violently shaking hands. Half of it spilled onto her knees and soaked into her long johns, a detail she would have to keep in mind if she found herself in the vicinity of fire any time soon.

Which she had every intention of doing. Only about a quarter of the big can's contents sufficed to fill the bottle. The rest was available for other purposes.

First she was careful to get the lid screwed firmly back onto the bottle and stow that in her pack. Then she fished out a couple of the matches she'd packed earlier and stuck them into her mouth. She stood up and hoisted the pack around onto her back. During all of these exertions, she had come upon an old flashlight with nearly dead batteries, so she set it on the floor, aimed toward the stairs, and left it turned on. That enabled her to turn off her own flashlight. Gas can in one hand, she ascended the stairs as quickly as she could without making a lot of noise. Being chased around the Schloss by Ershut would be bad, and being cornered in the basement would be worse, but being caught by him in midstairway was the worst she could think of.

She stopped at the top of the stairs, appalled for a moment by the unpleasant thought that Ershut might be right on the other side of the door, waiting for her. That was enough to make her reach up above her shoulder in an exploratory way and verify that the handle of the big butcher knife was in a place where she could grab it.

She waited there in the dark until she was certain she heard a boom from farther away in the Schloss: probably Ershut kicking open a door in one of the guest wings.

She pushed the door open and waited for some kind of disaster, or at least nearby movement; but the place was quiet except for the crunching boom of another door being kicked in.

She felt her way around two corners and entered the tavern. By the faint red glow of her flashlight shining through the flesh of her hand, she found her way through the dining area to the end of the room that was dominated by the bar and the TV and the plush sofas and chairs arranged before it. A nest of empty chip wrappers and soda cans told her where her uncle had been vegging out at the moment Jones had come to pay a call on him.

She hated to do it, for she knew how Uncle Richard loved this place. But the foam in this furniture would burn better than anything else, once it got going. She spilled a long trail of stove gas down the length of the sofa and across the laps of the adjoining chairs, then dumped what was left in a puddle on the floor.

Before lighting the match, she stepped over to a window that afforded a view to the north side of the property and verified her suspicion that Jahandar—or at least someone with a flashlight—was posted there, right in the middle of the road, at the place where it ramped down to the top of the dam.

Ershut was continuing to make his location obvious. He was nowhere near her.

She pulled a match from her mouth, lit it, and threw it. Too fast, for it missed the target and went out on the carpet. The second one caught and the flames spread with shocking effect, blinding her night-adjusted eyes. To Jahandar or anyone out on the road, it would be as bright as sunrise, even with the blinds drawn. It seemed inadvisable to emerge from a door anywhere near that, so she made her way round to the guest wing where Ershut did not seem to be. This was just a long straight hallway, aimed generally southward, lined with doors to guest rooms on both sides. Moving at the best jogging gait she could manage with the heavy pack on her back, she went straight to its end, punched out through the emergency exit there (fighting a ridiculous feeling of good-girl shame that it should never be used except in an actual emergency) and moved as directly as she could in the direction of the nearest cover: the edge of the forest along the banks of the Blue Fork, about a hundred feet away.

She was finding it surprisingly easy to see where she was going without benefit of flashlight and thought for a second that this was because of the fire light shining out from the tavern's windows. Then she understood that the eastern sky was beginning to brighten. Whoever had written "the darkest hour is before the dawn" apparently had not spent much time in the Northwest, where, for hours before it actually breached the horizon, the sun scattered vague blue light off the underside of the cloud cover.

A bell started ringing. She wondered if she'd caused this to happen by using the emergency exit. But the power was off, so it couldn't be that. The bell was not an electrical device. It sounded like an actual, physical piece of metal being struck by a flailing hammer. The sound was thready and faltering, as though whatever contraption drove it was already on its last legs. For all that, it carried clearly through the still air of the valley.

A stocky man—Ershut—was silhouetted against the glowing windows of the tavern as he ran in front of them. He had gone outdoors when he'd realized that the building was on fire. He was headed for the front, zeroing in, she guessed, on the source of the noise. She lost him in the darkness. Then she returned her gaze to the windows, noting a dramatic fall-off in the intensity of the light.

The sprinklers must have come on inside the tavern. They were rigged up to some kind of device on the front of the building:

water rushing through the sprinkler pipes turned a little wheel that smacked the bell, sounding the alarm even when electrical power was shut off.

The big windows of the tavern began to explode: someone attacking them with a sledgehammer or a rifle butt, venting smoke. Dim flares of orange light shone through in places that weren't covered by the spray patterns of the sprinkler system. A few minutes later Zula heard the roaring hiss of a fire extinguisher being operated in short bursts and saw those little fires being snuffed out one by one. The bell continued to sound even after the fire had been put out, and it would keep doing so until the system ran out of water or was shut off by operating a valve somewhere.

She had made these observations while moving furtively through the woods, favoring north-facing slopes so that she could get a view down over the Schloss. The sky was getting appreciably brighter. When she had arrived, she'd been able to see nothing except dim gleams of moonlight on roofs, and the pools of illumination cast by flashlights, but now she could see the entire compound, albeit in faint gray on gray, and she could see Ershut and Jahandar moving around even when they weren't using their lights.

All of which worked to her advantage but told her that she had better move deeper into the woods before it became light enough to making tracking her easy.

She moved another hundred yards back, troubled by the amount of noise she made as she forced herself and the bulky pack through undergrowth. Then she turned back and looked again, since she had picked up bright lights in her peripheral vision.

A car was coming down the road, approaching the dam. She was thrilled to see it and then horrified by the certainty that whoever was inside it was about to be gunned down.

Instead, though, Jahandar approached, waving arms, bringing it to a stop at the far end of the dam. His rifle was slung on his shoulder. He bent down to engage the driver in conversation.

This must be the scrubs—the backup team. The day before yesterday, they must have driven the RV back to Elphinstone and parked it in a campground somewhere. When Zula had made her break, Jahandar or Ershut must have reached these people by phone or walkie-talkie or something, told them to come quick. The car's rear doors opened up, and a man got out from each side, pulling a bag out behind him, slinging it over his back.

After a few minutes' more conversation, the car went into movement again, pulling around in a U-turn, and headed back down the road toward Elphinstone.

She heard a pop behind her: the snap of a twig.

She turned around to see Sayed stealing up on her, about thirty feet away.

He was looking right at her. On his feet he was wearing the pink Crocs she had left behind at the campsite. He was movingly awkwardly because of the Crocs and because his hands were occupied by a black pump-action shotgun.

Her movements were no less awkward. But she knew she had to stay out of the range of that weapon, and so she backed away from him. Realizing he'd been sighted, he picked up his pace and began to stumble forward, flailing the gun around dangerously, dropping to his knees as the Crocs slipped on the steep loose ground, spitting and making little exclamations as branches caught him in the face.

The straps of her pack suddenly jerked violently at her shoulders. She thought she'd backed into a tree, that its branches had snagged the pack, spun her around.

Then she went down facefirst. She threw out her hands in an attempt to break the fall, but the palms of her hands skidded outward and she ended up spread-eagled on her belly. The weight of the pack was on her back. A moment later, this was joined by a weight much heavier. A weight that was moving.

"Got her!" said Zakir. His voice was coming from high above her; he was kneeling on her backpack or something. But then there was a sudden violent reshuffling and his entire weight bore down on her with force that might have cracked her ribs. It was certainly squeezing all the air out of her lungs.

"Bitch, how does it feel to be dead?" he asked her.

She only had one move, which made choosing much easier.

Bending her elbow sharply, she brought her right hand back to her left shoulder, groped upward a couple of inches, found the handles of the knives, picked the big one. It was almost wedged in place by Zakir's weight, but she jerked it free with a convulsive movement. Then, without pause, she reversed the movement and stabbed straight backward, aiming for the sound of his voice.

He gagged on his own scream and rolled off her. As he moved she felt the knife handle twist in her hand. She maintained her grip on it, jerked it out, felt blood spray. She planted both hands and pushed herself up on hands and knees, then rolled away from him, ending up seated on her haunches.

Zakir was kneeling on the ground with both hands clapped over his mouth. His forearms were turning red. Blood began to stream off one elbow, then the other.

She heard an exclamation. Not from Zakir, who had been robbed of the power of speech. She looked up to see Sayed standing there in his Crocs, no more than ten feet away, holding the shotgun slack in his hands, staring in horror at Zakir.

She was definitely within that gun's killing range now. She had half her own weight strapped to her back, and she was sitting down, immobilized by the pack.

For the first time in quite a while she didn't have any particular idea as to what she should do. She was tired of coming up with ideas.

She and Sayed stared at each other for a few moments. He glanced down at her hand and saw the bloody knife.

He probably wanted to go to the aid of Zakir, who was slumping back against a tree, deflating as blood and breath ran out of him. But he didn't want to come in range of the knife. He ought to just blow her away with that shotgun. But he couldn't quite bring himself to do it.

So it was a standoff.

Something flashed through the air behind him. Sort of like a bird, except that it weighed about as much as Zula. But the quality of its movement—a strange, almost supernatural combination of speed and silence—was akin to that of a bird.

Sayed went down on his face as if he had been struck by a car. The shotgun flew out of his hands and went bouncing and rolling across the ground toward Zula.

She was so preoccupied with that one detail that she saw nothing else until she had jerked her arms free from the pack straps and flung herself forward to scrabble the weapon up out of the thick layer of old brown pine needles and leaves in which it had come to rest.

Then she stared up into the golden face of a huge feline, regarding her from perhaps six feet away. The animal had blood on its fangs. It had planted both of its feet on Sayed's back; each of its claws was embedded in a spreading disk of blood. But most of the blood came from the back of Sayed's neck, which had been destroyed; the animal had struck him with a flying leap, and bitten all the way through his cervical spine, in the same instant.

She remembered that she had a shotgun in her hands. She aimed it at the cougar. For her mind, belatedly switching into animal taxonomy mode, had identified this as one. The same one, no doubt, that had been skulking around the camp last night and going after the raccoons earlier. She wondered if Sayed had had the presence of mind to chamber a shell and flick the safety off. She pulled back with her right hand, saw the yellow gleam of a shotgun shell in the breech, pushed it closed. Glanced back up at the cougar. Found the safety with her thumb, glanced down to see it had been left on, flicked it up until a red dot showed. Red, you're dead. Looked back up at the cougar. It was making no effort to come after her, but it was definitely paying close attention, snarling, making it clear she wasn't wanted.

It was guarding its kill.

Keeping the shotgun in her right hand, aimed at the cougar, she squatted down, thrust her left arm through a pack strap, and heaved the burden up onto her back. This irritated the cougar, sending it into a little fit of squawling and posturing. But Zula was definitely backing away now, increasing the distance.

Something caught her knee. She saw with horror that it was Zakir's bloody paw, not so much trying to hold her back as imploring her for aid. She kicked loose from him and moved away. Not until she was perhaps a hundred feet distant did she shoulder the pack properly and fasten its hip belt.

Her hearing had gone all funny during this, but when it went back to normal, she noted that Ershut or someone seemed to have gotten to the bell and stifled it. It was still making a dim pocking noise, but the bell wasn't clanging anymore and probably couldn't be heard from more than a few hundred yards' distance.

This made it possible to hear two sounds that had previously been obscured by the ringing of the bell. One, behind Zula now, was Zakir screaming. Apparently he had got his voice working again. His cries had an inchoate gargling sound. The other was a motor coming down the road from the direction of Elphinstone.

Zula was pretty sure it was a Harley-Davidson.

Chet was coming. He had heard the fire bell and was coming to see what was the matter.

Zula had drawn him here by setting the fire, and now they were going to kill him.

She heard Jahandar's voice, shouting into a walkie-talkie or a phone. As he spoke, Zula caught sight of him retreating from the dam, taking up a position behind a corner of the main Schloss buildings.

Chet wasn't in view yet, but the headlight of his chopper was illuminating the trees along the road perhaps half a mile away, and she could hear the engine throttling up and down as he took the familiar curves.

FROM THE DAY that Chet had made the decision to settle down and bind his fortune to that of Dodge and his crazy Schloss project, not an hour had gone by without his thinking, and usually worrying, about some aspect of the building and its grounds. This was his life now. It was not a bad life. But part of the job was getting up in the middle of the night and running into the place to put out fires.

Not literally. There had never been a serious fire in the place and he doubted that there ever would be, given the capabilities of the sprinkler system that they had, at shocking expense, installed in every room of the complex. But it was useless against *metaphorical* fires: petty burglaries, leaky roofs, starlings in the eaves, bears and raccoons getting into the Dumpsters. Once the staff had grown to a size where he could delegate a lot of that, he had acquired the property a few miles up the road and built his own cabin on it, so that he could live close enough to the Schloss for convenience, but far enough away to get his mind off its myriad chores and troubles.

The one exception was Mud Month, when all the staff went on vacation. Nothing could be delegated then; either Chet or Dodge had to be on call 24/7 until they all came back.

Dodge was there now. Had been for a few days. This had given Chet an opportunity to relax, catch up on his reading, go on a few motorcycle rides with the surviving members of the Septentrion

Paladins. He had just returned from one such ride, up the west shore of Kootenay Lake, a few hours before sunset. After grilling a steak and killing half a bottle of cabernet, he had collapsed into bed early and slept well. But in the hour before dawn he had found himself lying awake, convinced he was hearing something from up the valley: a jangling bell.

That fucking sprinkler system had sprung another leak.

It couldn't be an actual fire. Had there been an actual fire, the alarm system would have detected it, summoned the fire department, and sent a text message to his phone. Sirens would be screaming by his cabin already. And Dodge would be calling him.

No, something must have whacked a sprinkler head and set the thing going. Right now water was spraying in torrents around one of the Schloss's rooms. It had happened before. It was always a huge mess. It was probably Dodge, up early in the morning, chasing a stray bat around with a badminton racket, flailing in the dark, not thinking about the delicate sprinkler heads. Now he was alone in the Schloss in the wee hours, dark and wet and furious and humiliated, too proud to call for help.

Chet dragged himself out of bed, peed, and pulled his motorcycle leathers on over his pajamas. Not very dignified, but only Dodge would see him, and he had no secrets from Dodge. He strode out into the patch of gravel between his cabin and the road. The chopper was there. It was dirty and tired, needed to have its oil changed. Riding it through the dark, he would be uncomfortable and cold. A sane man would take the SUV that was parked right next to it. But Chet on a whim had decided to ride the bike. What the hell, he was up anyway and about to spend the whole day dealing with Dodge's mess. It couldn't get a hell of a lot more uncomfortable than that.

He bestrode the Harley, kicked it into life, fishtailed it around in the gravel, and headed out onto the little access road that led down to the highway from his property. This was a former mining road, bladed once a year after the spring thaw had finished turning it into a rutted gully. So it would never get any worse than it was today. Feeling his way into the hyperbola of light cast by the chopper's headlamp, he put all his attention, for the first couple of minutes, into staying out of the deepest channels that had been carved into it during the weeks since the snow had begun to thaw. His slow progress was a blessing in disguise; if he went any faster, clots of semi-frozen mud would hurtle up from the tires and glue themselves onto the insides of the bike's fenders.

As he neared the bank of the river, the trees thinned out and afforded him a clear view of the eastern sky, which had gone all pink and pearly. He was tempted to shut off the headlamp and run dark, the way he had used to, back in the old days. Back before the accident. But the accident had put sense into him, if having corn-stalks shoved into your brain could be so called. And living in these parts he had learned that this was the very time of day when crit-ters were about: it was light enough that they could see what the hell they were doing, but not so light as to make it easy for preda-tors to spot them, and so this was the hour when a lone biker was most likely to kill himself by T-boning a moose in the middle of the road. Predators would be out too, looking for crepuscular prey with their big glowing eyes and listening with their twitching radar-horn ears. The Selkirks were oversupplied with apex predators: bears of two types, wolves, coyotes, cougars and various smaller cats, just to name the four-legged ones—to the point where their station on the food pyramid no longer seemed like an apex so much as a plateau or mesa. If striking a deer on your chopper was bad, what adjective could be applied to striking a grizzly who was stalking a deer?

So he kept his light on as he turned south onto the road and built his speed only slowly, giving the tires a quarter mile of free running on the clean blacktop so that they could shed their furry husks of cold mud. Then he opened up the throttle and began to carve the turns toward the Schloss, picking up speed when there was a long clear stretch of road ahead of him, throttling it back a little when he approached blind curves where deer might be grazing in the low rich undergrowth that came to life, at this time of year, in the sunlit ditches and verges that lined the road cut.

In a few minutes—not long enough, really, since he had begun to enjoy the ride—he swept around the broad leftward curve into the shadow of Baron's Rock and felt the road angle downward beneath him as it made its plunge for the dam. It broadened, here, into a turnaround for vehicles too long and heavy to cross, and a sort of informal parking area for motorists who wanted to fish in the river or picnic on their tailgates while enjoying the view of the

Rock, the river, and the stone turrets of the Schloss rising up above the trees on the other side.

Because of trees and landscaping, the view of the Schloss did not really open up until one was halfway across the dam. At that point, Chet—who was not going very fast anyway—relaxed his throttle hand and let the bike drop to an idling pace. He had noticed some things that struck him as a bit odd. The alarm bell was still ringing, but it had a flat, muffled sound, as if something had been jammed into it. Why hadn't Dodge just shut the valve, and turned the thing off, to prevent further water damage to the building? Another thing was that there were no lights on in the place at all. Of course, since Dodge was here alone, you wouldn't expect a lot of lights to be burning. But you'd expect at least *some*, especially if Dodge were scurrying around the place trying to deal with a busted sprinkler head.

But what really got his attention, and told him that something was seriously out of whack, was the smell. The smell of burnt plastic that he associated with house fires. Moreover, there was enough light now to make it obvious that milky smoke was lingering in the trees and the river valley.

So there actually *had* been a fire.

Why hadn't the alarm system—the electronic one—sent out a call?

For the same reason that the power was out?

But the alarm system had battery backup that was supposed to keep running for a whole day.

Maybe the phones were out too?

Chet's first thought was to run into the Schloss and try to find Dodge, but he'd heard too many stories of people who did that, trying to be heroes, and succumbed to smoke inhalation and died along with the people they were trying to save. He had to at least summon help before doing anything else. He brought his chopper to a stop at the Schloss end of the dam and pulled his phone out of his pocket.

NO SERVICE said the screen.

Another oddity. The Schloss had its own cell tower. The coverage here ought to be fantastic. But apparently it had gone dead too.

What could account for so much going wrong all at once?

He was pondering the question when he heard a clear gunshot.

It was some distance away, and he was pretty certain that it was a shotgun, not a rifle.

His instinct was to get the hell out of there, so he got his hand on the throttle, twisted it up, shifted into gear, let go the clutch. The rear tire started spinning in the loose dirt and dead needles that covered the pavement, and he took advantage of that to fishtail the bike's rear end around and get it pointed back across the dam.

He was just about to let her rip and go blasting across when he noticed two figures running toward him across the turnaround. They had emerged from hiding places in the trees. Something was weird about their gait. Their legs were moving properly, but their arms weren't pumping.

Their arms weren't pumping, he saw, because each of them was carrying a handgun in a two-handed grip. And they were looking right at him.

To get across the dam he would have to ride directly at these guys, whoever they were, as they stood in his path. They would have plenty of time to empty their magazines at him.

He'd already done a one-eighty. He kept the momentum going and turned it into a three-sixty, which was to say that he got himself turned back around with the dam behind him and the Schloss to the front. Fleeing into the Schloss itself wasn't going to work. Whoever these guys were, they'd already gone into the place, done whatever they wanted to do to Dodge—some old drug-running grievance?—cut the power and the phone lines, set fire to it. He needed to put some distance between himself and them. He aimed the bike, not at the Schloss, but down the road that ran past it, and wrenched the throttle to max and popped the clutch and actually stood her up on her rear wheel, doing a wheelie as he accelerated onto the road.

As he went by the Schloss he saw in his peripheral vision a shape like a lily, made out of yellow-orange light, and realized that he was staring into the muzzle of a rifle that was firing at him: a rifle with a flash arrester on the end of its barrel, channeling the flame into six equiangular jets, like petals. The rifle let loose one, two, three, four rounds, producing a hammering noise with each one, and behind him he could hear the sharp *poppity-pop* of those gunmen on the dam, letting loose everything they had in their magazines.

A rightward bend in the road put some trees between him and the crazy men who were trying to kill him. He finally had the presence of mind to shut off the bike's headlamp. His arm moved heavily. He had a vague memory of taking a blow a few seconds ago, a rock thrown up by one of his tires or something. It must have deadened a nerve. His body was old and overused and suffered strange infirmities from time to time.

A light was flashing in the trees, and bobbing as it flashed. Coming down a slope. Headed, not for him, but for a point on the road ahead of him.

The light bounced onto the road, then swung upward to illuminate the bearer's face. It was too far away for him to resolve it clearly, and he didn't want to get much closer. He was out of shotgun range and out of pistol range, but if this person had a rifle—

"Chet! It's me! Zula!"

He gunned it forward and stopped next to her. As he drew closer, he noted with interest that she was carrying a pump shotgun.

"We thought you were dead," he said.

"I'm not."

"Where's Dodge?"

"Not here. Come on, we have to get moving."

"No shit." Because he could now hear the voices of the gunmen, who were running after them.

Zula safetied the shotgun. She was wearing a large, haphazardly made-up pack. She got a foot on one of the passenger pegs, then swung her leg over and sat down. As soon as he sensed the weight of her body against his back, he let out the clutch and began moving down the road again, just at a running pace at first—so the gunmen wouldn't be able to gain any more ground—then faster, once he felt as though Zula had got her balance and wasn't liable to flip off the bike backward.

There was a while, then, when all they did was ride. Chet liked that part of it, riding along the road in the dark, a salmon-colored light spreading over heaven's vault above, Zula's arms around his waist.

They didn't talk at all until they reached the turnaround just short of the wrecked mine complex where a million old gray planks were trying to avalanche down into the river. From here they could ride up a short ramp to the bike and ski path, which the Harley could easily negotiate. But it seemed reasonable to stop.

"I don't see any choice but to keep going," Zula said.

"There's nothing *there*," Chet said, nodding down the trail.

"Except the U. S. of A.," she pointed out. "And you know how to get there, right?"

"Not on *this* thing! This'll only take us as far as the tunnel."

"But that's a few more miles between us and the jihadists," she pointed out.

"What did you call them?"

"And you know how to go beyond that point. On foot. Right? You used to do it with Richard."

"Oh, it's been years, girl."

"But you know. You know the way. And they don't. So we can outdistance them."

"We should wait for them to pass us. Then double back."

"They'll be looking for that. They're smart. They'll post someone to guard the crossing at the dam."

"Still, if we stayed up in the trees, moved through the woods—"

"Listen. Some of those guys have Richard. They have Dodge."

"Dodge is okay?"

"As far as I know. Anyway, they're south of us. They don't have a motorcycle. We can just about catch them."

"Why the hell would we want to *catch* them!?"

"All I have to do is show myself to Uncle Richard—let him know they don't have me hostage any more—and then he's free, he can run into the woods, get away from these guys."

Chet said nothing. Not because he didn't agree. But because he was having difficulty concentrating.

"I have to go save his life," Zula said. Sounding almost matter-of-fact. *Ah, I see I failed to make myself clear . . . here's the situation . . . I have to go save his life.*

It gave him something to focus on. "Well, since you put it that way, I'll take you to the tunnel," he said, and he let the bike rumble off the end of the road and onto the loose gravel of the trail.

By the time they made it to the end, he was aware, somehow, that he had blood coming out of him. He couldn't remember how he knew this, how he'd first been made aware of the fact. There was a dim dreamlike memory of the girl on his back—Zula—mentioning it to Chet, and Chet laughing it off and just cranking up the throttle a little higher.

Then he noticed that he was lying on the ground staring up into a blue sky.

Had they crashed?

No. The Harley was parked next to him. Zula had rolled out a camping pad. He had been lying on it, dozing. Covered with a sleeping bag.

She squatted next to him and pulled the sleeping bag away to expose the right side of his torso. His shirt was missing. Bare skin shrank from the cool air. She regretted what she saw, but she wasn't surprised by it. She'd been looking at it while he lay there.

"How long have we been stopped here?" he asked.

"Not too long."

He was too embarrassed to come out and ask what was wrong with him. He felt that it must be obvious.

She did something involving a bandage. She had a pathetic little first aid kit.

"Stop it," he said gently. "It's a waste of time."

"Then what do you want to do?"

"Send you on your way. Save Dodge. I'll follow."

"You'll . . . follow?"

"I can't go near as fast as you. But there's no reason for me to just stay here. I want to die on the forty-ninth parallel."

She was squatting on her haunches with her arms crossed over her knees. She looked south, into the sunlight, toward the border. Then she dropped her head onto her forearms and sobbed for a while.

"It's okay," he said.

"No, it's not. People are dead." She raised her face, let herself tumble back onto her bottom, stretched her legs out next to Chet. "I didn't kill them. But they're dead because of things that I did. Does that make sense? Peter. The pilots. The people in the RV. They'd all be alive if I'd decided differently."

"But you're not helping the killers," Chet said. Something about lying on the ground, combined with her outburst, had revived him a little, made him feel almost normal.

"Of course I'm not helping them."

"You fired that shotgun, didn't you? To warn me."

"Jahandar—the sniper—was drawing a bead on you. Yes. I warned you by firing the shotgun."

"So you're fighting against them."

"Of course I am. But what's the point, if it just leads to a different set of people getting killed?"

"Too heavy a question for me," he said. "You just do what you can, pretty lady."

She tried to fight it, but the corners of her mouth drew back into a smile. "You call all women that."

"It's true."

"It's been a while since I heard that kind of talk."

Chet shrugged demurely.

"Well," Zula continued, "all those people died for nothing unless I help Richard escape. And then we can go for help. But I have to get to the border first. And I need your help for that."

"American Falls," Chet said. "That's where we're going."

"How do I—do we—get there?"

He turned his head, raised his good arm, gestured at the ridge that rose above them to the south: a blade of cream-colored granite, patched with snow, skirted by a ramp of boulders that had been flaking away from it and thundering down into the valley for millions of years. The trail had taken them up onto the ridge's middle slopes, flying on creosoted stilts over the rubble fields, and terminated at a place where a wall of sound rock jumped out of the talus. The tunnel had been blasted straight into it, aimed horizontally through the heart of the ridge.

"We use the mine tunnels to get past this bad boy. See, we don't have to hike over the top. That would take days. It'd kill me. Hell, it'd kill you. No. We use the tunnels. That's what Richard discovered. That's his secret. We go out the other side. Then down the river to the falls. Latitude forty-nine north. That's where I stop, and you keep going."

"Then let's go," she said, "if that's what you want."

"Yes. It's what I want."

THE TUNNEL WAS large enough to accommodate a narrow-gauge train, which was to say that a car could have driven into it with room to spare. To prevent just that sort of behavior, the owners had fabricated a massive steel gridiron, bolted into the rock, that blocked the passage. The barrier was situated about ten meters inside the entrance of the tunnel. That ten meters was a tornado of lurid graffiti and an ankle-deep trash heap of discarded beer bottles, chip bags, knotted condoms, and drained batteries. Just at the entrance was a fire ring; Zula, acting in Sherlock Holmes mode, verified that its ashes were still blazing hot. They were only a couple of hours behind Jones and company.

In the middle of the gridiron was a man-sized door. This had clearly been locked and vandalized, chained and vandalized, welded shut and vandalized, so many times as to threaten the integrity of the entire structure. Now it stood slightly ajar and Zula's flashlight, shining through the grid, revealed that the graffiti and trash on its opposite side were only a little less prevalent. Her nose caught a pungent and familiar odor: fresh spray paint. Playing her flashlight over the steel plate on the door, she saw a few characters in Arabic. She couldn't read them. She touched one of the glyphs and fresh green paint came away on her fingertip.

"Careful!" called Chet, strolling along slowly in her wake.

"Why?"

"They used to booby-trap it."

"*Who* did!?"

"Back in the day," Chet said, "the business got a little competitive. A little nasty. Crazy people got into it. People who'd kill you. That's when Dodge and I decided to go straight."

Zula painted the light beam up and down the length of the door crack, and noticed, way up at the top, a steely glint. Piano wire. It had been made fast around the vertical bar that served as the edge of the door, and routed horizontally across the gap between door and frame, across the grid and all the way to the tunnel wall. There it disappeared into a mound of trash that had been piled up in the corner formed by the wall and the steel grid.

By the time she finished piecing this all together, Chet had caught up with her and was following the wire with his own eyes as he leaned against the gridiron, breathing raggedly and gurgling as he did so. "Holy crap," he said, "I didn't actually expect to see it."

"You think there's something hidden in that trash pile?"

"Must be."

In a pocket of his leathers, Chet was carrying a Leatherman that included pliers and a wire cutter. After insisting that Zula go back outside and stand with her back to the mountain, he reached up, snipped the wire, and pushed the gate open—she could hear the massive hinges groaning. "All clear," he announced, after counting to ten. "But before we go through, I'm going to take a little rest here while you go back to my bike and get something."

The something turned out to be a massive cable lock. Zula fetched it back into the tunnel and helped Chet thread it through the bars of the gridiron and the gate, locking it securely behind them.

After that, they proceeded with extreme caution, which was not that difficult anyway since Chet couldn't move very fast. Once they got past the drifts of party trash that cluttered the floor near the grid, there weren't that many places to hide booby traps. And if the first one was anything to go by, Jones would have marked them all with spray-painted warnings so that the follow-up group—presumably Ershut, Jahandar, and anyone else deemed worthy to follow—wouldn't run afoul of them. So her nose became extremely sensitive to the sharp perfume of spray paint, and her eyes keen for the fluorescent green color that Jones had been using.

After a few minutes, they came to a place where the tunnel terminated in a rock wall pierced by a mouse hole just big enough for Chet to walk upright. "See, this thing was an adit," Chet was explaining, "which is what the miners call a tunnel that runs horizontal, flat enough that you can run rail cars on it. Straight into the ore body in the heart of the mountain. Only this first part of it, here, got expanded for the railway. But now we're going into the adit proper." There was another pileup of trash and another steel door, barring the entrance to the adit, that had been jimmied open and left hanging askew. It would have been a natural place to put another booby trap. But Zula did not see or smell spray paint, and Chet's minute inspection of the trash and the door revealed nothing suspicious. They stepped into the much more confined space of the adit and discovered that, as always, revelers and graffitists had been there first.

"Third one on the right," Chet intoned, then coughed and hacked up something dark which he spat against the wall. The physical effort of the coughing left him woozy, and he leaned against the stone for a few moments, then stumbled forward, insisting on leading the way.

Zula wanted to ask *Third what on the right?* but reckoned she would see soon enough and didn't want to put Chet to the trouble of talking. She got a clue when they passed a hole in the wall, and she shone her light into it to see another adit leading away into what she gathered was the ore body. They had clearly entered into a sort of rock that was different from what they'd seen at the surface: darker but laced through with veins of color and a-sparkle with crystalline growths, especially in those places where water seeped out of cracks and trickled along the gutter carved into the adit's floor. Only a few moments later they went by another, similar landmark, and perhaps twenty meters farther along, after passing momentarily through rock of a different sort, they reentered the ore body and came to adit number three. Which Zula could have guessed just by nosing it out, since the odor of spray paint had become strong again. This time several lines of script had been scrawled across the wall next to the side passage.

They stopped here so that Chet could gather his strength. He had been consuming water at an alarming rate and still complained of thirst. "You go down this adit for, I don't know, a hundred feet, and you'll come to a shaft in the floor of a chamber. Should be a steel ladder. Used to be a hoist, but it's busted now. Down the ladder all the way to the bottom. About fifty rungs. That gets you into an adit that takes you out to another intersection like this one."

"Does this mean you're not coming with me?"

"Just a figure of speech," he said, after a pause to consider it. "Just gathering my energy for that damned ladder."

It was more or less as Chet had predicted. The chamber at the end of this adit contained a surprisingly large machine that must have been brought down in pieces and assembled here. Its most prominent feature was a giant, rusty wheel with cables running over grooves in its rim and descending into the hole below. Obviously the thing hadn't moved in eons and so Zula, had she been a recreational spelunker, would have given up and turned around at this point. But Chet insisted, and more Day-Glo-green graffiti affirmed, that there was a way down. She followed him around to the back side of the machine. She began to collect that the shaft below them was circular in cross section, but that the circle had been parceled out into a bundle of separate squarish or rectangular passageways. The largest of these was in the middle and was serviced by the giant wheel, but smaller ones seemed to be reserved for other purposes such as cabling, ventilation, dumbwaiter-like rigs for carrying ore, and the ladder that could be used when nothing else was functioning. Chet gave the top of this a good careful look, inspecting for booby traps. Then he undid his belt, threaded it through the wrist loop on his flashlight, and rebuckled it so that the light would dangle in front of his crotch and the beam would shine downward. He began to descend the ladder with such speed that Zula feared he was falling, rather than climbing. She got the sense that he just wanted to get this over with. Perhaps he was expecting to find a booby trap at the bottom and wanted to set it off long before she got there. This didn't give her a lot of incentive to move quickly. Gripping her flashlight in one fist so that it shone downward, she began to descend the ladder, and quickly found herself in an environment that would have been violently claustrophobic had she been disposed to such feelings. Space in the shaft was apparently precious and the engineers didn't want to sacrifice any more than was absolutely necessary to this purpose. Her pack kept getting wedged against the wall behind her, or hung up on brackets, forcing her to push back a little wave of panic each time.

"I think there's another booby trap," she said, passing by a fresh annotation in green spray paint.

"I saw it too," he announced. "Hold on for a second."

She stopped and forced herself to look down. Chet was hanging from a rung near the bottom, unfolding his Leatherman. She heard a crisp snip as it severed a piano wire, and then several seconds of absolute silence as they both waited for a detonation.

"I think we're good," he announced.

They had made no effort to hide this one: it was a curved rectangular slab, simply lying on the floor at the base of the ladder, lashed into place with zip ties. "Claymore," Chet announced. "Aimed straight up. Would have taken out anyone on the ladder."

"How are you doing?" Zula asked him, since there didn't seem to be much more to say on that topic.

"Not bad!" Chet said, sounding a bit surprised. "Going to sit down and take a little rest. I'll meet you at the drift intersection up thataway." He waved his flashlight beam down one of three adits that radiated away from the base of the shaft. "Go about a hundred feet, we'll be taking the second adit on the left."

Zula had been noticing that Chet's condition improved markedly when something happened to trigger an adrenaline surge and declined during uneventful parts of the journey. At the moment he seemed quite energetic, so she was surprised that he was now requesting a break; but perhaps this was just his polite way of saying that he wanted her to leave him alone so that he could take a leak. Certainly he had been drinking enough water. So she walked up the adit to the second hole on the left and smelled and saw more graffiti. But she smelled something else as well: a current of fresh air coming down from that direction.

She tried shutting off her flashlight and letting her eyes adjust, and she convinced herself that she could see faint gleams of daylight ricocheting from the tunnel's moisture-slickened walls.

Which was obliterated by a wash of glare from Chet's flashlight. He had finished his potty break, or whatever, and was bringing up the rear. Moving heavily again, lurching frequently to the side, as if he needed the wall of the adit to hold him up. He had zipped up his leather jacket as if to ward off a sudden chill.

"This is the way out," Zula said, announcing as much as asking it.

"You can find the way out from here," Chet confirmed. "Just go slow and look for booby traps."

He allowed her, now, to lead the way. She moved forward about fifty feet, then waited for him to catch up, then did it again. She came to another intersection, but it was obvious which way to go, for light and air were unmistakably coming up the tunnel now. She began to proceed at an extremely deliberate pace, just barely staying ahead of Chet. There was no point in getting too far out in front of him, since she just had to wait for him to catch up, and going slowly gave her more time to look for booby traps. They came to what must be the main adit leading southward out of the mine and found a flatbed car that was still capable of rolling down the rails bolted into its floor. Zula, after inspecting it for piano wires and Claymore mines, insisted that Chet sit down on it. She got her hands on his shoulders and pushed him along down the rails for a surprisingly long time, the brightness ahead of them increasing every time they came to a bend in the tunnel, and finally came around a curve and were blinded by the almost direct light of the sun shining into the mine's southern entrance. It seemed an obvious place to put a third booby trap, and they were too dazzled to see, so they waited there for a few minutes, eating snacks and letting Chet guzzle another bottle of water. Then Chet got to his feet, and they took the tunnel's last hundred yards one cautious step at a time.

The last booby trap was a simple tripwire stretched from wall to wall at ankle level, just a few yards short of the exit, where hikers impatient to get out of this place would be tempted to break out into a long stride. Chet insisted that Zula step over it and then get all the way out of danger before he snipped it with his Leatherman. He was afraid that it was some sort of particularly fiendish IED that would detonate when the wire was cut. But nothing happened, and Chet staggered out of the tunnel a few moments later looking like the ghost of a miner who had died in the heart of the mountain a hundred years ago.

They had traveled less than a mile as the crow flew, but entered into a different world. Zula inferred that the prevailing winds must bring wet air from the Pacific up from the south to deposit loads of rain in the valley that now stretched out before them. For the air was palpably moister than what they'd been breathing on the Schloss side of the ridge, and the vegetation was of an altogether different biome. They had entered the mine in an arid wasteland of talus and emerged in the middle of something that was close to being a rain forest.

And a wilderness. There was no graffiti, no party trash at this end. A fire ring stood nearby, and around it were some flat spots where it looked as though backpackers might pitch tents when they ventured up here. But compared to the other side, only a short drive from the town of Elphinstone and a short hike from the comforts of the Schloss, this place was out in the middle of nowhere, a shred of territory caught between the U.S. border and the nearly uncrossable barrier of the ridge that now rose up behind them. Had the views been more spectacular, it might have attracted backpackers and mountain bikers anyway. But better vistas were to be had for less work in places like Glacier and Banff, not so many hours' drive away, and so this place had been left alone, save by cross-border smugglers and international terrorists. Patches of snow, rounded by the spring melt, spread in the trees all around them and lapped up the slopes of the mountain, contributing to a general runoff that seeped through mud and trilled down small watercourses into cold gurgling brooks that came together, perhaps a mile below, into a river that hurtled south down the valley; and though they couldn't see it from here, they could hear the roar of the cataract that almost coincided with the border, not marked on maps, but known to the few people who lived in these parts as American Falls.

OLIVIA HAD BEEN warned, of course, that working for MI6 would not be romantic. Not, in other words, the way it was in the movies. It was a bit embarrassing that this needed to be mentioned at all. No one who was worldly and intelligent enough to work for MI6 would really think it would be like a James Bond movie, would they?

So she had expected grinding tedium and deeply unromantic situations from the very beginning. For the most part, her time in Xiamen had amply fulfilled those expectations. The flashy bit at the very end had been anomalous to say the least.

And yet none of this careful hope deadening and expectation crushing on her trainers' parts had fully prepared her for the job of traveling from Wenatchee to Bourne's Ford on public transportation. She'd been lucky to reach the bus station in Wenatchee just a few minutes before the coach to Spokane was scheduled to depart. It was running half an hour late. No big deal. She bought a ticket with cash and climbed aboard a tired intercity bus reeking of mildew and air freshener and sat on it for several hours, watching the high desert of central and eastern Washington State go by, trying not to make too much of an impression on the down-at-heels senior citizens and migrant laborers sitting around her. A few hours later she disembarked at the bus and train station in downtown Spokane: a city she was certain had fine characteristics but that looked bleak and anonymous from street level at nightfall. It was ten degrees colder here than it had been on the coast. The next bus for Bourne's Ford didn't leave until tomorrow morning. She couldn't check into a hotel without presenting ID and thereby sending up a flare, so she walked to a reasonably nice Italian restaurant and had a long slow dinner that she paid for with cash. Then she walked to a cinema and caught the last showing of a comedy that, she guessed, was aimed at teenagers. This disgorged her into a parking lot at one in the morning. Everything was closed. Not even bars were open. Caught in the open, she just kept walking, trying to look purposeful. If she had to walk for five hours, it wasn't the end of the world. She was wearing comfortable flats and the energy expended by walking would keep her warm enough, despite the fact that she was underdressed for the weather. But after about two hours, as she was trudging up a seemingly endless commercial strip, she noticed a Perkins Family Restaurant that was open twenty-fours. She went into it and ate the most colossal breakfast she had ever had in her life, spent about an hour reading a single used copy of *USA Today,* then paid for the meal, went out, and hit the streets again.

By six in the morning the sky was getting light, joggers were out, and Starbucks cafés were beginning to open their doors. She killed another hour in one of those and then hiked back to the bus station, where she caught an 8:06 bus headed for Sandpoint and Bourne's Ford. This was much like the first one, except with a certain hard-to-pin-down air of Wild West mountain-man craziness about it. The Wenatchee-Spokane run had been a simple matter of getting across a sparse desert, irrigated in some places, therefore with a generally farmlike vibe. She had noticed, as they'd drawn closer to Spokane, that trees were beginning to survive, just isolated specimens at first, then clumps, then small forests. But northward from Spokane the forest cover became continuous, the highway began to bound up and down considerable slopes, and the businesses and dwellings along it stopped feeling like farms and began feeling like outposts. Decidedly eccentric signage began to show up: billboards inveighing against the United Nations, and hand-lettered jeremiads about the existential threat posed by the federal budget deficit. But of course she just noticed those things because she was looking for them; it was mostly fast-food joints and convenience stores like anywhere else in America, interspersed with clusters of vacation homes (wherever there was a lake or a nice stretch of river), ranches (where the land was open and flat), or outbreaks of Appalachian-style rural poverty. Sometimes they'd jump over a ridge and pass through what she thought was out-

and-out wilderness, until she saw the zigzagging tracks of the logging roads.

Then suddenly they were passing through a rather nice town, which she learned was Sandpoint, and which had all the indicia—brewpub, art gallery, Pilates, Thai restaurant—of a place where Blue State people would go to enjoy a high standard of living while maintaining nonstop connectivity and assuaging their guilty consciences in re global warming, fair trade, and the regrettable side effects of Manifest Destiny. The bus stopped there for a bit; many passengers got off, and only a few got on. For, as was obvious from looking out the windows, northern Idaho was not a place where anyone could sustainably live unless they had access to a vehicle of some description, so the market for public transit was correspondingly tiny and mostly limited to juveniles, very old people, shaggy men who appeared to be one step above vagrants, and women in ankle-length *Little House on the Prairie*–style dresses—apparently members of some very traditional religious sect.

An hour later she was in the considerably smaller and less Blue Statish town of Bourne's Ford, and half an hour after that—for it turned out to be a bit of a walk—she was in its Walmart.

She had been waiting for the point in the journey where the crazy would begin: when she'd step over some invisible threshold separating commonsensical America from the subculture where Jacob Forthrast, his family, and his neighbors lived their lives. So far, it had been more of a slow blend than a threshold. The Walmart definitely made her feel that she was getting warmer. She happened to enter through the part of it that was a huge grocery and drug store: all by itself, probably larger than any store in the United Kingdom. It was the sort of place that encouraged its customers to buy in bulk, and the shopping carts were sized accordingly. Still, they were not large enough for some of the customers: a hulking Grizzly Adams type, openly wearing a semiautomatic pistol on his hip, was pushing one overloaded cart and dragging another behind him, both piled with huge sacks of dog food, beans, bacon, macaroni. The next aisle had been all but taken over by a family of those long-dress-wearing people: Mom, two teenaged daughters, a smaller girl, a toddler boy strapped into the basket and another being chased around by a young man who was either the father or an elder brother. The men wore normal clothes: no funny hats or facial hair for them. They were running a train of three carts, and Mom was checking her way through a laser-printed list that ran to four pages. But none of the other customers was really distinguishable from what you'd see in a grocery store anywhere else in the United States, or the United Kingdom for that matter.

So she hadn't really found the crazy yet. But with a little introspection—and she had lots of time for that, as she made her way across acre after acre of machine-buffed Walmart floor space—she saw that what she was really looking for was a way for this journey to be something other than utterly and perfectly banal. If the police had chased her and Sokolov away from the shooting scene in Tukwila; if they'd been forced to abandon the car in the Cascades and make their way north through the mountains; if she had been pursued through the dark streets of Spokane by members of a drug gang; if the mountains of northern Idaho were infested with crazy Nazis; then all of this would have been more than what it was. But none of those conditions obtained, so this was nothing more than the most tedious imaginable way to spend two days, getting across one of the easiest-to-cross borders in the world between two relatively calm and docile countries.

Or so she had just about convinced herself when she strayed into the part of the store where the flat-panel TVs were displayed, and she noticed a hundred shoppers all standing still with their backs to her, gazing at live television coverage of some event.

The TVs were not all tuned to the same channel; some were showing Fox, some CNN, some local channels from Sandpoint or Spokane. But all of them were covering the same story and broadcasting similar images: a road, seen from a helicopter, in a generally green and open landscape. The road was broadening from two to several lanes as it approached a structure that looked like a tollbooth. All the lanes were filled with stopped cars. In the middle of this traffic jam was a gray hole. A crater. Like a meteor strike. Cars around the edge of it had been crushed, shredded, punched away from the center, and were still smoking despite streams of water being played on them from nearby fire trucks. The traffic jam was surrounded by flashing aid vehicles and infested with stretcher bearers. Still forms in body bags were lined up to one side.

She worked her way in close enough to see the banners across the bottoms of the screens:

EXPLOSION IN OKANAGAN.
B.C. BLAST.
TERROR AT AMERICA'S DOORSTEP?

A ground-level camera angle showed Canadian and American flags streaming in the breeze right next to each other. This seemed to be the favored backdrop for on-the-scene reporters, who, Olivia inferred, must be all standing right next to one another talking into their microphones. With several of them going at once, she found it difficult to tell one sound bite from another. She was hearing a lot of the coded phrases uttered by "Breaking news" reporters to admit that they didn't really know what was going on. But from time to time, one of them would launch into a recap "for viewers just joining us." Olivia inferred from a couple of these that the explosion had taken place in Canada, just a few meters short of the U.S. border, and that the thing she'd mistaken for a tollbooth was actually the border crossing. A vehicle stopped there, waiting for inspection, had exploded with what was obviously terrific violence. The death toll was already pushing a hundred, not counting bodies that had been completely vaporized, and rescue workers were still prying open smashed cars with the Jaws of Life and searching the collapsed wreckage of both Canadian and American buildings.

The studio-bound anchorpersons, interviewing the correspondents on the scene, asked the obvious questions: Do we have a description of the vehicle carrying the bomb? Of its passenger or passengers? But it was pretty clearly hopeless. The vehicle and its occupants would have been invisible, anonymous to all except those who were stuck in traffic near it; and anyone who'd been near it would be dead.

"I'VE NEVER BEEN so sad to be right," Olivia said to Sokolov, when she found him pushing a cart down an aisle in the camping and outdoors section. She fell in step next to him and cast an eye over the contents of his cart, wondering whether this was totally random stuff that he had thrown in there to perfect his Walmart shopper disguise or things he actually intended to buy: 5.56-millimeter cartridges, a water purification device, jerky, bug repellent, a camouflage hat, heavy mittens. Freeze-dried meals. A roll of black plastic sheeting. Parachute cord. Batteries. A folding bucksaw. Camouflage binoculars.

"You refer to explosion?" Sokolov said.

"Yes. I refer to explosion. Did you have any trouble getting here?"

In response, Sokolov just looked at her warily, uncertain whether she was asking the question tongue-in-cheek.

"Never mind," she said, and walked with him for a few more paces. "I'm just trying to work out whether I'm to be the hero or the goat, when I get back to London."

"Goat?"

"The one who gets blamed for screwing it up."

Sokolov merely shrugged, which she did not find comforting. *There are always fuckups, and there is always a goat. Sometimes the goat is you.*

"Is diversion," he announced.

"Ooh, that's an interesting thought. Why do you think it's a diversion?"

"Extreme size of explosion. Ridiculous. Purpose is to turn bodies into vapor, destroy evidence."

"You think Jones sent some guys to blow themselves up in a conspicuous place, drawing all of the attention—"

"Jones is crossing the border right now," Sokolov said, "in Manitoba." He shrugged again. "We are wasting time."

It turned out that Sokolov really did want to buy all that stuff. Not because he envisioned any particular use for it. He just believed in stocking up on such things, on general principles, whenever an opportunity presented itself.

He would fit in well here.

What he *really* wanted to buy was mountain bikes. He'd already cruised the bicycle aisle—evidently he had gotten here hours ago—and made his selections. She couldn't argue with his logic. They needed to get to Jake Forthrast's compound on Prohibition Creek—or "Crick" as the Iowans insisted on pronouncing it. It was thirty miles as the crow flew, longer on the roads they'd be taking. There were no buses. But on bicycles, they could make it before nightfall if they set a decent pace.

Olivia now understood what Sokolov meant by *We are wasting time.* He was saying, *I could do this ride in two hours. With you, pumping away on your little girl-bike, it will take four.*

Anyway, buying the stuff was no problem—if there was anything spies were good at, it was carrying lot of cash—and so it all led to a kind of festive scene out back of the Walmart in which they removed the new mountain bikes from their big flat boxes, put them together, and heaved the corrugated cardboard into a Dumpster. Sokolov, spurning the very idea of purchasing bottled water, filled several of his new containers with water from a hose bib, and put parachute cord and bungee cords to work strapping the other gear to the bikes' cargo racks. She would have found it fun had she not seen what she'd seen on all those televisions.

Then they were on their way, pedaling north. Heading for the proverbial hills.

THE CLOUDS PARTED just long enough to show them incontrovertible evidence that it was cold down there.

Seamus had forgotten about cold.

He was going to have to buy four jackets. One of them an XXXL. Four hats, four pairs of gloves.

When was the last time he had paid his credit card bill?

Never mind, Marlon would spring for it. How much of a dent could four jackets make in his net worth, compared to chartering this jet? Not only would Marlon buy the jackets, but he would make sure that they were stylish. Cutting-edge ski parkas, or something. Maybe all in the same style and color, so that they could look like the Fantastic Four.

Dumbfounded with fascination, Seamus began to explore that analogy as they made their final approach. The stewardess—each bizjet came with one, apparently—made a final pass through the cabin, picking up half-eaten plates of sushi and empty cocktail glasses.

Quite obviously, Csongor was the Thing. Seamus was Reed Richards, the gawky father figure, weirdly flexible, always scurrying around arranging stuff. Marlon was a Human Torch if ever there was one. Yuxia was—

Invisible Girl? If only.

The jet touched down and came to a brisk stop. Seamus sensed a little wave of depression sweeping through the Four. Chartering this jet, climbing onto it illegally at the air base outside of Manila, and blasting into the sky—for these jets really hauled ass, once they got going—had been the most exhilarating thing ever. Even Seamus, who went into combat against terrorists for a living, had been thrilled. Actually landing in the sodden gray landscape of Joint Base Lewis-McChord was a corresponding letdown.

Long experience flying around the world on airplanes had conditioned him to relax, for it would be another half hour before they actually made it off the plane. But of course, this was not true in the case of a bizjet. He smelled damp, piney air coming in through the open door and realized that nothing was preventing him from climbing off.

"Thanks for the ride, Marlon," he said, standing up and bashing his head on the ceiling again.

"Thanks for getting me out of there," Marlon returned, grinning, and climbing up into a prudent stoop.

Seamus held up his index finger. "Don't thank me until we get through the next fifteen minutes."

"LET ME GET this straight," Freddie's boss had said, over the hyperencrypted voice conferencing link from Langley. Never a great thing to hear from the lips of someone considerably above you in chain of command.

"We're not asking for any money," Seamus had broken in, before Freddie could say anything.

"Noted," the boss had said. "Always a plus."

"Not asking you to print passports or diddle any paperwork."

"The whole point," Freddie had put in, perhaps a bit nervously, "is to leave no paper trail at all."

"Two Chinese and a Hungarian, just basically parachuted into CONUS with no paperwork whatsoever."

"The Hungarian is legit, he has a visa."

"Two Chinese then."

"Yeah."

"Given that Chinese illegals are being shipped into the Port of

Seattle by the containerload, it seems like it would hardly make a dent."

"That's the spirit!" Seamus had said. "And these are not your baseline economic migrants. They're going to be running major corporations inside of a fortnight."

"Not without green cards."

"I think I'm going to marry the girl. That would take care of her status."

Freddie had turned to look at him incredulously. "Does *she* know this?"

"She has no idea. Just a feeling."

"A feeling on *your* part."

"Halfway there. Pretty respectable progress."

"What I'm really getting at," the boss had said, "is whether you have any kind of long-term plan for these people—other than matrimony—that would lead to complications down the road."

"Let's not focus on hypothetical complications," Seamus had said. "Let's focus on the fact that these people have been in physical contact with Abdallah Jones, rammed his vehicle, shot him in the head, been tortured by him, in the very, very recent past. Seems worthy of a free ticket to Langley, don't you think? Can't we buy these kids a cup of coffee at least?"

"We can buy them a cup of coffee in Manila," the boss had pointed out.

"Only at the risk of them getting arrested," Seamus had returned. "At which point information is going to start gushing out like Jolly Ranchers from a ruptured piñata."

"It would be easy at this end," the boss had said, "provided they land at a military base. Getting them on a plane at your end, without passing through formalities, is outside of my scope."

"Disavow all knowledge of our actions," Seamus had said, "and we're home free." He glanced for confirmation at Freddie, who turned the corners of his mouth down—he was very good at this—and nodded.

"Easiest decision I ever made. Consider yourself disavowed."

NONE OF WHICH really gave Seamus any idea of what to expect, twenty hours later, descending the wee, steep staircase to the hangar floor. Joint Base Lewis-McChord, was a combined army/air force facility, actually rather important to the global war on terror in that it was the home of the Stryker Brigades so heavily used in Afghanistan, as well as being an important special forces base. Seamus knew it well. It was about an hour's drive south of Seattle, on a huge tract of forest whose soil and climate made Seattle's seem arid by comparison.

What he was seeing now was like something from a David Lynch film in its surreal starkness. The jet, apparently on orders from the tower, had taxied directly into a small hangar that was otherwise completely empty. Powerful lights were on, as if trying to drive away the misty gray dimness flooding in through the hangar doors, which were rumbling shut, apparently driven by electric motors.

Nothing else was in here except for a maroon minivan with a BABY ON BOARD sticker in the window and an assortment of SUPPORT OUR TROOPS ribbons scattered around its liftgate. Standing next to the minivan was a man in civilian clothes. His bearing and haircut would have marked him as a military man even if Seamus hadn't already known who he was: Marcus Shadwell. A major in a locally based special forces unit. Seamus had been in some funny places and situations with Marcus.

None funnier than this, apparently. "Where are they?" was how Marcus greeted him.

"They're on the fucking plane, Marcus. What did you think, we bungeed them onto the roof rack?"

"Let's get a move on," Marcus said. "My orders are to get you off this base and into the civilian world." He held up his hands, palms out, and pantomimed backing away. Then he whisked his hands together as if washing them.

THEY ENDED UP at a regional airport a few miles away, outside of Olympia, only because it was big enough to support a couple of car rental agencies. Seamus went in and grabbed an SUV. His credit card was good for that much, anyway. Marcus helped them transfer their absolutely minimal baggage from his minivan into their new ride as Marlon and Yuxia huddled in the backseat, chafing their arms and shivering. Csongor, by contrast, seemed very much in his element and looked around at everything curiously to a degree that Seamus found slightly irksome. There was a U.S. customs office at the airport, and Seamus was troubled by a paranoid fear that some armed and uniformed agents would swarm out of it and demand to see papers.

But no such thing happened.

"I'm out of here," Marcus said.

"Appreciate it. Maybe we can catch up later," Seamus said. But Marcus already had his back turned and was hustling toward the open driver's-side door of his family van as if he expected gunfire to break out at any moment.

Driving at exactly the speed limit—difficult for him—Seamus got them out onto the interstate and backtracked a few miles to a strip mall complex out in the middle of nowhere, which he had noticed, and taken the measure of, as Marcus had driven them out into the civilian world. It was anchored by a Cabela's outdoor superstore, where he reckoned they could get warm stuff. But this, like every other Cabela's, was surrounded by restaurants and other small businesses that fed off the stream of Cabela's traffic without actually competing with the mother ship.

They ended up in a teriyaki joint, confronted by live news coverage of the car bomb explosion on the Canada/U.S. border, showing on a flat-panel above the cash register with the sound turned down.

This, then, became the topic of the conversation Seamus had with the boss at Langley. He spent most of it outside, strolling up and down before the windows of the teriyaki place, watching the Thing, the Human Torch, and Not-so-Invisible Girl snarfing their teriyaki. Above them, pictures of the crater and the body bags on the TV. Out here, the rain was spitting into his face, which seemed fitting somehow.

"I'd say this operation is all over," said the boss, "except for writing reports."

"I don't believe that," Seamus said. "This thing with the car bomb is obviously . . ."

". . . a diversion that Jones used to draw attention from his real plans." the boss said, finishing his sentence.

This left Seamus speechless, an unusual state of affairs for him. "You got that too?" he finally asked.

"Yes," said the boss. "You are not the only person in the world who knows what a diversion is."

"But in that case . . ."

"It is of no practical relevance, at least for the next ninety-six hours—probably more like a week—because it *worked,* Seamus. Like it or not—whether it's a diversion or not—the fact is that when a terrorist blows himself up at a border crossing and takes a hundred and fifteen U.S. and Canadian citizens with him, then that is what the FBI and the Mounties and everyone else in the chain of command are going to be focusing all their energies and personnel on for a while."

"So what do you want me to do?"

"You've got a car?"

"Yeah."

"You've got money? Credit cards? Everyone's healthy?"

"Everyone's fucking great."

"Then start driving east," the Boss said. "Show the kids Mount Rushmore along the way, and by the time you make it here, maybe I'll be able to devote some resources to debriefing your friends. And Little Bighorn, while you're at it. Foreigners eat that shit up."

"What about Olivia? What's she up to?"

"Olivia!" the boss exclaimed. "She's lucky that guy blew himself up."

"Why does that make her lucky?"

"Because, (a) it proves she was right, and (b) it gives the FBI and the local cops something to focus their energies on besides complaining about what she did in Tukwila."

"What is Tukwila, and what did she do there?"

"I'll explain when you get here."

"What's she doing now?"

"I have no idea," said the boss. "And believe me, that's a good thing."

THE CABELA'S SHOPPING spree went down pretty much as Seamus had envisioned it, except that they all ended up in camouflage. Because camouflage was what they sold at Cabela's. If you wanted ski parkas in sleek designs and eye-catching colors, you had to go somewhere else.

Seamus inferred that hunting culture in China was not well developed. "Is this where the soldiers go to buy their uniforms?" Yuxia inquired, gazing at rack after rack, acre after acre of floor space devoted to all manner of clothing in several distinct state-of-the-art camo patterns. Her confusion was understandable; she'd just entered the country through a huge military base, and Seamus had not been very diligent about explaining where the boundary lay between it and the civilian world. He had to spend a few minutes explaining to her and Marlon that lots of people hunted here, and even more liked to cop a certain stance or attitude about it, using camouflage as a cultural signifier, and this was where those people came to buy clothes. Marlon, Csongor, and Yuxia could, in other words, buy anything they wanted in this store without laying themselves open to the accusation that they were improperly wearing the uniforms and insignia of the armed forces of the United States. Once she had pushed through an initial barrier of culture shock, Yuxia found this amusing.

The Fantastic Foreigners were also dumbfounded by the size and variety of the gun section, and in this way they lost another forty-five minutes to culture shock, pure and simple. Seamus could tell that Csongor was lusting after a 1911, but fortunately the paperwork would have made purchasing such a thing impossible, and so the relationship had to remain platonic for now. Because of the unusual way in which they had entered the country, Seamus had been able to carry his own sidearm—a Sig Sauer—the whole way, but he had ended up with only one clip, and so while the others were distracted with running in and out of dressing rooms, he purchased two additional empty clips and four boxes of rounds, as well as a holster that he could use to carry all of that crap around under his jacket. He did not really expect that he would have to use, or even draw, his weapon while driving these people across the country and showing them Mount Rushmore. But the fact was that he had the gun, and he needed a way to carry it around safely and securely and not too obviously. It wouldn't do to have it rattling around loose in his backpack.

Having settled all of that, he rounded up Yuxia, who was mugging in front of a mirror in a ghillie suit that made her look like the Littlest Ent. She had gotten a little giddy, which he put down to a combination of jet lag, culture shock, and emotional trauma over having been ripped from the bosom of her family and homeland. On this side of the Pacific there were, of course, many persons of Chinese ancestry whose ancestors had come over to this country in the most fucked-up circumstances imaginable, and he supposed that if this adventure were better organized, maybe with some psychologists on its advisory board, he'd be getting Yuxia in touch with the relevant support groups. But as it was they were just going to have to get in the SUV and start driving, and she was going to have to suck it up for a while, and he was going to have to keep an eye on her.

So that was what happened. Csongor rode shotgun. Yuxia crept into the way back, burrowed into a deep warm nest of newly acquired camo gear, and crashed. Marlon sat in the center of the middle seat, blocking Seamus's line of sight out the rearview and watched America go by with all due curiosity. Seamus felt vaguely like one of those ex-military guys who gets a job as a celebrity body-guard and finds himself driving rock stars around.

He was feeling some unaccountable need to get clear of the Seattle-Tacoma metro area, so he headed east over the mountains and then down into the desert. At which point it seemed as though nothing stood between him and the Atlantic Ocean, and so he went into serious road-trip, put-the-hammer-down mode, and bombed down I-90 as if there was no tomorrow. White line fever got him most of the way across the state. But then certain real-world issues—the limited size of his bladder and of his fuel tank—began to interfere with the dream. He was seeing a lot of signs for some place called Spokane. He'd heard of it. It turned out to be a decent-sized city with the usual complement of strip malls and chain hotels. None of them looked absolutely perfect, and so he kept driving anyway, and found that he had passed into Idaho without really leaving Spokane; the city had thrown a pseudopod of exurban development across the border, groping out in the direction of a place called Coeur d'Alene. It was there that Seamus finally spotted the inexpensive chain hotel of his dreams, embedded roughly in the center of an eight-hundred-mile-long development that included, within a few hundred yards of the hotel entrance, a twelve-pump gas station/convenience store complex and a restaurant that looked as if it might have microbrews on draft. Presenting

his credit card—which, unbelievably, had not been canceled yet—
he rented three rooms: one for Yuxia, because she was a girl. One
for Marlon, because he was, ultimately, paying for everything and
so it seemed that he ought to have his own room. And one that he
would share with Csongor, since he and the Hungarian seemed to
have developed an understanding that verged on friendship.

They agreed to meet in the lobby an hour later and walk over to
the restaurant-that-might-have-good-draft-beer.

Seamus happened to come down to the lobby first and found
himself with nothing to do except scan the rack of travel brochures
by the registration desk: promotional literature for ski areas, amusement parks, gold mine tours, fishing and jet-skiing on the nearby
lake. He grew bored and sat back down. But his mind was troubled
in a way that it hadn't been when he had entered the lobby. He got
back up and went over to the rack and scanned it again, trying to
make out what he'd seen there that had subliminally irritated him.

He found it, finally, on the third slow pass through the rack: the
word "Elphinstone."

It was on a cartoonish, schematic map of something called the
International Selkirk Loop: a circuit of American and Canadian
highways, straddling the border, that, to judge from the numerous pictures, passed by lots of pretty lakes and through some nice
mountain scenery. This brochure badly wanted Seamus to understand that a person could drive this loop on a motorcycle or an RV
over the course of a leisurely day or two, see a lot of natural beauty,
eat tasty food, buy cool stuff. It was, in other words, a tourist brochure, and fundamentally of no interest whatever to Seamus.

Except for that one word "Elphinstone."

That was the name of the town where Richard Forthrast had
his cat skiing resort. The place where he had gone missing a couple
of days ago.

Correction: Seamus had no proof that he had gone missing per
se. He had abruptly stopped playing T'Rain. Pretty thin evidence,
that. But it had been something like twenty-four hours—difficult
to tell exactly, what with the time zones and all—anyway, a hell of
a long time—since Seamus had checked in on Egdod. And to judge
from what the boss had said, Olivia had been dealing with troubles
of her own, related to someone, something, or somewhere called

Tukwila. Jones, or more likely his minions, were blowing shit up on the border, drawing every cop in the world to the epicenter. So it seemed a good bet that no one had been attending to the *somewhat* Mysterious Case of the *possibly* Missing Online Gaming Entrepreneur in a while. Seamus hadn't been thinking about it, at least not at a conscious level, since getting these people illegally into the country had been foremost in his thoughts, and he had just been going on instinct and impulse for at least a day. When stuck in the American embassy in Manila with three illegals liable to be arrested and deported at any minute, it's hard to focus on hypothetical events that might be taking place near the Idaho/B.C. border.

But now he was here. Literally, he was on the map. For when he pulled the Selkirk Loop brochure out of the rack, Coeur d'Alene became visible on the map, down toward the bottom. His eyes began jumping back and forth, top to bottom: Elphinstone, Coeur d'Alene. Elphinstone, Coeur d'Alene.

The only problem being that horizontal line drawn through the middle of the Loop: the Canada/U.S. border. No way was he getting Marlon and Yuxia across that.

But maybe he didn't need to. Maybe what he was looking for was coming to him.

"Seamus?"

He looked up. Csongor was there, and Marlon, and Yuxia, all freshly showered and looking like the Xiamen branch of the Lynyrd Skynyrd Fan Club. He had the sense that they'd been looking at him for a while, wondering when he was going to snap out of it.

"Are you hungry?" Csongor continued. Not that he gave a shit; *Csongor* was hungry.

Now, some part of Seamus was wondering why these kids didn't just walk over to the restaurant and order food, if that was what they wanted. But he had dragged them to this place and created a situation in which they were totally dependent on him—appointed himself the Dr. Reed Richards of this little band of superheroes—and he had to step up to his responsibilities.

"Yeah," he said. "Just thinking about tomorrow's program of activities."

"Yay," Yuxia said. "Activities!" She translated this abstraction into Mandarin, and Marlon nodded, a little uncertainly.

Csongor was unsure to what degree Seamus was being sarcastic, and he was now watching with heightened vigilance. "What did you have in mind?" he asked.

"Well," Seamus pointed out, "we're dressed for hunting."

"We don't have guns."

"Speak for yourself."

Csongor was now watching very carefully. Seamus broke eye contact and returned his attention to the rack for a minute. "Just kidding," he said. He scanned an index finger across a row, looking for something he'd noticed earlier.

There it was. He snapped the brochure out, then turned toward the exit. "Let's eat," he said.

But the others were having none of it. They bunched behind him, peering over his shoulder or around his elbow to read the cover of the brochure he'd just pulled from the rack: SELKIRK HELICOPTER TOURS.

AFTER HE'D LED the terrorists through the mine and out the other side, Richard was aware, at some level, that he really needed to start in on the sell job of his life: he needed to get Abdallah Jones to believe that making it past American Falls would be no picnic and that his skills as guide were still—in the parlance of old what's-his-name, the CEO of Corporation 9592—mission critical. That Richard still had world-class value-added here.

But Richard could not bring himself to do this, for exactly the same reason that, when Corporation 9592 had grown to a certain size, he had become listless during meetings and allowed himself to drift to the periphery of relevance. Richard was, at bottom, a guy who did stuff. A farmer. A plumber. A Barney.

What he wasn't so good at was manipulating the internal states of other humans, getting them to see things his way, do things for him. His baseline attitude toward other humans was that they could all just go fuck themselves and that he was not going to expend any effort whatsoever getting them to change the way they thought. This was probably rooted in a belief that had been inculcated to him from the get-go: that there was an objective reality, which all people worth talking to could observe and understand, and that there was no point in arguing about anything that could be so observed and so understood. As long as you made a point of hanging out exclusively with people who had the wit to see and to understand that objective reality, you didn't have to waste a lot of time talking. When a thunderstorm was headed your way across the prairie, you took the washing down from the line and closed the windows. It wasn't necessary to have a meeting about it. The sales force didn't need to get involved.

Hence his recent surge of reinvolvement in the company, sorting out various troubles attributable to the Wor. The Wor had given him something to do and he had just gone out and done it. Likewise looking for Zula. As long as there had been doors to hit with sledgehammers, he'd been all over it. Later in that project, when it had become a matter of maintaining the "Where's Zula?" Facebook page and politicking with cops, he had become listless and of no use.

And now this: Jones had wanted help finding his way through the mine tunnels or else he would kill Zula. Richard had packed a sleeping bag and some spare clothes and applied himself to getting that done. They had punched through it while the sun was rising and emerged on the south slope to enjoy a view that in other circumstances he'd have found immensely pleasing: the low sun setting fire to torn diaphanous curtains of mist rising from stands of ancient cedars, the distant roar of the falls, swollen by snowmelt, the Selkirks and the Purcells and other ranges of mountains rambling off into the distance, affording peeks at deep blue lakes and cavernous valleys. The granitic mass of Abandon Mountain rising out of its rampart of talus, just a few miles south of the border, its sheer eastern face glowing in the rich golden light of the early sun.

Mission accomplished. Jones, or any idiot for that matter, could see right across the border now, would understand that Richard could simply be shot in the head and left here and they'd find some way of getting down past the falls and into the United States without his assistance.

It was time, in other words, to call out the sales force, take Jones to lunch, begin gardening personal contacts, shape his perception of the competitive landscape. Forge a partnership. Exactly the kind of work from which Richard had always found some way to excuse himself, even when large amounts of money were at stake.

Yet now his life was at stake, and no one was around to help him, and he still wasn't doing it. He simply couldn't get past his conviction that Jones could go fuck himself and that he wasn't going to angle and scheme and maneuver for Jones's sake.

Maybe because all that behavior ultimately seemed like groveling to him. That was *really* his problem: deep down, he believed that all such people were grovelers.

They took a little break at the mine's exit to enjoy the view, to set the last booby trap, to brew tea, to pray, and to try to get phone reception. Reasonable enough; it seemed as though the whole Idaho panhandle were directly visible from here, and there had to be a cell tower *somewhere* in that. The experiment would have been over very quickly if there'd been no reception at all, but it seemed that some of the jihadists were able to get one bar if they stood in a particular attitude in a particular place and held the phone a certain way and invoked various higher powers. Richard was tempted to make a sour analogy to pointing oneself in the direction of Mecca, but he didn't think it would do much for his life expectancy. Their rituals became ludicrous after a certain point. Because none of these guys had an ironic modern attitude, none saw the humor.

No, strike that. Almost all of them had been living under cover in the Western world and were as capable of seeing the humor as any fourteen-year-old American sitting on his couch watching *South Park* reruns and sending snarky tweets to his friends. But they'd made a conscious decision to turn their backs on all that. Like smokers or drinkers who'd gone straight, they were more dogmatic about this than anyone who'd come to that place naturally. Only Jones had the self-confidence to let himself be amused, and that was how he and Richard ended up making eye contact.

"So," Richard said, after he and Jones had enjoyed the moment, "you going to put a bullet in me now, or should I show you the easiest way to get past American Falls?"

"I'm happy with the arrangement in its current form," Jones said. "If that changes, you'll be the first to know. Assuming you see it coming."

"Well, you raise an interesting question there, Abdallah. *Would* I see it coming? Is it going to be one of those slow beheadings? Or just an unannounced shot to the head?"

Richard now watched in some degree of fascination as Jones actually mulled it over. "Other things being equal," he said, "I'd prefer to give you some opportunity to pray first, perhaps write out a statement. But if we find ourselves trapped in some awkward situation, there may not be time for that."

"Is that a little incentive program you just laid out for me? A built-in penalty for awkward situations?"

"The incentive program, as I'm sure you understand, is all about Zula. Because of the regrettable lack of phone reception, we have not been able to check in with our comrades. You may assume that she is still alive and that you may keep her in that condition by keeping us out of awkward situations and doing other things for us."

"Does that mean that if you'd been able to get bars, you'd have given the order to kill her?"

"There is no fixed plan. We assess our situation from hour to hour."

"Then assess this: we're sitting in an exposed place up here. Anyone down there in those valleys could see us. What are we waiting for?"

Jones acted as if he hadn't heard this. "Is that Abandon Mountain?" he asked, nodding south.

"Yes."

"Roads connect to its opposite side."

"The lower slopes, yes. That's the way out."

"Let's go then," Jones said, rising to his feet and dusting off his bum.

Richard had just tasked him: told him that they had to move away from this exposed position. Jones, not wanting to bow to Richard, had pretended not to hear it. But a few moments later he had done what Richard had suggested, as if it had been his own idea. Now *that* was the kind of psychological program that Richard could get involved in, if he could only find, or create, more opportunities to develop it.

Such an opportunity came along rather soon, as they came to a place where they could see an obvious way to traipse off in the general direction of Abandon Mountain. Every greenhorn pot smuggler who came this way tried it, only to find himself in difficulties two hours later when he learned that this easy-looking trail led to a cul-de-sac. In order to *prove* that it was a cul-de-sac, it was necessary to expend another few hours probing for a way out of it, thereby wasting most of a day. And so here Richard actually did have to perform a little sell job, convincing Jones that it would really be much better for them if they turned aside from the obvious and easy path and instead spent the next couple of hours picking their way down a slope that, had it supported a proper trail, would have been an endless succession of densely packed switchbacks. But no one could have built a proper trail on this thing without using tactical nuclear weapons. It was a junk pile of fallen logs strewn over primeval talus and covered with a loose slippery froth of moss and decaying vegetation. After leaving a green spray-paint annotation at the top, they devoted four hours to clambering down it, covering all of about half a mile on the map.

Richard, back in his dope-carrying days, had made this trip three or four times before he had lost all patience with it. He had come here with nothing on his back except for food and a bedroll and devoted several days to finding a quicker and easier way down: the proverbial Secret Shortcut: an abrupt and chancy descent into a dry wash followed by a relatively quick and easy hike down a gully leading to a spot near the top of the falls. Had it not been for that discovery, his nascent smuggling career probably would have been snuffed out by the sheer unattractiveness of this part of the journey. But he felt no particular need to share the shortcut with Jones and his men. For now, they were stuck in a place that had no phone reception: a state of affairs that seemed to limit the amount of damage that Jones could do. The longer this lasted, the greater the chance that someone would notice the signs of his hasty departure from the Schloss and launch a proper investigation.

And there was also the fact that, like it or not, Richard was leading these people directly toward the place where Jake lived. He was doing all of this to save the life of his niece. It had all seemed easy until he had looked out from the mine's exit and seen Abandon Mountain. Now he was thinking pretty hard about the fact that, to save his niece, he was leading a band of terrorists straight toward a remote cabin containing two brothers, a sister-in-law, and three nephews.

The plan that took shape in his head, then, as they devoted the entire morning to clambering down into the valley of the river, was that he would slip away from camp tonight and make his way to Jake's place and warn them.

They took a long siesta at the side of the river, prayed some more, cooked lunch, rested sore muscles, and wrapped bandages around twisted ankles. Richard pulled his hat over his face and pretended to sleep, but in fact stayed awake the whole time working out the plan in his mind. They would make one more push after this break, and he would show them how to get around the falls: yet another surprisingly difficult operation. After that they would set up the evening's camp, and Jones would kill him or not. If not, Richard would try to get out of there after dark. The falls were deep in a rock bowl, covered with mist-fed vegetation so dense that not even GPS signals could get through. Forget about phones.

If only he had a flashlight.

Then he remembered that he *did* have one, a pinky-sized LED light attached to his key chain.

Water he could get from the river. Some energy bars might be useful, and he had a couple of those in his pack that he could slip into his pockets when no one was looking.

He had gone, over the course of a few hours, from utterly hopeless cynicism to toying idly with this nutball idea, to seriously working it out, to deciding that it was doable. That he *was* going to do it. When they got moving again, working their way down the river toward the falls, he was already thinking several miles ahead, trying to remember the way he would take tonight up out of the gorge and into the lower slopes of the mountain.

They crossed into the United States, a fact discernible only because of a moss-covered boundary monument that one of the jihadists nearly tripped over. The falls were just ahead of them and to the right. They worked their way downstream of the falls by crossing a high shelf of rock that looked down upon it from its east side. This terminated in a cliff that obliged them to descend to the riverbank in order to make any more southward progress. As Richard now explained, there was a way to scramble down from here; there had to be, or else it would never have been possible to make the return trip. But when going in this direction, the descent was considerably easier if you just used ropes. Richard had warned Jones of this well in advance, and so Jones had made sure to bring some good long ropes along. They paused up there for a short while so that some could enjoy the view down while others, who were good at such things (or claimed to be) made the rope fast to a giant cedar growing near the edge of the cliff. Half the men went down to reconnoiter. Then they sent Richard. Then the rest of them went down. He got the sense that this had been carefully thought out; they were becoming nervous that he might make a break for it and wanted to make sure that there were a few people at each end of the rope to keep an eye on him.

As soon as they reached the bottom, Jones gave an order to Abdul-Ghaffar, the white American jihadist, and nodded significantly at Richard. Richard was still absorbing this when Abdul-Wahaab ("the other Abdul" to Richard; apparently Jones's most senior lieutenant) drew his pistol, chambered a round, and aimed it at Richard's chest from maybe eight feet away. "I'd like you to stand with your feet about shoulder-width apart," said Abdul-Ghaffar in his flat midwestern accent. Out of his pack he was pulling a sheaf of black heavy-duty zip ties: not the skinny ones used to restrain unruly Ethernet cables in office environments. These were a quarter of an inch wide and a couple of feet long.

None of which seemed like the beginnings of an execution. Richard, tired and taken by surprise, had been caught flat-footed anyway. He stood as Abdul-Ghaffar had asked him to, and Abdul-Ghaffar knelt behind him and zipped four of the big zip ties around the top of each of his boots, stacking them to build a heavy cuff around each ankle. He slipped more zip ties under those cuffs and linked them in a chain, joining Richard's feet with a sort of hobble. When he was finished, Richard could move in six-inch steps, provided the ground was level. A similar treatment was then inflicted on his wrists, leaving maybe eight inches of space between them, but in front of his body, presumably so that he could open his fly to urinate, or convey food and water to his mouth.

This had all happened fast enough that his brain didn't really catch up until it was all over. They weren't going to kill him, at least not yet. But they seemed to have read his mind and anticipated that he might have thoughts of escaping. They searched him thoroughly now, presumably to make sure he wasn't carrying a pocketknife or nail clipper that he could use to cut his plastic bonds during the night.

And night came soon, for they were deep in a bowl and the sky was a slot above them, traversed by the sun for a mere few hours each day. They pitched their shelters on a flat shelf of rocky ground a quarter of a mile downstream of the falls and used river water to cook up a generous repast of instant rice and freeze-dried backpacking chow.

Richard could think of nothing else to do and so he went into the tent that been assigned to him, wriggled into his sleeping bag fully clothed and booted and, without much trouble, went to sleep.

THEY PEDALED THROUGH Bourne's Ford, slowly getting warmed up, pausing twice to adjust the bicycles and tighten up the loads. Like most American towns, this one had grown in a thin sleeve on a highway. Farmland took over behind the strip malls and fast-food outlets. Olivia had gotten the general picture that they were riding north in the valley of a river, which was off to their left, sometimes close enough to the road that they could get a good look at it, other times wandering off into the distance. It was not a fast-running mountain chute but a slow stream that meandered all over the place, but to judge from the intensity with which it was cultivated, it was excellent land. To their right, low hills developed out of the floodplain, blocking their view of what she knew to be much higher mountains in the main ranges of the Rockies beyond. To their left, the picture was altogether different, as green mountains rose abruptly from the flats just on the other side of the river. Traffic on the highway was light, and it seemed as though the majority of the license plates were from British Columbia. Except for the dark mountains brooding over it to the west, it might have been some idyllic midwestern landscape, and Olivia could see perfectly well why people who only wished to be left alone and live uncomplicated lives might come here from all over the continent and establish homesteads.

The farmlands were served by an irregular network of rural roads. One of these led to a bridge across the river. They turned onto it and crossed over the stream, heading now directly toward the mountain wall. Olivia now saw the wisdom of trying to make good time, since the sun was going to set at least an hour earlier as it fell behind the high ridgeline of the Selkirks.

The bridge connected with a north-south road set just inside the tree line, at an altitude where it would not be inundated by seasonal floods. Olivia was referring more and more frequently to a map that she had drawn by hand on a Starbucks napkin. For Jake Forthrast had given her some rough coordinates, but he did not seem to have an address per se; or if he did, he denied the authority of the U.S. government to make such assignments. They did not have to ride far before they came to an intersection with a blacktop road that plunged steeply down out of the west. It seemed to correspond to one Olivia had sketched on the napkin, so they shifted into much lower gears and began to ride up it. Tall trees closed in to either side. Half a mile later the road devolved into gravel. At the same time, it became considerably less steep, as it had taken to following the course of a tributary stream rushing down out of the mountains toward the big lazy river.

Olivia was continuing to be quite sensitive, or so she imagined, to the Crazy that she imagined must lurk up in these places. The Canadian border had become in her mind something like the end of the world, a sheer, straight cliff descending straight into the pit of Abaddon; as they crept asymptotically closer to it, the scene must become more and more apocalyptic and the people who chose to live there correspondingly strange. Which was, of course, utterly ridiculous, since what actually lay on the other side of that imaginary line was British Columbia, a prosperous and well-regulated place of socialized medicine, bilingual signage, and Mounties.

And yet the line was there, drawn on all the maps. Or rather, it was the upper edge of all the maps, with nothing shown beyond it. Since people—at least, before Google Earth came along—could not actually hover miles above the ground and see the world as birds and gods did, they had to make do with maps, which substituted for actually seeing things; and, in that way, the imaginary figments of surveyors and the conventions of cartographers could become every bit as real as rocks and rivers. Perhaps even more so, since you could look at the map any time you wanted, whereas going to look at the physical border involved a lot of effort. So perhaps it might as well be the end of the world, as far as some of the locals were concerned, and might affect the way they thought accordingly.

But now that they were actually riding up into those hills she found that human beings, and what they thought and did and built, were the least part of the place. It didn't matter how odd the locals were when there were so few of them, scattered over so much space that was so difficult to move around in.

Road signs, riddled by shotgun blasts and the occasional hunting round, insisted that they were on National Forest Service land and that the same agency was responsible for these roads. And indeed they frequently saw steep gravel ramps launching up into swaths of mountainside that were being logged or had been logged in the recent past. But from place to place they would enter upon a stretch of road that ran through relatively flat and manageable territory, frequently in proximity to river crossings. Small ranches occurred in such places, and sometimes several dwellings were collected into a sort of hamlet scattered through the pines and cedars. They were not close enough to call each other neighbors, but still there was a definite sense of placeness, even though these were not named and did not appear on maps. Some of the dwellings reflected a degree of poverty that Olivia associated with Appalachia, or even Afghanistan. But as they worked their way deeper and higher up the valley, such places became less frequent; or perhaps the elements had already destroyed them. For it was clear that, while one need not be rich, or even affluent, to survive in this environment, it was necessary to have some of the qualities that led to affluence when they were applied in more settled places. The cords of split wood neatly stacked under corrugated roofs, still amply stocked even at the end of the long mountain winter, and many other such details told Olivia that the same people, transplanted to Spokane, would soon be running small businesses and chairing civic organizations.

They rode into dusk and found their progress up the valley blocked by a pair of large dogs who had classified them as intruders. Each of these animals probably weighed more than Olivia. One seemed to have a lot of Newfoundland in him, but she could easily convince herself that the other was largely, if not entirely, a wolf. But both of them had collars, and both were well fed. "Do not look them in eyes," Sokolov suggested, dismounting and getting his bicycle between him and the animals. "Turn bike around, ride away if it gets bad." Olivia, feeling no urges whatsoever to behave heroically, reversed her bicycle's direction and kept one leg thrown over the saddle. Sokolov stood his ground. She knew that he could put these animals down with bullets to the brain from the pistol that he was carrying somewhere on his person, and that he was refraining from doing so only out of a desire not to offend their owners.

The dogs' barking eventually drew the notice of a man who came riding out from a nearby compound on a four-wheeled ATV. He did so, Olivia suspected, because he was too heavy to move about conveniently on his feet. He was armed with (at least) a large flip-knife and a semiautomatic pistol in a hip holster. He began shouting at the dogs as he drew closer, but it was difficult to get them calmed down, and so there had to be rather a lot of shouting and alpha-male drama before he could get them to sit down and shut up. The whole time he was keeping a sharp eye on Sokolov and, to a lesser extent, on Olivia.

She had no idea how these people would think about race. She had seen many more Native Americans than Asians today and guessed that she might be mistaken, by such people, for a member of one of the local tribes. But it didn't seem to be an issue with this guy; or at least it didn't make him any more suspicious and hostile than he was to begin with.

How he'd react to a man with a heavy Russian accent was impossible to guess.

Olivia set her bicycle down in the middle of the road, approached Sokolov, and tucked herself in under his arm. A woman who had been claimed by a dominant-looking male was a whole different organism from a woman who seemed to be up for grabs. Flattening her vowels and trying to sound as American as possible, she said, "We're looking for Jake Forthrast's place. He invited us to come and pay him a visit."

This changed everything. The man, who introduced himself now as Daniel ("as in The Book Of") wouldn't hear of letting them finish the journey on their bicycles; he rode back into his compound and emerged a few moments later driving a huge diesel pickup truck. Sokolov threw the bicycles into its back and rode with them while Olivia sat in the passenger seat with Daniel. From the way he had talked, she was expecting a long journey, but the distance covered, from there, was no more than a few miles. Somewhat adventuresome miles, as the road became steeper and worse the farther they went—giving Olivia the vibe that they really were approaching the

End of the World. But then they penetrated a narrow slot between a granite cliff face, astream with snowmelt, and a furious river and entered into a little dell, no more than a mile across, where four distinct homesteads had been built around a little body of water that Olivia guessed was there because of beavers. Directly across the water, and reflected in it, was a lone mountain, so close to them that they could be said to be on its southern approach.

The pond was ringed by a dirt road. In one place, another road led away from it, between two of the homesteads and farther up into the woods that grew on the mountain's southeastern flank. Daniel proceeded up that, moving slowly and being sure to exchange friendly waves with all the children, dogs, and homesteaders who had taken note of them.

The landscape now changed dramatically, becoming moister and cooler and cedar scented. A few hundred meters up the road they came to a gate, bolted together out of massive timbers, completely blocking the way. Posted on it were several documents, preserved under clear plastic. Olivia only glanced at these as she approached it, undid the latch, and hauled it open. For Daniel had assured her that it was permissible for them to do this. One of the documents was the U.S. Constitution, with several passages highlighted. Another was some kind of manifesto, apparently placed there for the edification of any federal agents who might come calling to collect taxes or gather census data. There were some favorite Bible passages as well, and a page of the Idaho State Code explaining precisely what a citizen was and was not allowed to do to an intruder in the defense of his own dwelling.

All of which was quite intimidating, and probably would have prevented her from going into the place at all, had she come here without a local guide; but Daniel seemed to think that he could make it past all Jake's defenses simply by honking his horn a lot. Dogs came out at a run. Olivia closed the gate behind the truck and leaped up onto its rear bumper; Sokolov hauled her up over the tailgate with several moments to spare before the arrival of their canine escort. They drove along for another minute or so, since Jake apparently didn't believe in having his front gate inordinately close to where he actually lived. The road bent around a spur of rock, and then the actual house came into view: tall and narrow by the standards of log cabins, perched on the opposite side of a creek bridged by a homespun log-and-plank span. The truck crossed it and pulled around to the back side. Spreading away from the cabin was a flat, partially cleared space complicated by livestock enclosures, gardens, and sheds. This rambled over some acres of ground until it came up against the base of a forested slope.

A boy with an axe was emerging from a woodshed. A woman with a long dress was stepping out onto a deck above them. Jacob and John Forthrast came around the corner of the building wiping black grease from their hands.

"Picked up a couple of strays," Daniel joked, jerking a thumb toward the back. Olivia stood up, since the truck had come to a stop. Automatic lights had been triggered by the truck's thermal signature and shone warm on her face. She was about to remind them of who she was when she heard Jake explain, "It's Olivia." Guessing, maybe, that John's eyes were not good enough to recognize her in the sudden light. She found it odd that she was considered to be on a first-name basis with this family.

"Oh, hello again, Olivia!" John exclaimed. "Who is your friend?"

"That's a long story—but he came here because he wanted to help Zula."

"Then he's a friend of ours," Jake said. "Welcome to Prohibition Crick."

Day 21

Richard went to sleep with ease and then woke up a couple of hours later feeling bad that he had done so. After several days' absence, the Furious Muses had hunted him down in this remote place and come after him with a vengeance. It made for a very crowded tent.

The jihadists might kill him in the morning. But it seemed unlikely. If that had been the agenda, they would have done it already and saved themselves all those zip ties.

If they weren't going to kill him, then in the morning they would make him guide them up the old smugglers' trail to Abandon Mountain and Prohibition Crick. In order for that to work, they'd have to remove the zip-tie hobbles. He would then have the option of trying to run away from them. It seemed likely that this would lead to pursuit, capture, and ceremonial decapitation.

So he was going to have to look for a place where he could get away from them suddenly, out of rifle shot range, in some manner that would make it difficult to track him.

A movie hero would have jumped off the cliff into American Falls yesterday. After a few tense moments, his head would have broken the surface of the river some distance downstream. Richard knew that this was not really a practical strategy. But there might be stretches of the river that he could conceivably use in a similar way, body-surfing through rapids.

The problem was that their route didn't really follow this river. The river ran south and west. Their destination was more easterly, and so their plan today was to hike down the east bank for about a mile and then clamber up an endless slope until they broke out above the tree line and found themselves on a rocky spur thrown out from the mountain. From there they'd traverse a talus field that constituted the peak's western slope and finally drop into the valley of Prohibition Crick. The only way Richard could make a quick getaway in that sort of country was to let gravity take him and skid or roll down a slope. Which might have been fun, or at least survivable, on a sand dune or a snowfield, but in this territory would just lead to slow death from broken bones and ruptured organs.

Still, he kept pondering it through the long hours of the night, since it was the only way to keep the F.M.s off his back. He readily agreed to their basic premise, which was that, since he was about to lead a band of heavily armed terrorists straight to the homestead where several of his close relatives were minding their own business, his own life was forfeit to begin with.

The obvious dodge was to lead them somewhere else instead. But there were limits to how far he could mislead them. Jones had quite obviously done his homework, interrogating Zula in considerable detail, poring over Richard's Wikipedia article, printing out hard copies from Google Maps. He had a very clear idea of where they were going. As a matter of fact, Jones could easily find his way all the way to Pocatello from here with no help at all from Richard, which made Richard suspect that he was now being kept alive, not as a guide, but as a hostage and possible subject of a gruesome webcam execution. He could already picture the YouTube page, Dodge kneeling on a rug with a sack on his head, Jones behind him with the knife, and, underneath the little video pane, the first of many thousands of all-capital-letter comments sent in by all the world's useless fuckwits.

No, at this point the only card he really had to play—the only way to help Jake and John and the others save themselves—was to warn them. Because until now Jones had shown no awareness whatsoever that the valley of Prohibition Crick was inhabited. He must have seen a few roofs peeking out of trees in the Google satellite photos, but he might have made the reasonable guess that these were just summer cabins for Spokane orthodontists, boarded up and quiet at this time of year. Even if he had known that people were living in them year-round, he couldn't have guessed—could he?—that these were the most heavily armed civilians in the history of the world—gun nuts on a scale that made Pathans look like Quakers.

Even gun nuts could be taken in a surprise attack, but if Richard could somehow make them aware that they were in danger, then they would be able to give a very good account of themselves.

The plan he finally arrived at, then, just as the roof of his tent was beginning to shed a few stray photons into his wide-open eyes, was that he would proceed docilely until he was within audible gunshot range of Jake's place, and then make a break for it. The jihadists would shoot at him, and probably hit him. But everyone in the valley would hear it.

And then all hell would break loose.

He actually dozed for a little while, maybe an hour or so, and woke up to see more light filtering through the tentcloth and to hear the hiss of a backpacking stove being lit up.

Something told him to get moving. He wriggled out of the sleeping bag, spun around on his butt, got his booted and hobbled feet out the door, and then inchwormed out onto the ground.

Only two of the nine jihadists were out here: the tall Somalian-Minnesotan named Erasto, and another guy whose name Richard could not seem to keep in his mind. An Egyptian with a dark, callused spot in the middle of his forehead, caused by contact with the ground during prayer. They were heating a pot of water, presumably to cook up some porridge. Richard waddled closer to the stove and held his zip-tied hands out near the pot to catch some of the warmth. Erasto was eating an energy bar, the Egyptian just staring off aimlessly into the distance.

Richard realized that he had to take a crap, and he had to take it now.

He stood up. Erasto watched him carefully. He looked over toward the crap-taking place, which was a hundred or so feet away at the base of the cliff they had yesterday descended with rope.

"You guys have any toilet paper?"

No response.

"Dude," Richard said, "I really gotta go. No fooling."

Erasto seemed incredulous-verging-on-disgusted that he was having to deal with such matters. "Jabari!" he said. This seemed to get the attention of the Egyptian. Richard seized on it as an opportunity to finally learn the guy's name. Jabari. As in jabber. As in jabbing someone with a knife.

Erasto was asking some kind of question. Jabari bestirred himself and began to sort through a nearby pack, apparently looking for the bumwad supply.

Richard was hopping from foot to foot, as best he could when hobbled. It was very much open to question whether he was going to make it to a suitable place in time.

"I'm going to start hopping toward a suitable place to take a crap," he announced. He was speaking as calmly as possible, since he didn't want to shout and give non-English speakers such as Jabari the wrong idea. "You can follow me, you can shoot me in the back, whatever. But something's got to give." The sentence was punctuated with an impressive fart, which proved a much more effective communication than anything that had been escaping from Richard's other end. Richard toddled around until his back was turned to Erasto and then began mincing across the campsite, moving away from the river and into the undergrowth that grew profusely between the bank and the base of the cliff. In about half a minute's hopping, cursing, farting struggle through the shrubs—which grew densely here, watered by the mist drifting from the falls—he came to a clear place, dotted with turds and flecked with used bumwad, at the base of the cliff.

"Cliff" was too simple a word to denote the geological phenomenon rising above him. It was not a sudden vertical wall so much as a rapid increase in the slope of the ground that became fully vertical, and even developed into a bit of an overhang, twelve or fifteen feet above. And it was not a simple monolith, but a junk pile of boulders, tenacious vegetation, and packed soil that just happened to be really steep. Its top was out of view, but he knew it to be about fifty feet above. Anyway, it was now sheltered enough that he felt he could take a decent crap and so he hopped up and down several times, reversing his direction by degrees, and began to fumble with his belt.

A roll of toilet paper in a Ziploc bag struck him in the chest, underhanded by Jabari from perhaps twenty feet away, and bounced to the ground at his feet. "Thank you," Richard said, stripping his trousers down. Jabari turned his back and retreated somewhat. Richard, looking at him through the tops of the shrubs as he squatted to obey nature's call, saw the Egyptian raising both hands and waving cheerfully to someone back in the camp; apparently someone, probably Abdul-Wahaab, wanted to know what the hell was going on and needed to be reassured that all was well.

Richard was just in the middle of letting it all go when a dark object dropped out of the sky and thudded to the ground right in front of him. He assumed at first that it was a short bit of a stick that had tumbled out of a tree on the top of the cliff. But on a closer look he observed that it was neatly rectangular.

It was, he now saw, a pocket multitool—a Leatherman or similar—in its black nylon belt holster.

"THIS IS ALL about making a case," Seamus said.

The automatic waffle machine emitted a piercing electronic beep, signaling it wanted to be turned over. Seamus reached out and flipped it. The Four were standing at the complimentary breakfast bar of their hotel in Coeur d'Alene. None of the others had ever seen an automatic self-serve waffle machine before, and so Seamus was giving them an impromptu demo of the best that America had to offer.

"I'm not sure how that phrase translates into Chinese or Hungarian," he went on. "What I'm trying to say is this. We are going to see my boss, who happens to live on the other end of the country. We have to drive because I can't get you guys on a plane without IDs. We happen to be in striking distance of a place where I think Jones might be crossing the border. Last time I logged into T'Rain—which was about half an hour ago—Egdod was still wandering across the desert, followed by a couple of hundred coup counters and curiosity seekers. Which supports my theory."

"It does?" Yuxia asked.

"Okay, never mind the part about Egdod. You either believe it or you don't. I happen to believe it. Anyway, I called this dude who has a chopper." Seamus patted the brochure for the dude in question, which was sticking out of his back pocket. "He is willing to take me up there to fly over the area. I'll only be gone for a couple of hours. We'll be on the road by midafternoon. Chances are we can still make Missoula tonight. You guys can hang out here, see a movie, whatever. Just don't get arrested or do anything that would call attention to your complex immigration status."

"I want to come with you," Yuxia said.

"There's not enough room in the helicopter."

"The brochure says it can carry up to four passengers," Yuxia said, and pulled another copy of the same brochure out of her jacket pocket.

During the awkward silence that followed, Seamus happened to look up and see Csongor and Marlon gazing at him expectantly. The waffle seemed to have been forgotten.

"The big one can take four," Seamus admitted. "I had my eye on the little one."

"What is it exactly you think you're going to be doing?" Csongor asked.

"Flying over the area I'm interested in. Taking pictures. Getting a feel for it."

"How would our being in the helicopter prevent you from doing that?" Marlon wanted to know.

Seamus shrugged. "Maybe it wouldn't."

Yuxia asked, "Are you just lying to us?"

"Why would I lie to you?"

The waffle maker squealed again.

"You're acting weird," Yuxia said. "Are you expecting to, like, land the chopper and have combat with Jones?"

"No, I am not going to have combat with Jones. That is not what this is about."

"Good," Yuxia said, "because if that is your plan, you should warn the pilot."

"YOUR WAFFLE IS DONE!" shouted a peevish breakfaster from across the room.

Yuxia elbowed Seamus out of the way, figured out how to open the waffle iron, and deposited its steaming load onto a plate. The squeal stopped.

Csongor wanted to try it now. He picked up a minicarafe of

waffle batter and poured it into the appliance and watched brood-ingly as it infiltrated the valleys between the bumps.

"Of course," Seamus said, "if I believed that there was any chance whatsoever of getting into a firefight with jihadists, it would behoove me to say so to the pilot."

"Behoove it would!" Yuxia agreed.

"So it is totally safe," Csongor said.

"As safe as flying around in a chopper can ever be," Seamus agreed. He did not actually believe a word of this, but he had been cornered.

"Whereas if we stay here, there's a chance that we'll get into trouble," Csongor pointed out. "You are responsible for us."

"Alas, yes."

"If the chopper has a breakdown, you get stuck up north, then we are here with no car keys, no hotel room, no ID . . ."

"Okay, okay," Seamus said. "You can come with me and stare at trees from a great height all morning."

RICHARD HAD SEEN that tool and its holster before. He was pretty sure it was the one Chet always wore on his belt.

It was about five feet in front of him. When he was finished emptying his bowels, he rolled forward onto his knees, then to all fours, stretched out, and coaxed it up off the ground with the tips of his fingers. Then he pushed himself back to a squat. He set the multitool down on the ground next to his foot, then picked up the Ziploc bag containing the roll of bumwad and pulled that open.

He could hear some of the other jihadists emerging from their tents in the campsite, a couple of hundred feet away. If they behaved true to form, they would begin the day by estimating the direction of Mecca, then kneeling on their camping pads and praying.

When he was finished using the toilet paper, he stuffed the roll back into the Ziploc bag. With one hand he wadded and rattled the bag, making noise that he hoped would cover the crackling sound of the Velcro on the Leatherman's holster—for he was using his other hand to jerk that open. He pulled out the tool and turned it inside out, making it into a pair of pliers with built-in wire cutters. These would make short work of the zip ties while producing a characteristic sound—a crisp pop that Jabari would certainly recognize, if he heard it. The roar of the American Falls and the rapids downstream of it might cover some of that sound, but still Richard was careful to cut the zip ties with the bare minimum of force required, sort of worrying the cutters through the plastic instead of severing them explosively. He removed only the ties joining his ankles and the ones joining his wrists, leaving in place the ones serving as cuffs.

He then closed up the multitool and was about to pocket it when he realized that a knife might come in handy. The device had several external blades, files, rasps, and so forth. Richard found the one with the sharpest and most traditionally knifelike blade and opened that up until it snapped into the locked position.

He set it on the ground, rose to a half squat, pulled up his trousers, and fastened his belt. Remaining in a crouch, he picked up the knife and began to walk along the relatively clear space that ran along the base of the cliff. Until now he had not bothered to look up because he knew that all he would see was an overhang several feet above him. But as he moved along the cliff's base he came into a zone only a short distance away where the overhang receded, and at that point he looked up, expecting to see Chet's face gazing down at him.

Instead he saw a frizz of black hair exploding out from beneath a stocking cap.

It took him several moments to understand that the person he was staring at was Zula.

She extended one arm and pointed, drawing his attention to something on the ground behind him: Jabari, who was coming to investigate.

Richard looked back up and saw her waving frantically, telling him to move farther away along the base of the cliff. She herself had risen from a squat and was beginning to move that way, exhorting him with gestures to follow.

Until now he had moved slowly, to hide the fact that he had removed his hobbles. But Jabari was closing in on the place where Richard had been taking his dump and would see the cut zip ties soon enough. Richard broke into a run.

Within a few moments he understood that Jabari was coming after him.

It was difficult to run, to keep an eye on Jabari, and at the same time to keep casting glances upward toward Zula. But at some point he realized that she was holding both hands out, gesturing at him to stop.

Which didn't make sense. Why would he want to stop?

He looked back and saw that Jabari was much closer than he'd expected. The Egyptian had drawn a semiautomatic pistol but not aimed it yet; he was still using both hands to flail away at undergrowth that was impeding his progress.

Richard looked up again and saw Zula at the very lip of the cliff with a bundle of sticks in her arms. She heaved it out into space.

Jabari stepped out of the undergrowth. He was perhaps ten feet from Richard, looking him up and down, amazed that he had gotten out of the zip ties.

Richard looked up again and saw a rickety construct unfolding in the space above them: two thin lines of parachute cord with sticks lashed between them at regular intervals.

A rope ladder.

Jabari had seen it too. He seemed only slightly more dumbfounded than Richard.

It had been all rolled up and was now falling and unrolling in a tangledy mess. The rung in the middle of the bundle was the longest and heaviest of them all, and its weight was helping to pull the whole roll downward and keep it straight. Richard understood that it was coming right at his head, and so he stepped back against the wall of the cliff, allowing it to fall down in front of him.

The ladder bounced to a stop, yawing and sashaying. Jabari was looking up toward the top, trying to see who had thrown it. He aimed his pistol nearly straight up in the air.

Richard couldn't see what Jabari was aiming at. But he did now notice a curious fact, which was that the bottom rung of the ladder—the heavy thing that had made it all unroll—was a black pump-action shotgun.

While Jabari was preoccupied with trying to identify threats at the top of the cliff, Richard stepped forward, got the weapon in his hands, flipped off the safety, and pulled the forepiece back slightly so that he could see into its breech. A shell was already chambered.

Maneuvering the weapon was not made any easier by the rattletrap skein of parachute cord and tree branches from which it dangled, but, at a range of three yards, this wasn't going to be a precision operation anyhow. He brought the stock up to his shoulder and drew a bead on Jabari.

The movement finally drew the Egyptian's notice. He looked down at Richard. At the same time he was beginning to lower the pistol. Not fast enough to make a difference.

"Sorry," Richard said, as they were making eye contact. Then he pulled the trigger and blew Jabari's head off.

SEAMUS HAD DEVELOPED a set of instincts around timing and schedule that owed a lot to his upbringing in Boston and his postings in teeming Third World megacities such as Manila, which was to say that he always expected it would take hours to get anywhere. Those habits led him comically astray in Coeur d'Alene at six thirty in the morning. They reached the municipal airport in less time than it took the SUV's windows to defog. The chopper place was just inside the entrance. Two helicopters, a big one and a small one, were parked on the apron outside a portable office. A pickup truck was parked in front of it, aimed at the big chopper, headlights on, providing supplementary illumination for a man in a navy blue nylon pilot's jacket who was sprawled on his back under the instrument panel, legs dangling out onto the skid, messing with wires. "Never a good sign," Seamus remarked, and parked in front of the portable office.

It was evident from the look and style of the place that it was not, first and foremost, an operation for making tourists happy. Their bread and butter was serving clients in the timber industry. When that flagged, they were happy to take people on joyrides. A hundred percent of their budget for that part of the operation had gone into the printing of the brochure. Which was a completely rational choice, since by the time their clients showed up here to discover what a bare-bones operation they were dealing with, the decision had already been made. No one, having come this far, was going to storm out simply because they weren't serving lattes and scones in a tastefully decorated waiting area.

Yuxia was all for dragging the man in the blue jacket out by his ankles, but Seamus talked her around to the point of view that everything would go better in the long run if they left him alone to finish his work. It was surprisingly chilly. They sat in the car and let the motor run until it got warm. Eventually the man oozed out of the chopper and climbed to his feet, holding an electronic box with a connector dangling from it.

Seamus got out of the SUV and greeted him. "Morning, Jack." Last names were not much in vogue around these parts.

"You'd be Seamus? I can tell from your accent." Jack was probably ex-military, now with a neatly trimmed red-brown beard slung under a round, somewhat pudgy face.

"Sparky trouble?"

"I thought this'd be a quick fix and we'd be in the air by now," Jack said, waving the box around, "but the connectors don't match up."

"Technology fails to work the way it's supposed to. What a shock."

"Anyway—how many you got?" Jack's eyes flicked over to the SUV. "I was going to put you in the 300." He half turned and jerked his head toward the smaller of the two choppers. "It's a little less comfortable but if you don't mind—"

"Not at all," Seamus said. "But how many passengers will it carry?"

"Two. Maybe three in a pinch."

"And the big one is definitely down."

"The 500 ain't flying today."

"Give me a sec."

Seamus got back into the SUV. "Change of plans," he announced. "Big chopper is busted. Little chopper can only take two or three of us. One or two have to stay behind here and wait."

"Obviously I cannot fit into that thing," Csongor volunteered, looking incredulously at the 300. "I would not enjoy it anyway."

Yuxia had taken to bouncing up and down in her seat, worried that she was about to be left behind. She looked as if she were about to jump out of the car, run over, and cling to the chopper's skids. Marlon, observing this, looked at Seamus and said, "I will stay and use Wi-Fi." For during the wait he had borrowed Seamus's laptop, logged on to a guest account that Seamus had set up for him, and discovered an unsecured network emanating from the portable office.

Seamus twisted the SUV's keys to the off position, killing the engine, then moved it to the accessory position so that the laptop could suck juice from the cigarette lighter jack. "No joyriding!" he warned them. Then he nodded at Yuxia, who jumped out onto the tarmac.

Before they departed, there was a discussion of flight plan and travel time. Jack estimated forty-five minutes each way to cover the eighty miles to the area that Seamus wanted to see, plus half an hour to forty-five minutes actually circling the area and looking around. It was now about quarter to seven. They should be back by nine, nine thirty at the latest.

The backseats of the 300 were decidedly short on legroom, and Seamus was glad Marlon had elected not to come. After a very cursory safety briefing, they crammed Yuxia into the back and Seamus took the copilot's seat up front. This would not win any prizes either for spaciousness or comfort, but was no worse than situations that Seamus had to put up with all the time when pursuing his career.

Jack walked around the chopper going through some preflight checks. Csongor emerged from the SUV to watch the takeoff. Jack climbed in, handed beat-up but serviceable headsets to Seamus and to Yuxia, then donned a somewhat nicer one of his own. He got these plugged into the chopper's intercom system and did a little sound check.

After a terse conversation with local air traffic control, Jack throttled the engine up and things got very windy and noisy for a few moments. Watching from not far away, Csongor hunched his shoulders and averted his gaze. The ground fell away below them. The 300 angled forward and began to pick up speed and altitude, headed north.

THERE WERE SOME nonobvious questions as to how Richard should manage ladder climbing while maintaining possession of the shotgun and the semiautomatic pistol—a Glock 27—that he had obtained from the dead Egyptian at the base of the cliff. Not the sort of challenge that would leave him scratching his head all day, but enough to slow him down a little. The Glock had no safety lever—the safety was built into the trigger. Theoretically it wouldn't fire accidentally. Richard shoved it into his jacket pocket and then zipped the pocket shut, not wanting the weapon to fall out during the climb. At some point during the excitement, he had dropped the knife; he was reminded of this when he felt something hard under the sole of his boot. He moved his foot and pried the tool up out of the cold damp loam, then set about slashing through the two lengths of parachute cord that secured the shotgun to the bottom of the ladder. One of them was tied around the end of its barrel, just behind the little brass bead that served as the weapon's sight, and the other around the narrowest part of its black plastic stock, near the safety. Dangling from the weapon was a complex of black nylon webbing that his overburdened mind processed and identified as some kind of tactical strap or harness. He did not have time to sort it out now and so he merely thrust one arm through it and confirmed that it wasn't going to fall off. Then he raised a knee, reached up, and applied his weight to the rope ladder.

This struck him as dicey in the extreme, and something he would never have done had a pack of furious, heavily armed jihadists not been running toward him through the woods. Or at least he assumed they were doing so; the blast of the shotgun had left his ears ringing, and he couldn't gather much information by listening. The parachute cord was all of about an eighth of an inch thick. Its rated strength, he knew, would probably be high enough that two strands of it would support his weight—somewhere north of 250 pounds—in theory. But if it had been damaged, or if Zula's knots didn't hold—

Never mind. He started climbing. Or rather, he started to pull rungs down toward him. The cord was stretchy and would not bear his weight at first. But after a couple of tries the rungs began to push back against his feet and to pull back against his fingers and he noted that the cliff face was moving downward. Once he had gained about ten feet of altitude, he was tempted to swivel his head around and look out over the space between here and the river to judge the progress of the jihadists, whom he assumed must have started running in this direction when they had heard the boom of the shotgun. But he didn't think it would do him any practical good and so tried to focus on climbing. He scaled a few more rungs and then risked a look up. The top of the cliff was dishearteningly far away. He had lost sight of Zula. But then something moved up there and he realized he'd been looking at her all along; she was lying on her belly with just her head sticking out at the ladder's top, lost in the visual noise of the forest towering over her head. Light gleamed in the lenses of her eyeglasses. She was looking out over the territory below and behind Richard, and what she saw was making her nervous.

"Throw me the handgun!" she called.

Richard stopped, leaned against the damp rock of the cliff face, patted his flank until he felt the hard heavy shape of the gun in his pocket, then unzipped it, pulled out the weapon, and lobbed it, swinging his arm as far outward as he could and putting a lot of oomph into the throw. He didn't want to see the thing clattering back down past him a moment later. Zula's face elevated as she tracked it, and then she was up on hands and knees and she disappeared from his view.

Until now Richard had been held against the cliff face—which was not completely vertical—by gravity. Now he arrived at a concavity, created by a heavy brow of rock that protruded slightly, perhaps fifteen feet above him. Climbing the rope ladder became much more difficult as his feet thrust forward into the empty space, causing his whole body to lean back, hanging from nearly straight arms. His progress slowed considerably, and he found himself escalating into something that approached panic, so eager was he to get past this part of the climb and get over that brow, where he fancied he might be sheltered from anyone shooting upward from the cliff's base. His movements became jerky and he started to swing. He saw too late that the strand of cord on the left side was being sawed at by a sharp edge of rock on the prominence above him.

The rock was nearly within his reach, about two rungs above him, when the left cord snapped. The ladder collapsed into a single strand of parachute cord with a series of sticks dangling from it. He swung to the right and his entire body rotated helplessly, causing the world to spin around him and giving him a view of the riverbank below: undergrowth thrashing madly all over the place as jihadists sprinted through it, calling out the name of Jabari. Farther distant he could see a tall figure clambering up onto a huge fallen log to gain some altitude and get a better view of the proceedings. It was Jones. His gaze went right to the bright spray of blood where

Jabari had fallen, then traveled up the rope ladder until he locked eyes with Richard.

Richard was not one to back away from a staredown, but he had other concerns at the moment and so he kicked his legs to get turned around, then flailed them until he had trapped a fallen rung between his ankles, and straightened his knees while pulling as hard as he could with both arms. He hand-over-handed his grip to a higher position, raised his knees, reestablished the ankle grip, and repeated the procedure.

Something whined past him and in the same instant made a sharp whacking noise against the rock back in the little concavity. Then it happened a couple more times, and he heard the reports of a gun from down below. There was no rational reason why this should make him stop climbing. On the contrary. But he couldn't help freezing up for a few moments.

A series of bangs sounded from closer, up above him. He looked up to see flashes of light spurting from the barrel of the Glock, just at the top of the ladder.

Another leg thrust, another hand-over-hand, and a desperate adrenaline-fueled reach gained him enough altitude to grip the first rung above the rope break. He got both hands on it, performed a chin-up, did more desperate pawing and kicking, finally got to a place where he could get his feet planted against the rock prominence. Then he covered a few rungs very fast.

The ladder had begun to jerk and dance madly, and he realized that someone at the base of the cliff was either climbing it, or else yanking on it trying to break the rope. He paused in his climbing long enough to pull out the knife and sever the remaining cord just beneath the rung that was supporting his feet. The ladder sprang out away from the cliff and fell from view. Watching this was a mistake, since it gave him vertigo. He saw muzzle flashes from below. But at the same time he drew courage from the fact that many of the sight lines connecting him to the flat ground between here and the river were blocked by the dense foliage of evergreen trees. Most of the jihadists were shooting blindly, or trying to draw beads on him through small gaps between branches, or running around trying to find a position from which they could do so.

It would not be accurate to say that a man of his age and weight could scamper, but he felt as if he scampered the last ten rungs and finally hurled himself on his belly at the top. Zula withdrew from her perch almost in unison with him and they ran for a hundred or more feet into the forest, side by side, before stopping. As if the bullets could chase them over the lip of the cliff and hunt them through the woods. But they couldn't, of course. Only Jones and his men could do that. And as Richard had understood the moment he'd seen it, the ladder had given them a long head start on the jihadists.

Then Zula got in front of him and pulled a sharp U-turn and body-slammed him and wrapped her arms around his torso and ratcheted them down like enormous zip ties. Her face was in his chest and she was sobbing. Which Richard almost felt was *his* prerogative, since *she* had saved *him;* but he wasn't about to make an issue of it. He was still so astonished by all that had happened in the few minutes that had elapsed since he had hopped away from the campsite to answer the call of nature that he could do very little but stand there dumbfounded and await the cardiac arrest that seemed as though it ought to be inevitable. He got the back of Zula's head in the crook of his elbow and pulled it firmly in against his chest, planted his feet wide, and breathed.

IT WAS SHE who recovered first. He heard muffled noises and realized that she was trying to talk. He relaxed his grip on her, saw her face turn up toward him. A miracle. Every time he saw that face for the rest of his life he would call it a miracle.

Her lips were moving.

"What?" he said.

"Chet's up above the falls," she said. "He's hurt badly."

"Crap," Richard said. "You know we have to get over to Prohibition Crick and warn Jake."

"Yes," Zula said, "I do know that. But I'm just saying." In her tone was a kind of incipient, Furious Muse–like shock that Dodge would even consider not going back to check in on Chet.

"Did those fuckers shoot him?" Richard asked, jerking his head back the way they had come.

"Different fuckers," she said. "But all part of the same group, as you may have guessed." She added, "I'm not even sure if Chet is still alive, frankly. He was looking pretty bad."

"Do you think you can find your way to Jake's from here?"

This set her back on her heels for a second. "You're saying we should split up? That I should run ahead to Jake's while you circle back and see how Chet is doing?"

"Just a thought. I know a shortcut; I can get back to where Chet is in no time."

"I think it's the only way," she admitted, looking like she was going to start crying again. A whole different kind of crying. The last jag had been letting go of terrible pent-up emotions. The coming one was sadness that she would have to go out on her own again so soon.

"The only thing is," Zula said, and stopped, looking embarrassed at what she'd been about to utter.

"I have to get word back to the re-u."

"Yeah."

"I have to tell the story that you survived Xiamen, you survived whatever the hell you've been through the last couple of weeks, and you went on alone to warn the others."

"Yeah," she said. "Which means you have to survive."

"I have to survive," he corrected her, "if you don't."

"That's true," she said, as if he had made some cogent point during a business meeting.

"The flip side is—"

"*I* have to survive if *you* don't," she said. "But you will. You always do."

"No one does always," he corrected her. "But I will try very hard to do so, knowing that only by surviving will I have the joy and privilege of telling your story to the world."

"It's not *that* great of a story," she said shyly.

"Bullshit. Hey, look. Chet's dying. The fucking terrorists are headed for Jake's. We have to put this plan into execution. Even if that is a miserable fact that would never obtain in a good and fair world. Agreed?"

"Yeah." She held up one gloved hand, palm out.

He met it with his hand. They clasped them tight for a few moments. "You've always been a sort of herolike figure to me," he told her.

"You've always been my . . . uncle," she answered.

"Honored."

"See you."

"Haul ass," he said. "And remember, if you just get close and then empty that clip into the air, that'll be enough to put Jake and his fellow wack jobs on red alert. Because it doesn't take much."

"Noted." And she turned her back on him and began to walk away. After a few steps, she broke into a run.

"This must be kind of obvious by now," he called after her, "but I love you."

She turned her head and gave him a shy look over her shoulder, then bent to her work.

CHET WAS VISIBLE from half a mile away, sprawled on a boulder like a skydiver whose chute had failed to open. A stream of blood was running down the side of the rock. Something ungainly dangled from one hand. As Richard trudged up the mountain—a procedure that seemed to take forever—he resolved it as a pair of binoculars.

All that time on the elliptical trainer was paying off. Any other portly man of his age would have dropped dead a long time ago. He couldn't remember the last time he hadn't been panting and sweating.

He had quite satisfied himself that Chet was dead when the arm moved, the body sat up, the binoculars rose to his face. Richard came very close to screaming, just as anyone would who saw a dead man taking action. It almost made him not want to come any closer. But the agonizing slowness of travel on talus gave him plenty of time to get his primitive emotions under control as he got closer.

"Hey, Chet," he said, when he was close enough to be heard. Chet had lain down again and not moved in a while.

"Dodge. You came."

"You say that like you're surprised."

"I know you're busy. Got a ton of stuff on your mind."

"There's always time for you, Chet. I've always tried to be clear about that."

"It's true. Appreciate it. Always have."

"Don't talk like that."

"Aw, Dodge, you know I'm a dead man."

"But you were a dead man once before—in the cornfield. Remember?"

"No. Had amnesia. Remember?" Chet laughed, and Richard grinned at him.

"That was when understanding came to me," Chet went on, "about the parallels and the meridians. The fact that we live in curved space. Parallels run straight. Meridians bend toward each other and at their beginnings and their ends they are all one. When the Nautilus—the first nuclear sub—reached the North Pole, it transmitted a message. You know what the message was?"

"No," Richard lied, even though he had heard Chet tell this story a hundred times to dumbfounded members of the Septentrion Paladins.

"'Latitude ninety degrees north,'" Chet said. "See, they couldn't specify their longitude, because there, all the meridians are one. They were on all the meridians, and so they were on none of them. It's a singularity."

Richard nodded.

"Birth and death," Chet said. "The poles of human existence. We're like meridians, all beginning and ending in the same place. We spread out from the beginning and go our separate ways, over seas and mountains and islands and deserts, each telling our own story, as different as they could possibly be. But in the end we all converge and our ends are as much the same as our beginnings."

Richard kept nodding. He was afraid his voice wouldn't work.

"Do you realize where we are?" Chet asked him.

"Somewhere pretty damned close to the border," Richard finally got out.

"Not just close. Look!" Chet said, extending an arm in one direction, then swinging it over his head like the blade of a paper cutter to point exactly the opposite way. Following it, Richard noticed a line of widely spaced surveyor's monuments tracking across the landscape.

"We're on the forty-ninth parallel," Chet said. "My feet are in the U. S. of A. and my head is in Canada." The look on his face said that this was enormously profound to him, so Richard only nodded and tried to maintain a straight face. "I'm barring the path. Their meridians are going to end here."

"Who are you talking about?"

Chet gestured vaguely to the north and then offered Richard the binoculars. Richard picked them up, adjusted them, planted his elbows on the border, and aimed them north toward the talus slopes angling down from the ridgeline. Gazing over them with his naked eyes, he was able to pick out a pair of human figures, spaced about a hundred feet apart, picking their way down over the rocks. With the aid of the binoculars he saw them clearly as armed men with dark hair, answering generally to the stereotypical image of jihadists. The one in the lead was burly and had a submachine gun slung over his shoulder. The one trailing behind was wiry and had a longer rifle slung diagonally across his back. A sniper.

"The rear guard," Chet said. "Trying to catch up with the main group." He chuckled and coughed wetly. Richard had a pretty good idea of what he was coughing up and so he avoided looking. Chet continued, "They're so focused on catching up they haven't bothered to look behind them."

Richard drew back from the binoculars in surprise, and his aging eyes struggled to pull focus on Chet. Chet was nodding at him, casting suggestive glances upward. He had coughed a thin mist of blood out onto his chin, where it had caught in the gray stubble. Richard found the jihadists again and then tracked higher up the slope until he saw something in motion. Difficult to make out because its coloration blended in with the tawny hue of the weathered rock. Moving like a drop of glycerin oozing from one boulder to the next. Maintaining a fixed gaze on this target, he raised the binoculars and inserted them in his line of sight. With a bit of searching he was able to focus on the thing and see it distinctly as a mountain lion making its way down from the ridgeline. Its eyes glowed like phosphorus in the light of the rising sun. Those eyes were fixed upon the two men struggling down the slope below it.

"Holy crap," Richard said. Chet went into another laughing/coughing fit. "These guys are *so* out of their element. Let's hope it catches up with them soon."

"It already did," Chet answered. "Zula told me that it already took down one of their stragglers."

"Huh. Man-eater."

"They're afraid of humans. Don't bother them, and they won't bother you," Chet said, mocking what a sanctimonious tree hugger would say. Cougars attacked humans all the time in these parts, and the obstinate refusal of nature lovers to accept the fact that, in the eyes of a predator, there was no distinction between humans and other forms of meat had become the subject of bitter hilarity around the bar at the Schloss.

In this Richard now perceived an opening. "Well, shit, Chet, that settles it. I can't just leave you here. That thing has probably smelled you already."

"Do I stink that bad?"

"You know what I mean. I can't just leave you here defenseless. If the jihadists don't get you, that mountain lion will."

"I ain't defenseless," Chet said. He unzipped his motorcycle jacket, which fell away to reveal a ghastly and peculiar state of affairs. His bottom-most garment was a thermal underwear top, now soaked with blood all along one side, and lumpy, either from bandages or from swelling. He had thrown his leather jacket on over this. But in between those two layers, he had affixed a large object to his chest: a thick metal plate, slightly convex, lashed to his body and suspended around his neck by a crazy and irregular web of parachute cord. Words were stenciled on the plate in Cyrillic.

"I think it says something like 'This side toward enemy,'" Chet said. Then, seeing incomprehension still written on Richard's face, he added, "It's a Russian claymore mine."

Richard had nothing to say for a few moments.

"If they can do it," Chet said, "so can I."

"You mean, blow yourself up?"

"Yeah."

"I never really saw you as a suicide bomber."

"It's not suicide," Chet said, "when you're already a dead man."

Richard could think of nothing to say to this.

"Now listen," Chet said. "It's time for you to get the hell out of here. You're already in range of that one with the rifle. Get you gone. Your meridian isn't finished yet, you've got a ways to go south yet. Me, I'm curving under to the pole. I can see it before my eyes. Those guys up there, they're going to reach it at the same time as I do."

"I'll see you there" was all Richard could get out.

"Looking forward to it."

Richard hugged Chet, trying to be gentle, but Chet hooked one arm around the nape of his neck and pulled him in tight, hard enough to press the claymore mine against his chest and scrape Richard's face with his bloody whiskers. Then he let him go. Richard spun away and began to move south. His vision was fogged by tears, and he practically had to go on hands and knees to avoid turning an ankle on the strewn rocks.

He knew that Chet was correct about the range of the sniper's rifle, and so his first instinct was to get out of the line of sight and of fire. This was easily enough done by taking advantage of the ruggedness of the terrain and occasional clusters of desperate trees. He wouldn't be able to move freely, though, until he reached the edge of the woods, which was about half a mile down the slope. On his way up to Chet's position, he had trudged and scrambled wearily up the broken and boulder-strewn terrain, various muscles screaming at him the whole way, since they had already taken enough abuse during the previous days' hiking. He had taken a somewhat meandering course between areas of melting snow. Now it seemed to him that those snowfields would afford him a quick way down. Quick, and a little dangerous. But now that he had said good-bye to Chet, he was feeling an almost panicky imperative to work south and warn Jake, perhaps reconnecting with Zula en route. So he crab-walked to the edge of a large area of snow that sloped down all the way into the woods. His feet lost traction immediately. Rather than letting himself fall on his ass, though, he leaned forward carefully and allowed himself to skid down the slope on the soles of his boots, a procedure known as a standing glissade. Essentially he was skiing without skis. It was a common enough practice, when slope and conditions allowed it, and his involvement in the cat skiing industry had given him many opportunities to practice. He covered the distance to the tree line in a small fraction of the time it would have taken him to pick his way down from rock to rock. En route he fell three times. The last fall was a deliberate plunge into a snowbank to kill his velocity before he slammed into the trees.

The snowbank was soft, and now sported a Richard-shaped depression that cradled his tired and battered body in a way that was extremely comfortable. The cold had not yet begun to soak through his clothing. He swiveled his head around and verified that the jihadists with the guns could not see him.

He was tempted to just lie there and take a nap. He stuffed a handful of snow into his mouth, chewed and swallowed it. His heart had been beating very fast during the glissade, and he saw no harm in relaxing in this safe place for a few moments, pacing himself, giving his body a little rest, letting his pulse drop to a more moderate level.

Which it didn't seem to be doing. He could feel a steady whomping in his chest and wondered if he was finally succumbing to some sort of cardiac arrhythmia.

But this seemed to be the opposite of that, since it had nothing *but* rhythm. Almost mechanical in its perfection. He pressed a hand to his chest under his left nipple and observed that this beating sensation had nothing to do with his heart.

It was coming from outside his body.

It was in the air all around him.

It was a helicopter.

He rolled up to his feet and staggered out into the open, waving his arms.

THE MOUNTAINS THAT now filled the windscreen, rising up from the flat valley to an altitude somewhere above their heads, looked familiar to Seamus. Not because he'd ever been here before; he hadn't. But he had been in mountain ranges like these all over the world. These were the sorts of mountains that insurgents loved to hang out in.

Insurgents did not care for spectacular snow-covered mountain ranges. Snow impeded movement and implied harsh cold. "Spectacular" meant "easy to see from a distance," and insurgents did not like being seen. Insurgents liked mountain ranges that sprawled over large reaches of territory. That crossed national borders. That were high and rugged enough to discourage casual visitors and impede the operations of police and of military forces, but not so high as to be devoid of tree cover or bitterly cold all the time. Many of the features that tourists liked, insurgents found positively undesirable—most of all, the presence of tourists. But Seamus could see at a glance that tourists would not choose to visit these mountains

when the Rockies were a few hours' drive to the east and the Cascades an equal distance to the west. These were low, forgettable
mountains, no good for skiing, carved up by logging roads, partly
deforested in a way that provided employment to the locals but was
considered unsightly by tourists.

No wonder all the right-wing wack jobs came here. No wonder
smugglers loved it.

Seamus felt weird. It wasn't hard to understand why. He always
felt this way when he was riding a chopper into mountains like
this. Because it usually meant going into combat. He had to keep
reminding himself that all the adrenaline flooding into his system
was going to be wasted. That if it *weren't* wasted—if something actually *did* happen—it would be a very bad thing given that the people
he was with were not geared, physically or mentally, for combat.

Assuming, reasonably enough, that these tourists would want
to see the highest mountains, the pilot carved a long sweeping turn
up a valley with a white thread snaking down its bottom: a river
violent with snowmelt. After a few minutes, this frayed into several
tributaries draining a few miles of high Selkirk crest. All the mountains along the crest proper were above the tree line and presented a
bleak prospect of barren rocky snags and crags reaching high above
vast talus fields where nothing would grow except the occasional
freak tree. They burned a lot of fuel in a short time gaining altitude and thudded over a low saddle between peaks, suddenly giving
them a view of many more insurgent-friendly mountains beyond,
stretching to the horizon, interrupted only by a long north-south
lake in the middle distance. Turning north again, the pilot made for
the border, following the slow curve of the ridgeline, passing some
especially prominent peaks. But during the last few miles to the
border, the ridgeline lost a couple of thousand feet of altitude and
plunged back below the tree line again. One bald peak jutted out
of it a few miles south of the border—Abandon Mountain, the pilot
called it—but other than that, it was scrub trees, patchy snowfields,
and talus ranging northward well into Canada. In the far distance,
the Selkirks leaped upward and became a truly magnificent range,
but that was in British Columbia, where, plainly enough, everything was bigger and better.

Seamus, though, had eyes only for the dark valleys that wriggled through the lower country below. This was out-and-out wilderness. A few old roads wandered through it, connecting to widely spaced mineheads or logging camps. But it was as wild and as untouched by humans as anything you could expect to see in the Lower Forty-Eight. And as the pilot, responding to Seamus's directions, slowed the chopper down and allowed it to shed altitude, those valleys began to take on depth that he hadn't noticed from farther above. As if he had just put on a pair of 3D glasses at a movie theater, he saw into the gorges of the rivers now and understood the steepness of the terrain. The fury of the rivers told the same story.

"What would you like to see?" the pilot asked him. For they had just been hovering there for a couple of minutes, admiring a jewel-like waterfall set in a deep misty bowl.

Seamus had been looking for paths. The spoor of insurgents sneaking along secret ways through the forest.

"The border," he answered.

"You're looking at it," said the pilot, pointing northward. "I don't want to cross it, but I'll take you right up to it if you want."

"Sure."

They passed over a partially forested slope rising up from the waterfall toward a wildly uneven plateau of boulders and snowfields and clustered trees. Above that rose a much broader and higher talus slope that, according to the pilot, was a mile or two north of the border and roughly parallel to it. The rock wall rising out of that was pierced in one place by a man-made opening, evidently the adit of an old mine.

"Someone painted the rock," Yuxia observed.

"Where?" Seamus asked.

"Right below us," Yuxia said.

Seamus's gaze had been directed horizontally and north, but he now looked straight down and saw that Yuxia was right. What he had identified, a few moments ago, as a gnarled tree, branches covered with brilliant green sprigs of new leaves, was, on closer examination, a snarl of acid-green spray paint on a rock. Like graffiti. Except impossible to make sense of.

He could see now the faint traces of a trail, leading down to the graffiti from the north, coming from the approximate direction of that old mine tunnel. On the talus it was nearly imperceptible, but from place to place he saw tufts of fresh litter, and in one location it was absolutely clear that someone had glissaded down a snowfield, carving two parallel tracks, still crisp at the edges, not yet blurred by a day's, or even an hour's, exposure to the warmth of the sun.

He followed the track upward and was shocked to see, some distance above it, a dead man spread-eagled on a rock.

"Holy shit," the pilot said, seeing it too.

"Let's get a better look at that," Seamus said, feeling that weird sensation again: the adrenaline coming back into his system. The chopper pointed its nose down and accelerated north.

They were passing over that grooved snowfield when Yuxia let out a gasp that was almost a scream. "He's waving at us!" she called.

"Who's waving at us?" Seamus returned skeptically. For the man on the boulder definitely wasn't doing any waving, and that was the only man Seamus could see.

"I think it's Zula's uncle," Yuxia answered. "I saw him on Wikipedia."

A crack, explosively loud, sounded from above them. Then two more.

"What the hell?" said the pilot in the weird silence that followed. Silence being, in general, a bad thing in a helicopter.

"We're being shot at," Seamus said. For he had heard similar noises before. In general, military choppers stood up to the treatment a little better than this one had. "They have taken out the engine. Bite down." He twisted around so that Yuxia could see his face, opened his mouth, inserted the helicopter company brochure, and bit down on it, keeping his lips peeled back grotesquely so that she could see his jaws clenched together.

Staring at him fixedly, she reached up with one hand, bit down on the end of her camouflage mitten, then pulled her naked hand out of it.

"Brace for impact," the pilot said. But halfway through this utterance, Seamus stopped hearing his voice in the headphones, because another round seemed to have gone through the middle of the instrument panel and fucked up the electrical system.

The pilot, to his great credit, knew what to do: he manipulated the controls in such a way as to make the chopper autorotate, converting some of the energy of its fall into passive spinning of the rotors that broke the descent marginally. That, and the fact that they landed at an angle on the snowfield, saved them. Even so, the impact was so sharp that Seamus felt his teeth jumping in their sockets. Because he was biting down, they didn't slam together and they didn't bite his tongue off and he hoped that the same was true of the others.

The chopper planted its nose in the snow and began to skid downhill like a big out-of-control toboggan. Directly in front of them were trees. Standing in front of the trees was—just as Yuxia had been trying to tell him—Richard Forthrast. A.k.a. Dodge.

He dodged.

The trees didn't.

THE TEN OR fifteen seconds between the appearance of the chopper in the sky above him and its coming to rest in the trees, only a few yards away from where he had thrown himself to the ground, presented Richard with an unbroken chain of never-before-experienced sensations that, in other times, he'd have spent several weeks sifting through and making sense of. There was something in the modern mind that would not stop saying, *If only I had caught that on video,* or *This is going to make the coolest blog entry ever!* Barring which, he at least wanted to just lie there for a few moments asking himself whether that had really just happened.

People were stirring behind the cracked and spalled windshield of the chopper. At a glance he guessed two. On further consideration, three: there was a small person, a woman, in the back. The pilot seemed unconscious or at least unwilling to move. The passenger next to him was a lanky man with strawberry-blond hair and a beard, and he was flailing around like a spider in a bathtub, trying to get free of several entanglements while being belabored from the rear by the backseat person, who couldn't get out until he did. And she—the voice, speaking what he guessed was Chinese, was clearly that of a female—very much wanted to get out. The man was dressed from head to toe in camouflage gear, which suggested that he had flown up here to get in some hunting. Wrong season for it, but perhaps he was a poacher who had come to this area specifically to get away from game wardens.

Richard looked up the slope, just to see whether the jihadist with the sniper rifle had come into view yet. Either he hadn't, or he was taking sniperlike care not to be seen. Anyway, they'd be in his sights soon enough, and Richard wanted to make the newcomers aware of that fact and get them free of the chopper. He staggered to his feet and sloshed through snow and undergrowth toward the downed machine's right side—only to be greeted by the muzzle of a semiautomatic pistol, which had appeared by some sleight of hand in the passenger's right hand and was now aimed right at him.

"Okay," Richard said, letting his hands be seen, "if I'd just been through that, I'd be a little jumpy too."

"It's not so much that," said the passenger. "It's the Mossberg 500 on the tactical sling." He nodded at said weapon, which was dangling from Richard's shoulder.

"Fair enough," Richard conceded.

"You're Richard Forthrast," said the passenger, and dropped the pistol's muzzle. Then he was distracted by a series of vicious kicks directed against the back of his seat.

"T'Rain player?" Dodge asked.

"Yeah, actually. But there's more going on here than just a random fan encounter. We have information about your niece. Or rather she does." He nodded toward the back. "I have never met her, but I hear she is a fine young lady."

"I just saw her an hour ago."

The kicking and thrashing stopped. A face peeked out from behind the rear seat.

"She's alive?" the young Asian woman asked.

GETTING OUT OF the chopper required some knife work, since parts of the instrument panel had been crushed upward, and sharp sheet-metal edges were catching on seat belts and on camouflage clothing. But eventually the man, who gave his name as Seamus, and the woman, Yuxia, extricated themselves and went around to the other side to look in on the pilot. He was awake now. Richard, conditioned by long exposure to Hollywood, was wondering when the chopper was going to burst into flames, but this seemed less and less likely as time went on. The fuel tank was not leaking, and there were no sources of ignition that Richard could see.

The pilot was reporting, rather calmly, that all parts of his body from his navel on down felt as though they had gone to sleep. Not in the sense of being totally numb, for he could move them and feel sensations, but in the sense of tingling like crazy. His spinal column, obviously enough, had been jammed by the force of the impact and perhaps suffered some vertebral damage that was messing with his spinal cord. He wasn't paralyzed. But he might be if they tried to move him around "like a bunch of fucking do-gooder shit-for-brains" as Seamus put it.

Yuxia and Seamus both seemed to have come through the crash with little trauma other than a good deal of hard banging around that would leave them stiff and bruised tomorrow. Adrenaline seemed to be taking care of the rest. That, and, in Yuxia's case, what looked like a serious endorphin rush generated by the awareness that Zula was alive—or at least had been an hour ago. While Seamus interviewed the pilot and tried to figure out what to do, Yuxia focused on Richard. "Your niece honors you very much."

"I just figured out who you are," Richard said. "She wrote about you on a paper towel."

Once he had made up his mind that the chopper was not going to explode, and taken into consideration the fact that they now had two firearms between them, he had begun to feel quite optimistic—as if it were all over now except for rounding up the bad guys and buying people plane tickets home.

"Are others on the way?" he asked Seamus.

"Other *what*? What are you talking about?"

"Like . . . reinforcements?"

"We're on our own," Seamus said.

"But you knew I was here . . . that the jihadists were here."

"If we'd known they were here, we would have showed up with the entire fucking Idaho National Guard. And once we got here, we would not have hovered in a place where we could get shot down by one asshole with a rifle."

Richard just stared at him.

"I'm doing this on my own," Seamus said. "Checking out a hypothesis. No one else believes me. I had only a vague suspicion Jones might have come this way until rounds started going through our engine block."

"Were you able to send out a distress call or—" Then Richard shut up, realizing he was making an ass of himself. He had seen the shoot-down. They had not had time to send out a distress call. "Okay, but at some point someone is going to notice that the chopper hasn't come back."

"It is a one-man operation. It might take hours. By then, it's all going to be over."

"What's all going to be over?"

"Whatever is going to happen now," Seamus said. "Where the hell is Jones, by the way?"

"The guys who just shot you down are the rear guard. Jones is farther south. I'm happy to show you the way. But first may I suggest that we think about the ones who are actually shooting at us?"

As Richard was saying this, Seamus's eyes wandered up the slope in the general direction of the bad guys in question. Then they snagged on something. "It looks like someone else is already on that particular case," he pointed out. "Dead man walking."

THE HIKE SOUTH to the border had involved a number of events that Ershut might have accounted disappointments, hardships, and setbacks had he grown up in an effete Western democracy. As it was, he could hardly be bothered to notice them. The only thing that had really disturbed him had been what had happened to poor Sayed. A long bloody trail through the woods had led to a small tree where Sayed's body had been dragged up three meters off the ground and stuffed in a fork between two branches. His head lolled forward, nose pressed against breastbone, since all the structure had been removed from the back of his neck. A neat hole had been carved in the front of his abdomen and his liver removed. The very weirdness of the spectacle had made it much more troubling to him than the body of Zakir, who had expired in a way that was extremely bloody but much more conventional.

From there, they had hiked back to their campsite, staying always on the path to prevent the man on the motorcycle from turning around and escaping from the valley. Ershut and Jahandar had taken turns: one guarding the path so that the other could trudge to the campsite above and gather all the things that he would need to complete the final phase of the journey. Then they had hiked up the valley, following the track of the motorcycle, dotted with occasional drips of blood. This had been the source of great satisfaction to Jahandar, who had been convinced that he had gotten one good clear shot off at the motorcyclist.

The trip through the ridge had not gone well, since the way through the tunnels had been barred by a motorcycle lock on the gate, and Jahandar's attempts to shoot it off had been unavailing. But only a soft and corrupt infidel would imagine that this would really prove an obstacle to two men such as Ershut and Jahandar. They had withdrawn from the mine and simply climbed over the top of the ridge, camping near the summit, where they could get a clear view in all directions, and then proceeding south as soon as it had become light. Ershut had slept poorly, remembering Sayed up in that tree, and wondering who or what had carried out the atrocity. Ershut was burly and abnormally strong, and yet he doubted that he could have carried the limp burden of Sayed that far up a tree that was lacking in convenient side branches. Its bark had been marked with deep gouges made by four parallel claws, causing Ershut to form the opinion that this had been the work of a predatory beast, stashing its kill in the tree fork to keep it up away from jackals or whatever jackal-like beasts might inhabit these mountains. Jahandar scoffed at the theory. He was convinced that this had been the work of a human, trying to put a scare into them by mutilating Sayed's body and leaving it up where they could not help but notice it.

In any case, they had slept lightly and kept their weapons near to hand. During his watch, Ershut was convinced he sensed something prowling around their camp, and once, sweeping his flashlight beam around him, he was certain that he saw, for a fraction of a second, a pair of gleaming eyes shining out of the darkness. But when he swept the beam back, they had already disappeared.

It might have made sense, then, for them to have kept a sharp eye behind them as they descended the ridgeline in the light of the early morning. But two things fixed their attention forward. One, a fusillade of gunshots that echoed from valley walls all around shortly after they began their hike. And two, a man lurking on a boulder down below them, occasionally visible for a few moments when he came awake and peeked over the top with binoculars. Jahandar occasionally drew a bead on this fellow through the telescopic sight of his rifle and reported that he did not seem to be armed. He was drunk or otherwise impaired, lying still for long periods of time and then moving about unsteadily. Jahandar might have set himself up in a sniper's perch and then waited for a good shot to come along and gotten rid of this man before they came anywhere near him, but the man seemed so helpless that there did not seem to be a compelling reason to do so. Perhaps they could get some information out of him when they descended to his altitude.

That discussion, anyway, was cut short by the approach of the helicopter and all that happened after Jahandar fired upon it. To their considerable frustration, it slid out of direct view, and so it was not possible for them to see if any had survived, or to fire upon them. First they would have to shed a good deal of altitude. They began to do so as quickly as they could manage, throwing off their packs to give themselves greater freedom of movement and hopping from rock to rock, occasionally surfing on small avalanches that they touched off in steep patches of finer-grained scree. Their general plan was that Jahandar would hang back and try to work around into a position where he could cover the downed helicopter; Ershut, who was carrying a submachine gun that would be effective only at much shorter ranges, would get down closer until he had reached a point where he could shoot from another direction. Once Ershut opened fire, the survivors—again, assuming that there were any—would naturally move into positions of cover, hiding behind rocks or trees, and Jahandar would be able to pick them off from his place of concealment high in the rocks. It was difficult to judge the direction from which sniper fire was arriving, so it was likely that they would all be dead long before they could figure out where Jahandar was—or even come to the understanding that they were being shot at from another direction.

So intent was Ershut on executing his part of the plan that he quite forgot about the strange loiterer with the binoculars until he had descended to near the bloodstained boulder where the man had been hanging out. But he was not there now. What had seemed from high above like a single piece of rock was actually an outcropping of stone that had been shivered into a number of huge slab-sided chunks that had tumbled onto the slope below, forming a little debris trail. Ershut recognized this as a convenient place for him to make his way down the slope without exposing himself to view from below, and he traversed over to it.

And that was when he realized that the man in the black leather clothing had not gone down the hill to investigate the chopper crash but merely concealed himself in a space between two of the boulders. The man came out as Ershut approached, holding his hands up above his head to show that he was unarmed.

He looked almost more horrible than Sayed. Sayed, at least, had been dead, and therefore in a state of repose. There had been no worries that Sayed was going to climb down out of his tree and advance upon them. But this man was staggering toward Ershut with a huge grin on his face. One side of him was all bloody, and his skin would have seemed white had Ershut not been seeing it against a background of snow; instead his flesh looked gray.

The man was saying something in English, which Ershut barely spoke at all. As he raved, he staggered forward, one unsteady pace at a time, closing the distance. Ershut was not especially troubled by this since the man was still a few meters away, and still keeping his hands up, and Ershut was covering him with the barrel of the submachine gun. He rather wished that the man would stop, however, simply because there was something disturbing about his color and the look on his face and the way he was talking.

Ershut glanced down the slope, trying to get a view of the crashed chopper. He could see the bent-back tips of rotor blades dangling above the end of the long skid mark in the snow. People were definitely moving around down there, looking up at him.

The gray man said something about America.

Ershut looked up and noticed that the gray man was gripping, in one hand, the end of a piece of string that disappeared into the sleeve of his motorcycle jacket. He straightened his arm, jerking at the string.

IT WAS A good thing that Olivia enjoyed looking at Sokolov, because his reactions had given her a lot *to* enjoy since their arrival at Jake's cabin. Clearly he had never even imagined that there were people in the world like this, living out in the middle of nowhere, disconnected by choice from the grid, surrounded by weapons, and living each day as if it might be civilization's last. During the bicycle ride from Bourne's Ford, she had tried to explain what they were getting into. Sokolov had nodded occasionally and even made eye contact from time to time. She had sensed, though, that he was only doing so to be polite. He did not really believe until he saw a woman in a long, old-fashioned dress with a shoulder holster strapped over the bodice carrying a semiautomatic pistol and two extra clips. From that point on, his reaction to everything was fascination and bemusement. Noting this, and choosing to interpret it in a favorable way, Jake gave him a quick tour of the place, showing off the water purification system, the ammo reloading bench, the stockpiles of food and antibiotics and gas mask filters, and the safe room—a reinforced-concrete bunker— under six feet of earth in the backyard. Sokolov watched Jake carefully, and Olivia watched Sokolov, and John, the elder brother, stomping along a few paces behind them on his artificial legs, watched Olivia watching Sokolov, occasionally sharing a wry look with her. Sokolov began to notice these exchanges of looks and to share in them, and so by the time they had gone inside, sat down around the table, held hands to say Grace, and tucked into a simple but generous and nutritionally balanced dinner, they all seemed to have arrived at a wordless understanding. Jake was a true believer. Elizabeth perhaps even more so. But Jake understood that not everyone saw the world as he did—not even his own brothers, with whom he was nonetheless quite close. This did not especially trouble him. In fact, he was even capable of making little self-deprecating jokes and drawing humorous comparisons between this part of the world and Afghanistan. John, for his part, seemed to have developed a facility for shutting his ears off whenever Jake began to talk what he deemed nonsense. If Jake needed to change the oil in his generator or fish wire through a wall to hook up a new electrical outlet, then John was right there with him, helping him get it done. And he had unlimited time and patience for Jake's sons, who clearly loved him. Olivia suspected that John was making a conscious effort to tell the boys, without explicitly saying anything, that if, when they grew older, they decided they wanted to rejoin the civilization that their parents believed to be utterly corrupt and doomed, they would always be welcome in his house.

In any case, John's ability to relate easily to these people without actually believing in any of what they believed provided a sort of template that Olivia was able to use in order to maintain cordial and even warm relations with them during the evening and through breakfast the following day. Because in most of their social interactions they were like any other basically happy and stable family.

Olivia provided a vague explanation of why she and Sokolov were here. Anywhere else, it would not have gone over very well. But Jake, no great respecter of borders and laws, readily agreed to show them the way to the Canadian border in the morning. The first few miles, he explained, could be a bit tricky, even if they had a GPS. As a matter of fact, the GPS could actually be more trouble than it was worth in that it would induce them to go in directions that would turn out to be dead ends. As a man who enjoyed hiking anyway, he was more than happy to guide them to a point along the flank of Abandon Mountain from which they would be able to see all the way to the border. They could do much of the journey on their mountain bikes. In places, they would have to carry them, which would be tedious work, but it would pay off later when they crossed over and made it through the old mine and found themselves on a nicely groomed trail leading all the way into Elphinstone. "On foot it's a three-day hike," he said. "With your bikes you can be sipping your lattes in downtown Elphinstone tonight."

Jake had a sturdy, unspectacular mountain bike of his own. So in the morning, after they had risen, showered, eaten a huge pancake breakfast, and packed their things, they set out in a caravan of four: Olivia, Sokolov, and Jake on their bicycles and John trundling along behind them on a four-wheeled all-terrain vehicle. The ATV carried the baggage at first, which made for rapid going during the first hour as they switchbacked up a trail that took them out of the valley of Prohibition Crick. This petered out as it reached the tree line. Jake began to lead them along a circuitous and, as advertised, completely nonobvious route on terrain that rapidly became almost impossible. Soon they had to traverse a long steep talus bank that was impassable for any wheeled vehicle, so at that point John shut off the ATV's motor and helped them load their gear onto the mountain bikes. John then switched off the engine, made himself comfortable on the ATV's saddle, and enjoyed a little snack while

Jake led Olivia and Sokolov across the traverse, sometimes pushing the bikes, sometimes carrying them, but never riding them. They were clearly making for a spur of cream-colored granite thrust out westward from the summit of Abandon Mountain. Perhaps a thousand feet below them, in the lee of that spur, were the remains of what Olivia took to be an abandoned mine: a roadhead, some old shacks devastated by weather, some rusted-out trucks and abandoned equipment. She understood Jake's warning now: if they'd had a GPS, they probably would have made for that site. But the road leading away from it went in the wrong direction and would take them miles out of their way. They only way to get past it was this arduous traversal of the slope high above. The spur seemed to bar their way, and she wondered how they would ever get past it, but Jake assured her that it was not as forbidding as it looked. And indeed as they struggled closer, Olivia was able to make out a series of natural ramps and ledges that seemed as though they would give much better footing than the loose talus. Seen from a distance, the spur had been foreshortened in a way that made it look very steep— almost a vertical cliff. But as they drew closer, she perceived that this had just been a trick of the eyes and that its slope was actually quite manageable.

This pleasing prospect only made the trip to it seem that much longer. But in due time they reached a place where they could finally stand on hard and reasonably level ground. Olivia was all for stopping there and having a little snack, but Jake talked her into clambering up over the spur. This they did easily, even riding the bicycles for part of the way, and finally attained the flattish top of the great outcropping, from which they could look back the way they'd come and see John still sitting on the red ATV a couple of miles behind them, as well as enjoy a previously hidden vista to the north.

Several miles away, their path was barred by a high ridge running approximately east-west that Jake assured them was north of the border. Far below them, and a little closer, was a dark green kettle in the terrain, producing a dim roaring noise and partly shrouded in humidity. This, Jake said, was American Falls, which, as the name implied, was just south of the border. Between those two landmarks, and making use of a compass, it was easy to envision the east-west line of the forty-ninth parallel running between them.

All they had to do was get there; and that, Jake said, was straightforward from here on out. He had printed out some maps of the area and added hand-drawn notations showing them useful landmarks and telling them what to avoid.

This, in other words, was where they would be parting company. Olivia thanked him, and even hugged him, hoping that she was not trespassing on any moral/religious boundaries by doing so. Sokolov shook his hand and thanked him politely but, as she thought, a trifle coldly. Later, maybe, she could find out what he really thought of Jake and his people. But maybe she was misreading the situation; perhaps the Russian's coolness, his evident haste to be finished with the pleasantries, was just him being focused on the mission (he would probably think of it as a mission) at hand: getting out of this country and figuring out what was going to come next. And for a man in that state of mind, being able to look out and see the border engendered a powerful urge to get moving and get it behind him.

So Jake turned back and coasted on his bicycle down the side of the spur to a place where it became positively dangerous and then hopped off it and resumed the arduous trudge back across the talus slope. Olivia, who had been known to harbor slight feelings of resentment when she found herself obligated to give a friend a lift to Heathrow, felt ashamed by comparison.

But she was with a man who had little time or patience for such ruminations, so they were on their way as soon as they could down a few swallows of water and finish their candy bars. The north side of the spur was a different proposition from the one they had just climbed, being flatter, smoother, and easier to move on at first. They were pushing and sometimes carrying the bicycles, picking their way down among huge shivered boulders, headed for a stretch of talus that would take them down into the tree line a couple of hundred meters below.

Olivia had been hearing a dim *whacka-whacka-whacka* noise for a few moments.

"Helicopter," Sokolov said, and drew into the shadow of a boulder, indicating with a look at Olivia that she might want to do the same. They laid the bikes on their sides and then squatted down.

A minute later, a small helicopter, moving at a leisurely pace,

traversed across the broad valley to the west of them, headed generally north. It slowed and descended as it drew closer to the falls and
hovered there for a couple of minutes. Then its tail elevated, and it
began to head north.

"Do you think they're looking for us?" Olivia asked. "They're
not cops."

Sokolov seemed to have been thinking quite hard about the same
question. He shrugged. "It is not how I would do it," he said. "But
someone is looking for something. It is better that we not be seen."

"In a few more minutes, we'll be down in the trees," she pointed
out, tapping a notation on Jake's map.

"Then let us go that way while they are looking at something
else," Sokolov suggested, and rose to his feet and picked up his bicycle.

The chopper, flying quite close to the ground now, had disappeared from view among the convolutions of the ridges and valleys.
Sokolov now set a pace that Olivia was barely able to keep up with.
He was too much the gentleman to leave her far behind, but she did
not want to make him stop and wait any more than was strictly necessary. They soon emerged from the boulder field and began to pick
their way straight down the talus slope toward the trees.

The footing was treacherous and demanded all her attention.
So she almost rear-ended him. He had pulled up short and was holding out a hand for silence.

"What?" she asked. She had veered to the left to avoid a collision
and now found herself nearly abreast of him.

"Shooting, maybe," he said.

They stood absolutely silent for a minute, then two, then three.
Finally Sokolov began to breathe more deeply and to show interest
in things around them. He hitched his bottom up onto the seat of
his bicycle, got a foot on a pedal, and eyed the slope below. Wondering if he could take it on wheels. Olivia was praying he wouldn't.

"Interesting that there is no more helicopter," he pointed out.

"Maybe they landed."

"Blades would still be moving, I think."

His sentence was punctuated by a sharp bang, impressively loud
even though it was at a great distance. Echoes continued to reach
them, reflecting from various slopes, for what seemed like a full
sixty seconds afterward.

Sokolov's eyes met Olivia's. He saw the uncertainty on her face. Read her mind, perhaps, as she got ready to put forth the theory that it was a big tree branch snapping, or a stick of dynamite going off in a mining operation.

"Ordnance," Sokolov said.

"I beg your pardon?"

"We are in some kind of little war." Then, seeing a look of incomprehension or disbelief on her face: "Jones is here."

SEAMUS DID NOT have a direct line of sight to what happened above, but his eyes saw a sort of blood comet hurtling upward just a moment before his eardrums were all but staved in. The comet expanded and faded to a bank of pink fog that, mercifully, was blown in another direction by the light breeze coming up out of the valley.

Yuxia was standing next to the helicopter, where she had been bantering with the pilot, trying to get his mind off his troubles. She had belatedly clapped her hands over the side of her head and was standing there with her mouth in an O, eyes darting around uncertainly. Richard Forthrast seemed to have been taken by a dizzy spell and sat down roughly on the ground and hugged his knees, staring in an unfocused way in the general direction of the explosion. Seamus noted with approval and interest that, even as Richard had been semicollapsing to the ground, he had taken care to manage the shotgun hanging from his shoulder, making sure that its barrel did not dig into the ground and get jammed with dirt.

"Care to fill me in on anything?" Seamus asked, when he felt as though he had some chance of being able to hear the answer.

"That was my friend Chet," Richard answered.

"The casualty on the rock?"

Richard nodded. "He had a claymore mine strapped to his chest. He was going to use it on those guys, if he got an opportunity."

"Well, I guess an opportunity presented itself," Seamus said. It was not an exquisitely sensitive thing to say. Richard's eyes jumped quickly toward his face, checking for signs of archness. But Seamus had said it, and meant it, quite seriously. Richard broke eye contact and squinted up the slope.

"The question is how many did he get?"

"There were two jihadists?"

"And one man-eating cougar."

Now it was Seamus's turn to look at Richard for signs of sarcasm. But the latter had deadpanned it.

"If the jihadists had a lick of sense," Seamus said, "they wouldn't have been standing right next to each other. We had better assume that at least one of them is still alive. And it is safest to assume that he is the sniper."

"And here we are with a shotgun and a pistol," Richard pointed out.

"What is that thing loaded with? Slugs or—"

"Buckshot," Richard said. "Four shells remaining."

"What are these words?" Yuxia asked.

"All the guns we have," Richard explained, "can only hit things that are close. Up above us, we think is a man with a gun who can hit things from far away."

Seamus considered it. "If there's anything to your Wikipedia entry, you know the way from here."

"That much of it is actually true," Richard said.

"If the three of us go together, the following will happen," Seamus said. "The sniper will come down here and—" He nodded toward the chopper and flicked his thumb across his throat, indicating the likely fate of the crippled pilot. "Then he will track us down the valley and try to pick us off one by one. So that's not what we're going to do."

"Who the fuck are you?" Richard asked him.

"A man in his element. Here's how this is going to go. I am going to find a blind where I can hang out. You two, Richard and Yuxia, are going to get out of here and try to find your way to safety. If the sniper comes here, I will kill him. If he follows you, then I will follow him. That's good for the pilot"—he nodded toward the chopper—"because he's got enough warm clothes and water and stuff to stay alive here for a little while as long as fucking jihadist snipers aren't coming after him."

"What about the man-eating lion?" Yuxia put in.

"Fuck!" Seamus said, and then immediately felt bad since it made Yuxia flinch. "I don't know. I'll warn the pilot. Tell him to keep the door closed."

A moment passed.

"What are you guys waiting for?" Seamus asked.

JUST BEFORE AWAKENING, she had dreamed of the flight from Eritrea, the six-month barefoot march into the Sudan and the quest for a refugee camp willing to take her group. The faces had faded from her memory, but the landscape, the vegetation, the feel of the march had stayed with her and become the continuo line underlying many of her dreams. Usually it was northern Eritrea, which they had marched through during the first days of the journey, when her mind had been fully open to the new sights and impressions that, once they hiked free of the caves in which she had spent her earliest years, seemed to present themselves to her every moment. The terrain was endless brown hills separated by the arroyos of seasonal streams and barely misted with scrubby vegetation. Nothing like the terrain she was running through now, densely grown with huge cedars and carpeted with ferns. But she knew that if she gained enough altitude, she would find herself in territory like what she and Chet had traveled through yesterday: steep, wide-open country where you could see for miles. And going there was not optional. If she stayed to the low moist valley of the river that flowed south from American Falls, it would lead her off in the wrong direction, taking her down into the basin of a major lake system that drained southward. It might be two days' hiking down into those lakes before she could reach a place where she could summon help. To reach Uncle Jake's, she would have to climb out of the valley and above the tree line to the lower reaches of Abandon Mountain, which she would have to traverse for several miles until she came to the headwaters of Prohibition Crick. That bit, she already knew, was going to be the desperate part: that was where she'd have to summon whatever it was the leaders of her refugee group had summoned on the worst days of their trek, when they were tired, short on food and water, and being pursued by men with guns.

The only thing that was going to make it possible was that she had a head start. The jihadists would have to climb farther out of the valley than she would. Even so, it was a long climb; and she feared that they would be able to narrow the gap, or even catch up with her, before she broke out above the tree line and into country where it would be impossible to hide.

So there was only one thing for it, and that was to run like hell and not stop for anything. She had grabbed all the water she had—the CamelBak pilfered from the Schloss, about three-quarters full—and as many energy bars as she could stuff into her pockets, and then simply lit out in the direction Richard had indicated. Down below, the jihadists were making it easy for her by shouting to one another and communicating on loud walkie-talkies.

Her first objective—which she achieved perhaps half an hour after parting from Richard—was to make contact with a trail that switchbacked up out of the gorge. The idea of following a marked trail was ridiculous in a way, since the jihadists would use the same route, and therefore be on her tail the entire way. But the terrain left no choice; the slope seemed nearly vertical when viewed from below, and it was a wildly uneven jumble of fallen, rotting logs. To bushwhack to the top would have taken days, if it were possible at all. Switchbacking up the trail, Richard had assured her, could be done in hours by a man carrying heavy cargo on his back.

She didn't reckon she had hours.

She slammed to a halt when the trail came into view, then retreated several paces and squatted in ferns to listen and think for a moment. While she was doing that, she sucked water out of the tube of the CamelBak and forced herself to eat a food bar. The sounds being made by the jihadists had become fainter during her run, which was of course better than the alternative, but still no reason to relax. If they knew what was good for them, they were talking less and running more, working their way down the bank of the river and looking for the head of this trail, just a few hundred yards below where she was now perched.

She had been peeling off layers as she ran, tying them around her waist, and was now dressed in a black tank top and cargo pants with the legs rolled up to expose her calves. She understood now that she would have to discard the outer layers. They would do nothing but slow her down. And they were bright pastel colors that could be seen for miles. The Girl Scout in her was screaming that it was a bad idea, that she'd become hypothermic the moment she stopped running.

But if she stopped running, she would be dead much sooner from other causes. So she dropped all those layers of fleece that Jones had bought for her at various Walmarts, stuffing them under a rotten log where men running up the trail would be unlikely to notice them, and went on with nothing except the clothes on her body and the water pouch slung on her back.

And then it was just switchbacks and switchbacks, seemingly forever. She struggled, every second, with the desire to slow down, to stop and take a rest, reminding herself over and over that the men behind her were used to scampering around Afghanistan like mountain goats. For all she knew, Jones was putting guns to their heads to force them to go faster. So she tried to remember what that was like—Jones putting a gun to her head—and to use that to eke out a little more speed. As much as fear told her to keep looking down, her brain told her to keep looking up, trying to make out the next leg of the switchback on the slope above her. For sometimes these things were designed as much for erosion control as for hiking efficiency, and there might be places where she could dash straight up the slope for, say, fifty feet and thereby cut off hundreds of feet of a switchback's apex. She perceived a few such opportunities and took them, arms flailing and legs scrambling as some part of her mind told her, *If I had only stayed on the trail, I'd already be long past this point!* Listening to that voice, then, she ignored a couple of such opportunities and then heard another voice saying, *If you had taken the shortcut, you'd be way ahead*. There was no getting away from those voices, so she tried to take each opportunity that looked worth it. The jihadists, she knew, didn't have to make such choices; they could split up and send half the group one way and half the other, let the best men win.

Which, if true, must mean that they were getting widely spread out on the trail below her. She wouldn't have to contend with all of them at once.

Thank God Jahandar had stayed behind. But she'd been taking a silent inventory of their weapons and seen other guns perfectly capable of killing at long range.

She had no concept of time's passage and had forgotten to count switchbacks. But she had the clear sense that the canopy overhead was thinning out, the light growing brighter, the switchbacks becoming less acute as the slope abated.

She got to a point where she simply could not run anymore, so she permitted herself to drop into a brisk walk while she drank more water—she hadn't been drinking enough, the CamelBak was only half empty—and ate another couple of bars. She was now on something that almost felt like a proper hike through the woods. Still gaining altitude but no longer with the sense of clinging to a cliff face. Gazing ahead and up-slope through increasingly common gaps between trees, she saw the high terrain that she had both longed for and dreaded all through the ascent, and towering above it the bare scarp of Abandon Mountain, which had nothing to recommend it as a tourist attraction unless you were a big fan of bleak. It looked like a science-fiction magazine cover, a mountain on some dead moon of Jupiter.

It was during this little respite that she heard the sound of a helicopter somewhere and debated whether she ought to run out into the open and flag it down. But it was hopeless; the chopper was a good distance away and the sight lines obscured by trees.

If only she had saved some of those bright pastel garments so that she could wave them in the air.

Speaking of which, the air was now bitingly cold on her shoulders. She bolted the last of her energy bar and forced herself to accelerate into a trot, then slowly build that up into a run.

She was just hitting her stride when she heard a sharp cracking boom. Because of the way it echoed around all the neighboring slopes, she found it difficult to judge direction. She was fairly certain, though, that it had sounded out of the direction from which she had just come. Miles away.

There was no one moment, no one place when she made the decision to go for it. The trees became thinner and thinner, the sight lines became clearer and longer, the ground angled more and more steeply under her feet. Minutes ago, she had been running across nearly level ground. But now she noticed that she was scrambling, almost on all fours, up a talus slope; looking back and down to judge her progress, she saw a good quarter of a mile of perfectly open ground behind and below her, terminated in the distance by a fringe of scrubby undergrowth that shortly developed into proper forest.

Down in that forest she could see movement. At least one man, possibly two of them. They were at most five minutes behind her:

a sufficient head start to keep her alive in the dense forest down below, but, up here, just enough to make it a challenging shot.

She snapped her head back around to scan the slope above her, hoping she might see a place to take cover.

In most ways, this place could not have been worse. During her geoengineering studies, she had learned all about the angle of repose, which was the slope that a heap of particulate matter naturally adopted over time; it explained the shape of an anthill, a mound of sugar, a pile of gravel, or a mountain of scree. The angle was different for each type of material. Its exact value was not important here. What was important was that the angle was everywhere the same, and so slopes made of such materials tended to be ruler straight. There were no mounds or bulges to hide behind.

And—as she kept being reminded—they were inherently unstable. As long as she remained on areas of larger rocks, her weight was not sufficient to break anything loose, but when she strayed into sandy or gravely areas she set off little avalanches. Nothing big enough to be dangerous, either to her or (unfortunately) those below her, but enough to give her the impression that she was climbing on a treadmill, burning energy but, like Sisyphus, going nowhere.

She had made it about two-thirds of the way up this sharpshooter's paradise when she began to hear guns firing from below. At first, a loose and irregular string of four or five pops, probably shots from a pistol. One of them whanged off a football-sized rock perhaps ten feet away from her and dislodged it. It went tumbling down the slope, neither picking up speed nor slowing down, occasionally loosening smaller stones but not setting off anything like a proper avalanche. So the shooter had missed her by a mile, which was to be expected with that sort of a weapon at this distance; but the mere fact of being shot at and of seeing bullets hit things nearby had frozen her in a low crouch for several moments—moments that, she knew, the slower members of Jones's crew were using to make up for lost time. She forced herself to keep scrambling, heading for a patch about twenty feet above her that seemed to include a few larger rocks—perhaps just enough that she could flatten herself behind them. This worked for all of about three seconds, until a hellish racket started up from below, so startling her that she planted a foot wrong, lost her footing, and fell hard, banging one elbow and nearly planting her face. The air around her was full of sharp dust and zinging fragments of rock. Someone down there had opened up with a fully automatic weapon. She hazarded a look down and saw, through a cloud of kicked-up rock dust, one of the jihadists planted there with a submachine gun braced on his hip. Not one of the bigger assault rifles, which fired high-velocity rifle rounds. This would be loaded with pistol rounds. Still perfectly capable of tearing up her body, of course, but intended for short-range work. Urban combat. Mowing down commuters on buses.

The shooter's companion—the one who had been firing the pistol a few moments earlier—shouted some advice at him, and he sullenly raised the weapon from his hip to his shoulder. Yes, he was actually going to try aiming it this time.

Zula got up and scrambled as hard as she could.

More shouted debate from below. The man with the submachine gun had been persuaded that he would get better results if he deployed its collapsible stock and braced it against his shoulder.

While this was being done Zula was putting everything she had into a frantic series of leaps and pounces. When frantic pawing didn't work, she paused, breathed, planted feet and hands on big rocks, and hurled her body upward.

The noise began again and then stopped; a hail of rock splinters peppered her back. Another burst then struck the slope above her, sending a few stones tumbling down, forcing her to dodge sideways for a couple of yards. Something tugged at the loose fabric of her cargo trousers, behind her thigh, and she dared not believe that a bullet had passed through it. A brief silence, and then several rounds chattered against a mosaic of bigger rocks, perhaps watermelon sized, just ahead of her: the shooter had figured out where she was going and was trying to drive her back. But she had already launched herself and could not have changed her course even if she'd had second thoughts. Something whacked her in the mouth. She landed on her belly and flattened herself on the upper side of this tiny collection of larger stones. She could not see the shooter; that was good. Rounds struck near her feet. She kicked wildly, bashing a few protuberant rocks out of the way, enabling her to settle her legs and her feet just a few inches lower. Important inches.

She was choking on something that was cold and sharp and

hard, and hot and sticky and wet at the same time. She hocked and spat and felt the hard thing leave her mouth, sending a jolt of pain up into her skull.

Actually it was two hard things, borne on a spate of blood and saliva: a chip of rock, about the size of a chickpea, but angular and sharp. And a tooth that it had apparently sheared off at its root when the rock chip had flown into her mouth, which had been open and gasping for air. Feeling with her tongue, she found a seeping hole where her right canine ought to have been. In front of that her upper lip was numb and felt huge. It was going to hurt soon, if she lived that long.

A few more bursts of fire swept across the tiny bulwark of stones behind which she was hiding, but to no effect, other than psychological. She could hear the men talking down below. Shouting, actually, since they had deafened themselves by playing with loud toys.

What would she do in their situation? Leave the one with the submachine gun below to keep her pinned in place with occasional bursts of fire. Meanwhile the one with the pistol could scramble up the slope and find an angle from which to shoot at her.

She said good-bye to her tooth, wiped her bloody hand on her shirt, then groped down the side of her body until she found the Glock in the cargo pocket of her trousers. This she pulled out and brought up in front of her face. She had no idea how many rounds it contained. Since she seemed to have some time, she ejected its clip and rotated the back of it into the sunlight so that she could see through the little holes in its back and count the bullets. This was a seventeen-round magazine that contained nine rounds at the moment; a tenth was already chambered. She shoved the clip back into the pistol's grip, made sure it was firmly seated, and slipped her finger carefully over the trigger, which was in its forward position: her weapon was cocked and ready to fire.

YUXIA ABOUT-FACED AND hurled herself down into the forest with Richard mounting the hottest pursuit of which he was capable. Seamus was very close to having his feelings hurt by the decisiveness with which the young lady had embraced, and acted upon, his plan. He had been assuming that there would be a lengthy and tedious transitional phase during which he would be obliged to convince her, against all of her soft womanly emotions, to leave him behind in this mortally dangerous situation: semiexposed, facing an enemy with a vastly longer-range weapon, yet unable to maneuver freely because of the requirement not to abandon Jack the chopper pilot.

In the minutes after she and Richard departed, Seamus had to keep himself busy moving about the area in a very specific manner, trying to situate himself so that the sniper above would (preferably) not be able to see him, or (barring that) not be able to get a good shot off at him. His camouflage clothing, ironically, was doing him very little good. The helicopter had come to a halt in a small and sparse collection of trees surrounded on three sides by a field of blindingly white snow. Unless he wanted to expose himself on that snow like a cockroach in a bathtub, he only had one way out, which was to move downhill into a little draw, lined with shrubs and scrubby little coniferous trees, that drained this part of the slope and eventually turned into a tributary of the river that plunged over the American Falls. This was the route that Yuxia and Richard had taken. There was little doubt in Seamus's mind that those two were safe, at least for the time being. He was hoping that the sniper would see the disturbance that they made in the low foliage as they hustled through it, hear them crashing through dry undergrowth and snapping branches with their feet, and decide to chase after them, which would bring him directly across Seamus's field of fire. The sniper couldn't possibly know how many surviving people were in this party, and he couldn't know how many had just run down the draw; with luck he would assume that they had *all* run off and feel no inhibitions about giving chase openly.

Seamus found a place that suited him, where he was able to settle himself into a little depression in the ground and peer uphill between tree trunks. He had pulled the hood of his jacket up over his head and cinched its drawstring tight, covering his hair and as much as possible of the oval of his face. This interfered with hearing and peripheral vision but seemed preferable to giving the sniper a nice round flesh-colored target. Sunglasses hid his eyes. He settled in to wait.

The thing with Yuxia meant nothing, he convinced himself. It wasn't like she had been living in normal circumstances for the last couple of weeks. Even before recent events, she had been decisive and strong-minded, probably to the point where people in her village considered her a little weird. He could see that much. All this stuff with the Russians, with Jones, the Philippine excursion, the chopper crash—it had just made her more so. She just wanted to get out of this alive.

Having satisfied himself as to that, he began questioning his judgment in re the matter of Jack the pilot. If the only objective was to keep Jack's spine stabilized until medical help could be brought in, then leaving him tightly strapped into his seat was probably a good move. But in these circumstances, leaving him there, exposed to observation and to fire from above, seemed downright ghoulish.

Jack was moving his arms. It wasn't clear why. Trying to actually do something? Or just flailing around in agony? A lot of times, trauma did not actually hurt. The pain came later. Maybe this was happening to him now. It was difficult to see what was going on in there. The chopper's windscreen was a casserole of cracks and shards.

"Seamus," Jack called, "I need to get out of here."

"Fuck!" Seamus said under his breath.

"Seamus! Help me, man! I'm in a lot of pain!"

Seamus was biting his tongue. He wanted to tell Jack to shut up, but he had no idea how close the sniper might be, whether he could hear anything that Seamus might say.

But Jack was already making it pretty obvious that someone else was down here with him and that his name was Seamus.

He heard the distinctive and never-to-be-forgotten sound of a high-velocity round passing through the vicinity, and a sharp pop/tinkle from the direction of the chopper, and, on its heels, the crack of a rifle shot from up the slope.

The temptation here, of course, was to engage in sudden movement, which was exactly what the sniper would be looking for. Seamus contented himself with swiveling his eyeballs to examine the chopper. It was such a wreck that it was difficult to see clear evidence of its having been newly shot. But as he was watching, he heard the bullet sound again and saw another round impact the fuselage, behind the cabin, below the engine. Searching its vicinity, he now saw the previous bullet hole, just a hand's breadth away.

Another hole appeared, between the first two.

The fucker was using the chopper as a target to zero his sights. No, wait. What was that smell?

"Gasoline!" Jack cried. "The tank is ruptured, I'm getting the hell out of here, Seamus!" And Seamus saw Jack lurch free as he undid his harness. The sudden movement caused him to scream. Seamus, like anyone else who was not a complete sociopath, felt sympathy for Jack and wanted to help him, or at least to call out some encouraging words. But those lovely altruistic instincts were completely suppressed, at the moment, by tactical calculations. Jack was actually doing the right thing, without any help, or even encouragement, from Seamus. If Seamus were to move or to call out now, he'd be giving the sniper exactly what the sniper wanted, and he wouldn't be doing Jack any good at all.

Because—if Seamus were reading the situation correctly—the sniper suspected that there was another person down here, another person who was named Seamus and who was assumed to be able-bodied. That much he could have guessed from overhearing Jack. His plan had been to draw Seamus out of cover by creating an implicit threat to cremate the helpless pilot.

Now that Jack was moving, though, the sniper had to shoot at him directly in order to create a threat. And this was difficult since much of the helicopter was between him and the target. Jack had tumbled out the chopper's side door and collapsed to the ground in a manner that could not have been pleasant for him. He was now dragging himself downhill, headed for the draw, albeit very slowly, his fear of the burning gasoline overriding the pain in his back.

The gasoline was ice cold and would be more difficult to ignite than usual. Merely shooting at it from a distance might not do the trick and would waste bullets. Seamus, a connoisseur of high-speed gun photography, knew that a plume of still-burning gunpowder and hot gas would erupt from the barrel of his Sig when he fired a round and probably set fire to the fuel—if he could get close enough.

Unfortunately, he was something like twenty feet away from the chopper.

Jack was moving commendably for a man with a serious spinal injury, dragging himself down the slope on his elbows.

Seamus stood up. He just stood straight up and gazed directly up the slope for perhaps two seconds and got an excellent view of the sniper, who was ensconced on a rock in the seated position, rifle at the ready, but gazing over the top of his scope, taking in a general view of the scene. The sniper reacted quickly, raising the weapon and getting his eye socketed into the scope, trying to find Seamus with it. But as Seamus knew perfectly well, these things took time. Seamus had a pretty good idea of how long they took. The transition from normal vision to the world as seen through the scope was jarring and confusing to the visual system no matter how many times you practiced it; the scope was never aimed in exactly the right direction, you had to swing the barrel around to bring the target into view, and there was a tendency to overmove it when you were hurrying to catch up with something that was moving rapidly.

And Seamus was definitely doing that. Having fixed an image of the sniper in his mind, he spun and ran toward the chopper, not in a straight line but in a series of zigzagging lunges, like Nate Robinson driving through a zone defense, and when he reached a place where he could see the side of the chopper wet with streaming gasoline, he aimed his Sig right at it, hurled himself forward, planted his feet for a quick reversal, and pulled the trigger three times as fast as his finger would move. Without pausing to observe the results, he spun away and shoved off with all the force he could muster in both legs, gaining himself an immediate distance of maybe six or eight feet. He dove to his belly and skidded across a stew of melting snow and icy mud that was suddenly growing bright, as though Venetian blinds had been opened to let the rays of the sun invade this little copse of trees. A couple of downhill somersaults got him clear of the burning wreck while (he hoped) putting out any fires that might have started on his back. Then he crawled into the draw, following the rut that Jack had made a few moments before.

He caught up with the stricken pilot in a location that was actually rather good: a water-worn cleft, forming a bottleneck in the draw, overgrown with vegetation, difficult to see or to shoot into. They were only a stone's throw downhill from the chopper but, tactically, it was a whole different world.

Seamus motioned for Jack to stop and make himself comfortable. He did not aim his Sig at the pilot, but he certainly made no secret of the fact that it was right there in his hand, ready to fire. "If you make another fucking sound, I'll shoot you dead," he said.

"Sorry, but those are the rules. Do you understand the rules?"

Jack nodded.

"Sniper has a predicament," Seamus said. "He suspects we are still alive. This makes him want to stay behind and take care of us. But he knows that we sent other people on ahead of us. He needs to catch up with them and kill them. I am betting that the psychological impact of what just happened will be that he says, 'Fuck it, I'm going to go look for the other guys.' He will bypass this draw, which looks scary to him because it equalizes the odds—his long gun doesn't do him any good, he has to get close, within range of this." Seamus gave the Sig a little flick of the wrist. "He'll go past us. I'll follow him. You'll stay here. If you want, you can make your way back to the chopper after it stops exploding, and throw some sticks on the fire and warm yourself up."

Jack nodded again.

"Now, I can't see shit from here, so I have to crawl up out of this hole and look around. We'll get you help as soon as we can. Got that?"

Jack nodded.

"Good luck. I hope you never again have a day that sucks as hard as this one." Seamus safetied his pistol, holstered it under his arm, and began to crawl up out of the draw on elbows and knees. When he reached a place where he could lie still, he burrowed as best he could into dry leaves and pine needles, and waited, motionless. But he didn't have to wait long before he saw the sniper walk past, tromping and skidding awkwardly in the snow, moving parallel to the tree line, just far enough away that hitting him with a pistol would have been a miracle shot. He was looking nervously into the trees as he went. He knew, or at least suspected, that he was in view of someone who had every intention of following him. But Seamus had guessed right: the sniper simply couldn't wait any longer. He had pressing business down-valley.

The obvious trick would be for the sniper to hike out of sight, stop, conceal himself, and wait until Seamus blundered into his sights. Seamus, accordingly, took his time and moved, when he did decide to move, in the cover of the foliage that lined the draw. Beyond the bottleneck where Jack was hiding, it broadened steadily until it developed into a valley, snow-free and heavily forested. Over the next quarter of an hour, Seamus, without exposing himself, was able to track the sniper's footprints in the snow. But eventually the trail led down into the forest, forcing Seamus to up his game a little bit and begin tracking the sharpshooter like wild game. Before he made his plunge into the valley, he paused for a few moments to take a good look around, get his surroundings fixed in his head, make sure that he wasn't missing anything that could be important later. Such as another contingent of jihadists bringing up the rear. It would be embarrassing to fail to notice such a thing.

He did not see another contingent of jihadists. But he was troubled by the feeling that he had seen something moving across the snow, roughly following the path that the sniper had taken. He saw nothing. He swept his gaze up and down the length of the trail that the sniper had left and convinced himself that nothing was on it. From place to place, though, it passed over a patch of khaki-colored rock that had been left exposed by the melting sun, and it had to be admitted that such places were excellent for the concealment of anything that happened to be light brown in color. After a while, with some hard looking and almost as hard thinking, he convinced himself that something might be crouching up on one of those patches, looking back at him, waiting for him to take his gaze away so that it could go back into motion.

Which might be for real, or just his imagination. But if it were for real, he could sit here all day staring at it and nothing would ever happen. So he turned his back on it and stalked into the forest.

DURING HER TIME among the jihadists, Zula had often been bemused by the slapdash and informal way that they went about certain activities. In this she recognized some of her own heritage: a mind-set and a collection of habits that had eventually been drilled out of her by Iowans. It had something to do with the way that such people assessed risk. Some might call it fatalism born of religious doctrine; others might point out that persons growing up in regions where war, disease, and famine were chronic conditions would naturally have a different set of instincts and reactions where danger was concerned.

And so when the pistol-carrying jihadist strolled out into the open and began to hike up the open slope directly toward Zula, she was not quite as dumbfounded as she might have been, had she never been around people who manifested the Third World attitude toward risk.

It could be that the man simply did not understand that Zula was armed. She had not fired the weapon recently, certainly had not showed it to them. He imagined that he would simply be able to walk up the slope, get close to her, and shoot her.

Or perhaps the plan was to take her prisoner again?

It didn't matter. The result was the same: a moment was approaching in which Zula—lying prone, and reasonably well sheltered behind rocks—would place this man's center of mass in her sights and pull the trigger. The closer she let him get, the easier the shot would be. As the Girl Scout in her might have predicted, she was getting cold, and her hands were beginning to shake. So she had to fight the temptation to shoot early. Better to wait for him to grow larger in the sights of the gun. But if she let him get too close, he might see the pistol in her hands.

She was lying on her side, having plastered her body into a tiny depression. It was awkward and uncomfortable. But the man below, sweeping the area with submachine-gun fire, had not been able to hit her with anything other than rock fragments, and that argued for not moving. Some little shift in position that might feel inconsequential to her could have the result of exposing some part of her body to fire.

Still—it was tempting. Her view of the man with the pistol was blocked by the pattern of the rubble. If she jackknifed, moved forward just a bit, she'd be able to see him clearly, brace her arms on a sort of flat tablet of rock a few feet away, get off the shot from a greater, and safer, distance.

Those were her thoughts while she waited and grew cold and shivery and stiff. She wondered what had caused the huge explosion she had heard earlier. Chet setting off the Claymore mine seemed like the obvious explanation. She wondered what that implied about the fate of Chet, and about Richard who had gone to look for him. She wondered what the story was on the helicopter, and whether it would be coming back.

Her meditations were interrupted by new movement, seen in the corner of her eye. She had been looking directly at the jihadist with the pistol, visible only from the shoulders up, struggling up the same scree slope she had climbed a little while ago. She now turned her head to see that the man with the submachine gun had been moving too, trying to get a new angle.

His eyes locked with hers for a moment. He looked excited and raised the weapon to his shoulder, taking aim.

She wriggled forward, moving to the new position a couple of yards ahead. The man with the pistol was startlingly close. He was flailing his arms, trying to maintain his balance. She stretched out her arms on the rock and lined up the front and rear sights, then swung them onto the dark form of the climber.

A single loud noise sounded from *above* her. Her ears suggested as much. The climber's face proved it. For his immediate reaction was to freeze and look up the slope.

She pulled the trigger, felt the pistol jerk as its action cycled, saw the shell casing tinkle onto the rocks nearby.

The man was just standing there with a sort of *Oh shit* look on his face, and she thought for a moment that she must have missed him. But then he tried to sit down, which wasn't going to work when facing up a steep slope. His legs flew up in the air before his ass had even touched the ground, and he began to turn back-somersaults down the mountain, gathering speed as he went.

She twitched her head around to look at the man with the submachine gun. But he was gone. Raising her head carefully, she found him at the base of the slope, lying spread-eagled.

The edge of the wood now lit up with muzzle flashes from two different weapons: freshly arrived jihadists who had witnessed all of this. But if they were firing at Zula, they were missing by a mile.

Answering fire now came from above: single shots, fired deliberately. These seemed to discourage the shooters below. Zula rolled on her back, rested her head on that flat rock, tried to figure out where it was coming from. The obvious answer was a large mass of solid stone, about the size of a city block, that jutted out from the ramp of talus. She inferred that it had a flattish top and that someone was up on top of it with a long gun.

Then her eye was drawn to movement. Along the side of that outcropping, someone was waving a piece of cloth. A T-shirt. Zula turned to look at this and, after a few moments, waved back.

A person emerged into view and began to make huge beckoning motions toward Zula. *Run to me.*

Zula had no idea who it was. She got up and began running anyway. She was tired of being cold and she was tired of being alone, and she was willing to try anything. Even if some risk was involved. Call it fatalism. But the piercing bangs that sounded overhead—high-powered rifle rounds lancing down into the tree line from the top of the rock—seemed to give the men below second thoughts about coming out to shoot at her.

SOKOLOV'S IMMEDIATE REACTION to the loud bang was to shed his backpack, open it up, and begin assembling the assault rifle that Igor had taken from Peter and that he had taken from Igor. The logic of this move was far from obvious to Olivia. They were only a couple of miles away from a country in which possession of this gun would be spectacularly illegal. They had not seen another living soul today, other than the Forthrasts. But Sokolov was firm in his conviction that what they had heard was not a mining blast but the detonation of a tactical military device and that they were now in a state of open war with unseen and unknown enemies.

Olivia saw, then, how it all made sense. She had known it all along, really, but had suppressed it out of a sort of bureaucratic instinct: the fear that she would never be able to sell the idea in a meeting. Of course Jones would interrogate Zula, read Richard's Wikipedia entry, learn about the smuggling, go to his place near Elphinstone, use Zula as leverage to make Richard guide him across the border. And of course the explosion at the border crossing yesterday had just been a diversion.

He was here, now.

How long had Sokolov known it? Until the moment of the blast he had betrayed no suspicions that they might be hiking into a free-fire zone with a gang of heavily armed jihadists. But she saw now that he had been expecting this all along.

Had he been playing her?

It was more complicated than that, she suspected. He had been playing the odds. There were good reasons for Olivia and Sokolov to cross the border. They could have done it anywhere. Sokolov had favored the crossing point that was most likely to produce a meeting with Jones.

They spent a quarter of an hour—though it seemed much longer—staging a tactical retreat back up the slope, through the boulder field, to the top of the rocky spur where they had parted company with Jake.

Inside Sokolov's pack was a smaller bag, just a thin nylon stuff sack, made to hold a wadded-up sleeping bag. Once Sokolov had found a convenient place to lie prone on the top of the rock, he pulled this out by its drawstring and set it down on the rock. It clattered. It was full, she realized, of hard, heavy objects with corners. Once he had finished assembling the rifle, Sokolov zipped the bag's drawstring open and dumped it out on the rock. It contained half a dozen curved plastic boxes: ammunition clips for the rifle. From their weight it was obvious that they were loaded.

Sokolov had gotten to Bourne's Ford before her, made the rounds of local gun stores, bought all of this stuff, and loaded the clips. Just to be ready.

Okay, so he had been playing her. She found that it didn't really bother her. Because, in a sense, she'd been playing him too. Hoping that something like this would happen.

In any case, there was little time for these metaphysical considerations. Sokolov—who had belly-crawled to the edge of the big flat rock—called her forward and got her to see what was going on below them: a young woman, brown-skinned, black-haired, in a tank top and cargo pants, scrambling up the slope in obvious fear for her life. Bursts of submachine-gun fire from a location that, at first, they were unable to see. By the time they had repositioned themselves to a place where Sokolov could get the man with the submachine gun in his sights, that man had stopped firing and was biding his time while a companion flailed and scrabbled up the slope with a pistol in one hand.

"Go down," Sokolov commanded her, "and get Zula."

This—more than the helicopter, the sudden appearance of the assault rifle, the shocking blasts of the submachine gun—snapped Olivia's head around.

"That's *her*!?"

Sokolov pulled his face away from the rifle's sight and turned to give her a certain look that was very male, and very Russian.

"Okay," she said, "but what about the guy with the pistol?"

"Zula is going to kill him," Sokolov said.

"Seriously?"

The look again. "Seriously. But then. Only a short time—what do you call it—a *window of opportunity*—when she can run to safer place. I will fire suppression."

ALL THE CHINESE people Richard had ever met had been sophisticated urbanites, so he had been half expecting that he would end up carrying the girl Yuxia on his back. But it became clear almost immediately that she was half mountain goat, or whatever the Chinese equivalent of a mountain goat was. This was made evident by the fact that he was always seeing her face. Because she was always ahead of him and frequently turned around to see what was taking him so long.

He was afraid that *she* was going to ask *him* whether he needed any help.

On one of those occasions, only a couple of minutes after they started running, she got an awed look on her face. Richard already felt as though he knew Yuxia, partly because of Zula's description of her in the paper towel note. Her face was expressive and handsome, but not given to unguarded moments. Much of the time she had a keen and interested look about her, and frequently she flashed a knowing grin, as if enjoying a private joke. Frank astonishment was not something she would allow herself to manifest unless it was a really big deal. So Richard faltered and turned around, taking a couple of backward steps in an amazed, staggering gait. A mushroom cloud of yellow fire was turning inside out as it sprang into the air above the site of the chopper crash.

"I'm sure it's okay," he blurted out, turning back around and placing a gentle hand on her shoulder, encouraging her to get turned around and moving again. She recoiled, and not in a stop-harassing-me-you-dirty-old-man way. She had taken more damage in the chopper crash than she wanted to let on. When she did turn around, she did so stiffly, and Richard understood that the spryness he had been envying her for was at least partly an act, a willed refusal to show pain. Because she didn't want men covering for her. Because chivalry sometimes came with a price.

"I didn't get to know Seamus very well during the five minutes I spent watching the chopper crash and so forth," Richard said, lengthening his stride and trying to draw the suddenly indecisive Yuxia along in his wake, "but he struck me as a smart guy who knows what he's doing, and I don't think that he would just hang around next to something that was getting ready to explode."

She had started moving again, perhaps a little stung to see that a lumbering old man had gained several meters on her. He saw the stiffness in her neck now, the preoccupied look of someone who was working on a major headache.

"Listen," he said, after a minute, "there's no telling how long we are going to be running around in these mountains being chased by jihadists, and so I would like to introduce you to our new friend and traveling companion, Mr. Mossberg."

Yuxia looked around theatrically, doing most of it with her eyes since the neck didn't like to move. "I don't see him," she said.

"Yes, you do," Richard said, and displayed the shotgun. Some part of him was aghast at the possible consequences of supplying Yuxia with a pump-action shotgun and the knowledge of how to use it, but, in general, this all felt right. "Have you seen these things in movies?"

"And video games," she said. "You pull back on the slider."

"Yeah. It's called a forearm, for some reason. With this kind, sometimes you have to pull back hard—a soft pull doesn't work."

"It's okay, I'm strong," she said.

"Red, you're dead," he said, showing her the safety and flicking it back and forth a couple of times, alternately hiding and exposing the red dot. "Here, you try it. Just remember to keep your finger like this." He showed her how he was keeping his index finger pointed forward along the side of the stock, not allowing it to touch the trigger.

"Oopsy daisy," she said, nodding.

They had slowed to a brisk walk, but he deemed it a reasonable risk; it was important for her to know how to work this thing. He got the harness untangled from his clothing and handed her the gun, noting with approval that her index finger went naturally to the right place. "Pull the forearm back a little and you can see that there is a shell ready to fire," he said.

"Shell equals bullet."

"Shell is a word we use to mean a piece of ammunition, but here it's not a bullet. It's a lot of little balls." He used his hands to pantomime them spraying outward. "Very powerful. But you have to be close, or the balls will spread out and miss the guy."

"How close?"

"Twenty meters or less. And it helps if you aim it."

She looked at him, not sure if he was being sarcastic. "I'm serious," he said. "Put it to your shoulder, keep your cheek on the stock—the handle—and look down the barrel. Both eyes open."

Yuxia came to a stop so that she could practice this, taking aim at a tree about ten yards away. "I want to shoot it," she remarked, finding it funny and fascinating that she wanted this.

"Someday you can come to my family reunion and do all the shooting you want," he promised her. "Not now. We only have four shells. And we don't want Jahandar to hear us."

"Okay, I guess I'll give it back to you," she said, sounding quite sullen. He looked sharply at her, and she flashed a grin. *Fooled you!*

"Probably a good idea," he said. "He'll shoot the one with the weapon first. Then you have to take it from me, and hide, and wait for him to come close."

This remark seemed to take all the joy out of the situation, so they picked up the pace now and devoted all their attention to covering ground. He was surprised by the apparent speed with which they made it back to the spot where he had parted company with Zula earlier. This seemed like a natural place to take a break, or at least slow down, and take stock of their situation.

"I am glad I had so many free waffles," Yuxia remarked, eyeing Richard.

"I'm running on fumes," he confessed.

Yuxia didn't seem to find this very reassuring. Richard straightened up and patted his belly. "Fortunately, I have a lot of stored energy."

Yuxia gazed clinically at his gas tank.

"In another half an hour or so, we'll be at a trail. A long climb up many switchbacks."

"Switchbacks?"

"Zigzags. At that point, you should probably go on ahead. I'm just going to slow you down."

"Who gets the gun?" she asked.

He thought about this question for a few moments. His brain was tired and working slow.

Then he understood that the question wasn't meant to be answered. It was an impossible choice. They had to stay together.

Which meant that he needed to get off his ass.

"Thank you," he said, and forced one foot to pass in front of the other.

"Is this where Zula went?" she asked him.

"I hope so. But Jones and the others probably followed her."

"And now we are following them."

"And Jahandar is following us."

"If that is true," Yuxia said, "I hope Seamus is following Jahandar."

She seemed enormously comforted by that idea, so Richard held his tongue rather than speculate about the mountain lion that might be serving as the death train's caboose.

"I am sooo glad Zula is alive," Yuxia said, a few minutes later. Richard got the clear idea that she was trying to get his mind off how exhausted and sore he was. "I thought she was dead. I cried so hard."

"So did I."

"I asked her questions about her family," Yuxia said, "but she did not answer very much. Now I get it; she didn't want the others to hear such information."

"Smart girl. She didn't want them to know about me."

"We found out about you later," Yuxia said. "Big game man."

"Yes. I am a big game man." *Being stalked by a big game hunter.*

"Tell me about your family," Richard suggested.

"Aiyaa, my family! My family is sad. Sad, and maybe in trouble."

"Because of what happened to you?"

"Because of what I *did*," she corrected him. "It didn't all *happen to* me."

"When the story comes out," he said, "it will all be fine."

"If we don't get killed," she corrected him, and picked up her pace so dramatically that he lost her in undergrowth—her camouflage outfit was very effective—and had to break into a jog for a few paces.

"Look, someone left clothes!" she announced a long sweaty while later and tugged on a loose sleeve that was peeking out from beneath a fallen log.

"Zula's," he said, catching up with her and recognizing the garment. "She ditched all the stuff she didn't need. Getting ready for the climb."

"The climb is next for us?"

"It starts now," he said, and stepped past Yuxia, bushwhacking through a few more yards of undergrowth until he broke in upon the switchback trail.

During his sporadic, Furious Muse–driven efforts to lose weight, he had been forcefully reminded of a basic fact of human physiology, which was that fat-burning metabolism just plain didn't work as well as carbo-burning metabolism. It left you tired and slow and confused and dim-witted. It was only when he was really stupid and irritable—and, therefore, incapable of doing his job or enjoying his life—that he could be certain he was actually losing weight. So it was in that state that he began to shamble up the switchback trail. But even in his flabbergasted condition, he was soon able to pick up on a basic fact of switchback geometry that was about to become important. Two hikers who might be a mile apart from each other on the trail might nonetheless find themselves separated by only a hundred yards of straight-line distance as one zigged and the other zagged. Assuming that Jahandar was chasing them—which was what they *had* to assume—they might have started out with an excellent head start. And he hoped that they had preserved that head start by moving as fast as they were able. And yet the moment might come, a minute or an hour from now, when they might look down, and Jahandar might look up, and they might lock eyes on each other from a range that was easily within rifle, and maybe even within shotgun, distance.

Richard wished he could have bullshitted himself into believing that Jahandar would not be aware of this fact. But Jahandar looked like a man who had spent his whole life on switchbacks, and who well understood their properties.

He saw, then, how it was all going to work out. And he understood that his confusion, his laggardliness, his irritability, were not all due to the fact that he was hungry. This was his brain trying to tell him something.

And if there was one thing he had learned in his ramshackle career, it was to pay close attention to his brain at such times.

His brain was telling him that their plan was fucked.

Their plan was fucked because Jahandar was going to catch up with them—had probably been doing so the entire time—and was going to reach the place where he could shoot up the slope from another switchback. Hell, he could just set up a sniper's perch, get his gun propped up on something nice and solid, make himself comfortable, and wait for Richard and Yuxia to pass back and forth above him, zigging and zagging up the mountain like a pair of lame ducks in a shooting gallery.

I love you, but I'm tired of being the girlfriend of the sacred monster. This had been the last thing that Alice, one of his ex-girlfriends, had said to him before ascending into the pantheon of the Furious Muses. It had taken him a while to decode it—Alice hadn't been in a mood to wax discursive—but he'd eventually figured out that this, in the end, was the reason that Corporation 9592 had no choice but to keep him around. Every other thing that he had done for the company—networking with money launderers, stringing Ethernet cable, recruiting fantasy authors, managing Pluto—could be done better and more cheaply by someone who could be recruited by a state-of-the-art head-hunting firm. His role, in the end, had been reduced to this one thing: sitting in the corner of meeting rooms or lurking on corporate email lists, seeming not to pay attention, growing ever more restless and surly until he blurted something out that offended a lot of people and caused the company to change course. Only later did they see the shoals on which they would have run aground if not for Richard's startling and grumpy intervention.

This was one of those times.

The only thing that made any sense at all was to stop, look for cover, wait for Jahandar to catch up with them, hold fire until he came within twenty yards, and try to take him down with the shotgun before he could shoot back.

"Stop," he said quietly.

"You okay, big guy?" Yuxia asked.

"Fantastic," he assured her. "But here is where we have to stand and fight."

"I am so in favor of that," she said. "Do I get to shoot one of these motherfuckers?"

"Only if I die first."

. . . .

CSONGOR ABRUPTLY SHIFTED the SUV into gear, punched the gas, and rumbled out of the parking lot. He had been running the motor to feed juice into Marlon's laptop.

"What the—?" Marlon asked, as he watched his Wi-Fi connection disappear. Csongor couldn't tell whether Marlon had cribbed this phrase from comic book word bubbles or was making an arch reference to Chinese nerds who naively picked up snatches of English dialog in this way. It was hard to tell, sometimes, with Marlon.

"Something is wrong," Csongor said.

"I thought you said you couldn't drive this thing."

"I can't drive it *legally*," Csongor said.

"Oh."

"But I can make it go, as you see."

"I was transferring money," Marlon said. Not in a whiny, complaining way. Just making sure Csongor knew that his important work had been interrupted.

"You've been transferring money for three hours," Csongor pointed out, "while I have been looking at the clock and the map." He rattled an Idaho road map that Seamus had bought at a gas station yesterday. "There is no way that those guys should still be gone. The da G shou can wait for their money; they've waited this long."

Because he had been studying the map, Csongor knew how to get them out of Coeur d'Alene and on the road north to Sandpoint and Bourne's Ford. He followed the route, scrupulously observing all the traffic laws to minimize his chances of being pulled over. He did not think that a Hungarian driver's license would pass muster in these parts.

"Maybe they just found something interesting to look at."

"That's not the point," Csongor said. "A helicopter can only carry so much gas—it can only stay in the air for a certain amount of time."

He sensed Marlon looking at him incredulously.

"I googled it," Csongor explained, "when you went out to urinate."

"Okay . . ."

"I know what you are going to say next: maybe they had

mechanical trouble and had to land. But in that case they should have called us and told us that they would be late."

"How late are they?"

"Very late."

Marlon was still looking at him expectantly.

"Mathematically," Csongor said, "the helicopter is out of gas." He glanced at the dashboard clock. "Fifteen minutes ago."

"Maybe we should call—"

"Call who?" Csongor asked, with a kind of cruel satisfaction. For he had gone down the same road in his mind and found only dead ends. He waited for Marlon to work his way to the same non-conclusion.

They blew through what seemed to be an important road junction at the extreme limit of the greater Coeur d'Alene metropolitan area and went bombing north on a nice straight open highway. It was turning into a beautiful day.

"So what are you going to do?"

"*We* are going to go to Bourne's Ford, which is only a few miles from where they were flying, and go to the Boundary County Airport, and ask the people there if they know anything about a missing helicopter."

About half an hour later they found themselves crossing a long causeway over a lake. Before them was the town of Sandpoint. Csongor noticed Marlon craning his neck to get a sidelong view of the speedometer. Glancing down, he saw that he was going ninety.

"It is not kilometers per hour," Marlon informed him. "In the metric system, you are going at something like five thousand."

"Not quite that fast," Csongor said, but he did relent and drop down to eighty.

A minute later, he explained, "I believe Seamus went up there to find Jones. This was his real plan. But he could not say this out loud. Then Yuxia asked why she could not go along, if it was only a sightseeing trip. Seamus was trapped."

"Yuxia is good at such things."

"What do you think of her?" Csongor asked. "Is she your girl-friend?"

"For a while I was thinking maybe," Marlon admitted, "but then I decided she was my sister."

"Huh."

"China is funny. One child per family, you know. We are all looking for siblings."

Csongor nodded. "It is a much better system," he said, "than the one we use in Hungary."

"Why?"

Csongor looked across at Marlon. "Because you get to choose."

Marlon smiled. "Ah."

Csongor turned his attention back to the road.

"Your brother in California," Marlon said.

"What about him?"

"Are you going to go and visit him?"

"Do you want to see California?"

He could hear Marlon beaming. "Yes."

"It is probably a better place for you," Csongor said, "than for me. If I go, I will take you. You can be the star. I will be your—"

"Bodyguard?"

"Fuck that. I was thinking entourage."

"California, here we come!" Marlon exclaimed.

Csongor thrust a stubby finger out the window at a road sign that said CANADA 50 MI/80 KM. "We are going wrong way," he pointed out. "Before California, we have to get into trouble. Then out of it."

Marlon shrugged. "But that is what we do."

Csongor nodded. "That is what we do."

BY THE TIME Csongor had finished slowing down from highway speed, they were halfway through Bourne's Ford and in danger of blowing past it altogether. As a way of giving them some time to get their bearings, Csongor pulled into a gas station. Using some American cash from his wallet—for Seamus had passed out a bit of spending money—he fronted the cashier $40, then strolled back to the SUV and began to pump fuel into it. The way that the gas pump worked was slightly unfamiliar and made him feel inept and conspicuous. But eventually he figured out how to latch the nozzle in the on position, and then he leaned back against the side of the vehicle and crossed his arms to wait for its enormous tank to fill. Marlon had made a quick toilet run and was already ensconced back in the passenger seat, scanning the airwaves for open Wi-Fi connections.

A blue Subaru station wagon turned in off the highway and pulled up on the opposite side of the pump island. Its front was thickly speckled with the dried corpses of insects. Bundles of stuff had been lashed and bungeed down to its roof rack. Since it was so clearly not from around here, Csongor glanced at its license plate. It was from Pennsylvania.

It sat there for a while with its engine running, and Csongor could just barely hear the muffled sounds of a discussion going on inside of it. The tail end, he suspected, of a long-running argument among tourists who had been cooped up together in this small vehicle for far too long.

Then the driver's door swung open and a man climbed out: a Middle Eastern fellow with a close-cropped beard and dark wrap-around sunglasses. He went to the cashier and gave him some paper money, then returned to the Subaru and began to pump gas into it.

Another man, an African with a slender angular look that reminded him of Zula, got out of the backseat, went inside, and used the toilet. When he emerged, he was carrying a large-format paperback with a red cover, which he had apparently just purchased: *Idaho Atlas and Gazetteer.*

Noting movement in the corner of his eye, Csongor looked up the SUV's flank to the passenger-side rearview mirror, which Marlon had adjusted so that he could use it to stare Csongor in the eye. The look on his face said: *Can this really be happening!?*

Csongor looked off in some other direction and responded with a nod.

He had decided that he wanted to be the last vehicle out of this gas station, so when he was finished pumping the gas, he went back inside as if he intended to use the W.C. Instead of which he lurked in the back of its little convenience store area, pretending to be unable to make up his mind as to which selection he ought to make from its dizzying variety of jerky and keeping an eye on the blue Subaru.

"Selkirk Loop," said the clerk wonderingly, gazing out at the same thing. "Brings in all kinda people."

The driver removed the nozzle from the side of his car. Csongor advanced to the cash register, spilled out some bags of jerky and two water bottles, and yanked an *Idaho Atlas and Gazetteer* out of the rack for good measure.

"Those are hot sellers today," the clerk remarked.

Csongor said nothing. The clerk had pegged him as an American, and he saw no reason to call that into question by opening his big mouth.

Now the Subaru's driver came in to use the toilet, and Csongor had no choice but to go outside, get into the SUV, and start it up. He pulled out onto the road, went about half a block down a commercial strip, and entered the parking lot of a fast-food place. This turned out to have a drive-through, and so, on an impulse, he drove into it and placed an order for a couple of hamburgers. He drove around the back in a big U and paid at the window. The SUV was now pointed back out toward the street.

While the man at the window was stuffing their order into a bag, Marlon said, "There!" and Csongor glanced out to see the blue Subaru cruising past them at a safe and legal velocity.

He was a bit anxious that they might have lost their quarry as a result of the fast-food gambit, but a few moments later, when he gunned the SUV back out onto the street, sucking deeply from a bucket-sized serving of Mountain Dew, he was able to see it clearly a few hundred meters ahead, making its way peaceably through a series of stoplights.

The next bit felt touch-and-go, since, depending on the lights, they sometimes seemed to fall far behind and other times drew uncomfortably close. But it had become obvious that these men were heading north out of town. Marlon used these minutes to flip through the *Atlas and Gazetteer* and find the relevant map.

"North of here, a few kilometers, is an intersection," Marlon announced. "If they go straight, then they are headed for Canada, and it means nothing. But if they go left, across the river, then they are trying to reach the place where Seamus and Yuxia were flying to this morning."

"Is there some other way we can cross that river?" Csongor asked. "So we won't be following them so obviously?"

"Yes. Turn around here."

And thus they turned back, dropping away from direct pursuit of the Subaru, and went back into the middle of the town and crossed over a different bridge. A few minutes later they were headed west, seemingly direct into the mountains; but just before the terrain became really steep, Marlon directed Csongor to make a right turn onto a gravel road that ran due north, heading generally parallel to the river. During his three hours of intense boredom at the flight center, Csongor had flipped through the vehicle's manual enough to learn how it could be shifted into four-wheel drive, so he took a moment to do this, and then went blasting up the road at an insane pace for some miles. He did not think that there were any cops around here to pull him over; and if they did, he would simply claim that there were terrorists in the area, driving a blue Subaru.

Come to think of it, they should have done that before leaving Bourne's Ford. But their own illegal status had put them in an awkward frame of mind, never knowing when to hide from the authorities and when to call out for their help. They didn't *know* that those men were terrorists. They might have been innocent tourists. When Marlon had said, a few minutes earlier, that they might go straight at the intersection and head north into Canada, presumably to enjoy the Selkirk Loop, it had sounded perfectly reasonable to Csongor and he had wondered at his foolishness for harboring this racist stereotype that the men were terrorists.

And now he was here in the middle of nowhere cursing himself for his failure to recognize the obvious.

They crested a minor rise in the highway in time for Marlon to pick out the blue Subaru crossing the bridge. It had made the left turn and was headed into the mountains.

Marlon opened his mouth to say something, but Csongor had caught it too. "Fuck!" he said.

"This is the part where we get into trouble?"

"Evidently. Make sure you don't lose sight of it," Csongor said, and then devoted all his attention and energy to keeping the SUV from drifting off the road. For its suspension was being thrashed so hard at the moment that it was a rare moment when all four of its wheels were actually touching the ground.

"Here," Marlon said, a minute later. They were approaching a fork, a smaller gravel road headed up a valley to the left.

"This is where you saw them turn?"

"I didn't see them," Marlon said.

"Then how can you be sure?"

"Because they left a trail in the air," Marlon said, "like a jet."

And indeed, Csongor now saw that the air above the little side road was milky with dust that had been churned up by the Subaru's tires a minute earlier. Whereas, when he looked north along the riverside road, the air was clear.

A sign, rusted and snowplow-bashed and riddled with shotgun pellets, stood at the junction. PROHIBITION CREEK ROAD, it said.

"Here goes," said Csongor. He swung the steering wheel and gunned the motor.

ZULA'S RISING TO a crouch and sudden scramble toward the base of the rock elicited several bursts of gunfire from down below, each of which was answered by a crisp rifle shot from the top of the rock above. The shooters below, who she imagined were firing from a standing position after sprinting up the last few switch-backs, did not really have time to situate themselves and draw a proper bead on her; she thought she might have heard a few of the insane-bumblebee noises that apparently signaled the near approach of high-velocity rounds. But the going here was much easier than below, partly because of the gentler slope and partly because the footing was better—more hard rock and less random boulder pile. She forced herself to cover at least a hundred feet before risking a look back. The tree line was no longer visible. She experimented with rising out of her crouch and saw it slowly peek back over the horizon, then dropped her head before anyone could draw a bead and pull a trigger. She ran now in a hunched-over posture, headed for that frantically waving T-shirt, and covered another couple of hundred yards before looking back again. She was now able to stand all the way upright without exposing herself. Winded and banged up, the cold dry air sending an ice pick into the root of her shattered tooth with each breath, she permitted herself to quick-walk the last bit, and finally came within conversational distance of the T-shirt waver.

She had hoped, in a completely irrational way, that this might be Qian Yuxia, but she had known this was not the case from a hundred yards out. The voice that greeted her now spoke in an English accent: "Is that Zula?"

Zula, not trusting herself to speak, just nodded her head and grimaced. The English woman came out to greet her and met her with a handshake at the base of the huge rock. "My name's Olivia. I'm so sorry about your lip; is that as painful as it looks?"

Zula rolled her eyes and nodded.

"I wish I could tell you we had an ambulance—a helicopter—*something*—but there's none of that, I'm afraid. We've got a bit of a walk ahead of us. Do you feel up to it?"

"Who's we?"

"The man up there," Olivia said, momentarily shifting her gaze to the top of the rock, "is known to you, I believe. Name of Sokolov."

"Someone needs to get that guy a first name," Zula lisped.

"I know, it seems a bit gruff to go round calling him that."

"What the hell is Sokolov doing here? Other than the obvious, I guess."

"I believe he feels he owes you something."

"You could say that." Zula was following Olivia's lead now, as they climbed up along the side of the big outcropping. The slope here had become steep again, and Zula could see the skid marks in the gravel where this Olivia person had sledded down.

"There's a bit coming up," Olivia said, pointing up the slope, "where we'll need to keep our heads down. Coming back in view of the fellas down below."

Zula looked back and nodded.

"He never intended for things to get quite so fouled up," Olivia said, returning to the topic of Sokolov. "Was keeping an eye on you. Didn't want you hurt."

"I had sort of gotten that vibe, but it was hard to tell."

"Then, when Jones entered the picture, I'm afraid our man Sokolov took it quite personally. In other words, I don't think it's about you anymore."

"I'm perfectly happy for it not to be about me."

"All right then, are you ready?"

"I guess so," Zula said, though in truth she could hardly have been more exhausted.

"One good push over the top." And Olivia began churning her

feet in the scree, setting off little avalanches that Zula had to hop over. Their progress through this last exposed bit was probably not as nimble or as quick as Olivia had pictured, and Zula, becoming stuck at one point, risked a look back and verified that they were now in view of the tree line again. But the distance was so great that the shot would have been impossible without a scoped rifle, and the shooters down there seemed to have become thoroughly demoralized by Sokolov's policy of firing high-velocity rounds down into their muzzle flashes. The next time Zula glanced back, all she could see was rocks, and then she and Olivia enjoyed a fairly easy scramble up a little chute and out onto the broad and generally flat top of this giant outcropping.

Until now Zula had had only a vague idea of where she was on the larger map, which had been fine since she'd had very little leisure to think about grand strategy. But from here the whole thing became plain. Abandon Mountain was at her back. Looking outward and down over the territory from which she had just ascended, she was facing generally west. Off to the right, a few miles away, was the ridge through which she and Chet had passed yesterday via the old mining tunnels. To her left, a long, gently curving talus slope spanned a distance of a couple of miles to a long ridge thrown out southward from the mountain. She knew from Richard's description that if she traversed that slope and popped up over that ridge she would descend into the valley of Prohibition Crick and find Jake's place.

She collected all these impressions while following Olivia, at an exhausted, shambling pace, across the top of the rock toward the precipitous edge from which Sokolov had been shooting at the jihadists. The farther Olivia went, the more she tended to hunch over, then crouch, then crawl. Deeply tired of such inefficient forms of locomotion, Zula balked at going farther. She advanced slowly to the point where she would have to begin crawling on hands and knees, then stopped and squatted on her haunches, stretching out her wrecked thigh muscles and her calves. About thirty feet away she could see the soles of Sokolov's boots, heels up and toes down, as he lay prone at the cliff edge, peering through the scope of a tricked-out AR-15 rifle that looked oddly similar to the one Peter had kept in his safe. Olivia was lying on her side next to him, talking into his ear, and he was nodding and making little remarks back to her. Something in Olivia's body language—the almost total relaxation with which she lay next to him—told Zula that she was watching a sort of intimate moment, which made her feel awkward. But after a few moments, Olivia began to inchworm back from the precipice, and Sokolov turned his head and gazed back at Zula with his blue eyes. An American would have made some sentimental gesture here, made it mawkish, but Sokolov contented himself with the tiniest nod and a suggestion of a wink. Zula responded by raising her hand and twitching her fingers in a suggestion of a wave. This was plenty for Sokolov, who snapped his head back around and returned to his occupation.

Olivia led her to a place where she and Sokolov had stashed a couple of mountain bikes. These were loaded with gear, much of which was now irrelevant—or perhaps of greater use to Sokolov than to them. All of this Olivia stripped off and left lying on the ground. They had come well supplied with water and food, a good deal of which went into Zula's mouth while Olivia was sorting through the rest. A first aid kit contained some over-the-counter painkillers, which Zula consumed at greater than the recommended dosage. Olivia helped Zula adjust the height of her seat post—she was apparently going to use what had been Sokolov's bicycle—and led her on a short ride up this outflung spur of rock toward the summit of the mountain. In a minute or so they came to a place where they could ramp down onto the faintest trace of a trail that tracked horizontally across the talus slope in the direction they wanted to go.

Their traversal of this seemed endless. It was enlivened at the beginning by some shots fired, apparently at them, from far below. It seemed that the jihadists were probing southward, trying to avoid or to outflank Sokolov's position by moving through the woods. An abandoned mining camp down at the bottom of the slope looked like it would provide lots of cover for the jihadists, if they could only reach it. But Olivia and Zula were far out of range, and Sokolov was continuing his policy of trying to pick off anyone who took shots at them, and so within a few minutes Zula had stopped worrying about gunmen and turned all her attentions to the project of just making it through the next hour or two. Part of the time they were able to ride the bicycles in their lowest gear, which was very low indeed, but for the most part it was more efficient to push or even carry the machines. Olivia insisted it was worth it, that the bicycles would come in very handy once they got through this part of the journey. Zula did not respond and hardly cared; she had descended into some numb and semicomatose state where all that was going on around her seemed to have been shone dimly onto a screen by a failing projector with a bad sound system.

But in time they made it to a place from which they could look down a clear and reasonably well-defined trail into a valley lined with dark green forest, and Zula remembered Uncle Richard's story about how he had long ago happened upon Prohibition Crick after a miserable, hot slog across an exposed and sun-blasted slope. She felt she knew the way down out of some family instinct, and she ignored Olivia's solicitous questions and polite suggestions that they stop for water and food. She threw a leg over the saddle of her bicycle and let gravity begin pulling her down into that valley, squeezing the brakes every second or two, making sure she didn't run out of control. She could hear Olivia following her in like style. This trail had lots of switchbacks too, but downhill switchbacks on a bicycle were, of course, pure ecstasy compared to uphill on foot, and so she did nothing but enjoy the ride and feel her spirits rise and her energy return for the first few minutes. Then Olivia's voice intruded on her awareness, warning her of something. She skidded to a halt and listened. Below them, an engine was snarling: not a chainsaw, but some sort of vehicle, a dirt bike or four-wheeler.

"That might be your uncles," Olivia said. Probably the wrong advice for Zula, who responded by releasing the brakes and letting the bike run downhill at a speed that was on the edge of being out of control. She managed to slow it down just enough to avoid spinning out at the next switchback, got it fishtailed around, built up speed again, and then had to slam the brakes hard to avoid a head-on collision with a camo-painted four-wheel ATV coming up the other way.

Uncle Jake was driving and Uncle John was riding on the jump seat in back, and both of them were carrying rifles and wearing preoccupied expressions. The transformation that came over their faces when they discovered Zula blocking their path was, she hoped, something she would remember for the rest of her life and tell people about at the re-u.

RICHARD HAD, OF course, packed for the trip hastily, Jones following him around the Schloss aiming a pistol at him and telling him to go faster. There'd been no shortage of warm clothes to choose from. All of it had been skiwear; the Schloss was not about hunting. He was now wearing a yellow parka and red snow pants, with white gloves and a blue hat. Underneath were a green flannel shirt and blue jeans. So he could make himself slightly less conspicuous by shedding the outerwear, at the cost of freezing to death.

Qian Yuxia was wearing just what the doctor ordered for this sort of affair: head-to-toe camouflage. When Richard pointed out the disparity, more out of black humor than anything else, she immediately offered to swap with him. But this would have taken a lot of time; her clothes wouldn't have covered much of his body; and it would have left her either freezing to death in her underwear or else a blaze of primary colors in Jahandar's telescopic sight.

She then offered to take the gun, find a good place to hide, and blow Jahandar away when he happened by. Which Richard would not have taken seriously had it been proposed by certain other women of Yuxia's age and stature. In her case, he found it entirely believable. But it would have been the first time she had ever fired a gun. She would only have one chance. She would have to wait until he came very close; if she misjudged the distance and fired too soon, she'd miss him, or just wound him lightly, and then he would tear her apart with high-velocity rounds while Richard watched helplessly from a hiding place. Not really the way Richard wanted to spend his last few minutes on earth.

They were running out of time, talking too much. Yuxia was becoming sort of a problem in that she simply would not be satisfied with anything less than an active role in the death of Jahandar. Faint rustling noises were sounding from down the slope, which could be explained in many different ways, but it was most prudent to assume that this was the approaching sniper.

They settled it like this: Richard moved downhill off their current switchback and crouched behind the root-ball of a huge tree that had toppled straight down the slope. The root-ball was at least twelve feet in diameter, a scraggly sunburst of enormous but shallow roots, interstices caulked with brown mud and with moss. It rose above him as an almost vertical wall. He could not have been more totally shielded from view; Jahandar could peer up the slope all he wanted, he could ascend the switchback that ran about ten yards below where Richard was crouching and never get any suggestion that Richard was there. By the same token, however, Richard couldn't see Jahandar.

Yuxia meanwhile maneuvered to a place directly uphill of Richard where she could squat in some undergrowth and peer out, almost impossible to see from below. She had a panoramic view of the slope beneath her and could look Richard in the eye from a distance of perhaps fifty feet. She would wait and watch for Jahandar to pass just below Richard, and raise both hands in the air at the moment when the sniper was immediately below the root-ball, moving laterally along the switchback below it.

Richard waited, watching Yuxia's face and listening to the sounds of the forest.

Ten minutes passed of what was very close to bliss, as far as Richard was concerned.

Zula was alive. He had seen her. But that didn't explain the bliss. After all, Chet was dead. Moreover, there was a seriously injured chopper pilot awaiting rescue up on the ridge. Any happiness he felt for Zula ought to have been outweighed by sadness for them.

So that wasn't it.

He was in beautiful wilderness that he had known for almost forty years, just sitting and waiting, alert and alive, banged up, half in shock, but probably soaked in endorphins and adrenaline for just that reason. And no one could reach him via phone or email, Twitter or Facebook, and bother him. His whole mind, his whole attention was focused on one thing for the first time that he could remember.

Occasional bangs sounded from higher up: people shooting at each other, he reckoned. Most of it sounded tentative, exploratory. What did John call it? Reconnaissance by fire. But then came a prolonged exchange, scores of rounds being fired, some from semiautomatic and others from fully automatic weapons, and he had the sense that it had come to a head somehow.

He knew that one side of this small war had to be Jones and his jihadists, but who was on the other side? Had the cops finally arrived? If so, why didn't they have helicopters?

These ruminations caused his attention to waver for some time, while also making it difficult to hear more subtle noises emanating from the trail below.

He became aware that Yuxia was gesticulating furiously. Which gave him a pang of guilt, since he got the idea that she had been signaling to him in a more discreet way for some time and that he had failed to notice it and forced her to make herself obvious.

She got a stricken look on her face and dropped from view.

A mighty crack sounded from what seemed like just over Richard's shoulder, and mud and moss exploded from the slope just behind where Yuxia's head had been a moment earlier.

Jahandar must have come up the trail behind Richard and passed all the way behind him, then looked uphill and seen Yuxia waving her arms.

He heard the bolt of the rifle being worked, ejecting the spent casing, chambering a new round. Then the rustle of clothing. Then the sound, amazingly crisp and distinct in the clear, quiet air, of a revolver's hammer being pulled back and cocked.

Why was Jahandar switching to a handgun?

Because he'd seen Yuxia gesturing, trying to get someone's attention down below. From that, he knew someone had to be down here, hiding. Waiting for him. And the obvious place to hide was the root-ball only a few yards away from where Jahandar was standing. The sniper rifle was not going to do him any good in that sort of a fight.

Slow, subtle rustling now as Jahandar stepped off the path, into the foliage, looking for a way to come around Richard's flank.

Richard had checked the shotgun a hundred times to verify that a shell was chambered, and forced himself not to do so again, since doing so would make a noise. He looked down and inspected the safety lever to make sure that the red dot was showing. It was ready to fire.

He had nestled himself back into a hollow among the dead tree's roots, which might not be the best situation since it was constraining his field of view, limiting his arm swing. He was considering how to improve this state of affairs without getting killed when his glance fell on a round stone, about the size of a baseball, that hundreds of years ago had gotten caught up in the root system of this tree and was now sticking out of the clotted mud down by his knee. Remembering a trick he had played as a boy, stalking and being stalked by John in the ravine of the farm crick, he acted now without thinking. Until this point he had been mired in a kind of psychological cold molasses. But now he just reached down with his left hand, found the rock, pulled it free from its mud matrix, and underhanded it into some shrubs about five yards off to his right. It flew soundlessly and probably invisibly, then rustled through the bushes and struck the ground with shocking and sudden noise. Jahandar responded immediately, firing a round at it, recocking. This gave away his position: too far off to the right for Richard to get a clear shot without moving farther away from the root-ball. Reckoning that it was now or never, Richard shoved off against the roots with his butt, pivoting around his planted right foot as his left swung around like the leg of a compass tracing a ninety-degree arc. At the same time he was bringing the shotgun up, getting the barrel and the bead aligned with the pupil of his eye, wondering when the hell Jahandar was going to swim into his sight picture. Finally he saw Jahandar in his peripheral vision and realized he had not pivoted far enough; he gave his hips an extra twitch. His left foot was coming down, a bit sooner than he'd have liked; he tried to raise the knee, delay the footfall, give himself some extra rotation, but the result was that the toe hooked on a root and torqued badly. He was falling to his left now, balance lost, still lacking a solid plant for the left foot, which came down hard and uncontrolled on whatever happened to be there. Whatever it was, it was slippery and uneven and made his foot twist around in a way that it wasn't supposed to. He felt no pain, yet. He had glanced away from Jahandar for just a fraction of a second. He now returned his attention to the sights. Jahandar was gone. He had executed some sort of dive-and-roll back onto the trail. Richard was tempted to fire blindly but held his finger away from the trigger, mindful of the limited number of shells in the magazine. Reconnaissance by fire wasn't going to work for him.

Getting low seemed to be a good idea and so he let himself drop, which was already happening anyway: his ankle was badly messed up, and the first spike of pain had just made it up his leg to his brain. He took his left hand off the shotgun's forearm and let its barrel go vertical for a few moments as he tumbled back onto his ass, using his left hand to break the fall just a bit.

Then he looked up to see Jahandar staring at him through a gap between dangling roots, no more than ten feet away. Jahandar was just in the act of bringing his revolver up to bear on Richard.

Richard, who had been so much at gravity's mercy an instant ago, now found it too weak and slow to bring the shotgun's barrel down as fast as he would like. Rather than wait here to get shot, he twitched his body sideways, flinging himself down onto his back and then his side, rolling away. A younger man on better terrain might have rolled all the way over and come back up firing, but Richard bogged down in rocks and tree roots about halfway through this maneuver and found himself in the worst possible situation of having to get up on hands and knees with his ass pointed squarely in Jahandar's direction and the shotgun down in the mud. How could anything go so badly wrong? It was just like John's Vietnam stories, the ones he told when he was drunk and weeping. A pistol was *banging, banging, banging*. Richard wasn't dead yet. His mind had registered something odd about that banging, but he hadn't had time to think about it yet. An eternity later he fell heavily onto his ass, finally facing toward the enemy, finally with the shotgun up where he wanted it. He expected to see Jahandar still aiming the revolver his way, fire spurting from the barrel and all but scorching Richard's nylon parka, but the jihadist had turned to look downhill and had crouched down so that only the curve of his back was showing.

The banging hadn't come from Jahandar's pistol. It must be Seamus, firing from farther way.

Richard, taking advantage of the slope, rolled up onto his feet, got a clear view of Jahandar's center of mass, aimed the shotgun, and fired. He then collapsed facefirst into the root-ball as his ankle gave way beneath his weight. A broken-off root jabbed him in the eye. His hand came up involuntarily, and the shotgun tumbled into his lap. He heard himself letting out a brief scream.

In the silence that followed, a gentle footfall, very nearby. He looked up with his one operant eye and saw nothing but the forest moving alongside him. The shotgun slid out of his lap as if moving under its own power.

Qian Yuxia jerked the forearm back. Sharply. A spent shell flew out and bounced off Richard's head. She rammed it home, then raised it to her shoulder. Someone said, in a gurgling voice, *"Allahu akbar,"* but the final syllable was buried in the shotgun's muzzle blast.

"Nice," pronounced a voice. The voice of Seamus. "But don't stand so fucking close to him next time. I almost nailed you."

"Dream on," said Qian Yuxia.

SOKOLOV WATCHED THE departure of Olivia and Zula with a vast sense of relief: an emotion that he would, of course, never be able to share, or even hint at, with those two estimable females. By this point he had seen enough of them to know that they were cooler under pressure, and better to be with in a tight spot, than 999 out of 1,000 women. But their presence obliged him to divert a significant fraction of his attention into being considerate of their needs, responding to their inquiries, and keeping them alive. In most other circumstances it would have been no trouble at all, and more than repaid by the pleasure of their company. But this business now was going to be formidable trouble, and he needed to think of it to the exclusion of all else.

The environment was, on the whole, markedly Afghanistan-like. The jihadists would feel at home here, would instinctively know how to move, where to seek cover, how to react. Sokolov, of course, had done his time in Afghanistan. But that was long ago, and most of his work since then had been of a decidedly urban character. Advantage Jones.

There were more of them. Sokolov was alone, at least until such time as Zula and Olivia could get back to the compound where the fanatics—those American Taliban—lived with all their guns and their stockpiles of ammunition and materiel. Even then, it was not clear to what extent those people could form themselves up into an effective force on short notice. It was clear that Zula's relatives were well armed and that they had the marksmanship part of the curriculum well covered. But military recruits spent only a small portion of their time actually shooting at targets; other forms of training were ultimately more important. Even supposing that they did come out from their bunkers with their assault rifles and their expensive knives, they might be more hazard than help to Sokolov. He had no way of communicating with them. They were as likely to identify him as foe than as friend. Soon he might have not just one but two groups of well-armed mountain men trying to kill him. Advantage Jones.

Sokolov was operating completely alone, which, while it technically placed him at a numerical disadvantage, conferred another sort of benefit in that he did not have to coordinate his actions with anyone else. No communication meant no foul-ups. The tiniest bit of cover could be used to advantage. Advantage Sokolov, provided he kept his distance and avoided getting surrounded.

So that—not getting surrounded—was what the Americans called the Name of the Game. Zula's startling emergence from the wilderness had obliged him to give away his position. Had it not been for that, he'd have waited for all the jihadists to expose themselves on the slope below and then spent the morning picking them off.

According to Olivia—who had obtained the information from Zula—the size of Jones's contingent had been nine this morning. One of them had somehow been killed hours ago. During the action just concluded, Sokolov and Zula had each accounted for one. That left six unaccounted for. It was possible that Sokolov's suppressing fire had hit someone down in the trees, but he doubted it.

Another detail: Zula reported that a rear guard of unknown size—quite likely no more than two men—was an hour or two behind Jones's main group. But one of them was a sniper.

Which raised the question of whether any of the men down below Sokolov might be so equipped. He had engaged in several exchanges of fire with them so far, but with so many opponents, all concealed in the forest, spraying rounds at him from different directions, it had been difficult for him to take a census of their weapons. From sound alone it was obvious that most of them had submachine guns or assault rifles. But the infrequent firing of a bolt-action sniper rifle could easily have gotten lost in all that noise. Some of them might have been packing scopes in their bags, and for all he knew they were down there right now mounting better optics on the weapons that he knew about. Sokolov's gun was pretty and expensive, with a nice scope on it, but its barrel and its ammunition imposed certain inherent limitations on its effective range. In a sniping duel against a man armed with a proper long-range weapon, he would lose.

Earlier, Olivia had assisted him by bringing a sleeping bag, food, and water right up to the edge of the rock where he had made his little nest. It had become comfortable to a degree that was actively endangering his life; he was reluctant to move from this location that had already been made known to the enemy. As a first step toward abandoning it, he wriggled back to a spot from which he could not be seen from below, then devoted a few minutes to teasing a sleeping bag out of its nylon sack and loosely restuffing it into his parka. He pulled the hood up and made sure that it was packed tight enough to keep it round, then poked his sunglasses into it and wrapped a scarf around the lower part of its "face." The whole time he was doing this he was feeling a moderate sense of embarrassment at playing such a cheap trick. But he had read all the old propaganda stories about the snipers of Stalingrad and knew that they had achieved much with a repertoire of simple gambits such as this one. When it was complete, he crawled forward, pushing the effigy before him so that its head would pop into view over the edge of the rock long before Sokolov himself became exposed.

A mirror would have been nice to have at this point, but he lacked one. He had to use his ears. The result of the experiment was a fusillade of reports from perhaps four different weapons, most of them firing multiple rounds in semiautomatic mode, which was to say that they were shooting one bullet per trigger pull rather than simply opening up with bursts. They were, in other words, aiming. Perhaps Jones had finally made it to the top of the trail and imposed some discipline. Rounds cracked into the rock near the effigy, others whined overhead. Sokolov closed his eyes and listened for the slow, heavy cadence of a bolt-action rifle firing high-powered rounds. A jerk ran down his arm as the effigy took a bullet in the head, and he heard a plasticky clatter as the sunglasses fell out and bounced down the cliff face below.

So at least one person down there was a good shot with a properly zeroed assault rifle. But if they had a sniper's weapon per se, they had decided not to use it; and that was, in these circumstances, an odd decision. Zula had told Olivia that there was a sniper in the rear guard. Perhaps he had all the good stuff with him.

Or perhaps a fantastically good long-range weapon was aimed at his location at this very moment and its operator, having detected Sokolov's pathetic masquerade through his excellent telescopic scope, had elected not to show his hand.

Taking only what he thought he'd need to survive the next few hours, Sokolov pulled back from the edge of the rock. Jones's vanguard might have been idiots, but Darwinian selection had now removed them from the battle, and the only people left down there were the smart and cautious remainder, probably being led personally by Jones. They'd not expose themselves to his fire again. If they were feeling extraordinarily feisty, they might look for a way to outflank his position and get him in a cross fire, but this would take half the day, and they must know they didn't have that long. The tree line stretched south all the way to—well, to wherever the hell these men needed to go. Moving through the forest was slow and awkward, but preferable to being shot at from above. That, Sokolov was quite sure, was what they would do. They would only post some sort of rear guard to keep an eye out for him and make sure he didn't fall on them from behind.

His understanding of the local geography was not perfect, but he had the general sense that, on their way out to the open highways of the United States, they would pass near to the compounds of the American Taliban. Had it not been for the fact that Olivia and Zula were headed for one of those compounds right now, Sokolov might have been tempted to set up a blind and wait for the stragglers Zula had warned him of. The American survivalists, after all, could take care of themselves, and Sokolov was not above feeling a certain "plague on both your houses" attitude toward these groups.

But as it was, he felt obliged to pursue these men. They would already have a considerable head start. He ought to be able to erase this, however, by moving through open territory and proceeding generally downslope.

He ran over the top of the big rock, following roughly in the tracks that Zula and Olivia had made a bit earlier, and then began working his way judiciously down the talus slope. Below he could see the abandoned mining facility. He had not examined this carefully when he and Olivia had passed above it a few hours ago. Now he confirmed his vague memory that the place was overgrown with scrub trees and high weeds. For it was situated right at the edge of the zone where it was possible for vegetation to survive. Beyond it was the mature forest through which the jihadists were moving, or would be soon.

He was exposed on this slope, but it offered enough scraps of cover that—being that he was a lone operative, not a platoon—he could move from one to the next, throwing himself down when he reached them and making little stops to listen and observe. For about the first half of his progress down the talus field, he neither saw nor heard a thing. The jihadists—assuming they were coming this way—had been forced to work their way around a lobe of the mountain, traveling two kilometers to cover one kilometer of straight-line distance. Sokolov was just hurtling somewhat recklessly down the southern face of that landform, so it was to be expected that he would not see them at first. The seventeen-year-old buck private in him just wanted to sprint all the way to the bottom and take cover in the old mine buildings strewn invitingly around the base of the slope. The veteran wanted to creep on his belly from one cover to the next, never rising to his feet, never exposing himself. In the early going, the buck private won the argument, but as he lost more and more altitude, the verge of the forest began to seem more and more fraught with hazards and the veteran's approach began to take over. He was lower down now, more on a level with any possible attackers, and this made it easier to find cover.

He came to a point where he could definitely hear the jihadists making their way through the trees, and then it became a matter of calibration: he didn't have as far to travel now, but he had to do it more carefully. They did not appear to think that he was nearby. Perhaps they believed that, in shooting the effigy atop the rock, they had killed Sokolov. Perhaps they had become confused as to geography. In any case, they did not know that he had come around from another direction to engage them, and as long as they remained in that state of ignorance he had a huge advantage that could be lost in an instant if he behaved indiscreetly. And so the last part of Sokolov's journey was a reenactment of the very worst moments of his special forces training: he spent the whole time crawling on his belly, at first over sharp rocks and then over sopping ice-cold mud overgrown with thorny and poky vegetation.

But this got him, at last, into the precincts of the mining camp, which was a generally flat bottomland at forest's edge, really a kind of sump that had accepted more snowmelt in the last few weeks than it could absorb. It extended perhaps fifty meters from the base of the slope to the edge of the true forest and several hundred meters in the direction parallel to the slope, and it was scattered with abandoned trucks, trailers, shacks, and one structure that seemed to be an actual log cabin. Sokolov gravitated to the latter. Its cedar-shake roof had long since fallen in to cover its floor, and windblown pine needles and other such debris had collected in the lee of its walls, almost a meter deep. Sokolov burrowed into the needle pile, then reached around him and arranged the stuff to form a mound of camouflage, nothing showing except for the snout of his Makarov.

Then he relaxed and sipped from his CamelBak tube. Ten minutes later, he was listening as Jones, probably standing no more than twenty meters away, gave orders to his men. Sokolov's Arabic was rusty. Even without the half-remembered vocabulary he had managed to retain, he could guess what Jones was saying, simply based upon the tactical realities of the situation. He was telling some of his men—probably no more than two of them—to find suitable cover in this mining camp and keep an eye on the slope above. Anyone trying to make his way down that slope should be tracked until he was close enough to make for easy shooting, then shot. Anyone taking the high road should be harassed with long-range fire, which might not hit the target but would at least give him something to think about while warning Jones and the others that they were being shadowed from the commanding heights.

Jones then moved on with the main group.

The ones he'd left behind talked to each other in low tones for a minute and then began to explore the camp, looking for places where they could take cover and wait. Sokolov was now convinced that there were exactly two of them.

One of them walked straight into the cabin. He was a tall slender East African man, quite young. Sokolov shot him twice in the chest and then, while the boy was standing there wondering if this was really happening, once in the head.

Having had plenty of time to inventory the escape routes from this structure, he exploded from under the pile of pine needles, got a leg up on an old table, and vaulted through a vacant window opening. He was fairly certain that this placed most of the log cabin between him and the other jihadist, who was out familiarizing himself with an abandoned truck. Moving around to a location from which he could see said truck, he unslung the rifle, brought it up, and fired four rounds through its sheet metal, distributed through the part of the cab where a terrified man would be likely to throw himself down.

Answering fire came out of weeds ten meters from the truck and forced him to drop into a lower crouch. Looking back up a moment later, he saw a man in full sprint toward an outhouse. Getting a moving target centered in his sights, at this distance, that fast, was impossible. Instead he drew a solid bead on the outhouse and fired four more rounds through it. The bullets would pass all the way through the structure and out the other side, probably not hitting anything but keeping the runner honest.

He then embarked on a retreat toward the edge of the woods. The fight had begun too soon: less than a minute since Jones and the main group had departed. They would come back, they would figure out where he was, and they would surround him. Given more time, Sokolov would have won the duel with the man hiding behind the outhouse. As it was, he had no choice but to make himself scarce in the most excellent hiding place he could find, and wait for them to move on.

On cue the other four jihadists came running back out of the woods firing undisciplined bursts. The man behind the outhouse called for a cease-fire and then stood up, exposing himself in a manner that verged on insolent. This man was both good and brave: he was daring Sokolov to take a shot at him and give away his position. Sokolov, inching out of the mining camp on his back, was tempted. But he was making an obvious track in the mud that they would soon find and follow. His only purpose for the next quarter of an hour was to get into the woods and run and hide. If he survived that, the jihadists would begin moving again, and his pursuit of them could resume.

THE SUV BOTTOMED out in a dip, angled sharply upward, and vaulted a sharp rise, nearly jumping into the air. In the same instant, they came in view of a wide spot, just ahead, where a smaller road forked off to the left and strayed up into the mountains. Two vehicles had taken advantage of this to pull over to the side of the road. One was the Subaru wagon they'd been tailing. The other was a dust-caked Camry. Both vehicles' doors were hanging open, in perfect position for them to be sheared off by the bumper of the onrushing SUV. Men had emerged from both cars and were holding an impromptu conference around the back of the Camry. Some were looking at maps spread out on its rear window. One had a laptop open on the Subaru's hood and was pointing something out to another. A man was pacing up and down the shoulder of the road, talking into a very large phone. No, on second thought that thing was a walkie-talkie. Most of them were smoking. There were at least eight of them—more than could be counted at a glance. All their heads turned to look in alarm at the SUV, which fishtailed wildly at the top of the rise as Csongor twitched the steering wheel. For a moment, nearly airborne, the big vehicle had practically no grip on the road. Then it slammed back down onto its suspension.

"Left!" Marlon shouted. "Go left!"

Csongor gunned it up the little road that forked off to the left. As they blew past the parked vehicles, Marlon gave them a cheerful grin and a friendly wave. These pleasantries were not returned. Csongor felt the tires losing traction for a moment as he shifted course, and all the muscles in his neck and back went hard as he imagined bullets coming in through the tailgate. But then they were on their way up the little side road, going considerably slower now as this one was even steeper, windier, and rougher than the one they'd just turned off of. "Just keep going," Marlon said.

"I get it."

"They have guns."

Csongor turned to look at him. "You saw guns?"

"No. But when we came over the hill, their hands moved." He pantomimed a jerk of the elbow, a reach of grasping fingers toward a concealed weapon.

"Crap. So now there's, what, eight of them?"

"At least."

"Where was that Toyota from?"

"Some place with a lot of dirt."

Csongor had been gradually tapering the SUV's speed down to little more than a walking pace. They had rapidly gained altitude and now found themselves creeping along the edge of a slope so steep that some might accuse it of being a cliff. In any case, it was too steep for trees to grow on, so Marlon now had an excellent view down toward the river and the main road that snaked along its bank. "Okay, they are moving again," he announced, from this Olympian perspective.

"We must have spooked them."

"We should turn around and go back," Marlon said, "because this road goes friggin' nowhere."

But Csongor, lacking Marlon's view to the side, had been scanning the territory ahead and begged to differ. "These roads are for the men who cut down the trees," he said. He was unsure of the English term for that occupation, and even if he had known it, Marlon might not have recognized it. "They go all over the place." And indeed, in another few hundred meters—once they had gotten clear of an out-thrust lobe of mountain that accounted for the steep slope—the road forked again, the left fork winding up a valley into the mountains, the right plunging downhill. Csongor took the latter. A few seconds later they passed through another such intersection and found themselves on a short spur that dropped straight down to rejoin the road along the river. Once again they were following a dust trail. But it was so dense now that they could not see more than a hundred or so meters into it; the Subaru and the Camry might be just ahead of them, easily close enough that they could shoot back out their windows and hit the SUV. Csongor had to steady his nerves by reminding himself that the dust was even thicker in the wake of those vehicles; they could peer back out their rear windows all they wanted, but they wouldn't be able to see anything, not even a vehicle as big as this one.

Along a curve of the river they caught sight of the lead vehicle—the Camry—just a short distance ahead of them, and Marlon exhorted him to drop back a little bit, lest they be spotted.

"What the hell are we going to do when we get to the end of the road?" Csongor asked.

The question elicited a slack-jawed, distracted expression from Marlon. It occurred to Csongor that Marlon, born and raised in a colossal, densely packed city, had no instincts that were useful for being out in the middle of fucking nowhere.

"Hide," Marlon said, "and wait for them to come back out. Then we follow them out. When we get to that town, we stop and call the cops."

"We could just do that here."

"There's no place to hide here." Marlon spoke an evident truth; the road was a narrow graveled ledge trapped between a mountain and a river.

But Marlon's rejoinders had been coming more and more slowly, and after this one he went silent for a while.

"We should start looking for a place to hide," Csongor offered, just trying to be agreeable. "Maybe there will be something up here." For the valley was now broadening, as if the river were about to divide into tributaries. The distance between the road and the riverbank grew rapidly, and soon their view of the stream was blocked by dense coniferous forest, brightened here and there by the fresh shoots and buds of deciduous trees. The general trend was uphill, but the terrain was flatter than what they had passed through minutes before; they seemed to have found their way into some high, broad valley among the mountains. Until seeing this, Csongor had supposed that they had ventured beyond the limit of civilization and entered into wilderness, but now he understood that they had merely been driving through a natural bottleneck. Cleared land, livestock, mailboxes, and houses began to complicate their view.

"We should keep going," Csongor said. "Maybe there is a town or something."

"There is no town on the map," Marlon said, fixated upon the *Atlas and Gazetteer*. "Just a mountain, name of Abandon. Then Canada."

"Then maybe we should just pull into one of these places and ask for help," Csongor said. He slowed down and took the next right, turning into a driveway that ran into the woods for a few meters—just enough to accommodate a stopped vehicle—before terminating in a gate.

"TRESPASSERS WILL BE SHOT," Marlon said, reading words spray-painted in foot-high letters on a sheet of plywood that covered most of the gate. "What is a trespasser? Some kind of animal?"

"It's us," Csongor said, throwing the SUV into reverse and gunning it backward onto the road.

They proceeded without further discussion for a kilometer or so, then slowed down as they approached a whorl of dust filling the whole road cut, from tree line to tree line. Csongor took his foot off the accelerator and let the SUV idle forward. The windshield was a dusty mess, so he motored his window down and leaned out to get a clear view.

This made it possible for him to see that a big vehicle—a pickup truck, red—was stopped in the oncoming lane, pointed toward them. No silhouette was visible behind its steering wheel. This struck Csongor as deeply wrong.

A figure emerged from the dust, walking up along the driver's side of the truck. Behind him was a second man, moving in the same way. The first of them reached the driver's door and pulled at the handle but found it to be locked. He then reached in through the window, which was apparently open, and got it unlocked. This was accompanied by some strange pawing gestures that caused little cascades of sparkly bits to tumble out of the window frame and scatter on the ground.

"Broken glass," Marlon said.

The man hauled the door open and then backed away, as if aghast at what he was seeing there. He paused for a moment, pulled a walkie-talkie from his belt, and said something into it. Then he reholstered the radio and nodded to his companion. The two of them bent forward as one and reached into the truck's cab, then hauled back.

What they dragged out of the cab was clearly recognizable as a limp human form even though its head had been blown apart into a soggy mushroomlike thing trailing gray stuff that had to be brains. The feet came out last; clad in a pair of high-topped work boots, they bounced off the truck's running board and then hit the ground heels first.

"Shit, Csongor. Csongor! CSONGOR!" Marlon was calling.

Csongor was so transfixed by the sight of the body that he had stopped paying attention to the two living men who were dragging it by the arms. He now noticed, dully, that those men were staring directly up into his face from no more than about ten meters away.

Then he felt something come down hard on his knee and sensed the steering wheel moving free of his hands. The SUV surged forward, veered left, then right, then left again. The corpse-dragging men were filling the windshield; then they disappeared beneath the edge of its hood and the vehicle thumped and bucked as it smashed them back into the pavement and rolled over them.

Csongor looked down to see Marlon's left hand on his knee, shoving his foot down into the gas, and his right hand on the steering wheel. Marlon had flung himself sideways across the SUV's cab and was practically in Csongor's lap.

"I got this," Csongor said. "I got it! Fine!" Marlon relented and wriggled back into the passenger seat.

"Maybe we should go back and get their guns," Marlon suggested.

"That's how it would work in a video game," Csongor said, which was his way of agreeing. He allowed the gas pedal to come up off the floor for a moment.

Then Marlon hollered as the rear end of the Subaru became visible just ahead of them. Men were standing around it, looking up in alarm. Csongor twisted the wheel to avoid them. Then remembered that these were the guys they wanted to run over. Tried to correct the error. Felt the vehicle tilt beneath them as it went up on two wheels.

In his peripheral vision, something was coming at him. He looked out Marlon's window to see that it was the road, hinging straight up into the glass. Marlon was spinning away from it, bringing his hands up to protect his face.

That they had rolled over was obvious enough. What didn't become obvious for several moments was that they had rolled over *all the way* and ended up sitting upright on all four wheels, sideways on the road, rocking gently from side to side on the suspension.

Csongor looked out his open window and saw jihadists (it was time to start calling them that) reaching into their garments, just as Marlon had pantomimed a few minutes ago.

He swung the wheel. "Get down!" he said.

Glass was breaking all around him. His door had been sprung off its hinges during the rollover. He pushed it open to provide some space for him to lean sideways. Looking straight down at the road, using its edge as a guide, he got the SUV pointed in what he hoped was the correct direction and punched the accelerator.

A few moments later he sat up straight, just in time to see that he was making for a head-on collision with a fat man riding down the middle of the road on an all-terrain vehicle, a rifle in his lap. Some mutual swerving occurred, and they just avoided hitting each other.

He looked over to see that Marlon was, at least, moving. He had banged his head on something during the rollover and was bleeding from a laceration, stanching it with a wad of *Gazetteer*.

The road went into a gentle leftward curve. Rustic houses went by them, mostly on the right.

Some of them began to look familiar, and he understood that he was driving in circles. The road had terminated in a big loop. There was nowhere he could go from here.

Except, possibly, up a driveway? He had to do *something* because the jihadists would be coming soon—might be running laps on the same loop already—and they had him bottled up here, at the head of the valley. He paused at the entrance to one driveway, saw a white man coming down it holding an assault rifle. An assault rifle! He gunned it forward to the next driveway, but this one was blocked, just off the road, by a gate. No place to hide from vengeful jihadists.

The driveway after that seemed to wind off into the woods for some distance. Csongor, reacting without thinking, turned down it, praying that the move wasn't being observed by any of the people who were pursuing them. Because this not was a decision he could take back; he couldn't assume that there was a handy infinite loop at the end of *this* road.

It went around a single bend and terminated in a massive timber gate. Csongor crunched it to a stop, then took advantage of a little wide spot that had been cleared, just in front of this barrier, to make it possible for wayward vehicles to turn around. Even so, getting the SUV reversed in such a tight spot required many back-and-forths. During a few of these, he found himself gazing curiously out his window at a panoply of documents that had been laminated in weatherproof plastic and stapled to the wood. None of them seemed to be direct threats to kill him. They were more in the way of legal filings and political/religious manifestos.

A word passed in front of his eyes that took a moment to sink in. When it did, he stomped the brake. Reversed the vehicle's direction. Then crept back the way he'd come, as slowly as he could make the vehicle move. Scanning the documents on the gate, unwilling to believe he'd actually seen it.

"What is *up*, bro?" Marlon demanded. Then he called out "Aiyaa!" as Csongor stomped the brake again, jerking the vehicle, and him, and his aching head.

"I think I get it now," Csongor said.

"Get what?"

"What's happening."

He was staring at a document—a sort of open letter—signed at the bottom. The signature was so neat that you could actually read it. It said, JACOB FORTHRAST.

UNCLE JOHN DROVE the all-terrain vehicle back toward Jake's cabin with Zula sitting on the luggage rack behind him. Jake rode her bicycle. Olivia and Jake chivalrously suggested that those two ride on ahead as fast as possible, the bicyclists catching up as soon as they could. John, though, was averse to any plan that involved splitting up; and the intensity of his reaction as much as proved that he was recollecting something that had not worked out very well in Vietnam. The journey back was therefore carried out in a tortoise-and-hare mode, the ATV running forward for a few hundred yards and then idling along while Jake and Olivia caught up with them.

During these pauses, John would try to communicate with persons not present. The people who lived around Prohibition Crick had gone there specifically to get off the grid, and so excellent phone reception was not among their priorities. They were not the sort to look benignly on phone company technicians crawling around the neighborhood hiding cables under the ground and setting up mysterious antennas to bathe every cubic inch of their living space with encoded emanations. In spite of which, you could sometimes get one bar if you stood in a high, exposed place in just the right posture. But they were in some combination of too far from the down-valley cell towers and too deeply trapped in the folds of Abandon Mountain's lower slopes for this to work.

John also had a walkie-talkie, which Jake and members of his family tended to take along with them as a safety measure when they ventured into the wilderness on hunting and huckleberry-picking expeditions. This was of a common brand, pocket-sized, and notoriously fickle when used in the convoluted landscape of the Selkirks; sometimes they could reach people from twenty miles away, sometimes they were no better than shouting at each other. John's first few efforts to reach Elizabeth back at the cabin were unavailing.

After that, Zula took the device from him and hit on the idea of trying some of the other channels. The device was capable of using twenty-two of them. John had left it set on channel 11, which was the one that the Forthrast family was in the habit of using. Zula hit the Down button and indexed this all the way to 1, pausing on each channel for a few moments to listen for traffic. Then she worked her way back up to 11 and attempted to hail Elizabeth a few more times, with no results. Then up to 12. Nothing. Then she moved up to 13. A barrage of noise came out of the thing's tiny speaker, and she had to turn the volume down. Several people were trying to transmit on the same channel all at once, and all of them were shouting.

"Why is channel 13 special?" she called back to Jake, who was jogging along about fifty feet behind the ATV.

"Community emergency channel," he said. "Why?"

"I think there's an emergency."

"That's why Elizabeth hasn't answered," John suggested. "She must have switched over to 13." He gunned the ATV ahead and gave Zula a few hundred yards' rough ride to a spot where the trail swung around a root of the mountain and gave them a view—albeit distant, dusty, and cluttered by trees—down into the valley. Sporadic gunfire and sounds of roaring engines were spiraling up from below.

The voices on channel 13 were a bit clearer now, but still fragmentary as different transmissions stepped on each other. A man kept breaking in to insist on the need for radio discipline. "Cut the chatter!" "Copy." "Pennsylvania plates . . ." "Come again?" "Multiple vehicles . . ." "Black SUV, two subjects . . ." "Frank is dead, repeat, they ambushed him in his truck . . ." "Camry . . ." "Full auto . . ."

It required a minute or two for Zula to absorb this. She assumed at first that word of Jones's approach had preceded him into the valley and that she was listening to the sounds of the community preparing to be invaded from out of the north. But this could not be reconciled with all that she was hearing about vehicles—vehicles that had to be coming up out of the south.

"He must have friends," she concluded, "come up here to meet him."

John knew who *he* was, and approximately what *he* was doing, because Zula had been giving him an update during the ride. He considered it and shrugged. "It's not like he was going to hitchhike around the U.S. He'd have to have confederates. I guess they're here." He thought about it some more, gazing back at Olivia and Jake who were huffing and puffing along in their wake. "I wonder what they were expecting. Probably just empty logging roads. Jake's community doesn't have a name, doesn't show up on maps. Still, it's odd that they would come in shooting."

Jake had not heard the radio traffic, but the gunfire coming up out of the valley was clear enough, and he had a look in his eye that Zula hoped she'd never again see on a loved one's face. He was up here, and his wife and children were down there, where the fighting was.

John saw it too. "They know what to do," he reminded his kid brother. "You can be sure that they're bunkered down and they're fine."

"I have to get down there," Jake said.

Without a word John hopped off the ATV, turning it over to Jake. Zula rolled off the back and came up on her feet, a little unsteady but feeling much better.

Jake turned off the trail and began plunging down the slope, cutting across switchbacks wherever he could.

"It's about one click from here," John said. "Descending steep slopes is not my strong suit. I suggest you healthy young ladies proceed together and I'll bring up the rear." Slung over his back had been a hunting rifle of the old school, with a brown wooden stock and a telescopic sight. Zula knew he had carried it along only in case he needed it to deal with an enraged bear. He now stripped this weapon off his shoulder and held it out to Zula. "Pump action," he said. "Thirty ought six, four rounds in the magazine."

Some part of Zula—the small-town upbringing—wanted to say, *Oh no I couldn't possibly,* but she stifled it; the look on the face of her uncle—who, for all practical purposes, had been her father for the last fifteen years—said that he would not brook any argument. She remembered, just for an instant, the day that the meth heads had come to the farm to steal their anhydrous ammonia.

So she only uttered a single word, which was "Thanks."

OLIVIA TURNED OUT to be pretty spry—more than a match, anyway, for Zula in her current condition. They hewed mostly to the trail and occasionally crossed tracks that had been carved across it by Jake in his impetuous plunge. Zula's expectation that Jake would soon get far ahead of them turned out to be wrong. When the ATV moved, it moved faster than they could run, but he seemed to spend an inordinate amount of time hung up on obstacles or working his way around slopes too steep for it to negotiate. Its sound was always there, just a bit ahead of them, occasionally drowned out by gunfire. Some sort of weird, inappropriate family-competitive instinct made Zula want to catch and surpass it. But before this happened, they came in view of the cabin itself, its green sheet-metal roof nestled among the peaks of the surrounding trees, and then it became all about getting there as fast and as directly as possible.

Jake and his family had gone through the forest within a hundred-meter radius of the cabin and removed all small scrubby undergrowth and pruned away the dead, ladderlike branches that tended to project from the trunks of mature conifers. This was supposedly an anti-forest-fire measure; it would prevent blazes from storming through the dry understory and consuming the house. It had the side effect of vastly increasing visibility. In the natural woods of these parts, you couldn't see farther than a few dozen yards because of all that clutter, but from the windows of Jake's cabin you could see all the way to the edge of the zone they had cleared. Which made Zula suspect that it was also a tactical measure, making it more difficult for people to sneak up on them through the woods. Whatever its purpose, the upshot was that when Olivia and Zula burst into that zone, they suddenly had a clear view all the way to the back of the cabin, where Jake had just finished jumping off the ATV. He made straight for the cellar door, a pair of heavy-gauge steel hatches mounted on an angled frame of reinforced concrete.

Zula watched as those doors opened and Elizabeth, strapped with a shotgun in addition to her usual Glock semiautomatic, came out to throw her arms around her husband and give him a kiss.

But it was not a long, fond sort of reunion, for her next act was to grab Jake's face between her hands and tell him something that looked very important. As she spoke, she turned her head signifi- cantly toward the front side of the cabin.

Jake nodded, gave Elizabeth a peck, and stepped back. Elizabeth backed down the steps and hauled the doors closed on top of her- self. Zula, now sprinting through the trees no more than fifty paces away, had an impulse to call, *No, wait for us!* But she was too out of breath to make any sounds other than gasping, and—on second thought—being trapped in a bomb shelter with Elizabeth and the boys did not actually sound that appealing.

Jake meanwhile had unslung his rifle and chambered a round and gone into a style of movement that he must have learned by attending a tactical rifle combat seminar or else by watching DVDs of action films. The gist of it was that he kept the rifle aimed in the same direction as he was looking, and he tended to go very cau- tiously around corners.

Zula managed to call out, "Coming at you from behind, Uncle Jake!" since there was something in his body language that suggested he might not take kindly to being surprised.

He turned back and made a shushing gesture, then ventured around the corner of the building and disappeared from their view.

Zula was trying to make sense of it. Lots and lots of armed bad men in front of the cabin would call for Jake to go down below with his family and to gather Zula and Olivia with him. So whatever was in front couldn't be that bad.

"I want to see what is there," Zula said, breaking stride, and making a lateral move, swinging wide around the same side of the cabin up which Jake was creeping. "I might be able to help." She swept the rifle down off her shoulder.

"May I join you?" Olivia said between gasps for air.

"Of course." Olivia seemed to be joining her in any case.

The ground was uneven, the sight lines interrupted not only by tree trunks but by piles of firewood and outbuildings. They were moving in a wide swing around the property while Jake advanced in a straight line up the side of the cabin. So an anxious and confused minute passed as they tried to get Jake back in view without exposing themselves to whomever might be coming up the driveway. They ran afoul of chicken-wire enclosures that the Forthrasts had erected to keep rabbits away from their vegetables, coyotes and lynx away from their chickens, wolves and cougars away from their goats. But finally Zula swung into position where she was able to see Jake from the waist up, standing in his driveway, leveling his rifle at a target nearby, and shouting.

Zula stood up cautiously. Two heads came into view, down at the level of Jake's waist. Were they kneeling? Both of them had their hands on tops of their heads, fingers laced together.

One of them looked awfully familiar. But what she was thinking could not be real. Checking to make sure that the safety was engaged, she raised the rifle and used its telescopic sight to peer at the one on the right. A big man, not much shorter than Jake even on his knees. Burly. Close-cropped copper hair and a sunburned neck.

"OMFG," she said.

"Two men are coming in through the gate," Olivia said, "and I don't much like their looks."

Zula panned the rifle down the length of the driveway until the crosshairs found the big timber gate. This was ajar. A half-wrecked SUV was partly visible through it, blocking the road. And just as Olivia had said, two men had just circumvented the vehicle and were now coming around the edge of the gate. They perfectly matched the profile of the jihadists Zula had been hanging around with for the last three weeks. One of them had a pistol drawn, the other had a carbine, which he now raised to his shoulder, apparently drawing a bead on Jake: the most obvious target. And the most vulnerable.

Zula got the crosshairs on the latter and pulled the trigger. Nothing happened.

"Look out!" Olivia screamed.

Zula flicked the safety off and tried it again. The shot apparently missed; she was breathing hard and she hadn't really braced herself properly. But it had a remarkable effect on the two jihadists, who jumped back around behind what they perceived as the shelter of the gate and threw themselves down on the ground.

Shouting now from the driveway. She clearly recognized Csongor's voice, and she understood his tone: *Are you crazy? We're the good guys!*

"The Asian gentleman," said Olivia, "I recognize from his hoops career in Xiamen. Marlon, it must be. And may I assume that the big lad is the famous Csongor?"

Lady, who the fuck are you? was what Zula wanted to say. Instead, what came out was: "Uncle Jake!" Zula came into the open, calling, "Let them in! It's okay!"

Two heads—Marlon's and Csongor's—turned around to look in her direction. They seemed astonished. Especially Csongor.

"Go! Go!" Jake said, pivoting to face the gate. Moving somewhat uncertainly, Csongor and Marlon took their hands off their heads and clambered to their feet. They began moving toward the cabin. Jake went the other way, getting well clear of them and raising his AR-15 to his shoulder. He was aiming it straight down the driveway toward the gate. He fired a spread of several rounds, then began backing up, keeping his sights centered on the gate while closing the distance between himself and his house. Zula meanwhile had braced herself against a tree and obtained a clear view of the same target, ready to fire again if either of the two jihadists should show themselves. But nothing happened. Nothing moved.

WHAT HAD HAPPENED to Richard Forthrast's ankle was clearly a sprain, not a break. He could hop and hobble, but not walk. This created an interesting situation for Seamus. Not that the situation hitherto had been devoid of fascinating qualities. According to Richard, they were only a few minutes' walk (for an able-bodied person, anyway) from breaking out into an open space where they would be able to move south, traversing the western face of the mountain, and drop down into a valley where Richard's brother lived in a cabin. Richard wanted Seamus to leave him behind and move in that direction as fast as possible, because he was worried that Jones's main group was about to attack the place.

Which Seamus was more than willing to do. He was suffering a bit of survivor's guilt, having left Jack the chopper pilot behind earlier in the day, and getting ready, now, to abandon the lamed Richard. This was made a lot easier by Richard's insistence that he should just get on with it, and that he, Richard, could take care of himself in the meantime.

Yuxia was a different matter. Seamus had sort of imagined that she would be a good girl and hang around to look after Richard and keep him company. That being in a chopper crash and being chased through the American wilderness by a fanatical sniper might have sated her taste for adventure, at least for one morning. Barring that, that the heavy psychological aftermath of having just killed a man with a shotgun blast from point-blank range might have left her with a need to sit in a quiet place for a while and think about what it all meant.

But no, everything in her face and body language said that she was going with Seamus. That she was kind of irked by the stupid deliberation that Seamus had been displaying, in the sixty seconds since Jahandar had gone to meet his seventy-two black-eyed virgins, and that if Seamus spent any more time thinking it through, she might just grab a weapon and take off without him.

The inevitability of Yuxia's participation in the operation's next phase caused Seamus to think about its details a bit harder. It sounded as though they would be traversing a slope in the open, where they could be shot at from a distance by men with good rifles.

"Is there any way of getting to the same place without going across an exposed slope?" he asked Richard.

"It can be done through the woods," Richard allowed, nodding off the trail into some formidable-looking forest. "Much more slowly." He thought about it. "I heard some shooting from that direction a minute ago."

"So did I. Either Jones met with opposition, or he decided to ambush a meth lab."

"Up here, a marijuana grow would be more likely. Too far from the road for a meth lab."

"Anyway, they seem to be going through the woods," Seamus said, "which would slow them down."

"If you take the high road," Richard said, "you'll be way up above them. You'll be able to reach cover if you have to. And you'll have the advantage if you are packing the A.I." For he had recognized Jahandar's rifle and assumed Seamus had done the same.

"The high road it is," Seamus said, trying to put a lot of decisiveness into his voice, as a way of appeasing Yuxia, who was bouncing around in her camo like the little sidekick bruin in the old Yogi Bear cartoon. "Which gun, or guns, would you like me to leave you with?"

"You can take them all, if your intention is to shoot lots of bad guys with them."

"I should have mentioned that it was a trick question," Seamus continued. "We are being tailed by a mountain lion that is most definitely *not* as afraid of us as we are of it."

"I know." Richard looked around. "As much as I covet the A.I., in these woods, I can't see far enough for its excellent qualities to be of any use beyond assuaging certain masturbatory gun-nut impulses."

"What about the shotgun?" Seamus asked.

"Yuxia should take that. She knows how to use it, and it looks cute on her." This, at least, elicited a dimpled grin from Yuxia as she basked for a few moments in the scrutiny of the two men.

"No argument."

Seamus approached the pellet-riddled corpse and rolled it over. "Here's a wheel gun, if you can believe it."

"I *thought* it sounded like a six-shooter," Richard said.

"Five-shooter, more like. Large caliber." Seamus dropped to his knees and studied the revolver, which had been concealed under Jahandar's body and was now lying in the middle of the trail. He carefully uncocked it, then held it up. "Trophy piece. Must have taken it off a dead American contractor."

"Seems like just what the doctor ordered for last-ditch cougar defense. I'll take it. You get the A.I."

"Done," Seamus said. Less than a minute later, he and Yuxia, regeared and rearmed, were jogging up the switchbacks.

DURING THE QUARTER of an hour that Sokolov spent fleeing from the jihadists and hiding in a cold and wet place beneath a fallen log, he thought about age. These ruminations were triggered by all that he had done in the last half hour or so. He had created an effigy, seen it shot to pieces, run across a big rock, and then made a helter-skelter descent of a large open slope. Twenty times he had dived and rolled into cover on a surface consisting largely of big sharp rocks, each of which had left some kind of mark on him, some of which had inflicted bone bruises that would take weeks to get better. Another twenty times he had dived and rolled in ice-cold mud. He had sprinted into an unfamiliar abandoned mining camp with no idea of what he was going to do, then found an ideal place to take cover and taken advantage of it. He had rested there for all of about three minutes before blowing it by shooting the tall African jihadist, whereupon he had been obliged to abandon the position and go into another intense fugue of running, diving, vaulting, rolling, and hiding in uncomfortable places.

All this effort, all these risks taken and damages sustained, had achieved one thing for him, which was that he had killed exactly one of his numerous foes.

Now, had he been a seventeen-year-old, he'd have harbored foolish and unrealistic expectations of what could really be achieved in a situation such as this one, and he'd have believed that the payoff for all that work and risk and pain ought to have been greater than bagging one enemy. Driven by that misconception, he would have been slower to abandon the log cabin, slower to give up on the hope of shooting the man who had hidden behind the outhouse. He would have adopted a combative stance toward the main group of jihadists who had come running back to the camp. As a result, they would have surrounded him and killed him. All because he was young and imbued with an unrealistic sense of what the world owed him.

On the other hand, had he been a few years older than he really was, or not in such good physical condition, then all the running and diving and exposure to the elements would have felt much more expensive to him. Unsustainable. Disheartening. And those emotions would have led to his making decisions every bit as fatal, in the end, as those of the hypothetical seventeen-year-old.

So, as loath as he was to be self-congratulatory, he saw evidence to support the conclusion that he was at precisely the right age and level of physical conditioning to be undertaking this mission.

Which, viewed superficially, seemed like a favorable judgment. But with a bit more consideration—and, as he hid beneath the tree and listened to the jihadists beating the bushes, he did have a few minutes to think about it—it was really somewhat troubling, since it implied that all the operations he had participated in during his career before today had been undertaken by a foolish boy, in over his head and surviving by dumb luck. Whereas any operations he might carry out in the future would be ill-advised excursions by a man who was over the hill, past his prime.

He really needed to get out of this line of work.

But he'd been saying that ever since Afghanistan, and look where it had gotten him.

After a while, he heard Jones calling out to the others, telling them to give up the search. The need to press on outweighed the desire to take vengeance on the man who was stalking them. Sokolov waited until he could no longer hear the jihadists moving around, then emerged from his cover very carefully, beginning with a quick bob of the head followed by an immediate retreat. When several such ventures failed to draw fire, he began to feel some confidence that they had not left anyone behind to kill him when he emerged from cover, and he moved more freely. But he had the uncomfortable sense that they were now way ahead of him, and he began to consider how he could make up for lost time. Jones and his crew had made the decision to move through the forest, which was slower than going across the high country above the tree line, and so an obvious way that Sokolov might make up for lost time would be to go back into the mining camp and then continue to move through the scrubland just outside the limit of the trees.

This involved some slogging, since the ground here at the base of the slope was saturated with runoff. After several minutes of slow progress, he was reminded of his foolishness by a sound from high above: scraping and banging rocks. He went into the best cover he could find, which was a clump of bushes that seemed to thrive in the boggy soil, and then looked up in time to see a minor avalanche petering out on the talus slope, perhaps a thousand meters above him: just a few rocks that had been dislodged by someone or something and tumbled for a short distance before coming to rest. This gave him an idea of where he should look, so he swung his rifle up and peered through its scope, starting at the place where the rocks had stopped moving and then tilting up until he could see the faint horizontal scar of the trail. With a bit of panning sideways, he was confronted with the arresting sight of a man, sitting on the ground, and aiming a rifle right back at him! His first reaction was to flinch and get deeper into cover, which caused him to lose the sight picture. Even as he was doing so, however, his mind was processing what he had glimpsed and noting a few peculiarities.

Chief of these was that the rifle's bolt handle had been jutting perpendicularly out from the side of the weapon, which meant that it was not in condition to fire.

And—unless his memory was playing tricks—the man had been holding the weapon oddly. His right hand was not where it ought to have been—not in a position to pull the trigger.

Slightly emboldened by these recollections, he reacquired the sight picture and verified it all. This time, as soon as he had the other man in his sights, the guy pulled his head away from his scope, revealing a European-looking face. Not that this proved anything. But there was something in the set of that face that did not say "paleface jihadist."

This guy, whoever he was, was on Sokolov's side. He had seen Sokolov from above, probably tracked him through his telescopic sight, and identified him as a friendly. He had triggered the little avalanche as a way of getting Sokolov's attention. And he now wanted to communicate.

He grinned and looked off to the side. A moment later his face was joined by that of a young Asian female.

Very familiar-looking.

Sokolov had been trained for more than two decades to remain absolutely silent in battlefield situations, but he could not prevent an expression of surprise from escaping from his lips when he recognized this person as Qian Yuxia.

The man with Yuxia now began gesturing with his hands. It was impossible to communicate well in this manner. Russians and Americans—he guessed that this fellow was American—used different systems of hand signs. But the gestures were eloquent enough. The man was envisioning a sort of pincer movement. He and Yuxia would proceed along the high road, Sokolov would likewise continue doing what he was doing, and they would converge on the jihadists at the target, which Sokolov assumed to be Jake Forthrast's cabin.

All of which was obvious enough. And even had it not been obvious, it was more or less mandatory; neither of them had much choice as to where they would go and what they would do next. That wasn't the point.

The point was that they should try to avoid killing each other by accident during the fight that was going to begin in a few minutes. And Sokolov thought it was an excellent point.

"THIS WAY!" ZULA called, for Csongor and Marlon were preceding Jake up the driveway, headed for the cabin. Zula could see through the scope of the rifle that the jihadists had parked a couple of vehicles athwart the driveway's entrance, up where it joined the road. They had posted a few men behind those vehicles and in the surrounding woods, apparently to fire at any neighbors or inquisitive police who might try to come after them. The main group, numbering perhaps five, were running toward the gate, using the half-wrecked SUV as cover. When they got there, they'd be able to shoot down the driveway and pick off anyone standing out in the open.

Olivia had seen the same thing. "Get behind cover!" she was calling. "Come toward me!"

The men were all slow to hear and respond. They had a lot on their minds. Olivia switched into Mandarin and called something out in a high sharp tone that made Marlon's head swivel around and look right at her. He seemed to come to his senses then and grabbed Csongor's sleeve and hauled him toward the sound of Olivia's voice. Csongor was too big and had too much momentum to be diverted by this alone, but he could be steered, and within a few moments he and Marlon were both storming through the belt of woods and undergrowth that ran along the edge of the driveway. They burst out into the semicleared space where Zula and Olivia were. A few seconds later, Jake followed in their wake. Zula collected most of these impressions through her ears, since her gaze was still fixed through the scope at the gate. She had pumped a new round into the rifle. The magazine had only held four to begin with. Muzzle flashes lit up the view through her scope, and several rounds zipped through the foliage over her head.

"I'm covering the gate," Jake announced. "You should pull back, Zula."

Zula turned to see Jake kneeling behind the bole of a large tree, aiming his rifle through what she could only assume was a gap in the brush. He fired a round, studied the result, fired two more. Then he glanced up at her and used his eyes and his chin to indicate the direction he thought she should go.

"Over here, Zula!" Olivia called. Zula bent low and scurried into a gap between a goat pen and a net-enclosed structure where Jake and Elizabeth cultivated raspberries. A few seconds later, she had emerged into an open space behind the shed where the goats took shelter from the mountain weather. Olivia, Marlon, and Csongor were there.

It was awkward to say the least. Csongor took a quick step toward her, then faltered.

Why did he falter?

Because she was carrying a rifle?

Because her face was a horror show?

Because he wasn't sure whether she fancied him?

She searched his face for clues and got no answers, other than a powerful, unfamiliar, and situationally inappropriate feeling of pleasure that he was alive and here.

Two bangs sounded from up the hill. Then a third. Then a whole lot of other bangs in return.

"Uncle John," Zula explained, in the silence that followed. "I left him with the Glock."

Olivia said, "So, at the risk of stating the obvious, they're coming to shake hands with that lot." She tossed her head in the direction of the driveway, which was all of a sudden sounding like a free-fire zone. Zula peered around the edge of the shed and saw Jake retreating toward them.

"What is going on?" asked the voice of Elizabeth, coming out of the walkie-talkie. "Someone fill me in."

Zula raised the device toward her face and was about to say something when Jake came in range of her, lashed out with his left hand, and ripped it out of her grasp. "Lock it down, baby," he said. "Don't wait for us."

"Where are you?"

"Tell me you are in lockdown, and I'll answer your question," Jake responded testily.

A few moments' radio silence followed. Jake turned to look at the others. "We're cut off," he said. "There's no way we can get to the cabin before these guys do."

"Done," Elizabeth confirmed.

"The safe room is sealed," Jake announced, then pressed the transmit button on the walkie-talkie again. "Okay. We're behind the goat shed. I'll try to update you from time to time. Can the boys hear me?"

"Yes, they're right here gathered around me."

"Be brave and pray," Jake said. "I love you all, and I hope I'll see you soon. But until you see my face in the security camera, don't unlock those doors no matter what happens."

ONCE HE WAS certain that no one could see him, John sat down and began to descend the slope on his ass. His artificial legs were very nice—Richard bought him a new pair every few Christmases and spared no expense—but they were worse than useless when going downhill. Even when he was moving in ass-walking mode, all they did was get hung up on undergrowth anyway, so he paused for a minute to take them off and rub his sore-as-hell stumps. He reached around behind his back and stuffed them into the open top of his knapsack, then resumed inchworming down the mountain. Progress was slow, but—considering the switchbacks—actually not a hell of a lot slower than walking upright. In normal circumstances, he'd have been chagrined by the loss of personal dignity, but he was alone, and since his head was no more than a couple of feet off the ground, no one could see him in any case.

It was probably this detail that saved his life, since the advance scout moving ahead of Jones's main group was doing a commendable job of passing through the forest quietly, and John—whose hearing was not the best—didn't become aware of him until he was only twenty feet away.

John, of course, had been using his hands for locomotion. The Glock that Zula had given him was in his jacket pocket.

The scout would have blown by too quickly for John to take any action, if not for the fact that some shots sounded from below, and caused the scout's stride to falter, and drew his attention. Standing with his back to John, he looked down toward Jake's cabin and raised a walkie-talkie to his mouth. He was a close-cropped blond man with a scar on the back of his head. John had the Glock out by this point. The shot was so ideal that he got a little ahead of himself, raising the weapon in both hands and thereby disturbing his perch on the slope. He felt his ass starting to break free and managed to squeeze off one round before he became discombobulated and slid down a yard or so to a new and more stable resting place.

The scout had turned around to see him and probably would have killed him had his hand not been occupied by the walkie-talkie. As it was, all he could do was shout some sort of warning into it before John fired two more rounds into his midsection and brought him down. His body spiraled around the trunk of a tree and skidded down the slope for a few yards. Abandoning all pretense of quiet movement, John skidded down after him, using his ass as a sled, and probably breaking his tailbone on a rock about halfway down. This sent such a jolt through his body that it spun him into an ungainly, sprawling roll down the hill as things spewed out of his pockets and backpack in a sort of avalanche-cum-yard-sale. But he got to the jihadist and stripped him of his weapon before any of the others could get there to investigate. This was a very nice piece, a Heckler & Koch submachine gun, fully automatic. John was not familiar with it. Without his reading glasses he couldn't make sense of the little words stamped into its metal around the controls. But with a bit of groping around and experimentation he was able to figure out how to charge it and how to take off the safety.

An anxious voice blurted from the jihadist's walkie-talkie. But at the same time John heard the same voice saying the same thing from a few yards away.

The approaching man heard it all too, and now began to use the walkie-talkie as a way to home in on his friend's location, keying the mike every couple of seconds and listening for the answering crackle of static. John, somewhat desperately, grabbed the device and flung it away from him as if it were a live grenade. But the oncoming jihadist did not seemed to be fooled; apparently he head heard John's clothes rustling with the sudden movement. He did not stop. John aimed toward the sound and pulled the trigger. A short burst of rounds chortled from the weapon. Poorly aimed and unlikely to hit anything; but John, unfamiliar as he was with this gun, had not been a hundred percent certain that it was in a condition to fire when the trigger was pulled, and he needed to get past that.

The jihadist, perhaps ten yards away but completely obscured by ferns and scrubby little trees, reacted instantly by diving down the slope: a desperately dangerous move, but a logical one, if he'd had reasons to doubt the security of his position. For John now had no idea where the man was, and given the density of the undergrowth, that would continue being true until he gave away his position by moving.

Speaking of which, John's position was nothing to write home about either, and anyway he had given it up by firing the weapon. Making a reasonable guess as to where his opponent had rolled and tumbled, he edged down the slope a little more, trying to move as quietly as possible, which meant slowly. He became aware as he was doing this that more than one person was moving through the woods around him.

He was sitting very still, trying to listen for their movements, when a boot slammed into the side of his Heckler & Koch and pinned it to the ground. Since John was holding on to it firmly, this shoved him down on his side. He turned his stiff neck and looked up to see a man's face staring down at him from six feet above.

Or maybe a bit more than six feet. The man was tall. Black fellow. Not that John had any problem with blacks. He had always been happy to judge other men on their own unique qualities as individuals.

He looked kind of familiar. John had seen his picture recently.

Abdallah Jones was gripping a pistol in one hand and, in the other, one of John's artificial legs, which had skidded down the slope in advance of him.

"Too pathetic for words," Jones said.

"Fuck you and the goat you rode in on," John returned.

Jones bent down, raised the leg above his head, and brought it down toward John's face like a truncheon.

WHEN THE GUNFIRE started in earnest, Sokolov abandoned stealth and broke into a run. There was no point in sneaking around in the woods anymore. Jones had not left anyone behind to snipe at him.

The jihadists were in full flight toward Jake's compound now, shooting at anything that moved, just trying to make their way out to a road so that they could get clear of this area before the police locked it down. Or at least that was the vision that Sokolov constructed in his head. It occurred to him to wonder how Jones expected to escape. Was he planning to commandeer vehicles? Or did he have confederates scheduled to rendezvous with him? The latter seemed a much better plan, and thus far Jones had planned rather well. It was also the most pessimistic scenario from Sokolov's point of view, since it meant that Jones would have reinforcements, presumably armed with all that the gun shops of the United States of America had to offer. They would probably make directly for the Forthrast compound, since that was the most-difficult-to-fuck-up instruction that Jones could possibly give them. Men in situations like this one were largely instinct-driven, and their instinct would be to gravitate toward something that looked like a shelter and that would serve as an obvious rallying point.

As he drew closer to the compound, he began to hear more small-arms fire. He rounded a hillside and found himself only a couple of hundred meters from the cabin. Had it not been for the trees he'd have been able to see it clearly. As it was, he could glimpse a corner of roof, a chimney top with a lightning rod projecting from it, the whirling anemometer of the little home weather station that Jake and his sons had mounted up there. Gunfire and shouting were coming from out in the driveway. And other sounds of battle from nearer—the hillside leading down from the high trail. But there did not seem to be anything emanating from the cabin itself, which made him think that he had arrived before either Jones's hikers or the U.S.-based drivers had managed to occupy the place.

And so he decided that he would occupy it first. Its walls were solid logs, almost half a meter thick, sufficient to stop most of the rounds that the jihadists' weapons were firing.

He plunged down the hill and across a short stretch of level ground until he reached the edge of the area that Jake had cleared. This was going to become a very dangerous place in a few seconds. It might already be. He dropped to his belly and crawled several meters to a spot where he could take shelter behind a recently felled tree, not yet cut up for firewood. Its trunk was too skinny to hide him or to stop bullets, but its innumerable small dead branches, spraying out in all directions, created a visual screen. He crawled down the length of it, getting a bit closer to the cabin, then raised his head cautiously and, when this failed to draw fire, spent a few moments looking into the cabin's windows. He saw no smashed-out panes, no faces peeking round the edges of window frames—no signs, in other words, that it had yet been occupied. He could still make out two identifiable groups of gunmen moving around the property, converging generally on the cabin—but not there yet.

He got to his feet and sprinted for the cabin's back door.

TO PARAPHRASE A familiar proverb, Seamus had been provided with a hammer—a rather good sniper rifle—and now he was looking for nails. He and Yuxia had spent the last few minutes descending the trail that, judging from evidence (lots of recent footprints and ATV tracks) led down into wherever it was that everyone was converging—a cabin, according to some hasty directions supplied by Richard, owned by Richard's brother Jake and occupied by family members, including women and children, who ought to have no part in this quarrel.

In his haste to get to the bottom of the slope, Seamus nearly caught up with Jones's main group. Alerted, almost too late, by a few gunshots from just below—gunshots that were evidently not intended for him—he threw himself down, got situated in a prone firing posture with reasonable cover, flipped the lens caps off the ends of the rifle's scope, and got it ready to fire.

He had also run some distance ahead of Yuxia, who now caught up with him and didn't have to be told that she should throw herself down next to him so as not to present a target.

Now if one of those assholes down below would only make a target of himself. This was the rub of the hammer/nail problem. If Seamus hadn't come into possession of the rifle, he'd have brought a completely different skill set into play, moving down the slope as stealthily as possible in search of shorter-range combat opportunities. Instead, here he was, frozen in a fixed position that was too far out of the action to be of any use.

A movement caught his eye through a gap in the foliage. Yuxia saw it too and pointed. By the time he had flicked his eyes in that direction, whatever he'd glimpsed was gone. He lost interest, reckoning that none of these jihadists would ever show himself twice in the same place. But then a little gasp from Yuxia told him he'd guessed wrong. He swung the rifle in that direction, peered through the scope, waited for a few seconds, and then, finally, saw it clearly.

But it wasn't what he'd expected. Not a head. Not a gun. Not a hand. But a foot. A disembodied boot on the end of a rod.

Holding the rod about halfway along, a gloved hand. It descended sharply, then came back up again.

Seamus risked climbing up to his knees, so that he could get a better view. It took a moment to get the scene recentered in his scope. This time he was able to see the arm attached to that hand. Following it down, he identified the face of none other than Abdallah Jones.

He was just about to pull the trigger when his sight picture was obscured by the head and shoulders of another man who had entered the scene, gesticulating like crazy, trying to get Jones's attention. Seamus lifted his eye from the scope, trying to see what this other jihadist was looking at, but his view of the world was limited to a single narrow aperture between tree branches, and whatever had got this man so excited was far out of his view.

So he exhaled, dropped his eye back to the scope, made sure the crosshairs were still on the man's back, and pulled the trigger. The rifle went off like a motherfucker and the jihadist sprang forward as if he had been kicked in the back. He dropped out of view, revealing Jones, who Seamus fondly hoped might have been struck by the same bullet. But the bullet had either fragmented in the first man's body or else caromed off a vertebra and gone off in another direction.

There might be some alternate, parallel universe, designed to the exact specifications of snipers, where Jones would now freeze with terror long enough for Seamus to work the bolt, chamber another round, and fire. But not here. Jones dove and rolled and was long gone before Seamus was in a position to shoot again.

"They know we're here," Seamus said.

"Ya think?"

"We just have to proceed with caution, is all I'm saying."

"Why was that man waving his arms?"

"Could have been anything," Seamus said, "but I'll bet he saw Sokolov."

"DON'T SHOOT!" OLIVIA cried, for Jake Forthrast, attracted by movement in his peripheral vision, had swung his AR-15 around to bear on a man sprinting in a zigzag pattern across his backyard, headed for his cabin. Olivia had just recognized the man as Sokolov.

"Thank you," Jake said, and turned instead to aim in the general direction of some gunshots sounding from the base of the hill. Some of the jihadists were up there, trying to bring down Sokolov. A single very sharp crack sounded from higher up the slope.

"They've got a sniper," Jake said. But at almost the same moment they could hear excited voices from where Jones and his men had gone to ground, apparently saying much the same thing.

"Maybe *we've* got a sniper," Csongor suggested.

"Maybe," Jake said, "but who the hell?"

Olivia heard all of this as if from a great distance, focused as she was on Sokolov. About halfway through his run he had disappeared from her view, hidden behind the corner of the cabin, and she had no way of knowing whether he had found shelter there or been brought down by that clatter of fire from the woods. But then a curtain moved in an upper-story window. He was too smart to expose himself where she, or anyone, would be able see his face, so she saw nothing more than this subtle movement; but that alone gave her confidence that the one behind that curtain was him. "I believe he made it," she said. "He's in the cabin."

Glass shattered in the front of the house and a series of bangs sounded. A scream of dismay erupted from the driveway.

"So it would appear," Zula said.

"What do we do now?" Marlon wanted to know.

"As far as I'm concerned," Jake said, "if you all can just hole up somewhere and not get killed, well, that's the best you can reasonably hope for."

"I'm all in favor of not getting killed," Olivia said, "but what are *you* going to do, Jake?"

"My neighbors are probably headed this way right now, loaded for bear," Jake said. "If they just blunder into the middle of this, they'll be mowed down—they have no idea what they are getting themselves into. I'm going to work my way back out to the gate and do what I can to prevent that from happening."

A jihadist sprinted out of cover, making a run for the rear of the house—apparently thinking that he could get in through the back door while Sokolov was shooting out the front. He thudded up the porch steps, grabbed the doorknob, and found it locked. Zula was getting into position to aim her rifle at the man. Before she could do anything, however, his head snapped forward as if he were trying to head-butt his way through the door. He slid and crumpled to the deck and lay there twitching. The echo of another sharp bang resounded from above.

"Definitely *our* sniper," Marlon concluded.

Jake had already departed, taking advantage of these distractions to run for the cover of a woodpile some yards away. From there he was quickly able to make his way off the property, or at least out of their field of view. More bangs sounded from the upper-story windows of the cabin, as Sokolov was apparently moving from window to window taking aim at any targets that presented themselves: sometimes shooting out the back at Jones's group, other times out the front at the ones trying to come up the driveway. The latter seemed more numerous and better armed. Jones's contingent had lost a few members and also had to contend with the sniper firing down on them from the hillside behind.

"They are coming closer to us," Marlon said. His face was turned toward the back side of the property, his ears tracking the purr of a submachine gun, firing in occasional bursts that got a little nearer each time. Each of those bursts caused damage to a window or a window frame on the cabin's upper story, and those targets were migrating slowly along the back and around the corner of the building. The dark weathered surface of the logs was splintering to reveal blond wood underneath, as if the place were being swarmed by invisible chainsaws.

Sokolov popped up in the window where he had twitched the curtain earlier, and fired two rounds before ducking back down to avoid a long burst of fire. So it would seem the owner of the submachine gun was working his way through the property, dodging around the side of the cabin in a wide arc, probably trying to connect with his brothers in the driveway without exposing himself to fire from either Sokolov or the sniper. The farther he got without being cut down, the more likely it was that others would follow in his wake and that the four behind the shed—who were armed only with Zula's rifle and the pistol that Jake Forthrast had handed to Csongor—would find themselves confronting all that remained of Jones's group, who were few in number but armed to the teeth. And no doubt pissed. All four of them assembled this picture in their minds over the course of a few moments and instinctively drew away from the approaching shooter, seeking cover around the corner of the shed or behind tree trunks. But the news was not particularly good from the driveway side either. The jihadists in front were communicating with those in back using walkie-talkies. While Sokolov had been focusing all of his attention on Jones's group, trying to prevent them from coming around the side and tangling with Zula, Olivia, Marlon, and Csongor, the attackers in the driveway had begun to move up toward the cabin.

Zula, prone behind a cedar tree and gazing over the sight of the rifle, trying to catch sight of the agile shooter with the submachine gun, was growingly conscious of a rhythmic *thud-thud-thud* that was growing to fill the air and shake the ground. Focused as she was on other matters, she had not given it much thought at first. She now recognized it as the sound of a helicopter. It had come in at higher altitude but was now making a low and slow pass over the compound. She rolled over on her back and looked almost vertically upward at the belly of a chopper passing maybe a hundred feet overhead. Men were peering out the windows, trying to make sense of what was going on down here. As it passed by and banked around, she was able to see markings of the Idaho State Patrol.

It made a lazy swing over the back forty and then came around to the front and hovered above the driveway.

A streak of fire lanced up out of the trees near the gate and struck it near the tail rotor. The back half of the chopper disappeared for a moment in a spike of white fire. What was left of it began to pinwheel, descending rapidly. It dropped out of Zula's view, and a moment later she heard it crash into the driveway, and fusillades of gunfire as the jihadists on that side poured rounds into its wreckage.

SOKOLOV UNDERSTOOD THAT the rocket-propelled grenade had been intended for him. Pinned down by his fire from the upper story of the cabin, the jihadists had sent a man back to get the device out of the trunk of a car. He had been stealing through the woods, trying to get into position to fire a grenade through a window, when the chopper had appeared overhead and presented him with an even more tempting target. And so he had played his hand and ruined the surprise.

The next RPG would be headed his way as soon as the jihadist could reload.

The back of the cabin sported screened-in decks on both the ground level and the upper story; Elizabeth, last night, had referred to the latter as a "sleeping porch." Sokolov vaulted through a shattered window and landed flat on the deck of the sleeping porch. If any of the jihadists out back had noticed this—and they probably had—then they knew that they now had a shot at him. Not a good shot, for if they were close, they'd be firing upward through the two-by-four decking of the porch; and if they were farther away, their view would cluttered by furniture. But their surplus of ammunition would make up for many of these deficiencies. Sokolov's life expectancy up on this deck was well under sixty seconds.

Or at least that was the state of affairs before the upper story of the cabin exploded. The man with the RPG knew what he was doing: with two shots he had brought down a helicopter and essentially decapitated the building that Sokolov had been using as a sniper's perch.

Sokolov now became part of a large mass of rubble—mostly logs—finding its way to the ground. The sleeping porch peeled away from the side of the house and toppled, and he of course fell with it and struck the ground with less violence than might have been expected. But logs, and a considerable part of the roof structure, came after, and Sokolov's world grew dark and confined, and when he tried to move his right leg, it budged not at all, but responded only with weird tingling sensations that he knew as harbingers of serious pain.

. . . .

SEAMUS'S QUEST FOR nails to hit with his hammer had been petering out as the would-be nails either died or fled, making their way
around the side of the cabin and taking cover behind the numerous
trees, small structures, and woodpiles that complicated that swath
of the property. It became obvious that he needed to relocate to a
position farther down the slope. And yet he hesitated. He knew that
Yuxia would insist on coming with him, and he did not want to
bring her into what would clearly turn into a vicious, short-range,
tree-to-tree kind of affair, your basic hatchet fight in a dark cellar.
He was trying to think of some way to broach this topic with her
when he noticed the chopper making its pass over the back of the
compound, just above treetop level—which meant it was nearly on
a level with Seamus. Had he been one of the bad guys he could have
taken out both the pilot and the copilot with a single round through
both of their helmets. As it was, he levered himself up on his elbows
and simply watched it fly by with the cynical and helpless attitude
of the experienced combat veteran. For it was obvious that the two
troopers in the chopper had no idea how much danger they were in.
They had probably flown up here in response to a vague, excited telephone report of shots fired in the woods: something that must happen all the time in these parts. Assuming that it was nothing more
than poachers, or kids screwing around with their dads' guns, they
were making a low and slow pass over the area, just to put the fear
of God into the hearts of the miscreants. After which they would
fly home and spend the afternoon drinking coffee and writing up a
very dull report.

They were going to die.

The copilot was swiveling his head from side to side, scanning
the ground below, occasionally turning to an angle from which Seamus might—just might—show up in his peripheral vision. If only
Seamus were not clad from head to toe in camouflage.

Seamus jumped to his feet and did a few jumping jacks. He
unzipped his parka, turned it inside out, began waving it over his head.

The chopper turned its tail rotor toward him, like a dog presenting its ass to be sniffed, and began to cruise away.

Seamus noticed something red on his arm, just above the elbow,
and looked down curiously to see that a chunk of flesh was missing
from it.

Yuxia jumped to her feet and fired the shotgun. Pumped it, ejecting the spent shell, and chambering the last one.

ZULA HAD BEEN having miserable bad luck with the rifle. The jihadists seemed to be quite good at staying behind cover. She had fired another round but apparently not hit anything. She had just two left.

Olivia had sprung to her feet when the top half of Jake's cabin had disintegrated, and she had taken a few paces toward its still-settling ruins before Marlon had jumped up and tackled her to the ground. He was lying next to her now, a consoling hand on her shoulder, talking to her.

Zula flinched, sensing movement nearby, and looked back to see that it was Csongor, approaching on hands and knees. He flopped down, pressing against her. Her body responded to the contact as if it were just him being companionable. But her mind understood that he was making himself a human shield to protect her from any shots that might come from the direction they were most concerned about.

"You don't have to do that," she said.

"Ssh," he said. "It is very logical."

"Oh really?"

"Yes. You have to use your rifle to get the guy with the big weapon— I guess it must be rocket-propelled grenade? But you can't do that if this asshole over here"—he waved the pistol vaguely in the direction from which they'd been hearing the bursts of the submachine gun—"is shooting at you. So I'll take care of him."

She was about to take issue with this when a racket sounded from above their heads. They looked up, blinking their eyes against a descending haze of wood dust, to see a ragged line of fresh bullet holes in the wall of the shed.

Zula met Olivia's eye for a moment.

"Scatter!" Zula cried, and rolled up and ran around to the other side of the shed. She heard Olivia relay the command to Marlon and then felt and heard their footfalls and their ragged breathing as they sought other cover.

She was looking around trying to figure out where Csongor had ended up when a fusillade, the longest and the loudest yet, sounded from the driveway, up near the gate. Cringing against the shed wall, she understood that this had to be Jake and the neighbors, mounting some kind of organized assault. They'd be moving up the driveway, which meant that the remaining jihadists on this side would have to retreat toward the house.

Had Jake and his group seen the RPGs? Did they understand what they were up against?

Zula, summoning energy she had no right to have, risked getting to her feet and running several yards to the cover of the woodpile that Jake had used earlier. Throwing herself down, she raised her head cautiously and tried to scope out the scene in front of her.

In this environment, so filled with irregular natural forms, anything straight and smooth captured the eye. She saw one such thing now, projecting outward near the base of a tree. Definitely a manmade shape. But not a rifle. She suspected that it might be the stock of the RPG launcher. It was wiggling around, as if its operator were getting ready to use it.

Getting ready to fire a grenade into the middle of the group that Jake was leading up the driveway.

She was too low. She sat up, leaned against the side of the woodpile to steady her aim, and drew a bead on what she'd just been looking at.

From this higher vantage point she was clearly able to see the head and shoulders of a man, crouching against a tree with his back to her, holding a loaded RPG on his shoulder.

She got the crosshairs between his shoulder blades and took up the slack in the trigger. Then she heard a loud crack and felt something crash down on top of her head.

THE MAN WITH the submachine gun had been maddeningly elusive. When the four had scattered at Zula's suggestion, he ought to have fired wildly in all directions, trying to hit at least one of them. This, at any rate, would have made things easier for Csongor. Instead, the jihadist had prudently held his fire, probably realizing that in such a melee he was only going to waste ammunition.

Csongor was confident that he had found reasonably secure cover. Since he was a large target with a small gun, he didn't fancy his chances in a running-and-shooting duel with a small, elusive person carrying anything fully automatic. So, as difficult as this was, he lay very still and very quiet, and simply waited for the other guy to make a move.

Nothing happened for a minute or so, other than the sound of shots coming from the driveway.

But then the man just stood up, perhaps ten meters away, and fired a burst from his hip. He examined the results, then raised the weapon to his shoulder to fire at something with better aim.

The man was shooting at Zula.

Csongor pressed himself up to one knee, raised the pistol, and fired half a dozen rounds. By the time he was finished, the man was gone: dead or fled to cover, it was difficult to say.

ZULA HAD BEEN struck by a hunk of firewood that had been dislodged from the top of the pile by what she guessed was a poorly aimed burst of fire. It would leave a nasty bump but nothing serious.

Trying not to think about what this meant, she lined up her shot again and saw the man with the RPG, still about where he had been before, squatting on his haunches, bouncing up and down a little, pivoting and moving from time to time as he evaluated different targets.

Then a change came over him. He had been restless, nervous, but now had settled down into the attitude of a cat getting ready to pounce. Through the scope she could see his eye making itself comfortable in the weapon's sight, his finger finding the trigger.

She pounced herself by pulling her trigger first.

Nothing happened. She understood now that her finger must have contracted against the trigger and fired a shot when the piece of wood had struck her on the head. The chamber was empty.

She pumped the weapon, chambering her last round, quickly lined up her shot again, and fired. Lifting her head from the sight she saw the man sprawling forward, and a jet of fire leaping from his shoulder as the RPG was launched. It caromed off the ground a few yards in front of him, spiraled into the air, and went screaming away.

. . . .

"OKAY," SEAMUS SAID, "I guess you can come with me. Just save the last shell for something really important, okay?" And with that he plunged forward down the slope at a run, cradling the rifle in his good arm and letting the damaged one dangle. Blood streamed down it freely and dribbled from his fingertips. He nearly tripped over the body of the man who had shot him, and who had been destroyed by Yuxia's shotgun blast. Jones must have sent this guy back to track down the annoying sniper and kill him, which Seamus had almost made too easy by jumping up and presenting himself as a target.

Though, on the other hand, that might have saved his life. Had he stayed down, the stalker would have drawn closer before opening fire. By doing jumping jacks in plain view, Seamus had made himself irresistible, and the stalker had given way to the temptation to open fire at longer range than his pistol could really hit anything at.

"Should I take his gun?" Yuxia asked, thrashing along a few yards behind him.

"Good idea, honey," Seamus called back. "Know that if you pull the trigger, it will fire."

"Okay."

"On top of it is a moving slide thingy that will jump back and bite a hunk of flesh from your hand if you keep holding it that way."

"Mmmkay," she said, a bit absently.

"I'm serious. Move your hand down."

She did so, finally.

"You all right?" Seamus asked.

"We are running in the open."

"You're welcome to stop at any time," Seamus pointed out, a little testily. "We are doing this because the end game of this thing is happening right now, and we are no longer near the place where it's happening. I need an angle, and a shot."

"You are bleeding on the ground."

"Excellent place for it."

They ran for a couple of hundred yards through the open space along the perimeter of the cleared compound, seeing no jihadists who were alive. Something spectacularly bad had happened to the cabin, but Seamus saw and understood it only dimly. He was, he realized, probably going into shock. And he was a little ashamed of that, since the wound on his arm ought not to have been such a big deal. His act of running down the hill and into the compound had, in a way, been a semiconscious tactic to put it out of his mind and get him focused on something else.

"I see the fucker," he announced. The head of a tall man had popped up into view perhaps a hundred yards away. Advancing to the next tree, he leaned against it, to steady the upcoming shot, and then dropped to his left knee.

He hadn't *planned* to drop to a knee; it just happened. His right leg had buckled.

Something heavy had been slapping against his thigh with each stride. Something in his right pants pocket. When he dropped, his right knee came up, and that pocket got squeezed as the front of his trousers creased, and a large amount of warm fluid gushed out of it and washed over his right buttock and ran down his thigh.

He glanced down for the first time in a while and observed that he had also been shot on the right side of his abdomen and that blood had been running out of the wound this whole time and accumulating, for some reason, in his pocket.

He was lying on his back, and Yuxia was standing above him with her hands clapped over her mouth. She might have let out a bit of a scream.

He thrust the rifle up into the air with his good arm. "Shoot him," he said. "Shoot Abdallah Jones."

CSONGOR MOVED FORWARD cautiously to see whether he had managed to hit the man with the submachine gun. He heard a slight rustle and looked over to see Abdallah Jones, just standing there looking at him. Csongor moved his pistol around to bear on Jones. Jones brought a Kalashnikov around and aimed it at Csongor, at the same moment.

The range was greater than Csongor was comfortable with. His hands were shaking.

"You," Jones said. "If it were anyone else, I'd have already pulled the trigger. As it is, I'm just standing here dumbfounded. How the hell, Csongor? It is Csongor, right?"

"Yes."

"What the hell are you doing here?"

"The story is complicated."

"Shame, that. Because I really would love to hear it. But there is, of course, no time." He raised the Kalashnikov to his shoulder.

A crack sounded from off to the side. The sniper again. Jones looked in that direction, but showed no ill effects; the sniper had somehow missed.

Csongor dropped to the ground and began firing blindly through foliage.

Several rounds came back in his general direction, but this was nothing more than Jones firing to keep Csongor's head down. It worked. The next time Csongor felt brave enough to lift his head, Jones was nowhere to be seen.

From over near the cabin, he heard the drone of a small engine starting up.

He stood to see Jones astride an all-terrain vehicle. Jones spent a few moments figuring out the controls, then got the thing turned around and headed around the side of the house, trying to make it out to the road.

SOKOLOV WAS IN worse pain than he'd ever experienced, and he reckoned that he might lose the leg before this was all over. Had even considered pulling out his knife and self-amputating. Other than that, however, he was not doing that badly. No bullets had struck him. He had not suffered serious trauma during the collapse of the sleeping porch. The actual deck of the porch, which had thudded into the ground right next to him—a blunt guillotine blade that would have pinched him in half, had he landed wrong—had formed a pocket; all the logs and other debris that had rained down on top had been held up above the ground by its planking, which had been crumpled and compressed but not altogether driven into the ground.

So he was fine. He just couldn't move. The heap of logs provided several large apertures through which he could look out and view his surroundings, and he had experimented with aiming the rifle through these. But no targets had presented themselves.

Until, that is, he heard the ATV starting up.

He could not actually see the ATV—his view in that direction was blocked by a sizable chunk of the cabin's roof—and so he assumed that this was Jake, come back to reclaim his vehicle.

It idled for a few moments. The driver revved its motor and put it into gear, then began to ride it around the side of the cabin, circumventing the debris pile in which Sokolov was trapped.

Through a gap between logs Sokolov caught a brief glimpse of the driver's head. Jones.

He thrashed around, sending a shocking wave of pain up his leg, and twisted into a position from which he could fire the rifle through another gap. He expected that Jones would be passing by very soon.

Which Jones obligingly did, and Sokolov pulled the trigger a few times as the vehicle came into view.

The engine stopped with a mechanical crunch, and Jones cursed. Unfortunately the vehicle's momentum had carried it out of Sokolov's sight. He heard Jones climbing off and unlimbering his Kalashnikov. The end of the weapon's barrel appeared for a moment, silhouetted on the edge of Sokolov's aperture.

But the gunshots that he heard next were not Kalashnikov rounds fired from nearby, but pistol shots from a greater distance. Not just one, but two pistols firing round after round.

TOTALLY EXPOSED AT the base of the rubble pile, harassed by poorly aimed rounds from faraway pistols, unable to seek cover in the log heap because he knew that an armed man was lurking back in there, Jones rolled to his feet and broke into a run, heading away from the cabin, back the way he had come. When it became obvious what he was doing, Yuxia broke from cover and went charging after him, screaming curses and firing the pistol wildly until it was out of ammunition. But by that time, Jones had disappeared into the forest at the base of the hill.

A FEW MINUTES after Seamus and Yuxia left him behind, Richard forced himself to get on his feet and begin hobbling up the trail. He had swallowed as much ibuprofen as his system could handle and he had swaddled the sprained ankle in strips of fabric cut from Jahandar's garments. A long tree branch, trimmed and whittled, served as a walking staff. The high road—the climb up to the top of the big flat rock, followed by the long traversal of the talus slope—would be many hours of misery for a man in his condition. But there was another way of getting to Jake's, a low road leading along the edge of the forest, through the old abandoned mining camp and then around a spur of the mountain into the valley of Prohibition Crick. It seemed much the better choice. So he split off from the trail shortly before it pierced the tree line, and hobbled south through the woods. He had feared that this would turn into an endless, toiling death march, but once he found his stride, he began to make reasonably good time—not a hell of a lot slower than if he hadn't sprained his ankle.

The first leg of the journey, from the trail to the old mining camp, presented some difficult going in places. At one point, he was forced to range up and down a slope looking for the easiest place to traverse it. In the end, he found the spot by noticing a trail that had been pounded into the ground by several people who had gone before him. It was obvious from the freshness of the traces and the litter left behind that he was now following literally in the bootprints of Jones's contingent of jihadists. Once he worked his way through the difficult bit, which involved a certain amount of scooting along on his butt, keeping his staff planted to prevent him from avalanching down the hill, he came out into a stretch of more level ground that, if memory served, would lead eventually to the mining camp. Here the jihadists' trail spread out, as they had formed a broad front while reconnoitering the level ground. Richard chugged along freely in their wake, planting his staff with each stride.

His mind wandered. He now dared to believe that everything was going to work out okay, that Zula would have made it safely to Jake's by this point, and that he would get there soon. That Jones would slip away into the Idaho/Montana wilderness, or else be captured, and that life for the Forthrasts would return to normal. Which got him to thinking about all the email, all the tweets that would be waiting for him, all the things left undone. And as part of all that, it occurred to him to wonder what Egdod was up to. Because, come to think of it, Richard had been logged on as Egdod when Jones had severed his Internet link. Egdod would have reverted to his bothavior, which in his case would mean trudging for thousands of miles across T'Rain, trying to get back to his mountaintop palace. This would, to put it mildly, draw lots of notice in that world. He wondered how many high-level characters had showed up to attack Egdod, and whether any of them had succeeded in bringing the old man down. He tried to recollect what the landscapes looked like between Carthinias and Egdod's home zone. He envisioned the aged wizard wading through swamps, trudging doggedly across deserts, scaling mountain ranges, and walking through forests.

Kind of like Richard was doing. Egdod, of course, carried a wizard's staff, just a simple stick, no fancy carvings or jewels. Just like what Richard was carrying now. Egdod's beard was long and white, where Richard's was just a couple of days' gray stubble. And Egdod, of course, had no need to carry a huge, looted revolver in his waistband. Hell, Egdod didn't even *have* a waistband. But despite all of those differences, Richard still found something hugely enjoyable about the fact that, at the same moment, both he and Egdod were wandering alone across their respective worlds, seeing everything close up in a way that they rarely had a chance to. Getting back in touch with the terrains from which they had sprung, autochthonously, early in their lives.

And possibly beset by unknown enemies. Richard, in his reverie, had quite forgotten to keep an eye out for the mountain lion. He executed a slow pirouette around his staff, just to see if anything was hunting him. But of course the whole point of being hunted was that you didn't know it was happening. He stood still for a minute or two, just listening, just being aware of the place. Enjoying the moment. Because very soon this part of his life would be over, and he'd be descending into the valley of Prohibition Crick the way he had done on that autumn afternoon in 1974 with a bearskin on his back. Except that instead of finding a hidden smuggler's cabin, he would find a nice modern cabin with Internet, full of people who would all want to talk to him.

When he was good and ready, he turned back around and followed the jihadists' muddy footprints out of the trees and into the open plateau of the old mining camp.

A solitary man was walking toward him, a couple of hundred meters away, with a rifle slung over his shoulder. He was moving with the weary, hitching gait of a man who knew he ought to be running but simply could not summon the energy. Occasionally he spun around and walked backward for a couple of steps, much as Richard had done just a few minutes before when he had been worried about the cougar. Unlike Richard, he was also scanning the sky. And indeed, now that Richard was out in the open, he noticed the sound of at least one helicopter.

The man turned forward again and froze, staring directly at Richard. It was Abdallah Jones.

Richard considered reaching around behind his back and drawing the revolver, but even with its long barrel and large caliber, it was useless at this range. No point, then, in letting Jones know that he was armed. Using the staff to ease his descent, he dropped to one knee. He and Jones were now looking at each other through a haze of scrub brush. Jones was bringing up his rifle: a Kalashnikov. Richard dropped to both knees, then to all fours, then scurried to a different position just as a few exploratory rounds hummed through the air above him and pelted into the mucky ground behind.

It was difficult to move in this way without making the brush wiggle, which would give Jones a way to track where he was. And in any case he was leaving a mashed-down trail that Jones could simply follow until he had a clear shot. Richard, looking behind him, saw that trail and noted its embarrassing width and, even here, heard the voice of a Furious Muse reminding him that he needed to lose weight. Zigzagging would break the trail up into short segments and make it more difficult for Jones to just drill him in his fat ass while strolling along in his wake. But it would also slow him down. So he very much needed to find proper cover and to take shelter there and force Jones to expose himself.

Calling to mind the last prospect he had enjoyed before he'd noticed Jones, he recalled a tumbledown log cabin that ought to be about fifty yards away from him now. It was not terribly far from the edge of the woods; and he could get into the trees with a short, very painful sprint from where he was now. He crawled, therefore, toward the woods, pausing occasionally to listen, hoping to get a fix on Jones's location.

Which Jones obligingly provided by calling out: "Who's your sneaky little friend, Dodge?"

Richard got to his feet and sprinted toward the woods, then dove as soon as he began to hear gunfire. Actually "sprint" was an awfully optimistic way to describe his movement; for Richard, it meant simply that he was moving as fast as he possibly could. Several rounds passed nearby, or so he judged from the weird sounds that seemed to be tearing up air molecules in his vicinity. From the place where he landed, it was a short belly crawl through mud into the trees. There he felt safe in getting up to a crouch and moving along through the forest until the old log cabin was visible just a stone's throw away.

He could see Jones, tracking him at a leisurely pace through the part of the camp where he'd been running, diving, and crawling just a few moments earlier. Jones's attention, quite reasonably, was directed mostly forward into the woods. But he kept turning to look back in the direction from which Richard had emerged into the camp a minute before. Richard took advantage of one such moment to hop out from cover and "sprint" perhaps half of the way from the tree line to the cabin, keeping an eye on Jones as he was doing so. Eventually Jones noticed him and brought the Kalashnikov around. Richard then dove again and belly-crawled the rest of the way to the cabin with rounds from Jones's rifle humming through the air. If Jones had been carrying unlimited ammo, he could have laid down a lot more fire, and almost certainly hit Richard. But he seemed to be conserving his rounds. Which was a good thing. But it did cause him to wonder what had gone wrong, for Jones, in the last few hours. Why was he backtracking, alone, with depleted ammunition? What had been happening at Prohibition Crick this morning?

Once he had reached the safe side of the cabin, Richard got to his feet and shambled wearily into its front door and, in the sudden darkness, tripped over something soft that turned out to be the dead body of Erasto. Flies were already getting to it. Where did flies come from in situations like this?

Controlling a powerful urge to throw up, Richard patted the corpse down looking for weapons. But someone had already done this and relieved his departed comrade of everything except one ammunition clip for a pistol that was no longer here.

Richard knee-walked over the rotting remains of the building's collapsed roof to a vacant window, popped his head up for a moment, and withdrew it. Jones had altered his course and was walking directly toward the cabin now, holding the rifle up at his shoulder, ready to fire.

"Another Forthrast holed up in the ruins of another log cabin, waiting to die," Jones said. "You people are consistent, I'll give you that. Unfortunately I don't have an RPG, like the one we used on your brother's place, but the results are going to be the same: a pile of dead meat in a ruined shack."

Richard, as a younger man, might have been powerfully moved by this sort of talk. As it was, he was largely ignoring the meaning of the words themselves and using them mostly as a way to keep track of Jones's position. He had pulled out the revolver, checked its cylinder, verified that it was loaded with the full five rounds. He got his thumb on its massive hammer and drew it back until it cocked.

"You see," Jones said, "when you make the mistake of letting me get this close, the grenade doesn't need to be rocket propelled."

Richard was sitting on the floor beneath the window, gazing up into the shaft of light coming in through it, and saw an object fly in, bounce across the opposite wall, and tumble to the floor— which was actually the former roof. It bounced and came to rest almost within arm's reach. Richard rolled toward it. His hand closed around it at the same moment as his conscious mind was understanding what it was: a grenade. It would have been clever, he later supposed, to toss it *back* through the same window at Jones, but the easy and obvious—and quick—throw from here was out the cabin's vacant doorway. So that was where he threw it, and he was relieved to see it disappear from direct shrapnel line of fire beyond the poured concrete front stoop. It went off, and for a few seconds afterward, Richard's life was all about that.

But only for a few seconds. He had waited too long, been too conservative; he had escaped the effects of that grenade only through dumb luck. He got to his feet, a little unsteadily, not just because of the ankle but the brain-stirring effect of the blast, and stood with his back to the wall next to the window. Through the opening he could see a narrow swath of what was out there, but Jones wasn't in that swath. Getting the revolver out in front of him, he pivoted around his good foot and presented himself in the window opening long enough to get a wide-open view outside the cabin.

Jones was at about ten o'clock, and lower down than Richard had been expecting, since he had apparently thrown himself down to await the results of the grenade. He was just clambering to his feet, and when Richard caught his eye, he made a sudden sideways dive toward the cabin. Richard swung the revolver laterally, trying to track the movement, but his elbow struck the frame of the window at the same moment as he was deciding to pull the trigger. The revolver made a sound that would have seemed loud, had a grenade not just gone off, and a bullet drew a trace through weedy foliage about a foot away from Jones's head. Jones was bringing his rifle up to return fire, but Richard was already withdrawing from the window. He pulled back so quickly, in fact, that he lost his balance and tumbled onto his ass.

He and Jones were now no more than four feet apart, separated only by the log wall of the cabin.

Richard could squat there and wait and hope that Jones would move into just the right position so that Richard could fire through a gap between logs. Or he could go out the way he had come in, move around the side of the cabin, and try to shoot around the corner. Or he could present himself in the window again and just fire from point-blank range.

He was cocking the revolver again when Jones opened fire with his Kalashnikov. Richard's whole body flinched, and he very nearly let the hammer slip. But no rounds seemed to be passing through the cabin. Nor could they, really, given Jones's location. So what the hell was Jones shooting at?

It came to him then that he was overthinking this.

This was a *shoot-out*. Nothing could be simpler. But he was making it too complicated by trying to use his wits to work the angles, figure out some clever way to dodge around the essential nature of what was happening, to get through to the other side without getting hurt. His opponent, of course, simply didn't give a shit what happened to him and was probably a dead man anyway— which gave Jones an advantage that Richard could match only by adopting the same attitude. It was an attitude that had come naturally to him as a young man, taking down the grizzly bear with the slug gun and doing any number of other things that later seemed ill-advised. Wealth and success had changed him; he now looked back on all such adventures with fastidious horror. But he had to revert to that mind-set now or else Jones would simply kill him.

All of this came simply and immediately into his head, as though the Furious Muses had chosen this moment to give up on being furious for once—perhaps forever—and were now singing in his ears like angels.

Richard stood up in the window, holding the revolver in one hand now, and swung it out and down.

Jones was right there, sitting on the ground, leaning back against the wall of the cabin, aiming his rifle, not up at Richard, but out into the open space beyond. He had been shooting in that direction for some reason.

He glanced up into Richard's eyes.

"It's nothing more than a great bloody cat!" Jones exclaimed.

Richard pulled the trigger and shot him in the head.

He cocked the revolver again and stood poised there for several seconds, looking at the aftermath to make sure he was not misinterpreting the evidence of his eyes, out of wishful thinking. But Jones was unquestionably dead.

Finally he raised his gaze from what remained of Jones and looked up and out over the field of weeds and overgrown scrub beyond. It was by no means clear what Jones had been marveling at in the last moment of his life. For fresh green leaves had not yet begun to bud out, and the hue of the place was the tawny umber of last year's dead growth. Finally, though, Richard's eyes locked on something out there that was unquestionably a face. Not a human face. Humans did not have golden eyes.

The eyes stared into Richard's long enough for Richard to experience a warm rush of blood to his cheeks. He was blushing. Some kind of atavistic response, apparently, to being so watched. But then the eyes blinked, and the cougar's tiny head turned to one side, ears twitching in reaction to something unseen. Then it spun around, and the last Richard saw of it was its furry tail snapping like a whip, and the white pads of its feet as it ran away.

THE FORTHRAST FARM
Northwest Iowa

Thanksgiving

Richard had been spending a lot more time at the farm lately, mostly because he had been named executor of John's will. Since Alice was still alive, this was much less complicated than it might have been—he didn't have to sift through *all* his older brother's property, only the bits that were of no use or interest to Alice. This meant tools, weapons, hunting and camping gear, and some clothing. Richard distributed all of it among John and Alice's four sons and sons-in-law. Only a few odds and ends remained. Of these, the most difficult for Richard to deal with—speaking here of emotional difficulty—were the artificial legs. Owing to Richard's habit of buying John a new pair whenever he read about some fresh innovation in that field, there were a lot of them, piled up like cordwood in a corner of the attic. During a weepy afternoon of sorting through them, Richard hit on an idea: an idea that might not really make that much sense on a practical level, but somehow felt right. He got in touch with Olivia, who said that she "knew how to reach" Sokolov. A few emails passed back and forth containing measurements and photographs. The finding was that Sokolov's height, weight, leg length, and shoe size were a close match for John's, and so by the end of the day Richard was down at the local UPS depot shipping several very expensive carbon-fiber right legs to an address in the United Kingdom. Custom stump cups and other modifications would, of course, be needed, but the result was that Sokolov got something a bit nicer than what he would have been issued by the National Health Service.

At eleven in the morning, after they had all come back from the memorial service—a ceremony honoring not only John but Peter, Chet, Sergei, Pavel, the bear hunters, the RV owners, and two of Jake's neighbors—Zula hooked her laptop to the big flat-screen on Grandpa's porch, and they made a Skype connection to Olivia in London. She had just returned to her apartment after work and was looking every inch the smartly turned-out intelligence analyst. Once the connection was made, she insisted that Zula put her face up to the little camera above the laptop screen and display her new artificial tooth, which was indistinguishable from the one that had been knocked out, and the lip in front of it, which bore a hairline scar and a little notch. The notch, Zula explained, was fixable, but she had decided to keep it. Olivia heartily approved and pulled back her hair—which she'd been growing in—to show off what she described as the "Frankenstein" scar that had been incised on her scalp in Xiamen.

These preliminaries out of the way, Zula backed away from the camera. Olivia made some approving remark about her church dress. Zula responded with a mock-demure curtsy, then smoothed the garment in question under her bottom as she settled into the couch right next to her grandfather. "My goodness, who are all these fine gentlemen?" Olivia exclaimed. "What company you keep, my dear!" For sitting on Zula's other side was Csongor, dressed up in a hastily acquired black suit from the big and tall section of Walmart. With the timeless awkwardness of the suitor embedded deep in enemy territory, he reached one arm around and laid it on the back of the couch across Zula's shoulders. A slapstick interlude followed as his hand came down on Grandpa's oxygen tube and knocked it askew. Fortunately Richard had had time to read all the instruction manuals for Grandpa's support system and get trained in how to make it all work, so he jumped up in mock horror and made a comical fuss of getting it all readjusted and then offered to perform CPR on his dad. It was unclear just how much of this Grandpa was actually following, but his face showed that he understood that it was all meant to be amusing.

"How about you?" Zula asked, when things had calmed down a bit. "What sort of company are *you* keeping, honey?"

Olivia seemed to have set her laptop up on a kitchen table. She rolled her eyes and sighed as if she had been caught out in a great deception. Her hands got big as they reached for the laptop. Then her apartment seemed to rotate around them, and they were greeted with the sight of Sokolov, dressed in a bathrobe, drinking a cup of coffee and reading a book through a pair of half-glasses that made him seem oddly professor-like. This elicited a cheer from the group in Iowa. He lifted up his coffee mug and tipped it toward them, then took a sip.

"Isn't it a bit late in the day, there, to be getting out of bed and having your shower?" Richard asked lewdly. Sokolov looked a bit uncertain, and off-camera they could hear Olivia feeding him some scraps of Russian. When he understood the jest, he looked tolerantly into the camera and explained, "Just came back from gym." He then leaned back in his chair and heaved his leg up onto the table. It occasioned a moment of silence from those watching on the sofa. Finally Richard said, "It suits you."

"Is small price," Sokolov said. "Is very small price." The workings of the video chat linkup made it difficult for them to know who he was looking at, but Zula got the sense that the look, and the words, were intended for her.

"We all had some things to pay for," Zula said, "and we paid in different ways, and it wasn't always fair."

"You had nothing to pay for," Sokolov said.

"Oh," Zula said, "I think I did."

The silence that followed was more than a little uncomfortable, and after giving it a respectful observance, Olivia edged around into view, standing behind Sokolov, and said, "Speaking of which, what do we hear from Marlon?"

"We're going to Skype him later," Csongor said. "It is early in the morning, yet, in Beijing."

"He doesn't work all night anymore?" Olivia said wonderingly.

"Nolan has him on banker's hours," Richard said. "Oh, he was up as recently as a few hours ago, playing T'Rain, but we're going to let him catch a little shut-eye before we confront him with *this*." And he made a gesture down the length of the couch.

"I think it's a very nice lineup to be confronted with," Olivia said, "and I'm sorry H.M. government doesn't observe Thanksgiving, or I'd be there." She glanced down. "We'd be there."

"Immigration," Sokolov said darkly.

"We'll get that sorted," Olivia assured him.

Gunshots were heard from outside. It was difficult to know how the sounds came through the Skype link, but the expression on Sokolov's face changed markedly.

"It's nothing!" Zula exclaimed. "Here, I'll show you!" She got up, picked up the laptop, carried it as close to the window as its cables would allow, and aimed it out in the direction of the crick.

To Richard, in truth, it was quite a bit more than nothing. He'd been dreading it for half a year. It was impossible for him to hear the sound of guns being fired without thinking of things he didn't want to remember. In Seattle, he and Zula had been seeing the same doctor for treatment of posttraumatic stress.

But lurking in the house all day wasn't going to make that better, and going out to participate was unlikely to make it worse. And so after they wrapped up the Skype call with fond words and promises of future transatlantic visits, all of them except for Grandpa put on warm clothes and ear protection and shuffled out toward the crick. Jake was there, and Elizabeth, and the three boys. They had taken a week off from the cabin-rebuilding project to drive out from Idaho and check in with the extended family and lay flowers on John's grave. The boys, homeschooled in the wilderness, had been an awkward fit with the crowd of mostly affluent suburban midwesterners who made up the re-u, but here they were in their element, moving up and down the line assisting their cousins with jams, giving them pointers in marksmanship. It was a relatively still day, which was a blessing for outdoorsmen, even though it meant that the wind turbines were not doing much.

Richard was examining one of those—he'd learned a lot more about them, now that he was handling some of John's residual business affairs—when he saw an SUV turning off the highway into the gravel drive that led to the farmhouse. About a hundred feet in, it stopped at the checkpoint that the state patrol had set up, nominally to stop terrorists from coming here to wreak revenge on the Forthrasts, but also to keep media from coming in and making nuisances of themselves. Richard could not see through the windshield at this distance, but he could tell from the body language of the state trooper that the driver was one deserving of respect. The gate was opened and the SUV waved through. It came down the driveway with a searing noise, a plume of dust rising in its wake.

"They're here," Zula told him, her voice muddy through the earplugs. For she had apparently seen the same thing.

"I have to warn you," Richard mentioned, "that he's the most outspoken and cheerful colostomy patient who ever lived."

"That's good, right?"

"Cheerful is good. Outspoken can be a bit of a problem. Especially if he can't keep his mouth shut about it during Thanksgiving dinner." He looked at his niece. "His mouth, and his other orifices. See, now I'm doing it too."

"Maybe he'll be better behaved when he's sitting next to Yuxia," Zula suggested. "It's just temporary, right?"

"What? Him and Yuxia? Who knows?"

"I was actually thinking of the colostomy."

"That's temporary," Richard agreed. "The jokes about it, however, are eternal."

They were strolling, side by side, toward the road. "How about you and Csongor?" Richard asked, glancing over his shoulder at the Hungarian, who was squeezing off rounds from a pistol while Jake critiqued his form.

"It might be permanent," Zula said. "Who knows? If he can make it through today, and he still wants to have anything to do with me and my family, then maybe we can talk."

"He's made it through harder things than today."

"This is differently hard."

The SUV pulled off the road a few yards away, and the driver's-side window rolled down. "That's a relief," Seamus called. "I was afraid my bag had overflowed, until Yuxia pointed out that we were driving past a hog confinement facility."

Yuxia had jumped out of the passenger side before the SUV even came to a full stop, and now engaged in a full body-slam greeting with Zula and an exchange of squeals so loud that it actually caused the noise-canceling electronics in Richard's ear protectors to engage. Richard exchanged a look with Seamus and pantomimed reaching up with both hands to turn the knobs on the device all the way down.

"Glad your clan in Boston was willing to lend you to us for the holiday," Richard remarked, shaking Seamus's hand. Seamus had climbed out of the vehicle and unlimbered himself to his full height.

"They're afraid of barnyard humor," Seamus said, "so they sent me to one. We're going to see them around Christmas. Yuxia wants to perform serious reconnaissance on my culture before getting in any deeper."

"Have you kissed her yet?"

"She's elusive," Seamus admitted. "If I were to presume any-thing—to act like I was *entitled*, you know—she would tear me a new—"

"Don't say it."

"To answer your question, Dodge, I think she wants my alimen-tary tract back in one piece before she comes into contact with any part of it. But there has been a bit of progress on that front. Not what you'd look for in an American girl. But you have to proceed with caution when dealing with a Big-Footed Woman."

Zula and Yuxia had just discovered that they were wearing the exact same style of winter boots, which made their feet look very big indeed. They were milking that for more hilarity than Richard would have thought possible.

"Ready to go in and give thanks?"

"You know it," Seamus said.

ACKNOWLEDGMENTS

Several persons deserve thanks and credit for having helped me when my progress was impeded by my ignorance. None of them, however, deserves any blame for cases where I got something wrong. Chief among these is Josh D'Aluisio-Guerrieri (葛佳旭), the consummate modern China hand; his skills at translation and cultural navigation made this book far better than it would have been had I been left to my own devices (I am also indebted to Charles Mann for allowing me to tag along with him and Josh on a trip that was originally intended as a research expedition for Charles's book *1493* but that I was allowed to, in a small way, hijack). Deric Ruhl saved me from one embarrassing blunder having to do with the workings of the Makarov, then went on to read the entire manuscript and offer extensive and very useful comments about firearms. I daresay he may have invented a new literary niche: ballistics copy editor.

George Dyson helped with fishing boat lore, Keith Rosema with flight plans, and George Jewsbury did a bit of Russian translation. John Eaton and Hugh Matheson helped fill out the picture of British Columbia by cheerfully supplying background information about cat-skiing resorts and mining operations, respectively.

Having put the reputations of the above people in play, I must reiterate that there are places in the book where I may have misinterpreted their advice, or simply chosen to ignore it for storytelling reasons, and so none of them should be blamed for any defects.

Somewhat in the same vein, a word about geography: the advent of Google Earth makes it easy to call up high-resolution maps of any place on the planet and compare them against the descriptions in a work of fiction. Anyone who attempts this with *Reamde* open on their lap is wasting his or her time. There is an Abandon Mountain in northern Idaho, and something that goes by the local and informal name of American Falls, but I have taken vast liberties with their descriptions here. There is no Prohibition Crick, as far as I know. In short, none of the geographical description in *Reamde* can be expected to tally with the real world or its high-quality digital representations, and so readers are encouraged to enjoy it as what it is—a work of fiction—and leave it at that.